Also by Christina James

In the Family

CHRISTINA JAMES

ALMOST LOVE

SALT

CROMER

PUBLISHED BY SALT PUBLISHING
12 Norwich Road, Cromer, Norfolk NR27 0AX

© Christina James, 2013

The right of Christina James to be identified as the author of this
work has been asserted by her in accordance with Section 77 of the
Copyright, Designs and Patents Act 1988.
This book is in copyright. Subject to statutory exception and
to provisions of relevant collective licensing agreements, no
reproduction of any part may take place without the written
permission of Salt Publishing.

Salt Publishing 2013

Printed in Great Britain by Clays Ltd, St Ives plc

Typeset in Sabon 9 / 10.5

ISBN 978 1 907773 46 4 paperback

1 3 5 7 9 8 6 4 2

*For Chris and Annika, always appreciated
for their alert and perceptive reading*

CHAPTER ONE

IT WAS THE boozy night before the conference, towards the end of the evening, and Alex, who was neither sober nor completely drunk, was heading for bed. It had been a long day and she had not enjoyed the pre-conference dinner. She'd had to look after the speakers, an irascible bunch of eccentrics who had taken a dim view of the wine waiter's capabilities; they'd complained to his face in loud, alcohol-charged voices that had gradually tipped over into unpleasantness. The argument was about credit cards. Alex had been sitting at the far end of the long speakers' table, and she hadn't caught the start of it. The waiter, a youth of about nineteen, was standing there stolidly, holding the card machine in his hand and woodenly absorbing their opprobrium . Nevertheless, Alex was afraid that someone from the hotel management would come diving into the fracas and there would be a scene.

Without enquiring what exactly had gone wrong, Alex had smoothed things over by herself paying for their wine. As she was keying in her PIN, the thought had crossed her mind that their indignation might have been a ploy to get the extra alcohol buckshee. She dismissed it as uncharitable – less because she did not think that it might be true than because she did not want to descend into a depressed state of cynicism ahead of two days in the company of these people.

She had intended to leave the hotel dining-room immediately dinner was over and headed for the shallow staircase that led past the maitre d's desk to where the lifts were. Oliver Sparham suddenly emerged from the small bar where everyone was now gathering. He was one of the more civilised delegates whom she had managed to bounce into acting as conference chairman on the following day. Grasping her elbow, he asked her if she would join him for a drink. She was both too dazed and too polite to refuse; she knew that she owed him for the task that he had agreed to (and, more to the point, which he had yet to perform). She nodded consent and allowed him to steer her, still holding on to her elbow, past the knot of people gathered at the bar's double doors and into the inner drinking sanctum itself. She knew that many of the conference delegates would now be ensconced in this room until the hotel closed it at 2 a.m.; she was determined not to be among them.

"There's a table over there with two seats free," said Oliver. "You go and claim it, and I'll buy you a drink. What will it be?"

At least these words gave her an excuse to shake him free. Her mind was fuzzy with wine and fatigue. What could she ask for that would not give her a blinding headache the next day?

"Prosecco," she said. "Just a small one." She tried to smile at him. He nodded and trotted off, his face pink under the lights, his spectacles gleaming, evidently unaware that her response was barely lukewarm.

She sat on one of the red velvet upholstered stools at the small, cockly table that he had indicated and, picking up a beer mat, slowly began to shred it. Someone said close in her ear: "Bored again, I see. It's an occupational hazard at these events. Mind if I join you?"

She knew it was not Oliver before she looked up; glancing across at the bar, she saw that he was still queuing and some way from being served. She had not recognised the voice, however, so when she turned to meet the eye of her new companion she was surprised to see that it was Edmund Baker, the Heritage Officer for South Lincolnshire and currently Honorary President of the Society. His voice must have sounded strange because he'd been drinking. She sighed inwardly. Edmund was famous for being a bore when he was sober; when he was drunk, his stupor-inducing talents were almost legendary.

"Hello, Edmund," she said offhandedly. "Did you have a good dinner?"

He wrinkled his long nose rather comically.

"So-so," he said. "I got saddled with Lois Merton. Not much of a looker, is she? Even if she has got the equipment up top." He mimed two enormous breasts, accompanying the gesture with the exaggerated leer of a schoolboy.

"Really, Edmund, that is a disgraceful comment. I'd rather you talked to someone else if you can't behave any better." She smiled, though, in spite of herself.

"I'll behave if you let me talk to you," he said. "Can I buy you a drink?"

"Oliver's getting one for me; and in fact he was sitting just there. You'll have to give that seat up to him when he comes back."

"Yes, ma'am," he said, pulling another schoolboy face. His hair was silver-white. Alex wondered what colour it had been in his youth. She guessed sandy, which meant that he probably hadn't been as attractive then as he was now.

She gulped inwardly. Had the thought just flitted through her brain that Edmund could be in any way attractive? She'd always found him difficult to deal with and very boring on occasions; and actually quite asexual. When Oliver came back with her drink, she would down it as quickly as she decently could and go to bed. Her judgment had been impaired by the booze.

"What's up?" said Edmund. He was evidently in a good mood. She saw that he was clutching a large scotch.

"Nothing," said Alex. "I'm just tired, that's all." She cast around for something to talk about. Afterwards, she could never quite understand why she had shared her pet project with Edmund.

"Since you're there," she began, "there *is* something I'd like to talk to you about. It's all those cases of old finds we're holding at the Archaeological Society. I'd really like to organise a project to classify them, before all sense of where they came from gets lost forever. Some of them are beyond classification already. The trouble is I don't have the time – or even the knowledge, for some of the stuff – to do it myself. I'd need to set up a research project, probably involving academics and students, over a period of time. And I'd need a joint project manager, because I'm away so much. So it would have to attract some quite substantial funding. I thought you might be able to help me to get it: point me in the right direction, advise on writing a proposal, that sort of thing. I know you have more experience in attracting money than I do."

Edmund looked at her for a long moment, swirling the scotch in his glass as he did so.

"I could help you with more than securing the funding," he said unexpectedly. "I'd be happy to work with you on it, if you'd let me be joint project manager. It would be good to find out if we work well together. I'll be retiring soon, and I'll need something else to fill my life with. I've often toyed with the idea of setting up a little business with you."

Alex was taken aback. She tried to think quickly. Edmund was much older than she was – as he said, he was close to retiring, which made him more than twenty years her senior – and, although she'd long dreamed of setting up a sort of research consultancy for archaeological projects, she'd always thought that if she made a go of it, it would be a business that Tom might like to work in as well. Even Tom couldn't spend his whole life doing social work. But, counter-intuitively, she suddenly found something appealing in the idea of working with Edmund.

Oliver came back with their drinks before she could reply. Edmund launched himself to his feet, swaying a little.

"Alex says that this is your seat," he said. "Don't let me interrupt anything. Ah, I see there's another chair over there. I'll just fetch it."

He turned his back. Oliver handed Alex her glass of Prosecco, pulling a face as he did so.

"Sorry," he said. "That's what happens when you leave a girl on her own; she becomes a maiden, or perhaps I should say matron, in distress. How long has he been boring you?"

"He hasn't been here for very long, and actually he hasn't been boring me at all." She meant to sound surprised, but she realised as soon as she spoke that she had delivered the sentence rather aggressively.

"Oh. Well, to quote Edmund, 'Don't let me interrupt anything.' If you're happy talking to him, I'm quite willing to leave you two alone. I have no wish to play gooseberry," he added, smirking slightly.

"Don't be ridiculous. And don't go, either. There's no reason why the three of us shouldn't have a perfectly civilised conversation. We're all far too old for playground squabbles."

"You're right there. Especially Edmund."

"Especially Edmund what?" said Edmund, returning in triumph with a spindly gilded chair that looked as if it would not take his weight.

"Nothing," she and Oliver said together. They both giggled.

"I see. Talking about me behind my back, were you?" said Edmund. He spoke genially, without rancour. Alex reflected that she had never seen him in such a good mood.

Oliver launched into test-delivering a series of little vignettes that he had prepared by way of introducing the speakers the next day. Alex thought that they succeeded in being quite as humorously malicious as he had intended, but she could hardly concentrate on what he was saying and she wished he would lower his voice; she knew that his performance tomorrow would fall flat if too many people overheard in advance what he was planning. Edmund didn't contribute to the conversation at all, which was unlike him, but she was grateful for it. She knew that he could be both rude and tactless if he was feeling cantankerous. But he continued to swirl the whisky in his glass, smiling and nodding almost beatifically. Afterwards, it occurred to her that he had been very drunk. She herself was quite drunk by this time. The room had taken on a surreal quality; voices rushed at her and then retreated; a wicked little pang that she'd felt in her forehead while she was shredding the beer mat was growing into a Goliath of a headache. Her replies to Oliver, as he showed off his genial but lethal character-assassination skills and asked mock-modestly for reassurance that he was delivering 'what she had anticipated', became ever more perfunctory. Edmund continued to grin and swirl, and then suddenly downed what was left of the whisky.

"Anyone want another drink?" he asked.

"Not for me, thanks," said Oliver. "It's time I went to bed. I need to have a clear head tomorrow. So does Alex, don't you, love?"

Alex watched Edmund's eyes widen and knew, with a shock, that he thought that Oliver was trying to proposition her, whereas she was quite certain that all he meant to do was release her from Edmund so that she could go to bed; her own bed, in the magnificent suite that was always allocated to her in recognition of her hard work in organising the conference, but which she barely saw because her every waking hour had to be spent elsewhere. It was because she could not bear to give Edmund grounds to believe this inference that she made herself accept his offer of yet another drink. Oliver stood up and made a waving gesture.

"Have fun," he said. "I'll see you tomorrow. Bright and early, Alex, I hope. I've asked the AV people if we can do a quick run-through before breakfast."

Edmund also stood, swaying even more than when he had first approached her.

"I'll go and get those drinks," he said thickly. "Prosecco, was it?"

Alex nodded weakly. Her evening was turning into a disaster, yet one from which she felt powerless to extricate herself. She knew that tomorrow she would feel sick and hungover and that, when she got up, the day's programme of conference presentations and 'gala dinner' would seem to drag on endlessly before she could crawl into bed again. She desperately needed her bed now, but getting to it seemed harder than walking through a maze for the first time.

Edmund came back with a much larger glass of Prosecco than the one that Oliver had bought and what seemed to be at least half a tumbler of whisky on the rocks. He sat down heavily. She took the glass of wine from him and sipped it. He started talking about her idea again. Alex said little, but took a few more sips of the wine. Miraculously, the pain in her head lifted.

CHAPTER TWO

THE FOLLOWING MORNING, Alex awoke early with a thumping headache. You should know better at your age, she chastised herself. She let the familiar hangover remorse and self-disgust seep through her, and then tried to push them away. She lay inert in bed for a while, staring at the LCD figures on the hotel alarm clock. Pull yourself together, she chided. She made herself take in the clock's message, concentrating carefully in order to focus her eyes. The digital display read 06.15. Six fifteen! She could stay in bed for another thirty minutes before she had to get up and prepare for the day. She knew that she would be unable to sleep again. Shutting her eyes made her feel sick.

Something niggled at the back of her mind: some reason why she had more cause to dread the day ahead than the knowledge that she must spend its entirety hobbled by the pain caused by too much alcohol. Of all the kinds of suffering, it was the one that nobody with an ounce of self-respect would acknowledge, so she would just have to put a brave face on it.

Besides the drinking, what else had happened during the early hours? She thought back over the events of the previous evening . . . and remembered Edmund. She could recall the conversation in the bar. After it had become unbearably noisy, she had asked Edmund if he would like to come to her sitting-room to discuss further his suggestion that they should work together. After that, her memories were hazy, with gaps.

She remembered Edmund standing over her as she sat in one of the leather armchairs with her feet tucked up under her. Why was he standing? He had extended a trembling hand to stroke her hair. She had looked up at him and said something, but could not remember the exact words. She did recall their substance: it had been something about Christine; Christine, his wife, whom she had never met. It seemed unlikely, but she thought she might have asked him if he loved Christine. Whatever her question, she could remember his response quite clearly. He said, "Yes, of course," but in a clipped, almost strangulated, way, as if signalling either that this was a considerable achievement, or that his love was necessarily qualified in some way. He had then withdrawn his hand very precipitately, and left.

My God, she thought, had Edmund made a pass at her? It would certainly explain the fear with which she was facing the day ahead. It must have been that; otherwise, why had he disappeared so quickly? And what an idiot she had been; she could understand why even Edmund, the least sexually interesting of men and, as far as she knew, one of the least interested in sex, would mistake the signals sent out by a half-drunk woman who had invited him back to her room. That the sitting-room and bedroom were quite separate was hardly a convincing defence.

She hauled herself out of bed. She knew she would have to try every trick in her repertoire to combat her mental and physical wretchedness. She lay on the floor and tried to relax her limbs in preparation for some gentle yoga. She managed the 'tense yourself, relax' technique all right, but, as soon as she closed her eyes, waves of nausea swept over her again. She got up slowly, sat on the edge of the bed for a while and then turned on the television.

A bomb had gone off in Oslo, wrecking the railway station. At least one hundred people had died and the casualty figures were climbing rapidly. She stared at the screen for a while, gazing in horror at images of wrecked cars piled on top of each other and huge twisted chunks of masonry, followed by some jumbled footage of people lying in the streets, blood-speckled and injured or running hysterically with stretchers bearing the dead and wounded. She pointed the remote again. She knew she was being cowardly, but she was not yet in a fit state to take in an international catastrophe.

She walked over to the glass balcony doors and flung open the curtains. The hotel had originally been an eighteenth-century country house and her room overlooked a flagged courtyard. Holding back the gauzy net and peering down, she saw what was unmistakably a column of cigarette smoke curling up towards her. Someone must be standing in front of the French window on the ground floor. She could not see who it was. She tried moving to the far right hand side of the glass in an attempt to catch a glimpse of a head or arm, but still could make out nothing except the regular curlicues of smoke. She did not doubt that it was a man. If she opened the door and went to stand on the balcony, she would be able to see him, but he would almost certainly hear the doors opening and look up at her. Her curiosity was not keen enough to make her want to expose herself to view, dressed as she was only in a short nightshirt, the depredations of the night before unconcealed by make-up and her hair all over the place. She dropped the net curtain and propelled herself towards the bathroom.

Twenty minutes later, having showered and washed her hair and dressed in the smart navy suit that she had bought especially, with make-up applied and her outfit discreetly complemented by gold stud earrings and a slender gold chain, she felt a little more able to face the world. She drew back the net covering the balcony doors and unlocked and opened them. She stepped out onto a narrow stone platform bound by tall piano-leg-shaped columns and a sturdy rail of Portland stone and into sunlight that was already quite strong, despite the earliness of the hour. Below, she saw a white delivery van arrive. Painted in black on its side, in letters that were made to resemble elaborate handwriting, was the legend *Gourmet Sea-foods Ltd. Proprietor: E. Gregory* and a telephone number and website address. A man got out and opened the back doors of the van. He loaded himself up with three large cardboard boxes and disappeared into the hotel with them. Otherwise, the courtyard was deserted. The secret smoker had vanished.

Alex went back into her room and looked at her watch. It was just after 7 a.m. She decided that she couldn't face meeting anyone for breakfast – especially not Edmund or Oliver. Although she wasn't the slightest bit hungry, a light snack might help her to get through the morning better. She called room service and ordered croissants and coffee. Smoothing her skirt carefully, she perched on the end of her bed and pointed the remote at the television again. A politician and a well-known historian sat hunched on sofas intended to make them look casual. They talked about the situation in Norway. The politician was very red in the face and kept saying, 'If you'll let me finish . . .' whenever the anchorwoman or the historian tried, however courteously, to interrupt him. The result was a stultifyingly tedious, one-sided harangue about how such a situation could never arise at home while the present government was in power, because. . . .

She was about to consign him to oblivion when, quite suddenly, the interview was concluded and the anchorwoman announced that the news would now continue with regional items 'where you are'. Welland Manor was, of course, some thirty miles from 'where Alex was' usually and fell within a different local television region from the one at home. Nevertheless, as she always enjoyed local news more than the national news because it was more about people, less about big business and political set-pieces, she decided to watch it.

The first item was about hunting and the second about the wedding of a local woman who had married her soldier fiancé despite his having been terribly disfigured during the invasion of Iraq. After a third clip on local authority cuts and the consequent reduction in bus services and provision for pre-school children, the newscaster – a dapper, bald little man with a strong local accent – was in the process of returning viewers to the main newsroom when he interrupted himself with a 'breaking news' announcement.

"We have just heard that Dame Claudia McRae, the archaeologist, has disappeared from her home in suspicious circumstances. Police were called to her house early this morning after Guy Maichment, her nephew, failed to reach her by telephone. Because she is elderly and quite frail, Mr Maichment decided to check on her. When he reached her house, which is situated in Teapot Lane, about five miles from the village of Welland, near Helpston, he found the front door wide open. Dame Claudia was not there, but there were no signs of a struggle. Dame Claudia, if you are safe and well and watching this programme, City of Peterborough Police would like to appeal to you to contact them immediately. The police would also like to talk to anyone who has had contact with Dame Claudia over the past forty-eight hours. Dame Claudia pioneered the use of archaeological dating techniques based on the semantic development of ancient languages and is particularly well-known for her work in the Middle East, especially in the region known to bible scholars as Mesopotamia, and for deciphering the text of what has become known as the McRae Stone." Pictures of the house were shown. It looked like a story-book thatched cottage, its walls washed pale pink. It was surrounded by trees and apparently stood in a very isolated location.

Claudia McRae. Alex did not know her, but she had met her once. She had heard her speak at a lecture when she was a student and had been introduced to her briefly afterwards. Miss McRae must have been about seventy at the time; a bulky, arrogant woman, as far as Alex could remember. She had announced her retirement shortly afterwards. Some of the conference delegates would undoubtedly have been past colleagues and acquaintances and had probably looked up to her when younger. Alex herself had found her theories about semantic dating fascinating and had read several books and papers by Claudia McRae before she had attended that lecture. In some ways, she had regretted going to it; the woman had seemed so much less distinguished than the corpus of work that she had produced. Perhaps that was being unfair: it is bound to be difficult to live up to the expectations of your admirers when your work has become a legend.

There was a tap at the door. Alex thrust her feet into her black court shoes and opened it. A white-jacketed waiter stood before her, bearing a tray.

"Where would you like me to leave this, Madam?"

Alex indicated the desk, walking ahead of him to move the cardboard folder containing the day's schedule of events. He put it down carefully and asked her to sign a chit.

"This is also for you, Madam," he said. "It was left with the night porter early this morning."

He handed Alex a thick vellum envelope embossed with the Welland Manor's coat of arms.

"Thank you."

He inclined his head and left the room slowly. When he finally reached the door, he closed it quite smartly behind him. Too late, Alex realised that he had been expecting a tip.

She glanced at the television screen again. The national anchorwoman was back. She had just finished summarising the news headlines and was handing over to the weather forecaster. Alex snapped the remote again, relishing the instant peace that this brought. She sat down at the desk and poured herself coffee. Sipping it carefully, she thought that perhaps her headache was easing. She looked at her watch: seven-thirty. There was still half an hour before she had to meet Oliver in the conference suite. If she could eat at least one of the two croissants that the waiter had brought, and drink the orange juice as well as the coffee, she might make a passable recovery.

She was topping up her coffee when her eye fell again on the envelope that the waiter had handed her. She had barely registered what it was when she had taken it from him, distracted as she had been by Claudia McRae, her own hangover and the slight feeling of unease that she always experienced when being served by over-attentive hotel staff. She sighed. It was probably connected with the contretemps over the wine yesterday evening. She hoped that it would be nothing more controversial than, perhaps, a routine – and probably insincere – apology from the sommelier. The flap of the envelope had been sealed down, not just folded. She ripped it open, creating an untidy ragged gash in the expensive, cream-laid paper. Inside, there was a single sheet of the hotel's notepaper. Like the envelope, it was of expensive, cream-laid vellum and had been neatly folded into three so that it fitted the envelope exactly. She opened it out and smoothed it down flat on the desk. The hotel's address and crest, printed in the same discreet grey-blue in which they appeared on the envelope, but magnified to about twice the size, were centred at the top of the sheet of paper. Otherwise, it bore only two words: *Be Careful.* These had been inscribed in black ink right in the middle of the page, in a handwriting which attempted to copy Victorian copperplate. There was no date, and no signature: just this single curt message.

Alex sighed again. The missive aroused in her more irritation than alarm. It had almost certainly come from one of the curmudgeonly old men who had made such a nuisance of themselves yesterday evening. If so, how cowardly of the author not to identify himself! It flitted swiftly across her mind that, alternatively, it might have been written by someone who had seen her leave the bar with Edmund. But she didn't think that anyone besides Oliver had really been aware that they had been sitting together and he had headed for bed long before her own departure. She was all but certain that no-one had seen her enter the suite with Edmund: one of the clear memories that stood out from the blur of the events of the small hours was of Edmund glancing nervously up and down the corridor as they stood outside her room and she fumbled with the key-card. He would certainly have alerted her – and probably bolted – if anyone had been watching. In any case, she thought defensively, if they had been seen, what could anyone do about it? Tell Tom? Tell Christine? Neither featured at all in the lives of this group of archaeologists; and besides, exactly what was there to tell?

She looked at her watch again. It was 7.45 a.m. now: time to tackle the croissant. Taking small bites, she masticated the papery mass as thoroughly as she could and managed to swallow about half of it, her gorge rising slightly each time a morsel was dispatched. She spent five heroic minutes at this task, then swigged the last of the orange juice, downed some more coffee and went to the bathroom to brush her teeth and apply lipstick. She snatched up her handbag and the folder, inwardly declaring that she was as ready as she would ever be for what the day had in store. It was next to impossible to escape through the mock hallway that led out of her suite without consulting her reflection in its floor-to-ceiling mirror. She threw a sidelong appraising glance at her image and decided that it passed muster. With exaggerated bravado, she strode out of the room to keep her appointment with Oliver.

CHAPTER THREE

DESPITE THE FACT that it was an unspoiled morning and he was driving along some of his favourite country lanes in brilliant winter sunshine, Inspector Tim Yates was not happy. He thought that he had probably been sent on a fool's errand, for one thing; to a place near Helpston, as well, which was not, strictly speaking, in his territory. For another, he had had one of his rare disagreements with Katrin – OK, he conceded, as he rewound the events of the previous evening in his mind, it was a row . Katrin had been behaving strangely of late – she was not her usual sunny, rational, forgiving self. There had been a heated exchange, during which she had said that it was he who had been behaving thoughtlessly. She would say that, of course. Nevertheless, her comments had prompted him to embark on some unaccustomed moments of introspection. Perhaps she was right. Perhaps they both needed a holiday. Perhaps he would be in a better mood if Superintendent Thornton hadn't landed him with this bloody 'incident', or rather, non-incident. It would turn out to be a wild goose chase, he would put money on it. In the meantime, Detective Constables Juliet Armstrong and Andy Carstairs were investigating what appeared to be a contract killing that had taken place in Spalding the night before – a man had been found dead in Ayscoughfee Gardens, the cause of death apparently a single bullet through the forehead. Drugs, thought Tim. Drugs would be at the bottom of it; though it was odd that the man seemed to be a vagrant. He had been trying to persuade his superiors for months that there was evidence of an organised drugs gang at work in South Lincolnshire. Perhaps now they would believe him. Discovering the identity of the victim in the park could lead to the uncovering of a drugs network. If so, it would probably be the most important case that South Lincolnshire police had worked on for many years. And here he was, traipsing around the countryside looking for a vain old woman who had contrived to go missing.

His assessment of Claudia McRae's character was not entirely based on prejudice. As a history undergraduate, he had developed a passing interest in archaeology and, of course, he had heard of her. Dame Claudia McRae, as she was now. Most people had heard of her, even if they barely knew what archaeology was about. Her fame had been attributed to her having pushed back the boundaries of what the women of her generation were allowed to achieve; she had succeeded in gaining eminence in a science (art?) that had previously been a fiercely-guarded male preserve. Tim had read one of her books, however, and he suspected that vanity and a decided talent for self-promotion had also been major factors in her rise to stardom – not to mention her many friends in politics and other influential spheres. He did not deny the inventive virtuosity of the theories that she propounded; indeed, he found them fascinating, because they lent to archaeology the very quality which for him it had traditionally lacked: the power to recreate the voices of the past. But her prose style was thumping and arrogant and she allowed no room for doubt that she was right. Some of her hypotheses were based on extremely tenuous interpretations of tiny examples of barely-decipherable scraps of ancient writings whose languages could not be fully reconstructed. It was therefore difficult to say that she was wrong (particularly as she was the pre-eminent 'expert' in her field), but for a trained mind it was equally difficult to swallow that all of her theories were irrefutable. Remarkably, no-one of either her own generation or the one succeeding it had publicly challenged her writings, though conversely she had never received much acclaim from her peers. He wondered if a new young crop of would-be famous archaeologists was now busily casting a sceptical eye on the corpus of her work and coming up with alternative explanations for her 'findings'. If so, he hoped that they would be diligent in researching the many accounts of recent discoveries that could no doubt be cited to provide a legitimate pretext for undertaking such a project and, also, that they would apply absolute integrity to whatever counter-arguments they might come up with. Otherwise it would just be the usual academic tit-for-tat refined slanging match, of no practical use to anyone. Thank God he had turned his back on all of that and chosen to become a policeman.

The thought cheered him. His mood was lightened further when his mobile phone chirruped its 'text message waiting' ditty and, pulling over into a lay-by, he saw that the message was from Katrin. It read simply: 'Sorry. XXX.' He texted her back. 'My fault. XXX'. The day was already beginning to look a great deal brighter.

The last leg of his journey took him deep into the country lanes beyond Helpston. He made a few wrong turns, cursing equally the inadequate map which he had printed from the Internet and the local council's failure to signpost the maze of tiny lanes in which he found himself. Claudia McRae's cottage, when eventually he reached it, stood at the end of a narrow unmetalled farm track which gradually petered out altogether, so that for the last two hundred yards or so he was just driving on hard mud.

The house itself was a confection, almost too picture-book pretty with its thatched roof and rose-coloured walls. Its walls were bowed with age and seemed to grow up out of the grass – there was evidently no proper garden, nor even a boundary fence – and it bore more than a fleeting resemblance to the picture of the cottage into which Hansel and Gretel had been lured in the edition of Grimm's Fairy Tales from which his grandmother had read to him as a child. Taking the analogy further would turn Claudia McRae into a witch. If the cap fits, thought Tim.

There was a police car and a battered Citroen parked in front of the house. Tim parked his own car – a BMW and also battered – at some distance from them and walked up the slight slope to the house. The front door was wide open. A police cordon had been looped through stakes set in a box shape around the entrance. Wary of contaminating evidence, Tim shouted out 'Hello?', feeling faintly foolish as he did so.

A uniformed policeman appeared from somewhere behind the house. He was carrying a plastic bag and was followed by a slightly-built man of about fifty who held up his head with an almost aristocratic bearing, although he was dressed in very shabby, dirty clothes. Tim recognised the policeman.

"PC Cooper?" he said. "Have they sent you out here as well? Don't City of Peterborough Police have any coppers of their own, for God's sake?"

Gary Cooper grinned. "It was Superintendent Thornton's idea, sir," he said. "He thought you would appreciate working with one of your own team, so to speak."

Tim rolled his eyes. "Heaven preserve me if the Superintendent has started getting in touch with his feminine side. What next?"

"When you've finished your banter," said the slightly-built man quietly, but with unmistakable, if contained, hostility, "my aunt has disappeared and I think that you should lose no time in setting about finding her. If you are able to, that is. It is already several hours since I first called for help and nothing at all constructive appears to have happened yet."

Tim took an instant dislike to the man, but he knew he must guard against showing it. Both Katrin and Juliet Armstrong had told him that his opinions of other people could often be read only too clearly in his face. Not a good trait in a policeman.

"Mr Maichment?" he said, extending his hand. "Detective Inspector Tim Yates, South Lincolnshire Police."

Guy Maichment placed his slight and none-too-clean hand in Tim's and let it linger there limply for a moment before withdrawing it.

"Delighted," he said. "Now, if you will come into the house, I'll show you what I found when I arrived here during the night."

"About what time was that, Mr Maichment?" Tim asked.

"Just before 1 a.m. Why do you ask?"

"Rather late to be visiting an old lady, wasn't it?"

"I've already explained several times that I was trying to reach my aunt by telephone during the whole of yesterday evening. She's in quite good health for her age, but obviously not strong. She usually has someone with her – Jane Halliwell, a sort of companion and secretary rolled into one – but Miss Halliwell is not here this week."

"Do you know where she is?"

"I believe that she is on holiday abroad somewhere."

"So you haven't been in touch with her to ask if she might know where your aunt could have gone?"

"I haven't been in touch with anyone, except you people," Guy Maichment said peevishly. "The policeman whom I spoke to on the telephone told me just to stay here and not touch anything until someone arrived to help."

"Which policeman was that?" asked Tim, directing his question to Gary Cooper.

"Superintendent Little, of the City of Peterborough force, sir. Mr Maichment's call was taken very seriously. Superintendent Little was alerted and dealt with the matter personally. He sent a panda car here straight away."

"I would expect Roy Little to take a call from me 'very seriously'," said Guy Maichment. "He is a friend of my aunt's." He almost preened himself.

"Presumably there was a policeman – or even two – from Peterborough. Where are they now?"

"There was a policeman and a policewoman, sir. I've written down their names. They left just after I got here. They asked Mr Maichment some preliminary questions, I believe, and now they've gone to check the hospitals and old people's homes in the area."

"I see." Tim didn't actually see at all. If Superintendent Little was so keen to help, and a friend of the family to boot, why involve South Lincolnshire Police? And why had Superintendent Thornton agreed? Tim was here now, however, and there was work to do. He would get to the bottom of whatever Thornton was up to later.

"Let's go into the house now, shall we, as Mr Maichment suggests?"

Gary Cooper produced some white overshoes from his plastic bag.

"Best to wear these, then, sir. SOCOs haven't got here yet."

"You've called the SOCOs in? That was a bit precipitate, wasn't it?"

"You'll see why, sir."

Tim took the shoes and eased into them. PC Cooper lifted out more shoes for himself and Guy Maichment, who made quite a palaver of putting them on. Tim had the strange feeling that he was enjoying himself.

Gary Cooper ducked under the police cordon. Guy Maichment hopped over it nimbly, close on Gary's heels. Tim himself hurdled it in rather an ungainly way and followed them both through the open door of the house. They each halted abruptly and stood a few paces back from the left-hand wall in the poky, corridor-like entrance hall. Both turned simultaneously to face the wall itself, as if to signpost to Tim what he was supposed to be looking at.

Tim prided himself on not being easily shocked, but the spectacle that confronted him made his heart turn over in disbelief. At first he could see very little: the entrance hall to the cottage was dark and gloomy. It was dingily painted and unlit by external windows. After a few seconds, his eyes adjusted a little, enabling him to make out the crescent of colour that arced across the wall as if daubed by an abstract artist or a naughty child. Exactly what he was looking at dawned on him at the same moment as PC Cooper switched on the light. The low wattage bulb cast shadows, distorting the daub so that the smear appeared to stand out from the wall like a bas-relief.

"Christ!" he said.

"Yes, sir," said Gary Cooper. "There can't be much doubt about what it is. The SOCOs will take swabs, of course, but I'd say that the fine spray of little droplets nearest to the door confirms it pretty well."

"A trajectory of blood consistent with someone having staggered towards the wall after the cutting of a major artery – possibly in the throat?"

"Yes, sir," Gary Cooper responded again. "That would be my opinion."

"I'm glad that you both agree," said Guy Maichment sardonically. "What I want to know is, whose blood? Is it my aunt's? Did she hurt herself while running away from an attacker? And where is she now?"

"Whether it was your aunt or someone else who sustained the injury that resulted in that, Mr Maichment, it is unlikely that they were able to run anywhere. In all probability they collapsed or were on the point of collapsing as soon as it happened. As you see, the mark is quite high on the wall. Is your aunt a tall woman?"

"She's well-built, but not particularly tall. I suppose that there's a chance that the blood isn't hers?"

Tim spent a second appraising Guy Maichment before he answered – not enough time to worry him, but long enough for Tim to note his expression and try to understand his demeanour. Despite his posh haughtiness, which Tim was beginning to think might be assumed, he seemed to be inappropriately excited, even gleeful, about the mystery that he had found himself caught up in. Correction, thought Tim: Guy Maichment had actually *announced* the mystery, though there was plenty of evidence, of course, to support the action that he had taken. Not everyone would stir themselves to visit an elderly aunt in the middle of the night simply because she wasn't answering her telephone; measured by the norms of civilised society, someone who did so would normally be praised for sensitivity, not suspected for motive. Certainly, most responsible people would have telephoned the police, just as Guy had done, if they had found the old lady's house empty, the front door open and what was apparently a significant quantity of blood smeared on the wall. There was something strange about Guy, nevertheless. Perhaps he was just behaving unnaturally because the adrenalin was still surging. Unlike PC Cooper and me, he can't have had much experience of missing persons, let alone lurid blood stains, Tim thought. His innocence could be believed in; for now.

"We can't even be certain that it *is* blood until some tests have been done," he said, continuing to meet Guy's eye. "But I agree that it looks like it. It will take more tests to establish *whose* blood – and then we shall only be able to use the results to eliminate people, rather than pinpoint the actual individual. Unless, of course, they have a criminal record and their DNA is recorded on the national database. I imagine that someone will know what your aunt's blood group is?"

"She doesn't like doctors very much, but I'd say that her doctor is bound to have a record of it, because she travelled abroad so much. She will have had to agree to injections, possibly blood tests, both before and after some of the expeditions that she went on."

"Do you know her doctor?"

"Not personally, but I know her name. It is Dr Rentzenbrinck. I believe her first name is Marianna, but I can check. Her telephone number will probably be in my aunt's address book."

"Do you know where to find it?"

"Oh, yes. She keeps it by the telephone in the parlour. Ringing people up is one of her great pleasures: she has many friends throughout the world and she doesn't sleep well. And she virtually never goes out in the evenings. That's why I thought it so odd that she didn't answer the phone last night."

"How many times did you try?"

"Oh, several. At least four. On the first occasion, the phone was engaged, which made her later failure to respond even odder. Of course, it could just have been someone leaving a message via BT callminder, or whatever it's called. I use an old-fashioned answering machine myself. My aunt is surprisingly up-to-date in some ways."

"Has anyone checked for 1571 messages?" Tim asked PC Cooper.

"No, sir. Would you like me to do it now?"

"No. Leave it until the SOCOs have tested it for prints."

Guy Maichment's swarthy face changed colour.

"But my fingerprints will be on it," he said. "I used it when I telephoned the police. In any case, why would an intruder want to use the telephone?"

"I don't know why – they probably wouldn't, in fact. But it's our job to check. We can eliminate your prints, Mr Maichment, and those of your aunt. So don't worry about that."

"I don't know how long fingerprints last. If it's more than a few days, Jane's will be on it as well."

"We can eliminate any of the fingerprints of people who have used the phone legitimately, if we know who they are, and then see what, if any, we have left," Tim explained patiently. "What else did you touch? I'm assuming that you didn't put your hands on the wall – this wall, I mean?" He waved a hand at the red smear.

"Good God, no." Guy Maichment recoiled. "I can't stand blood, actually. Why would you think I'd touch *that*?"

"Just checking," Tim said again. "You might have been groping for the light switch, for example. Did you turn the light on? Could you tell us exactly what happened, and what you did, in the order in which you did it, if you can remember? I'm sorry if you have already been over it with PC Cooper," he added, as Guy Maichment began to look affronted again.

"We didn't talk about it in detail," Gary Cooper said quickly.

"Well, I'd like to understand the detail now," said Tim. "Should we stand outside again? We can't sit down here, but we can go and sit in my car if you like; or in the panda car."

"I don't mind standing, but I should like to get away from that," Guy Maichment said, gesturing at the wall. "It gives me the creeps."

They filed out into the sunshine. Guy Maichment bent to remove the overshoes.

"I'd leave those on for the moment, Mr Maichment. We'll need to go back into the house eventually. When you're ready, PC Cooper will take notes."

Guy Maichment cleared his throat.

"I came in the car. I have a Land Rover as well, but it needs some rep[airs after a problem when I was on my latest landscaping contract. I drove up the track quite slowly; the car is quite noisy, and if my aunt had been asleep I didn't want to alarm her by waking her up suddenly. When I reached the house everything was in darkness. As you can imagine, it is very dark here in the woods at night, even when there is a full moon. There was a crescent moon last night, so it wasn't bright. I dipped the headlights and drove as near to the front door as I could – to about where the panda car is standing now. I'm not sure what I intended to do next. I have a key, but I should have been reluctant to alarm her by unlocking the door during the night. I know that sounds stupid, since I had made the journey on purpose to check that she was OK, but I suppose that really I'd hoped to find the downstairs lights on. She sometimes stayed up half the night and often slept in a chair rather than going to bed.

"I was still wavering about what to do when I saw her cat. I had parked to the right of the house, you understand, so I didn't have a direct view of the front door. But I saw the cat slink round the side of the building. He was approaching from the back garden. I watched him closely; I like cats and I thought I was probably watching him hunt. When he reached the front wall of the house, he crept along it, keeping in very close. I could still make him out – by the light of the dipped headlights I could see the front of the house and a few feet beyond it – when suddenly he disappeared. I was sure it wasn't simply because I'd taken my eye off him; one moment he was inching along the wall, the next he had gone. I thought that perhaps my aunt had opened the door to let him in, so I got out of the car to see if she was there."

He paused and swallowed, then passed the back of his hand across his forehead. It was an affected gesture, Tim thought, as if Guy Maichment were trying to conjure up some more appropriate signs of emotion than the ones he had shown so far.

"You don't happen to have any water, do you? My throat is very dry."

"I've got an unopened bottle of water in my car," said Gary Cooper.

"Would you mind getting it?" said Tim. He was quite pleased to have the opportunity to observe Guy Maichment out of role, as it were, for a few seconds.

"You must be feeling tired, sir," he said. "I'm sorry that I have to put you through all this. You will appreciate that in order to find your aunt I need as much detail as I can get from you while it is still fresh in your mind. As you pointed out, time is of the essence."

"I quite understand. I suppose it has just hit me, that's all."

Tim gave him a casual look. Guy's eyes still glittered unnaturally brightly, like a child's at a birthday party. Perhaps this was genuinely his way of coping with stress. It seemed odd, somehow, but no doubt a psychologist would say otherwise. Tim might contact one to see, or consult one of his many psychology books. It was a subject which fascinated him.

Gary Cooper came back with a small bottle of Evian water. Guy took it from him – not so much as a murmur of thanks, Tim noted – wrenched the cap off it and drank thirstily. He supposed that was fair enough: the man had been here for several hours and had presumably consumed nothing since the previous evening.

"So," he said, "you got out of the car. Did you lock it?"

"No. I wouldn't have locked it while it was parked at my aunt's, but as a matter of fact I rarely do. It's such an old heap that I'm pretty confident that no-one will try to steal it."

Tim inclined his head. This wasn't the right time to give a lecture on the dangers of 'twocking'.

"So what did you do?"

"I took the torch from the dashboard and switched it on. Then I left the car and followed where the cat had gone. I walked in close to the side of the house, as he did."

"Any particular reason for that?"

"Not really. I suppose that I felt that what I was doing was quite eerie; to follow in the cat's footsteps made it seem a bit more . . . normal."

"Indeed," said Tim. Whatever the state of Guy Maichment's psychological health, he was not great on logic. "Did you find the cat?"

"No. But when I reached the door, I found it open. I was right in my assumption that the cat had been let into the house. Just not by my aunt."

"That's an interesting way of putting it."

"What do you mean?"

Shit, Tim thought. I've put him back on the defensive again. He tried to smile reassuringly.

"Oh, nothing much: you must forgive me, I'm obsessed with terminology; it's a bit of a hobby of mine. If I had been telling your story, I'd probably have said that the cat had got into the house and when I reached the door I found that it was open. Do you have any reason to believe that the cat was let in?"

Guy Maichment shrugged. "Someone must have left the door open."

"I agree: but the question is, when? Do you have any reason to believe that the cat was let in by someone while you were watching it? Did you notice whether the door was open when you first arrived?"

"The answer is 'no' to both questions," said Guy huffily. "If I'd seen that the door was open to start with, naturally I shouldn't have wondered whether it was the right thing to do to go into the house. I'd have jumped out of the car as quickly as I could and gone to see what was wrong. My aunt may be a little eccentric, but she certainly isn't in the habit of leaving her door wide open in the middle of the night."

"Did you see or hear anyone else at all?"

"No. No-one."

"So you went into the house. You say that you didn't turn the lights on. Why was that?"

"I thought that if there was an intruder inside I would stand a better chance of apprehending them if they didn't know where I was."

"But you didn't turn the torch off?"

"No."

"Why not?"

Guy Maichment shrugged again, but he was calmer now. He smiled self-depreciatively.

"Scared, I guess. I didn't stop to think it through properly, but I was pretty alarmed. I don't pretend to be a hero."

"Once you were in the house, did you call out to your aunt?"

"No. By then I had already decided that something was wrong."

"Because the door was open?"

"Yes."

"When did you first see the blood – or whatever it is – on the wall?"

"Not until after I came back downstairs. I turned the lights on after I searched the house."

"So you searched the whole house by torchlight?"

"Yes."

"Did you start with the upstairs rooms?"

"Yes."

"Why was that? If there had been an intruder in the house and they were still downstairs, they could either have got away or trapped you. And what about your aunt? You said that she sometimes sleeps all night in a chair. Didn't you think that she might have been doing that last night? In which case, she would have been very frightened if she'd woken up to hear someone moving around upstairs. Much more frightened than if you'd rung the doorbell."

Guy Maichment shot Tim a look of pure loathing. Tim noted that the pupils of his eyes shrank rapidly, while the irises, normally hazel, took on an iridescent yellow hue. The yellow faded as suddenly as it had appeared when Maichment tamed his stare. He evidently hoped that his anger had gone unnoticed. He dropped his gaze and attempted another of his "I-was-doing-my-best-but-was-out-of-my-depth" shrugs. Tim kept his eyes steadfastly fixed on Maichment's face throughout this performance. He was beginning to lose patience. It was clear that the man had something to hide and he was tired of pussyfooting around. He stopped himself from directly challenging Maichment by recalling the day on which Katrin and Juliet Armstrong had each separately told him that he gave himself away too easily. Instead he waited. Guy Maichment compressed his lips, and ran his tongue around the top one. He took another swig from the water-bottle.

"To be honest, I don't know why I went upstairs first. The doors to all the downstairs rooms were closed, and the staircase leads straight up from the hall, as you see. It just seemed the natural thing to do."

"I see. How many rooms are there upstairs?"

"Three. My aunt's bedroom, Jane Halliwell's room and what Claudia calls the box-room. It actually has a single bed in it, but there's a lot of junk in there as well. When guests stay, Jane usually moves out of her room into the box-room for a few nights."

"Isn't there a bathroom?"

"Yes, but it's downstairs; it's part of the extension at the back of the house. As you can imagine, there was no bathroom when the house was built, nor for centuries afterwards, as far as I know. My aunt didn't build the extension herself. I think it was added in the 1930s."

"So you went upstairs, still with the lights off, still shining your torch, and looked in all of the rooms?"

"Yes."

"Which one did you start with?"

"My aunt's bedroom. I knocked on the door and said, 'Claudia, it's me, Guy. Don't be alarmed. I've just come to see that you're all right. May I come in?'"

"Was there any response?"

"Of course there wasn't. As you are perfectly aware, she's disappeared."

"So then you entered the room?"

"Yes. I knocked again, a little louder, and then I went in. I could see immediately that she wasn't in the bed. I walked round the bed, in case she had fallen on to the floor. There's a walk-in cupboard – her 'closet', she calls it – on that side of the room, beyond the window. I opened the door and shone the torch in there as well. I thought there was an outside chance that she might have hidden in there, if she'd been alarmed by something."

Tim nodded.

"And after that?"

"I went into Jane's room. It's much smaller, with no large cupboards, so I just stood in the doorway and swung the torchlight around. I don't think I've been in it once since Jane came to live here, but it is just as I'd expect her room to be: pin-neat, with nothing left out at all. Then the box-room. As I've said, it's full of junk. The bed is made up, but piled with stuff at the moment: it looks like old curtains. And all the usual boxes that my aunt refuses to get rid of. It was pretty obvious that there was no-one lurking in there."

"Then back downstairs again?"

"Yes. I came down the stairs by torchlight and opened the door to the parlour. It was there that I decided to turn on the lights. The parlour is cluttered and I was afraid of tripping over something. In any case, I was pretty convinced by this time that I was alone in the house – though it did cross my mind . . . ." Guy Maichment paused abruptly.

"Go on, Mr Maichment. What crossed your mind?"

"It did occur to me that she might have died, or had a stroke, or something."

"Quite a natural thought. In fact, if it hadn't been for the open door, I'm guessing this would have been the thought uppermost in your mind?"

"Yes, I suppose so."

"So what did you find in the parlour?"

"Nothing unusual at all. My aunt is not a tidy woman; the room looks much as I would have expected it to, especially as she has been on her own this week. But there is no sign of a disturbance, or of her having left in a hurry. The same goes for the other rooms. There is an office leading out of the parlour – I think it was a dining-room in times past – and the extension leads out of the office. It's really just the bathroom and conservatory."

"There must be some kind of kitchen?"

"Yes, but it's separate from the rooms I've just been talking about. You get to it through the other door that leads out of the hall."

"Did you go in there as well?"

Guy Maichment hesitated.

"Not until . . . afterwards."

"After what?"

"I returned to the hall, intending to explore the kitchen, as you suggest. But I was using the lights now. I had to feel along the wall for the hall light – I couldn't remember where the switch was – I know that it is over the little bureau that stands opposite the door, but I couldn't remember exactly where. I found it, anyway, and I was about to go into the kitchen when something made me turn round and look at that wall." He shuddered, a little theatrically, Tim thought.

"What made you turn round, exactly?" Tim asked crisply. "Was it a noise of some kind?"

"Oh, no." Guy Maichment eyed Tim with a contemptuous look which suggested his profound sense of his own superiority. "It was just a feeling. I have always been very sensitive."

"Indeed. So seeing the mess on the wall prevented you from going into the kitchen?"

"It didn't *prevent* me exactly: it just made me focus very clearly on what I ought to do next. I decided to telephone the police immediately."

"Very sensible," said Tim drily. "So you went back into the parlour?"

"Yes. I called nine nine nine. The woman who answered said that what I had told her could not be classed as an emergency as such, but when I mentioned Roy Little she promised to talk to her superior. I must say that Roy called me back very promptly indeed," he added, almost with a simper.

"At what time was this?"

"Do you mean my original call, or Roy's call back?"

"Either or both. From what you say, they were very close together."

"Oh, yes. I didn't look at my watch, but my guess is that it was about 4.30 a.m. While I was making the first call, I could see that the moon was dipping behind the clouds. It rained briefly afterwards."

"Do you own a mobile phone, Mr Maichment?"

"Of course. I carry it with me everywhere. It would be impossible to do my job without it."

"So you had it with you last night?"

"Certainly."

"In that case, why did you use the landline? If I were in someone else's house, even someone I knew quite well, I wouldn't use their phone without their permission unless I had no alternative."

Again the shrug. "Force of habit, I guess. I never use the mobile when I'm at home myself. I suppose it's a kind of hangover from the days when calls on the mobile were much more expensive. Nowadays, of course, they tend to be cheaper than ordinary calls, but one doesn't always think clearly, especially in trying circumstances; one's habits tend to become a little ingrained. Besides, my aunt wouldn't have minded."

He made himself sound like a pensioner, thought Tim, when he was probably fifty at the outside.

"After you made the call, did you just sit and wait until Superintendent Little rang you back? Or did you do something else for however many minutes it was?"

"I just waited. I sat quietly in one of the armchairs. To be honest, I was beginning to feel the effects of all I'd been through up until that point. A kind of dizziness came over me, so I needed to rest. I also wanted to get some instructions about what I should do next," he added virtuously. "I didn't want to do anything that would destroy evidence that might help to find my aunt."

"And after Superintendent Little spoke to you?"

"I remained seated for a while, and then I decided to look in the kitchen. Roy Little said that I should touch as little as possible, but he didn't forbid me from touching anything at all, so I thought it would probably be all right. I must admit to being a bit apprehensive about what I might find in there, and I loitered outside the door for a few seconds before I could pluck up courage to turn the handle. But it was – is – fine. Some of the usual clutter that my aunt creates, but nothing to suggest a struggle."

"And no body lying on the floor?" said Tim, with a hint of satire.

Guy Maichment looked affronted.

"That's in very poor taste, if I may say so. And quite unnecessary. If there had been a body, obviously we wouldn't all be standing here, thinking about what might have become of my aunt. Would we?"

It was on the tip of Tim's tongue to retort that that would depend on whose body it was. He thought better of it, however, in part because he was more interested in the car which he could now hear approaching. He turned to face the track at the same moment as the first glimpse of a small white van appeared through the trees. He recognised it immediately as the vehicle used by Patti Gardner and her team of SOCOs.

CHAPTER FOUR

ALEX SUSTAINED HER veneer of jauntiness as she entered the conference room, though her heart was still quailing at the prospect of the day ahead. She saw that Oliver was already waiting for her. He was sitting at a table near to the podium with his back to her, his long legs stuck out to one side of the table, his fingers absent-mindedly playing with what looked like a piece of plastic. The tables had been arranged 'cabaret style', as the events manager of the hotel had suggested: a break with tradition that had at once appealed to Alex and filled her with alarm when she considered the reaction that it might provoke amongst the old guard.

Oliver turned to look at her as the swing door banged behind her and rose to his feet. He was sucking a sweet. He held out the packet.

"Love hearts," he said, brandishing the twist of transparent paper with which he had been toying. "Why is it that hotels seem to think that conference delegates have suddenly regressed to late toddlerhood and need fortifying with the sort of sweets that one saw on the pocket-money counter of the corner shop, circa 1960? Or is it just the pernicious creeping American influence, do you think, of trivialising everything? Want one?" he added, taking another himself. He scrutinised the inscription on the next sugared sweet in the packet. "Wonder girl," he read. "How appropriate! You must take it now!"

Alex laughed and brushed his hand away.

"Certainly not!" she said. "It's far too early in the day to be eating sweets." She looked around her. "I see that the technicians aren't here yet, despite all the fuss that they made about getting the equipment tested and all the rehearsals over by eight-thirty. I don't suppose you've seen them, have you?"

"No. I've only just arrived myself. I daresay I could switch on the sound system and a mike on my own, though. It can't be that difficult."

"I wouldn't if I were you. They're certain to make us pay if anything gets broken. I suggest we give them another five minutes and then, if they still haven't turned up, I'll go in search of the events manager and ask him to page them. It's the sort of thing that he loves doing: you can just tell."

Oliver scrutinised the love heart again.

"Sure I can't tempt you?" he said. "No, really," said Alex. "To tell you the truth, I felt a little the worse for wear when I got up this morning."

"Indeed?" Oliver's curiosity was almost palpable. "You surprise me! I've always thought of you as being picture-perfect at these events. Overindulgence doesn't fit my notion of you at all."

Alex could not think of a suitably witty riposte, so she didn't reply. She couldn't tell if Oliver's incredulity was genuine; he might well have been mocking her.

"I blame myself, actually," he continued. "I should never have left you in Edmund's clutches. The man is such a bore – in every sense of the word, if one disregards the spelling. He's enough to turn anyone to drink. I do hope that you managed to get rid of him eventually?"

"We spent the night in separate beds, if that's what you mean," said Alex curtly.

Oliver looked abashed. She decided to change the subject.

"Did you ever meet Claudia McRae?" she asked.

"Of course. I went on some of her digs when I was a student. It's funny that you should ask, because, as a matter of fact, she lives close by to here and I dropped in on her yesterday. Why do you mention her? Do you think we should have invited her to the conference? I must admit that it crossed my mind to suggest it, although she is quite frail now and extremely eccentric. Many people feel that her theories have been discredited – including, I am quite certain, some of our esteemed fellow delegates. If she'd come, it could have caused a bit of a ruckus."

"You saw her yesterday?"

"Yes. Only for half an hour or so. I dropped in for a cup of tea, that's all. I've always kept in touch with her, though it must be several years since we last met. You seem surprised."

"You obviously didn't see the news this morning."

"I never watch so-called 'breakfast television'. Another detestable American habit, with a name to match. Why? What did I miss? Something about Claudia?"

"She's disappeared. The police are treating it as suspicious."

"Disappeared! But how could she have? She was at home yesterday, and certainly not planning on going anywhere. In fact, she seemed quite lost – tired out, disorientated, almost – but I put that down to the fact that her paid companion wasn't there. Claudia was always hopeless at practical things, even in her heyday. I had to make tea for her yesterday, because it was clear she was never going to gather herself together enough to make it for me. What you say is worrying. Do you mind if I go to my room to listen to the news headlines? Perhaps I ought to talk to the police as well."

Alex was faintly amused by Oliver's penchant for placing himself in the midst of a drama; she had watched it happen before. She knew from long experience that his sense of theatre could always be relied upon. However, the diversion was short-lived; it did not take her long to realise that Oliver might be right. The police might well want to speak to him.

The swing door banged boisterously. Three men clad in black T-shirts and jeans burst in.

"Hi! I'm Archie, and this here is Baz, and Gully. We're the sound guys. Sorry we're late. Ready to roll now, though."

"If you'll excuse me," said Oliver. "I did get here on time, as you specified, but I'm afraid something rather urgent has come up now that I have to attend to."

Archie looked affronted.

"Suit yourself," he said. "You wanted the rehearsal. Don't blame us if your gig doesn't go according to plan."

"My 'gig', as you put it, might not happen at all if you don't learn to behave with a bit more respect."

The technical team stood and faced him across the expanse of white-cloth'd tables, arms folded, lowering like a bunch of trainee matadors who had just cornered an elderly bull.

Alex put her hand on Oliver's arm.

"Please," she said. "I can see that you're upset, but it's no skin off their nose if the conference goes badly. I don't think you need to rehearse very much; just make sure that your mike is working and adjusted to the right height for you. Then you can go and listen to the next news bulletin on the radio, if that's what you want to do and, if you think it's necessary, call the police. There's plenty of time before we start – until nine-thirty, it's just coffee for people who weren't here last night."

Oliver nodded.

"Sorry," he said. Alex was surprised to see his face contort briefly, as if he might burst into tears. "You're right. I am upset. I'm amazed at how upset, actually. It's not as if Claudia and I are particularly close these days and, God knows, we crossed swords enough times when we were working together. She rarely got on with anyone that she worked with, actually. It's just that – well, she's frail now, and very elderly, and I think sad about what's happened to her reputation. I can't bear the thought of something frightening having happened to her – or, worse, that she's wandered off by herself somewhere and hurt herself or been attacked by some vagrant or something." He smiled briefly. "If I'm honest, I suppose it's myself I'm concerned about, not just Claudia. She represents what I did in my youth, you see; what many of my generation of archaeologists did, in fact, because of her. Whether or not her theories were right – and opinions will always differ on that point – her passing will mark the end of an epoch."

Alex took his hand and held it for a few seconds.

"I think I understand," she said, "but do try to look on the bright side. From what I've heard, she's only missing: there's no evidence to suggest that she's dead or that someone's holding her against her will. I wish I hadn't told you about it, in a way; it might have saved you some worry, if by the time you turn on the radio they're announcing that she's back where she belongs and that the whole episode was a false alarm."

Oliver in turn squeezed her hand and let go of it gently.

"Thank you," he said. "Comforting as ever, Alex. But somehow, this time, I doubt that you're right."

CHAPTER FIVE

IT WAS 12 noon. The clock over the old stable block was cranking its way through twelve strokes, each one accompanied by background whirring noises, as if this might be its last effort before giving up the ghost.

Detective Inspector Tim Yates had already negotiated at some speed the long winding lane that led from the main road to the hotel courtyard, and was now parking his ancient BMW more sedately on the cobbles that fronted the central façade of the building.

The geography of the hotel was confusing. Tim walked around the courtyard once, trying various doors, including one that yielded when he turned the handle but which led only to banked tiers of trestle tables folded flat and towers of chairs stacked six or eight high. Emerging from the courtyard itself, he followed a gravel path which eventually led him to a temporary signpost – it was an aluminium stand of the kind used by musicians – on which someone had wedged a sheet of cardboard with CONFERENCE > RECEPTION printed on it in capital letters. Following the sign, he reached an insignificant wooden door which, when he passed through it, brought him immediately into a vast mock-mediaeval hall. A staircase and various passageways led out of it.

Set squarely in the middle of the flagged stone floor, dwarfed by its surroundings, was one of the hotel's evidently ubiquitous trestle tables. A banner bearing the words *Spalding Archaeological Society* had been unfurled behind it. On the table itself were arranged the few name badges left for latecomers to the conference. The many gaps between them indicated that most of the delegates had already registered.

An epicene little man was seated behind the table. He rose when he saw Tim, scrutinised the policeman's face and frowned.

"Can I help you? I'm not sure that we've met."

"I'm quite certain that we haven't. I'm Detective Inspector Yates, South Lincolnshire Police."

The little man's freckled face broke into a smile.

"Oh! That's a relief. I was wondering if I'd left someone out. When I was making the name badges, I mean. One does check the list very carefully, of course, but these things happen and I'm positive that I'm acquainted with all the delegates who have yet to arrive. Wing-Commander Francis

Codd," he added, extending his hand. "Retired now, of course. I like to help out on these occasions."

Tim took the proffered hand and shook it briefly.

"But, dear me," said the Wing-Commander, frowning again, "Police, you say? I do hope that nothing is wrong." He gestured at the remaining name badges. "There hasn't been an accident, has there? No-one delayed because they've been hurt?"

"Not as far as I know," said Tim. "I've come at the request of one of the delegates, Oliver Sparham. Do you know him?"

"Yes, of course I do. He has kindly agreed to act as our Chairman today. And he is always a very active member of the society. Most generous with his time."

"Could I speak to Mr Sparham? I'd ask you to take me to him, but it would probably be less disruptive if we could talk here."

"What? Yes. But no: the final session before lunch is in full swing, and Oliver is chairing it, as I said. Would you mind terribly if I asked you to wait for a few minutes? I can hardly drag the poor man off the stage."

Tim was still debating with himself about how he should respond to this when the heavy swing doors to the right of the Wing-Commander opened and a slender, dark-haired woman emerged from the passageway beyond.

"Oh, Mrs Tarrant, how opportune! This is a policeman who wants to speak to Oliver. I've explained that he is busy at the moment. Do you know when he might be available?"

The slight woman moved rapidly over the stone flagstones towards Tim, her high heels clicking in a businesslike way. She, too, held out her hand, which Tim noticed was very small, and adorned with a narrow wedding-band on which sat another, broader, ring in which was set a single, pale, square-cut blue stone: an aquamarine, perhaps.

"Inspector Yates? I'm Alexandra Tarrant, the secretary of the Archaeological Society. Oliver is expecting you; he's told me why he asked you to come. He has just introduced the final speaker of the morning, so his formal duties are over until after lunch. I'll fetch him. We placed his chair as near to the edge of the stage as possible, so that he would be able to slip away quite discreetly. Fortunately, Dr Pfleger is showing some slides at the moment, so the room is in semi-darkness."

Tim nodded.

"Thank you. It is very considerate of you."

She had clear grey eyes set in an oval face, with a slightly turned-up nose and small but determined chin. She looked a little weary, he thought, but she was very pretty.

"Not at all," she said. "I don't know Claudia McRae myself, but many of our delegates do. Naturally, they are shocked by what they've heard on the news and, if any of them can help you, they will certainly want to do so. Oliver was an assistant of hers when he was a young man. He thought that you'd like to know that he saw her yesterday."

"He's right about that, of course. He may have been the last person to see her before she disappeared."

There was a small silence, after which she laughed nervously.

"That's what Oliver himself said. I'll fetch him now."

"Thank you."

As her clicking heels retreated, Tim turned his attention towards the Wing-Commander again. Since the latter had clearly not been warned in advance of his visit and therefore was also not aware of its purpose, he expected the old man to be agog with curiosity. Not so. Francis Codd was now bent forward, tranquilly engaged in arranging the remaining name badges in a neat row with no gaps, and in the process displaying the mass of overlapping freckles that topped his round, bald head. He had either been unable to hear the interchange between Tim and Alex Tarrant or had discreetly refrained from listening to it.

Alex Tarrant returned quickly. A tall man loped in her wake. He had thick, greying hair and the slightly stooped posture that is common in the very tall. He wore round, gold-rimmed spectacles, from behind which twinkled intelligent, even humorous, light-brown eyes. He, too, extended his hand. Tim took it.

"Oliver Sparham."

"Mr Sparham," Tim said. "Thank you for calling me."

An observant man, thought Tim, and not a killer. He had wondered: the old policeman's adage, that the last person to have admitted to seeing a victim alive was probably also their killer, was not so much a cliché as a truism. There was a certain type of killer who could not resist involving himself in the subsequent police investigation, no matter how dangerous to himself this might be. Oliver Sparham was not such a person; Tim would stake his life on it, even though he had only just met the man. He caught his breath inwardly, even so, for he had just admitted two things to himself: firstly, that he believed that Claudia McRae was dead and secondly that she had been murdered.

"Should we sit down?"

"If you'll excuse me," Alex Tarrant said with a smile, "I really need to get back."

Tim indicated a cluster of rather ugly, 1960s-style square leather chairs that had been arranged around a huge inglenook fireplace. It was the most comfortable-looking area in the massive room, and had the added advantage of being out of earshot of Francis Codd.

As if he could read his mind, Oliver Sparham said:

"You don't need to worry about old Frank. He lives in a world of his own most of the time. He likes a life of complete order. If he finds it hard

to cope with the idea of a policeman disrupting the serenity of the conference, he'll just edit it out; pretend it's not happening. He certainly won't
want to confront the idea of Claudia's disappearance."

Tim smiled. He was rather warming to Oliver Sparham.

"Did – does – he know her?"

"I expect so. He's been interested in archaeology all of his life, so she
must have crossed his path at some point, even though she has not had
dealings with our society for many years."

Tim nodded. He made a mental note to return later to that: throwaway
comment or useful clue?

"It was very good of you to contact us about your visit to Miss McRae.
It could make a great deal of difference to whether she is found safe and
well or not. People often don't realise the significance of something they
have heard or seen in relation to a missing person or a crime, or they only
think about it weeks after the event, when the police have found out for
themselves – or not, of course. In either case, it is often too late."

Oliver shrugged.

"I take that as a compliment. Thank you."

"What is your job, Mr Sparham?"

"I'm terribly sorry, didn't I say? If I'd been calling you from work, I
should have introduced myself straight away. I'm the County Archaeologist for Lincolnshire. Not every county has one: just those with outstanding monuments, or where there have been significant archaeological digs.
Lincolnshire has always been of pivotal strategic importance, because of
its long coast line and, from the Middle Ages, the sheep farming. Lincoln
was a very important city six hundred years ago; and a little after that,
incredible though it may seem now, the port of Boston was one of the
four wealthiest in the country. My office has supervised some exciting
digs in recent years that demonstrate the county's importance before it
even existed as such. We have excavated a Roman villa near Fishtoft and
a mediaeval merchant's house in Kirton. Then there are the gravel pits
near Maxey, which have yielded up the remains of woolly mammoths
and some quite interesting flint implements. But the real reason that my
post continues to exist, especially in this time of local authority spending
cuts, is because of the power and prestige of the Spalding Archaeological
Society. It was founded in the seventeenth century by some eminent clergymen scholars and supported financially by a number of rich gentleman
dilettantes. Among them was one of my ancestors, as a matter of fact.
Perhaps because of its age, and certainly because of its long association
with some of the country's most brilliant scientists and historians – Isaac
Newton was a member – as an organisation it still carries a lot of clout in
archaeological circles."

"That's the society whose conference this is?"

"Yes. I'm not one of its employees – in fact it only has one paid employee, Mrs Tarrant, whom you've just met – but I'm expected to work closely with it. There are others employed by the local authority who interact with it as well as me. One of them is a colleague whom I've known since we were both students. His name is Edmund Baker. He works in the architect's department. He's the Heritage Officer; it covers a broader remit than just archaeological sites. Part of his job is to slap preservation orders on buildings of historical or architectural interest, to make sure that people don't tear them down or stick plastic conservatories on them, that sort of thing. He's currently President of the Society – each president assumes the role for a three-year period, though they can be invited to serve for a second term. Edmund is quite new in the post, as a matter of fact. The role is quasi-executive – more than honorary, but it carries no fee. "

"Interesting. And is Dame Claudia a member of the Archaeological Society?"

"As a woman, she can't be a full member. I think that she must have been an honorary member in the past, but, quite frankly, Claudia and organised groups of any kind just don't mix. She can pick a fight with a paper bag; or could, perhaps I should say."

"We have no proof that she is . . ."

"Oh, good God, I didn't mean that. Heaven forbid. It's just that when I saw Claudia yesterday, some of the fight seemed to have gone out of her. Of course, she is very old now."

"Tell me about your visit yesterday."

"Yes; that is why you've come, isn't it? I'm sorry; I seem to have sidetracked you with a lot of other stuff."

"On the contrary, it is I who have been asking the questions. It's always useful to get a feel for the background of a victim, or someone who's disappeared for no apparent reason. As you yourself have realised, what you have to tell me about yesterday might be important; there may be some detail that you can recall which will lead us straight to her, or at least explain why she has gone."

Oliver frowned.

"It's hard to believe that, much as I would like to. It was such a banal sort of meeting. I just dropped in for tea and a chat, you know. But I'll try to remember the minutiae, if you think that will help."

"Did she know that you were coming? Was she expecting you?"

"Yes and no. I phoned her only an hour or so before I got there; just before I left the office, actually. I worked until lunchtime yesterday. To be honest, I'd been in two minds about going to see her at all; I didn't know if she knew about the conference and I thought that if I were the one to tell her about it she might be upset that she hadn't been invited as a guest speaker or something. But the opportunity to call in on her was too good to miss. I was close to her at one time, a sort of pupil of hers, and I'm quite aware that even Claudia can't go on forever. She must be into her nineties now."

"Ninety-three, I believe. So, although it was a last-minute decision, you didn't decide to surprise her?"

"No. Old people don't like surprises, do they? And I thought that she might have been working on something, old though she is. She still publishes the odd paper. I like to respect people's working time. I get very annoyed myself when I am disturbed if it scuppers my plans to get something done."

"How did she sound on the phone?"

"Just the same as usual: Booming, mannish voice; a little combative, but her fierceness was directed not at me but at a kind of confusion that was frustrating her. Pleased to hear from me, I think; she made no attempt to discourage me, which she certainly would have done if I'd been unwelcome. She warned me that she'd been on her own for a few days and that the place was in a bit of a mess. She said that she couldn't cope with housework in the way that she used to. I thought that she probably meant this as a joke. Claudia has never been the slightest bit interested in things domestic, aside from her immediate creature comforts and, as far as I can recollect, she always used to live in a tip. Even on digs she was messier and more chaotic than most people."

"And when you arrived?"

"The state of the house wasn't too bad at all. I'd been prepared for some real squalor, but there was only surface untidiness. I put that down to the companion's influence. Jane something."

"Jane Halliwell. Do you know her?"

"No. Claudia said that she was some sort of academic, though not, I think, an archaeologist. I forget her subject: current affairs or something like it. Anyway, she doesn't do it any more. She's given it up to look after Claudia. If you didn't know Claudia, you might think the woman was on the make."

"Why do you say that?"

"Well, Claudia's not short of a bob or two, you know. Aside from what she's made from her lectures and writing, her father left her quite a lot of money. He was a barrister, I think. However, I'd say that Claudia's much too astute to be taken in by a confidence trickster; but what I mainly meant was that no-one would take Claudia on unless they really cared for her. The task would be too daunting!"

Tim grinned.

"So – tell me what happened when you first arrived. Did you ring the doorbell?"

"I didn't need to. It was a sunny day and the door was wide open.

Actually, Claudia had told me that it would be; I forgot that until just now. It didn't surprise me; I think she's a little claustrophobic. Years of living outside. And she's probably not as steady on her pins as she was, so not having to answer the door would have been easier for her, and possibly less embarrassing. She's very proud. She'd told me to go straight in, so I did. I just knocked once on her sitting-room door, for form's sake, and went in."

"Had you been to the cottage before?"

"No. Claudia's been living there for only a few years. The last time I saw her she still had the town house in Stamford."

"How did you know which was the door to the sitting-room?"

Oliver shrugged.

"There were only three doors leading out of the hall. I just chose the one on the left. If it had been the wrong one, I would have tried the others."

"So you went straight into the room and she was already there? Did you notice anything unusual about the hall, on your way in?"

"Yes, I went straight in, and no, I didn't. Did I miss something? I'm usually quite observant."

"Not as far as I know. I was just checking – since the door had been left open." The police had not included information about the spray of blood on the hall wall in the news bulletins that they had issued. Tim debated confiding in Oliver Sparham and immediately rejected the idea. The fewer people who knew about it the better, at least until they had established whose blood it was. Besides, there was no point in distressing him unnecessarily.

Oliver Sparham paused, and then continued.

"It struck me as being quite dark in there, especially at first, because I'd just walked out of bright sunlight. But I saw her immediately. She was sitting in an armchair by the fireplace. She has a very distinctive profile: a massive, square face, with thick hair cut short, almost like a man's old-fashioned short back and sides, and a very short neck. But you'll have seen the photographs."

Tim nodded.

"Her head was drooped forward a little, but she lifted it with a jerk when she heard the click of the latch on the door. I suppose she had been dozing. I remember thinking that there was not much wrong with her hearing. She had a stick propped against the chair and grabbed it. I could see that she was struggling to get to her feet, so I told her to stay where she was. I must say that it was a shock, seeing her so immobile."

"You told her to stay where she was? Were those the exact words that you used?"

"No, of course not. I said, 'Dear Claudia, please don't get up for me.' Then I went across to take both of her hands and I bent down to kiss her."

"What did she say to you?"

"Something quite clichéd, I think: 'Oliver, it's been too long', or something like that."

"And how did she seem?"

"Quite different from how I remembered her from the last occasion on which we'd met, yet just the same, if that doesn't sound too ridiculous. She was as physically robust as ever in appearance – one would say 'overweight', if one wished to be unkind – but she seemed frail, somehow. I don't mean her obvious difficulty with walking. It was more of a mental weakness. She wasn't as certain as she'd always been whenever I'd been with her before. The Claudia I know has always dealt in absolutes. She was famous, as you're probably aware, for sticking to her opinions and defending them against all comers. Not that we discussed much to do with work, either hers or mine, but I sensed a hesitancy in her, a diffidence, that I would never have expected to encounter. It was as if she no longer trusted herself. And yet there was that underlying anger that I've also mentioned. Am I making sense?"

"Not especially, though I think I do understand the contradictions that you are trying to convey. What exactly did you talk about? The surface conversation, I mean."

"She asked me about the conference. I felt a bit embarrassed, to be honest: to have had an eminent archaeologist on our doorstep and not to have invited her even to part of it, seemed to me to have been a breach of etiquette. But I have to admit that I didn't suggest it to Alex when she was putting the programme together and she is almost certainly too young to have known anything of Claudia beyond what she may have read in a few outdated textbooks when she was a student. By the time that Alex went to university, Claudia was well on her way to being marginalised – though not by everyone, of course. She had and still has – will always have, in all probability – her supporters."

"Ah, now that does interest me. I've heard this said several times now: that her views have become 'marginalised'. What exactly does that mean?"

"I don't know how interested you are in archaeology, Detective Inspector, but the best way I can describe it is as a never-ending jigsaw puzzle. If you're lucky, you find a few pieces that fit together. More frequently, you find one or two tantalising pieces that seem to belong together, yet present so many contradictions that you're not sure. Perhaps worst of all, you may find some pieces of a puzzle that someone else has already tried to assemble – it may have been half a century ago, or even several generations since – and you are either seduced by their theories, thus reducing your ability to work out your own independently, or you're utterly convinced that they are wrong and develop a new theory which flies in the face of all that they have said. Then you are bedevilled by the fact that their version is the accepted one, and the one that appears in all the books. And then there is the curse of history, of documentary evidence, patchy though it often is as far as archaeology is concerned. As I'm sure you are aware, not all documentary evidence provides a correct, unvarnished version of the truth; it is more likely to be the version that its author was anxious to sell to posterity."

"As it happens, I do understand what you're talking about, even if I operate from the other side of the fence: I studied history at university. It is, as Churchill pointed out, usually written by the victors."

"Yes – or by the 'church victorious'."

"Indeed. But how does Claudia McRae – who was elevated to the title of Dame Claudia, after all, and whom one might therefore assume to have been received into the ranks of the Establishment at some point – fit in with all of this? She was hardly an outsider by the end of her career, was she?"

"Not in the sense that you mean. But you have to take into account the period at which Claudia became an archaeologist and how archaeology has since developed, as a discipline and as a science, during her working life. Claudia was remarkable for breaking into what until then had largely been a man's world, for developing a theory that enabled archaeological classification to run side by side with what we know of the development of languages and even for helping to build that seductive bridge between archaeology and history which eludes most archaeologists, by offering a means through which its links with history can be explored."

"But? I'm sure that there is a but in all of this?"

"But Claudia is of her time, nevertheless. Although she was not a plunderer in the material sense, she belongs more to the era of Lord Caernarvon and Howard Carter than to the school of academically-educated archaeologists, myself included, who came to the subject in the 50s, 60s and 70s or later. Claudia has had little formal education and certainly never studied at a university. That doesn't mean that she isn't intelligent; she has a formidable intelligence, but hers is not a trained mind. By this I mean that she has not been schooled to think in the same way as the last two generations of archaeologists have been taught. I should perhaps add here, for better or for worse. What I am trying to say is that although Claudia developed some fascinating theories – such ingenious ones, indeed, that they took the world by storm – she cut corners in a way that probably did not strike her as being intellectually dishonest. She did not exactly fabricate evidence, but she did tend to ignore things that did not fit in with the pieces of the jigsaw that she had discovered; and she was fiercely protective of her ideas once they had been published. If anyone challenged them, she took it as a personal affront. Claudia is a prima donna. She doesn't want to be involved in collaborative effort, however prestigious it may be; she has to be the celebrity, the person at the head of it all. As she has grown older, she has seen it as her right to exist as a living legend, immune to any kind of questioning or scrutiny."

"Do you think that the attitude that you describe could have created real enemies? People who would dislike her enough to want to hurt her?"

"Not physically hurt her, no. Marginalise her, certainly. But Claudia has effectively marginalised herself. As I've said, she's not a team player and she has not attended conferences and symposia for a very long time. Archaeologists are notorious for not writing up accounts of their field-work, so if you take yourself off the lecture circuit, you quickly lose touch with what is going on."

"Though you say she was interested in the conference that's happening here?"

"In a sort of way. She knows a lot of the people who are here, myself and Edmund included. And she was curious about Alex, the secretary of the Archaeological Society and our conference organiser, as you know – but mainly I suspect because she doesn't know her. If she was interested in seeing the conference programme itself, she didn't say so."

"What else did you talk about?"

"Most of the conversation was about people that we both know, but it progressed in a very desultory sort of way. She seemed confused. She muddled me with Edmund several times. And she kept on closing her eyes. She offered me tea on at least three separate occasions; the third time, I got up and made it myself, and some for her, too. That may have been her intention all along, perhaps, but I don't think so: it was more as if she were running through the social niceties because she remembered them, but without any idea of how to carry them through; a bit as if she were drugged. She could have been taking some kind of medication, I suppose."

"Did she at any point indicate that she intended to leave the cottage?"

"Not at all. She was anticipating Jane Halliwell's return this weekend. She was really looking forward to it. I asked if anyone was helping her in the meantime and she said that her nephew was 'keeping an eye out', whatever that means."

"She didn't say anything else about her nephew?"

"No."

"Does anything at all out of the ordinary spring to mind? Did she talk of anyone else, or receive any calls while you were there?"

"No; no-one; and no. My whole time there could barely have exceeded forty minutes. I couldn't stay longer. I'd promised Alex that I'd get to the hotel by late afternoon to help here with various things and I'd already left the office much later than I'd intended."

"How did you part?"

"I kissed her again and she gave me a quick peck in return. Claudia was never very tactile or emotionally demonstrative. I said that I would keep in touch better than I had in recent years and make sure that I saw her again this year. She just nodded. Nothing seemed to exercise her mind especially, except having the front door left open. She particularly asked me not to close it. She became quite agitated at the thought that I might forget."

"I see. I assume that you did leave it open?"

"Yes, I did."

"And you came straight here to the hotel afterwards?"

"Yes."

"At what time did you arrive here?"

"If that monstrosity of a clock in the courtyard is correct, it was at exactly 5 p.m. The clock was striking as I parked the car."

"Thank you. Is there anything else at all that you can think of that might help us to find Dame Claudia?"

"Not offhand. If there were anything, of course I should tell you. I'd like to see her safely restored to her friend and nephew as much as you would."

"I have no doubt of that, Mr Sparham. May I give you my card? If anything else should cross your mind that you think might be even remotely useful, please let me know."

CHAPTER SIX

ALEX'S DAY HAD taken on a surreal hue. First of all she had awoken barely able to recollect the events of the night before, grateful not to find Edmund lying beside her in the bed; then she had had to prepare for the main day of the conference with a debilitating hangover, which she had just about managed to overcome when she had had to calm Oliver down enough to persuade him not to abandon his role as chairman; finally, there had been the whole Claudia McRae business. It was true that the morning's programme had run reasonably smoothly, but there had been a listlessness, almost a mass depression, hanging over the proceedings. All of the delegates were in a subdued mood following the news of Dame Claudia's disappearance, so that the morning had gone like clockwork in more ways than one: according to plan, but mechanically, as if everyone were merely going through the motions. Finally, just before lunch, Oliver's policeman had arrived. Now lunchtime itself was upon her and she knew that she was going to have to face up to Edmund.

She had caught his eye across the 'cabaret-style' tables once or twice that morning. The first time he had looked away quickly, clearly embarrassed. The second time he had beamed at her an imploring smile, his blue eyes as open and bashful as an errant schoolboy's.

Even more bizarrely, 'boy' was how he actually referred to himself when they each forced themselves to talk. It was during the ten minutes or so between the last session and lunch, a mini-networking break which most of the delegates used for one single purpose only. Indefatigable topers as they were, three quarters of them had hurried or drifted towards the bar, an extended arrangement set up especially for the conference which ran the full extent of the main residents' lounge. She spotted Edmund sitting at one of the tables farthest from the bar, peering into his laptop. Quietly she moved across the room and sat down next to him.

He looked up as if startled, though she was pretty certain that he had been aware of her as soon as she entered the room. He flashed her another sheepish grin and then stared back into the depths of the computer screen again, as if his life depended on what he saw there.

" 'Never apologise, never explain,' as my mother used to say," he whispered, his voice almost too low for her to hear. "Nevertheless, I am sorry," he added, "and I want you to know that I am not a bad boy."

Alex shrugged in a way that she recognised as theatrical.

"We should forget about it," she said. "Put it down to the fact that we'd both had too much to drink."

Edmund bristled.

"I wasn't that far gone," he said. She didn't know whether he was defending his ability to take his liquor, or whether he did really . . . what? . . . 'fancy' her? Sincerely wish to have an affair with her? Or an even more serious relationship? Or was this just his way of beating a retreat with as much dignity as he could scrape together?

She looked across at his computer.

"What are you doing?" she asked.

"Writing my annual report. An interminable process, always, but it's been particularly bad this year. It's riddled with politics – not so much about what we have achieved, but what we *could* have achieved if we'd had more money. But I've got to include plenty about what we *have* done, as well: this government's not so much interested in checking that value for money has been delivered as in clawing money back, but if it has any suspicion that the former is in doubt, it will have no compunction in swooping down on the modest funds that we're allowed. Why do you ask?" he added.

Alex smiled inwardly. It was obvious that she was making small-talk, trying to get them over the awkwardness of the night before.

"No reason. I just wondered why you had to spend every spare moment of the conference working. What's that?" she added, as his screen-saver flashed on.

"It's a motor-bike; one which I am almost certainly going to buy."

"A motor-bike!"

"You don't need to sound quite so surprised. I rode one when I was young."

"Sorry! But that *is* why I'm surprised. People do ride them when they're young. Then they have children . . ."

"Grow up, you mean? Or alternatively die on them, in some cases." He chuckled sardonically. "You're right, of course. It's just a silly whim and I'm not going to try to defend it. It's something that I want to do, though, and that I *am* going to do," he added defensively, as if rehearsing what he would say to someone who might try to stop him.

"What does your wife think?"

"Krystyna? She isn't very happy about it, but mainly because of the expense. I've told her that I will pay for it by backing horses, though, which has mollified her a little."

"Backing horses?" said Alex, trying not to sound astonished. She was really shocked this time. She knew it was prim of her, but it was the way that she had been brought up. Backing horses was sinful, according to her

parents: the way of the devil. No good could come of it. She began to see
Edmund in a new light. Beneath that respectable, boring exterior there was
evidently an edgy degeneracy, a desire to flirt with seediness, that made him
seem almost dangerous. She was half-appalled, half-fascinated.

"I see that you're scandalised," he said. "For that, I do apologise."
She felt foolish.

"I'm not scandalised," she said, "but I need to adjust my ingrained prejudices slightly. My family were Methodists: swearing, drinking, smoking
and gambling were all regarded as the handiwork of the Devil. Gambling,
especially. I was taught that it was a pernicious habit and bound to lead
to misery."

"Well, that's not far wrong, actually," said Edmund reflectively.
"Krystyna would certainly agree with you."

Suddenly Alex felt queasy. She didn't want to know any more about
Edmund's louche hobbies. She changed the subject.

"I didn't know that your wife's name was Christina," she said. "I always
thought that it was Christine. It's a beautiful name: poetic. It reminds me
of Christina Rossetti."

"It's not spelt like that, unfortunately. Krystyna is Polish. Her name is
spelt with a 'k' and two 'y's.

"Quite exotic, then."

"Perhaps, though you probably wouldn't think her so if you met her.
There are three of them, actually: Krystyna and her sister Birte, and a
brother, Tomas. And they have an aged mother, Jelena, who is still alive.
The two girls are very exercised about Jelena's welfare. They try to rope
Tomas in, but he is an evasive character: they give him tasks to carry out
and, if he doesn't want to do them, he simply disappears. They're not an
odd family, exactly, but they find it hard to fit in. Living in this country,
I mean."

"I see," said Alex, though she was finding this conversation increasingly perplexing. Talking to Edmund was like peeling away the layers of
an onion: he was dull, then amorous, importunate, then conciliatory, then
'wicked' and, finally, a man who spoke of his wife in a curiously detached
way, as if she were a rather unsatisfactory specimen that he had been asked
to dissect. He did not heed the edge that had crept in to Alex's voice.

"It's not her fault, of course," he continued. "It's the clash of cultures.
It's not so much that she can't cope, as that she feels compromised. You
can see it sometimes when there's a conversation going on. You look at
her, and she's genuinely puzzled, as if she's contributing to the dialogue,
but not part of it, if you understand me. As if she's saying what she thinks
she ought to say, for form's sake."

Alex nodded. She could understand what he was saying now. What
remained difficult, alienating, even, was his apparent detachment from

his marriage. She supposed that this conversation – it was in truth more of a monologue – could have been prompted by a not particularly subtle attempt by Edmund to indicate that he was still available, to demonstrate that he was willing to pick up from where they had left off last night. But instinct told her that this was not correct. His next comment, murmured sotto voce to himself, confirmed her in this belief. It was more as if he were trying to work out the place that he had reached in life, to comprehend how he had arrived at where he now found himself.

"She is a very pretty woman. She was beautiful in her day. We were both in our thirties when we met, both thinking it was time we married. And she wanted children. Why she couldn't find someone else to give them to her, I'll never quite be sure."

"Are you going in to lunch?"

Alex flinched, startled, while Edmund, still lost in whatever reverie he had just conjured up, looked up vacantly, his blue eyes clouded with some less than satisfactory thought. It was Oliver, leaning in to them across the wings of Alex's lounge bar chair.

"Oh, Oliver, you made me jump!" she said, as lightly as she could. "Has your policeman gone?"

"Which policeman?" asked Edmund truculently. "Why are the police here?"

"Yes, he's gone," said Oliver. "Nothing to concern yourself about, Edmund. He only came because I happened to call in on Claudia yesterday on my way here. I thought that the police should know that I had visited her, as it was so close to the time at which she disappeared. But I daresay I wasn't much help really."

"Oh, God, yes – Claudia. I'd almost forgotten the reason for the lingering malaise that seems to have taken over this conference," said Edmund spitefully.

"I wouldn't go so far as to say that," said Oliver, looking at Alex's stricken face. "It has an excellent programme. It has delivered all that was expected of it so far. It's just that the delegates are understandably melancholy about Claudia. Most of us have met her, after all, and some of us – like you and me – know her very well. When did you last see her, incidentally?"

"Oh, how should I know?" asked Edmund crossly. He packed up his computer, shoving it and its power supply untidily into his holdall, got up and headed for the French windows which led to the terrace outside. He stumped off, trailing his gammy leg slightly.

Oliver sighed.

"Curmudgeonly as always, I see, but at least he's running true to form. Shall we go into lunch?"

CHAPTER SEVEN

IT WAS FIVE-THIRTY that afternoon and Alex was back in her room at last. She hoped that she might slip into bed to take a few minutes' sleep before the conference dinner and then thought better of it. Her hangover had disappeared completely, but in its wake had left her in the grip of such intense fatigue that she feared that if she were to lie down she would not wake again that day.

Instead, she decided to call Tom. She was feeling guilty about him, although logically speaking there was no need, aside from her having failed to reach him yesterday evening. It was not her fault, after all, that Edmund had tried to seduce her, nor had it been the first time during her marriage that she had been propositioned. She and Tom had laughed about some of the other occasions. She wondered if she would tell Tom about Edmund and decided that probably she wouldn't.

She took her mobile from her handbag and was surprised to see the display light up before she had pressed the keys. It was Tom, calling her first – a rare event, as the received view in the Tarrant household was that she should always be responsible for their calls when they were separated.

"Everything OK?" he said. Usually, that was her question; in fact, often Tom couldn't wait for her to get off the phone.

"Yes," she said cautiously. "Why do you ask?"

"No reason – except that some female archaeologist has disappeared. The news has been full of it. I thought that it might be one of your lot."

"Well, she isn't one of 'my lot', as you put it," she snapped, exasperated, "though some of the delegates do know her – as you would expect."

"There's no need to get shirty. It's not my fault if I don't understand who's in and who's out in your crowd. Put a bit of a dampener on the conference, has it?"

She listened carefully to the tone of his voice and decided that he was trying to show sympathy rather than to exult.

"Not really. Well, yes, I suppose it has, in a way. Everyone's very subdued."

"From what you've told me about some of those malevolent old men, it's probably not a bad thing."

"What sort of a day did you have?"

"A difficult one, since you ask. You remember that I told you about the Herrick Old House scheme?"

"Vaguely," said Alex, wracking her brains. "It's a work creation scheme, isn't it? For juvenile delinquents?"

"That's more or less right, though we don't use the term 'juvenile delinquents' any more. It was the brainchild of Lord Herrick after his son died of a drugs overdose. Its aim is to help young people, particularly those who have admitted that they have drugs problems. It's a foundation that he's set up in conjunction with opening the other Herrick House – the one he lives in – to the public. The outbuildings have been completely restored and Herrick House now has a working home farm, buttery, stables and laundry. Young people are trained in the traditional skills needed to run these facilities. They then either give demonstrations on the estate when the house is open or work in the facilities when the house is closed. The estate sells the produce and services, mostly to the local community, but sometimes to shops and enterprises further afield. The young people are paid proper wages for their efforts, even though it's not usually much above the legal minimum. Lord Herrick is planning to extend the scheme to the gardens once renovation work in them has been completed."

"It all sounds wonderful – exemplary paternalism which presumably creates some kind of income for his lordship in the process. So what's the problem?"

"There's no problem with the scheme as such. It was a brilliant Idea, and one that is being monitored with the intention of rolling out similar plans elsewhere in the country. My problem is that I sent two of my most promising lads to work on the home farm and they've now been discovered to be in possession of Ecstasy – and not only that, but allegedly caught trying to sell it to some of the visitors to the attraction."

Alex giggled.

"That was very enterprising of them!"

"For God's sake, Alex, it's not like you to be so irresponsible! You know how serious this is, especially for kids who already have a record. These two are both on probation. They'll probably get custodial sentences now. And, needless to say, his Lordship wants to ban them from his property. They'll certainly never be allowed to set foot on the Herrick Estate again and, in all probability, neither will anyone else recommended by the youth service."

"Sorry," said Alex. "I didn't mean to laugh. It's been a strange day. Is there anything you can do to mollify Lord Herrick? Do you know how they came by the drugs? Can it be explained as a temporary lapse?"

"That's part of the problem. They both swear blind that they had no knowledge of the drugs, which were found in their rucksacks, and therefore can't explain how they got them. Typical responsibility-evading replies, I know, but I'm disappointed even so; particularly with the elder of the two: I'd have expected better of him. They weren't actually caught in the act of selling the drugs, but they were packaged for the street, apparently in a very professional way. "

"How was it discovered?"

"Just during a routine search. A random check is carried out on two or three of the trainees every day. It was one of the conditions that Lord Herrick laid down when he set up the foundation."

"So they would have known that the chances of their being caught were high?"

"Yes, they knew the score. All of the trainees go through an induction process at the Centre, and a further refresher session when they actually start work on the estate."

"And you say that at least one of them now normally behaves responsibly. How bright are they?"

"Better than average. I hand-picked them and a few others because the scheme has only just started and I wanted to choose kids who'd make a good impression."

"Well, either they aren't such reformed characters as you'd thought, or they're telling the truth. From what you say, there's a fifty-fifty chance of either. If I were you, I wouldn't assume automatically that they are lying. Stranger things have happened than kids having drugs planted on them."

"You sound like the Delphic Oracle! But thanks for the advice. It's not like me not to keep an open mind, as you know, but I've been so disappointed, not to say embarrassed, over this that I may have allowed my own feelings to cloud my judgment. I'm not going to be able to budge Lord Herrick unless I can find some concrete evidence of their innocence. And I can't for the life of me think what anyone could hope to gain from planting the drugs on them. When are you coming home, by the way?" he asked, audibly brightening up as he changed the subject.

"I should be back by tomorrow lunchtime. It's the conference dinner tonight and the AGM tomorrow morning first thing. I'm planning to cut it as short as possible and I'm guessing that in any case the delegates won't want to spin it out. Their current mood is too downbeat. They'll probably all have left the hotel by about 10 a.m. I've got a few things to sort out after that, but I should be able to get away myself by soon after eleven; and the drive back shouldn't take much more than three quarters of an hour."

"You're surely not planning to work at the Society tomorrow afternoon?"

"No, but I need to call in briefly, to return some stands and things. After that, I shall come home to work."

"Meet me for lunch? At the White Hart? You seem to have been gone

for ages and I can afford to take a longer lunch break than usual tomorrow."

Alex tried not to sigh aloud. It was flattering that Tom was missing her,
but at the moment she felt that she would never want to eat – or drink –
again. And she knew that having to sit through the protracted rituals of the
conference dinner this evening would not improve her mood.

"Would you mind if we just both went home? I'll pick some things up
from the delicatessen on the way."

"OK, sure, if that's what you'd prefer," said Tom. He sounded surprised
rather than offended. "I'll see you here, then, at around one o'clock?"

"That should be fine," said Alex wearily. "I've got to go now. I need
to change."

"Don't let me keep you. I love you. Take care."

"You, too," said Alex, as she put the phone down.

She peeled off the navy blue suit, and let it drop to the floor. She was
about to head for the shower when she realised that her bedroom curtains
had not been drawn. Although she may have been protected from view
by the floor-length nets, they were pretty sheer, and she suspected that,
as it was almost dark, it would be possible for someone standing outside
to see into the room now that she had switched on the lights. Quickly
she snapped the lights off again and went to draw the heavy drapes. She
noticed that the french windows were still open a few inches. She didn't
close them; she would be bound to feel hot when she returned from the
dinner. She leaned briefly into the dusky evening, enjoying the rush of cold
air on to her face. As she did so, she became aware of something moving
in the courtyard below. Quickly, she stepped to the other window to get a
clearer view, but whatever it was had disappeared around the side of the
building before she could glimpse it again.

CHAPTER EIGHT

THE SEARCH OF the woods that surrounded Dame Claudia's house yielded no spectacular results – no knife bearing whomever's blood was smeared across her hall wall, no discarded clothing in the undergrowth. Unless it had been buried very deep and the freshly-dug soil camouflaged so expertly that it could escape the noses of sniffer dogs, there was no body. One or two small items had been found which probably were not related to her disappearance: a black leather button with long tails of thread attached to it and a badge depicting a swastika. Tim thought that the latter might have been lost from a child's dressing-up kit, but he sent it for analysis, anyway. He asked Juliet to try to find out what sort of garment the button had been torn from. On the whole, the search had been disappointing.

Since they could not obtain primary evidence that might help to explain why Dame Claudia had vanished, Tim determined to gather more background stuff. He was beginning to realise that they did not have enough objective information about Dame Claudia and how she had lived her life – just conflicting views from a number of people who probably had their own reasons for presenting her in a certain way – and he therefore now asked Juliet to find out as much about her as she could. "The private as well as the professional woman, if you can," he had said.

Juliet thought to herself that this shouldn't be too difficult. There were many drawbacks to investigating the disappearance of famous people, but always one bonus: they left a trail of information in their wake wherever they went. She was well aware that Claudia's glory days had pre-dated the Internet, but, even so, you never knew what online searches might turn up. People were always digitising the most arcane old rubbish. Juliet was a past mistress at ferreting out the obscure details that made up the building blocks of other people's lives.

She began with straightforward Google searches about Claudia's activities. She found details of some of the digs that Claudia had led in the Middle East in the 1930s and, occasionally, the archaeological reports that had followed on from them. Until 1938, the main geographical areas in which Claudia had worked were the region that the newspapers called 'Mesopotamia'; then it was the North of Scotland and the Orkney Islands. Juliet was familiar with the word 'Mesopotamia' from school scripture lessons, but she did not know what its modern-day equivalent was called.

Further searches revealed that it has no exact modern equivalent: the term was used to describe a very large region which today would include parts of modern Iraq, Iran, Turkey and Syria. That Claudia was familiar with this part of the world was significant enough for Juliet to download some of the reports and newspaper articles that gave accounts of how Claudia's digs were funded, who accompanied her and what she had discovered while working on them. Juliet skim-read some of these, thinking perhaps that she might find references to entanglements with Islamic extremists or other groups who might have had cause to resent Claudia's presence or her activities in their country. However, she could discover no controversies: just tedious accounts of the day-to-day work at consecutive sites in the desert, none of which seemed to have yielded anything of spectacular interest to the lay person. Claudia's involvement with the local populace appeared to be minimal; some local labour was employed to carry out removal of soil and for porterage, but most of Claudia's entourage on these expeditions appeared to consist of young academics or student volunteers from England or, less commonly, other European countries. Her sponsors were nearly always scholarly foundations, mostly British. She also received some donations from benefactors, the list of whose names sounded like a roll-call from Burke's Peerage.

The northern expeditions were fewer – Claudia had worked on sites in Scotland and the Orkneys twice in the years 1938 and 1939 – but had produced more exciting results. The star among these was the discovery of a fifth-century rune stone – a kind of Orkney version of the Rosetta stone – which was unearthed during the late autumn of 1938, just as the dig was about to halt for the winter. Claudia published several articles on this in the winter of 1939; she was clearly very excited about the find herself and also, Juliet suspected, determined to publish as much about it as possible before her peers and colleagues could air their views.

Juliet noted that the style and nature of her writing changed abruptly in the Orkney 'McRae Stone' articles. Previously, although she had been a reasonably good documenter of her digs, the conclusions that she had drawn had often been florid and imaginative and, to Juliet's eye at least, did not illustrate the caution and scrupulous rigour usually associated with academic argument. She had been a very early proponent of 'feminist archaeology', not only arguing that women as well as men could have made the stone and bronze artefacts that she and her team had discovered, but that they were just as likely as men to have used them for hunting and battle. Juliet herself was not averse to listening to a good feminist argument, but she could not help feeling that, if men had been so marginalised in pre-history and very early written history, it was difficult to explain the transformation that had taken place by the time that whole documents began to appear. Although she was not a historian, she knew there was little evidence of matriarchal societies having existed in the ancient Middle East.

However, in her articles on the McRae Stone, Claudia had attempted something quite different. Although the theories that she was proposing were still colourful, and must undoubtedly have been controversial at the time, she was manifestly trying to present them in a much more scholarly fashion. She built step-by-step arguments which were underpinned at each stage by allusion to her findings and carefully explained her interpretation of the significance of each one of them. The broad-brush approach had gone. Although some of the logic she employed still seemed to Juliet to be tenuous, she saw that these articles were Claudia's attempt to become accepted by the establishment. Prior to this, she had been a rogue woman in a man's world, a socialite outsider who had thumbed her nose at the coterie of male archaeologists who believed that, because they had had the privilege of being formally educated, only they had the right to contribute to the corpus of archaeological knowledge. Now she wanted to be of that world and she had to raise her game by showing that she had the right kind of incisive mind. The newspaper articles and reviews from this period suggested that, although her work would always be controversial, she had succeeded.

None of them spelt out that Claudia's interpretations of the McRae Stone languages were inspired by what Juliet recognised as an extreme variety of fascism.

If Claudia had had strong political convictions prior to the discovery of the stone, they were not reflected in her work. Now her purpose seemed to be to prove that the 'super-race' theory could be endorsed by how early peoples used language.

The Orkney collection of papers was published very quickly, in the space of the few months immediately preceding the outbreak of the Second World War. Most of them described the McRae Stone and hypothesised about its significance in some way. They were published in *Archaeologica Orkneia*, a learned journal owned by a small local history publisher taken over in the 1970s by a political foundation that had subsequently digitised most of its publications and made them available free on the Internet. The last of Claudia's McRae Stone articles, published in the spring of 1939, had a co-author: Doctor Elida Berg. Juliet immediately googled her name.

Doctor Berg had evidently been a famous academic. She had worked at Oslo University and her name had been given to one of the public lecture theatres built there between the wars. Juliet could find little about the exact role that she had occupied at the university, nor her dates of tenure, but a search produced a number of learned articles, some of which were available free of charge, others only by subscription. Most were in Norwegian. Juliet printed out some of the free ones and saved the URLs of others in her 'favourites', thinking that she might need to have them translated. She skimmed quickly through the fifty or so pages that she had printed. Some contained tiny photographs. One was of an archaeological dig: it was very blurred and the features of its subjects indistinct; nevertheless, the forms of two ladies could be made out, both squatting in a trench, their faces in shadow from the broad bush hats that they were wearing. One was heavily built and untidily dressed; the other was slender and looked rather well-groomed, despite the circumstances. Both were looking straight at the camera and smiling. Juliet could understand enough from the Norwegian caption to confirm that the photograph depicted Doctor Berg and a 'colleague', Miss Claudia McRae.

Returning to her Claudia searches, Juliet discovered that Claudia had abandoned the last of her Mesopotamian digs early in 1938, leaving it unfinished. She announced when she left that she had no plans to return and attributed her failure to complete the excavation of the site to lack of funds. Juliet reflected that, prior to this, Claudia always seemed to have been able to attract funds from rich men and foundations, but the excuse might have been genuine, given that Europe and the Middle East were about to be plunged into war. Perhaps Claudia had been advised – or warned – to relinquish the site by the Foreign Office. It was equally possible that she had found something – or someone – else that drew her elsewhere.

Tim dropped by at that moment.

"Having fun?" he asked. "Have you found any skeletons in Claudia's closet?"

"That's a funny thing to ask about an archaeologist," said Juliet, "but the answer is, maybe. The impression I'm getting is that in her heyday Claudia was a volatile and emotional woman who was quite keen on giving her work universal significance by combining her findings with the creation or endorsement of pseudo-disciplines and movements. First among these was a version of the Aryan ideal, but derived from the notion of a perfect language rather than physical superiority."

"She was right wing, then?"

"I think so – though she may not have expressed her beliefs in that way to herself. Her work is such a strange mixture of erudition and specious pleading that it is difficult to tell. Since you're here, can you tell me whose side Norway was on during the war?"

"As a country, officially it was neutral. However, it was occupied by the Germans and, in practice, many Norwegians were Nazi sympathisers. There were reprisals after the war: some of them were prosecuted for treason."

"What about academics? Which side would they normally have been on?"

Tim shrugged.

"Both, I suppose. There were some famous socialist academics who resisted the Germans. Why do you ask?"

"Because I think that the whole tenor of Claudia McRae's work may have been altered by a relationship that she developed with a female Norwegian academic: a woman called Dr Elida Berg. I don't know much about her yet. I've found some journal articles that were written by her, but they're all in Norwegian. We need to get some of them translated. I suspect that they peddle similar theories about race, class and language that Claudia's own work tries to do at this time. It's quite unlike what she wrote before about 1938 – which was when she and her team discovered what has become known as the McRae Stone, incidentally. Have you heard of it?"

"I'm not sure – it rings a vague bell. Do you know for sure that Claudia was in Norway during the war?"

"No, I'm still checking."

"Well, carry on – don't let me stop you! And thank you for doing this. I suppose that she didn't have to be in Norway in person in order to adopt these views," he added, almost to himself. "The woman that you speak of could have come here. Or they could just have shared ideas, however academics did that then: by post, I suppose, or telephone? And conferences, when there wasn't a war on?"

Juliet laughed.

"I'll let you know, sir," she said. "Don't put thoughts into my head that I can't prove. I need to stay objective about this."

She carried on with her work. Despite trying a variety of search techniques, she could find very little about Claudia's activities during the war. Perhaps she was not working as an archaeologist then, but had been assigned to some kind of war work. There wasn't much available on Dr Elida Berg for these years, either, but there was no reason to believe that she had left her post at the University of Oslo. Its curriculum was evidently undisturbed by the German occupation. However, if she published any papers in the years 1939 – 1948, the searches were not flagging them up, which was strange considering how prolific Dr Berg had been in the previous decade.

By the mid-1950s, Claudia was a sort of archaeological superstar. She had become the figurehead of a prototype feminist movement which was also supported by a new generation of self-consciously egalitarian male academics. There were many black-and-white pictures of Claudia in full flood at academic symposia and conferences. By the 1960s, she had gathered around her a coterie of adoring young men. Two of them had already figured in the police investigation: Oliver Sparham and Edmund Baker. Juliet was not particularly surprised by this revelation: Tim had already noted that each of them had a long-term association with the vanished woman and she had expected their names to crop up eventually. The contexts in which they featured seemed innocuous enough: they had participated in digs that had taken place in both the UK and Europe. There were the usual pictures of them standing knee-deep in trenches wearing shorts and sunhats. In some of the photographs, Claudia was posing with them or looking on benevolently as they wielded their shovels. (By the mid-1950s, she had become a bulky, shapeless woman, though still striking of countenance, who dressed most of the time in workman's overalls.) But the accounts of the digs that Edmund and Oliver and the other young men had worked on were innocent of any political message that Juliet could divine; most were matter-of-fact accounts of excavations that had taken place at the sites of prehistoric farming communities, including some in the Orkneys. There had been no more finds of the calibre of the McRae Stone. Most of the accounts managed to mention the Stone, presumably to increase readership of these later digs by lending archaeological 'sex appeal', but none recapitulated Claudia's semantic theories in detail.

This did not mean that Claudia was not still actively propounding her views, however. During the 1950s and 1960s, she had been invited to give a succession of high-profile public lectures – the Sir Maximus Wheelwright Memorial and BBC Longbourne Lectures in England, the keynote presentation at the Holyrood House Symposium in Scotland, the opening speech at the Fine Gael Conference in Ireland. She had also, rather peculiarly, been presented with the Prix Femina Vie Heureuse Anglaise in 1962 for her writings, though Juliet believed – and her researches confirmed – that this award was usually conferred only on writers of fiction, drama and poetry. Juliet could find no explanation on the Femina magazine's website for its departure from tradition, but the award had evidently increased Claudia's reputation yet further. In 1963, she was made a Fellow of the Royal Society of Literature and, in 1965, a Fellow of the Royal Society of Arts. She gave a series of radio broadcasts on her work in the Orkneys in 1968 and, in the early 1970s, she was the chief commentator for a long-running BBC Two television programme entitled *Digging up Britain's Past*. Her fame seemed to have reached its apogee at this point. She was given an honorary doctorate by the University of Cambridge, the first British university to offer archaeology as a degree, and also accepted one from Cardiff University. She was made a Dame Commander of the Order of the British Empire in the New Year's Honours list in 1975. Thereafter, mention of her and her publications and appearances began to drop off.

There was something missing from this glittering roll-call of achievements, Juliet realised. Aside from the honorary degree from Cambridge, which had been presented by a Vice-Chancellor who dabbled in archaeology, there were no accolades from the chief luminaries of the discipline of archaeology itself. Juliet did not know who they were, but was correct in her assumption that they would be easy enough to find. Further Google searches revealed that eminent archaeologists usually belonged to, and were accorded honours by, at least one of three august and long-established organisations: the Society of Antiquaries, the British Archaeological Association and the Royal Institute of Archaeology. A painstaking trawl of their past and present members and of the honorary memberships that they had conferred yielded no mention of Dame Claudia's name. Juliet reflected that Claudia had been active in her field a long time ago and such organisations did not necessarily post records of all their past members. Nevertheless, the absence of any mention on their websites of such a seminal twentieth-century archaeologist was strange. Juliet recalled Oliver Sparham's comment, as reported by Tim, that Claudia and organised societies did not mix. Apparently, she had briefly been an honorary member of the Spalding Archaeological Society, but was now estranged from that, too. Juliet sensed that if she could find out why Claudia had not been honoured by her chosen profession it might shed some light on the mystery of her disappearance.

A first step would be to find out what kind of messages Claudia had been promoting to her vast and ever-growing popular audiences between the end of the war and the mid-seventies. An initial search brought up more journal articles, for some of which only the abstracts were available to non-subscribers. However, some were also reproduced online in full. Juliet skimmed two or three of these and discovered that the hypotheses that they were presenting were identical to those of the immediate pre- and post-war articles that she had already found; some were even couched in exactly the same language. She knew that this was odd; her experience of academic didacticism was limited to what she had read during the course of her own reasonably conscientious undergraduate career, but even this cursory acquaintance with the workings of erudition had demonstrated to her that academic theories rarely stood still. Most academics modified and embellished their theories and hypotheses over time, or were constrained to do so by the publication of the counter-theories of their peers. In contrast, what Claudia had divined from the discovery of the McRae Stone and her interpretation of its writings had been frozen in time. In 1978, her conclusions, and even the way in which she expressed them, were almost exactly the same as they had been in 1938. Although quite intricately argued (but with what Juliet considered to be a flawed logic), they could be summarised in a single sentence: that several languages had developed alongside each other in prehistoric Northern Europe, one of which was far superior in its 'purity' and power of expression to the others, and that the speakers of this language had become a super-race whose descendants now inhabited Northern Britain, parts of Scandinavia and other Northern European countries.

She wanted to hear Claudia's own voice propounding this theory and tried to find one of her radio or television broadcasts. She couldn't locate either. However, by typing the words 'Claudia McRae' into YouTube, she came upon something more startling than she had anticipated.

Juliet had located a film – or, to be more accurate, a podcast – of some kind of ceremonial occasion. It began with a grainy picture of several hook-nosed, grave and elderly men sitting at a table on a podium. Then the camera moved jerkily to capture a shot of the audience: row upon row of people seated in a huge auditorium. They appeared to be predominantly male, although the poor quality of the podcast made it difficult to establish this for sure. A few of the faces were framed with long hair, so probably belonged to women.

The men on the podium were speaking in a language that Juliet did not understand, but which she knew from the titles at the beginning of the podcast was Norwegian. They each rose in turn to give a short speech, encouraged by the smiling faces of the others. As each individual concluded his speech and prepared to resume his seat, his fellows led the audience in a booming roar of applause. Finally, the tallest and most distinguished-looking of them – the one who appeared to be the Master of Ceremonies – strode temporarily out of view. When the camera picked him up again, he was standing behind a lectern at the far end of the podium, beaming and clapping his hands, which were held ostentatiously aloft as the whole auditorium erupted once again.

A powerfully-built, untidy woman clambered up the three or four steps of the podium. The Master of Ceremonies ceased clapping and stretched out his hand, which she took in her own and pumped up and down. The Master of Ceremonies said a few more words and returned to his place among the dignitaries.

The stout woman planted herself squarely behind the lectern and adjusted the microphone. She began to speak. Her first few words were delivered in Norwegian. Then she began to speak in English. At first her words, although obviously delivered full-strength to a microphone, were difficult to distinguish, but when Juliet adjusted the sound regulators on the headphones that she was wearing she could hear them more clearly.

Dame Claudia McRae was obviously accepting some kind of honour. However, the speech that she was making was far from gracious. She was happy to receive the award 'on behalf of the work that she had done, and on behalf of her staunch supporters and like-minded thinkers', but she warned that others were out to sabotage their work, and that they would need to exercise vigilance at all times. To Juliet, her words sounded paranoid, but they seemed to go down well with the audience. Despite the stern tone of the speech, it was relatively short. When it had ended, the audience rose as one and gave her a standing ovation. The roar of the clapping was deafening. Then the Master of Ceremonies appeared again and presented her with a gold statuette and an envelope. Juliet knew from the snippets that she had gleaned from the speech that she had just heard that the envelope contained a cheque for $100,000 to enable Claudia's work to be continued.

The camera zoomed in on her at that moment and managed to capture a close-up of her face. Her great age, which had previously been camouflaged by her robust figure and booming voice, suddenly became apparent. Who was going to carry on her work, Juliet wondered? Surely no-one would give so large a donation to a nonagenarian in the belief that she would herself continue to work as an archaeologist in the field.

Almost immediately, she discovered what might have been the answer to her question. As the applause died down, a man younger than those seated appeared at the steps of the podium and extended his hand to help Claudia walk back down them. Juliet noticed for the first time that she had propped a stick against the lectern and that she was a little unsteady on her feet. A well-groomed woman in early middle age was standing behind the man. Juliet did not know for sure who the man was, but she could guess: from Tim's description, she had just been watching footage of Claudia McRae's nephew, Guy Maichment. The woman would be her companion, Jane Halliwell. It was only natural that they would have been present at such a prestigious event, of course; it would have been stranger if they hadn't. What Juliet had really been hoping to see were the faces of some of the other members of the audience; people known to the police, perhaps, or faces that might crop up again later in the investigation (Juliet had a good memory for faces). However, the quality of the podcast was so poor that this would not be possible. The only faces that she could see at all clearly were those of the Master of Ceremonies, the two people waiting for Claudia at the foot of the podium and Claudia herself. Watching the podcast – which Juliet's researches had told her was of Claudia's last public appearance – had not been a total waste of time, however. It had shown her that feelings ran high in the world which Claudia inhabited; so high, in fact, that it was conceivable that even these distinguished and respectable people would resort to violence in order to impose their opinions on others. They were like missionaries, thought Juliet: unenlightened missionaries, convinced not only that their views were the correct ones, but determined to ensure that everyone else thought so, too.

CHAPTER NINE

TIM YATES WAS sitting at his desk. As usual, it was tidy, but his in-tray was packed tight with documents that required his sign-off (top shelf) and documents that he ought to read (bottom shelf). He sighed. This morning, City of Peterborough Police and South Lincolnshire Police had joined forces to carry out a fingertip search of the woods that surrounded Claudia McRae's house. He was impatient to get results and hated being chained to paperwork. He debated whether he should join them, and decided that he would compromise; he would work on the top in-tray until lunchtime and then drive out to Helpston.

He drew out the first set of papers and started work, but he felt restless and after five minutes got up and began walking around his office, at first aimlessly. Eventually he gravitated towards the window and looked out. The police station, a late Victorian building that resembled a mini version of Lincoln Gaol crossed with Tattershall Castle, stood black and minatory at the head of the Sheep Market, so that he had a clear view of the whole of the triangle that had originally been the market. The latter had now been adapted to serve as a shopping area and car park. As a historian, he was curious to know why the nineteenth-century inhabitants of the small, law-abiding, prosperous market town had decided that they needed such a forbidding symbol of law and order as this grim building to be erected at their expense. What was even more curious was that the police station at Boston was identical.

He had often noticed that people were still intimidated by the exterior of the building. Pedestrians tended to hurry past it. Few passers-by felt impelled to look up at its windows. If they did, the windows themselves were set so deep into the walls that it was impossible to tell if someone was staring back out at them, which was unnerving; and, in his opinion rather absurdly, all of the windows, even the ones on the second and third floors, were barred. Nor were ordinary members of the public encouraged to penetrate to the interior of the building. People reporting lost keys, missing dogs and stolen bicycles were required to ring a bell set in a side wall and talk through a hatch to a duty officer.

Today was not a market day and it was still early. A few people could be seen passing, hastening to work; the occasional car made its way slowly around the large car park that now occupied the whole space of what had once been the circular animal auctioning area and disappeared. The car park itself was all but deserted.

A public toilet had been built at the extremity of the car park furthest from the police station. It was a 1950s concrete structure, squat and ugly. As Tim's eye played idly over the whole scene, he noticed someone lurking at the corner of the toilet block. Whoever it was stood motionless, hands in pockets. Tim squinted to get a better view. It was a thick-set man, dressed unremarkably in jeans, an anorak and trainers. He was wearing a woollen hat with the hood of the anorak pulled over it, so that his face was obscured in shadow. There was nothing in the least unusual in his appearance, but his behaviour was strange. What struck Tim was that the man's eyes were fixed permanently on the police station. He never changed his line of vision, never dropped his gaze to the ground.

DC Juliet Armstrong knocked and entered the room.

"Good morning, Juliet. Could you just come over here a minute?"

She raised her eyebrows, but did as he asked.

"Do you see that bloke over there – by the toilet block? Have you seen him before?"

Juliet stepped past him to the window and peered out across the market square.

"I can't see very well without my specs – but I don't think whoever it was is still there. Do you mean him?" She added, pointing at a figure that was walking rapidly away from the toilet block, and about to disappear from sight. He was holding a mobile phone to one ear.

"I guess I do," said Tim. "I thought he looked suspicious, but perhaps not. Just my warped mind dreaming up conspiracy theories!"

Juliet smiled. There was no denying that Tim could be over-imaginative.

"I came to tell you that Ms Halliwell is here, sir, and would like to see you if you can spare the time."

"Do you mean Jane Halliwell? How did you manage to conjure her up? You can't be serious about if I can 'spare the time'! She's probably top of my list of people to talk to in the McRae case, now that we appear to have got all we can from the nephew. But I thought that she was on holiday abroad, and unreachable?"

"Apparently only the first part of her holiday involved cruising up and down the Norwegian fjords, and she reached dry land again yesterday. The second part of it was to have been spent in Oslo, but someone texted her about Claudia McRae's disappearance and she came home as soon as she could get a flight. She seems very distressed – and she seems nice, too. It would be kind to see her."

"Yes, of course I'll see her. Give me five minutes and bring her in, will you?"

"In here, sir, rather than one of the interview rooms?"

"Certainly in here. She isn't a criminal, is she? And, Juliet, I'm sure she'd like some proper coffee."

Tim flushed as he said it.

"You should be ashamed of yourself!" said Juliet as she made her exit. But he noted that she was laughing.

Jane Halliwell, when she arrived, was very pretty, in a timeless sort of way, and elegant. Tim could think of no other words to describe her. Immaculate, perhaps. He was surprised. She was of medium height, with brown eyes and a heart-shaped face that wore rather a sweet expression, although at the moment it was quite troubled and her eyes looked pink. She had probably been crying. Her thickish blonde hair was styled in an immaculate shining bob. She wore a well-pressed light wool suit in some neutral shade – taupe, he believed it was called – with black patent leather accessories. Her clothes looked expensive in an understated way.

Tim had learnt from Guy Maichment that Jane kept Claudia's house and her affairs in good order, so he had not expected the paid companion to be large, untidy and undomesticated, which was how everyone who knew Claudia seemed to describe the archaeologist: rather the opposite. But he certainly didn't think that Jane would be . . . well, glamorous. A stick-thin, meek little woman with mousy hair turning grey would have fitted his notion of a woman in her line of work exactly. His next thought, one that leapt unbidden into his mind, was that this woman didn't look like a lesbian. He chided himself mentally for his prejudice, but he did allow himself to wonder why Jane seemed so well-to-do.

"Ms Halliwell, thank you for coming. Please take a seat," he added, after they had shaken hands. Her hand was small, the bones so delicate that he was afraid of crushing them. He gestured towards one of the four chairs placed at his meeting table and emerged from behind the desk to claim one of the others, pausing on his way to pull out her chair for Jane. She inclined her head slightly. She was clearly accustomed to such minor attentions. "I'm DI Yates. I'm in charge of the enquiry into Dame Claudia's disappearance."

Jane Halliwell may not have been meek, but she did present herself as being rather engagingly nervous. She gave a little start at the word 'disappearance', and looked up at him with her limpid brown eyes. She clasped both her hands together, then dropped them down on to her lap.

"I really cannot believe that this has happened," she said. "I feel as if I'm living in a nightmare. Tell me, Detective Inspector," she said, reaching across the table to place her hand on his arm in a confidential manner, "do you have any idea – any idea at all – of who might have done this?"

"Might have done what, Ms Halliwell? We are not certain yet that a crime has been committed, or indeed that a third party was involved."

"Oh, but Guy said . . ." She halted suddenly. Her hand flew to her lips.

"Oh dear, I'm afraid that that was indiscreet. You probably told him not to discuss it with me, didn't you? Don't go blaming him; it was my own fault entirely. He said that he didn't want to gossip about it, but of course I felt I needed to know as much as possible. Please don't tell him that I gave him away."

"Have you already seen Mr Maichment?" Tim asked. "DC Armstrong told me that you had come straight here from the airport."

"I have, but Guy was kind enough to offer to pick me up. As you can imagine, it was impossible for us to avoid the subject – impossible to concentrate on anything else, actually."

"I can imagine," said Tim, "and I have no objection to your knowing details that we aren't releasing to the Press. But if, as you imply, Mr Maichment is being less discreet than we have very strongly advised him to be, we may have to see him again and convey the message somewhat more forcefully. I hope that this won't go any further than yourself. I must emphasise that disclosure of all but the bare facts could jeopardise Dame Claudia's safety and that it is best to say as little as possible to anyone until we have located her. I shall have someone get in touch with Mr Maichment to reinforce this. Is he waiting for you outside?"

"No. He had to go on. I told him that I would take a taxi back to the cottage. I'm sure that you won't need to tick him off. He is perfectly aware of the gravity of the situation and devoted to Claudia, as I'm sure you have already found out. It would also be a kindness to spare me his wrath," she added, somewhat imploringly.

"A taxi all the way to Helpston would be expensive, but I'm afraid that it won't be possible for you to return to the cottage at the moment. It has to be kept intact as a possible crime scene. Of course I shall be asking you to accompany me there at some point – perhaps later today, if you are not too tired – to see whether you think that anything is missing or there is something unusual you can spot. In the meantime, is there somewhere you can stay? If not, we shall have to ask you to check into a hotel."

"I don't have many friends of my own living in this area. Of course I know some of Claudia's acquaintances, but they are mostly quite elderly and I should feel uncomfortable imposing myself on them. I guess it will have to be an hotel, therefore. I'd rather that it were closer to Helpston than Spalding. I don't want to be too far away in case Claudia comes back. There's a place quite close to the cottage – by some coincidence, there was an archaeological conference taking place there earlier this week, I believe."

"I think you're referring to Welland Manor. I shall be happy to have someone take you there after we've finished talking. "

"Will I be able to take some of my clothes from the cottage when I visit it with you? Most of the things I took with me need laundering and some are quite unsuitable for the present weather."

"Not today, unfortunately. Once the Scene of Crime Officers have finished their work – and they could take several days – I should be able to allow you to collect some possessions. If Dame Claudia hasn't returned by then, that is."

Jane Halliwell made a little moue of discontent; it was apparently intended as an expression of wry humour. Tim had the passing thought that it was odd, but he had more pressing matters to address than Jane Halliwell's mood or her notions of correct behaviour.

"What exactly has Guy Maichment told you?" he asked.

"Very little – and that's the truth. Nothing that you haven't told the media, I'm sure, except for the smear of blood. He did impress upon me that that should be kept secret." She shuddered. "It sounds quite horrible. Does it mean that Claudia has been injured?"

Tim engaged in a quick internal debate about how much of the truth to reveal.

"Not necessarily," he said. "In fact, probably not. But it does indicate that someone else was in the house after Oliver Sparham saw her in the late afternoon on Tuesday. Whether the blood is linked directly to her disappearance is impossible for us to say, until we can understand why and how she vanished."

Jane Halliwell blinked several times, as though confused.

"But surely . . . but it is likely that the two events are connected, is it not?"

"As I say, I don't know. Weighing the balance of probabilities, I'd say you're right. Tell me, when did you last speak to her?"

"I think it was yesterday . . . no, no, of course not, I mean Tuesday. The days seem to be running into each other! And I didn't go to bed last night. Yes, it was on Tuesday – in the early afternoon. I just called her briefly, because it was our last day on the cruise and I was about to go to a lecture on the history of the fjords. She told me she was expecting a visitor."

"How did she seem?"

"Quite excited at the prospect of seeing Oliver Sparham again. Otherwise, perfectly normal, I'd say."

"Did she mention Oliver Sparham by name?"

"Yes – I think so. She must have done, otherwise how would I have known?"

"Mr Maichment could have obliged you with this detail as well."

"No, I don't think he did. Claudia told me herself that it was Oliver."

"Did she mention anyone else by name during the course of the conversation?"

"Only Guy. She said that he had been very good about keeping in touch with her during my absence."

"Did she talk about her health or give you cause for concern about her well-being?"

"Not at all. I should have been in touch with Guy myself if she had."

"What else did you talk about?"

"Nothing else. As I've said, it was a short call – I had only a few minutes before the lecture started. I told her that I would call her properly when I reached Oslo."

"When was that?"

"In the early hours of yesterday morning. The boat was already moored when we awoke. The passengers had breakfast on board and then disembarked. We had all been booked into a hotel in Oslo by the tour company."

"Did you try to call her yesterday?"

"No. I learned of her disappearance on the news. She's well-known in Scandinavia – she's done a lot of work there. I tried to call Guy, but could not reach him. I decided pretty quickly that I would come home as soon as I could get a flight. The tour operator was actually very helpful in arranging one for me."

"Did you keep trying to call Mr Maichment?"

"I tried a couple more times, that was all. After that, I was too busy trying to arrange my departure, or, of course, actually flying. I did send him a text message, though. I didn't receive his reply until I landed at Luton. It simply said that he would be there to meet me. I was very grateful, as you might imagine."

"Indeed. Can you tell me how Dame Claudia was when you left for your holiday? Did she seem ill or depressed?"

"Not at all. In fact, I rather thought that she was looking forward to being on her own for a while. Claudia is well advanced in years, as you know, and quite infirm; she would be utterly unable to live alone for any length of time. But she is fiercely independent."

"One final question, Ms Halliwell, before we let you go and get some rest: did you take your holiday alone or were you accompanied?"

Jane Halliwell flushed.

"I – I should prefer not to answer that question, Detective Inspector. I can't imagine why you are asking it. How can my answer possibly help you to find Claudia?"

"You are more intimate with her than anyone else in her life. In fact, it would probably be true to say that your lives are intertwined, would it not?"

She eyed him suspiciously. She seemed affronted.

"I'm not quite sure what you may be implying. But if you say that because you have heard some rumour that Claudia and I are lovers, you can take my word for it that there is absolutely no truth in it."

"I was not implying anything, Ms Halliwell. I am just asking you for anything that can help us to find Dame Claudia. You don't have to answer my question. But I'm sure that you can see that knowledge of the whereabouts of intimates of both yourself and Dame Claudia at the time of her disappearance could be helpful."

"Very well. I can see in that case that my answer might be helpful. I wasn't on my own, Inspector; I was accompanied by a gentleman friend whom I am not willing to name. All that you need to know is that I met him just before we embarked at Southampton and left him when I departed from Oslo. He has never met Claudia and although she is aware of his existence she does not know his identity. Will that do?"

Tim nodded.

"Thank you," he said. "I don't think we can usefully detain you here any longer. It will be more helpful for everyone if you try to get some sleep. Would you like to phone the hotel for a room? Once you've made the booking, DC Armstrong will call for a police car to take you there. Perhaps you could leave your mobile number with us. We'll call you as soon as we can to arrange the visit to the cottage. Could you also let us know if you have any plans to move away from the area? We shall need to know your whereabouts while we are working on this case. We're bound to need to come back to you for more information about Dame Claudia and her friends and acquaintances."

Jane Halliwell stood up and smoothed down her immaculate pencil skirt. She held out the birdlike hand again. Tim stood up and grasped it lightly.

"Thank you very much indeed, Detective Inspector," she said. "I can't say that you have put my mind at rest, but I am impressed with the thoroughness with which you are dealing with Claudia's disappearance. Of course I am not intending to leave the area – nothing could be further from my thoughts. As I've already explained, my intention is to be as near to the cottage as possible against Claudia's return. I can only hope that there is a simple explanation for all of this. Though I must say . . ." – her voice rose, and she dabbed at her cheek just below her eye – "I have wracked my brains to think of what it might be and come up with an absolute blank!"

Tim nodded sympathetically. Juliet went to put a tentative arm around Jane. He watched with interest as she shook it off; almost imperceptibly, it was true, but, however slight the action, it was still rejection of an offer of compassion. An interesting woman, he decided. He wondered exactly how much she knew about Claudia's professional life and her friends. He guessed that not much escaped Jane Halliwell's notice.

"Oh, DC Armstrong," he called after Juliet's retreating back, "could you come back when you've assisted Ms Halliwell? There are a couple of things I need you to help with."

CHAPTER TEN

"WELL, WHAT DID you make of her?" Tim asked when Juliet returned some twenty minutes later.

"Quite a brave lady," said Juliet. "She's obviously very upset, but trying to help as much as she can by adopting a practical approach."

"Is that really what you think?"

"Yes, sir. Otherwise I wouldn't say it."

Tim laughed. "Of course not. I should know better. But didn't you find anything at all odd about her?"

Juliet considered, her head on one side in an attitude that he knew well.

"Not exactly odd," she said slowly. "I found her surprising in some ways. The way she was dressed, for one thing, and that general air that she has of being quite wealthy. She doesn't quite square with my notion of the lady's companion."

"Go on," said Tim.

"She seems too independent – too well-educated, almost. But I guess that's an absurd thing to say, because Claudia McRae is no ordinary little old lady wanting someone to fetch her slippers and entertain her with fireside chatter. I'm sure that there is strong intellectual stimulus on both sides."

"There'd have to be, wouldn't there, if you lived out in the wilds as they do, miles from the next house, and hardly ever went anywhere? But talking of stimulus – why do you think she went out of her way to tell me that she wasn't a lesbian?"

"She didn't actually say that, sir. She said that there was no truth in the rumour that she and Claudia McRae were lovers. That doesn't mean that either or both of them couldn't have female lovers."

"Of course you're right," said Tim. "I hadn't thought of that."

"But even so, the chances are that Ms Halliwell is not gay. She mentioned her gentleman lover, after all."

"Now it's my turn to split hairs. She didn't say he was a lover: just that she was with him, and that she'd prefer not to reveal his name. She made a great fuss of keeping it a secret. Didn't you think that there was more to that than met the eye? She seemed determined to draw attention to this man by keeping his identity mysterious."

"I didn't quite see it like that, sir."

"How did you see it?"

"I just assumed that she'd gone on holiday with a married lover and that she refused to say who he was to protect his marriage."

"That would be one explanation, I suppose."

"What other explanation could there be?"

"What? Oh, I can think of several. The person concerned could really have been a woman, for a start; or, man or woman, it could have been someone that she didn't want to name to the police, not because she was protecting a third party, but because it was part of some kind of plan. Or the relationship is an innocent one, but she wants us to think there is more to it. Or possibly, even, she was on the cruise on her own, but wanted us to think that she was accompanied."

Tim had wandered over to the window and he stood with his back to Juliet.

"I can find out from the cruise company whether she shared a cabin with anyone and, if so, where and when they boarded. I believe that the boat stops in Rotterdam and Copenhagen to pick up passengers after it leaves Southampton. The British tourists embark first."

"Good idea," said Tim, turning round briefly. "Do that, will you? And, even if she had a single cabin, get hold of the entire passenger list. It might tell us something. It's worth a try, anyway."

"Yes, sir," said Juliet. She turned to leave.

"He's there again," said Tim excitedly, pointing through the window. "I thought I saw him. He's walking this way now, so we might get a look at his face. Come quickly, I want you to see him."

Juliet hastened to the window. The thick-set man in the hat and hooded anorak was passing on the other side of the road, just a few yards from where they stood. He was still wearing the hat, but the hood was down now.

"Do you recognise him?" said Tim.

"I'm not sure that I do," said Juliet. "His face looks familiar, though."

"Damn!" said Tim. "I thought you'd be sure to know who he was. I'm certain that I've seen him somewhere else myself. Keep a look out for him, and let me know if he comes past here again, will you?"

CHAPTER ELEVEN

LATER THAT MORNING Juliet knocked on Tim's door again.

"I have the results from Forensics."

"And?"

"The blood is certainly human; and it isn't Dame Claudia's."

"How do you know?"

"Her doctor told me her blood group when I called her yesterday. Claudia's is O positive. The blood on the wall was A positive. It also belonged to a man."

"There can't be any doubt about it?"

"None."

"Can you find out Guy Maichment's blood group for me? And Oliver Sparham's?"

"I can if you think it will help," said Juliet doubtfully. Tim realised that he had stopped her in her tracks.

"Why do you say that?"

"Because we've been told that the arc of blood on the wall came from an artery. Its owner sustained a very serious, if not a fatal, injury. Whoever he is, he won't just have a little scratch."

"Of course. I wasn't thinking. In that case, I've no idea whom it could belong to. Have you?"

"Not yet. But I do have something else that might help us to find out. The tour company has sent me the passenger list from Jane Halliwell's cruise. I haven't had time to work through it yet, except to check that Jane was on board. And she did have a single cabin – a deluxe outer cabin with a window."

"So we don't know who her gentleman companion was?"

"Not yet. I shall have to work through the list carefully to try to find out his identity."

Tim was aware that Juliet loved puzzles of this kind. He didn't like to dampen her enthusiasm – and in this instance he knew that she was right; it was definitely worth checking the list to try to identify Jane's 'friend'. Nevertheless, he felt obliged to advise caution. She had been known to waste her energies on wild goose chases that had lasted for days.

"She may still have invented him. Look by all means, but don't spend too much time on it. And do tell me why you think that there's a link between the cruise guest list and the blood on the wall – I'm always fasci-nated by your hunches," he added, to soften the blow when he saw Juliet's face fall.

"You'll probably think that it's very tenuous – I suppose that it is. But Blood Group A is the most common blood group in Norway."

"I'm sorry; I don't follow."

"The bulk of Jane's holiday was in Norway, either cruising up and down the fjords, or stopping off at towns along the way. As far as I can tell, Dame Claudia spent most or all of the Second World War in Norway and some of her friends were very right wing, especially a Dr Elida Berg who dropped from view before the war ended. And although three quarters of the people on that cruise were British or Dutch, most of the others were Scandinavian, Norwegians especially. I can start with the male Norwe-gians: find out if any of them has a criminal record, at least."

"I think I can see what you're getting at," said Tim slowly, "though there are some leaps of logic in there that defeat me. And if Jane herself has a right-wing Norwegian friend, might he not equally be someone that she just met when she was there? Not someone who went on the cruise at all?"

"That's a possibility. But she said that she was accompanied on the cruise by a friend."

"That doesn't mean that she was telling the truth."

"Of course not. But as you know, an accomplished liar sticks as closely to the truth as possible."

"I thought that you liked her?"

"I do – did. But there was something about her that didn't add up. I didn't understand why she wanted to incarcerate herself in that house in the wood, especially when she had quite a successful career. So I decided to find out a bit more about her. It wasn't difficult – I just made enquir-ies at Lincoln University. She's still a research fellow there and publishes stuff through her old department occasionally. I wanted to know what her subject was."

"And?"

"Politics. Extreme right-wing politics – she wrote her thesis on the rise of Fascism in Europe. In the university website's profile of her she claims to be a dispassionate researcher who embraces no political affiliations of her own. But having read some of the stuff that she's written, I think that that is doubtful."

Tim whistled.

"So I may pursue my line of enquiry, at least for a reasonable time, to see if I can get any further results?"

"Yes," said Tim. "For a reasonable time. Well done, Juliet." Her deep-set eyes behind the unattractive spectacles were shining.

"There's one other thing, sir."

"Yes?"

"I've printed off several papers that were written by Dr Berg in the 1930s, but they're all in Norwegian. Do I remember that you once told me that Katrin speaks some Norwegian?"

"She does, but I'm not sure that she would be able to translate academic stuff. The language might be too specialised. You could give her a try, though. You don't have to ask me; I'm not her boss." Tim sounded tarter than he intended.

"Thank you, sir," said Juliet, eyeing him keenly. "It was just a courtesy. I'll phone her this afternoon. I can e-mail the papers to her, but perhaps you wouldn't mind taking the print-outs home with you, always assuming that she'll do it."

"Of course," said Tim. "Leave them in an envelope on my desk. And now I must catch up with Thornton. I've got to convince him that we're on to something and ask him to get us more help."

CHAPTER TWELVE

TIM AND KATRIN had recently bought a house on the Edinburgh estate, a post-war housing development that had been built partly to replace houses that had been damaged by bombs, partly to provide new accommodation for the town's burgeoning professional class. Their house had been described as a 'chalet bungalow' by the estate agent. This apparently meant that it was a bungalow with one bedroom tucked away under the eaves that had to be reached by means of a folding stepladder, as well as the two downstairs bedrooms. The bathroom, kitchen and sitting-room were all downstairs. The 'dining-room' was an alcove in the sitting room, which ran the length of the house. It was entered from the hall through double sliding glass doors. The hall itself was large enough to contain some plants in large pots, an old-fashioned hall-stand (an heirloom from one of Tim's grandmothers) and a cat basket.

Tim passed Katrin's car in the drive and entered through the front door as usual. The muted noise of a television turned down low was coming from the sitting-room. Katrin was curled up on the sofa, her eyes glued to the screen.

"Hello, darling," said Tim. "I'm glad we've both got home on time, for once."

"Shhh," said Katrin, holding up her hand in admonishment, "and look!"

Tim perched on the arm of the sofa and focused on what she was watching. It was a close-up of Superintendent Thornton, his uniform spick and span, his hair brushed severely off his forehead. He was reading from a prepared statement. All that could be seen of his audience was a couple of dozen microphones of varying sizes and textures arrayed at the bottom of the screen. He completed his statement and glared at the phalanx of microphones.

"Any questions?" he asked gravely.

The camera zoomed away from him, to show the front row of a large crowd of journalists.

"Have the police made any progress on this case yet?" asked one reporter in an impertinent voice.

"I'm not at liberty to answer that question."

"Superintendent, what do you yourself think has happened to Dame Claudia?"

"It would be foolish in the extreme for me to speculate. No police officer would do that – as I'm sure you are aware."

"Superintendent, is there any truth in the rumour that bloodstains were found at Dame Claudia's cottage?"

Only Tim, who knew his mannerisms so well, recognised the look of fury that fleetingly crossed the Superintendent's face before he composed his features into his usual media-repelling frown and answered smoothly.

"None whatsoever. Now, if you'll excuse me, I must draw this press conference to a close."

"Wait for it," Tim groaned, smiling ruefully. "If he hasn't called my mobile in the next five minutes, I'll be amazed."

Superintendent Thornton's back was seen retreating through a door. The camera turned its attention to the anchorman.

"The police would like to appeal to anyone who has seen Dame Claudia, or who has any information that may lead to her whereabouts, to contact them immediately. Please call South Lincolnshire Police on . . . ."

"Good God!" said Katrin.

"What?" asked Tim, alarmed. He turned to face her. She was staring fiercely at the screen again. Returning to it himself, Tim saw the photograph of Dame Claudia that Guy Maichment had given him at their first meeting. It was a relatively recent three-quarters picture of her dressed in trousers and a baggy jumper. She was wearing her spectacles and a large gardening hat. The photo was slightly out of focus, but the TV camera zoomed in again in an attempt to portray her face in as much detail as possible.

"Is that her?" Katrin demanded. "The woman that you've been looking for?"

"Claudia McRae? Yes, of course. I'm surprised you haven't seen that picture before. It was on the news last night as well and it's been plastered over the papers."

"You were out yesterday evening and I didn't bother with the news; I didn't see the paper, either. But, good God!"

"Why do you keep saying that? What's wrong?"

"I was in Boston today, and I swear that I saw that woman."

"You couldn't have done!"

"Why not? Are you saying that because you think that she's dead? You don't have any proof of that, do you? And besides, I'm quite certain. There can't be two people like her living in this area. She wasn't wearing the hat, but she had spectacles on, and she was dressed in trousers and some kind of bulky coat."

"Was she alone?"

"No. She was walking with a stick – she seemed to have some difficulty in walking – and someone was helping her. She was holding on to his arm."

"She was with a man? Can you describe him?"

"Yes. He was middle-aged and not very tall. And quite thickset. But I didn't see his face – it was turned towards her."

"What was he wearing?"

"Fairly nondescript clothes. I'm sorry – I don't sound very observant, do I? I would have taken more notice if I'd known who it was. But his clothes were very ordinary: dark-coloured and casual. That's all I can remember."

"Where was this?"

"There's a little passageway beside the hospital. They came out of it and walked towards the disabled car park."

"Did anyone else see them?"

"I suppose they must have. It was mid-morning; it was quite busy. I was walking – I'd had to park in the Tunnard Street car park, because the one in Sibsey Road was full. I wasn't really close to them, but I'm quite certain it was the woman in the photograph."

"Did she look happy? Oppressed? Did you hear her say anything?"

"No to all of those questions. If anything, she looked frail. She was finding it difficult to walk and she was concentrating hard. The man was encouraging her. She seemed to trust him well enough."

Tim's mobile started ringing. He rolled his eyes to the ceiling.

"Yes, Superintendent. Yes, I saw it – I saw your interview just now. No, no idea whatsoever. No, that's not possible. I think that the most likely explanation is that he was guessing. I'm certain that the SOCOs wouldn't have given anything away. Yes, I know it's infuriating – I was annoyed myself. But you handled it very well, sir. There's something else I have to tell you. It's urgent," he added, as the tirade issuing from the mobile continued. It subsided gradually.

"I'm at home, sir. Katrin's here, too, and she says that she saw Claudia McRae this morning, in Boston. I don't know – where was it, exactly?" he asked, turning to Katrin. "I'll put you on speak," he added.

"In the disabled car park near the Pilgrim Hospital," said Katrin flatly.

"Are you quite certain?" crackled the disembodied voice.

"Yes, absolutely certain. Tim's already asked me that." Katrin sounded sullen and unforbearing – not at all her usual self, Tim thought. He looked at her more closely. Her eyes were red-rimmed and her face was very pale. Even Superintendent Thornton had caught the peevishness of her tone.

"Would you mind coming in to the police station? Now?" he asked. "Both of you."

"Of course," said Tim. "I was almost on my way anyway."

Katrin sighed.

"So much for an evening in together," she said, more or less to herself. "I'll be with Tim, sir," she added. "Just give me a few minutes to change." For the first time, Tim noticed that she was wearing her dressing-gown. "Goodbye, sir," he said. "We'll see you shortly." He switched off the phone.

"Are you all right?" he asked.

"Since you ask, no I'm not," she replied. "But I daresay that it will keep until Thornton's bled me dry of any information that I might have. What happens to you after that? Will you go rushing off to Boston?"

"Not if you don't want me to," said Tim. "You come first, of course."

They both knew that, within the context of what had just happened, this simply wasn't true.

CHAPTER THIRTEEN

TIM WAS DRIVING along the winding road to Helpston for the second day running. He was trying to concentrate on the traffic, which was not heavy, but he was aware that most of the other vehicles on the road were as idiosyncratically driven and therefore potentially lethal as was usual in this part of the world. The farmers naturally assumed that they had a supreme right to trundle along, gouging holes into the surfaces of the highways with their outlandish and often ill-maintained vehicles as they plied the modern version of their ancient occupation, an occupation made newly mysterious by their seeming hardly ever to take these vehicles into the fields. Essentially, their attitude was that all other road-users were there on sufferance and had to take their chance. Already Tim had almost collided with a harrow that was protruding far to the right of the ancient Land Rover that was towing it, unmarked with flag or lantern, as he tried to overtake. City of Peterborough police should do something about these farmers, he thought sourly. He knew that he was being unfair, however. The farmers in South Lincolnshire were just as ungovernable, if less visible offenders. This was partly because their land was more remote and often accessed via B roads that attracted little other traffic; partly because they were professionally adept at extracting money from the EU and so were able to maintain much newer, more roadworthy vehicles. He dropped behind the Land Rover, screwing up his eyes to try to see the road beyond it more clearly. There was no prospect of his being able to overtake: the road was too winding.

A glance to his left told him that he was passing the Herrick estate. Still dominated by a massive country house, with a park that stretched as many miles as when it had been bestowed by a grateful queen, and still bounded by the same neat sixteenth-century stone walls, it had been built by Giles Herrick, an Elizabethan courtier whose descendants had continued to serve country and monarch right up to the present. He wondered idly how they had managed to escape the death duties that had rudely ejected so many noble families from their ancestral seats in the twentieth century. Service and royal patronage still counted for something, he supposed. And the house was open to the public, of course – that post-war source of manna for the aristocracy. Curious that in the sixties and seventies the working classes, in the new-found affluence that had provided them with mass-produced cars and 'disposable income', had chosen to spend their Sunday afternoons gawping at the treasures amassed by descendants of the hierarchy that had oppressed their ancestors. He supposed that there was a certain triumph to be gained from tramping through rooms thus exposed to common scrutiny, especially if you knew that their owners were cowering in some other part of the house, disdainful of the sweaty crowds but needful of their precious cash. Yet he did not really believe that those early visitors had made their jaunts in this spirit. Their attitude had rather been one of respectful reverence. He remembered being taken to Witham Abbey by his mother in the early eighties, when he was still at primary school, and how thrilled she had been when the Duke of Botolph himself had deigned to spend some minutes talking to the bus-load of ladies who were making their day more memorable by spending their husbands' hard-earned pounds in His Grace's souvenir shop. He had signed the apron that she had purchased. When she reached home again, one of her first tasks had been to embroider the Duke's signature in black silk so that it would not come out in the wash. As long as the pinny lasted, she could show her friends a perpetual record of the fact that His Grace had spoken to her. And what had he said? Nothing, as far as Tim could remember, except: 'Would you like me to sign that?' He had not asked her name. He had certainly not acknowledged the small boy standing at her side. Odd thing, the English reverence for titles. Even more remarkably, it rubbed off on foreigners. Katrin was a great royalty lover and never missed televised events that featured the royal family.

Katrin. She was the problem lurking at the back of Tim's mind, the reason why he was obliged to force himself to concentrate on driving properly. Their relationship had become strained. To have said that she, normally the most sanguine and even-tempered of women, was experiencing 'mood swings' would have been an understatement. Her moods did change, but merely from sad resignation to downright unhappiness. There were no high points. She no longer had any enthusiasm for the small treats or pleasures that he might suggest and she often seemed close to tears. He had tried to talk to her, but she had just stone-walled him. She had variously said that there was nothing wrong, that he was imagining it, or that she was just suffering a touch of the winter blues and that he was making her feel much worse by constantly talking about it. He could not understand it; their courtship and the first two years of their marriage had been so blissfully happy. Aside from the fact that he adored her and that she had given him every reason to believe that she reciprocated as wholeheartedly, he had counted himself blessed in finding a wife who understood the demands and the savagely unsocial hours that working as a policeman entailed. That Katrin worked as a police researcher represented the perfect solution in Tim's eyes. She could share in his experiences and enjoy confidences that he would not have been able to disclose to an ordinary civilian without herself taking on the irregular hours and the frayed nerves that went with the territory. Katrin was the homemaker, the warm, funny and beautiful woman to whom he had always looked forward to returning at the end of the day, however long it had been. That is, until a couple of months ago, when things had started to go wrong without warning.

Tim suddenly felt that he could not bear it. He knew that to lose Katrin, even to lose the wonderful intimacy that they had shared, would destroy him; yet he felt helpless. If she continued to keep him at arm's length, what could he do to restore their happiness?

The events of the previous evening had made matters considerably worse. He had taken Katrin to the police station at Spalding to make a statement to Superintendent Thornton. Boston Police were contacted, and they immediately checked the Pilgrim Hospital for anyone answering to Claudia's description. The hospital drew a blank – and its administrators could only grudgingly be persuaded to trawl through their records again, having already done so earlier in the week at Juliet's request. An announcement about the sighting, with a further plea for witnesses to come forward, had been broadcast on local radio and on Look North. No-one responded.

Katrin was shown photographs of the only two men in the district known to be current associates of Claudia – Guy Maichment and Oliver Sparham – and could not make a positive identification of either of them as the man who had been accompanying Claudia. Nor was she able to help put together a convincing Identikit picture. Her lack of confidence was disconcerting.

Superintendent Thornton had been very tolerant – even tactful, by his standards – but it was clear that he thought that Katrin had been mistaken. He had tried not to indicate this.

"Don't worry," he had said, patting her arm, "it's early days yet. We may very well get some responses tomorrow. And you're obviously exhausted, my dear. You should go home and get some sleep."

Under the circumstances, Tim saw that no useful purpose would be served by his going to Boston himself. By this time it was almost 11 p.m. As Thornton said, if anything came of the broadcasts, it would be better dealt with in the morning or, if it was urgent, by the Boston police on the ground. He drove Katrin home. Both were silent during the short journey.

"Drink?" asked Tim, when they were through the door.

"No, thanks. I think I'll go straight to bed."

"Are you OK?"

"I suppose so."

She did not meet his eye. Instead, she fetched a glass of water from the kitchen tap and disappeared upstairs with it. Tim sat in the cold sitting-room for an hour, drinking whisky, before he joined her. She was already asleep. She was still sleeping at 7 a.m. the next day when he left for work.

Pondering all of this, Tim realised with a start that he had almost over-shot the turn-off to the road to Guy Maichment's house. He slowed down. The Land Rover towing the dangerous harrow was still immediately in front of him. It also began to slow down and, at the last minute, to indicate left. Although he had not visited it before, Tim knew that Guy's house was the sole property standing beside a metalled road that gradually petered out into a dirt track. The track led to an area peppered with disused gravel pits. Its location, in light woodland, and isolated situation were not dis-similar to those of Claudia McRae's house. It therefore occurred to Tim that Guy Maichment was probably the driver of the Land Rover.

Keeping a prudent distance, he followed the Land Rover down the road. As he did so, he passed a series of water-filled gravel-pits. They were enclosed by a barbed-wire fence with a gate set in it that faced the last of the pits. A narrow cinder path ran round the circumference of the entire enclosed area. On a sign beside the gate the words 'Painton's Fisheries: licence holders only' had been inscribed in large block letters. A much older sign with an arrow pointing to the right announced more gravel pits. Tim remembered vaguely that when he was a child the bones of woolly mammoths and other prehistoric animals had been discovered in these pits. At that time the gravel works were still operational, but they had fallen into disuse quite soon afterwards. An enterprising person had evidently converted some of them into an organised fishing ground.

As the dirt track took over, the edge of the protruding harrow that the Land Rover was towing rose up on to the bank of the dyke that separated the fishing compound from the road, cutting down in its wake the small bushes that had been planted there. The driver of the Land Rover carried on without slowing down, though he must have been able to feel the drag on his tyres as the machinery battled its way through the long grass and scrub. When he reached the end of the track he turned a half-circle so that the Land Rover was standing parallel to the house, facing the woodland beyond. Tim parked the BMW half on the road, half on the bank of the left-hand dyke, so that if any other vehicle approached it would be able to get past.

The driver of the Land Rover jumped out smartly without looking across at Tim and walked quickly into the house, slamming both the gate and the door as he went. Tim was irritated by this. Unless Guy – or whoever it was – was a very poor driver indeed, he or she must have seen him in the wing mirrors as he followed the Land Rover down the track and must surely also have realised that Tim's was the same car that had been tailing his for miles. He came to the conclusion that Guy was trying to make a point. Exactly what point was less clear; aside from being a manifestation of his sulky and rather arrogant nature, it was probably intended to convey how little time he had to waste on policemen. Such a gesture would be wasted unless Guy decided not to answer the door. He'd better not, thought Tim to himself, his anger rising.

He took a deep breath and told himself to keep calm. After a few seconds, he got out of the BMW slowly and shut and locked the car quietly. Crossing behind the Land Rover, he opened the low gate in the fence that bounded Guy's garden and walked up the straight concrete path to the house. It struck him in passing how bleak this garden was, even allowing for the fact that winter was not kind to gardens. To call it austere would be generous; unadventurously conventional might be more accurate. The nondescript concrete path bisected two almost identical plots of land, in each of which was planted a grass patch and an arrangement of small box hedges shaped like noughts and crosses frameworks. If this garden contained flowers in the summer, they would have to be annuals or border plants so small that they died down completely in the winter. Tim considered what he knew of Guy's choice of career. How many professional gardeners planted their own plots so drably?

The house was also a surprise: a squat building with terracotta-washed walls and a flat roof with an unattractive overhang fashioned of thick concrete, it looked as if it had been constructed from a post-war pre-fab to which a large-ish extension had been added afterwards. The windows were sliding panels of glass of the kind found in Victorian railway carriages; the door, of some type of wood shoddy such as hardboard or chipboard, looked as if it could have been broken open with a single well-judged kick. It was an extremely ugly, not to say scruffy and down-at-heel building, and not the type of residence that Tim would have expected the self-regarding Guy Maichment to occupy.

There was no doorbell. A lion's head knocker, itself incongruous in such a setting, had been set high up on the door, but when Tim reached up to tap it he found that it had stuck to the blistering green paintwork. He was about to rap on the door with his knuckles when he heard footsteps approaching. He turned and saw Guy Maichment standing immediately behind him, almost too close for comfort. Guy was dressed in a voluminous waterproof of the kind that horse-riders wear on wet days and a pair of knee-length leather boots. He was carrying a tree-lopper.

"Good morning, Detective Inspector Yates. This is a surprise."

"Mr Maichment," said Tim, tipping his head forward slightly, since the tree-lopper made shaking hands awkward. "Not much of a surprise, surely – unless I'm mistaken, I've just followed you home."

Guy Maichment looked puzzled.

"I've been here all morning," he said. "I've been cutting branches off the trees at the back of the house to let in more light." His brow cleared suddenly. "Oh, you mean that you were following the Land Rover. I heard

Jared come back in it just now."

"Who's Jared?"

"Just a local man who works for me on occasions. In fact, I hope to have some pretty regular work for him shortly. He's been into Peterborough to buy some supplies for a job that we're doing."

"What kind of job?"

Guy Maichment looked Tim levelly in the eye.

"A landscape gardening job. You do know that landscape gardening is my profession?"

"Yes, I believe you mentioned it when we first met. This Jared isn't very sociable, is he? He got straight out of the Land Rover and went into the house. He must have seen me following him."

Guy shrugged.

"He is a bit anti-social. But I must say I hardly think he's at fault on this occasion. He would almost certainly have thought that any visitors would be for me."

"He has a key to your house, does he?"

"No. But the door's not locked when I'm here. He's probably in the kitchen, making himself some tea. Would you like to meet him?"

"Not especially," said Tim, "but I should like to have a further conversation with you about your aunt, if you don't mind. Should we go inside?"

Guy Maichment propped the lopping tool against the side of his porch and, squeezing past Tim without touching him, flung open the door with an expansive movement and made a sweeping gesture with his left arm to encourage him to enter. Tim could not tell whether it was meant ironically or not.

Inside, Guy Maichment's house was almost preternaturally tidy. The hall was bare of all furniture save for a doormat and a small mirror on the wall. Guy divested himself of the long raincoat and the quilted gilet that he was wearing beneath it and stowed them carefully in the cupboard under the stairs. He motioned Tim into what was evidently the main downstairs room of the place. Tim had realised by now that his abode was considerably smaller than Claudia's.

The living-room was one of the most functional rooms that Tim had ever seen. It was furnished with a small cottage suite consisting of two fireside chairs and a two-seater settee, a coffee table, a standard lamp and a glass-fronted bookcase. A brass screen stood in the fireplace. There was an oblong Chinese rug before it that made a small green oasis in a desert of sanded and polished wooden floorboards. That was all. There were no pictures, no vases or other ornaments, no flowers and no plants in pots. There wasn't even a television.

"The TV's in the kitchen," said Guy, as if reading Tim's mind. "Ah, there goes Jared," he added, as someone passed quickly by the window.

"Pity. If he'd still been in the kitchen, I'd have asked him to make some tea." Tim looked across, but caught only a glimpse of a navy-blue windcheater.

"Don't worry on my account," said Tim, not altogether sincerely. It seemed that Guy had no intention of doing so. He sat in one of the fireside chairs. The room was extremely cold, and it contained no radiator or any other form of heating that Tim could see besides the fireplace, which was clearly not in use.

"Now," said Guy, rubbing grubby palms on his trousers, "tell me more about my aunt. Or rather, about what you've discovered about her disappearance. I'm assuming that you haven't dropped by to tell me you've found her?" he added with a glint in his eye, his voice heavy with irony.

"Unfortunately not," said Tim with studied blandness.

"But you have more information? I understand that yesterday the police were searching the woods near her house?"

"Yes, but unfortunately they didn't find much – nothing, in fact, that might be connected directly with your aunt. However, DC Armstrong, whom I think you may have spoken to on the phone, has been doing a little bit of desk-based research. She's discovered some quite interesting things about your aunt's past."

Guy Maichment gave out a loud guffaw, which sounded forced and was incongruous, coming from such a usually quiet, taut and ironical man.

"Oh, well done, Inspector! So my aunt had an interesting past, did she? And it's taken you several days to find that out. Really, you must excuse me if I'm beginning to lose confidence in you. She was the most famous female archaeologist of her generation, for God's sake – in fact the only female archaeologist of any note. The only British one, that is. She led digs in the Arab countries before the war, and she was subsequently in Nor . . . in Scandinavia, when some of the most important ship burial digs took place there. She has lived a life packed full of adventure. And you're here to tell me that it was interesting!"

"I'm not referring to her accomplishments as an archaeologist, Mr Maichment, fascinating though I'm sure those are," said Tim quietly. He paused to look Guy Maichment in the eye. Guy held his gaze, but with a look that was neither relaxed nor amused, though it tried to be both. Tim thought that he saw alarm, even fear, stalking Guy. "Tell me, did you know that your aunt was associated with some extremely right-wing political groups?"

Guy looked away and turned his gaze to the fireplace.

"I'm not quite certain what you mean by 'extremely right wing', Detective Inspector. I suspect that you and I might disagree if we were to try to define such a term. I am, of course, aware that Claudia's most groundbreaking work sought to tie her findings – some of them very spectacular findings – to sociological and anthropological hypotheses which were open to dispute. Not to put too fine a point on it, some of her critics thought that she embroidered the conclusions which she drew beyond the basis of the actual facts that she was able to record. Her methods were popular just before and just after the war; but, as archaeology became more allied to science and as science rapidly improved to the extent that it could enable many statements to be made with certainty that had only been educated guesses before (and, of course, vice versa), her views became discredited in some quarters. Unjustly, in my view. We're still subject to creative ideas, even in these scientific times, and often some notion that's been dressed up by 'science' is just as unprovable as an idea put forward by an amateur. And Claudia's work on early languages was actually quite ingenious. It still deserves to be taken seriously."

"I agree with you there," said Tim, not wishing to draw out the hostility that he knew was never very far from the surface when he was speaking to Guy. He chose the most innocuous of Claudia McRae's theories, as retailed to him by Juliet, in an attempt to maintain Guy's good will. "These ideas of which you speak: are they related to her convictions as an early feminist?"

"Goodness, Inspector, you *are* well-informed! It's true that when Claudia was a young woman and still trying to make her name as an archaeologist she picked up and ran with the premise that the role of pre-historic women had been underestimated by the historians that followed them, because by the time that history was first recorded the societies that recorded it were mostly patriarchal. Claudia's argument was that women and men must have contributed more equally in very primitive times in order for communities to survive, but as far as I know there was little evidence to support this, save Claudia's observations on the way that some flintheads and other tools had been fashioned. Anthropologists were quick to point out that she was in any case applying twentieth century values to cultures that may, for all we know, have revered the woman's role as bearer of children and homemaker. I've read some of that early stuff and I think that it was pretty jejune. No, what I was referring to were the much more sophisticated arguments that she constructed from her work on the McRae Stone. Since you've been delving into her past, Detective Inspector, you must have found references to it? It was undoubtedly the most important find of Claudia's career."

Tim nodded. "The Northern Rosetta," he offered, to indicate that he understood the reference. "Can you explain to me, broadly speaking, what your aunt's 'sophisticated arguments' consisted of?"

Guy Maichment leaned forward in his chair, earnest and engaged.

"They were at once quite simple, in being easy to grasp, and linguistically very complex. I couldn't begin to go into the detail – even if you were interested in it, I am no expert myself. As you say, the McRae Stone, which was discovered during a dig in the Orkneys (ironically, Claudia hadn't even wanted to take that dig on, but she agreed to do it because she'd been evacuated from the Middle East in the run-up to the war, so she was at a bit of a loose end), was similar to the Rosetta Stone, in that it bore the same inscription in three different languages. One of them was a Celtic language symbolised by runes that had already been partially deciphered by others – romantically, it has sometimes been called Thari, or 'the language of the Druids'. The other two languages were both forerunners of Gaelic – one she called proto-Gaelic-Norse and the other proto-Gaelic-Scots. By carefully transcribing all the words that she had of these languages and carrying out painstaking work on the probable roots of each of them, she was able to attribute to them a kind of hierarchy of semantic richness and sophistication which she believed to be a reflection of how noble and cultivated the people who spoke them were."

"I see. So she conferred upon the people who spoke what in her view was the best of these languages the attributes of a master-race?" Tim was being deliberately provocative. Guy Maichment blinked and looked across at him sharply, but his reply was urbane enough.

"I wouldn't put it quite like that, Inspector. But you're on the right track."

Tim bowed his thanks and decided to surprise Guy by changing tack. He would keep his most important piece of information until last.

"Tell me, Mr Maichment, have you heard of a Norwegian academic called Dr Elida Berg?"

Guy Maichment examined his knuckles.

"No, I can't say that I have. Why? Is she an associate of Claudia's? If so, I should tell you that Claudia has supervised and collaborated with scores of people, academics and others, and that I'm aware only of a tiny proportion of them, mostly those relating to the latter part of her career. You must remember that Claudia was well into her forties when I was born."

"Indeed," said Tim. "Nevertheless, I thought that you might have come across Dr Berg. For one thing, she and Dame Claudia wrote a number of joint papers on the McRae Stone after its discovery and you might have read some of them. More importantly than that, we have reason to believe that Dame Claudia may have spent the Second World War living with Dr Berg, who was working at a Norwegian university at the time."

Guy shrugged. "It's perfectly possible. As I've said, I don't know – it was before my time. You know of course that my aunt is gay. But quite honestly, Detective Inspector, interesting as it may be to review my aunt's life and work and even to discuss her friends, I don't see where this is leading us. In fact, I feel inclined to say that if your investigations don't take a more direct turn very shortly, I shall be in touch with Roy Little again and ask him to remove you from this investigation."

"As you wish, Mr Maichment. I am perfectly aware that you are able to exert influence in that quarter. However, I should also like you to consider this: Although Norwegian by birth, Dr Elida Berg was a Nazi sympathiser who eventually had to 'disappear'. We're not sure exactly why, yet. Your aunt, on the other hand, continued to live in Norway until some time after the end of the war, when she returned to the UK. Her celebrity as an eminent archaeologist continued to increase."

"Another set of irrelevant points, Detective Inspector, unless I am missing something. My aunt can hardly be expected to have been account- able for the political views of her colleagues."

"I quite agree. But what interests me is that it is from this period – or, more specifically, from the period just before the war when your aunt col- laborated with Dr Berg on the papers about the McRae Stone – that your aunt's publications become much more tightly argued and scholarly. As you said yourself, before that they were rather florid and naïve. And she continued to employ this more erudite style throughout the fifties, long after Dr Berg disappeared, though it has to be said that she didn't develop her arguments very much thereafter."

"So? Perhaps she was a good pupil. Perhaps the original work was so good that she could not make many material additions to it."

"Perhaps, Mr Maichment. And perhaps there were other reasons. We may never know, but, if we can find out, I think that we may be able to solve the mystery of your aunt's disappearance."

Guy Maichment regarded him stonily. "Is that all, Detective Inspector?"

"Not quite," said Tim. "There is one other thing. A very reliable witness says that she saw your aunt in Boston yesterday morning, being escorted by a man."

Guy Maichment was visibly disconcerted: his face blanched; he seemed to gasp for breath.

"Why have you only just told me this?" he demanded, with clumsy indignation – almost certainly feigned, Tim thought. "Why aren't you there now, searching for her?"

"I'm sorry to startle you, sir. Of course we began extensive enquiries in Boston straight away, but so far they have yielded nothing. Although your aunt was seen near the hospital, she has not been admitted there; and, if anyone else saw her, they have not reported it to the police."

"So it might not have been her at all?"

"It might not; although the witness is convinced that it was."

"What about the man? Do you have a description?"

"Unfortunately not. He had his face turned away from the witness."

"Why didn't she – you did say the witness was a woman? – call the police, or seek help?"

"She didn't realise that it was your aunt until afterwards. She had not seen a photograph of her until one was shown after the police press conference was televised early yesterday evening. Were you watching, by any chance?"

"I – No. No, I didn't know about it. I don't watch much television. But if this woman couldn't identify the man and no-one else has said that they saw my aunt, don't you think that her claim sounds a little far-fetched? Surely she must have been mistaken – or perhaps even making it up. I've heard that there are people who do such things, who deliberately get themselves involved in high-profile enquiries of this kind by pretending to have useful information."

"There are such people," said Tim, "and although we think that this witness is reliable it is also possible that you are right."

"Who is she, anyway?"

"I cannot tell you that at the moment, sir. If she should ever have to testify about what she saw in court, you would find out her identity then."

Guy Maichment raised his eyebrows and shrugged as if to conjure the return of his slightly off-colour urbanity. He escorted Tim to the door without saying another word beyond a curt goodbye.

"Goodbye, Mr Maichment. We shall, of course, keep you informed if there are any more developments."

CHAPTER FOURTEEN

TIM DROVE BACK to Spalding more slowly than he had come. He knew that Guy Maichment had a difficult and unpredictable character. Nevertheless, he was convinced that there was more to Guy's reaction to Katrin's sighting of Claudia than scorn for the police investigation. It had made Tim certain that Katrin had really seen her in Boston. That Guy had been rattled until he had discovered that the anonymous witness had not got a look at Claudia's companion's face was beyond question. It would be tempting to conclude that this was because Guy himself had been escorting his aunt, but there were other likely explanations, including the possibility that Claudia was being held by a person whom Guy feared.

Tim parked the BMW in the station car park and ran up the stairs to his office. Somehow he was going to have to convince Superintendent Thornton that a full-scale search should be mounted in the Boston area.

He had intended to petition the Superintendent immediately, but, when he reached the top of the stairs, Juliet was standing there.

"Good Morning, Juliet. A lot of water seems to have passed under the bridge since we spoke late yesterday afternoon. I assume you know about the sighting in Boston?"

"Yes, sir. You think that it was genuine, then?"

"I'm certain that it was genuine." Tim narrowed his eyes. "Has Thornton been suggesting otherwise?"

"No, not exactly. He's just being cautious, I think."

Tim decided to let this pass.

"Any more news from the Boston police?"

CHAPTER FIFTEEN

ALEX SPENT THE days after the conference writing the first draft of her proposal. She knew that eventually she would have to consult Edmund about it, but she fought shy of contacting him yet. Although they were not lovers, they were no longer the ordinary colleagues that once they had been.

The deadlock was broken by chance. She and Tom were temporarily sharing a car. (Tom ran an ancient Sunbeam, to maintain which he periodically had to scour the country for spare parts; once again, it was out of action.) On the Tuesday following the conference, he had taken her to a trustees' meeting at the Peterborough Museum in her own elderly but reliable Volkswagen. He promised to return for her some hours later, after he had driven himself back to Spalding. He had to attend a case conference about a child who was considered to be at risk.

When Alex had been invited to become a trustee of the museum she was at first reluctant to accept, mainly because of the size of her workload at the Archaeological Society, but also because she saw it as a foray into rival territory that she did not particularly wish to make. However, the Archaeological Society's committee had persuaded her that to accept would be in its interests, because it would demonstrate its support for other local historical foundations. The Society had passed most of the three centuries of its existence as a self-consciously aloof and haughtily-exclusive organisation, but its present-day members were not as well-heeled as their forbears and were consequently unable to provide it with the same levels of private financial support that had helped to make it at once distinguished and snobbish. Its leading lights, Oliver Sparham among them, had to bid for national grants in order to maintain its glory and in doing so had woken up to the fact that government funding was unlikely to be forthcoming for self-styled élites. Reluctantly, therefore, they had been prevailed upon to share its treasures and occasionally to make an effort to give it a profile within the wider community. From the point of view of the committee, sparing the Society's secretary for occasional well-publicised duties at the museum was an easy sacrifice to make. Despite the extra burden that it added to her workload, Alex had allowed herself to be persuaded.

She was vaguely aware that Edmund also had some kind of relationship with the museum, though he was not a trustee, and so far had not attended any of the meetings at which she herself had been present. When she entered the imposing boardroom a few minutes after the meeting had started (Tom was incapable of being early for anything), she was somewhat disconcerted to see Edmund's face among the half-dozen or so that turned to greet her. Worse still, although there were several spare places at the table, the board papers had already been distributed and the neat pile awaiting her had been placed before the chair next to Edmund's own, which happened also to be the one nearest the door. If she had moved the papers to take them to another space at the table, she would have caused a disturbance, so she had little alternative but meekly to occupy that seat. Edmund moved back her chair and created a minor kerfuffle by ostentatiously moving his own papers to give her more room.

"Would you like some tea?" he enquired. She tried to meet his bright blue eyes, but he immediately looked away.

"No, thank you," she said in a stilted voice. "Water is fine." The chairman, Dr Ratcliffe, poured her a glass and passed it. She took it with a shaking hand. "I'm sorry I'm late," she added.

"No matter," muttered Dr Ratcliffe, scrutinising her suspiciously. Hers had not been an appointment of which he had approved. "We're no further than signing off the minutes of the last meeting. I trust you have no amendments that you wish to table?"

Alex shook her head. Every meeting proceeded in the same way, at a snail's pace, the agenda items barely changing from one six-month period to the next. She settled down in her chair, resigning herself to an afternoon of boredom tinged with the discomfort caused by Edmund's proximity.

They plodded through the agenda until they came to the 'donations' item. This was always the penultimate topic that they discussed, just before 'A.O.B.' Alex suspected that 'donations' occupied this place in the proceedings because Dr Ratcliffe was a compulsive collector who could not bear to turn away any gift to the museum, however slight its interest or dubious its authenticity; by this stage, the trustees had been reduced to such a state of ennui that all they could think of was how to remove themselves from the boardroom as swiftly as was decently possible. Consequently, despite the fact that the museum's storerooms were groaning with items that would never be displayed, some of which were disintegrating for lack of proper curation (a heritage-conserving point usually higher up the agenda, but producing no practical plan of action), they almost always agreed to accept all of the donations that the museum had been offered.

Dr Ratcliffe worked his way solemnly through the list of items which had been offered, a copy of which was included in the trustees' sets of papers. Alex, still embarrassed by Edmund's presence, had contributed little during the course of the afternoon and was even more anxious than her fellow sufferers for the meeting to end. However, she was now forced to emerge from the carapace of introspection that she had built around herself: an opinion was required from everyone present. She became aware that Edmund was very excited about something on the list. He was fidgeting and tapping his pen against his writing-block, but not, Alex was certain, because he wanted to get away. She had sat through enough meetings with Edmund to know that he was both agitated and gearing himself up to speak. Her suspicion became a certainty when he cleared his throat.

"As I said at the beginning of the meeting," Dr Ratcliffe intoned, looking over his spectacles like a headmaster checking that all of his charges were paying attention, "we are fortunate to have with us today the Heritage Officer for South Lincolnshire, Mr Edmund Baker. I am sure that you will all agree that Mr Baker has made an invaluable contribution to this meeting and I should like to renew our very sincere invitation to him to attend all of our meetings. However, I am now able to disclose," he looked around him, changing from headmaster to impresario, "I am now able to disclose that Mr Baker has a particular reason for being here today. It concerns the final item on this list, Item 8: the papers of the Honourable Esther Lockhart, widow of the Reverend Victor Lockhart, which Mrs Lockhart's great-great niece, Violet Wood, would like to donate to the museum. The papers did not belong to the Reverend Lockhart, but to Mrs Lockhart's first husband, who was both a clergyman and an enthusiastic antiquary. As it happens, besides documenting his archaeological work, the papers include quite an interesting collection of mid-nineteenth century ephemera and some family letters and other documents about the clergyman's parish; but they do not, strictly speaking, belong in Peterborough." He paused. "I say 'strictly speaking', because Miss Wood herself *does* live in Peterborough, but the papers relate to the parish of Kirton, near Boston. Also, as it happens, Mr Baker is particularly interested in documents relating to this parish and has already built up quite a collection of them for the South Lincolnshire archives. Mr Baker is therefore proposing that, in his role as Heritage Officer for South Lincolnshire, he should purchase the Honourable Esther Lockhart's papers for the district. The sum he is offering – five thousand pounds – is a generous one. It would make a significant contribution to some of the preservation work that we need to carry out, which we have already discussed at some length. I have raised the matter with Miss Wood, and she is happy for the transaction to proceed. She is a Friend of the Museum, and feels that raising funds in this way would be as worthy a way of remembering her great-great aunt as keeping the papers here. Now, does anyone wish to object to Mr Baker's proposal?"

Alex shot Edmund a look that he was not quick enough to deflect immediately. She saw that he was excited and agitated, certainly, but above all he seemed to be afraid. Afraid of what, she could only guess: was it that his bid for the papers might not succeed? It would be unlike Edmund to get personally involved with any aspect of his work, even the prospect of making an acquisition that he coveted. Why he wanted these papers was also a mystery. Both the Archaeological Society and the county and district archives had dozens of collections of the amateur musings of eighteenth and nineteenth century clergymen; one set more or less would make little difference to either's store of knowledge. As for paying five thousand pounds for them, it was a ridiculously generous offer. £500 would have been munificent.

"I suppose that the papers have been properly valued, by an independent expert?" It was Mrs Munson speaking. She was a stout, mannish lady of about seventy who showed an instinctive distrust of any initiative that was proposed to the trustees, even if it was a straightforward gift of money.

Edmund flushed brick red.

"Not exactly," he said hoarsely, pausing to clear his throat, "but Dr Ratcliffe and I have encountered collections of papers like this on many previous occasions and he is aware that the offer, as he has said, is a very generous one. In fact, the price that I am offering is somewhat above the market value – simply because I wish the Kirton papers to be as complete as possible, you understand."

"Dr Ratcliffe, is that the case? Has the museum itself ever bought collections of this kind in the past, or had them valued?"

"Not archaeological papers. We bought the collected natural history papers of a Victorian cleric some years ago. Natural history tends to command a higher price than archaeology. It is because the papers are usually illustrated. I seem to remember that the collection that I mention included some very fine illustrations."

"Indeed. So the price that the museum paid for that collection would give us a clue as to whether the price offered by Mr Baker is fair?"

"I would say so."

"Do you know how much we paid?"

Dr Ratcliffe shifted uneasily in his chair. "As it happens, I did look it up. I was anticipating the question, as it were."

Alex looked from Dr Ratcliffe to Edmund. "They've cooked this up between them," she thought.

"Well, how much was it? Don't keep us in suspense: I'm sure we all want to go home," said Mrs Munson, glowering at everybody.

"It was . . . hmm," Dr Ratcliffe cleared his throat . . ."um, twelve hundred pounds."

"I see," said Mrs Munson sardonically. "So Mr Baker's offer would appear to be a very good one indeed, as far as the museum is concerned. So good that one wonders if one has a duty to inform Mr Baker's employer of the extent of his generosity. I assume that the money is to come from the heritage fund, Mr Baker?"

"Of course," said Edmund, his voice even croakier. He swallowed, then opened his mouth to say something else, but Dr Ratcliffe, his aplomb suddenly restored, held up his hand.

"I think that we have debated this enough," he said. "Mr Baker has explained why he is prepared to offer so much – on behalf of the heritage fund – in this instance. In my opinion, it provides what I believe is called a win-win opportunity for both the Kirton collection and the museum. I propose that we vote on it. As you so wisely point out, Mrs Munson, it is time that I drew this meeting to a close. Who is in favour of the sale?"

Four of the six trustees immediately raised their hands. Alex and Mrs Munson did not.

"Who is against it?"

"I am not against it, as such," said Mrs Munson. "I should just like a little more proof that we really are doing as well as possible out of it."

"I think I should abstain," said Alex. "I have vested interests in both the Kirton collection, through my work with the Archaeological Society and the district archive, and, of course, the museum; so it is not appropriate for me to vote."

Dr Ratcliffe nodded in an exasperated way.

"Very proper," he said. "Quite right." He turned away from her and addressed the room.

"I am pleased to announce that the majority of the trustees are in favour of the sale. I don't therefore need to use my casting vote, but, for the record, I am in favour also. Motion passed."

Alex looked sideways at Edmund. He had folded his hands on his pile of papers and was trying to look calm, but his face had gone from puce to pale and there were beads of sweat on his forehead.

"Thank you," he said. "I am grateful."

He was trying to sound low-key, but she did not miss the catch in his voice. She doubted if anyone else noticed; even as Dr Ratcliffe was asking if anyone had any other business, the trustees were rustling their papers together and pushing back their chairs.

"Then I declare the meeting closed!" said Dr Ratcliffe. "Edmund, a word, if I may?"

"Of course," said Edmund. Alex got up to leave with the others.

"Oh, Alex, must you go? I had hoped to have a quick word with you, too. This won't take a moment."

"Tom is coming to pick me up, but he'll probably be late. I'll wait in the foyer. If he comes on time, I'll have to disappear, because there's no parking round here. He's going to call me when he arrives."

"OK. I'll be with you shortly."

The day was seasonally squally and it was cold waiting in the museum foyer. Alex stood as far away from the revolving door as possible as people came and went, 'bringing the cold with them', as her mother used to say. She had been waiting for ten minutes when Tom called her mobile.

"Hello? Tom?"

"Darling, I'm so sorry. Is your meeting over? Are you waiting?"

"It finished only ten minutes ago, so yes I am waiting, in the foyer as we agreed, but I haven't been here for long. Where are you?"

"I'm still in Spalding. There was an unexpectedly nasty turn of events after the case conference this afternoon, so I haven't been able to get away. I can't get away now, in point of fact; I'm needed at the police station shortly."

Alex sighed. This was so typical of Tom. He always gave his juvenile delinquents priority over everyone else. He sounded more strained than usual, though – as if he were worried about more than just the fact that she would be annoyed.

"Is anything wrong?"

"What? No. Yes. I don't know – probably. As I've explained, I can't get away. Do you think you can find some other way of getting home? I'm sure that the bus ride would be too miserable to contemplate, but could you perhaps find a taxi?"

Alex didn't know whether to laugh or lose her temper. Only Tom could suggest that she ran up the expense of a twenty-mile taxi ride when there was an adequate bus service available, however tiresome it might be.

"Don't worry," she said, trying not to let an edge creep into her voice. "Edmund Baker is here. I'll see if he intends to drive home straight away and, if he does, I'll ask him if he minds taking a little detour via Spalding. I'm sure he won't refuse."

"What if he does – or if he's going somewhere else?" asked Tom. Worried, thought Alex, but obviously not worried enough to put her first. She laughed as brightly as she could. "He won't – and I'm sure he won't be," she said. "If by any chance he can't help, I'll manage."

"OK, thanks," said Tom. "I love you." Testing the water, now, thought Alex grimly, at the same time catching the sound of Edmund's unmistakeable heavy tread coming down the staircase. It was the perfect excuse not to repeat Tom's words to her exactly. "Me too," she said in a low voice. "Got to go. Take care." She switched him off before he could reply.

"Alex, thank you for waiting," said Edmund, who was still finding it difficult to meet her eye, but otherwise seemed to have recovered his equilibrium. "Do you fancy a drink? Oh, I forgot, Tom's likely to appear at any moment, isn't he?"

"Not any more," said Alex wryly. "He's got caught up in another of his cases. As you know, in Tom's book, any 'underprivileged' juvenile criminal takes priority over us more advantaged citizens, his wife included. So the answer is yes: drink, dinner, whatever you like. The night is young, as they say, and I very much doubt if I'll see Tom before midnight."

Edmund looked at her quizzically. This time he did meet her eye.

"It's not like you to sound so bitter," he said. "I thought you were proud of Tom and his work."

"Oh, I am. I'm just tired, I guess, and a little bit fed up with never knowing whether he'll meet me or not when he promises to. To add insult to injury, he's driving my car at the moment. The Sunbeam needs a new alternator, or some such thing – vintage 1956, of course. As a matter of fact, I was going to ask you if you'd run me home – if you're planning on going home yourself, of course, and if you don't mind going a little out of your way?"

Edmund seemed to hesitate for a few seconds; then he smiled broadly.

"I'd be delighted," he said. "And I like your idea of having supper together, too. Where would you like to go?"

"Probably best to stay in Peterborough – there's more choice here. I don't eat here very often, but I seem to remember that there's a passable Italian just round the corner from the cathedral."

"Fine by me. It's a bit early to eat now, though." Edmund looked at the flashy square watch that Alex had disliked since she had first noticed it at an Archaeological Society meeting years before. "Barely half-past five. Should we go for a drink first?"

"On condition that you let me pay," said Alex, "and also that you let me get the drinks. I haven't forgotten the last time that you bought me a drink; you're not to be trusted."

He had the grace to blush.

"All right, but the dinner is on me." Damn, thought Alex. I let myself in for that.

CHAPTER SIXTEEN

EDMUND SEEMED TO know Peterborough well; much better than Alex herself. Holding her arm lightly, he guided her through the winding side streets that led away from the museum until they reached a rather bijou pub called the Queen's Head. It was very small and very old and stood, surprisingly, in the middle of a residential terrace. The pub looked older than the houses that surrounded it.

Inside, it was almost too warm, with old-fashioned card tables crammed up against each other and plush-covered stools for the patrons to sit on. The landlord nodded at Edmund as they entered.

"I come here quite a lot," he said quickly, though she found the fact that he had offered her an explanation odder than if he hadn't bothered. "I found it once when I was taking a walk after I'd been to the museum. It's a good place to relax in."

Alex laughed. "What would you like to drink?"

"Since I'm driving later and I shall certainly drink wine with dinner, I'd better say half a bitter. Don't let me stop you choosing something with a little more kick to it."

"I've told you, I intend to be good this evening."

Nevertheless, when she reached the bar, she felt rebellious. She had intended to suggest to Tom that they should eat out that evening because she knew that she would need to unwind. There was no reason why her evening should be spoilt by Tom's job – or, to put it more truthfully, his inconsiderateness.

"Half a bitter, please," she said, "and a vodka and tonic."

The landlord had poured her a double before she could stop him. "On the house," he said, with a wink, as he uncapped a bottle of tonic water. "I've not seen Edmund with a lady before . . . and he's a good customer."

Alex was annoyed at the assumptions that the man was clearly making, but decided that there was no point in being unpleasant. She thanked him curtly for the drinks. She wouldn't have to come here again, after all, and they'd be leaving for the restaurant in a few minutes.

Edmund was sitting at a table with his back to her, talking to someone on his cellphone. He sounded irascible. "Well, that's all there is to it," he said. "I can't come home until later. Something's come up." He switched the phone off and put it in his pocket. Alex was surprised. Did he talk to

'Krystyna' like that?

"Was that your wife?"

"No. One of my sons. He's staying with us for a few days. I don't know where Krystyna was – Callum didn't say. No doubt he will pass on my message to her."

Alex sat down opposite him. She passed him the beer.

"Well, cheers," she said. "I feel as if I've bunked off school. No-one will know where we are for the next few hours."

"Cheers," he said, clinking her glass. "What made you say that?"

She laughed. "I really have no idea. I suppose just being entirely free from responsibility, free to do something secret, even if it is just having dinner with an old friend, has a certain appeal; especially after that bloody awful meeting. Talking of which, why on earth do you want the Lockhart papers so badly? You must have seen dozens of country vicar collections. What makes those so special?"

His manner changed immediately. He was clearly annoyed that she had asked.

"If you must know," he said tautly, "I wanted them for us. There's some work that I've started on that will be hugely enhanced by what's in those papers, mundane though they might be," he added unconvincingly.

"For us?" Alex tried to keep the incredulity and rising panic from her voice. "What do you mean, for 'us'?"

"Oh, don't worry," said Edmund. His tone was threaded with sarcasm now. "I'm not trying to wreck your marriage or persuade you to elope with me. It's simply some work I'm doing to increase our chances of getting the money that we want for our museum project. I can't explain properly yet -you'll just have to trust me. I'm confident that I've made a breakthrough that will ensure that we get the funds, but I need the Lockhart papers to do it. They're the missing piece of the jigsaw."

Alex took a sip of her vodka.

"You're talking in riddles," she said, "and of course it is impossible for me to understand. But I do feel that I should point out that it is unethical of you to use the heritage fund to over-pay for the Lockhart papers, however much you may want them and however beneficial they may be to 'us'."

"Don't be silly. You could credit me with a little more integrity than that. I wouldn't dream of using the heritage fund to pay for a personal project."

"You're not spending your own money on them?"

"Not exactly, no. But I promise you that no public money will change hands. Bill Ratcliffe and I decided that it was best to deceive the trustees in that respect, and only in that respect, to get them to agree to the sale without a lot of pointless argument. But everything else is entirely above board."

"Hum," said Alex. "I'm not sure that that shows great integrity, either. But I am willing to believe that the purchase will create a 'win-win' situation , as Dr Ratcliffe so engagingly puts it. And to be quite honest, I can't be bothered to think about it any more. As you know, I was coerced into becoming one of the museum's trustees, much against Dr Ratcliffe's own wishes as well as my own, and its projects don't lie very close to my heart. Let's talk about something else."

Alex knew that it was her own fault that she drank the second vodka and tonic. She felt the vodka burn her throat; her head was already swimming as she tied the belt of her trench-coat and picked up her handbag.

Edmund held out his arm in rather an old-fashioned, courtly way once they were outside on the street again; not entirely because she was feeling dizzy from the vodka and a little sick from lack of food, she accepted it. It was beginning to rain, and the pavements shone darkly. They walked quickly and in silence. Alex felt uneasy. She was familiar, of course, with Edmund, but the intimacy which they now seemed to be sharing was strange, obviously wrong. At one point she tried to pull her arm away from his, but he had it clenched tightly and did not release her. She felt relieved when finally they reached the restaurant.

CHAPTER SEVENTEEN

IT WAS LATER than they had realised. Perhaps because it was a Monday, perhaps because it was raining, the restaurant was already crowded when they arrived. It was only a small place, having eight or possibly ten tables, and through the misted windows they could see that all were occupied, as was the sofa next to the cash desk where hopefuls waited patiently for a vacant space.

"It looks as if we're out of luck," said Alex.

"The evening's still young. You said that you didn't have to be home until midnight, didn't you?"

"No, I said that Tom probably wouldn't be back before then. I certainly want to be in bed earlier than that – I have a busy day tomorrow. Besides, I don't know that Tom will really be as late as that and I don't want to worry him." Alex was getting cold feet.

"He's sure to call you if he gets back first," said Edmund, leading her through the door. However, her intuition proved to be right. Immediately they entered the restaurant, they were surrounded by two or three waiters, all speaking excitedly in varying degrees of broken English. After a few seconds, the patron, a stereotype of the short, stout Italian proprietor, pushed his way through to them and informed them in comprehensible English that they would be unable to accommodate any more diners that evening.

Alex pulled a wry face. She was half disappointed, half relieved.

"I guess it's home for each of us, and toast and tea before bed," she said. "We'll feel virtuous tomorrow, at any rate."

"You don't want to go in search of another restaurant?"

"There really isn't time," she said.

"Well, you shan't go supperless. I have another solution."

"What is it? Fish and chips?" She laughed, glad to inject some lightness into the conversation.

"Not quite – you'll see. First we need to go back to the car."

"You're sure that this isn't going to take a long time?"

"Absolutely certain. It will be almost as quick as going straight home. And it will give me the opportunity to show you something."

"Now I'm intrigued! How far away is the car?"

"Not far at all. I've left it in the big multi-storey car part in the shopping centre. Are you OK to walk?"

She laughed again. "What else do you propose? That I wait here until you come back?"

"If you like. I'm sure the Italian gentleman would allow you to prop up his bar for ten minutes."

She shook her head.

"Your sudden onset of chivalry is worrying! But I'll come with you, if you don't mind."

He offered his arm again, but she declined, walking beside him but apart from him now. She was suddenly quite tired and realised that she was cold and hungry, too; but she did her best to match his pace, which grew more rapid as they approached the car park.

Edmund had at least one thing in common with Tom, she reflected: neither of them was a car snob. Tom's car at least had the virtue of being unusual, however inconvenient that turned out to be when it broke down, but Edmund's elderly Saab was simply a rust-bucket. However, when Edmund opened the passenger door, she saw that, inside, it was immaculate: the leather seats were clean and polished, the mats on the floor scrubbed and there were no empty soft drinks bottles or more unpleasant food detritus tossed on the back seat or in the door-pockets, as was invariably the case with Tom's car. Edmund handed her in with some ceremony. The absurdity of the situation made her giggle.

"What's the matter?" he asked huffily. She read his mood and was sober in an instant.

"Nothing, really. I'm just light-headed from too much booze unaccompanied by food."

"Get in quickly, then." He slammed the door shut almost before she had moved her coat out of its way.

Edmund drove at speed through the city and out beyond the shopping centre. He slowed down when they came to a modest residential area and cruised sedately through the streets of terraces and between-the-wars semis. He was peering through the rain-spattered windscreen, apparently intent on finding somewhere he only half-remembered. Several times they ended up in a cul-de-sac or he saw that they were approaching the ring road and reversed the car to travel back in the direction from which they had come, before again plunging into yet more side-streets and badly-lit thoroughfares. His jaw was set, his frown one of annoyance as much as concentration. Alex decided not to risk an attempt at conversation, not even to ask if she could help by looking out for the street name that he wanted. Instead, she kept her eyes on the rain-washed windscreen, just occasionally shooting him a sideways glance. It was when employing this tactic that she saw his face suddenly light up in one of his beatific smiles. Edmund was at his most engaging when he looked like this.

"There it is!" he exclaimed. "It's on an old corner shop site and it hasn't changed at all!"

Alex could barely see through the rivulets of rain. "What am I looking at?" she asked.

"That!" said Edmund, taking his hand off the wheel and pointing with his index finger. "Croxley's. It's an upmarket fish shop. I used to bring my first girlfriend here. Rock salmon was a speciality then. I wonder if they still sell it!"

He jumped out of the car. He was gone for some time; when he returned he was smiling broadly. He carefully lifted a small brown carrier-bag over the back of the seat and placed it on the floor behind Alex.

"It's unbelievable!" he said. "The place hasn't changed a bit. Apparently old man Croxley is still alive, though it is his son, Terry, who runs it now. And they still do rock salmon!" he added triumphantly.

"So you bought some?"

"Of course. And some coke. There's a small bottle of rum in the dashboard that I always keep for emergencies, so we can have rum and cokes, just like I used to when I was a teenager. A pity we're not under-age as well; it would make it taste even better."

"I don't know where this secret place is that you're proposing to take me to, but can we get there soon, please?"

He started up the car and slowly rounded the corner. Alex saw that they were now on a main road and about halfway down a steepish incline. Once more Edmund was peering intently through the windscreen. He switched the wipers to double-speed.

"This road leads straight down to the river; and the bridge that I'm looking for should be a little to our left, when we reach the bottom of the hill."

Alex sighed. She could no longer recollect why she'd agreed to this wild goose chase. She yearned despairingly for the warmth of her own kitchen.

When they entered the next street Alex could see the bridge some yards to their right. As they drew closer, she saw that it was a Victorian railway bridge, solid and ornate in finely-crafted cast-iron. The river bank adjacent to it was wide and flat. Edmund parked next to a squat structure that had been erected next to the bridge.

"We have to get out now, but it is only a few steps to shelter. I have an oilskin in the boot if you would like to borrow it?" He placed his hand solicitously on her arm. She shook it off, apparently by accident, by unclasping her seat-belt.

"I'm sure I'll be fine," she said, wondering why her vocabulary seemed to have shrunk to so few words. "If you want me to make it to the bridge, my mac should keep me dry; but I warn you, Edmund, that I think it's unlikely that I'm going to want to stay there for long. If it is wet or cold, or muddy underfoot, I'm going to get straight back into the car and ask you to drive me home. Is that understood?"

"Certainly. But you won't be disappointed. Now, could you hand me the bottle that you'll find in the glove compartment, before you get out?"

She opened the door of the glove compartment and fished about inside it, eventually bringing out a quarter-bottle of Captain Morgan which she handed to Edmund without comment.

He put the rum bottle in his pocket and handed her out of the car before reaching into the back to lift out the brown paper carrier bag of food. She caught a whiff of chips fried in dripping. The smell was delicious. Despite the absurdity of the situation, Alex found her spirits lift.

"I'm afraid I don't have an umbrella," said Edmund. "Can you just make a dash for it?"

"Where to? Under the bridge?"

"Yes – keep to the left. There's a path all the way down so it shouldn't be too muddy."

Although the street lights behind them cast some light on the path, Alex could not see well enough to feel confident in running. Instead, she walked as swiftly as she could, looking down at her feet all the time. Gusts of wind-bearing rain were coming from the direction of the river. They swept her hair into her eyes and quickly made it damp, but she reached the shelter of the bridge in a couple of minutes without feeling drenched or frozen. At first she could not see Edmund – he had stopped to rummage in the boot of the car – and she felt a surge of panic. But then she heard his distinctive plodding footsteps coming down the path and saw his thickset silhouette approaching.

"I was worried you had abandoned me," she jested, her voice slightly shrill.

"As if I would do that! I'm sorry if I alarmed you, though. I was looking for the bottle of coke. It had fallen out of the carrier. I found it – and these, too!" Triumphantly, he held out two plastic cups for her to see. "Leftovers from a dig, I guess! I've got my electric storm-lantern, too, so we're in luck!"

It was surprisingly light under the bridge. At first Alex could not understand why; then she saw that there were lozenge-shaped lights set all along the archways and the inner wall.

"Is this what you brought me to see? It's dry, I grant you, and I can see well enough; but it's hardly the warm and cosy spot that you suggested. It looks as if it's used as a billet for tramps, as well." She indicated a heap of rags topped by an ancient sleeping-bag that had been abandoned near the footpath.

"Probably," said Edmund, glancing at it, "But actually this isn't all. Come with me."

He transferred the coke bottle and cups to the carrier bag, and hung it on his arm so that he could carry it and the storm lantern with his left hand. Holding Alex's hand with his right, he proceeded to climb with her up the slope towards the ceiling made by the bridge until they reached a ledge that jutted out near the top.

"Are you OK?" he asked, as he hauled Alex up the last few inches of the slope. She nodded, breathless and a little afraid of the height. "Sit down for a moment. It's quite safe. Then we're just going to move along this ledge a little way, and we're there."

"We're where?"

"That's what I want to show you. It's what I discovered when I was young. There's a small room set into the side of the bank here. I think it must have been built by the workmen for shelter when they were constructing the bridge. That in itself is interesting enough; but what really fascinated me when I found it was that it has been fashioned out of all sorts of debris from the past. I suppose it was just stuff that they unearthed when they dug the foundations. There are definitely some Roman tiles incorporated into it and some carved stones from a mediaeval building."

"But are you the only person who knows about it? It sounds very unusual. Surely it should be declared a site of archaeological interest and preserved for the city?"

Edmund shrugged.

"I did write to the curator of the museum at the time – who, you'll be amused to know, was almost a Bill Ratcliffe clone. But I was only in my teens and I suppose he didn't take me seriously. The museum has always been more interested in documents and artefacts than archaeological sites. Anyway, I never heard back from him and as far as I know no-one ever inspected it to see if it was of interest."

"So you kept it to yourself?"

"Not entirely. As I told you, I brought my first girlfriend here – with some food from Croxley's!" He waved the carrier bag. "It was when I decided that I wanted to be an industrial archaeologist. I realised that there is so much unexpected information to be yielded from old buildings and other constructions."

"Was she interested?"

"Who?"

"Your girlfriend."

"She was at first – we came here a few times. But her mother didn't like me and she certainly didn't like my proposed choice of career. Janet was a county sort of girl and always destined to marry a rich farmer."

"Is that what happened to her?"

"I believe so," said Edmund, in a voice which discouraged further questions. "We lost touch. Now, should we eat the food while we're sitting here, before it goes cold, or would you like to see the room first? It's snug in there."

"Let's eat the food first. I'm not cold – and it will make exploring easier if we don't have too much to take with us."

"OK." Edmund carefully removed two wrapped packages from the carrier bag and unrolled them. He placed one on Alex's lap and gave her a plastic fork. "Ambrosia," he said.

Alex thought that she had probably settled for a lot less than 'ambrosia', but she was really hungry now and attacked the food with gusto. She had to admit that the rock salmon was delicious. She had nearly finished her supper when Edmund passed her one of the plastic cups. She could feel the coke fizzing against her face as she bent to sip it. The kick from the rum was so strong that she swung out her free arm involuntarily, and knocked the packet containing the remains of her chips down to the ground below.

"Pity!" said Edmund, looking down. "Here, have some of mine."

"No thanks, I've had plenty. But you were right: the food was delicious."

"Cheers!" said Edmund, touching her plastic cup with his own. She took several swigs of the rum and coke. It was very strong indeed, but she was enjoying it and had soon drained the cup.

"Another?"

"Not yet. If you want me to make it to your secret room I'll at least need not to be too tipsy to keep my balance."

"Very true." He laughed, and downed his own drink. "Are you ready to see it, then?"

She nodded. He worked his way along the ledge, and she crawled after him. She looked down at the towpath once; it was quite a long way down, but she didn't feel afraid. Dutch courage, probably, she reflected. She could see the scattered chips. The paper that had contained them had disappeared, blown away by the wind.

Edmund shone the lantern at a spot above his head.

"There should be a sort of wrought-iron door just here somewhere," he said. "There it is! I hope that I can shift it. I should probably have thought to bring some tools from the car as well." He stood up.

"Careful!" said Alex.

"It's OK – I'm more agile than I look. Can you just take the lantern? Shine it there, while I give this a push."

She knelt on the ledge, her feet tucked under her, and did as he asked. She could see the door now. It was more like a grating on a hinge. It consisted of five or six twisted wrought iron bars set into wood. Edmund gave it a series of hefty pushes and gradually it edged open.

"Not as difficult as I thought it would be," he said, although she could see the perspiration on his forehead. "Give me the lantern. I'll go in first."

She passed the lantern to him and he disappeared for a few seconds.

"It's perfect," he said, his head emerging again. "Just as I left it last time – I've been back a few times since I started working in this area, but not for several years now. Would you like to come in? You really need to stand, but don't worry – give me your hand and I'll make sure you don't slip."

Alex was not afraid, but she held out her hand anyway and he pulled her gently to her feet.

"That's it. Now just edge your way round here – careful, mind your head – now just stoop a little – that's it – and we're there. I'll push the door to so that we keep warm."

"Don't close it completely!" said Alex, suddenly fearful that Edmund might not be able to open it again from the inside. If they got trapped here no-one would ever find them.

"Don't worry, it opens both ways. But there, I'll leave a little gap, just to please you."

He had set the lantern on the floor. It cast quite a lot of light and also created shadows in the confined space that they were now occupying. Alex took stock of her surroundings. What Edmund had said was true: it was a small, perfectly-constructed room. The floor was flagged with pieces of tile of different shapes and sizes, but beautifully fitted together. Some of them were patterned. She could not see them clearly enough to judge how old they were, but she guessed that Edmund's claim that they were Roman was probably correct.

"Look at this!" he said excitedly, picking up the lantern and holding it against one of the walls. She saw that an engraved stone block had been embedded in the brickwork.

"What is it?" she asked, drawing closer.

"It's a carving of a face. I think it's mediaeval, but I've never been able to puzzle out exactly which period it comes from. What do you think?"

"It's amazing," said Alex. "I don't think that it's mediaeval, though. It reminds me more of . . ."

"Hush!" said Edmund, holding up his hand.

Normally the action would have irritated her, but he sounded so urgent – and so worried – that she stopped talking immediately, and listened. She could hear them quite clearly: the sound of footsteps on the towpath below, echoing as someone walked under the bridge.

"It is just someone walking by," she whispered.

"No," he whispered back, "It isn't. I heard the footsteps walk along the towpath beyond the bridge, then turn and walk back again. They are pacing the ground below us now. They aren't moving on."

Alex listened.

"You're right. But what is there to be afraid of?"

Edmund shrugged and attempted a smile, but she saw that his face was taut with fear.

"I just don't want anyone to find this place, that's all. We mustn't give ourselves away." He reached out a hand to take hers and she saw that he was shaking. She realised that he was not telling her the whole truth and normally that would have made her angry, but his fear had infected her and she too felt terrified. She gripped his hand.

"What's that?" she whispered.

"I can't hear anything."

"Neither can I; but I can smell cigarette smoke. Whoever it is, is still there."

"You're right. I can smell it, too."

They crouched in silence. After a while they heard a scuffing sound; then the footsteps again. An arc of light swept across the doorway and vanished, then swept back towards them. The smell of rising smoke was stronger now.

"They've got a torch," whispered Alex.

"It's all right – you can't see the doorway from below, even in daylight."

The arc of light came and went again. And once again. Then, slowly, the footsteps continued along the towpath. This time they did not return.

"They've gone!" said Alex quietly, but no longer whispering.

"Shh!" said Edmund. "We'll stay a little longer. It's going to take us a while to get down from here and I want to make quite sure first that they aren't coming back."

"Why are you so frightened?"

"No particular reason," said Edmund evasively, "except that it's dark and lonely on the river bank and anyone prepared to walk along there on a night like this is probably up to no good. It's not fear, so much as apprehensiveness – and as I said, I don't want anyone else to find this place. Another drink?"

Unnerved by the whole experience, Alex held out her cup. Edmund sloshed it half-full of rum and then added a little coke. It was even stronger than the first drink, but she didn't protest. She drank it rapidly, feeling her head swim before she had even finished it. Edmund had downed his in one go.

"Another?"

"Not yet," she said. "Don't forget we've got to climb back down to the path. I'd rather not be too drunk; it would be nasty, falling down that slope on to the footpath."

Edmund nodded, but poured more rum for himself. She noticed that he added no coke. He was sipping this drink more slowly, however. She caught his expression by the light of the storm lantern. Craven was the word that occurred to her. She decided to try to take his mind off whatever was frightening him so much.

"You really should tell the museum about this place – or the county, if the museum's not interested – and get it properly excavated. It's very unusual."

"I know that. I feel reluctant to do so, though. Over the years, I've come to regard it as my special place. It's a secret that I've barely shared."

"You've never brought Krystyna here?"

"God, no, she wouldn't be interested. Neither my career nor my personal interests are of any concern to her. I'm just a walking bill-payer. Still, I suppose that's what the word 'husband' meant originally – or an approximation of what it meant, anyway."

"You sound very bitter . . . and I'm sure that you exaggerate. She must be quite proud of you and what you have achieved."

"I wouldn't bank on it. As you must yourself realise, archaeology is fascinating to few people except archaeologists – discounting the charisma enjoyed by the television charlatans, of course. My marriage hasn't been successful, but it's my own fault; I married a pretty face and there's the end of it. And to be quite honest, I'm responsible for the fact that we've grown so far apart from each other, too. I had an affair about ten years ago and, although she claims to have forgiven me, our life together has never been the same since. The trouble was," he added slowly, meeting Alex's eye, "I told her that it was over when it wasn't. So of course, when she found out, I had to finish it all over again. It was touch and go for a long time. It was why I took this job, actually. I decided to row for dry land, and here I am." He smiled sardonically.

"I see," said Alex.

"What about you and Tom? Is he interested in what you do?"

"Not as much as I'd hoped. He's more bound up in his social work than I ever thought he would be. I'd always hoped that we would do something together – in fact, I had thought that the work that I mentioned to you might be the start of a joint business . . . oh, you needn't look like that. There's no way that he would ever have agreed to it. I've come to realise that lately. So I guess that we will grow apart, too, in time; we have nothing much in common and I'm less interesting now that I have ceased to be one of his rescue projects."

"Now who's sounding bitter?"

"I really don't mean to. I'm very fond of Tom. I suppose that expecting him to get too deeply involved in what I do would have been asking the impossible. What's the time?"

Edmund held his flashy watch face against the bulb of the storm lantern.

"Good God, it's almost eleven o'clock. I had no idea that we had been here so long."

"We must go," said Alex, scrambling to her feet. "Tom will be getting worried. And I guess Krystyna will, too, despite what you say."

Edmund ignored the last comment. "I'll go first," he said, suddenly cautious again. He pulled open the barred door and edged out on to the ledge, swinging the lantern both ways and peering down. Alex followed him out, getting down on all fours once she had left the safety of the secret room.

"There's no-one down there," said Edmund. "I'm going to go first. Follow in my footsteps exactly after I've got to the bottom and then if you slip I'll be able to break your fall."

For a heavy man, he was surprisingly nimble. He made it down the slope in two or three giant strides and stood with arms outstretched at the bottom.

"Come now," he said. "Turn round, so that you're coming down backwards. There are some small cracks and crevices in the bank that you can use as handholds and footholds – you'll see them. There's quite a big hole under the ledge, just where you are now. Turn round and find it first with your foot."

Nervously, Alex obeyed.

"Now stretch down with your other foot – that's it. Feel that? You can get a toehold there. And again. That's it – well done. Now you can turn round and jump."

She turned and jumped almost in one action, more suddenly and forcefully than either of them had anticipated, so that inadvertently she hurled herself into his arms and pushed him backwards at the same time. He fell on his back on the towpath, and she landed on top of him. Both burst out laughing.

"Are you all right?" she gasped.

For answer, he took her head in his hands and kissed her. She did not draw back. He stroked her face and kissed her again.

"Alex," he said. "It wasn't the drink last time, and it isn't now. I love you. I mean it."

She raised her head, and looked at him.

"I mean it. I don't expect you to say that you love me – yet. But please give me a chance."

Troubled, she tried to think rapidly about what he might be proposing and what the consequences would be. Her mind flooded with contradictory emotions – her disappointment with Tom, her knowledge of Edmund's less pleasing ways, his difficulties with people, the double infidelity that he had just confessed to and, even more, the fact that he was evidently hiding something from her that spelt trouble – something dishonest, illegal, dangerous, she could not tell what; or possibly nothing at all, something that he had just magnified in his own mind and over-dramatised. After this flurry of thought, she surprised herself with her reply.

"Yes," she said. "All right. I will."

CHAPTER EIGHTEEN

ALEX AND TOM lived in a maisonette in an eighteenth-century town house in Spalding. It was a three-storey building; the ground floor was occupied by a building society. There was no front entrance, but as Edmund drove around the roundabout in the Sheep Market Alex could see that the lights were still on in the living-room.

"Where should I drop you?" asked Edmund.

"At the top of Chapel Lane, by the railway station," said Alex.

"Are you sure? It's very dark now; and the streetlights down there are dim."

"It's as near as you can get in a car," said Alex. "I'll be fine; if there's anyone lurking, I can always call Tom. It looks as if he's at home now, and not in bed."

"All the same, I don't like to leave you."

"What do you suggest? That I ask you in for coffee?"

"No," said Edmund, flushing. "When shall I see you again?"

"Call me tomorrow at the Archaeological Society and we'll work something out," said Alex.

"OK, I will."

He had parked the car by this time. He leant across and kissed her clumsily and then, reaching out, turned her face to his and kissed her again on the lips. She responded half-heartedly before drawing away.

"What's wrong?"

"It's too risky here. Tom may come looking for me and just about everyone who lives round about knows who I am."

"Sorry. I didn't think. Alex?"

"Yes?"

"I did mean it, you know. I love you."

She nodded and got out of the car, trying to smooth down her trenchcoat as she did so. She hadn't looked in a mirror since they'd left the pub, but she guessed that she was pretty dishevelled. She slammed the car door, giving Edmund a cursory wave, and headed into the blackness of Chapel Lane. Edmund was right – it was scarily dark and she was rarely, if ever, out on her own at this time. She increased her pace, at the same time trying to walk as quietly as possible. She looked over her shoulder a couple of times, but no-one was following her and, even though the street lamps were inadequate, she could see that the alleyway ahead was deserted. She gave herself a little shake; she was becoming as paranoid as Edmund.

Alex made herself try not to think too much, but to concentrate her efforts entirely on getting to the warmth and safety of home. Her mind was jangling, however, constantly trying to say something to her, overloaded as it was with shame, with joy, with mistrust, with apprehension and also an unarticulated whisper at the back of her mind that she was playing a sham role. Part of her wished that Edmund had never made this second overture to her and she had no idea why she had responded in the way that she had. It wasn't just the drink, yet she was as aware of his faults as ever. She knew that she had no intention of jeopardising her marriage and that Edmund would be a much more impossible person to live with than Tom. Yet part of her was unwilling to let him go – she would not do so yet, anyway. She did not delude herself that theirs could be a relationship that would last, even in a clandestine fashion. Perhaps she was just flattered by his attention. If so, she despised herself for her own shallowness. Even more unwelcome were the thoughts of Tom that kept intruding. She kept on telling herself that she was not prepared to risk losing him, even though she knew that she was tempting fate in the most blatant way. She pushed all these thoughts away as she neared home.

Number 24a Chapel Lane was about halfway along the alley. As she approached the tall blue gate that led into the yard that the Tarrants shared with the building society, she paused to fumble in her bag for her keys. There were two keys: a rather heavy silver Chubb key for the gate and a Yale for the lock upstairs. She kept them in an inner pocket in her handbag; since both the handbag and its lining were black, in the poor light she could not see properly to unfasten the zip. She fished around and found the leather tab on which they hung, pulling on it hard so that the keys jerked out of her hand and into the open gutter that ran down the side of the alley. As she stooped to pick them up, something landed beside them in the rainwater that was streaming down the gutter. There was a flash of red, then a sizzling sound. Alex straightened up and jumped back in one movement, at first startled, then terrified. She looked around her. She could see no-one; but there was the distinct smell of cigarette smoke in the air. She tried to peer into the black recesses of the doorway of the Wesleyan chapel that gave the passage its name, but she could see nothing. She bent again and scrabbled for the keys, snatched them from the gutter and hastened the last few steps to the yard door, fumbling in her panic as she unlocked the door and scrambled through it. Once on the other side, she locked it again quickly, leaning back on it momentarily to catch her breath. The switch to the outside light was set in the wall right beside the door but she dared not turn it on. She knew the stone staircase that led to the maisonette well enough, anyway, and hurtled up the steps, not pausing until she reached the flat area at the top. At the same moment, someone snapped on the kitchen light and opened the kitchen door.

"Alex?"

"Tom!"

She flung herself into his arms so that he stepped back into the kitchen with the force of her weight; then, breaking away from him, she quickly banged the door shut, turned the key in it and slid the bolt.

"Whatever is the matter? And why are you so late? My God," he added, taking a closer look at her, "has someone attacked you?"

"No," she said. "I thought I heard someone in Chapel Lane, that was all. It was too dark to see."

"Why are you so . . . dishevelled? Your clothes are covered in mud."

"I had supper with Edmund and he took me to see a . . . an archaeological site that he's interested in. But it started to rain and we both got wet; and I stumbled over at one stage." The words came tumbling out, disingenuous half-truths.

"I see." Tom paused. Alex did not look at him. "And Edmund brought you home, did he?"

"Yes. I told you that I would ask him."

"You did indeed. But I didn't expect you to come back in this state. Whatever was he thinking of, taking you round archaeological sites in the rain, dressed like that? And I suppose it was dark when you went, too?"

"Yes. But, Tom, it was my fault that I went. I agreed to it. I'm a grown woman, after all. Edmund didn't coerce me in any way."

Tom looked at her curiously.

"I should hope not. But he could at least have walked you to the door when he brought you home."

"He offered. I told him not to."

"You should have called me, then. I've been trying to call you for the last hour. Is your mobile switched off?"

"I think it is," said Alex, as if she couldn't remember. "I turned it off for the museum meeting and I don't remember switching it back on again."

Tom laughed shortly.

"You talk about me being absent-minded. Try and remember another time, will you? I've been worried about you."

He unbuttoned her coat as if she were a child.

"Let's get you out of this muddy coat. Take your shoes off as well – there are some thick socks here. Put them on to warm up your feet and I'll fetch you a fleece. Are you up for a drink? There's so much that I want to tell you about what happened today."

Alex nodded and allowed herself to be petted and gently bullied. Normally she would have been furious that Tom had already forgotten her tale of someone lurking in the alleyway or discounted it as a figment of her imagination, and depressed that he was not more curious about her own day. As it was, the less he enquired about how she had spent the twelve or so hours since she had last seen him, the better. She put on the socks and the fleece like a dutiful schoolgirl.

"Go through into the living-room," said Tom, pouring whiskies. "I've lit the fire. I decided it was not too late to do it, even though it was after ten when I got in, because I hoped that you'd feel up to talking." Tom's earnest face was alight with enthusiasm and importance. "You're going to be absolutely fascinated by this. It is the most amazing thing that has happened to me in all the years that I've been working."

Alex sighed inwardly. She was not certain, but she thought that she had heard this from Tom on at least one previous occasion.

CHAPTER NINETEEN

ALEX AND TOM were sitting together on the sofa in front of the open fire in their living room, each nursing a substantial whisky. Alex's head was beginning to pound from the vodka and rum that she had drunk earlier, but she sipped at the whisky anyway. She had curled her legs up on to the seat of the sofa and Tom was absently-mindedly stroking them. It should have been comforting, but she wanted him to stop; she knew that she had already compromised their intimacy.

Tom moved his hand to stroke her cheek and she flinched slightly.

"What's wrong?" he asked. "You don't mind staying up to talk to me, do you? If you're too tired, we'll go to bed now. It's just that my head's buzzing with what's happened. I know I won't sleep if I don't talk about it."

"No, I'm fine," Alex said, trying to conceal her weariness. "You've made me curious now. Do carry on."

"Well, I'm sure you've heard me talk about the Padgett family?"

Alex nodded. Tom's casebook was seldom without an open file on one or other of the Padgett children. They belonged to a large West Indian family that lived in a sprawling but dilapidated rented house in Little London. The council paid for it, because they did not have a council house big enough to accommodate all of the Padgetts. Mrs Padgett occasionally took on some seasonal work at the neighbouring farms, but apart from that the family had no acknowledged income except what they received from the DHSS. There were ten or eleven Padgett children, all of them of school age, and most, it was reputed, with different fathers, all of whom were distinguished by their absence. Certainly there had been no man present in the household since Tom had first been introduced to it half a decade ago and sporadic attempts made by the Child Support Agency to strong-arm maintenance for some of the children never got off the ground. All of the children were too young to work, though the teenaged ones rarely attended either school or college. Mrs Padgett – who was an engaging lady, handsome in a big-boned way, with an infectious laugh – had been prosecuted for their non-attendance several times and had even been threatened with prison, but, as she said, who would look after a family like hers if she were 'put away'? She actually cared for the children very well: they did not go hungry and were always clean and well-dressed. She blamed LeRoy Padgett, her oldest son, for getting in with the wrong crowd and acting as a bad influence on his siblings. LeRoy himself was quite a prepossessing character. He was always sunny and cheerful when he was found out. He had a series of convictions for minor crimes: shoplifting, taking a bicycle without the owner's consent, under-age drinking.

"Is it LeRoy Padgett again?" Alex asked.

"No, surprisingly, this time it isn't: it's his brother Thobias. Though of course LeRoy is almost certainly mixed up in it, too. There isn't much that goes on in that family that can't be traced back to LeRoy in some way."

"I don't think I've heard you mention Thobias before."

"I probably haven't. I've met him several times, of course, when I've visited the Padgetts, but he's only just reached the age of criminal responsibility. In fact, that was the root cause of the problem this time. There has been a series of breaking and entering cases, most of them at the houses along the road to Spalding Common, which of course is close to where the Padgetts live. The police suspected LeRoy – I think they suspect LeRoy whenever a petty crime takes place in the area now – but LeRoy swore that he had nothing to do with the break-ins. Then Thobias was caught in the coffee bar in Bridge Street, paying for a milk shake by peeling £20 from a roll of banknotes. The proprietor called the police while he was still on the premises."

"And it was stolen money?"

"Not as such, no, as it turns out. But they thought it was at the time. They took Thobias to the police station and asked me to meet them there. Thobias was there with Mrs Padgett – her name is Marlene – and they were both terrified. Shaking scared."

"Not surprising, really."

"Well, yes, most parents who have children that age – and the children themselves – would be frightened if they found themselves on the wrong side of the law. But not the Padgetts. Marlene's been at the police station – and in court – in similar circumstances many times with LeRoy, and it has barely ruffled her. Her reaction today was totally out of character."

"Did you find out why?"

"That's what I'm coming to. The police kept on asking Thobias where he got the money from. His story varied each time, and it was transparently obvious that he was lying. They were the usual unimaginative lies that we always get on these occasions: that he had found the money, that it had been given to him by an older boy to look after, that he'd earned it doing odd jobs – even though he had almost £2,000 in his possession and clearly could not have come by it in any credibly honest way. Etcetera, etcetera. The policeman who was questioning him was getting quite rattled and I thought was beginning to be too rough with a child of Thobias's age. I suggested that he put a temporary halt to the interview while he and I had a quick word and when we were outside the interview room, I warned him that if he intimidated the boy I would have to take the matter further. I also said that I thought that he should be allocated a solicitor before any more questions were asked.

"The policeman – his name is DC Carstairs, and I think I've met him before somewhere – not only agreed with me, but said that as it was now so late in the evening he would let the child go home with his mother, on condition that both they and I returned the next day, when there would have been time to appoint a solicitor. I thought that this was the only sensible solution, but when it was suggested to Marlene and Thobias they were both terrified. She said that if we sent Thobias home with her, she was sure he would be killed and the whole family put at risk. We tried to calm her down – DC Carstairs had some more tea sent in and I told her that she must be overwrought by the day's events and hinted that perhaps her imagination was working overtime. I tried to put my arm round her, but she pushed me away and became completely hysterical. Thobias shrank away into the corner. At first he lay slumped on the floor with his eyes closed, but after a while he started rocking backwards and forwards and banging his head against the wall. It really upsets me when children do that," he added. "I've seen it on a few occasions. It means that they've reached the end of their tether; that they can't cope any longer and can't see any way out."

Tom sounded so anguished that Alex was moved to respond genuinely for the first time since she had reached home. She put down the whisky glass, felt for his hand and caressed it. She could see that her sudden act of compassion had brought Tom close to tears.

"You take it all so much to heart," she murmured. "I know it's hard, but you should try to distance yourself a little. You can't let your job blight your life."

Tom pulled his hand away.

"It's not my life that's being blighted," he said gruffly. "You of all people should understand. Most of the kids that I see don't stand a chance. Every so often one of them manages to break out of the vicious spiral of slovenliness, apathy and petty crime that they were born into. But mostly I can only help them so far. It's not even as if they are evil – it's so naïve of people to think that they were born different from us. Sure, they've got a warped set of values, but so would we have, probably, if we'd grown up in the same surroundings."

Alex had heard this before and it irritated her. Tom verged on the sanctimonious when he talked like this, even though she knew that the pain he felt was genuine, and she hated it even more when he dragged her own upbringing into his musings. Her parents had been thoughtless, self-centred and unkind, but her father had held down a job and neither of them had ever broken the law.

"Carry on with your story, Tom," she said crisply.

"OK." He swallowed. "DC Carstairs was getting angry again. He said that unless Thobias told us why he was so upset, there would be no reason not to send him home, subject to the conditions that he had mentioned. He also wanted to know what else Marlene and Thobias could expect. Did they want to spend the night in the cells? He doubted if they would enjoy that and, in any case, the police station was not a hotel.

"Marlene pulled herself together a bit then. She said that she had to get home to her other children; that she had left her daughter Coleen in charge, but that the girl wouldn't be able to cope without her all night. She repeated that it was Thobias alone who was in danger and that he would jeopardise the safety of the rest of the family if he spent the night with them. DC Carstairs wasn't having any of this; he clearly thought that Marlene was trying to offload the boy for some reason. I'd begun to believe her by this time, though. I'm sure that Marlene transgresses all sorts of accepted moral norms – she may even be a petty criminal herself – but over the years that I've known her I've become convinced of one thing. According to her own lights, she loves her family and looks after them as best she can. I was therefore prepared to believe that she was genuinely afraid for Thobias. I asked DC Carstairs if we could have another quiet word outside the interview room. He asked a woman PC to come in and stay with the Padgetts and I said to him what I've just said to you. Reluctantly, he agreed that the police had a duty to protect Thobias if he were really in danger and not just trying to create a melodrama because he had some kind of half-baked idea that this would get him out of trouble.

" 'But I need a reason for protecting him if we are going to go to the expense of doing it,' he said. 'If I let you go back in there and talk to him on your own, do you think you might be able to get some sense out of him?'

" 'I can try,' I said.

"So he accompanied me back to the interview room and called to the woman PC who was standing outside. I don't know where they went – I had the feeling that they hadn't gone far, which I suppose was fair enough. By this time, Thobias was sitting on Marlene's lap like a small child, sucking his thumb, and she was cradling him. She herself was calm and sensible now. She looked at me imploringly. I felt sorry for her, even though I know she knows how to lay it on thick.

" 'Please, Mr Tarrant,' she said, 'Please help us.'

"I took a chair and faced her from the other side of the table. I made her meet my eye. 'Marlene,' I said, 'you have got to help Thobias and yourself by telling the police exactly what you know. Thobias has managed to get himself into some serious trouble, hasn't he?'

"She nodded, and the tears spilled from her eyes. 'He not a bad boy,' she said. 'He just run a few errands because LeRoy ask him – and to get a bit of spend for himself. He don't have no idea what he getting into. Even LeRoy don't know.'

" 'Where is LeRoy?' I asked.

"She shrugged. 'Gone to ground somewhere – what he do when there trouble, unless police get to him first. He got friends everywhere. I don't know where he is half the time.'

" 'Tell me what you know, Marlene,' I said. 'We won't bother Thobias again for the moment, because he's clearly too upset. I understand that he probably hasn't told you everything. But you must know something?'

"She nodded.

" 'Like I say, he think it just running errands. It *was* running errands, sort of. And LeRoy offer to lend him his new bike. He been trying to have a go on that bike and pestering the daylights out of me to get one for him, since the day LeRoy come home with it.'

" 'Did you give LeRoy the bike?'

"She looked at me, rolled her eyes, and laughed.

" 'Hell, no, where you think I get money for that? Must cost two hundred pounds, maybe more. LeRoy been working for one of the farmers out Pinchbeck way. Say he save some money from his earnings and the farmer pay the rest, so he can get to work on time.'

"I didn't mention that LeRoy should have been in school. I didn't want to sidetrack Marlene when she was about to tell me about Thobias.

" 'So LeRoy offered Thobias a share of his bike if he would run some errands? Did he say Thobias would get paid, as well?'

"She nodded. 'Ten pounds for each package he deliver, but only if he never look at what inside and bring parcel he get back unopened.'

" 'Why didn't LeRoy take the job on himself? He's not usually slow to turn a fast pound, is he?'

"She grinned. She's obviously proud of her jaunty eldest son, even though she knows what he does is often wrong; he causes her a lot of heartache.

" 'LeRoy say he too old. Say Thobias the right age – they want a little kid.'

" 'Too *old*? How could LeRoy be too old?'

"She shrugged.

" 'I tell you what he say. He say Thobias the best person, because he not twelve. He is now, though. His birthday on Sunday.'

" I was beginning to understand now: LeRoy had chosen Thobias because he was below the age of criminal responsibility.

" 'Marlene,' I said, 'What else can you tell me? Do you know who the people were that Thobias was working for?'

"She became suddenly wary, and shrugged again.

" 'I tell you what I know . . . what Thobias tell me. You ask LeRoy if you want more.'

"I nodded. I could see that she was very afraid of these people, whoever they were. I also realised that the police would want to question Thobias again as soon as he was in a fit state to answer.

"'Wait there, Marlene,' I said. 'I'm going to fetch the policewoman again. I'm going to suggest that we take Thobias somewhere safe for this evening and that they arrange for a police car to take you home.'

"She smiled, relieved, when I was talking about Thobias, but mention of the police car almost precipitated another fit of hysterics.

"'No police car!" she said. 'Not been seen in one!'

"'It's OK,' I said quickly. 'No-one's going to make you do anything you don't want to do.'

"I went to the door. I was not surprised to see that the policewoman was waiting just a little way down the corridor.

"'Could I have a further word with DC Carstairs?'

"'I'll call him. I don't want to leave the interview room unwatched. We know the Padgetts – they've escaped before when we've been questioning them.'

"'I expect you mean LeRoy Padgett,' I said. 'The boy in there is his younger brother and I don't think that he'll try to escape; as you saw when you were in there, he's actually terrified that you're going to let him go.'

"She nodded, and turned to make a call on her mobile.

"DC Carstairs returned almost immediately.

"'Would you mind coming with me to another interview room, Mr Tarrant?' he said. 'It won't take long.'

"'I don't like to leave Mrs Padgett on her own. I promised her I'd be back immediately.'

"'It's all right: DC Armstrong will go and sit with her again.'

"I wasn't sure about this. The police don't realise how intimidating they can be, even to a woman like Marlene, who's had plenty of brushes with them in the past.

"'I promised Mrs Padgett . . .'

"'It's all right,' he repeated, quite sternly, I thought. I'm quite aware of how the police view people like me. We're useful to them and annoy them in about equal measures. They always think that we should take a stronger line with the kids than we do. I saw that I had no alternative but to follow him.

"'Take a seat,' he said, gesturing at a chair. We were in a room identical to the one in which Marlene and Thobias were waiting. 'Did you manage to get any particle of the truth out of them?'

"I resented his way of putting it, but I tried not to show it.

"'Marlene has told me as much as she knows,' I said. 'It isn't a great deal, but apparently Thobias's older brother, LeRoy, who I know is well-known to the police, persuaded him to run some errands. His reward was ten pounds per errand, plus the use of LeRoy's bike, which apparently he covets. There was one condition, which I'm sure will interest you: the assignments were two-way. Thobias was expected to pick up a return package, as well as deliver the one entrusted to him, and he was on strict instructions not to open any of the packages. From what Marlene says, I think that they chose Thobias for the task because he was under the age of criminal responsibility – at least, he was when all of this started. His twelfth birthday was last Sunday. I'm certain that she was telling me the truth, though she may still be holding something back.'

"'You've done a brilliant job – thank you. Well done. She's certainly been telling the truth. I can vouch for that."

"'As I said, I didn't think she was lying: but what makes *you* so certain? You weren't even listening to her – or were you?'

"'No, I wasn't,' he said. 'While you were talking to Mrs Padgett, I was taking a call from Forensics. They confirmed what I suspected when I took the bank-notes from Thobias: that there are traces of cocaine on them.'

"It didn't take me long to understand the significance of what he was saying, because I was half-expecting it, or something like it. As far as I knew, the Padgetts had never been involved in serious crime, but Marlene's and Thobias's extreme fear had already told me that they were out of their depth this time.

"'So the money was used to pay for drugs and Thobias was acting as a courier both for the drugs and payment for them?'

"'Probably. I'd guess so. It may be that there was some kind of money-laundering activity going on, but I don't think so. They wouldn't involve a child in that – it would be the next stage in the process.'

"'What happens now?'

"'Thobias is going to have to be interviewed again, properly, with a solicitor and a child psychiatrist present. What we urgently need to know is who asked him to do this – aside from his brother, I mean. Don't worry, we won't alarm him any more than we need to. He will be treated with kid gloves from now on. The seriousness of this puts a whole new complexion on the matter – and especially on where he spends the night. He and his mother are right to be worried. If he's got mixed up with a drugs ring, his life could very well be in danger; as could the brother's. We need to find him, as well.'

"'I think that Marlene is telling the truth when she says that she doesn't know where LeRoy is. For one thing, if she doesn't want Thobias to go home with her because she fears for the safety of the other children, pre-sumably she isn't hiding LeRoy.'

"'I think you're right. If I thought she had LeRoy, I'd have the premises searched. As it is, it's probably best to let her go home on her own, in case the house is being watched.'

"'She said that herself, when I said that you would send her home in a police car.'

"He gave me a wry look. I realised that the admiration I'd gained from my interviewing technique had just evaporated.

"'Ladies like Marlene don't accept lifts in police cars,' he said.

"'What about the boy?'

"'The boy is a bit of a problem. We can't allow a child to stay in the cells overnight, so he'll have to go somewhere else; and for his own safety he'll have to be accompanied by a policeman. We can smuggle him out of here in a van easily enough, in case we're being watched by whoever's after him, but it's a question of where to take him. Is there any suitable accommodation that you have at your disposal – say, when homeless children suddenly turn up?'

"'That doesn't often happen in this part of the world, I'm glad to say – it's more common in London. But of course we do have to take children into care unexpectedly – quite frequently, actually, if their parents are found unfit to look after them or there is only one parent and he or she is unexpectedly given a custodial sentence. If it's late in the day, we can't always find temporary foster parents. Sometimes we take children who've been stranded in some way to spend the night in the sick bay at Herrick Old House, near Sleaford. The sick bay's quite a pleasant, self-contained unit and it keeps them away from the other children there until they've calmed down and we've decided what to do with them.'

"'What's it like, this place? Would there be space to accommodate a policeman as well?'

"'Yes, if the warden will have him. I'm surprised you haven't been to it – the inmates aren't exactly angelic, so I would have expected you to have encountered a few of them. It's on the site of old manor house, but essentially a Victorian workhouse, now run by the council as a children's home. It's a bit of a monstrosity, actually; but as I say, the sick bay's OK. It's been modernised. It's in one of the wings, in a sort of mock turret. There are several beds in the dormitory and a kind of day-room. The whole thing's quite self-contained – it was designed in case any of the children needed to be quarantined – and access is via a single stone staircase, though there is a fire escape, too.'

"'So the policeman would be able to hear if someone was approaching?'

"I nodded. It was this simple question, not the Padgetts' histrionics, that brought home to me the real danger that they were in.

"'It sounds as if it will do. How do we get them in? Can you telephone someone?'

"I looked at my watch.

"'It's after 9 p.m.,' I said. "The warden's not always there at this time. She has a room at the house for when she does nights, but she doesn't live in. If it's one of the nights that she isn't working, there will be a house-master in charge.'

"'Can you call them and see?' He gestured to the telephone that stood on a shelf on the wall.

"I nodded again. 'It's all right,' I said. 'I've got the number programmed into my mobile.'

"'Don't give them all the details. Just say that we have a child who's appearing before the juvenile court and we need to keep him in a safe place. Tell them that there'll be a policeman with him, but don't explain any further. We can pay for the accommodation, incidentally, if that helps.'

"'OK.'

"I called the number and, after a couple of rings, one of the older children answered, but she fetched Eric Westerman quite quickly. He's the senior housemaster there. I was quite pleased that it was him; he's a matter-of-fact bloke and takes most things in his stride. He was fine about Thobias – less sure about the policeman – and asked me if I would come with them. We had the phone on speak, so that DC Carstairs could listen. He nodded vigorously, so I agreed to go as well, though I must say I was beginning to get really tired by then. I didn't relish the prospect of a trip out to Sleaford. I was worried that you'd get home before me and be worried about me, too."

"What did you tell the mother?"

"I just told her that the police would look after Thobias overnight and asked her to return to the police station tomorrow, at around 10.00 a.m., by which time I hoped the solicitor would have arrived. She's given me her mobile number; I offered to call her tomorrow, to let her know when everything was ready, but she said that she wanted to come back as early as possible to check on Thobias."

"Acting on behalf of Thobias sounds like a tough job! Are there special solicitors to represent children?"

"There are in London, but not here. Not enough cases. I've suggested that they ask Jack Lewis if he's free. I've worked with him on quite a lot of probation cases; he's gentle-mannered and prepared to listen to a child psychologist."

"You will ask Marie, I suppose?"

"Yes, if she can come. I know you don't like her, but she's the best we've got in this area – and tough enough to stand up to the police if they start questioning too aggressively. She'll probably get more information out of Thobias than they will, in any case."

Alex nodded. Marie Krakowska was a big-boned Polish woman who called a spade a bloody shovel and had uncouth table manners. On the few occasions on which they had met – mainly at semi-social functions organised by Tom's team – Alex had not hit it off with her. However, she knew that Tom respected Marie's professionalism and she was prepared to accept his judgment. It was just that she could not imagine Marie winning the confidence of damaged children.

"What about Thobias?"

"I'm quite worried about him. DC Carstairs called in the policeman who's looking after him tonight – PC Cooper. He was very good with the boy; either he's got children himself, or he does a lot of youth work. But Thobias had completely turned in on himself. He wouldn't speak to anyone and he kept hiding his head, either by covering his face with his hands and arms or by sitting facing the wall. He was still rocking himself, too; if he was sitting against the wall he hit the back of his head on it, or his forehead if he was facing it."

"Poor kid! Did he go to Herrick Old House, then?"

"Yes. Marlene helped us get him to his feet and PC Cooper took him to a back entrance with a blanket over his head. We put him straight into a police van. The police vehicle compound is surrounded by a high fence – I'm sure that no-one could have seen him getting into it, even without the blanket. There was a driver as well as PC Cooper – it hadn't occurred to me, but he wouldn't have wanted to take a police vehicle with him to keep overnight at the children's home. He sat in the rear of the van with Thobias."

"It all seems so surreal! Did you go with them?"

"No, I didn't, in the end. DC Carstairs said that if I were to follow the van in the car, I'd only be drawing attention to myself. I rang Eric again and he was fine about it – I think it had just taken a while for him to adjust to the idea of having them there. I said that I would go and see him soon – even if the police won't let me tell him much, he deserves some kind of explanation, not to mention thanks."

"So that was the last that you saw of them?"

"Yes; but I've heard from both Eric and PC Cooper. They got there safely and are installed in the sick bay. Thobias went straight to bed, apparently. Eric persuaded him to drink some warm milk that contained a mild sedative, so I hope that he'll get some rest."

"What happens next?"

"I'm not entirely sure. DC Carstairs will call me tomorrow. He's going to contact Jack Lewis and I'll get in touch with Marie first thing. My guess is that we'll then all meet again at the police station. They'll probably have already collected Thobias from the home by then – I hope so, because that's what I told Marlene. She'll be there as well, of course."

"I'm so sorry that you have to get involved in all of this . . . and I'm desperately worried that you might be in danger as well."

"It's my job; and I doubt if I'm in danger from the people who are after Thobias. In my admittedly limited experience of criminal gangs, they won't waste time on peripherals such as me; not unless I try to obstruct them in some way. I'm finding it all much more difficult than I would have expected, though. It's probably because the kids I deal with have not often been involved in organised crime. It makes me feel sick to think of it – and grubby, somehow. Corrupting a little kid like Thobias and then terrifying him out of his wits. The whole thing stinks."

Alex looked at Tom intently. The day's events had been momentous for both of them, though she knew that she couldn't tell Tom that. She sensed that they had reached a watershed in their lives. If she acted quickly, perhaps she could set them on a different course together.

Tom met her eye.

"Why are you looking like that?"

"Tom," said Alex, "have you ever thought about doing something else? You've given enough years of your life to other people. As you say, situations like today's really bring it home to you how squalid it all is. Isn't it really time to let someone else take the reins now? Would you like perhaps to consider setting up a business together instead?"

"What sort of business?" said Tom warily.

"It's something I've mentioned before – I've been thinking about it again lately."

"If you mean that archaeological curating notion, you can forget it. I don't see how it could conceivably give us an income long-term, unless we were prepared to move around the countryside living in the vicinity of museums that needed help. And, quite frankly, I don't relish that sort of life – or that sort of work. I've tried to explain to you before: things don't interest me, even very ancient and hallowed things. It's people that I care about."

"You don't have to sound so shirty!"

"I suppose I don't; but you could have chosen a better moment. When I say that the job makes me feel sullied, it's on behalf of children like Thobias who have never stood a chance. Thobias and kids like him need my help. If anything, what's happened today makes me more determined than ever to keep on being there for them."

CHAPTER TWENTY

TIM HAD JUST spent an hour making a half-hearted attack on his in-tray. Extreme ennui made him go in search of coffee, as much for the exercise as the end result. He hoped he had covered all the urgent items pending, because he wanted to arrange to spend the afternoon at the cottage with Jane Halliwell.

As he rounded the corner to the corridor that led past the interview rooms, he came upon a group of people bunched together. They were completely obstructing his route. He saw immediately that one of them was Andy Carstairs. Andy had just opened the door to the interview room and was trying to shepherd the others in. As Tim walked closer to them, he saw that Gary Cooper was also one of the party. He was holding a small black boy by the hand. A very large black woman – presumably the child's mother – was holding his other hand. She was flanked by an equally large woman with a china-doll complexion and white-blonde hair brushed back off her face. This woman was perhaps the most incongruous of the whole group. She was dressed in a kind of peasant bodice, which was cut low on her protuberant bosom, and a floor-length skirt that might have been fashioned from a horse-blanket. Her large, broad feet were shod in black lace-up boots. Tim had never seen her before, he was sure of that. Bringing up the rear were a wily little man with a lined face and thick, unruly hair that stuck out at right angles from his head in silvery tufts and a rather flabby middle-aged man with sad brown eyes and a placating expression. He was dressed much more casually than all of the others except the boy. No prizes for guessing who he is, thought Tim. He has 'social worker' written all over him.

Andy Carstairs continued to hold open the door for this motley group until he had ushered them all in. Tim caught his eye.

"Interesting bunch you've got there, Andy," said Tim, sotto voce. "Presumably it's the kid that's in trouble? Are you sure you've gathered enough people to support him? What's he done, anyway?"

Andy smiled at the sarcasm.

"Not my fault that we need all of them," he said. "The copper is extra – and would probably actually rather be somewhere else. He's already spent the night looking after the kid. But the kid's traumatised by what's happened to him and he's rather taken a shine to PC Cooper, so we're hoping that he'll be able to help us get some sense out of him. You can guess why the others are there: child-friendly solicitor, child-friendly educational psychologist, child-friendly social worker, and the kid's mother. It won't be my fault if he doesn't get off."

"But get off what? Either he's done something serious, or you've got a real sledgehammer and nut situation there."

Andy Carstairs looked guilty.

"Superintendent Thornton made me promise not to bother you about it. He says he wants you to focus exclusively on the lady archaeologist."

Tim guessed immediately.

"He's not here on drugs charges by any chance, is he?"

"Not exactly – look, sir, I have to go now," he said, as the elderly man's head poked round the door. "I'll tell you more later – confidentially, if that's all right with you."

Tim realised that the old man was watching him, so he nodded and walked on. Inside he was seething. It was one thing having Thornton remove him from a drugs case because he thought his time could be spent more profitably (and even if Tim disagreed with this, he had already realised that there was a lot more to the McRae disappearance than trying to find a confused old lady who had somehow wandered off); it was quite another to tell him that his hunch that there was a major drugs cartel operating in the area was a figment of his imagination if there was clear evidence to the contrary. There could be few other explanations for Andy Carstairs' having assembled all those people in an interview room and provided police protection for the child the night before. He was annoyed with Andy, too. Did he think that Tim would be stupid enough to believe that it took six adults to question a juvenile about some petty offence? 'Not exactly', indeed! He would ask Andy what his game was at the first available opportunity.

As he entered the canteen, he almost collided with Superintendent Thornton. This was a surprise. Thornton was rarely to be encountered in such egalitarian surroundings; he preferred to get the women in his detail to wait on him. Less surprising was that when he met Tim's eye, he looked away again in a decidedly shifty manner.

"Ah, DI Yates," he said, quickly recovering his composure and eyeing Tim severely. "Did you receive my press release?"

"No, sir," said Tim. "But I've only just left my office. If you've sent it, I expect it will be waiting for me when I get back. I'll turn it round as quickly as I can."

"No need for that – I'm really just showing it to you as a courtesy, for information. No time to be lost, you see. I've already sent it to the main newspapers."

Tim's pale complexion flushed scarlet.

"But I thought that you wanted me to approve it?"

"I should have appreciated that if you'd been there, certainly; but, as I say, time was of the essence. I want to avoid having the press pack here if I can. No time for them at present and I don't want anyone to let something slip that we don't want to get out. Much better to keep them informed at one remove."

Tim decided not to retort; it would only take his mind off more important things. On one level, he could even concede that Thornton was right. The Superintendent had overcome his embarrassment now. He was still barring Tim's passage to the canteen.

"What are your plans for today?"

"I've been catching up with some desk-work. I want to spend the afternoon at Helpston with Claudia McRae's companion."

"Good idea!" The Superintendent was a little too ready with his approval.

"Incidentally, sir . . ." said Tim.

"Yes?"

"Do you know anything about what's going on in the large interview room this morning?"

"What? Oh. I believe that DC Carstairs is dealing with a young offender."

"Not drugs-related, is it?"

"Now don't start on that tack again, DI Yates. You've got enough to do without bothering with DC Carstairs' workload. I recommend that you get off to Helpston as soon as you can. I don't want Roy Little breathing down my neck."

CHAPTER TWENTY-ONE

TIM HAD INTENDED to ask Juliet to accompany him and Jane Halliwell to Claudia McRae's cottage, but at the last minute he changed his mind and decided that he would go by himself. He could not explain his reason for this, especially not to Juliet, who had been carrying out mundane enquiries to support the investigation for practically the whole of the previous two days and was understandably miffed to have been denied this more interesting task. But he had an uneasy feeling about Jane – she was almost too good to be true, yet oddly inauthentic; and, although Juliet had found the short film that showed Jane at some kind of right-wing meeting, he knew that she did not altogether share his concerns about her. Juliet normally had a sharp eye for detail and a finely-tuned sense of mood and integrity. He told her that he had every confidence in her ability to pick up on unusual reactions that Jane might display. Nevertheless, he wanted to observe Jane for himself as she entered the cottage for the first time since her return. He also wanted Juliet to try to find out more about the passengers on the Norwegian cruise and, if possible, to establish whether Jane had gone ashore for any length of time. And there was more work to be done with Forensics.

"You are so much better at all that nitty gritty stuff than I am," he said, smiling sheepishly. "You know that I'd only lose my temper."

Juliet frowned, but managed the ghost of a smile before she walked away.

Tim had no sooner left than the telephone on his desk began to ring. Juliet knew that eventually it would divert to either the desk sergeant or to Tim's mobile, but since she was near she decided to answer it.

"Good afternoon. Detective Inspector Yates's telephone."

"Hello, who is that?" asked a pleasant female voice with a slight foreign inflection. Juliet recognised it immediately.

"Katrin?" she asked. "Is that you? It's Juliet Armstrong speaking."

"Yes it is me. Hello, Juliet. Where is Tim? I really want to speak to him."

"Unfortunately he's just left. You could try his mobile."

"I have done that. I think it's switched off – it's going straight to message mode."

"That's probably because he's on his way to meet a witness. He'll be driving to meet her now – he should be with her in half an hour or so.

Unless he turns the phone on briefly to collect any messages before he reaches her, he'll probably not be able to respond for a couple of hours. Can *I* help you in any way?"

"No," said Katrin uncertainly. Juliet thought that she sounded close to tears. "Not unless he gets in touch with you before I can reach him. If he does, will you let him know that I need to talk to him?"

"Yes, of course. I hope that nothing's wrong?"

Juliet heard a strangled sound before Katrin rang off abruptly. She held the receiver in her hand for a few moments, before replacing it carefully. She had met Katrin only a few times – she was based at Holbeach police station, where the South Lincs force's small research unit had been set up – but she liked her tremendously. Tim's entire team were united in liking his wife and appreciating his good fortune in having married her. They were such a warm and well-suited couple that their happiness seemed to rub off on to other people. But Juliet reflected now that Tim himself had been unusually taciturn over the past few days and had lost his temper on a couple of occasions. She had put this down to the stresses of the Claudia McRae case, but now she suspected that there might be a more personal reason. She hoped with the deepest sincerity that nothing had gone wrong with the marriage. She considered leaving a message on Tim's mobile to tell him that Katrin was trying to contact him, but thought better of it. Katrin herself was certain to have left a message, so further prompting from Juliet was likely to be seen as interfering.

"Oh, God," she said, as she sat down heavily at her own desk. She had not realised that she had spoken the words aloud until Andy Carstairs looked up.

"Something troubling you?" he said. "Apart from the usual, that is – too much routine work on a case that's going nowhere." He grinned to show that he was being sympathetic.

"No; nothing at all, really. Just bogged down, as you guessed. Thanks for asking."

She turned away, and shuffled through her notes until she had found the telephone number of the ferry company. The number for Forensics was already programmed into her phone.

CHAPTER TWENTY-TWO

FOR THE TENTH time Alex searched through her wardrobe. She was trying to find something to wear to the dinner of the one-day conference that she was attending with Edmund. The dresses that she usually wore to the Archaeological Society conferences were all too matronly, the frocks that accompanied her to France when she was on holiday with Tom too skimpy for the time of year. She held a flame-coloured backless dress with a halter neck against her for the fourth time.

"That's a gorgeous outfit. My favourite."

Alex jumped. Tom had entered their bedroom soundlessly and she had not noticed him.

"You're not going to wear that for one of your old farts' dos, surely?" Tom continued, prowling restlessly round the room before he stretched out on the bed. Alex snatched a pile of newly-ironed underwear out of reach of his shoes.

"It isn't one of their 'dos', as you put it. It's an international conference for society secretaries and officials – people like me. Some of them work for very renowned organisations, so they're quite eminent, as well as much better paid than I am. I wanted to wear something decent to the dinner – so as not to show myself up, as much as anything." Even to herself her words sounded feeble and unconvincing. Tom looked at her suspiciously.

"You always look lovely," he said, after a pause. "And you know as well as I do that most of them *will* be old farts – lecherous ones, in all probability. There's no need to encourage them by wearing a frock like that. Do you know anyone else who's going?" he added, with studied casualness.

"Only Edmund," said Alex.

"There you are, you see!" Tom sounded triumphant, but also relieved. He evidently didn't regard Edmund as a threat. "The old fart personified. And there's probably a lecher hiding under all those layers of boring society procedures and archaeological detail, too."

"Nonsense!" said Alex, attempting a laugh. "You surely hadn't forgotten about it, though, had you? I've written the dates on the planner in the kitchen. I shall be out only for tomorrow night. I get back late on Thursday – too late for dinner," she added.

"Now you mention it, it does ring a vague bell. In Scotland somewhere, isn't it? At a fancy golf course or something."

"Yes. Roundberry. Not my kind of place, really."

"Well, I daresay you'll cope. How are you getting there? By train?"

"Goodness, no. It would take forever – and I'd have had to travel today and stay overnight tonight as well, because it starts at 11.00 a.m. tomorrow. Edmund and I are catching an early flight to Glasgow from Luton. He's coming to pick me up. We'll leave his car at the airport and he's booked a hire car at Glasgow."

"Good Lord! What time does he intend to get here?"

"About 5.00 a.m. We decided that would give us time to get to Luton and park the car in good time. The flight leaves at 8.30."

"Very cosy," said Tom. There was no mistaking his tone this time. "Well, it will be chilly up there, so may I suggest that you wear something a little more substantial than that dress, even if the place is centrally-heated?"

"I don't have time to buy anything new," Alex said defensively.

"You don't need anything new! Your wardrobe is bursting with clothes. Let me choose something."

This time Alex's laugh was unforced.

"This sudden interest in my clothes is quite overwhelming. You've never before given the slightest indication that you take any notice of what I wear."

"Ah, well, you see, I'm more observant than you think," said Tom. He sprang to his feet and began leafing through the rail in her wardrobe.

CHAPTER TWENTY-THREE

THE FOLLOWING EVENING Alex was sitting across the table from Edmund at dinner wearing a black knitted, sequin-spangled, silk jumper with a low neck and a long black velvet skirt. Tom's choice of clothes, though hardly sexy, was at least not frumpy. In fact, she felt quite elegant compared to the other guests. Aside from the other delegates at the conference – about thirty of them and almost all, as Tom had predicted, men of 'a certain age' – the guests at the hotel were mostly rich elderly golfers with heavily made-up wives in tow, some of them wearing floaty chiffon creations that were rather too uncomfortably like parodies of her red dress.

They were having dinner quite late by Scottish standards. Contrary to what she had assumed, no formal conference dinner had been arranged. Instead, the conference delegates had been invited to join the other guests at a time of their own choosing and, consequently, most of them had opted to eat earlier and were now propping up one of the several residents' bars in the hotel.

Edmund placed his hand over hers.

"You're looking very lovely," he said. She allowed it to rest there for a while, before gently drawing her own hand away.

"What's the matter?" he said. "Don't you like me to do that?"

"It's not that I don't like it; it's just that I don't want anyone to see us. There are too many people here that we know for us to be able to make displays of affection in public."

Edmund nodded and withdrew his hand altogether.

"Did you ring home?" he asked.

"Yes, but Tom was out. He's working on a complicated case at the moment. I doubt if he'll even notice that I'm not there."

"Then he doesn't deserve you," said Edmund. He was obviously trying to sound gallant, but the words came out a little unctuously.

"What about you? Did you call your wife?" Alex could not bring herself to say 'Krystyna'. It would sound impertinent, somehow.

"Yes, but she wasn't there either. Visiting her mother, probably. As I think I've told you, she and her sister suffer from an unhealthy preoccupation with the minutiae of their mother's life. In reality, the old girl's as tough as old boots. They should just leave her to get on with it. I think that Krystyna needs her more than the other way round. She usually goes there when she's becoming depressed."

"Does she suffer from depression?"

"Yes, unfortunately. They all do: the sister and brother as well. I think it may have something to do with that sense of rootlessness that I told you about. They don't quite fit in here – despite all their charm. Anyway, let's change the subject. If you decide what you're going to eat, I can choose some wine."

Alex had been determined not to drink too much on this occasion, but, as they started their second bottle of wine, she reflected that alcohol seemed to have become an indispensable prop to their relationship. She was enjoying Edmund's company, though; and its illicitness, which had worried her so much at the end of the evening that they had spent in Peterborough, was not disturbing her unduly. "Thou shalt not be found out," she thought ruefully. The devil's commandment. She could hardly doubt that her more relaxed attitude stemmed less from her having been engulfed by an overwhelming passion for Edmund than from the feeling of security that she had gained from being almost 400 miles from home. As she also knew, once they had sunk the second bottle of wine, the caution that compelled her to reject his caresses in public would have evaporated completely. They would have to retire to avoid scandal. That she was not booked into a suite, as she had been at the Society's conference, caused her a small tremor of apprehension. It looked so much more blatant to invite a man to her bedroom, even though she knew it was what they were both anticipating.

Edmund was drinking more slowly than usual and she felt that he was taking extra care to make the conversation interesting. He had put aside his habitual combativeness and was talking to her earnestly about the best ways to label artefacts that had not been properly classified upon discovery. As this was at the heart of the 'big project' which they had now agreed to take on together, she felt touched, because she knew that he was trying to tell her that some of the logistical difficulties that worried her most could be overcome. She sipped the wine and smiled, catching his eye.

He halted in mid-sentence.

"What's the matter? Am I boring you?"

She laughed, a silvery, tinkling laugh that she hardly recognised as her own, and patted his sleeve.

"No, of course not. I'm just touched by how seriously you're taking the project."

"Of course I'm taking it seriously," he said. "Everything depends on it!"

"Not everything, surely?" Her flirtatiousness evaporated. Was he implying that he expected her to leave Tom? If so, she must be careful not to fall into the trap. She knew that she was not ready to change her life so irrevocably.

Edmund's voice was taut.

"Well, everything eventually. We're both proposing to give up our jobs, aren't we? A great deal hangs on our success. For me more than for you, perhaps."

"I'm not sure that I follow you."

Edmund flushed and bit his lip. He took a long swig from his water glass.

"I . . . just meant that I have to support two people, that's all. Krystyna no longer works, as I told you; and, even when she did, she was only a part-time teaching assistant at a primary school. Stupidly, she has never paid into a pension scheme – despite good advice from me on the subject, I might add."

He was blustering, thought Alex: changing the subject.

"I've been thinking that we might not have to hand in our respective notices until we're pretty sure that the business idea is going to work," said Alex smoothly.

Edmund steepled his fingers and regarded her over the crown that he had made.

"How do you propose to do that, without cheating on your employer – and requiring me to cheat on mine?" he enquired severely.

"I'll ask the board of the Archaeological Society to approve our taking a sample of uncategorised artefacts. We can try to attribute them to the correct period by working after hours. I'll say that you are willing to help. We can present it as a pilot study, to see if a full classification project is achievable and then suggest that the work is put out to tender after the pilot is successful – which it will be, if what you're telling me is correct." She shot him a challenging smile.

"Not a bad idea," he said, his words belying the eagerness with which he spoke, "but what if the tender process produces a better offer than ours?"

Alex let out a peal of laughter, entirely genuine this time.

"You don't know them as well as I do! There's no way that they'll want to go out to tender if a viable proposal is put on the table in front of them – especially if I'm the person who is suggesting a way of getting the classification work done. I can just envisage the board meeting at which it will be discussed. It will be a time for courteous speeches and fulsome compliments – and probably a suggestion that I continue to work part-time as the secretary. They hate change so much that I'm convinced that this is how they'll react."

"But that isn't what you want, is it? To work part-time, I mean. I thought that you wanted to concentrate on building the business and espe-

cially on making this project successful so that we can offer our services
to other societies and museums."

"That *is* what I want, in the long run; but you're absolutely right to
suggest that we should minimise the risks if we can. This means steering
a middle course until we are sure that the business can be made to work.
That would be the time to consider resigning altogether."

Edmund nodded slowly. He still seemed to be testing what she had said
in his mind; yet she also sensed that he was relieved to hear her words.

"Alex?" he said, taking her hand again.

"Yes?"

"Do you think that they will allow us to remove some of the boxes from
Broad Street? To work on them, I mean?"

"Gosh, you are good at jumping from the general to the particular! I
don't see why not. We should have to ask them, of course, and we may
have to guarantee the safety of the boxes by taking out insurance. But
none of the items has much intrinsic value, especially in their unclassified
state. Their value is bound up with the Society's own reputation as an
able curator of the region's prehistory. So I'm guessing that the answer
will be 'yes'."

"That's wonderful!" said Edmund, his expression suddenly his hallmark
beatific. He picked up the half-bottle of wine that remained, and waved it.

"Shall we adjourn?"

Alex nodded . . . and lowered her eyes.

"Your room or mine?" she asked quietly.

"Oh, yours, I think," said Edmund. "It wouldn't be very gentlemanly
to let a lady go creeping around the corridors in the middle of the night,
would it?"

Alex did not reflect at the time that this was a very Edwardian way
of conducting a love affair, but when she awoke the next morning to
find herself alone, she realised that it had its advantages, especially as her
mobile phone began to ring almost as soon as she had opened her eyes.
She hauled herself out of bed and retrieved it from her handbag, which
was lying on the floor among her discarded clothes. She pressed the green
button with some trepidation, but it wasn't Tom: just someone from the
garage calling about her car.

She looked at her watch. It was almost 7.30 a.m. The conference didn't
start for another two hours, but now that she was awake she didn't feel
like going back to bed. She decided to take a quick shower and go for a
brisk walk. She had a lot to think about.

It was a beautiful clear frosty morning. Quickly she walked beyond the
perimeter of the park and golf course to the fields beyond. She wanted to
get away from the immediate vicinity of the hotel because she suspected
that Edmund might also plan an early morning stroll. Despite the cold, the

sheep were grazing on the sparse grass in the fields. Out of sight, further down the valley, she could hear a cowman whistling to his herd.

She had been walking at speed. The moment that she paused to take in the view, she realised how fierce the cold was. She had forgotten her hat, so she pulled up the hood of her duffle-coat and curled her hands within her woollen mittens so that her fingers gained warmth from her palms. She didn't have a hangover, but her head felt woolly with that curious half-absent sensation that drinking too much often causes. She was also shivery and extremely hungry. She removed one of her mittens and fished in her pocket. She found half of a Bounty bar and sucked on it, trying to make it last.

She needed to confront herself before she could face the day – indeed, before she could either face Edmund or speak to Tom. Her mother's voice rose unbidden in her imagination: "Just what do you think you are doing, young lady?"

What was she doing? Last night had been pleasant – perhaps more pleasant than she had anticipated. Edmund had been a considerate and tender lover, anxious to please and receptive to her demands. He had been neither boisterous nor perfunctory, either of which would have made her feel cheap. He had also not been madly passionate – but neither had she. She knew that neither of them could claim the excuse of having been overtaken by the throes of a passion beyond their control. It had been pleasant – she returned to the word. But more fulfilling or more enjoyable than sleeping with Tom? That depended. Tom, absent-minded and arousing himself from the toils of sleep, could be a trial; but Tom at his best, engaged and focused? No. Tom was the better lover: more sensitive, more imaginative and, most importantly, an infinite extension of herself.

So why the affair with Edmund? It was not as if it had taken her by surprise. On the contrary, she could have nipped it in the bud immediately if she had tried – had indeed done so after the Archaeological Society conference, until, almost perversely, she had allowed it to be resurrected again. No, that was too kind to herself to be truthful: she had *encouraged* its resurrection. She could not deceive herself otherwise. There had been no good reason for spending that evening in Peterborough with Edmund. She could have taken a taxi, as Tom had suggested, or persuaded Edmund to drive her home straight away. She had known, or at least guessed, to what it would lead. So why had she done it?

For the adventure, she decided; and then, more harshly – because she had to be as unforgiving of herself as possible in order to get to the truth – out of vanity. She had been flattered by Edmund's attentions . . . and by his confidences. And, to be fair, she had enjoyed talking to him – had enjoyed being permitted to glimpse below his verbose, pedestrian exterior to find that the 'real' Edmund was someone rather more interesting. The 'real'

Edmund was not as morally correct as she had supposed, either. Did this shock her? Not on balance. Doubts crept in, though, when she considered this. She was not convinced that she understood Edmund. She was even less convinced that she knew why he had sought her out. What did he hope for beyond the obvious thrill of a transitory affair?

She knew that Edmund was not about to leave Krystyna for her. This made her both sad and dissatisfied – irrationally, because she herself had no intention of leaving Tom. The difference was . . . she held herself in check for a moment while she analysed whether she was about to embark on some specious pleading favourable to herself again . . . the difference was that Edmund had made it abundantly clear to her that his marriage was a shell; a sham, really. He would be prepared to leave Krystyna, of that she was sure, if he fell properly in love. But Alex had no doubt that she was not the special person that had eluded him for his whole life; nor did she try to persuade herself that Edmund had said that he would not ask her to leave Tom out of respect for their marriage. Perhaps he did just want a fleeting affair, after all. Wasn't that what most men wanted?

She could not believe that that was all. There was the business idea, of course. Edmund had been keen on this – almost obsessed by it – right from the start. Strange that she'd never thought of involving him, but that was because she'd always conceived of it as a venture for her and Tom, something on which they could work together and be happy together. That clearly wasn't going to happen now. She felt suddenly tearful.

She thrust her hands into her pockets and began to walk back to the hotel.

CHAPTER TWENTY-FOUR

ANDY CARSTAIRS WAS having a frustrating time. Thobias Padgett was a quick learner; like his elder brother LeRoy, he had an intuitive understanding of how to play the system.

Thobias was now sitting in solemn state with an entourage of protective adults, each one determined to shield him from police brutality and any other rude intrusions upon his sensitive young mind. Thobias accepted their attentions with the impervious grace of a plump young Buddha. Andy detected no recurrence of the hysterical fear that the child had displayed on the previous day. The only sign of possible inner turmoil was that he was still quite taciturn. His demeanour was calm, even dignified, and the troupe of attendant adults was clearly impressed. They seemed to have forgotten that he and they were crammed into this room because he was suspected of being a petty criminal who had stumbled into a bigger crime by accident. Andy sighed. In his opinion, Thobias was a devious little bastard who had been all too quick to cotton on to the fact that he could run rings round all of them and stick a finger up to the police in the process.

Marlene, wearing a woollen dress patterned with horizontal black, purple and yellow stripes that lent her more than a passing resemblance to a giant bumblebee, was holding Thobias's hand and stroking it tenderly. Like her son, she had sussed out her audience quickly to find ways of playing up to its expectations. The whole group was seated at the small oblong table that occupied most of the room: five larger-than-average adults and one diminutive youth; all of them except Andy, who paced back and forth the short distance from wall to wall like a caged cat. He paused and folded his arms.

"Now, Thobias," he said, his voice as warm as he could make it, "I want you to think very carefully. Exactly when did you last see LeRoy?"

Thobias made a quick sweep of all the faces intent upon his answer and decided that it would be in his best interests to comply.

"When he said I could borrow his bike," he said in a subdued voice.

"When was that? Which day of the week?"

"The day that he asked me to do the job."

"Can you remember which day of the week it was?"

The child gazed at him.

"Come on, Thobias, it can't be that difficult to think back. Which day of the week was it?"

Thobias studied the thumb of his right hand, and put it in his mouth. Marlene continued her rhythmic stroking of his left hand.

"Well, at least give me an answer, even if it's only to tell me that you don't remember." Andy had inadvertently raised his voice; in fact, he was almost shouting in his exasperation. Thobias's eyes filled with tears. His face crumpled. Jack Lewis sprang to life.

"DC Carstairs, I'm going to have to ask you to be much more sensitive to the child's state of mind. You know that he has been badly frightened and he is undoubtedly traumatised by his experiences. It is very important that he learns to rely on us now. He must be able to think of us as friends who will keep him safe. Browbeating and bullying will not help. I shall take steps to ensure that his feelings are respected. If you find that his understandable reticence taxes your patience too greatly, I'm sure that Superintendent Thornton can be asked to provide someone else. A lady detective, perhaps."

Andy raised his eyes to the ceiling, then lowered them and tried to catch Gary Cooper's eye. Gary looked away quickly. Andy fervently hoped that this was because he regarded the situation as ludicrous and not because he had been drawn into the magic circle of child-worshippers.

"I'm sorry if you think that I have been too precipitate," he said. "Perhaps Marlene – Mrs Padgett – can help. Mrs Padgett, can you remember when LeRoy last came home?"

Marlene adjusted her countenance to convey that she was concentrating with some ferocity. Her velvet forehead furrowed.

"Well, now, it may be Sunday."

"It either was or it wasn't," snapped Andy. He saw Jack Lewis shift uneasily in his seat, and adopted a more emollient tone. "You must be able to remember – try to use some memory props to think back." Marlene stared blankly. "I mean, think about what you *do* remember about Sunday. What did you cook and who was there when you ate? Did you provide LeRoy with any meals?"

"Not right sure. Always I cook for everyone, an' LeRoy, but he don't always show up."

"But he does still live with you?"

"Do usually. He not home now."

"So you said yesterday. Do you know when LeRoy last went to school?"

"Not since holidays, I think. I tell 'im about court order an' all."

"But he has been living at home for most of the time since he was last at school?"

"I tell you. He mostly with us. Only when trouble he go away."

"Mrs Padgett, did you know about the errands that LeRoy sent Thobias on?"

"Not sure, no."

"What does 'not sure' mean?"

"Well, I see them whisper together. Then, when LeRoy go out, Thobias come and tell me LeRoy promise to lend him his bike. My little boy overjoyed!" She is laying it on with a trowel now, thought Andy, but no-one else in the room seemed sceptical.

"But he didn't tell you why LeRoy said he could borrow the bike?"

"Not 'til after, when policeman bring him home. He say then about the errand. He scared – he know he done wrong – a good boy, really. LeRoy a good boy, too," she added, instantly detracting from the credibility of her opinion of Thobias.

"What happened to the bike?"

Thobias burst into tears.

"LeRoy will kill me," he said.

Gary Cooper volunteered an answer.

"The bike was lost when Thobias visited the milk bar," he said. "Thobias told me about it last night. He propped it up against the wall of the milk bar, which is right next to some waste ground. He said that he'd only intended to pop in for a minute to get some hot chocolate. But when the proprietor saw the wad of notes that he was carrying, he insisted on detaining Thobias and called the police. When he was allowed outside again the bike had vanished.

"It was you pigs made me lose it," said Thobias defiantly, half-sobbing through scanty tears.

"Hush, Thobs," said Marlene soothingly. "All be fine, you see." It was as if she'd taken on the demeanour of the social workers by being in close proximity to them.

"Thobias," said Andy, squatting on his haunches so that he could look up at the boy's face, "you were caught because you were going to pay for the hot chocolate that you bought in the milk bar with money from the parcel that you'd been given to carry back. You'd been given strict instructions not to look inside that parcel. What made you disobey?"

"The paper tore," said the child, looking shifty, "so I could see inside. I was only going to take one of the twenties. They'd never of known. 'Sides, LeRoy never paid me, so they owed it me."

"Who would never have known? Who owed you the money, Thobias?"

"LeRoy and . . . the others."

"Which others, Thobias? Can you tell me their names?"

The boy fell silent again, his face a smooth mask.

"I said, which others, Thobias!" Andy was standing up straight again. He was almost shouting. Thobias began to whimper again.

"DC Carstairs, I am going to have to ask you again to go easier on the boy. You can see that you are upsetting him and you must be perfectly aware that you are exceeding what is permitted by law, especially when the interrogation is of a minor."

All of the other adults in the room fixed their eyes on Andy. He knew that Thobias was also watching him through the splayed fingers of his free hand. It made Andy's blood boil.

"All right," Andy said, smacking his own forehead with the flat of his palm. "Would you like to try to talk to him, Tom? You had some success yesterday."

"Marie's the professional child psychologist," said Tom Tarrant. "That's why we asked her here. She'll know better than anyone else how best to talk to him in this more formal situation. Thobias, you do know that everything that you are saying is being recorded, don't you?"

Thanks for that, thought Andy. Jack Lewis had already explained this to Thobias and Andy had announced that the tape recorder was on when he had pressed the switch. But there was nothing like ramming home the point to make the child clam up completely.

Marie Krakowska stood up and rustled round the table in her prickly wool skirt. She hitched it up a little to reveal striped scarlet and beige stockings, and knelt on the floor just in front of Thobias's chair. She sat back on her heels and rested her substantial buttocks on the cushion of cloth that this action had created. Marlene still had hold of Thobias's left hand. Marie now proceeded to stroke the wrist of his right one.

"Thobias," she said softly, staring at the child hypnotically with her pale blue eyes, "Look at me."

Thobias fixed his eyes on the floor.

"Thobias, you do as the lady says, now. She nice lady."

Thobias did not look up. Unexpectedly, Marlene let go of his hand and in the same movement raised her own to give him a smart clip round the ear.

Pandemonium broke out. Tom Tarrant rushed round the table to help comfort Thobias, who was shrieking at the top of his voice. Marie had already lifted him down from the chair and was pressing him into her ample broderie anglaise-frilled bosom. Marlene herself was crying noisily in response to Jack Lewis's quiet admonishments.

Andy groaned. "Heaven give me strength!" he exclaimed. "We're none of us likely to get any sense out of the kid now."

"Is it all right if I go?" PC Cooper asked. "They're searching the woods at Helpston and I've been detailed to join them."

Andy nodded. "Sure, you get off," he said. "Thanks for your help with this."

"Jammy devil," he added sotto voce as Gary edged past him. PC Cooper managed to look solemn but there was the glimmer of a smile in his eye. The door closed behind him.

CHAPTER TWENTY-FIVE

TIM HAD ARRANGED to meet Jane Halliwell in the foyer of the Welland Manor hotel. It was strange to be returning there only a few days after he had met Alex Tarrant and interviewed Oliver Sparham. The archaeology conference was long over, its members dispersed, and the hotel seemed much more run-down and desolate than when they had filled it with their eccentric presence. Jane was waiting for him. She was dressed in a long camel coat and brown leather knee-length boots. There was a silk scarf knotted with faux carelessness around her neck. Even he, unversed in fashion as he was, recognised it unmistakably as a purchase from Hermès.

He had deliberately left Jane to her own devices to see whether she would make the first move. He thought that if she had asked for news or whether she might visit the cottage it would give him further insight into her character. He was slightly surprised by her silence, since he had suggested that he might be asking her to accompany him to the cottage on the same day that she'd visited the police station. Several days had now gone by. Jane had kept silent. He had not been able to gauge her reaction when he had called her that morning to apologise for not having contacted her earlier, with the request that she accompany him now. There was a brief silence before she spoke; then she was courteous forbearance itself: "Oh, that is quite all right. I know that you have a great deal to do. And this afternoon is perfectly convenient for me."

Now he was stretching out his hand in order to receive the same birdlike handshake that had distinguished their first meeting. He thanked her again.

"Ms Halliwell – I hope that you are better rested than when we last met? I should like to thank you again for co-operating."

"It is not only my pleasure, Inspector, but the least that I can do while you are trying to find Claudia." She withdrew her hand and looked at him intently. "I take it that there is no news?"

"I'm afraid not. We've searched the entire area for clues and contacted all the hospitals. Like you, Guy Maichment could not think of many close friends whom she might have taken it into her head to visit, but we have contacted everyone on the small list that he provided. Her professional contacts are legion, of course, but her disappearance has been so well-publicised that I doubt whether any of them could be unaware that we are looking for her or would be irresponsible enough to harbour her secretly.

What do you think?" he asked suddenly, deciding to put Jane to the test a little.

She blinked, but continued to meet his eye.

"I think it's highly unlikely. Claudia and I have been living a very secluded life for several years. I go away to meet friends occasionally, but she never does; and she rarely has visitors, apart from Guy. She mainly keeps in touch with people by telephone. But I've told you this before."

"Quite. Shall we walk to the car?" asked Tim, indicating that she should precede him. She nodded and walked so briskly across the flagged floor, her high heels tapping the stones in a businesslike manner, that he had to hurry to get to the door first in order to open it for her. Once in the courtyard they fell into step beside each other. Tim continued to talk in a conversational way.

"How long have you known Dame Claudia?"

"Oh – let me think – it must be the best part of a decade. But I've only been her secretary-companion for about five years."

"Have you lived with her all of that time?"

"Yes, since I took the job. Not before. You've seen where we live, Detective Inspector. It is a very isolated place. It would have been impossible for me to have lived with her and continued in my former occupation."

"What was your former occupation, if you don't mind my asking?"

"Of course not. I was a lecturer at Lincoln University. That was where I met Guy. He was a mature student. He was taking a course in landscape design so that he could set up his own business. We shared various interests, so I met him socially on a number of occasions. He talked about his aunt quite a lot – as you may have gathered, they have a kind of love-hate relationship. Guy is often exasperated by her, but he is also very proud of her. I had heard of her myself and asked if he could arrange for us to meet. She hadn't bought the house at Helpston then; she was living in a terrace in Stamford. But she didn't like small town life and was already looking for somewhere else. I believe that it was Guy who subsequently found the cottage for her. They are very alike in some respects. They both like to live in deserted places."

"And you don't?"

"I manage. I need to get away from solitude more than they do. I don't mean for holidays; the Norwegian trip was my first holiday in three years. But I do like to visit the theatre and cinema and to go to libraries and bookshops. I make a point of keeping in touch with civilisation. However, it is peaceful where we live. Was, perhaps I should say." She gave a bleak little laugh.

"This is my car," said Tim, unlocking it. He noted that she was more expansive than when they had first met and, despite her last comment, seemed to have unwound yet further during their short walk across the courtyard. As they began the slow journey to the old lodge gate, he resumed his gentle questioning.

"So she offered you the job after she moved to Helpston?"

"Yes; quite a long time afterwards."

"You will forgive me for saying that it's difficult to understand why you accepted the offer. What attraction could acting as the companion of an elderly woman – even a very eminent one – hold for someone who has an established position in a university?"

"I am not her nursemaid, Detective Inspector. I am employed as her secretary-companion, with the emphasis decidedly on the secretary part. I accepted her offer without hesitation because I happen to believe in her life's work. She has a closely-guarded secret to which only Guy and I are privy. I will tell it to you so that you understand the situation completely, but I must first ask you to respect that it is strictly confidential."

"I am happy to keep anything that you may tell me secret unless I believe that it will further jeopardise her safety. Or yours, of course."

Jane Halliwell gave him one of her level looks. She paused, then announced with some éclat:

"Claudia is working on a book which draws together all of her past work, and that of others, to create a comprehensive exegesis of her semantic theory. I am helping her to do it. Her brain is as bright as ever, but, as we've already discussed, she rarely leaves the house, so she cannot check references in libraries; and she is too old – and possibly too contrary – to learn how to access library materials through the internet. She doesn't type, either. My role is therefore that of researcher, secretary, editorial and occasional amanuensis, rolled into one. She doesn't want anyone to know that she is writing the book, because she wants to spring it on the world as a total surprise. It will be both her swansong and the crowning work of her career. It will also vindicate her and turn the tables on the many establishment figures – men, mostly – who have ridiculed or discounted her writings over the past fifty years and more."

"I see," said Tim. He wished that he could think of something more imaginative – more responsive – to the gushing fanfare of Jane Halliwell's announcement than this terse sentence, but no other words sprang to mind. He could feign no enthusiasm for the project. "Thank you for telling me," he added.

They had left the grounds of the hotel and were driving sedately along the main road to Helpston, their progress hindered by the inevitable tractor in front. Tim debated whether to ask Jane directly about Dame Claudia's politics and decided that he would not risk alerting her to his interest in them. He needed more time to consider the implications of her revelation about the book. If indeed she occupied as central a role in

Claudia's work and was as enthusiastic about her theories as she claimed, it was likely that Jane herself held strongly right-wing views. Not that there was any crime in that. But the unease that he had felt at their first meeting was not dissipated by her new-found talkativeness.

"We have not been able to stage a reconstruction of Dame Claudia's last hours before she vanished," he said, "because we have no idea what she did after Oliver Sparham left her at about 4 p.m. It would be useful to know how she normally spent her time. Could you describe to me a typical day in her life – in both your lives?"

"I can try. You should be aware that we don't have a strict routine. I know that many writers religiously devote certain hours of the day to their work. Claudia doesn't have the temperament for that; she is too undisciplined and disorganised. But she works for quite a long period every day – it could be in the morning, the afternoon, or the evening – and she almost always gets up early, often before 7 a.m. She herself says that this is a legacy from the time when she worked in the desert before the Second World War, when she had to make the most of the early morning before the heat of the sun became too oppressive. But Claudia is quite a romantic and a great mythologiser of her own past. I suspect that these days she gets up early because she doesn't sleep too well. Her arthritis is severe and plagues her, especially when she is lying down."

"Her nephew told me that she sometimes sleeps all night in an armchair."

"That may be true when I'm not there – which is rarely, as you know. When I am there, I usually manage to persuade her to go to bed – though often it is very late when she retires."

"That must be tiring for you. Do you get up as early as she does?"

"Rather earlier, usually. Depending on the weather, I like to go for a run, or a brisk walk, in the woods before we have breakfast. I'm quite keen on keeping fit and I have little other opportunity for exercise."

"Do you prepare the breakfast?"

"Sometimes. Sometimes Claudia does it while I'm out. I actually prefer to do it myself because she's so messy. But she means well, and I don't like to be unkind when she is willing to make the effort."

"And afterwards you both begin to work?"

"As I've said, Claudia has no regular routine. I certainly always work in the mornings myself. If Claudia is not ready to dictate – she dictates to me two or three pages at each of our sessions on the actual book – she may wish to read parts of her previous works, or those of others, in order to refresh her memory. I help her to do this by taking notes as she requires, or marking certain passages for us to refer back to again. I may even read aloud to her. Sometimes she doesn't want to work at all. On these occasions, I catch up with the typing or the checking of references. But she'll then need me to work with her later on. Usually in the afternoon, but occasionally in the evening."

"What does she do when she isn't working?"

"When I first came, she was quite active. She would go for short walks in the woods or do some gardening. She could drive the car then, too, though I'm not certain that she's ever taken a driving test. But I'm afraid that the arthritis has curtailed most of these activities; and, of course, Guy looks after the garden now. She spends most of her free time listening to the radio or to records. She's got a big vinyl collection. She watches television occasionally, but not very often. She much prefers the radio. And she reads newspapers when we can get them, but no newsagent will deliver so far out, so we are dependent on Guy to bring them when he visits."

"Doesn't it distract you if she's listening to the radio when you're trying to work?"

"I usually work in the conservatory when Claudia doesn't need me. She stays in the sitting-room most of the time now."

"Does she ever work without you? When you were in Norway, for example, would she have carried on writing a little by herself or would she have simply planned to take a break until your return?"

"She wouldn't have done any actual writing without me," Jane said, a little emphatically, Tim thought. "But she may have done some reading. She might even have made some notes – though she would have been more likely to have used her Dictaphone."

"That's interesting," said Tim, his tone conveying the opposite. He was racking his brains, trying to conjure up a complete picture of Claudia's sitting-room. Dictaphone? He was sure that he would have remembered if one had been found. The SOCOs would certainly have recorded its presence if it had been there and taken any tapes away for analysis. He would check their inventory and also double-check the cottage himself when he and Jane arrived.

"Tell me," he said, "how much of the book is there still left to write? I appreciate that it is a weighty work and will be taking a long time to complete. You have been working on it for – how long? Five years now?"

"About four years," said Jane. "There was a lot of planning to do and information to track down, before we started. But if you're thinking that we must be near to publication, you are correct. The book is three-quarters finished now. Of course, there will still be a lot of checking and proofing to do when the first draft is completed."

"Is the publisher Dame Claudia's usual one? The MacLachan Press, I believe?" Tim was indebted to Juliet for this piece of information.

"Not . . . exactly."

"Oh?"

"We may offer it to a commercial publisher eventually; and as you say, the MacLachan Press has first refusal on her work. But initially the plan is to print it ourselves, for private circulation only. Publishing is much easier and cheaper these days, since the invention of digital printing and e-books." Jane contrived rapidly to climb out of a tense moment by offering this airily expansive general observation.

"Indeed. But it seems a pity to deny this work – Dame Claudia's magnum opus, no less – to the world at large."

"Her work is caviar to the general, Detective Inspector, as her critics have proved," said Jane Halliwell briskly. "Ah, here we are. It would seem that some of your colleagues have arrived before us."

Despite the fact that of course he knew that he had taken the turn-off to Claudia's cottage, Tim had not been paying attention to the last leg of their journey. He followed the direction of Jane's line of vision and saw Patti Gardiner's small white van parked neatly at the side of the road.

Jane got out of the car slowly and smoothed down her coat. She took an almost theatrically deep breath and grimaced deprecatingly at Tim. He felt impatient at what he recognised as feigned apprehensiveness, but managed to conjure up a brief smile of encouragement.

"Come on," he said. "There's nothing to be afraid of. Apart from the unpleasant smudge on the hall wall, which you know about, and some residual mess from the fingerprint dusting, I'm pretty certain that the place is much as you left it."

She nodded, reciprocating with an equally wan smile of her own, and followed him up the path. He knocked on the door of the cottage to ask to be admitted. One of the SOCOs – not Patti – opened it. The electric light in the hall was switched on. Jane hung back.

"Come on," he said again, more gently. "I'm sorry, but I have to ask you to do this."

Jane nodded again, and stepped over the threshold. She turned immediately to fix her eyes on the wall.

"My God!" she said precipitately. "I feel sick!"

Tim would have bet money that she would make such an exclamation. Patiently, he took her arm and led her in the direction of the kitchen. "Let's just get past it," he said. "Then I'm sure you'll be fine." Privately, he thought that the trajectory was much less evil-seeming now that it had darkened from red to deep brown. He doubted that it could really have produced such a distressing effect on a rational woman like Jane. The lady with the vapours act did not suit her.

"Would you like some water?" he asked, indicating the bottles and plastic cups that had been placed on the kitchen table by the SOCOs. She shook her head.

"You'll find the kitchen less untouched than the other rooms. We've left the dirty crockery in the sink and on the work surface, as we found it, but the SOCOs finished here quite quickly. Besides Dame Claudia's, the only prints we found in here were your own, Mr Maichment's, and Oliver Sparham's. All quite legitimate."

"Why do you say that Oliver Sparham's were legitimate?" she asked sharply.

"Because he told us that he had come in here to make himself and Dame Claudia a cup of tea and this is corroborated by the two cups that we found in the sitting-room, one of them bearing his prints only, the others those of both of them. Do you know Mr Sparham?" he added.

"Not personally, though I've seen photographs of him. I know that he was one of Claudia's disciples when he was young. I understand that subsequently he drifted away from her, though. He decided to play safe and opt to support more conventional theories than hers – in fact, to support no theories at all. Nowadays Oliver Sparham is what I would call an empiricist: he will have no truck with anything except the scientific evidence produced by digs."

"Speaking as a historian, I would say that seems a sensible approach."

"It's a very desiccated approach," said Jane Halliwell with vehemence. "And actually not one that's well supported by historians. Look at the Marxist interpretations of the English Civil War, for example, and the fascinating books that were written because of them."

"A bit before my time, I'm afraid," said Tim. "I'm a post-modernist myself – which is how I guess Oliver Sparham might also describe himself. But are you saying that he has shown hostility towards Dame Claudia?"

"Not personally, no. But he has failed to endorse her work in his writings, even though it was she who gave him his first start in life."

"Has he actively criticised her?"

"No, not as such. I suppose he has some conscience left. It's what he doesn't say that counts. In fact, he hardly mentions her at all in any of the stuff that I've read by him. And there are no half-measures with Claudia's thesis: you either accept it or you don't. Personally, I see his behaviour as a betrayal. Claudia took – takes – a more lenient view. Of course, she still thinks of him as a young man who has his way to make in the world, whose own ideas are barely formed."

"Indeed." Tim smiled as he recollected the silver-haired and rather urbane and distinguished figure whom he had met and interviewed at Welland Manor. "May I take it that you don't see anything out of place in the kitchen? If so, would you come into the conservatory?"

The conservatory was reached by what had originally been the back door of the cottage. It had been built against the back wall of the house, so that it was more of a glorified lean-to than a structure in its own right. Like the sitting-room, it faced east. It was cold and, for a room that consisted of glass on three sides, dark in the winter. Like the rear sitting-room window, it was overshadowed by the yew hedge that grew just a few feet beyond it. It contained two rattan chairs that had seen better days and a modest table with a wooden chair tucked beneath it. The table bore a telephone extension and what Tim recognised to be a fairly old-fashioned PC. He gestured towards them.

"Is this where you work?" he asked.

Jane Halliwell nodded. "Yes," she said. She shivered. "It's cold in here – I'm the only person who uses this room, so I suppose that it hasn't been heated for a while. I have an electric radiator that I use in the winter. It makes it quite cosy."

"I don't see it now. Nor any of your books and papers. Where do you keep those?"

"All the research materials are replaced in the sitting-room when I'm not using them, so that Claudia can find them easily. I gave her the radiator to use while I was away so that she would still be warm if neither she nor Guy managed to light the fire."

"I see. Well, we haven't found anything in this room: almost all the prints are yours. It seems quite bare, though. Is there anything missing?"

"Nothing. I don't like a cluttered room to work in. In fact, I can't stand clutter at all."

"Quite. Well, I'm afraid that inspecting the sitting-room won't be as easy to accomplish. As I'm sure you know, it contains quite a lot of . . . things. I need you to work through them as carefully as you can, to try to see if anything is missing. Or, for that matter, if there is anything new among the items that you haven't seen before." Tim decided that 'clutter' was too pejorative a word, even though Jane Halliwell had used it herself. "And I'm also afraid that I'm going to have to ask you to step through the hall again. But you know that already."

Jane nodded and passed back through the kitchen and the hall with some speed, ostentatiously averting her gaze from the stain on the hall wall as she went.

Patti Gardiner, wearing a white SOCO suit, was crouching on the floor of the sitting-room when they entered. She was working through the deep pile of the black and grey hearthrug, parting the tufts painstakingly with her latex-gloved hands. She had her back to them and did not look round immediately. "I'll be with you in a minute," she said over her shoulder. "I've just found something that might be interesting. Got you!" she added, pouncing with a pair of tweezers. She extracted something from the rug, and placed it in a small plastic bag, deftly sealing the grip-lock fastening in a continuation of the same motion. She stood up slowly, massaging the small of her back, and turned round.

"I've been crawling about on the floor for too long," she said conversationally. "It plays havoc with my . . . Detective Inspector Yates!" she said, as she saw that it was Tim standing there. "I'm sorry. I thought that you were Jo. I didn't know that you were coming today." She flushed.

There was a slight pause. Patti had been Tim's girlfriend very briefly when he had first joined the South Lincs force. It had not been a serious relationship as far as he was concerned, but they were both aware that Patti had felt differently. She bore him no grudges, but conversations between them were usually quite strained. She shifted her gaze from Tim to Jane Halliwell, who, Tim noticed, was taking in the situation with some curiosity.

"No, I spoke to Jo. I'm sorry – I should have asked her to tell you." Then, in a more conversational voice, he said, "Patti, this is Ms Jane Halliwell. She is Dame Claudia's secretary-companion. Ms Halliwell, this is Patti Gardiner, who is heading up the Scene of Crime Officers team in this case. She is looking for any forensic evidence – of an intruder, for example."

Jane extended her bird-like hand again. Patti removed her glove to shake it.

"I am indebted to you," said Jane, rather haughtily. "Thank you so much for the work that you're doing."

Patti shrugged. "It's what I get paid for. And I like my job."

"What did you say you had just found?"

"It's a hair. A silver hair. Not the only one I've found here, but the only one like that. I've collected quite a few of what I'm fairly certain are Dame Claudia's hairs and your own – I've matched them to the hairbrushes in your rooms – but this one is different. It probably has nothing at all to do with the case – it could have been there for months – but it's worth checking."

"I suppose so," said Jane Halliwell. She sounded doubtful, almost scornful.

"I've brought Ms Halliwell to look through the rooms in the house to see if she can notice any missing items, or any new ones, since she was last here. Will we be in your way if she comes in here next? And should we be wearing white suits? I'm sorry – I thought you'd probably be finished inside the house now. When I talked with Jo yesterday she said that she'd started on the garden."

"Yes, she has, and I'll be joining her shortly. I just wanted to give this room one last going over, because it is so clut . . ." – Patti looked at Jane Halliwell – "because there is so much in here that I wanted to be sure that I hadn't missed anything. I've nearly finished – if you could just give me another ten minutes that would be great. And no, you don't need to wear suits now. As I've said, there's virtually nothing left to do here."

"Of course I am happy to wait," said Jane Halliwell. She turned to

Tim. "If the forensic search of the house is more or less complete, does that mean that I can return home?"

"Not yet, unfortunately," said Tim. "We shall need to wait for the analysis of the SOCO team's work first. If we find evidence that one of the rooms in the house may indeed be a crime scene we may have to preserve it as it is, in the hope that the criminal will be apprehended and brought to trial. In such a case the trial judge may wish to bring the jury to visit it."

"I see," said Jane crisply. "But it could take years to apprehend the criminal – or they might never be caught. Would that mean that I could never come home?"

Tim smiled.

"I see that you are somewhat sceptical of police capabilities," he said. "But the answer is no. We may preserve the cottage as a possible crime scene for a reasonable time, but not indefinitely. And Patti's work may yield nothing further, though there is still the bloodstain to explain. Despite it, we are still hoping, like you, that Dame Claudia may return safely – though it would be misleading of me to deny that the likelihood of that diminishes with every day that passes. If she is safely found, of course you may return here immediately. If she isn't, I can't give you an answer at present."

Jane Halliwell nodded with a resigned air. She's forgotten to look sad, Tim thought.

"In that case, may I take some clothes with me when I leave? As I think I've explained, I have very little with me at the hotel that is suitable."

Tim looked at Patti.

"I don't see why not," she said. She smiled at Jane. "Your room has been dusted for prints and I can't find anyone's there except your own, nor any evidence of anyone else's having been in there except you – not even Dame Claudia. You should be able to take away what you need now."

"Thank you," said Jane. "Perhaps I might do that immediately, while I am waiting for you to finish here?"

Tim nodded. Jane left the room with some alacrity. Her footsteps could be heard mounting the polished wooden stairs. Tim would have liked to see her reaction as she passed the bloodstain again but not much of the hall was visible from where he was standing.

Patti replaced her glove, wiggling her fingers until it became a second skin. She waited until Jane Halliwell could be heard moving about in the room immediately above them and pushed to the door of the sitting-room. She moved closer to Tim and whispered, "I don't trust her."

"Neither do I," Tim whispered back. He was rather pleased by the naturalness of this gesture, Patti's professional interest in Jane apparently having dispelled her customary awkwardness. "What makes you say it, though?"

"Just a hunch," said Patti. "She doesn't seem worried enough, somehow."

"Have you found a tape-recorder in here? I understand that Dame Claudia sometimes uses one when she is working, but I don't recollect having seen one when I was here before."

"No," said Patti. "No, I'm sure there isn't one here now. We'd certainly have found it."

CHAPTER TWENTY-SIX

TIM ESCORTED JANE Halliwell back to the Welland Manor Hotel in time for her to keep the hair appointment which she had told him about. "Thank you," she said as she got out of the car. Tim had read somewhere that society women were trained at finishing schools to swivel themselves round on their buttocks when emerging from a car, in order to be able to stand up elegantly and to allow their skirts to fall immediately into place. Whether or not this was true, it was certainly a talent that Jane Halliwell had perfected. Tim remained in the driver's seat for a minute and then realised that she was waiting for something.

"May I have my bag?"

"Oh, of course," he said. "I was forgetting." Jane had packed a large leather holdall while he had been talking to Patti. "Let me help you with it."

"There's really no need," she said in her gracious voice. "I can easily run for the hotel porter."

"I'll carry it to the reception area for you," said Tim levelly. "The porter can take over from there." Of course she had intended that he should do this. Not for the first time he found her disingenuousness irksome.

The bag was heavy. She must have stuffed it very full of clothes. He wondered what she had put in it. It had crossed his mind at the time to ask Jo or Patti to accompany her when she was packing it, but he knew that she would certainly have objected to this and it was important to keep her on side, at least for the moment. Patti had searched her room thoroughly before her visit and said that it contained nothing but clothes and books. If there had been something incriminating in the bag, only she would have understood its significance. But I'm being absurd, thought Tim. There is no reason to think that she was implicated in Dame Claudia's disappearance. She hadn't even been in the country at the time. She had a cast iron alibi. Maybe that had been the whole point of the Norwegian excursion?

"You're looking very disapproving, Chief Inspector," said Jane lightly. "I suppose you think it is frivolous of me to want to have my hair done at such a time. But the fact is I've been brought up to take care of my appearance and I'm certain that the newspapers are going to catch up with me sooner or later. I don't want to be photographed looking like a fishwife. Oh, you needn't worry – I won't tell them anything that you don't want me to. Besides," she added in a lower voice, "even if it is frivolous, it's a diversion. It helps to take my mind off all of this." Tim thought he saw her lip tremble.

Despite the play for sympathy, he took his leave of her rather brusquely.

"I'll leave the bag here," he said, as they reached the hotel entrance. "Thank you for coming to the cottage today. I know that it must have been difficult for you. I realise you didn't think anything was missing or out of place, but something may come to you later. If it does, please get in touch. You have my card?"

She nodded.

"Goodbye, then. Of course, we'll let you know if there are new developments or if it is decided that you can return home."

Jane Halliwell nodded again and disappeared into the hotel, leaving the bag outside the door. Tim turned to see the porter emerge to retrieve it as he walked back to his car.

Tim looked at his watch. It was not quite four-thirty. It had been his intention to go back to the office to see if Juliet had made any progress, but he realised that, unless she'd had a breakthrough, she would have left for the day by the time he arrived. He sat in the car and called her number.

"Juliet? It's me. I'm at Welland Manor. I've just dropped Jane Halliwell off. What? No, no help at all. I'm calling because I wanted to know if you'd got anything more out of Forensics. Tomorrow? Are you absolutely certain about that? Well, I'd hoped for something today, but I suppose we'll just have to wait. What about the ferry company? Tomorrow as well? OK, well, thank you. And well done," he added, belatedly aware that Juliet would blame herself for disappointing him.

"There is one other thing, sir."

"Oh?" She could hear Tim sounding hopeful.

"It's nothing to do with the case. In fact, it's personal to you, sir, so if you think it's none of my business, just stop me. It's about your wife."

"Katrin? Has she been in touch with you?"

"Not intentionally. She called you shortly after you left. She seemed very upset about something. I suggested that she left a message on your mobile, but of course you will know whether she did or not."

"I haven't checked it for messages," Tim said. "I'll do it now."

He rang off, leaving Juliet uncertain whether or not he was grateful for her interference. He dialled 1 for his mobile voicemail service. There were no messages. He speed-dialled Katrin's mobile number, then thought better of hitting the green button. He needed to see her. Whatever it was that was upsetting her it had been going on for too long now. He decided to go home and make her talk to him about it. If he drove straight there now he and she would probably arrive more or less together.

CHAPTER TWENTY-SEVEN

AFTER EDMUND DROVE her home from their assignation in Scotland Alex did not see him again for almost a week. She did not try to contact him, partly because she had yet to make the first move in their new relationship, but mainly because she was embarrassed about the night that they had spent together. In retrospect, she did not feel that it had been the modest success that she had at first believed and she suspected that Edmund took a similar view. He had not asked when he could see her again as they parted – though admittedly this was probably because he had insisted on walking her to the outside gate of her flat after she had told him of her fright the last time he had dropped her there; as soon as she had inserted her key in the lock, the external light was switched on and Tom had appeared at the top of the stairs. Edmund had given her a chaste kiss on the cheek and departed precipitately.

Tom ran down the steps to take her case. He kissed her briefly on the lips.

"Was that Edmund?" he asked off-handedly. "He didn't hang about, did he?"

"He wants to get back to his wife. She's been depressed – it's something she suffers from every so often, apparently."

"I'm not surprised. It must be tedious, being married to him. Poor woman."

Alex didn't reply. She couldn't decide whether Tom was behaving strangely or not. Tom didn't know Edmund very well; he had no reason to dislike him, nor could she recall that he had shown any antipathy for him in the past. She prayed that Tom had not become suspicious of their relationship.

"How's work?" she asked, as soon as they reached the kitchen. "Has any more happened in that child drugs case that you told me about?"

Tom brightened visibly.

"It's funny you should mention that, because, as a matter of fact, I have been working on it again today. I think I told you that the police and my colleagues and I failed to get much more sense out of Thobias Padgett. It was decided to take him to a safe place until more evidence could be gathered about the drugs gang. He's staying at Herrick Old House for a while. Apparently, he's doing well there. It just demonstrates to me what a bad influence the older brother, LeRoy, has been on him. Marlene Padgett herself says that she has no control over LeRoy. But she may have more in future, because LeRoy was found badly beaten up in the graveyard of St Mary's church at Surfleet yesterday. He's been taken to hospital and a police guard put on his ward. If I was spooked by how frightened Thobias was, his reaction was minor compared to how scared LeRoy is. One thing's for sure, he's not going to say who hit him. He's almost out of his mind with fear. He's been heavily sedated and I've been advised that he'll be prescribed Xanax when he wakes up. But I've never seen anyone so disturbed. I think he may be permanently damaged mentally."

"Poor child," said Alex automatically, half her mind elsewhere. "Will he come under your care?"

"Probably not. The Padgett family as a whole has been assigned to me, but LeRoy will need specialist care. He'll probably be put on probation, too. Eventually he may have to stand trial. I don't know. As I've said, he may not be up to it mentally."

Inwardly, Alex felt a huge surge of relief. Those first few minutes had been dangerous, but she had succeeded in diverting Tom's attention elsewhere.

"I think I'm ready for bed," she said. "I seem to have been awake forever."

"You go up. I'll be with you as soon as I've locked the door."

CHAPTER TWENTY-EIGHT

THE NEXT FEW days passed tranquilly enough. Alex spent most of her time beginning to consider exhibits for the series of open days that would be held at the Archaeological Society the following summer. It was the Friday afternoon of the week following the conference in Scotland and she was just thinking of tidying her desk and going home when the outside buzzer rang. She turned on the intercom.

"Hello?"

"Ah, Alex, I hoped you'd still be there. Can you let me in? I've got some good news."

Feeling apprehensive about the nature of Edmund's 'good news', Alex pressed the button that released the door-catch. Edmund was with her in a moment. He kissed her hairline quickly, but it was evident that further pursuit of their romance was not uppermost in his thoughts. He sat heavily in the Victorian studded-leather captain's chair that faced her desk, the twin of the one in which she herself was seated.

"I've just come from the trustees' meeting," he said.

"Oh," said Alex. She had forgotten about the trustees' meeting or, to be more accurate, she had blotted it from her memory. The trustees of the Archaeological Society met three times a year. She attended two of the meetings, but not this one. Ostensibly, one meeting was held without her annually so that matters relating to her salary and performance could be discussed freely, but the fact that the trustees still chose to keep up this tradition after she had been several years in the post made her feel both vulnerable and resentful. She was certain that they used the meetings to criticise, probably at length, and she knew them to be such a crabbed bunch, with such arcane prejudices and priorities, that she would probably want to hand in her notice if she were privy to some of the notions that they chewed over when she was not there to defend herself.

"Was it a useful meeting?" She eyed Edmund warily.

"Very useful." He chuckled. "You don't need to look like that. I know you're paranoid about what we might say behind your back, but all the comments about you were very complimentary. And what was said about me, too, as it happens." He preened a little. "That's why I've come."

"Go on. I'm all ears."

"Don't be sarcastic. It doesn't suit you. I told them about your idea – the business idea, I mean. And they agreed to it. For both of us."

"That's wonderful news!" said Alex. She got up and came round the desk to give him a swift embrace. Inwardly, she was already dreading the prospect of telling Tom. "But how soon can we take it on? I've started work on planning the summer opening programme now. And you must be planning all the heritage activities for next year yourself. I can't see that we will be able to resign until next autumn now."

"That's all taken care of, too," said Edmund triumphantly. "They've agreed that you can spend up to one day per week of your salaried time on it and as much time as you like during evenings and weekends. I doubt that the council will want to release me in the same way, as there won't be anything in it for them, but the Archaeological Society is also happy for me to contribute as much as I can at evenings and weekends."

"I'm not sure that I understand," said Alex slowly. "The idea was to set up a business that would generate enough profit to pay us. I wanted to use the Archaeological Society as a first customer, perhaps offering them a discount, but not to provide the service free. And what do you mean by 'there won't be anything in it' for the council? What will there be in it for the Archaeological Society – besides getting the benefit of work done in our personal leisure time free of charge?"

She stopped talking until Edmund would meet her eyes and she saw that he finally did so with difficulty. She also saw that he was about to bluster. She sighed.

"Oh, Edmund," she said. "What have you let us in for?"

"I haven't 'let us in' for anything that you don't want to do," he said crossly. "You haven't given me time to explain properly. As I said, the trustees were very complimentary about you and they made it clear that they don't wish to lose you. What they're offering is actually quite gener-ous: they are prepared to pay you for one day a week to pursue this idea of yours. Naturally they expect a bit of a quid pro quo . . ."

"Which is?" Alex interrupted. Edmund cleared his throat.

"They'd like a stake in the business, if it's successful. In fact, they'd like to become its major shareholder – allowing you and me some shares, as well, of course. Then, if the proposition can be translated to other socie-ties and museums, they'd like you to continue to run it as a business but also to continue your work here, with an assistant secretary to help you."

"But that isn't what I meant to happen at all, and certainly not what we agreed!" exclaimed Alex, dismayed. "Effectively speaking, it means I'll just carry on being an employee, presumably with a bigger salary and also a dividend from the new business, but an employee nevertheless. It isn't what I want to do!"

"Calm down," said Edmund. "You need to take a long-term view of this. First of all, they're not asking you to come to any formal arrangement until the first project – the classification of their own artefacts – is complete; so we won't be trapped into doing anything prematurely. Secondly, they're offering you a risk-free opportunity to try out a business idea. Finally, if we accept this offer, it is going to go a long way to helping us to explain it to Krystyna and Tom. Krystyna is likely to be upset about the idea of my giving up my job straight away – as you know, she has virtually no money herself. And I think it would make Tom suspicious about us if we were both to jack in our jobs at the same time to pursue an untried concept together. If we do it by stages, they are both much more likely to accept it."

"Do you think that Tom is suspicious already?"

"How should I know? I hardly ever see him. He certainly didn't greet me when I saw you home the other night – he must have seen that I was there, or heard me say goodnight to you, anyway. And if I were him, I'd be suspicious – I'd be convinced that everyone was trying to get into bed with you."

Alex knew that this was meant as a compliment, but she thought that it made her sound like a tart. Nothing was working out as she had intended. She felt all her energy and enthusiasm for the business idea ebbing away.

"OK, so I accept that some of what you're saying makes sense. But won't we be trapped by our own success? Assuming that the project for the Archaeological Society succeeds, won't we then be committed to sharing the future business with its members?"

Edmund shrugged.

"You're crossing your bridges before you come to them, Alex. It's not like you. Where's your entrepreneurial spirit? They haven't asked for any paperwork yet, or any formal commitment at all. We can work out what to do about that when the time comes. I really think that we should agree to this. We'll never get such an opportunity again."

"I'd like some time to think it over – and to discuss it with Tom."

"Of course. It's the weekend now, anyway. Perhaps we can talk again on Monday?"

"I'm not here on Monday. I'll call you on Tuesday. Will you talk to Krystyna about it, as well?"

"I should like to get it settled on Monday if possible. Where are you going?"

"I've got the day off to see a friend. One of my old university friends – she's based in Ireland and is just here for a few days. I'm going to meet her in London."

"Are you taking the train?"

"Yes, but from Peterborough. The service back to Spalding is too infrequent – it doesn't give me enough flexibility."

"Can I meet you at Peterborough station in the evening? We could go for supper. I could book that Italian restaurant that you like."

"I can't make the commitment at the moment. If Carolyn wants me to eat with her, I shall accept. I'll text you on Monday."

Alex stood up, and collected her coat and scarf from the hat-stand by her window. She scooped up her handbag from the floor and tucked a box file under her arm.

"I have to go now," she said. "One of Tom's colleagues is coming to supper."

Edmund gave her a hug and a peck on the lips. He didn't release her immediately. He might have been encouraging a warmer embrace, but she didn't respond. She wasn't in the mood. She pulled away as soon as she could.

"What's the matter?" he said.

"Nothing. Everything." said Alex. She was close to tears.

"I'm sorry if I've upset you; I didn't mean to. I think that you've been working too hard. It's the end of the week, as well. You need to take more time off, relax more. Look at you with that file – taking work home as usual. What is it, anyway?"

"It's an inventory of all the collections. It's been very badly done – at some point in the 1950s. It was bashed out on an old pica typewriter. It isn't comprehensive; it just lists the collections under the names that they were given then. There are details about some of the main pieces – the things that have been individually insured, but there aren't many of those. Some of the stuff has just been packed up in boxes which haven't been opened for a hundred years or more. But the catalogue's moderately useful – for example, it gives the location of each collection."

"Really? I had no idea that the Society was so well-organised."

"Well, it is – up to a point. Some of the collections – the ones considered to be most financially valuable – are kept in the cellar here. The rest are in the warehouse that we own in Broad Street; I'm sure you know about it. It's been the subject of discussion at some of the AGMs. It actually houses most of the stuff that is really difficult to classify – prehistoric flints and arrowheads etc."

"Are you saying that the collections have been stored in more or less the same locations since the 1950s? That's amazing!"

"It's for longer than that. The warehouse in Broad Street was donated by a Victorian benefactor – I believe he was a clergyman with an independent income – and he had a carpenter make special stalls for keeping the collections in. Similar stalls were built in the basement here – but you've seen them, haven't you?"

"I've been down to the basement, certainly, but it's so chocka with stuff, I didn't realise that there was any order to it. What about new acquisitions, though? How do they fit into this static arrangement?"

"There was space left at the time, in both places. There haven't been many acquisitions since the 1950s – or rather, not many that have been brought to the Society. That's probably why the inventory was taken then. As you know, our policy now is to maintain large collections in situ when possible. For example, we paid for some showcases when those Iron Age axeheads were found in Stamford and installed them in the public library there. The rationale is that they belong to the people of Stamford and should be enjoyed by them."

"You don't sound very convinced!"

"I'm not, particularly. I don't think that people take much interest in small isolated collections like that – they're not spectacular enough, if you like. And really not very exciting, except to archaeologists. On the other hand, societies and museums can't take on everything – we're already creaking at the seams here and we have stuff that hasn't seen the light of day for many years. Though I do try to rotate the displays on open days as much as possible."

"Is that why you're taking that file home? To plan the open days?"

"Yes. I've started working on them, but I don't have a theme yet. The problem is that last year's theme was the Vikings. It's just about the sexiest topic in archaeology and a hard act to follow – especially as they were dominant in this area, so there was plenty to exhibit. And I was able to borrow that helmet from the British Museum. We raised a lot of money with the Viking Exhibition. I don't see how I'm going to be able to match it this year."

"How about 'Gentlemen Archaeologists'? After all, it was those eighteenth and nineteenth century dilettantes who made the Society great."

Alex burst out laughing.

"Really, Edmund, you mustn't get carried away by your own interests. Do you honestly think that groups of schoolchildren will be grabbed by an exhibition with a title like that? It could be based on a celebrated individual – people are always curious about the famous. I'd thought about focusing on Isaac Newton, who was a founder member. We have quite a few of his personal possessions, which would make it interesting. But apparently my predecessor mounted a display called 'Four Great Men of Lincolnshire' the year before I came, and of course Newton featured in that. I had wondered about doing something on the occult – that's always a popular subject and we've got a surprising amount of stuff on it. There are some relics from the cult of Mithras that were found at the Roman Villa at Fosdyke and, as you probably know, in the eighteenth century, Lincolnshire had its own version of the Hellfire Club. Your gentleman clerics weren't averse to dabbling in a little bit of magic, either – especially towards the end of the nineteenth century, when it almost became respectable. Madame Blavatsky and all that. And there were some weird political ideas associated with some of them. What's wrong?" she said, suddenly catching sight of a change in Edmund's expression.

Edmund's face had flushed to an unattractive brick colour. It seemed to have frozen into a mask.

"I certainly wouldn't choose that," he said. His voice was disapproving, but it also trembled. "As you said, the exhibitions have to attract school parties. I think you might get a lot of flak if you start introducing kids to Satan."

Alex laughed again, genuinely amused this time.

"How extremely old-fashioned of you! I'm sure that we don't have anything here as disturbing as some of the online games that they play. But you're looking so prim about it that it almost tempts me to do it." She planted a kiss on his cheek. "Come on, Edmund, we're both tired out and this is a pointless conversation. Go home and talk to Krystyna about the business idea. And I'll talk to Tom. We'll both sleep on it, and I promise to reach my decision by Monday."

CHAPTER TWENTY-NINE

Alex did not broach to Tom the subject of going into a business partnership with Edmund. When she had had time to think about it, she wasn't sure that embarking upon a new business venture was actually what Edmund said he had negotiated with the trustees; what they seemed to be proposing was just a dressed-up extension to her job. There might therefore be no need to talk to Tom about it at all. Besides, she and Tom were enjoying an unexpectedly pleasant weekend together. She reflected wistfully that it had been more like the weekends and holidays of their early married years; she was not about to cast a shadow over it by mentioning Edmund.

Marie Krakoswka and her partner, Max, dined with them on the evening after her visit from Edmund. Despite Alex's reservations about Marie, she had to admit that she and Max had been extremely good company. Tom had relaxed visibly and, unusually for him, had then decided not to work over the next two days. On Saturday, he had taken Alex for a pub lunch followed by a long walk on the marshes. While holding Tom's hand, she had watched a heron flapping slowly over the reed-beds and felt a sudden access of pure happiness. She told herself that she would remember the moment for the rest of her life. On Sunday they had lingered over breakfast and then set out on a 'grave-grubbing' expedition, as Tom good-naturedly put it, to read the inscriptions on the graves in the older part of Spalding cemetery. It was the first time in years that he had spared the time to share her interests. Alex herself was discovering a talent for living her life in compartments. While she was with Tom, she hardly gave Edmund a thought. She and Tom went to bed early on Sunday evening and made love lazily and slowly.

She awoke after Tom had left for work on Monday morning and enjoyed the luxury of getting up gently, of taking a long leisurely bath instead of her usual hurried shower and of dressing in serviceable but pretty clothes for her day in London. She was quite excited by the prospect of a day of freedom in 'town' and looked forward to seeing Carolyn again.

Predictably, Carolyn was late. Alex had suggested that they meet for an early lunch in a tapas restaurant near to Euston station and had sent Carolyn the URL for directions. The restaurant was one of her favourites. Its unpretentious plain wooden tables and chairs were offset by the wonderfully kitsch pseudo art-deco bar, which was shaped like the hull of a boat and studded with pieces of enamelled broken mirror in flamboyant shades of turquoise. The food was delicious, based mainly on authentic Spanish seafood and vegetable dishes, with a range of starters made from fine Iberian hams and delicate shavings of pungent cheese. Alex had always come here alone or to meet her girlfriends and this in itself contributed to her current exhilarating sense of liberation. Her mood was light-headed and frivolous. These feelings were overlaid by the even more seductive sensation that today she could forget all of her worries and responsibilities.

She was telling herself this, and debating whether to enhance the holiday mood by ordering a glass of the strong white Rioja that was one of the house specialities, when Carolyn suddenly burst through the door, carrying a collection of up-market carrier bags and dragging her suitcase behind her.

Carolyn was the sort of woman Alex would have loved to have been bold enough to be. She did not watch her weight, she had never stayed with a man for more than a few years, had no intention of ever 'settling down' with one and, although she made quite a lot of money as a freelance recruitment consultant, was in no way wedded to her job. She divested herself of her fake fur coat, also leaving the suitcase by the coat-rack, and hauled the carrier bags across the room to the table where Alex was sitting and dropped them on the floor; she flung her arms around Alex and said: "It's lovely to see you. I'm so sorry I'm late. One thing and another happened and then I couldn't get a taxi in Oxford Street." She stood before Alex, plump, glamorously made-up, heavily perfumed and slightly dishevelled, her thick hair dyed raven black and arranged in a slickly-shaped, feathery bob. She was wearing a short, gauzy red dress and four-inch black patent stilettos. Only Carolyn could consider this apparel to be suitable for a shopping expedition in London on a fiercely bitter winter's day.

Alex returned the embrace, and gestured towards the carrier bags.

"You look as if you've been having a good time."

"Absolutely out of necessity," said Carolyn. "I've got no clothes that fit. I've gone up a dress size – one of the hazards of getting old. It will creep up on you, you'll see."

Alex laughed. Carolyn did a good line in irresponsible, fluffy female. It did not fool Alex for a minute.

"Don't be ridiculous!" she said. "I'm only six months younger than you – remember? I just don't have such a sweet tooth, that's all."

"Very kind," said Carolyn, "but I think that what you really mean is that you have more willpower. Or perhaps that I have zilch willpower." She shrugged happily. "It probably amounts to the same thing."

"Whatever the truth of that," said Alex, "and I suspect it's more down to genes, I don't intend to exercise any willpower at all today. First we are going to have a wonderful lunch. Then we are going to go to a gallery,

or to the shops, or just please ourselves all afternoon. Then we shall have
dinner, if you wish. And then, if you haven't got anything that you have
to do tomorrow, I suggest that you might like to come home with me and
stay the night."

Carolyn pouted.

"I'd love to do all of that, Alex," she said. "And I can't wait to catch
up with your news. But the fact is, this trip isn't just for pleasure. I'm
here because I'm recruiting on behalf of a client for a new appointment
and unfortunately I've arranged to do some early evening interviews with
him later on. So I've got until about five o'clock. I suggest that we have
quite a long boozy lunch here and tell each other all we know. I'll come
to stay another time," she added. "It would be heaven to get away for a
few days."

Alex's heady mood was punctured immediately. She saw her grand
plan for the day melting away and snatched somewhat desperately at
what remained.

"OK," she said levelly. She smiled at Carolyn in a fixed way which
did not convince her friend. Carolyn had always been a sharp observer.

"There's no need to look like that!" she said, touching Alex tenderly
on the arm. "I'm doing my best by you. I can't help it if I need to work
or manage the eccentricities of clients like Vernon Matthews any better
than I do."

"Sorry!" said Alex, suddenly realising that it was not disappointment that she was experiencing, but fear: fear that she would have to see
Edmund again this evening now that Carolyn would not be able to furnish
her with an excuse not to. "I'm being ridiculous," she muttered, half to
herself. Of course she did not have to see Edmund if she didn't want to.

Carolyn was scrutinising her.

"Are you OK?" she said.

"Yes, of course. Sit down and I'll order some wine. They do a very nice
white Rioja here."

"Sounds good," said Carolyn, taking the chair opposite Alex's. She
shoved some of her parcels under the table and piled the rest of them on
to the free seat beside her. "But that last comment wasn't meant for me,
was it? Why are you being 'ridiculous', Alex, my love? You're the most
sensible person that I know!"

"Not any more, I'm not. Tom sends his love, by the way."

"Ah, yes, Tom. Your sensible husband. I take back what I said – *he's*
the most sensible person I know, by several miles." She leaned in to the
table, her beautiful flecked golden eyes searching Alex's. "You're not
having an affair, are you?"

"Really, Carolyn, your sixth sense is outrageous," said Alex, laughing
uneasily.

"So you *are* having an affair? Well, congratulations. It should shake Tom up enough to appreciate you, if nothing else can. But I'm surprised in one way: I'd always thought of you as Mrs Married Fidelity personified. Who is it, by the way? I'm amazed you've had the opportunity to meet anyone, the sort of life you lead, poking about among holes and ruins. I suppose he must be a farmer. Did you find a hoard of something ancient on his land and exchange his priceless treasure for your own?"

Alex threw back her head and laughed without restraint, simultaneously knocking the order pad from the hand of the waiter who had silently materialised at her side.

"Oops!" she said, retrieving the pad and handing it to him, her face flushing red with the effort. "I didn't mean to do that." She gave a little giggle by way of apology. "Could you bring us a bottle of the white Rioja? And a jug of tap water?"

The waiter nodded gravely. She pushed aside her laughter and regarded Carolyn more soberly as he retreated to the turquoise bar.

"That's not quite as prescient," she said, "though even more outrageous. He isn't a farmer, but I did meet him through work. He's actually someone I've known for a long time – someone whom I considered quite asexual until recently. And Tom doesn't know about him, of course. There is no point in hurting him. As a matter of fact, Tom's been angelic just recently – attentive and wanting to share in my interests, just as he did when we first met."

"Which suggests to me that he does know, or at least suspects," said Carolyn. "But don't let me interrupt. And 'asexual' is a word that sets my alarm bells clanging – it makes this bloke sound too cerebral to be bothered much with sex! You still haven't told me who he is. Lover boy, I mean. I must say you don't seem head over heels with him. If it were me I'd hardly be able to speak one sentence without mentioning him. "

"I know that to be true," said Alex. "But I also know that the next time we met you'd be similarly unable to stop talking about his successor."

"Oh, touché," said Carolyn, rolling her eyes. "Well, at least that way I don't get hurt. Not often, anyway. But you keep on sidestepping me. What is the man's name, for God's sake?"

"Edmund Baker," said Alex. "He's an archaeologist. He works for the council and is paid by the Heritage Commission."

"I might have known. 'Eminent in his field', is he? Or one of those distinguished-looking academics who have slightly gone to seed and are always hell-bent on getting their own way? He is older than you, I take it? If he's younger, I really take my hat off to you."

"Yes, he's older than I am. Quite a lot older, in fact, so no doffed hats for me on that score. I'm not sure that 'eminent' is the right word to describe him and he's certainly not academic – or distinguished-looking.

He's more of an administrator than a scholar. But you're probably right about him liking to get his own way."

"Well, watch that, my love, particularly as you seem to be saying that the whole thing's just about having a fling." The wine arrived, and she poured out two glasses while the waiter was setting down the water-jug. "If he's unscrupulously self-interested, and deeper in than you are, he might just leak the situation to Tom in the hope that Tom'll leave you. And you could easily end up worse off than you are now. I take it that this Edmund is also married?"

Alex felt her scalp crawl. From the start she had dreaded Tom's finding out about Edmund, precisely because she did not know how he would react. Or rather she did: Tom would be silently outraged and instantly unapproachable. He would be capable of walking out in seconds and leaving everything behind that they had shared together. And, if she were honest with herself, she was much more dismayed by contemplating the break-up of her marriage than by the prospect of hurting Tom's feelings. She wondered again why she had felt impelled to take the risk with Edmund.

"Don't," she said, gulping down a large swig of her wine. "Yes, he's married. Not very happily, I think, but he's given no indication that he wants to leave her; or to come between me and Tom, for that matter. Actually, I think that our romance came out of our professional connection, rather than the other way round. He wants to work with me – permanently work with me, I mean. In that respect, we probably went too far by mistake – or accidentally, at any rate. The two types of relationship got mixed up, somehow."

Alex had said this to comfort herself, to make the vivid mental picture of Tom leaving her recede, but, as soon as she had spoken the words, she realised that they were true, at least on her side. Yet again she circled back to the same question that had nagged at her ever since the Archaeological Society conference: why had Edmund made that first pass at her? She was convinced that it had been more than the alcohol talking, especially when he had renewed his pursuit of her weeks later, but she was less persuaded that Edmund was motivated by love.

"You've gone quiet on me again," said Carolyn. "And although I've been telling you to have a fling for years, from the clues that you're giving me I'm far from convinced that your Edmund is a good thing. It's probably my fault that we've jumped right into the middle of your story, but can we start again? Tell me from the beginning. Then I'll understand. And we'd better order some food first – we're halfway down this bottle of wine already. I don't want you passing out before you've TOLD ALL." She exaggerated the last two words, pulling a clown's face as she did so. Alex laughed again, but sadly, now.

Two hours and a second bottle of wine later, Alex had told her story. It had taken a long time, because she wanted to explain both the facts and her own feelings to Carolyn as precisely as she could; and also because Carolyn interrupted frequently with exclamations and observations (some of them penetrating) of her own.

"Well," said Carolyn at length, having been uncharacteristically silent for some moments after Alex had concluded, "you certainly have got yourself deep into an intrigue here." She picked up Alex's hand, which was lying limply on the edge of the table, and stroked it a few times before replacing it carefully.

"What do you mean? And what do you think I should do?"

Carolyn frowned.

"I'm not sure," she said. "There's something about all of this that just doesn't fit. Oh, I don't mean that I don't think you're gorgeous or that I'd ever be surprised that someone could fancy you. And I'm not criticising your morality, either; you've been a saint for far too long since you married Tom. But Edmund Baker doesn't sound like a budding Lothario to me and he doesn't seem particularly smitten by you, either. Are you sure he doesn't just want something from you and sees embarking upon an affair as the easiest way of getting it?"

"What could he possibly want from me? His status in the world of archaeology is significantly greater than mine and he certainly earns more than I do."

Carolyn frowned some more.

"He could be going through a late male menopause, I suppose. It could just be sex, plus an old man's vanity, testing himself to see if he can 'pull' a younger woman. But I still think that there's more to it than meets the eye. What about the business opportunity that you described? Do you think that's what it's all about?"

"Hardly! I must admit that I hadn't considered Edmund as a business partner – and it was certainly he who talked me into working with him, not the other way around. But he didn't need to sleep with me to achieve it. By the same token, if I hadn't thought it would work, that he was my lover would have made no difference. As it is, his idea of joining me is probably what will make the idea workable, because Tom's made it clear that he's not interested."

"I still think that he's after something. Perhaps it's something that he hasn't asked for yet – something that you don't know about. Or perhaps he does just want to have an affair and I'm wrong. Talking of which, how do you feel about it? Really feel about it, I mean? Do you want it to continue, or would you be relieved to put a stop to it? I must say it doesn't sound as if it's been very romantic so far and I can't think of any other reason for going on with it."

Alex wanted to burst into tears. She covered her face with her hands. Carolyn tugged gently at her wrist.

"I'm sorry," she said. "I didn't mean to upset you."

"It's OK. I need to pull myself together. To answer your question, I don't know what I'm doing. I don't know if I agreed to it out of boredom, out of vanity, as you say – it isn't only old men who are vain – or from a kind of despair, because of where Tom and I appeared to be with our marriage. But I'm not sure about any of this. Tom and I have just had a wonderful weekend. And when Edmund first tried to proposition me, I turned him down. I guess that the real truth is that I just fell into it."

"Don't worry – it happens more often than you think. It happens to me all the time, actually. The thing to do now is to just fall out of it – and quickly. When will you see him again?"

"I'm not sure. He wanted to meet me off the train this evening for supper in Peterborough. I told him that I would probably be having dinner with you in London. He said he'd text me to check."

"And has he?"

"I don't know," said Alex, taking her mobile from her bag. "No. Not yet."

"Can you text him and say that you can meet him after all? But don't go to dinner with him. Go for a drink at the station buffet – or at the hotel. There's a hotel over the road from Peterborough Station, isn't there? And finish it then. Tell him you still value him as a colleague and all that stuff."

"What about the business idea?"

"You can still do that. Tell him you'd like to work slowly – try out a few ideas on your own before you bring him in. If he doesn't agree, postpone the whole thing and then start again in six months or so when all this is part of the past. Will that work?"

"Yes," said Alex doubtfully. "It will work well as far as our jobs are concerned, because we're both starting to plan for the busiest period of the year. But I'm not sure whether Edmund will want to agree, especially as he's come to the arrangement with the trustees now."

"It's your idea, don't forget, not his. You don't have to be corralled into doing what Edmund wants. Go to see the trustees yourself, if necessary. They like you, don't they?"

"I suppose they do – as much as they like anyone. They're the biggest bunch of misanthropes that were ever gathered together under the pretext of sharing similar interests. Misfits is probably a better word, actually. They're well-heeled misfits."

"Well, use your charm, sweetie. You've got plenty." Carolyn looked at her watch. "My God, it's almost four o'clock. I'm going to have to dash. I need to take all my stuff back to the hotel and freshen up a bit before Matthews arrives. I'll get the bill."

"Let me pay," said Alex. "It's the least I can do after spending the whole time we've had together talking about myself."

"Certainly not," said Carolyn. "It can be my treat." She winked. "Well, Matthews's treat – he'll be picking up the bill for this, though he won't know it."

Carolyn sashayed up to the turquoise bar in her black patent stilettos, swaying just a little now that she had consumed a bottle of wine. When she had paid, she returned to Alex, who was now standing by the table, and kissed her on both cheeks.

"Now, remember," she said. "Be strong. Be firm and kind with him and don't let him talk you into changing your mind. I'll call you tomorrow."

Alex nodded obediently and followed Carolyn to the door.

"By the way," said Carolyn, as she donned her coat and gathered up her parcels and the suitcase, "do you know that woman archaeologist that's disappeared?"

"Vaguely," said Alex. "I met her once. And I've read quite a lot of the books and papers that she's written. Edmund knows her, too."

"He would do, I suppose. Very odd case. She's almost certainly dead, I'd say."

"Why do you think that?"

"Common sense. People don't just disappear like that and turn up perfectly well again later on, do they? Not often, anyway. And not old ladies who can barely walk."

CHAPTER THIRTY

ALEX DIDN'T RECEIVE a text message from Edmund. She did not keep her promise to Carolyn, either. She couldn't face talking to Edmund tonight. She wanted to go home, take a bath, relax with Tom, pour some wine, retail to Tom an edited version of her day. The train she had caught was the first of the evening commuter services from King's Cross to Peterborough. The other passengers were mostly male businessmen and office workers. They were either talking loudly on their mobiles or slumped untidily in their seats sipping like babies at lidded plastic cartons of tea and coffee, the odd one swigging from a can of lager. Alex closed her eyes, willing the journey to be over.

The train was delayed for twenty minutes outside Peterborough. The female guard announced on the tannoy a 'signalling problem' and apologised for 'any inconvenience', as if most of the passengers were expected to be quite content just to sit there. Incensed by this nonchalance, the occupants of Alex's carriage grew restless and disgruntled. They began to complain to each other in loud voices. Alex dreaded being drawn into their futile rebellion and tried to indicate that she was otherwise engaged by attempting to call Tom to tell him to wait supper. She could not get a signal. She closed her eyes again.

When the train finally shuffled into Peterborough Station, a heavy rain had begun to fall. Alex was wearing only a lightweight jacket and she hurried along the platform, her head down. In a few seconds, she was soaked, wet strands of her hair clinging itchily to her face, her trousers uncomfortably wet just above her knees where the jacket finished. She presented her ticket to the surly clerk at the barrier and was preparing to sprint for the car park when she felt a hand on her sleeve. At first she thought that someone was brushing against her by accident and pulled away to her right. But the hand remained, its grip tightening. She turned, brushing away the strands of sodden hair from her eyes and saw Edmund standing beside her.

"I thought you were going to text me. Or call," she said, defensive because she knew that she had been relieved that he hadn't.

"I thought you were going to call me if you decided not to dine with your friend," he countered, emphasising the last word.

"I didn't know until the last minute that she had an appointment this evening. Besides, I need to get home to see Tom."

"Oh, you do, do you?" His tone was cutting. "Very cosy. Lunch with the dear friend, supper with the loving husband, is it?" He was almost sneering at her. His grip on her arm tightened.

"Why are you being like this, Edmund? You can see that I'm soaked, and I'm cold and tired, too. I need to go home."

He released her arm and took hold of her by the shoulders, so that she was forced to look at him.

"I'm sorry," he said, suddenly deflated. "Can't you see that I'm desperate, Alex? I need you, too. Come for a drink, at least. We have to talk."

"OK. Just one drink, though. I agree that we should talk."

He preceded her to the automatic doors, waiting on the other side for her to emerge. Then he took her hand. It was a curiously intimate gesture and it made her feel unsettled. In her head, she repeated Carolyn's advice like a mantra. She could and would curtail the strange romance upon which she and Edmund had embarked. She would try to preserve their professional relationship, but she wanted to pursue the business idea on her own at first. Edmund must surely agree. Their liaison could not have made him any happier than it had made her and she would not appear to be cutting him out of the business partnership, just postponing it.

He held open the door of the Station Hotel and she took the opportunity to draw away from him. Outside, the hotel's grim and grimy architecture proclaimed it to be mid-Victorian. Inside, it had become suspended in a 1950s time-warp. The reception area consisted of a tall booth like a pulpit whose dark polished wood panels concealed from view any activity that might take place behind it, and, unless they made an effort to show themselves, also the identity of the person standing there. Alex could just see the curly dark top of a man's head. It was bent forward, presumably over some book-keeping task. The man did not look up or greet them. They therefore made their way to the lounge unimpeded and unescorted. It was a room furnished with fat red plush sofas and solid round tables set about with sturdy plush-upholstered chairs. The dusty red curtains were looped back to reveal elaborate but dingy nets. A sole waitress stood to attention beside a vast ungainly sideboard. She was middle-aged and lumpy. She wore a black dress on which a tiny frilled apron had been superimposed. It looked as if her whole ensemble had been sewn together into a single garment and she had come upon it by rummaging through a dressing-up box. She remained stock-still until they had selected a table and seated themselves, then advanced with her order pad.

"What would you like?" asked Edmund humbly.

"Tea, please," said Alex firmly.

"No afternoon teas after four-thirty," said the waitress uncompromisingly. She spoke with an unattractively strong local accent.

"I don't want afternoon tea. Just a cup of tea."

"This room's for bar snacks after six," said the waitress triumphantly "or drinks from the bar. You can have tea or coffee with food," she added helpfully. "Would you like to see the menu?"

"Yes, please," said Edmund. The woman retreated temporarily to her sideboard.

"You know that I don't want supper," said Alex in a low, furious voice. "Order for yourself if you like."

"Of course I don't want to eat alone," said Edmund snappishly. "Will you at least have some wine?"

Alex nodded, defeated. When the waitress returned, Edmund waved away the menu and asked for the wine list.

"A bottle of Merlot, please," he said.

"You'll have to drink most of it yourself," said Alex. "I've been drinking already today and I have to drive home."

"OK, fine. I'll just pour you a glass and you can dilute it, or drink water with it as you please. A jug of water, as well, please," he added to the waitress.

The conversation was taut while they were waiting for the drinks to arrive.

"Did you have a good time with your friend?" Edmund asked, after a protracted silence.

"Yes. But we could only have lunch as she had to work later on."

"You're very late back in that case."

"It was a long lunch." There was another silence.

"How are things at home?"

"Fine. Tom's working hard, but he's managing to make time for me, too. For us, I should say. What about you?"

Edmund shook his head. "Krystyna's very depressed," he said. "I've not seen her as bad as this before."

"Has she seen a doctor?"

"Yes, he's prescribed some form of medication. It's not very strong – not strong enough, probably. But she won't take Valium any more. She says it makes her feel like a cardboard cut-out."

"Perhaps you should spend more time with her."

"Perhaps. The fact is I no longer love her. There's no reason for it – she's a perfectly nice woman and she's forgiven me completely for that affair I had ten years ago. But there it is."

The waitress arrived with an opened bottle of red wine and a jug of water on a tray. She slid the tray carefully on to the small round table that separated them.

"I'll be straight back with some glasses," she said, stumping off again.

"Do you think that she knows about us?"

Edward's blue eyes irradiated alarm. "Christ! What made you suggest that?"

"It's not such an outlandish suggestion, is it? You may have been very careful, but it's possible that she suspects something. After all, as you've just said, it's happened before."

"You certainly know how to hit below the belt, don't you? You're hardly whiter than white yourself. But no, I don't think she does suspect. If her behaviour last time is anything to go by, she wouldn't suffer in silence. She'd come straight out with it and accuse me."

The waitress returned, bearing four glasses on her tray. She unloaded them slowly, one by one. She was obviously intrigued by the couple she was serving and took her time. Alex thought that she'd probably caught some snippets of their conversation.

"Thank you," she said, as the woman hoisted the water jug aloft, "we can serve ourselves now."

The waitress eyed her suspiciously.

"Would you like to taste the wine, sir?" she said to Edmund with almost ceremonial politeness.

"What? Oh, yes, I suppose so," he replied distractedly. The waitress shot Alex a triumphant glance. Alex did not respond. She just wanted to be rid of the woman as soon as possible.

Edmund downed the splash of wine that he had been poured and set the glass back on the table. He was about to seize the bottle when he realised that the waitress was still hovering.

"Is it all right, sir?"

"Hmm? Yes, yes, thank you." Edmund took the mock-leather pocketbook from her and signed the chitty. He placed two pound coins on top of it and closed it before handing it back to her.

"Thank you, sir." The woman gave a curious little bob before she walked away. Alex could hardly believe her eyes; she realised that she had just witnessed a curtsey, albeit a brief one. She wished that it had been Tom sitting opposite her so that they could have shared the joke. Edmund seemed not to realise and she couldn't be bothered to explain it to him.

"Will you have some of this?" he said to her now, waving the bottle at her.

"Just half a glass," said Alex, her tone softer. His face was bleak. She regretted what she had said about Krystyna.

"What did you want to talk about?" said Edmund, swirling his wine in the glass. Alex sensed that he wanted to down it in one go and was trying to make himself wait for as long as possible before he did so.

"The business idea," said Alex. She blurted it out quickly, knowing that if she thought about it too much she would chicken out of discussing it.

"You're not getting cold feet, are you?" The words came out accusingly, rattled off one after the other like machine-gun bullets. "I sincerely hope not, because I've really stuck out my neck with the trustees so that you can do it."

"I know that, and I'm very grateful," said Alex more gently. "And no, I'm not getting cold feet. I just think we should take it slowly, that's all. We both need to prepare for the busiest time of year at work and neither of us wants to let anyone down. I think we should start small, now that the trustees have agreed to it. Just do it in our own time, perhaps for a year or so. And I was wondering if it might not be better for me to go it alone at first just to see if it works. If it does, of course I should like you to join me later, as we've already said."

Edmund put his head in his hands for a few seconds. When he raised his eyes to meet hers, he seemed close to tears.

"Whatever you say. I can alter the arrangement with the trustees now that it's been broached. I'm sure that they will be very grateful to retain all of your official services for the summer. Just don't give me the brush-off, that's all. This means so much to me. You mean so much to me," he added, a second too late.

"I can see that," said Alex, not without irony. Apparently he did not pick up the edge in her tone.

"Besides," said Edward. "There's quite an important project that I'd like to get my teeth into. I want to do it on my own, if you don't mind. When it's finished, it can be a surprise for you. It will put the business on the map; that I do assure you." He was suddenly animated, more fully engaged than she had ever seen him and also, she could see, fearful of what her reaction to this might be.

"That sounds very intriguing," she said as archly as she could. "I'm not sure that I can wait to be surprised – I might die of curiosity before I find out what it is. Couldn't you just give me a little clue?"

Edmund took in the new playfulness of her tone and immediately echoed it.

"No," he said teasingly. "But I do promise you that I'll start on it straight away, in order to keep you in suspense for as short a time as possible. I'll start tomorrow, in fact. I'll come to the Archaeological Society after work and begin then."

Alex immediately felt uneasy, though she couldn't explain why. All they were proposing to do was to catalogue boxes of flints and bones after all. What could be the harm in it?

"All right," she said. "Just for an hour, though. I don't want to be there too late tomorrow."

"You could have a key cut for me if you like."

"You know that I need permission from the trustees to do that."

"Yes, of course. Don't bother, then. An hour should be fine for making a start. And Alex?"

"Yes?"

"I know we've been going through a rough patch and I'm certainly not the world's greatest lover, but I do love you. Please don't take that away from me."

Alex sighed. She was cold and tired and had no energy left to argue.

"All right," she said, "but we shall have to see how it all works out – for both of us. And with Krystyna and Tom, as well." She rose and put on her jacket. "Now, I really must get home," she said. "And so should you."

Edmund stood up and kissed her near to her mouth, but with closed lips. He sank back down into his seat again. He had drained the first glass of wine without her noticing and now poured himself another.

"And don't sit here drinking until you're not fit to drive," she added.

He raised his glass to her.

"No," he said, "I won't."

CHAPTER THIRTY-ONE

THE SUN WAS shining when Alex awoke the next morning. She turned to face Tom and found that he was already awake, his arm propped up on his elbow. He smiled at her.

"Happy?" he asked. She nodded and thought to herself that, if it were not for her foolish entanglement with Edmund, it would have been the truth.

"I'm sorry I was late back last night," Tom continued. "I half expected you to stay out for supper with Carolyn, so it was frustrating to get your message. I was tied up with the Padgett case again and you know that I can't work nine to five on that."

Alex nodded.

"There's no need to apologise; I'd have stayed with Carolyn until halfway through the evening if she'd been free. She's got an exacting client at the moment, someone who insisted on meeting her for a working dinner at short notice."

Tom burst out laughing.

"Is that what Carolyn calls her assignations these days?"

"It wasn't an assignation. It was . . ." Alex frowned and found herself also laughing good-humouredly. "You could be right," she said. "Who knows? I don't think Carolyn is often deceitful, but she may have told me a little white lie to spare me the humiliation of being stood up. And she loves intrigue, as you know. She's probably very amused that I was so gullible."

Tom kissed her on the nose.

"I'm glad you're gullible," he said. "And so is Carolyn, probably. Have you noticed that she has no friends like herself? None of the rest of you runs her life in triplicate, carries on clandestine affairs and generally wraps her personal life in secrecy and double-dealing in the way that Carolyn does."

"I suspect that none of us has either the energy or the talent for it!" said Alex, with a pang.

Tom kissed her again, then sat up and swivelled round so that his legs and feet were hanging out of the bed.

"I must get up," he said. "I need to be back at the office by eight to read up the Padgett case notes before we have another meeting. It's early, though; you don't need to stir yourself yet. If you want to stay in bed a little longer, I'll bring you some tea and toast."

"That's sweet of you," said Alex, "but it would do me good to get up early, too. I intended to do some work over the weekend and I've got quite a bit of catching up to do if I'm going to get the plan for the summer displays ready for the committee later this week."

Tom sniffed.

"I'd think they were a ridiculous bunch if I didn't find them and their behaviour quite sinister. I don't understand why you have to submit a plan to them. They never argue with it, do they?"

"No, but they could do, in theory. They're meant to be responsible both for the safekeeping of the Society's possessions and for its good reputation."

"Rubbish! Its reputation isn't what they're thinking of. They just want to make sure that you choose something popular enough to replenish the coffers. Get their paws on the cash, in other words."

Alex sighed.

"You're probably right. I sometimes wonder why I'm wasting my life on this!"

Tom leaned over to kiss her again.

"No more mood swings!" he said. "You know very well that you get a huge kick out of your job. The same as I do."

"Go and have your shower. I'll just read in bed for a few minutes until you come out. Or would you like me to make *you* some tea?"

"Don't worry. I can buy some tea and a muffin in the canteen."

CHAPTER THIRTY-TWO

ALEX ARRIVED AT the Archaeological Society just before 8 a.m. She was carrying the bulky file that she had taken home the previous weekend. She tried to wedge it between her hip and the door while she fumbled in her bag for her keys, but the file slipped away from her and bounced down the two steps to the pavement. A few of the papers that it contained had not been secured and they slalomed untidily across the path. The furthest of them lay fluttering in the gutter.

"Fuck!" said Alex under her breath. She swung her open handbag over her shoulder and bent to retrieve the documents.

"Let me help you."

Alex looked up to find Edmund standing over her. She blenched.

"Sorry – did I startle you?"

"Not really: I just wasn't expecting to see you."

"I said that I would come today."

"I know, but I had thought that you would come this evening. You must have left Holbeach quite early."

"I did. I've taken the day off because I wanted to come to see you this morning and I'm accompanying Krystyna to the doctor's this afternoon."

"Is she worse?"

"I don't think so; but she was pretty bad in the first place. At least she's seen sense and agreed to ask for some more powerful medication."

"So you're going with her in case she changes her mind?"

"Something like that," said Edmund grimly. Alex did not pursue it.

Edmund collected the papers and lifted the file from the step.

"Here you are," he said. "I'm afraid I can't put the loose sheets back – I don't know where they came from."

"They were just held by a clip at the front of the file – not very well, obviously. Thank you," she added, shoving the pages back between the boards of the file. "Would you hold it again while I unlock the door?"

"Tea?" she enquired, when they were both inside.

"No, thank you, I don't have time. I need to go and look at some of the stuff that has been archived in Broad Street. I've come to ask you for the key."

"This is a bit precipitate, isn't it?"

"Why? I told you that I have a special project that I want to carry out.

I give you my word that it will benefit both of us – and the Archaeological Society, too."

"I'm not sure that I should let you have the key."

"I don't see why not. I'm the President, after all."

"I suppose that's true." Alex paused for a moment. She was unhappy about giving Edmund access to the archive without quite knowing why. As he pointed out, he had more right than most people to request it. She decided that she couldn't refuse.

"You'll need the burglar alarm code, too. I'll write it down for you. And I'll have to ask you to complete our standard consent form for researchers. You must undertake not to remove or damage any of the Society's artefacts or papers and to leave everything in the archive exactly as you found it."

"That's hardly necessary, is it? I am an officer of the society – even if only a temporary one."

"So you keep saying, but we ask everyone to comply – as I'm sure you know. You'd be the first to complain if I allowed anyone else into the archive without signing. I'll get you a copy of the form now; I'm sure you must have read it before, so it won't take you a minute."

"What if I do want to remove something – temporarily, of course?"

"We don't normally let anyone take the artefacts away unless it is another society or museum that wants them for an exhibition. Individuals aren't usually allowed to take them except for scientists who have been requested to carry out dating tests or experts asked to establish authenticity. We do let researchers take papers home with them sometimes, if there's a lot for them to get through. Usually we only allow the material out for a very short time – a few days, or a week. They need permission – from me, and from one or more of the trustees, depending on what it is. They have to sign another document and pay for temporary insurance if we decide that it's advisable. I've only allowed papers out two or three times, though. I don't get asked very often. And I've never had to call on the trustees to give their permission for documents to be borrowed because the ones that have been requested have not been of great monetary value. Not many of the documents that the Society owns are. Some of the artefacts are valuable, of course; I'm sure that you've been at meetings where we have debated the risk factors involved in lending certain items."

"I suppose I must have been. I don't really remember. I'd certainly forgotten how bureaucratic it all was! And I thought that we were bad at the Heritage Foundation!"

"Well, you'd be the first person to say that we should safeguard our legacy, if it weren't for the fact that this happens to be something that inconveniences you. I'll walk over to Broad Street in a couple of hours, if you like, to see if there are any papers you'd like to borrow. If there are, it will probably be something that I can authorise myself. It *is* papers that you're interested in, isn't it?"

"Hm? Yes . . . yes, of course."

"Do you know what you're looking for? Otherwise it will be a needle and haystack job. As long as you have a reasonable idea of what you want to find, the archive plan should help you. There is a copy of the plan inside the desk at the entrance to Broad Street, but I can give you one for your own use now. The lighting there isn't very good, so it might help you to work out where to search while you're still here."

"Thanks. Yes please, I'd like to see the plan now."

"I'll find the consent forms at the same time."

Alex stood precariously on her desk chair, trying to reach a pile of box files high on the shelves behind her.

"Can I help you with that?" Edmund asked rather lamely.

"Yes, if you would," she said, as she struggled with recalcitrant folders for the second time that day. "I'm not sure which of these boxes contains the forms and the plans. I'm pretty certain that both will be in them somewhere. Can I pass them to you one by one?"

Edmund took the dusty boxes from her and piled them precariously on her desk.

"There's one more file, up there on the top shelf, but I can't quite reach it," said Alex, stretching up. The chair moved and she nearly lost her balance.

"For goodness sake, come down now," said Edmund pettishly. "I don't want to be responsible for your breaking your neck. If we need that top file I'll get it myself."

Alex found the plan of the Broad Street archive almost immediately.

"Here you are," she said to Edmund. "When you get there, you'll see that the chapel has been divided into twelve stalls, each of which contains shelves and space for hanging files. Some of them have cupboards or pigeon-holes as well for storing bone tools and shards of pottery, that kind of thing. All of the papers have been filed meticulously under subject headings and there are card-indexes which catalogue each paper within collections of documents individually. Most of the cataloguing work was done in the 1950s, I believe by a retired schoolmaster who belonged to the Archaeological Society, and his wife. The papers are catalogued according to when they were received by the Society and where they came from. There is no proper dating of any of the artefacts, as you know, but some attempt has been made to record either where they were found or who donated them. Nothing has been moved since, but of course there have been some new acquisitions. Most of these are stored in the basement here – they haven't been nearly as meticulously catalogued – but the final two stalls at Broad Street also contain some of the more recent uncatalogued material. Do you know how long the documents you are looking for have been in the Society's possession?"

"I think that they date from the middle of the nineteenth century," said Edmund.

"Well, you should be OK, then." Alex smiled, trying to catch his eye, but he looked away immediately.

"Yes," he said. "Let us hope so." He spread the plan out on her desk, and began to pore over it at once. Meanwhile, Alex searched through all of the box files without finding the consent form.

"I can't find those forms," she said, as she closed the final file. "They may be up there, right on the top shelf. Someone had a hundred or so printed years ago. What I really need to do is to create my own digital copy so that I can just print them out when I need them. I've found some used forms here in this file, so I could do that."

"You don't expect me to wait while you do it, though, do you?" Edmund did not even try to smile.

"No, I suppose not," said Alex, slowly. "I'll give you the key and the burglar alarm code now. Bring the key back before lunch and I'll have the consent form waiting for you then."

"Thank you."

Edmund folded up the archive plan and placed it carefully in his inside pocket. He took from Alex the key and the slip of paper bearing the alarm code and pocketed them, too.

He had reached the door of Alex's office before he turned and hurried back to place a perfunctory kiss on her cheek.

"I'll see you later," he said.

Alex spent the morning working on her summer exhibition plan. Just before midday, she created a Word document version of the consent form and printed it out. She looked at her watch. It was almost three hours since Edmund had left her. It was less than a ten-minute walk to Broad Street, so he would have been looking at the archives for more than two hours. It would soon be time for him to go back to Holbeach for Krystyna's appointment. Alex hoped that she could trust him to return the key. She wouldn't put it past Edmund to pocket the key and go home, then turn up tomorrow and explain airily that he hadn't had time to give it back immediately. She still felt uneasy about having given him access to the archive, although she hardly knew why. He was the County Heritage Officer, for God's sake! If she had asked any of the other trustees, of course they would have agreed to it. They probably would have been as impatient with the formalities as Edmund was himself.

Alex sighed. Tom was right. They were an insufferable bunch of vain old men . . . and Edmund was one of them – younger than most of them and with some redeeming qualities, but still an irascible old buffer at heart. The thought struck her that she had always considered them corrupt, but in a petty way; she knew them to be the sort of people who would fail to query restaurant bills from which some items were missing, or disguise rounds of drinks for their friends on expenses claims. She did not believe that Edmund would stoop to this kind of behaviour. She did wonder, however, whether he might not be capable of some grander evil.

She decided that she would take a walk to Broad Street, ostensibly to ask him to sign the form but also to retrieve the key. She placed the consent form in an envelope and wedged it into the side pocket of her handbag. Stepping out into surprisingly warm winter sunshine, she enjoyed the heat of the sun on her face. It was the warmest day she could remember after many miserable weeks of rain and cold.

As she turned the corner from Westlode Street into Broad Street, she saw Edmund's battered car parked half on the pavement and half on the road. She was surprised; she had assumed that Edmund had left his car in the big car park at the bus station and made the journey from the Archaeological Society to the chapel on foot. He must have returned to the car park after he had left her. She shrugged. Perhaps he had moved the car in order to be ready to leave for Holbeach when the time came. She looked at the car again and saw Edmund emerging from behind it. He slammed the boot shut and walked rapidly back into the chapel. Alex was still a considerable distance away from him and could not see what he was doing. She quickened her pace and was within a few feet of the car when Edmund emerged from the chapel again, carrying one of the large grey files from the archive. He paused when he saw her.

"Alex, hello! I thought I had told you not to bother to come here. I'm sure you have better things to do."

"You didn't actually say that, Edmund, but I would have come anyway, to help you to lock up, and to save you the journey back to the Archaeological Society. I've brought the form for you to sign. Where were you going with that file?"

"I was just going to bring it to you, to ask you if I might sign it out. I've found the collection of papers that I want."

"I'm glad about that," said Alex severely. "What are they?" She squinted at the small rectangular label, trying to make out the faded inscription in the schoolmaster's impeccable italic script. *Kirton Parish Papers, 1830 – 1870* she read. There was something familiar about it, though she could not think what it was.

"Just some local history papers relating to the Boston area. As you know, I am particularly interested in the local gentlemen historians of the period."

Alex remembered the trustee meeting at Peterborough Museum.

"Not more about the Reverend Lockhart?" Edmund hesitated, evidently a little ill at ease.

"I believe that he is mentioned, but one would expect that – he was one of the foremost clergyman antiquaries of the county."

"I seem to recollect that you didn't paint him in quite such a rosy way when you were purchasing his papers from the museum."

"Perhaps not, but I assure you that I paid more than a fair price for those papers. They are not of any interest or value except within the context of local study. Just like the ones I have here. In fact, these are probably rather less valuable than the Lockhart papers, as they consist of a mish-mash of notes from several antiquaries who were active at the period. I'm assuming that you won't consider them to be too valuable to be removed from the archive temporarily?"

"I shall need to look through them, to make sure that each paper contained in the file has an index card. But I think it's unlikely that I shan't be able to release them on my own authority alone."

Like wine being poured into a carafe, Edmund's face filled from the chin with the deep purplish red that Alex had seen on previous occasions when he was ruffled. He fiddled with his cuff in order to consult his watch.

"Must you do that now? I don't have time to wait; I have to be back in Holbeach in half an hour."

"That's all right; leave the file here and I'll check the card index for you now. You can either come back for it today or tomorrow morning, whichever you prefer. I'll call you if I think there'll be a delay in granting permission; but as I've already said, I think that is unlikely."

"Alex, please, I'm anxious to get on with this now and I doubt if I'll be able to come back today, because this visit to the doctor's bound to have an adverse effect on Krystyna's state of mind. Can't I just sign the form and take the file for a few days? I give you my word that I won't remove anything from it."

Alex felt compromised. She knew that if Edmund had been any bone fide researcher in a hurry she would almost certainly have said yes. She doubted his motives, yet she found it impossible to show that she didn't trust him.

"Oh, all right," she said. "But you have to sign the form – here it is – and I'm going to say that the papers have been loaned to you for six days. That means you have to return them first thing next Monday. Is that OK?"

Edmund nodded. He was already scribbling his signature on the form as she spoke.

"By the way," she said as playfully as she could. "I thought I saw you putting something in your boot when I turned the corner just now. You aren't absconding with some of the Society's possessions, are you?"

"Don't be ridiculous," said Edmund, frowning. "You should know better than to ask that."

He opened the nearside rear door of his car and placed the file carefully on the back seat, wedging it in place with a travel rug.

"Thank you for this, Alex," he said, affable again. "You won't regret it, I promise you; I shall have something very exciting to show you soon." He bent to kiss her cheek again, a little more tenderly than on the earlier occasion in her office.

She put her hand on his arm.

"Good luck this afternoon, Edmund," she said. "I do hope that the doctor will be able to help Krystyna."

His brows knitted again.

"I doubt very much whether anyone can help Krystyna now," he said, "but one has to make the effort, I suppose. No stone left unturned, eh?" He gave her one of his sunny smiles, then climbed into the car and started the engine.

Alex watched him drive off. His last comment could hardly have been more inappropriate. She felt shocked by its coarse joviality. She could only excuse it by supposing that Edmund was trying to conceal some deeper feelings of despair and anxiety.

As his car rounded the corner and disappeared, she suddenly remembered that he had not returned the key to the chapel. It was an oversight, she supposed, but an annoying one. She would have to ask him to return it tomorrow. She could not allow it to be missing for six days. It would give her the opportunity to ask him to bring the file of documents back with him so that she could check them against the catalogue cards.

She returned to her office, dispirited and uneasy. She knew that she would have to spend the rest of the afternoon completing the summer schedule if she were to get it off the ground, but her heart was no longer in it.

CHAPTER THIRTY-THREE

THAT AFTERNOON ALEX left two separate messages for Edmund, one on his office landline and one on his cellphone. On each occasion she asked him to get in touch with her as soon as possible to arrange the return of the key to the archive. She had tried to sound as calm and matter-of-fact as she could, despite the anxiety which nagged at her. She fervently wished that she had not let him have the key. It was unlikely that it would be needed, she knew, but what would she say if one of the trustees visited and asked to see the archive? She cursed her own carelessness for not having had a duplicate key made.

She still had not heard from Edmund at six o'clock that evening. She debated whether to call him at home, but told herself that it would be too much of an infringement of his privacy, especially as she knew that Krystyna was unwell. No, she thought fiercely, despising her own dishonesty, that isn't the reason; it's because I'm afraid of having to talk to Krystyna if she should herself take the call.

Alex walked home slowly, depressed. She would put an end to this charade of a liaison. Carolyn had been right. Carolyn was usually very clear-sighted about other people's emotional entanglements.

Alex shivered as she turned into the Chapel Lane passageway. Since the episode with the cigarette butt, she had been nervous about walking the last few steps from the end of the passage to the yard gate. Today the street lights had come on, however, and there were several people in view, some using the lane as a short-cut to the Pied Calf pub. If she thought about it logically, she knew that she was safe here. She hated this wretched feeling of apprehension that kept her held in its grip and she believed that it, too, could be traced to the start of her relationship with Edmund. 'Self-esteem', she murmured; that elusive quality so beloved of the self-help books that Carolyn swore by. It was unfair to blame Edmund for her loss of it; she had been his accomplice every step of the way. Well, she would change that.

She already had the key to the yard gate in her hand when she rounded the corner. The gate was always locked except when she and Tom or the people who worked in the building society below the flat were coming or going; none of them ever left it unlocked, let alone open.

Alex stood stock still in the middle of the path, then clutched suddenly at the wall for support. The yard gate was swinging on its hinge.

"Are you all right?"

A motherly woman wearing a pill-box hat fashioned from some kind of hairy synthetic material had grasped her gently by the elbow.

"Yes," said Alex. "No. The gate's open."

The woman followed her gaze. Her face was thick with powder, her chin bristly. She regarded Alex with watery, curious eyes.

"Do you live there?" she asked.

"Yes, and the gate is always closed. We keep it locked."

"Well, perhaps someone forgot. Is your husband in?"

"Yes, I think so," said Alex. She looked at her watch. It was almost six-thirty. Tom would be sure to be home by now.

"Well, if I were you, I'd go in and ask him to make you a cup of tea. Put your feet up for a while. You probably need a little rest." She had a gratingly sing-song voice.

"I – thank you," said Alex. The woman meant well, but Alex couldn't stand to be patronised. She had to get away from her.

"You'll be all right, now?"

"Yes, of course," said Alex. She walked sedately to the gate and then looked round once before she crossed the threshold. The woman gave an encouraging little wave, gloved hand held to shoulder height, fingers wiggling, then turned and continued on her way.

Alex raced up the steps.

When she reached the door of the flat, it also was hanging open.

"Tom?" She called. "Tom!" She was almost screaming now.

There was no reply. If Tom had been inside the flat, he must surely have heard her.

The telephone started ringing. There was an extension in the kitchen. Alex steeled herself to walk through the door and answer it. If the flat had been burgled, surely the intruder would not still be inside? The open door, the open gate: both suggested a hurried departure. Someone still inside the building would have covered their tracks better.

She needed to know where Tom was. She made herself walk into the cool dark room. She snapped on the light. She inhaled the familiar nutty smell of the old wooden work-bench. She found it hard to focus her eyes, partly because she had just come in from the street, partly because she felt faint. She seized the receiver just as the phone stopped ringing.

Alex replaced the receiver carefully, as if it were made of glass. She hovered uncomfortably beside the open doorway. She did not know what to do. She was afraid of going further into the flat unaccompanied, afraid to stay where she was. She stared at the phone as if it were an oracle, and saw an old envelope standing next to it, propped against a bottle of olive oil. She snatched it up. On it Tom had scrawled: "Just called in briefly – hoped you might be home early. Padgett case again – sorry.

Back late. Tx."

Alex knew now that she must search the flat. She crept silently along the narrow hall to the sitting room, and edged her way through the door, which was standing ajar. It squeaked horribly on its rusty hinge as she pushed it.

The sitting-room was as they had left it that morning, their coffee cups from the night before still on the hearth, one of Tom's social worker magazines tossed untidily on the sofa. The pendulum of the long case clock, an heirloom from Tom's family, moved steadily back and forth, clicking slightly with each measured movement.

There was only one other downstairs room – the dining-room – and its door, as usual, was firmly closed. She knew that it had a habit of sticking, so she pressed her shoulder against it and turned the handle suddenly to get some leverage. She burst into the room rather suddenly, making more noise than she had intended.

Inside, she found another serene, deserted space with no evidence of recent use. She and Tom barely went into the dining-room during the week. It seemed to be just as she had left it when she'd cleaned it the previous weekend, except that the freesias that she had placed in a crystal vase on the Victorian gate-legged table were beginning to die and had dropped some of their blooms onto its polished top. They had scattered a faint trail of yellow pollen.

Alex listened intently. If an intruder was still on the premises, he – or she – would be sure to have heard her now. She could detect no unsettling sounds, nothing that might indicate that she was not alone. The upstairs rooms presented the greatest challenge. If she had surprised someone on the first floor, she thought she would have stood a chance of running out of the flat, or at least have been able to attract attention by pounding on the sitting-room window that overlooked the Sheep Market. On the second floor she would be trapped – the two bedrooms were three storeys up, their windows small and set deep into the thick walls, so that it was impossible to look into them from the street below. And the steep narrow staircase was the only way out.

There was no going back. She took her mobile from her handbag and held it in her hand. She would speed-dial Tom's number as soon as she heard a sound. She edged her way up the stairs, stopping to listen frequently, but she could hear nothing.

Both bedroom doors were ajar. Alex went into the guest room first. She had stripped the bed after Marie and her partner had stayed on Friday night. The quilt was rolled into a neat sausage in the middle of the bed, the discarded sheets and pillowcases in a pile near the window, just where she had left them. Alex looked fleetingly at the cupboard that had been built into the wall many decades before, but she knew it to be filled with linen-laden shelves. There was not the space to conceal a person, not even a child.

The bedroom that she shared with Tom was the last room left. It was a big room with a walk-in cupboard. She would have to search it carefully, perhaps get very close to a would-be assailant. Her fear was acute. She was terrified by what she might find on the other side of this door.

Unlike the dining-room's, its door it was loose-fitting; someone had removed it from its hinges decades ago, and re-hung it so that it opened inwards. It had a small panel of frosted glass let into it in the centre, high up, presumably to allow a glimmer of natural light to filter through to the landing. Alex stretched up and tried to look through the small opaque window. She could discern the outline of the bed and her cheval mirror. There seemed to be no movement in the room.

She opened the door slowly, inadvertently rattling the round brass doorknob, and stood, framed, in the doorway.

The bed had been made. This was certainly not her doing – she knew that she had left the quilt furled at the bed's foot – but it was possible that Tom had taken into his head to neaten it when he had left the note.

Alex dropped to her hands and knees and looked under the bed. There was nothing but dust and discarded novels.

She got up, and moved across to the closet, pulling its door open suddenly as she had the sitting-room door downstairs. She put her hand into each of the two rails of dresses and suits, parted them and searched the floor beneath them. There was no evidence that they had been tampered with.

Unless there was someone cowering in the tiny bathroom next to the kitchen, she had established that she was alone in the flat. Perhaps there had been no intruder; perhaps her alarm had been caused by Tom himself. Could he have been so preoccupied with the Padgett case that he had left both the gate and the flat door not only unlocked but wide open? Alex was doubtful, but she had to acknowledge that it was possible.

She walked slowly back to the top of the stairs. She was about to descend them when the outside door banged loudly. Alex caught her breath and ran towards the sound. If there was an intruder and he or she had either succeeded in hiding from her or had returned, she had no option but to confront them now.

She burst into the kitchen. The outside door that led into it had banged shut. The kitchen itself was empty. Alex flung open the only other door that led from it: the bathroom, too, was unoccupied.

Cautiously, she moved to the outside door and opened it. She took a few steps outside. The flat roof was deserted save for the few shrubs that she grew in tubs and the ornate wrought iron table at which she and Tom sat and drank coffee on warm weekends. She peered over the staircase railings, but could see no-one.

Someone had slammed the door, though; she was convinced of it. It was dark now, but the evening was still, with no hint of a breeze. The door had closed like a thunderclap. Someone had pulled it hard; they had deliberately slammed it shut to frighten her.

The phone started ringing again. She reached it much more quickly this time. It was still ringing when she lifted the receiver. She said 'Hello?' There was a click, then nothing. The caller had hung up, though it had rung only three times.

Alex turned to rest her back against the work-bench.

"Oh, Tom," she thought. "Come home soon."

Then she raised her eyes and screamed.

CHAPTER THIRTY-FOUR

ALEX HAD NEVER met her neighbours. The top floors of the eighteenth-century town-house to the right of theirs were not inhabited, but used as the storeroom for the Chinese restaurant below them. The top floors of the building to the left had been converted to a maisonette similar to theirs; there was a solicitor's office on the ground floor below it. Access to this maisonette was via a small private door next to the solicitor's solid portal in the Sheep Market. As Tom and Alex's entrance was in Chapel Lane, they had never bumped into the people who lived next door.

Alex had forgotten that, like the putative intruder, she had left the yard gate open. When her screams brought footsteps hurrying up the outside steps, she did not hear them. It was with renewed terror that she suddenly became aware that someone was pounding on the kitchen door. Pulling herself together a little, she realised that no adversary would be likely to knock.

She opened the door. A tall, stout young man was standing there, his florid complexion glowing with the effort of the sprint he had just made. He was wearing chef's whites. Now that he had arrived he seemed abashed, uncertain of what to do next.

"Are you all right?" he asked. "Only I thought that I heard screaming."

Alex nodded, and then burst into tears.

"What's going on?" asked another voice. Alex became aware of the vague shape of a woman standing on the rooftop courtyard, someone who had positioned herself well behind the figure in white.

"Who are you?" asked Alex. This couple may genuinely have been trying to help, but she felt that she could trust no-one.

"We live next door," said the woman, stepping forward. Alex saw that she was heavily pregnant. She wore jeans and a large black jumper stretched tightly over her bump. "Steve was just on his way to work and I said I'd walk round with him, for some fresh air. He cooks at the Pied Calf. We heard screams and saw that the gate was open. I've never seen that gate open before," she added.

"No, it is usually kept locked," Alex agreed.

"But are you all right? Is there someone in there giving you a hard time?" asked Steve.

Alex realised that he was insinuating that she might be a battered wife.

The idea would have been amusing if she had not felt so fragile.

"No-one else is here," she said. "I've just had a bad fright, that's all. It's all right – I'm over it now. I'm really grateful to you for taking the trouble to come, though. I apologise for the screaming: I feel embarrassed by it."

"Can we help?"

"I'm not sure that you can. I just need my husband to come home."

"Well," said the girl, advancing a little, "Steve's got to go to work now, but I can stay with you until your husband comes, if you like. My name's Wendy." She held out her hand. Alex took it briefly.

"That's very nice of you . . ." she said. She was going to refuse the offer, but she paused. She would give a great deal not to be left alone at the moment, even though this small rotund young woman was no stronger than she. Wendy misinterpreted her hesitation for diffidence and clambered down the kitchen steps to give her a hug.

"Don't . . ." Alex began. At the same moment, Wendy turned round to face the kitchen window.

She did not scream, but the colour drained from her face. She held her hand to her forehead, shielding her eyes with her fingers.

"God!" she said.

"What is it?" demanded Steve sharply. He was over the threshold and standing in the middle of the kitchen floor in a single stride. He turned to follow Wendy's line of vision. He did not have to search for what had sickened her.

"Jesus!" he said. "Is that real?"

"It looks it," said Alex.

A thick smear of blood arced its way across the kitchen wall from the window to the door.

"If it is blood, whose is it? Where *is* your husband?" asked Steve suspiciously. It took Alex a moment to understand his line of reasoning: in a heartbeat she had morphed from potential victim to potential murderer.

"He's working late. He's a social worker and he's dealing with a difficult case at the moment." Alex drew in her breath sharply and clapped her own hand over her mouth. "Surely it can't be his blood?" She said to herself, her horror returning. "He left me a note. Oh, Tom, I hope you're all right."

"Can I sit down somewhere?" said Wendy.

"Yes, of course – go through into the sitting-room," said Alex.

"Just there on that step will be fine," said Steve, gesturing towards the hall door. He put his arm round Wendy's shoulder, and led her across the room. She heaved herself on to the step, her legs splayed.

"Does your husband have a mobile? Can we call him?"

"Yes – thank you." Alex realised that she was still clutching her own mobile in her hand. "Here – I can never remember the number, but it's saved under 'Tom'."

Steve pressed the speed dial. Alex waited anxiously. There was no reply.

"What now?" she said. She felt powerless to do anything, all energy and even the power of any but the most basic thinking leached out of her.

"I think that we should call the police right away," said Steve grimly.

Alex's phone began to ring. She held out her hand to take it from Steve, but he answered it himself.

"Hello?"

"Who is that?" Alex could just make out that it was Tom's voice. He sounded truculent and worried.

"Tom! Thank God," she said.

"I'm a neighbour, though I don't think that we've met," said Steve. "There's been an ... I suppose you'd call it an accident ... in your flat."

"An accident? Is my wife there? Could you let her speak to me?" Tom was shouting now. Alex could hear him clearly. She held out her hand for the phone.

"Tom? I'm so glad that you're all right!"

"Why wouldn't I be all right? What about you? The guy who took the call said that there's been an accident. Is he really a neighbour?"

"Yes, I think so," said Alex, trying to smile at Steve. "He's been trying to help."

"What's happened?"

"When I came home, I found both the yard gate and the flat door unlocked and open. I assume you didn't leave them like that?"

"Don't be stupid – of course not. Have we been burgled?"

"Not as far as I can see. I've looked in every room."

"You shouldn't have done that on your own. You should have called the police. Is that all?"

"Almost. Nothing appears to have been taken, but something has been left. There's a ... there's what seems to be a big smear of blood across the kitchen wall, near the door. Did you see it, when you came home to write your note?"

"Of course I didn't! And I'm quite certain that it wasn't there then. I would have noticed it."

"What time did you leave?"

"I don't know – about five-thirty, I think. But that's irrelevant. Alex, you've got to call the police – get them to come round straight away. I've no idea what's going on, but it seems to me that there are only two possible explanations: either someone broke into the flat and in the process got hurt, or else someone is trying to frighten us. Either way, the police have got to know. Do you still have the number of that detective that you told me about – the one who came to see you when that woman archaeologist went missing?"

"Yes. Yes, I'm sure I do. Can't you come home, Tom? I'm afraid. I'm really upset about this."

"Yes, I'll come home now – but I'm in Sleaford again, so it will take me a while to get there. You must call the police before I get there – as soon as I've rung off, OK? Could you put that – the neighbour – on again?"

"His name's Steve. Yes, here he is." Alex handed back the mobile.

"Hello, Steve, this is Tom Tarrant again. Listen, I'm sorry that I was a bit abrupt with you just now – it was because I was worried. I hope you understand. Steve, I've told my wife to call the police. Can you stay with her until they arrive?"

"I'm a chef at the Pied Calf. I should have started work five minutes ago. They'll be stuck without me."

"Just until the police get there. They should come pretty quickly – the police station's so close. Please, Steve. If you lose any pay through this, I'll be glad to make it up. Can you call them and explain? Not the details, but say that a neighbour is in trouble and needs help."

"OK," said Steve, doubtfully.

CHAPTER THIRTY-FIVE

TIM WAS IN trouble. It was nearly two weeks since Claudia McRae had disappeared and police attempts to find her had made no significant progress. Today he had been berated by Superintendent Thornton after a sharply critical phone call that the Superintendent had himself received from Superintendent Little. Guy Maichment had apparently complained that the police investigation was being conducted in an incompetent manner. He had hinted that Tim himself had displayed prejudice towards his aunt because of her sexual orientation; the sub-text of his comment was that Tim was not particularly committed to finding her. Superintendent Thornton had given him until the end of the week to make a breakthrough. After that, he said, they would have to 'review the situation'. Tim knew that this was Thornton-speak for relieving him of his leadership of the case. He was desperate for this not to happen, although the irony of it was not lost on him. He had not wanted the case at first and now he did not want to lose it.

Alex Tarrant's call was an added complication and one that he barely had time for. Tim remembered her with the vivid clarity with which a man remembers a woman to whom, in a fictional time and place, he might have allowed himself to feel attracted. When they had first met, her appearance at that gloomy and strange hotel and their subsequent conversation had enabled him to perceive the thread of logic that ran through the arcane and eccentric world which she inhabited. Oliver Sparham had also made sense, but he was still a fully paid-up member of the archaeological crew. Alex had seemed to stand at right angles between them and the rest of the world, occupying a role somewhere between that of protector and servant. It was not just her beauty and her efficiency that had impressed him; he had also admired her openness and evident integrity.

Under any other circumstance, therefore, he would have been delighted to have received a call from her, but this evening he cursed his luck that she had managed to catch him before he had left the office for the day. He wanted to take home all the notes from the McRae case and review them methodically. He had also resolved that tonight he would confront Katrin. He – and she – had pussyfooted around her malaise for too long. He was determined to make her tell him the truth about it, however unpalatable that might be for him. He was aware that forcing it into the open might create a catastrophe; he had already considered the unthinkable, that whatever it was might spell the end of his marriage. But he could no longer bear to pretend that the huge gulf that now yawned between them did not exist. Knowledge of it tore daily into his mood. Still he could neither guess its cause nor fathom whether he himself shared the responsibility for creating it. He thought that Katrin's behaviour indicated that he was to blame in some way. It could be something that he had said or done or, more probably, not said or not done.

He contemplated the alternative explanation: that Katrin herself was guilty of some fault that she could not or would not discuss and had become sullen with a transgressor's resentment. But he could not believe this to be the truth. He was certain that she would not have betrayed their relationship in an overt way – by taking a lover, for example. No, their estrangement must have been caused by something that had passed between them. He racked his brains. If this were so, it was something that had escaped his attention entirely; some stupid blunder of his own, perhaps, which he had failed even to register because, as usual, he had been preoccupied with his job.

He had always tried not to be smug when other policemen confided in him their difficulties with wives and girlfriends and he had believed that he would never share the same fate. Katrin was an insider who understood the pressures of his work. He had felt secure in the knowledge that she did not have the kind of dependent personality that required a partner always to show up for meals, always to share joint plans for the evenings and weekends. Now he was not so sure. For the first time since he had become a policeman, he felt resentful of the price that his career exacted. It was not just that it demanded the use of his every waking hour; it was the claim that it laid on his character. It made him intolerant, self-centred and, he feared, at times unreasonable. He knew that it was an age since he had put Katrin first when work had called. Even someone as flexible and forgiving as she would be likely to become disillusioned at some point.

And now there was this SOS from Alex Tarrant. The call she had made to his mobile was not especially coherent. At first he had thought that she was merely reporting a random break-in. He had been about to transfer her to the duty desk at the police station when, hesitantly, she had mentioned the blood stain. Immediately he knew that there must be a link to the Claudia McRae case. It followed that Alex Tarrant was at risk, even if he did not have enough information to understand where the danger lay. She must be protected; she might also be able to provide him with the break-through that he so desperately needed.

She had clearly been very shaken. She said that she feared that the person who had been in her flat would return, but she obviously did not have the knowledge to make the connection with Dame Claudia's disappearance. Immediately he arranged for Juliet Armstrong to go and sit with her and sent a message that he would be with them himself in less than an hour. First he would call in at home to see Katrin. The showdown for which he had steeled himself would have to be postponed, but at least he could demonstrate to Katrin that he cared.

He let himself in through the front door, calling out 'Hi!' in a voice which to himself sounded falsely cheerful. He was gratified to receive a subdued but not hostile response: 'Tim?'

Katrin was in the kitchen. He hoped against hope that she was not in the process of preparing an elaborate meal which he would be unable to stay to consume. Katrin when well was an enthusiastic cook.

The kitchen was typical of that of many houses built just after the war and therefore not its home's best feature. It was square but small, with a north-facing window that let in little light. It was necessary to cook by artificial light on all but the brightest days of the year, when the rays of the sun, welcome intruders, would sometimes manage to slant obliquely through the panes. There was no sunshine now. The dull yellow of the strip light failed to penetrate to the corners of the room, but it managed to cast a subdued glow over Katrin's bent head, drawing out the glints of auburn which threaded through her dark-brown hair. She was seated at the tiny table which, together with two modest wheelback chairs, was all the furniture that the room could accommodate. An untouched cup of tea stood in front of her, the dark tan surface of the liquid already coagulated.

'Tim?' she said again, dully. 'I thought that you were going to be late tonight?'

'I was – I am,' said Tim awkwardly. 'I've come home sooner than I intended, but I'm going to have to go out again. I'm really sorry. I wanted to spend the evening with you.'

'It doesn't matter,' she said listlessly. 'At least I won't have to cook now. I was just wondering how to summon up the energy.'

'I'd gladly have taken you out somewhere,' said Tim. 'We'll do it tomorrow, instead. But you will eat something, won't you?'

She sighed. 'I suppose so. I can always knock up a sandwich for myself.'

'I'll make you a sandwich, if you like.'

'Don't worry, I can do it myself. If you've got to go out again, you might as well go straight away. You'll be back quicker. But it was nice of you to offer,' she added. She gave a half-smile. Tim took her hand.

'I'm so worried about you,' he said. 'You don't seem to be happy any more and I don't know what to do about it.'

He hadn't meant to blurt out his concern quite like this, and he realised immediately that it had been a mistake. Initially, his words seemed to bring her close to tears, but, worse still from his point of view, her face quickly recomposed itself and adopted the shuttered look that had become only too familiar to him in recent weeks.

'Don't worry about me,' she said. There was asperity in her tone now. 'I'll be all right. I may be in bed when you get back: I think that I'm in need of an early night.'

She drew away her hand. Tim opened his mouth to answer her, trying to think of something reassuring and loving to say, but no words came. He met the blankness of her gaze, and tried not to flinch.

'OK,' he said. 'I won't disturb you if you're asleep.' She nodded.

As he climbed back into his car, he wondered what, exactly, she had meant by her last comment, and, indeed, what he had intended to convey with his reply. He always tried not to wake her when he came in late and as far as he knew he usually succeeded. She had never mentioned being disturbed before. Had she intended to mean that he should sleep in the spare room? Had he tacitly agreed to such an arrangement? Had her final nod been one of complicity?

CHAPTER THIRTY-SIX

HE ARRIVED AT the Tarrants' flat at the same time as Tom Tarrant. Tom, a slightly overweight, balding man, had come hurrying along Chapel Lane as Tim reached the yard gate. He held out his hand. 'Detective Inspector Yates, thank you for coming.'

Tim was puzzled for a moment, though the other man's face did seem vaguely familiar.

'I'm Tom Tarrant,' he explained. 'I've seen you on television, talking about Claudia McRae.'

Tim grasped the proffered hand. It turned out to be limp and sweaty.

'Are you just coming home now? You haven't seen your wife since the break-in?'

'No. I've been working in Sleaford today. I came as soon as she called me. It was my idea for her to get in touch with you.'

'I see,' said Tim. He followed Tom Tarrant up the steps to the door of the maisonette. Tom opened the door and looked behind it immediately.

'My God!' he exclaimed. 'Who would want to do *that*?' Tim felt a little irritated by the theatricality of the words until he was himself facing the cause of Tom's outrage. The blood smear was thicker and deeper than the gory daub at Claudia McRae's cottage. It seemed almost to have been gouged into the plaster.

'You haven't seen that before, sir, I take it?'

'Of course not!' said Tom. 'Do you think that if I had I would have gone out as if nothing had happened?'

Juliet Armstrong appeared in the kitchen doorway.

'Good evening, sir,' she said. 'Mrs Tarrant is in the sitting-room.' She turned her head towards the wall. 'Ugly, isn't it? Someone must be pretty sick.'

Tim followed her down the short, dark corridor. Tom Tarrant was close behind. Juliet paused when she reached the sitting-room door.

'Would you like to go first, sir?' she said to Tom. He nodded, and squeezed past them both. Tim knew that Juliet had been right to extend this courtesy, but, as it made it impossible for him to witness the first moments of Tom's reunion with Alex, from his point of view it was to be regretted. By the time that he had rounded the door, Alex was already embracing Tom, her face hidden against his shoulder. Tom caught Tim's eye and gently released her.

"Alex, Detective Chief Inspector Yates is here." She turned to face Tim immediately, holding out her hand, which was cooler and much slimmer than her husband's. Her face was pale and she was clearly very upset.

"Please, sit down," she said. "I do hope that you won't think that this is a fuss about nothing."

"On the contrary, Mrs Tarrant, I think that we should take this intrusion very seriously. For your own safety, you should probably have called us before you decided to search the flat. Your kitchen will have to be cordoned off as a crime scene, but no doubt you were expecting that. Aside from the mark on the wall, are there any other signs of intrusion? For example, do you think that drawers or cupboards have been searched, or that any items have been removed?"

Alex shook her head.

"There's nothing else, as far as I can tell. Tom might like to check as well, but I can't see that anything has been disturbed. What is that on the kitchen wall, Inspector? Is it really blood, or does it just look like blood? Surely it can't be someone's idea of a joke?"

"I'm afraid that I can't answer your questions now. We try not to speculate about motive, because it can mislead us and waste time. However, I think that I can say that I'm convinced that we're dealing with something more serious than a joke in poor taste."

"Do you think that someone was actually hurt here?" asked Tom Tarrant.

"I think it unlikely that anyone was hurt *here*. There is no blood on the floor and if someone had been wounded at that height of the wall they would have had to have been standing on something several feet off the ground. I'm not a forensic expert – we'll find out what they think – but I'd say that the smear of blood is too thick to have spurted from an injury. Sorry," he added, as Alex Tarrant shuddered. "I think that it has been daubed on the wall by someone trying to convey a grotesque message and that its profusion is part of the message. Whoever did it is trying to frighten you."

"Well, they've succeeded," said Alex.

Tom Tarrant looked annoyed.

"I'm sorry," he said. "You're talking in riddles as far as I'm concerned. If you're right, what can the message be about, for God's sake? And why not just tell us whatever it is, instead of operating in this bizarre way?"

"I may not be right," said Tim, "and I've probably said too much already, given that I told you that I wouldn't speculate. But I'll just add that being able to create fear gives the perpetrator a great deal of power; most people are more afraid of what they don't know, or don't understand."

"I suppose you're right," said Alex. "What do we do now?"

"I'd like you each to talk us through your last entry into the flat in detail, starting with you, please, Mr Tarrant. I mean when you called in earlier, of course, not when you came in with me just now. Do you mind if we record what you say? We'll take notes as well."

"No, that's fine," said Tom. "I don't have much to tell you, really. I'm a social worker, based in Spalding, but I travel around this area quite a bit, because I specialise in caring for disturbed children. There's a particular case that I'm working on at the moment – by chance, it also involves the police – and late this afternoon I realised that I would have to travel to the children's home in Sleaford where one of my clients is being held under curfew."

"I thought I'd seen you before!" said Tim. "You were at the police station a few days ago, with Andy Carstairs, weren't you? Helping him to interrogate the child in the drugs investigation?"

"That's right: Thobias Padgett is the boy's name. His elder brother, LeRoy, is also involved. I'd prefer not to use the word 'interrogate', by the way, especially in a case which involves children. Ours isn't a police state, as far as I'm aware."

"Just a figure of speech," said Tim quickly. "DC Carstairs has told me a bit about the case. I think he's familiar with the Padgett family."

"They're well known both to the police and to social services, though the children aren't neglected. The mother, Marlene Padgett, is doing a good job at bringing them up, according to her own standards, anyway. It's a large family and as the boys get older they run rings round her."

"I'm sure you're right," said Tim. "To get back to where we left off: you realised that you would have to travel to Sleaford and stay there until when?"

"I thought that I'd probably get back here at about 9 p.m. So I called in to tell Alex that I'd be late."

"Why didn't you just phone her?"

Tom shrugged. "It was almost five-thirty and I thought that she'd probably be at home already. I did try calling her mobile, but I got the engaged tone and decided not to leave voicemail. Alex is very bad at picking it up, for one thing. I'd managed to park my car just round the corner, so it was almost as easy to come home to see if she was here and, if not, to leave a written message."

Tim nodded.

"Where exactly was your car parked?"

"At the end of Chapel Lane, just on the corner. You're allowed to park there for thirty minutes."

"So you locked your car and walked down Chapel Lane," said Tim. "Were you carrying anything?"

"No. I had some case notes with me – the ones I have here, now – but I left them in the car."

"Did you see anyone? Bump into anyone you know, or notice anyone following you?"

"I certainly didn't see anyone I knew and I didn't look behind me to see if I was being followed. It wouldn't have occurred to me. There were people about – mostly walking across from the Bus Station to the Pied Calf – but none of them seemed to be taking any interest in me; nor I in them, for that matter."

"So you couldn't describe any of them clearly?"

"I . . . No. I was in a hurry and not really paying attention."

"When you reached your flat, what did you do?"

"First of all, I took out the key to the yard gate. It's always kept locked."

"Who has keys to it?"

"Alex and me, of course; and the people who work in the building society."

"Do they have a key each?"

"No, I don't think so. The manager has a key, but the other staff mainly use the front entrance to come and go. They just need to use the yard gate when it's time to take the dustbins out to Chapel Lane for collection; oh, and one of them sometimes comes on a bike and uses the key to get into the yard, to leave the bike there. And the landlord has one, of course."

"Who is the landlord?"

"The building society itself administers the property for the actual landlord. We don't know the identity of the owner."

"I take it that neither of you has lost a set of keys lately?"

"No," said Tom. "We have only one set each."

"OK," said Tim. "So you let yourself into the yard. Was there anyone there?"

"No, of course not. If there had been, it would have been unusual and I'd have mentioned it already."

"So no-one was there from the building society? Was its door closed?"

"Yes, I'm sure that it was; it almost always is. And I didn't see any of the staff. It was just after 5.30 by that time; they would probably all have gone home by then."

"How do you know what time it was?"

"I looked at my watch when I parked the car. If Alex had been here, I thought I might have stopped to have a cup of tea with her and I didn't want to get a parking ticket."

"So you saw nothing at all unusual and walked up the steps to the flat. Did you lock the yard door behind you?"

"I . . . No. No, I don't think I did. I can't be sure, but I don't always when I'm popping in quickly."

"Someone could have followed you in, then?"

"I suppose so, but I didn't see anyone when I was on my way out again."

"All right. So you opened your kitchen door – presumably this has a different key?"

"Yes, a Yale, with a deadlock. And yes, I unlocked the door, went into the kitchen and called Alex."

"She didn't reply?"

"No. You know she didn't."

"What did you do then? Did you go looking for her?"

"No. I knew that if she'd been there, she would have heard me. I had no reason to stay, therefore."

"You said you would have liked a cup of tea. Did you make one?"

"No, I wasn't desperate. I'd have had one with Alex, but just to be companionable before I went out again."

"So you left her a note. Did you have to go in search of something to write it with?"

"No, I took a piece of discarded paper – an old envelope – from the wastepaper bank and wrote on it with one of the pencils in the tub beside the telephone."

"You were facing the far wall? The one opposite the window?"

"Yes."

"Did you look at the wall opposite – the one with the window?"

"I suppose that I must have."

"But do you remember looking at it specifically?"

"No. But I'm sure that that mark couldn't have been there then."

"What makes you so certain?"

Tom Tarrant shrugged. "I don't know – a kind of sixth sense, I guess. I'm sure that something would have drawn me to it if it *had* been there. I get a feeling when things aren't quite right – I'm not making myself out to be anything special. A lot of people do."

Tim didn't disagree. He knew that what Tom had offered was not a rational explanation, but he also knew that what he had said was often true. People *did* get a feeling if something was not quite right with familiar surroundings.

"So you left the note, walked out of the kitchen, locked the door, went back down the stairs, seeing no-one in the yard, and out into Chapel Lane and locked the yard gate behind you?"

"Yes, precisely that."

"You're quite sure that you locked both the door and the gate?"

"As sure as I can be. I wasn't particularly preoccupied, nor even in a great hurry, and I've never left either of them unlocked before. Besides, the Yale lock fastens to of its own accord – it's only the deadlock that requires you to turn the key. Even if I'd forgotten to lock it, I'd hardly have left it standing wide open."

Tim nodded.

"And then you walked back down the passage to your car, again unaware whether you were being followed or not? And you just started up the car and drove off to Sleaford, believing everything at home to be normal."

"Yes."

"Thank you."

Tim turned to Alex.

"Mrs Tarrant, could you describe your day?"

"What, all of it? You mean from this morning onwards?"

"If you don't mind," said Tim.

"I got up after Tom – he had to leave early – but I was still at work early myself. I was letting myself in to the Archaeological Society when I met Edmund Baker on the steps. He'd come to ask me for access to some papers that he wanted to research. I opened the door and took him into my office with me. I offered him tea, but he said that he was in a hurry, so I gave him the key to the archive and he left."

"The archive is in the same building? The one in which you work?"

"No, it's in Broad Street. There's an old chapel there that is used as a kind of overflow store for the Society's possessions – papers, mainly. It's been in use since the 1950s. Strictly speaking . . ." Alex hesitated.

"Go on, Mrs Tarrant. Strictly speaking, what?"

"Strictly speaking, I shouldn't have let Edmund have the key, because he hadn't signed the indemnity papers. But he's closely involved with the Society, and a member of the Heritage Council, so I overlooked it."

"Why wouldn't he sign the indemnity form?"

"Oh, there was nothing sinister about it. It was simply that I couldn't find the forms. They're printed, you see – we don't have an online version. It's antediluvian, I know, but the Society doesn't claim to be at the forefront, technologically speaking. It's ironical, I suppose, considering that some of the most forward-thinking scientists and artists of the past were members."

"Couldn't he wait for you to find the form? Or come back another time?"

"He said that the work was urgent and he'd already driven over from Holbeach. And I knew that he had personal reasons for needing to get away by lunchtime."

"What sort of personal reasons?"

"They're – confidential," said Alex. She glanced at Tom, who was regarding her quizzically. "I don't mean confidential as far as I'm concerned," she added. "Edmund confided a personal problem to me that he needed to sort out this afternoon and I feel that I should respect his confidence."

"Fine for now," said Tim, "but if we feel later that revealing whatever it is may be instrumental to this enquiry we shall expect you to do so. After he'd gone, what did you do?"

"I spent some time recreating the form in digital version – I found some that had already been filled in – so that I would be able to print it out and ask him to sign when I saw him again."

"You expected that to be later this morning?"

"Yes. I thought that he would come back to the Society before lunch, to return the key. I worked on my summer events programme until midday and, when Edmund had still not appeared, I decided to walk to Broad Street, taking a form with me, so that I could at the same time ask him to sign it and to return the key before he left. I knew that he would not be able to stay into the afternoon."

"Because of the 'personal problem' that you've described?"

"Yes."

"Did you see him?"

"Yes, he was just leaving. He wanted to borrow one of the files of papers."

"Did you say that he could?"

Alex gave a short laugh. Tim could not tell whether it was meant to be relaxed or ironical.

"Yes, against my better judgment."

"Why do you say that?"

"Because he should have asked the trustees for permission to take something away from the archive; and also to sign another form and, if necessary, to take out insurance, before he did so. Those are the Society's rules. It's obvious why they exist."

"But you let him take the papers anyway?"

"Yes."

"Even though you had misgivings about it?"

"Yes."

"Can you explain why?"

"No, not exactly. It was partly because Edmund was in such a hurry – he seemed flustered and I allowed myself to become flustered, too. And partly because I felt sorry for him – I didn't wish to put even more difficulties in his way."

"You mean, besides his personal ones?"

"Yes."

"So he left with the papers. What did you do?"

"I went back to the office and carried on working on the summer programme."

"Did you receive any visitors or take any telephone calls?"

"No."

"Did you make any calls yourself?"

"No. That is, only to Edmund."

"Why did you call him?"

"Because I'd forgotten to ask him to return the key to the archive. I was – I am – worried about that. I shouldn't have let him have it and, although it's unlikely that anyone else will want access to the chapel before I can get the key back, I could get into trouble with the trustees if they find out that the key is missing."

"I see. How many times did you call Edmund Baker?"

"Three or four."

"At his office?"

"No, I knew he wouldn't be there this afternoon. I called his mobile. I wasn't actually expecting him to be able to reply until later this afternoon or this evening. I knew that he'd be busy. I left several messages for him."

"All messages about the key?"

"Yes."

"They all said more or less the same thing?"

"Yes."

"Why did you call him so many times? Did you doubt that he would get back to you?"

"No, not really. But although I didn't want to sound panicky, I wanted him to understand the seriousness of the situation – that it was serious for me, anyway."

"Has he been in touch with you yet?"

"No. At least, I don't think so."

"Why do you say that?"

"Because after I found the – whatever it is on the kitchen wall – the telephone rang. I answered it and the caller rang off – I may not have got to it in time. But then my mobile started ringing and I answered it immediately, but again the caller rang off. It was an undisclosed number."

"You think that it might have been Mr Baker?"

"It could have been."

"We can check that later. If you don't mind, I'd like you to continue with your account of your day. You say that you worked all afternoon on your summer programme and, apart from yourself breaking off to make the calls to Mr Baker, there were no interruptions. When did you leave your office?"

"At about five-thirty. I don't know exactly, but it can't have been much after that."

"And you walked straight home?"

"Yes."

"It can't have taken you more than ten minutes to get back here from the Archaeological Society."

"It is about a ten-minute walk. I may have taken a little longer, because I stopped to call Edmund once more on my way. But that won't have held me up for more than a minute or two."

"I'm sorry to ask this question of you, too – but is there any possibility that you were being followed?"

"No, I don't think so. I stopped to lean against the wall at the top of the passage while I found Edmund's number and I'd have noticed if anyone had been hovering close to me. When I got no reply, I didn't bother to record a further message. I put the phone away and walked down Chapel Lane until I saw that the yard gate was open."

"That worried you?"

"Yes."

"What did you do?"

"I did something quite out of character, actually. I spoke to a stranger, someone I'd never seen before. A woman – an elderly woman – asked me if I was OK and I told her that I knew that something was wrong because of the open gate."

"What did she say?"

"She tried to comfort me, in a vague sort of way. She clearly thought that I was mentally ill, or at least overwrought. She asked if my husband was at home and suggested that I should go in and put my feet up while he made me a cup of tea."

"That was rather strange advice, wasn't it, under the circumstances? And quite a coincidence that your husband had been there a few minutes earlier, hoping to do almost exactly what she suggested?"

"It didn't occur to me that she was strange. I was much more preoccupied with the open gate."

"Would you recognise her again? Or be able to piece together an Identikit picture of her?"

"Possibly," said Alex doubtfully.

"Did she definitely walk away?"

"Yes. She hovered for a while, I thought to make sure that I was all right, and then she walked away towards the town centre – very slowly, but she was quite old."

"And despite your fear, you decided that you would go into the yard and continue up the steps to the flat."

"Yes."

"Can you tell me why you were so afraid? After all, at this stage, all you had found was the open gate. It could easily have been left open by mistake, by one of the building society people, or by Tom in a hurry."

Alex paused.

"It's just one of several things that I don't have an explanation for that have happened to me recently. They're probably not connected – they're probably all coincidences – but they've made me more jumpy than usual."

"I'm not much of a believer in coincidences," said Tim. "Can you give us more detail?"

"Yes, can you?" said Tom. "It's the first I knew about it." His tone was suspicious. Alex flushed. Tim thought for a moment that she was embarrassed, but it became apparent that her face was instead bright with anger.

"You did know," she said tautly. "I told you about the episode in the passageway. You were too preoccupied with your precious juvenile delinquents to take it in."

Tom opened his mouth to retaliate, but Tim interrupted him.

"Tell me what happened in the passageway," he said. "And about the other incidents as well. You say there were several?"

"Yes," said Alex. She was already embarrassed by her bad-tempered retort. "The first was at the conference – at the hotel that you visited to interview Oliver Sparham. I was standing on my balcony early in the morning and someone was smoking a cigarette beneath it – just out of my sight. I wouldn't have believed it to have any significance, if a message had not arrived on my breakfast tray. It said 'Be Careful'."

"I'm sure you didn't tell me about *that*," said Tom.

"I probably didn't. At the time, I thought that it was just an ill-bred comment from one of the Society delegates – there had been some kind of altercation about paying for wine the night before, which I'd had to sort out. But when I thought about it afterwards – after the episode in the passageway – I decided that perhaps it had been intended as something more personal, more specifically directed towards me."

"What happened in the passageway?"

"I'd been at a meeting with Edmund Baker and came back late in the evening. It was dark in Chapel Lane and I dropped my keys in the gutter – it had been raining and the keys had dropped into flowing water, so I was anxious to retrieve them quickly. As I bent down, someone threw a cigarette end into the water, just in front of me. It could have hit me. I looked round quickly, but I couldn't see anyone. They may have been hiding in the chapel doorway – I didn't wait to find out. I just let myself in as quickly as possible. Tom came out of the kitchen and stood at the top of the steps almost immediately afterwards."

"Do you recall this now, sir? If so, did you see anything?" Tim asked Tom.

"Yes, I do remember it, but Alex didn't tell me about the cigarette until we were inside."

"You didn't go out again to look?"

"No. She was tired and as far as I was concerned it was an isolated incident. I thought that it might have been teenagers playing a prank or even just a passing drunk who hadn't noticed her and had pitched the cigarette end into the dark."

"So, if you're right about their being connected, there were three incidents altogether? There were no others?"

Alex shook her head, but did not meet Tim's eye. It crossed his mind that she was hiding something. Alex was thinking that she should tell him about the cigarette smoker who had frightened Edmund when they had visited his secret place, but she knew that this was impossible while Tom was there. Even if he hadn't been present, she didn't want this policeman to suspect that her relationship with Edmund was anything more than professional. It could only cause trouble.

"What do you think, Detective Inspector? Do you think that someone was threatening Alex with these incidents?"

"It's difficult to say. Aside from the break-in, the note is the most concrete evidence that someone was trying to frighten you. Do you still have it?"

"I'm not sure – I think so. If I've kept it, it will be in my office, with the other papers from the conference."

"Perhaps you might look for it tomorrow. I'll drop by for it, or DC Armstrong will. So, where were we? You climbed the steps to the flat and found the kitchen door open. Was it wide open?"

"Yes, it was bent right back on its hinge."

"You were already afraid by then, but you still went into the kitchen?"

"Yes."

"Why didn't you try to get help?"

"It honestly didn't occur to me. And I wanted to know if Tom was there; I thought that it was possible he'd been taken ill. That could have explained why the gate and the door were both open."

"What happened when you entered the kitchen?"

"I called Tom's name, but there was no answer. Then the phone started ringing. I didn't know whether I should answer it. I couldn't see it, for one thing; I needed to turn on the light and I couldn't decide whether or not this was a wise thing to do. So I hesitated for a few moments and then turned it on. The phone stopped ringing as I picked up the receiver, but almost immediately my mobile started instead. I answered it pretty quickly, but the line went dead. And then I saw Tom's note, saying that he would be late."

"Did you notice the marks on the kitchen wall at that point?"

"No. I was still thinking about Tom – even though I also thought that there might still be an intruder in the flat, I wanted to make sure that Tom wasn't here. I looked in every room, but of course I didn't find him; there was no evidence that anyone had been in any of the rooms, either. As I said when we spoke on the phone, there is nothing missing or out of place. If it weren't for that horrible mess on the wall, I should believe that Tom was mistaken and that he had left the place wide open in a fit of absent-mindedness."

"So, having searched every room, you returned to the kitchen?"

"Yes. And that was when I noticed the bloodstains – or whatever they are – on the wall."

"You can't therefore be certain that they weren't put there while you were searching the other rooms?"

"No – but I assume . . ."

"Since Mr Tarrant also says that he did not see them when he was in the kitchen a few minutes earlier, we can't discount this as a possibility. Could someone have been hiding in the outside area when you came up the steps?"

"Yes – I suppose so; it would be possible for someone to conceal themselves behind the garden furniture – or simply to walk across from the outside area of the maisonette next door."

"Isn't there a wall between the two properties?"

"Yes, but it isn't high: it's more of a boundary marker than anything. We've never tried to cross it, and neither have the people in the other maisonette, as far as I'm aware, but only because we've never had reason to. But, my God, the thought of someone out there while I was inside makes my blood run cold!"

"What did you do when you saw the stain on the wall?"

"I screamed. It was another reaction that is quite out of character for me. It had some effect, though, because the young couple who live next door came to see if I was all right."

"Do you know them?"

"I didn't until today. But they've left their name and telephone number. They were very helpful; they called Tom for me."

"Why didn't they stay with you?"

"The young woman did stay, sir, until I arrived," said Juliet. "Her husband is a chef – he had to go to work."

"So you have their details?"

"Yes, sir. Their names are Steve and Wendy Allsop. As Mrs Tarrant says, they've left their telephone number."

"We'll need to see them again this evening," said Tim. "We don't want this story going the rounds, if we can help it. Mrs Tarrant, thank you for giving us so much detail. You've been extremely helpful. I'm afraid that we're going to have to bring a Scene of Crime forensics team here now." He turned to include Tom in the conversation. "Is there anyone that you can stay with tonight? It is likely to be noisy and uncomfortable for you, even if they start with your bedroom."

"There's a colleague that I can ask," said Tom. "I mean Marie," he added to Alex. She nodded.

"I suggest that you tell her as little as possible about what has happened," said Tim. "In particular, please don't reveal any specific details, for example about the open gate and door, or the smearing on the wall. Particularly not that. Please also be prepared to talk to us again tomorrow. We have your mobile numbers – we'll contact you again as soon as we can. Juliet, could I have a brief word?"

"Of course, sir."

She followed him out of the kitchen and down the area steps to the yard.

"I am going to stay here to brief the SOCOs. I'd be grateful if you would call on Mrs Allsop and also find out when it will be possible to talk to her husband. I'd like you to see him tonight, as well, if you can."

Juliet nodded.

"What do you make of all of this?" he asked.

"I'm not sure. I think that Mrs Tarrant is telling the truth, yet she also seems to be holding something back – if that makes sense, sir."

"I agree. Have you noticed how often Edmund Baker seems to crop up in her life – at least in the version of it that she gave to us?"

"Yes, sir; but they work in the same profession. It could just be coincidence."

"There are too many coincidences in this case. The Tarrants have links to Claudia McRae and to Thobias Padgett, as well. As a police force, we're conducting two major investigations at the moment, and they seem to be involved – apparently as innocent parties – in both of them. Don't you think that that's odd?" Without waiting for her reply, he added: "Tomorrow, I think that I'll pay a visit to Mr Edmund Baker."

CHAPTER THIRTY-SEVEN

Detective Inspector Tim Yates arrived at the station at 7.30 a.m. the next morning. His intention had been to go straight on to the flat in Chapel Lane to wait for the SOCOs, who were scheduled to turn up at the start of their working day. He felt relatively happy and well-rested; he had reached home the previous evening to find Katrin in bed and sleeping, as he had expected. After some deliberation, he had eschewed the spare room and undressed as soundlessly as he could to climb in beside her. She had stirred a little and curled herself against him in her usual way. Although by the time he woke in the morning she had turned away from him and was stretched out precariously close to the edge of the bed, this was her normal behaviour. He got up quickly, without disturbing her; she was clearly in need of a lot of sleep at the moment.

Tim sensed that some of the accord, if not the passion, was returning to their marriage. As long as she did not hold some deep grudge against him, as long as the marriage itself was secure, he felt that he could tackle any other catastrophe. He would take Katrin to a really nice restaurant in the evening: try to discover what was troubling her. He berated himself a little for the clodhopperish way in which he had tried to force confidences from her yesterday evening, but self-immolation was not his forte. His mood was again sanguine as he swung the BMW into the station yard.

His bright plans for the day proved to be short-lived. He had yet to reach his office when he was waylaid by Superintendent Thornton.

"Ah, Yates, could you come to my office? Would you care for some tea?" Thornton added, swivelling his eyes across to the open-plan office area inhabited by Tim's team. The desks were all empty. "It looks as if we shall have to make it ourselves," he added.

Tim grinned. "That's all right, sir, I'm happy to do it," he said, more to save himself from having to drink the Superintendent's tea than to avoid impairing Thornton's dignity. "I'll be up with it shortly, if you'd care to go on ahead."

Superintendent Thornton nodded approval.

Tim was still waiting for the kettle to boil when Juliet Armstrong came into the kitchen.

"Want a cup?" he asked. She shook her head. "My mother's staying at the moment, so I'm awash with tea," she said. "I've got a bit of paperwork to do, but I think that when it gets to 9 o'clock I'll go to the Archaeological Society to take a formal statement from Alex Tarrant."

"Good idea. See if you can get more out of her than we did last night. I'm sure that she's holding something back. Talk to her some more about Edmund Baker, if you can make it seem relevant and not too prying. I'm sure you'll know how to handle it subtly."

"Thank you," said Juliet. Tim did not miss the irony in her tone. "Do you really think that she's in danger, sir?"

"It's difficult to say. I must say I'm very uneasy about the blood smear. I'm going to put a policeman on duty at the Archaeological Society for a few days, at least until the smear has been analysed, but you know as well as I do that if we can't get any direct proof that someone's threatening her, I'll have to stand him down again. Thornton will be the first to point out that we don't have the staff to put on protection details unless we can make a very compelling case. As it is, I won't be able to extend the protection to evenings and nights. Let's hope that husband of hers doesn't get so engrossed in his work that he fails to come home at a reasonable hour."

"Quite," said Juliet, smirking.

"Talking of Thornton, I'm supposed to be taking him some tea."

"That's very noble of you."

"Not really. He would have asked you if you'd been here – I could see he was casting around for you. He wants to see me about something, so I'd better get up there."

Tim seized the two mugs of tea that he'd made while they were talking.

"Good luck!" Juliet called after him.

"There you are!" said Superintendent Thornton. "I thought you'd been milking the cow." He laughed at his own witticism. "Shut the door, Yates. And sit down. Tell me, what are your plans for the day?"

"You'll have seen the summary report that I e-mailed last night, sir, about the break-in at the flat in Chapel Lane. I'm convinced it's connected with the Claudia McRae case. I thought I'd go there first to see how the SOCOs are getting on. Then I plan to go back to Helpston, to interview Guy Maichment again. He's Claudia McRae's nephew."

"I'm aware of who he is. I've read your reports and I've got his name from Roy Little, as I told you yesterday. As you know, I'm keen for you to get on with the McRae case; progress on it has been far too slow so far. Far too slow. But there's something else that I want you to do before you tackle Mr Maichment. You can leave the SOCOs to their own devices; you know that they won't want you there and it's unlikely you'll get any results from their work today."

Tim was annoyed. He wanted to ask the SOCOs some particular questions about the blood stains – or whatever they were – and he was afraid that the evidence might be destroyed without providing the answers unless he intervened.

"What is it you want me for, sir?" he asked blandly. Long experience had taught him not to challenge Thornton's instructions head-on.

"There was an incident at a level crossing early yesterday evening. Mac-Fadyen has written a short report and circulated it, but you may not have picked it up yet."

"I saw it in my in-box, sir, but I haven't read it."

"Well, I suggest that you do so now. A woman got out of a car that was waiting at the crossing and threw herself into the path of an oncoming train."

"Jesus! Was she killed?"

"What do you think? At first it looked like a straightforward suicide, if there is such a thing. Her husband said that she just got out of the car before he could stop her and ran towards the train. Apparently the woman – her name was Krystyna Baker – had a history of mental illness and was very depressed. In fact, she and the husband had just been to see a doctor when the incident occurred."

"I'm not sure why you need me to get involved in this, sir. Isn't it a job for the coroner?"

"It would be, if it weren't for the fact that a young lad has since come forward to say that both the woman and the man got out of the car and that she appeared to be running away from him. The lad couldn't say whether or not she was pushed, though he thought she might have been. Whether she was or not, his testimony certainly raises the possibility that either she was murdered outright or her death was engineered. But there are further complications."

"Yes, sir?" said Tim, thinking that Thornton had introduced plenty of 'complications' already.

"The lad in question is an inmate of the children's home in Sleaford. It appears that his talents include embroidery of the truth."

"Should we take any notice of his statement, in that case?"

"I think we have to be reasonably sure that there is no substance in it before we dismiss it out of hand. We'll need to interview the train driver and anyone else who was near the front of the train when it happened. British Transport police have already taken an initial statement from the train driver – he was pretty shocked last night, as you can imagine – but they're seeing him again today, and I've asked MacFadyen to sit in on it. I've also asked him to try to get further witness statements from the train passengers. Fortunately the transport police had the presence of mind to take the details of those travelling in the first coach."

"I'm not sure what you want me to do, in that case, sir."

"Aren't you, Yates? I should have thought it was fairly obvious. I want you to interview the lad – with an appropriate adult present, of course. But, even more to the point, I want you to interview the woman's husband, see whether you think he's above board. The job should suit you; it's one for which you've had plenty of practice lately."

"I don't follow."

"The chap – the husband – is another of those archaeologists," said the Superintendent. "It's very unlikely that this incident is related to the Claudia McRae case, but I must say that these people are getting very troublesome. Who'd have thought that people who grub in the ground all the time could make such a nuisance of themselves?"

Tim would have smiled at Superintendent Thornton's latest expression of peevish outrage that a group of members of the public was not performing according to expectations if he had not been too busy putting two and two together.

"What did you say the woman's name was, sir?"

"Krystyna Baker. Krystyna's spelt in some foreign way, with a 'K' and lots of 'ys'."

"And the husband's name? Is it Edmund?"

Superintendent Thornton consulted the notes on the desk in front of him.

"Yes. Yes it is. Is he known to us already?"

"I don't think he's got a criminal record, if that's what you mean, sir; though of course we'll check. But I have met him before. You may remember that I interviewed the County Archaeologist – his name is Oliver Sparham – at the Welland Manor Hotel shortly after Claudia McRae disappeared, because he'd called in on her the day before on his way to a conference at the hotel. I was briefly introduced to Edmund Baker at the same time."

"An interesting coincidence – although, since every archaeologist in the area was probably at that event, not a very significant one."

"No. But Edmund Baker's name has cropped up again very recently. Last night, in fact, when I was taking statements from Alex Tarrant and her husband about their break-in. She mentioned Edmund Baker several times. She seems to have been seeing rather a lot of him lately."

"She's not an archaeologist as well, is she?"

"Not exactly, but she works with archaeologists: she's the Secretary of the Archaeological Society. It's in one of my McRae reports. As I said in my report of the break-in at her flat, it's the smear on the wall that concerns me. It's too similar to the one in Claudia McRae's cottage not to be connected with it. Either they were both left by the same person, or that in Mrs Tarrant's flat was daubed by someone who knew about the first one. You will recall that we didn't make information about the McRae smear public, so only a few people know of it."

"I hadn't quite realised its significance when I read your report of the break-in," said the Superintendent, with a guilty edge to his voice. Tim would have placed a bet on his not having read either report properly. "There are far too many coincidences here for my liking. I don't believe in coincidences."

"Neither do I, sir."

"Well, perhaps what we've just discovered together will make you a little more accommodating about carrying out my request to see this Edmund Baker. Do you think that Mrs Tarrant is having an affair with him?" he added in a prurient tone.

"It had crossed my mind. Either that or he's intimidating her in some way. Her husband seemed suspicious of their relationship. She herself admitted that she'd let him have access to the Society's archive and take something away from it without going through the correct procedures – though she implied that she was just doing him a favour."

Superintendent Thornton had lost interest. As Tim had observed on previous occasions, he had the attention span of a gnat.

"Yes, well go and talk to Edmund Baker, will you? There seems to be more to him than meets the eye. Show some respect for his bereavement, though. I don't want him accusing us of insensitivity."

"Of course." Tim was irritated, but tried not to show it.

"And Yates? In view of all the 'coincidences', perhaps you had better call in on the SOCOs on your way. You'll be better at spotting any further similarities between the two cases than they will. We don't want them destroying any evidence that might help to find Dame Claudia, do we?"

"No, sir. Thank you. Good idea, sir."

CHAPTER THIRTY-EIGHT

ALEX AWOKE EARLY in a room with a low ceiling. She was lying in an old-fashioned iron-framed bed covered with a patchwork quilt that smelt of joss sticks. Tom was beside her, still sleeping deeply. For a moment, she wondered where they were; then she remembered that she and Tom had turned up on Marie's doorstep late the night before, like a couple of waifs begging for a roof over their heads, and had of course been enveloped in Marie's voluminous hospitality. This included being pressed to consume rather more Portuguese brandy than was wise on an empty stomach (although, when Marie discovered that neither of them had eaten, she had also produced a huge platter of bread and cheese accompanied by various pickles), with the result that she suspected that her feeling of disorientation was not entirely caused by the trauma of the evening before and finding herself in a strange bedroom.

Tom stirred. He propped himself on one elbow.

"What was all that about Edmund Baker last night?" he said.

"I don't remember that Edmund was singled out," said Alex. "What were you thinking of in particular?"

"Nothing *particular*," said Tom truculently. "Just that it seems that every time something *non-routine* happens in your life, Edmund Baker has been there to hold your hand."

"Really?" said Alex. "I hadn't noticed. Perhaps you're right, but before you read too much into it, just understand that from my point of view, Edmund is an inconvenience. He's barely one step ahead of the other unreasonable old men that I have to deal with."

"You expect me to believe that?"

"I don't see why not. It is the truth."

"Go back to sleep, Alex, and wake up when you have a better story to tell. And stop being so naïve. I can tell you for a fact that you've convinced that policeman that you and Edmund are lovers."

"I don't care what he thinks. I can assure you, though, that if that is what he thinks, he is wrong."

"Wrong?" Tom echoed her with what was approaching a sneer.

"Just what are you saying, Tom? Because if you're accusing me of infidelity, as if things weren't bad enough already, I can tell you that I can't put up with any more. Either you believe what I say, or I go. There's no halfway house. I can't put up with you trying to pick a fight on top of everything else that has happened."

Tom's face caved in.

"I'm sorry," he said. "I don't want to put more pressure on you; of course I don't. But I don't understand your relationship with Edmund, either – or rather, I don't understand the way that it has developed over the past few months. You barely had a word to say about him before the last Archaeological Society conference. In fact, when you did mention him, I got the distinct impression that you disliked him. Now his name seems to crop up all the time and apparently you eat supper with him or go to meetings with him at the drop of a hat. Can you tell me why?"

Alex turned her head away from him.

"I don't know. It's not something that I'd noticed. I guess that at the moment we share more projects than we did in the past. It's probably just a temporary thing. I'm sorry if you've found it unsettling." Even to herself her words did not sound convincing.

Tom manifestly was not convinced, but he backed down.

"I'm sorry, too. I have no right to make unfounded accusations. I was already under pressure from the Padgett case before this break-in, or whatever it was, happened. That the police think that you might be in danger only makes it worse. Do you think that it has anything to do with Edmund?" Tom hesitated before he put the last question, but he felt compelled to ask it, even if it irritated Alex again.

"I can't think why it should, but then I have no idea what I've done to make someone want to frighten me, either."

There was a low rap at the door.

"I have brought tea," called Marie's sing-song voice. "I'll leave the tray just outside the door."

Alex smiled.

"You're too good to us, Marie," she said, raising her own voice a little. "We're not on holiday – we're not even invited guests, but gatecrashers."

"Nonsense. No gatecrashers allowed here. You are honoured guests – you would not be here otherwise. It's six-thirty," she added more briskly.

"God, is that all?" said Alex in a low voice to Tom. She collapsed back against the pillows. "We could have slept for another half-hour. I still feel exhausted."

"I'm sorry that she woke you so early, but it was because I need to get up myself. Marie and I have to leave for Sleaford in about three quarters of an hour."

"Padgetts again?"

"Yes. I'm a bit concerned about DI Yates: he said we should stay close in order to be contacted. He might be annoyed to find that I have travelled so far."

"Sleaford's not a million miles away."

"No, but I doubt if DI Yates will take that view if some copper has to be detailed to come out to me there."

"I think that's unlikely; they're more likely to summon you back to Spalding. They've got your mobile number, haven't they?"

"Yes. Now I must get up and see if the bathroom's free for me to take a shower; and I haven't brought a dressing-gown."

"Neither have I, but Marie has left one out for us." Alex gestured towards the tent-like, cerise-coloured cotton robe hanging on the back of the bedroom door.

"I'm not wearing that!"

"What choice do you have?"

"It won't fit me!"

"Of course it will. We could both get into it!"

CHAPTER THIRTY-NINE

ALEX DOZED WHILE Tom showered. She was vaguely aware of his returning to their bedroom, where he dressed quickly and left without saying goodbye to her. She was resolved to believe that this was because he did not want to disturb her rest, as she appeared to be sleeping. However, he usually kissed her, sleeping or awake, when he left for work before she did. She had a nagging fear that he had not forgotten their conversation about Edmund. She hoped that he was too preoccupied with the Padgett case to dwell on it further.

She stayed in bed for another fifteen minutes, until she heard the front door slam and footsteps retreating on the gravel outside as Tom and Marie departed. Max, Marie's boyfriend, was working away somewhere, so she knew that now she had their house to herself. She swung her legs to the side of the bed, and reached down for the dressing-gown, which Tom had tossed onto the floor. She was arranging it around her shoulders when she heard her mobile ringing. At first she could not locate where the sound was coming from; eventually, she remembered that the phone was in her handbag, which was standing on the stripped-down Victorian dressing-table that occupied one corner of the room. She snatched it out of the bag before the caller could ring off. As she did so, she saw Edmund's number come up on the screen. She looked at her watch, which she had left with her rings and earrings on the table-top the night before. It was not yet seven-thirty – well before office hours. She thanked fate that Edmund had not rung before Tom's departure, even though Tom knew that she was expecting a return call from him. Edmund must be allowed to intrude into Tom's conscious as little as possible from now on. It dawned on her at the same time that Edmund could not have been the mystery caller of the night before; she had forgotten that his mobile number was programmed into her phone.

"Edmund!" she said. "Thank you for calling me back. I'm sorry about all the messages that I left yesterday, but I was worried that you still had the key to the archive. But please do keep it today, because something dreadful has happened . . ."

"You don't know then?" Edmund's voice was dull. "I thought perhaps you might have watched the local news, either last night or this morning."

"No, I haven't had the chance. Was there something about the break-in? I'm surprised, because I thought that the police were trying to keep it as quiet as possible."

"What break-in? I don't know about a break-in!" It would have been the same old peevish Edmund of before their affair, if he hadn't also sounded so weary. Alex reflected with grim humour that they appeared to be entirely at cross-purposes with each other. Perhaps this had always been the case. She decided to humour him. He obviously had no time for her troubles at present.

"What should I have heard about on the news?"

Edmund sighed deeply, and said in a very low voice: "About Krystyna. I went with her to the psychiatrist yesterday afternoon – I took her in the car. We had something of a . . . of a disagreement on the way home, when the car was standing at a level crossing, and she jumped out. She ducked under the barrier and threw herself under an oncoming train."

"She's dead?"

"What do you think? Most people come off worse when they pick a fight with hundreds of tons of steel travelling towards them at sixty miles an hour."

"Oh, Edmund, I'm so sorry!"

"Are you? Perhaps you should have thought of that before you led me on. She told the shrink that she suspected me of having an affair. I denied it, of course."

Alex did not protest against the accusation. She had a more important matter to address.

"Did she say that she thought you were having an affair *with me*?"

"No. If she had her suspicions, she didn't say so. It wouldn't have been like her to make wild accusations. Why do you ask? Are you worried that she might have got in touch with your precious Tom?"

"The thought did cross my mind, mainly because of something that Tom himself said today."

"Well, he won't find any proof now, whatever he may think."

"No, though we must be careful in the future."

Edmund groaned.

"I don't think that we have a future, to be honest, Alex, do you? I'm not sure that we ever did. It was just a sour dream, a silly make-believe relationship. And I'm ashamed of it now that Krystyna's dead. I wouldn't want to insult her memory by carrying it any further."

"I agree entirely," said Alex, though she was smarting at his sanctimonious tone and more than a little aggrieved that she had allowed him to take the initiative in breaking off their liaison. She told herself to be more gracious. Edmund had just suffered bereavement, after all, and in the most horrific of circumstances. That he was feeling guilty about the shortcomings of his relationship with his wife was perfectly natural.

"What were you saying about a break-in?"

"Someone broke into our flat last night, just before I got home from work. Tom wasn't there – he was working."

"Did they take anything?"

"Not as far as we can tell. The police have sealed it off as a crime scene, so we've had to spend the night with one of Tom's colleagues."

"A *crime scene*? Why?"

"I – I can't say."

"It seems a bit extreme, for a burglary, especially one in which nothing was apparently stolen. I've been burgled myself in the past and usually it's difficult enough even to get them to take it seriously. There must be some reason why they're taking it to such extremes."

"I suppose there must," said Alex. "I'm not an expert on the law. Talking of rules, though, I'd really appreciate it if you could get the key of the archive back to me by tomorrow. As you know, I broke several of the Society's rules by letting you take it and the file. I'm sorry to ask you for it when you have so much on your plate; you can post it to me if you prefer."

"Yes, Alex, I'll post it to you," said Edmund shortly. "Of course, it's absolutely the most important thing on my mind at the moment." His tone was vicious. "I'll do it now." Before she could reply there was a quiet click and silence.

CHAPTER FORTY

EDMUND BAKER LIVED in a tall, three-storey Edwardian terrace on the main Spalding to Holbeach road. The houses were built of red brick elaborately faced with stone and decorated with wooden gables and finials. They resembled old-fashioned dolls' houses and were sometimes disparagingly called the 'dolly houses' by the residents of the far less grand private housing estate that now abutted them. The builder who had bought the plot in 1908 had been planning to live in one of the houses himself and had chosen it because at the time it had been on the extreme outskirts of Holbeach, overlooking the fields, but now it was surrounded by other streets and very much part of the town. There were eight houses in the terrace, each one fronted by a small garden with a straight path to the front door.

Edmund's house was number seven, second to the end nearest to the town. It looked less well-cared-for than the others. The black-and-white paintwork was shabby and blistering in places; the garden contained several drooping standard roses, unsupported and in urgent need of rescue from the burgeoning weeds.

Tim had checked the extent to which Edmund had already been subjected to police questioning since his wife's death. As Superintendent Thornton had unnecessarily pointed out, it was essential that he should tread carefully, and not just for compassionate reasons. If Edmund Baker had committed a crime, he must not be given the opportunity to put up a smokescreen of righteous indignation by playing the bereaved husband. Luckily for Tim, the desk sergeant at Holbeach police station had told him that the statement that had been taken from Edmund on the previous evening was 'adequate for an accident' (whatever that meant), so there would be no more need for the local police to disturb Mr Baker unless further evidence emerged. No-one had called on him today. Of course, he would still have to attend the inquest when it took place.

The desk sergeant offered to e-mail the statement to Tim, but he had already received it from Superintendent Thornton. It had struck him as a peculiarly detached and desiccated account of the violent death of a spouse, but that might partly be accounted for by the stolid prose of the policeman who had written it.

Taking his cue from other residents of the terrace, he parked the BMW half on, half off the pavement. He got out and stood looking up at the six front windows of the house for a minute or so. He could discern no sign of life, but that did not mean that Edmund Baker might not be standing back from one of the elegantly-narrow upstairs windows and watching. Tim opened the rickety gate to number seven and made the short walk (about three strides in his case) to the substantial front door, which was protected from the elements by a small porch. A door-pull hung against one of the pillars of the porch. It was apparently of pre-Great War vintage, but proved still to be in sombre working order. He yanked it, and after some seconds heard its dirge-like bell tolling deep inside the house.

Tim was about to mount the step to the porch when his foot encountered something soft and crinkly. Looking down, he saw three or four slender sprays of flowers done up in cellophane. He took hold of the card attached to one of them. 'From the Reynolds next door', it said. 'Sleep well, Mrs Baker'. He was in the process of flipping over one of the other cards, which also had 'Mrs Baker' handwritten at the top of it, when the massive and rather grubby black-painted door opened abruptly. A man of middle height and stocky build with thick white hair and piercing blue eyes emerged from the house and came to stand opposite him in the porch. As Tim was still standing on the path, he was unable to look Edmund Baker in the face without peering up at him, an experience that he found a little disconcerting. Their eyes met. Edmund gave him a stony look and then shifted his gaze to the flowers.

"My God!" he said. "Whoever put those there? What an extraordinary idea! Why didn't they ring the bell or, more to the point, wait until the funeral?"

"I think that they're meant as a tribute to Mrs Baker, sir – they're intended to show sympathy for her, and for you. And my guess is that your neighbours didn't want to intrude by ringing the bell."

"From the neighbours, are they? Probably just being nosy in that case. Talking of which, who are you and why have you come? I think I've seen you before somewhere, haven't I? Are you from the undertaker's?"

Tim produced his identity card.

"Detective Inspector Tim Yates, South Lincolnshire Police," he said, feeling like a parrot. How many times did he say this during the course of a single week? He wondered if he could have a tape-recoding of it made, perhaps one that would play when he pressed a button on his key-ring.

"I thought I'd seen you before. You came to talk to Oliver Sparham after Claudia disappeared, didn't you? At the conference?"

"Yes," said Tim. "But I don't recollect that we were introduced."

"We weren't. You were too busy listening to Oliver's story and being impressed with Alex Tarrant. Why are you here now? Is it something more to do with Claudia?"

"No. It's closer to home than that, Mr Baker. I'd like to ask you a few more questions about exactly what happened to your wife yesterday. I'm sorry to bother you with this again – I realise that you've already made a statement to the police, which I've read, and I know that talking about her . . . accident again must be distressing for you. Please accept my condolences for your loss. Evidently your wife was a well-respected lady." Tim gestured at the flowers.

"Yes, well if they'd shown how much they valued her a bit earlier, perhaps she'd still be with us now. I can't think what more there is to say about the episode and I certainly don't want to stand out here and talk about it. You'd better come in."

"Thank you, sir," said Tim. "Should I gather these up for you?"

"What? No, leave them where they are for the moment. I think that's what they want, isn't it? To be allowed their ostentatious display of 'sympathy'? Otherwise there'd be no point in doing it."

Tim decided not to argue with Edmund Baker's views on neighbourliness. He had more important things to discuss and did not wish to start an irrelevant argument. He stepped over the flowers, standing awkwardly as he held out his hand for Edmund Baker to shake. Edmund touched his fingertips briefly before turning away. He disappeared into the house so quickly that Tim was afraid that the door would close again if he did not himself leap through it with speed.

He found himself standing in a small rectangular hallway with a black-and-white tiled floor. There was a strong musty smell. It was quite dark; a single dim light bulb was set in the high ceiling, its modest effort diminished further by its heavy dark-red shade. Tim's eyes took a short while to accustom themselves to the gloom. Gradually he made out a staircase rising precipitately almost immediately in front of him. Beside it was a narrow passageway with two doors leading off to the right and another at the end of it. He took in that the décor was dingy in the extreme before refocusing quickly on his host. Edmund Baker was well ahead of him now and disappearing into the second of the two rooms on the right. Tim hurried after him. By the time that he reached the door, it was closing slowly. Tim reached it in time to stop the catch from fastening and knocked gently.

"Mr Baker? May I come in?"

"Don't be ridiculous!" said Edmund Baker, flinging wide the door again. "Of course! Why do you think that I have come in here?"

It was a good question, Tim thought, and not one that he could easily answer after he had entered the room and taken in what faced him there.

His senses were assailed with a witch's brew of filth and foul smells. As a policeman of some ten years' standing, he had had plenty of first-hand experience of domestic squalor, but rarely at such sordid levels, and never before in a house like this. He was confronted with the kind of unsavoury turmoil that he had come to associate with drugs squats or the houses from which the very elderly, after years of trying to cope on their own, were finally persuaded into care. Crumpled sheets of newspaper, used cups and plates (some still bearing the congealed remains of meals), half-empty wine and medicine bottles and fast-food packaging were jumbled together on the floor and on all the available flat surfaces. Closer scrutiny revealed that the debris was even more unpleasant than he had first thought; the heaps of detritus also contained used sticking plasters, piles of dirty clothes, and opened cat-food tins. The single sofa bore an unsteady pile of books and magazines topped with a yellow tea-towel that had been folded like a bandana. It was encrusted with something dried-on and dark. Trails of spilt liquids criss-crossed the floor tiles. The stench of decay was over-powering.

Edmund Baker responded to the surprise that Tim could not conceal with a look of sardonic amusement.

"Not a pretty sight, is it? I must apologise for bringing you in here. Unfortunately, the kitchen is even worse. You do know, I take it, that my wife had been clinically depressed for some time before her death?"

"I saw in your statement that when she died you were returning together from a visit to a psychiatrist. I'm also aware that severely-depressed women sometimes cease to take an interest in themselves or their homes. Was there no-one who could help her when she became ill?" It was the most tactful way he could devise of asking Edmund why he himself had not attempted to put right the worst of the disorder and, indeed, to insinuate the question of whether he had attempted to support his wife in any way whatsoever.

"Our sons both left home some time ago. In spite of the flowers outside, she was not on intimate terms with the neighbours. I work long hours myself, whereas, after her retirement from a part-time teaching post it was her job to maintain the house. We had a cleaner when she was working." The final sentence sounded defensive; all the same, Edmund Baker evidently thought that his insistence on maintaining this division of labour was justified, and not negotiable in the event of illness. "I must admit, though," he added, half to himself, "I hadn't realised quite how bad a state the downstairs rooms were in. I've been out in the evenings a lot lately and my office is upstairs. The upstairs of the house is in better order; she was still changing the beds, for example." Tim noted his use of the plural.

"When did you first become aware of your wife's illness, sir?"

"This time around, two or three weeks ago. She told me of it herself – she's been depressed before, and recognised the symptoms. If she hadn't told me I'd still have found out, because she was close to both her mother and her sister and they are very interfering."

"Did you notice nothing wrong yourself, sir?"

"Not exactly. Krystyna could at no point during our marriage have been described as an upbeat person and she'd been subdued on and off ever since she retired. In retrospect, retirement wasn't a wise move for her. She'd been complaining of fatigue and she was only a couple of years off pensionable age – though she had neglected to pay into the pension fund, so there was nothing to lose on that score. I didn't stand in her way, therefore, when she said that she wanted to pack in. You behold the result."

"Would you say that you were on good terms?"

"As good as most people who've been married as long as we have. When she wasn't depressed, I still enjoyed her company, up to a point. I must admit that her depressed moods irritated me. I thought that she should pull herself together – engage in some useful activity to give point to her life. I don't just mean catching up with the housework, obviously. I wouldn't say that we were close, if that's what you mean."

"Did you talk to her doctor?"

"No. She saw the doctor on her own. It was only when she was referred to the psychiatrist that I got involved. I offered to go with her to keep the appointment."

"Understandably, you were concerned about her health?"

"Yes, of course I was. I also wanted to make sure that she wasn't being sold down the river by the guy. He wasn't available on the NHS and I didn't want her to rack up massive bills unless he could convince me that he was doing her some good."

"Indeed. Can you talk me through the events of yesterday afternoon? Were you here with her all day?"

"No. I was working in the morning. I was . . . I had to go to Spalding on business. I promised Krystyna I'd get back here in time to drive her to the psychiatrist. I knew it would take us more than half an hour to get there. Her appointment was for 3 p.m. and I think I got back here just after two."

"Where is the psychiatrist based?"

"At Rauceby." Edmund's face reassumed the same defiant expression that it had presented when Tim had first entered the room. Tim was aware that this was because Rauceby was a mental hospital for severely-disturbed patients, and that Edmund would know that he knew it.

"She was a voluntary patient?"

"Yes, obviously; otherwise she wouldn't have been allowed home. She was just an outpatient. But I think that this time the doctor might have sectioned her – for her own good – if she hadn't agreed to treatment. As I said, she had a history of depression. She was actually an inmate at Rauceby some years back, when she was 'ill' the first time round."

"Did you stay with her when she saw the psychiatrist – what is his name, by the way? I understand from what you've said already that it was a man?"

"No. He wanted to see her on her own. He said that she'd be less inhibited without me and that was how he always worked, in any case

– on a one-to-one basis with the patients. But I insisted that he saw me afterwards, to give me a reasonable account of his diagnosis. His name is Dr Bertolasso."

"Oh, yes. As it happens, I've met him myself. He was very helpful with a case that I was working on last year. He was working at Birmingham University then."

Edmund was plainly annoyed by this revelation. He shrugged.

"I'm glad that you found him so amenable. Don't ask me to explain the terms of his employment – he may hold several jobs, for all I know. I noticed last time Krystyna went there that the more eminent staff were the ones who only showed up occasionally. More than one iron in the fire, no doubt."

"What was his diagnosis? A brief summary will do – I don't want to ask you to betray any specific confidences."

"You can be quite sure that I wouldn't. She was my wife, after all," said Edmund sanctimoniously. "He agreed that she was depressed – he hardly needed his string of fancy qualifications to be able to tell me that. He also said that she was suffering from acute anxiety. Apparently the two conditions – depression and anxiety – are not the same, though they're often related. Depression can sometimes exist without anxiety and vice versa. He said that the anxiety might prove harder to treat than the depression and that medication – for both – was the only option, as she'd already had electric shock treatment. Apparently, they can't repeat that."

Tim nodded. Although he had no training in psychiatry, he was an enthusiastic student of psychology, and knew that what Edmund Baker was saying had the ring of authenticity.

"Did he give her a prescription while you were there?"

"Yes; and afterwards we collected it from the pharmacy at the hospital. I was keen for her to start the treatment as soon as possible."

"May I see the drugs?"

"They're still in my car. I'll get them for you when you leave. She didn't take any of them. There wasn't time."

"Was Mrs Baker with you when you talked to Dr Bertolasso?"

"No. As I've said, I wanted to see him on my own. Krystyna waited in the anteroom outside his office."

"Did you discuss his diagnosis when you began the drive home?"

"No. She was quite unreachable. I tried talking to her about general things – the weather, what we might have for supper – but she barely answered me. At first she just stared straight ahead of her; then she turned her head away, so I couldn't see her expression, and looked out of the window."

"Did she say anything at all during the journey?"

"Nothing beyond some mechanical 'yes' and 'no' answers to my com-

ments. I'd given up trying to engage with her long before we reached Holbeach."

"Would you say that there was an atmosphere in the car?"

"I don't really know what you mean by that. The situation was quite
tense, I suppose, as you may imagine, under the circumstances. We didn't
have a row as such, but the barrier between us was as great as if there had
been one, if you see what I mean."

"I do see," said Tim, sadly. There was a pause. He was aware that
Edmund Baker was scrutinising him and he pulled himself together. Their
situations were not comparable; he must not make the mistake of identifying with the man before him.

"I know that this is painful for you," he continued more briskly, "but
can you tell me what happened when you reached the level crossing?"

"Of course." There was a curious flatness to Edmund Baker's tone
which made Tim think again of the statement that he had provided to the
Holbeach police. Perhaps it was his way of coping with grief.

"We were approaching the crossing, but some way off, when the lights
started flashing. There were two vehicles ahead of us. The first of these,
a small car, could definitely have got through, but its driver was cautious
and halted. The other vehicle was a lorry – not a juggernaut, just a local
delivery lorry. I think that it was carrying builders' materials. Of course it
had to stop as well, as did we."

"Did you or Mrs Baker say anything to each other at that point?"

"I think I may have made some exclamation of annoyance. As I've
explained, I wanted to get her home and started on the medication. I'm
pretty sure that she didn't respond."

"And then she just got out of the car?"

"Yes."

"Were her movements hasty or panicky, or did she just get out as
usual?"

"The latter. But it was still an odd thing to do. She had no reason to get
out that I knew of."

"You're quite sure of that, sir?"

"What are you implying? Yes, quite sure." The last words were uttered
with some emphasis.

"And then she walked up to the crossing – or did she run?"

"She walked – she was walking quickly, but not running."

"And you just sat in the car and watched her?"

"Yes, at first. I wasn't really watching her – I was just shocked for
a moment, totally surprised by her behaviour. Surprised into a kind of
temporary inertia. I couldn't see her once she had rounded the near side
of the lorry."

"What did you think she was going to do?"

"I really had no idea. But then I heard the train coming and I was suddenly very scared of what she might do . . . what she might intend to do."

"So then you got out of the car yourself. Did you run towards her?"

"I ran towards where I thought she was. I had to approach her from the other side of the lorry. When I drew level with the cab, I could see her on the other side of the small car – it was a little Fiesta. She was almost at the barrier. I ran towards her and she ducked under it." He closed his eyes, though his voice remained curiously flat. "There was nothing that I could have done."

"So you didn't touch her?"

"I reached out towards her, but she was already through the barrier."

"Thank you, sir. I apologise again for putting you through this. I understand that the woman in the car was unable to corroborate your version of events?"

"So I believe. She told the police that she could see what was going to happen and simply hid her face in her hands."

"The lorry driver couldn't confirm the details, either. He said that he had been reading his newspaper."

"I believe that that is what he said. I wasn't looking at him. There is no reason to doubt that he is telling the truth, though, is there?"

"No reason at all, sir. But, as neither he nor the lady driver saw what happened in Mrs Baker's final moments, we may have to rely on your account."

"Is there any reason why you shouldn't?"

Tim gave him an appraising look.

"None that I am aware of, as yet," he said. "I'm very grateful for sparing me so much time, Mr Baker. I've nearly finished now; there's just one more thing. Again, forgive my insensitivity: when you came home, did you find a note from your wife?"

"A note? What sort of note? Oh, you mean some kind of farewell . . . no, nothing like that. Nothing at all."

"Thank you. If you could show me the medication that Dr Bertolasso prescribed, I shall leave you in peace."

"Certainly. It's in the car. I'll go and get it."

On the spur of the moment, Tim said: "I'd like to accompany you, sir, if that's OK?"

Edmund Baker shrugged.

"I suppose so," he said. "It's parked in the back alley; you'll have to come through the kitchen."

Tim followed him out of the room. Edmund Baker paused before he opened the door at the end of the hall corridor.

"Don't say I didn't warn you," he said. "About the mess, I mean."

They entered a rectangular room which was dominated by a large, old-fashioned range. The rest of the kitchen had been modernised. The walls were lined with double rows of white cupboards, and an 'island' had been built in the middle of the floor. It was topped with an oval work surface into which a double sink had been fitted. Both sinks and all of the surfaces in the room were piled high with dirty pans and crockery. The twin steel waste-bins that stood on either side of the island were overflowing with rubbish. The chairs were festooned with sour-smelling dishcloths and tea-towels. The floor was covered with food debris, some of it ancient and rotting.

"This way," said Edmund over his shoulder. "Be careful when you're walking through the garden. It's a brick path and it gets slippery."

The rear garden was long and narrow, but of a good size. Several apple trees were growing at some distance from the house. There was a vegetable garden, which appeared to have been recently dug over, and some fruit bushes. There was less evidence of the neglect and decay that permeated the rest of the house.

A 1930s brick garage stood at the far end of the garden. A short path led from it to a five-barred gate, which was padlocked. Edmund Baker unlocked it and led Tim out into the street. His car was parked in front of the gate, half on the pavement and half off it, just as the cars on the main road had been parked. It was an ancient, rusting Saab. Tim doubted that it would pass an MOT, but challenging the car's roadworthiness was not why he was there. Not at the moment, anyway. It might prove a useful way of curtailing Edmund's activities later if there seemed to be any foundation in the suspicions raised by the boy on the bicycle.

"You don't garage the car, then, sir?" he said conversationally, as Edmund unlocked the driver's door and thrust his upper body awkwardly into the car in order to release the lock on one of the rear doors.

"I used to. Unfortunately, the garage is full of my archaeological equipment now. I don't like leaving the car on the street." Edmund emerged from the car and opened the rear-side far door. Tim looked in and saw that a large green box had been wedged onto the back seat. On top of it was a thick white paper package fastened with sellotape. There was a picture of a flagon on the side of it. Edmund grabbed hold of the package and handed it to Tim.

"This is what Dr Bertolasso prescribed. As you can see, Krystyna never opened it."

Tim took the package. "May I keep this, for the moment?" he asked.

"Certainly. You can keep it for good, as far as I'm concerned. I won't have any use for it."

"I will send you a receipt for the package." Tim peered into the car. "That's an impressive-looking box you have there. I'm surprised you managed to get it into the vehicle. Is it something to do with your work?"

The expression that crossed Edmund Baker's face was hard to define. It could have been one of peevishness, but, if Tim had been pushed for an opinion, he would have said that Edmund was afraid of something. His reply, when it came, was hesitant.

"Yes, in a way. It's more connected with my hobby than my work – but the two are intertwined. The box contains some papers that I've borrowed from the Archaeological Society."

"Ah, yes. Mrs Tarrant mentioned something about it when we interviewed her yesterday."

"Alex? Why have you been talking about me to Alex?" Edmund's reaction was decidedly panicky, but masked with a veneer of irritation. His voice had risen angrily.

"The conversation was not principally about you, Mr Baker. We asked Mrs Tarrant to describe her movements of yesterday when we were investigating a break-in at her flat. She happened to mention that she met you yesterday morning."

"Oh, yes, I remember that she told me about the burglary now. I'm sorry; I didn't really take in what she was saying when we spoke."

"That's perfectly understandable – you've had plenty to think about besides her problems. So Mrs Tarrant has been in touch with you today?"

"I phoned her this morning, in response to several calls that she made to me yesterday."

"She said that by mistake she'd allowed you to keep the key to the Archaeological Society's archive. Was the call about that?"

"Yes. It was an oversight. I didn't mean to keep the key. Alex was making a great fuss about it. Strictly speaking, she shouldn't have let me have it, but if the trustees had found out they wouldn't have minded. I am well known to them. Anyway, to put her mind at rest, I said that I would post it to her."

"I see. Well, thank you, Mr Baker, for all your help. Once again, I'm sorry that I had to intrude on your grief. There is one other thing: are you planning on going away in the near future?"

"Of course not. There is the funeral to organise – and my work to do. It's a very busy time of year at work for me, actually."

"Quite. But if you should change your plans, I'd be grateful if you'd let us know – just in case we need to talk to you again."

"Very well. Although I have absolutely no more information that could be of use to you."

"That's probably true, sir. But it's surprising how often people recollect things of importance later, in cases of this kind."

"Suicides, you mean?"

"Yes, suicides. And sudden deaths of all kinds. Goodbye, sir." Tim held out his hand. Edmund Baker took it, more forcefully than when they had first met, and pumped it up and down a couple of times, without speaking. Tim smiled at him and walked to the top of the short street. He turned briefly at the corner. Edmund Baker was still standing on the pavement, apparently lost to his surroundings, his eyes fixed on the ground.

Once back in his own car, Tim opened the package. Inside were two oblong boxes. He saw that one of them contained sleeping tablets, the other a course of Librium. He inspected the leaflet inside the box. It was a fairly low dosage. He would need to check with Dr Bertolasso, but it did not seem to him to be the kind of treatment that would be prescribed to someone who was acutely depressed and on the verge of being sectioned.

CHAPTER FORTY-ONE

WHEN TOM TARRANT had said that he didn't want to annoy the police by making them send a copper to fetch him, he evidently had not realised that there was a close professional connection between Detective Inspector Tim Yates and Detective Constable Andy Carstairs; in fact, he seemed to have assumed that they worked in entirely different divisions and hardly entered each other's orbits at all. This may have been because he had failed to recognise that, although the Padgett brothers were children, they were facing serious criminal charges. He apparently thought that Andy Carstairs, even if he were a plain clothes policeman, was employed as a sort of youth worker whose role approximated in some way to that of a community constable.

This was Andy's own interpretation when he met Tom Tarrant and Marie Krakowska at the children's home that morning. He himself had been there for almost an hour and was eagerly awaiting their arrival so that he could pass on a request from Tim Yates.

"Mr Tarrant," said Andy, "Thank you for getting here so early. And you, too, Ms Krakowska. I understand that the Padgett brothers have to have some kind of routine medical examination and that we won't be able to question them immediately after breakfast, as we had hoped. I apologise that you had to get up so early, therefore. However, I do have a favour to ask on behalf of DI Yates; if you agree to help, your early start won't have been wasted."

"DI Yates?" said Tom. He looked astonished. "Do you work together, then?"

"Yes, sir. There aren't many detectives working in the South Lincolnshire force. Our crime rates don't warrant it, I'm pleased to say. Do you know DI Yates?"

"I met him for the first time yesterday evening. He was introduced to my wife recently when he was conducting an enquiry that involved one of her colleagues, so it was he she telephoned when she found that our flat had been broken into."

"Indeed?" said Andy. "He didn't mention it, but it probably explains why he has asked me to request your help. There's a boy living here who witnessed an accident at a railway crossing yesterday – it was a fatality – and DI Yates would like you to help me to question him about it."

"I'm assuming that the boy is considered to be vulnerable?"

"I believe so; I believe that he may also be unreliable, which is one of the reasons why we need professional help."

"Marie is the child psychologist. She'll probably get a better account from him than I can; but I should warn you that neither of us has a built-in lie detector. As I'm sure you're aware, some of the children here come from appalling backgrounds: homes where being able to lie well is an essential survival technique. And despite the best efforts of their carers, cared-for children don't get the individual attention that children brought up in stable homes receive. If they find themselves the centre of attention, they may therefore – shall we say – embroider the truth? Just to keep their place in the limelight for as long as possible."

"Please do not encourage the detective constable to judge this boy prematurely, Tom," said Marie frostily. She turned an exaggerated smile upon Andy, her blue eyes fierce. Andy reflected that she was that rare thing in his experience, an attractive large lady. "I shall be happy to help you, DC Carstairs. Do you know the name of the boy?"

Andy opened a thin cardboard file and consulted the notes inside it.

"His name is Lyle Scott. Do you know him?"

Tom Tarrant rolled his eyes heavenwards. "We'll be lucky if . . ."

"Tom, please," Marie Krakowska cut in again. "We know all of the children here, DC Carstairs. Lyle is one of the more challenged ones, but I believe that his heart is in the right place."

Andy looked at Tom Tarrant again. It was difficult to read the expression on his face. However, it was clear that he would not cross Marie again.

"Thank you for agreeing to help, Ms Krakowska," said Andy. "I'd be grateful if you'd both be present – though I stress that the boy is not in trouble and we want to keep it as informal as possible. To give you a bit of background, Lyle was out on his bicycle yesterday. I understand that he had travelled much further than he is allowed to by his carers; in fact, he ended up in Holbeach in the later part of the afternoon, though he says that he got lost and did not intend to go so far. Whatever the truth of that – and I don't blame the lad if he's telling a white lie to get out of being grounded; most boys would do the same – he was at the level crossing on the main road in Holbeach, waiting for a train to pass through, when he witnessed a fatal accident. As a matter of fact, it was probably a suicide and may possibly even have been . . ."

"Thank you, DC Carstairs," said Marie Krakowska firmly, the Polish lilt in her voice becoming more pronounced. "That is enough background, I think. What you have told us is very useful, but, if you wish us to help you to question Lyle as a witness, we should listen to what he has to say now. I understand that you were not there yourself?"

"No, of course not. If I had been, we wouldn't want to speak to the boy now. "

"Then we should listen to Lyle, without any kind of gloss from you, if you will forgive me. That is the only way of getting at the truth, as I'm sure you will agree. You are fortunate that neither Tom nor I knows any of the details. Therefore it is still possible for us to be unbiased."

"Marie is right," said Tom Tarrant. "But please don't let it worry you! She doesn't mean that we will necessarily be taken in by Lyle, if he isn't telling the truth; just that, if we are to help you – and him – we should be allowed to make an independent assessment."

"Of course," said Andy, inclining his head. "I am very grateful to you . . . and I'm certain that DI Yates would be impressed by your strict approach to getting at the truth!"

When Lyle arrived Andy got quite a shock. He had expected him to be an undersized boy with the pinched face and shifty look typical of children who have spent too long drifting about the streets, having to stick up for themselves when picked on by older domineering youths, before finally being taken into care. But the boy who knocked politely on the door and waited to be invited in before he entered was neither runty nor undernourished. He was thick-set without being fat and powerfully built, like a rugby player. He had a square-ish face and black hair combed back to reveal a high forehead culminating in a widow's peak. His brown eyes met Andy's without flinching, but his gaze was tinged with no discernible insolence. Andy saw that he was very well-dressed. He was wearing Diesel jeans and Nike trainers. His black sweatshirt was emblazoned with the Armani logo, so was presumably a copy – but a good one.

"Come in, Lyle," said Andy. "Thank you for agreeing to help us again. We just want to run through what you told the policeman you saw last night, to make sure that he's written it all down correctly and in case you manage to think back and remember anything else. I believe that you know Ms Krakowska and Mr Tarrant?"

Lyle nodded. He gave them an apparently open, guileless smile. Marie smiled broadly back. Andy noticed that Tom Tarrant looked uncomfortable, but he also managed an uncertain smile.

"Hello, Lyle," said Tom in a firm voice.

"Hello, sir. Hello, Ms Krakowska."

"Sit down, Lyle," said Andy. "Now, just to reassure you once more, we know that you biked further than you were supposed to yesterday, but, as PC Chakrabati said last night, we're not here to question you about that, or to get you into trouble. I've been assured by the warden that you won't be punished here, either."

"I didn't know I'd gone so far, I was enjoying it that much," said Lyle. It was a simple statement: there was no attempt at whining or self-justification. Andy saw that Tom Tarrant was observing the boy very closely.

"It's easily done," said Andy. "I've gone farther on my bike than I thought I had myself sometimes. You told me a bit about your bike ride yesterday, so I don't think we need to repeat that again. It was fairly uneventful until you got to Holbeach, wasn't it?"

"I was just riding along," said Lyle. "I didn't see anything special." The boy was almost too ingenuous. Tom Tarrant continued his scrutiny.

"Quite," said Andy. "What happened when you arrived in Holbeach?"

"I was gobsmacked when I saw the Holbeach sign. I didn't know I'd gone so far. I wasn't sure that I could get back before supper. I turned round to go back the way I'd come. I didn't get far before the crossing gates closed. I thought of dodging round them to save a bit of time, but then I decided, best not." He looked virtuous. Andy wondered if this was a bit of 'embroidery'. He glanced at Lyle's statement of the previous night and noted that this detail had not then been included.

Marie Krakowska nodded encouragingly.

"Very wise," she said.

"So you decided to wait," Andy continued. "Can you tell me exactly where you were waiting?"

"On the pavement by the gate. When I got off the bike, I moved it on to the pavement."

"Any particular reason why you did this?"

"There was a lorry in the queue. It was very close to the kerb. I thought it best to get right out of the way." Lyle continued to look virtuous.

"Can you describe the lorry?"

"It was an old bashed-up lorry with an open back. Full of builder's tackle."

"Was it the vehicle nearest to the gates?"

"No. There was a car in front of it: a little Fiesta, with a lady in it."

"What about the car behind the lorry? Did you get a clear view of that?"

"Yes. I was standing alongside it when I got off the bike. Like I said, the lorry was right in against the pavement, so I had to get off the bike and hoik it on to the pavement so's I could walk up closer to the gates."

"What kind of car was the one behind the lorry?"

"An old one of some kind. A red one. I didn't take that much notice."

"What about the people inside that car? Did you notice them?"

"I looked into the car and saw that there were two of them – a man and a woman. The windows were closed, but I could see they were having a row. The woman looked very upset. She was screeching at him. I could hear the screeching but not what she was saying."

"What about the man?"

"I didn't see him as clearly."

"So you just walked past their car, to get as close to the gates as you could?"

"I didn't want to be caught staring. I know better than to poke my nose in when folks is rowing." Lyle said this with feeling. Andy almost smiled. He would vouch for it that the comment did not constitute an instance of Lyle's prowess at 'embroidery'.

"How close to the gates did you get?"

"Very close. As near as I could without touching the barrier."

"Could you see up and down the track?"

"Some of the way. Not far enough to know whether the train was close or not. That's why I didn't try to dodge through them."

"About how long do you think you were waiting?"

"It seemed like fuckin' ages. But it was probably only three or four minutes."

"Before the train came?"

"No. Before I heard a lot of scuffling behind me. I turned to see that the woman in the old car had got out. The man had got out as well – he was holding on to her. Then they disappeared around the other side of the lorry. When I could see them again, they were almost level with me, but in front of the Fiesta. The train was coming now – I could hear it. The lady in the Fiesta hid her face in her hands. I think she thought that the woman was trying to throw herself under the train and the bloke was trying to hold her back. But he wasn't, see. I saw him. He pushed the woman. She went straight under the train."

For the first time, the boy faltered. His face paled. It was this as much as the matter-of-factness of his account – there were no fancy flourishes in this part of it – that persuaded Andy that he could be telling the truth.

"Thank you, Lyle. You are quite certain of that? You don't think that you could have made a mistake?" It was Tom Tarrant talking. Lyle's face grew even paler. It took on a shut expression. He swayed slightly.

"Would you like some water?"

The boy nodded. Marie Krakowska rose and bustled about. She poured water and placed the plastic cup in front of Lyle with exaggerated care. He snatched it up and swiftly drank most of the contents. Marie stroked his hand.

"Are you OK, love?"

"Yes," said Lyle, regarding her with open-eyed innocence. He shot Tom Tarrant a poisoned look.

"What happened next?" said Marie.

"The train ran right over her. I hardly heard a bump. I moved back a bit from the crossing. I didn't want to see . . . what was there. The bloke started making a big fuss right away. He was shouting, calling out for help."

"Did he ask you to help him?"

"No. I don't think he noticed me. He banged on the cab door of the lorry first. The lorry driver opened it after a bit – I think he might have been asleep. They were talking, but I couldn't hear what they were saying. The woman in the Fiesta had got out of her car, but she didn't speak to them. She just stood there with her hands over her mouth, saying 'Oh my God'. She was pathetic," he added contemptuously.

"What next?"

"Take your time, Lyle," interposed Marie. "We know that this is difficult for you. You're doing very well. Don't be rushed, now."

"I just stood there, watching. I felt a bit – blank – if you know what I mean. The cops showed up very quickly. Two in a car, one on a motorbike. And a bloke from the railway. The train had only been gone for a little while. I didn't move because I didn't want to look at the – at what was on the crossing."

"Did the policemen speak to you?"

"The one on the bike did. The other two had taken the bloke to sit in their car. The one on the bike asked the lady in the Fiesta and the lorry driver to pull their vehicles over to the side of the road. Then he noticed me. He asked me if I had seen anything."

"That was when you gave the statement that I've got here?"

"Yes. Then we hung around for a bit. An ambulance came, but I didn't see what it did – I don't think it stayed long. Then two police vans. The policeman who'd talked to me said that one of them had come to take me home. He put the bike in the back. The road was still closed when we left."

"That was all?"

"Yes. The policeman in the van brought me back here and came in to talk to the warden, so's I didn't get into trouble. I didn't sleep last night," he added plaintively. Andy observed that this was his first obvious ploy to gain sympathy.

"You've done very well," said Marie again.

"Will he get put in prison?"

"I don't know, Lyle. It depends on whether it was an accident or not. It's not for us to speculate."

"He means guess," put in Tom Tarrant. Lyle regarded him without expression.

"I know that, sir." He turned back to Andy. "It weren't no accident. I've just told you. Don't you believe me?" His voice was rising.

"I believe that you've described to us exactly what you think you saw," said Andy. "We shall be taking other witness statements as well."

"But no-one else saw it like I did!" Lyle was almost shouting now. "The others weren't looking. You don't believe me, do you?" He banged the table with his fist.

"Yes, I do believe you, Lyle. But I still have to gather as much information as I can. There may have been people on the train who saw what happened."

Lyle blew a raspberry.

"Fuck you, then," he said. He stood up and strode to the door, knocking over what remained of the water as he went.

"Come back here at once, Lyle," said Tom. Lyle did not look round. He rushed headlong through the door, banging it behind him.

"I'll go after him," said Marie. "As you see, DC Carstairs, his self-confidence is fragile. He tends to react badly when the truth of what he says is called into question." She spoke as if Andy had taken a whip to the boy.

When she'd gone, Andy sat down wearily.

"God," he said. "These 'damaged' children. They do my head in. I don't know how you ever get anywhere with them."

"We don't, always. We can only try our best," said Tom. "And, over time, we can sometimes help them to lead normal lives. But they're never cured completely. I tried to warn you about Lyle but, as you see, Marie is very protective of children like this."

"Rightly so, of course. Do you think that Lyle was telling the truth?"

"I just don't know. He sounded very plausible, as you'll probably agree. But he is a skilful liar, and he's misled us on previous occasions."

"Do you know why he is here? He seems different from the other cared-for children I've met. He's better spoken and better dressed; and appears to be better nourished, too."

"I'm not at liberty to discuss his case in detail, unless it proves to be of direct importance to your investigation. Then we must obtain permission from the warden or his legal guardian, if it isn't the warden. I'm sure that this would be forthcoming, provided of course that any information is treated in the strictest confidence. I can see that it could be of benefit to Lyle if his account were to be believed; however, it would be unfair to him, and very detrimental to his recovery, if he were exposed in court as an unreliable witness."

"You're saying that I can't depend on the truth of his evidence unless it is corroborated by someone else?"

"What do you think, DC Carstairs? In any case, is that the right question to ask? In my experience, few coroners or judges would take the word of a minor in care against that of an adult male of previous good character, even if other circumstances were stacked up against the latter. For what it's worth, Lyle's outburst at the end of the interview may be attributable to a sense of moral outrage at perhaps not being believed, which in turn would suggest that he is telling the truth. But this may be what he wants us to think. He is a very accomplished liar and a competent emotional blackmailer. Before you turn against him, I should add that his background contains enough privation to account for precisely why he has developed such skills, even if it does not excuse them."

"I'm not making any judgments, sir. But I should like a little more clarity from you, if you can manage it. Am I to understand that you don't think that Lyle's evidence can be relied upon at all?"

"I'm not prepared to say that. Just that you should treat it with caution."

Andy sighed. As a cut-and-dried man himself, he hated all nuance. Why couldn't the truth be straightforward for everyone?

CHAPTER FORTY-TWO

DESPITE HER ANXIETY about the break-in and the pity that she felt for Edmund's unknown wife, Alex's heart was lighter than it had been for weeks as she took her shower and prepared for work. Her still-born affair with Edmund had been nothing more than a piece of vanity born out of temporary disillusion with her marriage and her job. She was relieved that it had finished so abruptly and infinitely grateful that, although Tom might have his suspicions, as Edmund had said, he would be unlikely to discover anything incriminating now. There were loose ends to tie up, of course; she wondered what Edmund had really told the trustees about the business proposal. She resolved to ask to see them herself as soon as possible. She hoped that Edmund had not suggested to them that she was dissatisfied with her work at the Archaeological Society.

Marie had left a spare key which Tom had agreed that Alex should take, as he was expecting to spend most of the day with Marie. Alex slipped it carefully into her bag before emerging from Marie's house and shutting the door behind her. As she did so, her mobile rang again. She did not recognise the number. She pressed the green button quickly, before the caller could ring off.

"Hello?" she said cautiously.

"Alex?" It was Carolyn's voice.

"Carolyn! I've got so much to tell you."   .

Alex had to catch a bus to get to the Archaeological Society from Marie's house. She made it to the bus shelter at just after ten minutes past eight, but when she consulted the timetable was peeved to discover that she had narrowly missed the 8.10 bus to Spalding. She would have to wait another twenty-five minutes for the next one.

There was no-one else waiting with her and she felt exposed standing there alone. She was still fragile from the previous evening's events and full of emotions that she could not precisely define about Edmund. She reflected that, were it not impertinent for her to register any kind of feeling about the death of a woman whom she did not know but had certainly wronged, she would be in a state of shock over Krystyna Baker's death. Patently this was not because she could sincerely mourn Krystyna as a person; it was because she had always felt afraid of the deaths of people associated with those that she knew and the way in which they underlined the transitoriness of life, the precariousness of the status quo. Of course their loved-ones' lives were catastrophically changed, but hers too was altered, if more subtly. Krystyna Baker's death was an assault on her security.

She looked up to see a large white van drive slowly past the bus stop. She thought that she had seen it before, but could not be certain. She watched it cruise slowly out of sight, relieved when it passed from her view.

A vicious little eddy of wind whipped around the bus shelter, making her shiver. She looked at her watch. It was 8.17. She decided that if she were quick she would have time to walk back to the newsagent's in the next street to buy today's paper and return to the stop in time to catch the 8.35 bus.

The woman at the newsagent's was apologetic: the national newspapers had yet to arrive. She couldn't understand why they were so late; this had only happened once before in all the years that she had been running the shop etcetera, etcetera. But the *Spalding Guardian* had come, if Alex would like to buy a copy of that? She hadn't managed to write the headlines up on the board yet, but Alex might like to know that it contained the full story of the poor lady who'd died at the level crossing in Holbeach yesterday. Alex had probably seen it on the news?

Alex shook her head. She was annoyed by the woman's chit-chat and found her method of peddling this news distasteful. Nevertheless, she acknowledged to herself that she would like to know more about how Edmund's wife had died. She scooped up the top newspaper from the pile and handed over the money.

There was a photograph of the level crossing on the front page. All it showed was the crossing itself, cordoned off with police tape, with a police-man standing in front of it. The actual story was reported on Page Eight, presumably because most of the paper had already been typeset when this fresh news had come in. There was no picture of Krystyna. Alex folded the paper so that she could read the article as she walked.

It did not tell her a great deal that she didn't already know. Krystyna was described as a "fifty-nine-year-old retired teaching assistant and mother of two, originally from Denmark, whose husband was the well-known County Heritage Officer, Edmund Baker". It said that Edmund had been with her when she died, that they had been waiting at the cross-ing when she got out of the car and that her death was 'probably a tragic accident', although there would be an inquest and the actual cause of death would be determined by the coroner. There was no mention of the place from which Krystyna and Edmund had been returning, nor any hint of her illness. One of Krystyna's neighbours had been interviewed and said that she was a 'pleasant, shy lady who kept herself to herself'. The article was quite short, and concluded with the information that police wished to talk to any witnesses who had either been waiting at the crossing or were passengers on board the 16.04 train to Spalding. There was a number to call for anyone who thought that they might be able to help.

Alex had slowed her pace as she read. She glanced to her right when she reached the turning into the road of the bus stop and saw that the bus was already bearing down upon her. She sprinted the three hundred yards or so to the stop and managed to arrive there just as the first of the two other people now waiting had boarded to pay his fare. The second, a kindly old man with bushy eyebrows, said: "You go first, ducky. You look as if you need a sit-down."

Alex, breathless, smiled her thanks. She was fumbling in her purse for the exact change when she heard the old man, who had now mounted the platform behind her, exclaim.

"I'll be blowed if it isn't the third time that van's gone by since I've been stood here. I can't think what the feller is about. If he's got lost, he only needs to ask me for directions."

Alex raised her head sharply. The white van was just passing the bus. There was a female passenger sitting beside the driver and she caught the woman's eye momentarily before they both looked away. Annoyed with herself, Alex looked again, but the van was already some distance beyond the bus; it disappeared at speed around the next bend. The passenger had seemed vaguely familiar. Had it been someone that she knew or not? Troubled, she took her ticket and hurried to find a seat. She was grateful for her visit to the newsagent's. Instinctively she sensed that it had saved her from some kind of unpleasantness, possibly even from danger. All her anxieties from the previous day returned.

CHAPTER FORTY-THREE

ALEX WAS STILL feeling ruffled and fearful when she arrived at the Archaeological Society. She was pleased when she remembered that Francis Codd had asked her if he could drop by later on to look at some documents relating to his latest research topic. Under normal circumstances she found his company exasperating, but today she dreaded the thought of having to spend the next eight hours alone in that sombre old building.

For a couple of hours she worked at adding to her notes for the summer programme, but her heart was not in it. Francis had said that he would arrive at about midday. She decided that she had better tidy up the nineteenth and early twentieth century issues of *Fenland Notes and Queries* before he arrived. She knew that she could count Francis among her supporters, but he was still one of the most punctilious and fussy members of the Society. Finding the journals out of sequence – as they inevitably were, because none of the members except Francis ever replaced them correctly – always infuriated him. Alex was often impatient of such tasks, but today she thought that routine work was just the panacea that her jangled nerves yearned for.

She started sifting through the volumes. The whole collection occupied one of the huge book-cases in the library. Each year's four issues were bound together. As usual, some of the volumes had not been replaced in the correct order, though not as many as she had feared. Whole decades stood in line, impeccably regimented and chronologically ordered. The disorder belonged mostly to the 1860s publications. Several of the volumes were out of sequence and the one containing the issues for 1869 had apparently disappeared completely. Alex sighed as she tidied them. She would have a cursory look on the other shelves for the missing volume, but she knew from experience that it was likely to have been well hidden within the library itself or illicitly borrowed by a member who was working on a particular topic. If the former, the hiding-place was likely to be too ingenious for Alex to be able to seek it out successfully; if the latter, the tome would almost certainly be returned, though not in time for Francis Codd's visit. Alex hoped that his quest today would not relate to the 1860s.

The society's hundred-and-fifty-plus years' collection of *Fenland Notes and Queries* had been uniformly and anonymously bound, first in red morocco, and then, from about the turn of the twentieth century, in cheaper dark red boards. Each volume was labelled only on the spine and only with the dates of the issues that it contained. However, the same enterprising librarian who had first raised the funds for and then meticulously catalogued the materials in the archive had also placed a postcard in each of these volumes that summarised its contents. Thinking that it might help her to understand what attractions the 1869 volume could hold for a library cheat, Alex drew out the card from the book of 1868.

Many of the subjects listed represented the perennial fare of this publication – theories about the provenance of ancient roads and ditches, linking surnames to place-names, the everlasting arguments about how to date accurately early artefacts of flint and bone which, she thought ironically, were still rumbling on today. Alex turned the card over. The summaries continued on the reverse side. The last one of all caught her eye. It was entitled *An Account of a Recent Meeting with Mr Charles Darwin, to Explore his Thoughts and Views on Natural Selection.* The contributor was identified as the Reverend Jacob Sparham.

The Reverend Sparham, she knew, was one of Oliver Sparham's ancestors. He had been quite a renowned antiquary in his day. She had discussed him with Oliver more than once. Oliver had said that he was still celebrated in the Sparham family for sticking to his less than orthodox views. The church had taken a dim view of some of these and had threatened to defrock him more than once. At this point in his narrative Oliver, a born raconteur, usually chuckled, but left the rest of the story mysteriously untold. So far, therefore, Alex had not discovered the nature of the reverend's unorthodox opinions. She decided to read the article to see if she could find it out.

She quickly became absorbed in the clergyman's account of his meeting with Darwin. It had probably been encouraged by the great sage in the hope that it would help him to sell his forthcoming book. As the article mentioned at every possible opportunity, *The Origin of Species* was scheduled for publication the following year. Most of the piece took the form of an interview with Darwin in which he expounded the key conclusions of his seminal work and described some of the observations that had caused him to arrive at them. None of this interchange contained material of which Alex was unaware, though she suspected that the Reverend Sparham had simplified and therefore blunted some of the finer points of Darwin's argument.

It was the author's postscript to his account of the interview that arrested her attention. Jacob Sparham's main antiquarian interests, as his readers were evidently expected to know, lay with the history of the early Christian church and how it both compared with and deviated from the early history of other major religions. Although the postscript contained a very condensed version of his deliberations on this subject, it was apparent that he considered that early Christians possessed not only a moral, but also an intellectual, superiority to those who practised other religions. In short, he argued that, by virtue of their beliefs, Christians were likely to be physically stronger and mentally more agile than those of other faiths and he annexed Darwin's observations and theories as further proof of this. Alex was puzzled; the irony that similar arguments had caused Darwin himself to lose his faith was not lost on her. She also saw that as the reverend's exegesis continued, his thinking became at once more muddled and more fanatical. Despite his ardent, not to say shrill, expressions of the superiority of the Christian religion, he also celebrated the 'totemic power' of certain artefacts belonging to other religions. By this point, he had deviated completely from any discernible reference to Darwin, though he was still invoking the evolutionary sage's name, presumably to give authority to his own eccentric viewpoint.

Jacob Sparham's final paragraphs railed at the Spalding Archaeological Society itself, berating it for some real or imagined insult connected with a donation that he said that he had made. As a young man, he had travelled widely and had visited churches, shrines and temples dedicated to many different religions. He had collected various artefacts during this time and had donated some of them to the Archaeological Society. Of these, there was one that he claimed to be beyond price, but the trustees of the day, although they had accepted the gift, had chosen not to display it, because it did not 'fit' with their criteria. The collections on display had always to consist of artefacts or documents that had been discovered, created or produced in East Anglia. In the opinion of the reverend, only those of a narrow-minded, culturally-impoverished outlook could adopt such a philistine stance. Alex smiled grimly. The man might have been unbalanced in some ways, but he had hit the nail on the head there. It was a situation that still persisted, perhaps the most robust of all the Society's customs and legacies.

Tantalisingly, the Reverend Sparham's 'account' concluded with this statement. Beneath it, in italics, the editor, or perhaps the author himself, noted that his proposed gift would be the subject of a more extensive article in the next issue. The article would have appeared in the journal published in the first quarter of 1869: it was therefore contained within the missing volume.

Alex was at once fearful and fascinated. She began to make connections. What was it that the policeman had said? That he didn't believe in coincidences. Alex was rapidly coming to the conclusion that she didn't believe in them, either. If the 1869 volume of *Notes and Queries* didn't turn up – and she would send out a stiff notice to all members asking for its immediate return once she had searched the library properly – she would borrow the article from another library. In the meantime, although the key to the archive was not yet back in her possession, she did have the inventory. She also had the slip that Edmund had signed for the file that he had taken.

She was on her way back to her desk when the doorbell rang. She hesitated before she went to answer it. Still cautious, Alex opened the spy-hole in the door. Through the grille she could see Francis Codd standing on the step, looking disgruntled.

"What kept you?" he said as she let him in. "It's bloody freezing out there." He certainly looked windswept. Strands of grey-white hair were sticking out from the sides of his freckled pate. Alex's spirits lifted. She rejoiced in the fact that Francis's behaviour was, for Francis, perfectly normal.

"Would you like a cup of tea?"

"I suppose so. I can't stop and chat, though. I've got to get on."

Alex's smile broadened. Francis had been retired for at least fifteen years. Months went by when his archaeological interests lay completely dormant; then he would conceive of a new 'project' and immerse himself in it as if there were no tomorrow. He had been a member of the society since he was a schoolboy; he knew the publications that it owned and the possessions that it housed better than any other living person.

"If you're going to work in the library, I'll bring your tea to you there. You haven't by any chance borrowed one of the bindings of *Fenland Notes and Queries*, have you?" said Alex as conversationally as she could, while Francis divested himself of his ancient duffle coat. He bristled immediately.

"What? Of course not. You know that I observe the rules scrupulously. Has one of them gone missing? We must be more vigilant. Install security cameras, perhaps." Despite his final comment, Alex knew that his intention was to reproach her for what he perceived as her too lax guardianship.

"I expect that someone's working with it at the moment and they've concealed it in the library so that it'll be there next time they come," she said soothingly. "A childish trick, but there's no harm done as long as they put it back. The members don't usually thieve; in fact, never, in my experience."

"I disagree that there's no harm done. A collection of papers such as *Notes and Queries* is quite spoilt if it's incomplete, even temporarily. I hope it's not in the sequence that I want to look at," he added fiercely.

"It's the volume for 1869."

"Well, that's some consolation. My period is much later than that – I'm interested in the Edwardian archaeologists – the immediate predecessors to men like Howard Carter. It's my view that it was their work – done for the most part before the First World War – that paved the way for the modern professional. Of course, most people would disagree," he added combatively. "Received opinion suggests that there weren't any real professionals until Mortimer Wheeler, perhaps even later than him. But I beg to differ. As you know, I've carried out an extensive survey of the Victorian gentleman archaeologists, and my research has led me to observe that . . ."

"Have you come across the writings of a cleric and antiquarian called Jacob Sparham?"

"Yes, of course. If I hadn't read about him, I'd still have heard of him, because Oliver Sparham bores the pants off everyone talking about the man. I'm surprised you haven't heard him. He pretends there was some great mystery about the fellow, who was an ancestor of his; but actually the reverend was just a charlatan or, to take a more charitable view, a crackpot rural clergyman in search of infamy."

"Why do you say that?"

"Fellow was a proto-fascist. He also wrote a lot of disconnected drivel about comparative religion, about which he knew less than you would expect of a man of the cloth. But the stuff was inflammatory – and became more so. Sparham achieved some kind of posthumous fame in the 1930s among archaeologists who doctored accounts of their finds to tie in with the racist ideas of Oswald Mosley. Of course, by calling him a fascist, I'm guilty of an anachronism: the term hadn't been invented then. But like many crackpots, he tried to affiliate his work to that of the great thinkers of the day, which in his case meant Charles Darwin. His writing achieved brief fame – or notoriety, depending on your point of view – after he met Darwin. All the stuff that he wrote before that – and there were reams of it – was pure drivel. Is there something by him in the volume that's gone missing?"

"There may be. I'm not certain, but there's an article by him in the final 1868 issue of Notes and Queries that ends with a note suggesting that there will be a more substantial offering from him at the beginning of 1869."

"That's round about the time he met Darwin – fortuitous, you might think, just as Darwin was about to become famous. Sparham was an unashamed sycophant. But he died soon after they met. If you're interested in what he wrote, have a look at some of the earlier Notes and Queries. He was prolific in the 1850s and 60s. You'll soon tire of it, though. Halfbaked pseudo-religious drivel." Francis sniffed contemptuously. "Now, I must get on."

CHAPTER FORTY-FOUR

ALEX HAD ONLY just ushered Francis Codd off the premises when the doorbell of the Archaeological Society rang again. She was astounded to see Edmund standing on the step.

"Edmund! I didn't expect you to come here again until after . . ."

"Thank God Codd has gone at last," said Edmund brusquely, pushing past her into the entrance hall. He made no attempt at a greeting, far less any sign of affection. He spoke rapidly. "I've brought back the key, and the papers that I borrowed. I have another favour to ask: would you mind keeping the papers here in the library until I've finished with them? It's more convenient than my keeping on going back to Broad Street – it's very difficult to work there. And," he added, with a trace of sarcasm, "I'm sure you won't run foul of the trustees as long as the documents are at one of the Society's premises; especially at its headquarters, where they will be safeguarded most tenderly by its appointed châtelaine."

Alex chose to ignore the jibe.

"I suppose that will be all right, unless someone else wants to look at them. But, Edmund, you must be exhausted. I'm so sorry about . . . what's happened." She laid her hand gently on his arm. "Won't you sit down for a few minutes?"

"I don't have time. The boys will be at the house in a couple of hours to help me to organise the funeral. I need to get this business with the papers sorted out now." He paused, and gave her a suspicious look. "Who would want these papers, anyway?"

"No-one that I know of," she said in a timid voice, somewhat taken aback. Then, recovering her composure and trying not to sound irked, she added. "As you're perfectly well aware, I'm just trying to fulfil my commitment to safeguard all of the Society's possessions and to make sure that members have access to them when they require it. Since I don't know what's in those documents, I have no idea whether anyone else will want to see them in the near future or not. It's unlikely, but the possibility is there."

"Uh-huh," said Edmund off-handedly with unfaked absent-mindedness; he clearly was not paying attention to what she was saying. "I'll back the car up to the door. Perhaps you wouldn't mind helping me to carry the stuff in."

"Of course," said Alex, rather more coolly. Even making allowances for his bereavement, she could hardly tolerate his rudeness. "It's only a few files, after all. I can probably manage to carry all of them in myself, as you're in such a hurry."

He flicked her a sidelong glance.

"I took rather more than I signed for," he said evasively. "There was a tin box that I thought looked interesting and I forgot to record the catalogue entry for it when I was signing. I haven't had chance to go through it, though, with all its little packages. It certainly belongs to the period that I'm working on, but with what has happened to Krystyna, it will have to wait until later." He gave a forced little laugh.

Alex felt that, under the circumstances, she couldn't bear to quibble about his leaving with her a box that ought to have been returned to Broad Street; she would at least have the contents available for others, should anyone want them. She shrugged.

"Right, I'll get the car," said Edmund

"Wait . . . I'll help you."

He was already walking away from her. He half-turned to negotiate the steps and strode out into the street, his gammy knee causing him to limp slightly, so that he cut rather a pathetic figure. Alex watched him walk out sight and waited until his battered red car came into view. Edmund reversed carefully up the one-way street. He parked the car immediately in front of the steps that led to the front door. He leapt out, still truculent.

"We'll need to be quick, I don't want to get a parking ticket," he said breathlessly, looking over his shoulder as if he expected a policeman to appear at any moment. Alex was smitten with a sudden urge to laugh. Coming from a man whose wife had died the previous day in horrific circumstances, the comment was shockingly banal.

"Don't worry, vehicles have the same right to deliver here as to the other shops and businesses in the street."

Edmund was busy wrenching open the nearside rear door of his vehicle and evidently did not hear her. He thrust his head and the top half of his body into the car. He appeared to be struggling with something that had been wedged on to the back seat. After a protracted tussle, he emerged briefly, his face angry and puce-coloured.

"I'm going round the other side to give it a shove. Could you hold your arms out beside the seat, to catch it if I can slide it towards you? You won't need to take the whole weight of it: I just need you to stop it from tipping over and getting damaged."

Still feeling that she had wandered into a farce, but now increasingly troubled both by Edmund's lack of courtesy and his consuming obsession with the box, Alex did as she was bidden. Edmund gave the box a final vigorous push and it slid partway on to her outstretched arms. As he had indicated, she was not taking its full weight, but still its heftiness made her gasp.

"All right?" asked Edmund. "I'm coming straight round to take it from you. When I've got it, you go round the other side and push the rest of it into my arms. Don't worry, I'll catch it."

"I'm sure it's too heavy for you. Can't we ask someone to help?"

"There's no time!" Edmund was almost shouting now. "Just do as I say!"

Alex crawled on to the back seat and was preparing to hoist the box into Edmund's arms when she heard a voice say:

"Can you manage that, Mr Baker, or would you like me to help?"

She looked up sharply to see Detective Inspector Tim Yates standing over Edmund as he crouched on the pavement. Edmund added further to her unease by greeting the policeman with a kind of merry sarcasm.

"Detective Inspector Yates! There can't be too many people who can boast the pleasure in the same day!"

"I could say the same, sir," said Tim blandly. "The offer of help is here if you want it."

"Thank you, Inspector Yates, that would be kind," said Alex quickly, trying to cover up Edmund's rudeness. She wondered if the policeman would consider his behaviour to be as bizarre as she did herself.

Tim positioned himself alongside Edmund. Alex gave the box a final shove, and together the two men supported it as it tumbled out of the car.

"I can carry it up the steps by myself," said Edmund tersely, offering no thanks. "I carried it out from the old chapel, so I know that I can manage it."

"But there are no steps there," said Alex.

Edmund ignored her. With two or three clumsy movements he succeeded in flipping the box over, and grasped the handles at either side. He half-staggered under its weight. Despite his remonstrations, Tim moved forward to support its underside. "Let go of the handle nearest to me," he said, sliding his hand beside Edmund's into the solid leather bracket. Edmund was clearly annoyed by the action, but he had no option but to co-operate. They walked up the steps in unison, holding the tin box roughly level. They paused at each step before continuing.

"God knows what you've got in here," said Tim as they reached the top of the flight. Edmund shrugged theatrically.

"I don't know what's in there, either," he said. "I haven't managed to find out."

"Where now?" asked Tim.

"Through the lobby, into the entrance hall, and then take the first door on the right," said Alex. "You'll have to turn sharply to get through the door. If you could put it under the long table immediately inside the door, it won't get in anyone's way."

The situation was so absurd that it made Tim want to laugh. He noticed, however, that Alex Tarrant's expression was serious, even anxious. With a considerable amount of further heaving and pushing, they navigated the lobby, the hall and the library door and finally lowered the box onto the floor in front of the table. Together they pushed it out of sight.

"Thank you so much," said Edmund, huffily polite at last. "I suppose that you've come to ask me some more questions?"

"Not at all, Mr Baker. I had no idea that you'd be here. It's Mrs Tarrant that I've come to see."

"What? Oh. Oh, about her burglary, I suppose. Well, if you don't need me, please excuse me. I have to go to meet my sons."

"I'll show you out," said Alex.

While Tim awaited Alex Tarrant's return, he took in his surroundings. The library was a large oblong room, a little gloomy even with the lights on – there was also some natural light, but it was supplied by very small internal windows set high in the walls. All four walls were lined with massive glass-fronted bookcases, some containing elaborately-bound volumes in red or brown leather tooled in gold. He had seen books like these in country house collections. Some of the bookcases housed plainer sets of cloth-bound books labelled in black or green ink. Some reached as high as the windows; others were shorter, their flat tops adorned with eighteenth-century renderings of the busts of classical authors. Cicero, Livy, Homer, Aristophanes and Julius Caesar – all looking remarkably similar, their eyes blank, their curls adorned with marble crowns of laurels – were identified by silver plaques embedded in their marble necks. It was a place of restrained opulence, designed as a fitting environment for gentlemen to study or quietly dream or snooze without forfeiting the comforts of home. Did any of the gentleman-founders study seriously, Tim wondered, or were they all dilettantes? Whatever the answer, they deserved some credit both for establishing the Society and for funding it so well that it was still flourishing more than a quarter of a millennium later. Tim reflected that if he had been born in a different age, he might have enjoyed the life of a gentleman scholar. He pulled himself up sharply. The limited knowledge that he possessed of his antecedents was enough to tell him that if he'd been born in the eighteenth or nineteenth, or even the first half of the twentieth, centuries, the only career open to him would have been to follow the plough.

Alex Tarrant had re-entered the room so silently that he did not hear her.

"Penny for them, Inspector. Have you visited the Society before?"

"No, though I've often meant to. I'm a History graduate and I've always been intrigued by this place. Perhaps I might consider joining the Society. How much are the fees?"

She regarded him coolly. She seemed amused.

"Joining the Society is a little more complicated than just paying a fee," she said. "Its constitution allows a maximum of one hundred members at any one time. When a vacancy becomes available, two existing members have to nominate and second any new prospects. The other members can veto the applications if they wish – they are allowed two weeks in which to do so. If there are more prospective members than there are places available, but no-one objects to any of the prospects, the places are allocated by vote."

"There are no female members?"

"No. Ladies can be honorary members, and one of our annual dinners is a 'ladies' night'. Not all that many ladies come to it, though. Many of our members are confirmed bachelors . . . and there are some widowers, of course."

"I see. Strange, then, that they appointed a woman as Secretary."

She gave an ironic smile.

"Not really. It's an administrative role and women make good administrators, as you may have noticed. We work hard and are less likely to cause trouble than men! You would be correct, though, if you've deduced that I'm the first female Secretary in the Society's history. It would also be true to say that some of the members were a little dubious about my ability to match up to the job." There was an edge to her voice.

"Does that worry you?"

"Not especially. It does annoy me that though I've been doing the job for four years they still choose to review my performance in my absence. I doubt that they'd try to get away with that if I were a man."

"But you like the job?"

"Very much. Otherwise I wouldn't have come here."

"You didn't come to Spalding because of your husband's work?"

"No, the other way around. Tom could get work almost anywhere. It's like being a teacher – everywhere needs social workers. As a matter of fact, he was worried that the post he accepted here might not have been demanding enough after his work in the East End. But South Lincolnshire seems to have more than its fair share of problem children – as I'm sure you could have told me, Detective Inspector."

Tim nodded.

"Is there a possibility that your flat was broken into by one of the kids that he's dealing with?"

"I think that's unlikely. He's on their side, don't forget."

"Just sounding you out. I've been in two minds about saying this to you, Mrs Tarrant, because I don't want to worry you unnecessarily, but there is circumstantial evidence connected to your break-in that suggests that it might have been carried out by whoever visited Claudia McRae's house on the night that she disappeared."

"You must mean that hideous mark on the wall – there isn't any other evidence."

"There was a similar defilement at Dame Claudia's cottage, yes. We haven't made it public, so I'd be grateful if you'd keep the information to yourself."

"Is it blood?"

"In the case of the cottage, yes; human blood, but not hers; we haven't been able to identify to whom it belonged yet. The scrapings that were taken from your kitchen wall have still to be analysed."

"But you think that that is blood as well?"

"I'm trying to keep an open mind until we know. It certainly looks like blood, but that's where the similarity ends – unless we can find something that connects you with Dame Claudia. As far as we know, her house wasn't broken into, for one thing – apparently, it was her habit to leave the front door open. But most importantly, no-one disappeared or was abducted from your address. Tell me," he added, looking keenly at Alex, "is there any link at all between you and Claudia McRae that you can identify? Something that could make someone want to intimidate you?"

Alex looked troubled.

"There's no obvious link that I can think of. Of course, we are in a similar line of work, though not *very* similar – she is a famous archaeologist and, as I've just said, I'm an obscure administrator. I heard her speak when I was a student, but I was never introduced to her; for all I know, she is totally unaware of my existence. Some of the Society members knew – know – her, but I don't recollect ever having discussed her with any of them – not until Oliver Sparham said that he'd seen her on the day that she disappeared, anyway. "

"What about Edmund Baker?"

Alex flushed and hesitated. Tim appeared not to notice.

"Edmund and Oliver were students together, I believe, and I think that they both went on digs with her. Oliver was certainly one of her protégés. That's why he was so upset when he heard the news about her. I assume that Edmund also knew her well, at least when he was young, but he has never discussed her with me."

Alex started fiddling with some folders on the table. She looked uncomfortable. Tim decided to take a chance on probing further.

"I hope that you won't mind my asking, Mrs Tarrant, and you are fully within your rights not to answer, but I can't help wondering whether Edmund Baker is rather more than a colleague to you?"

"Just exactly what do you mean to imply by that, Detective Inspector Yates?"

She had taken a few steps back from Tim. She was trying to sound stern and unapproachable, but instead the timbre of her voice was tremulous and the words came tumbling out raggedly.

"I'm not implying anything and I apologise if I have offended you. Let me put it another way: are you quite sure that there is nothing in your dealings with Edmund Baker that could make him wish to harm you?"

Her shocked look was genuine.

"Edmund? Of course not. You saw how abrupt he was with me just now. He's always been what I would call curmudgeonly and naturally his wife's death must have hit him hard. But I regard him as a friend and I've always believed that he has the Society's interests at heart."

Tim noted that she had not given him a straightforward reply.

"Thank you. I'm sorry that you found my question so disturbing. I'll assume that I was barking up the wrong tree. There is one other thing that has been puzzling me – though, as you don't know Dame Claudia, I realise that you may not be able to help."

"What is it?" She had regained her composure as soon as Tim had stopped talking about Edmund Baker. As at the start of the conversation, she now seemed very anxious to co-operate.

"You have explained to me that the Society accepts only male members, but why wasn't Dame Claudia even made an honorary member? As you say, she is a very distinguished archaeologist and lives locally."

"You know more than I do, Inspector. I don't know whether she was made an honorary member or not – I should have to look it up. Who told you that she wasn't?"

"Oliver Sparham."

"Well Oliver would know. It sounds as if a conscious decision was made not to offer it to her. I suggest that you ask Oliver himself for more details. He still seems very upset about her disappearance, so I'm sure he'd like to help as much as he can."

"Thank you; I will ask him. DC Armstrong will be dropping by later, to ask you a few more questions about the break-in."

After DI Yates had gone, Alex sank down into one of the library's leather-clad chairs. She felt deeply disturbed by the conversation about Edmund. She wondered why she had defended him to the policeman, though of course she knew the answer: her purpose had been less to protect him than to prevent Tom's discovery of their affair.

She didn't know whether Edmund would be capable of harming her or not. His behaviour towards her had been odd from the beginning. With hindsight, she could not understand why their affair had started at all.

Tim Yates walked to the end of the street and paused to look back at the Archaeological Society. He wondered what secrets it had guarded over the centuries and what might still be hidden behind its tranquil façade. Of one thing he was quite certain: Alex Tarrant had not told him the truth about Edmund Baker.

CHAPTER FORTY-FIVE

TIM'S INVITATION TO Juliet to accompany him on his third visit to Guy Maichment had been an afterthought. It was a spur-of-the-moment attempt to reward her for the hard work she had put in to research Guy's background and his relationship to Jane Halliwell. Once he had thought of it, he was almost tempted to send Juliet to interview Guy on her own, to see if she could get further than he. He was well aware that her subtly-nuanced approach was more likely to yield results than his own more direct manner, especially as there had been an undercurrent of hostility in both his previous meetings with Guy.

Almost tempted, but not quite. Guy was a man of secrets. There might be some entirely innocent explanation for his secrecy – it might just be the result of a personal predilection for extreme privacy – but Tim doubted it. He believed that there was much more to Guy Maichment than met the eye and that what was hidden was probably unpleasant. He doubted that Guy would run the risk of attacking a policewoman, but it would still be irresponsible to allow Juliet to travel alone to the cottage at Helpston.

Later that afternoon they set off together in Tim's car, aiming to arrive at around 4.30 p.m., a time at which Guy had previously indicated he would have finished work. It was some time since Juliet had found herself completely alone with Tim. Once the BMW had left the outskirts of Spalding behind and Tim had turned it on to the windy and rainswept Cowbit High Bank, Juliet decided to make the most of their privacy by bravely raising the topic of Tim's wife.

"How is Katrin?" she asked, cursing the tremor that she could not keep out of her voice. "I haven't seen her lately."

Tim kept his eyes fixed on the road ahead.

"As a matter of fact, I haven't seen much of her either," he said. "This case is getting in the way of my personal life a bit, as no doubt it is getting in the way of yours."

His tone was not welcoming, but Juliet decided that now she had raised the subject of Katrin she would pursue the conversation until he cut it off.

"Forgive me for mentioning it, but by chance I took a call from her a few days ago and I thought that she sounded . . . unhappy. It may have been my imagination, of course, but if not I wondered if there was anything I could do to help." She finished her final sentence lamely, noting that even to herself it sounded as if she were prying.

"She is unhappy, bloody unhappy," said Tim fiercely, gripping the wheel with intensity and still staring at the road. "But since I don't have the slightest idea why and she doesn't see fit to confide in me, I think it unlikely that you would get very far with her, even if I were to encourage you – which I won't," he added tersely.

"OK. Sorry," said Juliet in a strangled voice. They drove along in silence, Juliet unhappily embarrassed by her blunder, until they reached the turn-off to Guy Maichment's house. Tim drew the car into the verge and halted.

"I'm sorry that I snapped at you," he said. "You're quite right about Katrin – there *is* something seriously wrong with her and it was perceptive of you to pick it up from a single phone call. But whatever it is, she's buried it deep. She doesn't want me or anyone else to find out about it. So thank you for your offer of help – it was kind of you, and I know you well enough to believe that you had the best of intentions, but it's highly unlikely that you would be able to get anywhere with her."

Juliet nodded. "Sorry," she said again.

"Don't keep on apologising: there's no need. Let's go and tackle Mr Maichment, shall we?"

Juliet nodded again, still embarrassed. She guessed that Tim had embarked on this further conversation in order to put her at her ease before they saw Guy, rather than because he was genuinely not offended. She cursed her own impetuosity. It was not the first time that her benevolent instincts had got her into trouble with Tim.

Guy Maichment's house had a deserted, almost derelict, air about it, although both of his vehicles were parked on the square of hard standing alongside it. Tim rapped on the door, first with the knocker, then with his knuckles, but no-one came to answer it. He was about to try the back door when Guy himself suddenly rounded the corner carrying a large cardboard box. When he saw Tim, he placed the box carefully on the bonnet of the Land Rover and removed from his mouth the leather tab that bore his car keys, which he had been carrying between his teeth.

"DI Yates, what a surprise!" he said without enthusiasm. "And your lady colleague, as well. Do you have news of my aunt?" He asked the question in the same sardonic manner that he had put it on the occasion of their last meeting.

"I'm afraid not," said Tim mildly, "but we were hoping that perhaps you could spare the time to answer a few more questions. This is DC Armstrong, by the way. I think you have already met."

"I believe so," said Guy, scrutinising Juliet so intently that she felt her colour rising. "What sort of questions and how long will they take? As you can see, I'm somewhat busy at the moment."

"I do see," said Tim. "I hope you're not thinking of going away, sir? As I mentioned when your aunt first went missing, as her next of kin we need you to stay close by while this enquiry is progressing. You and Miss Halliwell, too, as her other close contact."

"Well, I'm certainly not planning to go anywhere with Jane," Guy Maichment said. His attempt at a joke hung uneasily in the air. "And I'd have told you about the change in my whereabouts if you had not called today. I'm not going far. I'm just going to live on the Herrick Estate for a few weeks, that's all. I believe that I told you that I had a big contract in the offing? It's been signed now. It's to restore all the gardens on Lord Herrick's estate to how they were in the eighteenth century."

"I see. Congratulations. But is it entirely necessary for you to stay there? It can't be more than half an hour's drive, surely?"

"It isn't absolutely necessary, but I expect to have to get up very early in order to make the most of the daylight. Besides, I understand that his lordship is an early riser and will often want to visit the works before breakfast. Naturally I should prefer to be there myself on such occasions. He has therefore very kindly offered me the loan of one of the estate cottages that is standing empty. I doubt that my temporary change of address will inconvenience you in any way. The Herrick Estate is nearer to Spalding than this house is, should you need to talk to me."

"Indeed. You said that you had intended to inform us of this change in your plans and we're grateful for that. When do you think you might have told us?"

Guy Maichment looked annoyed.

"It isn't a change in my plans – I have known that it was going to happen for several months and I'm certain that I mentioned it to you before. Once the arrangement had been firmed up, I confess that it slipped my mind that I needed to tell you about it, but I should certainly have got round to it. There is a list of people whom I have to inform and you would have featured on it."

"Well, we've saved you the trouble, now, sir, haven't we? And we'll try not to delay you for too long as you're obviously so busy. We can ask our questions out here. No need to invite us in."

Guy Maichment swallowed. Suddenly he seemed nervous.

"We may as well stay out here. The place is virtually shut up now and there are no nosy neighbours to 'accidentally' overhear."

"Quite. As you know, we still have no proof that your aunt's disappearance was the result of foul play, though I would now suggest – and my superior officer agrees with me – that, on balance, she was probably taken away by someone, either with her consent or forcibly. Otherwise I think we should have found her by now."

"Are you quite sure of that, Detective Inspector?" Guy was in goading mode again, his tone once more heavy with sarcasm. Tim succeeded in keeping his temper.

"Not entirely sure, of course not. But I'm reasonably confident that we should have found her if she'd just wandered off, perhaps confused, or if she had met with an accident."

Guy's expression was difficult to read; it was as if he did not know how to react. Eventually he gave one of his shrugs and tried to resume his habitual air of superiority.

"I'm glad that we appear to have drawn the same conclusion, even though it's taken a while," he said, "but I fail to see how this might enable me to help you to pursue your case. Of course, if there is anything more I can do to help you to find my aunt, I shall be only too happy."

"I'm quite confident of that," said Tim. "You may remember that, last time we met, I mentioned that we – I say 'we', but it was actually DC Armstrong who carried out the research – had discovered that your aunt had links with some right-wing political groups when she was younger and you told us that you knew nothing of this because it was before your time?"

"So? That was the truth."

"I'm sure that it was the truth, in the sense that you were not born when the political activity of which I speak was at its height. As I didn't press the point, I suppose it would have been too much for me to expect that you would volunteer that Jane Halliwell – who, as I'm sure you know, is actually *Dr* Jane Halliwell – was a lecturer in Politics at Lincoln University when you were a student there."

"I did know that; of course I did."

"Did you also know that Dr Halliwell has made a particular study of the same right-wing group that your aunt became involved with during the Second World War?"

"Detective Inspector, as you know I studied landscape gardening at university. I . . ."

"Before you say any more, I should tell you that DC Armstrong has also unearthed the fact that you made a radical change to your plan of studies when you were at Lincoln. You may have graduated in landscape gardening, but I believe that the course that you originally enrolled in was Twentieth Century Politics? And that Dr Halliwell was your tutor?"

Guy looked uncomfortable, but his reply was sharp and openly defiant.

"What if it was? Jane herself tells people that she met Claudia through me. She's probably said it to you. As for my studies in Politics, I should have thought that it was blatantly obvious that they came to an end long ago. I changed courses. This wasn't to put up some kind of smokescreen, but because I had become profoundly disillusioned with the subject. I also decided that I wanted to become an expert in something that could be of practical use in making a career. After that initial false start, I haven't wavered from my chosen course of action, as I think you must agree."

Tim ignored this curious half-request for his approval.

"Tell me, Mr Maichment, are you party to the subject-matter of the book that Dr Halliwell is helping your aunt to write?"

"Not precisely. I have a vague idea of what it's about."

"Would you say that it could be described as an extension of Dr Halliwell's own published work?"

"No. It is not concerned with Jane's work at all. It is true that it was conceived of by Jane, but as a tribute to Claudia. Jane's intention has always been to create a maximum opus that will both reflect and commemorate Claudia's career. Jane will supply the formal academic skills that Claudia lacks in order to give the work the greatest possible credibility."

"So you are saying that what Dr Halliwell is providing is no more than general academic guidance and the benefits of her evidently formidable skills as a researcher?"

"More or less, yes."

"And the discipline which she served for the entirety of her academic career was totally irrelevant to Dame Claudia's decision to engage her?"

"I really have no opinion on that. I'm not closely enough involved. You would have to ask . . ."

"Your aunt?"

"I *was* going to say that, Inspector. A temporary lapse of concentration, coupled with some wishful thinking, perhaps. And if I may say so, it is a little more than wishful thinking on your part if you think that this line of enquiry can take us any closer to finding her. The way in which you keep prodding away at me and Jane seems to me to be not only vindictive but negligent. I'm going to have to ask Superintendent Little if more can't be done to speed up this investigation."

"You would be quite within your rights to do that, Mr Maichment; as he would be within his either to refuse your request or to endorse it."

Guy Maichment gave a slight bow.

"Well, if you'll excuse me, I have to get on. I'm starting work at the Herrick Estate tomorrow, so I need to make sure that I have everything there that I need, as well as ensuring that this place is shut up securely."

Guy Maichment moved the box that he had deposited from the bonnet to the back of the Land Rover. He placed it carefully alongside several other boxes that had already been lined up there, together with a sports bag and a large oilskin roll, from which the heads of several gardening tools protruded. A collapsible theodolite had been strapped to the side of the sports bag.

Once his hands were free, Guy placed them on his hips and stood to watch the two police officers start their walk back to Tim's car. When they had reached the BMW, he jumped into the Land Rover and reversed it off the hard standing, at the same time manoeuvring it so that it faced forward on the track, looking towards the main road. Juliet Armstrong gave one quick backward glance as Tim started up the engine of his car. Guy was still sitting in the driver's seat of the Land Rover, watching them intently.

Juliet was silent until they reached the main road. She gripped Tim's arm.

"Can you stop at the next lay-by, sir? There's one in a few hundred yards."

"Yes, of course. Is something wrong?"

CHAPTER FORTY-SIX

TURNING OUT OF the office at the end of her day, Alex decided to visit the flat before she caught the bus back to Holbeach. Suddenly feeling very tired, she was debating whether she should, after all, walk straight to the bus station, when a white van drew up alongside her. The driver opened his window. He was a stocky man with a square, lined face. He was wearing a knitted woollen hat.

"Excuse me . . ." he said. He had a slight foreign accent.

Alex turned to face him. At the same instant, an unseen man grabbed both her arms and pinioned them behind her. Her first instinct was to scream, but her invisible assailant, who was very strong, swiftly moved his left hand to cover her mouth. He kneed her in the small of her back.

"Shut up," he hissed in her ear. "Don't make a fuss. I've got a knife."

The van driver sat and watched. His expression was quizzical, detached.

Alex was dragged to the back of the van and bundled inside it. She was pushed face down on to a pile of plastic crates. Her wrists were tied behind her back. The smell of fish was offensive. There was a sharp sting in her leg. She collapsed into the darkness.

CHAPTER FORTY-SEVEN

TIM AND JULIET sat and waited in the lay-by until Guy's Land Rover had rattled past them. If he noticed them, he did not betray it. Juliet saw that his face stared straight ahead. He was frowning slightly, rapt in thought; he was driving too fast for the road.

They sat motionless for a few minutes longer. Tim started the engine again and turned the car round to head back to Guy's house. He parked alongside the hard standing. Guy's Citroen was still there. They both got out of the BMW. Squatting on his haunches, Tim studied the ground underneath the Citroen and saw that Juliet's sharp-eyed observation had been correct. The earth had been disturbed recently.

Tim stood up.

"Well done," he said. "We need to get digging as soon as possible."

"Won't we need a search warrant?"

Tim considered for a few seconds.

"I'd say it was a borderline case for one. The standing is quite a long way from the house, so it would be hard for Maichment to claim that we're invading the privacy of his home, but we will have to move the vehicle."

"What if we don't find anything and he complains to Superintendent Little?"

"That's a risk I'm going to have to take. I don't want him to come back here until we've finished."

An hour later, the breakdown truck that Tim had requested arrived. At almost the same time, a police car pulled up alongside it. Two uniformed policemen got out and fetched picks and shovels from the boot. A dog handler's van turned up a little later.

Tim was about to give them all instructions when his mobile rang. He saw at once that it was Katrin.

"Katrin, can I call you back? We've just . . ."

"Tim, listen to me, this is important. I've been translating those papers that Juliet sent. My Norwegian isn't brilliant, but it's good enough for me to be able to understand that in one of them Dr Berg was writing about genetic experiments."

"What do you mean, 'genetic experiments'? This was well before the discovery of DNA, wasn't it?"

"I don't know, but that isn't what the paper's about. It's about some experiments that took place in a children's home. The children were mostly gypsy or Polish refugees who got separated from their families when they fled from Germany and the Netherlands. She carried out some intelligence tests on them and compared the results with the scores achieved by Norwegian children."

"It sounds like another incarnation of the super-race theory that underpins Dame Claudia's theories about the McRae stone. But you're not suggesting that Elida Berg was another Mengele? I know that mind games can be as cruel as physical abuse, but normally they don't endanger life. Is there any suggestion that she also conducted physical experiments on the children?"

"Not exactly, but . . ."

"But what?" Tim was conscious that he had raised his voice. "I'm sorry, Katrin. I don't mean to sound aggressive: it's just that this is really important."

"It's all right – I know that. No, there's nothing in the paper – or in any of the papers that she wrote, as far as I can see – to suggest that she was involved in Mengele-like experiments. But I've done a little bit of additional research of my own. I've dug up some contemporary newspaper articles and I've also found an old cinema newsreel. The home for child refugees where she carried out the intelligence tests was burned down shortly after she finished her work there. She was suspected of arson, or at least of plotting with others to set fire to it, but the police were unable to find concrete proof and the case was dropped quite quickly. Nevertheless, that is why she disappeared. No-one has heard from her since then – the year was 1947 – although equally there is no evidence that she died at that time. She could have lived for many decades afterwards under an assumed name. She spoke several languages and could have found less high-profile academic work in another European country – as a teacher, say. At the end of the war and for several years afterwards there were so many homeless people trying to prove their identities that an intelligent woman like her would have had little difficulty in acquiring a new set of papers. She probably had influential friends who could help her, as well. It's improbable that she's still alive now, though not impossible. If she is, she would be about ten years older than Claudia McRae, which would make her 102 or 103."

"Katrin, thank you. I'm not sure what the exact significance is, but I'm sure it's an important breakthrough."

"There's one other thing."

"Yes?"

"She had a close relationship with a young girl, who may have been her daughter, or an adopted daughter. The girl was a toddler at the time of Elida's disappearance. The newspaper articles don't say much about her, but I've tracked her records as far as I can. I'm not absolutely certain of this, but I think that she's the same person who appears in accounts of digs that were carried out by Claudia McRae in the 1950s."

"What makes you suspect that?"

"It's the name. The girl's name was Abigail. It was an unusual name to choose for a girl of any nationality at that time, but almost unheard of in Norway. The newspaper account refers to her as Abigail Berg. The name of the young woman who took part in the 1950s digs was also Abigail."

"Was her second name Berg?"

"No. It was .."

"Let me guess: McRae?"

"No, Tim, you're jumping the gun, as usual. It was Maichment. Abigail Maichment."

"Should the break-down truck tow the car off the standing now, sir?" asked Juliet. "It will be getting dark soon."

"What? Oh, yes, please. I'm sorry to have kept everyone waiting. And, Juliet, thank you for sending those papers to Katrin. It's helped her to unearth some fascinating stuff – I'm not sure what it all means yet, but we can talk about it later. Let's get on with this now."

The break-down truck driver had fixed a large hook attached to a rigid bar under the tow-bar of the old Citroen. He was a short, stout man and he stumped across to Tim and Juliet with a rolling swagger.

"Any chance of getting into the vehicle to release the hand-brake?" he asked. "It's been left in first gear, as well. There'll be no give in the wheels if I just tow it as it is. Could cause some damage."

"We don't have the keys, and there's no time to get them," said Tim. "See what you can do with it like that. If there's any damage, it'll be my responsibility. I don't want to break into it unless it's absolutely necessary."

"Whatever you say." The man shrugged and climbed back into his truck. He started edging it forward. At first the car didn't budge; it just rocked from side to side a little. The truck-driver increased the revs, but it continued to resist, whilst the truck's wheels failed to get a purchase. He climbed out of his cab again and headed for the small knot of policemen who were watching.

"D'you think you guys could give it a push from the front when I give the word? Just to get it moving." Tim watched, amused: here was a citizen not to be fazed by blue uniforms. The policemen sprang into action and lined up in front of the bonnet, probably feeling sheepish at not having themselves thought to offer help.

"Cheers!" the driver shouted, giving them the thumbs-up. He got back into his cab and wound down the window. He yelled across to Tim and Juliet.

"I'd get out of the way if I was you. I might not be able to control a sudden move forward. I wouldn't want to squash you!"

It was Tim's turn to look discomfited. He and Juliet stepped back several yards.

The truck driver increased the revs gradually while the policemen pushed. As he had predicted, after a few moments the truck gave a sudden lurch, tugging the car with it. The three policemen struggled not to fall flat on their faces. They grinned, dusting off their hands.

"D'you want me, gov'nor, or can I go?"

"I'd be grateful if you'd stay," Tim said. "We shouldn't take too long. We're going to dig here to see if we can find something that may have been buried. If there's nothing there we'd like you to move the car back to where it was again – as near as you can, anyway."

The man shook his head.

"Not sure about that," he said. "I'll do me best, though. I'll have to charge for the time, like, if I stay."

"Of course."

Tim inspected the area that the car had occupied. The earth looked newly turned over. It was packed down at the edges, where the car wheels had stood, but soft in the middle. It was bare of weeds or grass.

The policemen fetched shovels and started digging at once. The soil yielded easily; soon they had dug down to a depth of several feet. Tim was beginning to fear that he and Juliet had initiated a wild goose chase when one of the officers paused and stood up straight. He had been standing in the hole that they'd made, trying to clear away the loose earth that had fallen in from the sides. He was wearing heavy-duty rubber gloves so that he could scoop out the debris with his hands. The others peered down at him.

"There's something here!" he said. "I'm not sure what it is. It feels like some old sacking."

"Let me see," said Tim. There was not room enough for them both in the hole, so the uniformed officer clambered out. Disregarding the effect on his suit, Tim jumped in. He knelt and brushed away at the sacking with his bare hand. He uncovered quite a large expanse, enough to see that it was part of a piece of oiled sackcloth of the kind sometimes used to wrap tools. It appeared to be in good condition. He thought that he could also detect an unpleasant smell rising from the dug ground, though the whole garden was wet and dank, so it could just have been part of a more pervasive odour.

"I think we need the SOCOs here now," he said. "If we dig any deeper ourselves we may destroy some valuable evidence. Juliet, can you get them here as soon as possible?"

Juliet Armstrong took out her mobile. Tim returned to the breakdown truck driver.

"I don't think we'll need you again today," he said. "Thank you for waiting so patiently. We won't keep you any longer."

The man surveyed the knot of people standing around the hole with ill-concealed curiosity.

"I can stay if you like," he said.

"Thank you, but that really won't be necessary," said Tim.

Patti Gardner and Jo, her assistant, arrived less than half an hour later. As they donned their white suits and laid out the range of small tools like surgical instruments, Tim reflected that their work had a lot in common with that of archaeologists. It was ironical that they were now about to use archaeological-type techniques to dig up what he'd wager would prove to be the body of an archaeologist.

Patti and Jo scraped and dusted. Darkness was beginning to fall and the policemen were now taking it in turns to shine their torches into the hole. One of them approached Tim. He was flapping his crossed arms over his chest.

"It's blooming cold out here," he said. "I could do with a cuppa."

"What do you suggest? That we break into the house and help ourselves?"

"We could use some help now," Patti called across. Tim and Juliet hurried over to her, followed by the policeman.

By widening and lengthening the hole they had exposed a large area of the sackcloth material.

"There are several thicknesses of this, apparently in good condition," said Patti. "My guess is that it hasn't been here long – a few weeks at most. There's obviously something wrapped up in it. We don't know what it is, but it's something quite heavy. I want you to help by digging underneath it so that we can use ropes to haul the whole lot out."

It took another hour to accomplish this task. Darkness had fallen; the temperatures were dropping further. They were all chilled to the bone and tired. Nevertheless, the atmosphere was charged with a kind of macabre excitement. Tim himself almost hoped that Claudia McRae's remains would be found here. It would get Thornton off his back, for one thing; the case would turn into an open-and-shut one, for another, since Guy Maichment would hardly be able to assert his innocence. Establishing his motive would be a bit of a conundrum, though.

They had passed the ropes under the mass of sackcloth and were levering it out of the hole. The smell was getting stronger. Tim could no longer blame his imagination – everyone was suffering from the stench. Juliet was holding her gloved hands over her nose. Tim improvised with a paper napkin that he found in his coat pocket.

They laid the damp and noisome package on the mud track. Patti and Jo were wearing masks. Jo had spares which she passed around. One of the policemen held his hurricane lamp aloft so that it cast an arc of light over their spoils.

The sackcloth did not appear to be tied or fastened. It had been wrapped around what it concealed several times and folded over at both ends. Patti knelt beside it, then sat back on her haunches to consider.

"If this contains a decomposing body, we are likely to damage it considerably by rolling it over several times in order to remove it and preserve the sackcloth intact. Although I'm reluctant to damage any kind of evidence, I therefore think that I'm just going to cut it so that we can see what's there." She looked at Tim for approval. He nodded.

Patti produced a large pair of shears and made an incision in the centre of the mass. She slit it upwards to the end furthest from her. She repeated the process by cutting two further layers of cloth. Jo helped her to fold back the flaps that she had created. She was kneeling closer to the stuff than Patti at this point. She shone her torch into the aperture.

"Christ!" she said, falling back against one of the policemen's legs. He bent to hold her steady.

"What is it?" asked Tim.

"I'm sorry," said Jo. "It takes a lot to shock me. But I think you need to look for yourself."

Patti silently passed across latex gloves and Tim eased them on. He took the shears from her and clipped the cloth back further. They were all expecting his action to reveal a body; they were not disappointed. However, the corpse now lolling partially exposed from its sackcloth shroud was not that of an elderly woman. It was unmistakably male: the remains of a man who had been lying dead for at least a week, perhaps several weeks, but no longer; a man who had been all but decapitated.

CHAPTER FORTY-EIGHT

"Do you remember the reported break-in at the house in Chapel Lane?" Superintendent Thornton fixed Tim with a flinty eye.

"Of course I remember," said Tim. "It was only yesterday. Juliet Armstrong was detailed to interview Alex Tarrant, the woman who lives there. I met both her and her husband myself. I'd actually met her for the first time a few weeks ago, when I first started work on the McRae case."

"Yes," said the Superintendent, "you did. You told me. You also said that the daub on the kitchen wall made you think – with good reason, I might add – that the break-in was connected in some way to Claudia McRae's disappearance and that therefore Mrs Tarrant might be in danger. Or is my memory playing tricks?"

"No, sir, that is correct."

"So why wasn't she given police protection?"

"We thought about it. But she went to stay with friends in Holbeach – is still there, as far as I know. So we thought the risk was minimal. I saw her earlier today, as a matter of fact, at the Archaeological Society. She seemed in good form. Nothing's happened to her, has it?"

Tim asked the question with a growing sense of foreboding. He knew almost before he spoke what the answer was going to be.

"She's disappeared, that's what's happened to her. That was her husband on the phone. He was expecting her back at the friend's house by about 6 p.m. this evening and she hasn't turned up. He's tried calling her mobile, but it's switched off. Naturally, he's terrified that she's been hurt."

"It's barely 7 p.m. now," said Tim, flicking his wrist so that he could see his watch. "It's a bit early to . . ."

"No, DI Yates, it isn't 'a bit early to' anything. You know as well as I do that we're looking at a pattern here: daub on the wall followed by abduction. It may not be exactly the same pattern, I grant you – but perhaps something went wrong yesterday. Perhaps the intention was to kidnap her then, and whoever was after her was thwarted in some way – maybe by those neighbours arriving. Whatever the answer, I think that we should be under no illusion that Mrs Tarrant is in danger now – and we'd better find her double quick. There's already been enough muttering over the ineptitude of this force in discovering any clue that might lead to the discovery of Dame Claudia, but at least when we were notified of *her* disappearance she'd been gone for several hours. Assuming that Mrs Tarrant was safe at work until at least 5 p.m. and that she hasn't just wandered off somewhere – which is highly unlikely – if she is being kept against her will, it must be somewhere local and her kidnapper can only have a head start of just over an hour. He – or she – must be a person that we know about, if only we can work out who it is. I expect you to do that, Yates. Pronto. And to find her. I want that woman reunited with her husband before the end of the evening. Is that understood?"

"Yes. Understood."

Tim's heart sank. Thornton was right to blame him for putting Alex Tarrant in danger. In truth he had intended to send a policewoman to look after her for a few days, despite the staff shortages, and it had simply slipped his mind. If she were in danger now, it would be his fault.

"And Yates?"

"Yes, sir?"

"I suggest that you find this Guy Maichment while you're at it. It seems to me that he holds a lot of the cards here. Friend of Roy Little or not, I want to hear what he has to say for himself. For a start, we want to know whether he knew about that body you've just found."

"I've requested a warrant . . ."

"You have. And I've got it for you. Now you'd better go away and get on with it before Mr Tarrant arrives. He sounds as if he's in a fine state and he's clearly not feeling very well-disposed towards you. I can't say that I blame him, either. I'll deal with him."

"Thank you. But I would like to see him anyway – he may have some vital information for us."

"I very much doubt it; he hasn't seen his wife since the morning and he says that she was perfectly all right then. But you must let me be the judge of what he says. If he tells me anything of importance, of course I will pass it on immediately. You don't need to see him now. There will be an opportunity for you to apologise to him later."

"Yes, sir."

For once in his life, Tim was unable to think clearly. He went back to his office and sank down into his desk chair. He felt drained. He would have put his head in his hands if he hadn't been aware that Andy Carstairs was watching him with undisguised curiosity.

"Are you all right? Would you like some tea?"

Tim jerked his head up suddenly: Juliet! Juliet had to come back to the police station immediately. Between them they had assembled many pieces of the jigsaw, but they hadn't put them together. He hadn't paid enough attention to all the background stuff that Juliet had gathered and he hadn't had the opportunity to relay Katrin's messages about the Norwegian journal articles. Then there was Andy's work with the looked-after children and the drugs gang. He was suddenly certain that the two cases were connected.

He pulled his mobile out of his pocket to speed-dial Juliet's number. Before he could complete the action, the gadget glowed yellow and the same number appeared on his screen.

"Juliet?" he said. "I was going to call you. I need you here. Now."

"I'm not sure that . . ." she sounded breathless, but Tim was in no mood to find out why.

"I said I need you here, now. It's an emergency. Alex Tarrant has disappeared."

"Oh, no . . ."

"Juliet? Are you all right?"

"I'm fine. But it's the dog-handler . . ."

"What? You aren't making much sense. Can you get back here now, or not? Presumably there is still a police car there that can bring you. What does the dog-handler have to do with it?"

"The Alsatian got a scent. He kept on trying to lead his handler out of Guy Maichment's garden. Apparently he's quite a young dog and . . ."

"Get to the point."

"He led the handler to a spot close to the gravel pits. He found a shoe there . . . and a walking stick. Close by one of the pits, the one that's used as a fish farm."

"And?"

"They belong to Dame Claudia. I'm quite certain of it. In the most recent photograph that we have of her, she's wearing the same shoes and the stick is propped up beside her."

"So you think that she was pushed into the pit? Or that her body was dumped there?"

"I think that it's likely. We'll have to get it dredged."

"Well, get the Peterborough cops onto it, will you? It's time they took responsibility for some of this case. I still need you to come back here. It's even more important now. Whoever is holding Alex Tarrant is probably the same person who took Dame Claudia to that pit. We've got to find Mrs Tarrant before they harm her, too. And we've also got to find that little shit, Guy Maichment – always assuming that he and the kidnapper aren't one and the same person. And there are some things that I need to tell you – stuff that I've found out that may or may not help. I need you to put your mind to linking up all the evidence that we've got, so come with a clear head."

CHAPTER FORTY-NINE

ONE OF THE policemen from Peterborough drove Juliet back to the police station. She arrived at her desk breathless and uncharacteristically dishevelled. There were spatters of mud on her coat and the soles of her shoes were caked in black loam.

Although he had awaited her return with impatience, Tim had meantime been co-ordinating the searches for both Alex Tarrant and Guy Maichment. He'd put Andy Carstairs in charge of the operation on the ground. Police officers had been deployed across the Fens, helped also by reinforcements from Peterborough and North Lincs Police. Both Maichment's and Alex's photographs and descriptions had been circulated to the officers taking part, as well as details of Maichment's Land Rover, but the media had been given details about Maichment only and asked to broadcast them immediately. On balance, Tim had decided that Superintendent Thornton's instruction not to make public the details of Alex Tarrant's disappearance yet was probably the right one, even though he did not share his boss's rationale for withholding them. Tim had scant regard for the politics of the situation, but he believed that it was important to delay alerting Alex's abductor for as long as they could; panicky kidnappers were dangerously unpredictable. Nevertheless, it was a difficult judgment to make. He was acutely aware that if they didn't locate her in the next forty-eight hours, they would be lucky to find her alive. Tim explained all of this to Juliet as briefly as he could. "We're covering as wide an area as possible and alerting other forces, in case either Maichment or the person who's holding Alex Tarrant – which of course may be Maichment – tries to get away from this area completely."

"I don't think that's likely in her case," said Juliet. "If Alex Tarrant has been kidnapped, it must have been for a purpose. There has to be a motive. I think that she was taken either to stop her from finding out about something or to prevent her from obstructing some action. My guess is that if whatever it is goes according to plan, she will be released. And I think that it's likely she's being held somewhere local. Why would the person who's holding her run the risk of being spotted on a major road when there are so many tiny lanes and deserted outbuildings in this area? We could search the Fens for days without finding her."

"Let's hope that you're wrong about that, but right in thinking that she's still in South Lincs. We still have to cover the widest possible area, even so. That may help us to find Maichment. And Thornton's already furious because he thinks that I'm responsible for Alex Tarrant's disappearance. He has told me to spare no resource to get her back now. He hardly had to make the point, actually; I'm quite aware that I should have looked after her better." Tim's face creased with weariness. Juliet was indignant on his behalf.

"It's too glib of Superintendent Thornton to blame you. Does he know that we've found some of Claudia McRae's possessions at the gravel pit, by the way?"

"God, no, I suppose I should have told him at once. Go and let him know yourself, now, will you? It will come better from you, since you were there, and you can explain the delay in telling him by saying that you've only just got back. He probably has Tom Tarrant with him at the moment. He's expressly forbidden me to sit in on the interview, but he may let you join in. If he does, try to probe Tom for any information that you think might help us. Then get rid of him as soon as possible and tell Thornton about the new McRae development. But hurry back as soon as you can – I urgently need your help to make sense of some other information I have."

Juliet smiled briefly. It was typical of Tim to forget about her existence for days and then expect her to jump to attention and complete several tasks at once. Even more in character was his blithe assumption that she could take over an interview that had been set up by Superintendent Thornton himself. Tim might believe that she could hold sway with her superior interviewing skills, but the Superintendent would have other ideas.

She returned in less than half an hour.

"I think that you were right," she said. "Tom Tarrant seems to be able to offer very little that could shed light on his wife's disappearance. He made one cryptic comment, about feeling that she had recently distanced herself from him for a time, but, when the Superintendent asked him if he meant that she might have been having an affair, he backed off immediately. He said that their relationship was a very happy one and that he might have imagined that the problem. Anyway, he's adamant that they are now as close as ever again."

"Trust Thornton to blunder in flat-footedly and ask the question head-on! What kind of response did he expect? What about her friends? Did he ask about them, or whether Tom Tarrant thought that any of them might know where she is, or even perhaps that she might have gone to see one of them without mentioning it?"

"He did ask that. Apparently she has only one close friend, a woman who lives in Ireland. Her name is Carolyn Sheldrake. She's actually working in London at the moment and met Alex for lunch a few days ago. Tom got in touch with her as soon as he became alarmed. He established that

Alex wasn't with this woman and hasn't been in touch with her today."

"Did he tell you how to get hold of Carolyn Sheldrake?"

"He's given me her mobile number."

"Good. I'd like you to call her a bit later. But first I want you to look at this."

Tim produced the transcripts of the newspaper articles that Katrin had e-mailed to him and waited impatiently for Juliet to read them. Belatedly, he saw that he was making her nervous and moved a few steps away to look out of the window. Juliet deliberately took her time. She was a slow reader, but a meticulous one. Tim knew that she would remember almost every word of what she was reading; more to the point, she'd be able to compare it in equal detail with stuff that she had read days or even weeks before.

She looked up, thoughtful.

"I do remember some references to someone called Abigail," she said, "but not from the Elida Berg articles. And I didn't know her surname, nor that Claudia McRae had adopted her. I thought that she was just a girl who had accompanied Claudia on one of her digs in the 1950s. But, if her surname was Maichment, or for some reason she chose to take that name, I suppose that she could have been Guy's mother. I didn't find out why she went on the dig, but I do know that it turned out to be a disastrous experiment. Apparently, Abigail showed not the slightest bit of interest in archaeology and refused to earn her keep by doing any work whatsoever. However, there was plenty to fuel her principle pastime, in the form of an abundant supply of unattached young men. Claudia herself seems to have occupied a Gloriana-like place in the coterie of young male archaeology students who were born after the war. They vied to be selected for her expeditions; it is interesting that she rarely chose women to accompany her, despite her alleged orientation. But although the men presumably aroused no sexual feelings in her, it still rankled when Abigail began to flaunt her charms. Eventually, Abigail was sent home at her own request, apparently to attend a secretarial college. I don't know what happened to her after that."

"How did you find all this out? I assume that it wasn't written down in the blank pages of the family Bible?"

Juliet smiled.

"No. As a matter of fact, it wasn't difficult. I got most of it from Oliver Sparham, when he was showing me some old photographs of digs."

"Really?" asked Tim. "I didn't know that you'd been to see him."

"I haven't. He was at the Archaeological Society this afternoon when I called in to ask Alex Tarrant to sign her statement about the break-in."

"Interesting. He's a character that I've largely overlooked during this investigation. I liked him when I met him, as well. I'm sure that any information that he can provide will be trustworthy. I suppose I should have made more of his long-term acquaintance with Dame Claudia. It might be worth talking to him again. Not now, though. I'd like you to try to think more about the significance of all this stuff that we've dredged up from Dame Claudia's past – if it *is* significant. It could be totally irrelevant. But first of all I'd like you to call Carolyn Sheldrake. See if you can get any more out of her than Tom Tarrant could. Use my office – you'll need some peace and quiet."

Tim had barely finished his conversation with Juliet when Superintendent Thornton bustled into view.

"Ah, Yates. DC Armstrong tells me that there may be another body at the Helpston property. Excellent news if it's Dame Claudia's. What steps are you taking to have the gravel pits searched? I trust that there are already frogmen there now trying to find it?"

Tim ignored the Superintendent's callous satisfaction at the likelihood that the corpse would come in handy to tidy up the case.

"We've asked Peterborough police to continue with the search, sir. It's their patch, after all. They will send divers in, but probably not until tomorrow. If Dame Claudia's body is in one of the pits, she's beyond our help and our priority is clearly to find her killer. The only person whom we know to be associated with that place is Guy Maichment and, as you know, a massive co-ordinated search for him was set in train as soon as we found the unidentified male body. We're using the same team to look for Alex Tarrant, although of course we have no way of telling whether or not she is with Maichment."

"Is there no-one else at all whom we know to be associated with Maichment? What about that rather personable woman who came here a few weeks ago? Didn't you say that she was his aunt's housekeeper, or something?"

Jane Halliwell! Tim was furious with himself. How could he have forgotten her or how suspicious of her he had been? It was doubly galling that it was Thornton who had reminded him about her. However, the Superintendent's thoughts had already flitted grasshopper-like to another subject. Tim noted that the smile was fast fading from his face.

"I don't know the details of the operation that you've set up, Yates, nor do I particularly want to know them, but I stand by what I said earlier. I want Alex Tarrant to be returned to her husband this evening. Poor chap's in a terrible state." He changed subjects again. "I'm going to call Roy Little about the gravel pits now. No doubt his own coppers have briefed him – though if he gets the same level of co-operation from them as I 'enjoy' here, it's by no means a foregone conclusion."

He walked briskly away.

Tim called Andy Carstairs.

"Where are you, Andy?"

"I'm heading out to brief some of the Peterborough team."

"Are any of our lot in the vicinity of Welland Manor at the moment?"

"Gary Cooper's just left the cottage at Helpston. Why do you ask?"

"I want someone to bring Jane Halliwell in for questioning."

"I'll get in touch with Gary. Do you want him to caution her?"

"Not if she co-operates. I don't want to alarm her unnecessarily; and I actually don't yet have any idea of what she might be guilty. I'm certain that she's deeply involved in all of this, but I'm not sure in what way."

CHAPTER FIFTY

JULIET JOTTED DOWN a few notes for herself before calling Carolyn Sheldrake. Other than being Alex Tarrant's friend, the woman was a completely unknown quantity. Juliet did not like conducting important interviews by telephone with witnesses she had not met. If the situation hadn't been so urgent, she would have arranged to meet Ms Sheldrake in London. As that wasn't possible, at the very least she wanted to get her questions in the right order.

Carolyn Sheldrake proved to be an engaging and helpful witness. She seemed to be very open and genuinely worried about Alex Tarrant. She told Juliet that she had spoken only once to Alex since the break-in, when she had still seemed very shaken by it. She'd indicated that there were details that she was not allowed to disclose to Carolyn.

"Naturally I was curious," said Carolyn, "but I was much more concerned about the effect of whatever it was on Alex than on what it was in itself. I hope that it wasn't something very horrible?"

"It was quite unpleasant," said Juliet. "Mr Tarrant said that you had met his wife recently for lunch in London. Did you think that there was anything worrying her?"

There was a long silence before Carolyn Sheldrake cleared her throat. Still she did not speak.

"Ms Sheldrake? Did you find it difficult to answer my last question?"

"Not exactly difficult, no. But I should hate to betray a confidence . . ."

"Ms Sheldrake, Mrs Tarrant's life may be in danger. We have no idea where she is at the moment and this, coupled with the break-in, gives us good cause to think that someone intends her harm. If you can help to throw any light at all on what has happened to her, you must tell me."

"Do you promise not to tell Tom?"

"Everything that you tell me will be kept strictly confidential unless it hinders the investigation."

"I suppose that's as much as I can ask for. I just don't want to do anything to harm Alex's happiness."

"Please, Ms Sheldrake, we're losing valuable time talking about this."

There was another silence.

"OK. Alex was . . . not exactly upset when I saw her, but unhappy. She'd drifted into an affair which had proved unsatisfactory; from my outside perspective, it was difficult to see what the attraction was in the first place, but that is always the case in my experience – I usually find it impossible to explain the dynamics of sexual relationships, don't you? Anyway, Alex asked my advice and I said that I didn't like the sound of the man concerned and that she didn't seem very committed either to him or to the affair. She agreed with me – I think she was really just asking me to confirm what she already thought herself – and promised me that she'd break the relationship off that day. I didn't find out whether she actually did it, though, because I've spoken to her only once since then. Neither of us thought to bring up the subject of lover boy."

"Did she tell you the name of her lover?"

"Yes – it was someone she'd met through work – aren't they always! I'd never heard her mention him before. You'll have to give me a minute to try to think what he was called. I think his name was Edward . . . or Edmund, perhaps."

"Edmund Baker?"

"Yes, Edmund Baker. That was it. From Alex's description, he sounded a very pompous and self-interested man."

Tim was calling Andy Carstairs again, this time to ask him to send a policeman to bring in Edmund Baker for further questioning. Meanwhile, Juliet made tea for herself. It was many hours since she had eaten or drunk anything. A wave of faintness almost engulfed her. She shovelled an unaccustomed amount of sugar into the tea and gulped it down quickly.

She revived quickly. She went back to her desk and looked again at the translated newspaper articles and the other documents that Katrin had sent. Then she conducted a quick mental review of all the information that she had collected over the past weeks. There must be some common theme to this strange ragbag of happenings and circumstances: two abductions; smears of blood at the addresses of each of the people abducted; an unidentified man who had certainly been murdered; the suspicious death of the wife of Edmund Baker, the County Heritage Officer, at a railway crossing; Baker's affair with Alex Tarrant; archaeologists a-plenty, including the celebrated Dame Claudia McRae, the first of the abductees, who through ingenious analysis had expounded a right-wing interpretation of ancient cultures and had now almost certainly met her end in a gravel pit; her war-time relationship with a female Norwegian academic; the female academic's disappearance decades ago after a fire; Jane Halliwell, lecturer in right-wing Politics turned secretary-companion, who was helping Dame Claudia to complete a mysterious magnum opus; Guy Maichment, former student in right-wing Politics turned landscape gardener, who was also Claudia McRae's nephew; his mother, possibly called Abigail, possibly Dame Claudia's adopted daughter; Guy's own disappearance.

These people and events were certainly inter-related in some way. Then there had been the other case – the drugs case headed up by Andy Carstairs – elements of which seemed to have brushed up against the McRae case on several occasions; the cared-for teenagers working on the Herrick Estate, where Guy Maichment was also working, who had been caught with drugs that they swore they knew nothing about; the cared-for boy who saw Krystyna Baker go to her death; the involvement of the delinquent Padgett family, who had clearly been drawn into something deeper than they had bargained for; Tom Tarrant, social worker, also husband of Alex.

The two cases must be related . . . but what was the link?

Tim burst in upon her thoughts.

"I've just heard separately from Gary Cooper and Andy Carstairs. Jane Halliwell checked out of the Welland Manor Hotel this morning and left no forwarding address. Edmund Baker has also disappeared. Both of his sons are now at his house. One of them was out looking for him when I called; the other said that they have not seen him since this morning, though they didn't realise that he was missing until this afternoon. I saw him myself this morning, at the Archaeological Society, so they are probably telling the truth."

Juliet stared at him as if she was in a trance.

"It is the children!" she said. "The children at the Herrick home – they are in danger. I haven't worked out the details, but I'm certain of it!"

CHAPTER FIFTY-ONE

ALTHOUGH SHE HAD hit her head on the side of the van as she was pushed inside it, at no point was Alex entirely unconscious. The man who had grabbed her forced her down to her knees and swiped her across the back of her head. Coupled with the accidental blow, this almost knocked her out. She was dimly aware of having her face shoved down into a pile of fishy-smelling fabric. Her hands were still pinioned behind her in a rough male grasp. Her captor had large hands; he was able to hold both her wrists in one of them while securing her with some kind of restraint with the other. This turned out to be a makeshift handcuff of plastic ties. It was whipcord thin. She felt it dig into her flesh as he let her go, tossing her arms unceremoniously down on to her back as he did so. She tried to kick upwards with her legs in a hopeless bid to catch him in the face.

"Oh, would you do that?" He sounded grim. He grabbed her legs and fastened her ankles with a similar kind of device. While he was still kneeling beside her, he pulled back her head roughly and thrust a balaclava helmet over her face and hair. She realised that he had put it on back-to-front, because although it was dark in the van she had at first been able to make out dark shapes and outlines and now she could no longer see at all. The knitted helmet stank of beer and cigarettes and some nameless but horrible odour of unwashedness. She felt herself begin to retch.

"I would not bother if I was you," said the voice. "If you choke on vomit it is not my business." He spoke haltingly, as if he had to search for the correct words.

Alex tried to assume some vestige of dignity. She opened her mouth to speak, even though she was afraid that she would only be able to manage gibberish. The voice that came out was thin and high with fear, but coherent.

"I don't know who you are or why you want to frighten me," she said. "You'd better not try to hurt me, because there will be people looking for me very soon. I've been offered protection by the police. But if you tell me what it is that you want, I will honestly try to help you, if it lies within my power."

Her voice was muffled by the rancid wool of the headgear, but her captor seemed to understand. He appeared to find this short speech amusing.

"Very fine police protection turned out to be," he said. "Where are the policemen now? As for hurting you, that is up to you. If you help, you will be well. If you don't, we have guns. You must stay for a day, maybe a little longer; then perhaps you can go."

"Why?" said Alex, suddenly fearful that it was not herself that she should be worrying about. "What are you planning?"

"Stop talking," said the figure. She could feel his breath against her cheek; he must have been leaning over her. He stank of sweat and some other odour that she could not place – a burnt sackcloth kind of smell. "Turn yeer head this way."

She did as she was bidden. She felt one of the large hands lift the wool from the lower part of her face and clamp a great square of sticking-plaster across her mouth. In the same instant, the van bumped into movement. Too late, Alex realised that she had lost her only opportunity to scream out for help, dangerous though it might have been.

The van gathered speed quickly. Alex's fear was soon eclipsed by the extreme discomfort of having to roll helplessly on its floor as the driver cut corners and took bends too fast. Her arms and wrists strained against their bonds. Her knees banged against crates and van floor repeatedly, until she was certain that they must be bleeding. Her head ached from the blows and her mouth was dry. Because the plaster had been fastened tightly she could not swallow properly. And the pervasive stench of fish made her want to vomit.

During the drive she had no further contact with the man who had climbed into the van with her; nor did he speak to her again. She knew that he must still be there, because the van had been moving fast ever since he had gagged her and there was no way into the cab from the back, but he made no noise.

After some minutes the journey became smoother. She thought that it must be because they had left behind the town's network of small streets and continued along one of the country roads that lay beyond. She had no clue about where they were going. They could be heading for the A1 or penetrating deep into one of the fens. Alex closed her eyes and prayed for simple things: release from her pain, fear and nausea; above all, to be reunited with Tom again. She desperately wanted to be with Tom now, to fall into his arms with a clear conscience – or as clear a conscience as memory would permit.

Against all odds, she must have slept for a while. She was suddenly jerked awake as she became aware that the van was juddering to a halt. Nothing happened for a few seconds. Then she heard the driver's door open and the scrunch of heavy boots on gravel. The rear doors were yanked wide.

"Jared!"

It was the van driver's voice.

"Jared! Come out! Where is she?"

"Tied up on the floor."

"She better be all right. You didn't hit her?"

"You said not to. Just one small tap before I tied, to quieten. She's OK. I'll bring her inside?"

"Keep your fists to yourself in future. We'll take her in together. She'll have to be carried, because we'll need to keep her bound and her eyes covered. Wait with her while I ring the bell."

The footsteps marched away. They returned after a short interval.

"They're ready inside. Help me to turn her over."

Alex's original captor grabbed her by the shoulder and the waist together and flipped her on to her back.

"Gently, for God's sake!"

Pushing 'Jared' aside, the van driver thrust his arms under Alex's shoulders and the small of her back and hoisted her out of the vehicle. It flitted through her mind that now would be her last chance to struggle, but swiftly she reflected that she had no idea of where she was. It was unlikely to be somewhere she could get help readily. She lay inert in the man's arms, making herself as dead a weight as possible.

The tactic caused him no hindrance: the man was built like an ox. He strode across the gravel and up a short flight of steps with Alex in his arms. She felt a blast of central heating and could dimly discern lights though the dark wool that covered her face. They were entering a building. She sensed rather than heard a third person approach them.

"Good God!" said a new voice. "What have you . . ."

"Shhh . . ." said the van driver. "Don't let her hear you." Alex thought that she recognised the voice. She strained her ears for more, but no-one spoke again.

She was aware of being carried jerkily up several flights of stairs. The stairs must have been carpeted; the man's heavy boots made no sound. At intervals she knew that they had reached a landing, because the jerkiness stopped and briefly the man was able to take smooth, even steps – several of them, which suggested that the landings were quite large. On one of these occasions her bound feet brushed against something – a bowl, perhaps, or a vase – and released a fragrant smell.

Even though she could not see, Alex sensed a certain opulence about the building. Evidently she had not been taken to some dirty old warehouse or filthy shed to die an obscure and squalid death. She tried to take courage from this thought.

She thought that she had counted six flights of stairs when the man who was carrying her paused. She had not previously been aware that someone was following them, but now she felt a second person brush past. The man who was carrying her started to move again, but they were no longer climbing. There was no carpet now – his boots were clumping on wood. She thought that they must be traversing the length of a narrow corridor, because twice her feet brushed against a wall. He cursed under his breath and turned, apparently to enable him to walk sideways for a few steps. He seemed to be taking care not to hurt her. In the van she had been treated with careless, even vindictive, roughness. Something or someone must be influencing this change in approach. She tried to draw strength from this also.

"In here." It was said in a whisper, but she thought it was the same half-recognised voice she had heard earlier.

"Shut up," said her bearer curtly.

She heard a door being opened. Her bearer paused. Did the other person pass them? She felt herself being lowered on to a bed.

"Don't try anything," the man warned. "I'm going to take the gag off now, to let you have a drink. If you try to struggle or call out, you'll be sorry. Don't say I didn't warn you."

He hauled her into a sitting position. She heard him twist the cap of a plastic bottle and put it down. He ripped the sticking plaster from her face, leaving her lips and the skin around them sore and stinging. She felt him plonk down on the bed beside her. He seized her and encircled her with his left arm to hold her steady. He held the bottle to her lips with his right hand. She tried to duck away from it.

"Don't be stupid. This'll be your last chance to drink for a while."

"How do I know what it is?"

"It's just water. You heard me take the top off."

Alex hesitated, then nodded her head.

"All right – just a little."

He tipped some water into her mouth and she swallowed. He repeated the action twice.

"No more," she said.

"OK. Now I'm going to put a proper blindfold on you. I'll take the hat away. Don't look at me."

She nodded agreement. He lifted the hat and tossed it aside. The room was quite large. It was very dimly lit by a small table lamp that stood on an occasional table some distance from the bed. Alex found it difficult to acclimatise her eyes to the half-light, though she was desperate to see as much as she could before he deprived her of their use again. She blinked and made a huge effort to focus. She could see that the bed had an iron frame and that she was lying on a white coverlet. The wallpaper was patterned in an old-fashioned flower design, but it was too dark to be able to see the colours. The lamp on the table cast a halo of light which illuminated an engraving that hung above it. It was a three-quarters portrait of a nineteenth century gentleman wearing a frock coat. The picture was the last thing that Alex saw before the blindfold was fastened tightly around her head. It was made of a silky material and smelt freshly laundered.

The man got up. He propped her against the pillows. She sensed rather than heard him walk towards the door. She was aware of a brighter light penetrating from beyond as he opened it, then of this light's being shut off abruptly as the door closed. The blindfold was not thick. She could still make out the dimmer light from the lamp on the table. She wondered why the man had not switched it off. It was warm in the room, but she suddenly felt very cold.

CHAPTER FIFTY-TWO

TIM CALLED THE Herrick home immediately but could get no reply. Instantly he knew that Juliet's hunch must be correct; there was always someone there ready to answer the phone, day or night, because children were admitted into care at all hours. He called Andy Carstairs again.

"Where are you now?"

"I'm heading back towards Gosberton Clough. We've received a report of a white van driving at speed through Gosberton village at about 6 p.m."

"I need you to turn back immediately and get to Herrick House as soon as you can. Arrange for as many officers as you can get hold of to meet you there. I want you to cover the house from all sides, but don't try to go in and use extreme caution. We don't know exactly what's happening there, but something is very wrong. No-one is answering the phone and because of circumstantial evidence we have reason to believe that the children are in danger. We must evacuate them as soon as possible, but we don't know who may be in there with them or whether they're armed. I'm going to get authorisation for an armed response team to join you. Then I'll come out myself. I'll be there in less than an hour."

CHAPTER FIFTY-THREE

AFTER SHE HAD been abandoned face down on the bed, Alex was at first vigilant out of fear, but eventually she fell into a troubled doze. She dreamt of the blood splatter on her kitchen wall. The face of the woman she had encountered in Chapel Lane was floating in front of it, disembodied, grinning fiercely. "Put your feet up. Ask your husband to make you a nice cup of tea."

She could hear an unidentified noise in the background as the woman was speaking. It might have been the sound of slow footsteps. Alex stirred and half-woke. The footsteps weren't part of the dream. She could hear that someone was approaching the door of the room. As she pulled herself from sleep, she was gripped by an agonising pain across her shoulder-blades, a legacy of the hours that her arms had been restrained in such an unnatural position. Simultaneously she became aware that her bladder was full to bursting.

The key turned in the lock and the door was opened. Someone approached the bed – she sensed that it was a lighter and more nimble person than the man who had deposited her there. But it was a man – she could smell the sweet astringent aroma of Paco Rabanne. She knew immediately who he was. She felt sick with shock.

Gently he cut the ties that were binding her wrists and rolled her on to her back. He peeled back the sticking-plaster from her mouth. Her legs were still bound, but she succeeded in sitting up unaided. The light of the small table-lamp enabled her only to see his face dimly, but she had no need of further proof.

"Oliver!" she said.

"Hello, Alex," he said. "I am inexpressibly sorry about all of this."

She was simultaneously incredulous, furious and almost speechless with tumbling questions and demands. She could articulate only one of them.

"I need to go to the toilet," she said.

He whispered his reply: "Of course. That's one of the reasons that I've come. But please keep your voice down. Swing your legs to the edge of the bed and I'll cut the ties around your ankles, as well. I must warn you not to try anything, though. If you either lash out at me or try to escape I shan't be able to guarantee your safety. You'll have gathered that I am neither working on my own nor in control of the turn that events have taken. I want you to know that at no time have I sanctioned ruffianly or violent behaviour, nor any action that might result in injury or worse, especially to you. I have been very foolish; I'm trapped by something that I did years ago."

He bent to cut the plastic ties that bound her legs together. Fleetingly she thought of kicking him in the face, but his warning had convinced her that the action could only harm her.

He pointed to a door in the far wall.

"There's a kind of en suite washing closet with a lavatory through there," he murmured, his voice low.

Alex hauled herself awkwardly to her feet. She took a couple of steps and stumbled back against the bed. Oliver gripped hold of her.

"Steady!" he breathed. "Your muscles have stiffened up because you've been lying in the same position for so long. Would you like to take my arm?"

Alex pushed it away indignantly and hobbled towards the door that he had indicated.

"Don't turn on the light in there," he said quickly. Although he was still barely more than whispering, there was a tautness in his voice. "No-one must know that I've released you, even temporarily. If you leave the door open you should be able to see well enough from the light of the lamp."

Alex's anger was gobbled up by fear. The terror that she had felt during the van journey came flooding back, sapping her will. She did as Oliver bade her.

A large old-fashioned porcelain lavatory with an oversized cistern stood behind the door of the room that he had indicated. By leaving the door ajar she would be able to preserve her modesty, if not her dignity. She tried to pee as quietly as she could.

"Don't pull the chain," said Oliver in the same taut voice.

"You will at least let me wash my hands?" she hissed.

"No. Just come back here." He motioned her towards the small two-seater sofa which stood between the door and the bed. "Sit there for a while," he said. "Swing your arms and legs about to get the blood circulating in them again, but try not to make any noise." He listened intently, then went to the window and made a small chink in the curtains.

"They're not back yet," he was whispering again, "but we still need to keep quiet. We can't afford to take any chances. I think that they've all gone out, but I can't be absolutely certain of it. As soon as we hear them coming I'm going to have to tie you up again. I'm sorry."

"Oh, Oliver, for goodness sake!" sighed Alex, her irritation getting the better of her fear. "You're behaving as if we're acting out some kind of boys' own adventure."

"It would be like that," said Oliver, very quietly and gravely, "if it weren't for the fact that the people who took you are for real. And unlike comic strip super-heroes, once we cross them, we're finished. We shan't have the power to heal ourselves miraculously in time for the next episode."

"Do 'they', whoever they are, intend to kill us?" Alex's tone now matched his own in sombre gravity.

He paused.

"I think that you stand more chance of getting out of this alive than I do," he said. "I know too much about them; they won't let anything or anyone get in their way now. That makes me a liability. The fact that you know very little and – I'm guessing – don't at all understand what is going on can only help you, which is why I shan't tell you much. But there is no point in my pretending that they won't kill you if they think that it's necessary. One of them is actually quite capable of murdering you on a whim, if he feels like it."

Half an hour had passed. Alex remained on the sofa. Oliver was still jumpy, but less nervy than when he had first cut her bonds. Every few minutes he looked out of the window, making as small a gap in the curtains as possible. He listened intently each time he heard a slight noise. Evidently he thought that they were now alone in the house, but he wasn't certain enough to relax. After some time, he went to the small bathroom, flushed the toilet and returned with a glass of water, which he gave to her.

"I'm sorry I can't make tea. I'll need to tie you up again the minute they come back. They mustn't see any evidence that you've been free."

"I'm hardly free, am I?" said Alex, her voice heavy with irony. "And neither are you, from the way you're behaving. If we're both in danger, why don't we just leave now?"

"We'll never get away with it," said Oliver fearfully. "They'll hunt us down and kill us. Going along with them is the only chance we have of getting out of this alive."

"You're speaking in riddles, Oliver, and you know that I don't under-stand what you're talking about. I'm grateful for your refusal to tell me stuff that might endanger me even more, but I should at least like to under-stand why you've got mixed up with these people." She glanced again at the engraving on the wall. She was nearer to it now than she had been when she was lying on the bed.

"That's a picture of Jacob Sparham, isn't it? Your ancestor? Are we actually in your house?"

Oliver removed his spectacles and passed a weary hand across his face.

"Yes," he sighed. "I should have realised that you'd recognise the engraving. There's one like it at the Archaeological Society, isn't there? Don't let them know that you've found out where you're being held."

"I'm sick of hearing about 'them'," snapped Alex. "And I know you're not going to tell me who 'they' are. But what about the rest of it? How *did* you get involved? Does it have something to do with Claudia McRae? Was your visit to her house on the day that she disappeared as casual as you said it was?".

"Yes . . . No. Well, sort of. When I said that I hadn't seen Claudia for a long time before that visit, I was telling the truth. I actually had been back in touch with her again a few years ago, but only by e-mail. That companion of hers – Jane or Jean – got hold of me to ask me to contribute to a collection of occasional papers that she is planning to publish to accompany a new book by Claudia. She told me that this book would be the culmination of Claudia's life's work. I was a bit sceptical – Claudia was never any great shakes at writing – but I agreed to do it."

"How did this woman find you?"

"I don't suppose I'm that difficult to find. But it's interesting that you ask, because this Jane – I think her name *was* Jane – was quite coy when I asked her the same question myself. She'd reached me through Edmund Baker – he'd supplied her with my e-mail address. Reading between the lines, I had the impression that there was something going on between her and Edmund at the time."

"Really? That's incredible!" Alex's voice was high with shock. Her face paled, then flushed scarlet.

"Please keep your voice down!" said Oliver, panicky again. "It's not *that* incredible. Do you know something that I don't?" he added, regarding Alex more closely.

"No. No, of course not. Do carry on."

Oliver was suddenly hesitant.

"How much do you know about Claudia and her work?" he asked.

"I read some of her writings when I was a student. I know about the McRae Stone, of course."

"What did you think of her theory about that?"

"You mean the political gloss that she put on it? About one of the languages belonging to an early super-race? I can't say that I thought about it very much at all. I was much more interested in what she said about the actual languages – their structure and the etymology of the words. If I had any opinion, it was that the theoretical stuff was pretty far-fetched. Surely you didn't swallow it?" she added, as Oliver's expression changed.

"I think that it's all nonsense now. When I was a young man I was more impressionable. Naïve, I suppose you'd say. The fact is, Claudia belonged to some extremely right-wing political groups and she encouraged the young archaeologists who went on her digs to join them. I was quite under her spell in those days and I didn't think twice about it. It was only later that I realised how unpleasant these organisations were. Some of them were illegal, in fact."

"I'm surprised. I'd never have guessed that you were a . . . er . . ."

"Fascist, you mean? Well, it's there in my history." Oliver gestured towards the portrait of Jacob Sparham. "And in my genes, too, I guess. Jacob took Darwin's writings and twisted them to demonstrate that the world order of which he approved was both natural and inevitable. No claim for originality there – poor old Darwin has had social divisiveness laid at his door ever since he published the *Origin of Species*. But what I knew about Jacob fascinated me as a young man, so I suppose that when Claudia sounded me out I was quite receptive to her ideas. As a matter of fact, I rejected all that years ago, both emotionally and intellectually. I saw the light when I understood that it had contributed to the failure of my marriage. It didn't reject me, however. There was one extremist group in particular that Claudia had encouraged me to join. Once you've become a member of it, you've sworn lifelong allegiance. I wasn't an active member after I was about thirty-five, but I knew that it could – probably would – call on me again. And the call came."

"But you said that this Jane person contacted you through Edmund. Was he one of that group, too? He's always struck me as being quite left wing."

"I would agree with you. Edmund certainly wasn't interested in committing himself to any of Claudia's wider activities when we were students. He made it clear that he wanted to confine his association with her to the digs. I still think that he is involved with *them* in some way, though. I haven't quite figured out how. I suspect that it may also have something to do with Jacob Sparham."

"I'm not sure that I follow."

"Jacob was a wealthy man. He was an amateur antiquarian who travelled extensively. He brought back all sorts of artefacts from his travels; you will have seen some of them at the Archaeological Society, or at least the records of them, because I think that most of them have been archived. He left to the Society most of his professional papers and the artefacts that he hadn't already donated to museums. A lot of it was junk, the sort of stuff that a tourist might bring back from Egypt these days – fake Pharaonic pottery scarabs and so on. The souvenir industry was booming even then. But there was one thing that Jacob described in his journals that was apparently of great intrinsic value. He was quite enigmatic about what he did with it. It wasn't among the things that he left to the Archaeological Society in his will and I and other family members have been unable to find it, despite scouring this house and others many times over the years. Edmund was very interested in it indeed; you could say, obsessed. He asked me about it several times and he definitely thought that he was on the trail of it. I didn't believe that he could be, because we had been so thorough in our searches."

"What was it?"

"A swastika that Jacob acquired in Albania. It was made of red gold and said to be encrusted with blue diamonds."

"Did Edmund give you any idea why he thought he'd found a new lead?"

"Well, obviously, he hoped he'd get to the swastika before I did – or *them*. As you can imagine, they have designs on it, not only because of its value but because of what it represents. But he did drop some hints. Jacob had been engaged for a while to a woman from a fairly well-to-do local family. The engagement was eventually broken off, but Edmund seemed to think that either he gave this woman the swastika or told her where he had hidden it."

"It all makes perfect sense now . . ." Alex realised that she was voicing her thoughts aloud.

"What did you say?"

"Nothing. Nothing of importance, that is. Jacob's fiancée – was her name . . . ?"

Oliver cocked his head.

"Shhh," he said. "Did you hear that? Someone's coming. I'm going to have to tie you up again. Now!"

His tone of voice made Alex sick with terror again.

"Get on the bed! Quickly!"

This is not really happening, she told herself, as she lay down docilely on the bed and allowed Oliver to apply fresh plastic ties and sticking plaster. She no longer had time for Jacob Sparham, Claudia McRae or even Oliver himself, or their weird political views and unpleasant ways of celebrating them. She wanted to think only of Tom . . . and of being released.

Before Oliver had retied the blindfold, she felt light penetrate the curtains briefly and disappear. The next minute heavy footsteps could be heard pounding along the corridor.

CHAPTER FIFTY-FOUR

THE HERRICK CHILDREN'S home was a Victorian mansion that had been built on the site of the original Herrick House, a fortified manor that had been the seat of the Herrick family when they had been minor mediaeval gentry. This ancestral building had been retained for service as a dower-house after the first Lord Herrick was ennobled and made great by Elizabeth I. Now too rich a man to inhabit a humble manor-house, he had built the opulent Herrick Great House that his descendants still occupied on the lands at Stamford, newly bestowed on him by the queen; but he had been too sentimental about the old family home to abandon it completely. Always in use as a dower-house, it had survived into the first half of the nineteenth century, when a shortage of suitable widows had caused it to fall into a state of dereliction beyond repair. The Lord Herrick of the day had ordered its partial demolition and built a workhouse on the site, thus beginning a tradition of conservative philanthropy that still persisted in the Herrick family.

The building that was now being silently surrounded by police had therefore been constructed with security in mind – the workhouse had been designed to be a semi-prison – on a piece of land whose original fortifications were still in place. It rose up baldly from its man-made mound and was encircled by cast iron railings. These in turn were surrounded by a moat which, although dry and grown shallower with the passing of time, still offered protection to the house. Under the direction of Andy Carstairs, officers were stationing themselves at intervals in the scrubby land around it.

The tall iron gates had been closed and possibly also locked. The house was in darkness, though occasionally lights could be seen flickering deep inside the building, as if people were moving through it by torchlight. Andy himself was concealed behind a solitary oak tree that grew close to the approach road so that he would be able to see advancing vehicles. DC MacFadyen came ducking through the bushes to talk to him.

"There are several vehicles in the compound at the rear of the house," he said. "One of them is Guy Maichment's Land Rover. And there is a large white van."

"Is the compound inside the railings?"

"Yes. And the gates may well be locked, though I didn't get close enough to try them. It's difficult to guess how many of them are there, or in which part of the house; or where the children and their carers are, either. There must be quite a few of them if they can overpower those kids. Some of *them* can hold their own in a rough-house, believe me."

"They wouldn't give much trouble if the gang's armed. Even the most reckless kids won't want to argue if they're on the wrong side of a gun."

"We don't know for sure that they *are* armed, do we?"

"No, but there's a fair chance, if this is something to do with the drugs ring. The body that we found at Ayscoughfee had been shot."

"It would help if we had some idea of the lay-out of the house. Do you think we could get hold of social services in Spalding and ask whether they have a floor-plan? It might show us where they're likely to be holding the kids."

"There won't be time. When the response unit gets here, I think we're going to have to go in. But I've just remembered that Gary Cooper came and stayed the night here with that boy who was caught couriering drugs. He must have seen some of the inside of the house. I sent him to Holbeach to try to bring Edmund Baker in, but Baker wasn't there, so I told Cooper to get himself back over here. Do you know if he's got here yet?"

"I'll find out."

CHAPTER FIFTY-FIVE

By the time the two men entered the room, Alex was lying on the bed, handcuffed, foot-cuffed, blindfolded and gagged. Oliver had stayed with her.

"What are you doing in here?" said a rough voice. She recognised that it belonged to the man who had sat in the back of the van with her. He seemed to have forgotten his earlier instruction to Oliver not to speak in Alex's presence.

"I'd just come in to make sure that she hadn't tried anything. You told me to check on her every hour."

"Well, it can't have taken you very long. She's still just lying there. Didn't think she had much spirit. I'm surprised she hasn't asked to piss."

"Should I ask her if she'd like to use the bathroom now?"

"Nah. Just leave her. She can piss on the bed if necessary. You won't mind about that, will you?"

"I – no. Not for the sake of the bed. I'd prefer not to have to compromise her dignity, though."

"Listen, Mr Professor, she's got a lot more to worry about than her *dignity*, believe me."

"What's the matter?" Oliver was trying to sound casual, but Alex could hear the catch in his voice. "Aren't things going according to plan?"

"Not sure that I should tell you. I never believed that you were on our side. But if you must know, we've been held up. We can't find it. And now someone has alerted the cops." There was insinuation in the rough voice now, as well as menace.

"Well, I assure you that it wasn't me. I've been here all the time. Since you've cut off the phone and taken my mobile, that should be enough proof for you that I haven't contacted anyone. As if I would, anyway," Oliver finished lamely.

"Yeah, well, I don't want you to stay in here with her now that we're back. Get yourself downstairs, will you? Jared can wait outside the door here. You can make us some tea if you haven't got anything better to do."

Alex heard the door close. At first, she found it difficult to guess whether they had all left the room. After five minutes or so of complete silence, she divined that she was on her own once again. At intervals, she could hear someone shuffling about in the corridor beyond. She guessed that that was

Jared. Without being certain, she felt, from his fidgety, unpredictable and brutish manner, that he was the one who had overpowered and trussed her in the van, whereas the driver had given the impression of being, if ruthless and unstoppable, intelligent and perfectly at ease with himself.

"Rubbish," she thought, as she dozed off into merciful sleep again. "They're all crooks, all amoral. They don't have any finer qualities. None of them. Even Oliver, despite his punctilious concern. Like all of them, he's really just out to serve his own ends."

CHAPTER FIFTY-SIX

TIM YATES DROVE to Sleaford as fast as he could. He parked his car out of sight of Herrick Old House and was walking cautiously towards it when the semi-armoured vehicles carrying the response team pulled on to the verge behind him, hidden from the house by a tall laurel hedge.

Tim reached Andy Carstairs. "Do we know anything about who's inside? Or how many of them there are? Has anyone been seen? What about the children?"

"We've haven't seen anyone properly. There have been lights moving around in the building at intervals, front and back, and we've seen a few shadows. We think that Guy Maichment is in there, because his Land Rover is parked in the compound. We don't have any other names. There is a large white van in the compound as well, but it's showing false plates."

"No-one inside the house has tried to make contact?"

"No."

A short, wiry man joined them.

"DI Yates? I'm Sergeant Jubb."

He was not the big-boned commando type that Tim had been expecting. He spoke with a strong Lincolnshire accent.

"Do you know the names of any of the hostage-takers?" he asked.

"Only one. We think that their leader is someone called Guy Maichment."

"Do you know him?"

"I've interviewed him a couple of times, but not as a suspect. He is the nephew of Claudia McRae, the archaeologist who disappeared a few weeks ago."

"Has anyone tried to talk to him?"

"No. The officers we've brought here were told to make no contact until you arrived."

Sergeant Jubb nodded.

"How many officers do you have deployed here?"

Tim looked at Andy.

"About twenty," said Andy. "Some from our force, some from Peterborough. The North Lincs police are checking the roads and doing some other local searches," he added, for Tim's benefit.

Sergeant Jubb regarded Tim with keen blue eyes.

"Are you used to dealing with hostage-takers?" he asked. "I don't mean the psychological stuff. I don't have much time for that. Have you tried negotiating with any? Spoken to them through a megaphone?"

"No," said Tim reluctantly. He knew that he was going to have to make a rapid decision here and that whether the children were rescued could depend on the accuracy of his judgment. He took in the slight, sinewy figure standing in front of him. Sergeant Jubb was a policeman, but he could have been a soldier. Tim guessed that although he was not a rash or impulsive man, he was probably not someone who would have the patience to spend much time 'negotiating'. He would want to take the soldier's route to a swift and efficient outcome. In short, he was a legitimate killing machine.

"We'll have to assume they are aware of our presence. Do you want me to try talking to this Maichment? I've done this sort of thing before."

Tim hesitated.

"It's good of you, but I think I'd like to have a stab at it myself first. He's quite a complicated character and I have some idea of how he thinks. If I don't get anywhere, I'll ask you to take over."

Sergeant Jubb shrugged.

"Whatever you think is best. I wouldn't make too much of a meal of it, though. If we hang about too long, they'll think of ways of regrouping to make our job more difficult. And don't forget about those kids. We don't know what's happening to them while we're chewing the fat, do we?"

Tim swallowed. He knew what Superintendent Thornton would think and could hear the testy tone in which he would say it: "Don't get in out of your depth. Leave it to the professionals, Yates." The subtext would be: 'Let this guy make the running; then, if it all goes wrong, South Lincs police won't have to take the rap.'

Sergeant Jubb didn't waste time on trying to argue. His mind had turned immediately to the practicalities of action.

"If you're going to stand out there with a megaphone you'll need a helmet and a bullet-proof vest," he said. "I'll get someone to kit you out."

In less than five minutes, one of the armoured vehicles had pulled forward and Tim was dressed in a helmet and body armour and clutching a megaphone. While he was being prepared, Sergeant Jubb delivered a series of instructions in short, clearly-articulated sentences.

"Stand out to one side of the car, in the road so that they can see you clearly. Hold the megaphone in both hands or, if you want to hold it in just one of them, make sure that they can see you aren't holding a weapon in the other. Be calm. Speak clearly and simply. If they agree to let you speak to Maichment, ask him what they want. At some point you'll have to warn them that we're armed. Make it clear that we don't want to shoot, but say we will if we have to. Don't make any promises, but don't indicate to him that their situation is hopeless or say that they're bound to be caught. They must be allowed to think that there is a way out for them. Try to take enough time to think about the likely implications of your replies before you speak. If Maichment gets down to specific requests, I'll be here to advise you. We'll leave the doors open on your side and I'll crouch down behind. If you think that you're in danger, throw yourself flat on the ground and then get behind one of the doors or round the back. We'll be covering you."

"Thanks," said Tim. He swallowed again. As he walked slowly out into the road, he realised that he was terrified; the piercing fear that was shooting through his whole being almost paralysed him, so that his legs felt as if they were made of rubber. A vivid image of Katrin laughing up at him, sharing some private joke, flashed before his eyes. He should have told her about this operation. He should have made his peace with her, got to the bottom of what was troubling her. He should have said good-bye properly, in case . . .

He flung the thought to one side and turned on the megaphone. He refused to be intimidated by a little shit like Guy Maichment. He held up the megaphone, using both hands as Sergeant Jubb had directed. He kept it to one side of his face so that he could see the outline of the house in front of him. Suddenly a thick shaft of yellow light illuminated the central section of the house, including the main gate and the door beyond it. With a start, Tim realised that the headlights of the armoured response vehicle had been switched on. If anyone emerged from the house he would have a clear view of them now, whilst to them he would be invisible.

"Press on! Get started now!" Sergeant Jubb whispered with sibilant impatience.

"This is Detective Inspector Tim Yates," Tim enunciated in a voice that sounded strange filtered through the megaphone, but was clear and strong. "Can you hear me? I'm guessing that Guy Maichment is with you. If he is, I'd like to speak to him."

There was a prolonged silence. The beam of the headlights continued to light up the old house. No-one appeared. Nothing moved.

Tim's mobile started to ring. It was in his jacket pocket. He was wearing his jacket over the bullet-proof vest, so the mobile was within reach, but he could only answer it if he put down the megaphone. He hesitated.

"Ignore it!" whispered Sergeant Jubb. "It's probably nothing to do with this."

The phone stopped ringing.

"Try again," said Sergeant Jubb. "Tell him we're armed now. Tell him that if he doesn't answer you, we're coming in."

Tim was sweating. He knew that to 'go in' aggressively could cause deaths.

"Hello?" he shouted again. "Can you hear me? It's DI Yates. I want to speak to Guy Maichment. I am accompanied by armed police. We don't want to hurt you. We just want to talk."

The phone was ringing again.

"Leave it," said Sergeant Jubb. "Put the megaphone down and get into the back."

Tim did as he was told.

"Now look and see who was calling before you . . ."

Sergeant Jubb got no further before Tim's phone emitted the series of urgent beeps that indicated that a text message was waiting.

"What does it say?"

Tim screwed up his eyes in order to decipher the words that had appeared on the screen.

"DI Yates, take your men and leave. Do not interfere with our work here. If you don't do as we ask, Alex Tarrant will die. She is not here and you won't find her first."

The message was not signed.

CHAPTER FIFTY-SEVEN

ALEX COULD NOT sleep for long. She was more afraid now than at any time since they'd pulled her out of the van. If Oliver was to be believed, he was almost as much a captive as she was and powerless to help her. Even worse, he seemed to have no spark of defiance or initiative to expend on freeing them. Despite his warnings, she was disappointed that he didn't show a little more spirit. He was surely being melodramatic when he said that their captors were bound to catch up with them if they tried to escape. What did they have to lose, anyway? Oliver himself admitted that at least one of the gang was trigger-happy and not beyond killing for kicks.

Being deprived of the ability to see had sharpened her other senses. Somewhere far away, in a different part of the house from where she was being held, she could hear a mobile phone ringing. It made her think of her own cellphone. Guiltily, she realised that she had probably left it on her desk at the Archaeological Society. She felt abject with shame. Tom was always telling her to carry it and to leave it switched on. He'd said that she needed to understand that it was for own security; one day she would regret her cavalier attitude. If she escaped from here, she vowed that she would always remember it in future.

The mobile phone downstairs rang until it cut out. There was a brief silence before it started ringing again.

"Answer it this time," shouted the rough voice of the man who had entered the room shortly after Oliver had re-tied her bonds. "Answer it!" he shouted again. She heard another man shout back at him. The reply was curiously high-pitched, as if the speaker were trying to demonstrate resistance whilst fighting off a terrible fear. The rough voice rapped out another short sentence. It sounded like a command. The other voice replied. This time it sounded more like Oliver's. It was as if, against all odds, a little of his urbanity had been restored. It almost seemed as if he were taunting his aggressor.

There was another short silence, followed by the sound of a chair falling. This was quickly succeeded by the scrape of more furniture being moved. A glass or cup was smashed. The man stationed as guard outside the room in which Alex was being held stirred uneasily. She heard him walk to the end of the corridor.

"You are all right, Endrit?"

There was no reply. She heard the guard's footsteps retreat along the corridor. Gradually the sound receded until she could hear them no longer.

There was another shout, pursued almost immediately by a loud cracking noise. It took Alex a moment to realise that she had just heard gunfire. She was truly terrified now and shook as if from shock. She was very cold.

After the shot, the sound of a terrible keening burst in upon her. Once when she'd been out walking with Tom she had heard the unbearable squeal of an injured rabbit. She was reminded of it now. The difference was that she was certain that this wailing, although it sounded inhuman, came from a man. It continued for several minutes, bestial in its agony, until abruptly it stopped.

She heard a door crash open and glass shattering. A warning was shouted. More footsteps were coming up the stairs, several sets of them. Alex shut her eyes behind the blindfold. She clenched her hands, willed herself not to vomit against the gag.

Someone kicked against the door of her room. She heard it splinter and break as if it were made of nothing stronger than balsa wood. Alex tried to pass out, but her mind was too alert. Instead she waited, her whole body tensed against the impact, for the inevitable bullet to strike her. She knew there could be no way out now. She tried to think again of Tom, but her reason had been all but obliterated by her fear.

Someone caressed the side of her face. She flinched and tried to draw away. Even as she did so, she recognised dimly that the touch was gentler than her captors or even Oliver had managed. The hand stroked her face again. It was small, soft and cool. She felt herself being lifted into a sitting position. First the blindfold was removed, then the gag. Alex blinked in the dim half-light. The little lamp was still the only source of light in the room. She tried to focus her eyes on the person who was standing by the bed.

"Alex!" said a soft female voice. "Mrs Tarrant?"

"DC Armstrong!"

"Hello, Mrs Tarrant. We're glad to have found you. You're quite safe. I'm going to cut these plastic ties now. I didn't do it while you were blindfolded in case you struggled and hurt yourself. Are you ready?"

Alex nodded, speechless. Tears were streaming down her cheeks.

"Are you in pain? Did they injure you in any way?"

"No, I don't think so. Not deliberately, anyway. I'm sore and stiff from lying here for hours, and from being tossed around in their van while they brought me here. Otherwise I think I'm OK." Alex was speaking through her tears, trying to pull herself together.

Juliet Armstrong cut the ties with a Swiss Army knife.

"That's better. We're going to call for an ambulance, even if you don't think you're hurt. You're suffering from shock and you may have sustained other injuries as well. They'll probably keep you in hospital overnight, for observation."

"I don't really want . . ." Alex lay back, suddenly too tired to argue or even to make the effort to haul herself from the bed, hateful though it now was to her. She remembered Oliver and the terrible noise that she had heard.

"What's happened to Oliver?" she asked. "Is he all right?"

Deep inside her she knew what the answer would be even before she had asked the question.

"Mr Sparham has been shot. He was involved in a scuffle just before we broke in. We could hear it as we were approaching."

Alex noticed now that there was an armed policeman standing in the doorway. The shattered door hung at an odd angle, its hinges half torn off.

"Is he badly hurt?"

Juliet looked at Alex steadily, trying to gauge how much truth she could take.

"He's dead, isn't he?"

Juliet nodded.

Alex's face crumpled again. Suddenly she felt furious. She wanted to be able to blame someone for this nightmare.

"Did you kill him? The police, I mean?"

"No, he was dead when we got to him. He'd died seconds before. He was shot by one of the men who've been holding you. Probably the one that we didn't catch. We've arrested the other one."

CHAPTER FIFTY-EIGHT

TIM BIT HIS lip until it was hurting. He was acutely aware of Sergeant Jubb standing at his elbow, impatient and unyielding.

"What now?" he said.

"There's no option. We go in."

"What about the threat they've made to kill Alex Tarrant?"

"We'll have to take a chance on it. She is just one person. There are more lives to be saved in there." He noted the stricken look on Tim's face and added quickly: "It was probably all bullshit, anyway. How do we know that they're telling the truth? She might be in there with the other hostages or she might not be under their control at all. No-one's heard from her, have they?"

"No, but . . ."

"If they were really planning to use her as a bargaining counter, more than likely they'd have got her to speak to us while under duress. Panic in the voice, heartfelt plea, all of that stuff." He met Tim's eye steadily. "Believe me, we have to do this now. We've got no idea what's happening to those children in there."

"Just let me check with my superior."

As if on cue, Tim's mobile rang again. He put it on 'speak'.

"Thornton here. Give me an update. Have you got the children's home surrounded? Is Guy Maichment there? What about Alex Tarrant? Have you talked to any of the perpetrators?"

"Can we take it one step at a time, sir?" Tim was stalling now, trying to gain extra minutes in which to think. Out of the corner of his eye, he saw Sergeant Jubb spread his hands, palms up, in a gesture of exasperation.

Tim tried to ignore him and continued.

"Yes, we have about twenty officers hidden beyond the moat that surrounds the Home. We aren't armed, but armed response are here with" – he glanced at Sergeant Jubb and mouthed – "eighteen of you?" Jubb nodded. "With eighteen armed men. We think that Maichment is here, because his vehicle is parked within the compound, but we're not certain because the only contact he's allowed has been via a text message on my mobile. I've warned him through a megaphone that we're accompanied by armed officers, but he may not have been able to hear me."

"Did he call you?"

"Yes, sir; but I couldn't answer the call immediately, so I didn't speak to him directly. As I've said, he followed it up with a text message. According to Maichment, Alex Tarrant is not here, but she is being held by whoever these people are, at some location that only they know about. Maichment has asked us to withdraw – to go away from here completely. He is threatening to have Mrs Tarrant killed if we don't comply."

"What action do you propose to take?"

"Sergeant Jubb says that we should go in, sir. He says that there is no time left to try to negotiate. We don't know what might be happening to the children."

"I expressly forbid you to do that. We don't know if Mrs Tarrant is inside and I won't tolerate her being harmed in any way. Or Guy Maichment , either. I have given Superintendent Little my word."

"You've promised not to harm Guy Maichment?" said Tim incredulously. "But you had the warrant signed for his arrest on sight. Sir." Belatedly he remembered that he was talking to his superior.

"Quite so," said Superintendent Thornton. Sergeant Jubb raised his eyes heavenwards.

"Is he some kind of idiot?" he hissed.

Tim motioned him to listen. Thornton was still speaking.

"I don't disapprove of his being arrested, but I do draw the line at exposing him to danger. As Roy Little pointed out when we spoke just now, he may be a hostage himself. The body in the garden may have been placed there to frame him and all of his other actions may be accounted for by his being exposed to duress by his captors."

Tim groaned. "Heaven give me strength!" he said, sotto voce. Sergeant Jubb grinned wryly. They were on the same side now.

"So what is your instruction, sir?"

"Don't give up the attempt to parley. I'm organising trained hostage negotiators to be with you." He sounds like a nineteenth-century general, Tim thought with despair. And he's about as on the ball as one would be in this situation; he doesn't seem to understand the urgency at all.

"So, hold off until negotiators arrive. And keep me fully briefed. Is that clear?"

"Yes, sir, quite clear."

"Good. I'll leave you to it, then. I'm going to continue to supervise the search for Alex Tarrant. Now that I've thought about it, I think that it's highly unlikely that she's involved in your little fracas."

He rang off before Tim could speak again.

"Shit!" said Sergeant Jubb. "Is he always like this?"

"I'm not exactly sure what you mean," said Tim blandly.

"Of course you are. He's like something out of fucking Z Cars. Where's he been for the last forty-odd years?"

"What *are* we going to do next?" asked Tim, skating the issue. "We'll have to obey his orders in fact, if not in spirit."

"Agreed. Though we may need to respond if the situation changes suddenly."

"OK, I think you're right. We may not have any choice."

Tim was still talking to Sergeant Jubb when three figures quickly crossed to them, stooping as low as they could as they ran. Andy Carstairs was the first to reach the armoured vehicle. He edged his way to the open rear door next to which Tim was sitting and crouched down beside it. The two others hung behind.

"Andy! I thought I said that everyone should keep out of sight."

"We tried not to be spotted, sir. There's been no movement in the house that we could see for half an hour, so chances are they didn't spot us. You were asking for PC Cooper, so I thought you'd want to know that he's arrived. He's brought someone with him who has more knowledge of the interior than he does, someone who says he's willing to lead us in by one of the back entrances. Apparently the wing Cooper stayed in with the lad is more or less separated from the rest of the building, so we could have got trapped if we'd tried to get in by that route."

"Who is this person?"

"Mr Tarrant, sir. He's a social worker and . . ."

"I know quite well who he is. He probably *can* help by describing the inside of the house to us. But he's a civilian. We can't allow him to endanger himself by coming in with us. How did Cooper manage to pick him up, anyway? He was at the station with Superintendent Thornton earlier this evening. Cooper hasn't had time to make a detour to Spalding on his way here."

The untidy figure of Tom Tarrant suddenly loomed above Andy's head.

"Get down!" Tim exclaimed. "We're probably being watched and we don't know if they're armed."

Tom obediently crouched next to Andy.

"I heard all of that," he said. "I don't think that I owe you an explanation for my movements, Detective Inspector, but, for the record, I phoned Carolyn Sheldrake again. I told your lady colleague that she was Alex's closest friend. She told me that your colleague had been speaking to her and, after a bit of persuasion, that she had indicated that Alex had been worried about some aspect of her dealings with Edmund Baker. Carolyn didn't tell me exactly what had been preying on Alex's mind and I chose not to pursue it further. I don't have time to think about that at the moment. Obviously I thought that Baker might be able to give some clue about her disappearance. I found his address in a directory of archaeologists that Alex keeps. As you know, we're staying with friends in Holbeach at the moment, so it didn't take me long to nip round to Baker's house. I met

PC Cooper just as he was leaving. He told me that Baker's whereabouts are at present unknown. It was PC Cooper's idea that I should come here with him."

"Indeed." Tim didn't know whether to be pleased at Gary Cooper's use of initiative or annoyed that he had dragged a member of the public into what could become a violent stand-off. As if he could read Tim's thoughts, Tom Tarrant continued.

"He has told me the bare minimum of what is going on here, but I've gathered that the children are being held hostage and may be in danger. Under the circumstances, I hardly count as a 'civilian'. I have a duty of care to those kids that is equal to your own."

Tim was impressed. He had Tom Tarrant marked down as a fairly effete character; certainly not as someone who could be relied on to keep a cool head in a crisis.

"Very well, Mr Tarrant. We shall be glad of your help, though you will have to let us be the judges of how much risk we'll allow you to take. This is Sergeant Jubb, who is in charge of the armed response unit."

Tom exchanged a nod with the Sergeant.

"Time was that I would have disapproved of what you do. But after Dunblane, I realised that people like you can be essential to protect children when there are madmen on the loose. But please tell me," he added, with only the faintest unsteadiness of voice, "is Alex in there?"

"We don't know for sure, but we don't think so, sir."

Tom's relief was palpable. Tim decided that this was not the right moment to tell him about the text message.

"I suggest that you describe as fully as you can to Sergeant Jubb the layout of the interior, Mr Tarrant," he said, and left them to it.

CHAPTER FIFTY-NINE

Juliet Armstrong called for two ambulances.

"If one of the men escaped how do you know he won't come back, perhaps with others?" Alex asked fearfully.

"It's unlikely. But if he does, this house is now being guarded by a squad of armed police. As I said, you're quite safe now. I'm going to make you some tea. I want you to stay here until the ambulance comes. I don't think it's good for you to try to move too far. Sergeant Harrison will stay here with you." She indicated the policeman who had accompanied her. He was still standing in the doorway. He was holding his gun at his side. He grinned at Alex. She tried to smile back.

Juliet did not add that she wanted to protect Alex from the scene of carnage in the kitchen. The man who had failed to escape had lost quite a lot of blood before she had applied a tourniquet. Oliver's body was lying outstretched on the floor in the position in which he had died, his torso reduced to a bloody pulp.

Juliet returned with the tea and Alex thirstily devoured a cup of it. It was stiff with sugar. She still felt weak, but the hit from the sweet tea helped to dispel her apathy. She hoped that Juliet would be able to answer some of her questions.

"How did you find me? This is Oliver's house, isn't it? I've never been here before, but I know that it's right out in the fen beyond Gosberton Clough, miles from anywhere. Was Oliver some kind of suspect?"

"No, no at all," said Juliet, remembering with some irony Tim's conviction that Oliver was a man in whom they could place absolute trust. "I haven't been here before, either, but Mr Sparham is known to us. As you are already aware, he's been helping with the McRae enquiry. We thought he might be able to help further when you went missing, so we tried to call him. There was no reply. When I'd called him before, an answering machine had kicked in when he was out. This time there was nothing, as if the phone had been disconnected. Not a cause for concern in itself, but when reports came in of a white van speeding through Gosberton, I decided to investigate further. An extra armed response unit had just reported for duty at the police station, so I asked if they could escort me. Were you abducted by someone in a white van?"

"Yes, but Oliver wasn't involved in that, though I saw him earlier today.

He was waiting when I was brought here. It was difficult for me to be able to tell whether he had helped to kidnap me or not. He seemed to have a very strained relationship with the people who took me; yet he wasn't exactly being held prisoner either. He did tell me that to try to escape would be futile. He seemed to be talking about himself as well as me. He tried to protect me as far as he could. He set me free for a while when we were alone. Who are these people? Do you know?"

"We're beginning to get some idea. We think that there are two sets of people involved, the members of a right-wing political group and an Eastern European drugs ring. The drugs ring seems to be funding the political group, but we're not sure why. It must be in return for something. They're also providing the armed men, but we've only just begun to understand why the political group wants to use violence."

"When Oliver and I were here on our own he mentioned that he'd belonged to an extremist group when he was young and that however much he might try to refute them and their ideas, he would never be able to escape from them. It all sounded a bit far-fetched to me."

"It probably wasn't, if he was talking about the group that I'm thinking of. It's called The Ymir. Have you heard of it?"

"No," said Alex. "But I think that I know why Oliver was interested in it. One of his ancestors was Jacob Sparham. There's a portrait of him on the wall over there." She pointed to the engraving. "He was a Victorian polymath. He belonged to the Archaeological Society. He travelled abroad a lot, and brought back various artefacts that he donated. Curiosities, a lot of them, and tourist junk. He wrote extensively in *Fenland Notes and Queries* – it was a quasi-learned journal that published the thoughts and exploits of gentlemen dilettantes. As a matter of fact, I was looking for the set of journals belonging to his period earlier today and I couldn't find them. I mentioned it to Francis Codd, one of our oldest members. He told me that Jacob Sparham had written some extremely right-wing interpretations of Darwin. I think that's where Oliver's political interest came from. He said as much, in fact."

"What about Edmund Baker? Did he show right-wing tendencies, too?"

"No, not at all."

CHAPTER SIXTY

TIM'S MOBILE ANNOUNCED another text message: "We can see that you haven't left. I'm sorry that you aren't taking us seriously at all. That is a mistake."

What happened next sped by with the rapidity of a dream in which Superintendent Thornton and his instructions played no part. The front door, still brightly illuminated by the police beam, opened and a figure well known to at least two of those watching stumbled out and almost fell down the two front steps; the next moment it was engulfed in flames, rolling and writhing in fitful agony.

"Lyle!" Before Tim could react, Tom Tarrant dashed forwards into the light, screaming and crying as he ran to the gates, which he succeeded in opening. They had not been locked. Pulling his jacket off, he desperately flapped at the flames, before a shot rang out and he cried once and fell.

Tim ran forward too, forgetful of his own safety, but was overtaken by three roaring armoured vehicles, the first of which rammed the partially-open gate and smashed it aside. Dark figures poured out and burst through the door in seconds, disappearing inside with incredible speed. Tim covered the ground faster than he had ever run, with Andy and Gary close behind him. Together, they worked with hastily-removed jackets and body armour to extinguish the flames, though it was clear that Lyle was already beyond help. Other officers, catching up, were tending to Tom Tarrant, who was alive but appeared to be badly hurt. There was blood on his sleeve and his usually rather flaccid face was etched, gaunt and pinched, in the lights of the vehicles. He stared ahead dully as if he had been hypnotised.

"Mr Tarrant! Tom! Talk to me!" Andy Carstairs had turned away from the gruesome body on the step to where he would perhaps be more useful.

Tom took a long moment to register Andy's presence.

"I think you're suffering from shock," said Andy. "Take my coat. An ambulance will be here any minute." As he spoke, emergency vehicles, both ambulances and fire engines, with sirens blaring, sped up the road.

Only a few minutes afterwards, Sergeant Jubb and several of his colleagues emerged. They were walking with four captives, each handcuffed. Three of the men were poorly dressed and looked as if they had been sleeping rough. The fourth was Guy Maichment. Tim made to step forward as Guy was marched towards an armoured vehicle, then changed his mind.

He had nothing to say to the man.

He was suddenly filled with alarm. Where were the children? Had they survived?

Sergeant Jubb had broken away from his colleagues and was walking briskly towards him.

"The kids!" said Tim. "Where are they?"

Sergeant Jubb grinned broadly.

"Relax!" he said. "They'd all been shut in the annexe – the sick bay that Mr Tarrant described. The fire escape had been chained and, from the fuel cans by the only internal door, it looks as if they intended to burn them and their carers all together in there. It didn't work, did it? And your Mr Maichment is all in one piece for your gov'nor."

CHAPTER SIXTY-ONE

STILL WEARING A hospital gown covered by a drab housecoat provided by the WRVS, Alex walked slowly through the hospital corridors to the ward to which Tom had been taken after his operation. Although she felt fuzzy with the combined effects of shock and the tranquillisers that she had been prescribed, she had refused her own ward sister's kindly offer of a wheelchair with a nurse to push it. She didn't want to alarm Tom more than she had to. Besides, to succumb to such pandering would have made her feel a fraud. Shock hardly counted as a proper illness; it certainly was not to be compared with gunshot wounds and burns.

She longed to meet Tom yet was fearful, almost shy, of seeing him. She didn't know the extent of his injuries or how much they might have disfigured him. That her enquiries had been met by the nurses with reassurances but no detailed information did not fill her with confidence.

She didn't know what they would talk about or whether he was angry with her. It was possible that he might not agree to see her. She remembered the comment that she had made to Carolyn when they'd met in the tapas restaurant: that, if Tom felt betrayed, he was quite capable of turning heel and just walking away. She hoped that she was wrong and that he would be able to show more compassion than this. She hoped that he hadn't found out about Edmund. Above all, Alex hoped fervently that, like herself, he would want to put the nightmarish events of the past two weeks behind him and that what they had suffered would bring them closer together. Even to herself, this sounded like too much of a women's magazine kind of ending.

She didn't know how much Tom had been told about the circumstances of her disappearance and subsequent rescue. She doubted that she could have done anything to prevent the kidnapping, but he might not believe that. Instinct told her that not only had he guessed that she had had an affair with Edmund – he had hinted as much on several occasions – but that, in the course of trying to find her, he had also stumbled on evidence that proved it. She could think of no other reason why he would have wanted to visit Edmund after she'd disappeared. Both Juliet Armstrong and Carolyn had told her of this visit. It was because Edmund had not been at home and Tom had instead met PC

Cooper that he had joined the police at Herrick House and endangered his own life. Indirectly, she was responsible for his injuries.

She had been told that although a bed in intensive care had been reserved for Tom there had been no need to use it. That at least sounded positive. He had been taken to a small ward for overnight observation.

She seemed to have been wandering the hospital corridors for hours when eventually she succeeded in finding Tom's ward. She tried to push against the swing door. Immediately it was pulled open from inside the ward. A nurse emerged.

"Are you lost, love?" she said. "I've got a patient in here who is very poorly. He needs quiet. Which ward are you on? I'll show you the way back." The woman was kindly and well-meaning, but still patronising. Despite her fatigue and the tranquillisers, Alex bristled. She told herself to be polite.

"I'm not lost. I was told that my husband was here."

"What's his name? As I've said, there's only one patient in this ward. He's post-operative and must not be disturbed."

"It's Tom. Tom Tarrant."

The nurse looked doubtful. "Who sent you here? Were you involved in the incident as well?"

"No, I wasn't. I was admitted because . . . it was a separate incident. Dr Singh sent a message to me. He told me that Tom had had his operation and that I'd be able to see him now."

"If Dr Singh said so . . . I thought that Mr Tarrant was to have no visitors until tomorrow, but he's awake now. He's very sleepy still. I'll ask him if he feels up to seeing you."

Alex nodded and waited nervously. She told herself that it was ridiculous to feel so scared.

The nurse returned.

"He says he'd like to see you. He can't speak very well and he's extremely tired. I don't think you should stay for more than five minutes."

The ward was half in darkness. It was lit only by the anglepoise lamp that stood on the nurse's desk. The three beds nearest the door were empty. The curtains of the fourth had been three-quarters drawn. A small gap had been left. The nurse gestured.

"There he is."

The nurse looked in and then went to sit at her desk. Alex was aware that she was still being discreetly watched. She pushed back the curtain a little further. Tom was stretched on his back, his head and shoulders propped high against a bank of pillows. His chest was bandaged and his arm resting in a sling. He was wired up to a machine and a drip had been attached to his left arm. A dressing obscured part of his face, but his eyes and mouth weren't covered. His eyes were not closed but drooping shut, as if he were about to fall asleep. He looked ineffably sad and small, somehow. Not the big, untidy, slightly overweight man to whom she had been married for more than ten years.

He seemed not to know that she was there. He was more badly hurt than she'd expected.

She moved closer to the top of the bed. His hand was protruding from the bandages. She wanted to take it in her own, to kiss it, but she was afraid of hurting or startling him. She was outside his range of vision now. She stood beside him, weeping.

Tom's head jerked up from his chest. The rushing tears had taken her by surprise. She could not cry silently. She bit deep into her lip. She didn't want to distress Tom. She was afraid of being ejected by the nurse.

Tom tried to turn his head so that he could see who was there.

"Alex?" he mumbled. His voice was dry and rasping. She could barely make out the word.

"Tom," she replied in a low tremulous voice. "Tom." She touched his fingers lightly, her tears raining down on them.

"Alex, you're here! No one knew . . ."

"Don't try to talk." She gripped the fingers more tightly. She saw that Tom's eyes had also filled with tears.

There was no chair in Tom's cubicle. Alex urgently needed to sit down. It would require more strength than she possessed to go back to the nurse and ask for one; in any case, she wouldn't leave Tom until she had to. She half-collapsed on to his bed, balancing on the very edge of it so that she wouldn't hurt him.

"Alex."

"Don't talk."

"I want to."

She had to lean her head close to his in order to be able to hear.

"I'm sorry," he whispered, the rasping voice becoming more ragged as he struggled to enunciate the words. "I'm so sorry that I didn't trust you. And so happy to have you back."

So that would be her cross. To have inspired a trust in Tom that she hadn't earned. She knew that she would not disillusion him by telling him the truth. That would be the coward's way out. She was lucky to have this second chance, flawed though it would always be by the knowledge of her own transgression. Ever afterwards, she would look back upon those days with Edmund as having belonged to an enchanted time. He had been a sorcerer, albeit a drab one, who had played upon her vanity. How could she have persuaded herself, even briefly, that their false lie-filled liaison had ever approximated to love?

CHAPTER SIXTY-TWO

THREE DAYS AFTER the terrible night at Herrick Old House, Tim and his team gathered in his office to take stock.

Lyle, of course, was dead.

Tom Tarrant had been seriously hurt. His face would be permanently, if not terribly, scarred, but the bullet had passed through him without materially damaging vital organs. He appeared to be in good spirits.

Guy Maichment had sustained no physical injuries, but the experiences of the evening had unhinged him. He had been taken to the high-security psychiatric unit at Rampton pending his trial. Tim had not yet been allowed to interview him, but he understood that Guy was receiving treatment from Dr Bertolasso, whom Tim liked and respected. He was confident that the psychiatrist would allow police access to Guy if he could make a sufficient recovery.

Several of the men from the drugs ring, including the Jared Tim had once glimpsed when he had visited Guy Maichment's cottage, had been cornered and arrested by the police, but a man called Endrit, whose name Alex Tarrant had heard and mentioned to Juliet (enabling her to identify him as an Albanian wanted by the police forces of several countries), and probably others had gone to ground. It was unlikely that their less fortunate cronies, now in captivity, would give them away; the temporary protection offered by custody notwithstanding, to betray Endrit was probably literally more than their lives were worth. Unless DNA could be found that definitively linked the rest of the gang to the crimes, Tim doubted that any of them would be apprehended.

The casualties had multiplied. The man found in the makeshift grave at Maichment's cottage might, in fact, have been the first of those relating to the case. Dame Claudia McRae was almost certainly dead, although the painstaking dredging operation now under way at the gravel pits had so far yielded no body. Krystyna Baker was dead. Oliver Sparham was dead. Lyle had been the most recent victim.

Edmund Baker and Jane Halliwell had disappeared. Superintendent Thornton thought that they had slipped through the police net together and were keeping each other company in a cosy hideaway somewhere; for some reason, he favoured Scotland. Tim knew that Juliet did not subscribe to this theory, which to his knowledge was not founded on fact. She believed that Baker was probably dead and was equally convinced that Halliwell had indeed managed to escape. She would put her money on the woman's having been whisked to the safety of a bolt-hole in Norway; she guessed that The Ymir would have welcomed Jane into the safety of their underground network. Her mission might have failed, but she was now one of their own, in deed as well as thought. Tim was inclined to agree with Juliet's assessment. Edmund Baker had never subscribed to the right-wing theories that Oliver Sparham had so unthinkingly embraced in his youth. He had agreed to work with them because they had had some kind of hold over him. He had both outlived his usefulness and become an embarrassment. Tim thought it likely that he had suffered the same fate as the corpse they had found in the park at Ayscoughfee shortly before Claudia McRae's disappearance.

Tim dismissed as worthless the warped logic with which The Ymir tried to rationalise their ideas. He would not waste time trying to understand their point of view, but he knew that they, like other extremist political groups, were probably adept at dazzling impressionable recruits, as they had the young Oliver Sparham, with their false glamour. What was more puzzling was how they had managed to interest a hard-nosed bunch of Albanian thugs in their activities, even to the extent of securing funds from them. Why the same thugs had agreed to risk not only their freedom but also their lives in embarking upon the insane and tragic enterprise of firing a children's home was even more difficult to fathom.

Over the past two days, Ricky MacFadyen and Andy Carstairs had been interviewing Jared. Juliet had meanwhile joined forces with Katrin to pool all of the information that together they had collected in order to try to make it tell an accurate and logical story. Tim noted that Katrin appeared to be much happier now. Their old intimacy would need re-learning, but her tears and scolding for exposing himself to danger at Herrick Old House had been a promising start. He had yet to pluck up the courage to engage her in the heart-to-heart that he had planned before the McRae case had completely taken over his life. He was determined not to shrink from it now by convincing himself that the problem had dissolved with her recovery. She might have regained some of her old equanimity and sparkle, but he had to find out if she was truly happy again. The period in which she had shut him out had been too profoundly disturbing for him to be able to risk allowing an unknown grievance to continue to fester beneath a veneer of calm.

Juliet had twice interviewed Alex Tarrant. Alex had been a pliant and co-operative witness, almost abject in her apologies for not having told the whole truth about her relationship with Edmund when the police had interviewed her after the break-in. Juliet was beginning to like her; all the same, she wondered if Alex would have been so frank if Tom Tarrant had not been tucked out of the way in hospital. She seemed fiercely deter-mined to defend her marriage against further damage. She confided that, although she had at first thought otherwise, she was satisfied that Tom did not believe that she had been unfaithful to him. Juliet wondered if this could really be true; an alternative explanation might be that Tom Tarrant was a wiser man than first acquaintance might suggest. He might have divined that healing the hurt would be easier if they did not confront the details of her infidelity head-on. Nevertheless, Juliet sympathised with Alex, who had suffered a great deal because of her ill-judged peccadillo with Edmund; and in part, Juliet believed, unfairly. She had certainly been groomed by him so that he could win her co-operation; Juliet doubted if Alex herself would have made the first move. And Tom probably had not been a perfect husband.

Many tasks remained to be accomplished. The police would have to continue to try to locate Edmund Baker and Jane Halliwell, round up more of the drugs gang and establish the exact crimes that each of the perpetra-tors could be charged with. In order to crack on with this work, Tim had asked Juliet to prepare as complete and accurate account as she could of the likely sequence of events since Dame Claudia's disappearance, giving background information where this might be relevant.

This was why the team had now all crammed itself into the largest of the evidence rooms. Most clutched plastic cups of coffee; the windows had already misted over. Juliet hovered apprehensively in front of the jumble of desks. Tim had invited her to fill in the gaps with conjecture if she felt that this could be done without making too many wild assumptions. He realised he was taking a risk here. Most of his direct reports were deeply sceptical about making deductions that couldn't be absolutely proved; he congratulated himself that this was mainly because he had trained them well. Whilst he had every respect for Juliet's hypotheses, he also knew that self-confidence was not her strongest trait; if ridiculed, she would back down or simply be unable to continue. Individually, he had therefore warned the others not to pour too much scorn on what she said if they disagreed with her. As he had explained, obtaining as coherent an inter-pretation as possible of an apparently disjointed, sometimes bizarre series of events would be more likely to promote a break-through than if they were merely to internalise each of these events individually.

Tim had always to tread a delicate path when encouraging Juliet. If he was too overtly critical, she shrivelled; if he praised her too fulsomely, she became embarrassed. Having thus quietly worked in private to ensure that she wouldn't be squashed during the meeting, he therefore decided that now he would adopt a matter-of-fact approach.

"Good morning, everyone. As you know, I've asked Juliet to provide us with a rather unusual kind of briefing and it may prove to be a long one.

Juliet's researched a lot behind the scenes as well as following all the work that we've done in the field and I'd like us all to hear her overall perspective on what has been happening from the perpetrators' point of view. I've told her to make educated guesses when she can't supply all the answers from fact. Juliet, we're all ears."

With her usual meticulousness, Juliet had already posted photographs on the glass screens in the meeting-room and written under each one with white, blue and red marker pens. She had drawn a timeline across the top of the central screen. Tim was amused to see that it began with the year 1937.

Juliet stationed herself alongside the screens.

"Good morning," she said. She didn't sound as nervous as he'd feared. She indicated the time-line briefly. "I'm not going to talk you through this all at once," she said. "It'll make more sense if I refer to it in stages as we go along."

She touched the first photograph.

"As you all know, this is a picture of Dame Claudia McRae. She is the famous archaeologist who disappeared four weeks ago. Her disappearance was reported by this man," – she indicated a photograph of Guy Maichment – "her nephew, who works as a landscape gardener and has recently been commissioned to carry out extensive work on the Herrick Estate. He has a long-standing relationship with this woman," – she pointed to a photograph of Jane Halliwell – "who is employed as Dame Claudia's companion and secretary. Jane Halliwell was cruising in the Baltic and some of the Norwegian fjords at the time of Dame Claudia's disappearance. She claims to have been accompanied by a friend, whom we have assumed to be male. She gave no further details, but we have established that she occupied a single cabin. The cruise ship's passenger records have yielded no information that could enable us to deduce which of her fellow travellers might have been the friend. However, during the middle part of the cruise the passengers disembarked at Oslo for the afternoon. I think that she may have met this man there." Juliet briefly touched a rather blurred picture of a tall, balding man standing in front of a lectern. It was a still taken from the podcast that she had watched early in the investigation. "I have examined the ship's CCTV; there is a picture of someone resembling him standing on the quay beside Jane before she re-embarked."

"Why did she say that she was accompanied by a friend if it wasn't true?" asked Andy Carstairs.

"I can't say for certain, but possibly to suggest that her reason for taking the cruise was to pursue a liaison. She wanted to cover up her real reason. Ironically, it was her mention of the friend that led me to dig further; the cruise ship company helpfully provided the CCTV footage."

"Do we know the identity of the man?"

"Various tests have yet to be carried out, but if I'm correct I think that he was *this* man." Juliet turned to another screen on which were affixed photographs taken from several angles of the corpse that had been dug up at Guy Maichment's cottage.

"Wow," said Andy. "Perhaps he should have gone on the cruise after all. He looks like he could have used a holiday." He was gratified to raise a few titters from his colleagues. "Who is he?"

"If I'm right – the tests still have to confirm it, remember – his name is Andreas Jensen. He is one of the leaders of an extremist right wing group that has existed in Norway since the 1930s. It calls itself The Ymir. The original Ymir was a primeval god. In old Norse mythology, its body parts were supposed to have been used to fashion the whole world. The group chose this name to indicate its commitment to monolithic racial purity; the founder's raison d'être was to preserve the Norwegian race intact, unsullied by any immigrant blood. There are indications that The Ymir has extended its activities to other countries. There are now 'chapters' here and in some of the European countries more strongly committed to opposing the introduction of immigrant communities."

"Did the swathe of blood we found on the hall wall of Claudia McRae's cottage come from this man?"

"Yes. That is one of the tests for which we already have a result."

"So if you are correct about his identity, he died two or three days after he met Jane Halliwell?"

"Yes. Rather cleverly, Halliwell made sure that she herself was nowhere near the scene of the two crimes – Claudia McRae's abduction and this man's murder – at the time they were committed. But I think that she instigated both of them."

"Who do you think killed the man? Was it Guy Maichment?"

"I think that that's unlikely. Guy claims to be very squeamish, especially about the sight of blood. The murder victim's throat was cut from ear to ear in a single slashing movement that required considerable strength, as well as a brutal disposition. I think that he was probably killed by a drug-dealer called Endrit Grigoryen, or by one of his henchmen, called Jared, one of the gang members we managed to apprehend. He's not co-operating, of course, and I'd say that he's borderline psychotic. I'll come back to him and Alex Tarrant's abduction later."

"We've believed all along that when she first disappeared, Claudia McRae had been abducted rather than murdered and, as you know, there was a sighting of her some time afterwards, which suggests that she wasn't killed straight away. But you think that she's dead now, don't you?" It was Tim speaking. Juliet noticed that his reference to the sighting sounded a little forced and uneasy.

"I need to give you some background about Dame Claudia. When she started work as an archaeologist in the 1930s she won a considerable amount of popular acclaim as a young woman who had broken into a man's world. However, she had little formal education or grounding in the scientific archaeological methods that were beginning to be developed. Although she wasn't just a treasure-hunter, she favoured the approach of the gentlemen archaeologists of the generation that preceded hers, such as Howard Carter. Briefly, this involved clawing their way willy-nilly through earthworks and architecture to reach the artefacts that lay beyond. They weren't interested in the construction of the monuments and buildings that they destroyed in the process. All archaeological digs are destructive, but the modern ones keep painstaking records of each stage of the dig and try to destroy as little as possible.

"Claudia's family was wealthy. She could have attended university to gain the right academic credentials or apprenticed herself to one of the younger archaeologists of the time. However, she was temperamentally unsuited to sustained study and very proud of the fame that she had already acquired as a young woman who had broken through the magic male monopoly."

"Very mellifluous!" said Ricky. "See if you can surprise us with a few more poetic turns."

Juliet flushed and faltered.

"Can we try to get through this uninterrupted?" said Tim. "We appreciate your wit, but this is all quite complicated. We need to concentrate."

Juliet gave him an uncertain smile.

"She wanted full recognition for her work and therefore began to write for archaeological publications, at least the ones that would accept her articles. Perhaps because she experienced some difficulty in getting the articles accepted, she wrote at least two full-length books about the digs that she had organised in the Middle East in the late 1930s. The first of these was published in 1937. Her theory, based on a limited amount of fact, was that in ancient societies women carried as much weight as men; that although the division of work between the sexes was already developing, women still fought and hunted alongside their menfolk. As well as this, she claimed that the traditional female tasks, such as child-rearing, were more valued than in later, historical times. As I've said, the theory was based on a very selective interpretation of some of the artefacts and wall paintings that she'd uncovered. Her writing was treated with scepticism by many of the male establishment, but Claudia struck a chord with women just as forerunners of what became the feminist movement began to gain momentum.

"Claudia was determined to overcome male prejudice. Her opportunity came in 1938. She'd been planning a dig in the Middle East and had obtained the funding for it – she was adept at touching her late father's influential friends for money – when the Foreign Office stepped in and warned her that the situation in Europe was such that it would be too risky for her to carry on with the dig. I don't think that Claudia would have taken a blind bit of notice of this, but, because of the fuss made about it, much of the funding was also withdrawn. She was asked by Lord McLachlan, who was also her publisher, to carry out some excavations in the Orkneys instead, as a kind of consolation prize. At first she was reluctant to take the job on, but she finally accepted the offer, if with a bad grace. By this time, war had been announced in Europe and she had few other options if she wanted to carry on as an archaeologist in the field.

"To give her due credit, she carried out the two Orkney excavations diligently, with little help except from local labourers who were paid to do some of the soil carting, etcetera. Her efforts were repaid with the most fantastic stroke of luck – a once-in-a-lifetime find."

"The McRae Stone?" said Tim.

"Yes. That's what it became known as. It's also been called the 'Rosetta of the North'. Like the Rosetta Stone, it was inscribed with the same text in three different ancient languages. Even though war had been declared, its discovery generated a huge amount of interest, both in this country and abroad.

"As we've seen, Claudia was already good at making her finds fit her theories. She had previously used her work to embrace the cause of feminism. She now set about claiming that her analysis of one of these three languages demonstrated that the people who had developed it were of superior intelligence to those who spoke the other two. I don't know whether she thought of it first herself or whether someone suggested it to her, but what she was proposing was that the sophistication of this language indicated the existence of an early master-race."

"And the language was an early form of Norwegian?"

"Yes. And of course the master race concept was as topical then as feminism had been earlier. Claudia wrote one article in support of her theory that reads just like her earlier stuff. She sets out her ideas enthusiastically, almost with bombast. She'd done some nifty work on the semantics, but she offers little other evidence to support it.

"The next article was published a year or so later. It is remarkable how much her style had changed in the interim . . ."

"This was after the war had started properly?"

"Yes. The article was published early in 1941. The second article and all the subsequent ones about the MacRae Stone that Katrin and I have found and read are less floridly written and much more closely argued. They are almost self-consciously erudite, with footnotes citing other work that show an impressive knowledge of semantics and early Norse history. And they are phenomenally well-versed in post-First-World-War politics. I suspect that Claudia herself introduced the master race idea to make a bit of a splash, but whoever wrote those articles was in deadly earnest. They were fascinated by her theory and they definitely wanted to make it stick."

"You don't think that Claudia herself wrote the later articles, then?"

"I'm certain that she didn't. Katrin doesn't think so, either. I should have said that, by the time the second article was published, Claudia had left Scotland for Norway. She was invited to collaborate with an academic at the University of Oslo. The academic's name was Dr Elida Berg."

"How did she manage to leave the country in wartime?"

"I don't know. She may have travelled on a warship. Through her father, she had plenty of friends in high places. She achieved instant acclaim when she discovered the McRae Stone, which probably made them more disposed to help her. In peacetime, she would have had a perfectly legitimate reason for taking up the Norwegian offer, because the language that she had identified was a variant of old Norse."

"Do you think that Elida Berg wrote the articles?"

"I'm certain that they collaborated; in fact, I've found an article that they wrote jointly. Later I think that Dr Berg was mostly writing on her own, but publishing under Claudia's name. The writings not only become progressively more erudite, but more strident in the political conclusions that they draw. I haven't found absolute proof that Dr Berg belonged to The Ymir, but the stuff that she wrote under her own name strongly points to it, as does her behaviour. I think that she may have belonged to more than one extremist group."

"But why would Claudia McRae go along with all this extremist stuff? Was this woman her lover?"

"It's true that, by the 1950s, Claudia's associates believed that she was a lesbian. According to Oliver Sparham, who first met her in the late '60s, her sexuality was a kind of 'open secret' among her student followers, something that they joked about in private. But I've found absolutely no evidence that she had lovers of either sex and I'm far from convinced that she was a lesbian. Everything that I've read and heard about her suggests to me that she was more or less 'asexual', for want of a better term. If Claudia was in love with anyone, it was herself. I think that she developed a kind of starry-eyed adulation of Dr Berg's intellect, though. It was almost love, but not sexually inspired."

"Do you think that she was coerced into lending her name to underpinning the theories of The Ymir?"

"Not coerced. I think that she recognised the huge cachet that the association with Dr Berg gave to her work; she would have agreed to support The Ymir, and maybe other political groups, without thinking too much about what she was doing. She probably didn't worry about the deeper implications. This was her chance of obtaining academic endorsement and she wasn't going to let it escape her."

"What happened to Elida Berg?"

"That's a good question. In 1947 a children's home that had been founded near Oslo during the war to shelter child refugees was burnt down. Some of the children had been reunited with their parents in 1945 and 1946, but the vast majority were still at the home in 1947. They had either been orphaned or their families could not be traced. They mostly came from Eastern European countries: Poland, Yugoslavia, the Baltic states. Some were Jewish. Only a few escaped the fire. The Norwegian police established without doubt that the fire had been started deliberately. Although it had the hallmarks of an organised crime rather than one that had been committed by a crazed individual, no group came forward to claim responsibility. Eventually the police became certain that it was the work of The Ymir; I'm not sure exactly how. The upshot was that several academics were forced to leave the University of Oslo; they disappeared completely. Other members of The Ymir were rounded up and some were tried and shot for treason. The organisation had been working with the Nazis during the war.

"It was alleged that the motive for burning the children's home had been ethnic cleansing. The Ymir had tolerated the presence of the children during the war, but, when it became clear that they would be remaining in the country, where one day they would be likely to intermarry and have children of their own, it decided to murder them."

Giash Chakrabati, who had been dozing off while Juliet was talking about archaeology, sat up straight in his chair and whistled.

"You're going to tell us that there is a link between this and the attempt to fire Herrick Old House!"

Juliet nodded. She was about to continue when Andy Carstairs interrupted.

"This is all fascinating and I'm sure you're right about a lot of it. You've done a great job on the research and the story so far hangs together, as far as I'm concerned. But all of this happened before any of us was born. Claudia McRae must have come back to the UK long ago and carried on being a famous archaeologist. So why has it taken more than half a century for a copycat crime to be committed? And what happened to Elida Berg?"

"Elida Berg's disappearance continued to be of significance in Claudia's life. We don't know where Berg went to ground; given her extreme nationalism, I'd put my money on her having been concealed in a remote part of Norway; I don't think that she would have consented to exile herself elsewhere. The Ymir would have helped. They may have supported her financially, or she may have been given a new identity and worked in some unobtrusive and appropriate profession – as a schoolteacher or a librarian, for example. Whatever the circumstances, she still had access to a good academic library. I know this, because I'm pretty certain that all of the so-called 'semantic archaeology' papers that Claudia McRae published in the fifties and sixties were actually entirely or partly authored by Elida Berg. They were never completely accepted by the archaeological establishment, but this was no longer because Claudia didn't use the right style and provide appropriate references; each one was a superbly-argued piece of academic virtuoso. But other academics were wary of the writings, because even those well to the right of the political mainstream felt uncomfortable about the extremist views upon which they were founded."

"I read some of those papers myself when I was a student," said Tim. "I didn't notice the 'extremist views'."

The whole team howled with laughter.

"OK," he said, raising his hands palms up. "I let myself in for that. I was more naïve in those days."

"Probably not all that naïve," said Juliet. "You'd have had to know what you were looking for, and to have read a considerable number of the articles before you would have understood what was going on. You'd probably need to have dug deeper than the average undergraduate would have been likely to. For example, Katrin found recurring instances of some of the arcane symbols and totemic words used by The Ymir and, although the extremist stuff is present in all of them, it's skilfully argued. What I'm saying is that, over time, it would have made an expert uneasy; and that's probably why, although Claudia achieved tremendous popularity with the British public as well as with her own coterie of students, she never received the academic accolades that she felt that she deserved."

"What happened to The Ymir?"

"I'm coming to that. After the executions, the group went to ground. It didn't disband; from 1950 to about 1990 there were isolated instances of attacks on immigrant communities in Norway and other acts of extreme nationalism that police attributed to The Ymir. In one or two very high-profile cases – the murder in 1982 of a government minister whose parents had been immigrants, for example – it actually claimed responsibility.

"At some point in the early 1990s, it ceased to be an entirely underground movement. It tried to make itself respectable by developing a political wing that acted within the law."

"A bit like the IRA?" said Andy, who was now hanging on Juliet's every word, fascinated by the turn her account had taken.

"Exactly. Though with the difference that, as far as we can ascertain, The Ymir's cause did not have – it still does not have – a large popular following in Norway. It has always been an extremist group, supported by and for extreme nationalists. That's not to say that all the members of its political wing have been nutcases living on the fringes of society. They have included at least one government minister and others with high profiles: a banker, a journalist and, most worrying of all, a high-ranking soldier."

"Did the terrorist element fade away, also become 'respectable', or just carry on as it had always done?" asked Tim.

"I can't answer that for sure. Probably it either carried on as it had before, or the extremist element broke away into splinter groups in order to perpetuate the violence because they despised the political agenda as being too insipid. One way or another, the violent acts continued, although they became more sporadic – possibly because at intervals the extremist groups recruited new members who embarked upon bursts of evangelism before becoming receding again into anonymity. Most of the violent acts had to be planned and paid for, as well. The best of The Ymir's brains had joined the political wing. It was able to canvass for funds like any other political group, but what it did with them was monitored quite closely by the authorities. However, in addition to legalising the movement in Norway, the political arm was able to offer The Ymir the advantage of legitimately raising its profile in other countries. So-called overseas 'chapters' were set up. Some of these provided money, but until now it seems there has never been enough money to carry out a large-scale act of terrorism."

"From what I've read, groups like this often take years to raise the money they need to carry out their plans," said Tim.

"I don't think that The Ymir was an exception. Andreas Jensen was appointed political leader in 1994 and worked hard to obtain funds. Although we know that some wealthy individuals were attracted to The Ymir, in Norway, as in other European states, political donations over a certain amount have to be made public. This may have dissuaded donors. Whatever the reason, The Ymir was still struggling for funds in 1998 when he hit on the idea of offering his services as an occasional lecturer on right-wing politics at universities in the UK and elsewhere in Europe. I think that his aim was not just to raise the profile of The Ymir, but to interest potential funders who were perhaps less sensitive about being identified in Norway than his fellow countrymen were.

"Lincoln was one of the universities at which he gave his series of lectures. He was invited by a young female academic who became an immediate convert."

"Jane Halliwell?"

"Yes. My guess is that Jane was a very bright young woman searching for a cause. She was also an assiduous researcher. It wasn't easy to research the history of The Ymir – it still isn't, because so much of it hasn't been openly published – but somehow she managed to establish that Claudia McRae's writings about the McRae Stone had brought her into contact with right-wing groups, including The Ymir. She was already interested in Claudia because of what she had read of her theories about the super-race. She'd also – and as far as I know this really was a coincidence, though many of the encounters and friendships between individuals in this story were, I'm sure, engineered – recently enrolled a mature student on one of her courses whom she discovered to be related to Claudia."

"Guy Maichment?"

"Yes. Guy was in his thirties at the time. He'd studied several subjects at college and university – he'd never completed a course – and spent brief periods of time in various dead-end jobs. Claudia had been his main source of income since he'd left school. He'd managed to persuade her to let him enrol on the Politics course, with the intention of eventually himself becoming a lecturer. I don't know how she viewed this – whether he presented it as being what he really wanted to do this time or whether she said that it would be his final chance. He could have had some kind of hold over her."

"It seems odd that she was so indulgent. You'd think that long before she'd have told him to knuckle down and support himself. From what you say, she wasn't famous for her philanthropy."

"I'm coming to that. This time, Guy *did* knuckle down. He proved himself to be not just an adequate, but a brilliant, student of Politics. You're right, however. People who know them – and I've talked to several people, local farmers, and others, who've been with Guy and Claudia together – say that he was often quite disparaging about her; that on occasions he treated her almost with disdain. They say that she either seemed to be afraid of him or to feel that she owed him some debt. If this is true, it would explain why she spent so many years supporting him financially. Something I also wonder about, though even if we carry out blood tests we probably won't get conclusive proof, is whether Claudia is his aunt at all."

"Do you think that he may be her son?"

"No. No, I don't. It was one of the first ideas that I had, but Claudia quite liked flouting convention and she wasn't afraid of gossip. If she'd had an illegitimate child, I don't think she'd have taken the trouble to try to disguise the fact. Guy's name, Maichment, was Claudia's step-mother's surname. The stepmother was not much older than Claudia herself and her marriage to Claudia's father didn't last long. She reverted to her maiden name after she was divorced from him. Some time after this, she gave birth to a daughter who was baptised Abigail. The mother died – probably of alcoholism – in the early 1950s, when Abigail was a very young child. Claudia, of course, was away a lot on digs. She paid for Abigail to be cared for and go to boarding school when she was old enough. She was obliged to do so because of some complication in her father's will. Apparently the girl mostly stayed at the school even during the holidays, unless she was invited to friends' houses. She had little contact with Claudia until she was in her teens, when Claudia allowed her to attend various digs. Oliver Sparham remembered Abigail. He said that she made a complete nuisance of herself. Eventually Claudia got fed up with her and sent her back to England, where she had enrolled her on a secretarial course."

"So Abigail Maichment wasn't a blood relative of Claudia's at all?"

"I don't think so; but Claudia seems to have accepted her as a sister, in public at any rate."

"Do you think that Abigail was Guy's mother?"

"I've thought about this a lot, too, as well as collecting as much evidence as I can, and I don't think that she can have been Guy's mother. She never started the secretarial course. She was admitted to University College Hospital on the day after she arrived back in England and died there the same day. She'd contracted West Nile Virus."

"That doesn't necessarily rule her out as Guy's mother."

"No; but the dates don't fit. Guy was born in 1960. Abigail was thirteen or fourteen then. I realise that she was therefore old enough – just – to have been his mother, but her school attendance record is unbroken between the years 1956 and 1964, the year that she left. She went on the digs in 1964 and 1965 and died in 1965. Schools in those days didn't allow pregnant pupils to stay on; they were usually expelled, or just required to go away discreetly. But even if Claudia had somehow persuaded the school to keep Abigail, I can think of no reason why she would then have agreed to support the baby. The babies of young unmarried mothers were routinely put up for adoption in those days, and Claudia wasn't maternal. Besides, there is the coroner's report to consider."

"Which coroner's report?"

"Because Abigail died of a virulent infectious disease, there had to be a full post mortem and inquest. I've seen the coroner's report, and there is no evidence of her having given birth. The post mortem would have picked this up and would have mentioned it."

"So who do you think Guy's mother was – or is?"

"Again I can't say for certain, but I think that it's likely that his mother was one of the academics who went into hiding with Elida Berg after the children's home near Oslo was burnt down. The Norwegian authorities are trying to help me to locate a birth certificate for Berg. I don't know her date of birth, but judging from the photographs I've seen of her and Claudia together she was about ten years the elder, which would mean that she was born in about 1907. It could have been a few years after this, but, even so, it seems unlikely that she would have borne a child in 1960."

"And she was gay." Andy presented the comment as a statement, not a question.

"In all probability, though again I can't be certain. If she was gay and had a partner who had a child, that could explain why Claudia took the child on. Guy has a British passport but I can find no record of his birth certificate or early years. He first surfaces as a boarding pupil at Stamford School in 1971."

"You've said that Guy was often offhand with Claudia. How does that fit in?" It was Andy again.

"Again I don't have an answer. It's possible that he spent his early years with hard-core members of The Ymir who felt that Claudia had taken the soft option by dissociating herself from them."

"Yet both Claudia and Guy seem to have got on with Jane Halliwell, and Jane Halliwell and Guy also seem to have worked closely together?"

"I think that Jane cast herself as the peace-maker. She had to tread a fine line in order to insinuate herself into the activities of The Ymir. They don't trust easily and Claudia McRae probably didn't trust them, although her respect for Elida Berg may have remained undiminished. Jane demonstrated the extent of her commitment by giving up her academic career, but she still had to earn her spurs. In order to do this, I think that she almost pulled off a brilliantly-conceived coup that she'd thought up herself. The Ymir wanted a full-length work on Claudia McRae's semantic theory, with the emphasis to be placed on the super-race angle and conclusions drawn about the importance of maintaining linguistic, and therefore racial, purity. Jane undertook to act as Claudia's secretary and amanuensis, and at the same time persuaded Claudia that she was herself a sort of latter day Elida Berg who could help her to create a magnum opus that would both bring acclaim at the end of her life and an assured place in academic history. Claudia was tremendously flattered and completely taken in. Arguably, Jane could have pulled off this feat and given both Claudia and The Ymir what they wanted – I've been told by her former dean that her academic prowess is formidable – if it hadn't been for Guy's fundamentalism.

"Guy didn't just want the book to expound the Claudia-Elida arguments in such a way that they would have to be accepted as watertight and irrefutable; he wanted to demonstrate that the atrocities committed in 1947 and on subsequent occasions by The Ymir, which they believed were justified by their reading of the theories, should be recreated to be cited as modern-day examples.

"My guess is that Jane was uncomfortable with this at first. Her analytical mind will not have wanted to mix principles with practice in such a way. However, in the years between his enrolment as a Politics student and the time at which he began to plot the attack on the children's home, Guy had probably become a leading light in The Ymir. It is conceivable that he had been groomed for a terrorist role since childhood. Whatever the truth of that, Jane either persuaded herself or was persuaded by members of The Ymir that Herrick Old House should be burnt in emulation of the burning of the children's home in Oslo. That Herrick Old House is home to children from many different national backgrounds will have lent weight to Guy's plan. He is an emotional character and no doubt believed that it was 'meant to happen'."

"I'd forgotten that you said that Guy originally enrolled in Politics," said Tim. "What on earth made him change to landscape gardening?"

"I think that this may have been Jane's idea, too. She must have known fairly early on in their relationship that Guy intended to spend his life working for The Ymir and, although she probably thought that it was his intention to set up a new political arm in the UK, rather than engage directly in militant activities, she may have advised him to keep a low profile. I don't know why they hit on landscape gardening. Guy must be competent at it, because he has attracted some eminent clients; but there is no evidence that he is passionate about gardening. It may be that Jane hoped that some of his aristocratic clients might be enthusiastic enough about The Ymir and what it stands for to want to offer donations."

"Is there evidence that Lord Herrick is a supporter?"

"None at all. On the contrary, Lord Herrick is rather self-consciously philanthropic. Not only does he help to fund Herrick Old House, but he's set up a foundation to train young people from the home in trades and craft skills. Some of them seem to have got tangled up with the drugs gang that's been funding The Ymir's activities here. Tom Tarrant, Alex Tarrant's husband, was involved in disciplining them. But I think that the kids brought with them an unexpected complication. The drugs gang was using them and other local tearaways, like LeRoy Padgett and his brother, as couriers."

"Explain the drugs gang," said Tim. "Obviously you must be right when you say that they were involved; we know that they were in it up to their necks. They were responsible for Alex Tarrant's abduction, Oliver Sparham's murder and for most of what happened two nights ago at Herrick Old House. They were certainly the ones with the weapons. But why did they bother to get involved at all, let alone provide the funds? I just don't see what was in it for them. And I certainly don't think that someone like Endrit Grigoryen would suddenly turn evangelical and embrace the right-wing ideology of a half-crazed Norwegian political group."

Juliet looked nervous again.

"Thank you for more or less accepting what I have said so far. This is where I really do need a bit of willing suspension of disbelief," she said. "Endrit Grigoryen does want something from The Ymir; and interestingly enough, although it has nothing to do with right-wing politics, it is related to a belief system.

"May I just take you back to the 1960s on my timeline?" Juliet touched a point about a third of the way along the line that she had drawn. Against it, she had affixed photographs of Oliver Sparham and Edmund Baker.

"You will remember that I said that once someone has belonged to The Ymir, they cannot escape from it afterwards. They may back away from its activities and lead a perfectly ordinary life in every other respect, but The Ymir still regards them as members and keeps a distant watch on their activities. To a certain extent I believe this was what happened to Claudia McRae, although she was probably willingly in touch with Elida Berg until her death, which I guess from the documentary evidence – I mean of the articles that Claudia published – happened at some point in the late sixties or early seventies. After that, I think it likely that Claudia tried to dissociate herself somewhat from them, at least until Jane Halliwell appeared on the scene. Of course, for much of that time Guy was around to keep tabs on her anyway.

"Oliver Sparham was persuaded to join The Ymir in the late sixties, probably by Claudia herself, during one of Claudia's digs in the Middle East. Another of her young protégés, Edmund Baker, was also on that dig. Oliver was much closer to Claudia than Edmund, who had left-wing tendencies and no time for the political 'truths' that Claudia attempted to draw from her archaeological writings. If someone mentioned The Ymir and its ideology to him, which may or may not have happened, he will either have regarded it as nonsense or something to be shunned as totally alien to his own beliefs. I am quite certain that Edmund was never a member. Edmund's role in the whole of this story has been that of outsider. He has been protected from danger only by something that he came to know about during that dig, when he met Oliver for the first time. In fact, he seems to have got on well with Oliver then, though the friendship cooled quickly when they ceased to be students.

"At some point during that summer Oliver told Claudia and Edmund, and probably also some of the other people working with them, about one of his ancestors, Jacob Sparham, a wealthy clergyman who lived in the mid-nineteenth century and travelled extensively. Apparently he fancied himself as an antiquarian, and brought back from his travels a large number of artefacts, which he donated to the Archaeological Society in his will. However, he had no eye for what was a genuine 'antiquity' and what had been faked. In short, the locals at most of the places that he visited saw him coming and palmed him off with a lot of tourist tat, no doubt also charging him handsomely for it. He was, incidentally, very right wing; he was one of the first pedants to misinterpret Charles Darwin's theories by drawing a link between them and the concept of a master race. The Archaeological Society boxed up most of Jacob Sparham's stuff and stored it in an old chapel which it uses as an archive. Various archaeologists have asked permission to open the boxes in the intervening century and a bit and they've all said the same thing: that they contain nothing of interest. However, the records that Jacob himself kept describe a precious artefact that was not included in the donation. It's not clear how he acquired this artefact; although he was a clergyman, I think that it's likely that he stole it. Perhaps because he was travelling in Albania at the time, he felt that it was fair game. His writings often refer to the people that he encounters as 'backward' and even 'savage'."

"Well, tell us what it was," said Tim.

Juliet rolled her eyes. All the faces in front of her appeared to be spellbound. She was enjoying this unexpected burst of power.

"It was a swastika made of gold, studded with blue diamonds," she said. "It was quite large – Jacob Sparham said that it did not fit comfortably into his hand. No one knows how old it was. Sparham obtained it from a monastery that belonged to the Albanian Orthodox church. The monastery was founded in the tenth century, but the swastika was probably much older. It almost certainly came from India and could have been made several thousand years ago."

"How much would it be worth?"

"Blue diamonds are among the most valuable, because they're extremely rare. It's not possible to say how much the individual stones would be worth – it would depend on whether they were large or small, almost perfect or very flawed. But together they'd be worth a lot – millions, certainly. If the swastika was indeed an ancient jewel, it would be priceless."

"Are you saying that you think that the promise of the swastika was used as collateral? That Endrit Grigoryen said he would bankroll the chapter of the Ymir set up by Jane Halliwell and Guy Maichment because he wanted to retrieve the swastika for this monastery? Or did he just pretend this and intend to sell it when he got his hands on it?"

"I don't know. But maybe one of those things, or a mixture of them. As I've said, he'd made things more complicated than they needed to be by involving children from Herrick Old House as couriers. Some of the same children were also apprenticed to the Herrick Estate, which confused matters even further, but Grigoryen and Guy might not have known about this."

"I'm beginning to lose track of this now," said Tim. "Some of those kids are from eastern Europe. Why would Grigoryen agree to try to kill them?"

"I don't think he'd have had any compunction about that," said Juliet. "He's a pretty ruthless character. He's wanted in several countries for drug smuggling and exploiting children. I think that he was determined to get his hands on the swastika , whatever his reason for wanting it, and that he agreed to go along with Guy's lunatic plan to burn down Herrick Old House and its occupants as part of the deal."

"There seems to be no proof at all that this swastika exists or that if it does it's still here in Spalding. If it wasn't among the stuff included in Jacob Sparham's legacy to the Archaeological Society, he might have given it privately to someone who subsequently sold it, or to some other organisation."

"That seems to have been Oliver Sparham's view, at least until recently; as I've said, his family hunted for the swastika on various occasions and concluded that it wasn't among their possessions. But if it is as rare and valuable as I think that it is, it couldn't have been donated to a society or museum without there being some record of it. It would probably be famous, in fact."

"So what has managed to convince a hard-boiled desperado like Grigoryen that he's really on to a winner here?"

"You'll remember that Edmund Baker was a member of the dig when Oliver told the story about the swastika. Edmund was never one of Dame Claudia's inner circle, probably in part because he didn't subscribe to her political views. But he was fascinated by the tale itself and never forgot it. After he took the post of County Heritage Officer he became an avid collector of local history papers and other memorabilia, particularly ones relating to the Kirton area, where he was born. To anyone except an enthusiast, collections like this can seem quite tedious. They tend to be a mixture of old wills and property deeds and the published and unpublished musings of clergymen of varying degrees of talent. Edmund Baker's collection was probably no exception. But then he struck gold. Missing from his collection were the papers of a nineteenth-century clergyman called the Reverend Victor Lockhart. Edmund read an announcement in one of the smaller, more gossipy sections of *Fenland Notes and Queries* for the year 1868 that this clergyman's daughter, Charlotte Lockhart, had become engaged to Jacob Sparham. It was not the usual sort of announcement made in this journal; it may have been included because both Sparham and Lockhart were amateur antiquaries. The event itself was of little interest to Baker, but the final section of the article held him spellbound; it mentioned that, instead of giving his fiancée a conventional engagement ring, Sparham had presented her with a 'rare jewel' acquired on his travels. The engagement was subsequently broken off. There was no record of the nature of the rare jewel or what happened to it, but Baker clearly thought that it was the diamond swastika. He was convinced that the information would be contained within the Reverend Lockhart's papers. He searched for them for years, without success. Quite recently they turned up as a donation to the Peterborough Museum. Baker borrowed the money to buy them from the museum's trustees. Alex Tarrant was at the meeting when this was agreed."

"If Baker didn't get on particularly well with Dame Claudia and would have no truck with The Ymir, how did they find out that he had new information that might lead to the swastika?"

"Again this is conjecture, but I've been helped by Alex Tarrant, who has begun to think about Baker's erratic behaviour and how it might be explained. One of the things that he told her during their brief romance was that he'd had a fling with another woman a few years before and had promised his wife that such a thing wouldn't happen again. Alex thinks that this woman could have been Jane Halliwell."

"Why would Halliwell target Baker? Or are you telling me that she really fancied the guy?"

"I think that she set out to get him. He'd been so enthusiastic about the swastika on the dig – possibly even said that he intended to track it down – that Claudia McRae probably remembered and told Halliwell the story when they were working on their book. Halliwell will have been just as keen to get her hands on it as he was, either to present the thing as a sort of trophy to The Ymir, or to break it up for funds to support them; but she'd have quickly found out that at that time he had no proper information about it."

"So she used him in the same way that he subsequently used Alex Tarrant?"

"That's what I'm guessing."

"What did he hope to get from Alex?"

"I don't know. Neither does she. My guess is that when he worked through the Lockhart Papers, the trail led him to the archive at the Archaeological Society. Either he thought he could find more information there, or the swastika itself. He needed Alex to help him to get access to the archive, and he needed it quickly."

"Why the hurry?"

"Because, I conjecture, on the strength of his hunch he'd borrowed the money for the Lockhart papers from Jane Halliwell, who'd perhaps got it from Endrit Grigoryen, and time was running out for him. He didn't have the funds to pay Endrit back."

"I still don't get it. How much did he have to pay for this country vicar's papers? It can't have been a huge amount."

"He paid the Peterborough Museum the sum of £5,000."

"Hmm, too much, almost certainly, though you can see why he'd be prepared to do it. But even though it's a hefty amount, you'd expect someone at his stage of life to have been able to cover it."

"He couldn't cover that or many more bills and bank loans that were outstanding. It's likely that soon he would have had to sell his house. Edmund Baker is a compulsive gambler."

Someone knocked and entered the room. It was the desk sergeant.

"Excuse me, sir. I've just taken a call from Rampton. Apparently one of the other inmates attacked Guy Maichment about an hour ago?"

"Is he seriously hurt?"

"Apparently he's half-dead. He's been rushed to Retford Hospital. It's touch and go whether they'll be able to save him."

"Juliet, we're going to have to postpone this. Andy, you need to get in touch with the Nottinghamshire police. Maichment's going to need round-the-clock protection. I'll ask Dennis Bertolasso if someone can be posted beside his bed to take down anything that he might say."

CHAPTER SIXTY-THREE

GUY MAICHMENT DIED that night, without regaining consciousness. Juliet's version of the McRae case was respected by her colleagues as having provided them with the sanest interpretation of events that they were ever likely to receive, although, as Giash Chakrabati pointed out, they weren't dealing with very sane criminals. She didn't get the opportunity to complete it. Tim had been counting on their being able to prise some information from Guy.

On the following day the divers at the gravel pit retrieved the remains of a very aged woman. They were identified from dental records and from an old healed fracture in one arm as having belonged to Dame Claudia McRae. On the same day, the results of DNA tests carried out on the corpse that had been buried in Guy Maichment's garden showed conclusively that it was that of Andreas Jensen. The police made further progress during the next fortnight; they succeeded in rounding up several more members of Endrit Grigoryen's gang. Poorly educated and unable to speak much English, these men had been at a loss to know how to survive once Endrit summarily cut them loose. They almost seemed glad to have been caught.

Although it would probably never be possible to piece together all of the events that had led up to the intended firing of Herrick Old House, the new arrests and other information gathered from Oliver Sparham's and Edmund Baker's houses seemed to corroborate Juliet's hypotheses. When, after news of Jensen's death was circulated by the media, it was announced that the Norwegian government had stripped the political arm of The Ymir of its right to be recognised as a bona fide organisation and therefore to raise funds legally, Tim Yates concluded that she had probably been right about him, too.

The development helped to provide an explanation for his murder. Although no doubt he had steered close to the law, for the past twenty years Jensen had tried to legitimise the The Ymir by presenting it to the world as a political group that was entitled to hold opinions, like any other. Guy's mad plan to restore it to its 'roots' by precipitating it headlong into acts of terrorism and mass murder had almost certainly been opposed by Jensen, who had paid for this resistance with his life. Tim guessed that his visit to Dame Claudia's cottage had been to ask her to persuade her nephew to abandon his crazy activism. It might have been then that she realised belatedly that Guy and Jane Halliwell were manipulating her and that her nearly completed 'great work' would be published not to celebrate her, but to support The Ymir's ideology. She might have been distressed by Jensen's account of Guy's intentions and promised to help him. This alone would have been enough to seal her fate, but, once Jensen had been killed in her house, presumably by Grigoryen or one of his thugs, if Guy could not get her to be complicit in the murder, he would have been obliged to make her disappear. Although he was not especially fond of her, he would probably have baulked at agreeing to allow her own murder and arranged to have her held somewhere instead. Sadly, it might have been Katrin's sighting of her that finally precipitated her death. Tim was anxious that Katrin should not understand this, though he suspected that it was a futile hope.

Why Guy had not cleared up the mess after Jensen's death was a bit of a puzzle; perhaps it had genuinely been because he was too squeamish. Whether or not Oliver Sparham had been directly involved in Dame Claudia's disappearance was impossible to say. Tim persisted in his original reading of Oliver as an essentially honest and honourable man. He therefore chose to continue to believe Oliver's account of his last meeting with Claudia. Juliet was inclined to agree with him, but for the less visceral reason that what Oliver had said fitted in with the forensic evidence. The wall had been spattered with Jensen's blood much later than 4.30 p.m. in the afternoon before Claudia's disappearance. Oliver had had a watertight alibi from the time of his arrival at the conference at 5 p.m. until the early hours of the following morning, by which time Jensen had almost certainly been murdered.

Superintendent Thornton was reasonably happy with the progress made by Tim and his team, even though there had been a certain number of deaths that he would have liked to be able to transform into arrests. He was still exercised by police failure to locate either Edmund Baker or Jane Halliwell, and persisted in his fanciful notion that they had eloped to Scotland together. Although Alex Tarrant's statement included details of the conversation with Oliver in which he had said that he believed that Jane might have been the mystery woman with whom Edmund had first committed adultery, Tim could not see why a woman like Jane would impede her flight and run a greater risk of capture by yoking herself to a man for whom she probably had little regard. He did not dissuade Thornton from enlisting the help of the Scottish police, but at the same time he was pursuing a different line of enquiry. Police officers who had been randomly stopping vehicles on the night of the Herrick Old House incident had seen a car approach at speed, then suddenly slow down and reverse. It had turned precipitately and roared back into the darkness towards Star

Fen, which was not far from Sleaford. Two of them had seen the car quite clearly. Although they could not say what colour it had been, they had both agreed that it was an elderly Saab.

If the car had indeed been Edmund's, it was possible that when he saw that he might be stopped, he decided instead to join Maichment and Grigoryen's men at Herrick Old House. Tim thought that this was unlikely, however. All the other evidence suggested that Edmund would be running away from the Albanians. He probably didn't know of their plans to fire the children's home, in any case. He had always been an outsider and now became a fugitive from everyone, even his own family. His sons had showed little but contempt for him. After their mother's funeral, they had each returned to their jobs in distant places, seemingly careless of whether Edmund was found or not.

Tim was intrigued by the sighting, though, and convinced that it held the key to Edmund's whereabouts. A few days after the fire he drove to the place where the officers had been, turned round, as had the driver of the Saab, and took the road to Star Fen. It was a tiny hamlet. He remembered vaguely that he had visited it once before, searching for someone accused of embezzling money who had been seen at a rented cottage there.

Star Fen consisted of a single street with half a dozen houses and a few farm buildings. Three vehicles were parked in the street. None of them was a dark red Saab. Tim got out of the BMW and walked along the road for some distance beyond the houses, and back again. It was a place of familiar fenland scenery: neatly-tilled fields bounded by deep dykes, no trees, few shrubs or bushes. Not promising territory for concealing a strange vehicle.

He sauntered back to his car again. At first he had thought that the hamlet was deserted. Then he saw a man standing at the side of one of the houses, watching him intently. He was a well-built man in his twenties, with a lot of untidy dark hair and a swarthy face. He was wearing navy-blue overalls and gigantic green gumboots. He carried a grease-gun in one hand. As Tim drew closer, he saw that he had evidently been tinkering with the engine of an aged tractor that was jammed up against the side of the house wall. Tim decided that he would speak to him. As he crossed the road, the man came walking towards him with rapid steps.

"Have you come about the bike?" he said.

"No," said Tim. "What made you think I had?"

The man snorted. "Got copper written all over you. No-one's come about it yet. I thought that they might have sent you."

"No," said Tim. "But you're right, I am a copper." He produced the photograph of Edmund Baker that Gary Cooper had acquired from one of Baker's sons. "Have you seen this man hanging around here at all?"

The man held the photograph gingerly between greasy thumb and forefinger.

"Can't say I have. People don't hang around here, in any case. That's what's so odd about the bike. Thought that bastard next door might have taken it." He jerked his head back in the direction of the tractor. "But I'd have seen him with it by now. It's too close to home for him, anyway. Wouldn't be able to use it here, would he?"

"Are you telling me that you've had a bicycle stolen and you've reported it?"

"Not a 'bicycle'." The man pronounced the word mincingly. "A motor-bike. A Triumph. My pride and joy, it was. And the only way I had of spending a bit of time away from here. It's all right, like. But it gets lonely."

Tim was suddenly very alert.

"When was your motorbike stolen, Mr . . . I'm sorry, I didn't ask your name . . ."

"It's Sentance. Richard Sentance. Four days ago."

"You're sure about that?"

"Of course I'm sure. Cops all over the place that night, weren't there? Even come here once. I didn't know it had gone then, mind. Otherwise I'd have put them on to it."

"You're definitely talking about four days ago?"

"That's the one. When will someone come about it, do you think?"

Tim dredged up one of the many details of Alex Tarrant's statement. She'd said that Edmund had been keen on motorbikes; that he'd told her that he'd had one in his youth and intended to buy another. He certainly knew how to ride one.

"I'll make sure that someone comes to take a statement today. In the meantime, would you mind describing it to me as accurately as you possibly can?"

"I don't need to do that. I've got photos of it: dozens of them. You can take your pick."

CHAPTER SIXTY-FOUR

ARMED WITH THE photographs, Tim returned to the police station. He put out a search request for sightings of the motorbike to all the police forces within a fifty-mile radius. He decided that it would be better to search intensively in a small area at first and extend the radius further if this didn't work. He also asked local radio stations to broadcast descriptions of it. Edmund's photograph had already appeared on regional news programmes and their websites. Tim asked them to re-run, adding photographs of the motorbike as well. Then he contacted the police at Sleaford and asked them to search the dykes around Star Fen.

The last of these initiatives was the first to bear fruit. Towards the end of the afternoon, he received a call to say that a dark red Saab had been found almost submerged in a deep dyke about half a mile from the hamlet. Checks with the DVLA showed that Edmund Baker was the owner. It was not possible to say whether the vehicle had been pushed into the dyke deliberately or whether it had crashed as the result of an accident, though the force with which the front of the car had hit the bottom, the crumpled state of the driver's door and the fact that it had been left open suggested the latter. There was a sharp bend in the road at the same place which a driver not familiar with the area would have found difficult to negotiate if going at speed.

"But there's no body?" said Tim.

"No, we don't think so. We've walked along the bank for several yards with nets and poles and we've not found one. We'd have to have the dyke properly dredged to make sure."

"Do that, will you?"

Tim was also perturbed by Alex Tarrant's kidnapping. Unless Alex was withholding key information – which he doubted, after she'd come clean about Edmund – he couldn't understand why she'd been taken. Alex herself said that she'd been told that if she co-operated she'd be held prisoner only for twenty-four hours, but that afterwards something had seemed to go wrong and she'd been convinced that her captors would kill her. How could holding her – or killing her – possibly have made any difference to what he knew of their plans?

He decided to ask Alex if they could meet again. He knew from Juliet that she was still staying with her friends at Holbeach, although the blood splatter – which analysis had shown was from a pig – had been cleaned from her kitchen wall and she'd been told that she could return to the flat if she liked. He wasn't surprised that she was reluctant to do so, especially while Tom was still a patient at the Pilgrim Hospital. He called her mobile and, when she agreed to the meeting, offered to send a police car to fetch her.

"It's all right – I'll come on the bus. I want to call in at the Archaeological Society, anyway. I've got the doctor to sign me off today – I'll start back to work next week – and I'd like to pick up my mail."

CHAPTER SIXTY-FIVE

THEY AGREED THAT she would come to his office at about 3 p.m. Shortly after 2 p.m., she called his mobile. He recognised her number and answered it immediately. As soon as he pressed the green button, she mumbled: "DI Yates?" The rest of her words were engulfed by a burst of sobs.

"Mrs Tarrant? Alex? Are you in danger?"

He could hear her swallowing air, as if trying with great effort to compose herself enough to speak.

"Not in danger – no – but the Society . . ."

"Are you there now?"

"Yes."

"I'll be there in five minutes. I'll bring DC Armstrong with me."

When Tim and Juliet arrived at the Archaeological Society, the door to the street was gaping open. They rushed in and saw immediately why Alex Tarrant was so upset. The whole place had been ransacked. There were papers scattered everywhere: in the hallway, on the stairs, in Alex's office. Alex's desk had been upturned. It looked as if the contents of all the shelves on the wall behind it had been swept to the floor in an act of fury.

They found Alex in the library, where the scene of devastation was even worse. Several of the glass doors on the bookcases had been smashed and the books that they contained tossed in all directions. Shards of glass were everywhere. Only one of the sightless marble busts remained in place. Tim noted with grim humour that it represented Cicero. He doubted that he had been spared for his eloquence.

Alex was sitting at the massive table on the only upright chair. She was clasping her forehead, almost pinching it, with the fingers of her right hand. At first, Tim thought that she was merely surveying the many acts of vandalism with which she was surrounded. As he moved nearer, he saw that she was looking at something in particular. At her feet lay a massive, twisted heap of green metal that he recognised. A thick slew of papers spilled like a crude sunburst from beneath it. Various trinkets lay half in, half out of a sizeable cardboard box, some of them smashed.

She looked up as Tim and Juliet approached.

"Mrs Tarrant? Are you all right?" said Juliet.

"Yes, I'm all right." Her voice was immensely weary. "I guess I don't have to wonder what my life's work will be now. It will take years to restore all of this."

Alex rose to her feet and gestured at the mound of metal, papers and nineteenth-century gewgaws.

"It's like a curse," she said. "The curse of Jacob Sparham. That was the box that Edmund had borrowed. Someone was desperate to get into it. They must have thought that it contained that diamond swastika that Oliver told me about. I wonder if they found it."

"I very much doubt it," said Tim. "I imagine that whoever it was wrecked the place in a fury when they found that it wasn't there."

"Oliver always thought that it was an invention."

"Perhaps it was – or perhaps it wasn't . . . and Edmund Baker got to it first."

CHAPTER SIXTY-SIX

ALEX CONTACTED FRANCIS Codd, now the most senior of the trustees, to tell him about the ransacking. Tim had wanted to send in the SOCOs straight away, but Alex persuaded him that they would have to be accompanied by an expert in antiquarian books as they carried out their work, to make sure that the Society's library was not damaged further. He agreed to wait until the next day if she could find a suitable person by then. She made other calls, to the museum at Peterborough and to the Heritage Society. Eventually he persuaded her to return to the police station with himself and Juliet. She had just accepted his offer of tea when she suddenly caught sight of his clock.

"It's almost four-thirty! I need to catch the 16.45 bus to get to the hospital for visiting time."

"Don't worry," said Tim. "Someone will take you. We'll make sure that you get there. It will give us a few more minutes to talk."

Alex nodded her thanks and clasped her tea-cup in both hands.

"As I'm sure you know, we haven't managed to locate Edmund Baker yet. Do you have any idea where he might be?"

Alex frowned.

"No," she said. "And I don't think that I can help you. For a brief period, I thought that I . . . understood Edmund, but clearly I was wrong."

"He didn't confide in you? Tell you perhaps of favourite places that he liked to visit, or to which he might plan to retire?"

"No . . ." Alex stopped suddenly.

"You've thought of something?" asked Juliet, gently.

"Yes . . . although it seems too far-fetched for words. And it isn't a place where he would be able to hide for days at a time. He might choose it to hide possessions in, though. We were together one evening in Peterborough a few weeks ago – we'd both been to a meeting at the Museum and decided to go for a drink afterwards. Then we picked up some fast food from somewhere, and instead of eating it in the car, Edmund wanted to take me to a secret place that he'd known about since he was a boy . . ."

Because it was getting dark and Alex had to leave for the hospital, Tim decided not to follow up on the information that she had provided about Edmund's 'secret place' until the following day. Although she knew that it was part of a bridge that crossed the River Nene at Peterborough, her memory of its precise location was vague. They would probably have to drive around quite a bit before they located it. Alex had agreed to accompany them the next day, but she stressed that she didn't want to enter the secret room itself. Tim wondered whether this was because it would provoke unpleasant memories, or perhaps because she had some premonition about what they might find there now.

After her departure, he asked the Peterborough police if they would search the river bank for abandoned motorbikes. Their response was that they would prefer to do this in daylight, so he had no option but to contain his impatience and go home. It was the earliest he would have arrived home for weeks. Although he was not keen to embrace the opportunity, he knew that the time had come to talk to Katrin.

The fragrant smell of Pichelsteiner hit him as soon as he let himself into their small hall. The stew was one of Katrin's specialities. He found her in the dining-room, in the act of placing a small bunch of flowers on a table laid with white damask and their best cutlery. She was wearing a black silky top and dangling silver earrings. She appeared to be serene and was looking very pretty. She turned to kiss him.

"You look lovely," he said. "What's the occasion?"

"You said you'd be home on time tonight. That's worth celebrating in itself."

Tim tried not to look guilty. The conversation they had had that morning had completely slipped his memory. He had had a narrow squeak: if Alex Tarrant had not been visiting her husband in hospital, he might have been pacing the towpaths of the Nene with her now.

"Would you like a drink?"

"Yes please! I've just opened a bottle of Pinot Noir. It's in the kitchen."

He went to fetch the bottle and poured wine into the two delicately-wrought crystal glasses that she'd put on the table.

"Cheers! And thank you for all your help with the McRae case. We'd never have got to the bottom of it without you."

She chinked her glass very lightly against his own.

"It was Juliet as well as me. Joint effort."

"Katrin, I've been so worried about you. You seem your old self now, but I need to know why . . ."

"Don't, Tim. It's too painful. Don't spoil a nice evening."

"OK, but what if it happens again? What if I ..?"

"Don't," she said again, in a tone that brooked no contradiction. "It was nothing to do with you. Not your fault in any way. Can we just leave it at that?"

CHAPTER SIXTY-SEVEN

THE POLICE AT Peterborough kept their word. They began searching for the motorbike as soon as it was light the next morning. By 10.00 a.m. they had called Tim to say that they had found it, propped out of sight of the road against the river-facing fence of a small electricity substation on the river bank. There was a bridge nearby and evidence that someone had been sleeping rough underneath it, but from the state of the heap of rags they'd left it didn't look as if they'd been there recently. The policeman who'd found it e-mailed Tim a couple of photographs of the spot.

Alex Tarrant arrived shortly afterwards. Tim showed her the photographs.

"I'm not sure about the bridge," she said. "It was dark and raining when I was there. But the power-station looks familiar. And there were signs that a tramp had been sleeping under the bridge. Though I suppose that isn't unusual."

"No," Tim agreed, "but it looks as if this might be the place. Are you still up for coming with us?"

She seemed to shrink inside herself.

"I'm . . . not sure. If the motorbike has been abandoned, where do you think Edmund is?"

"I don't know, but I think that it's likely that he's left the area. We just want you to show us where this hiding-place is to see if he's left anything there, or traces of having been there himself."

"All right. But when I've pointed it out to you, I'd like to wait in the car."

"Of course."

Tim decided not to take the BMW. Instead, they all travelled together in a police car. Tim was in the front passenger seat and Alex sat with Juliet in the back. He chatted to the driver, but Alex and Juliet were silent.

Even before they had arrived, Alex knew that it was the right place. She recognised the back streets through which Edmund had driven that evening. Their police car drew in behind another already parked against the bank. There was a large object lying beside it. Two policemen were standing there. One of them was fumbling with a tarpaulin that he was trying to spread over the object.

"Is that the motorbike?"

"Yes, sir. There's a breakdown lorry coming to pick it up."

"This is Mrs Tarrant. She's going to show us a place under the bridge that Edmund Baker brought her to once. When she's pointed it out, I'd like one of you to bring her back here before we take a closer look."

"I'll come back with you," said Juliet quickly, speaking directly to Alex, who shot her a quick look of gratitude.

They proceeded along the muddy path in single file. Tim led the way, with Alex following. Juliet came too and one of the policemen. The other waited with the motorbike. At the foot of the path, Alex paused and screwed up her eyes so that she could see into the shadowy area under the bridge. She could almost visualise the chip paper blowing along the towpath, almost smell the cigarettes of the man who had frightened them by patrolling up and down.

"Are you OK?" asked Juliet.

"Yes," said Alex, with a shiver. Tim had gone on a few paces and she now followed, stepping over the sodden mass of old blankets and sleeping bag as she had on her previous visit.

Once they were standing under the bridge Alex looked up at the ledge that had been built high in the support wall. The ledge seemed higher, and the wall steeper, than she had remembered. She could see the grille clearly, about three quarters of the way along. It appeared to be tightly shut. It was flush with the surrounding masonry.

"That is the entrance," she said, pointing to it. "It looks more inaccessible than I remember, but I'm sure you'll be able to cope." She looked at Juliet. "I'd like to go back to the car now."

She turned and picked her way back across the wet rags until she reached the path. Juliet followed silently.

They'd been sitting in the back of the car without speaking for some minutes when Juliet said quietly, "Alex? Are you sure you don't know anything more about what happened to Edmund Baker? You seem very jumpy."

Alex met her gaze unflinchingly, her eyes clear and candid.

"No, I don't know any more. I've no idea what he did or had planned after the last time I saw him at the Archaeological Society. The day that he returned the metal box, when DI Yates helped to carry it in. The day I was taken . . ." She looked down at her hands. "I know it sounds corny, and perhaps you won't believe me, especially if you do find something hidden up there. But I've just got a horrible feeling about this place. It's not entirely owing to imagination. Someone followed us the night that Edmund brought me here. Someone he was afraid of."

Tim twisted his head round and squinted up at the grille. The ledge looked damp and was plastered with bird-droppings. He turned to the Peterborough policeman.

"Fancy scrambling up there?" he said.

"Not really, sir, but I will if you want me to. I'm better shod for it than you are." He shot Tim's brown leather half-brogues an amused look. Tim looked down self-consciously. He was aware that his footwear betrayed the dandy in him.

"Be careful. I'll come up if you need me. Try not to fall on me, though!"

The policeman grinned. He was a tall, heftily-built man who had appeared quite clumsy when he was fixing the tarpaulin around the motorbike. However, he shinned up the wall quite nimbly now and had reached the ledge in a few seconds. He edged along it towards the grille. Establishing that its hinge was on the left, he seized hold of the vertical bar opposite and gave it a pull.

"It looks as if this is going to be tough to open, sir. It's been well rammed into the wall."

He pulled out a penknife and worked it round the edges of the metal. He pulled hard again.

"You need something to lever it with," said Tim. "Are there tools in the panda car?"

The policeman shrugged. "Just the normal breakdown tools."

"Throw me the keys; I'll go and see what I can find."

Tim returned from the car with a tyre lever.

"Can you catch this?"

The policeman held out his hand in response. Tim tossed the lever into the air and he caught it. He set to work on the grille again.

"I can feel some give in it now," he said, after several minutes' hard work. Tim couldn't see him sweating, but he could sense it.

"Careful!" he said again.

The policeman gave the grille a final yank and pulled it open. He shone his torch into the aperture he had just revealed.

"Fuck!"

"What is it?" said Tim quickly.

"There's a body in here."

"You're sure?"

"I'm definitely sure. I'm surprised you can't smell it; it stinks!"

"Push the grille to without shutting it completely and come down as quick as you can. There may have been a build-up of toxic gases in there."

CHAPTER SIXTY-EIGHT

THE CORPSE BELONGED to Edmund Baker. Forensic evidence taken from the secret room and the post-mortem results revealed that he had been injured, probably by crashing his car rather than as the result of an assault. Whether he had died from his injuries, become accidentally trapped in the room or been shut in deliberately would always be a matter for speculation. In Tim's view, there was one overwhelming piece of evidence to prove that Edmund's death was accidental. Under his coat he had been clutching a swastika of what appeared to be red-gold set with blue diamonds. Lab tests showed that the jewel had actually been fashioned from pinchbeck and set with stones made from paste. It was a well-made piece, dating perhaps from the 1850s. An antiquarian jeweller said that its historical value would cause it to be worth about a thousand pounds. Either Jacob Sparham had been guilty of perpetrating a fraud or, more probably, he was the victim of one. His reputation for being taken in by the traders who preyed on Victorian tourists was well-documented.

Some days after the discovery of the corpse, two women turned up unexpectedly at the police station and asked to speak to Tim. They gave their name as Brodowska. The desk sergeant rang to ask Tim if he would see them. They said that it was about Edmund Baker. Tim had been on the point of refusing – he had already fielded several lunatic calls about the swastika – when he remembered that Baker's deceased wife had had a Polish-sounding name.

One of the women was elderly – he thought probably in her early eighties. She was accompanied by a middle-aged woman who reminded him of someone, even though he was sure that he'd never seen either of them before. They stood together just inside the door of his office. Neither accepted his gestured offer of a seat.

The middle-aged woman pointed at the elderly woman. She spoke in fluent English, though it was heavily accented.

"This is my mother, Jelena," she said. "Her English is not good, but she has something to tell you."

The elderly woman enunciated several sentences in a harsh, cracked voice. She spoke very haltingly. Although most of the time she was looking at the floor, she darted beseeching little looks at Tim every few words. She clearly thought that what she was saying was intelligible to him. She concluded with a kind of vehement crescendo, as if that had settled it.

"I'm sorry," said Tim, appealing to the middle-aged woman for help. "I didn't quite understand that. Could you repeat it for me?"

"She said that when she was a girl, she was taken to a children's home in Norway. It was a home for orphans; her parents disappeared during the war. The home was burned down. It was burnt deliberately. My mother was one of the few children who escaped. Eventually, she married my father, who was Danish. As a family we lived first in Denmark, then in England. We moved to England when my brother and sister and I were still children. My sister, Krystyna, was the only one of us to marry. She married the man called Edmund Baker, the man whose body is talked about in the newspapers. We didn't like him, but his marriage to Krystyna seemed all right until a few years ago he had an affair. She was bitterly upset. My mother wanted her to leave him, but she refused. They patched it up, but just recently Krystyna suspected that he'd been seeing the woman – the same woman – again. I don't know whether it turned her brain, but she became convinced – I should have said, she knew the story of the fire – she became convinced that Edmund had somehow got mixed up with the people who had started it. We thought it was crazy. Krystyna was certainly very depressed. But then she died and there was a boy who said Edmund had pushed her. And now we are wondering, could it be true?"

Tim sighed. He hardly felt able to cope with this. He pressed a button on his phone.

"Juliet? Do you think you could come in please? And could you possibly bring some tea. For four. Yes, for four."

CHAPTER SIXTY-NINE

TIM AND JULIET spent a good hour listening to the two ladies as they went over their story several times more. Their theories, although probably well-founded, could be of no use to the investigation, even if the two people with whom they were concerned had not been dead. However, he was well aware that what he and Juliet were actually doing was helping them to begin the grieving process as they tried to make sense of the extraordinary events that had befallen their family, some of them more than sixty years before.

Juliet was downstairs showing them out and Tim was just returning to his desk when Superintendent Thornton poked his head around the door.

"Ah, Yates. You must be pleased with the way the investigation has gone. Not many more loose ends to tie up now. The Edmund Baker problem has been nicely solved. If you can catch Grigoryen, I think we can consider you home and dry. I doubt if you'll find Jane Halliwell, but we don't know that she's actually committed any crimes, do we? She'll be far away now, in any case. I've always thought that she went to ground in Norway somewhere."

"Really?" said Tim. Even Superintendent Thornton picked up the twang of sarcasm.

"Yes, well, if there's nothing else . . ."

"There is one thing, sir."

Superintendent Thornton immediately looked suspicious.

"Yes?" he said discouragingly.

"I should like to know why Superintendent Little was so keen for us to investigate Dame Claudia's disappearance in the first place. Rather than his own force, I mean."

"Yes. Well, Roy's quite a sensitive man, as I'm sure you've discovered. You probably won't know that he was adopted. Some years ago, he tried to trace his real parents, and came to the conclusion that he was related to Dame Claudia. Not her son – her nephew, I think. The son of her half-sister, or something? So he felt that he couldn't take the case on. I've no idea what steps he took to find this out and I'm sure now that he must have been mistaken. We know who her nephew was, don't we?"

ACKNOWLEDGEMENTS

I SHOULD LIKE especially to thank Chris and Jen Hamilton-Emery for their inspiration, advice and encouragement and their unfailing hard work on my behalf; and my husband, Jim, for being a wonderful co-editor. I'd also like to thank the many people who read *In the Family*, the first of the DI Yates novels, who sent kind and enthusiastic comments. And my sincere thanks to booksellers and librarians everywhere.

For further information about Christina James, see www.christina-jamesblog.com; Christina may be contacted at christina.james.writer@gmail.com or https://twitter.com/cajameswriter

Danielle Steel

Wings

CORGI BOOKS

TRANSWORLD PUBLISHERS
61-63 Uxbridge Road, London W5 5SA
a division of The Random House Group Ltd
www.randomhouse.co.uk

WINGS
A CORGI BOOK : 9780552137485

First published in Great Britain
in 1995 by Bantam Press
a division of Transworld Publishers
Corgi edition published 1996
Corgi edition reissued 2008

Addresses for Random House Group Ltd companies outside
the UK can be found at: www.randomhouse.co.uk
The Random House Group Ltd Reg. No. 954009

Penguin Random House is committed to a sustainable future for
our business, our readers and our planet. This book is made from
Forest Stewardship Council® certified paper.

MIX
Paper from
responsible sources
FSC® C018179
www.fsc.org

Printed and bound in Great Britain by Clays Ltd, St Ives plc

Typeset in 11/12pt Monotype Plantin by
Phoenix Typesetting, Burley-in-Wharfedale, West Yorkshire

To the Ace of my heart,
the pilot of my dreams . . .
the joy of my life,
the quiet place I go to
in the dark of night
the bright morning sun
of my soul
at dawn . . .
the bright shining star
in my sky,
to my love,
to my heart,
to my all,
beloved Popeye,
with all my heart and love,
always,
Olive.

1

The road to O'Malley's Airport was a long, dusty thin trail that seemed to drift first left, then right, and loop lazily around the cornfields. The airport was a small dry patch of land near Good Hope in McDonough County, a hundred and ninety miles southwest of Chicago. When Pat O'Malley first saw it in the fall of 1918, those seventy-nine barren acres were the prettiest sight he had ever seen. No farmer in his right mind would have wanted them, and none had. The land was dirt cheap, and Pat O'Malley paid for it with most of his savings. The rest went to purchase a beat-up little Curtiss Jenny, it was war surplus, a two-seater plane with dual controls, and he used it to teach flying to the rare visitor who could afford a lesson or two, to fly a passenger to Chicago now and then, or take small cargo loads to anywhere they had to be flown to.

The Curtiss Jenny all but bankrupted him, but Oona, his pretty little redheaded wife of ten years, was the only person he knew who didn't think he was completely crazy. She knew how desperately he had always wanted to fly, ever since he'd seen his first plane on exhibition at a little airstrip in New Jersey. He'd worked two jobs to make enough money to pay for lessons, and he'd dragged her all the way to San Francisco to see the Panama-Pacific Exhibition in 1915, just so he could meet Lincoln Beachey. Beachey had taken Pat up in his plane with him, which had made it all the more painful for Pat when Beachey was killed two months later. Beachey had just made three breathtaking loops in his experimental plane when it happened.

Pat had also met famed aviator Art Smith at the exhibition, and a battalion of other flying fanatics like himself. They were a brotherhood of daredevils, most of whom preferred to fly than to do anything else. They only seemed to come to life when they were flying. They lived it, talked it, breathed it, dreamed it. They knew everything there was to know about all the intricacies of every flying machine ever built, and how best to fly it. They told tales and traded advice, and the most minute bits of information about new planes, and old ones, and seemingly impossible mechanics. Not surprisingly, few of them were interested in anything but flying, nor managed to stay in jobs that had little or nothing to do with flying. And Pat was always in the thick of them, describing some incredible feat he'd seen, or some remarkable airplane that somehow managed to surpass the accomplishments

8

of the last one. He always vowed that he'd have his own plane one day, maybe even a fleet of them. His friends laughed at him, his relatives said he was daft. Only sweet, loving Oona believed him. She followed everything he said and did with total loyalty and adoration. And when their little daughters were born, Pat tried not to let her know how disappointed he was that none of them were sons, so as not to hurt her feelings.

But no matter how much he loved his wife, Pat O'Malley was not a man to waste his time with his daughters. He was a man's man, a man of precision and great skill. And the money he had spent on flying lessons had paid off quickly. He was one of those pilots who knew instinctively how to fly almost every machine, and no one was surprised when he was one of the first Americans to volunteer, even before the United States had entered the Great War. He fought with the Lafayette Escadrille, and transferred into the 94th Aero Squadron when it was formed, flying with Eddie Rickenbacker as his commander.

Those had been the exciting years. At thirty, he had been older than most of the other men, when he volunteered in 1916. Rickenbacker was older than many of the men too. He and Pat had that and their love for flying in common. And also like Rickenbacker, Pat O'Malley always knew what he was doing. He was tough and smart and sure, he took endless risks, and the men said he had more guts than anyone in the squadron. They loved flying with him, and Rickenbacker had said himself that Pat was one of the world's great pilots. He tried to encourage Pat to stick with it after the war, there were frontiers to be explored, challenges to be met, new worlds to discover.

But Pat knew that, for him, that kind of flying was over. No matter how good a pilot he was, for him, the great years had come and gone. He had to take care of Oona and the girls now. He was thirty-two, at the war's end in 1918, and it was time to start thinking about his future. His father had died by then, and left him a tiny bit of money from his savings. Oona had managed to put a little money aside for them too. And it was that money he took with him when he went to scout around the farmlands west of Chicago. One of the men he had flown with had told him about land going dirt cheap out there, especially if it was unsuitable for farming. And that's when it had all started.

He had bought seventy-nine acres of miserable farmland, at a good price, and hand-painted the sign which still stood there eighteen years later. It said simply 'O'Malley's Airport,' and in the past eighteen years, one of the l's and the y had all but faded.

He'd bought the Curtiss Jenny with the last money he had left in 1918, and managed to bring Oona and the girls out by Christmas. There was a small shack on the far edge, near a stream, shaded by some old trees. And that was where they lived, while he flew anyone who had the price of a charter, and did frequent mail runs in the old Jenny. She was a reliable little plane, and he saved every penny he could. By spring he was able to buy a de Havilland D.H.4.A., which he used to carry mail and cargo.

The government contracts he got to do mail runs were profitable, but they took him away from home a lot. Sometimes Oona had to manage the airport alone for him, as well as take care of the children. She'd learned how to fuel the planes, and take calls concerning their contracts or charters. And more often than not, it was Oona flagging in someone's plane for them on the narrow runway, while Pat was away on a flight, carrying mail, passengers, or cargo.

They were usually startled to see that the person flagging them in was a pretty young woman with red hair, particularly that first spring, when she was very obviously pregnant. She had gotten especially big that time, and at first she'd thought it might be twins, but Pat knew for certain that it wasn't twins. It was his life's dream . . . a son to fly planes with him, and help him run the airport. This was the boy he had waited ten years for.

Pat delivered the baby himself, in the little shack he had slowly begun to add on to. They had their own bedroom by then, and the three girls were sharing the other room. There was a warm, cozy kitchen and a big spacious parlor. There was nothing fancy about the house where they lived, and they had brought few things with them. All of their efforts, and everything they had, had been sunk into the airport.

Their fourth child had come easily on a warm spring night, in scarcely more than an hour, after a long, peaceful walk, beside their neighbor's cornfield. He'd been talking to her about buying another airplane, and she'd been telling him about how excited the girls were about the new baby. The girls were five, six, and eight by then, and to them it seemed more like a doll they were waiting for than a real brother or sister. Oona felt a little bit that way too, it had been five years since she'd held a baby in her arms, and she was longing for this one to arrive. And it did, with a long, lusty wail, shortly before midnight. Oona gave a sharp cry when she looked down at it and saw it for the first time, and then she burst into tears, knowing how disappointed Pat would be. It was not Pat's long-awaited son, it was another girl. A big, fat, beautiful nine-pound girl with big blue eyes, creamy skin, and hair as bright as copper. But no matter how pretty she was, Oona knew only too well how badly he had wanted a son, and how devastated he was now not to have one.

'Never mind, little one,' he said, watching her turn away from him, as he swaddled his new daughter. She was a pretty one, probably the prettiest of all, but she wasn't the boy he had planned on. He touched his wife's cheek, and then pulled her chin around and forced her to look at him. 'It's no matter, Oona. She's a healthy little girl. She'll be a joy to you one day.'

'And what about you?' she asked miserably. 'You can't run this place alone forever.' He laughed at her concern, as the tears coursed down her cheeks. She was a good woman, and he loved her, and if they weren't destined to have sons, so be it. But there was still a little ache in his heart where the dream of a boy had been. And he didn't dare think that there would be another. They had four children now, and even this mouth to feed would be hard for them. He wasn't getting rich running his airport.

'You'll just have to keep helping me fuel the planes, Oonie. That's the way it'll have to be,' he teased, as he kissed her and left the room for a shot of whiskey. He had earned it. And as he stood looking up at the moon, after she and the baby had gone to sleep, he wondered at the quirk of fate that had sent him four daughters and no sons. It didn't seem fair to him, but he wasn't a man to waste time worrying about what wasn't. He had an airport to run, and a family to feed. And in the next six weeks, he was so busy, he scarcely had time to even see his family, let alone mourn the son who had turned out to be a beautiful, healthy daughter.

It seemed as though the next time he noticed her again, she had doubled in size, and Oona had already regained her girlish figure. He marveled at the resiliency of women. Six weeks before she had been lumbering and vulnerable, so full of prom- ise, and so enormous. Now she looked young and beautiful again, and the baby was already a fiery- tempered, little redheaded hellion. If her mother and sisters didn't tend to her needs immediately, the entire state of Illinois and most of Iowa could hear it.

'I'd say she's the loudest one of all, wouldn't you, m'dear?' Pat said one night, exhausted from a long round-trip flight to Indiana. 'She's got great lungs.' He grinned at his wife over a shot of Irish whiskey.

'It's been hot today, and she has a rash.' Oona always had an explanation as to why the children were out of sorts. Pat marveled at her seemingly endless patience. But she was equally patient with him. She was one of those quiet people, who spoke little, saw much, and rarely said anything unkind to or about anyone. Their disagreements had been rare in nearly eleven years of marriage. He had married her at seventeen, and she had been the ideal helpmate for him. She had put up with all his oddities and peculiar plans, and his endless passion for flying.

Later that week, it was one of those airless hot days in June, when the baby had fussed all night, and Pat had had to get up at the crack of dawn for a quick trip to Chicago. That afternoon when he got home, he found that he'd have to leave again in two hours on an unscheduled mail run. It was hard times and he couldn't afford to turn any work down. It was a day when he'd wished more than ever that there had been someone there to help him, but there were few men he'd have trusted with his precious planes, none he'd seen recently, and certainly none of the men who'd applied for work there since he'd opened the airport.

'Got any planes to charter, mister?' a voice growled at him, as Pat pored over his log, and went through the papers on his desk. He was about to explain, as he always did, that they could rent him, but not his planes. And then he looked across the desk and grinned in amazement.

'You sonofabitch.' Pat smiled delightedly at a fresh-faced kid with a broad smile, and a thatch of dark hair hanging into his blue eyes. It was a face he knew well, and had come to love in their turbulent time together in the 94th Aero Squadron. 'What's a matter, kid, can't afford a haircut?' Nick Galvin had thick straight black hair, and the striking good looks of the blue-eyed, black-haired Irish. Nick had been almost like a son to Pat, when he'd flown for him. He had enlisted at seventeen, and was only a year older than that now, but he had become one of the squadron's outstanding pilots, and one of Pat's most trusted men. He'd been shot down twice by the Germans, and both times managed to come in, with a crippled engine, making a dead stick landing and somehow saving both himself and the plane. The men in the squadron had called him 'Stick' after that, but Pat called him 'son' most of the time. He couldn't help wondering if, now that his latest child had turned out to be yet another girl, this was the son he so desperately wanted.

'What are you doing here?' Pat asked, leaning back in his chair, and grinning at the boy who had defied death almost as often as he had.

'Checking up on old friends. I wanted to see if you'd gotten fat and lazy. Is that your de Havilland out there?'

'It is. Bought that instead of shoes for my kids last year.'

'Your wife must have loved that,' Nick grinned, and Pat was reminded of all the girls in France who had pined for him. Nick Galvin was a good-looking lad, with a very persuasive manner with the ladies. He had done well for himself in Europe. He told most of them he was twenty-five or twenty-six, and they always seemed to believe him.

Oona had met him once, in New York, after the war, and she had thought him charming. She'd said, blushing, that she thought he was exceptionally handsome. His looks certainly outshone Pat's, but there was something appealing and solid about the older man that made up for a lack of Hollywood movie-star looks. Pat was a fine-looking man, with light brown hair, warm brown eyes, and an Irish smile that had won Oona's heart. But Nick had the kind of looks that made young girls' hearts melt.

'Has Oona gotten smart and left you yet? I figured she would pretty quick after you brought her out here,' Nick said casually, and let himself into the chair across from Pat's desk, as he lit a cigarette, and his old friend laughed and shook his head in answer.

'I kind of thought she might too, to tell you the truth. But she hasn't, don't ask me why. When I brought her out here, we lived in a shack my grandfather wouldn't have put his cows in, and I wouldn't have been able to buy her a newspaper if she'd wanted one, which she didn't. Thank God. She's one hell of an amazing woman.' He'd always said that about her during the war, and Nick had thought as much too when he'd met her. His own parents were dead, and he had no family at all. He had just been floating around since the war ended, getting short-term jobs here and there at various small airports. At eighteen, he had no place to go, nowhere to be, and no one to go home to. Pat had always felt a little sorry for Nick when the men talked about their families. Nick had no sisters or brothers, and his parents had died when he was fourteen. He'd been in a state orphanage until he'd enlisted. The war had changed everything for him, and he had loved it. But now there was nowhere for him to go home to.

'How are the kids?' Nick had been sweet with them when he met them. He loved kids, and he'd seen plenty in the orphanage. He had always been the one to take care of the younger children, read them stories at night, tell them wild tales, and hold them in the middle of the night, when they woke up, crying for their mothers.

'They're fine.' Pat hesitated, but only for a moment. 'We had another one last month. Another

,irl. Big one this time. Thought it might be a boy, but it wasn't.' He tried not to sound disappointed but Nick could hear it in his voice, and he understood it.

'Looks like you'll just have to teach your girls to fly eventually, huh, Ace?' he teased, and Pat rolled his eyes in obvious revulsion. Pat had never been impressed by even the most extraordinary female fliers.

'Not likely, son. What about you? What are you flying these days?'

'Egg crates. War junk. Anything I can lay my hands on. There's a lot of war surplus hanging around, and a lot of guys wanting jobs flying them. I've kind of been hanging around the airports. You got anyone working with you here?' he asked anxiously, hoping that he didn't.

Pat shook his head, watching him, wondering if this was a sign, or merely a coincidence, or just a brief visit. Nick was still very young. And he had raised a lot of hell during wartime. He loved taking chances, coming in by the skin of his teeth. He was hard on planes. And harder on himself. Nick Galvin had nothing to lose and no one to live for. Pat had everything he owned in those planes, and he couldn't afford to lose them, no matter how much he liked the boy or wanted to help him.

'You still like taking chances like you used to?' Pat had almost killed him once after watching him come in too close to the ground under a cloud bank in a storm. He'd wanted to shake him till his teeth rattled, but he was so damn relieved Nick had survived that he ended up shouting right in his face. It was inhuman to take the chances he did. But it was what had made him great. In wartime. But in peacetime who could afford his bravado? Planes were too expensive to play with.

'I only take chances when I have to, Ace.' Nick loved Pat. He admired him more than any man he had ever known or flown with.

'And when you don't have to, Stick? You still like to play?' The two men's eyes met and held. Nick knew what he was asking. He didn't want to lie to him, he still liked raising hell, still loved the danger of it, playing and taking chances, but he had a lot of respect for Pat, and he wouldn't have done anything to hurt him. He had grown up that much. And he was more careful now that he was flying other people's planes. He still loved the thrills, but not enough to want to jeopardize Pat's future. Nick had come here, all the way from New York, on the last dollar he had to see if there was a chance that Pat could use him.

'I can behave myself if I have to,' he said quietly, his ice blue eyes never leaving Pat's kindly brown ones. There was something boyish and endearing about Nick, and yet at the same time he was a man. And once they had almost been brothers. Neither one of them could forget that time. It was a bond that would never change, and they both knew that.

'If you don't behave, I'll drop you out of the Jenny at ten thousand feet without thinking twice. You know that, don't you?' Pat said sternly. 'I'm not going to have anyone destroying what I'm trying to do here.' He sighed then. 'But I have to be honest, there's almost too much work for one man. And there's going to be entirely too much for one, and maybe even two, if these mail contracts keep coming in the way they have. I never seem to stop flying anymore. I can't catch up with myself. I could use a man to do some of these runs, but they're rough, and long. Lots of bad weather sometimes, especially in the winter. And no one gives a damn. No one wants to hear how hard it is. The mail's got to get there. And then there's all the rest of it, the cargo, the passengers, the short runs here and there, the thrill seekers who just want to go up and look down, the occasional lesson.'

'Sounds like you've got your hands full.' Nick grinned at him. He loved every word of what he was hearing. This was what he had come for. That and his memories of the Ace. Nick needed a job desperately. And Pat was happy to have him.

'This isn't a game here. It's a serious business I'm trying to run, and one day I want to put O'Malley's Airport on the map. But,' Pat explained, 'it'll never happen if you knock out all my planes, Nick, or even one. I've got everything riding on those two out there, and this patch of dry land with the sign you saw when you drove in here.' Nick nodded,

fully understanding everything he said, and loving
him more than ever. There was something about
flying men, they had a bond like no one else. It was
something only they understood, a bond of honor
like no other.

'Do you want me to fly some of the long hauls
for you? You could spend more time here with
Oona and the kids. And I could do the night stuff
maybe. I could start with those and see what you
think,' Nick asked him nervously. He was desperate for a job with him, and scared he might
not get it. But there was no way Pat O'Malley
wasn't going to hire him. He just wanted to be
sure Nick understood the ground rules. He would
have done anything for him. Given him a home, a
job, adopted him if he had to.

'The night runs might be a start. Even though' –
he looked ruefully at his young friend. There were
fourteen years separating them, but the war had
long since dissolved the differences between them
– 'some nights that's the most restful place to be.
If that new baby of ours doesn't start sleeping
nights pretty soon, I'm going to start dosing her
with whiskey. Oona says it's a heat rash, but I
swear it's the red hair and the disposition that
goes with it. Oona's the only redhead I've ever
known with those quiet, gentle ways. This one is
a real little hellion.' But despite his complaints, Pat
seemed taken with her, and for the most part, he'd
gotten over his disappointment about not having
a son. Particularly now that Nick was here. His

arrival was just the godsend he had prayed for.

'What's her name?' Nick looked amused. From the moment he'd laid eyes on them, he'd loved their family, and everything about them.

'Cassandra Maureen. We call her Cassie.' He glanced at his watch then. 'I'll take you over to the house, and you can have dinner with Oona and the girls. I've got to be back out here at five-thirty.' He looked apologetic then. 'And you'll have to find a place to stay in town. There are some rooms to rent at old Mrs Wilson's, but I don't have a place for you to stay here, except a cot in the hangar where I keep the Jenny.'

'That would do for now. Hell, it's warm enough. I don't care if I sleep on the runway.'

'There's an old shower out back, and a bathroom here, but this is a little primitive,' Pat said hesitantly, and Nick grinned as he shrugged his shoulders.

'So's my budget, until you start paying me.'

'You can sleep on our couch, if Oona doesn't mind. She's got a soft spot for you anyway, always telling me how handsome you are, and how lucky the girls are with a lad like you. I'm sure she won't mind having you on the couch, till you're ready to rent a room at Mrs Wilson's.'

But he never had done either. He had moved into the hangar immediately, and a month later he'd built himself a little shack of his own. It was barely more than a lean-to, but it was big enough for him. It was tidy and clean, and he spent every spare moment he had in the air, flying for Pat, and helping him to build his business.

By the following spring they were able to buy another plane, a Handley Page. It had a longer range than either the de Havilland or the Jenny, and it could carry more passengers and cargo. Nick spent most of his time flying it, while Pat stayed closer to home, did the short runs, and ran the airport. The arrangement worked perfectly for both of them. It was as though everything they touched turned to magic. The business went beautifully. Their reputation spread rapidly through the Midwest. The word that two hotshot flying aces were operating out of Good Hope seemed to reach everyone who mattered. They handled cargo, passengers, lessons, mail, and within a very reasonable time, began turning over a fairly respectable profit.

And then the ultimate bit of luck occurred. Thirteen months after Cassie was born, Christopher Patrick O'Malley appeared, a tiny, wizened, screaming, scrawny little infant. But a lovelier sight his parents had never seen, and his four sisters stared at his unfamiliar anatomy in utter amazement. The second coming could have made no greater stir than the arrival of Christopher Patrick O'Malley at O'Malley's Airport.

A large blue banner was flown, and every pilot who came through for a month was handed a cigar by the beaming father. He'd been worth waiting for. Almost twelve years of marriage, and finally he had his dream, a son to fly his planes and run his airport.

'Guess I might as well pack up and leave,' Nick said mock glumly the day after Chris was born. He had just taken an order for a huge shipment of cargo to be delivered to the West Coast by Sunday. It was the biggest job they'd had so far, and a real victory for them.

'What do you mean, *leave*?' Pat asked, with a terrible hangover from celebrating the birth of his son, and a look of panic. 'What the hell does that mean?'

'Well, I figured now that Chris is here, my days are numbered.' Nick was grinning at him. He was happy for both of them about the baby, and thrilled to be Chris's godfather. But the one who had stolen his heart from the first moment he'd laid eyes on her was Cassie. She was just what Pat had said she was from the very first, a little monster, and everything everyone had ever said about a redhead. And Nick adored her. Sometimes he almost felt as though she were his baby sister. He couldn't have loved her more if she were his own child.

'Yeah, your days are numbered,' Pat growled at him, 'for about another fifty years. So get off your lazy behind, Nick Galvin, and check out the mail they just dumped out there on our runway.'

'Yes, sir . . . Ace, sir . . . your honor . . . your excellence . . .'

'Oh, never mind the blarney!' Pat shouted at his back, as he poured himself a cup of black coffee and Nick ran out to the runway to meet with the pilot before he took off again. Nick had been just what Pat had hoped from the first, a godsend. And there had been no funny stuff in the past year. He'd taken his share of chances flying in bad weather the previous winter, and they both made their share of forced landings and emergency repairs. But there was nothing really outrageous that Pat could complain about, nothing Nick did he wouldn't have done himself, nothing that truly jeopardized one of Pat's precious airplanes. And Nick loved those planes as much as Pat did. And the truth was, having Nick there had really allowed Pat to build up his business.

And that was just what they had continued to do for the next seventeen years. The years had rushed past them faster than their planes taking off from the four meticulously kept runways at O'Malley's Airport. They had built three of them in the form of a triangle, and the fourth, running north/south, bisected it, which meant that they could land in almost any wind, and never had to close the airport due to problems with planes blocking one of their runways. They had a fleet of ten planes now too. Nick had actually bought two of them himself, and the rest were Pat's. Nick only worked for him, but Pat had always been generous with him. The two were fast friends after long years of working together, and building up the airport. He'd asked Nick to become partners with him more than once, but Nick always said he didn't want the headaches that went with it. He liked being a hired hand, as he put it, although everyone knew that he and Pat O'Malley moved as one, and to cross one was to risk death at the hands of the other. Pat O'Malley was a special man, and Nick loved him as a father, brother, friend. He loved his children as he would his own. He loved everything about him.

But other than Pat's, families and relationships were generally not Nick's strong suit. He had married once in 1922, at twenty-one. It had lasted all of six months, and his eighteen-year-old bride had gone running back to her parents in Nebraska. Nick had met her on a mail route late one night, in the town's only restaurant, which was owned by her mother and father.

The only thing she had hated more than Illinois was everything that had anything to do with flying. She got sick every time Nick took her up, she cried every time she saw a plane, and she whined every time he left to go fly one. It was definitely not the match for him, and the only one more relieved than his bride when her parents came to pick her up was Nick himself. He had never been more miserable in his life, and he had vowed never to let it happen again. There had been women since, a number of them, but Nick always kept quiet about what he did. There had been rumors about him and a married woman in another town, but no one was ever quite sure if they were true or not, and Nick never even said anything to Pat. From his striking boyish good looks, he had become a handsome man, but no one ever knew his business. The women in his life were never obvious. There was nothing anyone could talk about, except how hard he worked, or how much time he spent with the O'Malleys. He still spent most of his spare time with them and their kids. He was like an uncle to them. And Oona had long since given up trying to fix him up with any of her friends. She had even tried to start something between him and her youngest sister when she'd come out to visit years before, she was pretty and young and a widow. But it had been obvious for years that Nick Galvin was not interested in marriage. Nick was interested in airplanes, and not much more, except the O'Malleys, and an occasional quiet affair. He lived alone, he worked hard, and he minded his own business.

'He deserves so much better than that,' Oona had complained to Pat for years.

'What makes you think that marriage is so much better?' Pat had teased, but no matter how convinced she was of what would be good for him, even Oona no longer broached it with Nick. She had given up. At thirty-five, he was happy as he was, and too busy to give much time and attention to a wife and kids. Most days, he spent fifteen or sixteen hours a day at Pat's airport. And the only other person there as much as Pat and Nick was Cassie.

She was seventeen by then, and for most of her life Cassie had been a fixture at the airport. She could fuel almost any plane, signal a plane in, and prepare them for takeoff. She cared for

27

the runways, cleaned the hangars, hosed down the planes, and spent every spare moment she had hanging out with the pilots. She knew the engines and the workings of every plane they had. And she had an uncanny sense of what ailed them. There was no detail too small, too intricate, too complicated to escape her attention. She noticed everything about every plane, and could probably have described almost everything in the air with her eyes closed. She was remarkable in many ways, and Pat had to fight with her most of the time to make her go home to help her mother. She always insisted that her sisters were there and her mother didn't need her. Pat wanted her out of his hair, and at home where she belonged, but if he succeeded in driving her off one day, like the sun, she'd be back at six o'clock the next morning, to spend an hour or two at the airport before school. Eventually, Pat just threw up his hands and ignored her.

At seventeen she was a tall, striking, beautiful blue-eyed redhead. But the only thing Cassie knew or cared about was planes. And Nick knew, without ever seeing her fly a plane, that she was a born flier. He sensed that Pat had to know it too, but he was adamant about Cassie not learning to fly. And he didn't give a damn about Amelia Earhart, or Jackie Cochran or Nancy Love, Louise Thaden, or any of those female pilots, or the Women's Air Derby. No daughter of his was going to fly, and that was final. He and Nick had occasionally argued over it, but Nick had also come to unde: stand that it was a losing battle. There were plenty of women in aviation these days, many of them quite remarkable, but Pat O'Malley thought that things had gone far enough, and as far as he was concerned, no woman would ever fly like a man. And no woman was ever going to fly his planes. Certainly not Cassie O'Malley.

Nick had taken him on more than once, and pointed out that in his opinion, some of the women flying these days were better than Lindbergh. Pat had become so apoplectic he had almost thrown a punch at Nick for that. Charles Lindbergh was Pat's God, second only to Rickenbacker in the Great War. In fact, Pat had had his picture taken with Lindy when he had landed at O'Malley's in 1927, on his three-month tour of the country. The photograph still hung, nine years later, dusty and much loved, over Pat's desk, in a place of honor.

There was no question whatsoever in Pat's mind that no woman pilot would ever top or even match Charles Lindbergh's skill, or his prowess. Lindbergh's own wife, after all, was only a navigator and radio operator – to Pat, Lindy was a kind of God, and to compare anyone to him was a sacrilege, and one he didn't intend to listen to from Nick Galvin. It made Nick laugh when he saw how excited Pat got about it, and he loved goading him. But it was an argument he knew he would never win. Women just weren't up to it, according to Pat, no matter how much they flew, how many records

29

they broke, or races they won, or how good they looked in their flight suits. Women, according to Patrick O'Malley, were not meant to be pilots.

'And *you*,' he looked pointedly at Cassie as she came in from the runway in a pair of old overalls, having just fueled a Ford TriMotor before it took off for Roosevelt Field on Long Island, 'should be at home helping your mother cook dinner.' It was a familiar refrain she always pretended not to hear, and today was no different. She strode across the room, almost as tall as most of the men who worked for him. She had shoulder-length red hair that was as bright as flame, and big lively blue eyes that met Nick's as he grinned at her mischievously from behind her father.

'I'll go home in a while, Dad. I just want to do some stuff here.' At seventeen, she was a real beauty. But she was completely unconscious of it, which was part of her charm. And the overalls she wore molded her figure in a way that only irritated her father more. As far as he was concerned, she didn't belong here. It was not an opinion that was going to change, and theirs was an argument that everyone had heard at least a thousand times if they'd ever been to O'Malley's Airport, and today was no different. It was a hot June day, and she was out of school for the summer. Most of her friends had summer jobs in the drugstore, the coffee shop, or stores. But all she wanted to do was help out, for free, at the airport. It was her life and soul, and the only time she worked anywhere else was when she was desperate for a little money. But no job, no friend, no boy, no fun could ever keep her away from the airport for long. She just couldn't help it.

'Why can't you do something useful, instead of getting in the way here?' her father shouted at her from across his office. He never thanked her for the work she did. He didn't want her there in the first place.

'I just want to pick up one of the cargo logs, Dad. I need to make a note in it.' She said it quietly, looking for the book and then the page that she needed. She was familiar with all their logs, and all their procedures.

'Get your hands off my logs! You don't know what you're doing!' He was enraged, as usual. He had grown irascible over the years, though at fifty he was still one of their finest pilots. But he was adamant about his philosophies and ideas, although no one paid much attention, not even Cassie. At the airport, his word was law, but his battle against women pilots and his arguments with her were fruitless. She knew enough not to argue with him. Most of the time she didn't even seem to hear him. She just quietly went about her business. And to Cassie, the only business she cared about was her father's airport.

When she'd been a little girl, sometimes she'd sneaked out of the house at night, and come to look at the planes sitting shimmering in the moonlight. They were so beautiful, she just had to see them. He had found her there once, after looking for her for an hour, but she was so reverent about his planes, so in awe of them, and of him, that he hadn't had the heart to spank her, no matter how much she'd scared them by disappearing. He had told her never to do it again, and had taken her back to her mother without saying another word about it.

Oona knew too how much Cassie loved planes, but like Pat, she felt it just wasn't fitting. What would people think? Look what she looked like, and smelled like, when she came home from fueling planes, or loading cargo or mail, or worse yet, working on the engines. But Cassie knew more about the inner workings of planes than most men knew about their cars. She loved everything about them. She could take an engine apart and put it back together again faster and better than most men, and she had borrowed and read more books on flying than even Nick or her parents suspected. Planes were her greatest love and passion.

Only Nick seemed to understand her love for them, but even he had never succeeded in convincing her father that it was a suitable pastime for her, and he shrugged now, as he went back to some work on his desk, and Cassie went back out to the runway. She had learned long since that if she stayed away from Pat, she could hang around for hours at the airport.

'I don't know what's wrong with her . . . it's unnatural . . .' Pat complained. 'I think she does it just to annoy her brother.' But Nick knew better than anyone that Chris didn't give a damn. He was about as interested in flying as he was in getting to the moon, or becoming an ear of corn. He hung out at the airport occasionally, to please his dad, and now that he was sixteen, he was taking flying lessons, to satisfy him, but the truth was, Chris didn't know anything, and didn't care, about airplanes. He had about as much interest in them as he did in the big yellow bus which took him to school every day. But Pat was convinced, or had convinced himself, that one day Chris would become a great pilot.

Chris had none of Cassie's instinct for it, or her passionate love of the machine, or her genius about an engine. He only hoped that Cassie's interest in planes would get his father off his back, but instead it seemed to make him even more anxious for Chris to become a pilot. He wanted Chris to become who Cassie was, and Chris couldn't. Chris wanted to be an architect. He wanted to build buildings, not fly planes, but as yet, he had never dared to tell his father. Cassie knew. She loved the drawings he did, and the models for school. He had built a whole city once out of tiny little boxes and cans and jars, he had even used the tops of bottles and all sorts of tiny gadgets from their mother's kitchen to complete it. For weeks she had been looking for things, bottle caps had disappeared, small tools, and vital utensils. And then it all reappeared in Chris's remarkable creation. Their father's only comment had been to ask him why he hadn't designed an airport. It had been an intriguing idea, and Chris still said he was going to try it. But the truth was, absolutely nothing about flying enticed him. He was intelligent and precise and thoughtful, and the flying lessons he was taking seemed incredibly boring. Nick had already taken him up dozens of times, and he had logged quite a few hours. But none of it interested him. It was like driving a car. So what? To him, it meant nothing. And to Cassie, it was life itself. It was more than that, it was magic.

She stayed out of her father's office that afternoon, and at six o'clock, Nick saw her far down the runway, signaling a plane in, and then disappearing into one of the hangars with the pilot. He sought her out a little while later, and she had oil on her face, and her hair was tied in a knot on her head. She had a huge smudge of grease on the tip of her nose, and her hands were filthy. He couldn't help laughing as he looked at her. She was quite a picture.

'What's funny?' She looked tired, but happy, as she smiled up at him. He had always been like a brother to her. She was aware of how handsome he was, but it didn't mean anything. They were good friends, and she loved him.

'You're funny. Have you looked in the mirror today? You're wearing more oil than my Bellanca. Your father is going to love that look.'

'My father wants me cleaning house in a housedress, and boiling potatoes for him.'

'That's useful too.'

'Yeah?' She cocked her head to one side, and w
an intriguing combination of absurdity and shee
beauty. 'Can you cook potatoes, Stick?' She called
him that sometimes and it always made him smile
as he did now when he answered.

'If I have to. I can cook too, you know.'

'But you don't *have* to. And when was the last
time you cleaned house?'

'I don't know . . .' He looked thoughtful. 'Ten
years ago maybe . . . about 1926?' He was grinning
at her and they were both laughing.

'See what I mean?'

'Yeah. But I see what he means too. I'm not
married and I don't have kids. And he doesn't
want you to end up like me. Living in a shack
off the runway and flying mail runs to Cleveland.'
His 'shack' was very comfortable by then if not
luxurious.

'Sounds good to me.' She grinned. 'The mail runs
I mean.'

'That's the problem.'

'*He's* the problem,' she disagreed. 'There are
plenty of women flying and leading interesting
lives. The Ninety-Nines are full of them.' It was
a professional organization founded by ninety-nine
female pilots.

'Don't try and convince me. Tell him.'

'It's pointless.' She looked discouraged as she
looked up at her old friend. 'I just hope he lets
me be out here all summer.' It was all she wanted
to do now that she was out of school until the end

35

August. It would be a long summer, hiding from him, and trying to avoid confrontations.

'Couldn't you get yourself a job somewhere else, so he doesn't drive us both crazy?' But they both knew that she preferred to do without any extra money at all than miss a moment at the airport.

'There isn't anything else I want to do.'

'I know. You don't have to tell me.' He knew the extent of her passion better than anyone else. He had suffered from the same disease himself. But he'd been lucky. The war, his sex, and Pat O'Malley had made it possible for him to spend the rest of his life flying. Somehow, he didn't think that Cassie O'Malley was going to be as lucky. In a funny way, he would have loved to take her up in a plane one of these days, just to see how well she would fly, but that was one headache he didn't need, and he knew Pat would kill him for it. Without meddling in Pat's family life, Nick had his own work to do, and there was plenty of it at the airport.

As Nick went back to his desk to clear up the last of his paperwork, he saw Chris arrive. He was a good-looking boy, a handsome blond with fine features like his mother's, and his father's powerful build, and warm brown eyes. He was bright and nice and well liked. He had everything in the world going for him, except a love for airplanes. He was working at the newspaper that summer, doing layouts, and he was grateful he didn't have to work at the airport.

'Is my sister here?' he asked Nick hesitantly. He almost looked as though he wished Nick would say no. He looked as though he couldn't wait to leave the airport. As it was, Cassie had expected him an hour before and she'd asked Nick impatiently half a dozen times if he'd seen him.

'She is indeed.' Nick smiled at him. He kept his voice low so he wouldn't irritate Pat, in case he overheard him. 'She's in the back hangar with some pilot who just flew in.'

'I'll find her.' Chris waved at Nick, who promised to take him up again in a few days, when he came back from a run to San Diego. 'I'll be here. I came out to practice my solos,' he said solemnly.

'I'm impressed.' Nick raised an eyebrow, amazed at how badly the boy obviously wanted to please his father. It was no secret to Nick that Chris really didn't enjoy his lessons. It wasn't that he was afraid, it was more that they just bored him. To him, flying meant nothing. 'See ya.'

Chris found Cassie easily, and she left her newfound friend very quickly once she saw her brother. She was quick to berate him. 'You're late, now we're going to be late for dinner. Dad'll have a fit.'

'Then let's not do it.' He shrugged. He hadn't even wanted to leave work as early as he had, but he knew she'd be furious with him if he didn't.

'Come on,' she blazed at him. 'I've been waiting all day!' She flashed an angry look at him, and he groaned. He knew her too well. There was no escaping Cassie when she set her mind to something. 'I'm not going home till we do it.'

'Okay, okay. But we can't stay up for long.'

'Half an hour.' She was begging him, pleading with him, turning her huge blue eyes imploringly to his gentle brown ones.

'Okay. Okay. But if you do anything to get us into trouble, Cass, I swear I'm going to kill you. Dad would have my hide for this.'

'I promise. I won't do anything.' He searched her eyes as she promised him, and he wanted more than anything to believe her, but he didn't.

Together, they walked toward the old Jenny their father had had for several years. It had been built as a trainer for the military, and Pat had told Chris he could use it now any time he wanted to practice. All he had to do was tell Nick, and he just had. Chris had a copy of the key, and he took it out of his pocket. Cassie almost salivated when she saw it. She was standing close to him, and she could feel her heart beat as Chris opened the door to the small open-cockpit airplane.

'Will you stop it?' He looked annoyed at her. 'I can feel you breathing on me. I swear . . . you're sick . . .' He felt as though he were helping an addict supply his habit as they walked around the plane, checking the wires and ailerons. Chris put on his flying helmet and goggles and gloves, and then got into the plane in the rear seat, and Cassie climbed in quickly ahead of him intending to look like a passenger, but somehow she didn't. She looked too knowledgeable, too comfortable, even in the front seat, especially once she put on her own helmet and goggles.

They both buckled in, and Cassie knew the plane was well fueled, because part of her deal with her brother was doing all the scutwork for him; and she had done it herself that afternoon. Everything was ready and she inhaled the familiar smell of castor oil that was characteristic of the Jenny. And five minutes later they were headed down the runway, with Cassie watching Chris's style critically. He was always too cautious, too slow, and once she turned around to signal to him to go faster, and pull up. She didn't care if anyone saw her. She knew that no one was watching now, and everything she knew, she knew from listening and watching. She had watched her father and Nick, transient pilots, and barnstormers. She had picked up some real skills, and a few tricks, and she knew flying by instinct and by sheer intuition. It was Chris who had had the lessons, and yet it was Cassie who knew exactly what to do and they both knew she could have flown the plane easily without him, and a lot more smoothly.

Eventually, she shouted at him over the sound of the engine, and he nodded, willing her not to do anything foolish. But they both knew exactly why they had come up here. Chris was taking lessons from Nick, and in turn he was giving Cassie lessons. Or, in fact, the way it had been working out, Chris was taking her up in the plane, and letting her fly it, and she was giving him lessons. Or just enjoying the opportunity to fly. She seemed to know how to do everything, a lot better than Chris did. She was a natural. And she had promised to pay him twenty dollars a month for unlimited opportunities to fly with him in their father's plane. He wanted the money to spend on his girlfriend, so he had agreed to do it for her. It was a perfect arrangement. And she had worked hard all winter, at odd jobs, baby-sitting, and loading groceries, and even shoveling snow to save the money.

Cassie handled the controls with ease. She did some S turns, and lazy eights, and then moved on to some deep turns, which she did carefully, and with perfect precision. Even Chris was impressed with her easy, careful style, and he was suddenly grateful to her for how good she would make him look, if anyone was watching him from the ground. She was a splendid pilot. She moved into a loop then, and then he started to get nervous. They'd been up together several times before, and he hated it when she did anything fancy. She was too good, too fast, and he was afraid she might get out of control completely and do something really scary. For twenty bucks, he wasn't willing to let her terrify him. But she didn't even notice him. She was concentrating on her flying. So he just glared at the back of her helmet, and watched her red hair fly in the breeze around it. And eventually, totally fed up with her, he tapped her hard on the shoulder.

It was time to go back, and she knew it. But fo. few minutes, she pretended to ignore him.

She wanted to do a spin, but there was no time and she knew Chris would have a fit if she tried it.

But in his calmer moments, he'd have had to admit that his sister was a very smooth pilot. Even if she did scare the pants off him more than half the time. He just didn't trust her. At any moment, she was perfectly capable of doing something really crazy. There was something about airplanes that went to her head and made her forget all reason.

But she lost altitude carefully, and then let Chris take over the controls again, before they landed. As a result, his landing was not as smooth as hers would have been. They touched down too hard, bumping awkwardly down the runway. She was trying to will him to land the plane properly, but Chris had none of her instincts and as a result he'd done a 'pancake' as he landed, hitting the ground hard after leveling off too high for a proper landing.

When they got out of the plane, both of them were surprised to see Nick and their father standing near the runway. They'd been watching them, and Pat was grinning broadly at Chris, while Nick seemed to be staring at Cassie.

'Nice work, son,' Pat beamed. 'You're a natural pilot.' Pat looked immensely pleased and overlooked the shabby landing, as Nick watched them. been watching Chris's face, but he was much re intent on Cassie as he had been from the moment she stepped out of the plane. 'How was it being up there with your brother, Cass?' her father asked her with a smile.

'Pretty good, Dad. It was really fun.' Her eyes danced like Christmas as Nick watched, and Pat led Chris back to the office, as Nick and Cass followed behind in silence.

'You like flying with him, huh, Cass?' Nick asked carefully as they sauntered toward the office.

'A lot.' She beamed at Nick, and for reasons best known to himself he wanted to reach over and shake her. He knew she wasn't telling the truth, and he wondered why Pat was so easily fooled. Maybe he wanted to be. But those kinds of games could be dangerous, even fatal.

'That loop looked pretty good,' Nick said quietly.

'Felt good too,' she said, without looking at him.

'I'll bet it did,' he said, watching her for a moment, and then, shaking his head, he went back to his office.

A few minutes later, Pat drove the kids home with him. When Nick heard their car leave, he sat at his desk, thinking of them, and the flying he had just seen. He shook his head with a rueful grin. He knew one thing for sure. Chris O'Malley had not been flying that plane. And he couldn't help smiling to himself, as he realized that somehow Cassie had found a way to fly. And maybe, just maybe, after

42

all her hard work to get there, maybe she deserve
it. Maybe he wouldn't challenge her for a while.
Maybe he'd just watch and see how she did. He
smiled to himself again, thinking of the loop he'd
seen her do. Next she'd be flying in the air show.
But why not? What the hell? Everything about her
told him she was a natural. She was more than
that. He sensed instinctively that woman or not,
she *needed* to fly, just like he did.

2

When Pat, Cassie, and Chris walked into the house that night, all of Cassie's sisters were in the kitchen helping their mother. Glynnis looked like Pat, and at twenty-five, had four little girls of her own, and had been married for six years. Megan was shy like her mom, and looked like her, though her hair was brown. At twenty-three, she had three sons, and had married six months after Glynnis. Their husbands were farmers, and had small properties nearby. They were decent, hardworking men, and the girls were happy with them. Colleen was twenty-two and blond, she had a little boy and a little girl, both were barely more than toddlers, and Colleen had been married for three years to the English teacher at the local school. She wanted to go to college, but she was pregnant again, and with three kids at home there was no way she could go anywhere, except if she took them with her. It wouldn't be fair to leave three kids with her mother

every day just so she could go to school, and he
father wouldn't have let her anyway. Maybe when
the kids were older. For the moment college was
only a dream for her. The reality of her life was
three babies and very little money. Her father gave
them small 'gifts' from time to time, but Colleen's
husband was proud, and he hated to take them.
But with his own wages so small, and a new baby
only a few weeks away, they needed all the help
they could get, and Colleen's mother had given
her some money that afternoon. She knew they
needed it to buy things for the baby. Depression
wages had hit the schools, and they could hardly
eat on what David made, even with regular gifts
from her parents, and food given to them by her
sisters.

All three of the girls were staying for dinner with
them, their husbands had other plans that night
and the girls came home to their parents often.
Oona loved seeing the kids, although having them
all home at once made the dinner hour unusually
chaotic and noisy.

Pat went to change and Chris went to his room,
while Cassie tried entertaining the kids and everyone else cooked, and two of her nephews thought
the dirt on her face was hysterically funny. One
of her nieces did too, and she chased all of them
around the living room pretending to be a monster.
Chris didn't appear again until dinner was called,
and he glared at Cassie when he did. He was still
annoyed at her about the loop she had done, but on

45

the other hand she had won his father's praise for him, so he didn't dare complain too much or too loudly. They were both getting what they wanted out of the arrangement. She wanted to fly, and he wanted the money. His father's praise was an added bonus.

Half an hour later, they all sat down to an enormous meal, of corn and pork, corn bread and mashed potatoes. Glynnis had brought the pork, and Megan the corn, and Oona had grown the potatoes. They all grew their own food, and when they needed more they bought it at Strong's. It was the only grocery store for miles, and the best one in the region. The Strongs were doing well, even in tough times, and theirs was a solid business. Oona said as much again as they finished the meal, and Cassie heard a familiar sound of wheels outside the house, almost as though on cue. It was easy to guess who it was, he dropped by almost every night after dinner, particularly now that they were both out of school for the summer.

Cassie had known Bobby Strong, the only son of the local grocer, since they were children. He was a good boy, and they had been good friends for years, but for the past two years they'd been more than that, though Cassie insisted she didn't quite know what. But her mother and Megan always reminded her that they had gotten married at seventeen, so she better know what she was doing with Bobby. He was serious and responsible, and her parents liked him too. But Cassie wasn't ready to admit to herself, or to him, that she loved him.

She liked being with him. She liked him, and his friends. She liked his good manners and gentle ways. His thoughtfulness, his patience. He had a kind heart, and she loved the way he was around her nieces and nephews. She enjoyed a lot of things about him, but he still wasn't as exciting as airplanes. She had never met a boy who was. Maybe there was no such thing. Maybe that was something you just had to accept. But she would have loved to know a boy who was as exciting as a 'Gee Bee Super Sportster' or a 'Beech Staggerwing' or a Wedell-Williams racing plane. Bobby was a nice kid, but he didn't even compare to an airplane.

'Hi, Mrs O'Malley . . . Glynn . . . Meg . . . Colleen . . . wow! Looks like it'll be pretty soon!' Colleen looked huge as she tried to gather up her kids to leave, and Oona helped her.

'Maybe tonight if I don't stop eating my mother's apple pie,' Colleen grinned. She was only five years older than they were, but Cassie felt as though they were light-years apart sometimes. Her sisters were all married and so settled and so different. She knew instinctively that somehow she couldn't be like them. She wondered sometimes if there was a curse on her, if her father had wanted a boy so badly that it had somehow damaged her before birth. Maybe she was a freak. She liked boys. She liked Bobby particularly. But she liked airplanes and her own independence a whole lot better.

Bobby shook hands with her father, and said hi to Chris, and all the little kids climbed all over him. Then a little while later her mother and the oldest sisters went out to the kitchen to clean up, and her mother told her not to bother, and just to go sit with Bobby. At least Cassie had washed her face by then, but you could still see traces of the grease that had been there before dinner.

'How was your day?' he asked with a shy smile. He was awkward, but likable, and he tried to be tolerant of her unusual ideas and her fascination with her father's airplanes. He pretended to be interested, and listened to her rattle on about a new plane that had come through, or her father's cherished Vega. But the truth was, she could have said anything, he just wanted to be near her. He came by faithfully almost every night, and Cassie still acted surprised when he did, much to her parents' amusement.

She was just not ready to face the seriousness of his commitment, or what it might mean if he persisted in visiting her. Only a year from now she would graduate, and if he kept dropping by like this, he might ask her to marry him, and expect to marry her as soon as they finished high school. The very thought of that terrified her and she just couldn't face it. She wanted so much more than that. Time, and space, and college. And the feeling she got when she did a loop, or a spin. Being with Bobby was like driving to Ohio. Safe, and solid and uneventful. He wasn't like flying anywhere.

And yet she knew that if he had stopped coming to see her, she would miss him.

'I went up in my dad's Jenny with Chris today.' She filled him in, trying to sound casual. Getting too serious with Bobby always scared her. 'It was fun. We did some lazy eights, and a loop.'

'Sounds like Chris is getting good,' Bobby said politely, but like Chris, airplanes didn't do much to excite him. 'What else did you do?' He was always interested in her, and secretly he thought her beautiful, not like the other boys who thought she was too tall, or her hair was too red, or liked her because her figure was great, or thought she was weird because she knew a lot about airplanes. Bobby liked her because of who she was, even if at times he recognized the possibility that he might not understand her. But that was endearing about him too. A lot of things were, which was why her feelings about him confused her. Her mother told her that she had felt that way about Pat at first too. Commitment was always hard, Oona said. And that made it even harder for Cassie. She didn't know what to think of what she felt for Bobby.

'Oh, I don't know . . .' Cassie went on to answer his question, trying to remember all she'd done. All of it had to do with airplanes. 'I gassed a bunch of planes, tinkered with the engine on the Jenny before Chris took it out. I think I might even have fixed it.' She touched her face self-consciously then with a grin. 'I got a lot of grease on my face doing it. My dad had a fit when he saw me. I couldn't get it

49

all off. You should have seen me before dinner!'

'I thought maybe you were getting liver spots,' he teased and she laughed. He was a good sport, and he knew how much her dreams meant to her, like college. He had no plans to go himself. He was going to stay home and help his father with their business, just as he did every day after school, and all through the summer.

'You know, Fred Astaire's new movie *Follow the Fleet* is coming to the movie theater this Saturday night. Want to go? They say it's a great movie.' Bobby looked at her hopefully, she nodded slowly, and smiled up at him.

'I'd like that.'

A few minutes later, the last of her sisters and their children left, and Cassie and Bobby were alone on the porch again. Her parents were in the living room. She knew they could see them from where they sat, but her parents were always discreet about Bobby's visits. They liked him, and Pat wouldn't have been unhappy if they'd decided to get married when she finished school next June. As long as they didn't get themselves into trouble first, they could spend all the time they wanted cooing on the front porch. It was fine with him. Better than having her hang around the airport.

Inside the house, Pat was telling Oona about Chris's loop that afternoon. He was so proud of him. 'The boy's a natural, Oonie.' He grinned and she smiled at him, grateful that he had finally gotten the son he had so desperately wanted.

On the porch, Bobby was telling her about his day at the grocery store, and how the Depression was affecting food prices all over the country, not just in Illinois. He had a dream of opening a series of stores one day, in several towns, maybe as far reaching as Chicago. But they all had dreams. Cassie's were a lot wilder than his, and harder to talk about. His just sounded young and ambitious.

'Do you ever think of doing something totally different, and not what your father does at all?' she asked him, intrigued by the idea, even though all she wanted was to follow in her own father's footsteps. But those footsteps were totally forbidden to her, which made them all the more appealing.

'Not really,' Bobby answered quietly. 'I like his business actually. People need food, and they need good food. We do something important for people, even if it doesn't seem very exciting. But maybe it could be.'

'Maybe it could,' she smiled at him, as she heard a sudden droning sound above, and looked up toward the familiar noise of the engines. 'That's Nick . . . he's on his way to San Diego with some cargo. Then he's stopping in San Francisco on the way back, to bring back some mail on one of our contracts.' She knew he was flying the Handley Page, she could tell just from the sound of the engines.

'He probably gets tired of that too,' Bobby said wisely. 'It sounds exciting to us, but to him it's probably only a job, just like my father's.'

'Maybe.' But Cassie knew different. Flying wasn't like that. 'Pilots are a different breed. They love what they do. It's almost as though they can't bear the thought of doing anything else. It's in their bones. They live and breathe it. They love it more than anything.' Her eyes shone as she said it.

'I guess,' Bobby looked baffled by what she was saying, 'I can't say I understand it.'

'I don't think most people can . . . it's like a mysterious fascination. A wonderful gift. To people who love flying, it means more than anything.'

He laughed softly in the warm night air. 'I think you just see it as very romantic. I'm not so sure they do. Believe me, to them, it's probably just a job.'

'Maybe,' she said, not wanting to argue with him, but knowing far more than she let on to. Flying was like a secret brotherhood, one she desperately wanted to join, and so far no one would let her. But for those few moments in the air today, when Chris had let her fly the plane, that was all that mattered.

She sat thinking of it for a long time, staring into the darkness off the porch, forgetting that Bobby was even there, and then suddenly, when she heard him stir, she remembered.

'I guess I should go. You're probably tired from gassing all those planes,' he teased her. But actually, she wanted to be alone, to think of what it had been like to fly the plane. It had been so exquisite for those few minutes. 'I'll see you tomorrow, Cass.'

'Good night.' He held her hand briefly and then brushed her cheek with his lips before he walked back to his father's old Model A truck with 'Strong's Groceries' written across the side. In the daytime, they used it for deliveries. At night, they let Bobby drive it. 'I'll see you tomorrow.'

She smiled and waved at him as he drove away, and then she walked slowly back into the house, thinking of how lucky Nick was to be flying through the night, on his way to San Diego.

3

Nick returned to Good Hope from the West Coast late Sunday night, after dropping off cargo and mail in Detroit and Chicago. He was back at his desk at six o'clock Monday morning, looking rested and energetic. It was a busy day, some new contracts had come in, and there was always more mail and cargo to be moved around. They had plenty of pilots working for them, and enough planes, but Nick still volunteered for the longer-range trips himself, and the more difficult flying. It gave him enormous satisfaction to get in a plane, and fly off into the night, especially in rotten weather. And Pat was the perfect balance for him. He was a genius at running the administrative side of their business. He still loved to fly too, but he had less time for it now, and in some ways less patience. It annoyed the hell out of him when something went wrong with a plane, or they were delayed, or their schedules got loused up. He had no patience at all for pilots' quirks and little tricks, and he made them toe the line and be 100 percent reliable, or they never flew again for O'Malley.

'Ya better watch out, Ace,' Nick teased him now and again, 'you're beginning to sound like Rickenbacker,' their old commander.

'I could do a lot worse, Stick. And so could you,' Pat would growl back at him, using Nick's old wartime nickname. His wartime history was every bit as colorful as Pat's. Nick had once fought the famed German flying ace Ernst Udet to a standoff, and brought his plane back safely even though he'd been wounded. But that was all behind them now. The only time Nick thought of the war was when he was fighting weather, or bringing in a limping plane. He had had a few close calls in the seventeen years he'd flown for Pat, but none as dramatic as his wartime adventures.

Nick was reminded of one of them late that afternoon, as they watched a storm brewing in the east, and mentioned it to Pat. There had been a terrible storm he'd gotten caught in during the war, and flew so low to the ground to get under the clouds, he had almost scraped the plane's belly. Pat laughed, remembering it; he'd given Nick hell for flying that low, but he'd managed to save himself and the plane. Two other men had gotten lost in the same storm and never made it.

'Scared the hell out of me,' Nick admitted, two decades later.

'You looked a little green when you got in, as

55

I recall.' Pat needled him a little bit, and they watched the ominous black clouds gather in the distance. Nick was still tired from the long flight from the West Coast the day before, but he wanted to finish his paperwork before he went home to sleep. And when he walked back into the office with Pat, after checking the condition of some planes, he noticed Chris in the distance, chatting with Cassie. They seemed intent in conversation and neither of them noticed him. He couldn't imagine what they were saying. Nor did it worry him. He knew that the weather was looking too ominous for Chris to want to go up with him or practice solo.

Cassie and Chris were still talking after Nick disappeared back into the office, and Cassie was shouting at him over the roar of some nearby engines.

'Don't be stupid! We only have to go up and down for a few minutes. The storm is still hours away. I listened to all the weather reports this morning. Don't be such a damn chicken, Chris.'

'I don't want to go up when the weather looks like this, Cass. We can go tomorrow.'

'I want to go now.' The dark clouds rushing past them overhead only seemed to excite her further. 'It would be fun.'

'No, it wouldn't. And if I risk the Jenny, Dad'll really be mad at me.' He knew his father well and so did Cassie.

'Don't be dumb. We're not risking anything. The

clouds are still way up there. If we go now, we can be back in half an hour, and be perfectly safe. Trust me.' He watched her eyes unhappily, hating her for being so persuasive. She had always done this to him. After all, she was his big sister. He had always listened to her, and more often than not it had resulted in disaster, mostly when she urged him to trust her. She was the daredevil in the family, and he was always the hesitant, cautious one. But Cassie never listened to reason. Sometimes it was easier just to give in to her than to go on arguing forever. Her blue eyes were pleading with him, and it was obvious she wasn't going to take no for an answer.

'Fifteen minutes and that's it,' he finally conceded unhappily. 'And I decide when we come back in. I don't give a damn what you think, if it's too soon, or you haven't had enough. Fifteen minutes and we're back. And that's it, Cass. Or forget it. Deal?'

'Deal. I just want to get the feel of the weather.' She looked like a girl with a new romance as she beamed at him, her eyes dancing.

'I think you're nuts,' he said grumpily. But it seemed easier to get it over with than to stand there yelling at each other till the storm broke.

They went out to where the Jenny was kept, rolled it out, and did the necessary checks on the plane itself, and then they hopped into their respective seats. Cassie sat in front again, and Chris took the instructor's seat behind her. In theory, just as before, she was only a passenger, and since they both had controls, no one could see who handled them, if it was Chris or Cassie.

A few minutes later, Nick heard the hum of the plane overhead, but he didn't pay much attention to it. He figured it was some fool, trying to get home ahead of the weather front right before the storm broke. For once, it wasn't his problem. All his pilots were on the ground, where he had told them to stay, after listening to a news bulletin half an hour before. But as he listened to the sound now, he could have sworn he could hear the Jenny. It seemed impossible, but he wandered over to the window anyway, and then he saw them. He saw Cassie's distinct red hair in the front seat, and Chris right behind her. He was flying the plane, or so Nick thought, and the wind buffeted them terribly and seemed to almost toss them away right after takeoff. They were moving with surprising speed, and then Nick saw them rise dramatically, probably caught in a sudden updraft. He watched them, amazed, unable to believe that Chris had been both brave and foolish enough to take off in a windstorm like this one. And almost as soon as they disappeared into the cloud hanging over him, Nick saw the rain splash down on the ground as though someone in the sky had turned on a faucet.

'Shit!' He muttered to himself as he hurried outside, watching for where the Jenny had been, but he couldn't see anything, and the storm front was moving fast now, with terrifying winds and a flash of lightning. Within minutes he was drenched, and there was no sign of Chris or Cassie.

Chris was fighting with the controls as they gained altitude, and Cassie had turned around and was shouting something to him, but between the storm and the engine's noise, he couldn't hear her.

'Let me take it!' she was shouting, and at last he understood, as she signaled him with gestures. He shook his head, but she kept nodding at him, and it was obvious that he was being overpowered rapidly by the forces of nature. The force of the wind and the storm were too much for him, and the plane was being tossed around like a child's toy, in his unskilled hands. And then, without saying a word to him, she turned her attention to the controls, and by sheer force, she overpowered him and took them from him. She began flying the plane with her stronger hands on the controls, and within moments, despite the ferocious winds, the plane had almost steadied. Chris stopped fighting her then, and near tears, he let his hands go slack on his set of the controls, and let her fly it. She knew less than he did perhaps, but she seemed to have a relationship with the plane that he couldn't come close to. And he knew that in his hands they would almost surely be destroyed. Maybe in Cassie's there was some hope. For an instant, he closed his eyes and prayed, wishing he had never let her talk him into taking off in the storm.

They were both drenched in the open cockpit, and the plane was rising and falling on terrifying downdrafts. They would drop a hundred feet or so, and then rise again, although more slowly. It was like being dropped off a building when they fell, and then crawling up the side again, only to be dropped again, like a paper puppet.

The clouds were almost black as Cassie fought with the stick, but she seemed to sense their altitude almost by instinct. She had an uncanny sense about what the plane would cooperate with, and seemed to work with it to get where she wanted. But they had no idea where they were anymore, how far they had gone, or exactly how high they were. The altimeter was going crazy. Cassie had some idea, but they had totally lost sight of the ground, and a rapidly moving line of clouds had disoriented them completely.

'We're okay,' she shouted encouragingly back at Chris, but he couldn't hear her. 'We're going to be fine,' she kept saying to herself, and then she began talking to the Jenny itself, as though the little plane could follow her directions. She had heard about some of her father's and Nick's tricks, and she knew that there was one that would get them out of this mess, if it didn't kill them. She had to trust her own instincts for this, and she had to be very, very sure . . . she was talking to herself, into the wind, as the plane began to drop dramatically. She was looking for the lowest edge of the clouds, and counting on finding it before they hit the ground, but if it was too low, and she dropped too fast, or if she lost control for a single instant . . . it was called scud running, and if you lost . . . you died. It was as simple as that. And they both knew it, as the little Jenny dropped toward the ground as quickly as Cassie would let it.

Their speed was terrifying by then, the howling of the wind deafening, as they flew through the inky wet blackness. It seemed like a bottomless place they were falling into, filled with horrifying sounds, and terrifying feelings, and then suddenly, almost before she knew, she sensed before she saw, both the treeline, and the ground, and then the airport. She pulled sharply on the stick, and pulled herself up just before they'd have hit the trees. They got lost in the clouds again for a moment or two, but she knew then where she was, and how to approach the airport. She closed her eyes just for a second, feeling where she was, and how fast she could drop, and again she saw the trees, but this time she was in full control. She came in just over them, as the wind tipped her wings, and almost knocked them over. She pulled up and circled the airport again, wondering if they could land at all, or if in the end it would be impossible because of the force of the unpredictable winds. She wasn't afraid, she was just thinking very quietly, and then she saw him. It was Nick waving frantically. He had seen what she'd done, seen her running just under the clouds, and almost hit the ground. She was less than fifty feet above it. He ran to where she should be, and tried to wave her in, on the farthest runway. The angle of the wind was just enough gentler there to allow her to make a breathtaking landing. The little Jenny screeched all the way down the runway, with the wind hard on their faces, and Cassie gritted her teeth so hard her face ached. Her hair was plastered to her head from the rain, and her hands were numb from clutching the stick, and Chris was sitting behind her with his eyes closed. They bounced hard when they hit the ground, and he opened them. He couldn't believe she'd brought them in, he had been sure they were as good as dead; he was still in shock when Nick came rushing up to them, and physically dragged him out of the plane, while Cassie just sat there shaking.

'What the hell are you two lunatics trying to do? Commit suicide, or bomb the airport?' They had come pretty close to the roof on the way down, but Cassie had decided that was the least of their problems. She was still amazed that she'd brought them in at all, and she had to fight to repress a grin of relief. She'd been so damn scared, and yet a part of her had stayed so cool. All she could do was think about how to get out of it, and talk to the little airplane. 'Are you crazy?' Nick was shaking him, and glaring at her, as Pat came running out from the airport.

'What the hell is going on here?' he shouted at all of them, as the wind buffeted them, and Cassie began worrying about the plane. She didn't want her turned over and damaged as they sat in the wind on the runway.

'These two fools of yours went out for a joyride

in this. I think they're trying to get killed, or destroy your airplanes, I'm not sure which, but they ought to have their butts kicked.' Nick was so furious he could hardly speak, and Pat couldn't believe what he was seeing.

He stared at Chris in utter astonishment. 'You went out in *this*?' He was referring to the weather not the plane, as his son knew.

'I . . . uh . . . I just thought we'd go up and come right down . . . and . . .' He wanted to whine as he had as a child, 'But, Daddy, Cassie made me . . .' But he said not a word as his father tried to hide his pride in him. The kid had guts, and he was a hell of a pilot.

'And you landed her in this? Don't you know how dangerous this kind of weather is? You could have been killed.' Pat couldn't hide the pride in his voice, it was beyond him.

'I know, Dad. I'm sorry.' Chris was fighting not to cry, and Cassie was watching her father's face. She knew only too well what she saw there. It was raw pride in the accomplishments of his son, or so he thought. It was meant for her, but it went to Chris, because he was a boy, and that was just the way things were. The way they always had been. Whatever she did in life, she knew she had to do it for herself, not for him, because he would never understand it or give her credit for it. She was 'only a girl' to him. That was all she ever would be.

Pat turned to look at Cassie then, almost as though he could hear her thinking. And then he looked at his son again with an angry scowl. 'You should never have taken her up in this. It's too dangerous for passengers to be out in bad conditions. You shouldn't have gone up yourself. But never take a passenger into weather like this, son.' She was someone to be protected, but never admired. It was her destiny, and she knew it.

'Yes, sir.' There were tears standing out in Chris's eyes as his father glanced at the plane, and his son, in fresh amazement.

'Put her away then.' And with that he walked away, and Nick watched Chris and Cassie put the plane away. Chris looked so shaken he could hardly walk, but Cassie was calm, as she wiped the rain off the plane, and checked the engine. Her brother only looked at her angrily and stalked away, determined never to forgive her for almost killing him. He would never forget how close they had come, and all because of one of her whims. She was completely crazy. She had proved it.

She put the last of her tools away, and she was surprised when she turned to find Nick standing just behind her. He looked very much like the storm she had just flown through. Her brother was gone, and her father was waiting for them inside the airport.

'Don't *ever* do that again. You're a damn fool, and you could have been killed. That little trick only works once in a while for the greats, and usually not for them. It won't work for you again, Cass. Don't try it.' But it had worked for him more than once. And years before, watching him, it had made Pat as angry as Nick was now. His eyes were like steel as he looked at her. He was furious, but there was something else there too. And her heart gave a little leap as she saw it. It was what she had wanted from Pat, and knew she would never get from him. It was admiration, and respect. It was all she wanted.

'I don't know what you mean.' She looked away from him. Now that she was back on the ground, she felt drained. The exhilaration was almost gone, and what she felt now was the backlash of the terror, and the exhaustion.

'You know damn well what I mean!' he shouted at her and grabbed her arm, his black hair matted around his face. He had stood staring up at her plane, willing her in, willing her to find the hole in the clouds, to make it. He couldn't have stood losing both of them, seeing them die, and all for a joyride. In the war, they'd had no choice. But this was different. It was so senseless.

'Let go of me.' She was angry at him. She was angry at all of them. Her brother who got all the glory and didn't know how to fly worth a damn, her father who was so obsessed with him he couldn't see anything, and Nick who thought he knew it all. It was their secret club, they had all the toys, and they would never let her play. She was good enough to fuel their machines and work on their engines, and get their oil and grease in her hair, but never to fly their planes. 'Leave me alone!' she shouted at him, and he only grabbed her other arm. He had never seen her like this, and he didn't know whether to spank her or hold her.

'Cassie, I saw what you did up there!' He was still shouting at her. 'I'm not blind. I know Chris can't fly like that! I know you were flying the plane ... but you're crazy. You could have gotten yourself killed ... you can't do that ...' She looked at him with such misery that his heart went out to her. He had wanted to beat her senseless for almost killing herself, and now instead, he felt sorry for her. He understood now as he never had before what she wanted, and how badly she wanted it, and just how much she was willing to do to get it.

'Cassie, please ...' He kept a grip on her arms and pulled her closer to him. 'Please ... don't ever do anything like that again. I'll teach you myself. I promise. Leave Chris alone. Don't do that to him. I'll teach you. If you want it so badly, I'll do it.' He held her close to him, cradling her like a little girl, grateful that she hadn't been killed by her foolish but daring stunt. He knew he couldn't have stood it. He looked at her unhappily as he held her close to him. They were both badly shaken by what had happened. But she only shook her head at him. She knew how impossible it was. This was the only way she could have it.

'My father will never let you teach me, Nick,' she said miserably, no longer denying that she had brought Chris in, instead of the other way around. Nick knew the truth, and she knew that.

66

There was no point lying to him. She had done it.

'I didn't say I'd ask him, Cass. I said I'd do it. Not here.' He smiled ruefully at her, and handed her a clean towel to dry her hair with. 'You look like a drowned rat.'

'At least I don't have grease all over my face for a change,' she said shyly. She felt closer to him than she ever had before. And different. She was drying her hair, as she looked at him again. She couldn't believe what she was hearing. 'What do you mean "not here." Where else would we go?' She felt suddenly grown-up, part of a conspiracy with him. Something had very subtly changed between them.

'There are half a dozen little strips we can go to. It may not be easy. You could catch a bus to Prairie City after school, and I could meet you there. In the meantime, maybe Chris would drop you off there this summer now and then on his way to work. I imagine he'd rather do that than risk his life several times a week flying with you. I know I would.' Cassie grinned. Poor Chris. She had scared the pants off him, and she knew it. But it had seemed like such a great idea, and for a few minutes it was fun. And after that, it was the scariest thing she had ever done, and the most exciting.

'Do you mean it?' She looked amazed, but in fact, they both did. He was a little startled himself at what he'd just offered.

'I guess I do. I never thought I'd do something like this. But I think maybe some instruction will keep you out of a lot more trouble. And maybe after you fly respectably for a while,' he looked at her pointedly, 'we can talk to Pat and see if he'll let you fly from here. He'll come around eventually. He has to.'

'I don't think he will,' she said gloomily, as they went back out into the rain to meet her father in his office. And then, just before they reached it, soaked again, she stopped and looked at him with a smile that melted his very soul. He didn't want to feel that way with her, and it startled him. But they had been through a lot that evening, and it had brought them closer together.

'Thanks, Nick.'

'Don't mention it. And I mean that.' Her father would have strangled him for giving her lessons. He tousled her wet hair then, and walked her into her father's office. Chris was looking shaken and gray, and his father had just given him a nip of brandy.

'You okay, Cass?' Pat glanced at her, but saw that she looked none the worse for wear, unlike her brother. But the responsibility had been his after all, and the hard part of landing back at the airport, or at least that was what her father thought, and Chris hadn't told him any different.

'I'm okay, Dad,' she assured him.

'You're a brave girl,' he said admiringly, but not admiring enough. It was Nick who had understood. Nick who had agreed to give her what she had always dreamed of. Her dream come true, and she was suddenly glad she had gone up in the storm, even if she had taken a hell of a chance. Maybe in the end, it had been worth it.

Pat drove Chris and Cassie home, and their mother was waiting for them. As soon as they sat down to dinner, her father told Oona the whole story. Or what he thought was the whole story, of how incredible Chris had been, how he had flown by sheer wit and nerve, and after the initial foolishness of going up in the storm, had brought them home safely. Their father was so proud of him, and Chris said nothing at all. He just went to his room, and lay on his bed and cried, with the door closed.

Cassie went in to see him after a while. She knocked for a long time, and he finally let her in, with a look that combined anguish and fury.

'What do *you* want?'

'To tell you I'm sorry I scared you . . . and almost got us killed. I'm sorry, Chris. I shouldn't have done it.' She could afford to be magnanimous now, now that Nick had agreed to give her what she had always wanted.

'I'm never going up in a plane with you again,' he said ominously, glaring at her like a much younger brother who had been used and betrayed by a wilier older sister.

'You don't have to,' she said quietly, sitting on the edge of his bed as he stared at her.

'You're giving up flying?' That he'd never believe.

'Maybe . . . for now . . .' She shrugged, as though it didn't matter to her, but he knew her better.

'I don't believe you.'

'I'll see. It doesn't matter now. I just wanted to tell you I was sorry.'

'You should be,' he fired at her, and then he backed down, and reached out and touched her arm. 'Thanks though . . . for saving our asses up there. I really thought we were done for.'

'So did I,' she grinned excitedly at him. 'I really thought for a while there it was over.' And then she giggled.

'You lunatic,' and then, admiringly, 'you're a hell of a pilot, Cass. You gotta learn right one day, and not all this sneaky stuff behind Dad's back. He's got to let you fly. You're ten times the pilot I'll ever be. I'll bet you're as good as he is.'

'I doubt that, but you'll be okay. You're a good straightforward pilot, Chris. Just stay out of the tough stuff.'

'Yeah, thanks,' he grinned at her, no longer wanting to kill her. 'I'll remind you of that, next time you offer to take me up and kill me.'

'I won't, for a while,' she said angelically, but he knew her better.

'What's that all about? You're up to something, Cass.'

'No, I'm not. I'm going to behave . . . for a while anyway . . .'

'Lord help us. Just let me know when you decide to go berserk again. I'll be sure to stay away from the airport. Maybe you ought to do that for a while too. I swear, those fumes have made you crazy.'

70

'Maybe so,' she said dreamily. But it was more than that, and she knew it. She had those fumes in her blood, her bones, and she knew more than ever that she would never escape them.

Bobby Strong came by after dinner that night, and he was horrified when he heard her father's tale, and furious with Chris a little later when he saw him.

'The next time you take my girl up and almost kill her, you'll have to answer to me,' he said, much to Chris's and Cassie's astonishment. 'That was a dumb thing to do and you know it.' Chris would have liked to tell him Cassie wanted to, he would have liked to tell him a lot of things, but of course he couldn't.

'Yeah, sure,' her younger brother mumbled vaguely as he went back to his room. They were all nuts. Bobby, Cass, his father, Nick. None of them knew the truth, none of them knew who was to blame and who wasn't. His father thought he was a criminal, and Cassie had them all bamboozled. But only Cassie knew the truth about that, and Nick, now that he had promised to give her lessons.

Bobby lectured her that night on how dangerous flying was, how useless, and how foolish; he told her that all the men involved in it were immature, and they were just playing like children. He hoped she had learned a lesson that night, and that she would be more reasonable in the future about hanging around the airport. He expected it of her, he explained. How could she expect to have any kind of future at all if she spent her life covered in grease and oil, and was willing to risk her life on a wild adventure with her brother? Besides, she was a girl, and it wasn't proper.

She tried to make herself agree with him, because she knew he meant well. But she was relieved when he left. And all she could think of that night, as she lay in bed listening to the rain, was what Nick had promised her, and how soon they would start flying together. She could hardly wait. She lay awake for hours, thinking about it, and remembering the feeling of the wind on her face, as she dashed beneath the clouds in the Jenny, looking for the edge, waiting to escape, just before they hit the ground, and then soaring free again, shearing the top of the trees, and then coming in safely. It had been an extraordinary day, and she knew that no matter what anyone said to her about how dangerous or improper it was, she would never give it up. Not for any of them. She just couldn't.

4

Three days after the storm that eventually turned into a tornado, ten miles away in Blandinsville, Cassie got up and did her chores and when she left the house, she told her mother she was going to the library, and then to meet a friend from school who had married that spring, and was expecting a baby. And after that she'd stop by the airport. She had packed an apple and a sandwich in a paper bag, and she had taken a dollar from her savings and hidden it in her pocket. She wasn't sure how much the bus fare would be, but she wanted to be sure she had enough to get to Prairie City. She had promised to meet Nick there at noon, and as she walked toward the bus terminal downtown in the summer sun, she was sorry she hadn't worn a hat. But she knew that if she had, her mother would have suspected something. She never wore one.

As she walked along, she looked like a long, lanky girl, going off to meet friends. She looked her age, but was extraordinarily lovely. She was even prettier than her mother had been, she was taller and thinner, and she had an even more impressive figure. But her looks were something that Cassie never thought about. Looks were something for other girls, who had nothing else in their heads, or girls like her sisters who wanted to get married and have babies. She knew she wanted children one day, or at least she thought she did, but there were so many other things she wanted first, things she would probably never have, like excitement and freedom and flying. She loved reading stories about women pilots, and she read everything she could about Amelia Earhart and Jackie Cochran. She'd read Lindbergh's book *We*, about his Atlantic solo in 1927, and his wife's book *North to the Orient* the year before when it came out, and Earhart's book, *The Fun of It*. All the women involved in aviation were her heroes. She often wondered why they could do what she could only dream of. But maybe now with Nick helping her . . . just maybe . . . if she could just fly . . . if she could just take off as she had the other day with Chris, and soar lazily into the sky forever.

She was so lost in her own thoughts that she almost missed her bus, and she had to run to catch it before it left her. She was relieved to see that no one she knew had gotten on, and the forty-five-minute ride to Prairie City in the dilapidated bus was uneventful. It had only cost fifteen cents, and she spent the entire trip daydreaming about her lessons.

It was a long walk to the airstrip after the bus dropped her off, but Nick had told her exactly how to get there. He had somehow assumed that she would get a ride from someone. It had never dawned on him that she would walk the last two miles to meet him, and when she arrived she looked hot and damp and dusty. He was sitting quietly on a rock, drinking a soda, with the familiar Jenny parked at the end of the deserted airstrip. There was no-one else around, just the two of them. It was a runway that was used occasionally for crop dusters, and had been put in originally in barnstorming days. It was only used occasionally, but it was in good repair. Nick had known it would be the perfect place for their lessons.

'You okay?' He looked at her with a fatherly air, as she pushed her bright red hair off her face, and held it off her neck. The sun was blazing. 'You look hotter than hell. Here, have something to drink.' He handed her his Coke, and watched her admiringly as she took a long swallow. She had a long graceful neck, and the silky whiteness of her throat reminded him of the palest pink marble. She was a striking girl, and there were times lately when he almost wished she weren't Pat's daughter. But it wouldn't have done him any good anyway, he reminded himself. He was thirty-five and she was seventeen, she was hardly fair prey for a man his age. But there were moments when it could have been tempting. 'What did you do, you goofball?' he asked, relieving the tension of the moment. It was odd being here, just the two of them, alone on their secret mission. 'Did you walk all the way from Good Hope?'

'No,' she grinned back at him, quenched by his soda. 'Just from Prairie City. It was farther than I thought. And hotter.'

'I'm sorry,' he said apologetically. He felt bad to have brought her so far, but it had seemed the perfect place for their rendezvous with her father's plane, for their secret lessons.

'Don't be,' she grinned, accepting another swig of his soda. 'It's worth it.' He could see easily in her eyes how much it meant to her. She was crazed over planes, and totally in love with fly-ing. It was exactly how he had been at her age, dragging from airport to airport to airport, happy to do anything, just to be near the planes and get a chance to fly now and then. The war had been like a dream come true for him, flying in the 94th, with men who had almost all become legends. But he was sorry for her, it wouldn't be that easy, particularly if Pat was determined to keep her from flying. Nick was hoping that one of these days he might sway him. And in the mean-time, at least he could teach her the important things, so she didn't kill herself doing crazy tricks, or scud running with her brother. He still shud-dered when he thought of her flying out of the clouds three days before, just barely above the ground and moving like a bullet. At least now she'd know what she was doing.

'Shall we give it a whirl?' he asked, waving at the Jenny. She was sitting there, waiting for them, an old friend, just as they were.

She was too excited to even speak to him as they walked down the airstrip to the familiar plane. She had gassed her a thousand times, cleaned her engine, lovingly washed her wings, and flown her half a dozen times with Chris pretending that he was taking his sister up for a joyride. But the Jenny had never looked as beautiful to Cassie as she did now. They did a walk around first, checked the landing gear to make sure he hadn't damaged it when he landed. She was a low plane with a broad wingspan and the feel of a larger plane, although she was a modest size, and she wasn't daunting to Cassie. And now Cassie gently stepped into her and buckled her seat belt. She knew that the skies would soon be hers, she had a right to them, just as they all did. And after that, no one could stop her.

'All set?' Nick shouted at her in the first noise of the engine. Cassie nodded with a grin, and he hopped in the seat behind her. At first, he would be flying the plane, and once they were safely in the air, he would turn over the controls to her. This time she wouldn't have to wrest them from him, as she had from Chris. This time it would all be aboveboard, and as they taxied down the runway, Cassie turned to look at him. Nick's was such a familiar face to her, and yet as she saw him now, she felt happier than she had ever been, and she wanted to throw her arms around his neck and kiss him.

'What?' She had said something to him, and at first he couldn't hear her. He didn't think anything was wrong, she looked too happy for there to be a problem. But he leaned forward so he could hear her better. His dark hair was blowing in the wind, his eyes were the same color as the summer sky, and there were lines around his eyes from where he squinted into the sunlight.

'I said . . . thank you! . . .' she shouted back at him, her eyes so filled with joy that it touched his heart. He squeezed her shoulder gently, and she turned forward again, and put her hands on the controls. But there was no question this time as to who was flying the plane. Nick was.

He pushed the throttle forward evenly, and used the rudder pedals. And a moment later, they lifted smoothly off the runway and rose easily into the air, and as they did, Cassie felt her heart soar with the old Jenny. She felt the same thrill she always did when she left the ground. She was *flying*!

He started a gentle turn to move away from the small airstrip, and then rolled the wings to level off, and touched Cassie on the shoulder. She glanced over her shoulder at him, and he pointed at her, indicating to her to take the controls now. She nodded, and as though by instinct, Cassie took over. She knew what she needed to do, and they flew easily through the bright blue sky, as though she had been flying all her life. And in some ways she had. He was amazed at her skill, and her natural instincts. She had picked up a lot of his own and her father's tricks, just by watching them, and she seemed to have a style of her own, which was surprisingly smooth and easy. She seemed totally at ease at the controls of the small plane, and Nick decided to see how much she could do on their first lesson.

He had her do turns and banks in different directions, first moving left and then right; he was going to tell her to keep the nose up, to maintain altitude, but she seemed to know automatically that the plane would fall during turns, and she kept the nose up without his telling her anything. Her natural sense for the plane was uncanny. She kept back pressure on the stick with a steady hand, and the nose stayed up in response to her movements.

He had her do S turns then, using a small dirt road as a guide, and he noticed as she did them, that she controlled her altitude easily. She seldom seemed to look at the instruments yet she knew when she needed to compensate, or rise higher in the sky. She seemed to fly primarily by feel and sight, which was a sure sign of a natural pilot. It was rare to see one like her, and he knew he had seen damn few in his lifetime.

He had her fly circles for a while, around a silo they spotted on a distant farm, and she complained at how boring it was, but he had wanted to check her precision. She was careful and precise, and astonishingly accurate, particularly for someone who had scarcely flown. And then finally, he let her try a loop, and the double loop she had wanted to terrify her brother with. But after that, he taught her how to recover from a stall, which was far more important. But she seemed to know that by instinct too. Her total calm going into the stall impressed him, as the Jenny began to fall nose down with alternate wings dipping. But within seconds, she released the pressure on the stick that had created the stall in the first place and in a totally fearless move, she allowed the dive to increase their airspeed. He had explained how to do it at first, but she seemed to have no trouble at all figuring it out, and no lack of courage in following the procedure. Most young pilots were terrified at the drop and the sudden zero gravity. Cassie was awed by none of it, as the Jenny plummeted briefly, and when the Jenny had gained just enough speed, she pushed the throttle, gave it power, and leveled out like a baby eagle, soaring gently back to where she wanted to be, without a murmur.

Nick had never been so impressed by anything he'd seen. And he made her do it again, to see if she could maintain the same cool hands and cool head, and quick reactions, or if it had just been beginner's luck. But the second stall and recovery were even smoother than the first, and she swooped him right back up again from a stall that even had him worried. She was good. She was very good. She was brilliant.

He had her do a few lazy eights then, an Immelmann, and their last lesson of the day was a spin recovery, which was not unlike the stall, but first she had to give it right rudder pedal to induce a spin to the right, and then left rudder pedal to recover. She did it perfectly, and Nick was grinning from ear to ear as he landed the plane, but so was Cassie. She had never had so much fun in her life, and her only complaint was that she had wanted to try barrel rolls and he wouldn't let her. He felt they had done enough for one day, and he'd told her they had to save something for next time. She wanted to learn a dead stick landing too, his specialty, which had earned him his nickname, but there was time for that too. There was time for everything. She was a fantastic student.

He sat in the plane for a moment, looking at her, unable to believe how much she had picked up over the years, just by watching. All those times Pat had taken her up with him, or that Nick had flown her somewhere, every moment, every gesture, every procedure had been absorbed, and somehow, by watching them, she had learned how to do it. She really was what he had suspected she was all along, the ultimate natural. A pilot who was born to fly, it would have been a sacrilege to keep her from it.

'How was I?' She turned in her seat after they'd stopped, and he killed the engine.

'Terrible,' he grinned at her, still unable to believe what he'd seen. She had a natural sense of their altitude, an uncanny sense of direction, an instinct for guiding the plane almost as much with her mind as with her hands. She had known exactly what she was doing. 'I don't think I could ever fly with you again,' he teased, but his face told her all she wanted to know, and she let out a whoop of joy on the silent airstrip. She had never been as happy in her entire life. And Nick was the best friend she had ever had. He had given her her life's dream, and this was only the beginning. 'You're good, kid,' he said quietly, and handed her another Coke he had brought with him. She took a long swig, saluting him, and then handed it back to her new instructor. 'But don't let that go to your head. Those can be dangerous words. Never be overconfident, never over trust yourself, never assume you can do anything you want to. You can't. This bird is only a machine, and if your head gets too big, the ground will get too close, and you'll wind up with a tree between your ears. Don't ever forget that.'

'Yes, sir.' But she was too happy to care about his warnings. She knew how careful she'd have to be, and she was prepared to be, but she also knew that she had been born to fly and now Nick knew it too, and maybe one day he'd convince her father. And in the meantime, she was going to learn every single thing she could and be the best pilot who had ever lived. Better than Jean Batten or Louise Thaden or any of the others. 'When can we do this again?' she asked anxiously. All she wanted to do was go up again, and she didn't want to wait long to do it. Nick was paying for the fuel, and she didn't want it to cost him too much. But like an addict, she wanted more soon, and he knew it.

'You want to do this again tomorrow, right?' He grinned at her. He had been the same way when he was her age. In fact, he had been almost exactly her age when he floated all over the country, after the war, trying to get jobs at airports, and finally came to Illinois to fly for his old friend Pat O'Malley.

'I don't know, Cass.' Nick thought about it for a moment. 'Maybe we could do this again in a couple of days. I don't want Pat to start wondering why I'm taking out the Jenny. I don't exactly fly her much.' And he definitely didn't want Pat to suspect them. He wanted her to get plenty of good solid lessons under her belt first, before they confronted him with her skill, of which there could be no question. She was a thousand times the pilot her brother was, a thousand times the pilot most people he had taught were. But they had to convince Pat of that, and they both knew that wasn't going to be easy.

'Couldn't you tell him you're giving someone lessons out here. He doesn't have to know it's me. Then you'd have an excuse to take her out whenever you want to.'

'And where's the money, miss? I wouldn't want your dad to think I'm cheating him.' They took a cut on each other's profits, when they used each other's planes, or sometimes if Nick took charters or taught on time he would have otherwise used flying for O'Malley.

Cassie looked crestfallen at this. 'Maybe I could pay you . . . a little bit from my savings . . .' She started to look seriously worried and Nick touched the bright red hair and ruffled it.

'Don't worry. I'll get her out. We'll do plenty of this. I promise.' Cassie smiled gently up at him, and his heart did a little flip. It was all the payment he needed.

He helped her step from the plane, and noticed that there was a shady tree nearby. 'Did you bring anything to eat?' She nodded, and they went to sit under it. She shared her sandwich with him, and he shared his Coca-Cola. He drank a lot of it, and unlike Pat, who liked a good whiskey now and then, Nick had never been much of a drinker. He spent too much time in the air to be able to afford to do much drinking. He was always getting hauled out of bed for an emergency somewhere, or a special mail flight, or a long distance cargo flight for anywhere from Mexico to Alaska. He couldn't have flown those runs if he'd been unexpectedly drunk or even hung over. And Pat was careful too. He never drank if he knew he'd be flying.

They talked about flying for a long time, and her family, and how much they had meant to him when he first came to Illinois. He said he had come out from New York just to work for her father.

'He was good to me during the war . . . I was such a kid . . . I was a damn fool too. I'm glad you'll never have to get into something like that, dueling it out at ten thousand feet with a bunch of crazy Germans. It was almost like a game, sometimes it was hard to remember it was real . . . it was so damn exciting.' His eyes shone as he talked about it. For many of them, it had been the perfect time, and everything afterward had paled in comparison. Sometimes she thought her father felt that way, and she suspected Nick did.

'It must make everything else seem awfully dull . . . flying the Jenny . . . or cargo runs to California in the Handley can't exactly be exciting.'

'No, it's not. But it's comfortable. It's where I need to be. I never feel as good on the ground, Cass, crazy as that sounds. That's my life up there.' He glanced up at the sky as he said it. 'It's what I do well,' he sighed, and leaned back against the tree trunk where they were sitting, 'the rest of it, I'm not so good at.'

'Like what?' She was curious about him; she had known him all her life, but he had always treated her as a child, and now that they were sharing the secret of her flying, for the first time, they seemed almost equals.

'I don't know. I'm not so great at marriage, people . . . friends . . . except other pilots and the guys I work with.'

'You've always been great to us.' She smiled innocently up at him, and he marveled at how young seventeen was.

'That's different. You're my family. But I don't know . . . sometimes it's hard to relate to people who don't fly, it's hard to understand them, harder

for them to understand me . . . particularly women.'
He grinned. It didn't bother him. It was the way his
life was, and he was satisfied with it. There were
ground people, those confined to earth, in their
bodies and minds . . . and then there were the
others.

'What about Bobby?' he asked her unexpectedly.
He knew about her boyfriend. He had seen him
often enough at the house when he stopped by
there to see Pat, or came to dinner. 'How would
he feel about you flying like you do? You're good,
Cass. If you learn right, you could really do it.'
But do what? That was the problem. What could
a woman do, except maybe set records? 'What
would he say?' Nick persisted.

'What everyone else says. That I'm nuts.' Cassie
laughed at him. 'But I'm not married to him, you
know. He's just a friend.'

'He won't be "just a friend" forever. Sooner
or later, he'll want to be a lot more, or at least
that's what your father thinks.' It was what everyone thought and she knew it.

'Is that so?' She sounded cool suddenly and Nick
laughed at how prim she was.

'Don't go getting all icy at me over it. You
know what I'm saying. It's going to be odd if
you want to be another Earhart. You're going
to have to live with it. That's not always easy.'
He knew that only too well. He knew a lot of
things he suddenly wanted to share with her. The
new dimension of their friendship both excited and

86

frightened him. He couldn't imagine where it might lead them.

'Why is it such a big deal?' she said plaintively, thinking of Nick's questions about Bobby. It didn't make any sense to her. What was so wrong about flying?

'I guess it's a big deal because it's different,' Nick explained. 'Men are made to walk around on the ground. If you want to fly around like a bird all the time, maybe they figure you should have feathers, or maybe they just figure you're weird. What do I know?' He smiled easily at her, and stretched his long legs out ahead of him. It was fun talking to her, she was so bright and young and alive, so excited about the life she had before her. He envied her that. Her life was filled with challenges to be met and fresh beginnings. Even at thirty-five, a lot of the excitement in his life seemed to be behind him.

'I think people are stupid about flying. They're just planes, and we're just people,' she said simply.

'No, we're not,' he said matter-of-factly. 'We're superheroes in their heads because we do something they can't do, and that most of them are afraid of. We're like lion tamers, or high-wire dancers . . . it's all very mysterious and very exciting, isn't it?' He made her think about it for a minute and she nodded, and handed his Coke back to him again. He took a swig and lit a cigarette, but he didn't offer her one. She might be learning to fly, but she wasn't that grown-up yet.

'I guess it is kind of exciting and mysterious,' she conceded as she watched him smoke. 'Maybe that's why I love it. But it feels so good too . . . it's so free . . . so alive . . . so . . .' She couldn't find the right words and he smiled. He knew just exactly what she meant. He still felt that way too. Every time his plane lifted off the ground, whichever one he was flying at the time, he always felt the same wild thrill of freedom. It made everything else seem bland and uninteresting. It had affected his whole life, what he did, who he saw, what he wanted to do. It had affected all his relationships, and one day it would affect hers too. He felt he should warn her somehow, but he wasn't sure what to say. She was so young and so filled with hope, it seemed almost wrong to warn her.

'It'll change your life, Cass,' was all he could bring himself to say. 'Be careful of that.'

She nodded, thinking she understood what he had said, but she didn't. 'I know' – and then she looked up at him, with eyes so wise it almost scared him – 'but that's what I want. That's why I'm here. I can't live on the ground . . . like the others.' She was one of them, she was telling him, and he knew it was true. It was why he had agreed to teach her.

They spent a long time talking that day, and he hated to leave her there all alone, to walk two miles back down the country road to where she'd catch the bus to home, but he had no choice. He watched her go, with a long wave, and a moment later he took off, and did a slow roll for her, to signal his leaving. She watched him fly for a long time, still unable to believe what he had done for her. He had changed her whole life in a single afternoon, and they both knew it. It was a brave undertaking for both of them, but one which neither of them could resist, for different reasons.

The long hot walk back to the bus seemed like dancing to her; all she could think about were the feats she had done, and the feel of the plane . . . and the look in Nick's eyes afterward. He was proud of her. And she had never felt better in her life.

She boarded the bus with a huge grin for the bus driver, and almost forgot to pay her fifteen cents. And when she got home, it was too late to go to the airport. She went home to help her mother instead, and suddenly even helping her didn't seem so terrible. She had fed her soul, and whatever price she had to pay seemed worth it.

She was quiet at dinner that night, but no one seemed to notice it. Everyone had something to say; Chris was excited about his job at the newspaper, her father had landed a new mail contract with the government, and Colleen's baby had finally come the night before, and her mother wanted to tell them all about it. Only Cassie was unusually quiet and she had the biggest news of all, but couldn't share it.

Bobby came by after dinner, as usual, and they talked for a while, but Cassie didn't seem to have much to say to him. She was lost in her own thoughts, and the only thing she really said to him was that she could hardly wait till the air show. It would be just after the Fourth of July that year, and Bobby had never been, but he thought this time he might come, and Cassie could explain all the planes to him. But to her, the prospect of going with a novice and explaining it all didn't seem very exciting. She would much rather have gone with Nick, and listened to him. But it never dawned on her then that the changes had already begun. That afternoon, she had set sail on a long, long, interesting but lonely voyage.

5

The lessons continued through July, in total secrecy. But the air show, and Cassie's elation over it, was definitely not a secret. They all went to the air show together, her entire family, Nick, some of the pilots from the field, and Bobby and his younger sister. It was exciting for all of them, but nothing was as important to Cassie as her lessons with Nick, not even the Blandinsville Air Show. By the end of July she had mastered a very impressive dead stick landing. She had also learned barrel rolls, splits, and clover leafs, and some even more complicated maneuvers.

Cassie was every flying instructor's dream, a human sponge desperate to learn everything, with the hands and mind of an angel. She could fly almost anything, and in August, Nick started bringing the Bellanca instead of the Jenny, because it was harder to fly and he wanted her to have the challenge. It also had the speed he needed to show her the more complicated stunts and maneuvers. Pat still didn't suspect anything, and in spite of the long bus rides and the long walk, their flying lessons were frequent and easy.

In August, Cassie and Nick were both deeply upset when one of the pilots who flew for her father was killed when his engine failed on a flight back from Nebraska. They all went to the funeral, and Cassie was still depressed about it when she and Nick had their next lesson. Her father had lost a good friend, and one of his two D.H.4s. And everyone was subdued at O'Malley's Airport.

'Don't ever forget that those things happen, Cass,' Nick reminded her quietly as they sat under their favorite tree, having lunch after a lesson on the last day of August. It had been a wonderful summer for her, and she had never felt as close to him. He was her dearest friend, her only real friend now, and her mentor. 'It can happen to any one of us. Bad engine, bad weather, bad luck . . . it's a chance we all take. You've got to face that.'

'I have,' she said sadly, thinking of the most wonderful summer of her life, which was almost over. 'But I think I'd rather die that way than any other. Flying is all I want to do, Nick,' she said firmly, but he knew that by now. She didn't need to do anything to convince him. He was sold on her abilities, her natural skill, her extraordinary facility to learn, and her genuine passion for flying. He was sold on a lot of things about her.

'I know, Cass.' He looked at her long and hard.

She was the only person he had been truly comfortable with in years, other than Pat and the men he flew with. She was the only woman who seemed to share his views and his dreams, it was just his bad luck that she was only a baby, and his best friend's little girl. There was no hope of her ever being more than that. But he enjoyed her company, and talking to her, and it had meant a lot to him to teach her how to fly. He had long since had her solo. 'What do you want to do about lessons once you start school?' he asked as they finished lunch. She was going back the following day for her last year of high school. It seemed hard to believe that she was already a senior. She had always been such a little girl to him, except that he had come to know her better than that now. In many ways, she was more adult than most of the men he knew, and she was very much a woman. But there was a child in there too. She loved to play pranks and to tease, she had an easy laugh, and she loved playing with him. In some ways, she was no different from the way she had been when she was a baby.

'What about Saturdays?' she asked pensively, 'or Sundays?' It meant they would fly together less frequently, but at least it would be something. They had both come to rely on these long quiet hours together, her unwavering faith in him, her trust in all he told her, and his pleasure at teaching her the wonders of flying. It was a gift they shared, each one enhancing it for the other.

'I can do Saturdays,' he said matter-of-factly,

and his tone didn't tell her that nothing could have stopped him from it. She was his star pupil now, but more than that, they were best friends, and partners in a much loved conspiracy that they both held dear. Neither of them could have given it up easily, nor did they intend to. 'I don't know about you walking two miles to the bus once the weather gets bad though.' He worried about her walking two miles alone sometimes, though she would have been annoyed at his concern. She was an independent spirit and she was convinced she could handle anything. But the thought of her alone on a country road made him faintly nervous.

'Maybe Dad'll let me borrow his truck . . . or Bobby . . .' Nick nodded, but the thought of Bobby bothered him too, and he knew that it shouldn't. He had no right to object to any of her suitors, but Bobby just didn't seem right for her. He was so dull, and so damn landlocked.

'Yeah. Maybe so,' he said noncommittally, reminding himself that he was twice her age, and Bobby wasn't.

'I'll work it out.' She smiled at him without a care in the world, and it was hard not to be dazzled by her beauty.

They both wondered sometimes how they could go on like this, meeting at the deserted airstrip for lessons. It had certainly worked so far, but they both knew it would be more difficult through the winter. If nothing else, the weather would be an enormous problem.

But surprisingly, it worked remarkably well, and they met regularly every Saturday. She told her father that she had a friend from school she was meeting to do her homework with, and he let her have the truck every Saturday afternoon. No one seemed to mind, and she always came back on time, with her arms full of books and notebooks, and in high spirits.

Her flying skill had improved still further by then and Nick was justifiably proud of her. He said repeatedly that he would have given anything to put her in an air show. Chris was already preparing for the next one, and he was precise and reliable, but unexciting, and he had none of the instinctive, natural skills of his sister. They both knew that if Pat hadn't been pushing him, Chris would never fly at all. He had admitted to Nick more than once that he didn't really like it.

Cassie and Nick sat and ate their lunch in the truck once the weather got cold, and sometimes if the weather was bright, they went for walks near the airstrip.

In September, they talked about Louise Thaden being the first woman to enter the Bendix Trophy race, and in October about Jean Batten becoming the first woman to fly from England to New Zealand. They talked about a lot of things. They sat on fallen trees and talked for hours sometimes, and as the months wore on, they only got closer. They seemed to agree about everything, although she thought he was too conservative politically, and he thought she was too young to go out with boys and he said so. She made fun of him, and he cherished her irreverence, and she told him that the last girl she had seen him with was the ugliest woman she had ever seen, and he told her that Bobby Strong was clearly the dullest. If he was a little more than serious, Cassie never knew it. They just loved to fly and talk, and share their views of life. Everything seemed so much in synch, their interests, their worries, their shared passion for all things that flew, even their almost identical sense of humor. It was always bittersweet when they left each other late on Saturday afternoon, because they knew they'd have to wait a week before they could meet again like this. And sometimes, he couldn't be there at all if he had a long cargo flight and couldn't get back in time. But that was rare, he had come to organize his flying schedule around their lessons.

On Thanksgiving, he joined her family, as he always did, and Cassie teased him without mercy. They always laughed at each other a lot, but their exchanges seemed a little sharper and more intimate than they had before their lessons. Pat told them they were an uncivilized pair, but Oona wondered if she was noticing something different. It seemed hard to believe after all these years, but they seemed closer than they'd ever been, and when Oona mentioned it to Colleen, she only laughed and said Cassie was just having fun. Nick was like her big brother. But Oona wasn't wrong. The time they had spent, and the things Cassie had learned, and their endless talks under the tree at the airstrip for the past six months, had inevitably brought them closer together.

Nick was lying on the couch, claiming that he was going to die from eating so much good food, and Cassie was sitting next to him, teasing him and reminding him that gluttony was a sin and he should go to confession. She knew how he hated to go to church, and he was pretending to ignore her, but smiling appreciatively at her, when Bobby appeared in the doorway, and came in brushing the first snow from his hat and shoulders. He was a tall, handsome boy, and just watching him, Nick felt a thousand years older.

'It's bitter cold out there,' Bobby complained, and then smiled warmly at everyone, though cautiously at Nick. There was something about him that made Bobby uncomfortable, though he wasn't sure what it was. Maybe it was just that he was always so familiar with Cassie. 'Did everyone have enough to eat?' he asked the room at large, proud of the fact that he had sent them a twenty-five-pound turkey. And everyone groaned in answer. They had invited him to come to dinner too, but he had wanted to be with his parents and sister.

He invited Cassie to go out for a walk, but she declined, and stayed to listen to her mother play the piano. Glynnis sang, and Megan and her husband joined in. Megan had just told them all that she was having another baby. Cassie was happy for her, but it was the kind of news that always made her feel alien and different. She just couldn't imagine herself getting married and having babies. Not for light-years anyway. It wasn't what she wanted to do with her life for a long time, if ever. But then what would she do with her life, she wondered. She knew she'd never be Amelia Earhart either, or Bobbi Trout or Amy Mollison. They were stars, and she knew she never would be. There seemed to be no middle ground out there. You either did what her sisters did, married right out of school, had kids, and settled down in a dreary life, or you ran away and became some kind of superstar. But there was no money for her to buy planes, or enter races and set records. Even if her father had been sympathetic to her cause, his planes were old and serviceable, but certainly not what you'd use to become world-famous.

More than usual lately, she had talked to Nick about what she was going to do with her life. In six months, she would finish school. And then what? They both knew there was no job waiting for her at the airport, and there never would be. She had talked to one of her teachers too, and she was coming closer to knowing what she wanted. If she couldn't fly professionally, and for the moment, she couldn't see how that was even remotely possible, at least she could go to college. She was thinking of becoming a teacher and much to her delight, she had learned that several teachers' colleges offered both engineering and aeronautics. In particular, Bradley College in Peoria. She was hoping to apply for the fall, and if she could get a scholarship, which her teachers thought was possible, she would major in engineering, with a minor in aeronautics. It was as close to flying as she could get for the moment. If she couldn't fly an airplane for a living, like a man, she could at least teach all about them. She hadn't told her parents yet about her plan but to her it seemed like a good one. Only Nick knew, but her secrets were always safe with him. He glanced at her warmly as he stood up to leave that night, with a disparaging look at Bobby, who was talking about his mother's prizewinning pumpkin pie. Somehow, Bobby Strong never failed to annoy him.

Nick kissed Cassie on the cheek, and left, and Bobby relaxed considerably once Nick was gone. The older man always made him nervous. But Cassie seemed distracted once Nick was gone. She looked like she had a lot on her mind, and she brushed Bobby off when he started to talk about graduation. She hated talking about it now. Everyone else had concrete plans, and she didn't. All she had were hopes and dreams, and secrets.

It was late when Bobby finally went home, and Chris teased her once he was gone, and asked her when they'd all be going to her wedding. Cassie only made a face and she made a gesture as though to hit him.

'Mind your own business,' she growled, and her father laughed at them both.

'I don't think the boy's wrong, Cassie. Two years of coming by almost every night must mean something. I'm surprised he hasn't asked you yet.' But Cassie was relieved he hadn't. She didn't know what she'd say to him. She knew what she was supposed to say to him, but it didn't fit into her larger plans for herself, which now included college. Maybe after that, if he stuck around that long. But waiting four more years seemed a lot to ask of him. At least she didn't have to worry about it for the moment.

She and Nick did plenty of flying for the next three Saturday afternoons, despite some fairly dicey weather. And two days before Christmas, they went up in the Bellanca and within minutes had ice on their wings. Cassie thought her fingers would freeze in her gloves as she held the stick, and then suddenly she heard the engine start to go, and felt it stall as they went into a dive, and everything happened incredibly quickly.

Nick had the controls, but it was obvious that he was struggling with them, and she held them firm along with him. They recovered from the dive, which was no small feat, but then the propeller died and she knew instantly what that meant. They were going to have to do a forced landing. The wind was shrieking in their ears, and there was no way for him to say anything to her, but she knew instinctively what he was going to do. All she could do was back him up, but suddenly she realized they were dropping too quickly. She turned and signaled him, and for an instant he started to disagree with her, but then he nodded, deciding to trust her judgment. He pulled up as best he could, but the ground came at them too quickly. For a second, she was certain they were going to crash, but at the last minute, he brushed the top of the trees, and somehow broke their fall. They landed hard, but were unhurt, and all they damaged was one wheel. They had been extraordinarily lucky and they both knew it, as they sat shaking, realizing full well how close they had come to dying.

Cassie was still shaking when they stepped from the plane, but it was as much from the cold as from the emotions, and Nick looked down at her, and pulled her hard into his arms, with a wave of relief. For several minutes he had been certain that no matter what he tried, he was going to kill her.

'I'm so sorry, Cass. We never should have gone up in this. There's a lesson for you. Never learn to fly with an old fool who thinks he knows better than the weather. And thanks for signaling me when we were going down.' Her uncanny sense about altitude and speed had saved them. 'I won't do that to you again, I swear.' He was still shaking too as he held her. It was hard to ignore what she meant to him, as he looked down at her and felt his heart beat. All he had wanted was to save her life, not his own. He would readily have given up his life for her.

And then she looked up at him and grinned, still folded in his embrace. 'It was fun,' she giggled and he wanted to strangle her as he held her.

'You're a lunatic. Remind me never to fly with

you again!' But she was a lunatic who meant everything to him, as he slowly released her.

'Maybe I should give you a lesson or two,' she teased. But instead she helped him tie the Bellanca to a tree, and put rocks under the wheels, and she gave him a ride back to her father's airport. No one there seemed to question their arriving together, and he told her to go home and get warm. He was afraid she'd get sick from the bitter chill. He was on his way inside to have a stiff drink of Pat's stash of Irish whiskey. Knowing that he had almost killed her that afternoon had still left him shaken.

'What have you been up to this afternoon?' her father asked when she got home. He had just come home with their Christmas tree, and her nephews and nieces were going to come and help decorate it and stay for dinner.

'Not much,' she said, trying to look casual, but she had torn her gloves towing the plane, and there was oil on her hands.

'You been out to the airport?'

'Just for a few minutes.' She suddenly wondered if he was on to her, but he only nodded, and stood the Christmas tree up in the corner with her brother's help. He seemed in good spirits, and not inclined to question Cassie further.

She took a hot bath, and thought about their close call. It had been frightening, but the odd thing was that she didn't think she'd mind dying in a plane. It was where she wanted to be, and it seemed a better place to die than any other. But nonetheless, she was very glad they hadn't.

And so was Nick. He was still deeply upset over what had almost happened. And at ten o'clock that night, he was dead drunk, as he sat in his living room, wondering how Pat would have ever survived it if his oldest friend had killed his daughter. It made him suddenly think twice about flying with her again, and yet he knew he couldn't stop. He just had to do it, not only for her sake. It was almost as though he needed to be with her now, needed her wit and humor, her wisdom, her big eyes, and the incredible way she always looked the first time he saw her. He loved the way she flew, the way she knew so much instinctively, and worked so hard to learn what she didn't. The trouble was, he had realized that afternoon, he loved too much about her.

The Christmas tree at the O'Malleys' was beautiful. The children had decorated it as best they could, and their aunts and uncles and grandparents had helped. They had strung popcorn and cranberry beads, and hung all their old handmade decorations. Oona made a few new ones each year, and this year the star of the show was a big handmade silk angel she hung near the top of the Christmas tree, and Cassie was staring up at it admiringly when Bobby arrived with a load of homemade gingersnaps and cider.

Her mother made a big fuss over him, and her sisters left shortly afterward to put their children to bed. Pat and Chris went outside to get more firewood, and Cassie found herself suddenly alone with Bobby in the kitchen.

'It was nice of you to bring us the gingersnaps and the cider,' she said with a smile.

'Your mom said you were crazy about gingersnaps when you were a little girl,' he said shyly, his blond hair shining and his eyes almost like a child's. And yet, in an odd way, he was so tall and so serious that there was something manly about him. He was just eighteen, but you could begin to guess what he might look like at twenty-five or thirty. His father was still a handsome man at forty-five, and his mother was very pretty. Bobby was a fine boy, and exactly the kind of person her parents wanted her to marry. He had a solid future, a decent family, good morals, good looks, he was even Catholic.

Cassie smiled, thinking of the gingersnaps again. 'I ate so many once, I was sick for two days and couldn't go to school. I thought I was going to die . . . but I didn't.' But she almost had that afternoon . . . She had almost been killed in a plane with Nick, and now she and Bobby were standing there talking about cookies. Life was so odd sometimes, so absurd and so insignificant, and then suddenly so thrilling.

'I . . . uh . . .' He looked at her awkwardly, not sure what to say to her, and wondering if this was a good idea. He had talked it over with his dad first, and Tom Strong had thought it was. But this was a lot harder than Bobby thought, especially when he looked at Cassie. She looked so beautiful, standing there, in a pair of dark slacks, and a big pale blue sweater, her bright red hair framing her face like one of her mother's white silk angels. 'Cass . . . I'm not sure how to say this to you, but . . . I . . . uh . . .' He moved closer to her, and reached out and took her hand in his, and they could both hear her father and brother stirring in the living room, but they carefully left the two young lovers alone in the kitchen. 'I . . . uh . . . I love you, Cass,' he said, suddenly sounding stronger and older than he was. 'I love you a lot . . . and I'd like to marry you when we graduate in June.' There, he had said it. He looked remarkably proud of himself, as Cassie stared at him, her face suddenly paler than it had ever been, and her blue eyes wide in consternation. Her worst fears had come true. And now she had to face them.

'I . . . er . . . thank you,' she said awkwardly, wishing she had crashed that afternoon. It would have been simpler.

'Well?' He looked at her so hopefully, wanting her to give him the expected answer. 'What do you think?' He was so proud of himself he could have shouted. But his excitement was not contagious. All Cassie felt was dismay and terror.

'I think you're wonderful' – he looked instantly ecstatic at what she'd just said to him – 'and I think you're really nice to ask me. I . . . uh . . . I just don't know what I'm going to do in June.' June was not the issue, marriage was, and she knew that. 'I . . . Bobby, I want to go to college.' She said it as she exhaled, terrified that someone else would hear her.

'You do? Why?' He looked startled. None of her sisters had, and her mother certainly hadn't before her, or even her father. His question was reasonable, and she wasn't even sure she had an answer. 'Because I can't fly professionally' hardly seemed like a good answer. And marriage right out of school had never seemed like a particularly appealing option.

'I just think I should. I was talking to Mrs Wilcox about it a few weeks ago, and she really thinks I should. I could teach after that, if I wanted to.' And I wouldn't have to get married right away, and have babies.

'Is that what you want?' He seemed surprised; he had never counted on her wanting to go to college, and it altered his plans for her a little bit, but she could be married and go to college too. He knew people who had done that. 'You want to be a teacher?'

'I'm not sure. I just don't want to get married right out of school, have kids, and never do anything with my life. I want more than that.' She was trying to explain it to him, but it was so much easier to explain it to Nick. He was so much older and wiser than Bobby.

'You could help me with the business. There's lots you could do at the store. And my father says he wants to retire in a few years.' And then suddenly he had an idea; it struck him as brilliant. 'You could study accounting, and then you could do the books. What do you think, Cass?'

She thought he was a nice boy. But she didn't want to do his books. 'I want to do engineering,' she said, and he looked even more confused. She was certainly full of surprises, but she always had been. At least she hadn't told him she wanted to be Amelia Earhart. She hadn't said a word about flying, only about school, and now about engineering. But that was a little crazy too. He wasn't sure what to tell his father.

'What'll you do with an engineering degree, Cass?' Understandably, he sounded puzzled.

'I don't know yet.'

'Sounds like you have some thinking to do.' He sat down at the kitchen table, and pulled her into the chair next to his. He was holding her hand, and trying to excite her about their future. 'We could get married, and you could still go to school.'

'Until I get pregnant. And how long would that be?' He blushed at her openness, and he clearly didn't want to discuss it with her any further. 'I'd probably never finish the first year. And then I'd wind up like Colleen, always talking about going back to school, and too busy having babies.'

'We don't have to have as many as they do. My parents only had two.' He still sounded hopeful.

'That's two more than I want for a long time. Bobby, I just can't . . . not now . . . not yet. It wouldn't be fair to you. I'd always be thinking about what I'd missed, or what I wished I had done. I can't do that, to either of us.'

'Does flying have anything to do with any of this?' he asked suspiciously, but she shook her head. There was no way she could tell him all that she had been doing. And that was a problem too. She couldn't imagine herself married to a man she couldn't confide in. Nick and she were just friends, but there was nothing she couldn't tell him.

'I'm just not ready.' She was honest with him.

'When will you be?' he asked her sadly. It was disappointing for him, and he knew his parents would be disappointed, too. His father had already offered to help him pick out and pay for the ring. But there would be no ring now.

'I don't know. Not for a long time.'

'If you'd already been to college, do you think you'd marry me?' he asked her bluntly and she was startled by the question.

'Probably.' She wouldn't have any excuse not to. It wasn't that she needed an excuse, and she did like him. She just didn't want to marry anyone. Not yet, and not now, and probably not for a long time, but suddenly Bobby looked hopeful.

'I'll wait then.'

'But that's crazy.' She was embarrassed at having encouraged him. How could she possibly know how she'd feel when she finished college?

'Look, I'm in love with you. It's not like I'm looking for a mail order bride to pick up in June. If I have to wait, I will. But I'd rather not wait the whole four years while you go to college. Maybe we could compromise in a year or two, and you could finish school once we were married. At least think about that, it doesn't have to be so terrible. And,' he blushed furiously, 'we don't have to have a baby right away. There are things you can do about that,' he said, almost choking. She was so touched by what he'd said to her, and by the generosity of his feelings that she put her arms around him and kissed him.

'Thank you . . . for being so fair . . .'

'I love you,' he said honestly, still blushing from the things he had just said to her. It was the hardest thing he had ever done, proposing to her, and being rejected.

'I love you too,' she whispered, overwhelmed by guilt and tenderness and a maelstrom of emotions.

'That's all I need to know,' he said quietly. They sat and talked in the kitchen for a long time, about other things. And when he left, he kissed her on the porch, feeling they had come to an agreement. The decision was not now, as far as he was concerned, but definitely later. And all he had to do now was convince her that sooner was better than later. It seemed a small task to him in the heat of the moment.

6

The class of 1937 walked slowly down the aisle of the auditorium of Thomas Jefferson School, the boys and the girls hand in hand, two by two, the girls carrying bouquets of daisies. The girls looked so lovely and pure, the boys so young and hopeful. Watching them, Pat was reminded of the boys who had flown in the war for him. They had been the same age, and so many of them had died, and to him they had all looked like children.

Together, the entire class sang the school song for the last time, and the girls all cried, as did their mothers. Even their fathers had tears in their eyes as the diplomas were handed out, and then suddenly, the ceremony was over and there was pandemonium. Three hundred kids had graduated and would go on to their lives, most of them to get married, and have babies. Only forty-one of a class of three hundred and fourteen were going on to college. Of the forty-one, all but one were going to the state university at Macomb, and only three of these were women. And of course one of them was Cassie, who was the only student going as far as Peoria, to attend Bradley. It would be a long haul every day, well over an hour each way in her father's old truck, but she was convinced it was worth it, just for the chance to take the aeronautics courses they offered, and some engineering.

Cassie had had to fight tooth and nail for it. Her father thought it was a waste of time, and she'd be a lot better off married to Bobby Strong. He was furious with her for turning him down, and he only backed off because Oona had insisted to him quietly that she was sure they would get married eventually, if they didn't push her. Cassie just needed time. It was Oona who had prevailed on him, and talked Pat into letting her go on to college. It certainly couldn't do any harm, and she had agreed to compromise and major in English, not engineering. If she graduated, she'd get a teaching degree, but she had still applied for a minor in aeronautics. No woman had ever applied for the course, and she had been told that she'd have to wait to see if the professor felt she was eligible for the class. But she was going to talk to him as soon as she got to school in September.

There was a reception at the high school after graduation, and of course Cassie had already gone to her senior prom with Bobby. He had seemed to accept his fate for the past six months, but the night they graduated, he talked to her about it again, just in case she'd changed her mind, and had second thoughts about college.

'No, I haven't,' she said with a gentle smile. He was so faithful to her, and so earnest, that sometimes he made her feel very guilty. But she had made a commitment to other things, and she didn't want to lose sight of them now, no matter how sweet he was, or how kind, or how guilty he made her feel, or how much her father liked him.

He left early that night, his grandmother was in town, and he had to go home and visit with her. Pat growled at Cassie after Bobby left. She was still wearing the white dress she had worn under her black gown, and she looked very pretty.

'You'll be a damn fool, Cassie O'Malley, if you let that boy slip through your fingers.'

'He won't, Dad.' It was the only thing she could think of to say to him. It sounded conceited, but it was better than saying she didn't care, which would really have enraged him. And the truth was, she did care. There were times when she thought she really loved him, especially when he kissed her.

'Don't be so sure,' her father railed at her. 'No man can be expected to wait forever. But maybe once you have your teaching degree, you won't care. Maybe you have it in mind to become an old maid schoolteacher. Now there's something to wish for.' He was still annoyed with her about this business of going to college. Instead of being proud of her, as the other two girls' fathers were, he thought it was foolish. But Nick was pleased for her that she was going. He had realized long since how bright she was, and how capable, and it didn't seem fair, even to him, to just push her into getting married and having babies. He was relieved too that she hadn't decided to marry Bobby Strong fresh out of school. That would have changed everything, and he couldn't have borne it. He knew that eventually things would have to change, but at least for now their sacred Saturdays were safe, and they would still have their precious hours of flying.

Cassie sat by the radio that night after everyone had left. She had been dying to do that all afternoon, but she knew how much it would have annoyed her father. Amelia Earhart had taken off from Miami that afternoon, with Fred Noonan, in a twin-engine Lockheed Electra. She was flying around the world, and the expedition had been highly publicized by her husband, George Putnam. Her trip had been oddly plotted because of the threat of war, and there were areas she clearly had to avoid. They had chosen the longest route around the world at the equator, and the most dangerous, overisolated, and underdeveloped countries, which offered few airfields and fewer opportunities for fuel. She had not set an easy task for herself, and Cassie was enthralled with all of it. Like many other girls her age, and half the world, Cassie was in love with the courage and excitement of Amelia Earhart.

'What are you doing, sweetheart?' her mother asked as she wandered past her into the kitchen.

It had been an emotional day for her, and she thought Cassie looked tired too.

'Just listening to see if there's any news about Amelia Earhart.'

'Not at this hour,' her mother smiled. 'There will be plenty of it in the news tomorrow. She's a brave girl.' She was more than a girl obviously, she was a month shy of forty, which to Cassie seemed fairly ancient. But in spite of that she was still exciting.

'She's lucky,' Cassie said softly, wishing she could do something just like Earhart was doing. She would have liked nothing better than to tour the world, setting records, and flying incredible distances over strange lands and uncharted waters. It didn't frighten her at all, all it did was excite her.

And she said as much to Nick the next day, after they'd flown turns around a marker over their secret airstrip.

'You're as crazy as she is,' he said, dismissing Earhart's folly with a casual wave. 'She's not the great pilot Putnam sets her up to be. She's crashed more than half the women who fly, and I'll bet you a dollar that in that Electra of hers she overshoots every runway. It's a heavy machine, Cass, and it's got the heaviest Wasp engine Lockheed would give it. That's more than a handful for a woman of her size and build. This trip is just a stunt to make her the first woman to fly around the world. It's been done by men, and it's not going to do anything to advance aviation, only to advance Amelia

Earhart.' He seemed unimpressed, but Cassie was undaunted.

'Don't be a jerk, Nick. You're just mad because she's a woman.'

'I'm not. If you told me Jackie Cochran was doing this, I'd say great. I just don't think Earhart has the stuff to do it. And I talked to a guy in Chicago who knows her, and he says she wasn't ready, and neither was the plane. But Putnam wants to squeeze all the publicity he can out of it. I feel sorry for her actually. I think she's being used. And I think she's being pushed into some lousy decisions.'

'Sounds like sour grapes, Nick,' Cassie teased, as they shared a Coca-Cola. Their flights together had become a beloved ritual neither of them would have missed for anything in the world. They had been going on for exactly a year now. 'You'll eat your words when she breaks all records,' Cassie said confidently as he shook his head.

'Don't hold your breath.' And then he smiled at her, his eyes crinkling in the corners, as they did when he was staring into the sun when he was flying. 'I'd rather put my money on you in a few years.' He was playing with her, but he also meant it.

'Yeah, sure. And my father will be taking the bets, right?' They still hadn't figured out how to tell him about Cassie's flying, let alone that Nick thought Cassie was one of the best pilots he knew. But he had promised her that one of these days, when the time was right, they would do it.

The Peoria Air Show was in two weeks, and he was working with Chris, who was as steady as ever, and as uninterested as he had always been. He was entering the air show only to please his father. He was going to try and set an altitude record, though he didn't think he really could. Stunts were not his strong suit, and the hotshot flying still scared him. But they had strengthened the structure of Nick's Bellanca, and put a turbo supercharger on the engine to increase its power.

'I wish I could fly in it too,' Cassie said longingly, and Nick wished the same thing right along with her.

'So do I. Next year,' he promised her, and when he said it, he meant it.

'Do you really think I could?' She looked overwhelmed with excitement. Though it was a year away, it was something to look forward to, even more than college.

'I don't see any reason why not, Cass. You fly better than any of the guys there. It would make quite an impression, dazzle 'em a little bit. Believe me, they need it.'

'There are some pretty good guys at the air show,' Cassie said respectfully. She had seen some great flying over the years, but she also knew that she could fly as well as, or better than, most of those men now. Cassie had seen some terrible tragedies over the years too. It was not unusual to have fatalities at the air show. Oona had finally forced Pat to give it up, because flying stunts at the air show was just too dangerous. But he loved to see it.

'Want to take me back up and give me some cheap thrills?' Nick asked after their lunch. Sometimes they went back up for another spin, if the weather was good and they had time, as they did that afternoon. 'You could use a little work on your takeoffs and landings in crosswinds.' They had also been working on takeoffs with power cutbacks.

'The hell I do. My landings are better than yours are,' she disagreed with a grin.

'Don't be so modest.' He ruffled her hair, and let her sit behind him this time, and as usual, she didn't disappoint him. She was fabulous. It was as simple as that. And he was sorry all over again that he couldn't put her in this year's air show.

But two days before the air show, Cassie was sitting glued to her radio, unable to believe what she was hearing. Amelia Earhart had gone down, somewhere near Howland Island in the South Pacific. It seemed incredible to her, and to everyone else who heard the news. All except her father, who repeated constantly for everyone to hear that women belonged in the kitchen, and not in planes, except maybe as Skygirls, and even that didn't seem suitable to him. But Cassie was reminded of what Nick had said too, that Earhart wasn't good at handling heavy planes, and there were several people who knew her well who said she hadn't been ready. It seemed like a terrible tragedy, and the government cooperated immediately with the search for her. But on the day of the air show, two days later, they still hadn't found her.

It dampened Cassie's spirits terribly, as she watched all the trick flying and the stunts at the air show.

'Cheer up.' She heard a familiar voice behind her. 'Don't look so gloomy.' It was Nick. He had a hot dog in one hand, and a beer in the other, and he was wearing a paper Fourth of July hat. The air shows were always festive.

'I'm sorry,' she apologized with a tired smile. She had been up for two days, listening for reports of Amelia Earhart. But there were none. Nothing at all had been found. She had totally vanished. 'I was just thinking about . . .'

'I know what you were thinking about. The same thing you've been thinking about since she took off. But it's not going to do you any good, getting sick over her. Remember, I told you a long time ago. There are chances we all take. We all know it. We accept them. So did she. She was doing what she wanted.' He offered her a bite of his hot dog, and she took it, looking pensive. Maybe he was right. Maybe she had a right to die that way. Maybe if she'd been given a choice of a ripe old age in a rocking chair, and a quick exit in a Lockheed, she would have preferred this. But Cassie still hated to think of her going down. It was the death of a legend.

'Maybe you're right,' Cassie said quietly. 'It just seems so sad.'

'It is sad,' he agreed. 'No one ever said it wasn't. It's sad when anyone goes down. But it's a risk we all take, and some of us love. You too.' He put a hand under her chin and reminded her silently of how much she loved to fly and how willing she was to take chances. 'You would do the same thing, given half a chance, you little fool. You ever try to go on one of those damn world tours, and I'll set fire to your plane. Count on it.'

'Thanks.' She grinned up at him, and then he tugged at her arm in excitement.

'Hey . . . take a look at this . . . there goes Chris . . . come on . . . come on . . . head up there . . .' He was heading for an altitude trophy in Nick's plane, and he almost disappeared as they watched him. He had good steady hands, and a seriousness that made him perfect for this kind of competition. He had none of Cassie's excitement or sheer grit; all he really had was endurance. And when he landed, Nick was amazed by how far he'd gone. They hurried over to where Pat and Oona and some of Cassie's sisters were standing with their children. Glynnis and Megan were both hugely pregnant again, and Colleen had been looking a little green around the gills of late, which had made Oona suspect she was pregnant again too, but hadn't yet said it. They were a prolific group. This would be the fourth for Megan and Colleen, the fifth for Glynnis.

'Good thing too,' Cassie whispered under her breath as she chatted with Nick, 'if I'm never going to have any. They can have all the kids they want, as far as I'm concerned.' Lately she had begun to think she never wanted a husband or children.

'You'll have kids too, don't kid yourself. Why shouldn't you?' Nick never believed her when she said she'd never marry or have children. She didn't really believe it herself. But she knew she didn't want any of that for a long, long time, if ever. All she wanted was airplanes.

'What makes you so sure I'll have kids, Nick?' she challenged him.

'Because you come from a family that multiply like rabbits.'

'Oh, thanks a lot.' She was still laughing when Bobby Strong found her, and glanced at Nick awkwardly. He always had the feeling that Nick didn't like him. Moments later, having said very little to either of them, Nick went off to hang out with the other pilots.

Half an hour later, they announced that Chris had won a prize for setting the altitude record. And her father was beside himself with excitement. He went off to find Chris, and Oona went to find drinks with the girls, and the younger children. Bobby stood watching the show with her, as tiny red and blue and silver planes did stunts and rolls, and lazy spins in the air, crazy eights, and double eights, and a few tricks Cassie had never heard of. Just watching them took your breath away, and more than once the crowd gasped as disaster seemed imminent, and then cheered when there was a last minute save. She was used to it, but it was always exciting.

'What were you thinking just then?' Bobby had begun watching her face. It had been filled with light and an expression of total rapture as she watched a plane do an outside loop; it was a stunt Jimmy Doolittle had invented ten years before, and it really impressed her. The pilot then finished with a flourish by doing a low-level inverted pass, away from the crowd, so no one was endangered. Bobby watched the look on her face with fascination. And then she turned and smiled at him, almost sadly.

'I was thinking that I wish I were up there doing that,' she said honestly. 'It looks like so much fun.' All she wanted was to be one of them.

'I think I'd get sick,' he said with equal honesty, and she grinned at him, as a vendor wandered by with cotton candy.

'You probably would. I almost have a couple of times.' She had almost spilled the beans then, and had to remind herself to be careful. 'Negative G's will do it to you. You get those in a stall, just before you recover. It feels like your stomach is going to fly right out of your mouth . . . but it doesn't.' She grinned.

'I don't know how you can like all this, Cass. It scares me to death.' He looked handsome and blond and very young as he stood admiring her, and she was growing, day by day, to be more of a woman.

'It's in my bones, I guess.'

He nodded, worried that that was true. 'That's too bad about Amelia Earhart.'

She nodded too. 'Yes, it is. Nick says that all pilots accept those possibilities. It can happen to anyone.' She looked up at the sky. 'Anyone here too. I guess they figure it's worth it.'

'Nothing's worth risking your life,' Bobby disagreed with her, 'unless you have to, like in a war, or to save someone you love.'

'That's the trouble' – Cassie looked at him with a sad smile – 'most pilots would risk anything to fly. But other people don't understand that.'

'Maybe that's why women shouldn't, Cass,' he said quietly and she sighed.

'You sound like my father.'

'Maybe you should listen to him.'

She wanted to say 'I can't,' but she knew she couldn't say that to him. She could only say that to Nick. He was the only human being who knew the whole truth about her, and accepted it. No one else really knew her. Especially not Bobby.

She saw Chris walking toward them then, and she ran to him. He was carrying his medal, his face was glowing with pride, and Pat was walking on air right behind him.

'First medal at seventeen!' he was telling anyone who would listen. 'That's my man!' He was handing out beers, and slapping everyone on the back, including Chris and Bobby. Chris was basking in his father's love and approval. Cassie was watching them, fascinated by how desperate her father was for Chris's success in the air, yet at the same time how adamant he was that she never get there. She was ten times the flier Chris was, or better still, but her father would never acknowledge it, or even know it.

Nick came over to shake hands with Chris, and the boy was elated by his victory, and then he went off with Nick to meet some of the other pilots. It was an exciting day for him, and a day Pat O'Malley had waited fifty-one years for. And as far as he was concerned, this was only the beginning. Instead of seeing that this was the top of Chris's skill, he wanted more. He was already talking about next year, and Cassie felt sorry for Chris then. She knew how much their father meant to him, and that no matter what it cost him, he would do anything to please him.

The O'Malley clan were in high spirits. They were almost the last ones to leave, and Bobby went home with them for dinner. Nick went out to celebrate with his flying friends, and he looked pretty well oiled by the time he left the field. But he knew Chris was flying the Bellanca back to O'Malley Airport, and he could hop a ride in Pat's truck, so he didn't have to worry about flying or driving.

Oona had cooked platters of fried chicken for them in the morning before they left, and there was corn on the cob, and salad and baked potatoes. There was a ham too, and she had baked blueberry pie and made ice cream once back at the house. It was a real feast, and Pat poured Chris a full glass of Irish whiskey.

'Drink up, lad, you're the next ace in this family!' Chris struggled with the drink, and Cassie watched them, feeling sad. She felt left out somehow. She should have been flying with them, and basking in her father's praise, and she knew she couldn't. She wondered if she ever would. But the only fate that seemed open to her was that of her sisters, having another baby every year, and condemned to their kitchens. It seemed a terrible life to her, although she loved them all, and her mother, but she would have rather died than spend her life the way they had.

Cassie noticed too that Bobby was very sweet to all of them. He was kind to her sisters, and adorable to all their children. He was a gentle man, and he would make a wonderful husband. Her mother pointed it out to her again when she was helping clean up in the kitchen. And afterward, she and Bobby went for a long walk, and he surprised her when he talked to her about flying.

'I was watching you a lot today, Cass, and I know what all that means to you. And you may think I'm crazy, but I want you to promise me you'll never do any of that crazy stuff. I really don't want you to fly. It's not that I don't want you to have fun. But I don't want you to get hurt. You know . . . like Amelia Earhart.' It seemed reasonable to him, and she was touched, but Cassie laughed nervously. The idea of promising anyone that she wouldn't fly made her shudder.

'I'm not going to fly around the world, if that's what you're worried about,' she said with an anxious smile. But he shook his head; he meant a lot more than that, and she knew it.

'That's not what I mean. I mean I don't want you flying at all.' He had only seen a glimmer of how dangerous it was, but watching the stunts at the air show had convinced him. There was no question that there were terrible risks in flying, and two years before there had been a terrible tragedy at the same air show. Bobby was no fool, and he knew the magic it held for her. Simply put, he didn't want to lose her. 'I don't want you learning to fly, Cass. I know you want to. But it's just too dangerous. Your father is right. And it's much too dangerous for a woman.'

'I don't think that's a reasonable thing to ask,' she said quietly. She didn't want to lie to him, but she also didn't want to tell him that she'd been flying regularly with Nick for over a year now. 'I think you have to trust my judgment on that.'

'I want you to promise me you won't fly,' he said, showing a strength and stubbornness she had never seen before. She was impressed, but she wasn't going to promise.

'That's unreasonable. You know how much I love to fly.'

'That's why I'm asking you to promise, Cass. I think you would be just the one to take chances.'

'Believe me, I wouldn't. I'm careful . . . and I'm good . . . that is, I would be. Look, Bobby, please . . . don't do this . . .'

'Then I want you to think about it. This is very important to me.' So is flying to me, she wanted to scream. It was the only thing she cared about, and now he wanted to take it from her. What was wrong with all of them? Bobby, her father, even Chris. Why did they want to take something away from her that she loved so much? Only Nick understood. He was the only one who knew, and cared how she felt about it.

Though at that exact moment, Nick Galvin was passed out cold in the arms of a girl he had met at the air show. She had bright red hair, and brightly painted lips, and as he nestled close to her, he smiled and whispered, 'Cassie.'

7

Cassie's schedule at Bradley was more demanding than it had been as a senior in high school, but she managed to juggle it anyway, and now she and Nick met twice a week, always on Saturdays, and sometimes on a weekday morning. Her father wasn't aware of her schedule, and it was easy for both of them. And she had started working as a waitress in order to repay Nick for the fuel, even if she couldn't afford to pay him for the lessons. But he had never expected any payment from her. He did it for sheer love and pleasure.

She was getting better each time they flew, refining some fine points, and flying every plane she could so as to learn their differences and their quirks. She flew the Jenny, the old Gypsy Moth, Nick's Bellanca, the de Havilland 4, and even the lumbering old Handley. Nick wanted her to fly everything she could, and he had her perfecting all her techniques and honing her skills with great precision. He had even taught her some rescue techniques, and told her all the details of some of his more illustrious forced landings and near misses while fighting the Germans. There was very little she didn't know about flying the Jenny or the Bellanca or even the Handley, which Nick had brought with him because it was so much heavier and harder to fly, and had two engines.

She spent less time at her father's airport now, since she had farther to go to school, but she still hung around whenever she could, and she and Nick would exchange a conspiratorial smile, whenever their paths crossed.

She was working on an engine one day, in a back hangar, when she was surprised to see her father walk in with Nick. They were talking about buying a new plane, and her father thought it might be too expensive. It was a used Lockheed Vega.

'It's worth it, Pat. It's a heavy plane, but it's a beautiful machine. I checked one out the last time I was in Chicago.'

'And who do you think is going to fly it? You, and me. And the others are just going to bring it down in the trees. It's a damn fine machine, Nick, and there aren't five men here I'd trust to fly it. Maybe not even two.'

But as her father said the words, Cassie saw Nick looking at her strangely, and then she felt terror run up her spine. She knew instinctively what he was going to do. She wanted to tell him to stop, but another part of her wanted him to do it. She couldn't hide forever. Sooner or later her father would have to know. And Nick kept talking to her about flying in the next air show.

'There may not be five men around here who can fly it, Pat. But I can tell you one woman who can, with her eyes closed.'

'What's that supposed to mean?' Her father growled at him, already annoyed at the mention of a woman who could fly anything, let alone a plane he wouldn't trust his own men with.

Nick said it very quietly, and calmly, as Cass watched them, terrified, praying that her father would listen. 'Your daughter is the best pilot I've ever seen, Pat. She's been flying with me for more than a year, a year and a half to be exact. She's the best damn pilot you and I have seen since 'seventeen. I mean that.'

'You *what*?' Pat looked at his old friend and associate in total outrage. 'You've been flying with her? Knowing how I'd feel about it? How dare you!'

'If I didn't dare, she would. She would have killed herself a year ago, terrorizing her brother into taking her up and letting her fly anything she could lay her hands on. I'm telling you, she's the best damn natural pilot you've ever seen, and you're a fool if you don't let her show you what she's got, Pat. Give the kid a chance. If she were a boy, you would, and you know it.'

'I don't know what I know!' he raged at both of them, 'except that you're both two damn lying fools, and I'm telling you right now I forbid you to fly, Cassandra Maureen.' He looked straight at her as he said it, and then at Nick. 'And I'm not going to put up with any nonsense from you, you damn fool, Nick Galvin, do you hear me?'

'You're dead wrong!' Nick was insistent, but Pat was too livid to listen.

'I don't give a damn what you think. You're a bigger idiot than she is. She's not flying my planes at my airport. And if you're fool enough to fly her in your own, somewhere else, then I lay the responsibility on your head if you kill her, and it's your own damn fault, if she kills you, which she will undoubtedly. There isn't a woman alive who can fly worth a damn, and you know it.' He had just knocked out, with a single blow, an entire generation of extraordinary women, and among them his own daughter. But he didn't care. That was what he believed, and no one was going to tell him any different.

'Let me take her up and show you, Pat. She can fly anything we've got. She's got a sense of speed and height that relies on her gut and her eyes, more than on anything she sees on the controls. Pat, she's terrific.'

'You're not going to show me anything, and I don't want to see it. Couple of damn fools . . . I suppose she's bamboozled you into all this.' He looked at his daughter with total fury. As far as he was concerned, it was all her fault. She was a stubborn little monster, determined to kill herself with her father's planes and right at his own airport.

'She didn't bamboozle me into anything. I saw her scud running a year ago, in that storm she got herself into with Chris, and I knew damn well he wasn't flying the plane. I figured if I didn't step in, she'd kill both of them, so I started teaching her then.'

'That was Chris flying in that storm last year,' her father argued defiantly.

'It was *not*!' Nick shouted back at him, furious now himself at how unreasonable Pat was prepared to be, and all to support an outdated position. 'How blind can you be? The boy's got no guts, no hands. All he can do is run straight up and down, like an elevator, just like he did for you at the air show. What on God's earth makes you think he could have gotten them out of that storm? That was Cassie.' He looked at her possessively, and he was surprised to see that she was crying in the face of her father's fury.

'It was, Dad,' she said quietly. 'It was me. Nick knew. He confronted me when we came down, and—'

'I won't listen to this. You're a liar on top of everything else, Cassandra Maureen, trying to take the glory from your own brother.' The force of his accusations took her breath away, and told her again how hopeless it was to try to convince him.

Maybe one day, but not now. And never seemed more likely.

'Give her a chance, Pat.' Nick was trying to calm him down again, but it was useless. 'Please. Just let her show you her stuff. She deserves that. And next year, I'd like to put her in the air show.'

'You're both daft, is what you are. Two brazen fools. What makes you think she wouldn't kill herself, and me, and you, and a dozen other people at the air show?'

'Because she flies better than anyone you've ever seen there.' Nick tried to stay calm, but he was losing control slowly. Pat was not an easy man, and this was a very volatile subject. 'She flies better than Rickenbacker, for chrissake. Just let her show you.' But he had uttered the ultimate sacrilege this time, in invoking the name of the commander of the 94th Aero Squadron. Nick knew he'd pushed too far, and Pat stalked off and left them, and went back to his office. He never looked back at them, and he never said another word to his daughter.

She was crying openly by then, and Nick came to put an arm around her.

'Christ, your father is a stubborn man. I'd forgotten how impossible he can be when he gets something in his teeth. But I'll get him yet on this one. I promise.' He gave her a squeeze and she smiled through her tears. If she had been Chris, her father would have let her show him anything at all. But not now, not ever, not her, because she was a girl. It was so unfair, but she knew that nothing would change him.

'He'll never give in, Nick.'

'He doesn't have to. You're eighteen. You can do what you want, you know. You're not doing anything wrong. You're taking flying lessons. So what? Okay? Relax.' And very shortly she'd have her own license. She was more than qualified for it. When Pat had started flying in 1914, he hadn't even needed a license to fly then.

'What if he throws me out of the house?' She looked terrified and Nick laughed. He knew Pat better than that, and so did she. He made a lot of noise, and he was limited in his ideas and beliefs, but he loved his children.

'He's not going to do that, Cass. He may make you miserable for a while. But he's not going to throw you out. He loves you.'

'He loves Chris,' she said glumly.

'He loves you too. He's just a little behind the times, and stubborn as hell. Christ, sometimes he drives me crazy.'

'Me too.' She smiled and blew her nose, and then she looked up at Nick with worried eyes. 'Will you still teach me?'

'Of course,' he grinned, looking boyish and full of mischief, and then he pretended to look at her sternly. 'And don't let everything I said go to your head. You don't fly like the leader of the great 94th,' he scowled at her, and then grinned. 'But you could be better than he was one day, if you'd

133

clean up some of those turns and listen to your instructor.'

'Yes, sir.'

'Go wash your face, you look terrible . . . I'll see you at the airstrip tomorrow, Cass.' He smiled at her. 'Don't forget, we have an air show to prepare for.' She looked gratefully at him, as he strode away, wondering what it would take to bring Pat O'Malley to his senses.

He had certainly not come to them that night when he refused to say a word to her at their dinner table. He had told Oona what she'd done, and her mother cried when she heard it. Pat had convinced her long since that women were not constitutionally or mentally cut out to fly airplanes.

'It's just too dangerous,' she tried to explain to Cassie later that night in her room. With her sisters married and gone, Cassie had long since had her own bedroom.

'It's no more dangerous for me than it is for Chris,' Cassie said through tears again. She was exhausted from fighting with them, and she knew she'd never win. Even Chris had said nothing in her defense. He hated getting into arguments with their parents.

'That's not true,' her mother countered what she'd said. 'Chris is a man. It's less dangerous for a man to fly,' her mother said as though it were gospel truth, because she'd heard it from her husband.

'How can you say that? That's nonsense.'

'It's not. Your father says that women don't have the concentration.'

'Mom, that's a lie. I swear. Look at all the women who fly. Great ones.'

'Look at Amelia Earhart, dear. She's a perfect example of what your father says. She obviously lost her direction, or her wits, somewhere out there, and she took that poor man with her.'

'How do you know their disappearance wasn't his fault?' Cassie said persistently. 'He was the navigator, not Earhart. And maybe they were shot down,' Cass said sadly. She knew she wasn't getting anywhere. Her mother was completely convinced of everything her husband had always told her.

'You have to stop behaving this way, Cassie. I should never have let you loll around at the airport all these years. But you loved it so, and I thought it would be nice for your father. But you have to give up these foolish dreams, Cassie. You're a college girl now. One day you'll be a teacher. You can't go flying around like some silly gypsy.'

'Oh yes, I can . . . dammit, yes I can!' Cassie raised her voice to her, and a moment later her father was in her room, berating her again, and telling her that she had to apologize to her mother. Both women were crying by then, and Pat was at his wit's end, and clearly livid.

'I'm sorry, Mom,' she said mournfully.

'And well you should be,' her father said before he slammed the door again. A moment later her mother left, and Cassie lay on the bed and sobbed, from the sheer frustration of dealing with her parents.

When Bobby Strong came by later that night, Cassie had Chris tell him that she had a terrible headache. He drove away looking concerned, after leaving her a note, telling her that he hoped she felt better soon, and he'd be back tomorrow.

'Maybe tomorrow I'll be dead,' she said glumly as she read the note her brother handed her. 'Maybe that would be an improvement.'

'Relax, Sis. They'll get over it,' Chris said calmly.

'No, they won't. Dad never will. He refuses to believe women can fly, or do anything except knit and have babies.'

'Sounds great. So how's your knitting?' he teased, and she threw a shoe at him, as he closed the door to escape her.

But by the next day she felt better again. She felt like herself, once she and Nick took off in the Bellanca. He didn't feel he should let her fly any of her father's planes now. She handled it skillfully as usual, and just being in the air with Nick lifted her spirits. Afterward, they sat in the old truck for a while, talking, and Cassie seemed subdued. She was still obviously upset about her father's reaction to her flying.

'As good as Rickenbacker, huh?' she teased Nick after their flying.

'I told you not to let it go to your head. I was just lying to impress him.'

'He sure looked impressed, don't you think?' Cassie grinned ruefully, and Nick laughed. She was a good sport, and sooner or later they'd wear Pat down. He couldn't keep his head in the sand forever, or could he?

Their flying schedule scarcely changed. The only time it did was when Nick had long cargo runs, or she had too much homework. But neither of them was anxious to miss their lessons, so they always worked their other obligations around them. And interestingly her father never asked either of them if they were continuing their lessons.

Nick joined them at Thanksgiving as usual; Pat was cooler than he normally was, to both of them. He hadn't forgiven either of them yet for what he considered their betrayal. At the airport, Nick was walking on eggs, and at home, Pat had scarcely said two words to Cassie since October. It was getting more and more difficult, but by Christmas he seemed to have relaxed again. And then finally, he relented totally when Bobby Strong handed Cassie a tiny diamond engagement ring on Christmas Eve.

Bobby said he knew it would be a long wait for her, but he'd feel better if they were engaged. He had been courting her for three years, and he didn't think it was too soon. He looked so earnest and so in love with her that Cassie just didn't have the heart to turn him down. She wasn't sure what she felt, other than confused, as she let him slip the ring slowly onto her finger. She had felt so guilty and so unhappy about everything, since her parents had made such a huge fuss about her flying. But the engagement seemed to mollify them, and restore her to their good graces.

They were very pleased. They announced her engagement to the rest of the family the next day at Christmas dinner. Nick was there too, and he looked surprised at the news, but he didn't say anything. He only looked at Cassie, wondering if this would change everything between them. But oddly, she didn't behave differently. She seemed no closer or more comfortable with Bobby now. And she was as easy with Nick as she ever had been. In fact, very little changed, Bobby only lingered a little longer on the porch before he left, but it wasn't what Cassie herself would have expected of an engagement. But Nick was still wondering about it the next time he saw her at their deserted airfield.

'What does that mean?' He pointed to the ring, and she hesitated for a moment and shrugged her shoulders. She didn't want to be mean, but she never seemed to react to anything the way people expected.

'I'm not sure,' she said honestly. She didn't feel any differently about him from the way she had before he put the ring on her finger. She liked him, she cared about him, but she couldn't imagine being more to him than she was now. She had gotten engaged mostly because it seemed to matter so much to Bobby and her parents. Most of all, it seemed to make a difference to him, and she understood that. 'I didn't have the heart to give it back to him.' She looked sheepishly at Nick as she kept an eye on the Bellanca. They had had a good flight that day, and she had learned some fine points about landing in crosswinds. 'He knows I want to finish college,' she said helplessly. But college wasn't really the problem.

'Poor guy. This is going to be the longest engagement in history. What is that? Another three and a half years?'

'Yes.' She grinned mischievously at him, and he couldn't help but laugh as he resisted an urge to kiss her. He was so relieved by what she'd said. He had felt sick when he first saw the engagement ring. He hated the idea of her being married to anyone, or even engaged, but Bobby wasn't much of a threat actually. Sooner or later Cassie would have to figure that out for herself, but then someone else would be. And he knew how much it would bother him when that happened.

'Okay . . . get your ass in gear, O'Malley . . . let's see another dead stick landing.' He was going to take her up again.

'You must think I'm going to spend half my life on the ground instead of in the air. Can't you teach anything else, *Stick*?' She emphasized the word. 'Or is that the only trick in your repertoire?' She loved teasing him, loved being with him, loved being with the only person in the world who really understood her. And better yet, if they could be flying.

This time he sent her up alone, and watched her land perfectly, dead stick, then again without a hitch, and finally, without flicking an eye or a wing in the crosswinds.

It really was a shame, he found himself thinking again, that her father refused to watch her fly. It would have given him so much pleasure.

'Ready to call it a day?' he asked, as they walked back to her truck, so she could drive home to Good Hope.

'Yeah, I guess so,' she said sadly. 'I always hate to come down. I wish I could go on forever.'

'Maybe you should be a Skygirl when you grow up,' he teased her again, and she swatted him with her gloves, but she looked sad. She really had no options. And if it weren't for Nick, she couldn't fly at all.

'Take it easy, kid,' he said gently. 'He'll come around.'

'No, he won't,' she said, knowing her father.

Nick touched her hand, and her eyes met his. She was grateful for all that he had given her, and his kindness. They had the kind of friendship that neither of them had ever found with anyone else. She was a great girl, and a good friend, and they had fun on their stolen afternoons at their airstrip. Nick only wished it could go on forever. He couldn't imagine not meeting her like this anymore, or not having her to fly with, and share his thoughts with. In all the important ways, she was the only person he really talked to. And he was her only friend too. The only tragedy, for both of them, was that there was nothing more ahead for them in the future.

She drove home alone late that afternoon, thinking of him, and it started to snow just after she got back. She went into the house and helped her mother cook dinner for the four of them, but her father was late. And an hour later, he still hadn't come home. Oona finally sent Chris out with the truck to find Pat at the airport.

Chris came back twenty minutes later to grab something to eat for him and Pat. There was a train wreck two hundred miles southwest of them, with hundreds of injuries, and they were asking for rescue teams from everywhere. Pat was organizing rescue teams at the airport, and he wanted Chris to help him. Nick was there too, and they were calling all their pilots in to fly. But three were home sick, and too ill to come in, and they hadn't been able to reach some of the others. They were still waiting for a few more to come in. Pat had told Chris to tell his mother they wouldn't be back all night. Oona nodded, used to this, and packed some food for them to eat at the airport.

'Wait!' Cassie said, as Chris started to go back to him. 'I'll come with you.'

'You shouldn't . . .' Oona started to object, but at the look on her daughter's face, she shrugged. There was no harm in it. All she could do was sit at the airport. 'All right. I'll pack something for you to eat too.'

She gave them a basket filled with food, and Cassie and Chris drove off, skidding on and off the old road on the property to the airport. It was an icy night, and the snow had been falling for two hours. She wondered if they'd even be able to take off. Conditions did not look good, and her father looked worried when she and Chris walked into his office at the airport.

'Hi, kids.' He pushed aside the food. He and Nick were talking anxiously about the planes they could use, and the men they needed. They were trying to send four planes with supplies and rescue teams. Everything and everyone were assembled, except for the pilots. And so far, they were still two men short, and they were trying to reach them. Pat was going to fly the new Vega himself with Chris. Although, if he'd had to, Pat could have flown solo. Another of their best men had come in, with his co-pilot, and they had each been assigned planes. But they needed two more men to fly the old Handley. It was tricky to fly and because of its age and size, it was wiser to have two men flying it in this kind of weather. Nick could have flown it alone but it wouldn't have been a wise decision. And he wanted someone good to fly it with him. Silently, he looked over at Cassie, but he said nothing.

They heard from two more men shortly after that. One was bone-tired after a sixteen-hour flight around the country, delivering mail in terrible weather, and the other was quick to admit that he'd been drinking.

'That leaves one,' Nick said unhappily. One man left they needed to hear from. He called in finally around ten, with a ferocious earache. 'End of the line, O'Malley,' Nick said pointedly. They were one man short for their mission. Pat read his mind easily, and began shaking his head, but this time Nick wouldn't listen.

'I'm taking Cassie with me,' he said quietly, as Pat started to sputter. 'Don't waste your time, Ace. There are hundreds of injured people waiting for help and supplies, and I'm not going to argue with you. I know what I'm doing, and she's coming with me.' The only other choice would have been to let her co-pilot the Vega with her father, and Nick knew he wouldn't let her do it. Nick grabbed his jacket and started moving toward the door, and he held his breath as Pat stared at him angrily, but made no objection.

'You're a damn fool, Nick,' Pat growled at him, but he said nothing more as they gathered their things, and he called Oona and asked her to wait for them at the airport.

Cassie followed Nick quietly out to the familiar plane, feeling something deep inside her tremble, and for just an instant she saw her father look hard at her with eyes full of anger and betrayal. She wanted to say something to him then, but she didn't know what to say, and a moment later, he was gone, with Chris, in the Vega.

'He'll be all right,' Nick said as he helped her to her seat, but she only nodded. Nick had stuck up for her, as usual; he believed in her, and he hadn't been afraid to say so. He was an amazing man, and she just hoped she wouldn't let him down as they flew the old plane in bad weather all the way to Missouri.

They did the usual check on the ground, and then checked inside carefully. She knew the plane well, thanks to Nick, and as she strapped herself in, she was suddenly excited at what they were doing and she forgot all about her father. They were carrying emergency supplies that had been brought to them at the airport. The other planes were also carrying supplies, and two doctors and three nurses. Help was coming from four states. There were nearly a thousand people injured.

Nick took off cautiously but smoothly. There had been no ice on the wings, and the snow had thinned. It had almost stopped as they reached their final altitude of eight thousand feet and flew southwest toward Kansas City. It was a two-and-a-half-hour flight for them, although her father and Chris would make it in a little over an hour in the Vega. It was turbulent most of the time, but it didn't bother Cassie or Nick. Cassie was stunned by the beauty of the night, and how peaceful it was to be at the controls in a night sky full of stars now. It was like being on the edge of the world, in an endless universe. She had never felt so small or so free or so alive as at that moment.

Nick let her fly the plane much of the time, and when they reached a good-sized field near the train wreck, he brought it in for a landing.

There were wounded everywhere when they got to the train, supplies being brought in, medical personnel trying to help people lying on the ground, children crying. Nick and Cassie and the others stayed to help until dawn, and by then the state police seemed to have everything under control. Ambulances and medical personnel had come from all over the state. People had driven, flown, they had come as soon as they could. And in the morning, Nick and Cass flew home with the others. She had scarcely seen her father all night, as they did everything they could to help the rescue workers.

The sun came up just as they took off, and on the way back Nick let her fly it herself, and she brought it in for a textbook landing in spite of heavy winds and slippery conditions on the runway. Nick shook hands with her as she turned the engines off, and congratulated her for a job well done. She was grinning broadly as she stepped off the plane, and she was surprised to almost collide with her father. He was standing right next to the plane, and he looked at Nick with tired eyes, as he barked a question.

'Who landed this plane?' It was his plane, and Cassie instantly sensed trouble.

'I did,' Cassie said quietly, ready to take the blame for any mistake she'd made. She took her flying seriously and calmly.

'You did a damn fine job,' he said awkwardly, and then turned and walked away. She had proven everything Nick had said, and they both wondered what Pat would do about her now. It was hard to say. There was no predicting Pat O'Malley. But as she watched him walk away, there were tears in her eyes. It was the only praise he had ever given her that had meant anything. And she wanted to shout she was so excited. Instead, she just grinned at Nick, and saw that he was smiling broadly. And they walked arm in arm back to the office.

Her mother had brought in coffee and rolls for all the men, and Cassie sat quietly drinking her coffee and talking to Nick about what they'd seen at the train wreck. It had been a long, rough night, but at least they'd been useful.

'So, you think you're a hotshot.' She heard her father's words as he stood next to her, and she looked up at him, but he didn't look angry anymore when their eyes met.

'No, Dad, I don't. I just want to fly,' she said softly.

'It's unnatural is what it is. Look at what happened to that poor fool Earhart.' Cassie had heard it all before and she was prepared for it, but she was in no way prepared for what he said next, and her jaw dropped as she glanced at Nick to make sure she'd heard him correctly. 'I'll give you some work out here, after school. Nothing big. Just the little jobs. I can't have Nick flying around all the time, wasting fuel and time, giving you lessons.' She grinned as she looked at him, and Nick let out a whoop as the other men glanced over at them in confusion.

She threw her arms around her father's neck, and Nick pumped his hand, as Chris walked over to his sister and hugged her. She had never been happier in her life. He was going to let her fly . . . her father was going to let her fly, and give her flying jobs to do at the airport . . .

'Just wait till the air show in July!' she whispered to Nick as she hugged him tight, and he laughed. Her father was in for a big surprise. But this was certainly a good beginning.

8

For the next six months, Cassie's days seemed to fly by. She drove to Bradley every day, worked at the restaurant three afternoons a week to pay for fuel when she flew with Nick. And she tried to get to the airport as soon as she could before nightfall. She did whatever she could to help there, but most of her work for her father, and flying, was done on weekends. And those were her happiest days. Nick even took her on some cargo runs to Chicago, Detroit, and Cleveland.

Her life had never before seemed as perfect. She missed her secret flying lessons with Nick sometimes, and the time they'd shared alone. But he taught her openly now, when they both had time, taking off from her father's airport. And although Pat never said anything to her, it was obvious that he approved of her style, and secretly he admitted to Nick once that she was a damn fine little flier. All of his obvious praise went to Chris, who tried hard, but really didn't deserve it. But it didn't bother Cassie anymore. She had everything she wanted.

The only problem she had was with her fiancé, who was aghast that her father had relented. But since he had, there was little Bobby could say, except to remind her constantly of his disapproval. Her own mother thought it was only a passing phase, something she would lose interest in once she and Bobby were married and had children.

The biggest news that spring was when Hitler took over Austria in March. For the first time, there was serious concern about war, although most people still believed Roosevelt. He said there would be no war, and America would never step in again if there was. Once had been enough. America had learned her lesson.

But Nick didn't think it was quite that simple. He had read about Hitler and didn't trust him. He also had friends who had volunteered to fly in the Spanish Civil War two years before, and he believed that soon all of Europe would once again be in terrible trouble. Nick could easily envision America getting involved again despite Roosevelt's promises and protests.

'I can't believe we'd get into it again. Can you, Nick?' Cassie asked seriously after they'd practiced for the air show.

'I can,' he answered honestly. 'I think we will too, eventually. I think Hitler is going to go too far, and we'll have to step in to support our allies.'

'That's hard to believe,' Cassie said. It was harder

still to believe that her father was actually going to let her fly in the air show. Nick had talked him into it, and more than anything, Pat was afraid of being embarrassed. He had already seen that she was safe, had good hands, and had been well taught, but what if she did very badly? What if she did so badly he couldn't hold his head up?

'Chris won't let you down,' Nick had encouraged him, and Pat had naively bought it. Nick was a lot surer of Cass, but he wouldn't have dared to say so to her father. Pat still wanted to believe that Chris had a great future in the air, and he refused to see how little Chris cared about flying. In all fairness, Chris didn't let him see his true feelings. He was afraid to.

And when at last the big day came, all of Nick's beliefs and predictions proved to be prophetic. Chris won the prize for altitude again, but Cassie took second for speed, on a straightaway, and first for a race on a closed-circuit course. As they announced the winners in the afternoon, Pat couldn't believe his ears, and neither could Cassie. She and Nick were dancing around like two children, hugging and kissing, and letting out whoops and screams. The local paper took a picture of her, first alone, and then standing next to her father. And Chris didn't begrudge her any of it. He knew how much it meant to her. It was her whole life. Pat couldn't believe what she'd done. But Nick could. He had always known it. And he wasn't surprised either when one of the turn judges said he'd never seen a pilot as good at high-speed pylon turns as Cassie.

'Well, you did it, kid.' Nick smiled at her, as he drove her home at the end of the day, after they had flown all her father's planes back to the airport.

'I still can't believe it,' she said, staring at him, and then looking into the distance out the window.

'Neither can your dad.' He smiled.

'I owe it all to you,' she said seriously, but he only shook his head. He knew better.

'You owe it to yourself. That's the one you owe it to. I didn't give you the gift, Cass. God did that. I only helped you.'

'You did everything.' She turned to look at him, feeling suddenly sad. What if he stopped teaching her now? What if they no longer spent time together? 'Will you still take me up sometimes?'

'Sure. If you promise not to scare me.' He told her what the turn judge had said then, with real pride in her.

She guffawed, and then she almost groaned when she saw Bobby Strong waiting on their front porch. He had been so afraid of what might happen to her, he had refused to come to the air show. There were things she had to reckon with there, but she never had the courage, and he never wanted to hear it. He didn't want to believe how much flying meant to her, how badly she wanted other things than being his wife and having babies. What she really wanted right now was to relive every moment of the air show with Nick and have him assure her that their time together wasn't over. But instead now she'd have to deal with Bobby.

'There's your friend,' Nick said quietly. 'You gonna marry him one of these days?' It was something he always wondered.

'I don't know,' she said honestly with a sigh. She was always honest with him. But her honest answers were not what Bobby wanted. She was nineteen years old and she didn't feel ready to tie herself to anyone, and yet it was what they all wanted for her. 'Everyone keeps telling me I'll change, that being married and having kids changes everything. I guess that's what I'm scared of. My mom says it's what all women want. So how come all I want is what I had today and a hangar full of airplanes?'

'I can't say I've ever felt any different,' he grinned, and then grew thoughtful. 'No, that's not true. I did feel differently when I was about your age. I tried like hell, but it didn't work. And I've been scared to death ever since. There's no room for both a family and planes in my life. But, Cassie, maybe you're different.' In a way he wanted her to be, but not for Bobby.

'My dad seemed to do okay at it,' she grinned back at him. 'Maybe we're both weird, you and I. Maybe we're both just cowards. Sometimes it's easier to love airplanes than people.' Except that she knew she loved him. He was the dearest friend she had, and she knew he had loved her since she was a child. The trouble was, she wasn't a child now.

'You know,' he nodded thoughtfully then, responding to her calling herself a coward, 'that's exactly what I said to myself today when I watched you do that triple loop followed by the inverted spin before you flipped into the barrel roll in the aerobatics race. I said to myself, gee, I never realized Cassie is a coward.' She burst into laughter at the expression on his face, and pushed him where he sat behind the wheel in his old truck.

'You know what I mean. Maybe we're cowards about people,' she said cautiously.

'Maybe we're just not stupid. I think being married to the wrong person is about as bad as it gets. Believe me, I tried it.'

'Are you telling me he's the wrong person for me?' Cassie asked him in an undertone as Bobby waited for her patiently on the porch. He had already heard that she'd been a two-time winner at the air show.

'I can't tell you that, Cass. Only you know that. But don't let anyone else tell you he's the right one either. You figure it out. If you don't, you'll be awfully sorry later.' She nodded at the unexpected wisdom of his words, and then hugged him again for all he'd done for her.

'I'll see you at work tomorrow.' She was going to be working at the airport all summer. Her father was going to let her quit her job at the restaurant and work for him, for a pittance. She wondered if her father would let her do cargo runs alone. She wondered if her performance in the air show was going to change things.

She hopped lightly out of the truck, with a last look at Nick, and then went to talk to Bobby. He had waited a long time for her, and he was pleased that she had won, but he looked annoyed as she hurried over. He had been worried sick all afternoon, working in his father's store, and terrified he would hear of a disaster at the air show. And now she looked as breezy as could be, as though she'd gone into town to go shopping with her sisters.

'It's not fair to me, Cass,' he said quietly. 'I was worried about you all afternoon. You don't know what it's like, thinking of all the horrible things that could happen.'

'I'm sorry, Bobby,' she said quietly, 'but it was a special day for me.'

'I know,' he nodded, but he didn't look pleased. None of her sisters flew, what was she trying to prove? He really didn't want her to keep on flying, and he said so. But now was not the time, and Cassie suddenly looked as angry as he did.

'How can you say that to me?' She had come too far now, the air show, her father, all those years of lessons with Nick. She wasn't coming down ever again now. She was up there. And she was staying, whether Bobby liked it or not. He figured that eventually he'd change her. But by the end of the summer he had come to understand that he had allied himself with a family of fliers, and blood ran thicker than engagements. For the moment, all he could do was ask her to be careful. And she was, of course, but not because of Bobby. She was just good at what she did. And she flew constantly. By fall, when Jackie Cochran won the Bendix Trophy race from Burbank to Cleveland, Cassie was starting to fly mail runs for her father. He was sure of her flying by then, and had had her fly him all over the state herself. He had finally admitted to Nick that he was right. It was a coincidence of course, and you couldn't really trust a female the way you could a male, but she was a damn good pilot. Of course, Pat never said as much to Cassie.

She stayed on at Bradley for her sophomore year, and worked at the airport all through the winter. She helped out on several emergencies, flew with Nick whenever she could, and by spring she was an accepted member of the team at the airport. She flew everywhere, short runs, long, and of course she was practicing again for the summer air show. She went out to practice sometimes with Nick, and their time together reminded her of their years of lessons. But now they had time to talk at the airport, while they worked, and more than once, she joined him flying cargo or mail runs.

She was still engaged to Bobby Strong, but his father had been sick all year, and he had more responsibilities at the store now. He seemed to be visiting Cassie less and less often. And she was so busy, sometimes she didn't even notice.

Hitler occupied the rest of Czechoslovakia in

March, and became more of a threat than ever. Once again, there was talk of war, and fear of an American involvement. Roosevelt continued to promise that it wouldn't happen this time. And Nick continued not to believe him.

When Charles Lindbergh returned from Europe in the spring of 1939, he was the most outspoken champion of America staying out of the war. And Pat was glad to hear it. He believed whatever the famed aviator had to say. To Pat O'Malley, the name of Lindbergh was still sacred.

'We don't belong in the next one, Nick. We learned our lesson in the last one.' Pat was adamant. He was sure the United States would never get pulled into another war in Europe. But there was already trouble between the Chinese and the Japanese. Mussolini had taken Albania. And Hitler seemed to be looking toward Poland.

But all Cassie could think of by then was the summer air show. She was hard at work learning rolls and turns, and some new aerobatics she'd seen at a small airstrip in Ohio where she'd gone with Nick. She was working on her speed, and practicing whenever she could spare the time. By June, she had finished her sophomore year, and she thought she was ready for the air show.

Bobby was annoyed about her participating in the air show again, but he had his own problems at the grocery store, and he had long since understood how impossible Cassie was about flying. They went to see the new Tarzan movie when it came out in

June, and it was the only respite they shared as she prepared for the air show.

Finally, at long last, the big day came, and Cassie was at the airstrip in Peoria with Nick at four o'clock in the morning. Her brother was coming in later with Pat, but he wasn't particularly enthused about flying in the show this year. He had been so excited about starting college at Western Illinois University at Macomb that he had hardly practiced. Pat was still pinning all his hopes on him, and despite Cassie's impressive wins the year before, he scarcely ever mentioned her entering the air show.

Nick helped her fuel the plane and check everything, and at six o'clock he took her out for breakfast.

'Relax,' he smiled at her, remembering how he himself had been the first time he'd flown in an exhibition show, after the war. Pat had gone with him and Oona had brought the kids to see him. Cassie had been there too of course, she was only two then. And remembering that suddenly made him feel old. The two had become so close since he had started teaching her to fly years before. They had developed a bond that they would never lose now. But the painful thing for him sometimes was forcing himself to remember that he was old enough to be her father. She was twenty now, and there were eighteen years between them. He still felt like a kid, and he looked far younger than his years, and Cassie accused him constantly of acting like a child. But the fact was, he was thirty-eight . . . and she was only twenty. He would have given anything to cut in half the difference between them. Not that she seemed to care. But he did. But then again, she was still the daughter of his closest friend, and nothing would ever change that. Pat would never have understood the bond or the closeness between them. Nick knew it was a hurdle they would never overcome, unlike her flying. Pat had gone that far, but he would go no further.

Nick ordered her a plate of eggs, some sausages, a side of toast, and a cup of black coffee. But she waved it away as soon as it appeared at the table.

'I can't, Nick. I'm not hungry.'

'Eat it anyway. You'll need it later. I know what I'm talking about, kid. Otherwise, you're going to go weak in the knees when you're doing loops and negative G's out there. Be a good girl and eat it, or I'll have to force it down your throat, and the waitress might not understand it.' He looked at her in a way that said how much he cared, and she grinned up at him happily.

'You're disgusting.'

'You're cute. Especially when you take first prize. I like that in a girl. In fact, I'm kind of counting on you to do that.'

'Be nice. Don't push. I'll do what I can.' But she wanted to win first prize too, maybe even several of them. For him, for herself, and more importantly, to impress her father.

'He loves you anyway, you know. He just can't stand admitting he was wrong. But he knows how good you are. I heard him tell a bunch of guys at the airport last week. He just doesn't want to tell you, that's all.' Nick understood him better than Cass did. For all his gruff ways and seeming outrage over women fliers, her father was desperately proud of her, and just as embarrassed to show it.

'Maybe if I stacked a bunch of prizes up today, he'd have to admit, finally, that I fly okay . . . to me, I mean, not just to a bunch of guys.' She still sounded angry when she talked about it sometimes. Her father was always bragging about Chris, who didn't even like to fly. It drove her crazy.

'Would it really make that much difference to hear the words?' Nick asked her, eating fried eggs and steak with her. He wasn't going to be doing loops, but he had ordered himself a healthy breakfast.

'Maybe. I'd like to hear them just for the hell of it. Just to see how it feels.'

'And then what?'

'I go back to flying for you, and him, and myself, no big deal, I guess.'

'And you finish college and become a teacher.' He liked to say the words, but they both knew that she didn't believe that.

'I'd rather teach flying like you,' she said honestly, taking a sip of hot coffee.

'Yeah, and fly mail runs. That's a great life for a college girl.'

'Don't be so impressed. I haven't learned a thing, except from you.' And she meant it. But they were interrupted before he could deflect her praise, by a group of young men who had just finished breakfast. They seemed to hesitate somewhere near their table, circling like young birds, glancing at Nick and eyeing Cassie.

'You know those guys?' Nick asked in an undervoice, and she shook her head. She had never seen them, and then finally one of them approached Cassie's table. He looked down at her, and then at Nick, and he looked suddenly very young as he got up the nerve to address them.

'Are you . . . Stick Galvin?' he asked hesitantly, and then he glanced at her, 'And Cassie O'Malley?'

'I am,' she answered before Nick did.

'I'm Billy Nolan. I'm from California . . . we're flying in the air show. I saw you there last year,' he blushed furiously, 'you were terrific.' He looked about fourteen and Nick almost groaned. He was actually twenty-four, but he didn't look it. He was blond and young, his hair stood up in a cowlick like a kid's, and his face was covered with freckles. 'My dad knew who you were,' he said to Nick. 'He flew in the 94th with you, he got shot down. You probably don't remember him . . . Tommy Nolan.'

'Oh, my God,' Nick grinned as he stuck out his hand, and invited Billy to sit down with them. 'How is he?'

'Pretty good. He's had a bad limp since the war, but it doesn't seem to bother him much. We have a shoe store in San Francisco.'

'Good for him. Does he fly anymore?' Nick

remembered him well, and the funny thing was that Billy looked just like him.

But Billy said he hadn't flown in years, and he was none too thrilled that Billy had caught the bug from him. His friends were standing watching him then, and Billy beckoned them over. There were four of them, all about his age, and all from various parts of California. For the most part, they looked like cowboys.

'Which races are you in?' they asked Cass, and she told them. Speed, aerobatics, and a number of others, which Nick thought was a little ambitious. But it meant so much to her, and she loved being in the air show so much, he hadn't wanted to dampen her spirits. She had waited a long time for this, and she really enjoyed it.

Billy introduced them to everyone, they were a nice bunch of guys, and for the second time that morning, Nick Galvin felt ancient. Most of the boys were fifteen years younger than he was. They were all closer to Cassie's age, and by the time they all left the restaurant, everyone was laughing and chatting, and talking about the air show. They were like a bunch of kids, going to the school fair, and having a great time.

'I ought to let you kids go play,' Nick grinned at them, 'but then again maybe Cassie might forget to fly. Maybe I'd better stick around to see that you all behave and remember the air show.' They all laughed at him, and most of them had a thousand questions about the 94th and the war, and the

Germans he had shot down before it ended. 'Hey, hold on a minute, guys . . . one at a time,' and he told them another story. They treated him like a hero, and they were all in high spirits when they got to the fairground. This was what flying was all about, the camaraderie, and the fun, and the people you met at times like this, the experiences you shared. It wasn't just about the long flights and the solitude, and the sky at night when you felt as though you owned the world. It was all of those things, the highs and the lows, the terror and the peace of it, the incredible contrasts.

They wished Cassie luck, and went off to check their plane. They were all taking turns flying it, and they were enrolled in different events. But only Billy was going to be flying against Cassie.

'He's nice,' she said easily, once they were gone, and Nick glanced at her over his shoulder.

'Don't forget you're engaged,' he said politely, and she laughed at the pious look on his face, which was very unlike him. Most of the time he had no interest at all in Bobby Strong, or her fidelity to him.

'Oh for heaven's sake. I just meant he was "nice," you know, as someone to talk to. I wasn't planning to run off with him.' She was fueling the plane, and wondered suddenly if Nick could be jealous. It was a ridiculous idea, and she brushed it off as soon as she thought it.

'You could run off with him, you know,' he persisted. 'He's the right age. And at least he flies. That might be refreshing,' he said innocently.

'Are you finding guys for me now?' She looked amused. 'I didn't know that was part of the service you provided,' she said calmly.

'The service I will provide will be to chain you to the ground if you don't prepare your plane right. Don't fool around, Cass. You're going to be putting a lot of stress on the plane, and yourself. Pay attention.'

'Yes, sir.' The games were over now, but for a fraction of an instant, she could have sworn that he was jealous, although he certainly had no reason to be. She was engaged to someone else, and they were just friends, and always had been. She wondered if it annoyed him to see her making friends with other pilots. He was very proud of all she'd done, and maybe that was what had been bothering him. It was hard to tell as he helped her check the plane. And then a few minutes later they saw her father and her brother. It was nearly eight o'clock by then. And the races started at nine, although her first event wasn't until nine-thirty.

'All set, Cass?' her father asked nervously. 'Did you check everything?'

'I did,' she said defensively. Didn't he think she was capable of doing it? And if he cared so much, why hadn't he come out to help her, instead of Chris? He could have been attentive to both of them, but he wasn't. All his concern was for Chris, who looked more than anything as though he wished he didn't have to be there.

He was in only one event this year, and Cassie hoped for his sake that he'd win it.

'Good luck,' her father said quietly, and then left her to join Chris across the airfield.

'Why does he bother?' she muttered as he walked away, and Nick answered gently.

'Because he loves you, and he doesn't know how to say it.'

'He has an odd way of showing it sometimes.'

'Yeah? Maybe it's because you kept him up all night when you were born. Maybe you deserve it.' She grinned at the answer he gave her. Nick always made her feel better about everything, and it was comforting to know that he'd always been there.

She saw Billy Nolan and the boys again before her first event. They were hooting and laughing and raising hell. It was hard to believe they were serious, but they had entered all the toughest races.

'I hope they know what they're doing,' Nick said quietly. They looked like a bunch of kids, but it was hard to tell sometimes. He had known some real aces who had looked like cowboys. But no one wanted to watch a tragedy, and that usually happened when people overestimated their skill, or didn't know their planes' limits.

'They must be okay,' Cassie said confidently, 'they qualified.'

'So did you,' he teased, 'what does that mean?'

'Jerk . . .' she laughed at him, and half an hour later she was on her way. It was almost her turn. There had already been some pretty impressive stunts in the air, some great gasps, a few screams. It was all in a day's work at the air show.

'Give 'em hell!' Nick called as he left her and she taxied off down the short runway in the Moth for the aerobatic event. And for the first time in years, he found himself praying. He hadn't been nearly as nervous for her last year, but this year he was afraid she might push too hard, just to prove something to him, or her father. She wanted to win more than anything, and he knew it.

She began with a few slow loops, then a double, and a barrel roll. She went through the whole repertoire backward and forward, including a Cuban eight, and a falling leaf, and as he watched her, each exercise was completed to perfection, and then she did a triple, and a dive, and somewhere near him a woman screamed, not realizing that in an instant, Cassie would recover . . . and of course she did. Perfectly. It was the most beautiful demonstration he had ever seen, and she finished it off with an outside loop, which delighted everyone. And Nick was beaming at her when she landed.

'Not bad for a start, Cass. Pretty clean.' His eyes shone right into hers as he praised her.

'That's all?' Her excitement and adrenaline turned instantly to disappointment, but he gave her a tight hug and told her she'd been terrific. 'You were the best,' he said honestly, and half an hour later, the judges confirmed it. Her father congratulated her politely when their paths crossed. But his praise was more for Nick than for Cassie.

He was proud of her. But it still irked him that she was showing up the men with her flying.

'You must have had a very good teacher.'

'I had a very good student,' Nick corrected him, and the two men smiled, but her father said nothing more to Cassie.

Chris's race was next, and he tried hard, but he lost. He didn't even place this time, and the truth was he didn't really care anymore. For him, his flying days were over. He was much more interested in his classes at school, and all things separate from planes and airports. He just didn't have the bug, and the only thing he hated about it was disappointing his father.

'I'm sorry, Dad,' he apologized after he parked the plane. 'I guess I should have practiced more.' He'd been flying Nick's beefed-up Bellanca, which Cassie was going to fly too.

'Yes, you should have, son,' Pat said sadly. He hated to see him lose when, with a little effort, he could have been a great flier, or so Pat thought. But Pat was the only one who thought of Chris that way. Everyone else knew the truth, even Chris, that he just wasn't a flier. But Cassie congratulated him anyway.

'Good job, baby brother. That was a pretty piece of flying.'

'Not pretty enough apparently,' he grinned at her, and then congratulated her for taking first prize in the previous event.

And a few minutes later she saw one of Billy

Nolan's friends take second place. He had done some very fine flying.

Cassie's next race was at ten o'clock and it was more difficult this time. It involved speed, and she was worried that the Vega couldn't do it. It was fast, but some of the racing planes were faster.

'She'll do it if you play her right,' Nick promised as he talked to Cassie right before takeoff. The Vega was a great plane and Cassie flew it well. Nick knew that for this race it was better than the Bellanca. 'Just keep cool, Cass. Don't let it scare you.' She nodded and said not a word as she taxied off, and a moment later she was in the air, and flying remarkably. Nick had never seen anyone more precise or faster, and she managed some extraordinarily complicated maneuvers. He couldn't take his eyes off her, and he noticed that Pat was watching her intently too. And so was a tall blond man in a blazer and white trousers. He was watching her very carefully through binoculars, and talking to a man who was taking notes. He was out of place and Nick figured he was probably from one of the Chicago papers.

Cassie won second prize that time, but only because she hadn't had a faster plane. She had overcome every handicap the Vega had, and Nick still couldn't believe it. He had never expected her to win that race, and she had placed handsomely. When she was down again, Billy came over and congratulated her. He had won third against her. They were a great bunch of fliers, and Nick liked what he had just seen of Billy. He was careful and sure, and he had won in spite of an inferior plane. Like Cass, he had pushed it to the limit.

She had two more races to fly that day. One at noon, which went well, and the last one in the afternoon, which was a race Nick would have preferred she hadn't entered. She and Nick had had lunch with Billy Nolan and his friends, Chris had joined them eventually, and when her father wandered by, she introduced them to the famous Pat O'Malley. He liked all the young boys, and Billy spent some extra time talking to him, telling him about his father. Pat remembered him well, and was sorry he had lost track of him in the past twenty years. He had genuinely liked him.

And then it was time for Cassie's race. When Pat heard that she had entered, he was furious, and his eyes blazed as he berated his partner.

'Didn't you tell her not to?' he barked at Nick, who looked annoyed and unhappy at Pat's reaction. He felt guilty enough for letting her enter it and Pat wasn't helping.

'She takes after her old man, Pat. She does what she wants.'

'She's got the wrong plane for that, and she doesn't have the experience to do it.'

'I told her that. But she's practiced a lot, and I think she's smart enough to let it go if she can't make it. She's not going to push it to the edge, Pat. I told her that myself.' He only prayed that she had listened.

The two men stood staring up at the s▇ unhappily, with Chris, and Billy and his friends and the man in the white trousers. It was a daredevil event, usually entered only by old stunt pilots with aerobatic planes, which Nick's Bellanca wasn't. But she had desperately wanted to try her hand at this event. It allowed her to show off all the stuff she did best, and pull off a miracle or two, if she could get the plane to cooperate with her at low altitudes. She knew it was going to be scary, but she was prepared to scrub the race if she really had to.

There were over a dozen moves she had to do, all of them impressive and frightening, and she went through the first half dozen of them without being a hair off. Pat was even beginning to smile as he watched her. And then on the final dive, she seemed to lose control. Her plane dove with its wings askew, and Nick wondered if she was panicking and had forgotten everything he had taught her, or maybe she had fainted. But she was doing absolutely nothing to save herself, nothing at all, and no one moved as they stared in horror at what was going to become a tragedy in a single instant. But suddenly, with a roar, she throttled the hell out of it, and pulled up, barely higher than the heads of the horrified crowd, and pulled out of it, soaring high and completing a triple roll that took everyone's breath away. She completed every move and did a final loop that won her the race hands down, without even hearing from the judges.

Nick had a lump in his throat the size of an egg

…d Pat looked gray, but as he realized what she'd …one, Nick wanted to throttle her for scaring him so badly. How could she terrify them that way? Even first prize wasn't worth it. He ran to where she taxied the plane and almost yanked her out of the cockpit.

'What the hell were you doing up there, you damn fool? Trying to kill yourself showing off? Don't you realize that another foot and you couldn't have pulled up?'

'I know that,' she said calmly, startled to realize that he was shaking. She had done everything intentionally and with flawless calculation.

'You're a lunatic, that's what you are! You're not human, and you have no right to be in a plane.'

'Did I lose?' She looked agonized and more than ever he wanted to shake her, as her father watched from the distance with a look of fascination. And as he watched Nick's face, he realized that he was seeing something there he had never seen before. He wondered if Nick even knew it.

'Did you *lose*?' Nick raged on, holding firmly to her arm. 'Are you *nuts*? You almost lost your life up there, and killed about a hundred people.'

'I'm sorry, Nick.' She looked suddenly contrite. 'I thought I could get away with it.'

'You did. Damn you. And it was the finest piece of flying I've ever seen, but if you ever do anything like that again, I'm going to kill you.'

'Yes, sir.'

'Good. Now get out of that damn plane, and go apologize to your father.'

But surprisingly, he was much kinder to her, although he had been as scared as Nick, and he was grateful that Oona wasn't there to see it. She had stayed home with Glynnis, who was pregnant again, and all five of her young ones had the measles. But Pat had seen what Nick had done, and he thought there had been enough said. Instead, he complimented her on her style and her courage.

'I guess Nick was right after all,' he said almost humbly. 'You're quite a flier, Cass.'

'Thank you, Dad.' He gave her a hug, and it was the greatest moment of her life as he held her.

They watched Billy Nolan fly again after that, and he won first prize in his last race too. Cassie had won a second and three firsts, which was better than she'd dreamed. And the newspaper kept taking her picture.

They were all standing around drinking beer and watching the last event, when suddenly Cassie saw Nick's jaw tighten as he stood beside her. She followed his eyes high into the sky, and saw smoke, and suddenly, like everyone else there, she looked frightened.

'He's in trouble,' Nick whispered to her. They all knew who it was. It was a young pilot named Jim Bradshaw. He had two babies and a young wife, and a plane that wasn't worth spit, but more than anything in life, he loved air shows.

'Oh, my God,' Cassie mouthed the words, as

they all watched in horror, as he began to spiral lazily, just as she had, but this was for real, and the plumes of smoke from his fuselage told them all that this was no stunt. This was a disaster. The crowd began to run away from where the plane appeared to be, and people started screaming. But Cassie found she couldn't move, all she could do was stare at it, the lazy bird falling head over heels, into the ground, and then suddenly it hit with a tremendous crash and an explosion. People ran from everywhere, and Nick and Billy were among the first there, trying to pull Jim from the wreckage, but it was too late. He was inhumanly burned, and it was obvious that he had died on impact. His wife was sobbing hysterically, and two of the women held her, as her mother held onto the children.

The ambulances were already there, but it was a somber end to an exciting day, a reminder to all of them of the danger they constantly courted.

'I guess we'd better go home,' Nick said quietly, and Pat nodded. Earlier that day, Pat had feared that Cassie might meet the same fate and he was ashamed to admit now how grateful he was that it had been someone else and not his daughter.

Billy came to say good-bye to them, as they loaded their three planes onto flatbeds, and tied them up firmly.

'I'd like to come out and see you at the airport before I go,' he said to Pat after they shook hands.

'Anytime. You going back to San Francisco?'

'Actually, I was wondering . . . I was kind of

hoping maybe you could use another pair of hands
. . . I . . . I wouldn't mind sticking around and doing
some flying.'

'We could use a flier like you, lad. Come by
and see me tomorrow morning.'

Billy thanked him profusely, and they all said
good-bye again. His friends were all going home the
next day, and Billy looked thrilled to be staying.

'What do we need another hotshot kid for?' Nick
asked Pat, with a look of annoyance.

'You planning to spend the rest of your life
flying nights?' Pat asked with a look of amusement.
'Don't worry. I don't think he's her type.' Her
father grinned ruefully and for the first time in
years, Nick blushed, and turned away from his old
friend. 'I might remind you though, Nick Galvin,
she's engaged to the Strong boy, and she'll marry
him eventually, if I have anything to say about it.
She needs a man firmly planted on the ground,
not up in the sky, like the two of us.' He meant
what he said, but what he'd seen in Nick's eyes
that day intrigued him. There was something very
powerful there, between the two of them, though
he suspected that Cassie was too young to know
it. But he also knew that Nick was wise enough
not to be carried away by his own emotions.

They headed for the O'Malley home then, where
Oona had promised to cook them dinner.

She was amazed to hear of Cassie's wins when
they got home. In most ways, it had been a good
day. But the death of Jim Bradshaw had spoiled it

for all of them, and then in the midst of dinner, Bobby had arrived, looking crazed. He burst into their living room, and apologized when he saw them all eating dinner. His eyes went to Cassie first, and he looked as though he were going to burst into tears. He looked so distressed that Oona rose as though to go to him, but he backed out of the room apologetically and stood in the doorway.

'I'm sorry . . . I . . . they told me there was an accident . . .' His eyes filled with tears again, and they all felt sorry for him. It was easy to see what he'd thought, and Cassie got up and went to him.

'I'm sorry. It was Jim Bradshaw,' she said softly.

'Oh, my God. Poor Peggy.' She was a widow at nineteen and alone with two children. Bobby seemed overcome at the thought of it, but what had upset him so terribly was the fear that it could have been Cassie who was killed. And no one he talked to seemed to know what had happened.

They went out to sit on the porch quietly, and Cassie closed the door. You couldn't hear anything from inside the room, but they could still see how distressed he looked, as he talked to her. And she just sat there and nodded.

He was telling her that he couldn't live like this anymore, just being engaged to her, not going anywhere, not getting married, and never being entirely sure if they even had a future. He knew that she wanted to finish school, but he wasn't sure he could wait two more years. His father was so ill now, and his mother was so dependent on him.

He seemed overwhelmed by all of it, and it was obvious to her that he needed her to help him. But it was equally obvious to both of them that she wasn't prepared to give up everything, and be what he needed.

'And this flying thing.' He looked at her, his eyes filled with anguish. 'I can't live like this. I keep thinking you're going to be killed . . . and today . . . you could have been . . . you could have been . . .' He started to cry and she put her arms around him and held him.

'Oh, poor Bobby . . . poor Bobby . . . it's all right . . . shhh . . .' It was like consoling one of her nephews. But she understood now that there was too much on his shoulders and she was only part of that burden. He desperately needed someone to help. He was only twenty-one, barely more than a boy himself, and he deserved so much more than she had to give, and they both knew it. As she comforted him, she gently slipped his ring off her finger, and pressed it into his hand. 'You deserve so much,' she whispered to him, 'you deserve everything, and I have a long, long road ahead of me. I know that now. I was never sure of it before, but I am now.' She wanted life and freedom and flying. And now that her father accepted her, maybe she could have all those things. But she couldn't give Bobby Strong what he deserved, and in truth it was the last thing she wanted.

'Are you going to keep flying, Cass?' he asked miserably, sniffing like a small child, while the members of her family in the main room tried to ignore them.

'I am,' she nodded at him. 'I have to. It's my life.'

'Don't get hurt . . . oh God, Cassie . . . don't get hurt . . . I love you . . . I thought you were dead today.' He was sobbing again and she felt terrible for him. She could only imagine what it must have been like. Just as it had been for Peggy Bradshaw.

'I'm okay . . . I'm fine . . .' She smiled up at him with tears in her own eyes. 'You deserve wonderful things, Bobby, not someone like me. Find yourself a good wife, Bobby Strong. You deserve it.'

'Will you stay here?' he asked curiously, and it seemed an odd question to her. She had nowhere else to go, and she had always lived there.

'Where else would I go?'

'I don't know,' he smiled sadly, holding her ring. He missed her already. 'You seem so free to me. Sometimes I hate our damn grocery store, and all the problems that go with it.'

'You're going to do great things,' she said confidently, sure that it was a lie, but he deserved all the encouragement she could give him.

'Do you really think so, Cass?' He sighed then, thinking of his life. 'The funny thing is I just want to be married and have kids.'

'And I don't.' She grinned. 'That's the trouble.'

'I hope you do one day. Maybe we'll find each other again,' he said hopefully, wanting to pursue the dream again. She had always seemed so exciting to him, maybe even too much so.

But she shook her head as she looked at him. She was wiser than he was.

'Don't wait for that. Go get what you want.'

'I love you, Cass.'

'I love you too,' she whispered as she hugged him again and then stood up. 'Do you want to come inside?' she asked, but he shook his head, tears bright in his eyes.

'I guess I better go.' She nodded, and he slipped the ring into his pocket. He stopped for a long moment, and looked at her again, and then he turned and hurried off the porch before he started crying again. And Cassie went back inside and sat down. No one asked her anything, but they could all guess what had just happened. Nick glanced at her finger, and he wasn't surprised not to see the ring. In fact, he was relieved not to see it. Now all he had to worry about was Billy Nolan.

9

The next morning, as Cassie lay in bed, thinking of the day before, she realized with a start that she was no longer engaged. She wasn't sure it changed anything, but suddenly she felt as though she didn't belong to anyone. It was partially very exciting, and in some ways suddenly very lonely.

But she had known all along it was wrong, she just hadn't had the courage to say it. But that night, it had seemed so cruel to go on torturing him, to make him wait another two years, and then tell him she still wasn't ready. She didn't think she ever would be, not for a life like his or for him, and now she really knew that.

She made herself breakfast, and saw a note from her mother, saying she had gone to take care of Glynnis's kids again, and she doubted if she'd be home in time to make dinner. Chris had left another note saying he'd be out with friends, and half an hour later, Cassie had showered, dressed, and gotten herself to the airport. She put on a clean pair of overalls and fueled some planes, and it was noon before she saw either Nick or her father.

'Sleeping till noon these days, Cass?' Nick teased. 'Or just resting on your laurels?'

'Oh, don't be such a smartass. I was here at nine. I was just doing some work in the back hangar.'

'Yeah? Well, I've got a run for you today, if you want it.'

'Where to?' She was intrigued.

'Indiana. A little cargo, and some mail, and a quick stop in Chicago on the way back. It shouldn't take too long. You should be home in time for dinner. You can fly the Handley.'

'Sounds good to me,' she grinned. He told her where to pick up the log, and her father came out of his office just then, and told Billy to load the cargo. He had appeared out of nowhere, and he had been working hard all day. And her father surprised her by telling him to go with her.

'I can go alone, Dad.'

'Sure you can. But he needs to learn our routes, and I don't like the idea of your flying into Chicago.' She rolled her eyes at him, and he made a face, but at least he wasn't objecting to her flying. Things were looking up, and Nick looked warningly at her and Billy, as though they were both naughty children.

'Behave yourselves, you two. No stunts, no rolls.' He turned to Billy then. 'And watch out for her double loops.'

'If she tries anything, I'll toss her out on her

ear,' Billy grinned, looking more than ever like everyone's brother.

And as they took off toward the plane, Nick stood for a minute and watched them. They looked as though they were enjoying themselves, but they looked like two kids. He couldn't imagine her falling for him, but stranger things had happened. And in fact, even if she didn't, it didn't change anything for him. He had no right to be chasing a girl her age, and he would never have done it. She deserved a lot more than life in a lean-to shack at O'Malley's Airport, and he knew it.

They had just taken off when a brand-new green Lincoln Zephyr pulled up, and a man in a gray double-breasted suit stepped out and looked around the airport. He looked pleasantly at Nick, and at the small building which housed their offices and was the airport.

'Do you know where I might find Cassie O'Malley?' he asked smoothly. He had wavy blond hair, and movie-star good looks. And suddenly, Nick wondered if someone was going to offer Cassie a movie career. This was the man he'd seen the day before at the air show, in the blazer and white trousers. And he didn't look like a reporter now. He looked like a businessman of some kind, or maybe an agent.

Nick pointed up at the sky. 'She just took off on a mail run. Can I help you?'

'I'd like to talk to her. Do you know when she'll be back?'

'Maybe seven or eight hours. Not before. I'd say she'll be back sometime tonight. Can I give her a message?'

He handed Nick a card. His name was Desmond Williams. And the card said 'Williams Aircraft,' with an address in Newport Beach, California. Nick knew exactly who he was. He was the young tycoon who had inherited a fortune and an aircraft company from his father. And he wasn't all that young, Nick decided, looking at him. He was pretty close to his own age. In fact, he was thirty-four. A lot too old for Cassie, according to Nick anyway.

'Will you be sure and give her my card? I'm staying at the Portsmouth.' It was the finest hotel in town, which wasn't saying much. But it was the best Good Hope had to offer.

'I'll tell her,' Nick assured him, dying of curiosity. 'Anything else?' Williams shook his head, and looked Nick over with interest. 'How did you like the air show?' Nick couldn't resist asking him. 'Not bad for a small town, eh?'

'Very interesting,' Williams conceded with a smile, and then sized Nick up again, and decided to ask him a question. Williams's whole style was very cool, everything about him was perfect and manicured, totally calculated and planned. He was a man who never made mistakes, or allowed himself to be swayed by emotions. 'Are you her instructor?'

Nick nodded with pride. 'I was. She could teach me to fly now.'

'I doubt that,' Desmond Williams said politely.

He had an Eastern accent despite his Los Angeles address. And twelve years before, he had graduated from Princeton. 'She's very good. She's done you proud.'

'Thank you,' Nick said quietly, wondering what this man wanted with her. There was something faintly ominous about him, incredibly cool, and strangely exciting. He was very good-looking and very aristocratic, but everything about him said that he meant business.

He didn't say another word to Nick then, but got back into the car he'd just bought in Detroit a few days before, and drove swiftly away from the airport.

'Who was that?' Pat asked as he came outside. 'He certainly kicked up enough dust. Can he go any faster?' The car was the latest wonder by Ford, with a V-12 engine.

'That's Desmond Williams.' Nick answered his question with a look of concern at his old friend. 'They're after her, Pat. I never thought it would happen, but I think it may now. She made just enough noise at the air show.'

'I was afraid of that.' Pat looked unhappily at Nick. He didn't want her exploited or used, and he knew how easy it would be for that to happen to her. She was beautiful and young and innocent, and an incredible flier. It was a dangerous combination, and they both knew it. 'Where is she?' Pat asked.

'She's gone. She and the Nolan kid took off just as he got here,' Nick explained.

'Good.' Pat glanced at the card in his hand, took it and tore it in half. 'Forget him.'

'You're not going to tell her?' Nick looked at him in amazement. No matter what he thought, he wouldn't have had the guts to do that. But on the other hand, he wasn't her father.

'No, I'm not,' Pat answered him, 'and neither are you. Right, Stick?'

'Yes, sir.' Nick saluted with a grin, and they both went back to work with a vengeance.

On the way back from Chicago Cassie turned the controls over to Billy, to see how he handled them. She was impressed by how good he was. He said his father had taught him at fourteen, and he had flown for ten years now. And from the way he flew, it was easy to believe him. He had sure hands, and a good eye, he flew steadily and well, and she knew her father would be pleased. Billy was going to be a great asset to the airport. And besides that, he was a nice guy, easygoing and intelligent, and very pleasant to be with. They'd had a good time that day, on the flight, trading stories.

'I noticed yesterday that you were engaged,' he mentioned conversationally on the leg home. 'But I don't see the ring today. You getting married soon?'

'Nope,' she said, thinking of Bobby. 'I'm not engaged anymore. Gave back the ring last night.' She wasn't sure why she was telling him, but he was there, and they were almost the same age, and she liked him. Besides, she didn't get the feeling he was interested in her. He just wanted to be friends, and that seemed comfortable and easy.

'Are you upset? Think you'll get back together?'

'Nope,' she said again, almost feeling sorry for herself now. 'He's a great guy, but he hates my flying. He's in a hurry to get married, I want to finish school. I don't know . . . it wasn't right, never was, I just never had the guts to say it.'

'I know what that's like. I've been engaged twice, scared the hell out of me both times.'

'What did you do about it?'

'The first time I ran,' he admitted honestly with his boyish grin and his face full of freckles.

'And the last time? You got married?' Cassie looked surprised, he didn't look like someone who'd been married.

'No,' he said quietly, 'she died, at the San Diego Air Show last year.' He said it very calmly but she could see the pain in his eyes.

'I'm sorry.' There was nothing else to say. They had all lost friends at air shows. And it was terrible, but worse for him if he had loved her.

'So am I. But I've learned to live with it, more or less. I haven't really gone out with anyone since, and I don't think I want to.'

'Is that a warning?' she grinned.

'Yeah,' his eyes were full of mischief, 'just in case you thought you could jump me at ten thousand feet. I've been scared to death the whole trip.' The way he said it made her burst into laughter, and five minutes later they were both laughing again.

By the time they got home, they were as easy with each other as old friends. As far as Cassie was concerned, there was nothing romantic about Billy Nolan, Cassie just liked him, and he was a terrific pilot. Her father had lucked out, and she thought Nick would like him too.

They landed at the airport about nine and Cassie offered him a ride to the boardinghouse where he was staying. His friends had gone back to California with their truck and their plane, and he had to save enough money to buy a car, which wouldn't be any time soon with the wages she knew her father paid. 'How long do you think you'll stay?' she asked him.

'I don't know . . . thirty, forty years . . . like forever?' He grinned.

'Sure.' She laughed at his answer.

'I don't know. A while. I needed to get away. My mom died, and with Sally last year, I just figured I needed to get away from California. I miss my dad, but he understands.'

'Lucky for us,' she smiled warmly at him. 'It was fun today. See you tomorrow.' She waved, and drove home. Her mother was home by then, and she made Cassie a sandwich. Her father was sitting in the kitchen, drinking a beer. He asked her how the flight was, and she told him how impressed she was with Billy's flying. She told him why, and Pat nodded, pleased by her report, though he'd have to see for himself. He told her to get some sleep after she'd had something to eat, and he never mentioned Desmond Williams's visit to the airport.

10

Cassie was lying under an Electra the next day, with grease all over her face after working on the tail wheel, when she looked up and noticed an immaculate pair of white linen trousers. She couldn't help smiling as she looked at them, they looked so incongruous here, and so did the handmade spectators where the trousers ended. She looked up in curiosity, and was surprised to see an attractive blond man looking down at her with a puzzled air. She was almost unrecognizable, with her hair piled up on her head, grease all over her face, and a pair of old blue overalls that had been her father's.

'Miss O'Malley?' he asked with a frown, and she grinned. She looked like a bad joke from vaudeville as her white teeth shone in the black face, and the polished-looking man couldn't help smilmg.

'Yes, I'm Miss O'Malley.' She was still lying on her back, looking up at him, and she suddenly realized she'd better get up and see what he wanted. She sprang easily to her feet, and hesitated to shake hands with him. He looked so clean and so exquisitely groomed, everything about him was perfection. She wondered if he wanted to charter a plane from them, and she was about to direct him to her father. 'Can I help you?'

'My name is Desmond Williams, and I saw you at the air show two days ago. I wanted to speak to you, if I may.' He looked around the hangar and then back to her. 'Is there anywhere we could go and talk?' She looked startled at the question. No one had ever come to visit her that way, and the only place to talk privately would have been her father's office.

'If you don't mind the noise of the planes, we could walk over near the runway, I guess.' She didn't know what else to offer him.

They began walking side by side, and she almost laughed thinking of how incongruous they must have seemed, he so beautifully clean, and she so incredibly dirty. But she forced herself to look serious. She had no idea if he had a sense of humor. She saw that Billy had caught sight of them by then. He waved, but she only nodded.

'You were very impressive at the air show,' Desmond Williams said quietly to her as they walked along the edge of the fields, and his shoes began to get very dusty.

'Thank you.'

'I don't think I've ever seen anyone win so many prizes . . . certainly not a girl your age. How old are you, anyway?' He was watching her very carefully, and he sounded serious, but he was quick to smile at her. She still didn't know what he wanted.

'I'm twenty. This fall I'll be a junior in college.'

'I see,' he nodded, as though that made a big difference. And then he stopped walking and looked at her pointedly before he asked his next question. 'Miss O'Malley, have you ever thought of a future for yourself in aviation?'

'In what sense?' She looked completely baffled, and all of a sudden she wondered if he had come here to ask her to be a Skygirl, but even to her, that didn't seem very likely. 'What do you mean?'

'I mean flying . . . as a job . . . as your future. Doing what you love best, or at least I think it is. You certainly fly as though you love it better than anything.' She nodded with a smile, and he watched her face relentlessly, but so far, he liked it.

'I'm talking about flying remarkable planes, planes that no one else has . . . testing them . . . setting records . . . becoming an important part of modern-day aviation . . . like Lindbergh.'

'Like Lindbergh?' She looked amazed. He couldn't mean it. 'Who would I be flying for? You mean someone would just give me these planes, or would I have to buy them?' Maybe he was trying to sell her a new plane, but Desmond Williams smiled at her innocence. He was glad that no one had gotten to her before him.

'You'd be flying for me, for my company. Williams Aircraft.' As soon as she heard the name, she realized who he was, and she couldn't believe he was talking to her and comparing her to Charles Lindbergh. 'There's a wonderful future out there for someone like you, Miss O'Malley. You could do great things. And you'd be flying planes that otherwise you'd never be able to lay your hands on. The best there is. That's quite a thrill. Not like these.' He looked around him disparagingly, and for a moment she felt hurt on behalf of her father. These planes were her friends, and her father's proudest possessions. 'I mean real planes,' Williams went on. 'The kind that world records are made in.'

'What would I have to do to get the job?' she asked suspiciously. 'Would I have to pay you?' No one had ever offered her anything like this, and she had no idea how it worked. She had always thought that important pilots had their own planes, it had never occurred to her that they were given or loaned by aircraft companies like his. She had a lot to learn, and he was more than willing to teach her. She was the first fresh face he had seen since he had taken over his father's business.

'You wouldn't have to pay me anything.' He smiled at her. 'I would pay you, and handsomely. You'd get your photograph taken all the time, you'd get a lot of publicity, and if you're as good as I think you are, you could become a very important figure in aviation. Of course,' he looked at her carefully, 'you might have to wash your face a little more often than you do now,' he teased and she suddenly remembered that she was probably covered with grease. She wiped her face on her sleeve, and was astonished at what she saw there. But he was even more impressed by the face he could see better now. She was exactly what he had been looking for. She was the girl of his dreams. All he had to do now was get her to sign a contract.

'When would I start?' She was curious, it was the most exciting thing she had ever heard, and she couldn't wait to tell Nick and her father.

'Tomorrow. Next week. As soon as you can get to Los Angeles. We would pay your way out of course, and give you an apartment.'

'An apartment?' Her voice almost squeaked as he nodded.

'In Newport Beach, where Williams Aircraft is. It's a beautiful spot, and you can get into the city in no time. What do you say? Do you want the job?' He had brought the contract with him, and he was hoping she would sign without waiting another moment. But she hesitated briefly as she nodded.

'Yes. But I have to ask my father. I'd have to give up school. He might not like that.' Particularly not for a flying job. Although he'd never been overly excited about her going to college. But he might not like this either.

'We could arrange for you to take classes, whenever you're free. But most of the time, you'll be pretty busy. There's a lot of good will involved, a lot of photography. And frankly, a lot of flying.'

It sounded utterly fantastic. 'Actually, I came by yesterday, but the man in the office said you were flying. I left my card with him, and asked for you to call me. You probably got back too late, but I thought I'd better come out here again just in case he lost my card.' He smiled a winning smile at her, as Cassie looked at him pensively.

'You gave it to a man?' It had to be Nick or her father.

'I did and I told him I was staying at the Portsmouth. Did you call me there? Maybe I just didn't get the message.'

'No, I didn't,' she said honestly. 'I never got the card or the message.'

'Well, there's no harm done. I'm glad I found you today. Here's the contract for you to go over with your father.'

'What does the contract say?' she asked innocently.

'It commits you to a year of test flights and publicity for Williams Aircraft, nothing more than that. I don't think you'll find anything wrong with it,' he said confidently. He somehow managed to convey, just looking at her, that this was a great opportunity and she would love it.

She held the contract nervously in her hands, wondering what it all meant and why he had really come here. It couldn't really be this simple.

'I'll show my father,' she said quietly. She wanted to ask him about it too. Why hadn't he and Nick told her anything about Desmond Williams's visit?

To give them the benefit of the doubt, maybe they had just forgotten. But something told her it was more than that. They had kept it from her. But why? It sounded so perfect.

'Why don't you think it all over, and we'll meet again tomorrow morning. How about breakfast at my hotel at eight-thirty? After that, I've got to head back to the West Coast. But hopefully you'll be there too in a few days.' He smiled, and she noticed that there was something very persuasive about him. He was very handsome and very cool, and he somehow made it sound as though she couldn't possibly resist him, and surely wouldn't want to. 'Eight-thirty tomorrow morning then?' he asked pointedly, and she nodded. They shook hands on it, and a moment later, he had walked back to his car and driven away. As she stood staring, the Lincoln disappeared into the horizon. She tried to remember everything she'd ever heard about Desmond Williams. He was thirty-four; he was one of the richest men in the world, and he had inherited an empire from his father. His company made some of the finest planes, and he was supposedly ruthless in his business dealings, she had read somewhere. She had seen a photograph of him with some movie stars. And in her wildest dreams, she couldn't imagine what he wanted with Cassie O'Malley.

She walked slowly toward the small building where Nick and her father worked, thinking of everything he had said, and what it might mean to her. It was an opportunity that clearly would never come again. She couldn't even bring herself to believe that it had come this time.

She walked in, in her father's old overalls, and he glanced up at her, with her streaked face, and disheveled hair, and asked her if there was a problem with the de Havilland, because if there wasn't they needed it at noon for a long run. But she wasn't paying any attention to him, as she stared at him. And in her hand she was holding the contract.

'Why didn't you tell me someone came to see me yesterday?' she asked, and he looked suddenly startled.

'Who told you that?' He was going to have Nick's head if he had betrayed him. But Nick was staring at them. He had seen the look on her face when she walked into the office.

'That's not the point. A man came here yesterday and left a card for me. And neither of you ever told me.' She turned angry eyes to Nick then, accusing him as well, and both men looked uncomfortable beneath her gaze. 'That's like lying to me. Why?'

Her father tried to look unconcerned. 'I didn't think it was important. I probably just forgot.'

'Do you know who he is?' She looked from one to the other of them, unable to believe that they had been that ignorant. 'He's Desmond Williams, of Williams Aircraft.' It was one of the largest manufacturers of airplanes in the world, the second biggest in the States. Desmond Williams was certainly what one could call important.

'What did he want?' Nick asked casually, watching her, but he already sensed what Williams must have said, from the way she was behaving.

'Oh . . . just to give me a bunch of remarkable planes to fly, you know, to test fly, set records in, check out for him. Nothing much. Just a little job like that for a whole lot of money, and an apartment.' The two men exchanged a dark look. This was exactly what they'd been afraid of.

'Sounds nice,' Nick said easily, 'what's the catch?'

'There is none.'

'Oh yes, there is,' Nick laughed at her. She was still a child, and he knew that he and Pat would have to do everything they could to protect her. Desmond Williams was flying around the country looking for publicity props, and once he had her, he would use her till she dropped, not just for test flights, but for everything else he could, newsreels, advertisements, endless photography. In Nick's opinion, she was just going to be another kind of Skygirl. 'Did he give you a contract?' Nick asked casually, and she was quick to wave it at him.

'Of course he did.'

'Mind if I have a look?' She handed it to him, and Pat glared at both of them. This was exactly what he had never wanted.

'You're going to say no to him, Cassandra Maureen,' her father said quietly as Nick pored over the contract. Nick was no lawyer, but it looked pretty good. They were offering her a car, an apartment, for her use of course, not as a gift; she was to fly anything they thought appropriate, doing test flights for them; and the second part of the contract said that she would be available for unlimited publicity in connection with their planes. She had to make herself available for social, state, and even national events, for photography at the drop of a hat. She would be counted on as a spokeswoman for Williams Aircraft, and they expected her to act accordingly. She couldn't smoke at all, or drink excessively, there was an allowance for wardrobe costs, and they were going to supply her with uniforms she could fly in. Everything was clearly spelled out. The contract was for one year, and they were offering her fifty thousand dollars for the year, with a renewable option for a second year, if both parties agreed, at a higher rate to be negotiated, within reason. It was the best contract Nick had ever seen, and an opportunity few men would have turned down. But the contract also made it clear, Williams Aircraft was looking for a woman. It could be an opportunity that would be hard to miss, in spite of the fact that she was going to be part pilot, part model. But he was still deeply suspicious of Desmond Williams.

'What do you think, Pat?' Nick looked up at him, curious about his reaction.

'She's staying right here. That's what I think. She's not going anywhere, and certainly not to California to live in an apartment.'

Cassie looked at him, blinded by anger over his not even telling her that Desmond Williams had come to see her. 'I haven't decided yet, Dad. I'm going to meet with him tomorrow morning.'

'No, you're not,' Pat O'Malley told his daughter firmly, and Nick didn't want to argue with him in front of Cassie. He thought there were plenty of possibilities for exploitation in the deal but it was still worth exploring. It would be fun for her, and she would fly incredible planes for the next year. It was very exciting. They were even testing planes for the military, and openly competing with the Germans, and the money she would make would take care of her for a long time. It seemed unfair to him to keep her from it, or not to at least consider it carefully.

'What about college?' Nick asked her quietly as her father stormed back into his office and slammed the door behind him.

'He said I could take classes there when I have time.'

'It doesn't sound like you will, at least not most of the time. When you're not flying, you'll be doing publicity.' And then, cautiously, 'Cassie, are you sure you want to do this?'

She looked at him thoughtfully. She had never wanted to leave home, but her life wasn't going anywhere. She liked hanging around the airport, and she had had a good time at the air show. But she didn't want to teach. She didn't want to marry Bobby Strong, or any of the other boys she'd gone to school with. What was she going to do with the rest of her life? She wondered sometimes. And even she knew that there was more to life than greasing and gassing her father's planes, and making short runs to Indiana with Billy Nolan.

'What am I going to do here?' she asked honestly.

'Hang around with me,' he said sadly. If only she could, forever. He would have loved it.

'That's the bad part of it, leaving all of you here. It would be perfect if I could take you all with me.'

'It says in the contract they'll lend you a plane to come home with now and then. I can hardly wait for that. How about bringing home an XW-1 Phaeton for a quiet weekend.'

'For you, I'd bring home a Starlifter if you wanted me to, I'd even steal one.'

'Now there's a thought. That might soften up your old man. We could use a few new planes around here. Maybe they'd like to give us one or two,' he joked, but he was feeling devastated at the thought of her leaving. She was so much a part of his everyday life, and they had done so much flying together in the past three years, he couldn't bear to think of her going to L.A. He had never expected anything like that to happen to her.

And neither had Pat. He had no intention of losing his little girl. It was bad enough that Chris had been talking about going to Europe to study architecture for a year or two. But that was still a few years away. This was now. And it wasn't Chris, it was Cassie.

'You're not going anywhere,' he reiterated again that afternoon, 'and that's final.' But in her mind, she was still going to make the decision. She talked to Nick about it again, and he could definitely see opportunities for them to take advantage of her, but there were so many benefits to her in the process that he wasn't at all sure it mattered. The money, the fame, the planes, the test flights, the records she could set, the benefits to her seemed almost endless. It would be impossible to turn them down. But he had no idea how she was going to convince her father.

She talked to Billy about it too, and he knew Desmond Williams from the West Coast, though only by reputation. Some people said he was a fair man, others clearly didn't like him. He had offered a job to a girl Billy knew from San Francisco and she had hated it. She had said it had been too much hard work, and she felt as though they owned her. But Billy confided to Cass that she had also been a miserable pilot. For someone like Cassie, it could be the opportunity of a lifetime.

'You really could end up another Mary Nicholson,' he said, citing one of the stars of the day. But Cassie couldn't imagine ever being that famous.

'I doubt it,' she said gloomily. The difficulty of the decision was driving her crazy. She didn't want to leave her home and family, but she also knew that she had very little else to stay for. And if she wanted to fly, Williams Aircraft was the place to be, no matter how many dumb photographs they took of her in her uniform, or how many interviews she had to give. She wanted to fly airplanes. And Williams had the best ones.

'Give it some thought, kid. You may not get another chance,' Billy advised her solemnly, and in their offices, Nick was telling Pat much the same thing. She was a brilliant pilot, and there was nowhere for her to go from here. She'd be hanging around the airport all her life, and flying dusty routes around the Midwest with a bunch of guys who would never fly as well as she did.

'I told you not to teach her to fly!' Pat roared at him, suddenly angry at everyone, Nick, Cassie, Chris, all of them. It had to be someone's fault. And the worst culprit of all was the devil himself, Desmond Williams. 'He's probably a criminal . . . going after innocent young girls, looking to rob them of their virtue.' Nick felt sorry for him. After all these years, and with almost no warning at all, he was about to lose his little girl. And Nick knew how he felt. He hated it as much as Pat did. But he also knew they had no right to hang onto her. She had to fly . . . like a bird . . . and it was time for her to soar with the eagles.

'You can't stop her, Pat,' Nick said quietly, wishing he could say how much it hurt him too. 'It's not fair. She deserves so much better than we have to give her.'

'That's your fault,' Pat boomed at him again. 'You shouldn't have taught her to fly so damn well.' Nick laughed at the reproach, and Pat helped himself to a slug of whiskey. He knew he wouldn't be flying that day, and he was deeply upset over losing Cassie. And he still had to tell Oona about Cassie's visit from Desmond Williams.

And when he did, that night, Oona was shocked. She imagined all sorts of terrible immoral things. She couldn't imagine Cassie living anywhere but home, certainly not in Los Angeles, living alone as a test pilot and a publicity spokeswoman for Desmond Williams.

'Do girls do that kind of thing?' she asked Pat unhappily. 'Pose for pictures and all that? Do they wear clothes?'

'Of course, Oona. It's not a striptease parlor, the man builds airplanes.'

'Then what do they want with our little girl?'

'Your little girl,' he said miserably, 'is probably the best pilot I've ever seen, including Nick Galvin, or Rickenbacker. She's the best there is, and Williams is no fool. He can see that. She put on a hell of a show two days ago, at the air show. I didn't want to worry you, but she almost killed herself, the little fool, pulled herself right out of a spin no more than fifty feet off the ground. I damn near died. But she did it, and never turned a hair. Did a lot of other crazy stunts too. But she did them perfectly. And he knew it.'

'Does he want her to fly stunts?'

'No, just to test planes, and set some records it she can. I read the contract, and it sounds fair. I just don't like the idea of her going away, and I knew you wouldn't either.'

'What does Cassie want?' her mother asked, trying to take it all in, but there was a lot to absorb in a short time. And they all knew that Cassie had to make a decision before morning.

'I think she wants to go. She says she wants to go. Or she says she wants the freedom to decide her own fate.'

'And what did you say?' Oona asked with wide eyes, and her husband grinned sheepishly.

'I forbade her to go, just like I forbade her to fly.'

'That didn't get you very far,' Oona smiled, 'and I don't suppose it will this time.'

'What should we say?' He turned to his wife for advice. He relied on her judgment more than he realized, and sometimes more than he wanted to. But he trusted her, particularly about their daughters.

'I think we should let her do what she wants. She will anyway, Pat, and she'll be happier if she feels she can make her own decisions. She'll come back to us, no matter how many planes she flies in California. She knows how much we love her.' They called her into their bedroom then, and Oona let her father tell her what they had decided.

'Your mother and I want you,' he hesitated and glanced at Oona for a second, 'to make your own decision. And whatever you decide, we're behind you. But if you go,' he warned, 'you'd better come back, and damn often.' There were tears in his eyes when he hugged her, and she clung to him and kissed her mother, who was crying.

'Thank you . . . thank you . . .' She hugged them both, and sat down at the foot of their bed with a sigh. 'It's been a hard decision.'

'Do you know what you're going to do?' Oona asked. Pat didn't dare ask her, but he already suspected what Cassie had decided as she nodded and looked at them with a shiver of excitement.

'I'm going.'

But leaving them was harder than she'd feared. She met with Desmond Williams at the Portsmouth the next morning, and signed the contract with him. She had black coffee and toast, she was too nervous to eat anything else, and the details of what he was telling her were so exciting that she kept getting confused. They were going to arrange a flight for her from Chicago to Los Angeles. There was an apartment, a car . . . uniforms . . . a chaperone when they felt she needed one . . . a wardrobe . . . escorts, a weekend place in Malibu she could use. A plane for her personal use, whenever she wanted to fly home. And the kinds of planes she had always dreamed about flying.

Her schedule began in five days. There would be a press conference, a newsreel, and a test flight of a new Starlifter right off the bat. He wanted her to show America just how good she was. But first he wanted to show her what his planes could do. He was going to spend the first two weeks with her, mostly flying.

'I can't believe it,' she said to Billy as they lay in the sun on an old unused piece of runway later that morning.

'You sure did get a big break,' he said enviously. But he was happy here, and for the moment he had no desire to go back to California.

'I'll be home in two weeks for a visit, no matter what,' she promised him and everyone else.

Her parents gave a big dinner for her the night before she left, with all her sisters and brothers-in-law, their kids, Chris, Nick, and Billy. Bobby wasn't there of course, although she had seen him two days before at Jim Bradshaw's wake. He had been talking quietly with Peggy, and holding one of her babies.

But it was Nick she stood next to all night, whom she couldn't bear to leave. She derived so much comfort and support from him, and had for so many years, that now she didn't know how she would survive without him.

The next morning everyone was at the airport when she left. Nick was flying her to Chicago in the Vega, and after she kissed her mother and sisters and Chris good-bye, she went over to her father. They both had tears in their eyes as he looked at her. He wanted to ask her to change her mind, but he would never do it.

'Thank you, Dad,' she whispered into his neck as he held her close to him.

'Be careful, Cassie. Pay attention. Don't ever get sloppy in one of those fancy planes. They won't forgive you for an instant.'

'I promise, Dad.'

'I wish I believed you,' he smiled, 'damn female pilot.' He was laughing then through his tears, and gave her another bear hug and then sent her off with Nick. Chris and Billy were waving from the runway too, when they took off, and Cassie heaved an enormous sigh. It had been harder leaving home than she had ever dreamed, and all she could think of were the people she was leaving there, instead of the places where she was going. And as she turned to look at Nick, her heart felt heavier still. She wanted to hold onto every moment she had with him.

'You're a lucky girl,' Nick reminded her on the way up, to take her mind off her family, who were still waving at her, 'but you deserve it. You've got what it takes, Cass. Just don't let those city slickers use you.' Desmond Williams was indeed pretty slick, but he also seemed both fair and honest. He had made no bones about what he wanted from her. He wanted the best pilot in the world, the best-looking, best behaved woman he could find to represent his product, he wanted new records set, and his planes unharmed and well viewed by the American public. It was a tall order, but she was capable of filling it for him, and he was smart enough to sense that. She was the best pilot he had ever seen, and good-looking too, and for him, that was a beginning. For Nick it was an end. But he

was more than willing to sacrifice himself for h
future. It was his final gift of love to her. First flying
and then finally, her freedom.

'Don't let them push you around,' Nick reminded
her; 'you're a great girl, and if they're too tough on
you, tell them to go to hell, and come straight home.
All you have to do is call, and I'll fly out to get you.'
It sounded crazy, but it was actually reassuring.

'Will you come out to see me?'

'Sure. Whenever I have a run out there, I'll take
a little detour.'

'Don't give the California runs to Billy then,'
she reminded him, 'be sure you do them yourself.'
He smiled at her admonition. She was suddenly
looking very nervous.

'I kind of thought you might like to see more of
him,' Nick said, speaking of Billy as nonchalantly as
he could, which meant not very. 'Was I wrong?' He
was relieved at what she had just said. But he had
already begun to suspect that Billy was a friend and
not a romance, just as her father had predicted. But
it was nice to hear her confirm it. What he wanted
from her was celibacy and total adoration, and he
knew how crazy that was. One of these days she'd
have to find a husband, and have kids, and he knew
it wouldn't be him, but he wished it could be.

'Billy and I are just friends,' she said quietly. 'You
know that.'

'Yeah. Maybe I do.'

'You know a lot of things,' she said wisely.
'About me, about life, about what matters, about

what doesn't. You've taught me a lot, Nick. You've made my whole life mean something to me. You've given me everything.'

'I wish I had, Cass, but I haven't done all that well myself. And no one deserves it all more than you do.'

'Yes, you have given me everything,' she said, her admiration obvious, her love for him even more so.

'I'm no Desmond Williams, Cass,' he said honestly. He had no pretense about him.

'Who is? Most people aren't that lucky.'

'You might be one day, Cass. You might become someone really important.'

'From being in newsreels and getting my picture taken? I doubt it. That's show-offy stuff, it's not real. I know that much.'

'You're a smart girl, Cass. Stay that way. Don't let them spoil it.'

They landed in Chicago after a little while, and he walked her to her plane, carrying her bag for her. She was wearing a navy blue suit that had been her mother's. It looked a little out of date, and it was too big for her, but it was hard to make Cassie O'Malley look anything but lovely. At twenty years of age, she took your breath away, with her shining red hair, her big blue eyes, her full bust and long legs, the tiny waist he loved to put his hands around when he helped her to the ground. But she was looking up at him now, like a child, and all he wanted to do was take her back to her mother. Her eyes were filled with tears, but she wasn't crying for them, she was crying for him. She didn't want to leave him.

'Come and see me, Nick . . . I'll miss you so much . . .'

'I'll always be there for you, kid . . . don't you forget that.'

'I won't,' she sniffed, and he put an arm around her and held her. He didn't say anything else to her. He just kissed the top of her head, and walked away. There was nothing else he could say, and he knew if he did, his voice would betray him, and he'd never leave her.

11

When the flight from Chicago landed in Los Angeles, there were three people waiting to meet her, a driver, a representative from the company, and Mr Williams's secretary. Cassie was a little surprised to see them. He had told her she would be met at the plane, but she hadn't expected to be met so officially, or by so many people.

On the drive to Newport Beach, the company representative gave her a list of appointments for the week, a review of their latest planes, a test flight in each of them, a press conference with all the most important members of the local press, and a newsreel. The secretary then gave her a list of social events she was expected to attend with and without any of several escorts, and a few with Mr Williams. It was more than a little overwhelming. But she was even more overcome when she saw the apartment they had rented for her. It was in Newport Beach, and it had a bedroom, a living room, and a dining room, all overlooking the ocean. It had spectacular views, and a terrace which surrounded it. The refrigerator was stocked, the furniture was beautiful, there were Italian linens in the drawers. And she was told that a maid would attend to her needs if she wished to entertain, and she would clean the apartment daily.

'I . . . oh, my Lord!' Cassie exclaimed as she opened a drawer full of lace tablecloths. Her mother would have given her left arm to have any one of them, and Cassie couldn't begin to imagine why she had them. 'What are these for?'

'Mr Williams thought you'd like to entertain,' his personal secretary, Miss Fitzpatrick, said primly. She was twice Cassie's age, and she had gone to school at Miss Porter's in the East. She knew very little about planes, but she knew everything there was to know about all things social, and the proper decorum.

'But I don't know anyone here,' Cassie laughed as she spun around, looking at the apartment. She had never dreamed of anything even remotely like it. She was dying to tell someone, or show them. Billy, Nick . . . her sisters . . . her mom . . . but there was no one here. Just Cassie, and her entourage. And when she looked in the bedroom, she found all her new clothes neatly arranged for her. There were four or five well-cut suits in an array of somber colors, several hats to match, a long black evening dress and two short ones. There were even shoes and some handbags. Everything was in the sizes she had given them. And in a smaller closet in the room, she found all her uniforms. They were navy blue, and looked extremely official. There was even a small hat that had been designed for it, and regulation shoes. And for a moment, she almost felt her heart sink. Maybe Nick was right. Maybe she was going to be a Skygirl.

Everything was so regimented and prearranged, it was all like a very strange dream. It was like being dropped into someone else's life, with their clothes, and their apartment. It was hard to believe this was all hers now.

There was a young woman waiting for Cassie too. She was neatly dressed in a gray suit, with a matching hat. She had a warm smile, lively blue eyes, and well-cut dark blond hair that hung to her shoulders in a smooth page boy. And she appeared to be in her early thirties.

'This is Nancy Firestone,' Miss Fitzpatrick explained. 'She will be your chaperone, whenever Mr Williams feels that one is needed. She can help you with whatever needs you have, handle the press, escort you to meetings and luncheons.' The young woman introduced herself to Cass, and gave her a warm smile as she showed her around the apartment. A chaperone? What would she do with her? Leave her on the runway when she tested planes? After seeing all of it, Cassie was beginning to wonder if she'd even have time to fly one.

'It's all a little overwhelming at first,' Nancy Firestone said sympathetically. 'Why don't you let me unpack for you, and then we can talk about your schedule over lunch?' Nancy said, as Cassie glanced around, feeling lost. She had noticed a maid in the kitchen making sandwiches and a salad. She was an older woman in a black uniform, and she seemed perfectly at home there. Far more than Cassie felt at the moment. She couldn't help wondering what she was going to do with all these people. It was obvious that they were there to help, and Desmond Williams had certainly provided every possible creature comfort. He had done more than that. He had provided a dream for her. But suddenly all she felt was desperately lonely among all these strangers. And Nancy Firestone seemed to sense that. That was why Williams had hired her. He knew her well, and had assessed instantly that she was just what Cassie needed.

'Are we going out to look at the planes today?' Cassie asked mournfully. At least that was something she understood, and she was a lot more interested in planes than in what she'd seen in her closet. At least the planes were familiar to her, and this glamorous lifestyle wasn't. She hadn't come to California to play dress-up. She had come to fly airplanes. And amid all the hats and shoes and gloves, and people who were there to take care of her, she wondered if she'd ever get a chance to fly one. Suddenly, all Cassie wanted was her simple life in Illinois, and a hangar full of her father's airplanes.

'We'll go out to the airfield tomorrow,' Nancy said kindly. She knew instinctively, and from everything Desmond had said, that she had to treat Cassie gently. This was a whole new world for her, and he had warned Nancy that she would be new to all this and probably a little startled at first, but she was also headstrong and independent. He didn't want her suddenly deciding that this wasn't for her. He wanted her to like it. 'Mr Williams didn't want to wear you out on the first day,' she smiled warmly, as they sat down and helped themselves to sandwiches. But Cassie wasn't hungry.

'You have a press conference at five o'clock. The hairdresser is coming here at three. And we have a lot to talk about before that.' She made it sound as though they were just two girls getting ready for a party, and Cassie's head was spinning as she listened. Williams's secretary, Miss Fitzpatrick, left the apartment then, after pointing to a stack of briefing papers Mr Williams wanted her to have about his planes. And she said tersely that Mr Williams would come by to pick her up between four and four-thirty.

'He's taking you to the press conference,' Nancy explained as the door closed behind Miss Fitzpatrick. She made it sound like a great honor, and Cassie knew it was. But it terrified her anyway. They all did. All Cassie could do by then was stare at Nancy Firestone in dismay and amazement. What was all this? What did it mean? What was she doing here? And what did any of it have to do with airplanes? Nancy read her face easily and tried to reassure her.

'I know it's a little startling at first,' Nancy smiled calmly. She was a pretty woman, but there was something sad in her eyes that Cassie had noticed the moment she saw her. But she seemed determined to make Cassie feel at ease in these unfamiliar surroundings.

'I don't even know where to start,' Cassie admitted to her, suddenly feeling an overwhelming urge to cry, but she knew that she couldn't. They were all being so good to her, but there was so much to absorb and understand, the clothes, the appointments, what they expected of her, what she had to say to the press. All she really wanted to do was learn about the planes, and instead she had to worry about how she looked and dressed, and if she sounded intelligent or grown-up enough. It was terrifying, and even Nancy Firestone's warmth was of very little comfort.

At first glance, it almost seemed as though they had brought her out for show and not for flying. 'What do they want with me?' Cassie asked her honestly as they sat looking out at the Pacific. 'Why did he bring me out here?' She was almost sorry she'd come now. It was just too scary.

'He brought you here,' Nancy answered her, 'because I hear you're one of the best pilots he's ever seen. You must be terrific, Cassie. Desmond doesn't impress easily. And he hasn't stopped talking about you since he saw you at the air show. But he brought you here because you're a woman too, and not just an amazing pilot. And to Desmond, that's very important.' In some ways, women were important to him. In others, they mattered not at all. But Nancy didn't explain that to Cassie. Desmond Williams liked to have women around when they served his purposes, but he attached himself to no one. 'He thinks that women sell planes better than men because they're more exciting. He thinks that women – women like you, that is – are the future of aviation. You're a terrific press bonus for him, and a great boost for public relations.' She didn't tell Cassie it was also because of her looks, but that was part of it. She was a real beauty, and if she hadn't been, she wouldn't have been there. Nancy knew he had been looking for someone like her for a long time, and he had talked to a lot of female pilots, and gone to a lot of air shows before he found her. This was an idea he had had for years, even before George Putnam discovered Amelia Earhart.

'But why me? Who cares about me?' Cassie asked innocently, still looking overwhelmed in spite of Nancy's encouragement and explanations. She still didn't understand it. She wasn't stupid, she was naive, and it was difficult for most people to conceive of a mind like Desmond Williams's. Nancy knew a lot about him, from her husband, before he died, testing one of Williams's planes, from the other pilots he knew, and from her own experiences since Skip had died. Desmond Williams had done a lot to help her. In many ways, he'd been a godsend. Yet there were things about him that were unnerving. There was a single-mindedness about him that was frightening at times. When he wanted something, or when he thought something would be good for the company, he would stop at nothing to get it.

He had been very good to her when Skip died, and he had done everything possible for her and her daughter. He had told her that she and Jane were part of the 'family,' that Williams Aircraft would take care of them forever. He had opened a bank account for them, and all of their needs would be provided for. Jane's education was assured, and Nancy's pension. Skip had died for Desmond Williams, and he would never forget it. He had even bought a small house for them. And drawn up a contract. She was to remain an employee of Williams Aircraft for the next twenty years, doing projects such as these, nothing too unreasonable, or terribly wearing. But projects that required intelligence and loyalty. He reminded her subtly of how much he'd done for them, and suddenly she knew she had no choice but to do what he wanted. Skip had left them nothing but debts and sweet memories. And now, after all he'd done for her and Jane, Desmond Williams owned her. He kept her in a pretty little gilded cage, he made good use of her, he was fair, or at least he seemed to be, but he never let her forget that he owned her. She couldn't go anywhere, she couldn't leave; if she did, they'd have nothing again. She had no real training for anything, she'd be lucky to get a job, and Janie would never go to college. But if she stayed, she could keep what he'd given her. And Williams saw something useful in her, just as he did in Cassie. And what he wanted he got. He bought it, fair and square, and he paid a high price for it. But there was no mistaking his ownership once the contract was signed, and the purchase complete. He was a smart man, and he always knew what he wanted.

'Everyone will care about you eventually,' Nancy said quietly. She knew more about his plans than she intended to share with Cassie. He was a genius at dealing with the press, and creating a huge concept from a very small one. 'The American public will come to love you. Women and planes are what's ahead of us now. Williams Aircraft makes the finest planes that fly, but to have that brought home to the public through your eyes, through *you*, is a very powerful thing. To have you identified with his planes will give them a special appeal, a special magic.' And Desmond Williams knew that. It was that that he wanted from Cassie. He'd been looking for years for a woman who embodied the American dream, young, beautiful, a simple girl with great looks, a good mind, and a brilliant flier. And much to everyone's amazement, he had finally found her in Cassie O'Malley. And what better fate for her? What more could she possibly have wanted? Nancy knew Cassie was a lucky girl, and even if there were strings attached eventually, even if he wanted lifetime fealty, he would make it up to her. She'd be famous and rich, and a legend, if she played her cards right. Even in Nancy's eyes, knowing just how tightly those strings could be tied, she thought that Cassie O'Malley was to be envied. Desmond was going to make her a star like no other.

'It's so strange though, when you think of it,' Cassie said, looking thoughtfully at Nancy. 'I'm no one. I'm not Jean Batten, or Amy Johnson, or anyone important. I'm a kid from Illinois who won four prizes at the local air show. So what?' she asked modestly, finally taking a bite of a perfectly made chicken sandwich.

'You're not "just a kid" anymore,' Nancy said wisely, 'or you won't be after five o'clock today.' She knew just how carefully Desmond had begun laying the groundwork from the moment she'd signed the contract. 'And just how do you think those other women got started? Without someone like Desmond to publicize them, they'd never have happened.' Cassie listened, but she didn't agree with her. Their reputations were built on skill, not just on publicity, but Nancy clearly believed in what Williams was doing. 'Earhart was what George Putnam made of her. Desmond has always been fascinated by that. He always felt that she was a lot less of a pilot than Putnam made her out to be, and maybe he was right.' Skip had thought so too, and as Nancy thought of it, she looked at Cassie sadly.

Cassie was intrigued by Nancy, though there was a lot she liked about her, and yet there was a part of her that seemed very removed. She seemed both enthusiastic about what lay ahead for Cassie, and maybe even a little bit jealous. She made it all sound like such a great deal, and she spoke of 'Desmond' as though she knew him better than she would ever have admitted. Watching her, Cassie couldn't help wondering if there was anything between them, or maybe she just admired him a great deal, and wanted to be sure that Cassie appreciated everything he had done for her. It was all a lot to absorb and analyze in one afternoon, as they sorted through Cassie's things, and Nancy tried to explain the importance of 'marketing' to her. Like Desmond, Nancy thought it was everything. It was what made people buy the products other people made. In this case, planes. Cassie was part of a larger plan. What she was, what she would be, was a tool to sell airplanes. It was an odd concept to her, and when the hairdresser arrived, she was still trying to understand it.

Nancy had told her about her husband by then, and Jane. She had explained, simply, that Skip had died in an accident the year before during a test flight over Las Vegas. She spoke about it very calmly, but there was something ravaged in her eyes when she spoke of him. In a way, her life had ended when he died, or she felt that way. But in a number of ways, Desmond Williams had changed that.

'He's been very good to me,' she said quietly, 'and to my daughter.' Cassie nodded, watching her, and then the hairdresser distracted both of them with her plans for Cassie's bright red mane. She wanted to give it a good trim, and have her wear it long, like Lauren Bacall. She even said she saw a similarity, which made Cassie guffaw. She knew Nick would have really laughed if he'd heard that, or at least she thought so. But Nancy took the hairdresser very seriously, and approved of everything she wanted.

'What exactly is it they want from me?' Cassie asked with a nervous sigh, as the hairdresser clipped and snipped with determination, and Nancy watched her.

She managed to glance at her new charge with a smile, and answered her as best she could.

'They want you to look pretty, sound smart, behave yourself, and fly like an angel. That about sums it up.' She smiled again and Cassie grinned at the description. Nancy made it sound surprisingly simple.

'That shouldn't be too hard. The flying part anyway; the behaving ought to be okay if it means don't fall down drunk or run around with guys. I'm not sure what "sound smart" is going to mean, that could be rough, and "pretty" could be hopeless,' Cassie grinned at her new friend. When she stopped feeling terrified over it, it was all very exciting. How did things like this happen? It was almost like being in a movie. There was a feeling of unreality to it that she just couldn't escape now.

'I get the feeling you haven't looked in the mirror in a while,' Nancy said honestly, and Cassie nodded.

'No time. I've been too busy flying and repairing planes at my father's airport.'

'You'll have to learn to look in the mirror now.' This was why Williams had so much faith in Nancy. She was tactful, ladylike, intelligent, she did what she was told, and she knew what was expected. Desmond Williams knew his people well and he always knew exactly what he was buying. He had never doubted for a moment that Nancy would be useful to him when they had signed their contract. 'Just smile and think that a few photographs won't hurt you. And the rest of the time you can fly anything you want. It's an opportunity almost no one gets, Cassie. You're very lucky,' Nancy encouraged her. She knew just what flying fanatics liked, and how to cajole Cassie into doing the things she didn't. Like the press conferences she was scheduled for, the interviews, the newsreels, and the parties Desmond wanted her to be seen at. Miss Fitzpatrick had even provided a list of escorts.

'Why do I have to go to those?' Cassie asked suspiciously about the parties.

'Because people have to get to know your name. Mr Williams went to a lot of trouble to have you included, and you really can't disappoint him.' She said it surprisingly firmly.

'Oh,' Cassie said, looking more than a little daunted. She didn't want to seem ungrateful, and she was already beginning to trust Nancy's opinions. It was all happening so quickly, and Nancy was her only friend here. And what Nancy said was true, Williams was doing a lot for her, and maybe she owed it to him to accept his invitations. Nonetheless, to Cassie, looking at the list, the social obligations seemed endless. But Desmond Williams knew exactly what he was doing. And so did Nancy.

When the hairdresser was finished, they all liked Cassie's hair. She suddenly looked more sophisticated, but it was both elegant and simple. And then the hairdresser helped Cassie to do her makeup. At three-fifteen she took a bath and at three forty-five, she put on her own underwear, and the silk stockings that had been left for her. And when she put on a dark green suit at four o'clock, she looked like a million dollars.

'Wow!' Nancy said, adjusting Cassie's blouse carefully and checking that the shoes matched her suit and handbag.

'Silk stockings!' Cassie beamed. 'Wait till I tell Mom!' She was grinning like a kid and Nancy laughed and asked if she had any earrings. Cassie looked blank and then shook her head. Her mom had a pair that had been her mother's, but Cassie had never owned any. Nor had her sisters.

'I'll have to tell Mr Williams.' Nancy made a note to herself. She needed a string of pearls too.

He had told Nancy exactly the look he wanted. No greasy overalls or work clothes. They could save that for one rare shot, maybe for *Life*, as part of a bigger shoot. But the look he wanted for her on the ground was pure Lady. Although all Nancy could think of as she looked at her was Rita Hayworth.

Desmond Williams arrived promptly at four o'clock, and he was very pleased with what he saw. He handed Cassie some photographs and details of the Phaeton and Starlifter she was going to fly that week, just so she could familiarize herself with them. And the following week she had some important tests to do on a high-altitude plane he was trying to convert for the Army Air Corps. But as she looked at the photographs, she couldn't help thinking of Nancy's husband. What if Desmond's planes were too dangerous, or the risks he wanted her to take were too great? Like all good test pilots, she tempered blind courage with caution. She wasn't afraid to fly anything, she decided, as she looked longingly at a photograph of the experimental Phaeton.

'You're going to let me fly *that*?' She beamed at him, and he nodded. 'Wow! How about right now? Forget the press, let's go fly.' She beamed at him happily, and suddenly all her earlier concerns and hesitations were forgotten.

He laughed. He loved the way she looked, and Nancy had let him know as he came in that Cassie had been completely cooperative with her. He was very pleased with both of them. This was the best publicity plan he had ever had, and he knew it. 'Never forget the press, Cassie. They can make or break your business. Or mine at any rate. We want to be very nice to them. Always.' He looked at her pointedly, and she nodded, still feeling completely in awe of him. He was wearing an impeccably cut dark blue double-breasted suit, and brilliantly shined handmade black shoes. His blond hair was perfectly combed and everything about him was starched, ironed to perfection, and spotless. He was the most beautifully groomed man she had ever seen. And she watched him with utter fascination. Everything about him was calculated and preconceived, thought out to the nth degree. But she was too young to understand that. What she saw was the finished product, what he wanted her to see. And that was what he wanted to teach her, to show the world just exactly the face he wanted. The smiling, sunny, small-town girl, who flew better than any man, and dared everything, and then came tumbling out of the cockpit with a big grin, and a shock of perfectly combed red hair. She was going to have every man in the country in love with her in six months, if it even took that long, and she was going to be every woman's idol. In order to do that, she had to behave perfectly, look spectacular, and fly planes that made the toughest pilots tremble. He had studied everyone else's mistakes, and he didn't intend to make any of the same ones. Desmond Williams was not going to fail, nor was Cassie, if he had any control over her at all. She was going to become the biggest name the country had ever seen. He was going to completely create her. And in her own small way, just by making her comfortable and keeping an eye on her, Nancy Firestone was going to help him. He wasn't going to have all his dreams shot down, by having Cassie get drunk, or swear at someone, or look like hell after a long flight or get involved with some bum. She was going to have to be perfect.

'Ready for the big time?' he smiled at her. She looked fine, better than that actually, but he could still see room for improvement. She had her own remarkable looks, but the suit was a little too big for her, and later Nancy would have to arrange for alterations. She was just a fraction thinner than he'd remembered, and her looks were stronger. She needed something just a little more glamorous, a little bit younger. And he hadn't realized when he'd met her in Good Hope that she had such a spectacular figure. He wanted to play to that without cheapening her, or even approaching the vulgar. But there was a look he wanted to achieve, and they were not quite there yet. But for a first run . . . she was doing fine.

And she did far better than he had expected at the press conference, in the large conference room next to his office.

Twenty members of the press had been hand-picked by him, the impressionable ones. The men who liked girls a little too much, the women. None of the great cynics. And then he introduced her.

She came in looking frightened and a little pale, and feeling a little strange in her new clothes and bright red lipstick. But she looked terrific in her new haircut and the green suit. And her natural good looks and warm nature sparkled.

She enchanted them. He had given them the information about the air show, and she was very humble about it. She explained that she had hung around her father's airport all her life, working on engines and fueling planes.

'I spent most of my childhood covered with grease. I only found out I had red hair when I got here,' she quipped, and they loved her. She had an easy style, and once she got used to them, she treated them like old friends, and they loved it. Desmond Williams was so ecstatic he couldn't stop grinning.

In the end, he had to tear her away. They'd have sat with her all night, listening to her stories. She had even told them about her father not wanting her to fly, and only convincing him after the night she flew in the snowstorm with Nick, to rescue the wounded at the train wreck.

'What did you fly, Miss O'Malley?'

'An old Handley of my father's.' There was an appreciative look from the knowledgeable members of the crowd. It was a hard plane to fly. But they knew she had to be good, or Williams wouldn't have brought her out here.

By the time she left them, they were calling her Cassie. She was totally unpretentious and completely ingenuous. And when she made the front page of the *L.A. Times* the next day, the picture of her was sensational, and the story told of a redheaded bombshell that was about to hit L.A. and take the world by storm. They might as well have written a banner headline that said, WE LOVE YOU, CASSIE! because it was obvious that they did. The campaign had begun. And from then on, Desmond Williams kept her very busy.

Her second day in L.A., Cassie 'visited' all his planes, and of course the press was there, and so were the Movietone people for a newsreel.

When the newsreel was released, her mother took all her sisters and their children to see it. Cassie wanted Nick and her father to see it too, but all she got was a postcard from Nick that said, 'We miss you, Skygirl!' which annoyed her. She knew what she looked like in the newsreel, in the uniform she had to wear, but she knew he had to be impressed by their planes too. They were nothing short of fantastic.

Her first flights were in the Phaeton they were working on, and then the Starlifter he had shown her. After that, he let her fly a high-altitude plane he was working on, to take extensive notes for their designers. She had gone to forty-six thousand feet, and it was the first time she'd ever had to use an oxygen mask, or an electrically heated flight suit. But she had been able to gather some very important information. Their goal was to convert the plane into a high-level bomber for the Army. It was hard work. And she scared herself once or twice, but she impressed the hell out of Desmond Williams. His engineers and one of his pilots had gone up with her, and they had described her flying as better than Lindbergh's. She was prettier too, one of them had pointed out. But that much Williams knew. What he was pleased to hear was that her flying skill was beyond expectation.

She set an altitude record her second week there and a speed record in the Phaeton three days later. Both were verified by the FAI and they were official. These were the planes she had always dreamed of.

The only thing that slowed her down was the constant press conferences and the photographs and the newsreels. They were incredibly tedious, and sometimes the press really got in her way. She'd been in Los Angeles for three weeks by then, and the press were already starting to follow her everywhere she went. She was becoming news. And although she tried to be pleasant to them, sometimes it really annoyed her. She had almost run over one of them the day before on takeoff.

'Can't you keep them off the runway for chrissake?' she shouted from the cockpit before takeoff. She didn't want to hurt anyone and they'd frightened her by getting so close to the plane. But the men on the ground only shrugged. They were getting used to it. There was a frenzy about her like none they had ever seen. Items were printed about her constantly, and photographs. The public ate her up, and Desmond Williams kept feeding them exactly what they wanted. Just enough of her to excite them and keep the love affair alive, but never so much that they tired of her. It was a fine art, and he was brilliant at it. And Nancy Firestone was feeding him all the little personal details they needed. And she continued to be a huge help to Cassie.

She was scheduled to do a commercial for a breakfast cereal for kids, and an ad for her favorite magazine, and when Nick saw it at the airport one day, he tossed it in the garbage. He was furious and railed at her father.

'How can you let her do that? What is she doing, selling breakfast cereal, or flying?'

'Looks like both to me.' He didn't really mind. He didn't think women belonged in serious aviation anyway. 'Her mother loves it.'

'When does she find time to fly?' Nick groused at him, and Pat grinned.

'I wouldn't know, Stick. Why don't you fly out and ask her?' Pat was surprisingly calm about all of it, now that she was out in California. The only thing he was sorry about was that she didn't have time to go to school, but she was flying some damn gorgeous airplanes. And he couldn't help being proud of her, though he never actually said it.

Nick had thought of flying out to see her several times, but he hadn't had time to get away. With Cassie gone, he seemed to be doing more flying than ever, in spite of the useful presence of Billy Nolan.

But business was booming at O'Malley's. And Pa recognized more than anyone that his daughter's sudden stardom probably hadn't hurt them. The reporters had turned up there a few times too, but there wasn't much fodder for them, and after a few photographs, and a shot of the house where she'd grown up, the wire-service guys had gone back to Chicago.

Cassie's life on the West Coast seemed to move even faster than her planes. She could hardly keep up with herself, between test flights, and short runs to check out new instruments on planes, and meetings with engineers to explain their aerodynamics to her. She had gone to a few development meetings too, to better understand what direction Williams Aircraft was striving for, and Desmond himself couldn't believe the extent of her involvement. She wanted to know everything there was to know about his planes. He was flattered and impressed, and he was enormously proud of his good judgment. He had inherited an empire, which he had doubled in size in an incredibly short timespan. At thirty-four, he was one of the richest men in the country, if not the world, and he could have had or done almost anything he wanted. He had been married twice, and divorced both times, had no children, and the only thing he cared about, or loved with any passion at all, was his business. People came and went in his life, and there was always plenty of talk about his women, but the only thing that mattered to him were his planes, and being at the very top of the aviation business. And for the moment, Cassie O'Malley was helping him get what he wanted.

He loved Cassie's remarkable understanding about planes, and her naive but clear perceptions about his business. She wasn't afraid to express herself, or even, when necessary, to confront him. He liked seeing her at meetings, liked the fact that she cared enough to be there. He was thrilled with the flying records she'd set too. She dared almost anything, within reason. The only thing she seemed hesitant about, and often balked at going to, were the social events, which he insisted were critical, and Cassie thought were nonsense.

'But *why*?' She argued constantly with Nancy Firestone. 'I can't stay out all night, and fly intelligently at four o'clock in the morning.'

'Then start later. Mr Williams will understand. He *wants* you to go out in the evening.'

'But I don't want to.' Cassie's natural stubbornness hadn't been left in Illinois, and she had every intention of winning. 'I'd rather stay home and read about his airplanes.'

'That's not what Mr Williams wants,' Nancy said firmly, and so far she had usually won the argument, but there were a few times when Cassie escaped her. She preferred walking on the beach, or being alone at night, writing letters to Nick, or her sisters, or her mother. She missed her family terribly, and the familiar people she had grown up with. And even writing to Nick made her heart ache. Sometimes she felt as though the air was being pressed out of her as she wrote to him and told him what she was doing. She missed flying with him, and arguing with him and telling him how wrong he was, or what a fool. She wanted to tell him how much she missed him, but it always sounded strange to her in a letter. And more often than not, she tore it up, and just told him about the planes she was flying.

She never mentioned her social life to him, or to anyone, it didn't mean anything to her, no matter how much they wrote about it in the papers. Nancy had found a lot of young men to escort her, most of whom knew nothing about planes, and some of them were actors who needed to be seen too. It was all about being 'seen,' and where she went, and who you were 'seen' with. She didn't want to be seen with any of them, and most of the time, they just posed for photographs and then took her home, and she would collapse into bed, relieved to be rid of them. The only thing she really loved about her new movie-star life was the flying.

And the flying was incredible. Sailing into the dawn in the Phaeton, breaking all records for speed, was the sweetest thing she had ever done, and probably the most dangerous. But much to her own surprise, with the incredible machines, she was honing her skills here. She was learning how to handle very heavy planes, learning how to compensate for any problems they had, signaling them to the engineers, and correcting them right along with them. Her input was valued here, her views, they admired the way she flew, and they understood everything she wanted. It was every pilot's dream to be in the seat she was in, and as long as she was in the air, there was no question about it. She loved it.

She was stepping out of an Army pursuit plane with a Merlin engine on it for more speed, one afternoon, after a short flight over Las Vegas to make some notes for the design team, when a hand reached up to her and helped her down, and she was surprised to see it was Desmond Williams. He was as impeccable as ever, and his hair blew a little off his face in the soft breeze and he looked suddenly less rigid, and much younger than the other times she'd seen him.

'Did you have a good flight?'

'I did. But the Merlin engine was disappointing here. It still didn't give us what we wanted out of this plane. We have to try something else. But I've got some ideas I want to kick around with the design team tomorrow. The plane was pulling to port on takeoff too, which is a real problem.' She always thought of his planes, and the problems they needed to conquer. At night she dreamed of them, and by day she pressed them to their limits. And as he glanced at her, he was more impressed than ever with what he was hearing. She was a gold mine.

'Sounds like you need a break.' He smiled at her, as she pushed her hair out of her eyes and smoothed her uniform. She still longed for her overalls sometimes, and the old days of never caring how she looked when she flew. To Cassie, it didn't matter. 'How about dinner tonight?'

She was surprised at the invitation, and wondered if he had something on his mind. Maybe he was unhappy with her. He had never invited her out before, and their dealings with each other had been strictly business.

'Is something wrong, Mr Williams?' She looked worried and he laughed at the question. She wondered if maybe he was firing her, and he shook his head and looked at her in amusement.

'The only thing wrong is that you work too hard, and have absolutely no idea what a miracle you are. Of course nothing's wrong. I just thought it might be nice to have dinner.'

'Sure,' she said shyly, wondering what it would be like to have dinner with him. He was so handsome and so perfect and so smart, and so rich, that he scared her. Nancy always said what good company he was, and how pleasant, and she seemed to know him well. But he still frightened Cassie more than a little.

'What do you like? French? Italian? There are some wonderful restaurants in Los Angeles. I imagine you've been to them all by now.'

'Yes, I have.' She looked him right in the eye, overcoming her shyness for a moment. 'And I wish I hadn't.'

'So I hear.' He smiled at her. 'I understand you've been chafing at your social schedule.' He looked almost fatherly for an instant, despite his age, and Cassie could see why Nancy liked him.

'That's putting it mildly. I just don't see why I have to go out every night if I'm going to fly for you at four o'clock the next morning.'

'Maybe you should get a later start,' he said practically, but she groaned in answer.

'That's what Nancy said. But flying is the important part. Going out doesn't matter.'

He stopped walking with her then, and looked down at her, and she was totally surprised to realize how much taller he was. In more ways than one, he was a man of great stature. 'It's *all* important, Cassie. All of it. Not just the flying. But the going out too. Look what the papers say about you . . . what the public thinks now . . . how much they love you . . . Look how much that means, how much access that gives you to them, how much weight you carry with the public after only a month here. They want to know what you eat, what you read, what you think. Don't ever underestimate that. It's the power of the American public.'

'I don't get it,' she said, looking like a kid, and he smiled at her. He already knew her better than that. He had an uncanny sense about people.

'Yes, you do,' he said quietly. 'You just don't want to. You want to play the game on your terms. But you'll get a lot more out of it in the end, if you play my way. Trust me.'

'Having dinner at the Cocoanut Grove, or Mocambo, isn't going to make me a better flier.'

'No, but it will make you exciting . . . glamorous . . . someone people want to know more about. It will make them listen to you, and once they're listening, you can tell them anything you want to.'

'And if I'm asleep at home in bed, they won't listen?' She grinned, but she had gotten his point, and she was intrigued by it, and he knew it.

'All they'll hear then, Miss O'Malley, is you snoring.'

She laughed at him, and he left her at the hangar a few minutes later. He had promised to pick her up at seven o'clock, and said he would tell her later where they were going.

She told Nancy who she was having dinner with when she got home, but she had already heard from Miss Fitzpatrick what her dinner plans were. There were no secrets at Williams Aircraft. And she suspected where he would take her, probably Perino's. Nancy helped her pick out a particularly sophisticated dress, and assured Cassie that it was just the sort of thing he really liked.

'Why do you think he wants to have dinner with me?' Cassie asked worriedly. She was still wondering if he was secretly displeased with her about something. Maybe he really was annoyed that she complained about going out at night, and wanted to scold her.

'I think he wants to take you out because you're so ugly,' Nancy teased. She had begun treating Cassie like her daughter. In some ways, Cassie was still a child, not unlike Janie. In fact, Jane and

Cassie had hit it off splendidly on the two occasions Nancy had invited her to dinner. She would have invited her more frequently, but Cassie never had time for a private evening. 'Now go wash your face and stop worrying. He's a perfect gentleman.' He always was, no matter what he wanted, business or pleasure. Desmond Williams had a brilliant mind and impeccable manners. What he did not have was a heart, or at least, that was what women said. If he did, no one had found it yet. But Nancy knew it was not Cassie's heart Desmond wanted. He wanted her loyalty, and her life, her mind, her judgment about planes, and her courage. It was what he wanted from everyone. He wanted everything, except what was really important. And in return, he would take care of her, in the ways he understood, with contracts and money.

Cassie was ready right on time, and he appeared downstairs in a brand-new Packard. He was a man who liked machines, and he had bought every exciting car there was to own, at one time or another. The Zephyr she'd seen him in back home had already been shipped to California.

She was wearing a slinky black dress Nancy had picked out for her, and black silk stockings and black satin platform shoes that made her look even taller. But he was still taller than she was, and her figure looked fabulous in the black dress. Her hair was piled high on her head in loose curls, and in the month since she'd been in L.A. she had learned to do her makeup to perfection.

'Wow! If I do say so myself,' Desmond beamed at her, as they headed toward the city, 'that's quite an outfit.'

'I was going to wear my overalls,' she grinned mischievously, 'but Nancy sent them to the cleaners.'

'I can't say I'm disappointed,' he teased back. They chatted easily all the way into town, about a new plane she knew he was designing. There were questions she had about the fuselage, and her queries about the design, as usual, impressed him deeply.

'How did you ever get to know so much about planes, Cass?'

'I just love them a lot. You know, like dolls, for some kids. I've just played with planes all my life. I put my first engine back together when I was nine. I've been doing it since I was a little kid. My father put me to work when I was five, but then he had a fit when I learned to fly. Engines were okay, but flying was for guys, not for women.'

'It's hard to believe.' He looked amused. To him, it sounded like the dark ages.

'I know.' She grinned, thinking fondly of her father. 'He's an adorable old dinosaur and I love him. He threw your card away that day, you know. The first time you came to the airport.'

'I thought he'd do something like that, he and his partner. That's why I came back.' He glanced over at her as they reached L.A. 'I'm glad I did. When I think what I would have missed. What this country would have lost. It would have been a tragedy.' He made it sound very dramatic, and she laughed. What he said was very frightening, but it always sounded like nonsense to Cassie. She knew her own worth, or she thought she did. She was a pretty good pilot, but she wasn't the oracle he pretended she was, or the genius . . . or the beauty . . . but Americans were already beginning to know different. They agreed with Desmond Williams.

'Where are we going tonight?' she asked with mild curiosity. She recognized the neighborhood, but hadn't guessed what restaurant. He told her they were going to the Trocadero.

And when they stepped inside, she saw instantly how glamorous it was, and how luxurious. The lights were dim, and the band was playing a rumba.

'You haven't been here yet, Cassie, have you?'

She shook her head, visibly impressed by her surroundings, and by being there with him. She was twenty years old, and she had never seen anything like that. 'No, sir,' she said, and he leaned closer to her and touched her arm.

'You could call me Desmond.' He smiled at her, and she blushed. It was odd being so friendly with him. He was so important, he was her boss, and he was so much older.

'Yes, sir . . . I mean, Desmond . . .' She was still blushing in the darkness as they were led to an important table.

'Of course Sir Desmond has a certain ring to it. I hadn't thought of that before.' He made her laugh easily, and he helped her order. He made her feel surprisingly comfortable, even though everything she was experiencing was new. But he never made her feel ignorant or foolish. He treated it all as a great opportunity for her, and for him. He always let her know how lucky he felt to be there with her. He was a master at the fine art of putting her at ease, and before their dinner came, he had her laughing and dancing, and completely comfortable with him. So much so that she danced in his arms as though she had been doing it for a dozen years, and when the photographers appeared after dinner, they got a wonderful photograph of her smiling up at him, as though she adored him.

She was uncomfortable about it the next day, when she saw the newspaper on her way to work. The photograph somehow managed to convey the impression that she was involved with him, which she certainly wasn't. But there was something very intimate about the way he looked at her, as she stood next to him, and yet nothing inappropriate, or even faintly romantic, had ever happened. He was her boss, the man who had 'discovered' her, and given her a great opportunity. And she was grateful to him for that. But there was absolutely nothing else between them. She wondered if anyone at work would make a comment about it, but no one did, until three days later when she got a call from Nick. He was flying a mail run to San Diego that night, and he could come up to see her the following morning. It would be Saturday and she was free to spend the day with him. She was supposed to go to a charity ball with one of Nancy's young friends that night, but for Nick, she'd gladly cancel.

'So, is Williams giving you the rush, or are you falling for him?' he asked bluntly after he told her he'd meet her at her apartment as soon as he came up from San Diego.

'What's that supposed to mean?' She was annoyed at his assumption.

'I was in Chicago yesterday, Cass. I saw the picture of you two in the paper. Looks pretty cozy.' There was an edge to his voice she'd never heard there before, and she didn't like it.

'I happen to work for him. And he took me out to dinner. That was it. He has about as much interest in me as he has in his engineers, so knock it off.'

'I think you're being naive. And those didn't look like work clothes.' He was angry and jealous, and sorry her father had ever let her come out here. The flying she was doing for Williams was too damn dangerous. But it wasn't just the flying he was upset about. It was the look on Desmond's face as he looked at her in the photograph in the paper.

'It was just a business dinner, Nick. He was just being nice taking me out. He was probably bored to death. And believe it or not, those are my work clothes.' She was referring to the slinky black dress she'd been wearing. 'My chaperone buys me everything, and they send me out every night like a trained dog to show off and get my picture taken. They call it public relations.'

'Doesn't sound like work to me. Or flying.' He was consumed with annoyance, and the loneliness of not having seen her in over a month. He had been aching to see her. But she hadn't had time to get home yet. It had shocked him to discover how much he missed her. He felt as though he'd lost a limb, or his best friend. And he didn't like the idea of Williams taking her out to dinner.

'We'll talk about it when you're here,' she said quietly, sounding more grown-up than she had at home. She had already changed, but she didn't know it. And she had already acquired a lot of big-city polish. 'How long can you stay?'

'I've got to be out by six o'clock. I've got to get back with some mail.' She was instantly disappointed, and she would have no excuse to cancel her 'date' to go to the ball to benefit children with infantile paralysis.

'Well, we'll make the best of it. Try and get here early.'

'As early as I can, kid. I'm not flying the fancy stuff you are.'

'You don't need 'em. The way you fly, you could fly egg crates and get more out of them than anything I see here,' she said warmly.

'Stop flattering an old man,' he said, sounding mellower than he had at the beginning of the call. 'I'll see you tomorrow.'

She could hardly wait, and she was up as usual at three-thirty, anxious for him to arrive. It seemed endless, before he rang her bell at seven-fifteen that morning. She flew down the stairs and threw herself into his arms so hard she almost knocked him down. He was stunned by the sheer beauty of her, and the force of her affection. She had missed him too, even more than she'd realized. She missed their confidences, and their long talks, and their flying.

'Hey, wait a minute, you . . . give a guy a chance, before you knock the wind out of me . . .' She was kissing him and hugging him, she was like a lost child who had finally found her parents. 'Hey, it's okay . . . it's okay . . .' There were tears in her eyes as she clung to him, and he held her so close he wanted never to let her go. She had never looked as good to him, or felt as good in his arms, and he had to force himself to step back and release her. He would have liked to stay that way forever. 'Wow . . . don't you look fine.' He smiled. He noticed the new haircut, and the makeup, and she was wearing beige slacks and a white sweater. She looked surprisingly like Hepburn or Hayworth. 'You don't look like you've been suffering,' he teased, and then he whistled when he saw the apartment. 'My, my . . . talk about hardship . . .'

'Isn't it great?' she beamed at him, and showed him around. He was very impressed, and he had to remind himself that this was the little girl he had known since she was a baby. This was not some movie star he had just met. This was Pat O'Malley's daughter.

'Looks like you got lucky, Cass,' he said fairly. But he also thought she deserved it. There was no reason for her not to have all this. But he still worried about her. 'Do they treat you right?'

'They do everything for me. Buy me clothes, feed me, I have a maid, she's the nicest woman you've ever met. Her name is Lavinia. I have a chaperone named Nancy, who buys me clothes and sets up everything for me, like all the events I have to go to, my escorts, the people I see.' She chatted on and Nick looked at her strangely.

'Your *escorts*? They set you up with men?' He looked startled, and none too pleased, as she served him the breakfast she had made for him, and fried some eggs while he waited.

'Sort of. But not really. Some of them aren't really . . . I mean . . . they don't really like women, you know . . . but they're friends of Nancy's, or she knows who they are. Some of them are actors who need to be seen, and we . . . I . . . we go to events, or parties and get our photographs taken together.' She looked embarrassed as she explained it to him, it wasn't the part of her work she liked best by any means, but after Desmond's explanation the other night, she was trying to accept it. 'I don't like doing it, but it's important to Desmond.'

'Desmond?' Nick raised an eyebrow as he ate the eggs she had made him. They were delicious. But the sudden mention of Williams in such familiar terms made him stop eating.

'He thinks public relations is the most important thing in business.'

'What about flying? Is that important to him, or do you even get to do that?'

'Come on, Nick, be fair. I have to do what they ask me to. Look at all this.' She waved around at the spacious modern kitchen and the rest of the apartment beyond it. 'Look what they're doing for me. If they want me to go out and have my photograph taken, I owe it to them. It's not such a big deal.' But he looked angry as he listened.

'That's bullshit, and you know it. You didn't come out here to be a model, or go to finishing school, Cass. And the only thing you *owe* them is to risk your ass testing their planes, and break any record you can. That's what you *owe* them. The rest is up to you, or at least it should be. Williams doesn't own you, for chrissake. Or does he?' He looked at her ominously, and she shook her head. He made her feel ashamed for going along with the plan. But she *did* feel she owed it to them, and she could also understand what Williams wanted. He wanted her to become a star, in order to further her career in aviation, and publicize his planes. That wasn't totally wrong, and the other women in aviation had done their share of it too. You did what you had to.

'I don't think you're being fair,' she said quietly.

'I think you're being used, and it makes me mad as hell,' he said, pushing his plate away, and then taking a sip of his coffee. 'He wants to use you, Cass. I can smell it.'

'That's not true. He wants to help me, Nick. He's already done a lot for me, and I just got here.'

'Like what? Take you out dancing the other night? How often has he done that?'

'Just that once. He was being nice. And he was trying to explain to me how important it is to do the social things too, because Nancy told him how much I hate it.'

'Well, at least I know you haven't been completely snowed by him. How often have you been out with him?' he asked pointedly, and she looked him square in the eye when she answered.

'I told you just that once. And he was totally polite and respectful. He was a perfect gentleman. He danced with me twice, and it just so happened that the second time he danced with me they took our picture.'

'And that was an accident, I suppose.' He marveled at her innocence. It was all so obvious to him. He had thought it a great opportunity at first, but only if their main focus had been on her flying. All this social nonsense, and going out, and courting the press told him something very different. It told him Williams was using her in a much broader sense. And he knew she was too young to understand it. And what more did Williams want from her? Did he want her for himself? As young and naive as she was, she would be inevitably dazzled by him and Nick suddenly realized he didn't like the prospect of that either. She was too young to be involved with a man like him. And besides, Desmond Williams didn't love her. Nick had said all this to Pat, and even suggested that Williams might have unsuitable designs on her, and he had tried to rile Pat up about it. But her father was under Oona's spell and she was completely enthralled to be seeing her daughter in newsreels. And Pat wouldn't have done anything to interfere with it. She was safe, she was well, and from what she said in her letters, they were treating her like royalty. She even had a chaperone, so how unsuitable could that be? And they were paying her a ransom on top of it. What more could she ask for?

'Don't you realize,' Nick went on, pressing her, 'that either the guy has the hots for you, or he set it up to look that way by taking you someplace where you'd be seen, and photographed. He probably tipped them off that he'd be taking you there. So now America has more than just a pretty face to fall in love with, they have a romance. Dashing tycoon Desmond Williams courts America's sweetheart from the Midwest, girl next door and flying ace, Cassie O'Malley. Cassie, wake up. The guy is using you, and he's great at it. It's working. He's going to make you the biggest name there is, just to sell his goddamn planes and then what?' That was what worried Nick. What if he married her? The thought of it made him feel sick, but he didn't say that.

'What difference does it make? What's wrong with it?' Cassie didn't see all the dangers he did.

'He's doing it for himself, for his business, not for you. He's not sincere. He doesn't give a damn. This is business to him. He's exploiting you, Cass,

246

and it scares me.' Everything about Williams, and
his plans for Cassie, scared him.

'Why?' That was what she didn't understand.
Why was he so against it? And why was he so suspicious of Desmond Williams? He had done only
good things for her, but Nick saw other dangers.

'Look what happened to Earhart. She got too big
for herself, she did something she never should have
. . . a lot of people thought she wasn't capable of
that last trip, and she obviously wasn't. What if he
sets you up for something like that? What if that's
what he's leading up to? You'll get hurt, Cass . . .'
He felt his heart squeeze as he thought of it, and all
he wanted to do was take her back to Good Hope
where he knew she'd be safe forever.

'He's not doing that, Nick. I swear. He has no
plans for me. At least not that I know of. And
I'm a better flier than she was anyway.' It was
an outrageous thing to say, and she laughed as she
said it. But Nick took her seriously, as he sat there
and watched her. She had gotten still lovelier in the
month she'd been away and she didn't even know
it.

'You are faster, as a matter of fact. And you don't
know what his plans are. This guy isn't doing it for
small potatoes. He's got his eye on the big time.'

'Maybe you're right,' she said, doubtfully.
Maybe he did have a world tour in mind. 'If he mentions anything about one, I'll tell you. I promise.'

'Be careful.' He frowned at her, still worried
about her, and lit a cigarette, as she closed her

eyes and sniffed the familiar fumes of his Camels. They reminded her of her father's airport . . . and of Nick . . . and the old days, of meeting at the airfield in Prairie City. Just sitting there with him made her desperately homesick, for him, and all the people she loved there. But she had missed him almost more than anyone.

In the end he relaxed, and enjoyed the fact that he was finally with her again. Being away from her for so long had almost driven him crazy. And day after day, he had thought of new plots that Williams might be hatching to exploit her. He finally stopped nagging her about Williams's plans for her, and the fact that she was being used, and they had a nice afternoon. They went for a long walk on the beach, and sat on the sand in the August sun, looking out at the ocean. It felt good just sitting side by side again, and they sat for a long time together in silence.

'There's going to be a war in Europe soon,' he said prophetically, when they started chatting again. 'The signs are as clear as that sun up there,' he said unhappily. 'Hitler won't be controlled. They're going to have to stop him.'

'Do you think we'll get into it eventually?' She loved talking to him about politics again. She had no one to talk to here. She was too solitary and too busy. Nancy talked to her about clothes, and her 'escorts' just posed for pictures.

'Most people think we won't get into it,' he said quietly. 'But I think we'll have to.'

'And you?' She knew him well. Too well. She wondered if that was what he was telling her. That he felt the same pull he had felt twenty years before. She hoped not. 'Would you go?'

'I'm probably too old to go.' He was thirty-eight, and not old by any means. But he could have stayed home if he'd wanted to. Pat was too old to fight another war. But Nick still had choices. 'But I'd probably want to.' He smiled at her, his hair flying in the salt air, as hers did. They were sitting side by side on the sand, their shoulders touching and their hands. It was so comforting to have him near her. She had relied on him for so long, and learned so much from him. She missed him more than anyone at home, and he had found that her absence was like a physical ache that still had not abated.

'I don't want you to go,' she said unhappily, looking into the blue eyes she knew so well, with the small crow's-feet beside them. She couldn't bear the thought of losing him. She wanted to make him promise he wouldn't go to another war in Europe.

'I couldn't bear it if anything happened to you, Nick.' She said it so softly he could hardly hear her.

'We take the same risks every day,' he said honestly. 'You can run into trouble tomorrow, so can I. I think we both know that.'

'That's different.'

'Not really. I worry about you out here too. Flying those planes is a risky business. You're dealing with high speeds, and heavy machines, and altered engines at unusual altitudes. You're looking for problems and trying to set records. That's about as dangerous as you get,' he said grimly. 'I keep worrying that you're going to crash somewhere in one of his damn test planes.' He looked at her seriously and they both recognized the danger. 'Besides, your dad says women pilots can't fly worth a damn.' He grinned and she laughed.

'Thanks.'

'I know what a lousy teacher you had.'

'Yeah.' She smiled up at him, and touched his face with her fingers. 'I miss you a lot . . . I miss the days when we used to hang out and talk on our runway.'

'So do I,' he said softly, and curled her fingers into his. 'Those were some special times.' She nodded, and neither of them said anything for a long time, and then they walked along the beach for a while and talked about family and friends back home. Her brother hadn't flown since the air show, and her father didn't seem to mind. Chris was busy with school now. Colleen was pregnant again. To Cassie, it seemed endless. And Bobby had started seeing Peggy Bradshaw. She was widowed and alone with two small kids, and Nick had seen him more than once, driving his truck to her little cottage.

'She'd be good for him,' Cassie said fairly, surprised at how little she felt for him. It was only amazing that they had been engaged for a year and a half. They never should have been. 'And now she'll hate flying as much as he does,' she said sadly, thinking of the horrifying accident at the air show. It had been so awful.

'You'd have been miserable with him,' Nick said, looking down at her possessively. He wanted to stay right here and protect her, from being used, or endangered.

'I know. I think I even knew that then. I just didn't know how to get out of it without hurting his feelings. And I really thought I was supposed to marry him. I don't know what I'm going to do,' she said, looking out at the horizon. 'One of these days everyone's going to want me to grow up and get out of the sky, and then what am I going to do, Nick? I don't think I could stand it.'

'Maybe you can figure out a way to have both one day. A real life, and flying. I never have, but you're smarter than I am.' He was always honest with her. Most of them made a choice. He had made his. And so had she, for the moment.

'I don't see why you can't have both. But nobody else seems to believe that. '

'It's not much of a life for the other guy, and most people are smart enough to know that. Bobby was. So was my wife.'

'Yeah,' she nodded, 'I guess so.'

They went back to her apartment after that, and talked some more. And he promised to tell her mother all about where she lived. And afterward she drove him to the airport. She got into the familiar Bellanca with him, and she almost cried.

It was like going home. She sat there with him for a long time, and then finally, she got out, once he was on the runway.

He looked down at her with the smile she had known and loved all her life, and she wanted to cry and beg him to take her with him. But they had their lives to lead. He had to get back to Illinois, and she had signed a contract with Desmond Williams. Most people would have died for what he had given her, but a part of her wanted to throw it all away and go home to where life was simpler.

'Take care of yourself, kid. Don't let them take too many pictures.' He smiled at her. He still didn't trust what Williams had up his sleeve. But he felt better about Cassie now that he had seen her. She had her head on her shoulders. And she wasn't being snowed by anyone. She also didn't appear to be in love with Desmond Williams.

'Come back soon, Nick.'

'I'll try.' His eyes held hers for a long time. There was so much he wanted to say to her, but this wasn't the time, or the moment.

'Say hi to everyone . . . Mom . . . Dad . . . Chris . . . Billy . . .' She was lingering, wishing he would stay. But she knew he couldn't.

'Yeah.' He looked down at her, wishing he could swoop her up with him. He had wanted to do that for a long time, but he knew now he never would. It wasn't in their destinies. All he had to do was learn to accept that. 'Make sure you don't run off with Desmond Williams. I'll come after you, if you do. Course your mama might shoot me for destroying your big chance.'

'Tell her not to worry,' Cassie laughed. That was one thing that she was sure would never happen. 'Tell her I love her.' And then as he revved up his engines, she had to shout at him. 'I love you, Nick . . . thanks for coming.'

He nodded, wanting to tell her he loved her too, but he didn't. He couldn't. He saluted her, signaled her to step back, and a few minutes later he was circling lazily and dipping his wings over the Pasadena Airport. She watched him as long as she could, until he disappeared, a tiny speck on the horizon.

12

Exactly two weeks after Nick's visit to L.A.,
Germany invaded Poland, and the world was
aghast at the destruction Hitler wrought there.
And two days after that, on September third,
Britain and France declared war on Germany. It
had happened at last; there was war in Europe.

Cassie called home to the airport when she
heard, but Nick was out, and her father was taking
some passengers to Cleveland. She had lunch with
Desmond that day, and he had spoken to the President only that morning. There was no question, the
United States was planning to stay out of the war
in Europe. And it was a relief to hear that.

She told him she wanted to go home anyway,
and Desmond lent her one of his personal planes
for the weekend. She had been planning to go home
for a weekend since July, and she never had any
free time. So this was the perfect opportunity, and
no one objected.

She landed at her father's airport late Friday night. She had left L.A. at noon, and got to Good Hope at eight-thirty local time. There was no one there, but it was still light as she came in on the long east-west runway, and taxied to a slow stop. She tied down her plane, and walked to the old truck she knew her father kept there. She hadn't told anyone she was coming. She wanted to surprise them. And she did. She slipped into the house after nine o'clock that night. Her parents were already in bed, and her mother almost fainted when she walked out of her room in her nightgown the next morning.

'Oh, my God!' her mother screamed, 'Pat!' He came running out of their room and grinned when he saw her.

'Hi, Ma . . . Hi, Dad . . . I thought I'd drop in and say hi.' She beamed at them.

'You're a sly one.' Her father hugged her with a broad smile, and her mother cooed and clucked, made her an enormous breakfast, and woke Chris, who was pleased to see her.

'What's it like being a movie star?' her father teased. He still wasn't completely sure he approved of it, but everyone in town seemed to think it was great stuff, and it was hard to ignore that.

'Nick said you live in a palace,' her mother said, as she looked Cassie over carefully. She looked healthy and well, and other than a good haircut and beautifully manicured red nails, she didn't look any different.

'It's a pretty nice place,' Cassie conceded with a grin. 'I'm glad to hear he liked it.'

They sat around talking about her life in Los Angeles for a while, and finally she got dressed and rode with her father to the airport. She was happy to see all her old friends, and Billy gave a huge whoop of glee as soon as he saw her. She put on a pair of old overalls, and walked out to work on one of the planes with him, and half an hour later she heard Nick's old truck drive in. And she looked up and grinned. But he didn't come out to the hangar to see her until lunchtime. She figured he was busy, and she'd see him in a while, but she was happy just knowing that she was near him.

'You guys sure start work late around here,' she teased when she first saw him. 'I'm at fourteen thousand by four A.M. every morning.'

'Yeah? How come,' he grinned, obviously elated to see her, 'you meet your hairdresser up there?' His eyes danced, and his heart was pounding as he looked at her. His feelings for her were beginning to worry him. Maybe it was just as well she was living in California. Lately, it was getting harder and harder to control what he felt about her.

'Very funny.'

'I hear the Movietone guys will be here at three' – he grinned at Billy and two of the other men – 'better get clean clothes on.'

'That'll be a nice change for you, Stick,' she shot back at him, and he leaned against the plane

256

she'd been working on with Billy, and gave her an appraising look. She looked better than ever.

'Did you bring your chaperone with you?' he teased.

'I figured I could handle you myself.'

'Yeah,' he nodded slowly, 'you probably could. Want to go have something to eat?' He invited her in an undertone, which was unusual. It was rare for him to take her anywhere. Usually, they just hung out together at the airport.

'Sure.' She followed him to his truck, and he drove her to Paoli's dairy. They had a lunchroom in the rear, and they made good sandwiches and homemade ice cream.

'Hope this'll do. It's not exactly the Brown Derby.'

'I'll manage.' She was just so happy being with him, she'd have gone anywhere and loved it.

He ordered roast beef sandwiches for them both, and a chocolate milk shake for her. All he wanted to drink was black coffee.

'It's not my birthday, you know,' she reminded him. She was still impressed that he had taken her out to lunch. She couldn't even remember the last time he'd done that. If ever.

'I figure you're so spoiled now, eating beef jerky in the back hangar wouldn't do it.' He shrugged, but he looked desperately happy to see her. They were halfway through lunch, and she noticed he wasn't eating much, when she realized there was more to it than just taking her out to eat.

He looked uncomfortable suddenly and a little worried.

'What's up, Stick? You rob a bank?'

'Not yet. But I'm working on it.' But the jokes ended there. He looked into her eyes and the moment she looked at him, she knew. And she said the words even before he did.

'You're going?' The words caught in her throat, and her milk shake soured instantly in her stomach when he nodded. 'Oh, Nick . . . no . . . but you don't have to. We're not in it.'

'We will be eventually, whatever they say. And I'll bet Williams knows it too. He's probably counting on it. He'll sell a lot of airplanes. I don't believe all this stuff about the U.S. staying out of it. And it doesn't matter if we do. They need help over there. I'm going to England to join the RAF. I made some inquiries, and they need all the guys they can get. I've got what they need, and no one really needs me here. They don't need a genius to fly mail runs to Cincinnati.'

'But they don't need you to get shot down in a war that's not yours.' Tears filled her eyes as she said it. 'Does Dad know?'

He nodded. He hated telling her. But he had wanted to tell her himself. He had told Pat that the minute he knew she was home, and Pat had agreed to let him tell her. 'I told him yesterday. He said he knew anyway.' And then he looked at her strangely. 'I'll be back, Cass. I've got a lot of years left to do this kind of thing. And who knows?

Maybe I'll grow up this time. There's a lot of things I never did with my life after the last one.'

'You can do them here, you don't have to risk your life in order to change what you don't like in your life here.'

'I don't like how lazy I've been, how easy I've made it on myself. I just cruised for the last twenty years, because it was easy. It went by so fast I forgot where I was. Now I'm here, I'm halfway through, or thereabouts, and I've wasted a lot of time. I'm not going to do that next time.' She wasn't sure what he meant, but it was obvious he had regrets about things he hadn't done, relationships he hadn't bothered with. He always thought he had time. And he did. But in some ways he had lacked courage. He had never wanted to get married again, or to care too much about anyone, or get too involved, or have kids of his own. He never wanted to risk anything on the ground. He didn't want to lose. But he didn't mind dying. It was an odd kind of cowardice peculiar to most of them; they were brave in the air, but on land they were terrible cowards.

'Don't go . . .' she whispered over the remains of their lunch. She didn't know what to say to stop him, but she wanted to more than anything. She didn't want to lose him.

'I have to.'

'No, you *don't*!' She raised her voice at him, and people turned around at other tables. 'You don't have to do anything!'

'Neither did you,' he suddenly raged back, 'but you've made choices with your life. I have a right to that too. I'm not going to sit here while they fight a war without me.' They took their battle outside and shouted at each other in the September sunshine.

'Are you so important then? You're the only flier who can do it right for them? For God's sake, Nick, grow up. Stay here . . . don't get yourself killed in a fight that's not yours, or even ours . . . Nick . . . please . . .' She was crying, and before he knew it, he was holding her and telling her how much he loved her. He had promised himself he never would, and now he couldn't stop himself any longer.

'Baby, don't . . . please . . . I love you so much . . . but I've got to do this . . . and when I come back, things'll be different. Maybe you'll be through playing Skygirl for Desmond Williams by then, and I'll have learned something I never figured out the first time. I want so much more than I have now . . . And, Cassie, I never figured out how to get it.'

'All you have to do is reach out and take it . . . that's all . . .' She was clinging to him, and he was holding her, and all she wanted suddenly was to go away somewhere with him and forget the war, but there was nowhere to run now.

'It's not as simple as all that,' he said slowly, looking down at her. There was so much he wanted to say to her, so much he didn't dare. And maybe he never would. He just didn't have the answers.

They walked back to his truck hand in hand, and when they got to the airport he drove to the hangar where they kept the Jenny. It was the plane he had taught her in, and she knew without a word where they were going. She got into the front seat, out of deference to him, since the instructor always sat in the rear seat, and a few minutes later they had done all their checks, and were taxiing down the runway. Her father saw them take off and he didn't say anything. He knew Nick must have told her he was going.

They reached the old airstrip, and Nick let her land, and they sat beneath their familiar tree. She laid her head against him, and they sat in the soft grass, looking up at the sky. It was hard to believe that there was a war somewhere, and Nick was really going.

'Why?' she said miserably after a while, the tears rolling slowly down her cheeks, and then her eyes met his and he thought his heart would break as he touched her face, and gently wiped her tears away with his fingers. 'Why do you have to go?' After all this time, he had told her he loved her, and now he was leaving, maybe even forever.

'Because I believe in what I'm doing. I believe in free men, and honor, and a safe world, and all those things I'm going to defend in the skies over England.'

'You did that once. Let someone else do it this time, Nick. It's not your problem.'

'Yes, it is. And I've got nothing important to do here. Even though that's my own fault.'

'So you're going because you're bored.' There was always a little bit of that in all men, that and the spirit of the hunter. But there were good motives there too, and she knew that. She just thought it was foolish of him to go now, and she didn't want him to get hurt. But he swore he wouldn't.

'I'm too good to get hurt,' he said, teasing her.

'You fly like shit when you're tired,' she said, not entirely believing it, but he laughed.

'I'll be sure to get lots of sleep. What about you?' he said, frowning. 'You're flying those damn heavy planes over the desert, don't think I don't know the chances you take testing them. Plenty of guys have gotten killed doing it, and they probably flew better than you do.' It reminded her of Nancy's husband when he said it and she nodded. She couldn't deny the dangers of her job, but she was good at what she did, and there were no Germans shooting at her over Las Vegas.

'I'm careful.'

'We all are. Sometimes that's not enough. Sometimes you just have to be lucky.'

'Be lucky . . . please . . .' she whispered to him, and he looked at her for a long time, and then without a word, he did what he had wanted to for so long, and never dared. What he had never let himself do, and thought he never would. But now he knew he had to. He couldn't leave without letting her know how much he loved her. He leaned down ever so gently, and kissed her. And she kissed him back as she had kissed no man before him. There had been no man . . . only a boy . . . and now, Nick, the man she had loved since she was old enough to remember.

'I love you,' he whispered into her hair, breathlessly, wishing there could be more, but he knew there couldn't. 'I always have . . . I always will . . . I want to give you so much, Cass . . . but I have nothing to give you . . .'

'How can you say that?' He broke her heart with his words. 'I've been in love with you since I was five . . . I've always loved you. That's all we need. I don't want anything else.'

'You should have lots more than that . . . you should have a house and kids . . . you should have a lot of things, like all the things they've given you in California. But they should come from your husband.'

'My parents never had fancy things, but they didn't care. They had each other, and they built my father's business from a pile of dirt. I don't care if we start with nothing.'

'I couldn't let you do that, Cass. And your father would kill me. I'm eighteen years older than you are.'

'So what?' She was unimpressed, all she could think of now was the fact that he loved her. And she didn't want to lose him. Not after all they'd been through.

'I'm an old man,' he tried to object unconvincingly, 'compared to you at least. You should marry someone your age and have a mob of kids like your parents.'

'I'd probably go crazy if I did. And I don't want a mob of kids. I never did. Just one or two kids would be fine.' With Nick, even the prospect of children wasn't as daunting as she had once thought it.

He smiled down at her tenderly as he listened to her, trying to talk him into something impossible. He was going to war, and she had a contract to fly planes in California. But he had to admit, he liked the sound of what she was saying. Maybe someday though he doubted it. He'd never be that lucky or that foolish. She deserved so much more than he could ever give her. 'I'd love to give you kids, Cassie . . . I'd love to give you everything I have to give. But I'm never going to have anything but a bunch of old planes, and a shack at the end of your father's airport.'

'He'd give you half of everything, and you know it. You've earned it. You built the business with him. You know he's always wanted you to be his partner.'

'It's funny, I was so young when I started out that I never wanted to be more than a hired hand, and now I'm sorry. Maybe you're doing the right thing with that crazy job of yours, Cass. Make a bunch of money, save it up, and come back where you belong with something to show for it. I don't have zip, and I never cared . . . until you grew up, and I realized

264

everything I didn't have to give you. That and the fact that I'm almost twice your age, and your father would probably kill me for this.'

'I doubt it,' Cassie said wisely. She was smarter than he was about her father. 'I've always thought he wouldn't be surprised. I think he'd rather I was happy than married to the wrong man and miserable.'

'You should be married to a man like Desmond Williams,' he said unhappily and she laughed at him. He hated the thought of it, but Williams had so much to give her.

'And you should be married to the Queen of England. Don't be stupid, Nick. Who cares?' She smiled at him, but he was unconvinced.

'You'll care, when you're older. You're just a kid. You think your sisters are so happy being poor, or your mother?'

'My mother never complains about anything, and I think she is happy. And maybe if my sisters stopped having babies every year they wouldn't be quite as poor.' Cassie had always thought they had too many children. One or two seemed sensible to her. But Glynnis was expecting her sixth, and Colleen and Megan their fifth, respectively. To Cassie it had always seemed excessive and a little scary.

He kissed her again then, thinking of the babies he would have liked to have with her, and never would. He would never allow himself the self-indulgence or the selfishness of marrying Cassie.

No matter how much he loved her, or maybe because he did. She deserved so much better.

'I love you, Nick Galvin. I'm not going to run away. Or let you run away from me. I'll come over and find you, if I have to.' And she would too. He knew it. 'Don't you dare. I'll have you kicked right out of England if I have to. And don't you dare let Williams talk you into some goddamn world tour. I just smell that's what he has in mind for later. Just like Earhart. But with the war in Europe now, you won't be safe anywhere, not in the Pacific, and not in Europe. Stay home, Cass. Promise me . . .' He looked desperately worried and she nodded.

'You too,' she said softly, and then kissed him, and he had to control himself as he felt her passion meeting his own. He lay on the ground next to her, holding her, wishing he could have her forever. 'When are you going?' she finally asked him hoarsely, as he lay next to her and held her.

He hesitated for a long time and then he answered. 'In four days.'

'Does Dad know?' She knew it would be hard on her father, and she was sorry now that she wouldn't be there to help him.

'He does. Billy said he'd take care of things. He's a good kid and a tremendous pilot. I think he just needed to get away from his father. Old flying aces sometimes make life difficult for their kids, but I guess you wouldn't know about that, would you?' She smiled, thinking of how impossible her father had been, but lately he seemed to have mellowed.

She sat up and looked down at Nick then, wanting to know where things stood between them. 'What does all this mean, Nick? We find out we love each other, and now you go? Now what? Now what am I supposed to do without you?'

'Same thing you did before,' he said firmly; 'go out and smile pretty for the cameras.'

'What does that mean?'

'Exactly what it sounds like. Nothing's changed. You're free. And I'm going to England.'

'Bullshit.' She raged at him. 'That's it? I love you, you love me, and nothing, so long, goodbye, I'm going to war, have a nice life, and see you when I get back. Maybe.'

'You got it.' He looked suddenly hardened, but he had made up his mind a long time ago, and he was not going to change it. For her sake.

'And then what? You come home, and if we're lucky we find each other again and start over?'

'Nope,' he said sadly. 'If you're lucky, we find each other again, and you introduce me to your husband and kids, if I'm gone that long, and if I'm not, then you just introduce me to your husband.'

'What are you? Crazy, or sick?' She looked outraged as she stared at him, suddenly wanting to hit him. What kind of game was this? But this was no game to him. Nick Galvin had promised himself years before that he wasn't going to let himself ruin Cassie's life just because he loved her.

'Haven't you been listening to me?' He was shouting at her in their secret place, but there was no one to hear them. They were safe here. 'I have nothing to give you, Cass. That's not going to change while I'm gone, and it's not likely to improve when I get back, unless I rob a bank or hit it lucky in Las Vegas. You're a lot likelier to make some money than I am.'

'Then go work for Desmond Williams,' she said angrily. How could he be so stupid!

'My legs aren't good enough. Look, you're a commodity to him. You're a genius in the air, and look good. You're a dolly who can fly; you're gold in the bank for him, Cass. I'm just another flyboy.'

'Why is that my fault?' she said angrily. 'Why are you taking it out on me? What did I do, aside from get lucky?' She was crying now, and shaking with rage and frustration. Why were men so unfair sometimes? It was exhausting being a woman.

'You didn't do anything. The trouble is neither did I for the last twenty years, except fly a bunch of old planes and hang out with your father. I had a good time, we did some good things, the best of which was teach you how to fly, or teach you not to crash may be more like it, you taught yourself to fly. But that's not enough, Cass. I'm not going to marry you with nothing in the bank and empty pockets.'

'You're a jerk!' she shouted at him through her tears. 'You own three planes, and you built my father a goddamn airport.'

'I may never come back, Cass,' he said quietly. That was part of it too. He was not leaving her hanging there, waiting for him. It wasn't fair, not at her age. 'That's a fact. I may be gone for five years. I may be gone forever. You gonna wait for that? With the life you have now, and the opportunities, that's what you want? To wait for a guy twice your age, who may leave you a penniless widow before you start? Forget it. This is my life, Cass. This is what I've made of it. This is what I want. I want to fly. No strings. No promises. That's it . . . forget it . . .'

'How can you say that?' she raged at him, but he looked at her very calmly.

'Easy. Because I love you so damn much. I want you to go out there and hit the jackpot. I want you to get everything you can get, fly everything you can lay your hands on, as long as you're safe, and I want you to be happy forever. I don't want to worry about your doing that, when I'm flying my tail off after some Kraut over the English Channel.'

'You're incredibly selfish,' she said angrily.

'So are most people, Cass,' he said honestly, 'especially fliers. If they weren't, they wouldn't do it. They wouldn't scare the hell out of the people they love, risking their lives every day, and killing themselves right under their loved ones' noses at air shows. Think of that. Think of what we do to the people we love.'

'I have. A lot. But you and I both know that, that's an advantage right there. We're even.'

'No we're not. You're twenty years old, for chrissake. You have a whole life ahead of you, and a great one. But I don't want you waiting for me. If I get back, and I win the Irish sweepstakes while I'm there, I'll call you.'

'I hate you,' she stormed, unable to move him or change his mind. Nick was as stubborn as she was.

'I figured that. I especially figured that when I kissed you.' He kissed her again then, and all her fury and her rage and her sorrow exploded through her in a wave of passion that he felt with equal flame. He would have wanted to change a lot of things, but he knew he couldn't. He wanted to hold her and make love to her till they both died of pleasure. But he forced himself to let go of her before it was too late to stop. And for both of them, that moment was coming closer.

'Will you write to me?' she asked breathlessly, a little while later.

'If I can. But don't count on it. Don't worry if you don't hear from me. That's just what I don't want. I don't want you waiting for me. It's the shortest love story in the world. I love you. The End. That's it. I probably should never have told you.'

'Then why did you?' she asked unhappily.

'Because I'm a selfish sonofabitch and I couldn't stand not saying it anymore. I had to fight myself not to say it each time we came here. And it almost killed me when I left you in California. I've needed to tell you for a long time. But it doesn't change anything, Cass. It's nice to know. Maybe for both of us. But I'm still going.'

They went round and round about it for a long time, but she couldn't convince him not to go.

And eventually, they flew back to the airport after kissing each other for a long time and nearly tearing each other's clothes off.

It was a long, sad weekend for her, and she spent a lot of time with him. And on Sunday afternoon when she left, it tore her apart as nothing before in her life had. Her father had sensed what was happening and he had talked to her before she left, but it hadn't really helped her. It made her feel closer to him, but it didn't change what was happening with Nick. She was in love with him, and he with her, and he was telling her to forget it. She didn't tell her father that in so many words, but he understood it.

'It's the way he is, Cass. He has to be free to do what he believes in.'

'It's not our fight.'

'But he wants it to be his, and he's good at it. He's a good man, Cassie.'

'I know that.' And then she looked unhappily up at her father. 'He thinks he's too old for me.'

'He is. I used to worry about him falling for you,' Pat admitted, 'but I think he'd do you a lot of good too. But you can't convince a man of that. He has to find it out for himself.'

'He thinks you'd be angry at him.'

'He knows that's not the truth . . . nor the problem . . . the problem is in his mind, what he believes, what he wants for you. You won't find the answers now, Cass. If you're lucky, he'll come back, and you can both work it out later.'

'And if he doesn't?' she asked sadly.

'Then you've been loved by a fine man, and you've been lucky to know him.' She clung to her father then, finding the lessons to be learned to be almost beyond bearing.

She said good-bye to her family at the house, and Nick drove her out to the airfield. He helped her untie her plane, and do all her ground checks, admiring the extraordinary machine she had brought with her, but as she revved her engines, he pulled her close to him and just held her.

'Take care of yourself . . .' she said, in anguish. 'I love you.'

'I love you too. Now be a good girl, and do some good flying. I can see now why they keep a chaperone with you,' he teased, to help lighten the moment. They had come very close to losing their heads more than once over the weekend.

'Write to me . . . let me know where you are . . .' she said, as tears ran down her cheeks like rivers.

He pointed to the sky with a sad smile. His eyes told her everything she needed to know, and he could no longer say to her. He was leaving her, and if he came back, who knew what the future held. There were no promises, no sure things. There was only now. And right now, at this very moment, he loved her as he had never loved anyone and never would again.

'Take it easy, Cass,' he said softly, as he stepped away from her. 'Keep it high.' He was smiling, but there were tears in his eyes too. 'I love you,' he mouthed, and then left the plane. She looked at him for a long painful moment, and her eyes were so full of tears she could hardly see as she taxied down the runway. It was the only time in her entire life when there was no thrill as she left the ground, and she slowly dipped her wings to him, and then headed west, as he watched her.

13

The first weeks after Nick was gone were difficult for Cass. Her mind was constantly on him, but she had to force herself to concentrate on other things when she was flying. She seemed to fly all the time, from morning till night, and in the month of September she set two more records in the Phaeton. By October, Poland had fallen completely into German hands. And Cassie knew that Nick was at Hornchurch Aerodrome, and assigned to a unit of fighter pilots as an instructor. He was training young pilots to do what he had done in the last war, and for the moment he wasn't flying missions himself. Her father claimed that his age might keep him out of it, but with his extraordinary reputation, he thought it unlikely. But at least for the moment, he was safe. He hadn't written to her, but he had gotten word to her father through another pilot, which was something.

Her life in Los Angeles was as hectic as usual,

and the photographers and social events seemed to be thicker than ever. But Desmond kept insisting on the importance of it, and he took her to lunch from time to time, to discuss his planes and her observations of them, which always astounded him, but also to encourage her about the importance of public relations. Their conversations were almost always about his planes, and he was always very businesslike with her. There was a mutual respect there too, and at times he seemed a little more friendly. But the only thing that ever really interested him was his business. And for someone who had such a strong interest in publicity, she was surprised that she so seldom saw anything personal about him in the papers.

He continued to be very generous with her, giving her a large bonus each time she set a record. And he encouraged her to fly all his planes. On Thanksgiving she went home in a Williams P-6 Storm Petrel; she was sleek and painted black and the sheer beauty of her totally amazed her father. She took him up in it, and offered Chris a ride too, but he said he was too busy. He had a new girlfriend in Walnut Grove, and he didn't want to waste any time at the airport. But Billy was more than eager to go with her. He had heard from Nick. It seemed as though everyone had, except Cassie. It was almost as though he were proving a point. But she had long since understood the message. It was just as he had said it would be in spite of all her pleas and protests. 'I love you. So long. End of Story.' And there was nothing she could do about it now, if ever. She talked to Billy about it late one night, and he told her Nick was the greatest guy he'd ever known, but the epitome of a loner.

'I think he's crazy about you, Cass. I saw it the first time I met you. I figured you knew it too, and I was surprised you didn't. But he's scared, I guess. He's not used to taking anyone with him. And he figured maybe he wouldn't come back this time. He didn't want to do that to you.'

'Great. So he tells me he loves me, and then dumps me.'

'He figures you should marry some hotshot in L.A. He said so.'

'Nice of him to decide that,' she complained, but there was nothing she could do. Talking to Billy helped. He was like another brother, except one who liked to fly as much as she did. He was planning to come out and see her in L.A. sometime before Christmas.

And when she left again, she promised to come home for the Christmas holidays. Until then, she had a lot to do. Williams was introducing two new planes, and she was an important part of those introductions. She was going to be doing test flights, and interviews, and posing for photographs. But she figured that by Christmas the worst of it would be all over. Desmond had already agreed to give her a week off between Christmas and New Year's.

The Russians invaded Finland the day she went back after the Thanksgiving holiday, and it was obvious that things were not going well in Europe. It worried her for Nick, but with her grueling schedule, she scarcely had time to keep up with the news.

She was relieved to know that, for the moment, Nick was just an instructor.

When Billy came out to visit her in mid-December, she took him up in their best planes. He was stunned by what she'd been flying.

'You've got some great stuff out here, Cass.' His eyes had lit up like Christmas when he saw the maritime patrol variant developed by Williams from an earlier transport, borrowing innovations from Howard Hughes's fabulous racer.

'They'd probably give you a job as a test pilot if you ever wanted it,' she suggested to him, but her father would probably be outraged by her luring him away. Pat was relying on him now, and Billy knew that.

'I couldn't leave him,' Billy smiled. 'Just bring one of these gals home for a visit now and then, and that'll keep me happy.'

But she introduced him to Desmond Williams anyway, and told him what an extraordinary pilot Billy was the next time they had lunch in his office. He showed some interest in him, but his real interest was in Cassie. He couldn't imagine another pilot who flew as well as she did. They talked a lot about the war in Europe these days too. He was hoping to sell planes abroad, and like Nick, he assumed America would get involved eventually.

'I think we'll get shamed into it by our allies,' he said calmly. It was exactly what had happened last time.

'I've got a friend over there now,' she admitted to him one day. 'He signed up as a fighter instructor for the RAF. He's stationed at Hornchurch.' It was one of those rare days when they talked about something more than business.

'He sounds like a noble man,' Desmond commented as a waiter poured coffee for them in his private office.

'No, just another fool like the rest of us,' she said ruefully and he laughed. They both knew that fliers were a special breed of people.

'And what about you, Cass? No grandiose ideas of noble plans? You've accomplished a great deal since you've been here. Does that give you any bigger ideas?' She wasn't sure what he had in mind, but he seemed to have an idea he wasn't ready to discuss yet.

'Not for the moment,' she said honestly. 'I'm happy here. You've been very good to me, Desmond.'

He couldn't help notice that she had grown up a lot in the five months since she'd been in Los Angeles. She looked very sophisticated, and very polished, in part thanks to Nancy's help. But Cassie had her own ideas about clothes now. She handled herself beautifully with the press, and the public adored her. Not enough of them knew her yet, for his taste, but in the spring, he wanted her to start doing a tour of local air shows. She wondered sometimes what difference that kind of publicity made and if it really sold airplanes. Most air shows seemed so local and small scale. But it was important to him, and he reminded her that he expected her to make a tour of several hospitals and orphanages for a Christmas newsreel.

'You should have time to do that before you go home,' he said firmly.

'Don't worry, I'll take care of it.' She smiled at him and he laughed. Her eyes were always full of mischief, and he found it very appealing. He knew how much she disliked his publicity ideas, and he always wondered if she would balk at them. But in the end, she always did what was expected of her.

'In January, we're flying to New York, by the way,' he said casually, but this time with a glimmer in his own eye. 'For a meeting between the queen of the cockpit, Cassie O'Malley, and the illustrious Charles Lindbergh.' She knew her father would be thrilled with that piece of news when she told him. Even she was impressed by that one, as she listened to Desmond explain it to her.

They were taking Desmond's brand-new plane, and Cassie was to fly a brief demonstration for Lindbergh, and then he would give both her and the plane his endorsement. He had already promised it to Desmond, and they were old friends. Like

Desmond, Charles Lindbergh knew the value of public relations. And besides Lindy was interested in meeting Desmond's legendary young pilot.

She managed to do her hospital tour as planned, and Desmond was extremely pleased with what they got of it on the newsreel. And then she went home on schedule, for a week. Her mother had influenza, but she managed to be up and around long enough to cook Christmas dinner for all of them, and her father was in fine form. Billy had gone home too, to see his dad in San Francisco. And Chris was all wrapped up in Jessie, his new girl in Walnut Grove, so there was no one for her to play with. But she was happy anyway. She went for a long walk on Christmas Eve, and to church that night with her sisters. She stopped at the airfield on the way back, to check on her plane. She always felt even more responsible for the ones she brought home, they were so valuable and they weren't hers. But it was fun to fly them.

She checked that no one had disturbed anything, that the windows were closed, and the engine was protected. Her father had cleared his best hangar for her, and she knew that all his friends would come to see the plane she'd flown home. Little by little, she was becoming a legend.

After she'd checked on the plane, she walked slowly back into the night air. It was cold and brisk, and there was snow on the ground. It reminded her of Christmases when she was a little girl, and she had come to the airport with Nick and her father.

It was hard not to think of him here. There were so many memories that Nick was a part of. She looked up at the sky, thinking of him, and almost jumped out of her skin when she heard a voice behind her whisper 'Merry Christmas.' She wheeled to see who it was, and gave a gasp when she saw him standing there in uniform, like a vision.

'Oh, my God . . .' She stared at him in disbelief. 'What are you doing here?' she asked Nick breathlessly as she flung herself toward him and he caught her.

'Should I go back?' he asked with a grin, looking handsomer than ever, as he held her and she hugged him.

'No. Never,' she answered as he clung to her as powerfully as she held him. He had never been happier than at this moment as he kissed her.

They were golden days. They talked, they laughed, they flew, they went for long walks, they even went ice skating on the pond, and to see *Ninotchka* with Garbo at the movies. It was all like a dream. Their time together was so precious and so short, it was idyllic. And although they sat and kissed and held each other for hours sometimes, he was adamant that no one know what had changed between them.

'My father knows anyway. What difference does it make?' She was always so matter-of-fact, but as usual he was insistent, and convinced he was right.

'I don't want to ruin your reputation.'

'By kissing me? How old-fashioned can you get?'

'Never mind. The whole world doesn't need to know you've fallen in love with an old man.'

'I'll be sure not to tell them your age.'

'Thanks.' But as usual, he was very stubborn. There were no ties, no promises, no future held out to her. There was only now, and the infinite exquisite beauty and pain of the moment. They kissed constantly whenever they were alone, and they were hard-pressed not to go any further. But the last thing he wanted to do now was leave her pregnant.

The day before he had to leave, he brought up the subject of the war. He said conditions in England were good, and so far he hadn't flown a single mission.

'They'll probably never put me out there at my age, and you'll get me back like a bad penny at the end of the war. And then you'll be sorry, my friend,' he warned her. But that was all she wanted.

'And then what?' She tried to pin him down, but he wouldn't let her.

'Then I talk you into marrying Billy, which you should be doing yourself, not an old goat like me.' At thirty-eight, he was hardly an old goat, but no matter what she felt, he was still convinced he was too old for Cassie. She wondered sometimes if he hadn't seen her in diapers if he might have felt different.

'I don't happen to love Billy, if you care,' she explained with a grin, as they walked by the lake.

'That's absolutely immaterial. You'll have to marry him anyway.'

'Thank you.'

'Don't mention it.'

'Should we warn him?' Cassie loved being with him, he always made her laugh, even when he made her cry, which he had done a lot lately.

'Eventually. Might as well let the boy relax for a while. Besides he might bolt if he knew.'

'How flattering!' She gave him a shove and he almost tripped on the ice. He gave her a push then too, and a few minutes later they were rolling in the snow again and kissing.

They were perfect days, and over too soon, almost as soon as they had begun. She flew him to Chicago, and he took the train to New York, and from there he would return to England.

'Will you be able to come back again soon?' she asked as they stood waiting for the train in Union Station.

'I don't know. That was kind of a fluke. I'll have to see what happens once I'm back at Hornchurch.' She nodded. She understood that.

There were no promises again, only tears, and the aching feeling of knowing that he might not come back and this could be the last time she ever saw him. He kissed her one last time before he left, and she ran beside the train for as long as she could, and then he was gone, and she stood alone in the station.

It was a lonely flight back to Good Hope, and the

next day she flew back to L.A., and her apartment. She was desperately lonely for him this time, and tired of the ache of worry and not knowing if he was all right, if he'd be back, and if they'd ever find a way to be together. She wondered if he'd ever get over the objections to the difference in their ages, it was so hard to know what would happen.

In January, she flew to New York with Desmond and his new plane to demonstrate it for Charles Lindbergh. There were lots of photographs and newsreels too. And after that, it was a long, lonely spring for her, despite the long flights, the constant tests, the checking and rechecking of new equipment. She was racking up quite a reputation, for her skill and passion for flying. And she had begun meeting some of the women she had only read about for years, like Pancho Barnes and Bobbi Trout. They gave her whole life new dimension. She spent time with Nancy and Jane Firestone too. It was fun being with them, although she realized eventually that she never became as close friends with Nancy as she had hoped to. Maybe there was just too much difference in their ages.

She had dinner again with Desmond one night in April, and he surprised her by asking if she was involved with anyone. Given the businesslike relationship they shared, it struck her as an odd question, but she told him that she wasn't, and Nancy was still lining up her 'escorts.'

'I'm surprised,' he said pleasantly.

'Just too ugly I guess,' Cassie smiled at him,

and he couldn't help laughing as she joked. And in truth, she looked more spectacular than ever. If anything, she had gotten more beautiful, and Desmond had never been as pleased with any of his plans or projects.

'Maybe you work too hard,' he said thoughtfully, looking her straight in the eye. 'Or is there someone at home?'

'Not anymore,' she smiled sadly. 'He's in England. And he's not mine,' she added quietly. 'He's his own. Very much so.'

'I see. That might change.' Desmond was intrigued by her, she was as good as any man at what she did, better perhaps, and far more serious about her work. She didn't seem to care at all about her social life, and even less about becoming famous. It was part of her charm, and part of what the public sensed, and why they loved her. In spite of her astonishing success and visibility in the past nine months, she had somehow managed to stay modest. He didn't know many women like that. He liked a lot of things about her, and he was surprised he did. It was rare for him to take a personal interest in his employees, except for unusual cases, like Nancy's.

'War does funny things to men,' he said. 'Sometimes they change . . . sometimes they realize what's important to them.'

'Yes,' Cassie said with a wistful smile, 'their bombers. I think fliers are a different breed of men. At least all the ones I know are. The women too. They're all a little crazy.'

'It's part of the charm.' He smiled at her, suddenly looking more relaxed than she'd ever seen him.

'I'll have to remember that,' she said, sipping her wine, and watching him. She wondered what made him tick, but there was no way of knowing. Even when he was being friendly, he was completely guarded. There was really no way of knowing him. He was careful to keep his distance. Nancy had told her that about him, and Cassie finally understood it.

'And then there are the rest of us.' He smiled at her again. 'Those who live on the ground. So simple, and so lowly.'

'I don't think I'd say that,' she said quietly, as he watched her. 'More sensible perhaps. More reasonable about what life is all about, more directed toward their goals. There's a lot of merit to that, I think.'

'And you? Where do you fall in all that, Cass? Up in the sky, or on the ground? You seem to live very successfully in both worlds, from what I've noticed.' But the sky was her preference, she lived to fly, and he knew that. All she did on the ground was pass time until she could get back in the air, and fly with the birds again.

And then he decided to spring his idea on her. It was still too soon, but not for the seed to be sown, like a precious baby. 'What would you think of a world tour?' he asked cautiously, and she looked up, startled. Nick had warned her of that, and its dangers. He had said that that was what Williams had in mind all along. But how could he have known? She looked puzzled as she struggled for an answer.

'Now? Wouldn't it be awfully difficult?' The Germans had already invaded Norway and Denmark, and they were advancing toward Belgium and the Netherlands at that moment. 'A lot of Europe would be inaccessible to us, and the Pacific is awfully sensitive.' It had affected Earhart's route, and that had been three years before. Things were so much worse now.

'We could probably get around it. It wouldn't be easy, but we could do it, if we had to. But I've always thought that was the ultimate. The round the world trip. If you did it right. It has to be carefully planned and brilliantly handled. And it's not for now of course. It would take at least a year of planning.'

'I've always thought it would be fantastic, but right now or even a year from now, I can't imagine how we'll do it.' She was intrigued by the idea, but nervous about it too, and mindful of Nick's warnings. But Desmond seemed so sure of what he wanted.

'Let me worry about that, Cass,' he said, touching her hand, looking excited for the first time since she'd known him. It was his dream. And he had shared it with her. 'All you'd have to do is fly the very best plane in the sky. The rest is mine to worry about. If you'd ever want to do it.'

'I'd have to give it some thought.' It would certainly change her life. Her name would be a household word forever, just like Cochran or Lindbergh, Elinor Smith, or Helen Richey.

'Let's talk about it again this summer.' They both knew her contract would be up for renewal then. And there was no reason why she wouldn't want to renew with them. She made no secret of the fact that she loved what she was doing. But the world tour was something else. It was her dream too, but Nick had been so adamant about her not doing it for Williams. '. . . He's using you . . .' she could still hear his words . . . 'Cassie . . . don't do it . . . it scares me . . .' But why not? What was wrong with it? And why shouldn't she? Nick was doing what he wanted, wasn't he? And most of the time, he didn't even bother to write her. She had only had two letters from him since Christmas. And they only told her what he was doing, and not what he felt for her. He was doing nothing to maintain his relationship with her. He thought it wasn't right for her, and he refused to encourage her, or ask her to wait for him. His letters were like bulletins from flight school.

Desmond had taken her dancing that night, and all he talked about as they whirled around the floor at Mocambo was his world tour. Now that he had shared it with her, he couldn't stop talking about it, and he felt sure that she would be as excited about it as he was.

He mentioned it to her again the following week,

not to press her about it, but just in passing, as though it were a secret they shared, a goal they both longed for. It was obvious that this was something that meant a great deal to him, and now that he had shared it with her, he felt closer to her.

And given how busy he was, Cassie was startled when he asked if he could take her out for her twenty-first birthday. She was surprised he knew, but he had armies of people to remind him of minor details. Details were important to him, the smallest element of anything fascinated him, and he thought it was the key between the ordinary and perfection.

Not having anyone special to celebrate with, Cassie was pleased he remembered. He took her to the Victor Hugo Restaurant, and then dancing at Ciro's afterward for an evening which touched her deeply. He had a birthday cake for her at the restaurant and served champagne both there and at Ciro's. He had obviously checked with Nancy Firestone about all of Cassie's favorite things, and the entire meal was planned around them. Her favorite dinner, her favorite cake, her favorite songs. She felt like a little girl having a magical birthday. And afterward he gave her a diamond pin in the form of a plane, with the number twenty-one on its wings, and the word Cassie on its side. He had had it made months before by Cartier. He told her that after she opened it, and she couldn't believe the trouble he'd gone to.

'How could you do that?' She blushed as she looked at it. She had never seen anything as beautiful, and somehow felt she didn't deserve it.

But he was looking at her very seriously. She had only seen him look that way at a plane that he was studying before he redesigned it. 'I always knew you'd be very important to me someday. I knew that the first day I met you.' He said it with total seriousness but Cassie laughed, remembering the moment.

'In the overalls with the grease all over my face? I must have made quite an impression.' She was laughing and holding the pin that seemed so remarkable to her. Even the propeller moved when she touched it.

'You did,' he admitted. 'You're the only woman I know who looks good in blackface.'

'Desmond, you're awful.' She laughed, feeling close to him. It was odd, but despite the distance between them, she felt friendly toward him. He was one of the few friends she had here. Other than Desmond, there was only Nancy, and one or two of the other pilots. But there was no one she spent any real time with. She respected Desmond enormously and all he stood for and worked so hard for. He believed in excellence, at any cost, to him, or to his company. He never settled for anything less than perfection. Just like the little plane she held in her hand as a gift from him. It was perfect.

'Am I awful, Cass?' he asked seriously after her

lighthearted comment. 'I've been told that by experts and they're probably right.' But he said it so disarmingly, she felt sorry for him. She realized he was a lonely man, in spite of his importance, and all the luxuries he had. He had no children, no wife, few friends, and according to the newspapers at the moment, not even a girlfriend. All he had were his airplanes and his business.

'You know you're not awful,' Cass said softly.

'I'd like to be your friend, Cass,' he said honestly, and held a hand out to her across the table. She wasn't quite sure what he meant, but she was deeply touched by all he'd done for her, and the gesture of friendship.

'I am your friend, Desmond. You've been very kind to me . . . even before this . . . I never really felt that I deserved it.'

'That's why I like you,' he smiled, 'you don't expect anything, and you deserve it all, even better than that.' He gestured to the tiny diamond plane in her hand, and then took it from her, and pinned it on her dress from across the table. 'You're a special girl, Cass. I've never known anyone like you.' She smiled at him, touched by what he had said, and grateful for his friendship.

He took her home that night, and walked her upstairs. He didn't ask to come in, and he never mentioned the world tour. But he surprised her by sending her flowers the next day, and calling her on Sunday and inviting her to go for a ride. It had never even occurred to her before what he might do on the weekends. She usually flew if she had time, or Nancy booked her into social events where she had to be seen with her long list of escorts.

Desmond picked her up at two o'clock, and they drove out to Malibu, and walked on the beach. It was a glorious day, and the beach was almost deserted. He talked for a while about his youth, his years in boarding school, and then at Princeton. He hadn't been home a lot during that time. His mother had died when he was very young, and his father had plunged himself into his business. He had built an empire, but in the process of building it, he had forgotten his only child. He had never even bothered to have Desmond home for vacations. He stayed at his various schools, first Fessenden then St Paul's, and then finally Princeton. By then, he didn't really care anymore, he went away on his own or with friends for his vacation.

'Didn't you have any family at all?' Cassie looked horrified at the story of his desperately lonely childhood.

'None. Both of my parents were only children. All of my grandparents were dead before I was born. I never had anyone except my father, and actually, I never really knew him. I think that's why I've never wanted any children of my own. I wouldn't have wanted to inflict that kind of pain on anyone. I'm happy as I am, and I wouldn't want to disappoint a child.' There was something very bleak and sad about him, and she understood him better now. It was the loneliness she had sensed, the isolation that had gone on for years. He had put it to good use, but how painful for him. And he still seemed so lonely.

'Desmond . . . you wouldn't disappoint anyone . . . you've been so kind to me.' He had been. Her contacts with him had been nothing but pleasant. He was the perfect gentleman, the perfect friend, the perfect employer. There was no reason why he couldn't be the perfect husband or parent. She knew he had been married twice previously and she also knew he had no children. Magazines she'd read made a big point of saying that there was no heir to his gigantic fortune. But now she knew why. He didn't want one.

'I married very young,' he explained, as they sat on the sand finally, looking out at the water. 'I was still at Princeton. And it was incredibly stupid. Amy was a lovely girl, and completely spoiled by her parents. We came back here when I graduated, and she hated everything about it.' He looked at Cass then with sudden amusement. 'I was the same age you are now, but with tremendous illusions about being grown up, and knowing what I was doing. She wanted me to move to New York, and I wouldn't. She wanted to be close to her family, and I thought it terribly strange. I took her to Africa instead, on safari, and then to India for six months. And then we went to Hong Kong, where she took the first ship back to her parents. She said I had tortured her and taken her to horrible places. She said she'd been held hostage with savages.' He smiled at the absurdity of it and Cassie laughed. He made it all sound very funny. 'By the time I got back, her father's lawyers had filed for divorce. I suppose I never understood that she wanted to be near her mother, and I wanted to show her something a lot more exciting.

'My next wife was a lot more intriguing. I was twenty-five, and she was a fascinating English-woman in Bangkok. She was ten years older than I was, and apparently she'd led a very busy life. It turned out that she was married to someone else, and he surfaced rather unexpectedly while we were happily living together. He was not pleased, and our marriage was annulled. And then I came back here and settled down eventually. I enjoyed some of it, but I'm afraid none of that sounds like real marriage. I've never really tried it right here, or done what was expected of me. And once I inherited the business, I had no time for all that nonsense. I had no time for anything . . . except the business. So here I am, ten years later, alone, and very boring.'

'I wouldn't call all that boring . . . safaris . . . India . . . Bangkok. . . It's certainly a long way from Illinois, where I come from. I'm the fourth of five children, and I've spent my whole life living on an airport, and I have sixteen nieces and nephews. You don't get much more mundane than that. I'm the first member of my family to go to college, the first woman to fly a plane, the first person to move away, although my father and mother came out from New York, and from Ireland before that. But it's awfully ordinary, and not in the least glamorous or exciting.'

'You're glamorous now, Cass,' he said quietly, watching her. He always seemed interested in her reactions.

'I don't think I am. I know I'm still the girl in the overalls, with grease all over her face.'

'What other people see is very different.'

'Maybe I just don't understand that.'

'You couldn't say we have an awful lot in common,' he said thoughtfully, 'but sometimes that works,' he said pensively. 'Actually, I'm not sure anymore what works. It's been so long since I even tried to figure it out, I can't remember.' She smiled, and suddenly she felt as though she were being interviewed, but she wasn't sure for what position. 'What about you, Cass? Why is it exactly that at the ripe old age of twenty-one and two days, you're not married?' He was only half teasing. He wanted to know just how free she was. He had never been quite sure, although she didn't seem to be too tied to anyone, except maybe the RAF pilot in England.

'No one wants me,' she explained easily and he laughed, and so did she. She was surprisingly comfortable with him.

'Try again.' He lay back on the sand, looking at her, completely amused by her, and very relaxed in her unaffected presence. 'Tell me something I'll believe.' She was far too beautiful for no one to want her.

'I mean it. Boys my age are terrified by women pilots. Unless they fly themselves, and then the last thing they want is competition from another pilot.'

'And what about boys my age?' he asked cautiously, as she remembered that he was four years younger than Nick, who was thirty-nine now.

'They seem to get upset about the difference in age. At least some of them do, the ones say . . . four years older than you are.'

'I see. They think you're immature?' But she wasn't that either.

'No, they think they're too old, but haven't come far enough in life and have nothing to offer me. They fly away to England and tell me to go play with kids my own age. No promises. No hope.'

'I see. And do you play with boys your own age?' He was intrigued by her story. He wondered immediately if it was her father's partner at the airport, but he didn't ask her. He assumed it was, after the way the fellow had tried to protect her from him that first day at the airport.

'No,' she said honestly. 'I haven't had time for any boys of any age. I've been too busy flying for you, and going to all the social events you think are important.' She also didn't want to be involved with anyone. She was too much in love with Nick to care about someone else, but she didn't say that.

'Social events are important, Cassie.'

'Not to me,' she smiled.

'You can't be easy to please, Miss Cassie

O'Malley. You've been out five nights a week with a different man each night for close to a year now. And no one has struck your fancy?'

'I guess not. Too busy, no time, no interest. They all bore me.' She didn't bother telling him that most of them were male models, or less than masculine actors. Not that it made a difference to her.

'You're spoiled.' He wagged a finger at her, and she laughed at him.

'If I am, it's all your fault. Look what you've done for me, apartments, clothes, all the planes I could ever want to fly, including a diamond one' – she smiled gratefully, she had written him a thank-you note only that morning – 'cars . . . hotels . . . fancy restaurants . . . who wouldn't be spoiled after all that?'

'You,' he said simply, telling the truth, and then he pulled her to her feet and they walked further down the beach in their bare feet telling each other silly stories. They had dinner at a little Mexican restaurant near her apartment, and he told her the food was terrible, but she loved it, and then he took her home and promised to call her the next morning.

'I go to work at four,' she said, 'I won't be here.'

'So do I,' he smiled, 'we must both work for the same tyrant. I'll call you at three-thirty.' She was surprised when he did. He was the oddest person. And so lonely. His stories of his childhood made her heart ache. It was no wonder he had never loved anyone, no one had ever loved him. It made her want to protect him, and undo it all, and yet at the same time he was always doing things for her. He was an unusual combination of warm and cold, invulnerable, and deeply wounded.

He picked her up at the airport that afternoon, and drove her home, but he didn't come in. And from then on, he called her every day, and took her to dinner several times a week in quiet places. He never did anything more than that, and Cassie never felt they were more than friends, but within a short time they were very good ones. He had never mentioned the world tour again, but she thought of it sometimes when she flew, and all of Nick's warnings. She thought he was crazy to have been so worried. Desmond had no desire to do anything that would harm her or push her. He wanted only the best for her. She was sure of that. More than anything, he was her friend now. He turned up at the oddest times, as she climbed out of a plane, or left for work at four in the morning. He was there for her, if she needed him, he never intruded on her, or asked for more than she wanted to give. He seemed to want so little from her, and yet she always sensed his presence.

He brought her new contract to her himself at the end of June, and this time she was amazed at what she saw in it. Most of the terms were the same, except that some of the social events were optional, and the money was doubled. He promised to let her test all their best planes, and wanted her to guarantee that she would do a minimum number of commercials per year. But then the last clause in the contract was the one that stunned her. It stated that for an additional hundred and fifty thousand dollars, plus any additional fees and benefits that accrued from it, he was offering her a world tour within the year, in the best plane they had, on the safest route that could be devised, to be embarked on, on the second of July 1941, almost exactly a year from then, on the anniversary of the day Amelia Earhart disappeared four years before. It was to be the publicity tour of all time, and she would undoubtedly set new records. The prospect of it was enormously tempting, but she thought she ought to discuss it with her father. She was going home that week anyway, for the air show.

'Do you think he'll disapprove?' Desmond asked her nervously before she left, looking like a boy who was terrified someone would take his favorite toy from him. And she smiled and tried to reassure him.

'I don't think so. He may think it's dangerous, but if you think it could be done safely, I believe you.' He had never lied to her, never cheated her, never fooled her. He had never disappointed her as a friend, or as an employer. And they spent a great deal of time together. Theirs was a strange relationship for a girl her age, and a man his, it was based only on business and friendship. Nothing more. He had never even tried to kiss her and yet he had wanted to know that she was free. And he had relaxed visibly when he heard she was, with the exception of Nick, who hadn't written to her in months. She knew how violently he would have disapproved of this contract. 'My father is pretty reasonable,' she reassured him.

'Cassie, I've always wanted to do this. But there was never anyone who could, or whom I would have trusted, or wanted to work with. I trust you completely. And I've never seen anyone fly a plane the way you do.' She couldn't help being flattered by what he said about her.

'We'll talk about it when I get back,' she promised him. She just needed a few days to think it out, but she was very tempted, and he knew it.

'You're not flying in the air show this year, are you?' He looked worried before he left her, but she was quick to shake her head. Her life was an air show every day, and she hadn't practiced. She just hadn't had time this year, although she was looking forward to going.

'No, but my brother is. God knows why. He doesn't really like to fly, he just does it to please my father.'

'He's no different than the rest of us. I did wrestling at Princeton, because my father had. It's the most disgusting sport in the world, and I hated every minute of it, but I thought he'd be delighted. I'm not sure he ever even knew, and when I think of all the stiff necks and bloody noses I got, not to mention the bruises.' She laughed at his description of it, and she promised him she'd call him from home and tell him about the air show.

'I'll miss you when you're gone, you know. I have no one else to call at three o'clock in the morning.'

'You can call me,' she said generously. 'I'll get up to talk to you, it's five o'clock there.'

'Just have fun,' he smiled at her, 'and come back and sign on for the world tour. But if you don't,' he suddenly said seriously, 'we'll still be friends, you know. I'd understand if you didn't want to do it.' The way he said it made her want to throw her arms around him and tell him she loved him. He was such a solitary soul, and he wanted so badly to do the right thing, and to be fair. He also wanted the world tour so desperately. She really didn't want to disappoint him.

'I'll try not to let you down, Desmond, I promise. I just need some time to think about it.' She was glad she didn't have to face Nick and listen to him erupt like a volcano.

'I understand.' He kissed her on the cheek before she left, and told her to wish her brother luck from him, and she promised she would when she saw him.

She flew home in one of Desmond's twin engine transports and wondered what her father was going to say about the world tour when she asked him. There was no doubt that it was somewhat dangerous, even without the war, and the problems in the Pacific; flying long distance like that could be disastrous if you didn't know what you were doing, or had incredibly bad luck and hit unexpected storms. Nobody had ever figured out what had happened to Amelia Earhart. The disappearance had no rational explanation, except perhaps that she'd run out of fuel and gone down without a trace. It was the only sensible reason anyone could come up with. The wilder theories had their fans, but Cassie had never believed them.

But the world tour gnawed at Cassie all the way home. Dangerous or not, she was aching to do it.

14

The Peoria Air Show was the same wonderful circus that Cassie remembered it to be. She had never been happier than when she stood there with Billy and her father. Her mother and the other girls were off somewhere with the children. And Chris was pacing back and forth nervously eating hot dogs.

'You're making me sick,' Cassie scolded him, and he grinned and bought some cotton candy.

All of their old friends were there, her father's cronies, and the younger flyboys. Most of the flying fanatics from miles around had come to visit the day before, at her father's insistence. The Peoria Air Show was an important event in aviation. There were even a couple of girls this year, in one of the tamer events. And Chris was going for his usual prize for altitude in the last race of the afternoon. It wasn't much of a showstopper, but they both knew it would please their father.

'Don't you want to try something, Sis? Dad could

lend you a plane.' The one she had flown east in was far too big, and far too clumsy. And also worth far too much money. And it was Desmond's. She had tested it for him right after she had gone to work for him, and they had only recently perfected her recommended changes. For a girl of twenty-one, she had a remarkably important job; everyone here knew how famous she was now and there was a lot of talk about her being there. At Desmond's suggestion, the wire services had shown up in full force to greet her.

But Cassie was quick to tell her brother she wasn't going to be in the air show. 'I'm not good enough anymore. I've been flying these boats all year long, Chris. Besides, I haven't practiced.'

'Neither have I,' he said with a grin. At twenty, he looked exactly like their father. He was doing well in school, and still intent on becoming an architect, if he could get a scholarship at the University of Illinois in another year or two. And for the moment, he spent every spare waking moment with Jessie. They were adorable and Pat said he wouldn't be surprised if they got married.

Billy looked no older than Chris did. He seemed to have even more freckles this year, but it was obvious from his performance in the first two races that, unlike her brother, he had practiced. He won first prize twice, and another one half an hour later, in three of the most difficult competitions.

'What have you been doing, practicing all year? Boy, you guys get a lot of time to fool around,' she teased with an arm around him, as a photographer from the wire service snapped their picture. Cassie was careful to give them Billy's name and spell it correctly, and to remind him that Billy had taken first prize three times so far that morning.

'And the day's not over yet,' he quipped with a wink at Cassie.

'What about you, Miss O'Malley?' one of the reporters asked her. 'No performance today?'

'I'm afraid not. Today is my brother's show, and Mr Nolan's.'

'Any romantic ties between you and Mr Nolan?' he asked pointedly and she grinned at him as Billy pretended to choke on his lemonade.

'Not a one,' she answered coolly.

'And what about you and Mr Williams?'

'We're the best of friends,' she said with a smile.

'Nothing else?' the man pressed on as her father wondered how she stood it. But she was very patient with him, and very gracious. Desmond had taught her well, and she felt an obligation to him to behave with the press here, although a little mischief with them might have been tempting. They took themselves so seriously, and of course Cassie didn't.

'Not that he's told me,' she said pleasantly, and then turned away to talk to some friends, and they finally left her.

'What pests they are,' Billy said with a look of annoyance. 'Don't they get on your nerves all the time?'

'Yes, but Mr Williams thinks they're good for business.'

'Was there any truth to that, by the way?' Billy asked when they were alone again. 'Anything between you and Williams?'

'No,' she said cautiously, 'we're just friends. I don't think he wants to be involved. I'm probably as close to him as he is to anyone. He's a very lonely man. I feel sorry for him sometimes,' she said quietly so no one else would hear her. But Billy was in no mood to be serious, and he was always irreverent about tycoons worth over a billion dollars.

'I feel sorry for him too. All that nasty old money he has to take care of. And all those movie stars he probably goes out with. Poor guy.'

'Oh, shut up.' She gave him a shove, and Chris came over to join them. He was eating again, and Cassie made a face watching him. He'd been eating like that since he was fourteen, and he was still as thin as a scarecrow. Jessie was standing right next to him, beaming up at him in silent adoration. She worked at the local library. She was a serious girl, and she gave all the money she earned back to her parents to help support her four younger sisters. And it was obvious to everyone that she was crazy about Chris. She was very sweet to all the O'Malleys, especially the younger children.

'Don't you ever stop eating?' Cassie asked him, with feigned irritation.

'Not if I can help it. If you time it right, you can pretty much keep eating from the time you wake up till you go to bed at night. Mom says I eat more than the entire family put together.'

'One day you're going to wind up a fat old man,' Billy warned him, with a wink at Jessie, who giggled.

They were all in a good mood, and there were a few really glorious feats, but none that matched Cassie's of the year before, her horrifying dive and last second recovery.

'I hated it when you did that,' Chris admitted to her; 'it made my stomach roll over watching you. I thought you were going to crash.'

'I'm too smart for that,' she said smugly. But she was glad he wasn't doing anything dangerous. Altitude never got anyone into much trouble. It wasn't very exciting either, but she was happy knowing he was safe, and not taking any chances.

'So what's happening in L.A.?' Billy asked during a lull, and she told him about her work and their new planes, but she didn't say anything about the world tour. She wanted to talk to her father about it first. And then she was going to mention it to Billy. She had been thinking about it a lot, and if she did it, she wanted him to fly with her. He was the best pilot she'd ever seen; even after a year in Los Angeles flying with some real greats, she still thought Billy was better.

He went back up after they chatted for a while, and won another first prize, to prove her point. And shortly after that, there was a near disaster when two planes almost collided, but there was a last minute save, and after some gasps and screams from the crowd, everything turned out all right. But it made everyone think of the year before, when Jimmy Bradshaw crashed at the air show. Needless to say, they didn't see Peggy there this year, but Cassie had already heard from Chris that she and Bobby Strong were getting married. She had no regrets about him at all. Her life had moved far past him. But she wished him well, and she was happy for Peggy.

Chris was standing with her just before his big event, and they were chatting about some old friends, and then they called his group to their planes.

'Well, here goes nothing.' He looked nervous, understandably, and he looked at Cassie and grinned, and she reached out and touched him.

'Good luck, kid. When you come back, we'll get you something to eat. Try and hang on till then.'

'Thanks.' He grinned at her as Jessie went to find one of her sisters.

And as he walked away, for no particular reason except that she was proud of him, Cassie shouted after him, 'I love you!' He turned and showed a sign that he had heard her, and then he was gone. And at last it was his turn in the small red plane as he climbed, and he climbed, and he climbed, and she watched him sharply. She thought she saw something then, and she narrowed her eyes against the sun, and she was about to say something to Billy. Sometimes she felt things even before she saw them. But before she could say anything, she saw what she had feared, a thin trail of smoke, and she found herself looking up at it, willing him to the ground as swiftly and as safely as he could get there. She wasn't even sure he knew what the problem was yet, but he did a moment later. His engine had caught fire, and a moment later he was plummeting to the ground faster than he had risen. There was no stopping him, no time to say anything. There were the familiar gasps that meant something terrible, as everyone waited. And Cassie was mentally willing him to pull up on his stick as he fell, and she clutched Billy's arm, but she never took her eyes off her brother's plane. And then he was down, in a column of flame, as she and every man at hand rushed toward him. But the flames were furious and the smoke pitch black. Billy reached him before anyone else and she was right beside him. Together they pulled him from the flames, but he was already gone, and every inch of him was burning. Someone ran toward them with a blanket to quench the flames, and Cassie was sobbing as she held him. She didn't even realize she had burned her arm very badly. She didn't know anything, except that Chris was in her arms, and he would never see again, or laugh, or cry, he would never grow up, or be rude to her, or get married. She couldn't stop crying as she held him, and she heard a guttural cry above her, as the plane exploded and threw shards of metal at the crowd. Billy was pulling on her to get her away, and she was still holding Chris as her father tried to take him from her.

'My boy . . .' He was sobbing . . . 'My boy . . . oh, God . . . no . . . my baby . . .' They were both holding him, and people were running and screaming all around them, and then powerful arms lifted Chris from her, and her father was led away, and in the distance she could see Jessie crying, and all Cassie knew was Billy was holding her, and then she saw her mother sobbing in her father's arms. And everyone around them was crying. It had been that way the year before, but this was worse, because it was Chris . . . her baby brother.

She was never sure what happened after that, except that she remembered being in the hospital, and Billy was with her. The arm didn't hurt at all, but people were doing things to her. Someone said it was a third degree burn, and they kept talking about the accident . . . the accident . . . the plane . . . but she hadn't crashed. She hadn't crashed in her plane, and she kept saying as much to Billy.

'I know, Cass. I know, sweetheart. You didn't do anything.'

'Is Chris okay?' She suddenly remembered that there was something wrong with him, but she couldn't remember what, and Billy just nodded. She was in shock. She had been since it happened.

They gave her something to sleep for a while, and when she woke up, the arm had started to hurt terribly, but she didn't care. She had remembered.

But Billy was still there, and they cried together.

Her parents were there too by then. They had come back to see her. Her mother was almost hysterical, and her father was heartbroken, and Glynnis and her husband Jack were there, but everyone kept crying. Glynnis told her Jessie had gone home with friends of Chris's, and her parents had had to call the doctor.

Because Chris was so badly burned, the casket was closed, and the wake was the following night at the funeral home in Good Hope. And the funeral was the next day at St Mary's. Everyone he had ever gone to school with was there, all his friends, and Jessie. She was in terrible shape, surrounded by her sisters, and Cassie made a point of going to kiss her. It was a terrible thing for a nineteen-year-old girl to live through.

Bobby Strong was there, and he came over and talked to Cass, but Peggy just couldn't. Some of Chris's friends from college had come too, and almost everyone who'd been in the air show, just as all of them had gone for Jim the year before. It seemed such an idle death, such a stupid way to die, climbing to the sky just to prove how far you could go, or worse yet, that you couldn't.

Cassie felt as though part of herself had died, and as she followed the casket out of the church, she and her father had to hold up her mother. It was the worst thing Cassie had ever seen, the worst thing she'd ever been through.

And it was only as they left the church that she looked up and saw Desmond Williams. She couldn't even imagine how he had known, and then she realized the wire services had been there and it was probably all over the papers. She was a star now, and her brother's death in an air show was big news. But she was glad he had come anyway. There was something comforting about seeing him there. And she reached out to him as they left the church, and thanked him for coming. She asked him to come to the house afterward, with their other friends, and once he arrived she could tell him how much his coming meant to her. He nodded, and then she started to cry, and he just held her in his arms, feeling awkward. He didn't know what to say or do, he just held her, hoping that was enough. And then he saw her arm, and moved her gently.

'Are you all right? How bad is it?' He had been very worried when he heard she'd been burned trying to save her brother.

'I'm okay. Billy and I pulled him out, and . . . and . . . he was still burning.' The image she created was so horrible that it almost made him sick. But he was reassured when she told him the doctors weren't worried about her. He told her he wanted it checked out in L.A. when she got back. And he made a point of talking to her parents, and chatting with Billy for a while. And then he left. He said he was flying back that night. He had just wanted to be there for her, and she was glad he'd come. It meant a lot to her, and she told him.

'Thank you, Desmond . . . for everything . . .' He didn't mention the world tour, but she knew it was on his mind. And she was still planning to talk to her father. But she had already told Desmond she wanted to stay home for a week or two, with them, and he told her to stay as long as she wanted.

She walked back outside with him, and he hugged her, and then he left, looking very somber. And when she went back inside, her father was crying and said that Chris had done it for him, and he should never have let him.

'He did it because he wanted to, Dad,' Cass said quietly. 'We all do. You know that.' It was true in her case, but not in Chris's, but she felt she at least owed her father that. 'He told me before he went up that he wanted to do it. He liked it.' It was a lie, but a kind one.

'He did?' Her father looked surprised, but relieved as he dried his eyes, and took another shot of whiskey.

'That was a nice thing you did for him,' Billy said to her later, and she only nodded, thinking of something else.

'I wish Nick were here,' she said quietly. And then Billy decided to tell her what he'd done.

'I sent him a telegram the night it happened. I think they're pretty reasonable about granting leave to volunteers. I don't know, I just thought . . .' He wasn't sure if she'd be mad at him, but it was obvious now that she wasn't.

'I'm glad you did,' she said gratefully, and stood around looking at their friends.

It was a miserable reason to get together. She

wondered then if Nick would come, if he could get away, or they would let him.

She sat for hours with her parents that night, talking about Chris, and the things he'd done as a child. They cried and they laughed, and remembered the little things that meant so much to them now that he was no longer with them.

The next morning Cassie dropped by the hospital, to have them look at her arm. They changed the dressings for her and then she went back to the house to sit with her father.

He hadn't gone to the airport since the accident, and Billy was taking care of things for him. Cassie stopped there on the way, and Billy asked her how her dad was.

'Not so great.' He'd been drinking that morning when she left him after breakfast. He just couldn't face what had happened yet. He only drank in moments of great stress or celebration, and when she went back, he was sitting alone in the living room and crying.

'Hi, Dad,' she said as she came in. She had lain awake all night, thinking of how she had resented Chris, of how often she had thought her father liked him better. She wondered if Chris had ever known it. She hoped not. 'How're you feeling?'

He just shrugged and didn't bother to answer. She talked about some of their visitors then, and about stopping to see Billy at the airport. But for once, her father didn't ask how things were there.

'Did you see Desmond Williams here yesterday?'

she said, groping for things to say to him as he looked up at her blankly. But at least this time he answered.

'Was he here?' She nodded, and sat down next to him. 'That was nice of him. What's he like, Cass?' Her father had talked to him briefly, but he didn't remember in the agony of the day.

'He's very quiet, very honest . . . hardworking . . . lonely.' They were odd things to say about the man she worked for. 'Driven, I guess, would be the right word. He lives for his business. It's all he has.'

'That's sad for him,' he said, looking at her, and then he started to cry again, thinking about the air show. The poor kid had been only twenty. 'It could have been you, Cass,' he said through his tears. 'It could have been you last year. I was never so scared as when I watched you.'

'I know,' she smiled, 'I scared the pants off Nick too, but I knew what I was doing.'

'That's what we all think,' he said gloomily. 'Chris probably thought so too.'

'But he never did know, Dad. He wasn't like us.'

'I know,' he agreed. They all knew it too. Chris had really never known what he was doing. 'I just keep thinking of how he looked when you and Billy pulled him out.' He looked sick as he thought about it, and not knowing what else to do, she poured him another drink. But by lunchtime, he was slurring and half asleep. And then finally, he dozed off, and she just let him sit there. Maybe the best thing

315

for him was to sleep. Her mother came back that afternoon with two of Cassie's sisters, and by then her father was awake and had sobered up again. Cassie made them all something to eat, and then they sat talking quietly in the kitchen.

It was odd being with all of them, and Cassie realized that they seemed to be waiting for something. It was as though the reality of Chris's being gone hadn't sunk in yet, and everyone was waiting for him to come home, or for someone to tell them it hadn't happened. But it had. It had been as bad as it could have been. It couldn't have been much worse, except if he had suffered.

Glynnis and Megan left when Colleen arrived, with all her kids, and the brief chaos did them all good, and then finally they were alone again. Cassie cooked dinner for her parents, and she was glad she was there with them. She had no idea yet when she'd be leaving. Her mother cried again at the end of the meal, and Cassie put her to bed, like a child, but her father seemed better that night. He was calmer and very clear-headed, and he wanted to talk to her after Oona had gone to bed. He asked her about her work, and if she liked it, what kind of planes she'd been flying, and about her life in L.A. He knew the year was up and he wondered if Cassie would stay in L.A. or come home now. With Chris gone, his concerns were more poignant.

'I've been offered a new contract.' Cassie answered his question directly.

'What's he giving you?' he asked with interest.

'Double what he paid me last year,' she said proudly, 'but I was going to send the difference to you and Mom. I really don't need it.'

'You might,' her father said gruffly. 'You never know what can happen. Your sisters have their husbands to take care of them, but you, and Chris . . .' And then he caught himself and his eyes filled with tears again as she touched his hand and he held hers tightly. 'I forget sometimes,' he said through his tears.

'I know, Daddy . . . so do I . . .' She had been thinking about Chris that afternoon, and wondered if he was in Walnut Grove with Jessie, and then she remembered. It was as though their hearts and minds just didn't want to accept it. She had talked to Jessie on the phone that afternoon, and she felt that way too. She said she kept listening for his truck. They all did.

'Anyway, I want you to keep the money,' Pat said firmly.

'That's silly.'

'Why is he paying you so much?' he asked with a worried frown. 'He's not making you do anything dishonest, is he, Cass? Or too dangerous?'

'No more dangerous than any other test pilot who works for him, and probably less so. He's got a big investment in me. I think he just thinks I'm useful to the company, because I'm a woman, and all the publicity . . . the speed records I've set are important for his planes.' And then she looked at him, wondering if it was too soon to tell him. But she wanted to tell him now. She wanted to sign the contract as soon as she went back. She had thought about it a lot in the last few days, in spite of Chris, and she knew what she wanted.

'He wants me to do a world tour, Dad,' she said quietly, and for a moment, there was a long silence while he absorbed it.

'What kind of world tour? There's a war on, you know.'

'I know. He said we'd have to work around it. But he thinks it could be done safely, if we plan our route carefully.'

'So did George Putnam,' her father said grimly. He had just lost one child, he didn't want to lose another. 'There's no way to do a world tour safely, Cass, war or no. There are too many variables, too many dangers. Your engines could fail. You could navigate wrong. You could hit a storm. A million unexpected things could happen.'

'But less so in one of his planes, and if I took the right man with me.'

'Did you have anyone in mind?' He thought instantly of Nick, but he couldn't go now.

Cassie nodded. 'I thought maybe Billy.' Pat hesitated while he thought about it, and then he nodded.

'He's good,' he agreed. 'But he's young,' and then he reconsidered. 'Maybe you have to be. No one older than you kids would be crazy enough to want to do it.' He almost smiled then, and Cass suddenly felt better. It was almost as though he had approved. And she wanted him to. She wanted to do it with his blessing. 'Is that why they're paying you so much?'

'No.' She shook her head. 'They'd pay me even more for the world tour.' She didn't even dare tell him how much. A hundred and fifty thousand would sound like the world to him, and it was. And she didn't want him to think she was doing it out of greed, because she wasn't. 'And there would be bonuses, and other contracts resulting from it, and endorsements. It's a pretty good deal,' she explained modestly. But even talking about those amounts of money scared her.

'It's not a good deal if you're dead,' Pat said bluntly, and she nodded. 'You'd better think about it carefully, Cassandra Maureen. It's not a game. You'll take your life in your hands if you do it.'

'What do you think I should do, Dad?' She was begging for his approval and he knew it.

'I just don't know,' he said, and then he closed his eyes, thinking about it. He opened them again, and reached for her hands and held them. 'You have to do what you need to do, Cass. Whatever it is your mind and heart tell you. I can't stand between you and a great future. But if you get hurt, I'll never forgive myself . . . or Desmond Williams. I'd like you to stay here, and never risk anything again . . . particularly after what just happened to Chris. But that's not right. You have to follow your heart. I said as much to Nick when he decided to go to England. You're young, it could be a great thing if you make it. And a terrible heartbreak for us, if you don't.' He looked at her long and hard, not sure what else he should say to her. It was her decision in the end. She'd been right to go to Los Angeles the year before, but he just didn't know now.

'I'd like to do it, Daddy,' she said quietly, and he nodded.

'At your age, I would have too. It would have been the greatest opportunity in my life, if anyone had offered it. But they didn't.' He smiled, and looked more like himself again. 'You're a lucky girl, Cass. That man has given you a great chance to become someone very important. It's a gift . . . but a dangerous one. I hope he knows what he's doing.'

'So do I, Daddy. But I trust him. He's too smart to take chances. He believes totally in what he's doing.'

'When does he want you to go?' Pat asked cautiously.

'Not for another year. He wants to plan it perfectly.'

'I like that,' Pat said. 'Well, think about it, and let me know what you decide. I wouldn't tell your mother for a while, if you decide to do it.' She nodded, and a little while later they turned out the lights and went to bed, but she was immensely relieved to have talked to him, and even more so that he hadn't gotten angry. He seemed to have finally accepted who she was, and what she was doing. He'd come a long way since he'd forbidden her to fly or take lessons. The memory of that made her smile now.

She talked to Billy about it the next day, and he went wild when she told him she had suggested him as her navigator and co-pilot.

'You want *me*?' he shrieked and then threw his arms around her neck and kissed her. 'Zowie!!!!'

'Would you do it?'

'Are you kidding? When do we leave? I'll pack now.'

'Relax,' she laughed at him, 'not for another year. July 2, 1941, to be exact. He wants to do it on the anniversary of the day Earhart went down. It's a little spooky but he likes that.' It had to do with publicity, and in that, she trusted Desmond's judgment.

'Why so long?' Billy sounded disappointed.

'He wants to plan it carefully, build it up, test the right plane. He's thinking about our using the Starlifter, which would be tremendous publicity for it, for distance and endurance.' That was really what it was all about, but if they made it, their lives would never be the same again. And she already knew that there was fifty thousand dollars in it for Billy, and she told him.

'I could sure have a good time with that, couldn't I?' But like Cassie, it wasn't the money that appealed to him, it was the excitement and the challenge. It was the same thing that appealed to Desmond, and had even sparked a flicker of excitement in her father. 'Well, let me know what you do.' And like her father, he suspected that she had already made the decision. She had, but she was trying it on for size, thinking about it, trying to be sure she wanted to make the commitment. Working for Desmond for another year was one thing, that was an easy choice, but agreeing to do the world tour was entirely different, and she knew it. She knew how great the risks were, and the benefits, if she made it. Imagine what Earhart would have been if she had succeeded. It was hard to imagine her legend being even stronger than it was, but it would have been. If only . . .

Billy left on a quick hop to Cleveland that afternoon, and her father was still at home, so Cassie volunteered to stick around and close the office. She put some papers away for them, and then she put on a familiar pair of overalls and went out to gas some planes. She had nothing else to do, and it would save Billy some work in the morning.

She had just finished the last of them, and put away some tools, when she saw a small plane coming in on the main runway. The little plane didn't seem to hesitate. It came right in, and then taxied toward the far hangar. She wondered if it was a regular, it had to be. She didn't know all of them anymore. He seemed to know exactly where to go, and what to do. She watched him for a minute, but the sun was in her eyes. And then she saw him. It couldn't be . . . it couldn't . . . but it was. He had come home to them. It was Nick. And she was crying as she ran toward him. She flew into his arms and he held her there, careful of her bandaged arm. It brought it all back to be there with him, the sorrow and the pain, and the shock of losing Chris mingled with the pleasure of seeing Nick now. He kissed her long and hard, and she felt safe and at peace suddenly, knowing he was home now.

'They let me go as soon as I heard,' he explained when they came up for air. 'But I had a hell of a time getting to New York. I had to fly out of Lisbon, I got in last night, and I chartered this crate in New York this morning. I never thought I'd make it. The damn thing barely got off the ground in New Jersey.'

'I'm so glad you're here.' She hugged him again, so relieved to see him. And he looked incredibly handsome in his RAF uniform. But also very worried.

'How's your dad?'

'Not great,' she said honestly. 'He'll be glad to see you. I'll drive you over now. You can stay with us.' And then she almost choked on the words, 'You can have Chris's room . . . or mine. . . I'll sleep on the couch.' Billy was living in Nick's old shack, and it would have been close quarters with both of them there.

'I can sleep on the floor,' he grinned. 'It's not a problem. The British aren't known for their comfortable barracks. I haven't had a decent night's sleep since last September.'

'When are you coming home?' she asked, as she drove him to her parents' house.

'When it's over.' But it wouldn't be over soon. Now that France had fallen three weeks before, Hitler had control of an even larger chunk of Europe. And the British had their hands full keeping him from trying to take what was left of the French fleet in North Africa. Their problems were far from over.

Nick inquired about her arm, and she admitted it hurt, but was getting better.

They had arrived at the house by then, and her father was sitting in a chair on the porch looking doleful.

'Got a cot for a soldier, Ace?' Nick said quietly as he stepped onto the porch and walked swiftly to his old friend and embraced him. The two men cried, sharing each other's pain, and Cassie left them alone to talk and fix them some dinner. Her mother had gone to bed with a terrible headache. She was still taking it very hard, understandably, he had been her baby, and so young. He was only twenty.

Cassie made them both sandwiches and poured them beer, and her mother had made a big salad in case they wanted it. It was enough. None of them were very hungry. And as they ate, Nick told them about what was happening in Europe. He had heard tales of the fall of France three weeks before, and the heartbreaking fall of Paris. The Germans were everywhere, and the British were afraid Hitler would try to take them next, and there was some fear that he might succeed, although no one said it.

'Are they letting you fly missions yet?' Pat asked, smiling at the memories of their days together at the end of the last war.

'They're too smart for that, Ace. They know I'm over the hill.'

'Not at your age. Give 'em time. When things get hot for them, they're going to throw your behind into a fighter and kiss you good-bye in a hot minute.'

'I hope not.' It made Cassie angry listening to them. They all loved war so much, and as far as they were concerned, it was all right to take chances, as long as they were the ones who did it.

She left them talking on the porch late that night. She would have liked to talk to Nick too, but she knew her father needed him more. And she had time. Nick was there for three days. She would see him in the morning.

Her father finally went to his office the next day, and he was pleased to find everything in good order. Billy had taken good care of the planes. Cassie had taken good care of his desk, and his pilots were all standing by waiting for directions. It did him good to come back, and halfway through the morning, Cassie was surprised when Desmond called her. He asked if it was okay to talk, and she stepped in and closed the door to her father's office.

'It's fine. You're nice to call.'

'I've been worried about you, Cass. But I didn't want to intrude at a time like this. How's the arm?'

'I'll be fine.' She didn't want to worry him by

telling him how bad it really was, but so far it was healing nicely. 'Is everything all right there?' she asked, feeling guilty for staying away for so long. She had been gone almost a week now, but he had told her not to rush back. She apologized again, and he told her to stay as long as she wanted.

'How are your parents?'

'Not great. But my dad came to work today. I think it'll do him good, especially once someone makes him mad about something. It'll take his mind off his troubles.' He laughed at what she said, and asked if she'd given the world tour any more thought, and she smiled and said she had. 'I talked to my father about it.'

'I imagine he was thrilled to hear about it right now. Your timing wasn't exactly the best, Miss O'Malley.' He almost groaned at the thought of her telling him now. He could just imagine what he must have said. But she surprised him.

'Actually, he wasn't all that opposed to it, after we talked about it for a while. I think he's worried about a lot of things, but he was surprisingly reasonable. I think he sees it as a great opportunity for me. He told me I had to make up my own mind.'

'And have you?' he asked, holding his breath. He had been frantic about her since she left. And he was surprised at how much he missed her. And he was even more worried she might not come back to L.A. or renew her contract after her brother's death. She was an important part of his life now.

'Almost,' she told him tantalizingly. 'I just want to think it out while I'm here. I'll tell you the minute I get back, Desmond, I promise.'

'I can't stand the suspense.' And he meant it. It was driving him crazy.

'I think you'll find the answer worth waiting for,' she teased and he grinned. He liked the way she sounded. And he couldn't help thinking of how she looked, as he talked to her. She had even looked beautiful at the funeral with her ravaged face and heavily bandaged arm, but it seemed wrong to think so.

'Promises, promises. Hurry up and come home, I miss you.'

'I miss you too.' She said it as she would have to a friend, as she would have to Chris, or to Billy. She missed talking to him at the crazy hours when they were both awake, and about the things they both cared about, his airplanes.

'I'll see you soon, Cass.'

'Take care. Thanks for calling.' She hung up and went back outside to her father and Nick. Her father asked her who had called and she told him Desmond Williams.

'What did he want?' Nick asked, looking annoyed.

'To talk to me,' she said coolly. She didn't like the way Nick had asked the question. He was acting as though he owned her. And for a man who hadn't even bothered to write in three months, that was pushing his luck, or so she thought.

'What about?' Nick persisted.

'Business,' she said bluntly and changed the subject.

Pat smiled then and walked away. He could see a storm gathering, and he could only smile. She was definitely an O'Malley.

'How's the arm?' Nick asked when they were alone again.

'So-so,' she said honestly. 'It's starting to hurt like hell, which they claim is a good sign.' She shrugged and looked up at him then, and invited him to take a walk with her. He agreed and they strolled to the far edges of the airport.

'What are you doing these days, Cass?' He sounded gentler than he had a few minutes before, and her heart melted again the minute he came near her, and put an arm around her.

'The same stuff. Flying planes, pushing limits. My contract is up this week. They've offered me a new one.'

'Same terms?' he asked bluntly.

'Better.' So was she.

'Are you going to do it?'

'I think so.'

And then Nick asked a question she hadn't expected. 'Are you in love with him, Cass?' He looked worried as he asked, and she smiled at the bluntness of the question.

'Desmond? Of course not. We're friends, but that's all. He's a very lonely person.'

'So am I, in England.' But he didn't sound sorry

for himself as he said it. He sounded angry about Desmond, and jealous.

'Apparently not lonely enough to be bothered writing to me,' she said tartly. She hated not hearing from him, especially since he wrote to her father sometimes, and to Billy.

'You know how I feel about that. There's no point stringing you along, or our getting tied up with each other, Cass. There's no future in it for you.'

'I still don't see why not. Unless you don't love me. That I could understand. This I can't. This is crazy.'

'It's very simple. I could be dead next week.'

'So could I. So what, we're fliers. I'm willing to take my chances on you. Are you willing to take them on me?'

'That's not the point and you know it. If I do get lucky and survive, which would be lucky for me, and maybe not so lucky for you, then what? You live in a shack and starve for the rest of your life? Congratulations to the big winner. I'm a flier, Cass. I'm never going to have a hill of beans. I never minded till now. I never paid attention, just like Billy isn't. He's having a good time. So was I. I still am. Then what? It's no future for you, Cass. I won't do that. And your father would kill me if I let you do that to yourself.'

'He may kill you sooner if you don't wind up with me. He thinks we're both crazy. Me for loving you, and you for running.'

'Maybe he's right. Who knows, but that's the way I see it.'

'And what if I save some money?' It was an interesting question.

'Good for you. Enjoy it. I hope you do. You're practically a movie star these days. Every time I see a newsreel from home now, you're in it more than Hitler.'

'Gee, thanks.'

'Well, it's true. Williams sure knows what he's doing. So what are you asking me? If you get rich thanks to him, am I willing to live off of you? The answer is no, if that's the question.'

'You don't make anything easy, do you?' She was beginning to get annoyed. He made everything impossible. Heads I win, tails you lose. He had loaded the dice, and she just couldn't win a round, and she was getting sick of it. 'Are you saying that if you'd saved some money over these past few years, then you'd come home and marry me. But since you didn't, if I make some money, that's not okay. Is that it?'

'You've got it,' he said smugly. He had decided not to ruin her life, and he was determined to do everything he had to to stick by it. 'I don't live off women.'

'You don't make much sense either. You're the only man I've ever met who's more stubborn than my father. And he's at least beginning to make sense in his old age. Just how long do I have to wait with you?' she said impatiently.

'Till I get soft upstairs,' he said with a grin, 'and it won't be long now.' He was tired of arguing with her. All he wanted was to put his arms around her and kiss her. It drove him up the wall when he saw her in the newsreels. He wanted to shout, 'Hey, that's my girl!' But she wasn't. He wouldn't let her be. She was his best friend's daughter, and the girl he'd been in love with since she was three. Try explaining that to a bunch of guys in the RAF. It had knocked him off his feet to realize that. Two or three of them had her on their walls as pinups.

'Get over here,' he said gruffly, as she stood several feet away with her arms crossed, tapping her foot at him. 'And don't look at me like that.'

'Why not?' She scowled at him.

'Because I may be a complete jerk, and I may want you to marry someone half my age and have ten kids, but I still love you, Cass . . . I always will, baby . . . you know that.'

'Oh, Nick.' She melted at the sight of him, and as he pulled her into his arms all she wanted was him. They stood together and kissed for a long time, forgetting all the words and the arguments and the problems. And then they walked slowly back to the airport. Her father saw them from where he sat in his office, and he figured they had worked things out. He wondered when they were going to get smart and figure out that they had something rare and important. But they were both stubborn as hell, and he wasn't going to get into it with them. He wondered if she had told Nick about the world tour yet, and what he would say. But it was only the next day that it came up, as they were all three sitting in Pat's office.

'What are you talking about?' Nick looked confused. Pat had referred to it, and Nick had no idea what he was saying.

Pat looked at his daughter then and raised an eyebrow. 'Aren't you going to tell him?'

'Tell me what? Oh great. So what's the big secret?' He knew she wasn't in love with someone else or even seeing anyone, although he had told her to, and she had had a fit over his telling her that. And she certainly wasn't pregnant, since he pretty much knew she was a virgin. There had never been anyone in Cassie's life except Bobby, and Nick. And all she and Bobby had ever done was a little light kissing on the porch. And Nick would never have touched her. 'So what's the deal here?'

She decided to tell him herself. It wasn't a fait accompli yet. But she was as good as sure. And she was going to tell Desmond when she went back to L.A. that she was going.

'I've had a very interesting offer from Williams Aircraft.'

'I know. For another year. You told me,' he said smugly, but Cassie only looked at him and then slowly shook her head as Pat watched her.

'No. For a world tour. A year from now. I've been thinking about it, and I talked to Dad about it before you got here. But I wanted to make up my own mind before I told you.'

'A *world tour*?' He exploded onto his feet with a look of outrage.

'That's right, Nick,' she said calmly. She didn't tell him the price attached to it, because that wasn't why she wanted to do it. And saying it sounded vulgar.

'I told you that's what that sonofabitch had in mind right from the beginning. Goddammit, Cassie, don't you ever listen?' He raged at her, swinging at the air with a pointing finger. 'That's what the newsreels are all about, and the constant publicity. He wanted to make you into a name, and now he's going to exploit the hell out of you, and risk your life. There's a war going on, how the hell do you think you're going to do it? Even if you do figure out some insane route, which I doubt. Goddammit, Cass, I won't let you do it!'

'That's my decision, Nick,' she said quietly. 'It's not up to you. Any more than your joining the RAF was mine. We make our own decisions.'

'Oh, great. So what is this? Revenge? Because I volunteered? Or because I don't write you? Don't you understand what this guy is doing? He's using you, Cass. For God's sake, wake up, before he kills you.' Nick was in a total rage over what Williams was doing, and Cass refused to see it.

'He's not going to kill me. That's ridiculous.'

'Are you crazy? Do you know how dangerous that trip is, with or without the war? It's suicide. And you won't make it. You don't have the endurance or the experience.'

'I do now.'

'Bullshit, all you do is fly test flights. That's nothing like it. When was the last time you flew long distance?'

'Last week when I came here. I do it all the time, Nick.'

'You'll kill yourself, you damn fool. And what about you?'

He turned to Pat with a look of fury. 'You're willing to let her do this?'

'I'm not happy about it,' Pat said sadly. He had just lost a son after all, but he had learned a lot in recent years, and much of it from Cassie. 'But she's old enough to make up her own mind, Nick, for better or worse. I don't have a right to make her decisions for her.' Cassie wanted to cheer when she heard him.

'What happened to you?' Nick looked stunned. 'How can you say that?'

'Because I've grown older and wiser, and maybe you need to too. On the one hand you tell her she's on her own, you won't marry her because you're too old for her or God knows why and then you want to tell her what to do. It doesn't work that way, Nick. And even if you marry her, she may not let you tell her what to do. It's a new generation of women out there. I'm learning fast. And I'm damn glad I got Oona when I did, I can tell you. They're a complicated lot, these newfangled women.'

'I don't believe you. You sold out. You've let her talk you into this.'

'No.' Pat was adamant. 'She hasn't even told me if she's going yet. This is her decision, Nick. All hers. Not yours, or mine. I don't want to be the man who kept her from it, if I stop her, and you shouldn't either.'

'And if it kills her?' Nick asked bluntly.

'Then I'll never forgive myself,' Pat answered honestly. 'But I still have to let her do it.' There were tears in his eyes as he said the words, and she walked over and kissed him.

Nick was staring at her when she turned to him again. 'Well, *are* you going to do it?' Both men held their breath while they waited, and then she nodded, and Nick looked as though he might cry.

'Yes, I am. But I haven't told Desmond.'

'No wonder he called yesterday,' Nick groaned in anguish. He couldn't believe she was going to do it. He had taught her himself. He knew that she was capable of great things, but not this ... not yet ... not now ... and maybe never.

'He called to see how I was, and how Dad was.'

'How touching.' And then he looked at her in fresh rage. 'And that'll be the next thing, won't it?'

'What will?' She didn't understand him and neither did Pat, but Nick was off on a new tangent.

'More publicity. More stunts. It was no accident last year when he took you to that restaurant to go dancing and had his picture taken with you. It kept things exciting in the press, mysterious ... but he'll have to go a lot further than that now, to make things interesting, to keep it going. How much do you want to bet he'll ask you to marry him?' Nick said in a complete rage over it, and Cassie looked at him in disgust, and her father in amusement. He had never seen his old friend have a jealous fit before but that was clearly what this was, and it amused him.

'That's the most disgusting thing I've ever heard,' Cassie accused him, but he was sure of it.

And Pat shared wise words with him. 'If you've told her you won't marry her under any circumstances when you get back, and you won't even write to the girl now, what exactly do you expect? For her to enter a convent for the rest of her life, or stay a virgin? She has a right to a life, Nick. If not with you, then with someone else. And he seemed a decent man, if you ask me, whatever commercial motives he might have over this trip, or about his publicity. He's selling airplanes. He has to do what he can to make them interesting, and if having them flown by a pretty girl, who happens to be a damn fine pilot, I might add, works for him, then more power to him. And if you don't want to marry her and he does, then I don't think you've got much to say about it, do you?' Cassie had to hide a smile as she listened to him. She had never heard her father make a speech like that, and the best part of it was that he was right. But Nick didn't want to admit it.

'He doesn't love her, Pat . . . I do.'

'Then marry her,' Pat said quietly, and walked out of the room, to give them some time alone. They needed it more than any two people he knew, but an hour later they were still fighting and had gotten nowhere. He was accusing her of either being naive or leading Desmond on, and she was accusing him of being infantile. It was a hell of an afternoon, and by the end of the day, both of them were exhausted. And Nick had to fly back to New York in the morning.

They talked almost all night, and nothing was resolved. He kept reminding her that he was a thirty-nine-year-old man and he was not going to marry a child, and destroy her life.

'Then leave me alone!' she shouted at him, and went to bed finally, and the next morning before he left they were both still angry at each other.

'I forbid you to fly on the world tour,' he told her before he took off in his chartered plane, and she begged him to be reasonable and not give her ultimatums.

'Why can't we forget it for right now? It's not for another year, and you're leaving and going back to England.'

'I don't care if I'm flying to the moon, I don't want you to sign that contract.'

'You have no right to say that. Stop it, Nick!'

'No, I won't, goddammit, until you agree not to do it!'

'Well, I'm going to!' She shouted at him, her red hair flying in the wind, as he grabbed her and yanked her toward him.

'No, you're not.' He kissed her hard on the lips, but they both came up fighting.

'I am.'

'Shut up.'

'I love you.'

'Then don't do it.'

'Oh, for God's sake.' He kissed her again, but nothing was resolved by the time he left, predictably, and as he took off, she stood crying next to the runway. And five minutes later, she stormed into her father's office. 'That man drives me nuts.'

'You two are going to kill each other one of these days. It's a wonder you haven't yet,' he said, smiling. 'Stubborn as two mules. It really will be a shame if you don't get married one day. You deserve each other. Either of you would wear anyone else out.' And then he looked at her seriously for a long moment. 'Do you think he's right, that Williams might ask you to marry him for publicity for the trip?'

'No, I do not.' She looked incensed. 'The man is terrified of getting involved with anyone. He's had two disastrous marriages. And I think if he ever did marry again, it would have to be for love.'

'I hope so.' But he felt better to have heard her say it. 'Has he shown any particular interest in you, Cassie?' Other than coming to Chris's funeral, which he had thought was damn fine of him, and he said so.

'Not really. We're just friends. Nick doesn't know what he's talking about.'

'Well, you could do a lot worse, if you don't marry that lunatic on his way back to England. I swear, he'll be the death of me one day. He and I used to have rows like that in the old days. Stubbornest sonofabitch I ever met.' Cassie didn't disagree with him, as she went back to the house to check on her mother.

She left Illinois the following week, and returned to Newport Beach, to her apartment, and to work, and to sign her new contract for another year at twice the money. And on her first day back, she went to talk to Desmond alone in his office.

'Is something wrong?' he asked nervously, standing up quickly as she came in. He always did that for her when she entered the room, and she liked it. 'Fitzpatrick said it was urgent.'

'That depends on how you look at it,' she said quietly. 'I thought you'd want your answer about the world tour.' But he suddenly sensed from the look on her face that she didn't want to do it, and he could feel his heart sink.

'I . . . I understand, Cass . . . I thought probably after your brother . . . I don't suppose your parents were pleased . . . it wouldn't be fair to them . . .' He was trying to accept her decision gracefully, but it was a huge disappointment for him, and very painful. He wanted this so badly. He wanted to be part of it, and to help her do it.

'No, it wouldn't be fair to them,' she agreed. 'And my dad wasn't pleased.' They had agreed not to tell her mother yet. 'But he said it was my decision entirely, so that's how I made it.' He didn't say a word as he looked at her, and she came a step closer. 'I'll do it, Desmond.'

'What?' he whispered.

'I'll do the tour. I want to do it for you.'

'Oh, my God.' He sank back into his chair with his eyes closed, and then he looked up and saw her. He leaped to his feet and came across his desk to kiss her. It was a chaste kiss, but it held all the fervent gratitude that he felt for her. Nothing had ever meant more to him. And nothing would ever again be as important. He would see to that. He had a thousand plans, and he was going to share all of them with her. They had an incredible year ahead of them. And as he sat down and started telling her, he held tightly to her hand, and kept thanking her. And she was happier than ever that she had decided to do it. To hell with Nick. This was her life.

15

The publicity for the world tour began almost at once, with a huge announcement at a press conference in Newport Beach. This was followed by a series of announcements and brief lectures given by Cassie, all orchestrated and organized by Desmond. She spoke to men's and women's groups, political associations, and clubs. She was interviewed on radio, and there was a special newsreel just about her. Within two weeks the press was saturated with news of her coming tour. And then suddenly in mid-August Cassie was forced right off the front pages, by the escalation of the war in Europe. The Battle of Britain had begun, the blitz as it was called. The Luftwaffe was pounding England, in the hope of destroying it. And she knew without any doubt, just by being there, that Nick was in danger. No matter how angry at him she was, the news terrified her, and all she could think of now was Nick.

She called her father to see if he'd heard from

him, but of course he hadn't, even by the end of August.

'I don't see how anything could get out, Cass. You just have to know he's all right. I'm listed as his next of kin. I'll hear if anything happens.' It was small encouragement, and her father had agreed with her that he was sure that by now they had pressed Nick into active service. He wouldn't be teaching anymore, he'd be flying bombers or fighters. The Luftwaffe's entire goal was to destroy the RAF, so Cassie knew Nick had to be fighting to defend it. And knowing that worried her constantly. It seemed even more awful now to have left each other on such bad terms. She only hoped that he would be safe. Nothing else mattered.

Despite the war, Desmond continued to plan the tour very carefully, and with incredible precision. They had agreed on the plane she would take, and it was already being prepared and equipped with extraordinary new instruments, extra fuel tanks, and long-range tracking devices. With Desmond's meticulous attention to detail, Cassie felt sure that they were proceeding safely.

The only real difficulty they had, and major change, was with their route, because of the war in Europe. By 1940, the war had spread to too many places. There were areas of the Pacific that weren't safe, large parts of North Africa, and of course all of Europe. It had become impossible to think of circling the globe now. But there were still extraordinary records to be set, and enormous distances to cover. And with Desmond's heightened interest in warplanes, he was anxious to prove the reliability of his aircraft over vast expanses of ocean. In essence, they were going to circle the Pacific, doing eight legs in ten days, and covering fifteen thousand five hundred and fifty miles. Their plane was to fly from Los Angeles to Guatemala City, and from there to the Galápagos. From the Galápagos to Easter Island, and then on to Tahiti. From Tahiti to Pago Pago, and then on to Howland Island, where Desmond already had a brief ceremony in mind, to honor Amelia Earhart, and from Howland they would head for Honolulu. There would be celebrations there, of course, and he planned to meet them, and then he would fly back with them to San Francisco, for the final triumphant leg of their tour. He was disappointed not to have her circle the globe, but the Pacific tour, as he called it now, accomplished many of the same things. The world tour would just have to come later, after the war in Europe was over. And flying nearly sixteen thousand miles would establish almost all the same things for Cassie's reputation, and that of his airplanes. Cassie was impressed too by how sensibly he'd made the adjustment. In some ways, it disproved all the terrible things Nick had said about Desmond. He was not a madman, determined to kill her. Certainly that year, no one, mad or otherwise, would have attempted to fly through Europe.

Desmond arranged more press conferences for

her in the fall, and saw to it that she was always in the news. He wanted all the attention possible focused on her. It was also a good diversion for people from the war in Europe. This was something wholesome and hopeful and exciting, and she looked so beautiful in every photograph that everyone was in love with her and wanted her to make it. People stopped her on the street now, and men hung out of cars to wave to her. People asked her to sign autographs. Nick was right in that sense, she was being treated like a movie star. But Desmond had slowed down her social life lately too. He seemed to want to keep her 'pure' and free of romantic gossip. Nancy Firestone was still working with her, but she no longer arranged for escorts. If Cassie went anywhere important now, she went with Desmond. He said he could keep better control of things if he was there. They went to openings and premieres in Hollywood, they went out dancing at night, and to the theater. He was good company, and she enjoyed being with him, and since he got up as early as she did every day, he was happy to go home early. It was the perfect arrangement.

Meanwhile, Britain was still being pounded mercilessly by the Luftwaffe. And Cassie knew that her father had finally heard from Nick, and he'd been safe as recently as early October. He was flying Spitfires in the 54th Squadron, and he was still stationed at Hornchurch Aerodrome. He almost sounded as though he was enjoying it, and he promised that if he had anything to do with it, the Brits would soon be kicking the shit out of the Germans. His only mention of Cassie was to tell Pat to give his love to his very unreasonable daughter. So the battle between them was not yet over, but at least he was alive, which was a huge relief to all the O'Malleys.

Even Desmond had been kind enough to inquire about his welfare, and she told him what she knew. But at least by November, the Luftwaffe seemed to be easing up a little bit. Until then, the bombings had been incessant and relentless. Children had begun arriving in the States to be cared for until after the war, and her sister Colleen had taken in two of them, which touched Cassie deeply. They were adorable, and the poor things were still completely terrified when Cassie saw them over Thanksgiving. Funnily enough they were both redheads just like she was. Annabelle was three and Humphrey was four. They were brother and sister, and their parents had lost their home in London, and had no relatives in the country. The Red Cross had arranged for them to come to New York, and Billy had flown there to get them. And he was shocked when the children asked him, on the way back, if he was going to bomb the airport.

Like everyone else, Cassie had fallen completely in love with them. Having the two children there gave her mother something to worry about and caring for them took her mind off missing Chris. It was particularly hard over Thanksgiving for everyone, but somehow they got through it, thankful for

345

each other. Cassie went to see Jessie then too, while she was home for Thanksgiving, and she seemed to be getting over it better than the O'Malleys. She was young and eventually, for her, there would be someone else, but Cassie would never have another brother.

She ran into Bobby and Peggy too. And Cassie had correctly guessed that Peggy was pregnant. She congratulated them, and Bobby looked as though he had grown up and flourished since he'd gotten married. His father had died, and the grocery store was his now. He was still dreaming of a chain of stores across Illinois, but for the moment he was more excited about the baby.

'And what about you, Cass?' he asked hesitantly. He didn't want to pry, and he'd heard about the tour, but he wondered what else she was doing with her life, other than flying.

'I'm pretty busy getting ready for the Pacific tour,' she said honestly. And he felt sorry for her. He had long since decided that she would probably never get married, or know the happiness he now had with Peggy.

The tour didn't seem like much to him, but it was amazing how many hours of every day it consumed, reading reports, checking out the plane, and double-checking every little change the engineers made. She was also making long-range trips to get ready for the actual tour, and familiarizing herself with the details of their route across the Pacific.

She explained it to her father while she was there,

and he was fascinated by all the preparations. He was anxious to see her plane, and she invited him to California to visit her, and see it. But he insisted he didn't have time, he was too busy at the airport. And he was about to get a lot busier. Billy had to be in Newport Beach right after Christmas to start preparing for the trip too. He was so excited it was all he talked about, and Pat growled constantly about what an inconvenience it would be to have him go away for seven or eight months. They were expecting the trip to take less than a month to complete but there would be press conferences and interviews afterward, if he ever came back at all. Like Cassie, he would become a hero and he would get much bigger offers than O'Malley's Airport. And Pat hated to lose him.

In December, Cassie tried to do a thousand things, before she went home again for Christmas. The days were never long enough, and finally she had to send Nancy out to buy toys for all her nieces and nephews and Annabelle and Humphrey. She bought her sisters' gifts herself, and for her brothers-in-law, and her parents. It made her sad to realize there was no gift for Chris this year, and there never would be. When he was a little boy she used to give him cars that she traded her dolls for. She would have done anything for him then, and now he was gone. She still couldn't believe it.

It was going to be a rough Christmas this year, she knew, but they were expecting it, and she was touched when Desmond came by the night before she left, to bring her a present. She had bought him a beautiful navy cashmere scarf that she'd picked out for him at Edward Bursals in Beverly Hills, and a handsome new briefcase from the Beverly Hills luggage shop where Nancy said he bought his luggage. She couldn't imagine giving him anything frivolous, like a loud tie or a baggy sweater. The very idea made her laugh. And she was thrilled when he liked his presents. They weren't personal, but they were useful, and he liked that.

The gifts he had given her reminded her, as always, of how thoughtful he was. He had given her the book *Listen! the Wind* by Anne Morrow Lindbergh, the famed aviator's wife, and a licensed pilot in her own right, and a lovely watercolor of the beach at Malibu, because he knew she loved it there. And then he handed her a smaller box, and she smiled as she unwrapped it.

'I'm not sure you'll like this one,' he said anxiously, which was unlike him. And then he stopped her and took her hand. 'But if you don't, Cass, just give it back, and I'll understand. You don't have to feel obliged to accept it.'

'I can't imagine giving anything back that you gave me,' she said kindly, and he let her start unwrapping it again. Beneath the red paper, there was a small black box, and she couldn't imagine what was in it. It was very small, and she guessed it had to be a very tiny object. And then he stopped her again and took both her hands in his own. He looked so pale, she was worried about him. This was so unlike him. It was almost as though he regretted giving her the gift at all, or was afraid of her reaction.

'I've never done anything like this,' he said, looking very nervous. 'You may think I'm crazy.'

'Don't worry,' she said gently. Her face was very close to his, and for the first time in a year and a half, she felt a strange current run between them. 'Whatever it is, I'm sure I'm going to love it,' she promised, speaking very softly, and he looked relieved, but still uncertain. He was a powerful man, but for this one moment, he looked so vulnerable. She couldn't imagine what was happening or why. She wondered if the holidays were hard for him, because he was alone. She felt sorry for him, as she thought of it, and then she smiled at him.

'Everything is okay, Desmond. I promise.' She wanted to reassure him. They were friends now. The long preparations for the Pacific tour had already brought them closer together.

'Don't say that until you look at my present.'

'All right, then let me open it,' she said calmly. He took his hands away then, and she opened the box finally, and all she could do was stare at the contents. It was a perfectly round, extremely large fifteen-carat diamond engagement ring, and as she stared at it in total disbelief, he slipped it on her finger.

'Desmond, I . . .' She didn't know what to say to him. She hadn't expected this. He had never even really kissed her.

'Whatever you do, don't be angry at me,' he begged. 'I never intended to do this . . . not this way . . . but . . . Cass—' He looked at her imploringly, so vulnerable suddenly, so open. 'I've fallen head over heels in love with you. I never expected to do that. I thought we'd just be friends, and then . . . I don't know what happened. But if you don't want to marry me, I'll understand. We'll just go on as we did before, we'll do the tour . . . Cass . . . please . . . say something . . . oh God, Cassie . . . I love you.' He buried his face in her hair, and she was overwhelmed with tenderness for him. She didn't love him as she loved Nick, that would have been impossible, but she loved him as one would a dear friend, or someone who needed you very badly. She wanted to make things right for him, to be there for him, to help him. Even to erase the pain of the past for him, if she could. But not for an instant had she ever thought of their getting married.

'Oh, Desmond,' she said softly, as he pulled away to look at her face and see what she was really saying.

'Are you angry at me?'

'How could I be . . . ?' She looked stunned more than anything. She had no idea what to say now.

'Oh, Cassie, God, how I love you,' he whispered and then kissed her for the first time, without waiting to hear if she would keep the ring, and she was startled by the extent of his passion. He was deeply emotional, in a way she had never even suspected. Everything was bottled up inside, and had been for years probably. He kissed her again, and she was surprised at herself when she responded, and was breathless when she pulled away from him. The entire experience was dizzying and she was confused by everything she was feeling. He was a far more powerful person than she was.

'I think this is supposed to be the engagement, not the honeymoon,' she said hoarsely, and he grinned, looking boyish and a little wild-eyed.

'Is it? Is it the engagement, Cass?' He couldn't believe what he was hearing. He wanted it to be, but she wasn't sure yet. This was all so unexpected.

'I don't know . . . I . . . I didn't expect this . . .' But she didn't look angry at him, and she hadn't said no yet.

'I don't expect you to love me immediately. I know about your friend in the RAF . . . if . . . if you think that . . . Cassie, you have to do what's right for you . . . what about him?' He had to know now. And she wanted to be honest with him.

'I still love him.' She couldn't imagine loving anyone but him. She had always loved him, as far back as she could remember. 'He says he'll never marry me . . . he left in a rage about the tour the last time I saw him, and I haven't heard from him since. I don't think I will.' She looked at him a little forlornly, remembering the last time she'd seen Nick. But everything with Desmond was so different.

'Where does that leave us?' he asked her gently. She looked at him and shivered. He was so good to her, so understanding. And she knew she couldn't abandon him now after all he'd done for her. But it didn't seem right to love one man and marry another. It wasn't fair to Desmond, more than anyone, but he seemed willing to accept the situation. And Nick would never marry her, that she was sure of. He was the stubbornest man alive. And she and Desmond had so much in common. They shared his business and the tour. Together they could do great things. And if she couldn't have Nick, then maybe all she needed was to be married to a good friend. It didn't seem possible to find another man she loved as she did Nick in one lifetime. And in time, she might come to love him as she did Nick, though she couldn't imagine it. But in many ways, she already cared about Desmond deeply. Marriage would be the ultimate bond between them. But it hurt to think of marrying anyone other than Nick Galvin.

'I'm not sure.' She looked at Desmond honestly. 'I don't want to short-change you. You've already had two marriages that cheated you out of what you should have had. I . . .' She looked into his eyes then, and saw all his desperate hope there. He was pleading with her, without saying a word, and all she wanted to do was please him. She wanted to help him, and be there for him . . . and maybe that meant she loved him.

'I know how much he must mean to you,' he said understandingly. 'I don't expect to replace him overnight, Cass . . . I understand . . . I just love you.'

'I love you too,' she said softly. And she did. She valued his friendship, and his loyalty. She respected and admired everything about him. He had done nothing but good things for her. Right from the moment they met he had been wonderful to her. And now he wanted to give her everything. He wanted her to become Mrs Desmond Williams. She couldn't help smiling at the idea. It was more than a little overwhelming.

'If it doesn't work for you, we'll get divorced,' he said, as though to reassure her. But she looked horrified at the suggestion.

'I would never do that.' She had her parents' marriage as an example. 'I don't mean to seem . . . ungrateful . . . or hesitant.' She was groping for the right words, as he watched her. His eyes never left hers, and she felt the power of his wanting bore through her. She was surprised at the sheer force of him, as he held her hand and sat next to her. She could feel the strength of his need for her, and everything he wanted to give her.

'I'll never hurt you, Cass. And I'll always leave you free to be your own person. You're too important to me to try and clip your wings. You can do, and be, anything you want if we get married.'

'Would you ever want children?' She was almost embarrassed to ask him. The question was so intimate, and their relationship never had been.

'They're not important to me,' he said honestly.

'But maybe some day, if that's what you really want, and you're not too busy flying. But I think that's something you really have to think about. You have a lot of important things to do with your life. Having children might be more appropriate for women like your sisters. That's their job. You have yours, and it's a very important one. But I'm not telling you I wouldn't have one. I just wonder if that's really what you want.'

'I've never been sure. I used to think I didn't.' And then with Nick, she had begun to think she would love to have his babies. She didn't feel ready to give up the idea forever. It was too soon, and she was too young to decide that, and he knew it.

'You've got plenty of time to make those decisions later. At twenty-one, it's really not all that important. And you've got the tour to think of.' It was that that brought them together. And now she could imagine feeling even closer to him, if they were married.

'Desmond, I don't know what to say to you.' She was near tears as he pulled her closer.

'Say you'll marry me,' he said, putting an arm around her shoulder and bringing her closer. 'Say you trust me . . . say that even if you're not sure now, you believe that one day you could really love me. I already do, Cass. I love you more than anyone or anything in my life until this moment.'

How could she deny that? How could she let him down, or run away from him? How could she spend a lifetime waiting for Nick when she knew he wouldn't marry her? Her father had told him as much the last time he'd been home. If Nick wouldn't marry her, he had no right to interfere with her future, or her decisions.

'Yes . . .' The word was barely more than a whisper as he stared at her in amazement. 'Yes,' she said it very softly, and without another sound, he kissed her. It seemed hours before he let her go again, and Cassie was trembling with emotion.

'My parents are going to be stunned,' she said, looking like a child suddenly, and then she had a thought. Everything was going to be so different.

'Why don't you come home with me for Christmas?' She wanted to take him home to her family. If they were going to be married, it was important to her that he meet them and spend time with them. Her parents didn't even remember meeting him when Chris died. And their announcement would certainly make for an unexpectedly happy Christmas for the O'Malleys.

But he looked uncomfortable at the invitation. He hadn't had a family Christmas in years. He no longer even missed them. 'Cass, I don't want to intrude, sweetheart. Especially not this year. It may be a lot for your parents to absorb. And holidays aren't my strong suit.'

But she looked terribly disappointed. 'Desmond, please. They'll think I made it up, and stole the ring.'

'No, they won't. I'll call you three times a day. Honestly, I have a ton of work to do. You know that better than anyone. And when you come back, we'll go skiing for a weekend.' The last thing he wanted to do was spend Christmas in Illinois with the O'Malleys. The thought of it made him desperately uncomfortable and nothing she said would persuade him.

'I don't want to go skiing. I want you to come home with me,' she insisted with tears in her eyes. She was suddenly overwhelmed by events and emotions. She was *engaged* to Desmond Williams. It was amazing. And through it all she tried to force herself not to think of Nick Galvin.

'I promise we'll go next year,' he said firmly.

'Well, I should hope so,' she said, shocked at the idea that they wouldn't. 'You're not just getting me, you're getting my family. And there are lots of us.' She beamed, warming up to the idea of announcing her engagement.

'There's only one of you,' he said intensely and then he kissed her again. And for a flash of an instant, she thought of Nick, and knew she had betrayed him. And as she thought of him, she remembered his warnings about Desmond. But he'd been wrong about him. Desmond was a decent man. He loved her and she knew that in time she would love him, and they would have a great life together.

'When shall we set the date for?' Desmond broke into her thoughts again as he poured her another glass of champagne. 'Let's not wait too long. I'm not sure I can stand it, now that you've said yes. You'll have to keep Nancy around to protect you.'

He smiled knowingly at her and she blushed as she smiled up at him.

'I'll be sure to warn her,' Cassie said softly. She was happy with him, she always had been, even now they were more like friends than lovers, except for the sudden fervor of his kisses.

'What about Valentine's Day?' he suggested. 'It's sort of corny, but I like it. What do you think?' He sounded as though he were planning the tour, but she didn't mind that. She was used to Desmond being in control of things, but she also knew that he respected her opinions.

It was all so romantic. She was marrying a man that any woman in the world would have given her right arm to be married to, and he wanted to marry her on Valentine's Day. How much more perfect could it get, she asked herself. Not much . . . except if Nick had felt any different . . . But she wouldn't let herself think that. She couldn't. She would hold onto the dream of him forever, but that's all it was now.

'Valentine's Day is less than two months away,' she said, looking startled. 'Will we have a big wedding?' She was looking down at her ring, and flashing it. It looked like a headlamp. Everything seemed so unreal. It had been a remarkable evening.

'Do you like it?' he asked, as he pulled her closer again and kissed her.

'I love it.' She had never even seen a diamond that size, nor had anyone she knew. It was beyond amazing. And so was Desmond Williams.

'In answer to your question,' he said, with a smile, as she flashed her ring at him again and sipped champagne, with a giggle, 'no, I don't think we should have a big wedding. I think we should have a very small one, with only special people in attendance.' He kissed her again, and explained, 'This may be your first wedding, my love . . . but it's not mine. I think the third time one ought to be discreet, so as to generate a minimum of comment.'

'Oh . . .' She hadn't thought of it, but he was right. And they couldn't be married in the church if he was divorced. She wondered if her parents would mind terribly, though her parents had never been very religious. 'What are you, by the way?' she asked innocently. She had never even thought to ask him. 'I'm Catholic.'

He smiled. She was still a child sometimes, and he loved that. 'I suspected that. I'm Episcopalian. But I think a nice friendly judge would do just fine, don't you?' Feeling herself swept away on his tides, she nodded. 'And you'll need a beautiful dress . . . I'd say, something short but very elegant, in white satin. And a hat with a small veil. It's a shame we can't order something from Paris . . .' Hats from Paris, fifteen-carat rings . . . marriage to Desmond Williams on Valentine's Day. Suddenly she was staring at him, wondering if she had dreamed it all, but she hadn't. He was sitting there, talking about white dresses and hats with veils, and she was wearing the biggest diamond she had ever seen, as she looked up at him, and tears filled her eyes. She looked like a child as she sat there beside him.

'Desmond, tell me I'm not dreaming.'

'You're not dreaming, my love. And we are engaged. And very soon, you'll be married to me, for better or worse, forever.' He looked ecstatic and triumphant.

'Do you want to get married here?' she asked quietly, leaning against him. It was too much to absorb, she almost felt weak looking at him, and suddenly she realized more than she ever had before, how powerful he was, and how handsome. He had a quiet sexuality that he kept in control at all times, but now she could sense his nearness to her, and his interest. He hadn't stopped kissing her since he'd proposed, and she was almost feeling dizzy.

'I think we should get married here. It's not as though we can have a church wedding in Illinois, Cass. I think this is simpler, more discreet, and requires fewer explanations.'

'I guess you're right. I hope my parents come.'

'Of course they will. We'll fly them out for it. They can stay at the Beverly Wilshire.'

'My mother will die.' She grinned.

'I hope not.' And then he took her in his arms again, and forgot all the arrangements. She was so young, so sweet, so pure, he almost felt guilty kissing her, and there was so much more he wanted now. But it was still too soon, and he knew it.

He seemed to have to force himself to leave that night, and he called her the moment he got home, and then again, as he always did, at three-thirty the next morning. They chatted like old friends, and it was exciting knowing that soon she would be his wife, and she would share his life forever. And together, they decided not to tell anyone, until she had told her parents. They both knew that the entire country would be very excited.

He took her to the airport himself and as usual, she had checked out a plane to fly home. But this time, he told her repeatedly to be careful.

'It hasn't affected my brain, you know. Or maybe it has.' She grinned, kissing him again. She noticed one of the ground crew watching them and smiling. 'It'll be all over the papers if you don't watch out.'

'Something more dramatic might end up in the papers, if you don't hurry up and marry me soon, Miss O'Malley.'

'You only asked me last night! Give me a chance to get a dress and some shoes for heaven's sake. You don't expect me to get married in my uniform, do you?'

'I might. Or less. Maybe I should have come to Illinois with you.' But he was only teasing. She knew he had too much to do to go anywhere, with all the plans for the Pacific tour. But she was still sorry he wasn't going.

'My parents are going to be disappointed that you didn't,' she said sincerely. Especially when they heard the news. She still couldn't believe it herself, even when she saw his ring on her finger. And she would never forget how sweet he'd been when he'd asked her.

'Fly safely, my love,' he warned her again, and a few minutes later he left the plane, and waved as he watched her from the runway. She took off easily, and the flight was smooth. She had plenty of time to think of him, and Nick, along the way. Her heart still ached for him, but he had made his choice, so had she. They both had to move on now.

The flight to Good Hope took exactly seven hours. She landed at dinner time and the first person she saw at the airport was Billy.

'Ready to come to California with me next week?' she asked, but she didn't need to. He was ready to leave that night. For weeks now, it was all he could think of. And then as she signed her log, he noticed her ring, and stared down at it in amazement.

'What's *that*? A flying saucer?'

'More or less.' She grinned up at him, feeling awkward suddenly. But she'd have to tell him sooner or later. 'Actually, it's my engagement ring. Desmond and I got engaged last night.'

'You *did*?' He stared at her in disbelief, knowing that was impossible. Or was it? 'What about Nick?'

'What about Nick?' she asked coolly.

'Okay . . . sorry I asked . . . but does he know? Did you tell him?' She shook her head in answer. 'Are you going to? Did you write him?'

'He doesn't write to me,' she said unhappily.

Why was Billy trying to make her feel guilty? 'He'll find out sooner or later.'

'Yeah I guess,' Billy said, confused by what she'd done. Ever since he'd met them, he had known how much she and Nick loved each other. 'He's going to be very upset, isn't he?' Billy said quietly and she nodded, fighting back tears. But she had made her decision, and she couldn't let Desmond down now. He wanted her to be his wife. Nick didn't. He had said so. But still, being back home made Nick all the more real, which only made it harder for her.

'I can't help Nick's being upset,' she told Billy quietly. 'He didn't want any ties to me when he left. He said he wanted me to marry someone else.' She looked at him sadly.

'I hope he meant it,' Billy said softly, and drove her home to her parents. Everyone was there waiting for her, and it was only a matter of moments before one of her sisters let out a scream, pointing at her finger.

'Oh, my God, what is it?' Megan asked, and Glynnis and Colleen pointed it out to their mother, who was playing with the children.

'I think it's a light bulb,' Colleen's husband explained.

'I think it must be,' Megan teased, as her parents exchanged a look. Cassie hadn't said anything when she called them.

'It's my engagement ring,' Cassie said calmly.

'I figured that much out,' Glynnis said. 'Who's the lucky guy? Alfred Vanderbilt? Who is it?'

'Desmond Williams.' Almost as soon as she said his name, as though on cue, the phone rang. It was Desmond. 'I just told them,' she explained. 'My sisters went into shock when they saw my ring.'

'What did your parents say?'

'They haven't had a chance to say anything yet.'

'May I speak to your father, Cassie?' Desmond asked gently, and she passed the phone to him, and after that, Desmond talked to her mother. Her sisters were all going wild by then, and her brothers-in-law were teasing her. She had just told them she was getting married in Los Angeles on Valentine's Day, and Desmond was going to fly her parents out for the wedding.

Her parents had come back from the phone by then. Her mother was crying softly, which she did a lot these days, and she hugged Cassie close to her. 'He sounds like such a nice man. He promised me he'd always take care of you like a little girl.' She kissed Cassie then, and Pat seemed pleased as well. The man had said all the right things to him. But when he was alone with his daughter that night, he asked her some questions, and he wanted to hear her answers.

'What about Nick, Cass? God willing, he's going to come back eventually. You can't stay mad at him forever, and you can't marry another man because you're angry at him. That's a childish thing to do and Mr Williams doesn't deserve it.' He had liked him on the phone that night, but he wanted to know that his daughter was being honest with him, and herself.

'I swear I'm not marrying him out of revenge. He just asked me last night, and he took me by surprise . . . but he's so alone . . . he's had such a rotten life. He's a decent person and he wants to marry me. And in a funny way I do love him, though not like Nick. We're friends and I owe him so much for all he's done for me.'

'You don't owe anyone that much, Cassie O'Malley. He pays you a salary and you earn it.'

'I know that. But he's been so good to me, Dad. I want to be there for him. And he knows about Nick. He says he understands. I think in time, Daddy, I could really come to love him.'

'And Nick? What about him?' He looked her straight in the eye. 'Can you tell me you don't love him?'

'I still love him, Dad,' she sighed. 'But nothing's going to change. He's going to come back and tell me why he can't marry me. He's too old, he's too poor. Maybe the truth is he doesn't love me. He hasn't written to me since he left. And before he left, he kept saying no strings, no ties, no future. He doesn't want me, Dad. Desmond does. He really needs me.'

'And you can live with that? Knowing you love another man?'

'I think I can, Daddy,' she said softly, but just thinking of Nick turned her knees to water. Being back here now made him all the more real to her.

But she knew she had to put him out of her mind now. For Desmond.

'You'd better be rock sure before you marry this man, Cassie O'Malley.'

'I know. I am. I'll be fair to him. I promise.'

'I'll not have you running around here, cheating on him, and going off somewhere with Nick, when he comes back. A married woman is just that in this house.'

'Yes, sir.' She was impressed by what he said to her and the way he said it.

'Marriage is a sacred vow, no matter where you get married.'

'I know, Daddy.'

'See that you don't forget it, and that you bring honor to this man. He seems to love you.'

'I won't let him down . . . or you . . . I promise.'

Her father nodded, satisfied with her answers. But there was another thing he wanted to ask her now. Maybe it was unfair, but he had to ask the question. 'Do you remember what Nick said before he left, about how Williams would try and marry you before the world tour, to publicize it? Do you think he's doing that now, or that he's sincere? I don't know the man, Cassie. But I want you to think about it for a minute and tell me.' Nick's words had rung in his ears that night, the moment Cassie said she was getting married to Desmond Williams.

She was only twenty-one after all, and still naive. Williams was thirty-five and a man of the world. It would have been child's play for him to fool her. But she shook her head as she thought of it. This time Nick was wrong. She was sure of it.

'I don't believe he'd do that to me. I think it's just coincidence. We've worked so closely ever since I said I'd do the tour . . . and he's so solitary, I think it just happened by accident. And I think it's only coincidence that Nick said it would. It was a mean thing for him to say. I think he was jealous.'

Pat nodded, anxious to believe her, and relieved, and then he had to smile at her in spite of himself. 'That's nothing to the fit he's going to have when he comes home and finds you married. I warned him of that.'

'I know you did. I don't think he wants to be tied to anyone . . . and certainly not me . . .' she said, but she seemed to accept her fate now. It was certainly a lucky one, and her father was pleased with what she'd told him.

He looked down at her tenderly on Christmas Eve, and held her hand in his own, and then he kissed her cheek. There were tears in his eyes when he spoke to her. And in hers when she heard him.

'Cassandra Maureen, you have my blessing.'

16

Cassie stayed at home until the morning of December 31, and then she and Billy flew back to Los Angeles together. It was emotional for everyone when they left. And this time, most of the family came to the airport, even little Annabelle and Humphrey. Cassie wanted to spend New Year's Eve with Desmond. And when she got back, he was waiting for her on the runway. He was wearing a navy blue coat, flapping in the breeze, and the sun was setting just behind him. He looked handsome, and tall, and very distinguished. He was an extremely aristocratic man, and together they made a striking couple.

Desmond climbed into the cockpit easily, and he startled her by kissing her on the lips, and smiling down at her before she had even left her seat. He barely even seemed to notice Billy, who looked away with a smile while they were kissing.

'Hello there, Miss O'Malley . . . I missed you . . .'

'Me too,' she said with a shy smile. She had had dinner with her entire family the night before, and everyone had toasted her on her engagement. They were all excited about her wedding in six weeks, and everyone wanted to meet him. Suddenly she was the one who had done well. She was the shining star. And her engagement ring sparkled impressively on her left hand as though to prove it.

'I have a surprise for you,' he said with a big smile, after finally greeting Billy. He was gathering up his things and ready to leave the aircraft.

'Not another surprise,' she beamed, leaning back in her seat. 'My life has been nothing but surprises for the past week.' It was hard to believe that they had only gotten engaged a week before. It already seemed as though she had belonged to him forever. She was already getting used to it, and she really liked it. He was an exciting man to be engaged to.

Nick had come to mind a lot when she was in Illinois, but she had forced herself to remember that he had wanted her to marry someone else. He had given her up intentionally, and Desmond wanted and needed her very badly. And she had every intention of being a good wife to him. She smiled up at him as she thought of it, and he kissed her again, and gently touched her face with his fingers. The ground crew waited outside respectfully. The word was already out among them. O'Malley was to be the next Mrs Williams.

'What's the surprise?' she asked excitedly while

Billy watched them. Williams certainly seemed to be crazy about her, but Billy still felt sorry for Nick Galvin. It was going to destroy him when he found out he'd lost her.

'We've got some friends outside,' Desmond explained, as he hung his head with a sheepish grin that made her smile. 'I'm afraid I've been so excited I've been doing a little too much talking . . . Some of the boys from AP want to get a picture of us together. Everyone wants to be first. And I told everyone you were away, but they just thought . . . I told them you were coming back tonight, and when I got here . . . there they were . . . do you mind terribly, Cass? Are you too tired after the flight? I just couldn't help telling them we were engaged . . . I'm so proud . . .' He looked more boyish and more vulnerable than ever. There were times when he looked like a tycoon, or a relentless businessman, and there were others when he looked like a little boy, and she wanted to put her arms around him.

'It's okay. I'm excited too. I told everyone in Illinois. I guess if the press was there, they'd have been on our doorstep morning, noon, and night too.' She stood up in the cramped cockpit, and picked up her flight bag with her log and her maps, and Desmond reached up and took it for her. And then he glanced at Billy, as though remembering him.

'You know, I don't suppose it would hurt to have your Pacific tour co-pilot on hand too. You're welcome to join us.' He invited Billy with a smile, but the younger man looked embarrassed.

'I don't want to intrude.'

'Not at all.' He insisted on including him, as Cassie combed her hair and put on lipstick.

Desmond stepped out of the plane first, and Cassie came out right behind him. And as she did, what seemed like a hundred flashbulbs went off, and she was almost blinded. She and Desmond both waved gamely at them, and then he turned around and kissed her. And as she stepped onto the runway with him, she was stunned to realize that there must have been twenty photographers waiting for them. They didn't even notice Billy.

'When's the big day?' the *L.A. Times* shouted at them as the *Pasadena Star News* crowded in for another picture. The *New York Times* took two more, and the *San Francisco Chronicle* wanted to know about the Pacific tour *and* their honeymoon.

'Wait a minute, wait a minute . . .' Desmond laughed amiably at them. 'The big day is Valentine's Day . . . the Pacific tour is in July . . . and no, we're not spending our honeymoon on the *North Star*.' It was the name she had chosen for her plane for the tour.

And then they asked a hundred more questions, and all the while, he stood close to her, smiling and laughing with the press, as she tried to catch her breath, and understand everything that had happened.

'I think that's all, boys,' Desmond finally said

good-naturedly. 'My little bride has had a long flight. We've got to get home and get her rested. Thank you for coming.'

They snapped a dozen more photographs as the couple got into his Packard, while one of the ground crew gave Billy a ride. And Cassie waved gamely as they drove away. Overnight she had become the bride of the year and America's sweetheart in a flight suit.

'It seems so weird, doesn't it?' Cassie asked, still struggling to absorb it. 'They act as though we're movie stars. Everyone is so excited.' People had stopped her on the street back home, just to ask about the Pacific tour, and they hadn't even known she was engaged yet.

'People love a fairy tale, Cass,' he said quietly as he drove her home, and he patted her knee as she sat beside him. He really had missed her. 'It's nice to be able to give it to them.'

'I guess. But it feels weird to be one. I keep thinking to myself I'm just me . . . but they act as though . . . I don't know . . . as though I were someone else, someone I don't even know . . . and now they want to know everything, they want to be part of it.' It was almost as though they wanted to own her. And the thought of that made her uncomfortable. She had tried to explain it one night to her father, and he had reminded her that it would get worse after the tour. Look at the price poor Lindy had paid . . . his infant son kidnapped and killed . . . the price of fame could be frightening. But Pat hoped that Desmond would protect her.

'You belong to them now, Cass,' Desmond said, as though he believed that. And stranger still, he seemed to accept it. 'They want you. It's not fair to hold back. They want to share in your happiness. It's a nice thing to give them.' Desmond always seemed to feel as though he owed a great deal to the public.

But she wasn't prepared for the intensity of their attention over the next six weeks until their wedding. She was followed everywhere, and photographed, at the hangar, in the office going over charts and maps with Billy, outside her apartment, on the way to work, in department stores, shopping for her wedding dress, and any time she appeared anywhere with Desmond.

She took Nancy Firestone with her everywhere now, and sometimes she even tried to hide, with a big hat, or a scarf and dark glasses. But the persistence of the press was astounding. They hung off fire escapes and ledges, dropped from awnings, lay under bushes and in cars. They popped out at her constantly, from everywhere, and by early February Cassie thought they would drive her crazy. And for once, Nancy was of fairly little help to her. With anything. As organized as she was, Nancy seemed to have a lot on her mind, and she seemed less interested than usual in the details of Cassie's wedding. Desmond had told Cassie not to worry about it, and he was having Miss Fitzpatrick and an assistant handle most of the details. Cassie had enough to do just dealing with the press, and getting ready for the Pacific tour. He didn't want her too distracted by having to organize her own wedding.

But when Cassie tried to talk to him about Nancy Firestone, he never took her seriously. She was trying to explain to him that she had the impression lately that Nancy was annoyed at her and she wasn't sure why. Nancy had been irritable and cool ever since she and Desmond had announced their engagement. And there was no rational explanation for it. Nancy herself seemed to spend less time with her, and on the one evening Cassie had invited her for dinner, she had insisted that she had to stay home and help Jane with her homework.

'I don't know what's wrong with her. I feel awful. Sometimes I get the feeling she hates me.' They had never gotten as close as Cassie had once thought they might when they first met, but they had always been on good terms, and enjoyed each other's company when they worked together.

'The wedding probably upsets her,' Desmond said sensibly, with the rationality of a man, analyzing the situation, 'it probably reminds her of her husband. So she's backed off so as not to get too involved, or upset. It probably brings up painful memories for her,' he said, smiling at his bride. She was so young, there were a lot of things she didn't think of. 'I told you, just work with Miss Fitzpatrick.'

'I will. And I'm sure you're right. I feel like a

moron for not thinking of it.' And the next time she saw her, she realized that Desmond's explanation fit completely. Nancy was short with her more than once, and a little brittle when Cassie asked her advice about some detail of the wedding. And from then on, for Nancy's sake, Cassie took Desmond's advice and kept her distance.

She did her best to cope with the press herself, but at times they were truly impossible to deal with.

'Don't they ever stop?' Cassie gasped one day, as she ran into Desmond's house through the kitchen, and collapsed into a chair, exhausted. She had been trying to move some of her things from her apartment, but someone must have tipped them off. They had arrived en masse before she ever got through the door, and from then on it was sheer circus.

Desmond came in the front door half an hour later, and they besieged him, and finally he convinced her to come out and pose for a few pictures with him and get it over with. He had a great way with them. He always gave them just enough to keep them happy.

'Are you nervous yet?' one reporter shouted at her and she grinned back at them and nodded.

'Only about you tripping me on my wedding day,' she quipped back, and they laughed and shouted at her.

'We'll be there.'

Desmond and Cassie went back inside a few minutes later, and after that the reporters went away, until the following morning.

Her parents arrived the day before her wedding day, and Desmond had arranged for a suite for them at the Beverly Wilshire. None of her sisters had come, finally. It was just too complicated with all of their children. And Cassie was especially touched that Desmond had asked Billy to be his best man. It was really going to be the home team at their wedding. Her father would give her away, even though the ceremony was being performed by a judge. And she had asked Nancy Firestone to be her matron of honor. Nancy had balked at first, claiming that one of her sisters really should be. But in the end, she'd relented after Desmond talked to her. They had selected a gray satin dress for her, and an exquisitely made white one for Cassie, by Schiaparelli. I. Magnin had made her a little hat to match, with a short white veil, and she was going to carry a bouquet of white orchids, lily of the valley, grown locally, and white roses.

Desmond had given her a string of his mother's pearls and a spectacular pair of pearl and diamond earrings.

'You'll be the bride of the year,' her mother said proudly as she looked her over at the hotel. There were tears in Oona's eyes, as she thought she had never seen Cassie look so lovely. She looked radiant, and very excited. 'You're so beautiful, Cass,' her mother breathed, and then added proudly, 'Every time I look at a newspaper or a magazine, we see your picture!'

And the next day was all that they had expected.

Photographers, reporters, and newsreel crews waited outside the judge's home where they were to be married. Even the international press were there. They threw rice at her, and flowers as the wedding party left to return to the Beverly Wilshire, where Desmond had arranged a small reception in a private room. There were even crowds outside and in the lobby of the hotel, because someone had leaked to the press that that was where they were going.

Desmond had invited about a dozen friends, and several of his more important designers were there, particularly the man who had designed Cassie's plane for the Pacific tour. It was an impressive group, and the bride looked like a star in a movie. She was the most beautiful thing Desmond had ever seen, and he beamed as they danced a slow waltz to the 'Blue Danube.'

'You look ravishing, my dear,' he said proudly, and then he smiled even more broadly. 'Who would have ever thought that the little grease monkey I met under a plane less than two years ago would have turned out to be such a beauty. I wish I'd had a picture of you that day . . . I'll never forget it.'

She rapped his shoulder with her bouquet and laughed happily as her parents watched her.

It was a perfect day, and after Desmond, she danced with her father, and then Billy. He looked very handsome in the new suit he had bought for the occasion. He was having a great time in L.A., particularly with all the money he was making. And he was enjoying some of the best flying he had ever done, in planes he had longed all his life to get his hands on.

'You have a wonderful daughter, Mrs O'Malley,' Desmond said warmly to his new mother-in-law. Cassie had bought her a blue dress the same color as her eyes, and a little hat to go with it, and she looked very pretty, and very much like her daughter.

'She's a very lucky girl,' Oona said shyly. She was so impressed by Desmond's elegance and sophisticated air, she could hardly speak to him. But he was very polite to her and very friendly.

'I'm the lucky one here,' he disagreed with her. And a little while later, Pat toasted them and wished them many happy years and many children.

'Not till after the Pacific tour!' Desmond qualified, and everyone laughed. 'But immediately thereafter!'

'Hear! Hear!' her father said proudly.

Desmond had decided to let the press in for a round of pictures of them. They were in the lobby anyway, and he thought it was better to do it in a controlled situation. They arrived en masse, led by Nancy Firestone, and they got a very pretty picture of the bride dancing first with Desmond, and then her father. They made a big deal about his being a flying ace from the last war, and Cassie gave them all the details, knowing it made her father feel important.

And then, finally, they escaped to a waiting

limousine in a shower of rose petals and rice. Cassie was wearing an emerald green suit, and a big picture hat, and the photographs of her afterward were spectacular, as Desmond lifted her easily in his arms, and put her in the limousine. They were both waving from the rear window as they drove away, and her mother was crying and waving. Her father had tears in his eyes as he stood beside her.

The newlyweds spent the night at the Bel Air Hotel, and the next morning they flew to Mexico, to a deserted beach on a tiny island off Mazatlan, where Desmond had rented an entire hotel just for them. It was small, but perfectly private. The beach was as white as pearls, the sun was brilliant and hot, there was always a gentle breeze, and at night they were serenaded by mariachis. It was the most romantic place Cassie had ever seen, and as they lay on the beach and talked, Desmond reminded her that some of the places she would go on her tour would be even lovelier and more exotic.

'But I don't suppose I'll be spending much time lying on beaches,' she smiled at him, 'or with you. I'll really miss you.'

'You'll be doing something incredibly important for aviation, Cassie. That's more important.' He said it firmly, as you would to a child who was not paying attention to her homework.

'Nothing is more important than we are,' she corrected him, but he shook his head.

'You're wrong, Cass. What you're going to do has far, far-reaching importance. People will remember you for a hundred years. Men will attempt to follow your example. Planes will be named for you, and designed after yours. You will have proven that plane travel over vast expanses of ocean can be safe, in the right aircraft. A myriad of people and ideas will be affected. Don't think for a moment that it isn't of the utmost importance.' He made it sound so serious, so solemn, that it didn't even sound like flying. And she wondered sometimes if he attached too much importance to it, like a game that had stopped being fun and had become so vital that people's lives depended on it. Hers did of course, and Billy's, but still . . . she never lost sight of the joy of it. But he did.

'I still think you're more important than anything.' She rolled over on her stomach in her new white bathing suit, resting on her elbows. And he smiled down as he saw her.

'You're too beautiful, you know,' he said, looking at the gentle cleavage between her breasts. She had a very exciting body. 'You distract me.'

'Good,' she said comfortably. 'You need it.'

'Shame on you.' He leaned down and kissed her then, and a little while later they went back to their room. He was amazed, and so was she, at how easily they had adjusted to each other. She had been afraid of him at first, and of what physical love might be, but he had surprised her by not forcing it, and spending their night at the Bel Air merely holding her, and stroking her, and talking about their lives, and their dreams, and their future.

They had even talked about the tour and what it meant to them.

It had allowed her to feel at ease with him, just as she always did. And it was only when they reached the hotel in Mexico the following afternoon that he permitted himself to undress her. He peeled her clothes gently away from her, and stood looking at her astounding body. She was long and tall and lean, with high round breasts, and a tiny waist that curved into narrow but appealing hips, and legs almost as long as his. He had taken her slowly and carefully, and in the past week, he had shown her the exquisite ecstasies of their joined bodies. And as with everything he did, he did it expertly and well, and with extraordinary precision. And she had been ready for him. She wanted to be his wife, and to be there for him, and to make love to him, and prove to him that someone loved him. She was healthy and young and alive and vital and exciting. He was much more restrained, but she pushed him to heights he had forgotten for a long time, and he found himself enjoying the unexpected youth and abandon she brought him.

'I don't know about you,' he said hoarsely, after they made love that afternoon, 'you're dangerous.' He enjoyed making love to her enormously, much more than he had expected. There was a warmth and sincerity to her, which added to her passion, surprised him and touched him.

'Maybe I should give up flying, and we should just stay in bed and make babies,' she said, and then she groaned at herself, thinking that she was becoming just like her sisters. It made her wonder if this was what had happened to them; it was just so easy to be swept away, in the arms of a man you loved, and abandon yourself to the pleasures of the flesh, and their obvious rewards, in the natural order.

'I always thought they were missing so much by marrying so young, and having so many kids,' she explained to him as they lay side by side on the bed, their bodies hot and damp and sated. 'But I guess I can see now how it happens. It's just so easy to let things be, to be a woman, and get married and have babies.'

But Desmond shook his head as he listened to her. 'You can never do that, Cass. You're destined for far greater things.'

'Maybe. For now.' If he said so. Right now, she felt as though she were destined for nothing more than his arms, and she didn't want more. That was enough for her. Just to be his. Forever. Her sudden introduction to the physical side of him had swept her to a place she had never known, or understood before, and she liked it. 'But one day I'd like to have kids.' And he had said he would be willing if that was what she wanted.

'You have a lot to do first. Important things,' he said, sounding like a schoolteacher again, and she grinned, and turned over to look at him and run a lazy finger enticingly around him.

'I can think of some very important things . . .'

she said mischievously, as he laughed and let her do as she wanted. The results were inevitable. And the sun was setting on their desert island when they fell from each other again like two bits of lifeless flotsam in the ocean.

'How was the honeymoon?' the reporters shouted at them from their front lawn as they got home. As usual, they had somehow learned when the Williamses would be arriving, and as the limousine drove up, the reporters rushed forward. Sometimes it made her wonder how they always knew where they would be and where they were going.

They could hardly get through the door into the house, and then as usual, Desmond stopped for a moment and spoke to them, and while he did, they snapped a thousand pictures. The one on the cover of *Life* the next week was of Desmond carrying Cassie over the threshold.

But from that moment on, for Cassie, the honeymoon was over. They had been gone for two idyllic weeks, and the first morning back, he woke her at three, and she was back in training in her *North Star* by four o'clock that morning.

Their schedule was grueling and she and Billy were put through their paces a thousand times. They simulated every disaster possible, taking off and landing with one engine, then two, flying in with both engines cut, and practicing landing on the shortest of runways and in ferocious crosswinds. They also simulated landings in all kinds of conditions, from the difficult to nearly impossible. They also simulated long distance flying for hours at a stretch. And whenever they weren't flying, they were poring over charts, weather maps, and fuel tables. They met with the designers and engineers, and learned every possible repair from the mechanics. Billy spent hours practicing with the radio equipment, and Cassie in the Link Trainer, learning to fly blind, in all conditions.

She and Billy flew hard and flew well; they were a great team, and by April, they were doing stunts that would have dazzled any air show. They spent fourteen hours together every day and Desmond brought her to work at four A.M., and picked her up promptly at six o'clock every night. He took her home, where she bathed, and they ate a quick dinner. Then he retired to his study with a briefcase full of notes and plans for the tour, and recently with requests for visas. He was also busy arranging for fuel to be shipped to each of their stops. And of course he was negotiating contracts now for articles and books afterward. Generally he brought papers for her to look over too, about weather conditions around the world, important new developments in aviation, or areas they would have to watch out for on the tour, given the sensitivities of the world situation. It was like doing homework every night, and after a long day of flying she was seldom in the mood to do it. She wanted to go out to dinner with him once in a while, or to a movie. She was a twenty-one-year-old girl, and he was treating her like a robot. The only times they went out at all were to the important social events that he thought were useful for her to be seen at.

'Can't we do anything that doesn't have to do with the tour anymore?' she complained one night when he had brought her a particularly thick stack of papers, and reminded her that they needed her immediate attention.

'Not now. You can play next winter, unless you've planned another record-setting flight. Right now, you have to get down to business,' he said firmly.

'That's all we do,' she whined, and he looked at her with disapproval.

'Do you want to end up like the *Star of the Pleiades*?' he asked angrily. It was Earhart's plane, and there were times when Cassie was sick of hearing him say it.

She took the papers from him, and went back upstairs, slamming her study door behind her. She apologized to him later on, and as always, he was very understanding.

'I want you to be prepared, Cassie, in every possible way, so there will never be a mishap.' But there were elements they both knew he wouldn't be able to anticipate for her, like storms, or problems with the engine. But so far, he had thought of everything, down to the merest detail.

Even Pat was vastly impressed by what she told him of their preparations. The man was a genius at planning and precision. And more so at public relations. Even if he was compulsive about all his plans, he had her safety in mind, and her well-being.

And as a reward for her hard work, he took her to San Francisco for a romantic weekend in late April, and Cassie thoroughly enjoyed it, except for the fact that he had set up three interviews for her when they got there.

Their publicity stepped up radically in May. There were press conferences every week, and footage of her flying in newsreels. She and Billy made appearances everywhere: on radio and at women's clubs. They did endorsements and posed for photographs constantly. She felt sometimes as though she had no life of her own anymore, and in fact she didn't. And the harder they worked, and the closer they got to the tour, the less time she and Desmond spent together. He even went to his club a few hours at night sometimes, just to get a breather. And more often than not, by late May, he read papers in his study until he fell asleep there.

She was so sick of it that he suggested she go home for a weekend in May, for a break, and she was relieved to go. She was also happy to see her parents. This time it meant not being with Desmond on her birthday, but he gave her a beautiful sapphire bracelet before she left and told her they'd be together for the next fifty. Even she didn't feel it was a tragedy to miss this one. She was too tense now before the tour to enjoy it much anyway. And she and Desmond seemed miles apart these days. All he cared about was the tour.

It was ridiculous; she was turning twenty-two years old, married to one of the most important men in the world. She was one of the most celebrated women herself, and she was feeling restless and unhappy. All Desmond talked about was the tour, all he wanted to do was read about it, all he wanted her to do was pose for pictures, and spend fifteen hours a day flying. There was more to life than that. At least she thought so, but he didn't seem to know she was alive these days. And in some ways, she wasn't. There was certainly no romance in their life. Just the tour and its myriad preparations.

'How much goddamned flying can we do?' she complained to Billy on the way home. He had decided to come with her for the long weekend. 'I swear, sometimes I think I'm beginning to hate it.'

'You'll feel better once we get under way, Cass. It's just rough waiting to go now.' The tour was only five weeks away, and they were both getting tense about it. Cassie could feel it. And on top of it, she had been married for three and a half months, and she felt as though she were no closer to Desmond than before they got married. Their nights together certainly weren't romantic, she thought to herself as they flew east, but she didn't say anything to Billy.

Instead they talked about the press conferences Desmond had set up in L.A. and New York. And he wanted them to go to Chicago for an interview after the weekend, but so far Cassie hadn't agreed to do it.

'God, it's exhausting, isn't it?' She smiled at Billy when they were halfway there. She was glad she was going home. She needed to see her parents.

'I figure that later we'll think it was all worth it,' Billy encouraged her, and she shrugged, feeling better.

'I hope so.'

They flew on in silence for a while, and then he looked at her. She had looked particularly tired and unhappy lately. He suspected that the constant pressure from the press was getting to her. They were a lot easier on him. But they devoured Cassie, and Desmond never seemed to protect her from them. On the contrary, he liked them.

'You okay, Cass?' Billy asked after a while. She was like a younger sister to him, or a very best friend. They spent almost all their time together every day, and they never argued, or snapped at each other, or got tired of each other's company. She was going to be the perfect companion for the Pacific tour, and he was gladder than ever that he was going.

'Yeah . . . I'm okay . . . I'm feeling better. It'll be good to get home and see everyone.'

He nodded. He had gone to San Francisco the week before, to see his father, who was so proud of him. He knew how much Cassie's family meant to her. She needed them right now, just as he had needed to see his father. And then, suddenly, alone in the plane, he found himself wanting to ask her something he had felt awkward asking her before. But she seemed very relaxed now.

'Do you ever hear from Nick?' he asked casually, and she stared out into the clouds for a long time and then shook her head.

'Nope, I don't. He wanted us both to be free. I guess he got what he wanted.'

'Does he know?' Billy asked quietly, sorry that things hadn't worked out for them. Nick was a great guy, and Billy had always sensed how much Cassie loved him. Right from the first day he'd met them. It was as though they belonged to each other.

'About Desmond?' she asked, and he nodded. 'No. Since he didn't want to write, I figured he'd just hear eventually. I didn't want to write and tell him.' She also didn't want to write him and upset the balance. Something like that could make you just loose enough to make a fatal mistake in a fighter plane, and she didn't want that. 'He must know by now. I know he writes to my dad sometimes.' But she had never asked Pat if he had told him. It was still too painful to even think about, and she forced him from her mind as they flew over Kansas.

The press was waiting for them as they touched down in Illinois. They had spent the entire day waiting for them at her father's airport. And she knew there wasn't going to be any peace anymore, not until after the tour. It was just too close now.

She did what Desmond always wanted her to, gave them plenty of time, lots of photographs, satisfied them by answering some questions, and then she called it a day, and said she was anxious to go home to her mother.

Her father had been waiting for her, and he posed for photographs with her too, as did Billy. And then finally, the photographers left, and she heaved a sigh of relief, as she and Billy threw their things into her father's truck, and he looked at her with a long, slow smile. But she had noticed as soon as they'd arrived that her father didn't look well.

'You okay, Dad?' He looked kind of gray, and she didn't like it. But she figured maybe he'd had influenza. She knew her mother had when they returned from California. And he worked hard for a man his age. Harder now that Nick was gone, and she and Billy, and Chris . . . He had to rely entirely on hired hands, and the usual nomadic crews of wandering pilots.

'I'm fine,' he said unconvincingly. And then he looked anxiously at his daughter. Oona said he should have told her on the phone, but he wasn't sure what to say. But she had to know now. Pat hadn't told Nick either. And amazingly neither had anyone else. He had only arrived the night before though.

'Something wrong?' She had sensed his hesitation. Billy was unaware of it, as he looked at the familiar landscape out the window.

'Nick is here,' he said all at one gulp, looking straight ahead.

'He is? Where is he staying?' she asked uncomfortably.

'At his own place. But I imagine he'll come by the house eventually. I thought I'd better warn you.'

'Does he know I'm coming?' Pat shook his head, and Billy watched her eyes. He had just heard what her father had said, and he hoped it wouldn't upset her too much.

'Not yet. He got in last night. He's just here for a few days. I didn't have a chance to tell him.' She didn't dare ask if he had told him she was married.

She said not another word, and a few minutes later she was in the arms of her mother. Billy carried in her things, and Pat took him into Chris's room. His things were still everywhere, and it was a shock to walk in and see it. It made Cassie's heart ache to look around. It was as though he would be home any minute.

She settled into her old room, and her mother had dinner waiting for them. It was a hot, simple meal of the things Cassie liked best, fried chicken, corn on the cob, and mashed potatoes.

'I'd be the size of this house if I lived here,' Cassie said happily between mouthfuls.

'Me too,' Billy grinned happily, and her mother was flattered.

'You've lost weight,' Oona reproached her with a worried frown. But Billy was quick to explain it.

'We've been working pretty hard, Mrs O'Malley. Test flights fifteen hours a day. Long distance runs all over the country, we're testing everything we can before July.'

'I'm glad to hear it,' Pat said.

And as Oona cleared the table and prepared to serve them apple pie with homemade vanilla ice cream, they heard footsteps on the porch, and Cassie felt her heart stop. She was looking at her plate, and she had to force her eyes up to look at him as he came through the door. She didn't want to see him, but she knew she had to. And when she did, he took her breath away. He was more handsome than he had ever been, with his jet black hair, brilliant blue eyes, and a dark suntan. She almost gasped when she saw him, and then she blushed bright red, and no one moved or said a word. It was as though they all knew what was coming.

'Did I interrupt something?' Nick asked awkwardly. He could sense the tension in the room, like another person. And then he saw Billy. 'Hiya, kid. How's it going?' He strode around the room to shake his hand, and Billy stood up, grinning, his face still freckled, his eyes alight with pleasure to see him.

'Things are great. What about you, Stick?'

'I'm starting to sound like a limey.' And then, inevitably, he looked down at her, and their eyes met. There was a world of sadness in hers, and a look of wonder in his. He had missed her more than he had ever wanted. 'Hi, Cass,' he said quietly. 'You're

looking good. Getting ready for the tour, I guess.'
The last newsreel he'd seen had talked about it, but
it was five months old. They were a little behind the
times at Hornchurch, for obvious reasons. He had
done nothing but fly for the last year, every moment, every hour, every second. That and pull the
bodies of dead women and children from burning
buildings in London. It had been a tough year, but
he felt as though he were being useful. It was better
than sitting here, picking corn from his teeth and
waiting for mail runs to Minnesota.

Oona offered him dessert, and he sat down cautiously. He could sense that he had interrupted
something, or that they all felt awkward with him.
Or maybe he just imagined it. He wasn't sure, but
he chatted amiably with Billy and Pat, and Cassie
said nothing. She went out to the kitchen to help
her mother. But she had to come back eventually,
while they all ate dessert. She didn't touch her apple
pie, even though her mother knew she loved it. Pat
knew what was wrong with her. And so did Billy.
But Nick had no idea what had happened.

He lit a cigarette afterward, and stood up and
stretched. He had lost a lot of weight too, and he
looked young and firm and lean and very healthy.

'Want to go for a walk?' he asked her casually.
But there was nothing relaxed about the question.
He knew something was wrong, and he wanted
to ask her himself. For a terrifying moment, he
wondered if she'd fallen in love with Billy. Nick
hadn't been home in almost a year, not since Chris

had died. It was just an odd quirk of fate that he had come back when she was here. But as always, he was glad to see her. More than that, it filled his soul with light and air, and all he wanted to do was kiss her, but she was holding back purposely and he knew it. He figured she was probably mad at him. He had made a point of not writing to her all year. He didn't want to lead her on. He had meant what he said when he left her.

'Something wrong, Cass?' he asked finally, when they reached the stream that ran along the far edge of her father's property. She had said not a single word until then.

'Not really,' she said softly, trying not to look at him, but she had to. She couldn't keep her eyes from him. No matter what she had told herself that year about being ready to move on, about caring for Desmond and his needing her, she knew without a doubt she was still in love with Nick, whether he loved her or not. That was the way it was between them. But she would never have betrayed Desmond. She remembered her father's words when she'd told him she wanted to marry Desmond. And she was going to honor her marriage, if it killed her. But it might, she realized, as she looked up at Nick. Just seeing him made her heart ache.

'What is it, sweetheart? . . . You can tell me . . . whatever it is, if nothing else, we're old friends.' He sat down next to her on an old log, and took her hand in his, and then as he looked down, he saw it. The thin line of gold on her third finger, left hand. She hadn't worn her engagement ring home this time, just her wedding band, that said it all, as his eyes met hers and she nodded. 'You're *married*?' He looked as though she had just hit him.

'I am,' she said sadly, feeling, despite all her explanations to herself, and the fact that he had told her to move on, that she had betrayed him. She could have waited. But she hadn't. 'I got married three months ago . . . I would have told you . . . but you never wrote anyway . . . and I didn't know what to say . . .' Tears rolled slowly down her cheeks, and her voice caught as she told him.

'Who? . . .' Billy had looked very uncomfortable with her, and they had come home together. Nick had always felt they were right for each other, and he was the right age. It was what he had wanted for her, but it hurt so damn much now thinking of it, it brought tears to his eyes. 'Billy?' he asked in a choked voice, trying to sound noble, but this time she laughed through her tears, and took her hand away gently.

'Of course not.' She hesitated for a long time, looking away, and then, finally, back up at him. She had to tell him. 'Desmond.'

There was an endless silence in the warm night air, and then a shout of disbelief, almost of pain, as he understood it. 'Desmond *Williams*?' As though there were ten others with the same first name. He stared at her in outraged agony as she nodded. 'For God's sake, Cassie . . . how could you be such a fool? I told you, didn't I? Why the hell do you think he married you?'

'Because he wanted to, Nick,' she said with a tone of annoyance. 'He needs me. He loves me, in his own way.' Though she knew better than anyone that most of the time there wasn't room in his life for more than planes and papers.

'He doesn't need anything but a flight director and a newsreel crew and you know it. I haven't seen a newsreel that's less than five months old in a year, but I bet he's pumped the hell out of marrying you, and you've spent more time posing for pictures than Garbo.'

'It's five weeks before the tour, Nick, what do you expect?'

'I expected you to have more brains, to see him for what he is. He's a charlatan and a bullshitter, and I've said it since the day I met him. He's going to use you until he's squeezed you dry, or fly you till you drop, or wind yourself around a tree somewhere in a machine that's too much for you. He cares about one thing: publicity and his goddamn aircraft company. The man is a machine, he's a publicity genius, and that's all he is. Are you telling me that you love him?' He was shouting at her, and she flinched as he stood right in front of her and cast aspersions on her husband.

'Yes, I do. And he loves me. He thinks of me constantly. He takes care of . . . sure he cares about his planes, and the tour, but he's doing absolutely everything to protect me.'

'Like what? Sending you with waterproof cameras and a frogman crew? Come on, Cassie, come off it. Are you telling me he hasn't publicized the hell out of your marriage? I haven't seen any of it, but I'll bet they have here. I'll bet you tossed your bouquet right at the cameras.'

'So what for God's sake?' He was closer to the truth than he knew, but Desmond was always telling her to cooperate and be patient, that the press was an important part of their life, and her tour. But she was sure he had not married her because of it. That was disgusting, and hearing Nick say that made her angry. What right did he have to criticize? He hadn't even written to her. 'What do you care anyway?' she fought back. 'You didn't want me. You didn't want to marry me, or write to me, or come home to me, or even offer me any hope if you did get back from the war. All you want to do is play ace in somebody else's dogfight. Well, go for it, flyboy. You didn't want me. You told me that. You just wanted to smooch around with me while you were here and then go off to your own life. Well, go for it. But I have a right to a life too. And I've got one.'

'No, you don't,' he said viciously, 'you have a figment of your imagination. And as soon as the tour is over, and he doesn't need the illusions anymore to feed the press, he's going to dump you so fast your head will spin, or maybe he'll keep you around and ignore you.' It was what he was doing now, but she knew it was because he had so much work to do before the tour. She wanted Nick to be wrong. Everything he said was unfair, because he was a sore loser and he was angry. And then he went on to make it worse as he took another step closer to her. He wanted to yank her right off the log and into his arms, but out of respect for her, he didn't. 'I hear he keeps half a dozen mistresses quietly stashed away, Cass. Has anyone told you that, or have you figured it out for yourself yet?' He said it viciously, but he also looked as though he believed it.

'That's ridiculous. How would you know anyway?'

'Word gets around. He's not the saint he appears to be, or the husband,' he said sadly. He wished he had married her himself, but it seemed so wrong to him when he left. It still did. But so did her being married to Desmond. 'The guy's a bastard, Cass. He probably doesn't love you at all. Face it. He's a showman and a con man. You didn't marry him. All you did was join the circus.' But hearing Nick say those things about Desmond frightened her so much all it did was make her want to strike out to stop him. She reached back to slap him with all her strength, but he was faster than she was. He grabbed her arm and pulled it behind her, and then he couldn't help himself. He kissed her harder than he ever had, harder than he would have dared at any other moment, but she wasn't a little girl anymore, she was a woman. And without even thinking, she felt herself respond to him, and for an endless piece of time, the two clung to each other in unbridled passion. It was Cassie who finally pulled away, with tears rolling down her cheeks. She hated what was happening to them, hated herself for what she had done to him, but it had seemed so right at the time to marry Desmond. Maybe she was wrong.

But that wasn't the issue now. The issue was Nick, and what they no longer had a right to.

'Cassie, I love you,' Nick said urgently as he held her in his arms again, but this time he didn't kiss her. 'I always have, I always will. I didn't want to ruin your life, but I never thought you'd do anything this stupid . . . I thought you'd wind up with Billy.' She laughed at the idea, and sat down next to him on the log again, thinking about the mess she'd created. She was in love with two men . . . or maybe only one . . . but she was obsessed with one, and married to another.

'Being married to Billy would have been like marrying Chris,' she laughed sadly.

'And being married to *him*?' he asked in a choked voice. He wanted to know now.

'He's very serious,' she sighed, 'everything he does is for the tour right now. I think he's doing it for me. I don't know, Nick . . . I thought I was doing the right thing. Maybe I made a mistake. I just don't know.'

'Cancel the trip,' he said urgently. 'Divorce him.' He was panicking. He would do anything. He would marry her if that was what she wanted.

But every fiber of his being told him she was in danger.

'I can't do that, Nick,' she said honorably. 'It wouldn't be fair. He married me in good faith. I can't walk out on him. I owe him too much now. He's got so much riding on this tour, he's invested so much in it, not just the plane . . .' It didn't bear thinking about.

'You're not ready for it.'

But she was. And she knew it. 'Yes, I am.'

'You don't love him.' He looked suddenly so young and so vulnerable. She wished she had waited for him, but she hadn't.

'I'm not in love with him. I never was. He knew that. I told him about you, and he accepted it. But I do love him. He's been too good to me for me not to love him. I can't let him down now, Nick.'

'And afterward? Then what? You're stuck with him forever?'

'I don't know, Nick. There are no easy answers.'

'They're as easy as you want them to be,' he said stubbornly.

'That's what I said to you two years ago, Nick, before you left. And you didn't listen to me either.'

'Sometimes things seem more complicated than they are. We make them that way, but we don't have to,' he said wisely.

'I married him, Nick, for better or worse. Whether I loved you or not. I can't abandon him, just because you say so.'

'Maybe not,' Nick said tersely, 'but he'll abandon

you one day, emotionally if not otherwise, when this is over. It's all for publicity. You'll see, Cass. I know it.'

'Maybe. But until then, I owe him something. And I'm not going to break my word, or betray him. He is my husband. He deserves better than the two of us defiling him. I won't do it.'

He looked at her for a long time, and then seemed to sag as the force of her words hit him. 'You're a good girl, Cass. He's a lucky man. I guess I've been a fool all along. I thought I was too old for you . . . and too poor . . . and too foolish. I was part right anyway.' And then he couldn't resist a cheap shot, 'How does it feel to be married to one of the richest men in the world?'

'No different than being married to you would have been,' she came back at him quickly. 'You're both spoiled boys who want everything your own way. Maybe all men are like that, rich or poor,' she said, meeting his gaze, and he laughed at her. She hadn't lost her spirit.

'Touché. I wish I could be happy for you, Cass, but I'm not.'

'Try. We don't have any other choice.' She had to live up to the choice she'd made. For all their sakes. She was an honorable woman. He nodded then, and eventually they walked back slowly, holding hands in the starlit night and talking. He realized more than ever what a fool he'd been, but he had made his decisions for her, and look what had happened. Her father had been right. He had set her free, and she had married someone else. But Desmond Williams . . . he hated everything he knew about him. And he was convinced to his bones that he was using Cassie. And she was much too young and innocent to know it. He was forty years old and he could read Desmond like the front page of the *New York Times*. And so far, Nick didn't like the headlines.

Cassie said good night to him on the front porch, and they didn't kiss again. And it was only after she had gone inside that Nick saw his old friend, quietly sitting in a chair and watching.

'Keeping an eye on me, Ace?' Nick asked with a tired grin, and sat down in a chair near him.

'I am. I told Cassie months ago I'll not have her defiling her marriage.'

'She's not going to. She's a good girl. And I'm a fool. You were right, Pat.'

'I was afraid I would be.' And then, in the partnership among men, he was honest with his old friend, the boy who had been his protégé in another war, a quarter of a century before. 'The worst of it for her is that she still loves you. You can see it. Is she happy with him?' Pat asked him conspiratorially.

'I don't think so. But she thinks she owes him everything.'

'She owes him a lot, Nick. There's no denying it.'

'And if she gets hurt?' Nick didn't want to say 'killed' to her father. But it could happen, and they knew it. 'What do we owe him then?'

'It's the risk we all take, Nick. You know it. She knows what she wants and she knows what she's doing. The only thing she's not sure about is you.'

'Neither am I. I still wouldn't have married her by now. I didn't want to leave her a widow.' He laughed emptily then. 'I thought I was too old for her, but hell, he's almost as old as I am.'

'We're all fools. I almost didn't marry Oona thirty-two years ago. I thought she was too good for me, and my mother told me I was crazy. She told me to go for the brass ring. I was right. She is too good for me . . . but I love the girl . . . to this day, I've never regretted a single day of our marriage.' It was more than he had ever said to her, and the advice was too late for Nick. For now anyway. But if Nick was right about Desmond tossing Cassie aside, maybe she'd be free again someday. It was hard to say now.

They sat on the porch together and talked for a long time, and Nick noticed when they stood up that Pat was a little breathless. That was something new for him, and Nick didn't like it.

'You been sick, Ace?'

'Ahh . . . nothing much . . . a little influenza, a little cough . . . I'm getting too fat, Oona's cooking's too good. I get breathless sometimes. It's nothing.'

'Take it easy,' Nick said with a worried frown.

'Tell yourself,' Pat laughed at him, 'shooting Jerries all day. I'd say you've got a lot more to worry about than I do.'

Nick nodded, grateful for the things Pat had said

to him about Cassie. 'Good night, Ace. See you tomorrow.'

Nick walked all the way back to his shack, and everything in it was dusty. He hadn't been home in a year, but it felt good to be there. Everything felt good to him, except the fact that Cassie was married. He still couldn't believe it. He lay in his familiar bed that night, aching for her, unable to believe that she belonged to someone else now . . . that sweet face . . . the little girl he had loved so much was no longer his, and never would be again. She was Desmond's. And as he fell asleep that night, the tears rolled slowly from his eyes and into his pillow.

17

The weekend at home turned out to be difficult for both of them. Cassie made every effort to stay away from Nick, but their world was too small. And they kept running into each other everywhere, at the house, at the airport, even at the grocery store when she did some shopping for her mother. And he tried to be respectful of her, for her sake, if not for Desmond, but it was impossible. They wound up in each other's arms again the night before she left. It was the night of her twenty-second birthday. He'd had dinner with her and her family. And all through the meal, they were inexorably drawn to each other like magnets. They knew it was their last night to see each other, and there might never be another chance again. The very thought of that made them panic.

'We can't do this, Nick,' she said after kissing him longingly. 'I promised Dad I wouldn't. And I can't do it for me . . . or to Desmond.' And the way the press followed her around, all she needed was a scandal. They had tried to get pictures of everyone at the airport today, but Nick had disappeared discreetly into his shack until the photographers left and then he emerged again, and she was grateful. She knew that Desmond would have been very upset to see Nick in the pictures. She hadn't told him Nick was home when she called him.

'I know, Cassie . . . I know.' Nick didn't argue with her. He didn't want to hurt her. They sat on the porch and talked. Her parents had gone to bed an hour before but they hadn't said anything when Nick had stayed to talk to Cassie. She was leaving the next day and it was their last chance to be together.

'Are you sure you're ready for the tour? Billy says your plane is heavy as hell.'

'I can handle it.'

He didn't argue with her about it this time. 'Is your route safe?'

'It better be. Desmond works on it every night until midnight.'

'That must be fun for you,' he said smartly, and then he smiled at her ruefully. 'Damn fool. You could have had Bobby Strong and be selling onions, and what do you do? You marry the biggest tycoon in the country. Can't you do anything right, Cass?' he teased and she laughed. There was nothing laughable about it, but if they didn't laugh, they'd cry. Just in the few days that they'd both been in town, it was obvious to both of them that they were cursed with loving each other forever. Each time they met, or looked into each other's eyes, the power of what they felt for each other brought them closer. There was no escaping it. And Cassie realized now that it wasn't something time would change. She and Nick were part of each other. They always would be. There was no denying it anymore. She had never loved Nick more, and now she had to live with the agony of loving Nick and not wanting to betray Desmond.

But on this last night, they both knew this was their only chance to be together, and perhaps their last one. He was returning to the war to risk his life again, and she was taking every chance possible, flying across the Pacific. It was too late for games, or even anger anymore. They just had to live with what they'd done. They had both been foolish, and they knew it.

'What are we going to do, Cass?' he asked unhappily, as they looked at a full moon in a starry sky. It was a perfect night to be in love, but their story was no longer simple. They both longed for the early days when they had spent hours together at the deserted airstrip. They could have done anything then. And instead, they had made such stupid choices, he to fight another war, and she to marry a man she cared for, but didn't love. She knew only too well that despite all her loyalty to Desmond, Nick was the only man she loved or ever would. Maybe one day it would change, but it hadn't yet, and she didn't think it would for a long time, if ever. She'd been kidding herself when she married Desmond, and now that she saw Nick again, she knew it.

'I wish I were going back to England with you,' she said sadly.

'So do I. There are no women flying in combat over there. Not yet anyway, but the limeys are pretty open-minded.'

'Maybe I should run away and join the RAF,' she said, only half serious. She couldn't see how she was going to live her life now. In a way, she was grateful for the tour. At least it would keep her busy, and away from Desmond.

'Maybe I never should have gone in the first place,' he said, surprising her totally. And listening to him worried her. If he lost heart now, he could get hurt. She had heard too many stories like that, of men who lost their girlfriends or their wives, and then got killed in action.

'It's too late to say that now,' she scolded him, 'you'd better pay attention to what you're doing.'

'Look who's talking,' he laughed, thinking of what she was facing in barely more than a month. The thought of her tour still worried him sick, as he invited her to take a walk with him, and they walked slowly from her parents' house toward the airport. It just seemed to act like a magnet for them. He told her what England was like for him, and she told him about the tour, and their route across the Pacific.

'It's a damn shame the war won't let you do a

proper one. I'd feel better than with those long stretches across the Pacific.' But that was where the glory was right now, and they both knew that.

They were at the airport while they talked of it, and almost without thinking, they wandered toward the old Jenny. It was a warm night, and the moon was so bright, they could see easily across the airport.

'Want to go for a ride?' he asked hesitantly. She had a right to tell him to go to hell, but they both knew she didn't want to. She wanted to be alone with him for a while, and forget her other life, and the fact that they had to leave each other again tomorrow. This time maybe forever.

'I'd like that,' she said softly. And without another word, she helped him push the plane out, and do their ground check. They sailed into the midnight sky easily, with all the familiar sounds and feelings. But there was something different about doing it at night. They were in their own world up there, a world full of stars and dreams, where no one else could touch or hurt them.

He hesitated only briefly at the old airstrip where they used to meet, and brought the little plane down easily in the moonlight. And then he shut the engine off, and helped Cassie from the plane. They had no idea where they were going, they just knew they needed to be together now, in their own world, away from everyone. And here it was so peaceful. Without thinking, they both wandered toward the place where they used to sit and talk for hours. She felt so much older now, and so much sadder. Her brother was gone, and she had lost all hope of being Nick's now. It was here that he had kissed her for the first time, and told her he loved her. It was the day he had told her he was joining the RAF. And they'd been making bad decisions ever since then.

'Don't you wish you could turn the clock back sometimes?' she asked, looking up at him as he watched her sadly.

'What would you do differently, Cass? Then, I mean?'

'I'd have told you how much I loved you a long time ago. I never thought you'd care because I was just a kid. I thought you'd laugh at me.' She looked beautiful as he watched her standing beside him.

'I thought your father would have me arrested.' It was strange to realize now that Pat wouldn't have disapproved of him, and they had loved each other for so long. And now she was married to someone else, it was all so crazy.

'My father might have you arrested now,' she smiled, 'but not then, I guess.' But she wasn't even sure he'd object now. He knew how much they loved each other, even though this was exactly what he had told her he didn't want her doing. But he had softened so much over the years. He was her closest friend now. Especially now that Nick was gone. Her father had been surprisingly understanding about everything she'd done. It still surprised her.

They walked over to their old familiar log, and the grass was damp. Nick took the old flight jacket off, and let her sit on it, and then he sat down beside her and took her in his arms and kissed her. They both knew why they had come here. They were grown-ups now. They didn't need permission, or have to tell lies. Not tonight at least. They were here because they loved each other, and needed something to take away with them.

'I don't want to do anything dumb,' he said as she nestled close to him, and he worried about her. It was the same worry he had had about her when he left for England. But things were just different enough now to warrant the risk, and in an odd way, this time he almost hoped he'd leave her pregnant. Maybe then she'd have to leave Desmond.

And as she lay down beside him, and felt his powerful arms around her, as he kissed her, she wished the same thing. But within moments, their future paled in comparison to their present. She felt hot flames shoot through her as they kissed, and within minutes, her silvery flesh shimmered next to his in the moonlight. It was a night that neither of them would ever forget, and they both knew it would have to sustain them for years, maybe forever.

'Cassie . . . I love you so much . . .' he whispered tenderly, holding her, feeling her body next to his in the warm night air. She was more beautiful than he'd ever dreamed as they lay with their clothes scattered in the dew around them. 'I was such a fool.' He lay on his side, looking at her, carving each moment in memory. In the moonlight, she looked like a goddess.

'I was a fool too,' she whispered sleepily, but right now she didn't care, as long as she could lie in his arms and be near him. This was all she wanted. For this one moment in time, this was all that mattered.

'Maybe one of these days, we'll both get smart . . . or lucky,' he said, but he doubted it. It was all too complicated now. All they had was this. Tonight. In the silver moonlight.

They lay side by side for a long time, and they made love again just before sunrise. They had both fallen asleep, and awoke in each other's arms, aching for each other in the balmy morning. The sun came up, smiling down at them, and this time he watched her graceful limbs kissed not by silver, but by the golden light of sunrise. And afterward, they held each other close for a long time, wishing they could stay there forever.

When they flew back to her father's airport, the sky was streaked with pink and gold and mauve, and they both looked peaceful as they tied down the Jenny. She turned to him then with a long, slow smile. She didn't regret anything they'd done. This was their destiny.

'I love you, Nick,' she said happily.

'I'll always love you,' he answered, and then he walked her back to her parents' house. They belonged to each other now. Theirs was a bond that could not be broken.

Her parents' house was quiet as they stood outside. It was still early, and no one was up as Nick held her in his arms, and stroked her hair, trying not to think of the future, or Desmond Williams. They stood there for a long time, not wanting to leave each other as he kissed her again, and she told him again and again how much she loved him.

He left finally when he heard her parents get up and move around. They had no regrets. They needed each other's strength to go back to their lives, with all the terrors and challenges they would be facing.

'I'll see you before I go,' she promised him in a whisper, and then she pulled him close to her again, and kissed him on the lips with agonizing softness. He wondered how he would ever leave her again, or watch her go, especially knowing that she was going back to her husband.

'I can't let you go, Cass.'

'I know,' she said unhappily, 'but we have to.' They had no choice now, and they knew it.

He left her then and she walked slowly into the room she'd lived in as a child, thinking of him, and wishing things were different.

She showered, and dressed, thinking of Nick, and then she had breakfast with her parents. And as Nick had seen earlier, she noticed that her father was having trouble breathing. But he insisted it was nothing. And as soon as they were finished eating, her father drove her and Billy to the airport. She promised to call her mother frequently before the tour, and maybe even to fly back once more if she could. But she wondered if Desmond would let her. Seeing her father look so pale made her think she ought to.

Nick was in the office when they arrived, and he looked at her long and hard as they said good-bye, and then he walked out to their plane with them, chatting idly with Billy. But every moment, Cassie could sense him close by, she could feel the satin of his flesh on hers, and their exquisite pleasure. The real bond they shared was time and love and caring, but with passion added to it, Cassie knew now that the flame of her love for him would burn forever.

'Take it away, you two,' Nick admonished them, thinking of the tour again. 'Watch out that she doesn't fly into a tree somewhere,' he warned Billy, and then shook his hand, while Cassie did their ground checks, and he watched her. Nick couldn't keep his eyes from her, and she loved feeling him near her.

She kissed her father then, while Billy settled in, and then there was no escaping it. It was time to say good-bye to Nick. Their eyes met and held, their hands touched, and then he pulled her into his arms and kissed her gently in front of the others. He didn't care anymore. He just wanted to be sure she knew he loved her.

'Take care, Cass,' he whispered into her hair after he kissed her. 'Don't do anything crazy on that tour of yours.' He still wished she wouldn't go but he knew he couldn't stop her.

'I love you,' she said softly, with eyes full of tears that told him everything she felt for him and mirrored everything he felt. 'Let me know how you are sometime.' He nodded, and she stepped up into the cockpit as he squeezed her hand for the last time. It was almost impossible this time to leave each other. Pat was watching them, sorry for both of them. But he said nothing to reproach them.

Her father and Nick were still standing there as they taxied down the runway in the huge Williams Aircraft plane she'd borrowed from Desmond. Once off the ground, she dipped her wings at them, and then they were gone. Nick stood staring at the sky for a long time, long after Pat had walked back into the airport, long after her plane had left the sky. All he could think of now was lying beside her in the moonlight. And in a way, he was relieved that the next morning, he'd be going back to the war. He couldn't stand being here now without her.

She and Billy didn't talk much on the flight back to L.A. Her mother had given them a thermos of coffee, and some fried chicken. But neither of them was hungry. Her eyes told a thousand tales, but he didn't ask her any questions for the first two hours. And then, finally, he couldn't stand the silence any longer.

'How do you feel?' She knew what he was asking her, and she sighed before she answered.

'I don't know. I'm glad I saw him. At least he knows now.' She was filled with hope and despair all at once. It was hard to explain it to Billy. At least Nick knew about Desmond now, but in some ways their time together had only made it harder for her to go back to California.

'How did he take it?'

'As well as he could have. He was furious at first. He said a lot of things.' She hesitated and then looked at her friend grimly. 'He thinks Desmond married me as a publicity stunt to make the tour more appealing to the public.'

'Is that what you think?' he asked pointedly, and she thought about it and hesitated. She didn't want to think that. 'Sounds like sour grapes to me. Maybe it's hard for Nick to admit to himself that the guy really loves you.' But did he? He was so cool to her now, so involved in the tour, and nothing else about her. What if Nick was right, she wondered. It was hard to know, hard to see clearly, especially after the night she'd spent with Nick at the old airstrip. But she knew for certain that she had to put that out of her mind now. She wanted to be fair to Desmond. And she had to think of the tour. She could work the rest out later.

But thinking of the tour reminded her again of everything she owed Desmond. Nick wasn't being fair, and she didn't believe that Desmond had other women. He was completely driven by his work, he was obsessed with it. In a way, that was their biggest problem. That, and Nick Galvin. But she was returning to L.A. determined to play fairly. She wouldn't allow Nick to cast a shadow of doubt on their marriage.

But from the moment she returned, Desmond did everything Nick had predicted. All he did was talk about the press, and the Pacific tour. He didn't even ask about her weekend with her parents. And in spite of herself, she found herself suddenly suspicious of Desmond's coolness, and his constant love affair with photographers and newsreels. She questioned him about some interviews he had scheduled for her, balking at the necessity of it, and the tensions between them were instantly apparent.

'What exactly is it you're complaining about?' he snapped at her nastily at midnight on the day after she got back from her parents. She was exhausted from flying a twelve-hour day, followed by five hours of meetings. And he had ended her day with a bevy of reporters and photographers to take her picture.

'I'm just tired of falling over photographers every time I get out of bed, or climb out of the bathtub. They're everywhere, and I'm tired of it. Get rid of them,' she said pointedly, with a look of irritation.

'What is it that you're objecting to?' he said angrily. 'The fact that you're the biggest name in the news, or that you've been on the cover of *Life* magazine twice this year? What exactly is your problem?'

'My problem is that I'm exhausted, and I'm tired of being treated like a show dog.' Nick's warnings were affecting her. And she realized that she was suspicious of Desmond. But she really was tired of reporters.

And Desmond very clearly didn't like being challenged. He was furious with her. After another hour of arguing pointlessly, he moved into the small guest room off his study. He spent the rest of the week sleeping and working there, claiming he had too much work to do to move back into their bedroom. But she knew he was punishing her for complaining. But in a way it was a relief, and it gave her time to sort out her own confusion. Being with Nick hadn't made things any easier, but she knew that part of that was her own fault.

Eventually, things calmed down again with Desmond. Tensions were high, and their nerves were raw because of the pressures of the tour, but he apologized to her for being 'testy.' He tried to explain the value of the press to her again, and she decided that Nick was wrong about him. There was a certain truth to what Desmond was saying. Publicity was an important part of the Pacific tour, and he was right, there was no point accomplishing it in silence.

Desmond was a decent man, she knew. He just had very definite opinions. And he obviously knew what he was doing.

But in spite of their peace treaty over the press, some things didn't improve. For months now, they had had no love life whatsoever. More than once, she had wondered if there was something wrong with him, or with her, but she would never have dared to ask him. All he thought about was the tour. The budding passion of their honeymoon was long since forgotten. She knew that some of that had made her more vulnerable to Nick. But she also knew that her love for Nick was something Desmond had no part in. But her lack of physical relationship with Desmond made it hard for Cassie to feel close to him, and sometimes she wished she had someone to talk to. She thought of saying something to Nancy Firestone, but ever since her marriage to Desmond, Nancy had put a very definite distance between them. It was as though she felt uncomfortable being friendly with Cassie since she was the boss's wife now. But with no friends except Billy, and Desmond so cool, it made Cassie feel lonelier than ever.

In spite of whatever tensions existed, everything moved ahead on schedule. They were within a week of the tour, and they were ready.

Photographers followed her everywhere chronicling her last week before the trip, every action, every meeting, every movement. She felt as though she was spending her entire life smiling and waving. There was no privacy, no quiet time with Desmond. Everything was the Pacific tour, and the endless preparations for it. This was her only life now.

It was also getting very exciting for all of them. Cassie could hardly sleep anymore. And they were down to five days when Glynnis called her late one afternoon, and reached her at the airfield. Cassie was surprised to hear from her, and wondered if anything was wrong.

'Hi, Glynn . . . what's up?'

'It's Dad,' she answered quickly. She started to cry before she could say another word, and a vise of steel clutched Cassie's heart as she listened. 'He had a heart attack this morning. He's in Mercy Hospital. Mom's with him.' Oh God . . . no . . . not her father.

'Is he going to be okay?' Cassie asked her oldest sister quickly.

'They don't know yet,' Glynnis said, in tears again.

'I'll come home as soon as I can. Tonight. I'll tell Desmond and start in a little while.' Without a moment's hesitation, Cassie knew she had to be there.

'Can you do that?' Glynnis sounded worried, but she knew she had to call her. They had told her at first that her father wasn't going to make it. But in the last hour he had stabilized, and they were cautiously hopeful. 'When do you leave on the tour?'

'Not for five more days. I've got time, Glynn. I'm coming . . . I love you . . . tell Dad I love him . . . tell him to wait . . . not to go . . . please . . .' She was sobbing.

'I love you too, baby,' Glynnis said, in the strong voice of her older sister, 'I'll see you later. Fly safely.'

'Tell Mom I love her too.' They were both crying

as she hung up the phone, and then she went to tell Billy what had happened, and that she was going home to see her father. Without hesitating for an instant, he said he'd go with her. They were inseparable these days, like Siamese twins. They had become like each other's shadows in the six months of training. Sometimes they even seemed to know what the other was thinking.

'I'll meet you back here in half an hour. Do me a favor. Gas up the Phaeton. I'm going to go tell Desmond.' But she knew he'd understand, Cassie thought. He knew how much her father meant to her.

But when she got to his office, she was in for a surprise.

'Of course you're not going,' he said coldly. 'You've got five days of training and briefings left, two press conferences, and we have to plot the final course according to the weather.'

'I'll be back in two days,' she said quietly. She couldn't believe he was arguing with her about something this important.

'You will not,' he said firmly, as Miss Fitzpatrick slipped out of the room discreetly.

'Desmond, my father had a heart attack. He may not survive it.' Obviously, he didn't understand, Cassie thought. But he did. Perfectly.

'Let me make myself clear, Cass. You're *not* going. I am *ordering* you to stay here.' He sounded like an air marshal in a war. It was ridiculous. He was her husband. What was he talking about? She looked at him in confusion.

'You're *what*?' He repeated himself for her benefit and she stared at him. 'My father may die, Desmond. I'm going home to him, whether you like it or not.' Something hardened in her eyes as she said it.

'Against my wishes, and not in one of my planes,' he said coldly.

'I'll steal one if I have to,' she said furiously. 'I can't believe you're saying these things. You must be tired, or sick . . . what's wrong with you?' There were tears in her eyes, but he was immovable. The tour meant everything to him. More than her father. Who was this man she had married?

'Do you have any idea how much money is riding on this tour? Do you care?' he spat at her.

'Of course I care, and I wouldn't do anything to jeopardize it, but this is my father we're talking about. Look, I'll be back in two days. I promise.' She tried to calm down again, and remind herself that they were both under a lot of pressure.

'You're not going,' he repeated coldly. This was ridiculous. What was he trying to do to her? As she looked at him, she started to tremble.

'You have no choice!' she shouted at him, losing control finally. 'I'm going! And Billy's coming with me.'

'I won't allow it.'

'What are you going to do?' She stared at him with new eyes suddenly. She had never seen him so heartless. He had never been cruel to her before. This was a new insight into Desmond. 'Fire us both? Isn't it a little close to the trip, or do you think you can replace us?' She was not amused by his behavior.

'Anyone can be replaced. Eventually. And let me explain something to you, Cass, while we're on the subject. If you *don't* come back, I'll divorce you, and sue you for breach of contract. Is that clear? You have a contract with me for this tour, and I intend to hold you to it.' She couldn't believe what she was hearing. Who was he? If he meant what he was saying, the man was a monster.

Her mouth opened as she listened to him, but no sound came out. Nick had been right. All that mattered to him was the tour. He didn't care about her or her feelings, or the fact that her father was dying. He would divorce her for canceling the tour. It was incredible. But so was everything he had just said to her.

She walked slowly to his desk, and looked at him, wondering if she even knew him. 'I'll fly the tour for you. Because I want to. But after that, you and I are going to have a serious conversation.' He didn't answer her, and she turned around and walked out of his office. She was threatening the only thing in his life he cared about, his precious Pacific tour. But the real shock was that it meant more to him than their marriage.

She said not a word to Billy as she climbed into the plane, and she signed the plane out properly. She suddenly felt like an employee and nothing else. Her face was taut and angry as they took off, and Billy watched her. She had wanted to fly, so he didn't offer to take the controls. It kept her mind occupied while she tried not to worry about her father, but he could see that she did anyway. But she looked angry more than worried, and he wondered what had happened.

'What did he say? . . . about our going, I mean . . .'

'You mean Desmond?' she said icily and he nodded. 'He said he'd divorce me if I didn't do the tour. And he'd sue me for breach of contract.' It had to sink in for a minute before Billy reacted.

'He said *what*? He was kidding obviously.'

'He was not kidding. He was deadly serious. If we cancel, he's going to sue the pants off us. Me, anyway. Apparently, the tour means a little more to him than I thought. This is the big time, Billy. Big investments, big money, big stakes, big penalties if we blow it. Maybe he'll sue our families if we crack up his plane for him,' she said sarcastically, as Billy listened in amazement. She sounded angry and bitterly disappointed.

'But you're his wife, Cass.' He was confused by what she was saying.

'Apparently not,' she said miserably, 'just an employee.' He had disappointed her terribly. But then again, families were not his forte. 'I told him we'd be back in two days. We're in deep shit, kid, if we aren't.' She grinned at him. They were in it now, up to their ears, but at least they were

423

together. She was grateful he had come with her. He was truly her only friend now.

'We'll be back in time. Your dad'll be fine.' He tried to reassure her.

But when they got to Mercy Hospital, Pat was anything but fine. Three nuns and a nurse were standing at his bedside, and a priest had just given him the last rites. All of his children and grandchildren were there, and Oona was crying softly.

Cassie cleared the kids out first, she sent them outside with Billy. She knew he could manage them, he was like the pied piper with kids, and one of her brothers-in-law volunteered to go with him. And then she hugged her mother, and talked quietly to her sisters. Pat wasn't rallying, and he hadn't regained consciousness since Glynnis called her. The doctor came to talk to her a few minutes after that, and he said that he was doubtful now that Pat would make it.

Cassie couldn't believe what she was hearing, or what had happened to him. She had seen him only four weeks before, and he hadn't looked great, but she'd had no idea that he was this sick. Apparently, his heart had been giving him trouble for a while, but he ignored it, despite Oona's pleadings.

Cassie and her mother and all three of her sisters sat with him all night, and by morning there was still no improvement. And it was only late the following day that he regained consciousness, and smiled briefly at Oona. It was the first sign of hope they'd had, and two hours later, he opened his eyes again and squeezed Cassie's hand and told her he loved her. All she could think of then was how much she had loved him as a little girl, how good he had always been to her, and how much she had loved flying with him . . . she thought of a thousand things . . . a hundred special moments.

'Is he going to be okay?' she asked the doctor when he came by that afternoon, and he said it was still too soon to tell. But after another sleepless night for all of them, miraculously, the next morning, as the nuns kept silent vigil with them, saying their rosaries, he stabilized, and the doctor said he was going to make it. It was going to be a long haul, and he predicted two months of solid rest, most of it at home in bed, and after that, with any luck at all, he'd be a new man. But he'd have to take care of himself, not smoke so much, and cut out the whiskey and Oona's homemade ice cream. It was the greatest relief in Cassie's life as she stood crying in the hallway with her sisters. Her mother was still in the room with him, breaking the news to him about the ice cream.

'Who's going to run the airport?' Megan asked as they stood in the hallway. Pat had no assistant these days, and ever since Nick and Cass and Billy had been gone, all the responsibility had fallen on his shoulders. The doctor thought it had probably contributed to the problem. There was no one else around to help him handle the airport.

'Do you know anyone?' she asked Billy in an undertone. He had stood staunchly by them for two days, just as Chris would have. He was almost like their son now. But he didn't know anyone to help out either. A lot of the younger pilots who used to float around had volunteered for the RAF after Nick did.

'I'm stumped,' he said, as she looked at him. They were due back in L.A. that night. They were leaving on the Pacific tour in three days. As Billy looked at her, he read her mind, or he thought he did, but he couldn't believe she would do it. 'You're not thinking what I think you're thinking . . . are you?'

'I might be.' She looked at him seriously. It was a big step. Particularly after what Desmond had said before they left. A very big step. A final one possibly. But the only one, as far as she was concerned. And if he wanted to divorce her for that, let him. This was her father. 'You don't have to stay with me though. You can go back so he doesn't get mad at you.' Things were going to get rough once she told him.

'I can't go without you,' he said calmly.

'Maybe he'll get someone else.' She was being naive, and Billy knew it, even if she didn't. After all the publicity she'd had for the past year, and all the careful orchestration, it would never have had the same impact without her, and Desmond knew that.

'What are you going to do?' Billy asked worriedly. He didn't want her to get hurt by her decision, but he also knew what her father meant to her, and what her priorities were. There was no doubt about what she was going to do, just about how she was going to do it.

'I'm going to call him and tell him to postpone it. He doesn't have to cancel it. Just postpone it. All I want is two months, three max, so Dad can get back on his feet, and I can stay here and run the airport.'

'I'll stay with you. Possibly permanently,' he grinned. 'We may both be out of a job in about ten minutes.' But it was more than a job to her, he realized. For Cassie it was her marriage. But after Desmond's threats the day before, she wasn't sure if she had a marriage anymore, or if she'd ever had. Maybe Nick had been right about him all along, or maybe Desmond had just let the emotions of the moment get away from him, and by now he was sorry. Interestingly, he had not called Cassie once, at home, or at the hospital, since she'd left. She hadn't heard a thing from him in two days. And when she called him five minutes later from the hospital switchboard, Miss Fitzpatrick answered her with a tone of ice and went to get him.

He came on the line to her almost immediately, and she was sorry about the lack of privacy in the hospital lobby, but it couldn't be helped. She had to tell him as soon as possible, and she didn't want to go all the way to the airport to talk to him from her father's office.

'Where are you?' were his opening words.

'At the hospital in Good Hope. With my father.' As though he didn't remember. He did not ask her about his father-in-law, or how she was. For all he knew, her father was dead by then, but he didn't inquire about him. 'Desmond, I'm sorry to have to do this.'

'Cassie, I'm not going to listen to what you're telling me,' he said in a tone of icy fury. 'Remember what I said to you when you left, and remember that I meant it.' She paused only long enough to catch her breath, and remind herself that this was a man she had married four and a half months before. It was suddenly difficult to believe it. He was everything Nick had said he was, and wasn't.

'I remember everything you said perfectly,' she shouted at him across a poor connection. 'And I seem to remember marrying you. Apparently, you've forgotten. There's more to life than world tours. I'm not just a machine, or a flyboy in a dress, or one of your employees. I'm a human being with a family and my father almost died two days ago. I'm not leaving him. I want you to postpone the tour for two or three months. I'll go in September or October. You figure out when. Make whatever adjustments you have to for the weather and the course. I'll do whatever you want. But I'm not going three days from now. They need me here. I'm not leaving.'

'You bitch,' he shouted at her, 'you selfish little bitch! Do you know what I've put into this, not only in money, but in time and love and effort? You have no idea what this means to me, or to the country. All you're interested in is your own pathetic little tawdry life with your seamy little family, and your father's embarrassing little airport.' He spoke with utter contempt for her, and for them, and she couldn't believe what she was hearing. What a heartless bastard he was to even say things like that to her. It was almost impossible to believe it. And as she listened to him, she felt a physical pain as she realized that she and Desmond Williams had never had a marriage. She had just been a tool to get him what he wanted.

'I don't care what you call me, Desmond,' she shouted across the lobby, indifferent to who heard her anymore. 'Postpone the trip, or cancel it. It's up to you. But I'm not going now. I'll fly anything you want in the fall, but I'm not going in three days. I'm staying with my father.'

'And Billy?' he asked furiously. He wanted to fire both of them, but he knew he couldn't.

'He's staying here with me, with my tawdry little family, at our embarrassing little airport. And I won't fly it for you next time, Desmond, without him. You've got us, if you want us. But later. Let me know what you decide. You know where to reach me.'

'I'll never forgive you for this, Cassie.'

'So I gather.' And then she couldn't help asking, 'What exactly is it you're so angry about, Desmond, as long as I've agreed to do it later?'

'The embarrassment, the postponement. Why should we have to put up with this childish garbage from you?'

429

'Because I could have gotten sick . . . because I'm human. That's it, why don't you just tell the press I'm sick or something.' She laughed shallowly, knowing that it was beyond impossible, at the moment. 'Tell them I'm pregnant.'

'You don't amuse me.'

'I'm sorry to hear that. I'm not finding you very amusing either. In fact, I'm finding you very disappointing. Call me, when you decide what you're doing. I'll be at the airport for the next two months. Call me anytime,' she said with tears in her eyes, and then hung up on him with a bang. She had wanted to tell him she was sorry for postponing the trip, but he had treated her so abominably that in the end she hadn't. She was sorry to have to postpone it, she knew it was hard on everyone involved, but she just couldn't let her father down now. He had always been there for her, and now she wanted to be there for him. But there were tears of anger and defeat in her eyes when she hung up the phone, and her hands were shaking. And as she put the receiver back in the cradle she happened to glance at the old nun who was running the switchboard. She was smiling at her, and she gave her a sign of victory from her seat at the switchboard.

'You tell 'em,' she growled. 'America loves you, Cass. They can wait another two or three months. Good for you for staying with your father. God bless you.'

Cassie smiled gratefully at her, and went back to report to Billy.

'What did he say?' he asked anxiously.

'I'm not sure yet. I told him to postpone it, and said that we'd fly it for him in September or October. He called me a lot of rude names. I wouldn't exactly say he was pleased. And I told him you were staying here with me, and that I wouldn't fly the next one without you. It's a package deal.' Billy whistled at the courage she had shown, and he patted her shoulder. 'But listen, if you want to go back, I understand. You can even fly it for him yourself if you want to.' There was a lot she needed to think about now. About the trip, about her marriage, about everything he had said to her, and the things he hadn't. He had exposed himself to her completely. There were not many illusions left. After four and a half months, their marriage was over. In reality anyway, but not in the papers.

What she hadn't counted on was Desmond arriving in Good Hope the next day, and bringing with him over a hundred reporters and two newsreel crews. He announced right from the steps of Mercy Hospital that due to circumstances beyond their control, the Pacific tour was being postponed until October. He explained that his father-in-law was critically ill, and Cassie couldn't leave him. She would be running her father's airport for him for two months, and then training again for the tour in September. He caught her completely by surprise and he proved once and for all that he was everything Nick had said he was. He was a total fake and a bastard. And through it all, he pretended to care deeply about her father.

But he hadn't even told her he was coming. He had just showed up at the hospital, asked for her, and when she came out to see him, looking surprised, she found him waiting with a lobby full of reporters. He had set up a full press conference on the hospital steps, without even warning her. And she looked haggard and exhausted and unprepared, which was exactly what he wanted. He wanted America to feel sorry for her, so they would forgive her for canceling the tour. But there was no question of it. They would forgive her anything. It was Desmond who wouldn't. She was so overcome, and so tired, and so emotional, and so angry at him, that she ended up crying when the reporters asked her about her father. It was exactly what Desmond wanted.

And when the press had left, he walked her outside and explained to her in no uncertain terms what he expected from her. She had exactly two months 'leave,' as he put it, from the tour. On September 1, she was to come back to L.A. to train again and attend briefings, and on October 4 they would leave on the same course, with some slight adjustments for weather. Any variation from that plan, or any failure on her part to appear in Los Angeles, as agreed, would result in a lawsuit. And to be sure she understood perfectly, he had brought contracts with him for her and Billy to sign, and he reminded her that he was flying back the plane she had arrived in.

'Anything else? Would you like my underwear or my shoes? I think you paid for them too. I left my engagement ring in L.A., but you're certainly welcome to it, it's yours. You can have my wedding ring too.' She slipped it off her shaking hand, and held it out to him with trembling fingers. Everything that had happened in the past few days was a nightmare. And he looked at her now, totally devoid of emotion. He was a man who felt nothing for anyone, not even the girl he had married.

'I suggest you leave it on until after the tour, so as not to cause any gossip. You can dispose of it quietly after that, if you like. That's up to you,' he said coldly.

'That's what this was all about then, wasn't it? It was all about a publicity stunt for the tour. America's sweetheart and the big tycoon. Why did you bother? And what happened to you? Why are you so willing to expose yourself now? Just because I postponed it? Is that such a sin? I know it's inconvenient, and expensive to change plans. But what if we'd had a problem with the plane . . . or I got sick . . . what if I did get pregnant?'

'There was never any danger of that, I can't have children.' He hadn't told her that either. He had let her think that it was an option, that they would have them one day, when she was ready. She couldn't believe how totally he'd misled her, and how willing he was now to admit it. He had shown his hand to her completely. But he didn't care. All he wanted from her was the tour; he knew that he could sue her, and destroy her publicly if she didn't do it. The stupid thing was that she didn't care what he did to her. All she cared about was that he had lied to her. He had asked her to marry him, told her he loved her, pretended he cared about her. He didn't care about anything except his tour, and the planes he would sell as a result. And the publicity he would derive from organizing it from start to finish.

'What do you want from me?' She looked at him sadly.

'I want you to fly. That's all I ever wanted from you. I want you to fly. And I want everyone to fall in love with you. Whether or not I did was never important.'

'It was important to me,' she said with tears in her eyes. She had truly believed him.

'You're very young, Cassie,' he said quietly. 'One day you'll be happy you did this.'

'You didn't have to marry me to make me fly the tour. I'd have done it anyway.'

'It wouldn't have had the same impact on the public,' he said without embarrassment. His marriage to her had been totally calculated. She wondered if he had ever cared for her for a single moment. She felt totally stupid now, gullible and used. It was embarrassing to think of their physical relations. Even their honeymoon had probably been a sham. And everything after that had been business anyway. He hadn't wasted much time on romance.

'You never took the tour seriously. Your postponing it now just proves that. I probably should have picked someone else, but you seemed so perfect.' He looked at her as though she had cheated him and she stared at him in amazement.

'I wish you had picked someone else,' she said, and meant it.

'It's too late now. For both of us. We have to go through with it. We've all gone too far now.'

'We certainly have.' She looked at him pointedly. Or at least he had.

He had nothing else to say to her, no apology, no regrets, no words of comfort. He just told her to be in L.A. on schedule on September first, and she and Billy signed their contracts. Desmond drove back to the airport then, and an hour later he was gone. He had gotten what he'd come for, their sworn promise, and a round of publicity using Cassie again. By the following week, the entire country knew about her father's heart attack, they'd seen her cry, they sympathized completely. It only made the tour more exciting.

And at Mercy Hospital, her father was bombarded with flowers and gifts and get-well cards. They had to give them away to other patients, and then start taking the floral arrangements away in trucks, to other hospitals and churches. Cassie had never expected a response like that. But Desmond had. As usual, he had known exactly what he was doing.

He kept feeding them stories regularly, and gave

435

interviews from L.A. about how hard Cassie was working, and what progress they had made on her plane. But interestingly, in August, one of the engineers discovered a potential flaw in one of the engines. They were doing wind tunnel trials at the California Institute of Technology when the engine burst into flame, and it caused untold damage to her airplane. It could be repaired, the press was told, but it had been providential that the tour had been delayed and she'd had to stay home with her father. The first Cassie heard of it was when she read the newspaper to Billy, and he whistled.

'Nice, huh? How would you have liked to be peeing on your number-one engine over the Pacific?' she said with a raised eyebrow.

'Give me enough beer, and I can do great things, Captain.' He grinned, and she laughed. But they were both concerned, and they spoke to the engineers several times over it. Everyone assured them that the problem had been taken care of.

It was a tough summer for her. She was still in shock over everything that had happened with Desmond. She thought of Nick a great deal, and she wanted to write to him, but she wasn't sure what to say now. In a funny way, it was hard admitting that Desmond was as bad as Nick thought he was. It made her sound so pathetic. In the end, she just wrote to him about her father, and said that the tour had been postponed, and that she'd always love him. She decided to tell him the rest later, the next time she saw him. She thought of volunteering for the RAF too, but she didn't want to think about that until after the Pacific tour. Maybe afterward, in November, she could fly over to see him. They hadn't heard from him in two months, though that wasn't unusual. The war in Europe was raging on and they could only assume he was safe since they hadn't been notified otherwise. She missed him constantly, and read everything she could about the air war in England.

Most of the fun had gone out of the tour for her. To be doing it under threat was very different from doing it for love, or as a shared project. But she knew it would be interesting anyway, and now all she wanted to do was get it over and done with. She could get on with her life then.

Her father made steady improvements after he went home. He lost some weight, he stopped smoking, and seldom drank, and he looked healthier and stronger day by day. And by the end of August, he came back to the airport. And he seemed better than ever. He was amazed at all that she and Billy had done, and grateful to him for staying with her. But it was his daughter who had won his heart, more than ever. She was a rare and marvelous girl, he said to everyone, she had postponed the Pacific tour just for him, as though they hadn't heard it. And she had told him nothing of her problems with Desmond. Nonetheless he had sensed long since that something was bothering her, and he wondered if it was Nick, or something else. It wasn't until the night before she left that she finally told him.

'Is it Nick that's bothering you, Cass?' He knew she was haunted by the man, and he was worried about how close they had obviously still been the last time she saw him. He was sorry things hadn't worked out for them. But she couldn't have waited for him indefinitely if Nick had told her not to. Pat had tried to tell him it was a mistake, setting her free like that, but young people never listen. Not that Nick was so young anymore. He was old enough to know a thing or two. But like most men, he was foolish when it came to women. . 'You can't pine for him, Cassie. Not married to another man.' She nodded, loath to tell him the truth. She was so ashamed of her own bad judgment. Desmond had taken her in completely.

'There's something you're not telling me, Cassandra Maureen,' her father prodded her, and in the end, in spite of herself, she told him. And he was stunned at what she said. It was everything Nick had warned them of and predicted.

'He was right, Dad. Completely.'

'What are you going to do now?' He wanted to kill the man. What a rotten trick to pull on a girl like her, to exploit her so totally for his own gain and glory.

'I don't know. Fly the tour, obviously. I really do owe him that. I wouldn't back out on him, though I don't think he knows that. I'll do it. And then' – she took a breath, there weren't many choices

438

– 'we'll get divorced, I guess. I'm sure somehow he'll make it look as though I did something terrible. He'll manipulate the press somehow to his advantage. He's much more complicated than I realized. And a whole lot meaner.'

'Will he give you anything?' her father wondered. He was a very rich man, and he could have paid her handsomely for her disappointment.

'I doubt it. I'll make my fee for the tour. He was going to reduce it because of the postponement, but he didn't. He considers that a major gift. I don't need more than that. I don't want anything from him. He's been generous enough.' And she could live for years on the career he had helped her achieve, that was payment enough. She wanted nothing more from Desmond.

'I'm sorry, Cassie. I'm so very sorry.' He was deeply distressed by what he'd heard from her, and they both agreed not to upset her mother.

'Just take care of yourself on the tour. That's all that's important now. You can sort the rest out later.'

'Maybe I'll fly bombers to England when I come back, like Jackie Cochran.' That June, she had co-piloted a Lockheed Hudson bomber to England, proving once and for all that women could fly heavy airplanes.

'Oh, be gone with you,' her father rolled his eyes with a groan, 'flying bombers to England. You'll give me another heart attack. I swear, you'll make me rue the day I ever took you up in an airplane. Can't you do something ordinary for a while, like answer phones somewhere, or cook, or help your mother clean house?' But he was teasing her, and she knew it. He knew there was no hope of her giving up the skies now. 'Fly safely, Cass,' he warned her before she left. 'Be careful. Watch everything, with all your senses.' He knew she was good at that. He had never seen a better pilot.

And the next morning when she left, they all cried at seeing her go, and knowing the danger of the Pacific tour. And Cassie and Billy cried right along with them. Pat and another pilot flew them to Chicago, and Billy and Cassie flew back to California commercially from there. It was pleasant actually, for a change. The Skygirls made a big fuss over her, and she and Billy sat and talked about their month of training. It had been peaceful for them, hanging out together at the airport all summer, just like the old days, only better. They were older now. They had interesting days ahead. And in spite of Desmond, Cassie was getting excited about the tour.

'What are you going to do about a place to stay when you get back to Newport Beach?' Billy asked her quietly as they flew back.

'I haven't thought of that. I don't know . . . I can't stay at a hotel, I guess.' She suspected Desmond wouldn't like that, because of the scandal. But she couldn't imagine staying in his house with him after everything that had happened. He hadn't called her once in the past two months, and the only letters from him were from his lawyers or his office.

'You can stay with me, if you want. If anyone finds out, we can say it's for training. What do you think?' Billy offered.

'I think I'd like to,' she said honestly. She had nowhere else to go now.

She went home with him that night, with some clothes she'd brought from Illinois, and some flight overalls. And she went to work with him the next day, in his old jalopy. With all the money he made, Billy still hadn't bought himself a decent car, and he didn't plan to. He loved his old Model A, even though at least half the time it never started.

'For a guy who flies the best airplanes in the sky, how can you drive a car like this?' she asked at three-thirty in the morning.

'Easy,' he grinned. 'I love it.'

They were hard at work by the time the sun came up, and they didn't finish until late that night. They were also scheduled for a practice night flight. Cassie didn't even see Desmond until the second day, and only then because she ran into him in a hangar near his office. She was surprised to see him there, but he was giving someone a tour, and he dropped by to see her afterward. He wanted to make sure she wasn't going to say anything inappropriate to the press. And he was no nicer to her than he had been the last time she saw him.

'Where exactly is it you're staying?' He had suspected she wouldn't come back to him, and he didn't really care, as long as she kept it quiet.

He had packed up all her things and put them in storage in coded boxes in one of the hangars. The only thing he didn't want was for her to create a scandal. But he also knew her well enough to know she wouldn't. She had too much integrity, too much pride. She wanted to do the Pacific tour for him, and do it right. She had no desire to do anything to hurt him.

'I'm staying with Billy,' she said with a dignified look, wearing one of her old flight suits.

'Just be discreet about it,' he said coldly. But he knew better than anyone that at this point even a tiff reported by the press wouldn't really hurt them.

'Obviously. I don't think anyone even suspects that I'm staying at Billy's.' She had thought about calling Nancy Firestone before that, but Cassie had been embarrassed to ask to stay with her and Jane. They weren't close anymore, and Billy had invited her to stay at his place. The one thing she couldn't have done was stay at a hotel. That would have wound up instantly in the papers, unless Desmond was there with her, which of course he wasn't.

Oddly enough, she ran into Nancy Firestone later that day, right after she had run into Desmond. Nancy was leaving work, and Cassie was running out to grab something to eat for herself and Billy, before coming back for a night of meetings.

'It's getting close, isn't it?' Nancy said with a smile. Everyone at Williams Aircraft was counting the days and the minutes. And Cassie looked tired and strained as she smiled and nodded. Seeing Desmond at the end of a long day hadn't done anything to lift Cassie's spirits. He was so unkind to her, so cold, it was impossible to imagine that there had ever been anything more than business between them. But at least Nancy was warmer to her than she'd been in a long time, and it was good to see her.

'It's getting very close,' Cassie smiled. 'How's Jane? I miss her. I haven't seen her in ages.'

'She's fine.' The two women stood looking at each other for a long moment, and Cassie suddenly realized that Nancy was looking at her strangely. She looked as though she wanted to say something to her, but she wasn't sure. And for an instant, Cassie wondered if she had ever done anything to offend her, if that was why Nancy had been so cool after Cassie had married Desmond. Or maybe she'd just felt awkward with Cassie's new position. The thought of it almost made Cassie smile. If that was what had bothered her, she could relax now.

'We should get together some time,' Cassie said warmly, trying to be friendly in memory of old times. It was Nancy who had made her feel at home when she'd first come to Los Angeles and was so lonely.

But Nancy only looked at her now, as though she couldn't believe what Cassie was saying. 'You still don't get it, Cass, do you?'

'Get what?' Cassie felt like a fool, but she had

too many other things on her mind to want to play guessing games with Nancy.

'He's not what you ever thought of him. Very few people know him as he is.' Cassie stiffened at the oblique mention of Desmond. She wasn't about to get lured into discussing him with Nancy. As far as anyone knew, he was still her husband.

'I don't know what you mean,' Cassie said coolly, looking the other woman over. And suddenly she realized that there was a great deal more here than she'd ever seen. There was anger, and jealousy, and envy. Was Nancy in love with him? Had she been jealous of Cassie? Cassie suddenly realized how naive she'd been, about all of them. It seemed as though none of them had been what they'd pretended.

'I don't think we should be talking about Desmond,' Cassie said quietly. 'Unless you'd like to discuss it with him directly.'

'That's a possibility,' Nancy said with a supercilious smile. 'I knew he wouldn't stay with you for long. It was all for show. Too bad you never figured that out, Cass.' But what did she know about all of it? What had Desmond told her?

Cassie blushed as she shrugged a shoulder. 'It's a little complicated for me, I guess. Where I come from, people usually get married for other reasons.'

'I'm sure he was taken with you. And you might even have hung onto him if you'd played your cards right. But he doesn't like to play with kids. More than anything, Cass, I think you bored him.' And then, as Cassie looked at her, she understood what she was saying. She understood all of it, and how vicious they had been to her, how rotten.

'And you don't, Nancy? Is that it?'

'It would appear not. But then again, I'm a little more mature. I play the game better than you do.'

'And what game is that?' Cassie wanted to know now.

'It's a game of doing exactly what he wants, when he wants it, and exactly the way he wants it.' To Cassie it sounded like a service business and not a marriage.

'Is that your contract with him? Is that how you got your house, and the college education for Janie? I always thought he was so generous. But I guess maybe there's more to it than meets the eye.' This was exactly what Nick had meant. Desmond Williams had mistresses, whom he paid handsomely to be on call for him, and do whatever he wanted. For Nancy, it had meant chaperoning Cassie around. And suddenly Cassie realized how much it must have irked her. In a way, if it hadn't been so disgusting, it might almost have been funny.

'Desmond is very generous with me. But I don't have any illusions about him,' Nancy said coldly, looking right at Cassie. 'He's never going to marry me. He's never going to get involved with me in public. But he knows I'm here for him. And he's good to me. It works out very well for both of us.' But suddenly, listening to the cold simplicity of it, the calculated emptiness that allegedly met

445

his needs, Cassie wanted to reach out and slap her.

'Was he with you when he was married to me?' Cassie asked in a strangled voice, terrified by the conversation.

'Obviously. Where do you think he went at night when he wasn't working? And why do you think he wasn't sleeping with you? I told you, Cassie, he doesn't like playing games with children. And he's not as evil as you think. He didn't think there was any point sleeping with you, or misleading you more than he had to. Everything was for the tour. In some ways, Desmond is a purist.'

'The bastard.' The words escaped Cassie without any thought on her part. But as she looked at Nancy, she suddenly hated her. And him. It had all been a game. For both of them. It was all part of the Pacific tour, and the grander scheme of things, all to sell airplanes.

Marrying her had been just one small part of the plan, for publicity, and all the while he'd been sleeping with Nancy. No wonder Nancy had been so cool to her once they married. And maybe, for a little while, Nancy had even been worried. She was ten years older than Cassie, and not nearly as exciting, or as pretty.

'Weren't you just a little bit afraid he might fall for me?' Cassie eyed her carefully, and was pleased to see the older woman squirm at the question.

'Not really. We talked about it. You're really not his type, Cass.'

'Actually, given everything I know, I'd say that's a compliment.' Cassie looked at her coolly. And then she decided to deliver a small blow to the opponent. 'You're not alone, you know. You're not the only one with an arrangement with Desmond.' She said it very confidently, and it was easy to see that she had made Nancy more than a little nervous. Her livelihood and her future depended on her 'arrangement' with Desmond.

'What's that supposed to mean?'

'There are others like you ... with houses ... with contracts ... with arrangements ... Desmond's not a man to be satisfied with one woman.' Cassie was rewarded with a look of terror.

'That's ridiculous. Who told you that?'

'Someone who knows. He told me that there are quite a number of others. You know, kind of like a little competition.'

'I don't believe you.' But her words reeked of bravado.

'I didn't believe any of it, Nancy. I do now though. Nice to see you,' she smiled. 'Say hello to Desmond.' And with that, she hurried back into the building. She didn't want anything to eat anymore. Nancy Firestone had ruined her appetite. She felt sick when she went back to find Billy in the hangar.

'Where's my dinner?' They both had to be in a meeting in less than half an hour, and he was starving.

'I ate it on the way back,' she quipped, but she

was looking deathly pale. He noticed it immediately and was worried.

'You okay, Cass? You look like you've seen a ghost. Did someone call about your dad?'

'No, he's okay. I talked to my mother this morning.'

'So what happened?' She hesitated for a long moment, and then sat down in a chair, and told him about Nancy Firestone, and everything she'd told her.

'That sonofabitch,' he commented through tightened lips. 'He really plays quite a game, doesn't he? Too bad he has to go around ruining other people's lives. It would be nice if he stuck to his own kind.'

'I guess he does, at least some of the time.' Nancy Firestone had certainly not been the friend she'd thought her. 'All I want to do after the tour is leave L.A., and go home for a while. I think I've about done it here. This is a little racy for me.' She looked drained as she looked up at him and he nodded. He felt sorry for her, she didn't deserve this.

And for Cassie, it explained why they never made love anymore and why he'd never had any real interest in her after the honeymoon. He had just gone on seeing Nancy, and God only knew who else. Maybe she was lucky he hadn't bothered spending time in bed with her. Maybe she'd have felt worse now if they had. She suspected she would have. What she felt now was betrayed, and more than a little foolish. The worst part was that she had really believed him. The bastard.

'So what do we do now?' Billy asked, worried about her. He kept wondering if, because of Desmond's betrayal of her, she would throw in the towel, with or without a contract. But she didn't do things that way. She had every intention of finishing what she'd started. And Billy admired her for it.

'We finish the race, kid. That's what we came here for. The rest was all icing on the cake anyway.' And for Cassie, for a while now, the cake had been poisoned. But nobody had ever called Cassie O'Malley a quitter.

'Good girl.' Billy gave her a hug, and took her out for a quick dinner. But she hardly touched it.

There was a press conference every week after that, and Desmond made a point of being friendly to her publicly. There was lots of bantering, some funny little stories about her, and a small show of affection. It was all very touching, if you didn't know what was really happening. And it was surprisingly believable, to anyone who didn't know them.

Cassie seemed more serious than previously, but that was easily explained by the pressures of the upcoming tour. She had an important task set before her. She was training hard, and Desmond reminded the press frequently that she had spent the entire summer taking care of her father.

'How's your dad, Cass?' one of the reporters asked her.

'He's doing great.' And then she thanked America for their gifts and cards and letters.

'It really helped him. He's flying again, with a co-pilot now,' she said proudly. They ate it up. Just the way they ate everything Desmond had fed them. She knew the game now. And Billy marveled at how good at it she was when he watched her.

'You okay?' he asked her in an undertone after one of their press conferences. Desmond had been particularly nice to her, and Billy could see afterward that he had really upset her.

'Yeah. I'm okay,' she said, but he knew how hurt she was. And how betrayed she felt. She hated the hypocrisy of it, the pure sham of it. She had nightmares at night. And once from the next room, where he slept, he heard her crying.

She never saw Desmond alone again, until the night before the Pacific tour. There had been a huge press conference that afternoon, and she and Billy had gone out for a quiet dinner at her favorite Mexican restaurant afterward.

When they got back, Desmond was waiting for them. He was sitting in his parked car, and when he got out, he let Billy know he wanted to talk to Cassie.

'I just wanted to wish you luck tomorrow. I'll see you there before you take off, but I wanted you to know that . . . well, I'm sorry things didn't really work out the way we planned.' He was trying to be magnanimous, but the way he did it made her very angry.

'What exactly *did* you plan? I was planning to have a life, and a husband and children.' He was planning to have a world tour, and a mistress, and a cardboard wife he'd drag out for newsreels.

'Then you should have married someone else, I guess. I was looking for a partnership. And not much more than that. This was business. But isn't that what marriage is, Cassie?' He tried to make it sound as though things just hadn't worked out, and not as though he had lied to her about everything, including being sterile. She could have lived with that, she could have lived with a lot of things, if he'd been honest with her. But they both knew he never had been.

'I don't think you have any idea what marriage is, Desmond.'

'Maybe not,' he said without embarrassment. 'To tell you the truth, it's not something I've ever really wanted.'

'So why bother? I would have flown this for you, without all the nonsense, the lies . . . the wedding . . . You didn't have to go that far. You used me,' she said, relieved that she had finally had a chance to say it.

'We used each other. You're going to be the biggest star in aviation there ever was two months from now. And I put you there. In one of my planes. It's a wash, Cass. We're even.' He seemed pleased with himself. It was all he wanted. She meant nothing to him. She never had. That was the hard part.

'Congratulations. I hope you enjoy it as much as you thought you would.'

'I will.' He was sure of it. 'And so will you. And so will Billy. We all win on this one.'

'If everything goes right. You're assuming an awful lot,' she said cautiously.

'I have a right to. You're flying a remarkable plane, and you're a great pilot. It doesn't take more than that. Except Lady Luck, and some fine weather.' He looked at her long and hard, willing her to do right by him, but offering her nothing in return except glory and money. Love wasn't part of his scheme of things. He didn't have it in him. 'Good luck, Cass,' he said quietly.

'Thanks,' she said, and walked upstairs to Billy's apartment.

'What did he want?' Billy asked suspiciously. He was worried that Desmond might have said something to upset Cassie.

'Just to wish us luck, I guess. In his own way. There's no one in there . . . I finally figured that out . . . the man's completely empty.' It was truer than she knew. There was no soul to Desmond Williams. Only greed and calculation, and an unfailing passion for airplanes, never people. She was just a tool, no different from a wrench to tune the engine. She was a vehicle to success, nothing more, a cog in one of his machines, and in fact, a very small one. He was the puppeteer, the designer, the spirit behind it. In his eyes, she was nothing.

18

The *North Star* took off, right on schedule, on the morning of October 4, as planned, with a crowd of hundreds watching. The cardinal of Los Angeles blessed the plane. There was champagne for everyone, and she took off into the horizon on a circuitous route that was designed to break distance records, and accommodate the vagaries of world politics at the moment.

They flew south first to Guatemala City, covering two thousand two hundred miles at one gulp, without refueling. And when they arrived, they checked their maps, the weather, and spent some time investigating the area, and talking to the locals. People were fascinated by the plane, and flocked to the airport to see them. Desmond had done his homework well. People all over the world knew of Cassie's journey.

The press were waiting for them en masse at the Guatemala City airport, along with ambassadors, envoys, diplomats, and politicians. There was a marimba band playing, and Cassie and Billy posed for photographs. No one had gotten as much attention since Charles Lindbergh.

'Not a bad life, huh?' Cassie teased him as they took off for San Cristóbal in the Galápagos the next day, a mere eleven hundred miles, which took them just over three hours in the extraordinary plane Williams Aircraft had built them. Desmond had gotten his first wish this time. They had just set a record for speed and distance.

'Maybe we should just stop somewhere for a vacation,' Billy suggested, and she grinned as they were met by Ecuadorian officials, American military personnel, and local natives. There were more photographers, and the governor of the islands invited them to dinner.

The trip was going beautifully, and they spent a day there, checking the plane over carefully, and checking maps and weather again. Things couldn't have looked better.

From the Galápagos, they flew another twenty-four hundred miles to Easter Island in exactly seven hours. But this time they met with unexpected winds, and narrowly missed breaking the record.

'Better luck next time, kid,' Billy joked with her as they taxied down the runway at Easter Island. 'That husband of yours is liable to burn our homesteads down if we don't get him some more records.' They both knew that Desmond had an eye on the Japanese who had been working on a plane for the past year which could fly nonstop from Tokyo to New York, a distance of nearly seven thousand miles, but so far they had encountered nothing but problems, and hadn't even made it as far as Alaska. Their first test flight was scheduled only a year from now. And Desmond had every intention of beating them to it, which was why these long distances across the Pacific interested him so greatly.

They found Easter Island a fascinating place while they refueled. It was filled with innocent, beautiful people and intriguing moai statues. There were stories that went back to prehistoric man, and mysteries Cassie would have loved to explore if she'd had the time to stay there.

They stayed on Easter Island for only one night, to rest up for the long leg the following day to Papeete, Tahiti. And this time they managed to just barely shave the record. They traveled two thousand seven hundred miles in seven hours fourteen minutes, without a single problem.

Landing in Tahiti was like arriving in Paradise, and as Billy looked out at the girls lined up along the runway in sarongs, waving at them and carrying leis, he let out a whoop of glee that brought Cassie to gales of laughter.

'My God, they're paying us to do this, Cass? Oh, baby, I don't believe this!'

'Behave yourself, or they're going to put us in jail if you go out there looking like that.' He was practically panting and drooling. He was like a big funny kid, and she loved flying with him. More importantly, he was an outstanding navigator and a brilliant mechanic.

In fact, he had picked up a noise he didn't like just after they took off from Easter Island. And after paying suitable homage to the local girls, he wanted to come back and check it out. When they cabled home that night, they mentioned it, but assured everyone that it was by no means a serious problem. They were giving them daily reports of their progress, and were relieved to be able to announce that they had just broken another record.

In Papeete, almost everyone spoke French, and Billy spoke just enough to get by. There was a dinner given by the French ambassador for them, and Cassie apologized that she had nothing to wear but her flight suit. Someone lent her a beautiful sarong instead, and she wore a big pink flower in her hair when Billy escorted her to dinner.

'You sure don't look like Lindy to me,' he said admiringly, putting an arm around her as they walked from their hotel to the embassy. But the relationship between them was strictly one of brother and sister. And as they walked along the beach afterward, talking about the trip, Cassie said sadly that she wished Nick could be there. Papeete was a magical place, and the people were wonderful. It was the most beautiful place she'd ever seen, and she resisted any comparison to her honeymoon in Mexico. That was a memory she wanted to forget now.

She and Billy sat on the beach late that night,

talking about the people they'd met, the things they'd seen. The dinner at the embassy had been impressively civilized, and even in a sarong she felt somewhat out of place, though less so than she would have in her wrinkled flight suit.

'Sometimes the things we do still stagger me,' Cassie said with a smile, fingering the flower she'd worn in her hair that evening. 'I mean how did we get so lucky? Look at the plane we're flying all over the world . . . the people we meet . . . the places we go . . . it's like someone else's life . . . how did I get here? Do you ever feel like that, Billy?' She felt so young sometimes, so old at others. At twenty-two, she felt like she'd had a lot of good luck, and not much bad luck, all things considered. But that was the way she saw things.

'I'd say you paid a high price for this trip, Cass . . . higher than I did,' he said seriously, thinking of her marriage, 'but yeah, I feel like that. I keep waiting for someone to grab me by the scruff of the neck, and say "hey, what's that kid doing here? He doesn't belong here!"'

'You belong here,' she said warmly. 'You're the best there is. I wouldn't have done this without you.' The only other person she could think of who she would have liked to fly it with was Nick. Maybe some day.

'It's gonna be over too soon, you know that, Cass. I thought of that when we got here. Zip . . . it's over . . . gone . . . you plan and practice and sweat for a whole year, and then whoops . . . ten days . . . it's over.' They were almost halfway there already, and Cassie felt sad thinking about it. She didn't want the trip to end so quickly.

They walked slowly back to their hotel after that, and she said something to Billy that surprised him. 'I guess I should be grateful to Desmond for all this . . . and I am . . . but in a funny way, it doesn't seem like his trip now. He told all those lies, and did all his scheming, but it's our trip. We're doing it. We're here. He isn't. Somehow, all of a sudden, he doesn't seem all that important.' It was a relief for her, and Billy was glad she wasn't tormenting herself about the rotten deal she'd gotten from her erstwhile husband.

'Forget him, Cass. When we go back, all of that will be history. You'll have all the glory.'

'I don't think the glory is ever what I wanted,' she said honestly. 'I just wanted the experience, to know I could do it.' But not enough to ruin someone's life for.

'Yeah, me too,' he agreed, but he was also realistic about the hullabaloo that would come later. 'But the glory won't be bad either.' He smiled boyishly and she laughed, and then looked at him seriously.

'I was going to file for divorce before we left, but I decided to wait until after the trip, just in case some nosy reporter got wind of it. I didn't want to screw things up by moving too soon. But all the papers are ready and signed.' She sighed as she remembered going to the lawyer's office.

It had been a painful experience telling him what had happened.

'What are you going to get him on?' Billy asked with interest. He could think of at least half a dozen things, none of them pleasant, starting with adultery, and ending with breaking Cassie's heart, if that was officially grounds for divorce now.

'I guess fraud, for a start. It sounds terrible, but the lawyer says we have grounds.' And then of course there was Nancy. 'I think we're going to try to come to some quiet, mutual agreement. Maybe a divorce in Reno, if he'll agree to it. At least then it would be over quickly.'

'I'm sure he will,' Billy said wisely. And then they left each other for the night, and met again over breakfast on the terrace the next morning.

'What do you say we tell them they can have their plane back, and we just stay here?' He smiled happily at her, eating an omelet and croissants, and a big cup of strong French coffee, all served by a sixteen-year-old native girl with a breathtaking figure in a pareu.

'You don't think you'd get bored?' She smiled as she sat down next to him. She liked it here too, but she was excited about moving on, to Pago Pago, and then Howland Island.

'I'd never get bored,' he said, smiling up at the girl and then glancing happily at Cassie. 'I think I'd like to end my life on an island. What about you?'

'Maybe.' She looked unconvinced, and then she smiled at him over coffee. 'I think I'll probably end my life the way I started it, under the belly of an airplane. Maybe they could build me a special wheelchair.'

'Sounds great. I'll build you one.'

'Maybe you'd better check out the *North Star* first.'

'You mean I can't lie on the beach all day?' He pretended to look shocked, but half an hour later, they were both going over the plane with a fine-tooth comb in all seriousness. The jokes were over. And predictably, the photographers, and the visitors, came to watch them.

They were carrying a huge load of fuel on the *North Star*, and very little else except emergency supplies, a radio, life jackets, life raft. They had everything they needed. And the temptation was great at each stop to bring home souvenirs from their travels. But they had no room, and they didn't want to weigh the plane down with a single ounce of anything that was not absolutely essential.

They shared a quiet dinner that night at the hotel, and watched an extravagantly gorgeous sunset, and then they took a walk on the beach and went to bed early. And the next morning, they took off for Pago Pago.

They made it in four and a half hours, and this time broke no records. But it was easy flying, all except for a small noise Billy thought he heard in one of their engines. It was the same thing he'd heard the day before, and it was oddly persistent.

Pago Pago was a fascinating place, though they

only spent one night, and they spent most of it at the airport. Billy wanted to find the cause of the noise that had been bothering him, and by midnight he thought he'd located it. It was annoying him, but he was still convinced it wasn't a major problem.

They cabled home again, as they did from every stop, and in the morning they left for Howland Island. They had already covered more than nine thousand miles, and in Cassie's mind they were almost there, though there were still more than three thousand miles between them and Honolulu. But they had already done more than half the trip, and knowing they were approaching Howland, where most people believed Earhart had gone down, made her nostalgic.

'What are you going to do after all this?' she asked Billy as they shared a sandwich two hours out from Pago Pago. The woman at the place they'd stayed had been very nice, and had insisted on giving them a basket of fruit and sandwiches, which turned out to be delicious.

'Me?' Billy thought about it. 'I don't know . . . invest my money somewhere, maybe like your father did. I'd like to run a charter service somewhere. Maybe even someplace crazy like Tahiti.' He had really loved Papeete. 'What about you, Cass?' They had nothing but time on their hands, as they shared the basket of food, and flew over the shimmering Pacific.

'I don't know. I get confused sometimes. Sometimes I think this is it for me . . . planes . . .

test flights . . . airports . . . that's all I want . . . other times I wonder if I should do other things, like be married, and have kids.' She looked sad for a moment, looking out at the horizon. 'I thought I had it worked out with Desmond, but I guess not. I don't know,' she shrugged, 'I guess I'll have to refigure it when we go home. I sure didn't win on this one.'

'I think you had the right idea, wrong guy. It happens that way sometimes. What about Nick?'

'What about him?' She still didn't have any of the answers. He had been so adamant about not marrying her before, but maybe now, after Desmond, it would be different. She still hadn't told him. And who knew when she'd see him again? Who knew anything now, except what they were doing right now. For the moment, life was very simple.

The stop at Howland was very emotional for her because of Amelia Earhart. She and Billy were carrying a wreath to drop from the plane just before they reached the island.

Billy opened a window for her, just as they came in to land, and she dropped it with a silent prayer for the woman she had never known but admired all her life. She thanked her for being an example to her, and hoped she had had an easy death, and a life that was worthwhile to her. Looking at lives like hers, it was hard to know what people felt, or who they really were. Now that Cassie had been devoured by the press, she knew that most of it meant nothing. But she felt an odd kinship with her idol as she and Billy landed quietly after a twelve-hundred-mile flight. It was so simple for them. It had gone so easily. Why couldn't it have been that way for Amelia Earhart?

Billy patted her knee as the plane came to a stop; it was easy to see all that she was feeling, and he loved her for it.

At Howland, there were photographers waiting for them, courtesy of Desmond Williams. And the expected parallels were drawn between Cassie and Amelia Earhart.

They were only planning to spend one night, before the nearly two-thousand-mile flight to Honolulu. And it was there that Desmond had planned ceremonies and events, awards and honors, press conferences and films, and even a demonstration of the *North Star* to the Army at Hickam Airfield. It sounded exciting to both of them, but it was also a little scary. Everything was so much simpler here. In some ways it would be the last night of peace they had for a long time. And Cassie hated the prospect of seeing Desmond again. Just thinking about it depressed her.

She was quiet when they had dinner alone that night, and with what lay ahead of them, Billy wasn't surprised, that and the fact that she was still feeling emotional about Earhart.

'It's scary going back to all of it again, isn't it?' she said after dinner, sipping a cup of coffee.

'Yeah . . . and exciting.' It was less complicated for him, he didn't have the strain of her history with Desmond. 'It'll all be over soon, in a great flash of light,' he beamed, 'like a Fourth of July firework display, now you see it, now you don't, catch the shooting star. We'll be famous for a minute, and then gone,' he said prophetically, 'until someone else flies farther and faster.' But they'd be remembered for a long time. Their fame wouldn't be gone as quickly as he thought. Desmond was right about some things, and what they were doing was important.

'This time tomorrow night, we'll be in Honolulu, Miss O'Malley,' he said, toasting her with a small glass of wine. He only had a few sips, knowing that the next day he'd be flying. 'Think of the fanfare, the excitement.' His eyes danced and she smiled wanly.

'I'd rather not. I go pale thinking of it. Maybe we should just go back, and surprise them by going home the way we came. Now there's a thought.' She laughed at the idea and he shook his head, amused by her. They always had a good time together.

'I'm sorry, Mr Williams, my pilot was confused, well, you know how it is . . . she's just a girl . . . girls can't really fly, everyone knows that . . . actually, she had the map upside down . . .' They were both laughing, amused at their own schemes, but the next day, when they took off, some of what she'd said proved to be prophetic.

They hit an unexpected lightning storm two hundred miles out, and after assessing the situation, and the winds, they agreed to go back to Howland

Island. And as they attempted to land, it grew to a tropical storm of surprising proportions, and Cassie couldn't help wondering if this was what had happened to Noonan and Earhart. But she had her hands full bringing the plane down in ferocious winds that almost blew them off the island. In the end, they came down hard and fast in a crosswind, and almost missed the runway. It took everything she had to bring the *North Star* down, and when they stopped, they were within inches of landing in the water.

'May I remind you,' Billy said casually to her as she fought to turn the plane around, 'that if you drop this airplane in the drink, we're going to be in serious trouble with Mr Williams.'

She couldn't help but laugh at his warning, and she wasn't entirely sorry to spend another night on Howland. It was far from an exciting place, but at least her life was peaceful. Perhaps for the last time. She couldn't imagine what it would be like for them after Honolulu.

By late that night, the storm had calmed down but they discovered early the next morning that it had damaged their direction finder beyond repair. She and Billy both felt it was safe to fly on anyway, but they radioed ahead to Honolulu that they would need a new one upon arrival. The day was sunny and bright as they left early for the eighteen-hundred-mile flight to Honolulu. But three hundred miles out of Howland, they ran into another problem. It seemed to be a problem with one of their engines. Billy was checking for an oil leak, with a quiet frown, and she was watching him, checking their gauges.

'Want to go back?' she asked calmly, keeping her eyes on her instruments.

'I'm not sure yet,' he answered, still puzzled.

He played with one of the engines for a while, listening, fixing, adjusting, and after another hundred miles out, he reassured her that everything was in control. She nodded and kept a close eye on the instruments, she wanted to be sure she agreed with him.

Cassie left nothing to chance, which was why she was so good. Billy appeared to be a lot more casual than she was, but he was also extraordinarily careful. And he had an uncanny sixth sense about flying, which was why she loved flying with him. They were a perfect team.

She changed her course slightly after that, to avoid some heavy clouds ahead, and what looked like rough weather. And it was early afternoon when he looked out at the autumn sky, and then at her compass. 'Are you sure we're heading right? It feels off to me.'

'Trust your compass,' she said, sounding like an instructor, as she smiled at him. It was the one instrument she always trusted and the only reliable information they had, since both the sextant and the direction finder had broken in the storm.

'Trust your eyes . . . your nose . . . your guts . . . and then your compass.' He was right, as it turned out. With a brisk wind they were slightly off course, but not enough to worry them, and then as she checked the instruments again, she looked up and saw smoke in their number-two engine and thin streams of fuel running back across the number one.

'Shit,' she muttered and pointed it out to him as she cut the power to the number-two engine and feathered the prop. They were already a long way from Howland. 'We'd better go back.' They'd been in the air for two hours, and were already out of radio contact.

'Anything closer than that?' He checked the map, and saw a small island. 'What's this?'

'I'm not sure.' She looked at it. 'It looks like bird shit.'

'Very funny. Give me a reading, where are we?' She read the compass off to him, while he looked out at the engine. He wasn't pleased with what he saw, or the knowledge that they were carrying four hundred gallons of fuel near the engine.

They flew on for a few more minutes and decided to try for the island they'd seen on the map. But Cassie was worried about putting the *North Star* down there. If the island was too small, the plane too large, they wouldn't make it. They agreed to land on the beach if they had to. They were out of radio range. Billy checked the engine again, but the news wasn't good. Then he put the headphones on and tried sending distress signals to any ships that might be near them.

467

But as they looked out the window, they both saw that the engine was burning.

'Happy birthday, Cass. And that's not a cake.'

'Shit.'

'Precisely. How far are we from Bird Shit Island?'

'Maybe another fifty miles, give or take a few.'

'Wonderful. Just what we need, another fifteen minutes with four hundred gallons of fuel in our armpits. Oh goody.'

'Go sing to yourself or something,' she said calmly.

'You have the worst ideas,' he said while flipping some levers, and checking the other engine. 'No wonder you can't get a decent job.' They were joking, but they were not amused. The *North Star* was in trouble.

Ten minutes later the island came into view, and they checked it out. No flatland. Nothing but trees, and what looked like a small mountain.

'How well can you swim?' he asked conversationally, handing her a life jacket as a matter of routine. He already knew that she was an excellent swimmer. 'Looks like we're going to the beach, eh, ducky?'

'Maybe so, cowboy . . . maybe so . . .' She was concentrating on holding the plane. It was starting to pull very badly. And the other engine had begun to smoke too. 'What do you suppose is happening?' They were both puzzled by what was going on, but they wouldn't know what till they reached the ground. And that was going to be soon now. At first Billy had thought the fuel lines were clogged, but that wasn't it. Something was defective.

'Too much lighter fluid maybe?'

'Well, don't light up a Lucky now,' she warned him, as she prepared to land. She circled the island twice, made a pass at the beach once, and took off again, with both engines burning. She knew she needed to dump fuel, but there just wasn't time now.

'You want to try for New York?' he asked calmly, watching her maneuver the heavy plane over the tiny island.

'I think maybe Tokyo,' she answered, never taking her eyes off what she was doing. 'Tachikawa is going to pay a fortune for the test flight.'

'Great idea. Let's try it. Who needs Desmond Williams?'

'Okay, here we go again,' Cassie said, concentrating on every detail. 'Christ, that beach is short dammit . . .' And the engines were hot and flaming.

'I hate to say this, my dear,' Billy said calmly, putting on his own life jacket, 'but if you don't get your ass down there soon, we are going to make a very embarrassing explosion on this island. It might make a very bad impression on the natives.'

'I'm working on it,' she said through her teeth.

'Want some help?'

'From a kid like you? Hell, no.' She came in as low as she could, and used all her strength on the stick; she was almost down, and had just overshot the beach when they hit the water. The plane came to a stop, and sank slowly into three feet of water, as she cut the switches, hoping it wouldn't explode but there was no guarantee now.

'Nice landing, now let's go. Fast.' He grabbed her to push her from the plane, before she could take anything. Instinctively, she reached for their emergency kit, while he struggled to get the door open. Both engines were on fire, and you could feel the heat in the cockpit. He had the door open by then, and shouted to her. 'Go!' He pushed her out and clear of the plane almost before she knew what had hit her. He had the log and a small knapsack in his hand that she knew held their money, and that was it. They waded through the water as fast as they could and headed for the beach at a dead run. They ran another fifty feet down to the end of it, and just as they reached it, there was an enormous explosion. They turned and watched as the entire plane was outlined in flames, and pieces of it flew into the trees and farther into the water. There was a huge tunnel of fire towering above it, from their fuel, and it burned for hours as they watched it in shocked fascination.

'So long, *North Star*,' Billy said, as the last of it disappeared into the water. All that was left was a shell of what had been. All those men and all that work, all those months and hours and calculation, ended in a moment. They had covered eleven thousand miles of their trip. And it was over. They were alive. They had survived it. That was all that mattered. 'And here we are,' Billy said conversationally, as he handed her a piece of candy from the knapsack, 'on Bird Shit Island. Have a great vacation.' She looked at him and laughed; she was too tired and too upset to cry, or scream. All she could hope was that someone would figure out that they were gone when they failed to reach Honolulu, and send the troops out looking. She knew all the efforts they'd made to find Earhart four years before. But she also knew how much outcry there had been at the expense. But if nothing else than for the publicity involved, and to recover the plane, she knew that Desmond would stop at nothing to find them. He'd call Roosevelt himself if he had to. He'd play heavily on the fact that she was America's sweetheart and people loved her. They would *have* to find her.

'Well, Miss O'Malley, what do you say we call room service and order a drink?' They had been there for four hours by then, watching their plane disintegrate along with their hope of leaving. Now they had to be rescued. 'It wouldn't have been a real record-breaking trip, if this hadn't happened,' he said confidently. He was sure that they would be rescued within a day or so, and it would be exciting in the telling.

'Desmond will think I did this as revenge,' she grinned. There was a funny side to it too. But barely. If they let themselves, they could have gotten seriously worried. She wondered if it had been like this for Noonan and Earhart, or if it had been more dramatic or quicker. Maybe they had died on impact. Or maybe they were still sitting on an island like this one. It was an intriguing thought, but unlikely. And not very hopeful.

'I kind of figured you did this as revenge too,' Billy commented casually. 'I can't say I blame you. I wish you'd have done it a little closer to Tahiti. The waitress was great-looking.'

'So has been every girl since L.A.' She was feeling less cheerful than he, but she was grateful for his sense of humor.

'Not here. Definitely not here.' The island was totally deserted.

They went on a reconnaissance mission then, and found a small stream, and a lot of bushes with berries. As desert islands went, it seemed fairly comfortable, with everything they needed. There were some fruits which they didn't recognize, but when they tried them that night they found they were delicious. It was strange being here, but it didn't seem so terrible, as long as they weren't stuck here forever. The prospect of that was more than a little frightening, but Cass wouldn't let herself think of it, as they lay side by side in a cave they found that night.

They were both awake for a long time, and finally, she decided to ask the question. 'Billy?'

'Yeah?'

'What if they don't find us?'

'They will.'

'What if they don't?'

'They have to.'

'Why?' Her eyes were huge in the darkness and he was holding her hand very gently. 'Why do they have to find us?'

'Because Desmond will want to sue you for the plane. He's not going to let you get away with this.' He grinned in the dark and she laughed.

'Oh, shut up.'

'See what I mean . . . not to worry.' But he rolled over and held her close to him, and he didn't tell her he was scared too. He had never been so frightened in his life, and there was nothing he could do for her but hold her.

19

Desmond was called in the middle of the night, exactly twenty-two hours after they had left their last destination. The local authorities were absolutely sure by then that the *North Star* had disappeared, and probably gone down in the Pacific Ocean. But there had been no sign, no signal. And no one had any idea what had happened.

'Damn.' He called everyone in to help. They had an emergency plan to implement. The Navy was called, the foreign authorities, the Pentagon. The flight of the *North Star* had made world news, and now everyone who had ever heard of her, and some who hadn't, wanted to find her.

There was an aircraft carrier in the vicinity of where she was believed to have gone down, and they dispatched forty-one planes, and called in two destroyers. It was not unlike the search that had gone on four years before, and they were better trained, and better equipped now. They made every conceivable effort, and deployed every man possible. The President called Desmond himself, and then the O'Malleys in Illinois. They were in a state of shock when they heard. They couldn't believe they might lose Cassie. And Oona was particularly afraid for Pat's heart, but he seemed to be taking it fairly calmly. He was desperately afraid for his daughter, but he had a lot of confidence in the armed forces. He only wished that Nick were there to help them.

The search went on for days, in an area that covered hundreds of miles, and all the while Billy and Cass were trying to keep each other's spirits up and eating berries. Cassie had gotten a case of raging dysentery, and Billy had badly scraped his leg swimming over some coral the morning after they crashed. But other than that, they were in pretty good shape. They had whatever fruit they found around them, and enough water. But no sign of anyone coming to rescue them. No plane. No ship. Nothing had even come close. Because Cassie had changed course slightly before they crashed, and because of the winds that had pushed them still further off course before that, the search was being conducted some five hundred miles in the wrong direction. Their radio had gone dead just before they went down and then been destroyed in the explosion, so they had no way of giving anyone their location. And there had been no ship in the vicinity at the time, to hear them. They weren't even sure where they were now. But they had no way to tell anyone even if they had known it.

In L.A. Desmond was doing everything he could to keep the search going. But the press was beginning to question the shocking expense of the search, and began to turn on Desmond. They played up the futility of looking for them, and the likelihood that they'd been killed in the crash or would be dead by now anyway. The search went on at full steam for fourteen days, and then occasional sweeps were made for another week. The search was then called off entirely two days after that, one month to the day of the date they had left Los Angeles. It was over.

'I know she's out there,' Desmond insisted to everyone, but no one believed him. 'She's too well trained. I don't believe it.' But experts assumed that something went wrong with the plane. There could have been some unknown, fatal defect. No one questioned her skill, but there was always the element of fate, or good fortune.

Her parents were devastated once they knew the search was being called off without finding Cassie and Billy. It seemed impossible to believe that they had lost yet another child, and so cruelly. Her mother lay awake night after night, wondering if Cassie was alive somewhere and they just hadn't found her. But her father felt it was unlikely.

Cassie and Billy had been lost for six weeks on Thanksgiving Day, and it was a gloomy holiday for everyone that year. They barely celebrated it at all. They just had a quiet dinner in the kitchen.

'I just can't believe she's gone,' her mother sobbed in Megan's arms. It was a terrible time for them.

And for Desmond it was the end of a life's dream. He tormented himself constantly over what must have happened. If only they knew . . . if only they could find something . . . but there was no debris, no evidence, no piece of the plane or of their clothing. It led him to hope they were still alive somewhere. And he hounded the Pentagon constantly, but for them, the search was over. They were convinced that the *North Star* had gone down without a trace and they were certain there were no survivors.

Cassie's photograph was everywhere, in magazines, and newspapers. Even six weeks after they disappeared, her identity seemed as alive as ever. The press had been devoted to Cass. And appropriately, Desmond portrayed himself as the grieving widower. He had no Thanksgiving that year. And neither did Nick in England. He had heard about Cassie's disappearance about a week after the plane had disappeared. It was such a major event, it had made headlines in England. He couldn't believe it when he heard the news. He had volunteered for the most dangerous missions, until someone had explained the situation to his commander. They had given him a three-day leave and asked him to take some time off. It was obvious to everyone that something was bothering him and he was just taking too many chances. Nick had argued with them, but they didn't want to hear it. He thought about going home for a few days, but he knew he couldn't face Pat yet, knowing what had happened. What a blind fool he had been. What a coward. He knew he'd never forgive himself for not marrying her, and keeping her from Desmond Williams. It never occurred to him that maybe he couldn't have, or that she had wanted to fly the tour more than anything. It was her decision too, and she was very independent.

But he figured Pat would never forgive him either. If he had married her, it might all have been different.

He had seen a photograph of Desmond coming out of a memorial service for Cassie, with a grim face and carrying a homburg. And he hated Desmond for giving Cassie the opportunity to kill herself, and the plane in which to do it. And he knew better than anyone that Williams had probably pushed her into the tour in the first place, all for his own glory. She had deserved better than either of them. He was more convinced of that now than ever.

And on the island with no name, Cassie served Billy berries and a banana and a handful of water for Thanksgiving. They had been living on the same diet for more than a month, and it only rained occasionally, but they were surviving. Billy had gotten an infection in the leg he'd scraped so badly on the coral reef, and he'd been battling with a fever. She'd had a few aspirin in their emergency kit, but they were long gone now. And she'd had some trouble with a spider bite, but other than sunburn, they were in pretty good shape, except for Billy's frequent fevers.

They had managed to keep track of the days since they'd crashed, and they knew it was Thanksgiving. They talked about turkey and pumpkin pie and going to church, and being with their families and friends. Billy was worried about his father being all alone. And Cassie kept thinking about her parents, and her sisters and their husbands and children, and how much she missed them. She talked about Annabelle and Humphrey, the two children from England. They made her think of Nick again. She thought a lot about him. All the time now.

'What do you suppose they all think has happened to us?' she asked as she shared a banana with Billy, and she noticed he was looking flushed again, and his eyes seemed very intense and a little sunken.

'That we're dead probably,' he said honestly. Lately, he hadn't been joking as much. All they could do was sit and wait, and think, and eat the same kinds of berries over and over. There was nothing else to eat on the island, and so far they hadn't been able to catch any fish. But they weren't starving.

There was a storm two days after that, and the weather seemed to turn cooler than it had been. She was still wearing her flight suit, but it was torn and not very clean and Billy only had his shorts and a T-shirt. Cassie noticed the morning after the first chill that Billy was shivering even in the sun.

'You okay?' she asked, trying not to look as worried as she felt.

'I'm fine,' he said gamely. 'I'll go get some bananas.' He had to scale up a tree to get them, but he couldn't even get off the ground this time; his leg was hugely swollen and oozing pus, and he was limping when he came back with one banana that had fallen.

She didn't know what to do for him anymore. The leg just kept getting worse, and she could tell that his fever was getting higher. She bathed the leg in salt water, but it didn't help at all. She had nothing else to give him. He dozed a lot that afternoon, and when he woke up, his eyes looked even more glazed than they had been. She laid his head on her lap after that, and stroked his forehead, and as the sun went down he began shaking from the chill again, so she lay next to him, and tried to keep him warm from the heat of her body.

'Thanks, Cass,' he whispered in the dark of their cave that night, and she lay holding him, praying that someone would find them. But it seemed almost impossible now. She wondered if they would be there for years, or just die there. It seemed unlikely they'd leave the island. She knew too well that the search had to have been called off by now. They were presumed dead, just as others had been before them.

His teeth chattered constantly during the night, and the next morning, he was delirious as she bathed his head with cool water. There was a storm that day, and she drank too much of the rainwater herself, and wound up with violent dysentery again. Between the berries and the water and the leaves they ate, she had it all the time now. She could tell from the way her flight suit fit that she had lost a lot of weight since they'd reached the island.

Billy never regained consciousness that day, and that night, she lay holding him, crying softly. She had never felt so alone in her entire life, and to make matters worse she felt she had a fever now too. She wondered if she had caught a tropical disease. Billy had an infection from the coral, but they both were very sick.

In the morning, Billy seemed better again, and a lot more lucid. He sat up, and walked around the cave, and then he looked at her and said he was going swimming. It was chilly outside, but he insisted he was hot, and he suddenly became very argumentative, and very powerful. She couldn't stop him. He waded out into the water where the burned hull of their plane was. Even the storms they'd had hadn't washed it away yet, and it lay there like a reproach, and a reminder of all they had had and lost. For Cassie, it was a final reminder of Desmond.

She watched Billy swimming past the plane, and then back again, and when he came out of the water, she saw that he had torn the other leg, but he didn't seem to feel it. He insisted it was nothing, and she watched him scale up the tree, and eat a banana. He seemed to have unusual energy, but an odd kind of dementia. She could tell that he wasn't himself from the things he said, and the way he looked at her. He was very nervous and very wild-eyed, and by nightfall, he lay shivering in their cave, talking to someone she didn't know about a car, and a candle, and a little boy. She had no idea what he was talking about. And late that night, he looked at her very strangely, and she wondered if he knew her this time.

'Cass?'

'Yes, Billy?' She lay holding him close to her; she could feel his bones, and his whole body shaking.

'I'm tired.'

'That's okay. Sleep.' They had nothing else to do, and it was very dark there.

'Is it okay?'

'It's okay . . . close your eyes . . .'

'They are,' he said, but she could see that they were open.

'It's very dark in here. Close your eyes anyway. You'll feel better tomorrow.' Or would they ever feel better, she wondered. She could feel her own fever rising again too, and she was shaking almost as much as he was.

'I love you, Cassie,' he said softly after a little while. He sounded like a child, and she found herself thinking of her nieces and nephews, of how sweet they were and how lucky her sisters were to have them.

'I love you too, Billy,' she said gently.

He was still curled up in her arms, when she woke up the next morning. Her head ached, and her neck was stiff, and she knew she was slowly getting as sick as he was. Billy was already awake, she thought, he was lying very still and looking at her; and then she gave a small scream as she realized that his eyes were open, and he wasn't breathing. He had died in her arms in the night. She was alone now.

She sat there looking at him for a long time, huddled next to him, not knowing what to do, and not wanting him to leave her. She sat crying, hugging her knees and rocking back and forth. She knew she had to do something with him, to take him away, or bury him, but she couldn't bear for him to leave her.

She pulled him slowly outside that afternoon, and dug a shallow grave with her hands, in the thicker sand near the rocks, and she laid him there. And all she could think of as she did was his telling her not long before that he wanted to end his life on an island. He had. But that all seemed so long ago. It was part of another life, in a place she would never see again. She knew that now. She knew she was going to die like Billy.

She kneeled down next to him, and looked at him, with his eyes closed, and his freckles so big on the thin face, and she touched his cheek for a last time, and stroked his hair.

'I love you, Billy,' she said as she had the night

before. But this time he didn't answer, and she covered him gently with sand and left him.

She sat alone in the cave that night, hungry and cold and shaking. She hadn't eaten all day. She was too sick to eat, and too sad about Billy. And she hadn't drunk water either. And the next morning, she felt weak and confused and she kept thinking she heard her mother calling her. Whatever she had, it was killing her, just as it had killed Billy. She wondered how long it would take, or if it even mattered. There was nothing left to live for now. Chris was gone. Billy was gone. Nick was lost to her . . . her marriage was over . . . she had crashed Desmond's plane . . . she had let everyone down . . . she had failed them.

She staggered out to the beach and fell down several times, and she was too weak to go up to the rocks and get water. She didn't care anymore. It was too much trouble to stay alive. And there were so many people talking to her now. She saw the sun come out, and she heard them, and as she stood up again, she saw a ship on the horizon. It was a very big ship, and it was coming closer. But it didn't matter, because they would never see her.

The USS *Lexington* was in the area on maneuvers. It passed through these islands regularly, but it hadn't been there in a while, it had been assigned to other positions. But Cassie didn't bother with it, she went back into her cave and lay down. It was too cold outside . . . too cold . . . and there were too many voices.

484

The *Lexington* continued to cruise by, and there were two smaller ships with it. It was the lookout on the smaller one who spotted the burned hull of the *North Star* bobbing in the water half a mile off the island.

'What is that, sir?' he asked an officer next to him, who smiled. 'It looks like a scarecrow.' It did, from that angle, in the distance. Part of it had gone down, but there was so little left that the skeleton managed to stay afloat, and with another look, the officer gave a series of rapid orders.

'Could it be the plane that O'Malley and Nolan were flying, sir?' the junior officer asked excitedly.

'I don't think so. They went down about five hundred miles from here, give or take a few miles. I don't know what that thing is. Let's take a closer look.'

They advanced slowly on it, and several more of the men focused binoculars on it, but when they got there, the skeleton eluded them, and dipped in and out of the water. But it was obvious now that it was part of a plane. Half the cockpit was still there, and one of the wings had been blown off. The other had burned down to the frame and melted.

'What does it say?' one of the men was shouting to the other.

'Get some men in the water now,' an officer commanded. 'I want that brought aboard.' And half an hour later, they had the remains of Cassie's plane spread out on the deck around them. There wasn't much left, but there was one piece that told it all. They had found it. It was painted bright green and yellow. Those had been her colors, they all knew, and the script read 'Star.' They called the captain down to examine what they'd found, and there was no question in his mind. They had found what was left of the *North Star*. It had been burned to a crisp, and it had obviously suffered a severe explosion. But there was no sign of life on it anywhere, or of human remains. They checked carefully. There was no sign of Cassie or Billy.

They radioed their companion ships, and still others in the vicinity, which by late afternoon were scouring the waters for bodies in life vests. They had radioed to shore as well, and there was a news bulletin in L.A., which Desmond heard before anyone called him. Pieces of the plane had been found, but there was no sign of life anywhere. They had been lost for seven weeks now. It was unlikely they were alive, but not impossible. The search for O'Malley and Nolan had been reopened.

Landing parties were organized to search all the surrounding islands. There were three of them, two of them fairly good-sized, and one of them so small as to be unlikely. There wasn't enough vegetation to keep anyone alive for a week, let alone a month, they decided. But the officer in charge told them to search it anyway. There was nothing though. No sign of life, no scraps of clothing, or utensils.

And as Cassie listened, she heard noises again, and then more voices. She wondered if Billy had heard all the same things before he died. She had

486

forgotten to ask him. There were whistles and bells and people calling, and then she realized she was about to die, when a bright light shone in her face. There were voices and people calling again, and that light right in her eyes. She drifted off to sleep again as she looked at it. It was just too much trouble to listen to them anymore. And then she felt them moving her. She was being carried somewhere, just as she had carried Billy . . .

'Sir! Sir!' The whistle shrilled sharply three times signaling for assistance, and four more men came running in the direction of the whistle. There was a small cave, and one of the men was standing there with tears streaming down his face.

'I found her, sir! . . . I found her . . .' She was barely conscious and babbling incoherently, and she kept calling Billy's name over and over. She was rail-thin, and desperately pale, but they all recognized the red hair and the flight suit.

'Oh, my God,' one of the officers said. She was filthy and smelled terrible, and she was obviously deathly ill, but she was alive, although barely. Her pulse was thready, her breathing was shallow, and he wasn't sure she was going to make it. He told the young ensign to signal for help. They put her in the boat quickly, and left three of the men to continue searching the island. They wanted to get her back to the ship as quickly as possible.

They were calling and shouting orders, and she was loaded onto the ship in a sling, and they signaled to the medical personnel on the *Lexington* to assist them. She wore an ID tag around her neck, which identified her correctly as Cassie O'Malley Williams. And within minutes, the Pentagon had the news, she'd been found, barely alive, but there was no sign of Billy Nolan.

But the search party left on the island took less than half an hour to find him. They took him back to the ship, and by then Cassie was already on the *Lexington*, though she was unaware of it. A team of two doctors and three medics were doing what they could to revive her. She was dehydrated and delirious and had an uncontrollable fever.

'How is she?' the captain asked the medical personnel that night.

'Nothing's sure yet,' the doctor said quietly, 'but nothing's lost yet either.'

Her parents had just been called by the Department of the Navy. And Desmond was called shortly after that. It went out over the wire services that night. It was a miracle. The nation's prayers had been answered. Cassie O'Malley had been found, in a cave on an island in the Pacific, in critical condition. It wasn't known yet if she would survive. But it was already known that Billy Nolan hadn't. His father had already been called in San Francisco, and he was crushed to hear the news. Billy was a hero at twenty-six, but he was gone. He had died only a day or two before they found him, they believed, though Miss O'Malley had been unable to tell them anything yet. She was unconscious.

In the O'Malley house everything was still, as

Oona and Pat sat staring at each other, unable to believe what they'd been told. Cassie was alive. And the *Lexington* was steaming toward Hawaii with her at that moment.

'Oh, Pat . . . It's like another chance,' Oona said breathlessly, 'like a miracle . . .' She smiled through her tears, praying for Cassie silently, her rosary beads in her hand, and her husband patted her hand gently.

'Don't get your hopes up. We already lost her once. She may not make it, Oonie. She's been out there for a long time, and you don't know what kind of shape she was in when they crashed. She may have been pretty banged up then, and that was more than a month ago.' She'd been on the ground for seven weeks since they went down. It was a long time to live on rainwater and berries.

They had none of the details yet, and even Desmond had had a hard time prying anything out of them at the Pentagon. They just didn't know enough yet to reassure him.

But the news the next morning from the *Lexington* wasn't very hopeful. She was still unconscious, her fever hadn't gone down, and there were complications.

'What the hell does that mean?' Desmond shouted at them. 'What kind of complications?'

'They didn't tell me, sir,' the woman on the phone said to him politely.

Cassie's fever didn't respond to any of the medication, and she was dehydrated to the point of death. She was still delirious, and had violent dysentery, and she had started passing blood, which the medics told one of the men was a sure sign it was all over.

'Poor kid,' one of the midshipmen said. 'She's the same age as my sister, and she can't even drive a car yet.'

'Looks like Cassie didn't drive so hot either,' one of the men joked, but he had tears in his eyes as he said it. The entire ship was talking about her, and praying for her, and so was the entire country, as well as the world.

In England, Nick had been called into his commander's office at Hornchurch. Word had gotten out eventually that he was extremely close to Cassie O'Malley, though no one knew the details.

And he had been in rough shape since her disappearance in October. They'd sent him back to flying missions eventually, but he'd been hard on all his men, and dangerously willing to take unnatural risks for too long now.

'I wouldn't get my hopes up excessively, Major Galvin, but I thought you ought to know. We've just heard that they found her.'

'Found who?' Nick looked confused. He'd been asleep after flying two night missions over Germany back to back, when they'd told him to see the commander.

'I believe the O'Malley woman is a friend of yours, isn't she?' Gossip was everywhere in the Army, all the way to the commander's office.

'Cassie?' Nick looked as though he'd gotten an electric shock as he realized what the commander was telling him. 'Cassie's alive? They found her?'

'They found her. She's in critical condition on one of your warships in the Pacific. It sounds as though she might not make it, from what I've seen so far. But we'll keep you informed of any developments, if you like.'

'I'd appreciate that, sir,' Nick said, looking pale, as the commander watched him.

'You look like you need a break, Major. This might be the right time, depending on what happens.'

'I wouldn't know what to do with it, sir,' Nick said honestly. He was afraid to go home now. For him, there was nothing to go home to. Cassie would be with Desmond if she survived . . . and oh God, he hoped so . . . he would be willing to sacrifice his own life to make that happen. He would have been willing to do anything, if she just lived . . . even see her with Desmond Williams for the rest of her life. Anything was better than knowing she had died, or fearing it as he had for the past seven weeks. He had given up hope in the last month. It was just impossible that they'd still be alive somewhere in the Pacific. 'Any word of her navigator?'

The commander nodded. They were all used to losing friends now, but this was a hard way to do it. 'He didn't make it, they found him on the island with her. I'm afraid I don't know the details.'

'Thank you, sir.' Nick stood up to leave, looking

exhausted but hopeful. 'Will you let me know if you hear anything else?'

'As soon as we do, Major. We'll call you at once.'

'Thank you, sir.' They saluted each other, and Nick walked slowly back to his barracks, thinking of Cassie. All he could think of, as he had a thousand times since May, was the night they'd spent at the airstrip in the moonlight. If only he'd held onto her, if only he'd been able to keep her from going . . . if only she'd live . . . for the first time in twenty years, he found himself praying, as tears rolled down his cheeks, and he went back to his barracks.

20

Three days after they had found Cassie in the cave, the *Lexington* steamed into Pearl Harbor. She had regained consciousness once, but lost it again. She was transferred to the naval hospital by ambulance. And when she got there, Desmond was waiting for her. He had flown over from L.A., leaving Nancy Firestone to control the members of the press who were waiting for her arrival in L.A.

The doctors gave Desmond a report when they first saw her, and Desmond then explained to the reporters what had happened. But they had still heard none of it from Cassie.

'Will she be all right?' they asked with tears in their eyes, and Desmond's tears matched theirs. He was obviously deeply moved by his wife's condition.

'We don't know yet.'

A little while later, he went out to see what was left of the plane, which had come in on the

Lexington too, and Desmond thanked the captain for bringing her home safely, as photographers snapped their picture.

'I only wish we had found her sooner. She's a great gal. We're all rooting for her. You tell her that as soon as she can hear you.'

'I will, sir,' Desmond said, as they took another picture of him with the captain. Desmond went back to the hospital after that to wait for news and after another hour or two, they finally let him see her. She looked ravaged by everything she'd been through and she had IV tubes in both arms, one giving her medication and the other glucose. But she never stirred. And he never touched her. He simply stood staring at her, and the nurses couldn't tell what he was thinking.

Billy Nolan's body was sent back to San Francisco that day, on a flight Desmond had arranged. And funeral services were set for two days later. And in churches everywhere, people were praying for Cassie.

It was the fourth of December by then, and all over the country, people were talking about Christmas, but all the O'Malleys could think about was Cassie, comatose in Hawaii. They called Honolulu every morning and night for news of Cassie's condition. Pat wanted to fly them there, but his doctor didn't advise it. He was even thinking of calling that miserable husband of hers to lend him a plane, but he had heard he was already in Honolulu. Desmond was milking it for all the publicity he could get out of it. And on December 5, the doctor at the naval hospital called them again. Oona dreaded it now when the phone rang, and at the same time she longed for it. She was desperate for news of Cassie.

'Mrs O'Malley?'

'Yes.' She recognized instantly the scratchy connection of long distance. 'There's someone here who'd like to talk to you.' She thought it was Desmond, and she didn't want to talk to him, but maybe he had news for them. And then she heard Cassie. Her voice was so weak she could hardly hear her, but it was her. Oona was crying so hard she couldn't even tell Pat what was happening.

'Mama?' Cassie said softly, and her mother nodded, and then forced herself to speak through her tears as Pat understood and began to cry too.

'Cassie? . . . oh, baby . . . oh, sweetheart . . . we love you so much . . . we were so worried about you . . .'

'I'm okay,' she said, and ran out of steam almost immediately. The doctor took the phone from her hand, and the nurse explained that Miss O'Malley was very weak, but she was doing much better. And then Cassie insisted on having the phone back again so she could tell her mother she loved her. '. . . and tell Daddy . . .' she whispered and he could hear her anyway, as Oona shared the receiver with Pat and he cried openly as he listened, '. . . I love him too . . .' She wanted to tell them about Billy, but she didn't have the strength, and the nurse took the phone away then. And a little while later they let her see Desmond. The nurse stayed in the room with them, as Cassie needed to be watched constantly. She was so weak that sometimes she even had trouble breathing.

Desmond stood beside her bed, and looked down at her unhappily. He didn't know what to say to her, except that he was glad she had survived. It was an awkward moment for them. Everything he should have felt or said was wrong because of their circumstances, but he was relieved that she was alive. And he couldn't help wondering if she'd been careless about the plane. Or had there been some fatal flaw they hadn't known about before she left? Eventually he would need to ask her, but this wasn't the moment.

'. . . I'm sorry . . . about the plane . . .' she said to him with effort, and he nodded.

'You'll do it again one day,' he said confidently, but she shook her head. She hadn't even wanted to do it this time in the end. She had done it for him, because she felt she had to. It had always been his idea, his dream, his project. And in the end, she felt she owed it to him. She would never do it again, not for him, not for anyone, and not without Billy. 'What happened?' he asked as the nurse looked on disapprovingly. She needed rest desperately, and no one was supposed to upset her, least of all her husband. The nurse had noticed that he hadn't even kissed her. And as he stood there, talking to her, he never touched her or went near her.

But Cassie was trying desperately to answer his question. '. . . first smoke, then fire in the number-two engine . . .' she explained painfully, '. . . then . . . fire . . . in the number . . . one . . . too far from land . . . too much gas . . . brought it down where I could . . . tiny island . . . hit the beach . . . after we got out . . . tremendous explosion . . .'

He nodded, wishing he knew what had caused the fire in the number two. But she couldn't tell him. The nurse told him then that she had exerted herself enough, and had to rest. He could come back later. He was very correct with everyone, and very well bred and polite, but he was as cold as ice, and he had never said a single kind word to Cassie. It was hard to believe he was her husband. Cassie wondered then as she watched him go, if it would have been easier for him if she had died. Now he'd have to face the world when she divorced him.

Cassie sat up in bed the next day, and called her parents again. She was still very weak, but she was feeling a lot better. She had contracted a tropical disease of some kind, but mostly she had suffered from dehydration, malnutrition, and exposure, and it would take time to get back to normal. She was so weak, she couldn't even sit up without assistance. That afternoon Desmond showed up with a few photographers, but the nurse refused to let him bring them in to Cassie. He threatened to report her to her superiors, and she said it made absolutely no difference to her. The doctor had said no visitors except immediate family, and that was all she would allow to see Mrs Williams.

He was furious and he left almost immediately, and Cassie burst into laughter. 'Thank you, Lieutenant Clarke. You stick to your guns.'

'I don't think you want to see the press.' Cassie still looked very thin and pale and very disheveled. They gave her a bath that afternoon, and she washed her hair, and she almost felt human again by that night. But fortunately, Desmond never came back to see her. He had been very proper with her, but it was obvious that his only interest in her recovery was what he could tell the papers. He had even told them about the lei the crew of the *Lexington* had left for her before setting sail that morning. Her survival had already been announced in newspapers around the world, and in Hornchurch, Nick had cried when his commander told him.

On Saturday, Desmond tried to get the press in to Cassie's room again, and once again, the indomitable Lieutenant Clarke managed to thwart him. It was becoming a game, and Cassie loved it.

'He seems awfully intent on letting the press in to see you,' Lieutenant Clarke said cautiously, wondering what Cassie saw in him, but she didn't dare ask her. Other than his good looks and expensive clothes, he seemed to have a heart of stone. The only thing he warmed to was the press, and certainly not Cassie. But that wasn't news to Cassie. She was only amused that her nurse was so good at annoying him. She didn't want to see anyone yet.

Except her parents. And they had decided to wait for her to come home, now that she was doing better.

Lieutenant Clarke walked her down the hall for the first time that afternoon, and the doctor said he thought Desmond could fly her home by the end of the week. She needed to build her strength up a little bit, and they wanted to be sure the fever didn't return. But so far it hadn't all day, and she felt a great deal better.

A few men recognized her in the hospital as she walked down the hall awkwardly, she was still so weak, and they shook her hand and congratulated her on her survival. She was a heroine just for being alive, and she wished more than ever that Billy was alive now. She had sent a telegram to his father in San Francisco, expressing her grief to him.

'We were all praying for you, Cassie,' people told her in the halls, and she thanked them warmly. Letters and telegrams were pouring in too. President and Mrs Roosevelt had even called her at the hospital. But it didn't seem fair to Cass that Billy hadn't made it, and she had. She felt terribly guilty and unhappy about it, and she cried whenever anyone mentioned him. She was still emotionally worn out by everything that had happened.

She was pensive as she sat in her room most of the time and the nurses didn't want to disturb her. They could see that she was still troubled, and exhausted by her ordeal. They knew only that her co-pilot had died, but they knew no other details. And Cassie wasn't talking about it to anyone. She did a lot of thinking, and some sleeping. And she found herself thinking of Nick, and wondering where he was. She had never had the opportunity to tell him how right he'd been about Desmond. But maybe it didn't matter anymore. They had their own lives to lead. He wanted his own life, and she needed time just to recover from all that had happened. But when she felt better she wanted to look up Jackie Cochran, and talk to her about the planes she had ferried to England.

Cassie called her parents again that night and she told them she'd be home soon, probably in another week, and she'd be home with them for Christmas. She had no reason to be in L.A. anymore, she didn't want to fly for Desmond, and she was sure he'd agree that she had fulfilled her contract to the best of her ability. It was all over.

Her parents told her on the phone that they had just gotten a telegram from Nick in England, telling them how thrilled he was that she had survived. But he had sent nothing to her, probably because of Desmond.

'Does it say when he's coming home?' she asked casually, and her father laughed.

'You're too sly for your own good, Cassie O'Malley.'

'He's probably married by now anyway,' she said lightly, but she hoped not.

'No sane woman would have him.'

'I hope not.' She laughed. She was in much better

spirits. And after a brief chat, she went to bed early. She had no idea what Desmond was doing in Honolulu. He never even came to see her. She supposed he was wining and dining the press, lining up interviews for her when she felt better. But he was in for a shock. She was going to do one final press conference for him, to tell them all what they wanted to know. And then she was going home and folding up the road show. It had cost too much. Billy, and almost her own life. She didn't know what she wanted to do now. But whatever it was, it was going to be on a more human scale than what Desmond had pushed her to in the last year. She had made a lot of money, but she had lost a dear friend, and almost her own life. This time the risks had come at too high a price. And she needed time to recover.

Lieutenant Clarke came in at seven o'clock the next morning, and woke her up when she pulled back the curtains and raised the shades. It was a beautiful day, and Cassie was anxious to get up and walk around. She even wanted to shower and dress, but Lieutenant Clarke didn't want her to overdo it.

She had breakfast at seven-fifteen, poached eggs and three strips of bacon. It was a far cry from their island diet of bananas and berries. She never wanted to see either one again, for as long as she lived. And as she finished her breakfast, she glanced over the morning paper.

She saw quickly that Desmond had been at it

again. He had granted an interview to the *Honolulu Star Bulletin* and told them all about her condition. He didn't say too much however about what had happened to her on the little island; she suspected that he didn't want to steal any thunder from a major press conference with her. He thought of everything. Except her well-being. It was all business and publicity, airplanes and profit. Nick couldn't have been more accurate in his perceptions and predictions.

She was still reading the paper when she heard the first plane overhead. She thought it was an exercise by the Navy pilots. The hospital was fairly close to the airfield. But then as she listened, she heard an explosion in the distance. And then more of them. Curious, she got up and walked to the window. And then she saw them, wave after wave of bombers. They were being attacked, she realized instantly, with astonishment. It was seven fifty-five on December 7.

The sky was black with planes and they seemed to drone on endlessly, as they flew over the harbor, and systematically bombed every ship they saw beneath them. They strafed the airport simultaneously, and destroyed whatever they found there.

Lieutenant Clarke came running in, and Cassie explained to her quickly what she was seeing. Without thinking, she ran to the closet, and found the clothes that Desmond had brought her. There wasn't much. But there was a skirt and a blouse and a pair of shoes, and she hurriedly took off her robe and nightgown and got dressed for the first time since she'd been there.

In the hospital, people were crowding into the hallways, and dashing around aimlessly. Nurses and orderlies were trying to keep patients calm, and almost instinctively Cassie joined them. They were under attack for an hour, and by then the *Arizona* was in flames, along with a number of smaller ships, and large parts of the harbor. Reports were coming in rapidly, many of them inaccurate. And the radio was explaining that they had been bombed by the Japanese, and it was only moments later when ambulances began bringing in the wounded. There were terrifying burns, and men covered in oil, others with head injuries, some with machine gun wounds, and many with traumatic shock. Nurses were running everywhere, and patients like Cassie were giving up their beds for the men who were being brought in from the harbor.

Cassie worked alongside Lieutenant Clarke tearing bandages, and clean pieces of cloth. She helped to hold wounded men in her arms, lifting them onto beds. She did anything she could to help, but before they could deal with half of the wounded men, the Japanese attacked again. And this time they got the *Nevada*.

Suddenly there were thousands of men, injured and half dead, bleeding from everywhere, streaming into the hospital, or taken to the hospital ship *Solace*.

Rebecca Clarke only looked up at her once with concern and admiration as Cassie worked tirelessly, helping the wounded. She was quite a girl. No wonder the country loved her.

'Are you all right?' the nurse asked her briskly, after Cassie had brought a particularly nasty burn case into a treatment room. The man was screaming and there was flesh hanging everywhere, and even some left on Cassie.

'I'm fine,' she said coolly. She remembered her brother and pulling him from the burning plane. She still had a scar on her arm from where the flames on his body had burned her. 'Just tell me what to do.'

'You're doing just what you need to,' Lieutenant Clarke said firmly. 'Don't stop unless you feel ill, and if you do, tell me.'

'I won't,' Cassie said, willing herself not to be sick as she helped the injured men, and a number of women. Civilians began coming into the hospital too. There were casualties everywhere, and after a while there was nowhere to put them. The second bombing lasted till just after ten o'clock, and then they were gone, leaving not only the island in shock, but the entire nation.

Cassie worked feverishly all afternoon, doing what she could, and she felt weak in the knees when she finally sat down at four o'clock. She hadn't stopped, and she hadn't eaten since breakfast. Lieutenant Clarke brought her a cup of tea, and together they checked the lobby for more injured. The last ones had been transferred to the *Solace* just an hour before. The hospital simply couldn't hold another body.

There was nothing left for her to do for the moment, except offer comfort where she could, and as she was doing that, Desmond arrived with a lone photographer beside him. All the others had gone to the harbor to see the damage there, but he had promised the young reporter a picture of Cassie O'Malley if he came with him. He strode across the lobby to her, as Lieutenant Clarke settled a young pregnant woman in a chair. She had come to inquire about her husband, and Lieutenant Clarke had just promised to find him.

'There she is' – Desmond pointed to her dramatically – 'darling, are you all right?' he asked, looking at her tenderly, as the photographer snapped a picture of her in her skirt and blouse that were covered with other people's blood, and all she could do was look at Desmond in disgust, and the photographer along with him.

'Oh, for chrissake, Desmond,' she railed at him in contempt, 'stuff it. Why don't you go do something useful instead of showing off for the press all the time? And you,' she wagged a finger at the camera, and the man behind it was too startled to say anything, 'why don't you go help someone, instead of standing around taking pictures of me? We've been bombed, you idiot. Get off your lazy ass, and drop your camera.' And with that she wheeled out of the lobby with Lieutenant Clarke, and she left the two men with their mouths open behind her. She had won Rebecca Clarke's heart forever that day. She knew that as long as she lived, she would never forget the tireless redhead, helping wounded men, treating burns. She had given up her private room to four of them, and had wheeled the cots in herself and made them with whatever sheets she could find, or steal, from other beds if she had to.

The director of the hospital thanked her himself that afternoon. And they found her a folding cot that she set up in a closet to get some sleep. They had sicker people to take care of now, people who needed them more, and she felt guilty taking any of their attention. She stayed on to help the next day, and they were told, not surprisingly, that the President had declared war on Japan on Monday. There was a cheer in the hospital when it was announced. And on Tuesday, she checked into the Royal Hawaiian Hotel, and called her parents. She had already called them once before to tell them she was all right, but now she wanted to let them know she was going to try and get home as soon as possible.

The hotel promised to try and get a cabin for her on the *Mariposa*, which was leaving on Christmas Eve. It was the first ship she could get, and the only thing she wanted to be sure of was that Desmond wasn't on it.

She had no sympathy for him at all, she thought he had behaved abominably. The only thing he was interested in was milking her story one more time. It was disgusting.

He came to see her that afternoon, and told her that the Pentagon had promised him a seat on a military flight to San Francisco in a few days, and he could arrange one for her too, since she was practically a national hero now, but she was adamant that she didn't want to go anywhere with him.

'What difference does it make?' He looked annoyed at how difficult she was being. It would look a lot better to the press if they went home together, although he could still explain it if she didn't. He could even claim that she was suddenly nervous about flying, or blame it on her health. But she was not amenable to any of his excuses.

'I've got real bad news for you, Desmond. The whole world is not watching you, or me, they're thinking about the war we just got ourselves into, though you might not have noticed.'

'Think of what you could do now for the war effort,' he said hopefully, thinking of the publicity opportunities for him, and for his airplanes. But as far as she was concerned, she had just done it, for three days at the naval hospital, not that he understood that, although Admiral Kimmel had personally thanked her.

'I'll do exactly what I want to do,' she said unpleasantly, 'and you're not going to advertise, trade, announce, use, or exploit it. You got that? We're finished. I completed my contract.'

'You most certainly did not,' he said smoothly, and she stared at him in disbelief.

'Are you kidding? I almost killed myself for you.'

'You did it for yourself, for your own glory,' he corrected.

'I did it because I love flying and I felt I owed it to you. I thought doing the tour for you was the honorable thing to do. Not to mention the fact that you said you'd sue me if I didn't, and I figured my parents didn't need that headache.'

'And do they now? What's changed?' Nick was right to the end. Desmond was vicious.

'I flew eleven thousand miles, I did my damnedest, I went down with your goddamn lousy plane, and managed to live forty-five days on an island the size of a dinner plate, while starving to death, I might add. And I watched my best friend die in my arms. Isn't that enough? I'd say it is. And I'll bet a judge would.'

'A contract is a contract,' he said coolly. 'And yours said you would fly fifteen thousand miles across the Pacific in my plane.'

'Your plane went up like a matchbook.'

'I have others. And your contract said you would do unlimited publicity and endorsements.'

'We're at war, Desmond. No one's interested. And whether they are or not, I'm not going to do it. Sue me.'

'I might. Maybe you'll give it some thought on the way back.'

'I wouldn't waste my time thinking about it. I'll

call my lawyer when I get back . . . for a number of reasons,' she said pointedly.

'We'll have to discuss that. By the way, you mentioned Billy in rather touching terms a little while ago . . . was that your *best* friend, or your *boy*friend. I'm not sure I understood you.'

'You understood me perfectly, you sonofabitch. And if you're talking adultery, why don't you discuss it with Nancy Firestone. She's very clear about calling herself your mistress. I already mentioned that to my attorney.'

For once, he blanched, and she was pleased to have gotten him upset for a change.

'I don't know what you're talking about.' He was furious with Nancy for talking to Cassie.

'Just ask Nancy. I'm sure she'll explain it to you. She was very direct with me.'

His eyes told her he hated her, but she didn't care. She never wanted to see him again after Honolulu.

She spent the next two and a half weeks volunteering to help at the naval hospital again and on the hospital ship *Solace*. It was devastating to see what had happened in the harbor. The *Arizona*, the *Curtiss*, the *West Virginia*, the *Oklahoma*, the *Chew*, the *Oglala* had all been hit by the Japanese, 2,898 had been killed, and another 1,178 had been wounded. It was devastating, and now the country was at war. She wondered what it would mean to Nick, if he would stay in the RAF, or join the American armed forces. Everything was still very confusing.

And when the *Mariposa, Monterey*, and the *Lurline* finally sailed on Christmas Eve, she was touched and surprised when Rebecca Clarke came to see her off, and thanked her for all her help since the bombing. Cassie had done nothing but work with the wounded since the Japanese had bombed Pearl Harbor.

'It was an honor to meet you,' Rebecca Clarke said sincerely, 'I hope you get home safely.'

'So do I,' Cassie said honestly. She was anxious to get back to Illinois to see her parents, and to see a lawyer and find out how she could best get out of all her obligations to Desmond.

She was relieved to see that no members of the press had come to see her off. But Desmond had left for San Francisco by military plane the week before, so they hadn't bothered. She was happy not to have flown with him even if this did take longer and was potentially more risky. They were traveling by convoy to ensure greater safety.

Lieutenant Clarke left her on the ship, and they set sail an hour later. Everyone was anxious about the trip, and afraid that the Japanese would come back and sink them. They had complete blackouts every night, and everyone had to wear their life jackets day and night, which was very unnerving. There were a lot of children on the ship, which made it noisy and stressful for the other passengers, but families who had relatives on the mainland were anxious to get away from Hawaii. It was too dangerous there now. Everyone felt sure they would be attacked again at any moment. The *Lurline*, the *Mariposa*, and the *Monterey* sailed quietly with an escort of destroyers, which accompanied them halfway to California, and then left them to complete the trip alone, as the destroyers headed back to Hawaii.

The ships were very quiet as they zigzagged across the Pacific to avoid submarines. There were no parties at night, no one was in the mood. They just wanted to get to San Francisco safely. And Cassie was amazed at how long it took. After flying everywhere all her life, traveling by ship seemed endless and incredibly boring. She hoped she never had to do it again, and the entire ship cheered as they came through the Golden Gate and into the port of San Francisco five days later.

She was even more surprised when she stepped off the gangplank, carrying her one small bag, and saw her father. She had traveled under the name of Cassandra Williams, and only a handful of people had realized who she was and talked to her. The rest of the time, she kept to herself and minded her own business. She had a lot of thinking to do, and some quiet mourning. But when she saw her father, relief turned to excitement. And her mother was right behind him.

'What are you doing here?' she asked with wide eyes that filled instantly with tears. They were all crying as they hugged each other, her mother more than anyone, but Cassie and her father too. It was the reunion she had thought of a million times on the island. And then as they hugged and talked, out of the corner of her eye, she saw Desmond. He had set up an entire press conference to greet her. There were at least eighty members of the press to welcome her and ask her questions. But as Cassie noticed them, she saw her father's mouth set in a hard line. He was having none of this. Desmond Williams had gone far enough, and he would go no further.

'Welcome home, Cassie!' a flock of reporters shouted at her, as her father grabbed her firmly by the arm, and propelled her through the crowd like a snowplow. Oona was following them closely, and Pat was heading for the car and driver he had hired to meet her. And before the reporters could say anything, she was being pushed into the car, and Desmond had come toward them.

'You're very kind,' her father was saying warmly to the members of the press, 'but my daughter's not well. She's ill and she's had a traumatic experience in the hospital at the bombing of Pearl Harbor. Thank you . . . thank you very much.' He waved his hat at them, shoved his wife into the car after his daughter, and climbed in behind both of them. And then told the driver to pull out as quickly as he could without hitting them. Cassie was laughing at Desmond's expression as they drove off. They had completely foiled him.

'Does that man never stop?' her father said irritably. 'Has he no heart at all?'

'None whatsoever,' she assured him.

'I don't understand why you married him.'

'Neither do I,' she sighed, 'but he was very convincing then. Until afterward; then he didn't think he had to hide his moves anymore.' She told him about his threats to go after her now with his lawyers.

'You owe him nothing!' Pat raged at her, incensed at what Desmond had told her.

'Mind your heart, dear,' Oona warned, but he had been fine since the summer. Even during Cassie's ordeal, he had held up surprisingly well. And now he was only angry.

'He'd better mind my fist, not my heart,' Pat said bluntly, as they drove back to the Fairmont. Her parents had taken a suite for the three of them, and they spent two days there celebrating her safe return. Before they went home, she went to visit Billy Nolan's father. It was a sad and difficult visit, and she told his father that Billy had died in her arms peacefully, and he hadn't suffered. But even knowing that, it was difficult to console him.

It dawned on Cassie afterward, that with the war now, there would be many young men like Billy dying. It was an awful thought. And she had never been as happy to go home as she was this time.

Her father had brought a co-pilot along, and flown the Vega out for her. Halfway back to Illinois, he turned the controls over to her, and asked her if she'd like to fly it. And much to his surprise, and her own, she hesitated, but he pretended to ignore it.

'It's not as fancy as what you're used to, Cass. But it'll do your heart good to fly again.' It was a nice plane to fly, and he was right, she loved the feeling of flying again. She hadn't been in a plane since she'd gone down in the *North Star*, two and a half months before. And it was odd to be flying now, but she still loved it. It was in her blood, just as it was in her father's.

She told him about the crash then on the way home, and she and her father discussed what might have caused the fire in the engines, but it was anyone's guess. Desmond had brought back what was left of the plane, and was hoping they could learn more about what went wrong. But it was unlikely they would find much, the explosion had been so powerful.

'You were damn lucky,' her father said, shaking his head, as she flew his plane for him. 'You could have been killed on the way down. You could have been blown to bits, or never found an island to light on.'

'I know,' she said sadly. But it still hadn't helped Billy. She couldn't get over that. She knew she'd never forget him and then as she helped her father put the plane in the hangar that night, he offered her a job at the airport. He said he could use some help with cargo and mail runs, especially now that every able-bodied young boy would be enlisting. Most of his pilots were older than that, but still there was room for her, and he'd love to have her, he said with a shy smile. 'Unless you're going to be doing a lot of advertisements for tooth powder and cars.' They both laughed at that one.

'I don't think so, Dad. I think I've had enough of all that to last me a lifetime.' She wasn't even sure she wanted to do air shows, not after Chris died. She just wanted to fly, nice easy runs, or even long ones.

'Well, I'd love to have you. Think about it, Cass.'

'I will, Dad. I'm honored.'

He drove them home after that, in his truck, and her sisters and their families were waiting for them at the house. It was New Year's Eve, and they had never looked better to her than at that moment. Everyone cried and hugged, and screamed, and the kids ran around like crazy. They all seemed to have grown, and Annabelle and Humphrey looked cuter than ever. It was a scene she had never thought she'd see again, and she broke down and sobbed as her sisters held her. She only wished that Chris could have been there . . . and Billy . . . and Nick. There were too many people missing now, but she was there. And they thanked God that night for His blessings.

21

The week after New Year's, Cassie started helping her father at the airport again. But before that, he took her to see an attorney in Chicago. He was an expensive one, with a good reputation, but her father said that she couldn't afford to see anyone less than that if she was going to defend herself against Desmond Williams.

She explained her situation to him, and he advised her that she had nothing to worry about. There wasn't a judge or a jury in the world who would feel that she hadn't fulfilled her contract in good faith, and at great risk and personal expense to herself. 'No one's going to take money from you, or put you in jail, or force you to fly for him again. The man sounds like a monster.'

'And that brings up another matter,' her father said pointedly. The divorce. That was more complicated, but not impossible by any means. It would take time, but it would be easy to say that their marriage had not survived the trauma of her ordeal, and surely no one would contest that. It would be even easier to accuse him of adultery and fraud. And the attorney intended to wave those flags at him. And he was sure he would get Desmond's full cooperation.

He told her to go home, and not to worry about it, and three weeks later some papers arrived for her to sign to set the wheels in motion. And it was shortly after that that Desmond called her.

'How are you feeling, Cass?'

'Why?'

'It's a perfectly reasonable question.' He sounded very pleasant but she knew him better than that. He wanted something. She thought maybe he had called to argue about the divorce, but she couldn't imagine why he'd want to. He didn't want to be married to her any more than she wanted to be married to him. And she wasn't asking for money. Much to her surprise, he had sent her the full amount he owed her for the Pacific tour, even though she hadn't completed it, after her lawyer contacted him and pointed out that trying to shortchange her would look very bad to the American public after all she'd been through. Desmond had been furious, but the check for one hundred and fifty thousand was safely put away in her bank account, and her father was well pleased that it was. She had more than earned it.

'I just thought you might like to do a little press conference sometime . . . you know . . . tell the world what happened.' She had planned to, at first, just once, but in the meantime, she'd decided against it. Her career as a movie star was over.

'They heard it all from the Department of the Navy, after they rescued me. There's nothing else to say. Do you really think they want to know how Billy died in my arms, or about my dysentery? I don't think so.'

'You can leave those parts out.'

'No, I can't. And I have nothing to say. I did it. We went down. I was lucky enough to come back, unlike Billy, unlike Noonan, unlike Earhart, unlike a lot of fools like us. I'm here, and I don't want to talk about it anymore. It's over, Desmond. It's history. Find someone else you can mold into a movie star. Maybe Nancy.'

'You were good at it,' he said nostalgically, 'the best.'

'I cared about you,' she said sadly. 'I loved you,' she said very softly, but there was no one to love there.

'I'm sorry if you were disappointed,' he said pointedly. They were strangers again. They had come full circle. And then he realized that pushing her was pointless. 'Let me know if you change your mind. You can have a great career if you ever get serious about it,' he said, and she smiled. It had gotten as serious as it gets, and miraculously she'd still survived it.

'Don't count on it.' She knew he hated people

like her. In his mind, she was a quitter. But she didn't give a damn what he thought now.

'Good-bye, Cassie.' End of a career, end of a marriage. End of a nightmare.

They hung up and he never called her again. Her lawyer told her that Mr Williams had agreed to the divorce, and even offered a small settlement if she would go to Reno. She didn't accept the money, she'd made enough flying for him, but she went to Reno in March for six weeks, and when she came back, she was free again. And predictably, Desmond released a statement to the press afterward that she had been so traumatized by her experience in the Pacific, that continuing their marriage had become impossible for her, and she was living 'in seclusion with her parents.'

'It makes me sound like a mental case,' she complained.

'So what?' her father said. 'You're rid of him forever. Good riddance.' The press had called a few times after that, and she always refused to talk to them or see them. They had written about her sympathetically, but they didn't pursue her for long. As much as they had loved her before the tour, they had other fish to fry now.

She certainly didn't miss them or Desmond. But she did miss her friends. With Billy gone, the airport was very quiet for her. She was so used to flying with him day after day, that it was odd now to be there without him. And by April, when she got back from Reno, all the young men she knew had either been drafted or enlisted. Even two of her brothers-in-law had gone, although Colleen's husband had flat feet and bad eyes and was 4-F and had stayed. But her two oldest sisters and their children were around the house most of the time now. And that spring, Annabelle and Humphrey's parents were killed in a bombing attack on London. Colleen and her husband had decided to adopt them. And thinking about it, Cassie almost wished that she could have them.

They had news from Nick now and then, but not very often. He was still in England, flying fighter raids now with a vengeance. And killing as many Germans as he could shoot out of the skies, 'just like the old days.' He was old for those games at forty-one, but with America in the war now, he had full military status in the American Army. He also didn't get leaves back to the States anymore. Not in wartime. Cassie knew that he was still at Hornchurch. He never wrote to her, only to her father. She had never written and told him of Desmond's betrayal and her divorce, and she still wasn't sure what to tell him, or if he'd care. She didn't know if her father had said anything, but she doubted it. Pat wasn't much at writing letters, or at discussing other people's business. Like all men, they discussed world events and politics. But she felt that one of these days, she ought to tell Nick herself what had happened. The question was when and how. She had to assume by now though that if Nick had still been interested in her, he'd have written. She hadn't seen him in almost a year now. And God only knew what he was thinking.

She didn't go out on dates, just with friends, or her sisters. And she worked hard for her father, at the airport. It was almost enough of a life for her, although she had to admit that she missed the thrill of flying Desmond's exotic planes now and then. But you couldn't have everything, and she liked her life just the way it was now. The press had started to forget her, they seldom called now, without Desmond prodding them, and she got an occasional request for endorsements, which she declined. It was a quiet life, and her father worried about her sometimes, and said as much to Oona.

'She's been through a lot, you know,' he said. They all had.

'She's a strong girl,' her mother said fondly, 'she'll be all right.' She always was. She was just quiet sometimes, and lonely without the people she'd grown up with. Her brother, Nick, Bobby, even Billy, who had come a little later. But she missed them, and the camaraderie they had all shared in different ways. Now she was just another pilot flying to Chicago and Cleveland, but it felt good to be with her family again. It brought her a great deal of comfort.

In August, she got a phone call that amazed her. Her father took the call, and handed it to her with a blasé look. He didn't even recognize the name, which made her want to shriek at him.

Some things never changed. It was Jackie Cochran.

'Are you serious?' She had thought he was kidding at first. She had just come in from a run to Las Vegas. It was hotter than hell. But when she got on the phone, Jackie Cochran said she wanted to meet with her if possible. She said she'd always admired her, and she asked her to come to New York to see her, if she could spare the time. 'Sure,' Cassie agreed, jotting down the pertinent details. She had agreed to fly there two days later. She had nothing else to do, since it was her day off. And maybe she could even do a little shopping, since she had her money from the tour in the bank, and had never spent a penny. The funny thing was she had wanted to meet Jackie Cochran for ages, but once she got settled at home again, she got lazy and never did anything about it.

She was thinking about inviting her mother to come to New York with her, but then she decided to go alone. She had no idea what Jackie Cochran would want, but she thought it might be something her mother would disapprove of.

And as it turned out, it was something that fascinated Cassie. She had admitted readily that she was bored at home, and eager for some more exciting flying. Eight months after she had been rescued in the Pacific, she was ready to spread her wings again and do something a little more exciting. And what Jackie Cochran had in mind was right up her alley.

Jackie wanted Cassie to take charge of forming

a small group of experienced women pilots under the Army Air Force Flying Training Command, to ferry planes to wherever they were needed in the war, for the moment. The women involved would fly as civilian pilots but have uniforms and honorary rank. Cassie was to start as a captain. There was another women's air corps too, the WAFS, Women's Auxiliary Flying Squadron, if she preferred it, being organized for domestic ferrying by Nancy Harkness Love, another extraordinary female pilot. But Cassie liked the idea of ferrying planes into England right past the Germans. She knew her parents were going to be upset if she left home again, but this was something she believed in. It served a purpose, it wasn't frivolous or self-serving, like her Pacific tour, which just made money for a lot of greedy people. This was something she could do for her country, and if she died . . . she was prepared to accept that. So had Chris . . . so had Billy . . . sadly, so had Bobby Strong by then. He had been killed six weeks after he enlisted. Peggy was a widow again, with four children now. Life was never simple.

The WAFS would begin training in September, for eight weeks in New Jersey, but she could hardly wait. It was time for her to be challenged again and for the first time, she would be flying with other women. She had never had the opportunity to do that.

Jackie Cochran took her to dinner that night at '21' and they talked about their plans. Cassie couldn't remember anything she had wanted to do more, not even the world tour when Desmond had first asked her. This was so different.

It was exactly what she wanted and what she'd been waiting for. For Cassie it was time to move on now. She was still smiling when she flew home the next day, thinking about it.

Her father was at the airport when she got in; he was singing to himself, and filing some papers in his office. She hated to ruin his mood, and she decided to wait and tell him after dinner.

'How was New York?'

'Great,' she beamed at him.

'Oh oh. Do I smell romance in the air?' He smelled happiness, but not romance. Airplanes, but not boys. She was right back to where she'd been in the beginning. In love with flying.

'Nope. No romance,' she smiled mysteriously. She was twenty-three years old and divorced, and she felt free and independent. And she was about to do exactly what she wanted.

She could hardly contain herself until that night after dinner, and when she told her parents, they stared at her in disbelief.

'Here we go again.' Pat looked angry even before she explained it. 'You want to do what now?' She had been swimming upstream all her life. It was nothing new for them, or to Cassie.

'I want to join . . . I did join the Army's Flying Training Command,' she said happily, and then she explained it to them.

'Wait a minute. You're going to be flying bombers to England? Do you know how heavy and hard to manage those are?'

'I know, Dad.' She smiled. She'd flown just about every difficult plane in the sky, when she'd worked for Williams Aircraft. 'I'd have a co-pilot.' She knew that would make him feel better.

'Probably another woman.'

'Sometimes.'

'You're crazy,' he said tersely, 'patriotic, but crazy.'

She looked at him hard then. He had to understand. She was grown-up and she had a right to do this. But she had also put them through a lot, especially in the last year and she didn't want to hurt them. She would have preferred to do it with their approval, but her mother was already crying.

'You and your damn flying,' Oona said unhappily to her husband, and he patted her hand apologetically.

'Now, Oonie . . . it's always made us a nice living.' And it had made Cassie a small fortune, but at what price glory.

She explained the Flying Command to them again, and they told her they'd think about it. But she had already signed the papers, she reminded them. Pat and Oona looked at each other. There was nothing left to do but support Cassie again. She was always doing this to them. Always putting herself out on a limb, and stretching to the limit.

'When do they want you, Cass?' her father asked, looking somewhat deflated. He hated losing her too. She was such a big help to him at the airport.

'I start in two weeks, on September first. In New Jersey,' and then she added gratuitously, 'If I were a man, I'd be drafted anyway.'

'But you're not, thank God. And you won't be. It's bad enough to have our sons-in-law over there. And Nick,' who was like a son to them.

'You'd be there if you could,' she pointed out to her father, and he looked at her very strangely. She was right. He would. And Nick had volunteered long before, and he would never have had to go this time.

'Why can't I? Why can't I do something for my country, for a change? Flying is all I know how to do, and I do it well. Why can't I offer that to this country? You would. Why should I be prevented from that because I'm a woman?'

'Oh God,' her father rolled his eyes, 'it's the Suffragettes again. Where do you get this from? Your mother and your sisters never talk about this nonsense. They stay home where they belong.'

'I don't belong there. I'm a flier. Like you. That's the difference.' It was hard to argue with her. She was smart, and she was right. And she was gutsy. He loved that about her. She had taught him a lot over the years, and he loved her more for it.

'It's dangerous, Cass. And you'd be flying Lockheed Hudson bombers. They're heavy planes. What if you go down again?'

'What if you go down tomorrow over Cleveland? What's the difference between the two?'

'Maybe nothing. I'll think about it.' He knew she was bored flying mail runs for him, after all the fancy flying she'd done. But at least she was safe here.

He thought about it for days, but in the end, as before, he didn't feel he had the right to stop her. And in September she left for New Jersey. Oona was proud of her too, and her parents flew to New Jersey with her.

'Take it easy, Dad,' she said when he left her. She kissed both of them good-bye, and her father stood smiling at her.

'Try not to embarrass yourself,' he said mock somberly and she laughed at him.

'Keep your tail up.'

'Mind your own!' He saluted her and was gone, and the next time he saw her he almost burst with pride. She was wearing her uniform, with a gleaming pair of silver wings, and she looked older and more mature than she ever had before. She had her long red hair tied into a neat bun, and the uniform looked sensational on her long, lean figure.

Her parents had come to New York because she was shipping out for England that weekend, though they'd only be there briefly. She would be going back and forth with planes, whenever they were needed somewhere else. But her first assignment was to report to Hornchurch with a bomber.

She had dinner with her parents the night before she left, and she took them to a little Italian restaurant she went to whenever she was in New York with the other pilots. She introduced some of them to her parents, and they could see that she had never been happier than she was now. Despite the hardships of the training she'd gone through, to Cassie, more often than not, it seemed like summer camp for female fliers. She liked the women she flew with, and the challenge of ferrying bombers through dangerous airspace suited her completely. She was used to difficult flying, and she liked the fact that she'd have to pay close attention. For this first trip, she had been assigned a male co-pilot, and they were going through Greenland.

'Keep an eye out for Nick,' her father had said when he left her at the barracks, and she had promised to write to them from England. She didn't think she'd be there long, but she didn't know yet. She would be doing some flying there, and she would have to wait for a return assignment. She might be there for as little as a week or two, or as long as three months. There was no way of knowing. But one thing she did know and that was that all through her training, she had thought of nothing but Nick Galvin.

She had done a lot of thinking, and she had made some decisions.

All her life she had had to wait for other people to make up their minds about her life, and she wasn't willing to let that happen anymore. She had had to pay her own brother to lie for her and take her up in the plane, so she could learn to fly it. She had had to wait for Nick to notice how badly she wanted to learn, and agree to give her lessons, hidden from her father. She had had to wait for her father to come to his senses years before, and let her fly from his airport.

She had had to wait for Nick to tell her he loved her, and then leave for the RAF. And she had had to wait for Desmond to let her fly his planes, and lie to her, and use her, and then finally tell her the truth of how little he cared for her. All her life she had had to wait for other people's decisions and manipulations. And even now, Nick knew where she was, he knew what she felt for him, but he never wrote her. The only thing he probably didn't know, since it had never been publicized, thanks to Desmond's good relations with the press, was that she had left him.

But she wasn't waiting anymore. It wasn't anyone else's decision this time. It was her turn. And ever since she had found out what a bastard Desmond had been, she had wanted to go to England. She had no idea what would happen when she got there, or what Nick would say. And she didn't care how old he was, or how young she was, or how much money he did or didn't have. All she knew was that she had to be there. She had a right to know what he felt for her. She had a right to a lot of things, she'd decided, and it was time for her to get them. This trip was one of them. It was just exactly what she wanted to be doing at that moment.

They left at five o'clock the next morning, and she found the flying challenging, though dull some of the time. She and her co-pilot chatted for a while, and he was impressed to realize who she was.

'I saw you at an air show once. You cleaned up everything. I think three firsts and a second.' It had been her last one. And he remembered correctly.

'I haven't done those in a while.'

'They get old.'

'I lost my brother at the one the following year, it kind of took the fun out of them for me after that.'

'I'll bet.' And then he remembered the trick she had pulled, with admiration. 'You almost ate it the time I saw you.'

'Nah, just looked like it,' she said modestly, and he laughed.

'Nervy broads. You guys are all the same. All guts and no brains.' He laughed and she grinned at him. To her, it was almost a compliment. She liked the guts part.

'Gee, thanks.' She smiled at him, and for an instant he reminded her of Billy.

'No problem.'

By the time they arrived over England, they had become friends, and she hoped to fly with him again. He was from Texas, and like all of them, had been flying since he was old enough to climb into the cockpit. He promised to look her up the next time he was in New Jersey.

They'd been lucky that night, there were no German pilots scouting for them. He'd gotten in a couple of dogfights before, and he was happy they hadn't for her first trip. 'No big deal though,' he reassured her. And much to her delight, he let her land the plane, and she had no problem, despite her father's dire warnings. It was wonderful being treated as an equal.

She took the paperwork to the office they had told her to report to.

They thanked her politely for the paperwork, and handed her a slip of paper with her billeting. And as she walked back outside again, the pilot she'd flown over with invited her for breakfast. But she told him she had other plans. She did, but she wasn't sure where to start looking. She had his address but it meant nothing to her. Not yet, at least. She pulled the piece of paper she'd written it on out of her pocket, and was staring at it, fighting the exhaustion of the flight, when someone jostled her, and she looked up first in irritation, then in amazement.

It was ridiculous. Things didn't happen that way. It was too easy. He was standing there, staring down at her, looking as though he'd seen a ghost. No one had warned him she was coming. And there Cassie stood, in uniform, looking into the startled eyes of Major Nick Galvin.

'What are you doing here?' He said it as though

he owned the place, and she laughed at him, her red hair framing her face as the autumn wind blew through it.

'Same thing you are.' More or less, except that his job was a lot more dangerous than hers. But they both had their jobs and their missions. And several ferry pilots had already been killed by Germans. 'Thanks for all the great letters, by the way. I really enjoyed them.' She tried to make light of the pain he had caused her by his silence.

He grinned boyishly at the comment. He could barely make himself listen to her, he was so over-whelmed with just seeing her again. The last time he had seen her was the morning after they had spent the night at their secret airstrip.

'I really enjoyed writing them to you.' He quipped back, but all he wanted to do now was reach out and touch her. He couldn't keep his eyes from her, his hands, his arms, his heart, his fingers. Instinctively, he reached out and touched her hair. It still felt like silk and looked like fire. 'How are you, Cass?' he said softly, as people in uniform milled around them. Hornchurch was a busy place, but neither of them seemed to notice. They couldn't keep their eyes off each other. Despite the hardships they both had been through, nothing seemed to have changed between them.

'I'm okay,' she answered him, as he led her to a quiet spot, where they could sit down on a rock wall for a few minutes, and talk. There was so much to say, so much to catch up on. And he felt guilty suddenly for his silence.

'I was worried sick about you when you went down,' he said, and she looked away, thinking of Billy.

'It wasn't much fun,' she was honest with him. 'It was pretty rough, and . . .' She had trouble saying it, and without thinking, he took her hand and held it in his own. '. . . it was awful when Billy . . .'

'I know.' She didn't have to say the words. He understood perfectly. 'You can't blame yourself, Cass. I told you that a long time ago. We all do what we have to. We take our chances. Billy knew what he was doing. He wanted to fly the tour with you, for himself, not just for you.' She nodded, knowing the wisdom of his words, but it was small comfort.

'I never felt right that I made it back and he didn't.' It was the first time she'd said that to anyone, and she couldn't have said it to anyone but Nick. She always told him all her feelings.

'That's life. That's not your decision. It's His.' He pointed toward the heavens, and she nodded.

'Why didn't you call when I got back?' she asked sadly. They had gone right to the important things. They always did. He was like that.

'I thought about it a lot . . . I almost did call a couple of times,' he smiled, 'when I had a pint or two under my belt, as they say here, but I figured your husband wouldn't like it much. Where is he now, by the way?' His question confirmed her suspicion and she smiled at him. It was funny sitting here, talking to Nick, as though he'd been waiting for her to arrive. It was all so simple suddenly. There they were, four thousand miles from home, and chatting on a rock wall in the autumn sunshine.

'He's in Los Angeles. With Nancy Firestone. Or someone like her.'

'I'm surprised he let you do this . . . or actually, I'm not,' Nick said, looking somewhat bitter. It had torn his heart out when he thought she was lost, and that bastard had risked her life to sell his airplanes. Desmond was the one he'd wanted to call, to tell him what a rotten sonofabitch he was. But he never did it. 'I guess he figured this stuff would look good in the newsreels. Patriotic. One of the boys. Was it his idea or yours?' He wanted it to be hers, because he wanted to respect her for it.

'It was mine, Nick. I've wanted to do this for a long time, since the tour. But when I got back, I didn't feel right leaving Dad. It was hard on him even now. There's no one left to help him. He might even have to hire a few women finally, except that most of them are joining the WAFS, or the Flying Training Command, like I did.'

'What do you mean you didn't feel right leaving him? Did you stay with them when you got back?' The bastard hadn't even had the decency to take care of her, and she must have been pretty sick after seven weeks starving on an atoll.

'Yes, I went back to them,' she said quietly, looking at him, remembering their one night of happiness in the moonlight. 'I left Desmond, Nick. I left him when Dad had his heart attack.' It was over a year before, and Nick was stunned to realize he'd never heard it.

'When I went back to L.A. after the last time I saw you, things were just the way you said they were. He kept pushing me, press conferences, test flights, interviews, newsreels. It was everything you said it would be, but he didn't show his true colors until Dad got sick. He "ordered" me to do the tour on schedule, and "forbade" me to go back and see my father.'

'But you went anyway, didn't you?' He knew the trip had been postponed, and had seen a newsreel of her at the hospital, so he knew that much.

'Yeah, I went anyway, and Billy came with me. Desmond said he'd sue us if we didn't do the tour, and he made us sign contracts promising that we'd go in October no matter what.'

'Nice guy.'

'I know. I never went back to him. He never even called me. All he wanted was for me to keep it from the press till I got back. And you were right about the women too. Nancy Firestone was his mistress. Apparently, the only reason he married me was to publicize the tour, just as you said. He said it wouldn't have had "the same impact on the public" without it. The marriage was a complete sham. And afterward, when they brought me back, he told me in Hawaii that I still worked for him, and he was going to sue me for not completing my contract. I'd promised him fifteen thousand miles in the *North Star*, and only made eleven before we went down. He figured he'd get some publicity out of me even then, but it was all over. Dad took me to a lawyer in Chicago, and I divorced him.'

Nick sat utterly amazed at what she was telling him, although the fact that Williams was a sonofabitch wasn't news to anyone, and certainly not Nick. But he was a lot worse than even Nick had suspected.

'How did you keep all that quiet before you left?'

'He's good at that. That's his business. When I went back to L.A. before the tour, I stayed at Billy's. No one knew anything. We left a few weeks after I got back from Good Hope anyway, and Desmond dressed it all up in clean linen. He's a real snake, Nick. You were right about everything. I always wanted to tell you that, but I wasn't sure what to say, or how to say it. At first, my pride was hurt, and I was ashamed to admit that the whole thing had been a farce. And then, I figured maybe you wouldn't want to know anyway. You were so definite about not wanting me. I don't know . . . I figured maybe it was better to leave it for a while. I kept hoping you'd come home and we'd talk, but I guess after Pearl Harbor, you couldn't.'

'We don't get leaves anymore, Cass. And what do you mean I was "definite about not wanting you." Do you remember that night?' He looked hurt that she would say that.

'I remember every minute of it. Sometimes that was the only thing that kept me going on the island . . . thinking of you . . . remembering . . . it was what got me through a lot of things . . . like leaving Desmond. He was so rotten.'

'Then why didn't you write and tell me?'

She sighed, thinking about it, and then she looked at him honestly. 'I guess I figured you'd just tell me again that you were too old and too poor, and that I should find myself a kid like Billy.' He smiled at the truth of it. He might just have been dumb enough to do that. But that was before she had almost died, before he had come to his senses. Just sitting there, looking at her, made him realize what a total fool he'd been when he left her.

'And did you? Find a kid like Billy, I mean?' He looked so worried that for a minute she wished she had the guts to make him jealous.

'I should tell you that I've been out with every man in seven counties.'

'I'm not sure I'd believe you.' He smiled and lit a cigarette, as he sat back against the wall, and looked at her with pleasure. It was so good to see her again. This was the little girl he'd always loved, all grown-up now.

'Why not? Think I'm too ugly for any man to take out?' she teased him.

'Not ugly. Just difficult. It takes a man of a certain age and sophistication to handle a girl like you, Cass. There aren't too many men in McDonough County who could do it.'

537

'You're so full of it. Does that mean you're t
right age these days, or are you still too old fo
me?' she asked him pointedly, wanting to know
just where they were going.

'I used to be. Mostly, I was just too stupid,' he
said honestly; 'they almost had to retire me when
you went down, Cass. I thought I'd go crazy, thinking about you. I went nuts for a while there. I should
have flown home as soon as I heard. Then at least I
could have been in Honolulu when you got there.'

'It would have been wonderful,' she smiled
gently, but she didn't reproach him. Not for
anything. She just wanted to know where they
stood now.

'I suppose Desmond was there with the reporters,' he said with a look of annoyance.

'Naturally. But I had a great nurse who kept
throwing them out of my room before they got
a foot in the doorway. She absolutely hated
Desmond. That was when he was threatening to
sue me for not fulfilling my contract. I think he's
convinced I blew up his plane on purpose. It was the
damnedest thing, Nick,' she said solemnly, 'both
engines caught fire. I don't think they've figured
it out yet, and I'm not sure they ever will.' She
looked far away for a moment as she said it,
and he pulled her closer to him.

'Don't think about it, Cass. It's over.' So were a
lot of things. A whole lifetime had ended for her,
and now it was time for a new beginning. He looked
down at her with a slow smile, feeling the warmth

of her next to him, and remembered a summer night almost two years before that had sustained him ever since then. 'So how long are you here for?'

'I get my orders on Thursday,' she said quietly, wondering what was in store for them, what he wanted from her, if it was going to be the same game as before, or if he had finally grown up now. 'I'll be here anywhere from a week or two to three months. But I'll be back pretty often. I'm in the overseas ferry squadron, that's what we do, taxi service from New Jersey to Hornchurch.'

'That's pretty tame for you, Cass. Most of the time at least.' He was relieved she hadn't found something more dangerous to do. She'd be just the one to do that. For Desmond, she had tested fighter planes to be adapted for the Army. But that was over.

'It'll do for now. What about you? Where are you now?' she asked him, with a look that searched his soul. There was no escaping her question.

At first he didn't understand what she was asking him, and then he laughed, and looked down at her. He understood perfectly. It was no accident that she had come here. The only coincidence was that he'd run into her so quickly.

'What are you asking me, Cass?'

'How brave are you? How smart have you gotten over here, risking your life against the Germans?'

'I'm smarter than I used to be, if that's what you're asking me. I'm a little older . . . just as poor . . .' He remembered his own words easily, and how foolish he had been when he said them. 'How brave are you, little Cassie? How foolish? Is this what you want? After everything you've done and had and been in the last two years, is this what you still want? Just me and the old Jenny? That's all I've got, you know. That, and the Bellanca. It's never going to be fancy.' But they both knew she'd had that and it wasn't what she wanted. She wanted him, and everything he meant to her. Nothing more now.

'If I wanted fancy, I'd be in L.A.'

'No, you wouldn't,' he said quietly, with the stubborn look she knew so well.

'Why not?'

'Because I wouldn't let you. I'll never let you go back to that. I shouldn't have let you go in the first place.' They had both learned some expensive lessons. But they were wiser now. They had both come far, and paid dearly for everything they learned and wanted. 'I love you, Cass, and always have,' he said quietly as he pulled her close to him, and she looked up at him and smiled. It was the face she knew so well, and had always loved since she was a child. The same lines around the eyes from squinting at the sun, the same face she had grown up with. It was a handsome face with character and purpose and kindness, the only one she wanted to look at for an entire lifetime. She had come here to find him again. And she had. With Nick, she had everything she wanted.

'I love you too, Nick,' she said peacefully as he

held her close to him, feeling the warmth of her, the nearness he had longed for so often. It had been hell being away from her, a hell he'd made for himself, and bitterly regretted, but didn't know how to get out of. It took Cass to come over and find him.

'And if either of us doesn't come back from this?' he asked her honestly. 'What then?' He still didn't want to ruin her life, tying her to him, and then dying. That was the price you paid sometimes for loving a flier.

'That's a chance we both take every day. We always have. You taught me that. If this is what we want, we have to have the guts to live with that. And each let the other do what they have to.' It was a high price to pay for loving someone, but they had always been willing to do that.

'And afterward?' He still worried about all that, but she had crossed those bridges long since, and she wouldn't have cared anyway if he'd had absolutely nothing.

'Afterward, we go home, my father retires eventually, and he gives us the airport. And if we live in a shack because that's all you've got, so be it. I don't care, and if we do, we'll change it.' This time he didn't argue with her. This time he knew it was enough for both of them. They had had more, and less, in their lives, and it didn't matter to them. All they needed was what they had, each other, and a sky to fly in.

He kissed her gently, and afterward she looked into the autumn sky and smiled, remembering the hours they'd spent in his old Jenny. She reminded him of her first loops and spins, and he laughed.

'You used to scare the pants off me.'

'The hell I did . . . you told me I was a natural.' She pretended to be insulted as they stood up and he walked her slowly toward her barracks. They had resolved a lot that morning.

'I just said that because I was in love with you.' He laughed happily, feeling like a kid again. She did that to him. She always had.

'No, you didn't. You weren't in love with me then,' she argued with a broad smile, wondering if he had been.

'Yes, I was.' He looked happy and at ease and young. And he felt immeasurable pride as he walked along with her.

'Really?'

They laughed and talked and teased like children. Suddenly, life was very simple. She had done what she had come here to do. She had found him, and everything he had always been to her. She was home at last. They both were.

THE END

IRRESISTIBLE FORCES
by Danielle Steel

What happens when lives that fit together like delicately balanced puzzles begin to pull in different directions?

For fourteen years, Steve and Meredith Whitman have sustained a marriage of passion and friendship. The only thing missing in their lives is children. When Meredith is offered an extraordinary job opportunity in San Francisco, Steve urges her to accept. Perhaps in California, he hopes, they can begin a family at last.

Then Steve's job keeps him in New York for months longer than planned. Weekends fall prey to their hectic schedules. Almost unnoticed, Steve and Meredith have begun living separate lives, and irresistible forces start to tear them apart...

Believe In Happy Endings

9780552145053

CORGI BOOKS

BITTERSWEET
by Danielle Steel

A moving portrait of a woman who dares to risk it all and embark on a new adventure.

India Taylor lives in a world of manicured lawns, piano lessons and Cape Cod summer vacations. With four wonderful children, India believes in commitment and sacrifice, just as she believes in Doug, the man she married seventeen years before. She chose this life over her award-winning career as a photojournalist, and it was a choice she has never regretted – until now.

India can't pinpoint when the price of the sacrifices she'd made began to seem high. But when she meets Paul Ward, a Wall Street tycoon, India begins to share her dreams with him. She hadn't planned to become Paul's friend, and anything more is unthinkable. When Paul urges India to reclaim her career, Doug is adamantly against it. But with Paul's encouragement India can slowly begin the painful but exhilarating journey of self-discovery.

Believe In Happy Endings

9780552145039

CORGI BOOKS

A BEAUTY FOR THE BILLIONAIRE

BY
ELIZABETH BEVARLY

MILLS
BOON

First Published in Great Britain 2017
By Mills & Boon, an imprint of HarperCollins*Publishers*
1 London Bridge Street, London, SE1 9GF

© 2017 Elizabeth Bevarly

ISBN: 978-0-263-92816-7

51-0417

Our policy is to use papers that are natural, renewable and recyclable products and made from wood grown in sustainable forests. The logging and manufacturing processes conform to the legal environmental regulations of the country of origin.

Printed and bound in Spain
by CPI, Barcelona

Elizabeth Bevarly is an award-winning, *New York Times* bestselling author of more than seventy books. Although she has made her home in exotic places like San Juan, Puerto Rico, and Haddonfield, New Jersey, she's now happily settled back in her native Kentucky. When she's not writing, she's binge watching British TV shows on Netflix or making soup out of whatever she finds in the freezer. Visit her at www.elizabethbevarly.com.

Prologue

There was nothing Hogan Dempsey loved more than the metallic smell and clink-clank sounds of his father's garage. Well, okay, *his* garage, as of the old man's death three years ago, but he still thought of it as his father's garage and probably would even after he passed it on to someone else. Not that he was planning on that happening anytime soon, since he was only thirty-three and had no one to leave the place to—his mother had been gone even longer than his father, and there hadn't been a woman in his life he'd consider starting a family with since…ever. Dempsey's Parts & Service was just a great garage, that was all. The best one in Queens, for sure, and probably the whole state of New York. People brought their cars here to be worked on from as far away as Buffalo.

It was under one of those Buffalo cars he was working at the moment, a sleek, black '76 Trans Am—a gorgeous piece of American workmanship if ever there was one. If Hogan spent the rest of his life in his grease-stained coveralls, his hands and arms streaked with engine guts, lying under cars like this, he would die a happy man.

"Mr. Dempsey?" he heard from somewhere above the car.

It was a man's voice, but not one he recognized. He looked to his right and saw a pair of legs to go with it, the kind that were covered in pinstripes and ended in a pair of dress shoes that probably cost more than Hogan made in a month.

"That's me," he said as he continued to work.

"My name is Gus Fiver," the pinstripes said. "I'm an attorney with Tarrant, Fiver and Twigg. Is there someplace we could speak in private?"

Attorney? Hogan wondered. What did an attorney need with him? All of his affairs were in order, and he ran an honest shop. "We can talk here," he said. "Pull up a creeper."

To his surprise, Gus Fiver of Tarrant, Fiver and Twigg did just that. Most people wouldn't even know what a creeper was, but the guy toed the one nearest him—a skateboard-type bit of genius that mechanics used to get under a car chassis—and lay down on it, pinstripes and all. Then he wheeled himself under the car beside Hogan. From the neck up, he didn't look like the pinstripe type. He looked like a guy you'd grab a beer with on Astoria Boulevard after work. Blonder and better-looking than most, but he still had that working-class vibe about him that was impossible to hide completely.

And Hogan should know. He'd spent the better part of a year when he was a teenager trying to keep his blue collar under wraps, only to be reminded more than once that there was no way to escape his roots.

"Sweet ride," Fiver said. "Four hundred and fifty-five CUs. V-8 engine. The seventy-six Trans Am was the best pony car Pontiac ever made."

"Except for the sixty-four GTO," Hogan said.

"Yeah, okay, I'll give you that."

The two men observed a moment of silence for the holy land of Detroit, then Fiver said, "Mr. Dempsey, are you familiar with the name Philip Amherst?"

Hogan went back to work on the car. "It's Hogan. And nope. Should I be?"

"It's the name of your grandfather," Fiver said matter-of-factly.

Okay, obviously, Gus Fiver had the wrong Hogan Dempsey. He could barely remember any of his grandparents since cancer had been rampant on both sides of his family, but neither of his grandfathers had been named Philip Amherst. Fortunately for Hogan, he didn't share his family's medical histories because he'd been adopted as a newborn, and—

His brain halted there. Like any adopted kid, he'd been curious about the two people whose combined DNA had created him. But Bobby and Carol Dempsey had been the best parents he could have asked for, and the thought of someone else in that role had always felt wrong. He'd just never had a desire to locate any blood relations, even after losing what family he had. There wasn't anyone else in the world who could ever be family to him like that.

He gazed at the attorney in silence. Philip Amherst

must be one of his biological grandfathers. And if Gus Fiver was here looking for Hogan, it could only be because that grandfather wanted to find him. Hogan wasn't sure how he felt about that. He needed a minute to—

"I'm afraid he passed away recently," Fiver continued. "His wife, Irene, and his daughter, Susan, who was his only child and your biological mother, both preceded him in death. Susan never married or had any additional children, so he had no other direct heirs. After his daughter's death in a boating accident last year, he changed his will so that his entire estate would pass to you."

Not even a minute. Not even a minute for Hogan to consider a second family he might have come to know, because they were all gone, too. How else was Gus Fiver going to blindside him today?

He had his answer immediately. "Mr. Amherst's estate is quite large," Fiver said. "Normally, this is where I tell an inheritor to sit down, but under the circumstances, you might want to stand up?"

Fiver didn't have to ask him twice. Hogan's blood was surging like a geyser. With a single heave, he pushed himself out from under the car and began to pace. *Quite large.* That was what Fiver had called his grandfather's estate. But *quite large* was one of those phrases that could mean a lot of different things. *Quite large* could be a hundred thousand dollars. Or, holy crap, even a million dollars.

Fiver had risen, too, and was opening a briefcase to withdraw a handful of documents. "Your grandfather was a banker and financier who invested very wisely. He left the world with no debt and scores of assets. His main residence was here in New York on the Upper East Side, but he also owned homes in Santa Fe, Palm Beach and Paris."

Hogan was reeling. Although Fiver's words were making it into his brain, it was like they immediately got lost and went wandering off in different directions.

"Please tell me you mean Paris, Texas," he said.

Fiver grinned. "No. Paris, France. The *Trocadéro*, to be precise, in the sixteenth *arrondissement*."

"I don't know what that means." Hell, Hogan didn't know what any of this meant.

"It means your grandfather was a very rich man, Mr. Dempsey. And now, by both bequest and bloodline, so are you."

Then he quoted an amount of money so big, it actually made Hogan take a step backward, as if doing that might somehow ward it off. No one could have that much money. Especially not someone like Hogan Dempsey.

Except that Hogan did have that much money. Over the course of the next thirty minutes, Gus Fiver made that clear. And as they were winding down what the attorney told him was only the first of a number of meetings they would have over the next few weeks, he said, "Mr. Dempsey, I'm sure you've heard stories about people who won the lottery, only to have their lives fall apart because they didn't know how to handle the responsibility that comes with having a lot of money. I'd advise you to take some time to think about all this before you make any major decisions and that you proceed slowly."

"I will," Hogan assured him. "Weird thing is I've already given a lot of thought to what I'd do if I ever won the lottery. Because I've been playing it religiously since I was in high school."

Fiver looked surprised. "You don't seem like the lottery type to me."

"I have my reasons."

"So what did you always say you'd buy if you won the lottery?"

"Three things, ever since I was eighteen." Hogan held up his left hand, index finger extended. "Number one, a 1965 Shelby Daytona Cobra." His middle finger joined the first. "Number two, a house in Ocean City, New Jersey." He added his ring finger—damned significant, now that he thought about it—to the others. "And number three..." He smiled. "Number three, Anabel Carlisle. Of the Park Avenue Carlisles."

One

"You're my new chef?"

Hogan eyed the young woman in his kitchen—his massive, white-enamel-and-blue-Italian-tile kitchen that would have taken up two full bays in his garage—with much suspicion. Chloe Merlin didn't look like she was big enough to use blunt-tip scissors, let alone wield a butcher knife. She couldn't be more than five-four in her plastic red clogs—Hogan knew this, because she stood nearly a foot shorter than him—and she was swallowed by her oversize white chef's jacket and the baggy pants splattered with red chili peppers.

It was her gigantic glasses, he decided. Black-rimmed and obviously a men's style, they overwhelmed her features, making her green eyes appear huge. Or maybe it was the way her white-blond hair was piled haphazardly on top of her head as if she'd just grabbed it in two fists and tied it there without even looking to see what she was doing. Or it could be the red lipstick. It was the only makeup she wore, as if she'd filched it from her mother's purse to experiment with. She just looked so…so damned…

Ah, hell. Adorable. She looked adorable. And Hogan hated even thinking that word in his head.

Chloe Merlin was supposed to be his secret weapon in the winning of Anabel Carlisle of the Park Avenue Carlisles. But seeing her now, he wondered if she could even help him win bingo night at the Queensboro Elks Lodge. She had one hand wrapped around the handle of a duffel bag and the other steadying what looked like a battered leather bedroll under her arm—except it was too skinny to be a bedroll. Sitting beside her on the kitchen island was a gigantic wooden box filled with plants of varying shapes and sizes that he was going to go out on a limb and guess were herbs or something. All of the items in question were completely out of proportion to the rest of her. She just seemed…off. As if she'd been dragged here from another dimension and was still trying to adjust to some new laws of physics.

"How old are you?" he asked before he could stop himself.

"Why do you want to know?" she shot back. "It's against the law for you to consider my age as a prerequisite of employment. I could report you to the EEOC. Not the best way to start my first day of work."

He was about to tell her it could be her last day of work, too, if she was going to be like that, but she must have realized what he was thinking and intercepted.

"If you fire me now, after asking me a question

like that, I could sue you. You wouldn't have a legal leg to stand on."

Wow. Big chip for such a little shoulder.

"I'm curious," he said. Which he realized was true. There was just something about her that made a person feel curious.

Her enormous glasses had slipped down on her nose, so she pushed them up again with the back of her hand. "I'm twenty-eight," she said. "Not that it's any of your business."

Chloe Merlin must be a hell of a cook. 'Cause there was no way she'd become the most sought-after personal chef on Park Avenue as a result of her charming personality. But to Hogan's new social circle, she was its latest, and most exclusive, status symbol.

After he'd told Gus Fiver his reasons for wanting to "buy" Anabel that first day in his garage—man, had that been three weeks ago?—the attorney had given him some helpful information. Gus was acquainted with the Carlisles and knew Anabel was the current employer of one Chloe Merlin, personal chef to the rich and famous. In fact, she was such a great chef that, ever since her arrival on the New York scene five years ago, she'd been constantly hired away from one wealthy employer to another, always getting a substantial pay increase in the bargain. Poaching Chloe from whoever employed her was a favorite pastime of the Park Avenue crowd, Gus had said, and Anabel Carlisle was, as of five months prior, the most recent victor in the game. If Hogan was in the market for someone to cook for him—and hey, who wasn't?—then hiring Chloe away from Anabel would get the latter's attention and give him a legitimate reason to reenter her life.

Looking at the chef now, however, Hogan was beginning to wonder if maybe Park Avenue's real favorite pastime was yanking the chain of the new guy, and Gus Fiver was the current victor in that game. It had cost him a fortune to hire Chloe, and some of her conditions of employment were ridiculous. Not to mention she looked a little…quirky. Hogan hated quirky.

"If you want to eat tonight, you should show me my room," she told him in that same cool, shoulder-chip voice. "Your kitchen will be adequate for my needs, but I need to get to work. *Croque monsieur* won't make itself, you know."

Croque monsieur, Hogan repeated to himself. Though not with the flawless French accent she'd used. What the hell was *croque monsieur*? Was he going to be paying her a boatload of money to cook him things he didn't even like? Because he'd be fine with a ham and cheese sandwich.

Then the other part of her statement registered. The kitchen was *adequate*? Was she serious? She could feed Liechtenstein in this kitchen. Hell, Liechtenstein could eat off the floor of this kitchen. She could bake Liechtenstein a soufflé the size of Switzerland in one oven while she broiled them an entire swordfish in the other. Hogan had barely been able to find her in here after Mrs. Hennessey, his inherited housekeeper, told him his new chef was waiting for him.

Adequate. Right.

"Your room is, uh… It's, um…"

He halted. His grandfather's Lenox Hill town house was big enough to qualify for statehood, and he'd just moved himself into it yesterday. He barely knew where his own room was. Mrs. Hennessey went home at the end of the workday, but she'd assured him there were "suitable quarters" for an employee here. She'd even shown him the room, and he'd thought it was pretty damned suitable. But he couldn't remember now if it was on the fourth floor or the fifth. Depended on whether his room was on the third floor or the fourth.

"Your room is upstairs," he finally said, sidestepping the problem for a few minutes. He'd recognize the floor when he got there. Probably. "Follow me."

Surprisingly, she did without hesitation, leaving behind her leather bedroll-looking thing and her gigantic box of plants—that last probably to arrange later under the trio of huge windows on the far side of the room. They strode out of the second-floor kitchen and into a gallery overflowing with photos and paintings of people Hogan figured must be blood relations. Beyond the gallery was the formal dining room, which he had yet to enter.

He led Chloe up a wide, semicircular staircase that landed on each floor—there was an elevator in the house, too, but the stairs were less trouble—until they reached the third level, then the fourth, where he was pretty sure his room was. Yep. Fourth floor was his. He recognized the massive, mahogany-paneled den. Then up another flight to the fifth, and top, floor, which housed a wide sitting area flanked by two more bedrooms that each had connecting bathrooms bigger than the living room of his old apartment over the garage.

Like he said, pretty damned suitable.

"This is your room," he told Chloe. He gestured

toward the one on the right after remembering that
was the one Mrs. Hennessey had shown him, telling
him it was the bigger of the two and had a fireplace.

He made his way in that direction, opened the door
and entered far enough to give Chloe access. The room
was decorated in dark blue and gold, with cherry furniture, some innocuous oil landscapes and few personal touches. Hogan supposed it was meant to be a
gender-neutral guest room, but it weighed solidly on
the masculine side in his opinion. Even so, it somehow suited Chloe Merlin. Small, adorable and quirky
she might be, with clothes and glasses that consumed
her, but there was still something about her that was
sturdy, efficient and impersonal.

"There's a bath en suite?" she asked from outside
the door.

"If that means an adjoining bathroom, then yes,"
Hogan said. He pointed at a door on the wall nearest
him. "It's through there." *I think*, he added to himself.
That might have actually been a closet.

"And the door locks with a dead bolt?" she added.

He guessed women had to be careful about these
things, but it would have been nice if she hadn't asked
the question in the same tone of voice she might have
used to accuse someone of a felony.

"Yes," he said. "The locksmith just left, and the
only key is in the top dresser drawer. You can bolt it
from the inside. Just like you said you would need in
your contract."

Once that was settled, she walked into the room,
barely noticing it, lifted her duffel onto the bed and
began to unzip it. Without looking at Hogan, she said,
"The room is acceptable. I'll unpack and report to the

kitchen to inventory, then I'll shop this afternoon. Dinner tonight will be at seven thirty. Dinner every night will be at seven thirty. Breakfast will be at seven. If you'll be home for lunch, I can prepare a light midday meal, as well, and leave it in the refrigerator for you, but I generally spend late morning and early afternoon planning menus and buying groceries. I shop every day to ensure I have the freshest ingredients I can find, all organic farm-to-table. I have Sundays and Mondays off unless you need me for a special occasion, in which case I'll be paid double-time for those days and—"

"And have an additional day off the following week," he finished for her. "I know. I read and signed your contract, remember? You have Christmas Eve, Christmas Day and Thanksgiving off, with full pay, no exceptions," he quoted from it. "Along with three weeks in August, also with full pay."

"If I'm still here then," she said. "That's ten months away, after all." She said it without a trace of smugness, too, to her credit. Obviously Chloe Merlin knew about the Park Avenue chef-poaching game.

"Oh, you'll still be here," he told her. Because, by August, if Hogan played his cards right—and he was great at cards—Anabel would be living here with him, and his wedding present to her would be a lifetime contract for her favorite chef, Chloe Merlin.

Chloe, however, didn't look convinced.

Didn't matter. Hogan was convinced. He didn't care how many demands Chloe made—from the separate kitchen account into which he would deposit a specific amount of money each week and for which she alone would have a card, to her having complete dominion over the menus, thanks to his having no dietary restrictions. He was paying her a lot of money to cook whatever she wanted five days a week and letting her live rent-free in one of New York's toniest neighborhoods. In exchange, he'd created a situation where Anabel Carlisle had no choice but to pay attention to him. Actually not a bad trade, since, if history repeated—and there was no reason to think it wouldn't—once he had Anabel's attention, they'd be an item in no time. Besides, he didn't know what else he would do with all the money his grandfather had left him. It was enough to, well, feed Liechtenstein.

Hogan just hoped he liked…what had she called it? *Croque monsieur.* Whatever the hell that was.

Chloe Merlin studied her new employer in silence, wishing that, for once, she hadn't been driven by her desire to make money. Hogan Dempsey was nothing like the people who normally employed her. They were all pleasant enough, but they were generally frivolous and shallow and easy to dismiss, something that made it possible for her to focus solely on the only thing that mattered—cooking. Even having just met him, she found Hogan Dempsey earthy and astute, and something told her he would never stand for being dismissed.

As if she could dismiss him. She'd never met anyone with a more commanding presence. Although he had to be standing at least five feet away from her, she felt as if he were right on top of her, breathing down her chef's whites, leaving her skin hot to the touch. He was easily a foot taller than she was in her Super Birkis, and his shoulders had fairly filled the doorway when he entered the room. His hair was the color of good semolina, and his eyes were as dark as coffee beans. Chloe had always had a major thing for brown-eyed blonds, and this man could have been their king. Add that he was dressed in well-worn jeans, battered work boots and an oatmeal-colored sweater that had definitely seen better days—a far cry from the fresh-from-the-couturier cookie-cutter togs of other society denizens—and he was just way too gorgeous for his own good. Or hers.

She lifted her hand to the top button of her jacket and twisted it, a gesture that served to remind her of things she normally didn't need reminding of. But it did no good. Hogan was still commanding. Still earthy. Still gorgeous. Her glasses had begun to droop again, so she pushed them up with the back of her hand. It was a nervous gesture she'd had since child-hood, but it was worse these days. And not just be-cause her big black frames were a size larger than they should be.

"So…how's Anabel doing?" he asked.

Of all the questions she might have expected, that one wasn't even in the top ten. Although he didn't strike her as a foodie, and although he'd already filled out a questionnaire she prepared for her employers about his culinary expectations and customs, she would have thought he would want to talk more about her position here. She'd already gathered from Ana-bel that her former employer and her new employer shared some kind of history—Anabel had tried to talk Chloe out of taking this position, citing Hogan's past behavior as evidence of his unsophisticated palate. But Chloe neither cared nor was curious about what that history might be. She only wanted to cook. Cooking was what she did. Cooking was what she was. Cooking was all that mattered on any given day. On every given day. Chloe didn't do well if she couldn't keep every last scrap of her attention on cooking.

"Anabel is fine," she said.

"I mean since her divorce," Hogan clarified. "I understand you came to work for her about the same time her husband left her for one of her best friends."

"That was none of my business," Chloe told him. "It's none of yours, either. I don't engage in gossip, Mr. Dempsey."

"Hogan," he immediately corrected her. "And I'm not asking you to gossip. I just…"

He lifted one shoulder and let it drop in a way that was kind of endearing, then expelled his breath in a way that was almost poignant. Damn him. Chloe didn't have time for endearing and poignant. Especially when it was coming from the king of the brown-eyed blonds.

"I just want to know she's doing okay," he said. "She and I used to be…friends. A long time ago. I haven't seen her in a while. Divorce can be tough on a person. I just want to know she's doing okay," he repeated.

Oh, God. He was pining for her. It was the way he'd said the word *friends*. Pining for Anabel Carlisle, a woman who was a nice enough human being, and a decent enough employer, but who was about as deep as an onion skin.

"I suppose she's doing well enough in light of her… change of circumstances," Chloe said.

More to put Hogan out of his misery than anything else. Chloe actually didn't know Anabel that well, in spite of having been in her employ for nearly six months, which was longer than she'd worked for anyone else. Now that she thought about it, though, Anabel was doing better than *well enough*. Chloe had never seen anyone happier to be divorced.

"Really?" Hogan asked with all the hopeful earnestness of a seventh-grader. *Gah. Stop being so charming!*

"Really," she said.

"Is she seeing anyone?"

Next he would be asking her to pass Anabel a note during study hall. "I don't know," she said. But because she was certain he would ask anyway, she added, "I never cooked for anyone but her at her home."

That seemed to hearten him. Yay.

"Now if you'll excuse me…" She started to call him *Mr. Dempsey* again, remembered he'd told her to call him *Hogan*, so decided to call him nothing at all. Strange, since she'd never had trouble before addressing her employers by their first names, even if she didn't prefer to. "I have a strict schedule I adhere to, and I need to get to work."

She needed to get to work. Not wanted. Needed. Big difference. As much as Chloe liked to cook, and as much as she wanted to cook, she needed it even more. She hoped she conveyed that to Hogan Dempsey without putting too fine a point on it.

"Okay," he said with clear reluctance. He probably wanted to pump her for more information about Anabel, but unless his questions were along the lines of how much Anabel liked Chloe's pistachio *financiers*, she'd given him all she planned to give.

And, wow, she really wished she'd thought of another way to put that than *He probably wanted to pump her*.

"If you need anything else," he said, "or have any questions or anything, I'll be in my, uh…"

For the first time, he appeared to be unsure of himself. For just the merest of moments, he actually seemed kind of lost. And damned if Chloe didn't have to stop herself from taking a step forward to physically reach out to him. She knew how it felt to be lost. She hated the thought of anyone feeling that way. But knowing it was Hogan Dempsey who did somehow seemed even worse.

Oh, this was not good.

"House," he finally finished. "I'll be in my house."

She nodded, not trusting herself to say anything. Or do anything, for that matter. Not until he was gone, and she could reboot herself back into the cooking machine she was. The cooking machine she had to be. The one driven only by her senses of taste and smell. Because the ones that dealt with hearing and seeing and, worst of all, feeling—were simply not allowed.

A ham and cheese sandwich.

Hogan had suspected the dinner Chloe set in front of him before disappearing back into the kitchen without a word was a sandwich, because he was pretty sure there were two slices of bread under the crusty stuff on top that was probably more cheese. But his first bite had cinched it. She'd made him a ham and cheese sandwich. No, maybe the ham wasn't the Oscar Mayer he'd always bought before he became filthy, stinking rich, and the cheese wasn't the kind that came in plastic-wrapped individual slices, but *croque monsieur* was obviously French for *ham and cheese sandwich*.

Still, it was a damned good ham and cheese sandwich.

For side dishes, there was something that was kind of like French fries—but not really—and something else that was kind of like coleslaw—but not really. Even so, both were also damned good. Actually, they were better than damned good. The dinner Chloe made him was easily the best not-really ham and cheese sandwich, not-really French fries and not-really coleslaw he'd ever eaten. Ah, hell. They were better than all those spot-on things, too. Maybe hiring her would pay off in more ways than just winning back the love of his life. Or, at least, the love of his teens.

Chloe had paired his dinner with a beer that was also surprisingly good, even though he was pretty sure it hadn't been brewed in Milwaukee. He would have thought her expertise in that area would be more in wine—and it probably was—but it was good to know she had a well-rounded concept of what constituted dinner. Then again, for what he was paying her, he wouldn't be surprised if she had a well-rounded concept of astrophysics and existentialism, too. She'd even chosen music to go with his meal, and although he'd never really thought jazz was his thing, the mellow strains of sax and piano had been the perfect go-with.

It was a big difference from the way he'd enjoyed dinner before—food that came out of a bag or the microwave, beer that came out of a longneck and some sport on TV. If someone had told Hogan a month ago that he'd be having dinner in a massive dining room at a table for twelve with a view of trees and town houses out his window instead of the neon sign for Taco Taberna across the street, he would have told that person to see a doctor about their hallucinations. He still couldn't believe this was his life now. He wasn't sure he ever would.

The moment he laid his fork on his plate, Chloe appeared to remove both from the table and set a cup of coffee in their place. Before she could escape again—somehow it always seemed to Hogan like she was trying to run from him—he stopped her.

"That was delicious," he said. "Thank you."

When she turned to face him, she looked surprised by his admission. "Of course it was delicious. It's my life's work to make it delicious." Seemingly as an afterthought, she added, "You're welcome."

When she started to turn away, Hogan stopped her again.

"So I realize now that *croque monsieur* is a ham and cheese sandwich, but what do you call those potatoes?"

When she turned around this time, her expression relayed nothing of what she might be thinking. She only gazed at him in silence for a minute—a minute where he was surprised to discover he was dying to know what she was thinking. Finally she said, "*Pommes frites*. The potatoes are called *pommes frites*."

"And the green stuff? What was that?"

"*Salade de chou*."

"Fancy," he said. "But wasn't it really just a ham and cheese sandwich, French fries and coleslaw?"

Her lips, freshly stained with her red lipstick, thinned a little. "To you? Yes. Now if you'll excuse me, your dessert—"

"Can wait a minute," he finished. "Sit down. We need to talk."

She didn't turn to leave again. But she didn't sit down, either. Mostly, she just stared at him through slitted eyes over the top of her glasses before pushing them into place again with the back of her hand. He remembered her doing that a couple of times earlier in the day. Maybe with what he was paying her now, she could afford to buy a pair of glasses that fit. Or, you know, eight hundred pairs of glasses that fit. He was paying her an awful lot.

He tried to gentle his tone. "Come on. Sit down. Please," he added.

"Was there a problem with your dinner?" she asked.

He shook his head. "It was a damned tasty ham and cheese sandwich."

He thought she would be offended that he relegated her creation—three times now—to something normally bought in a corner deli and wrapped in wax paper. Instead, she replied, "I wanted to break you in slowly. Tomorrow I'm making you *pot au feu*."

"Which is?"

"To you? Beef stew."

"You don't think much of me or my palate, do you?"

"I have no opinion of either, Mr. Dempsey."

"Hogan," he corrected her. Again.

She continued as if he hadn't spoken. "I just happened to learn a few things about my new employer before starting work for him, and it's helped me plan menus that would appeal to him. Which was handy since the questionnaire I asked this particular employer to fill out was, shall we say, a bit lean on helpful information in that regard."

"Shouldn't I be the one doing that?" he asked. "Researching my potential employee before even offering the position?"

"Did you?" she asked.

He probably should have. But Gus Fiver's recommendation had been enough for him. Well, that and the fact that stealing her from Anabel would get the latter's attention.

"Uh…" he said eloquently.

She exhaled a resigned sigh then approached the table and pulled out a chair to fold herself into it, setting his empty plate before her for the time being. "I know you grew up in a working-class neighborhood in Astoria," she said, "and that you're so new money, with so much of it, the Secret Service should be crawling into your shorts to make sure you're not printing the bills yourself. I know you've never traveled farther north than New Bedford, Massachusetts, to visit your grandparents or farther south than Ocean City, New Jersey, where you and your parents spent a week every summer at the Coral Sands Motel. I know you excelled at both hockey and football in high school and that you missed out on scholarships for both by *this much*, so you never went to college. I also know your favorite food is—" at this, she bit back a grimace "—taco meatloaf and that the only alcohol you imbibe is domestic beer. News flash. I will *not* be making taco meatloaf for you at any time."

The hell she wouldn't. Taco meatloaf was awesome. All he said, though, was, "How do you know all that? I mean, yeah, some of that stuff is probably on the internet, but not the stuff about my grandparents and the Coral Sands Motel."

"I would never pry into anyone's personal information on the internet or anywhere else," Chloe said, sounding genuinely stung that he would think otherwise.

"Then how—"

"Anabel told me all that about you after I gave her my two weeks' notice. I didn't ask," she hastened to clarify. "But when she found out it was you who hired me, and when she realized she couldn't afford to pay me more than you offered me, she became a little... perturbed."

Hogan grinned. He remembered Anabel *perturbed*. She never liked it much when she didn't get her way. "And she thought she could talk you out of coming to work for me by telling you what a mook I am, right?" he asked.

Chloe looked confused. "Mook?"

He chuckled. "Never mind."

Instead of being offended by what Anabel had told Chloe, Hogan was actually heartened by it, because it meant she remembered him well. It didn't surprise him she had said what she did. Anabel had never made a secret of her opinion that social divisions existed for a reason and should never be crossed—even if she had crossed them dozens of times to be with him when they were young. It was what she had been raised to believe and was as ingrained a part of her as Hogan's love for muscle cars was ingrained in him. Her parents, especially her father, had been adamant she would marry a man who was her social and financial equal, to the point that they'd sworn to cut her off socially and financially if she didn't. The Carlisle money was just that old and sacred. It was the *only* thing that could come between Hogan and Anabel. She'd made that clear, too. And when she went off to college and started dating a senator's son, well… Hogan had known it was over between them without her even having to tell him.

Except that she never actually told him it was over between them, and they'd still enjoyed the occasional hookup when she was home from school, in spite of the senator's son. Over the next few years, though, they finally did drift apart.

But Anabel never told him it was over.

That was why, even after she'd married the senator's son, Hogan had never stopped hoping that someday things would be different for them. And now his hope had paid off. Literally. The senator's son was gone, and there was no social or financial divide between him and Anabel anymore. The blood he was born with was just as blue as hers, and the money he'd inherited was just as old and moldy. Maybe he was still feeling his way in a world that was new to him, but he wasn't on the outside looking in anymore. Hell, he'd just drunk beer from a glass instead of a longneck. That was a major development for him. It wouldn't be long before he—

"Hang on," he said. "How does Anabel know I only drink domestic beer? I wasn't old enough to drink when I was with her."

"That part I figured out myself," Chloe said.

"There are some damned fine domestic beers being brewed these days, you know."

"There are. But what you had tonight was Belgian. Nice, wasn't it?"

Yeah, okay, it was. He would still be bringing home

his Sam Adams on the weekends. *So there, Chloe Merlin.*

"Is everything you cook French?" he asked. He wasn't sure why he was prolonging a conversation neither of them seemed to want to have.

"Still angling for that taco meatloaf, are we?" she asked.

"I like pizza, too."

She flinched, but said nothing.

"And chicken pot pie," he threw in for good measure.

She expelled another one of those impatient sighs. "Fine. I can alter my menus. Some," she added meaningfully.

Hogan smiled. Upper hand. He had it. He wondered how long he could keep it.

"But yes, all of what I cook is French." She looked like she would add more to the comment, but she didn't.

So he tried a new tack. "Are you a native New Yorker?" Then he remembered she couldn't be a native New Yorker. She didn't know what a mook was.

"I was born and raised in New Albany, Indiana," she told him. Then, because she must have realized he was going to press her for more, she added, with clear reluctance, "I was raised by my grandmother because my parents…um…weren't able to raise me themselves. Mémée came here as a war bride after World War Two—her parents owned a bistro in Cherbourg—and she was the one who taught me to cook. I got my degree in Culinary Arts from Sullivan University in Louisville, which is a cool city, but the restaurant scene there is hugely competitive, and I wanted to open my own place."

"So you came to New York, where there's no competition for that kind of thing at all, huh?" He smiled, but Chloe didn't smile back.

He waited for her to explain how she had ended up in New York cooking for the One Percent instead of opening her own restaurant, but she must have thought she had come to the end of her story, because she didn't say anything else. For Hogan, though, her conclusion only jump-started a bunch of new questions in his brain. "So you wanted to open your own place, but you've been cooking for one person at a time for… how long?"

She met his gaze levelly. "For five years," she said.

He wondered if that was why she charged so much for her services and insisted on living on-site. Because she was saving up to open her own restaurant.

"Why no restaurant of your own by now?" he asked.

She hesitated for a short, but telling, moment. "I changed my mind." She stood and picked up his plate. "I need to see to your dessert."

He wanted to ask her more about herself, but her posture made clear she was finished sharing. So instead, he asked, "What am I having?"

"*Glissade.*"

"Which is? To me?" he added before she could.

"Chocolate pudding."

And then she was gone. He turned in his chair to watch her leave and saw her crossing the gallery to the kitchen, her red plastic shoes whispering over the marble floor. He waited to see if she would look back, or even to one side. But she kept her gaze trained on the kitchen door, her step never slowing or faltering.

She was a focused one, Chloe Merlin. He wondered why. And he found himself wondering, too, if there was anything else—or anyone else—in her life besides cooking.

Two

The day after she began working for Hogan Dempsey, Chloe returned from her early-afternoon grocery shopping to find him in the gallery between the kitchen and dining room. He was dressed in a different pair of battered jeans from the day before, and a different sweater, this one the color of a ripe avocado. He must not have heard her as she topped the last stair because he was gazing intently at one photograph in particular. It was possible that if she continued to not make a sound, he wouldn't see her as she slipped into the kitchen. Because she'd really appreciate it if Hogan didn't see her as she slipped into the kitchen.

In fact, she'd really appreciate it if Hogan never noticed her again.

She still didn't know what had possessed her to reveal so much about herself last night. She never told anyone about being raised by a grandmother instead of by parents, and she certainly never talked about the desire she'd once had to open a restaurant. That was a dream she abandoned a long time ago, and she would never revisit it again. Never. Yet within hours of meeting Hogan, she was telling him those things and more. It was completely unprofessional, and Chloe was, if nothing else, utterly devoted to her profession.

She gripped the tote bags in her hands more fiercely and stole a few more steps toward the kitchen. She was confident she didn't make a sound, but Hogan must have sensed her presence anyway and called out to her. Maybe she could pretend she didn't hear him. It couldn't be more than five or six more steps to the kitchen door. She might be able to make it.

"Chloe?" he said again.

Damn. Missed it by that much.

She turned to face him. "Yes, Mr. Dempsey?"

"Hogan," he told her again. "I don't like being called 'Mr. Dempsey.' It makes me uncomfortable. It's Hogan, okay?"

"All right," she agreed reluctantly. "What is it you need?"

When he'd called out to her, he'd sounded like he genuinely had something to ask her. Now, though, he only gazed at her in silence, looking much the way he had yesterday when he'd seemed so lost. And just as she had yesterday, Chloe had to battle the urge to go to him, to touch him, and to tell him not to worry, that everything would be all right. Not that she would ever tell him that. There were some things that could never be all right again. No one knew that better than Chloe did.

Thankfully, he quickly regrouped, pointing at the photo he'd been studying. "It's my mother," he said. "My biological mother," he quickly added. "I think I resemble her a little. What do you think?"

What Chloe thought was that she needed to start cooking. Immediately. Instead, she set her bags on the floor and made her way across the gallery toward him and the photo.

His mother didn't resemble him *a little*, she saw. His mother resembled him a lot. In fact, looking at her was like looking at a female Hogan Dempsey.

"Her name was Susan Amherst," he said. "She was barely sixteen when she had me."

Even though Chloe truly didn't engage in gossip, she hadn't been able to avoid hearing the story of Susan Amherst over the last several weeks. It was all the Park Avenue crowd had talked about since the particulars of Philip Amherst's estate were made public, from the tearooms where society matriarchs congregated to the kitchens where their staff toiled. How Susan Amherst, a prominent young society deb in the early '80s, suddenly decided not to attend Wellesley after her graduation from high school a year early, and instead took a year off to "volunteer overseas." There had been talk at the time that she was pregnant and that her ultra-conservative, extremely image-conscious parents wanted to hide her condition. Rumors swirled that they sent her to live with relatives upstate and had the baby adopted immediately after its birth. But the talk about young Susan died down as soon as another scandal came along, and life went on. Even for the Amhersts. Susan returned to her rightful place in her parents' home the following spring and started college the next year. For all anyone knew, she really had spent months "volunteering overseas."

Until Hogan showed up three decades later and stirred up the talk again.

"You and she resemble each other very much," Chloe said. And because Susan's parents were in the photograph, as well, she added, "You resemble your grandfather, too." She stopped herself before adding that Philip Amherst had been a very handsome man.

"My grandfather's attorney gave me a letter my grandfather wrote when he changed his will to leave his estate to me." Hogan's voice revealed nothing of what he might be feeling, even though there must be a tsunami of feeling in a statement like that. "The adoption was a private one at a time when sealed records stayed sealed, so he couldn't find me before he died.

"Not that I got the impression from his letter that he actually *wanted* to find me before he died," he hastened to add. Oh, yes. Definitely a tsunami of feeling. "It took a bunch of legal proceedings to get the records opened so the estate could pass to me. Anyway, in his letter, he said Susan didn't want to put me up for adoption. That she wanted to raise me herself. She even named me. Travis. Travis Amherst." He chuckled, but there wasn't an ounce of humor in the sound. "I mean, can you see me as a Travis Amherst?"

Actually, Chloe could. Hogan Dempsey struck her as a man who could take any form and name he wanted. Travis Amherst of the Upper East Side would have been every bit as dynamic and compelling as Hogan Dempsey of Queens. He just would have been doing it in a different arena.

"Not that it matters," he continued. "My grandparents talked Susan out of keeping me because she was so young—she was only fifteen when she got pregnant. They convinced her it was what was best for her and me both."

He looked at the photo again. In it, Susan Amherst looked to be in her thirties. She was wearing a black cocktail dress and was flanked by her parents on one side and a former, famously colorful, mayor of New York on the other. In the background were scores of people on a dance floor and, behind them, an orchestra. Whatever the event was, it seemed to be festive. Susan, however, wasn't smiling. She obviously didn't feel very festive.

"My mother never told anyone who my father was," Hogan continued. "But my grandfather said he thought he was one of the servants' kids that Susan used to sneak out with. From some of the other stuff he said, I think he was more worried about that than he was my mother's age." He paused. "Not that that matters now, either."

Chloe felt his gaze fall on her again. When she looked at him, his eyes were dark with a melancholy sort of longing.

"Of course it matters," she said softly. "Your entire life would have been different if you had grown up Travis Amherst instead of Hogan Dempsey." And because she couldn't quite stop herself, she added, "It's…difficult…when life throws something at you that you never could have seen coming. Especially when you realize it's going to change *every*thing. Whatever you're feeling, Hogan, they're legitimate feelings, and they deserve to be acknowledged. You don't have to pretend it doesn't matter. It matters," she repeated adamantly. "It matters a lot."

Too late, she realized she had called him Hogan. Too late, she realized she had spilled something out of herself onto him again and made an even bigger mess than she had last night. Too late, she realized she couldn't take any of it back.

But Hogan didn't seem to think she'd made a mess. He seemed to be grateful for what she'd said. "Thanks," he told her.

And because she couldn't think of anything else to say, she replied automatically, "You're welcome."

She was about to return to the kitchen—she really, really, really did need to get cooking—but he started talking again, his voice wistful, his expression sober.

"I can't imagine what my life would have been like growing up as Travis Amherst. I would have had to go to some private school where I probably would have played soccer and lacrosse instead of football and hockey. I would have gone to college. I probably would have majored in business or finance and done one of those study-abroads in Europe. By now Travis Amherst would be saddled with some office job, wearing pinstripes by a designer whose name Hogan Dempsey wouldn't even recognize." He shook his head, clearly baffled by what might have been. "The thought of having to work at a job like that instead of working at the garage is…" He inhaled deeply and released the breath slowly. "It's just… A job like that would suffocate me. But Travis Amherst probably would have loved it."

"Possibly," Chloe said. "But maybe not. Travis

might have liked working with his hands, too. It's impossible to know for sure."

"And pointless to play 'what if,' I know," Hogan agreed. "What's done is done. And the idea that I would have never known my mom and dad or have the friends I've had all my life... The thought of all the memories that live in my head being completely different..."

Chloe winced inwardly at the irony of their situation. They both grieved for the unknown. But with him, it was a past that hadn't happened, and for her, it was a future that would never be.

"I need to cook," she told him. She pushed her glasses into place with the back of her hand and took a step backward. "I'm sorry, but..." She took another step back. "I need to cook. If you'll excuse me..."

"Sure," he said. "No problem." He didn't sound like there wasn't a problem, though. He sounded really confused.

That made two of them.

When Chloe turned to head back to the kitchen, she saw Mrs. Hennessey topping the last stair. Hogan's housekeeper reminded her of her grandmother in a lot of ways. She wore the same boxy house dresses in the same muted colors and always kept her fine white hair twisted into a flawless chignon at her nape. She was no-nonsense and professional, the way Chloe was. At least, the way Chloe was before she came to work for Hogan. The way she knew she had to be again if she wanted to keep working here.

And she did want to keep working here. For some reason. A reason she wasn't ready to explore. It was sure to be good, whatever it was.

Mrs. Hennessey announced to the room at large,
"There's an Anabel Carlisle downstairs to see you. I
showed her to the salon."

That seemed to snap Hogan out of his preoccupation with what might have been and pull him firmly
into the here and now. "Anabel is here? Tell her I'll
be right down."

"No, Mr. Dempsey, she's here to see Ms. Merlin."

Hogan's jaw dropped a little at that. But all he said
was, "Hogan, Mrs. Hennessey. Please call me Hogan."
Then he looked at Chloe. "Guess she refigured her
budget and wants to hire you back."

Chloe should have been delighted by the idea. Not
only did it mean more money coming in, but it also
meant she would be free of Hogan Dempsey and his
damnable heartache-filled eyes. She should be flying down the stairs to tell Anabel that she'd love to
come back to work for her and would pack her bags
this instant. Instead, for some reason, she couldn't
move. "Tell Anabel we'll be right down," Hogan told
Mrs. Hennessey.

The housekeeper nodded and went back down the
stairs. Chloe stood still. Hogan gazed at her curiously.

"Don't you want to hear what she has to say?"

Chloe nodded. She did. She did want to hear what
Anabel had to say. But she really needed to cook.
Cooking was something she could control. Cooking
filled her head with flavors and fragrances, with methods and measurements. Cooking restored balance to
the universe. And Chloe could really use some balance right now.

"Well then, let's go find out," Hogan said.

Chloe looked at him again. And was immediately

sorry. Because now he looked happy and eager and excited. And a happy Hogan was far more overwhelming, and far more troubling, than a conflicted one. A happy Hogan reminded her of times and places— and people—that had made her happy, too. And those thoughts, more than anything, were the very reason she needed to cook.

Hogan couldn't understand why Chloe looked so unhappy at the thought of seeing Anabel. Then again, Chloe hadn't really looked happy about anything since he met her. He'd never encountered anyone so serious. Even cooking, which she constantly said she wanted to do, didn't really seem to bring her any joy.

Then he remembered she'd never actually said she *wanted* to cook. She always said she *needed* to. For most people, that was probably a minor distinction. He was beginning to suspect that, for Chloe, there was nothing minor about it at all.

"C'mon," he told her. "Let's go see what Anabel wants." And then, because she was standing close enough for him to do it, he leaned over and nudged her shoulder gently with his.

He might as well have jabbed her with a red-hot poker, the way she lurched away from him at the contact. She even let out a soft cry of protest and lifted a hand to her shoulder, as if he'd struck her there.

"I'm sorry," he immediately apologized, even though he had no idea what he needed to apologize for. "I didn't mean to..."

What? Touch her? Of course he meant to touch her. The same way he would have touched any one of his friends, male or female, in an effort to coax them out of their funk. People always nudged each other's shoulders. Most people wouldn't have even noticed the gesture. Chloe looked as if she'd been shot.

"It's okay," she said, still rubbing her shoulder, not looking like it was okay at all.

Not knowing what else he could say, he extended his arm toward the stairs to indicate she should precede him down. With one last, distressed look at him, she did. He kept his distance as he followed her because she seemed to need it, but also because it gave him a few more seconds to prepare for Anabel. He'd known he would run into her at some point—hell, he'd planned on it—but he'd figured it would be at some social function where there would be a lot of people around, and he'd have plenty of time to plan. He hadn't thought she would come to his house, even if it was to see someone other than him.

What Mrs. Hennessey called a "salon," Hogan thought of as a big-ass living room. The walls were paneled in maple, and a massive Oriental rug covered most of the green marble floor. A fireplace on one wall had a mantel that was dotted with wooden model ships, and it was flanked by brown leather chairs—a matching sofa was pushed against the wall opposite.

Three floor-to-ceiling arched windows looked out onto a courtyard in back of the house, and it was through one of those that Anabel Carlisle stood looking, with her back to them. Either she hadn't heard them come in, or she, too, was giving herself a few extra seconds to prepare. All Hogan could tell was that the black hair that used to hang in straight shafts to the middle of her back was short now, cut nearly to her chin.

And her wardrobe choices were a lot different, too. He remembered her trying to look like a secondhand gypsy, even though she'd probably spent hundreds of dollars in Fifth Avenue boutiques on everything she wore. Today's outfit had likely set her back even more, despite merely consisting of sedate gray pants and sweater. But both showcased lush curves she hadn't had as a teenager, so maybe they were worth the extra expense.

As if he'd spoken his appraisal out loud, Anabel suddenly spun around. Although she looked first at Chloe, she didn't seem to be surprised by Hogan's presence. But whether the smile on her face was for him or his chef, he couldn't have said. "Hogan," she said in the same throaty voice he remembered. God, he'd always loved her voice. "Good to see you."

"You, too, Anabel. How have you been?"

She began to walk toward where he and Chloe stood in the doorway. She still moved the way she used to, all grace and elegance and style. He'd always loved watching her move. She was just as gorgeous now as she'd been when they were kids. Even more, really, because she'd ditched the heavy eye makeup and dark lipstick she used to wear, so her natural beauty shone through. Strangely, the lack of makeup only made her blue eyes seem even bluer than he remembered them and her mouth even fuller and lusher.

He waited for the splash of heat that had always rocked his midsection whenever he saw her, and for the hitch of breath that had always gotten caught in his chest. But neither materialized. He guessed he'd outgrown reactions like that.

"I imagine you've already heard most of the highlights about how I've been," she said as she drew nearer. "My divorce was the talk of the town until you showed up." She smiled again, but there was only good humor and maybe a little nostalgia in the gesture. "I should actually probably thank you for that."

"You're welcome," he said, smiling back.

It really was good to see her. She really did look great. So what if his heart wasn't pumping like the V-8 in a Challenger Hellcat, the way he would have thought it would be. People grew up. Hormones settled down.

With one last look at Hogan she turned her attention to Chloe.

"I want you to come back to work for me," she said, straight to the point. "I can pay you three percent more than Hogan offered you."

Hogan looked at Chloe. She still seemed shell-shocked from whatever the hell had happened between them in the gallery. She glanced at Hogan, then back at Anabel, but said nothing.

Cagey, he thought. She was probably thinking if Anabel was offering three percent, she could get more from Hogan. Fine. Whatever it took to keep Chloe on, Hogan would pay it. Especially if it meant Anabel might come around again.

"I'll raise your salary five percent," he told her.

Anabel looked at him, her lips parted in surprise. Or something. Then she looked back at Chloe. "I can go six percent," she said coolly. "And you can have the entire month of August off, with pay."

Again, Chloe looked at Hogan, then back at Anabel. Again, she remained silent.

"Eight percent," Hogan countered.

Now Anabel narrowed her eyes at him in a way he remembered well. It was her *I'll-get-what-I-want-or-else* look. She always wore it right before he agreed to spring for tickets for whatever band happened to be her favorite at the time, or whatever restaurant was her favorite, or whatever whatever was her favorite. Then again, she'd always thanked him with hours and hours of hot *I-love-you-so-much* sex. Well, okay, maybe not hours and hours. He hadn't been the most controlled lover back in the day. But it had for sure been hot.

Anabel didn't up her salary offer this time, but she told Chloe, "And I'll give you the suite of rooms that face the park."

Chloe opened her mouth to reply, but Hogan stopped her with another counteroffer. "I'll raise your pay ten percent," he said. He didn't add anything about a better room or more time off. Not just because she already had a damned suitable room and more time off than the average person could ever hope to have, but because something told him money was way more important to Chloe than anything else.

What she needed the money for, Hogan couldn't imagine. But it was her salary that had been the most important part of her contract, her salary that lured her from one employer to another. Chloe Merlin wanted money. Lots of it.

For a third time she looked at Hogan, then at Anabel. "I'm sorry, Anabel," she said. "Unless you can offer to pay me more than Mr. ...." She threw another glance Hogan's way, this one looking even more edgy than the others. Then she turned so that her entire body was facing Anabel. "Unless you can offer me more than…that… I'm afraid I'll have to remain here."

There was a brief expectant pause, and when Anabel only shook her head, Chloe made her way to the doorway. "I'll draw up a rider for my contract and have it for you this evening," she said to Hogan as she started back up the stairs.

And then she was gone, without saying goodbye to either of them.

"She is such an odd duck," Anabel said when Chloe was safely out of earshot.

There was nothing derogatory in her tone, just a matter-of-factness that had been there even when they were teenagers. She wasn't condemning Chloe, just stating the truth. His chef was pretty unique.

"But worth every penny," she added with a sigh. She smiled again. "More pennies than I can afford to pay her. Obviously, she's working for someone who's out of my league."

Hogan shook his head. "Other way around, Anabel. You were always out of my league. You said so yourself. More than once, if I remember."

She winced at the comment, even though he hadn't meant it maliciously. He'd learned to be matter-of-fact from her. "I was a dumb kid when we dated, Hogan," she told him. "I was so full of myself back then. I said a lot of things I shouldn't have."

"Nah," he told her. "You never said anything I wasn't thinking myself. You were right. We came from two different worlds."

"Even so, that didn't give me the right to be such an elitist. My parents just taught me their philosophy well. It took me years to figure out I was wrong."

Now there was a loaded statement. Wrong about what? Wrong about the prejudice her parents taught her? Wrong about some of the comments she'd made? Wrong about their social circles never mixing? Wrong about leaving him for the senator's son?

Probably better not to ask for clarification. Not yet anyway. He and Anabel had rushed headlong into their relationship when they were kids. The first time they'd had sex was within days of meeting, and they'd almost never met without having sex. He'd sometimes wondered if maybe they'd gone slower, things would have worked out differently. This time he wasn't going to hurry it. This time he wanted to do it right.

"So how have you been?" she asked him. "How are your folks? I still think about your mom's Toll House cookies from time to time."

"My folks are gone," he told her. "Mom passed five years ago. Dad went two years later. Cancer. Both of them."

She looked stricken by the news. She lifted a hand to his shoulder and gave it a gentle squeeze. "Oh, Hogan, I am so sorry. I had no idea."

He covered her hand with his. "You couldn't have known. And thanks."

For a moment neither of them said anything, then Anabel dropped her hand. She crossed her arms over her midsection and looked at the door. Hogan told himself to ask her something about herself, but he didn't want to bring up her divorce, even if she didn't seem to be any the worse for wear from it. Her folks, he figured, were probably the same as always. Maybe a little more likely to invite him into their home than they were fifteen years ago, but then again, maybe not.

But for the life of him, he couldn't think of a single thing to say.

"I should probably get going," she said. "I have a thing tonight. My aunt and uncle are in town. We're meeting at the Rainbow Room." She expelled a sound that was a mixture of affection and irritation. "They always want to meet at the Rainbow Room. Which is great, but really, I wish they'd expand their repertoire a bit. Try Per Se or Morimoto sometime. Or Le Turtle. I love that place."

Okay, she'd just given Hogan the perfect opening. Three different restaurants she obviously loved. All he had to do was say, *What a coincidence, Anabel, I've been wanting to expand my repertoire, too. Why don't you and I have dinner at one of those places? You pick.* And they'd be off. For some reason, though, he just couldn't get the words to move out of his brain and into his mouth.

Not that Anabel had seemed to be angling for an invitation, because she didn't miss a beat when she continued, "Ah, well. Old habits die hard, I guess."

Which was another statement that could have been interpreted in more ways than one. Was she talking about her aunt and uncle now, and their dining habits? Or was she talking about her and Hogan, and how she still maybe had a thing for him? It didn't used to be this hard to read her. And why the hell didn't he just ask her out to see how she responded?

"It was good to see you again, Hogan," she said as she took a step in retreat. "I'm glad Philip Amherst's attorneys found you," she continued as she took another. "Maybe our paths will cross again before long."

"Maybe so," he said, finding his voice.

She lifted a hand in farewell then turned and made her way toward the exit. Just as she was about to disappear into the hallway, Hogan thought of something to ask her.

"Hey, Anabel."

She halted and turned back around, but said nothing.

"If I'd grown up an Amherst…" Hogan began. "I mean, if you'd met me as, say, a guy named Travis Amherst from the Upper East Side who went to some private school and played lacrosse and was planning to go to Harvard after graduation, instead of meeting me as Hogan Dempsey, grease monkey…"

She smiled again, this one definitely nostalgic. "Travis Amherst wouldn't have been you, Hogan. He would have been like a million other guys I knew. If I'd met you as Travis Amherst, I never would have bothered with you."

"You bothered with the senator's son," he reminded her. "And he had to have been like those million other guys."

"Yeah, he was. And look how that turned out."

Good point.

"You take care, Hogan."

"You, too, Anabel."

She threw him one last smile, lifted a hand in goodbye then turned around again and made her way down the hall. He heard her footsteps gradually fade away, then heard Mrs. Hennessey open and close the front door for her. Then, as quickly as she'd shown up in his life again, Anabel was gone.

And as the front door clicked shut behind her, it occurred to Hogan that, just like last time, she never actually told him goodbye.

Three

Although Chloe had Sundays and Mondays off, she rarely used them to relax. She generally went out in the morning and often didn't return until nearly dark—or even after—but the hours in between were almost always devoted to things related to cooking. Sometimes she explored new shops or revisited old favorites to familiarize herself with what they had in stock or to pick up a few essentials. Sometimes she sat in on lectures or classes that addressed new methods or trends in cooking. Sometimes she checked out intriguing restaurants to see what was on their menus that she might adapt for her own. Sometimes she attended tastings of cheeses, charcuterie, beers or wines.

It was to one of the last that she was headed out late Monday afternoon when she ran into Hogan, who was coming in the back door. She'd been exceptionally good at avoiding him since last week when Anabel had tried to hire her back—the same afternoon she'd shared those odd few moments with Hogan in the gallery that had ended with her completely overreacting when he nudged her shoulder with his.

She still wanted to slap herself for recoiling from him the way she had. There had been nothing inappropriate in his gesture. On the contrary, he'd obviously been trying to be friendly. There was a time when Chloe loved having her shoulder nudged in exactly that same way by...friends. It had just been so unexpected, that was all. Especially coming from someone who wasn't...a friend.

And, okay, it had also been a long time since someone had touched her with anything resembling friendship. It had been a long time since anyone had touched her at all. She went out of her way to avoid physical contact these days. With everyone. It just wasn't professional. Among other things.

It was those *among other things* that especially came into play with Hogan. Because even an innocent touch like a nudge to the shoulder felt... Well. Not innocent. Not on her end anyway. Not since it had been so long since anyone had touched her with anything resembling friendship. Or something.

Which was why she had been super careful not to let it happen again. Since that afternoon, dinner every night had been nothing but serving, identifying and describing Hogan's food. No more sitting down at his table. No more spilling her guts. And certainly no more touching. She was his chef. He was her employer. Period. Thankfully, he finally got the message, because after three or four nights of her sidestepping every question he asked about her by replying with something about the food instead, he'd finally stopped asking.

At least, that was what she'd thought until she saw him today. Because the minute he stepped inside he smiled that damnably charming smile of his and said, with much friendliness, "Chloe, hi. Where you going?"

It was the kind of question, spoken with the kind of expression that was almost always followed by *Can I come, too*? He just looked so earnest and appealing and sweet, and something inside Chloe that had been cold and hard and discordant for a very long time began to grow warm and soft and agreeable.

Stop that, she told that part of herself. *Stop it right now.*

But that part wouldn't listen, because it just kept feeling better. So she did her best to ignore it.

"Must be someplace really nice," he added. "'Cause you look really nice."

Had she thought that part of her was only growing warm? Well, now it was spontaneously combusting. The man's smile just had that effect. As did the fact that he was wearing garage-issue coveralls streaked with machine oil, an outfit that should have been unappealing—and on anyone else in her social sphere, it probably would have been—but only served to make Hogan look even more handsome.

She'd always found the working-class hero too damnably attractive. Men who worked with their hands *and* their brains could, at the end of the day, point to something concrete that was actually useful to society and say *Hey, I did that with my bare hands*. Inevitably, that always made her think about what else a man like that could do with his bare hands—especially at the end of the day. And, inevitably, she always remembered. Men like that could make a woman feel wonderful.

She pushed her glasses up with the back of her hand—it was a nervous gesture, she knew, but dammit, she was nervous—and, without thinking, told him, "You look really nice, too."

Only when he chuckled did she realize what she had said and immediately wished she could take back the words.

But Hogan shrugged off the comment. "No, I look like I've spent the better part of the afternoon under a 1957 Mercedes-Benz Three Hundred SL Gullwing that belonged to my grandfather. Which I have been. *You* look really nice. So where you going?"

It was nice of him to say so, but Chloe was the epitome of plain in a black pencil skirt, white shirt, claret-colored cardigan and black flats—all of which she had owned since college—with her hair piled on top of her head, the way it always was.

"Thank you," she made herself say, even though she was uncomfortable with the compliment. "I'm going to a wine-tasting."

She thought the announcement would put an end to any idea he might have about joining her. She was still serving him beer with his dinner—though he had certainly expanded his horizons there—and was hoping to find a few wines at this tasting today that might break him in easily.

"Sounds like fun," he said. Even though he didn't sound like he thought it was fun. In spite of that, he added, "Want some company?"

Of course she didn't want company. Chloe hadn't wanted company for years. Six years, in fact. Six years and eight months, to be precise. Six years, eight months, two weeks and three days, to be even more precise.

"I mean, knowing about wine," Hogan continued, "that could help me in the Anabel department, right? I need to know this stuff if I'm going to be moving in her circles. Make a good impression and all that."

He wasn't wrong, Chloe thought. She knew for a fact that Anabel Carlisle knew and enjoyed her wines. She could invite Hogan to come along, if for no other reason than that. And what other reason could there be?

Even so, she hedged, "Actually, I—"

But Hogan cut her off. "Great. Gimme ten minutes to clean up and change clothes. Be right back."

She was so stunned by his response that it took her a minute to react. She spun around and said, "But—"

But she knew he wouldn't hear her, because he was already pounding up the stairs.

She told herself to leave before he got back and explain her disappearance later by saying she'd assumed he was joking so went her merry way. She really didn't want company today. Or any day. So why didn't she slip out the door and make her way up 67th Street to Madison Avenue, where she could lose herself in both the crowd and the sunny October afternoon? Why did her feet seem to be nailed to the floor? More to the point, why did a part of her actually kind of like the prospect of spending the rest of the afternoon with Hogan?

She was still contemplating those questions and a

host of others when he reappeared ten minutes later. The man was nothing if not punctual. And also incredibly handsome. So far she'd seen him in nothing but jeans and sweaters and greasy coveralls, but, having clearly taken a cue from her own outfit, he now wore a pair of khaki trousers, a pinstriped oxford and a chocolate-colored blazer. And in place of his usual battered work boots were a pair of plain leather mocs—not quite as well-worn as the boots, but still obviously, ah...of a certain age. Just like everything else he had on.

How could a man have inherited as much money as Hogan had and not have spent at least some of it on new shoes and clothes? Then again, who was she to judge? The last time Chloe bought a new article of clothing for herself, it had been for... Well, it wasn't important what she'd bought the dress for. It had been six years since she'd worn it. Six years, eight months, two weeks and six days, to be precise. And she'd gotten rid of it soon after.

As Hogan began to walk toward her, heat bloomed in her midsection again, only this time it was joined by a funny sort of shimmying that only made it more enjoyable.

No! she immediately told herself. *Not enjoyable.* What she was feeling was...something else. Something that had nothing to do with enjoyment.

As he drew nearer, she noticed he hadn't managed quite as well with his grooming as he had his clothing. There was a tiny streak of oil over his eyebrow that he'd missed.

"All set," he said when he stopped in front of her.

"Not quite," she told him.

His expression fell. "I've never been to a wine-tasting. Should I change my clothes?"

She shook her head. "No, your outfit is fine. It's a casual event. It's just that…"

He was within touching distance now, and she had to battle the urge to lift a hand to his face and wipe away the oil herself. The gesture would have been no more inappropriate than his nudging of her shoulder had been last week. For some reason, though, the thought of touching him in such a way felt no less innocent than that one had.

So instead, she pointed at his eyebrow and said, "You missed a spot of grease there. Over your left eyebrow."

He swiped the side of his hand over the place she indicated…and missed the streak by millimeters.

"It's still there," she said.

He tried again, this time with the heel of his palm. But again, he missed it by *that much*.

"Still there," she said again.

He uttered an impatient sound. "Do you mind getting it for me?"

He might as well have asked her if she minded picking him up and heaving him out the window. Did he really not understand that physical contact was a physical impossibility for her after the way she'd overreacted to being touched by him last week? Were they going to have to endure another awkward moment to make that clear?

Strangely, though, the thought of touching Hogan now was slightly less…difficult…than it should have been. Resigning herself, she reached toward his face. Hogan's gaze hitched with hers, making it impossible for her to untether herself. Those brown, brown eyes, richer than truffles and sweeter than muscovado, made her pulse leap wildly, and her mouth go dry. Finally, finally, her hand made contact with his face, the pad of her index finger skimming lightly over his brow.

Her first attempt to wipe away the smudge was as fruitless as his had been—not surprising, since she was barely touching him. She tried again, drawing her thumb over his skin this time—his warm, soft skin—and that was a bit more successful. But still, the stain lingered. So she dragged her thumb across it again, once, twice, three times, until at last, the spot disappeared.

She didn't realize until that moment how her breathing had escalated while she was touching him, or how hot her entire body had become. Her face, she knew, was flushed, because she could feel the heat in her cheeks, and her hand felt as if it had caught fire. Worse, her fingers were still stroking Hogan's forehead, lightly and idly, clearly not to clean up a speck of oil, but simply because she enjoyed the feel of a man's skin under her fingertips and didn't want to stop touching him yet. It had been so long since Chloe had touched a man this way. So long since she had felt the simple pleasure of warmth and strength and vitality against her skin. Even a fingertip.

Worst of all, Hogan seemed to realize exactly what she was feeling. His face was a little flushed, too, and his pupils had expanded to nearly eclipse the dark brown of his irises. Seemingly without thinking, he covered her hand with his and gently removed it. But instead of letting it go after maneuvering it between them, which she had thought he would do—which he really should do—he held on to it, stroking his thumb lightly over her palm.

The warmth in her midsection went supernova at that, rushing heat to her every extremity. So acute was the sensation that she actually cried out—softly enough that she hoped he might not have heard her... except she knew right off he did. She knew because he finally severed his gaze from hers...only to let it fall to her mouth instead.

For one insane moment she thought he was going to kiss her. She even turned her head in a way that would keep her glasses from being a hindrance, the way she used to when— The way a person did when they knew something like that was about to happen. That was just how far she had allowed her desire to go. No, not desire, she immediately corrected herself. Appetite. Instinct. Drive. It had been too long since she'd enjoyed the sexual release every human being craved. Hogan was a very attractive man. Of course her body would respond to him the way it did. It was a matter of hormones and chemistry. There was nothing more to it than that.

Not that that wasn't more than enough.

He still hadn't released her hand, so, with much reluctance, she disengaged it herself and took a giant step backward. Then she took a breath, releasing it slowly to ease her pulse back to its normal rhythm and return her brain to its normal thoughts.

"There," she said softly. "All better."

She hoped he would think she was only talking about the removal of the oil streak from his face. But *all better* referred to herself, too. Her physical self, anyway. The emotional parts of her, though...

Well. Chloe knew she would never be *all* better. Not with so much of herself missing. But she was better now than she had been a few minutes ago, when touching Hogan had made so much of her feel so alive. That feeling was just a cruel ruse. She knew she would never feel alive again.

"All better," she tried again, forcefully enough this time that she sounded as if she actually believed it. "We should get going," she added. "We don't want to be late."

Hogan watched Chloe escape through the back door, his hand still hanging in the air between them. And he wondered, *What the hell just happened?* One minute he was asking her to wipe away a smudge of grease—an action that should have taken less than a second and been about as consequential as opening a jar of peanut butter—and the next, they were staring at each other, breathing as hard as they would have been if they'd just had sex. Really good sex, too.

His hand was even trembling, he noted as he forced himself to move it back to his side. And his whole body was hot, as if she'd run her fingers over every inch of him, instead of just his forehead. What the hell was up with that? The only person who was supposed to be making his hands shake and his skin hot was Anabel. Certainly not a near-stranger with a chip on her shoulder the size of the Brooklyn Bridge.

He gave his head a good shake to clear it. Then he made his feet move forward to follow Chloe, who had already gone through the back door. Outside on 67th Street, she was standing near a tree with her back to him, her face in profile as she gazed toward Madison Avenue—though she didn't look as if she was in any hurry to get anywhere. In fact, her expression was kind of distant and dreamy, as if it wasn't tasting wine she was thinking about, but tasting…uh… something else instead.

Hogan shoved the thought away. He had to be imagining things. Chloe Merlin had made it clear that she wanted to keep her distance from him, physically, mentally, emotionally, spiritually and every other-*ly* there was. Ever since that day last week when she'd reeled away from him in the gallery, she'd been professional to a fault. Every effort he'd made to get to know her better—because he always wanted to know a person better who was working for him, the same way he knew the guys who worked for him at the garage— had fallen flat.

Then again, he'd never met anyone like Chloe, so maybe it was just because of that.

By the time he drew alongside her on the street, she was back to her regular cool composure. When she looked at him now, it was with the same sort of detachment she always did. Her red-lipsticked mouth was flat, and she straightened her glasses with her fingers this time, instead of the back of her hand, a much less anxious gesture than usual. But he still couldn't quite forget that erotic little sound of surrender that had escaped her when he dragged his thumb along the inside of her palm. It would be a long time before he forgot about that.

"We're going to a new restaurant on Madison Avenue, just around the corner from sixty-seventh," she told him. "*L'Artichaut*. They don't actually open until next week, so it will be nice to have a little sneak peek in addition to the wine-tasting."

It suddenly occurred to Hogan that there might be a charge for him to participate. "Is it okay if you show up with someone? I mean, I have my wallet, but I don't have a lot of cash on me."

It was something he might have said in the past, when not having cash on him was a fairly regular occurrence. Saying something like that now, in light of his new financial situation, made him think he sounded like he was expecting Chloe to pick up the tab for him.

"There's no charge," she said. "It's by invitation. And mine included a plus-one. I just didn't, um, have a plus-one to invite."

Wow. She really was a Park Avenue sensation if she got invited to stuff like this. Then the second part of her statement registered. And made him a lot happier than it should have.

"I hope you don't mind having one now," he said.

"It's fine," she told him. But she still didn't sound like it was.

"Now that all the legalities of inheriting my grandfather's estate have been settled, it's kind of hard for me to keep busy, you know? I mean, I don't really have to work anymore, and, as much as I liked working in the garage, I thought I'd like not working more. Isn't that what everyone wants? Even people who like their jobs? To not have to get up every day and go to work?"

"I don't know," she said. "Is that what everyone wants?"

Well, everyone except, apparently, Chloe Merlin. Then again, she'd never said she liked her work. She said she needed it. He still wanted to know what the difference was. "*I* always thought it was," he said. "I started working for a paycheck in my dad's garage when I was fourteen, cleaning up and manning the cash register and running errands until I was old enough to work on the cars. When I was in high school, I worked another job, too, at a market up the street from us, delivering groceries."

Because it had taken the income from two jobs to keep Anabel in the style to which she was accustomed. Not that Hogan regretted a bit of it. She'd been worth every extra minute on his time cards.

The point was that he'd been working hard for more than two-thirds of his life. When Gus Fiver told him how much money he had now, Hogan had realized he could sleep late every morning and stay up late every night and enjoy a million different pursuits. Problem was, he wasn't much of a night owl—he liked getting up early. And he didn't really have any pursuits. Not yet. He hadn't even been away from his job for two weeks, and already, he was restless.

"I don't understand how the idle rich handle being idle," he said. "It feels weird to have all this money I didn't work for. I don't want to be one of those people who gets everything handed to them, you know? I need to figure out a way to earn my place in the world."

"Some wealthy people who don't work keep themselves busy by finding causes to support and raising money to help them. You could become a philanthropist."

He shook his head. "I'd rather just have someone tell me who needs something and write them a check."

Which was something he'd actually started doing already. "There's nothing wrong with charity work," he hurried to add. "It's just not my thing. I'm not comfortable asking people for money, even if the money's not for me."

"But you are comfortable giving it away."

"Well, yeah. It's not like I need it. Just the income I get from my grandfather's investments has me set for life. Not only do I have that incredible house," he added, jabbing a thumb over his shoulder toward the place they'd just left, "but he left me three other houses to boot. The guy had four houses. Who needs that many?" Before she could answer—not that the question had really required an answer—he added, "And he collected cars. There are four parked under the town house and another eight in a storage facility in New Jersey. Not to mention another ten at his other houses. Twenty-two cars. Hell, even I think that's too many, and I've always wondered what it would be like to collect cars."

She almost smiled at that. Almost. It didn't quite make it into her eyes, though. Still, he guessed hearing some mook complain about having too many houses and cars was pretty funny. Her reaction made him feel better. Maybe they could get back on solid, if weird, ground again.

"So that was what you were doing this afternoon?" she asked. "Looking at the ones parked at the house?"

He nodded. "Yeah. They're in incredible condition. Maybe Philip Amherst wasn't a huge success in the father and grandfather departments, but the guy knew wheels. In addition to the Merc Gullwing, there's a 1961 Ferrari Spyder, a 1956 Maserati Berlinetta, and, just when I thought the guy was going to be one of those European snobs, I pull the cover off this incredible 1970 Chevy Chevelle SS 427 in absolute mint condition that's—"

He stopped midsentence, because Chloe was looking at him now with an actual, honest-to-God smile on her face, one that had reached her eyes this time, and the sight nearly knocked the breath out of his lungs. He'd been thinking all this time that she was cute. Quirky, but cute. But when she smiled the way she was smiling now, she was... She was a... She was an absolute... Wow. Really, really...wow.

But all he could manage to say was, "What's so funny?"

She looked ahead again. "I think you've found your purpose."

"What? Collecting cars?" he asked. "No, that's too much. I'm already having trouble justifying keeping them all."

"Then maybe you could do something else with cars," she suggested. "Start designing your own line."

He shook his head. "I don't have that kind of talent."

"Then invest in someone who does."

He started to shoot down that idea, too, but stopped. That actually wasn't a bad idea. He even already knew somebody he could put some money behind. The daughter of one of the guys who worked at the garage. She was still in high school, but the kid knew cars inside and out, and had some great ideas for what to do with them. No way could her parents afford to send her to college. But Hogan could. And there were probably dozens of kids like her in New York...

But he still needed to figure out what to do with

himself. Investing in the future generation was great and all that, but Hogan needed a purpose, too. He'd worked with his hands all his life. He just couldn't see himself never working with them again.

Chloe halted, and Hogan realized they were standing in front of their destination. Looked like, for now, at least, what he would be doing was spending a few hours in a French restaurant tasting wine he knew nothing about. A couple of months ago the idea of doing something like that would have made him want to stick needles in his eyes. Today, though, it felt like a good way to spend the time.

He looked at Chloe again, at how the afternoon sun brought out sparks of silver in her white-blond hair and how the breeze had tugged one strand loose to dance it around one cheek. He saw how the smile had left her lips, but hadn't quite fled from her eyes.

Yeah, tasting wine with Chloe Merlin didn't seem like a bad way to spend an afternoon at all.

Four

Since she began working as a personal chef five years earlier, Chloe had lived in some seriously beautiful homes, from her first job cooking for Lourdes and Alejandro Chavez in their charming Tribeca brownstone to Jack and Martin Ionesco's Fifth Avenue mansion a few years later to Anabel Carlisle's Park Avenue penthouse just weeks ago. All had been breathtaking in their own ways, and all of her employers had generously made clear she had the run of their homes in her off-time, be it their dens or their balconies or—in the case of the Ionescos—their home cinema. Hogan, too, had assured her she was welcome in any part of his house at any time.

But Chloe had never ventured out of her room in any of her previous postings unless it was to cook in her employers' kitchens or to explore the culinary aspects of their various neighborhoods. She'd always been perfectly content to stay in her room reading books, watching movies or searching the internet for articles—but always something about cooking. She'd just never had the desire to involve herself any further in the homes or lives of her employers beyond cooking for them.

So why did she feel so restless in her room at Hogan's house? she wondered a few nights after their excursion to the wine-tasting—which had ended up being surprisingly enjoyable. And not just because Hogan had been such an agreeable companion, either. He'd also proved to have a fairly sophisticated palate, something that had astonished him as much as it had Chloe, and he had discovered some wines he actually enjoyed, all of them labels she would have chosen for him. She would have put his until then unknown oenophilia down to his Amherst genes, but somehow she suspected that whatever made Hogan Hogan was the result of Hogan alone. In any event, Chloe had actually almost had fun that day. She couldn't remember the last time she'd almost had fun.

Which was maybe why she suddenly felt so restless in her room. A part of her was itching to get out and almost have fun again. And no matter how sternly she told that part of herself to stop feeling that way, that part of herself refused to listen.

She looked at the clock on the nightstand. It was nearly midnight. Hogan, she knew, always turned in before eleven. She knew this because she often went to the kitchen to make a cup of *Mariage Frères* tea about that time before turning in herself, and the house was always locked up tight—dark and silent save a small lamp in the kitchen she required be kept on so that she could make late-night forages for things like *Mariage Frères* tea. She was confident enough he was in his own room by now that she didn't worry about having already donned her pajamas. Or what passed for pajamas for her—a pair of plaid flannel pajama pants and a T-shirt for François and the Atlas Mountains, her latest favorite band.

Even so, she padded as silently as she could in her sock feet down the stairs to the third floor—slowing only long enough at the fourth to ensure that, yes, Hogan's bedroom door was closed, and all the lights were off—where there was a library teeming with books, even though she was fairly sure they would be about things besides cooking. There might be a novel or two in the mix somewhere, and that would be acceptable.

The only light in the library was what spilled through the trio of arched floor-to-ceiling windows from a streetlamp outside—enough to tell her where the largest pieces of furniture lay, but not enough to distinguish any titles on book spines. So she switched on the first lamp she found, bathing the room in a pale, buttery glow.

She went to the set of shelves nearest her, pushing her glasses up on her nose so she could read the books' spines. All the titles there seemed to have something to do with maritime history. The next grouping was mostly atlases. After that came biographies, predominantly featuring robber barons, autocrats and politicians. So much for fun.

She went to the other side of the room and began working her way backward. Toward the middle, she finally came across novels. Lots of them. To her surprise, she found a number of historicals by Anya Seton, whom her grandmother had adored. She plucked out a title from the mix she recognized as one of Mémée's favorites, opened it to the first page, read a few lines and was immediately hooked. So hooked that she didn't look where she was going when she turned around and stepped away from the shelf, so she inadvertently toppled a floor lamp.

It fell to the ground, hitting the marble with what seemed like a deafening crash in the otherwise silent room. Hastily, she stooped to right it. No harm done, she decided when it was upright again with its shade back in place. Just to make sure, she flicked it on to see if the bulb still worked—it did—then turned it off again. After that the room—and the house—were silent once more.

She opened the book and went back to her reading, making her way slowly across the library as she did, skirting the furniture until she arrived back at the lamp she had turned on when she first entered. She stood there and continued to read until she finished a few more paragraphs, then absently turned off the light, closed the book and began picking her way through the darkness toward the wide library entrance—which, since she wasn't yet accustomed to the darkness, she had to struggle to make out, so her steps slowed even more. The moment she made her way through it and into the adjoining study, however, someone surged up behind her, wrapping an iron-hard arm around her waist to pull her back against himself—hard.

Chloe screamed at the top of her lungs and, simultaneously, elbowed him viciously in the gut and stomped down as hard as she could on his foot. When his grip on her loosened in response, she lurched away from him so fiercely that her glasses fell from her face and onto the floor. She barely noticed, though, because all of her attention went to hurling the heavy hardback as viciously as she could in the direction of her assailant—and hitting him square in the face with it if the expletive he yelled in response was any indication.

She was opening her mouth to scream again and about to race for the stairs when her attacker cried out, "Whoa, Chloe! I'm sorry! I didn't know it was you!"

Immediately, she closed her mouth. Hogan. Of course it was Hogan. Who else would it be? The house, she'd learned her first day on the job, had more security than Fort Knox, something she and Hogan both appeared to have forgotten. Realizing that now, however, did little to halt the flow of adrenaline to every cell in her body. Her heart was hammering, her breathing was ragged, her thoughts were scrambled and her body was trembling all over.

"I thought you were an intruder," he said.

He, too, sounded more than a little rattled—she could hear him breathing as heavily as she was. But his eyes must have been better adjusted to the dark, because he made his way effortlessly across the study to switch on a desktop lamp that threw the room into the same kind of soft, golden light the library had enjoyed only moments ago. In fact, the study was pretty much a smaller version of the room she'd just left.

Hogan, too, was bathed in soft, golden light, something that made him seem softer and more golden himself. His nightwear wasn't much different from hers, except that he was wearing sweatpants, and his T-shirt read "Vinnie's House of Hubcaps." And where her shirt hung loosely on her frame, Hogan's was stretched taut across his, so that it hugged every bump and groove of muscle and sinew on his torso. And there was a lot of muscle and sinew on his torso. And on his arms, too. Holy cow. His shirtsleeves strained against salient biceps that tapered into a camber of muscles in his forearms in a way that made her mouth go dry.

The moment Chloe realized she was staring, she drove her gaze back up to his face. But that didn't help at all, because his hair was adorably disheveled, his cheeks were shadowed by a day's growth of beard and his bittersweet-chocolate eyes were darker and more compelling than ever. Something exploded in her belly and sent heat to every extremity, but not before much of it pooled deep in her chest and womb.

Why did he have to be so handsome? So magnetic? So damnably sexy? And why couldn't she ignore all of that? She encountered handsome, magnetic, sexy men all the time, and she never gave any of them a second thought. What was it about Hogan that made that impossible to do?

He was gripping a baseball bat about a third of the way up, but he loosened his hold and let it slip to the knob as he lowered it to his side. With his free hand, he rubbed a spot on his forehead that was already turning red—the place where the book had hit him.

"I am so sorry," she said. "I thought you were an intruder, too."

He looked at his fingers, probably to check for blood, and when he saw that they were clean, hooked that hand on his hip. "Don't apologize for defending yourself. It was a nice shot."

She tried to smile at that, but she was so rusty at smiling these days, she wasn't sure she succeeded. "Thanks."

"I heard a loud noise," he said. "I thought someone had broken in."

"That was me. I knocked over a lamp in the library. I came down to look for a book, and then I got so caught up in my reading that I didn't look where I was going. I didn't realize it was that loud. I mean, it sounded loud when it went down, but I thought that was just because the room was so quiet. I mean this house must have walls like a mausoleum, and—"

And she made herself shut up before she started to sound like an idiot, even though it was probably too late for that.

"No worries," he told her. "It's fine."

Oh, sure. Easy for him to say. He wasn't staring at some luscious blond wondering what he looked like under that T-shirt. And those sweatpants. And socks. And anything else he might be wearing. Or not wearing.

Oh, she really wished she hadn't thought that.

They stood there for another moment in silence, their gazes locked, their breathing still a little broken. Though hers was doubtless more a result of her thoughts than any lingering fear for her safety. Her physical safety anyway. Her mental and emotional safety were another matter at the moment.

Finally, Hogan said, "I think I need a drink." One more look at her, and he added, "You look like you could use one, too."

She told herself to say no. Then said, "I wouldn't say no."

He nodded once, leaned the bat against a wide, heavy desk then crossed to a cabinet on the opposite side of the study, opening it to reveal a fairly substantial bar. Without even having to look through the options, he pulled down a bottle of very nice bourbon, along with a cut-crystal tumbler—obviously, he'd spent some time in this room—then turned around to look at Chloe.

"What's your poison?" he asked. "This is all bourbon. Something else my grandfather collected, I've discovered. If you'd rather have a glass of wine, I can go down to the cellar for some."

But she'd already recognized a familiar favorite on the shelf and shook her head. "I'll have a couple of fingers of the Angel's Envy," she told him.

His eyebrows shot up at that. "I never would have pegged you for a bourbon drinker."

"We're even, then," she said. "I wouldn't have guessed you'd be one, either." She'd been surprised enough at how quickly he'd taken to wine.

"I wasn't before," he admitted. "But after exploring my grandfather's study and discovering the bar, I realized cars weren't his only passion. I wanted to see if maybe we had this—" he gestured toward the spirits behind him "—in common, too." He grinned. "Turns out we do."

He withdrew her chosen label and a second tumbler for her and splashed a generous portion from each bottle into their respective glasses. Then he made his way back to her and handed her her drink, which she accepted gratefully.

He lifted his glass in a toast. "Here's to nonexistent intruders."

She lifted hers in response. "I'll drink to that."

They clinked their glasses and did so with enthusiasm, but after one taste, both seemed to lose track of where the conversation should go next. Chloe tried to focus on the heat of the bourbon as it warmed her stomach, but the heat in Hogan's eyes kept distracting her. He was looking at her differently from what she was used to, as if he were seeing something in her face that wasn't there before.

She realized what that was when he said, "You're not wearing your glasses. Or any lipstick. You're cute in them, but without them…"

It was only his mention of her glasses that made her remember she'd lost them in the scuffle. She really didn't need them that badly—only for up-close work—and mostly wore them because they were another way to keep distance between herself and others.

"I lost them when you, uh…when you, um…" *When you pulled me back against your rock-hard abs and made me want to crawl under your shirt to see them for myself* was the thought that tumbled through her mind, but she was pretty sure it wasn't a good idea to say that out loud. Especially since, at the time, what she'd really been thinking was that she needed to run for her life.

Then again, maybe the two thoughts had something in common after all.

He must have realized what she was trying to say— and thankfully not what she was actually thinking— because he glanced over toward the door where the two of them had been embraced a few minutes ago. Uh, she meant *embattled*, not *embraced*. Of course that was what she meant. Then he strode to the entryway, looked around on the floor and found them with little trouble. He picked up the book on his way back to Chloe and brought them both to her.

"Thanks," she said as she took her glasses from him. She started to put them back on then instead settled them on top of her head. She told herself it was only because she was sure they needed cleaning after what they'd just been through. It wasn't to get rid of any distance that might linger between Hogan and herself.

He looked at the spine of the book before handing it to her, eyeing her thoughtfully when he saw the unmistakably romantic title.

"It was Mémée's favorite," she said. Then, when she realized he would have no idea who Mémée was, clarified, "My grandmother. Anya Seton was her favorite author, and when I saw all the books in the library by her, it made me think of Mémée, and I just—"

She'd just felt kind of lonely, she remembered, when she saw all the books that reminded her of the grandmother who passed away when she was in college. She thought about Mémée often—nearly every time she cooked—but somehow, seeing all those novels had roused feelings Chloe hadn't felt for a very long time. Or maybe it was something else that had done that. Since coming to work for Hogan, nothing in her life had felt normal.

"I thought reading it might make me feel closer to her," she said halfheartedly. Then, because she couldn't quite stop herself, she added, "I just miss her."

Hogan nodded. "I lost my folks young, too," he said. "How old were you when your grandmother died?"

"Nineteen."

"Which means you were even younger when you lost your parents."

"I never actually knew my parents," Chloe said, again without thinking. Wondering why she offered the information to Hogan when it was something she never discussed with anyone. She really must be frazzled by the whole intruder thing. Because even though she told her brain to stop talking, her mouth just kept it up. "My father was never in the picture—I'm not even sure my mother knew who he was—and not long after my mother had me, she sort of…disappeared."

Which was something Chloe *really* never talked about. Only one other person besides her grandmother knew about her origins. And that person was gone, too. What was possessing her to say all this to Hogan?

Whatever it was, it had such a hold on her that she continued, "My mother was troubled. Mémée did her best, but you can only do so much for a person who refuses to get help."

Hogan said nothing for a moment, then, softly, he told her, "I'm sorry." Probably because he didn't know what else to say. Not that Chloe blamed him. She wasn't sure what to say about her origins, either. Other than that they had made her what she was, so she couldn't—wouldn't—regret them.

"It's okay," she said. "Mémée was a wonderful parent. I had a nice childhood, thanks to her. I loved her very much, and she loved me."

Hogan gazed down into his drink. "So I guess you and I have something in common with the biological mother, what-if-things-had-been-different, kind of stuff, huh?"

Chloe started to deny it, started to tell him that her own upbringing would have been virtually the same if her mother had been healthy, then realized there was no way she could know that was true. Maybe her upbringing would have been better, maybe not. Who knew? But her mother would have been the one to mold her, not Mémée, and there was no way of even speculating about what shape Chloe would have taken. Would she have ever discovered her love of cooking under her mother's care? Or would she be passionate about something else now? Had her childhood been different, she might never have come to New York. She might never have met Hogan. Or anyone else.

"Maybe," she finally said. "But things happen to people every day that change their lives, many of them events that are out of their hands. Or by the smallest choices they make. Even opting to cross the street in one place instead of another could have devastating results if you get hit by a bus."

He smiled at that. "Yeah, well, I was thinking more in terms of our quality of life."

"You don't think you had quality of life growing up in Queens?"

"I had great quality of life growing up in Queens. The best. I'm kind of getting the impression that growing up here with the Amhersts would have left me at a disadvantage."

His response puzzled her. "Growing up in a breathtaking, multimillion-dollar home with unlimited funds at your disposal would have left you at a disadvantage?"

This time he nodded. "Sure. If no one here loved me."

Her heart turned over at the matter-of-fact way he said it. As if it was a given that he wouldn't have been loved here in this world of excess.

"You don't think your mother would have loved you?" she asked.

He expelled an errant breath and moved to sit in one of the leather chairs. Chloe followed, seating herself in the one next to it. She wasn't sure why—she really should be going back to her room and making the effort to get into bed—but something in his demeanor prohibited her from abandoning him just yet.

"I don't know," he said. "She was awfully young when she had me. She might have started looking at me as a liability who kept her from living the kind of life her friends did. She might have started resenting me. But I know my grandfather wouldn't have cared for me. His letter to me was—" he inhaled deeply and released the breath slowly "—not the warmest thing in the world. I mean, he wasn't mean or anything, but it was pretty clear he was only leaving his estate to me because the Amhersts dating all the way back to the time of knights and castles considered bloodline to be more important than anything else. He obviously wasn't happy about doing it."

He looked at something above the door. Chloe followed his gaze and saw an ornate coat of arms hanging there.

"The Amherst crest," he said. "There's one of those hanging in nearly every room in this house. Have you noticed?"

In truth, she hadn't. But when it came to physical surroundings, Chloe deliberately wasn't the most observant person in the world.

"No," she told him. "I suppose if there are that many, then bloodlines did indeed mean a lot to him."

"In his letter, he even asked that I consider legally changing my last name to Amherst so the direct line to the family name wouldn't die out with him. I guess he always figured Susan would forget about me and go on with her life. Get married and have other kids whose names she could hyphenate or something. Kids he could proudly call his progeny. His legacy. Instead of some grease monkey whose blue collar was stained with sweat."

"I'm sure Susan never forgot you, Hogan," Chloe said with absolute conviction. "And I'm sure she loved you very much. In a way, you were probably her first love. No one ever forgets or stops loving their first love."

He gave her another one of those thoughtful looks, the kind where the workings of his brain fairly shone in his eyes. His dark, beautiful, expressive eyes. "You sound like you're talking from experience."

She said nothing in response to that. She'd said too much already.

But her response must have shown on her face, too, because Hogan grinned a melancholy grin. "So there's some guy back there in your past you're still pining for, huh? The same way I've been pining for Anabel all these years? Is that something else you and I have in common?"

Maybe it was the bourbon. Maybe it was the pale, otherworldly light. Maybe it was the last lingering traces of mind-scrambling adrenaline. Maybe it was just the way Hogan was looking at her. Whatever it was, Chloe couldn't resist it.

"I'm not pining for him," she said. "I'll never get him back. He's gone."

Hogan's grin fell. He met her gaze levelly, and whatever he saw in her eyes made his eyebrows arrow downward and his jaw clench tight. "Gone," he repeated. "Gone like...he moved to another country?"

Chloe shook her head. It wasn't the bourbon. It wasn't the light. It wasn't the adrenaline. It was definitely Hogan this time and the way he was looking at her that made her say the rest.

"Samuel was my husband. He was a chef, too. We were going to open our own restaurant. We were going to have kids and teach them to cook, too. We were going to have a long life together, full of family and food. We were going to retire fat and happy in Lyon, and we were going to have our ashes scattered together in the Pyrenees. Instead, his ashes were scattered in Brown County State Park, where he and I had our first date when we were in ninth grade."

Hogan was looking kind of horrified now, confirming what Chloe already suspected—she had made her biggest mess yet. So she gripped her glass and downed what was left of its contents. Then she rose and carried it back to the cabinet from which Hogan had taken it. She started to leave it there for him to take to the kitchen with his own glass when he was ready. Instead, she picked up the bottle of bourbon that was still sitting on the bar and left with both it and the glass. It was definitely time to go back to her room and make the effort to get into bed. Somehow, though, she knew it was going to be a while before she actually made it to sleep.

Five

Hogan didn't expect to see Chloe the morning after she bared the depths of her soul to him. Not just because a person as private as she was would obviously be embarrassed about having revealed what she had last night, but because he knew firsthand what too much bourbon—even good bourbon—could do to a person. She'd looked pretty serious about making a dent in the bottle she'd taken back to her room.

So it surprised him when he went into the kitchen Friday morning to make himself breakfast and found her in there cooking. She was wearing one of her gigantic chef's jackets and gaudy pants—these decorated with silhouettes of pigs and the word "oink"—and had her hair gathered at the top of her head the way she always did. Her glasses were back in place, her red lipstick was perfect and she looked none the worse for wear for having been up late drinking and grieving for a man she would have loved for the rest of her life if he hadn't died far too soon.

He still couldn't believe she was a widow at twenty-eight. Had been a widow since twenty-three or younger, considering she'd been in New York cooking for people for the past five years. Though her revelation last night went a long way toward explaining why she was the way she was, cool and aloof and serious to a fault. Had Hogan experienced what she had, had he, say, married Anabel and then lost her so young, he would have been putting his fist through something every chance he got. And there wouldn't have been enough bourbon in the world to keep him numb.

Then he remembered that Chloe wasn't cool or aloof or serious to a fault. There had been moments since he'd met her when her veneer had cracked enough for him to see through to the other side. That day in the gallery when she told him his feelings of confusion about his place in the world were valid. That afternoon of the wine-tasting when she uttered that erotic little sound at the touch of his thumb. Last night when she fought like a tiger for her safety. Chloe Merlin had a sensitive, passionate, fiery soul, one that clawed its way out of wherever she buried it whenever her guard was down. Though, now that he knew more about her, he understood her guardedness. He just wished she didn't feel like she had to be so wary around him.

"Good morning," he said as he headed for the coffeemaker.

She jumped at the sound of his voice and spun

around, but her expression offered nothing of what she might be feeling.

"Your breakfast will be ready in ten minutes," she said in reply.

"Great," he told her. "But you know, after last night, you didn't have to—"

"Your breakfast will be ready in ten minutes," she repeated before he could finish, in exactly the same way.

"But—"

"Your breakfast will be ready in ten minutes," she said a third time, more adamantly. Then, to drive that point home, she added, "Have a seat in your dining room, and I'll bring it out to you."

Ah. Okay. So they were just going to ignore what happened last night and go back to the way things were. Pretend she never said all the things she said— and pretend he never saw her looking all soft and vulnerable and pretty.

Which should have been fine. They had separate lives that didn't need to intersect except for mealtimes or if he happened to run into her in the house at some point.

Like he had last night.

He guessed that was beside the point—Chloe's point anyway. And it was a good point. For some reason, though, Hogan didn't want to take it. He didn't want to forget last night happened. He didn't want to forget what she said. He didn't want to forget how she looked. And he didn't want to go back to their old routine and roles.

Chloe obviously did, though. So, without saying anything more, he poured himself a cup of coffee—

ignoring her frown, since, as far as she was concerned, that was her job—then went to the dining room to wait for his breakfast.

But when he sat down at the table—the same way he'd sat down at the table every morning for a few weeks now—he didn't feel any more comfortable than he had on any of the other mornings waiting for his breakfast. Maybe a legal document had made this place his house, but it still didn't feel like home. Maybe he never had to work another day in his life, but his life right now didn't have any purpose. Maybe he was eating better than he ever had before, but he didn't like eating by the clock and by himself. Hell, at least he'd had the Mets and the Knicks to keep him company before.

Hogan's point was that he didn't like having someone else fixing and bringing him his breakfast. Even if hiring Chloe to do just that had been—and still was—the best way to bring Anabel back into his life. Which was something he needed to be focusing his attention on. And he would. ASAP. Just as soon as he figured out a way to do it that would keep Anabel in his house for longer than the few minutes she'd been here last time.

For now, though, he'd just have to keep putting up with breakfast Chloe's way instead of making his own, the way he'd been doing from the time he was a preschooler splashing more milk out of the cereal bowl than into it all the way up to grabbing a cruller from Alpha Donuts on his way to work. That was breakfast for normal people. Breakfast wasn't—

Chloe arrived at his side and set a plate in front of him. Beside a couple of slices of melon settled into what he'd come to recognize as chard was a wedge of something layered with... Ah, hell. He was too tired to try to identify what all the layers were.

So he asked, "What's that?"

"*Tartiflette avec les lardons, le reblochon et les truffes noires.*"

"Which is?"

"Potato casserole with bacon, cheese and mushrooms."

Hogan sighed. Breakfast wasn't *tarti*-whatever. It wasn't even potato casserole with bacon, cheese and mushrooms. He started to tell Chloe he'd have breakfast out this morning. He could take the train to Queens and stop by Alpha Donuts to treat himself to a baker's dozen. He could visit the garage while he was in the neighborhood, maybe go back to his old apartment for a few things he hadn't thought he'd need here. And then he could grab lunch at Taco Taberna across the street before he came ho— Before he came back to Lenox Hill.

He glanced at Chloe. Up close, she didn't look as put together as he first thought. In fact, up close, he could see smudges of purple beneath red-rimmed eyes and a minuscule smudge of lipstick at the corner of her usually flawlessly painted mouth. Not to mention an expression on her face that was a clear mix of *I'm-the-fiercest-human-being-in-the-world* and *I'm-barely-holding-it-together.* She'd gotten up early on a morning when she probably felt like crap because she had to do her job. She'd dressed and hauled herself into work, even though she probably felt uncomfortable facing her boss. Hogan would be the biggest mook in New York if he left now.

"It looks delicious," he told her. "Thank you."

She looked surprised by his gratitude. This after he'd thanked her every time she brought him a meal. But she replied, as she always did, "You're welcome." Then she spun on her heel to return to the kitchen.

As he often did, Hogan turned around to watch her retreat. Usually, she headed straight for her sanctuary, head held high, her step never faltering. This morning, though, she moved sluggishly, her head dipping down. She even lifted her hand to her face at one point, and he was pretty sure she was wiping something out of her eyes.

He turned back around and looked at his breakfast. Even if it wasn't what he usually ate, it was, like everything else she'd cooked, very…artful. In fact, it was, like everything else she'd cooked, almost too artful to eat.

He suddenly wondered what chefs fed themselves. Did Chloe prepare her own breakfast as painstakingly as she made his? Or was she in the kitchen right now, jamming a Pop-Tart into her mouth without even bothering to toast it first? Would her lunch be a slice of reheated pizza? With maybe some Sara Lee pound cake for dessert? Hogan really liked Sara Lee pound cake. He missed Sara Lee pound cake. And, while he was at it, when did Chloe eat dinner anyway? Before or after she made his? Did she fix a double batch of everything? One for him and one for her? Or did she just throw together a ham and cheese sandwich to eat while she was waiting for him to finish? A real ham and cheese sandwich. Not a French one.

He was still wondering about all that as he picked up his fork and dug in to the potato whatever. And he wondered about something else, too: How did he convince his chef there was more to life than timetables and fancy potato casseroles?

By the time Chloe left for her grocery shopping Friday afternoon, she felt almost human again. A mid-morning nap—which she took completely by accident in Hogan's wine cellar when she lay down to look at the bottles on the very bottom shelf—had helped. What helped more was Hogan's acceptance that they pretend last night never happened. But what helped most of all was losing herself in the sounds and sights and smells of Greenmarket, scouring the farmers' stalls for what seasonal finds this early November day had to offer. She needed shallots for the *confit de canard* she would be making for dinner, Brussels sprouts and mesclun to go with, and pears for the *clafoutis* she planned for dessert.

She took her time as she wandered through the market, stopping at a stall whenever she saw a particularly delectable-looking piece of produce to wonder what she could make with it. The apples always smelled so luscious this time of year. And there was a vendor with maple syrup. Had to have some of that. Oh, and fennel! She hadn't made anything with fennel for a long time. Fennel was delicious in vichyssoise. Had to have some of that, too. And this would be the last of the tomatoes until next year. She should probably pick up a few and use them for something, too. Maybe a nice *tartine*...

By the time Chloe returned from Greenmarket, she had two canvas totes teeming with vegetables and fruits and other goodies, more than enough to get her through Friday and Saturday both. Enough, really, so that Hogan could have leftovers on Sunday if he wanted to fix something for himself while she was out doing something. Something that wasn't staying in Hogan's house. Something that kept her mind busy with thoughts that had nothing to do with Hogan. Or the way Hogan looked last night after she told him about Samuel. Or thoughts about Samuel, for that matter. Or anything other than food and its preparation. Its wonderful, methodical, intricate preparation that could keep even the most prone-to-wandering-to-places-it-really-shouldn't-wander mind focused on the task at hand.

She couldn't wait to get started on dinner.

She had just finished putting everything away—save what she would be using tonight—and was about to head to her room to change from her khaki cargo pants and baggy pomegranate-colored sweater into her chef's duds, when Hogan entered the kitchen carrying two white plastic bags decorated with the red logo of a local grocery chain.

"I'm cooking tonight," he said without preamble when he saw her. Before she could object, he hurried on, "I was in my old neighborhood today to stop by my old place, and I dropped in at the market where I used to shop, and—"

"Why did you have to go to the market there?" Chloe interrupted.

She didn't mean to be rude. She was just so surprised and flustered by his appearance in the kitchen again—save this morning, he hadn't ventured into the room once since that first day when he greeted her here—that she didn't know what else to say. And that could also be the only explanation for why she sounded not just rude, but also a tad jealous, when she said what she did.

Hogan must have heard the accusatory tone in her voice, too, because he suddenly looked a little guilty. All he said, though, was, "I needed a few things."

"What kind of things?"

His guilty look compounded. "Uh…things. You know. Personal things. Things I needed to get. That are personal."

"And you had to go all the way to Queens? Does Manhattan not have these personal things you needed?"

And could she just stop talking? Chloe demanded of herself. She sounded like a suspicious wife. Where Hogan went, what he bought, why he went there and bought it was none of her business. *For God's sake, shut* up, *Chloe.*

"Sure, I could have gotten them here," he said. "But C-Town is right up the street from the garage, and it was on the way to the train, so I went in there. For some things. And while I was there, I picked up some stuff for dinner. I thought I could give you a break."

A break? she echoed incredulously to herself. She hadn't even been working for him for a month, and already he was tired of her cooking? No one got tired of Chloe's cooking. Not only was it the best in New York, they also paid her too much to get tired of her cooking.

"Dinner is my job," she reminded him. "It's what you pay me to do. I don't need a break."

"I know, but I thought—"

"Am I not performing to your standards?" she asked.

Now he looked surprised. "What? Of course you are. I just—"

"Have I not cooked you acceptable meals?"

"Yes, Chloe, everything you've cooked has been great, but—"

"Then why do you suddenly want to cook for yourself?"

And why did she still sound like a possessive spouse? Bad enough she was grilling him about things she had no business grilling him about. She was only making it worse sounding like she thought she was entitled to do it. Even if she did have some bizarre desire to actually be Hogan's spouse—which she of course did *not*—it was Anabel Carlisle he wanted to cast in that role. Chloe was his *chef*. So why wasn't she acting like one?

Hogan didn't seem to be offended by her outburst, though. In fact, he suddenly looked kind of relieved. He even smiled. "No, Chloe, you don't understand. I'm not cooking for myself. I'm cooking for us."

Okay, now she was really confused. As weird as it was for her to be behaving like a scorned lover, it was even weirder for Hogan to be acting like a cheerful suitor. Especially one who could cook.

Before she could say anything else, though, he was emptying the contents of the bags onto the kitchen island. A pound of ground chuck, a couple of white onions, a bag of shredded, store brand "Mexican blend" cheese, a bag of tortilla chips and a jar of salsa—both of those were store brand, too—a packet of mass-produced taco seasoning, a bottle of mass-produced taco sauce and a half dozen generic white eggs.

She hastily added up the ingredients in her chef's brain and blanched when she calculated the sum. "Oh, my God. You're going to make taco meatloaf, aren't you?"

He was fairly beaming as he withdrew a burned and battered loaf pan.

"Yep," he said proudly. "In the sacred Dempsey meatloaf pan, which is the mother of all meatloaf pans. On account of it was my mother's. And it gets even better."

He spoke as if that were a paean.

What he withdrew from the second sack was a bag of frozen "crinkle cut" carrots, which he said would be divine with a glaze of butter and Sucanat—except he really said they would taste great stirred up in a pan with some margarine and brown sugar, both of which he was sure Chloe had on hand—then came a tube of prefab biscuits whose label proudly proclaimed, "With flaky layers!" And then—*then*—to her absolute horror, he withdrew the single most offensive affront to gastronomy any chef could possibly conceive: a box of—Chloe could scarcely believe her eyes—macaroni and cheese.

"But wait, that's still not the best part," he told her.

Well, of course it wasn't the best part. There was no *best part* of anything sitting on the counter. He could pull a rabid badger out of the bag, and it would still be better than anything he'd removed so far. But it wasn't a rabid badger he pulled out of the bag. It was far, far worse. A ready-made pound cake wrapped in tinfoil that looked dense enough to, if there were a few thousand more of them, build a garage, followed by a gigantic plastic tub of something called Fros-Tee

Whip, which self-identified as a "non-dairy whipped topping." Chloe couldn't help but recoil.

"I know, right?" Hogan said, evidently mistaking her flinch of repugnance for a tremor of excitement. "It's the greatest dessert ever invented by humankind."

This was going to be news to the creators of *crème brûlée, crêpes Suzette* and *soufflé au chocolat*.

"Look, I know you're not big on the processed foods," he said when he saw her looking at the assortment of, um, groceries. "But you're going to love all this. And I got the good kind of mac and cheese. The kind with the liquid cheese in the pouch, not the powdered stuff in the envelope."

Oh, well, in *that* case…

When she looked at him again, he was grinning in a way that let her know he was perfectly aware that the meal he was proposing was the complete antithesis of epicurean. But he clearly intended to prepare it anyway.

"Hogan, do you realize how much sodium there is in that pile of…of…?" she asked.

"I think 'food products' is the phrase you're looking for," he supplied helpfully.

Actually, she had been thinking of another word entirely. Even so, the *products* part of his suggestion, she would concede. It was the *food* part she found debatable. So she only reiterated, "Hogan, do you realize how much sodium there is in that pile?"

He grinned. "Chloe, I don't care how much sodium there is in that pile. No one cares how much sodium comes out of their grocery bags."

"People who want to live to see their first gray hair do."

"This—" he pointed at his purchases on the island "—is a lot closer to the typical American diet than that is." Now he pointed at the items from her shopping trip she'd left on the counter. "Not to mention the typical American diet is a lot easier to prepare."

"Ease does not equate to edible. Or enjoyable."

"It does when it's taco meatloaf."

"If this—" now Chloe was the one to point to the… groceries…he'd bought "—is the sort of thing you want to eat, then why did you hire me to cook for you in the first place?"

She knew the answer to that question, of course. He was using her to get Anabel Carlisle's attention. Chloe knew that because Hogan himself had said so and, hey, it hadn't made any difference to her. It was irrelevant. She worked for whoever paid her the most. That was rule number one when it came to choosing her employers. For some reason, though, it suddenly kind of bothered her to be used as a means to an end. Especially that end in particular.

Hogan's reply, however, had nothing to do with Anabel. In fact, it wasn't a reply at all. At least not to the question she'd asked.

"Come on. Let me cook dinner tonight," he cajoled. "Have you ever even eaten taco meatloaf?"

She gave him one of those *What do you think?* looks and said nothing.

"Then how do you know you won't like it?" he asked.

"Two words. Butylated hydroxyanisole."

"Gesundheit." He grinned again.

And damn that grin anyway, because every time she saw it, something in Chloe's chest grew warmer.

At this point, it was also spreading into body parts that really shouldn't be feeling warm in mixed company.

"I guarantee you'll love it," he told her. "If you don't, I promise I'll never invade your kitchen again."

She started to remind him that the room they were standing in was actually *his* kitchen, but hesitated. For some reason she did feel a little proprietary when it came to Hogan's kitchen. Certainly more than she had any other kitchen where she'd worked. She told herself it was because it was less sterile than most with its tile the color of the French Riviera and its creamy enamel appliances and its gleaming copper pots that dangled like amaranth from the ceiling and its gigantic windows that spilled more sunshine in one morning than she'd seen working for months in most places. From the moment she'd set foot in here, she'd coveted this kitchen. In the weeks that followed, she'd come to feel as if she never wanted to leave.

Though, if she were honest with herself, there were days, she supposed, when she wasn't sure that was entirely because of the kitchen.

"Fine," she conceded reluctantly. "You can cook dinner tonight."

"For us," he clarified.

Although she wasn't sure why he needed or wanted that concession—and although she wasn't sure it was a good idea for her to make it—Chloe echoed, "For us."

When Hogan had gotten the bright idea to cook taco meatloaf for Chloe, he'd been wanting something for dinner that was a taste of home—his real home, not his adopted one. He'd been lying under the chassis of a Dodge Charger at the time—one Eddie Deflorio was thinking of buying, to give it a once-over and make sure Eddie wasn't about to get shafted—when Eddie said something about Hogan's mom's taco meatloaf. And just like that, Hogan had been jonesing for it more than he had in years. And not just the taco meatloaf, but also the carrots and biscuits and mac and cheese his mom always made to go with it. And—it went without saying—some Sara Lee pound cake for dessert.

It had just felt so good to be back in the garage, surrounded by familiar sounds and smells and people, talking about familiar stuff—not to mention *doing* something—that Hogan had just wanted the day to go on for as long as it could. And he'd wanted to keep *doing* something. Even if it was making taco meatloaf. If he was going to do that, then he had to go up to his old apartment to get his mom's meatloaf pan. Then, once he was back in his apartment...

He'd just felt better than he had in weeks. He'd felt like he was home. Then he'd realized he wanted to share that feeling with someone. And the person that popped into his head was Chloe Merlin. She had shared something of herself with him last night and obviously wished she hadn't. Now he wanted to share something with her so she wouldn't feel like she had to hide her emotions. From him or anyone else.

What better way to share a piece of his neighborhood home with her than to bring a taste of Queens into a kitchen of Lenox Hill?

Thankfully, Chloe had hung around while he was putting together the meatloaf to tell him where everything was, even if he sometimes had to walk clear across the room to find what he needed. Mostly, she had sat on a stool sipping a glass of red wine, throwing out words like *monosodium glutamate* and *propyl gallate* and *potassium bromate*. But she'd at least poured him a glass of wine, too, and turned on some halfway decent music to cook by, even if he didn't understand a word of what was being sung.

He had managed to combine all the ingredients of the dish and make a fairly serviceable loaf out of it—even if it was a little bigger on one end than the other, something that, now that he thought about it, actually made it more authentic—and was ready to put in the oven, when he realized he forgot to turn on the oven to preheat it. Which, now that he thought about that, too, also made the experience more authentic. What didn't make it authentic was that he had no idea how to work the damned stove, because it was three times the size of a normal stove and had roughly a billion knobs on it.

"How do you turn this thing on?" he asked Chloe.

She had finally ended her indictment of the processed food industry and was now reading a book about somebody named Auguste Escoffier—in French. She looked up at the question, studying Hogan over the tops of her glasses for a moment. Then she pushed them into place with the back of her hand, set her book down on the counter and rose to cross to the stove.

"What temperature do you need?" she asked.

"Three-fifty," he told her.

She flipped one of the knobs, and the oven emitted a soft, satisfying hiss. "Give it a minute."

She looked at the meatloaf, still sitting on the kitchen island in its pan, surrounded by stray bits of onion and cheese, splatters of salsa and a fine dusting of taco seasoning. Okay, and also a little puddle of wine, the result of Hogan having an accident during a momentary wild idea to add some red wine to the meatloaf, thinking maybe that would make Chloe like it better. Fortunately, he came to his senses before doing it, mostly to keep his mother from spinning in her grave, but also because he wasn't sure he was ready to wing it in the kitchen just yet. Chloe looked back at him, took off her glasses and met his gaze levelly. *"Ce travail, c'est pas de la tarte, n'est-ce pas?"*

He had no idea what she said, but he was pretty sure by her expression that she was commiserating with him. He was also pretty sure that the reason he was suddenly getting kind of aroused was because she just spoke French. And call him crazy, but arousal probably wasn't a good idea in the middle of a kitchen when the meatloaf wasn't even in the oven yet. Which was *not* a euphemism for *any*thing sexual.

"Uh…" he began eloquently.

She emitted a soft sigh, folded her glasses and set them on the counter, then gave him another one of those almost-smiles he'd seen from her once or twice. And liked. A lot.

"Cooking isn't for the fainthearted," she told him. "It's harder than people think."

Yeah, and he was only using like five ingredients, most of which came out of boxes and bags. He couldn't imagine how much trouble Chloe went to whenever she prepared a meal.

"Thanks for your help," he said.

"I didn't do anything."

"You told me where to find the scissors. That was major."

She almost smiled again.

"And you poured me a glass of wine. That was really major."

"It was the least I could do."

"Thanks again."

They stood staring at each other for another minute, Hogan trying not to notice how beautiful her green eyes were, or how great she looked wearing something besides her giant chef clothes, or how her hair was longer than he first thought, falling past her shoulders in a rush of near-white silk. Those weren't things he should be noticing about his chef. They were things he should be noticing about Anabel. Things he doubtless *would* notice about Anabel, once the two of them got together again. Just as soon as he called her up and invited her to, um, do something. Which he would totally figure out. Soon.

"The stove is ready," Chloe said.

Stove? he wondered. What stove? Oh, right. The one they were standing right next to. That must be the reason he was suddenly feeling so hot.

"Isn't there a beeper or something that's supposed to go off to tell us that?" he asked.

She shook her head. And kept looking at him as intently as he was looking at her. "Not on a stove like this."

"Then how do you know it's ready?"

"I just know."

Of course she did.

"So I guess I should put the meatloaf in the oven,

then," he said. Not thinking about any kind of sexual euphemisms *at all*.

"I guess you should."

Hogan nodded. Chloe nodded. But neither of them did anything. Finally, she took the initiative and picked up the pan. Then she opened the oven and pushed in the meatloaf. Really deep. Pretty much as far as it would go. Hogan tried not to notice. He did. Honest.

"There," she said, straightening as she closed the oven door. "How long does it need to go?"

Oh, it needed to go for a very long time, he wanted to say. Hours and hours and hours. Maybe all night. What he said, though, was, "Sixty minutes ought to do it."

Chloe nodded. Hogan nodded. And he wondered how the hell he ever could have thought it would be a good idea to cook dinner for Chloe in a hot kitchen with an even hotter oven.

"I should probably clean up my mess," he said.

But there weren't enough cleaners in the world to take care of the mess he'd made today. He was supposed to be focused on winning back Anabel. But lately, he was hardly ever even thinking about Anabel. Because, lately, his head was too full of Chloe.

Yeah, Chloe. A woman who had pledged her life to a man she'd lost much too young. And who was still grieving for him five years later. And who would probably never want anyone else again.

Six

"So? Come on. What did you think?"

Chloe looked at Hogan from her seat on his right at his gigantic dinner table. He was beaming like a kid who'd just presented for show-and-tell a salamander he fished out of the creek all by himself.

"You liked it, didn't you?" he asked. "I can tell, because you cleaned your plate. Welcome to the clean plate club, Chloe Merlin."

"It was...acceptable," she conceded reluctantly.

He chuckled. "Acceptable. Right. You had second helpings of everything, and you still cleaned your plate."

"I just wanted to be sure I ate enough for an accurate barometer of the taste combinations, that's all."

"And the taste combinations were really good, weren't they?"

All right, fine. Taco meatloaf had a certain *je ne sais quoi* that was surprisingly appealing. So did the carrots. And even the biscuits. Chloe had never eaten anything like them in her life. Mémée had never allowed anything frozen or processed in the house when Chloe was growing up. Her grandmother had kept a small greenhouse and vegetable garden in the backyard, and what she hadn't grown herself, she'd bought at the weekly visits she and Chloe made to the farmers' markets or, in the coldest months, at the supermarket—but organic only.

Chloe had just never felt the urge to succumb to the temptation of processed food, even if it was more convenient. She *enjoyed* prepping and cooking meals. She *enjoyed* buying the ingredients fresh. The thought of scooping food out of bags and jars and boxes was as alien to her as having six limbs. It wasn't that she was a snob about food or cooking, it was just that...

Okay, she was kind of a snob about food and cooking. Clearly, her beliefs could use some tweaking.

"You know," she told Hogan, "I could make some taco seasoning myself for you to use next time, from my own spice collection. It would have a lot less sodium in it."

He grinned. "That would be great. Thanks."

"And salsa is easy to make. I could make some of that fresh, the next time you want to cook this."

"I'd love that."

"Even the biscuits could be made—"

"I have to stop you there," he interjected. "I'm sorry, but the biscuits have to be that specific kind. They're what my mom always made. It's tradition."

And it was a taste of his childhood. Chloe got that. She felt the same way about *gratin Dauphinois*.

"Okay," she conceded. "But maybe fresh carrots next time, instead of frozen?"

He thought about that for a minute. "Okay. I mean, we already changed those anyway, since that stuff you call brown sugar is actually beige sugar, and you didn't have any margarine. By the way, what kind of person doesn't have margarine in their kitchen?"

Before, Chloe would have answered a question like that with some retort about hexane and free radicals. Instead, she said, "Butter is better for you."

She managed to stop herself before adding, *And you need to stay healthy, Hogan.* Because what she would have added after that was *I need you to be healthy, Hogan.*

She refused to think any further than that. Such as *why* she needed Hogan to be healthy. She told herself it was for the same reason she wanted anyone to be healthy. Everyone deserved to live a long, happy life. No one knew that better than Chloe, who had seen one of the kindest, most decent human beings she'd ever known have his life jerked out from under him. She didn't want the same thing to happen to Hogan. Not that it would. The man looked as hearty as a long-shoreman. But Samuel had looked perfectly healthy, too, the day he left for work in the morning and never came home again.

She pushed the thought away and stood. "Since you cooked, I'll clean up. It's only fair."

Hogan looked a little startled by her abrupt an-nouncement, but stood, too. "You helped cook. I'll help clean up."

She started to object but he was already picking up his plate and loading it with his flatware. So she did likewise and followed him to the kitchen. Together they loaded the dishwasher. Together they packed the leftovers in containers. Together they put them in the fridge.

And together they decided to open another bottle of wine.

But it was Hogan's suggestion that they take it up to the roof garden. Although he'd told her on her first day at work the house had one, and that she should feel free to use it whenever she wanted, especially since he probably never would, Chloe hadn't yet made her way up there. She really did prefer to stay in her room when she wasn't working or out and about. Save that single excursion to the library—and look how that had turned out. When they made it up onto the roof, however, she began to think maybe she should reconsider. New York City was lovely at night.

So was Hogan's rooftop garden. The living section—which was nearly all of it—was a patchwork of wooden flooring and was lit by crisscrossing strings of tiny white lights woven through an overhead trellis. Terra-cotta pots lined the balustrade, filled with asters and camellias and chrysanthemums, all flaming with autumn colors from saffron to cinnamon to cayenne. Beyond it, Manhattan twinkled like tidy stacks of gemstones against the night sky.

Knowing the evening would be cool, Chloe had grabbed a wrap on her way up, a black wool shawl that had belonged to her grandmother, embroidered with tiny red flowers. She hugged it tightly to herself as she sat on a cushioned sofa pushed against a brick access bulkhead and set her wine on a table next to it. Hogan sat beside her, setting his wine on a table at his end. For a long moment neither spoke. They only gazed out at the glittering cityscape in silence.

Finally, Chloe said, "I still have trouble sometimes believing I live in New York. I kind of fell in love with the city when I was a kid, reading about it and seeing so many movies filmed here. I never actually thought I'd be living here. Especially in a neighborhood like this."

"Yeah, well, I grew up in New York," Hogan said, "but this part of the city is as foreign to me as the top of the Himalayas would be. I still can't believe I live here, either. I never came into Manhattan when I was a kid. Especially someplace like Park Avenue. I never felt the need to."

"Then how did you meet Anabel?" Chloe asked. "She doesn't seem like the type to ever leave Park Avenue."

He grinned that damnably sexy grin again. He'd done that a lot tonight. And every time he did, Chloe felt a crack open in the armor she'd worn so well for so long, and a little chink of it tumbled away. At this point, there were bits of it strewn all over his house, every piece marking a place where Hogan had made her feel something after years of promising herself she would never feel anything again. What she ought to be feeling was invaded, overrun and offended. Instead, she felt...

Well. Things she had promised herself she would never feel again—had sworn she was incapable of ever feeling again. Things that might very well get her into trouble.

"How I met Anabel is actually kind of a funny story," Hogan said. "She and a couple of her friends were going to a concert at Shea Stadium, but they pissed off their cab driver so bad on the way, he stopped the car in the middle of the street in front of my dad's garage and made them get out. She and the guy got into a shouting match in the middle of Jamaica Avenue, and a bunch of us working in the garage went out to watch." He chuckled. "I remember her standing there looking like a bohemian princess and cursing like a sailor, telling the cabbie she knew the mayor personally and would see to it that he never drove a cab in the tristate area again."

Chloe smiled at the picture. She couldn't imagine Anabel Carlisle, even a teenaged one, behaving that way. Her former employer had always been the perfect society wife when Chloe worked for her.

"Anyway, after the cabbie drove off without them, all us guys started applauding and whistling. Anabel spun around, and I thought she was going to give us a second helping of what she'd just dished out, but she looked at me and…" He shook his head. "I don't know. It was like how you see someone, and there's just something there. The next thing I knew, me and a couple of the guys are walking up the street with her and her friends, and we're all going for pancakes. After that she came into Queens pretty often. She even had dinner at my house with me and my folks a few times. But she never invited me home to meet hers."

There was no bitterness in his voice when he said that last sentence. There was simply a matter-of-factness that indicated he understood why she hadn't wanted to include him in her uptown life. That was gentlemanly of him, even if Chloe couldn't understand Anabel's behavior. She imagined Hogan had been just as nice back then as he was now. Anabel must have realized that if she'd become involved with him. Who cared what neighborhood he called home?

"It was her parents," he said, as if he'd read her mind. "Her dad especially didn't want her dating outside her social circle. She would have gotten into a lot of trouble if they found out about me. I understood why she couldn't let anyone know she was involved with me."

"If you understood," Chloe said, "then how come you're still unattached after all this time? Why have you waited for her?"

She thought maybe she'd overstepped the bounds—again—by asking him something so personal. But Hogan didn't seem to take offense.

"I didn't sit around for fifteen years waiting for her," he said. "I dated other girls. Other women. I just never met anyone who made me feel the way Anabel did, you know? There was never that spark of lightning with anyone else like there was that night on Jamaica Avenue."

Chloe didn't understand that, either. Love wasn't lightning. She did, however, understand seeing a person and just knowing there was something there. That had happened to her, too. With Samuel. The day he walked into English class in the middle of freshman year, she'd looked up from *The Catcher in the Rye* and into the sweetest blue eyes she'd ever seen, and she'd known at once that there was something between them. Something. Not love. Love came later. Because love was something so momentous, so stupendous, so enormous, that it had to happen over time. At least it did for Chloe. For Hogan, evidently, it took only a sudden jolt of electricity.

"And now Anabel is free," she said, nudging aside thoughts of the past in an effort to get back to the present. "You must feel as if you're being tasered within an inch of your life these days."

Even if he hadn't done much in the way of trying to regain the affections of his former love, she couldn't help thinking. She wondered why he hadn't.

He looked thoughtful for a moment. "I think maybe I've outgrown the fireworks part," he said cryptically. "But yeah. I really need to call her and set something up."

"Why don't you have a dinner party and invite her?" Chloe suggested. Wondering why her voice sounded so flat. She loved preparing meals for dinner parties. It was great fun putting together the menus. "You could ask her and a few other couples. Maybe she's still friends with some of the girls who were with her the night you met her," she added, trying to get into the spirit. And not getting into the spirit at all. "Other people would offer a nice buffer for the two of you to get reacquainted."

By the time she finished speaking, there was the oddest bitterness in Chloe's mouth. Maybe the wine had turned. Just to make sure, she took another sip. No, actually, the pinot noir tasted quite good.

"Maybe," Hogan said.

"No, definitely," she insisted. Because...

Well, just because. That was why. And it was an excellent reason. Hogan clearly needed a nudge in Anabel's direction, since he wasn't heading that way himself. He'd made clear since Chloe's first day of employment that he was still pining for the woman he'd loved since he was a teenager. He needed a dinner party. And Chloe needed a dinner party, too. Something to focus on that would keep her mind off things it shouldn't be on.

"Look, Chloe," he said, "I appreciate your wanting to help, but—"

"It will be perfect," she interrupted him. "Just a small party of, say, six or eight people."

"But—"

"I can get it all organized by next weekend, provided everyone is available."

"But—"

"Don't worry about a thing. I'll take care of all the details. It will be your perfect entrée into society, which, for some reason, you haven't made yet."

"Yeah, because—"

"A week from tomorrow. If you'll supply the names, I'll make the calls to invite everyone."

"Chloe—"

"Just leave it to me."

He opened his mouth to protest again, but seemed to have run out of objections. In fact, he kind of looked like the proverbial deer in the headlights. Okay, proverbial stag in the headlights.

Then he surprised her by totally changing the subject. "So what was it like growing up in… Where did you say you're from? Someplace in Indiana."

"New Albany," she replied automatically. "It's in the southern part of the state, on the Ohio River."

"I'm going to go out on a limb and say it probably

wasn't much like Manhattan," he guessed. "Or even Queens."

"No, not at all. It's quiet. Kind of quirky. Nice. It was a good place to grow up." She couldn't quite stop herself from drifting back into memories again. "Not a whole lot to do when you're a kid, but still nice. And Louisville was right across the river, so if we wanted the urban experience, we could go over there. Not that it was as urban as here, of course. But there were nights when we were teenagers when Samuel and I would ride our bikes down to the river and stare at Louisville on the other side. Back then it seemed like such a big place, all bright lights and bridges. Compared to New York, though…"

When she didn't finish, Hogan said, "You and your husband met young, huh?"

And only then did Chloe realize just how much she had revealed. She hadn't meant to bring up Samuel again. Truly, she hadn't. But it was impossible to think about home without thinking of him, too. Strangely, though, somehow, thinking about him now wasn't quite as painful as it had been before.

"In high school," she heard herself say. "Freshman year. We married our sophomore year in college. I know that sounds like we were too young," she said, reading his mind this time—because everyone had thought marrying at twenty was too young. Everyone still thought that. For Chloe and Samuel, it had felt like the most natural thing in the world.

"How did he…?" Hogan began. "I mean…if you don't mind my asking… What happened?"

She expelled a soft sigh. Of course, she should have realized it would come to this sooner or later with

Hogan. It was her own fault. She was the one who'd brought up her late husband. She couldn't imagine why. She never talked about Samuel with anyone. Ever. So why was she not minding talking about him to Hogan?

"Asymptomatic coronary heart disease," she said. "That's what happened. He had a bad heart. That no one knew about. Until, at twenty-two years of age, he had a massive heart attack that killed him while he was performing the physically stressful act of slicing peppers for *tastira*. It's a Tunisian dish. His specialty was Mediterranean cooking," she added for some reason. "We would have been an unstoppable team culinarily speaking, once we opened our restaurant."

Hogan was silent for a moment, then, very softly, he said, "Those are his chef's jackets you wear, aren't they?"

Chloe nodded. "After he was… After we sprinkled his ashes in Brown County, I realized I didn't have anything of him to keep with me physically. We didn't exchange rings when we married, and we weren't big on gift-giving." She smiled sadly. "Symbols of affection just never seemed necessary to either of us. So, after he was gone, I started wearing his jackets when I was cooking."

She had thought wearing Samuel's jackets would make her feel closer to him. But it hadn't. It wasn't his clothing that helped her remember him. If she'd needed physical reminders for that, she never would have left Indiana. But she'd been wearing them for so long now, it almost felt wrong to stop.

She reached for her wine and enjoyed a healthy taste of it. It warmed her mouth and throat as she swallowed, but it did nothing to combat the chill that suddenly enveloped her. So she put the glass down and wrapped her shawl more tightly around herself.

"I'm sorry, Chloe," Hogan said, his voice a soft caress in the darkness. "I shouldn't have asked for details."

"It's okay," she told him, even though it really wasn't okay. "It was a long time ago. I've learned to…cope with it. The money I make as a chef goes into a fund I started in Samuel's name that makes testing for the condition in kids less expensive, more common and more easily accessible. Knowing that someone else—maybe even a lot of someone elses—might live longer lives with their loved ones by catching their condition early and treating it helps me deal."

Hogan was being quiet again, so Chloe looked over to see how he was handling everything she'd said. He didn't look uncomfortable, though. Mostly, he looked sympathetic. He'd lost people he loved at a young age, too, so maybe he really did understand.

"I lied when I said the reason I came to New York was to open my own restaurant," she told him. "There's no way I could do that now, without Samuel. It was our dream together. I really came to New York because I thought it would be a good place to lose myself after he died. It's so big here, and there are so many people. I thought it would be easier than staying in a place where I was constantly reminded of him. And it's worked pretty well. As long as I'm able to focus on cooking, I don't have to think about what happened. At least I didn't until—"

She halted abruptly. Because she had been *this close* to telling Hogan it had worked pretty well until she met him. Meeting him had stirred up all sorts of feelings she hadn't experienced in years. Feelings she'd only ever had for one other human being. Feelings she'd promised herself she would never, ever, feel again. She'd barely survived losing Samuel. There was no way she could risk—no way she *would* risk—going through that again. No way she would ever allow someone to mean that much to her again. Not even—

"At least you did until I asked about it." Hogan finished her sentence for her. Erroneously, at that. "Wow. I really am a mook."

"No, Hogan, that's not what I was going to say." Before he could ask for clarification, however, she quickly concluded, "Anyway, that's what happened."

The temperature on the roof seemed to have plummeted since they first came outside, and a brisk wind riffled the potted flowers and rippled the lights overhead. Again, Chloe wrapped herself more snugly in her shawl. But the garment helped little. So she brought her knees up on the sofa and wrapped her arms around her legs, curling herself into as tight a ball as she could.

"You know how people say it's better to have loved and lost than to never have loved at all?" she asked.

"Yeah," Hogan replied softly.

"And you know how people say it's better to feel bad than to feel nothing at all?"

"Yeah."

"People are full of crap."

He paused before asking even more softly than before, "Do you really think that?"

She answered immediately. "Yes."

Hogan waited a moment before moving closer,

dropping an arm across her shoulders and pulling her to him, tucking the crown of her head beneath his chin. Automatically, Chloe leaned into him, pressing her cheek to his shoulder, opening one hand over his chest. There was nothing inappropriate in his gesture or in her reaction to it. Nothing suggestive, nothing flirtatious, nothing carnal. Only one human being offering comfort to another. It had been a long time since anyone had held Chloe, even innocently. A long time since anyone had comforted her. And now here was Hogan, his heat enveloping her, his scent surrounding her, his heart thrumming softly beneath her palm. And for the first time in years—six years, nine months, one week and one day, to be precise—Chloe felt herself responding.

But there, too, lay problems. After Samuel's death, she'd lost herself for a while, seeking comfort from the sort of men who offered nothing but a physical release for the body and no comfort for the soul. The behavior had been reminiscent of her mother's— erratic and self-destructive—and when Chloe finally realized that, she'd reined herself in and shut herself up tight. Until tonight.

Suddenly, with Hogan, she did want holding. And she wanted comforting. And anything else he might have to offer. She reminded herself that his heart and his future were with someone else. He was planning a life with Anabel. But Chloe didn't want a future or a life with him. She'd planned a life once, and the person she'd planned it with was taken from her. She would never make plans like that again. But a night with Hogan? At the moment a night with him held a lot of appeal.

She tilted her head back to look at his face. His brown eyes were as dark as the night beyond, and the breeze ruffled his sandy hair, nudging a strand down over his forehead. Without thinking, Chloe lifted a hand to brush it back, skimming her fingers lightly along his temple after she did. Then she dragged them lower, tracing the line of his jaw. Then lower still, to graze the column of his throat. His pupils expanded as she touched him, and his lips parted.

Still not sure what was driving her—and, honestly, not really caring—she moved her head closer to his. Hogan met her halfway, brushing her lips lightly with his once, twice, three times, four, before covering her mouth completely. For a long time he only kissed her, and she kissed him back, neither of them shifting their position, as if each wanted to give the other the option of putting a stop to things before they went any further.

But neither did.

So Chloe threaded her fingers through his hair, cupped the back of his head in her palm and gave herself more fully to the kiss. At the same time, Hogan dropped his other hand to her hip, curving his fingers over her to pull her closer still. She grew ravenous then, opening her mouth against his, tasting him more deeply. When he pulled her into his lap, wrapping both arms around her waist, she looped hers around his neck and held on for dear life.

She had no idea how long they were entwined that way—it could have been moments, it could have been millennia. Chloe drove her hands over every inch of him she could reach, finally pushing her hand under the hem of his sweater. The skin of his torso was hot and hard and smooth beneath her fingertips, like silk-covered steel. She had almost forgotten how a man's body felt, so different from her own, and she took her time rediscovering. Hogan, too, went exploring, moving his hand from her hip to her waist to her breast. She cried out when he cupped his hand over her, even with the barrier of her sweater between them. It had just been so long since a man touched her that way.

He stilled his hand at her exclamation, but he didn't move it. He only looked at her with an unmistakable question in his eyes, as if waiting for her to make the next move. She told herself they should put a stop to things now. She even went so far as to say, "Hogan, we probably shouldn't..." But she was unable—or maybe unwilling—to say the rest. Instead, she told him, "We probably shouldn't be doing this out here in the open."

He hesitated. "So then...you think we should do this inside?"

Chloe hesitated a moment, too. But only a moment. "Yes."

He lowered his head to hers one last time, pressing his palm flat against her breast for a moment before dragging it back down to her waist. Then he was taking her hand in his, standing to pull her up alongside him. He kissed her again, long and hard and deep, then, his fingers still woven with hers, led her to the roof access door. Once inside the stairwell, they embraced again, Hogan pressing her back against the wall to crowd his body against hers, their kisses deepening until their mouths were both open wide. She drove her hands under his sweater again to splay them open against the hot skin of his back, and he dropped a hand between her legs, petting her over the fabric of her pants until she was pushing her hips harder into his touch.

Somehow they made it down the stairs to Hogan's bedroom. Somehow they made it through the door. Somehow they managed to get each other's clothes off. Then Chloe was naked on her back in his bed, and Hogan was naked atop her. As he kissed her, he dropped his hand between her legs again, growling his approval when he realized how damp and ready for him she already was. He took a moment to make her damper, threading his fingers through her wet flesh until she was gasping for breath, then he drew his hand back up her torso to her breast. He thumbed the ripe peak of one as he filled his mouth with the other, laving her with the flat of his tongue and teasing her with its tip. In response, Chloe wove her fingers together at his nape and hooked her legs around his waist as if she intended to hold him there forever.

Hogan had other plans, though. With one final, gentle tug of her nipple with his teeth, he began dragging openmouthed kisses back down along her torso. He paused long enough to taste the indentation of her navel then scooted lower still, until his mouth hovered over the heated heart of her. Then he pressed a palm against each of her thighs and pushed them open, wide enough that he could duck his head between them and taste the part of her he'd fingered long moments ago.

The press of his tongue against her there was almost more than Chloe could bear. She tangled her fingers in his hair in a blind effort to move him away, but he drove his hands beneath her fanny and pushed her closer to his mouth. Again and again, he darted his tongue against her, then he treated her to longer, more leisurely strokes. Something wild and wanton coiled tighter inside her with every movement, finally bursting in a white-hot rush of sensation that shook her entire body. Before the tremors could ebb, he was back at her breast, wreaking havoc there again.

After that Chloe could only feel and react. There were no thoughts. No cares. No worries. There was only Hogan and all the things he made her feel. Hogan and all the things she wanted to do to him, too. When he finally lifted his head from her breast, she pulled him up to cover his mouth with hers, reaching down to cover the head of his shaft with her hand when she did. He was slick and hard, as ready for her as she was for him. But she took her time, too, to arouse him even more, palming him, wrapping her fingers around him, driving her hand slowly up and down the hard, hot length of him.

When he rolled onto his back to facilitate her movements, Chloe bent over him, taking as much of him into her mouth as she could. Over and over she savored him, marveling at how he swelled to even greater life. When she knew he was close to coming, she levered her body over his to straddle him, easing herself down over his long shaft then rising slowly up again. Hogan cupped his hands over her hips, guiding her leisurely up and down atop himself. But just as they were both on the verge of shattering, he reversed their bodies so that Chloe was on her back again. He grinned as he circled each of her ankles in strong fists, then he knelt before her and opened her legs wide. And then—oh, *then*—he was plunging himself into her as deep as he could go, thrusting his hips against hers again and again and again.

Never had she felt fuller or more complete than she did during those moments that he was buried inside her. Every time he withdrew, she jerked her hips upward to stop him, only to have him come crashing into her again. They came as one, both crying out in the euphoria that accompanied climax. Then Hogan collapsed, turning their bodies again until he was on his back and she was lying atop him. Her skin was slick and hot. Her brain was dazed and shaken. And her heart...

Chloe closed her eyes, refusing to complete the thought. There would be no completion of thought tonight. There would be completion only for the body. And although her body felt more complete than it had in a very long time, she already found herself wanting more.

Her body wanted more, she corrected herself. Only her body. Not her. But as she closed her eyes against the fatigue that rocked her, she felt Hogan press a kiss against the crown of her head. And all she could think was that, of everything he'd done to her tonight, that small kiss brought her the most satisfaction.

Seven

Chloe awoke slowly to darkness. She hated waking up before the alarm went off at five, because she could never get back to sleep for that last little bit of much needed slumber. Invariably her brain began racing over the list of things she had to do that day, not stopping until she rose to get those things done. Strangely, though, this morning, her brain seemed to be sleepier than she was, because it wasn't racing at all. There were no thoughts bouncing around about the intricacies of the asparagus-brie soufflé she planned for this morning's breakfast. No reminders ricocheting here and there that her savory and marjoram plants were looking a little peaked, so she needed to feed them. No, there were only idle thoughts about—

Hogan. Oh, my God, she'd had sex with Hogan last night. Worse, she had woken up in his bed instead of her own. Now she would have to sneak out under cover of darkness before he woke up so she could get ready for work and make his breakfast, then figure out how to pretend like there was nothing different about this morning than any of the mornings that had preceded it and *Just have a seat in the dining room, Hogan, and I'll bring you your breakfast the way I always do, as if the two of us weren't just a few hours ago joined in the most intimate way two people can be joined.*

Oh, sure. *Now* her brain started working at light speed.

Thankfully, Mrs. Hennessey had weekends off, so Chloe didn't have to worry about explaining herself to the housekeeper. Even if Mrs. Hennessey did remind her of her grandmother, who Chloe could just imagine looking at her right now and saying with much disappointment, *"Mon petit doigt me dit..."* which was the French equivalent of "A little bird told me," a phrase Mémée never had to finish because as soon as she started to say it, Chloe would always break down in tears and confess whatever it was she'd done.

And now she'd *really* done it.

Panicked by all the new worries rioting in her head, Chloe turned over, hoping to not wake Hogan. But the other side of the bed was empty. She breathed a sigh of relief...for all of a nanosecond, because her gaze then fell on the illuminated numbers of the clock on the nightstand beyond.

It was almost nine thirty! She never slept until nine thirty! Even on her days off! Which today wasn't!

By now she should have already finished cleaning up breakfast and should be sipping a cup of rose and lavender tea while she made a list for her afternoon shopping. She had completely missed Hogan's break-fast this morning. Never in her life had she missed making a meal she was supposed to make for an employer. How could she have slept so late?

The answer to that question came immediately, of course. She had slept so late because she was up so late. And she was up so late because she and Hogan had been… Well. Suffice it to say Hogan was a very thorough lover. He'd been even more insatiable than she.

Heat swept over her at some of the images that wandered into her brain. Hogan hadn't left an inch of her body untouched or untasted. And that last time they'd come together, when he'd turned her onto her knees and pressed her shoulders to the mattress, when he'd entered her more deeply than she'd ever felt entered before, when he threaded his fingers through her damp folds of flesh and curried them in time with the thrust of his shaft, then spilled himself hotly inside her…

Oh, God. She got hot all over again just thinking about it.

How could she have let this happen? She wished she could blame the wine. Or Hogan's unrelenting magnetism. Or the romance of New York at night. Anything besides her own weakness. But she knew she had only herself to blame. She had let her guard down. She had opened herself up to Hogan. She had allowed herself to feel. And she had lost another part of herself as a result.

No, not lost, she realized. She had surrendered herself this time. She had given herself over to Hogan willingly. And she would never be able to get that part of herself back.

She'd barely been able to hold it together after Samuel died. She'd had to tie herself up tight, hide herself so well that nothing outside would ever get to her again. Because losing something—someone—again might very well be the end of her.

She tried looking at it a different way. Okay, so she and Hogan had sex. So what? She'd had sex before. It was just sex. She'd been physically attracted to Hogan since the minute she met him. He was a very attractive man. Last night she'd simply acted on that attraction. As had he. But it was just an attraction. Hogan was in love with Anabel. He'd been in love with Anabel for nearly half his life. And Chloe still loved her late husband. Just because she and Hogan had enjoyed a little—okay, a lot of—sex one night didn't mean either of them felt any differently about each other today. It was sex. Not love.

So why did everything seem different?

She had to get out of Hogan's room and back to her own so she could regroup and figure out what to do. She was fumbling for a lamp on the nightstand when the bedroom door opened, throwing a rectangle of light onto the floor and revealing Hogan standing before it. He was wearing jeans and nothing else, and his hair was still mussed from the previous night's activities. He was carrying a tray topped with a coffeepot and a plate whose contents she couldn't determine.

"You're awake," he said by way of a greeting, his voice soft and sweet and full of affection.

Chloe's stomach pitched to hear it. Affection wasn't allowed. Affection had no place in a physical reaction. No place in sex. No place in Chloe's life anywhere.

"Um, yeah," she said, pulling the covers up over

her still-naked body. "I'm sorry I overslept. I can have your breakfast ready in—"

"I made breakfast," he interrupted.

Well, that certainly wasn't going to look good on her résumé, Chloe thought. Mostly because she was afraid to think anything else. Like how nice it was of Hogan to make breakfast. Or how sweet and earnest he sounded when he told her he had. Or the warm, fuzzy sensation that swept through her midsection when he said it.

"I mean, it's not as good as what you would have made," he continued when she didn't respond. "But I didn't want to wake you. You were sleeping pretty soundly."

And still, she had no idea what to say.

Hogan made his way silently into the dim room. He strode first to the window and, balancing the tray in one hand, tugged open the curtains until a wide slice of sunlight spilled through. Then he smiled, scrambling Chloe's thoughts even more than they already were. When she didn't smile back—she couldn't, because she was still so confused by the turn of events—his smile fell. He rallied it again, but it wasn't quite the same.

When he set the tray at the foot of the bed, she saw that, in addition to the coffee, it held sugar and cream, along with a modest assortment of not-particularly-expertly-cut fruit, an array of not-quite-done to far-too-done slices of toast, some cheese left over from last night and a crockery pot of butter.

"I wasn't sure how you like your coffee," he said. "But I found cream in the fridge, so I brought that. And some sugar, just in case."

When Chloe still didn't reply, he climbed back into bed with her. But since it was a king-size, he was nearly as far away from her as he would have been in Queens. Even so, she tugged the covers up even higher, despite the fact that she had already pulled them as high as they would go without completely co-cooning herself. Hogan noticed the gesture and looked away, focusing on the breakfast he'd made for them.

"It's weird," he said. Which could have referred to a lot of things. Thankfully, he quickly clarified, "You know what I like for every meal, but I don't even know what you like to have for breakfast. I don't even know how you take your coffee."

"I don't drink coffee, actually," she finally said.

He looked back at her. "You don't?"

She shook her head.

"Then why is there cream in the fridge?"

"There's always cream in the fridge when you cook French."

"Oh. Well. Then what do you drink instead of coffee?"

"Tea."

"If you tell me where it is, I could fix you—"

"No, that's okay."

"If you're sure."

"I am."

"So...what kind of tea?"

"Dragon tea. From Paris."

"Ah."

"But you can get it at Dean and DeLuca."

"Gotcha."

"I don't put cream in it, either."

"Okay."

"Or sugar."

"Noted."

The conversation—such as it was—halted there. Chloe looked at Hogan. Hogan looked at Chloe. She fought the urge to tug up the sheet again. He mostly just sat there looking gorgeous and recently tumbled. She told herself to eat something, reminded herself that it was the height of rudeness to decline food someone had prepared for you. But her stomach was so tied in knots, she feared anything she tried to put in it would just come right back up again.

Before she knew what she was doing, she said, "Hogan, about last night..." Unfortunately, the cliché was as far as she got before she realized she didn't know what else to say. She tried again. "What happened last night was..." At that, at least, she couldn't prevent the smile that curled her lips. "Well, it was wonderful," she admitted.

"I thought so, too."

Oh, she really should have talked faster. She really didn't need to hear that he had enjoyed it, too. Not that she didn't already know he'd enjoyed it. Especially considering how eagerly he'd—

Um, never mind.

She made herself say the rest of what she had hoped to get in before he told her he'd enjoyed last night, too, in case he said more, especially something about how eagerly he'd—

"But it never should have happened," she made herself say.

This time Hogan was the one to not say anything in response. So Chloe made an effort to explain. "I was feeling a little raw last night, talking about Samuel and things I haven't talked about to anyone for a long time. Add to that the wine and the night and New York and..." She stopped herself before adding *and you* and hurried on, "Things just happened that shouldn't have happened. That wouldn't have happened under normal circumstances. That won't happen again. You're my employer, and I'm your employee. I think we can both agree that we should keep it at that."

When he continued to remain silent, she added, "I just want you to know that I'm not assuming anything will come of it. I don't want you to think I'm under the impression that this—" here, she gestured quickly between the two of them "—changes that. I know it doesn't."

And still, Hogan said nothing. He only studied her thoughtfully, as if he was trying to figure it all out the same way she was.

Good luck with that, Chloe thought. Then again, maybe he wasn't as confused as she was. Maybe he'd awoken this morning feeling perfectly philosophical about last night. Guys were able to do that better than girls were, right? To compartmentalize things into brain boxes that kept them neatly separate from other things? Sex in one box and love in another. The present moment in one box and future years in another. He probably wasn't expecting anything more to come of last night, either, and he'd just been sitting here waiting for her to reassure him that that was how she felt, too.

So she told him in no uncertain terms—guys liked it when girls talked to them in no uncertain terms, right?—to make it perfectly clear, "I just want you to know that I don't have any expectations from this. Or from you. I know what happened between us won't go any further and that it will never happen again. I know you still love Anabel."

"And you still love Samuel," he finally said.

"Yes. I do."

He nodded. But his expression revealed nothing of what he might actually be feeling. Not that she wanted him to feel anything. The same way she wasn't feeling anything. She wasn't.

"You're right," he agreed. "About all of it. What happened last night happened. But it was no big deal."

Well, she didn't say *that*. Jeez. Oh, wait. Yes, she did. At least, she'd been thinking it before Hogan came in with breakfast. Looking and sounding all sweet and earnest and being so gorgeous and recently tumbled. Okay, then. It was no big deal. They were both on the same page.

She looked at the breakfast he'd prepared. She had thought getting everything about last night out in the open the way they had would make her feel better. But her stomach was still a tumble of nerves.

Even so, she forced a smile and asked, "Could you pass the toast, please?"

Hogan smiled back, but his, too, looked forced. "Sure."

He pulled up the tray from the foot of the bed until it was between them, and Chloe leaned over to reach for the plate of toast. But the sheet began to slip the moment she did, so she quickly sat up again, jerking it back into place.

"I should let you get dressed," Hogan said, rising from bed.

"But aren't you going to have any breakfast?"

"I had some coffee while I was making it. That'll hold me for a while. You go ahead." He started to back toward the door. "I have some things I need to do today anyway."

"Okay."

"And, listen, I'm pretty sure I won't be here for dinner tonight, so don't go to any trouble for me."

"But I was going to make *blanquette de veau*. From my grandmother's recipe."

"Maybe another time."

Before she could say anything else—not that she had any idea what to say—he mumbled a quick "See ya," and was out the door, leaving Chloe alone.

Which was how she liked to be. She'd kept herself alone for six years now. Six years, nine months, one week and… And how many days? She had to think for a minute. Two. Six years, nine months, one week and two days, to be precise. Alone was the only way she could be if she hoped to maintain her sanity. Especially after losing her mind the way she had last night.

She was right. It shouldn't have happened.

As Hogan bent over the hood of Benny Choi's '72 Mustang convertible, he repeated Chloe's assertion in his head again. Maybe if he repeated it enough times, he'd start believing himself. Chloe had been spot-on when she said last night was a mistake. It had been a mistake. An incredibly erotic, unbelievably satisfying mistake, but a mistake all the same.

She was still in love with her husband. First love was a potent cocktail. Nothing could cure a hangover from that. Hell, Hogan knew that firsthand, since he was still punch-drunk in love with Anabel fifteen years after the fact. Right? Of course right. What happened between him and Chloe last night was just a byproduct of the feelings they had for other people, feelings they'd both had bottled up for too long. Chloe had been missing her husband last night. Hogan had been missing Anabel. So they'd turned to each other for comfort.

Stuff like that happened all the time. It really was no big deal. Now that they had it out of their systems, they could go back to being in love with the people they'd loved half their lives.

Except that Chloe couldn't go back to her husband. Not the way Hogan could go back to Anabel.

"Thanks for coming in to work, Hogan," Benny said when Hogan dropped the hood of his car into place. "Now that your dad's gone, you're the only guy I trust with my baby."

Benny and Hogan's father had been friends since grade school. With what was left of Hogan's mother's family living solidly in the Midwest, Benny was the closest thing to an uncle Hogan had here in town. He was thinning on top, thickening around the middle and wore the standard issue blue uniform of the New York transit worker, having just ended his shift.

"No problem, Benny," Hogan assured him. "Feels good to come in. I've been missing the work."

"Hah," the other man said. "If I came into the kind of money you did, I wouldn't even be in New York. I'd be cruising around the Caribbean. Then I'd be cruising around Mexico. Then Alaska. Then… I don't even know after that. But I sure as hell wouldn't have my head stuck under Benny Choi's Mach One, I can tell you that."

Hogan grinned. "To each his own."

They moved into Hogan's office so he could prepare Benny's bill. Which seemed kind of ridiculous since Hogan wasn't doing this for a living anymore, so there was no need to charge anyone for parts or labor. With the money he had, he could buy a whole fleet of Dempsey's Garages and still have money left over. He knew better than to tell Benny the work was on the house, though. Benny, like everyone else in Hogan's old neighborhood, always paid his way. Even so, he knocked off twenty percent and, when Benny noticed the discrepancy, called it his new "friends and family" rate.

Hogan sat in his office for a long time after Benny left, listening to the clamor of metal against metal as the other mechanics worked, inhaling the savory aroma of lubricant, remembering the heft of every tool. He couldn't give this up. A lot of people would think he was crazy for wanting to keep working in light of his financial windfall, but he didn't care. Hogan had been working in this garage for nearly two decades, most of it by his father's side. It was the only place he'd ever felt like himself. At least it had been until last night, when he and Chloe had—

A fleet of Dempsey's Garages, he thought again, pushing away thoughts of things that would never happen again. He actually kind of liked the sound of that. There were a lot of independent garages struggling in this economy. He could buy them up, put the money into them that they needed to be competitive, keep everyone employed who wanted to stay employed and give everything and everyone a new purpose. He could start here in the city and move outward into the state.

Then maybe into another state. Then another. And another. This place would be his flagship, the shop where he came in to work every day.

And it would be a lot of work, an enterprise that ambitious. But Hogan always thrived on work. Being away from it was why he'd been at such loose ends since moving uptown. Why he'd felt so dissatisfied. Why his life felt like something was missing.

And that was another thing. He didn't have to live uptown. He could sell his grandfather's house. It didn't feel like home anyway, and it was way too big for one person. Of course, Hogan wouldn't be one person for much longer. He'd have Anabel. And, with any luck, at some point, a few rug rats to keep tabs on. Still, the Lenox Hill town house was just too much. It didn't suit Hogan. He and Anabel could find something else that they both liked. She probably wouldn't want to move downtown, though. Still, they could compromise somewhere.

The more Hogan thought about his new plans, the more he liked them. Funny, though, how the ones for the garage gelled in his brain a lot faster and way better than the ones for Anabel did. But that was just because he was sitting here in the garage right now, surrounded by all the things he needed for making plans like that. Anabel was still out there, waiting for him to make contact. But he'd be seeing her next weekend, thanks to Chloe's dinner party plans. Yeah, Hogan was *this close* to having everything he'd ever wanted.

Thanks to Chloe.

Eight

A week later, Hogan stood in his living room, wondering why the hell he'd let Chloe arrange a dinner party for him. It was for Anabel, he reminded himself. This entire situation with Chloe had always been about winning back Anabel.

Despite his recent encounter with Chloe—which neither of them had spoken about again—that was still what he wanted. Wasn't it? Of course it was. He'd spent almost half his life wanting Anabel. She was his Holy Grail. His impossible dream. A dream that was now very possible. All Hogan had to do was play his cards right. Starting now, with the evening ahead. If he could just keep his mind off making love to Chloe—or, rather, having sex with Chloe—and focus on Anabel.

He still wasn't looking forward to the night ahead, but he was relieved there wasn't going to be a large group coming. Chloe had only invited Anabel and three other couples, two of whom were friends of Anabel's that Chloe had assured him it would be beneficial for him to know, and one of whom was Gus Fiver and his date.

Hogan realized he should have been the one to plan something, and he should have been the one who invited Anabel to whatever it was, and he should be in charge of it. He also realized it should just be him and Anabel, and not a bunch of other people, too.

So why hadn't he done that? He'd been living in his grandfather's house for a month now, plenty of time for him to figure out how things were done here and proceed accordingly where it came to pursuing the love of his life. But the only time he'd seen Anabel since ascending to his new social status had been the day she came over to try and lure Chloe back to work for her. He'd thought about asking her out a lot of times over the last few weeks. But he'd always hesitated. Because he wanted the occasion to be just right, he'd told himself, and he hadn't figured out yet what *just right* was with Anabel these days.

Back when they were teenagers, they'd had fun walking along the boardwalk on Rockaway Beach or bowling a few sets at Jib Lanes or downing a couple of egg creams at Pop's Diner. Nowadays, though… Call him crazy, but Hogan didn't see the Anabel of today doing any of those things. He just didn't know what the Anabel of today did like. And that was why he hadn't asked her out.

Tonight he would find out what she liked and he *would* ask her out. Just the two of them. By summer, he promised himself again, they would be engaged.

Then they would live happily ever after, just like in the books.

"You're not wearing that, are you?"

Hogan spun around to see Chloe standing in the doorway, dressed from head to toe in stark chef's whites. He'd barely seen her since last weekend. She'd sped in and out of the dining room so fast after serving him his meals that he'd hardly had a chance to say hello or thank her.

Tonight her jacket looked like it actually fit, and she'd traded her crazy printed pants for a pair of white ones that were as starched and pressed as the rest of her. Instead of the usual spray of hair erupting from the top of her head, she had it neatly twisted in two braids that fell over each shoulder. In place of bright red lipstick, she wore a shade of pink that was more subdued.

This must be what passed for formal attire for her. Even though she'd promised him the evening wasn't going to be formal. He looked down at his own clothes, standard issue blue jeans, white shirt and a pair of Toms he got on sale. Everything was as plain and in-offensive as clothing got, and he couldn't think of a single reason why Chloe would object to anything he had on.

"You said it was casual," he reminded her.

"I said it was *business* casual."

He shrugged. "Guys in business wear stuff like this all the time."

"Not for business casual, they don't."

"What's the difference?"

She eyed his outfit again. "Blue jeans, for one thing." Before he could object, she hurried on, "Okay, *maybe* blue jeans would be okay for some business casual functions, but only if they're dark wash, and only by certain designers."

"Levi Strauss has been designing jeans since the nineteenth century," Hogan pointed out.

Chloe crossed her arms over her midsection. "Yeah, and the ones you have on look like they were in his first collection."

"It took me years to get these broken in the way I like."

"You can't wear them tonight."

"Why not?"

"Because they're not appropriate for—"

"Then what is appropriate?" he interrupted. He was really beginning to hate being rich. There were way too many rules.

She expelled a much put-upon sigh. "What about the clothes you wore to the wine-tasting that day? Those were okay."

"That guy who bumped into me spilled some wine on my jacket, and it's still at the cleaner's."

"But that was weeks ago."

"I keep forgetting to pick it up. I never wear it."

"Well, what else do you have?"

He looked at his clothes again. "A lot of stuff like this, but in different colors."

"Show me."

Hogan opened his mouth to object again. People would be showing up soon, and, dammit, what he had on was fine. But he didn't want to argue with Chloe. These were the most words they'd exchanged in a week, and the air was already crackling with tension. So he made his way toward the stairs with her on his heels—at a safe distance. He told himself he was only changing his clothes because he wanted to look his best for Anabel, not like the kid from Queens she'd chosen someone else over. He wanted to look like a part of her tribe. Because he was a part of her tribe now. Why did he keep trying to fight it?

He took the stairs two at a time until he reached the fourth floor, not realizing until he got there how far behind Chloe was. He hadn't meant to abandon her. He was just feeling a little impatient for some reason. When she drew within a few stairs of him, he headed for his bedroom and threw open the closet that was as big as the dining room in the house where he grew up. It had four rods—two on each side—for hanging shirts and suits and whatever, a low shelf on each side beneath those for shoes, and an entire wall of drawers on the opposite end. Every stitch of clothing Hogan owned didn't even fill a quarter of it. The drawers were pretty much empty, too.

Mrs. Hennessey had started clearing out his grandfather's suits and shoes before Hogan moved in and was in the process of donating them to a place that outfitted homeless guys and ex-cons for job interviews—something that probably had his grandfather spinning in his grave, an idea Hogan had to admit brought him a lot of gratification. But the housekeeper had left a few things on one side she thought might be of use to Hogan because he and his grandfather were about the same size. Hogan hadn't even looked through them. He just couldn't see himself decked out in the regalia of Wall Street, no matter how high he climbed on the social ladder.

Chloe hesitated outside the bedroom door for some

reason, looking past Hogan at the room itself. The room that was furnished in Early Nineteenth Century Conspicuous Consumption, from the massive Oriental rug in shades of dark green, gold and rust to the leather sofa and chair in the sitting area, to the quartet of oil paintings of what looked like the same European village from four different angles, to the rows of model cars lining the fireplace mantel, to the mahogany bed and dressers more suited to a monarch than a mechanic.

Then he realized it wasn't so much the room she was looking at. It was the bed. The bed that, this time last week, they were only a few hours away from occupying together, doing things with and to each other that Hogan had barely ever even fantasized about. Things he'd thought about a lot since. Things, truth be told, he wouldn't mind doing again.

Except with Anabel next time, he quickly told himself. Weird, though, how whenever he thought about those things—usually when he was in bed on his back staring up at the ceiling—it was always Chloe, not Anabel, who was with him in his fantasies.

In an effort to take both their minds off that night, he said, "Yeah, I know, the room doesn't suit me very well, does it? Even the model cars are all antiques worth thousands of dollars—I Googled them—and not the plastic Revell kind I made when I was a kid. I didn't change anything, though, because I thought maybe I'd learn to like it. I haven't. Truth be told, I don't think I'll ever stop feeling like an outsider in this house."

He hated the rancor he heard in his voice. Talk about first world problems. Oh, boo-hoo-hoo, his house was too big and too luxurious for his liking. Oh, no, he had millions of dollars' worth of antiques and collectibles he didn't know what to do with. How would he ever be able to deal with problems like that? Even so, being rich was nothing like he'd thought it would be.

"Then redecorate," Chloe said tersely.

"Oh, sure," he shot back. "God knows I have great taste, what with working under cars on a street filled with neon and bodegas and cement. Hell, apparently, I can't even dress myself."

She winced at the charge. "I didn't mean it like that."

"Didn't you?"

"No. I—"

Instead of explaining herself, she made her way in Hogan's direction, giving him a wide berth as she entered the closet.

"My stuff is on the left," he told her. "The other side is what's left of my grandfather's things."

He hadn't been joking when he told her everything he had was like what he had on, only in different colors. He'd never been much of a clotheshorse, and he didn't follow trends. When his old clothes wore out, he bought new ones, and when he found something he liked, he just bought it in a few different colors. He hadn't altered his blue jeans choice since he first started wearing them, and when he'd started wearing them, he just bought what his old man wore. If it came down to a life-or-death situation, Hogan could probably name a fashion designer. Probably. He just didn't put much thought into clothes, that was all.

Something that Chloe was obviously discovering,

since she was pushing through his entire wardrobe at the speed of light and not finding a single thing to even hesitate over. When she reached the last shirt, she turned around and saw the drawers where he'd stowed his, um, drawers. Before he could stop her, she tugged open the one closest to her and thrust her hand inside, grabbing the first thing she came into contact with, which happened to be a pair of blue boxer-briefs. Not that Hogan cared if she saw his underwear, at least when he wasn't wearing it. And, yeah, okay, he wouldn't mind if she saw it while he was wearing it, either, which was something he probably shouldn't be thinking about when he was anticipating the arrival of his newly possible dream. So he only leaned against the closet door and crossed his arms over his midsection.

Chloe, however, once she realized what she was holding, blushed. Actually blushed. Hogan didn't think he'd ever seen a woman blush in his life. He'd never gone for the kind of woman who would blush. Especially over something like a guy's underwear that he wasn't even wearing.

"There are socks and T-shirts in the other drawers," he told her, hoping to spare her any more embarrassment. Not that there was anything that embarrassing about socks and T-shirts. Unless maybe it was the fact that he'd had some of them, probably, since high school. "But I'm thinking you probably wouldn't approve of a T-shirt for business casual, either."

She stuffed his underwear back where she found it and slammed the drawer shut. Then she looked at the clothes hanging opposite his. "Those belonged to your grandfather?"

"Yeah," Hogan told her. "Mrs. Hennessey is in the middle of donating all his stuff to charity."

Chloe made her way to the rows of shirts, pants and jackets lined up neatly opposite his own and began to give them the quick *whoosh-whoosh-whoosh* she'd given his. She was nearly to the end when she withdrew a vest and gave it a quick perusal.

"Here," she said, thrusting it at Hogan with one hand as she began to sift through a collection of neckties with the other.

He accepted it from her automatically, giving it more thorough consideration than she had. The front was made of a lightweight wool charcoal, and it had intricately carved black buttons he was going to go out on a limb and guess weren't plastic. The back was made out of what looked like a silk, gray-on-gray paisley. It was a nice enough vest, but he wasn't really the vest-wearing type.

In case she wasn't reading his mind, though, he said, "I'm not really the vest-wearing ty—"

"And put this on, too," she interrupted, extending a necktie toward him.

It, too, looked as if it was made of silk and was decorated with a sedate print in blues, greens and grays that complemented the vest well. It was nice enough, but Hogan wasn't really the tie-wearing type, either.

"I'm not really the tie-wearing ty—"

"You are tonight," Chloe assured him before he could even finish protesting.

As if wanting to prove that herself, she snatched the vest from its hanger, leaving the latter dangling from Hogan's fingers. Before he knew it, she was ma-

neuvering one opening of the vest over both of those
and up his arm then circling to his other side to bring
the vest over his other arm. Then she flipped up the
collar of his shirt, looped the tie around his neck and
began to tie it.

She fumbled with the task at first, as if she couldn't
remember how to tie a man's tie—that made two of
them—but by her third effort, she seemed to be recovering. She was standing closer to him than she'd
been in a week. Close enough that Hogan could see
tiny flecks of blue in her green eyes and feel the heat
of her body mingling with his. He could smell her
distinctive scent, a mix of soap and fresh herbs and
something else that was uniquely Chloe Merlin. He
was close enough that, if he wanted to, he could dip
his head to hers and kiss her.

Not surprisingly, Hogan realized he did want to
kiss her. He wanted to do a lot more than kiss her, but
he'd start there and see what developed.

"There," Chloe said, bringing his attention back to
the matter at hand.

Which, Hogan reminded himself, was about getting ready for dinner with the woman he was supposed to be planning to make his wife. He shouldn't
be trying to figure out his feelings for Chloe. He
didn't have feelings for Chloe. Not the kind he had
for Anabel.

Chloe gave the necktie one final pat then looked
up at Hogan. Her eyes widened in surprise, and she
took a giant step backward. "I need to get back to the
kitchen," she said breathlessly.

Then she was speeding past him, out of the closet

and out of his room. But not, he realized as he watched her go, out of his thoughts. Which was where she should be heading fastest.

Hogan was surprised at how much fun he had entertaining near-strangers in his still-strange-to-him home. The wife of one couple who was friends of Anabel's had been in the cab with her the night Hogan met her, so they shared some history there. The other couple who knew her was affable and chatty. Gus Fiver and his date both shared Hogan's love of American-made muscle cars, so there was some lively conversation there. And Anabel...

Yeah. Anabel. Anabel was great. But the longer the night went on, the more Hogan realized neither of them were the people who met on Jamaica Avenue a decade and a half ago. She was still beautiful. Still smart. Still fierce. But she wasn't the seventeen-year-old girl who flipped off a cabbie in the middle of Queens any more than Hogan was the seventeen-year-old kid who'd fallen for her.

All he could conjure up was a fondness for a girl he knew at a time in his life when the world was its most romantic. And he was reasonably sure Anabel felt the same way about him. They talked like old friends. They joked like old friends. But there were no sparks arcing between them. No longing looks. No flirtation.

It was great to see her again. He wouldn't mind bumping into her from time to time in the future. But his fifteen-year-long fantasy of joining his life to hers forever evaporated before Chloe even brought in the second course. Which looked like some kind of soup.

"*Bisque des tomates et de la citrouille,*" she announced as she ladled the first helping into the bowl in front of Anabel.

"Ooo, Chloe, I love your tomato pumpkin bisque," Anabel said, leaning closer to inhale the aroma. "Thyme and basil for sure, but I swear she puts lavender in it, too." She looked at Chloe and feigned irritation. "She won't tell me, though. Damn her."

Chloe murmured her thanks but still didn't give Anabel the information she wanted. Then she circled the table with speed and grace, filling the bowls of everyone present before winding up at Hogan's spot. When she went to ladle up some soup for him, though, her grace and speed deserted her. Not only did she have trouble spooning up a decent amount, but when she finally did, she spilled a little on the tablecloth.

"I am so sorry," she said as she yanked a linen cloth from over her arm to dab at the stain.

"Don't worry about it," Hogan told her. "It'll wash out."

"That's not the point. I shouldn't have done it."

He was about to tell her it was fine, but noticed her hand was shaking as she tried to clean up what she'd done. When he looked at her face, he saw that her cheeks were flushed the same way they'd been in the closet, when she was handling his underwear. Must be hot in the kitchen, he decided.

"It's okay," he said again. Then, to his guests—because he wanted to take their attention off Chloe—he added, "Dig in."

Everyone did, but when Hogan looked at Anabel, she had a funny expression on her face. She wasn't looking at him, though. She wasn't even looking at the soup she professed to love. She was looking at Chloe. After a moment her gaze fell on Hogan.

"Your soup's going to get cold," he told her.

She smiled cryptically. "Not with the heat in this room, it won't."

Hogan narrowed his eyes. Funny, but he'd been thinking it was kind of cool in here.

The soup was, like everything Chloe made, delicious. As were the three courses that followed it. Everyone was stuffed by the time they were finished with dessert, a pile of pastries filled with cream and dripping with chocolate sauce that Anabel said was her most favorite thing Chloe made. In fact, every course that came out, Anabel had claimed was her most favorite thing Chloe made. Clearly, Chloe was doing her best to help Hogan woo the woman he had mistakenly thought was the love of his life. He wasn't sure how he was going to break it to her that all her hard work had been for nothing.

"We should have coffee on the roof," Anabel declared after the last of the dishes were cleared away.

Everyone agreed that they should take advantage of what the weather guys were saying would be the last of the pleasantly cool evenings for a while in the face of some inclement, more November-worthy weather to come. Hogan ducked into the kitchen long enough to tell Chloe their plans then led his guests up to the roof garden.

The view was the same as it was a week ago, but somehow the flowers looked duller, the white lights overhead seemed dimmer and the cityscape was less glittery. Must be smoggier tonight. He and his guests made their way to the sitting area just as Chloe appeared from downstairs. For a moment Hogan waited for her to join them in conversation, and only remembered she was working when she crossed to open the dumbwaiter. From it, she removed a tray with a coffeepot and cups, and little bowls filled with sugar, cream, chocolate shavings and some other stuff that looked like spices. Evidently, even after-dinner coffee was different when you were rich.

As Chloe brought the tray toward the group, Anabel drew alongside Hogan and hooked her arm through his affectionately. He smiled down at her when she did, because it was so like what she had done when they were kids. That was where the similarity in the gesture ended, however, because her smile in return wasn't one of the sly, flirtatious ones she'd always offered him when they were teenagers, but a mild, friendly one instead. Even so, she steered him away from his guests as Chloe began to pour the coffee, guiding him toward the part of the roof that was darkest, where the lights of the city could be viewed more easily. He didn't blame her. It was a really nice view. Once there, she leaned her hip against the balustrade and unlooped her arm from his. But she took both of his hands in hers and met his gaze intently.

"So how are you adjusting to Park Avenue life?" she asked, her voice low enough that it was clear she meant the question for him alone.

"I admit it's not what I thought it would be," he replied just as quietly. "But I guess I'll get used to it. Eventually."

He looked over at his other guests to make sure he wasn't being a neglectful host, but they were all engaged in conversation. Except for Chloe, who was busying herself getting everything set out on the table to her liking. And also sneaking peeks at Hogan and Anabel.

She was more concerned about the success of the evening than he'd been. He wished there was some way to signal her not to worry, that the evening had been a huge success, because he knew now the plans he'd made for the future weren't going to work out the way he'd imagined, and that was totally okay.

"I know it's a lot different from Queens," Anabel said, bringing his attention back to her. She was still holding his hands, but she dropped one to place her palm gently against his chest. "But Queens will always be here in your heart. No one says you have to leave it behind." She smiled. "In fact, I, for one, would be pretty mad at you if you did leave Queens behind. You wouldn't be Hogan anymore if you did."

"That will never happen," he assured her. "But it's still weird to think that, technically, this is the life I was born to."

She tipped her head to one side. "You have something on your cheek," she said.

Again? Hogan wanted to say. First the engine grease with Chloe, now part of his dinner with Anabel. Before he had a chance to swipe whatever it was away, Anabel lifted her other hand to cup it over his jaw, stroking her thumb softly over his cheekbone.

"Coffee?"

He and Anabel both jumped at the arrival of Chloe, who seemed to appear out of nowhere. Anabel looked guilty as she dropped her hand to her side, though Hogan had no idea what she had to feel guilty about. Chloe looked first at Hogan, then at Anabel, then at

Hogan again. When neither of them replied, she extended one cup toward Anabel.

"I made yours with cinnamon and chocolate," she said. Then she paraphrased the words Anabel had been saying all night. "I know it's your *most favorite*."

Hogan wasn't sure, but the way she emphasized those last two words sounded a little sarcastic.

"And, Hogan, yours is plain," Chloe continued. "Just the way I know *you* like it."

That, too, sounded a little sarcastic. Or maybe caustic. He wasn't sure. There was definitely something off about Chloe at the moment, though. In fact, there'd been something off about Chloe all night. Not just the soup-spilling when she'd ladled up his, but every course seemed to have had something go wrong, and always with Hogan's share of it. His *coq au vin* had been missing the *vin*, his *salade Niçoise* had been a nice salad, but there had hardly been any of it on his plate, his cheese course had looked like it was arranged by a five-year-old, and his cream puff dessert had been light on the cream, heavy on the puff.

He understood that, as the host, he was obligated to take whichever plates weren't up to standards, and he was fine with that. But that was just it—Chloe was *always* up to standards. She never put anything on the table that wasn't perfect. Until tonight.

Hogan and Anabel both took their coffee and murmured their thanks, but Chloe didn't move away. She only kept looking at them expectantly. So Hogan, at least, sipped from his cup and nodded.

"Tastes great," he said. "Thanks again."

Anabel, too, sampled hers, and smiled her approval. But Chloe still didn't leave.

So Hogan said, "Thanks, Chloe."

"You're welcome," Chloe replied. And still didn't leave.

Hogan looked at Anabel to see if maybe she knew why Chloe was still hanging around, but she only sipped her coffee and gazed at him with what he could only think were laughing eyes.

"So your coffee is all right?" Chloe asked Anabel.

"It's delicious," Anabel told her. "As you said. My *most favorite.* Somehow, tonight, it's even better than usual." She hesitated for the briefest moment then added, "Must be the company."

Even in the dim light, Hogan could see two bright spots of pink appear on Chloe's cheeks. Her lips thinned, her eyes narrowed and her entire body went ramrod straight.

"I'm so happy," she said in the same crisp voice. Then she looked at Hogan. "For both of you."

Then she spun on her heels and went back to his other guests. Once there, however, she turned again to study Hogan and Anabel. A lot.

"What the hell was that about?" Hogan asked Anabel.

She chuckled. "You really have no idea, do you?"

He shook his head. "No. Is it some woman thing?"

Now Anabel smiled. "Kind of."

"Should I be concerned?"

"Probably."

Oh, yeah. This was the Anabel Hogan remembered. Cagey and evasive and having fun at his expense. Now that he was starting to remember her without the rosy sheen of nostalgia, he guessed she really could be kind of obnoxious at times when they were teenag-

ers. Not that he hadn't been kind of obnoxious himself. He guessed teenagers in general were just kind
of annoying. Especially when their hormones were
in overdrive.

He studied Anabel again, but she just sipped her
coffee and looked amused. "You're not going to tell
me what's going on with Chloe, are you?" he asked.

"No."

"Just tell me if whatever it is is permanent, or if
she'll eventually come around and things can get back
to normal."

She smiled again. "Hogan, I think I can safely say
your life is never going to be normal again."

"I know, right? This money thing is always going
to be ridiculous."

"I didn't mean the money part."

"Then what did you mean?"

She threw him another cryptic smile. "My work
here is done." As if to punctuate the statement, she
pushed herself up on tiptoe to kiss his cheek then told
him, "Tonight was really lovely, Hogan. And illumi-
nating."

Well, on that, at least, they could agree.

"Thank you for inviting me," she added. "But I
should probably go."

"I'll walk you out."

"No, don't leave your guests. I can find my own
way." She looked thoughtful for a moment before nodding. "In fact, I'm really looking forward to finding
my own way in life for once."

She walked back toward the others. He heard her
say her goodbyes and thank Chloe one last time, then
she turned to wave to Hogan. As he lifted a hand in

return, she strode through the door to, well, find her own way. Leaving Hogan to find his own way, too.

He just wished he knew where to go from here.

Nine

Tonight was a disaster.

Chloe was still berating herself about it even as she dropped the last utensil into the dishwasher. There was just no way to deny it. The evening had been an absolute, unmitigated disaster. And not just the dinner party, where every single course had seen some kind of problem. The other disaster had been even worse. Hogan's reunion with Anabel had been a huge success.

Chloe tossed a cleaning pod into the dishwasher, sealed the door and punched a button to turn it on. It whirred to quiet life, performing perfectly the function for which it had been designed. She wished she could seal herself up just as easily then flip a switch to make herself work the way she was supposed to. She used to be able to do that. She did that as efficiently and automatically as the dishwasher did for six years. Six years, nine months and…and…

She leaned back against the counter and dropped her head into her hands. Oh, God. She couldn't remember anymore how many weeks or days to add to the years and months since Samuel's death. What was wrong with her?

And why had it hurt so much to see Hogan and Anabel together tonight? Chloe had known since the day she started working for Hogan that his whole reason for hiring her had been to find a way back into Anabel's life. He'd never made secret the fact that he still wanted the girl of his dreams fifteen years after they broke up, nor the fact that he was planning a future with her.

For Pete's sake, Chloe was the one who had been so adamant about throwing the dinner party tonight so the two of them would finally be in the same room together. She'd deliberately chosen all of Anabel's favorite dishes. She'd helped Hogan make himself more presentable for the woman he'd loved half his life so he could make a good impression on her.

And she'd accomplished her goal beautifully, because the two of them had laughed more than Chloe had ever seen two people laugh, and they'd engaged in constant conversation. They'd even wandered off as the evening wound down to steal some alone time together on the roof. Alone time Anabel had used to make clear that her interest in Hogan was as alive as it had ever been.

Chloe didn't think she'd ever be able to rid her brain of the image of Anabel splaying one hand open on Hogan's chest while she caressed his face with the other, the same way Chloe had done a week ago when she and Hogan were on the roof themselves. She knew what it meant when a woman touched a man that way. It meant she was halfway in love with him.

No! She immediately corrected herself. That wasn't what it meant. At least not where Chloe was concerned.

She started wiping down the kitchen countertops, even though she'd already wiped them off twice. You could never be too careful. She wasn't in love with Hogan. Not even halfway. She would never be in love with anyone again. Loving someone opened you up to too many things that could cause pain. Terrible, terrible, *terrible* pain. Chloe never wanted to hurt like that again. Chloe never *would* hurt like that again. She just wouldn't.

She wasn't in love with Hogan. She would never fall in love again.

Anyway, it didn't matter, because Hogan and Anabel were back on the road to the destiny they'd started when they were teenagers. His hiring of Chloe had had exactly the outcome he'd intended. He'd won the woman of his dreams.

Before long Chloe would be cooking for two. She'd serve Hogan and Anabel their dinner every night, listening to their laughter and their fond conversation as they talked about their shared past and their plans for the future. And she'd bring in their breakfast every morning. Of course, Anabel liked to have breakfast in bed most days. She'd probably want that for her and Hogan both now. So Chloe would also be able to see them every morning all rumpled from sleep. And sex. More rumpled from sex than from sleep, no doubt, since Hogan's sexual appetites were so—

Well. She just wouldn't think about his sexual appetites anymore, would she? She wouldn't think about Hogan at all. Except in the capacity of him as her employer. Which was all he was. That was all he had ever been. It was all he would ever be. Chloe had reiterated that to him a week ago. All she had to do was keep remembering that. And forget about the way he—

She closed her eyes to shut out the images of her night with Hogan, images that had plagued her all week. But closing her eyes only brought them more fiercely into focus. Worse, they were accompanied by feelings. Again. Feelings she absolutely did not want to feel. Feelings she absolutely could not feel. Feelings she absolutely would not feel. Not if she wanted to stay sane.

She finished cleaning up the kitchen and poured what was left of an open bottle of wine into a glass to take upstairs with her. As she topped the step to the fifth and highest floor of Hogan's house, her gaze inevitably fell on the roof access door across from her. Unable to help herself, she tiptoed toward it and cracked it open to see if anyone was still up there. She'd been surprised that Anabel left first, until she remembered her former employer often turned in early on Saturday night because she rose early on Sunday to drive to a farm in Connecticut where she stabled her horses.

There were still a few voices coming from the roof—Chloe recognized not just Hogan's, but Mr. Fiver's and his date's, as well. She wondered briefly if she should go up and check on the coffee situation then decided against it. She'd sent up a fresh pot and its accoutrements before cleaning up the kitchen, and Hogan had assured her he wouldn't need anything else from her tonight.

Or any other night, she couldn't help thinking as she headed for her room. He had Anabel to take care of any nightly needs he'd have from now on. And every other need he would ever have again. Which was good. It was. Chloe was glad things had worked out between the two former lovers the way they had. She was. Hogan would be happy now. And Anabel was a nice person. She also deserved to be happy. Now Chloe could focus completely on her cooking, which would make her happy, too. It would.

Happiness was bursting out all over. They were all hip deep in happiness. Happy, happy, happy. Yay for happiness.

Thank God she had the next two days off.

Hogan had always loved Sundays. Sunday was the one day of the week Dempsey's Parts and Service was closed—unless there was an emergency. He loved Sunday mornings especially, because he could sleep late and rise when he felt like it, then take his time eating something for breakfast that he didn't have to wolf down on the run, the way he did during the work week.

At least, that had always been the case before he became filthy, stinking rich. Over the course of the past month, though, Sundays hadn't been like they used to be. He hadn't been working his regular shifts at the garage, so how could one day differ from any other? And he didn't have to eat on the run anymore, so a leisurely Sunday breakfast was no different from any other breakfasts during the no-longer-work-week. No, he hadn't been completely idle since leaving Queens, but he hadn't had a regular schedule to keep. He hadn't had places he *had* to be or things he *had* to get done.

Yeah, he was putting plans into place that would bring work and purpose back into his life, but there was no way his life—or his Sundays—would ever go back to being the way they were before.

The thing that had really made Sundays even less enjoyable than they were before, though, was that Chloe was never around on Sundays. She never stayed home on her days off, and the house felt even more alien and unwelcoming when she wasn't in it.

This morning was no different. Except that, some-how, it felt different. When Hogan stumbled into the kitchen in his usual jeans and sweater the way he did every Sunday morning to make coffee, the room seemed even more quiet and empty than usual. He busied himself making his usual bacon and eggs, but even eating that didn't pull him out of his funk.

Too little sleep, he decided. Gus Fiver and his date had hung around until the wee hours, so Hogan had logged half the amount of shut-eye he normally did. Of course, last weekend he'd woken having only logged a few hours of shut-eye, too, and he'd felt *great* that day. At least until Chloe had told him what a mistake the night before had been.

He stopped himself there. Chloe. What was he going to do about Chloe? The only reason he'd hired her was because he wanted to insinuate himself into Anabel's life. And the only reason he'd planned to keep her employed in the future was because she was Anabel's favorite chef. Not that he intended to fire her now—God, no—but her reason for being in his house had suddenly shifted. Hell, the whole dynamic of her place in his house seemed to have suddenly shifted. Hogan for sure still wanted Chloe around. But he didn't want her around because of Anabel anymore. He wanted Chloe around because of, well, Chloe.

He liked Chloe. He liked her a lot. Maybe more than liked her. All week he'd been thinking about Chloe, not Anabel. Even before he realized his thing for Anabel wasn't a thing anymore, it was Chloe, not Anabel, who had been living in his head. He'd had dozens of nights with Anabel in the past, and only one night with Chloe. But when he piled all those nights with Anabel into one place and set the single night with Chloe in another, that single night had a lot more weight than the dozens of others. He wanted to have more nights with Chloe. He wanted countless nights with Chloe. The problem was Chloe didn't want any more nights with him. She'd made that crystal clear.

And there was still the whole employer-employee thing. He didn't want Chloe as an employee anymore. He wanted her as…something else. He just wasn't sure what. Even by the time he finished his breakfast and was trying to decide what to do with his day—other than think about Chloe, since that would be a given—Hogan had no idea what to do about her. Even after cleaning up from his dinner that evening, he still didn't know what to do about her.

Chloe evidently did, though, because she came into the den Sunday night, where Hogan was putting together a preliminary plan for a state-wide chain of Dempsey's Garages, and handed him a long, white envelope.

"Here," she said as she extended it toward him.

She was dressed in street clothes, a pair of snug blue jeans and a voluminous yellow turtleneck, her hair in a ponytail, her glasses sliding down on her nose—which she pushed up with the back of her hand, so he knew she was feeling anxious about something.

"What is it?" he asked.

"My two weeks' notice."

He recoiled from the envelope as if she were handing him a rattlesnake. "What?"

"It's my two weeks' notice," she repeated. "Except that I'm taking advantage of article twelve, paragraph A, subheading one in my contract, and it's really my two days' notice."

Now Hogan stood. But he still didn't take the envelope from her. "Whoa, whoa, whoa. You can't do that."

"Yes, I can. That paragraph outlines my right to an immediate abdication of my current position in the event of force majeure."

His head was still spinning from her announcement, but he found the presence of mind to point out, "Force majeure only applies to things beyond our control like wars or strikes or natural disasters."

"Exactly," she said.

He waited for her to clarify whatever was beyond their control, but she didn't elaborate. So he asked, "Well, what's the force majeure that's making you give me your two weeks'—correction, two days'—notice?"

She hesitated, her gaze ricocheting from his to the shelves of books behind him. Finally, she said, "Impracticability."

Hogan narrowed his eyes. "Impracticability? What the hell does that mean?"

"It's a legitimate legal term. Look it up. Now, if you'll excuse me, I have a cab waiting."

"Wait, what? You're leaving right now? That's not two days' notice, that's two minutes' notice."

"Today isn't over yet, and tomorrow hasn't started," she said. "That's two days. And my new employers have a place ready for me, so there's no reason for me to delay starting."

She still wasn't looking at him. So he took a step to his left to put himself directly in her line of vision. As soon as he did, she dropped her gaze to the floor.

"You already have a new employer?" he asked.

"Yes."

Of course she already had a new employer. Since she'd come to work for him, Hogan had had to fend off a half dozen attempts from people besides Anabel to hire her away from him, upping her salary even more every time. He hadn't minded, though, especially now that he knew where the money went. He would have done anything to keep Chloe employed so he could keep himself on Anabel's radar. At least, that was what he'd been telling himself all those times. Now he knew there was another reason he'd wanted to keep Chloe on. He just still wasn't sure he knew how to put it in words.

"Who's your new employer?" he asked.

"I'm not required to tell you that," she replied, still looking at the floor.

"You might do it as a professional courtesy," he said, stalling. "Or even a personal one."

"It's no one you know."

"Chloe, if it's a matter of money, I can—"

"It isn't the money."

She still wasn't looking at him. So he tried a new tack.

"Haven't your working conditions here been up to standard?"

"My working conditions here have been——" She halted abruptly then hurried on, "My working conditions here have been fine."

"Well, if it isn't the money, and it isn't the working conditions, was it..." He hated to think it might be what he thought it was, but he had to know for sure. "Was it the taco meatloaf?"

She looked up at that, but she closed her eyes and shook her head.

Even though he'd assured her he wouldn't mention it again, he asked, "Then was it what happened after the taco meatloaf?"

Now she squeezed her eyes tight. "I have to go," she said again.

Hogan had no idea how to respond to that. She hadn't said specifically that it was their sexual encounter making her situation here "impracticable"—whatever the hell that was—but her physical reaction to the question was a pretty good indication that that was exactly what had brought this on. Why had she waited a week, though? If their hookup was what was bothering her, then why hadn't she given her notice last weekend, right after it happened?

He knew the answer immediately. Because of Anabel. Chloe had promised before they ended up in his bed that she would arrange a dinner party for him so he could spend time with Anabel and cinch their reconciliation. She'd stayed long enough to fulfill that obligation so Hogan would be able to reunite with the woman he'd professed to be in love with for half his life. Now she figured he and Anabel were on their way to their happily-ever-after, so there was no reason for her to hang around anymore. And, okay, he supposed it could get kind of awkward if Anabel reentered his life after he and Chloe had had sex. Maybe Chloe just wanted to avoid a scenario like that. His anxiety eased. If that was the case, it wasn't a problem anymore.

"Anabel and I aren't going to be seeing each other," he said.

At that, Chloe finally opened her eyes and met his gaze. This time she was the one to ask, "What do you mean?"

Hogan lifted his shoulders and let them drop. "I mean we're not going to be seeing each other. Not like dating anyway. We might still see each other as friends."

"I don't understand."

Yeah, that made two of them. Hogan tried to explain anyway. "Last night she and I both realized there's nothing between us now like there was when we were kids. No sparks. No fireworks. Whatever it was she and I had fifteen years ago, we've both outgrown it. Neither one of us wants to start it up again."

"But you've been pining for her for half your life."

This part, at least, Hogan had figured out. He told Chloe, "No, the seventeen-year-old kid in me was pining for her. I just didn't realize how much that kid has grown up in the years that have passed, and how much of his youthful impulses were, well, impulsive. The thirty-three-year-old me wants something else." He might as well just say the rest. He'd come this far. "The thirty-three-year-old me wants some*one* else."

Okay, so maybe that wasn't exactly saying the rest. He was feeling his way here, figuring it out as he went. Chloe, however, didn't seem to be following him. So

Hogan pushed the rest of the words out of his brain and into his mouth. And then he said them aloud.

"He wants you, Chloe. *I* want you."

He had thought the announcement would make her happy. Instead, she recoiled like he'd hit her.

But all she said was, "You can't."

Now Hogan was the one who felt like he'd been hit. Right in the gut. With a two-by-four. But he responded honestly, "Too late. I do."

Her brows arrowed downward, and she swallowed hard. "I can't get involved with you, Hogan."

"Why not?"

"I can't get involved with anyone."

"But last weekend—"

"Last weekend never should have happened," she interrupted.

"But it did happen, Chloe. And you'll never convince me it didn't have an effect on you, the same way it had an effect on me. A big one."

"Oh, it definitely had an effect on me," she assured him. Though her tone of voice indicated she didn't feel anywhere near as good about that effect as he did.

"Then why—"

"Because I can't go there, Hogan. Ever again. I was in love once, and it nearly destroyed me. I never want to love anyone like that again."

"Chloe—"

"You've experienced loss," she interrupted him. "With both of your parents. You know how much it hurts when someone you love isn't there for you anymore."

He nodded. "Yeah, but—"

"Now take that pain and multiply it by a hundred,"

she told him. "A thousand. As terrible as it is to lose a parent or a grandparent, it's even worse when you lose the person you were planning to spend the rest of your life with. Losing someone like that is so… It's…"

Tears filled her eyes, spilling freely as she continued. "Or even if you lose someone like that in old age, after the two of you have built a life together, you still have a lifetime worth of memories to get you through it, you know? You have your children to comfort you. Children who carry a part of that person inside them. Maybe they have their father's smile or his way of walking or his love of cardamom or something else that, every time you see it, it reminds you he's not really gone. Not completely. A part of him lives on in them. You walk through the house the two of you took years making your own, and you're reminded of dozens of Thanksgivings and Christmases and birthdays that were celebrated there. You have an *entire life* lived with that person to look back on. But when that person is taken from you before you even have a chance to build that life—"

She took off her glasses with one hand and swiped her eyes with the other. "It's a theft of your life before you even had a chance to live it," she said. "The children you planned to have with that person die, too. The plans you made, the experiences you should have shared, the memories you thought you'd make… All of that dies with him.

"A loss like that is overwhelming, Hogan. It brings with it a grief that goes so deep and is so relentless, you know it will never, ever, go away, and you know you can never, ever, grieve like that again. *I* can never grieve like that again. And the only way to avoid grieving like that again is to never love like that again. I have to go before I'm more—"

She halted abruptly, covering her eyes with both hands. Hogan had no idea how to respond to everything she'd said. As bad as it had been to lose his folks, he couldn't imagine losing someone he loved as much as Chloe had loved her husband. He hadn't loved anyone as much as she had loved her husband. Not yet anyway. But even after everything she'd just said—hell, because of everything she'd just said—he'd like to have the chance to find out what it *was* like to love someone that much. And if Chloe's last few words and the way she'd stopped short were any indication, maybe there was still a chance she might love that way again, too.

"I'm sorry, Chloe," he said. The sentiment was overused and of little comfort, but he didn't know what else to say. "Your husband's death was a terrible thing. But you can't stop living your life because something terrible happened. You have to do your best to move on and make a different life instead. You can't just shut yourself off from everything."

"Yes, I can."

He shook his head. "No. You can't. And you haven't."

She arrowed her brows down in confusion. "How do you know?"

He shrugged and smiled gently. "Because I think you pretty much just told me you love me."

"No, I didn't," she quickly denied. Maybe too quickly. "I don't love anyone. I'll never love anyone again. I can't."

"You mean you won't."

"Fine. I won't love anyone again."

"You think you can just make a choice like that? That by saying you won't love someone, it will keep you from loving them?"

"Yes."

"You really believe that?"

"I have to."

"Chloe, we need to talk more about this. A lot more."

"There's nothing to talk about," she assured him. Before he could object, she hurried on, "I'm sorry to leave you in the lurch. My letter includes a number of recommendations for personal chefs in the area who would be a good match for your culinary needs. Thank you for everything."

And then she added that knife-in-the-heart word that Anabel had never said to him when they were kids, the one word that would have let Hogan know it was over for good and never to contact her again, the word that, left unsaid the way it was then, had given him hope for years.

"Goodbye."

And wow, that word really did feel like a knife to the heart. So much so that he couldn't think of a single thing to say that would counter it, a single thing that would stop Chloe from leaving. All he could do was watch her rush out the door and head for the stairs. And all he could hear was her last word, with all its finality, echoing in his brain.

Ten

Chloe stood in the kitchen of Hugo and Lucie Fleury, marveling again—she'd made herself marvel about this every day for the last three weeks—at what a plumb position she had landed. Her new situation was perfect for her—something else she made herself acknowledge every day—because Hugo and Lucie had grown up in Paris and arrived in New York for his new job only a year ago, so they were about as Parisian as a couple could be outside the City of Light. They didn't question anything Chloe put on the table, so she never had to explain a dish to them, their Central Park West penthouse was decorated in a way that made her feel as if she were living at Versailles and she was using her second language of French every day, so there was no chance of her getting rusty. *Mais oui*, all Chloe could say about her new assignment was, *C'est magnifique!*

So why didn't she feel so *magnifique* after almost a month of working here? Why did she instead feel so blasé? More to the point, why hadn't a single meal she'd created for the Fleurys come out the way it was supposed to? Why had everything she put together been a little…off? And now she was about to undertake a dinner party for twelve, the kind of challenge to which she normally rose brilliantly, and all she could do was think about the last dinner party she'd put together, and how it had resulted in—

Not that the Fleurys had complained about her performance, she quickly backtracked. They'd praised everything she set in front of them, and tonight's menu was no exception. Not that they'd tasted any of it yet, but, as Lucie had told her this morning, *"Ne vous inquiétez pas, Chloe. J'ai foi en vous."* Don't worry, Chloe. I have faith in you.

Well, that made one of them.

Lucie and Hugo didn't seem to realize or care that they were paying her more than they should for a party they could have had catered for less by almost any bistro, brasserie or café in New York. But Chloe realized they were doing that. And in addition to making her feel guilty and inadequate, it was driving her crazy. She just hadn't been at her best since leaving Hogan's employ. And the whole reason she'd left Hogan's employ was because she'd feared losing her ability to be at her best.

Well, okay, maybe that wasn't really the reason she'd left Hogan. But she was beginning to wonder if she'd ever be at her best again.

He'd called her every day the first week after she left, but she'd never answered. So he'd left messages, asking her to meet him so they could talk, even if it meant someplace public, because even though he didn't understand her desire to not tell him where she was working now, he respected it, and *C'mon, Chloe, pick up the phone, just talk to me, we need to figure this out.* As much as she'd wanted to delete the messages without even listening to them, something had compelled her to listen…and then melt a little inside at the sound of his voice. But even after hearing his messages, she still couldn't bring herself to delete them. Deleting Hogan just felt horribly wrong. Even if she never intended to see him again.

I want you.

The words he said the night she left still rang in her ears. She wanted Hogan, too. It was why she couldn't stay with him. Because wanting led to loving. And loving led to needing. And needing someone opened you up to all kinds of dangers once that person was gone. Losing someone you needed was like losing air that you needed. Or water. Or food. Without those things, you shriveled up and died.

I think you pretty much just told me you love me.

Those words, too, wouldn't leave her alone. Because yes, as much as she'd tried to deny it, and as much as she'd tried to fight it, she knew she loved Hogan. But she didn't need him. She wouldn't need him. She couldn't need him. And the only way to make sure of that was to never see him again.

Unfortunately, the moment Chloe entered the Fleurys' salon in her best chef's whites with a tray of canapés, she saw that her determination to not see Hogan, like so many other things in life, was completely out of her control. The Fleurys had invited him to their dinner party.

Or maybe they'd invited Anabel, she thought when she saw her other former employer at Hogan's side, and he was her plus-one. Whatever the case, Chloe was suddenly in the same room with him again, and that room shrank to the size of a macaron the moment she saw him. He was wearing the same shirt with the same vest and tie she'd picked out for him the night of his own dinner party, but he'd replaced his battered Levi's with a pair of pristine dark wash jeans that didn't hug his form nearly as well.

As if he'd sensed her arrival the moment she noted his, he turned to look at her where she stood rooted in place. Then he smiled one of his toe-curling, heat-inducing smiles and lifted a hand in greeting. All Chloe wanted to do then was run back into the kitchen and climb into a cupboard and forget she ever saw him. Because seeing him only reminded her how much she loved him. How much she wanted him. How much—dammit—she needed him.

Instead, she forced her feet to move forward and into the crowd. Miraculously, she made it without tripping or sending a canapé down anyone's back. Even more astonishing, she was able to make eye contact with Hogan when she paused in front of him and Anabel. But it was Anabel who broke the silence that settled over them.

"Oh, yum. *Brie gougères.* Chloe, I absolutely love your *brie gougères.*" She scooped up two and smiled. "I love them so much, I need to take one over to Hillary Thornton. Talk amongst yourselves."

And then she was gone, leaving Chloe and Hogan

alone for the first time in almost a month. Alone in the middle of a crowd of people who were waiting to try her *brie gougères* and her *choux de Bruxelles citrons* and the half dozen other hors d'oeuvres she'd prepared for the evening. None of which had turned out quite right.

"Hi," he said softly.

"Hello," she replied.

"How've you been?"

"All right." The reply was automatic. Chloe had been anything but all right since she last saw him. The same way her food had been anything but all right. The same way life itself had been anything but all right.

They said nothing more for a moment, only stood in the middle of a room fit for a king, as nervous as a couple of teenagers on their first date.

Finally, Hogan said, "What are you doing after the party?"

Again, Chloe replied automatically. "Cleaning up the kitchen."

He grinned, and Chloe did her best not to have an orgasm on the spot. "What about after that?" he asked.

"I'll, um… I'll probably have a glass of wine."

"Want some company?"

She told herself to tell him no. That she hadn't wanted company for years. Lots of years. And lots of months and weeks and days—she just couldn't remember precisely how many. But she knew she was lying. She did want company. She'd wanted company for years. Lots of years and months and weeks and days. She just hadn't allowed herself to have it. Not until one glorious night three weeks, six days, twenty hours and fifty-two minutes ago, a night she would carry with her forever. Even so, she couldn't bring herself to say that to Hogan.

"Anabel is friends with the Fleurys," he said. "She told me the view from their roof is spectacular."

"It is," Chloe replied.

He looked surprised. "So you've been up there?"

She nodded. She'd gone up to the Fleurys' terrace a number of times since coming to work for the Fleurys. She didn't know why. The New York nights had turned cold and damp with winter setting in so solidly and hadn't been conducive to rooftop wanderings. But wander to the roof she had, over and over again. The view was indeed spectacular. She could see all of New York and Central Park, glittering like scattered diamonds on black velvet. But it had nothing on the view from Hogan's house. Probably because Hogan wasn't part of the view.

"Maybe you could show me?" he asked. "I mean, once you've finished with your party duties. Anabel said the Fleurys' parties tend to go pretty late, and she hates to be the first to leave."

"She was the first to leave at your party," Chloe said.

"That was because she was a woman on a mission that night."

"What mission?"

Hogan smiled again. But he didn't elaborate. "What time do you think you'll be finished?"

Chloe did some quick calculating in her head. "Maybe eleven?"

"Great. I'll meet you up on the roof at eleven."

She told herself to decline. Instead, she said, "Okay."

He looked at the tray. "What do you recommend?"

What a loaded question. All she said, though, was "Try the tapenade."

She remembered belatedly that he probably had no idea what tapenade was and was about to identify the proper selection, but he reached for exactly the right thing. Her surprise must have shown on her face, because he told her, "I've been doing some homework."

And then he was moving away, fading into the crowd, and Chloe was able to remember she had a job she should be doing. A job that would fall just short of success because, like the hors d'oeuvres and so much more, nothing she did was quite right anymore.

Instead, the party went off without a hitch, and every dish was perfect—if she did say so herself. Even the moments when she served Hogan, where she feared she would spill something or misarrange something or forget something, all went swimmingly. By the time she finished cleaning up the kitchen— which also went surprisingly well—she was starting to feel like her old self again. Like her old cooking self anyway. The other self, the one that wasn't so focused on cooking, still felt a little shaky.

She had just enough time to go to her room for a quick shower to wash off the remnants of *Moules à la crème Normande* and *carottes quatre epices*. Then she changed into blue jeans and a heavy black sweater and headed for the roof.

Hogan was already there waiting for her. He'd donned a jacket to ward off the chill and stood with his hands in his pockets, gazing at the New York skyline in the distance. The full moon hung like a bright silver dollar over his head, and she could just make out a handful of stars higher in the night sky. Her heart hammered hard as she studied him, sending her blood zinging through her body fast enough to make her light-headed. Or maybe it was the simple presence of Hogan doing that. How had she gone nearly a month without seeing him? Without hearing him? Without talking to him and feeling the way he made her feel? How had she survived without him?

Although she wouldn't have thought he could hear her over the sounds of the city, he spun around the moment she started to approach. The night was cold, but the closer she drew to him, the warmer she felt. But she stopped when a good foot still separated them, because she just didn't trust herself to not touch him if she got too close.

"Hi," he said again.

"Hello."

"It's good to see you."

"It's good to see you, too."

A moment passed where the two of them only gazed at each other in silence. Then Hogan said, "So I looked up impracticability."

She barely remembered using that as an excuse to cancel her contract with him. How could she have wanted to do that? How could she have thought the only way to survive was to separate herself from Hogan? She'd been dying a little inside every day since leaving him.

"Did you?" she asked.

"Yeah. I even used a legal dictionary, just to make sure I got the right definition. What it boiled down to is that one party of a contract can be relieved of their obligations if those obligations become too expensive, too difficult or too dangerous for them to perform."

"That about covers it, yes."

He nodded. "Okay. So I thought about it, and I figured it couldn't have become too expensive for you to perform your job, because I was paying for everything."

She said nothing in response to that, because, obviously, that wasn't the reason she'd had to leave.

"And it wasn't becoming too difficult for you to perform your job," he continued, "since you were excellent at it, and you made it look so easy and you seemed to love it."

"Thank you. And yes, I did love it. Do love it," she hastened to correct herself. Because she did still love to cook. She just didn't love cooking for the Fleurys as much as she'd loved cooking for Hogan. She hadn't loved cooking for anyone as much as she'd loved cooking for Hogan. Probably because it wasn't just cooking for Hogan she'd loved.

"So if you didn't think your job was too expensive or too difficult to perform," he said, "then you must have thought it was too dangerous."

Bingo. Because loving anything—or anyone—more than cooking was very dangerous indeed for Chloe. Loving anything—or anyone—more than cooking could very well be the end of her. At least that was what she'd thought since Samuel's death. Now she was beginning to think there were things much more harmful to her—and much more dangerous for her—than loving and wanting and needing. Like not loving. And not wanting. And not needing. She'd spent six years avoiding those things, and she'd told herself she was surviving, when, really, she'd been dying a little more inside every day. Losing more of herself every day. Until she'd become a shell of the woman she used to be. A woman who'd begun to emerge from that shell again the moment she met Hogan.

"Yes," she told him. But she didn't elaborate. She still didn't quite trust herself to say any of the things she wanted—needed—to say.

"So what was getting too dangerous?" he asked. "Were the knives too sharp? Because I can stock up on bandages, no problem."

At this, she almost smiled. But she still said nothing.

"Then maybe the stove was getting too hot?" he asked. "Because if that's the case, I can buy some fans for the kitchen. Maybe get a window unit for in there."

Chloe bit back another smile at the thought of a portable air conditioner jutting out of a window on the Upper East Side and dripping condensation onto the chicly dressed passersby below. She shook her head again. And still said nothing.

"Okay," he said. "I was hoping it wasn't this, but it's the only other thing I can think of. It was all that fresh, unprocessed whole food, wasn't it? I knew it. Someday scientists are going to tell us that stuff is poison and that boxed mac and cheese and tinned biscuits are the best things we can put in our bodies."

"Hogan, stop," she finally said. Because he was becoming more adorable with every word he spoke, and that was just going to make her fall in love with him all over again.

Then she realized that was ridiculous. She'd fallen

in love with Hogan a million times since meeting him. What difference would one more time make?

"Well, if it wasn't the sharp knives, and it wasn't the hot stove, and it wasn't the allegedly healthy food, then what was it that made working for me so dangerous?"

He was going to make her say it. But maybe she needed to say it. Admitting the problem was the first step, right? Now if she could just figure out the other eleven steps in the How-to-Fall-Out-of-Love-with-Someone program, she'd be all set. Of course, falling *out* of love with Hogan wasn't really the problem, was it? Then again, she was beginning to realize that falling *in* love with him wasn't so bad, either.

"It was you, Hogan," she said softly. "It was the possibility of falling in love with you." Then she made herself tell the truth. She closed her eyes to make it easier. "No, that's not it. It wasn't the possibility of falling in love with you. It was falling in love with you."

When he didn't reply, she opened first one eye, then the other. His smile now was completely different from the others. There was nothing teasing, nothing modest, nothing sweet. There was just love. Lots and lots of love.

"You can't fight it, Chloe," he said. "Trust me—I know. I've been trying to fight it for a month. Trying to give you the room you need to figure things out. Trying to figure things out myself. But the only thing I figured out was that I love you."

Heat swamped her midsection at hearing him say it so matter-of-factly. "Do you?"

"Yep. And I know you love me, too."

"Yes."

For a moment they only gazed at each other in silence, as if they needed a minute to let that sink in. But Chloe didn't need any extra time to realize how she felt about Hogan. She'd recognized it the night they made love. She'd just been trying to pretend otherwise since then.

Hogan took a step toward her, close enough now for her to touch him. "Do you think you'll ever stop loving me?" he asked.

She knew the answer to that immediately. "No. I know I won't."

"And I'm not going to stop loving you."

He lifted a hand to her face, cupping her jaw lightly, running the pad of his thumb over her cheek. Chloe's insides turned to pudding at his touch, and she tilted her head into his caress.

"So here's the thing," he said softly. "If we both love each other, and neither of us is going to stop, then why aren't we together?"

She knew the answer to that question, too. Because it would be too painful to lose him. But that was a stupid answer, because it was going to be painful to lose him whether they were together or not. Okay, then because she would live in fear of losing him for the rest of her life. But that didn't make any sense, either, because if she wasn't with him, then she'd already lost him. Okay, then because…because… There had to be a reason. She used to have a reason. If she could only remember what the reason was.

"It's too late for us, Chloe," he said when she didn't reply. "We love each other, and that's not going to change. Yeah, it's scary," he added, putting voice to her thoughts. "But don't you think the idea of life without each other is even scarier?"

Yes. It was. Being alone since Samuel's death had been awful. Although she could deny it all she wanted, Chloe hadn't liked being alone. She'd tolerated it because she hadn't thought there was any other way for her to live. But she hadn't liked it. The time she'd spent living with Hogan and being with Hogan was the best time she'd had in years. Some years and some months and some weeks and some days she didn't have to keep a tally of anymore. Because she wasn't alone anymore. Or, at least, she didn't have to be. Not unless she chose to.

Hogan was right. It was scary to fall in love. No, it was terrifying. But the prospect of living the rest of her life without him was far, far worse.

"I want to come back to work for you," she said.

He shook his head. "Just come back. We'll figure out the rest of it as we go."

Chloe finally smiled. A real smile. The kind of smile she hadn't smiled in a long time. Because she was happy for the first time in a long time. Truly, genuinely happy. "Okay," she said. "But I'm still not going to cook you taco meatloaf."

Hogan smiled back. "No worries. We can share the cooking. I need to introduce you to the joys of chicken pot pie, too."

Instead of wincing this time, Chloe laughed. Then she stood up on tiptoe, looped her arms around Hogan's neck and kissed him. Immediately, he roped his arms around her waist and pulled her close, covering her mouth with his and tasting her deeply as if she were the most delectable dish he'd ever had.

Chloe wasn't sure how they made it to her bedroom on the first floor without alerting the dinner guests still lingering in the Fleurys' salon, since she and Hogan nearly fell down every flight of the back stairs on their way, too reluctant to break their embrace and shedding clothes as they went. Somehow, though, they—and even their discarded clothing—did make it. He shoved the door closed behind them, then pressed her back against it, crowding his big body into hers as he kissed her and kissed her and kissed her.

By now, she was down to her bra, and the fly of her jeans was open, and he was down to his T-shirt, his belt loosened, his hard shaft pressing against her belly. She wedged her hand between their bodies enough to unfasten the button at his waist and tug down the zipper, then she tucked her hand into his briefs to press her palm against the naked length of him. He surged harder at her touch, and a feral growl escaped him before he intensified their kiss. He dropped his hands to her hips, shoving her jeans and panties down to her knees, then he thrust his hand between her legs to finger the damp folds of flesh he encountered.

This time Chloe was the one to purr with pleasure, nipping his lip lightly before touching the tip of her tongue to the corner of his mouth. Hogan rubbed his long index finger against her again, then inserted it inside her, caressing her with the others until she felt as if she would melt away. With his free hand, he slipped first one bra strap, then the other, from her shoulders, urging the garment to her waist to bare her breasts. Then he covered one with his entire hand, thumbing the sensitive nipple to quick arousal.

Her breath was coming in quick gasps now, and her

hand moved harder on his ripe shaft in response. He rocked his hips in time with her touches, until the two of them were *this close* to going off together. Just as the tightening circles of her orgasm threatened to spring free, he pulled their bodies away from the door and began a slow dance toward the bed. The moment they reached their destination, she yanked Hogan's shirt over his head, tossed it to the floor and pushed at his jeans to remove them, as well. Taking her cue, he went to work on removing what was left of her clothing, too.

When she turned to lower the bed's coverlet, he moved behind her, flattening his body against hers and covering her breasts with both hands. But when she bent forward to push away the sheets, he splayed his hand open at the middle of her back, gently bent her lower, and then, slow and deep, entered her from behind.

"Oh," she cried softly, curling her fingers tightly into the bedclothes. "Oh, Hogan..."

He moved both hands to her hips, gripping them tightly as he pushed himself deeper inside her. For long moments, he pumped her that way, the friction of his body inside hers turning Chloe into a hot, wanton thing. Finally, he withdrew, taking his time and caressing her fanny as he did, skimming his palms over her warm flesh before giving it a gentle squeeze. He tumbled them both into bed, lying on his back and pulling her atop him, straddling him. Instead of entering her again, though, he moved her body forward, until the hot feminine heart of her was poised for his taste.

His tongue flicking against her already sensitive flesh was her undoing. Barely a minute into his ministrations, Chloe felt the first wave of an orgasm wash over her. She moaned as it crested, waiting for the next swell. That one came and went, too, followed by another and another. But just when she thought she'd seen the last one, he turned her onto her back and positioned himself above her.

As he entered her again, another orgasm swept over her. But this time, Hogan went with her. He thrust inside her a dozen times, then emptied himself deep inside her. Only then did the two of them fall back to the bed, panting for breath and groping for coherent thought. Never had Chloe felt more satisfied than she did in that moment. Never had she felt so happy. So contented. So free of fear.

Loving wasn't scary, she realized then. Avoiding love—that was scary. Loving was easy. So love Hogan she would. For as long as she could. Because, *oh là là*, living without loving wasn't living at all.

It was a hot day in Brooklyn, the kind of summer day that cried out for something cold for dessert. So Chloe decided to add *tulipes de sorbet* to the daily menu of her new café, *La Fin des Haricots*. They would go nicely with the rest of the light French fare the little restaurant had become famous for in Williamsburg over the last year and a half, and it would make Hogan happy, since it was a reasonable compromise for the chocolate ice cream he preferred.

They'd compromised on a lot over the last eighteen months. He'd sold his grandfather's Lenox Hill town house, along with Philip Amherst's other properties— save the one in Paris, of course, where they planned to spend the month of August every year, starting with their honeymoon last summer. Then they purchased a funky brownstone they'd been renovating ever since, and in whose backyard Chloe had planted a small garden and built a small greenhouse. Hogan's chain of Dempsey's Garages was fast becoming reality—he was already operating three in the city and had acquired properties for a half dozen more. And *La Fin des Haricots* was fast becoming a neighborhood favorite. They worked hard every day and loved hard every night, and on Sundays...

Sundays were sacred, the one day they dedicated completely to each other. Usually by spending much of it in bed, either eating or talking or loafing or— their favorite—making love.

Hogan's other passion in life was the scholarship fund he'd set up in his parents' names for kids from both his old and his new neighborhoods. He'd also donated significantly to Samuel's fund. The losses of their pasts would help bring happiness into others' futures, and that made the two of them about as rich as a couple of people could be.

Life was good, Chloe thought as she finished up the menu and handed it off to her head waiter to record it on the ever-changing chalkboard at the door. Then she buttoned up her chef's jacket—one that fit, since she had packed Samuel's away and wore her own now— and headed back to the kitchen. Her kitchen. She might still be cooking for other people, but it was in her own space. A space where she was putting down roots, in a place she would live for a very long time, with a man she would love forever. It still scared her a little when she thought about how much she loved her husband. But it scared her more to think about not loving him.

He met her at the end of her workday as he always did, on this occasion arriving at the kitchen door in his grease-stained coveralls, since it was the end of his workday, too. They ate dinner together at the chef's table, then, hand in hand, they walked home. Together they opened a bottle of wine. Together they enjoyed it on their roof. Together they made plans for their trip to Paris in August. And then together they went to bed, so they could make love together, and wake up together and start another day in the morning together.

Because together was what they were. And together was what they would always be. No matter where they went. No matter what they did. No matter what happened.

And that, Chloe thought as she did every night when they turned off the light, was what was truly *magnifique*.

* * * * *

If you love billionaires, pick up these books from New York Times *bestselling author Elizabeth Bevarly.*

THE BILLIONAIRE GETS HIS WAY
MY FAIR BILLIONAIRE
CAUGHT IN THE BILLIONAIRE'S EMBRACE
ONLY ON HIS TERMS
A CEO IN HER STOCKING

Available now from Mills & Boon Desire!

* * *

"I'm not asking you to marry me, Piper, or even date me," Jaeger replied.

This wasn't how the conversation normally went. He usually fielded the demands about when he'd be calling, when their next date would be. He didn't particularly care that the shoe was very firmly, and uncomfortably, on the other foot. "I was just wondering if you'd like to—"

"Hook up again sometime?" Piper tipped her head and the corners of her mouth lifted. When she exposed her neck he wanted to nibble on her collarbone, kiss that spot under her jaw. "Thanks, but no. Hooking up is not something I make a habit of. This interlude will be a lovely memory, but re-creating this back home won't work for me."

Piper stood up and pulled the knot on her robe, allowing the sides to fall open. With a small shrug the robe slid down her arms and then to the floor and she stood in front of him, gloriously naked. She straddled his thighs and gently touched his mouth with hers. "If this is all the time we have, then we're wasting it."

She was the perfect one-night stand; she'd let him off the hook with no drama and little fanfare and he should feel grateful, he thought, lowering her to the bed.

So then, why didn't he?

* * *

His Ex's Well-Kept Secret
is part of the Ballantyne Billionaires series—
A family who has it all...except love!

HIS EX'S WELL-KEPT SECRET

BY
JOSS WOOD

First Published in Great Britain 2017
By Mills & Boon, an imprint of HarperCollins*Publishers*
1 London Bridge Street, London, SE1 9GF

© 2017 Joss Wood

ISBN: 978-0-263-92816-7

51-0417

Our policy is to use papers that are natural, renewable and recyclable products and made from wood grown in sustainable forests. The logging and manufacturing processes conform to the legal environmental regulations of the country of origin.

Printed and bound in Spain
by CPI, Barcelona

Joss Wood loves books and traveling—especially to the wild places of Southern Africa. She has the domestic skills of a pot plant and drinks far too much coffee.

Joss has written for Mills & Boon Modern and, most recently, the Mills & Boon Desire line. After a career in business, she now writes full-time. Joss is a member of the Romance Writers of America and Romance Writers of South Africa.

Dedicated to Chris, taken too fast and too soon. Your family—and friends—lost an incredibly good man. You will be missed, bud.

Prologue

In the presidential suite of a boutique hotel on the Via Manzoni, the most luxurious hotel in Milan, Jaeger Ballantyne ran his hand down a slim female back, the bumps of her spine pearls under satin skin.

The fine cotton sheet covered Piper's hips and draped her butt. Jaeger couldn't stop touching her, loving the feel of her warm skin under his rough hand. He'd had women in his hotel room before, probably more than he should have, and while Piper was not the most beautiful female he'd ever had in his bed, she was certainly the most magnetic. Since the moment she'd stumbled into his life a day and a half ago, he'd thought of little else.

Exceptional gems—the cut and sparkle of diamonds, rubies, opals, emeralds and a dozen more—captured and held his attention. Women? Not so much. Like diamonds destined for the mass market, they were generally nicely cut and well polished but nothing exceptional. And when he did find one a cut above the rest, he enjoyed her and quickly moved on.

But for some reason, he kept thinking of Piper as a flawless, colorless diamond, the rarest type on the planet. Ridiculous, because he knew there was always another gem to discover, and he never lost his head over sparkly stones or the sweeter-smelling sex.

Piper Mills made him wonder if walking around headless was a risk he was prepared to take.

He should have been back in New York City already, Jaeger thought, irritated with his overthinking. He'd originally intended to be in Milan only for the previous evening. But when he'd seen Piper at the Milan branch of Ballantyne and Company, her long legs under a short skirt captured his attention. They'd been designed, he was convinced, to wrap around his hips.

The intelligence in her light green eyes intrigued him, and the splash of freckles across her nose charmed him.

Her body had him wanting to make her scream until the whole of Milan knew his name.

Piper had mentioned owning ten blue stones that family legend said were sapphires, but he was too fascinated by her face to pay much attention. Then she smiled and a tiny dimple in her right cheek flashed, and all thoughts of carats and color disappeared. His breath hitched, his vision swam and he knew he was not leaving the city until he'd taken her to dinner.

And to bed.

Fast-forward thirty-six hours and three dates—dinner, lunch and another dinner—and they'd shared some very hot, very fun sex. Jaeger's thumb ran over her right buttock, flirted with the curve at the top of her thigh and back up again.

Best day and a half of his life, by far.

Jaeger bent down and placed a kiss on the ball of her shoulder, pulling a long curl the color of a newly minted penny off her face.

Piper rolled onto her side, and when Jaeger looked into her eyes, he felt like he was walking in a mysterious forest. Her gaze bounced away from his face, ricocheted off his body and focused on the watercolor painting on the far wall. So the very sexy Ms. Mills wasn't very good with post-sex conversation. Why did that make him smile?

Piper sat up and pulled the sheet to her torso. "Um… this is awkward."

"It really doesn't have to be," Jaeger assured her.

Piper tucked the sheet under her armpits, pushed a hand through her hair and adjusted the sheet again. "Can we have a quick chat about why I was in Ballantyne and Company?" Piper asked.

Jaeger could think of a better use of their time, but if talking about her stones made her feel at ease, then he was all for it.

"Okay, let's talk sapphires." Jaeger rolled off the bed, snagging his boxers from the floor. He pulled them on and walked over to the bathroom to pluck a blindingly white cotton robe off the hook behind the door. He opened the robe and Piper, self-conscious, left the bed and hastily slid her arms into the sleeves. Jaeger turned her around, covered her up and tied the belt across her narrow waist.

Resisting the urge to lower his mouth to hers, Jaeger took her hand, led her into the living room of the suite and dashed the remains of a vintage Cabernet into a wineglass for her. Piper took the glass and curled up into the corner of the couch, tucking her bare feet, tipped with red-hot toes, under her butt. Along with every other inch of her body, he'd tasted those toes. He'd kissed his way up her calves, tasted the sweetness of her inner thighs, the heat and spice of her core.

And he desperately wanted to do it all again.

He would; the night wasn't over yet.

Deciding he needed a whiskey, he poured two fingers into a glass, sat down opposite her and mentally begged her to make it quick.

"As I said, I have some sapphires that have been passed down through my mother's family."

"How many stones are we talking about?" Jaeger asked, resting his forearms on his thighs.

"Ten. There were twelve, but my mom sold two, thirty years ago, to give my father the money to start his business."

He realized he knew nothing about her or her family. *You don't need to; you're not going to see her again.*

"Most of the stones are around an inch, some bigger, some smaller," Piper continued.

A sapphire longer than an inch? He didn't think so. "Are they cut? Uncut?"

"The smaller stones are cut. There's one that's…spectacular."

Jaeger knew people exaggerated, particularly when it came to gemstones. The stones were probably half that size. He looked at Piper and sighed when he saw the blissful look on her face. If she were anyone else, he would bluntly have told her the gems were probably fake. A cache of sapphires like she was describing would have been well-documented. Unless you enjoyed royal connections, exceptional and important gems were rarely passed down a family line.

Unaware of his skepticism, Piper held her wineglass to her chest, her eyes dreamy. "Oh, Jaeger, it's beautiful. A deep, dark blue, sleepy and velvety and just, God, gorgeous. I just want to touch it, hold it, look at it."

"It's difficult to comment on stones I haven't seen, but I wouldn't get my hopes up if I were you," he said, keeping his voice noncommittal.

"I have a photo of them. Could you look at it?" Piper asked.

Jaeger nodded and sighed when Piper bent over to pick up her bag. The cotton robe delineated her heart-shaped bottom, revealed the backs of her thighs. He felt his boxers tighten as his junk moved up to half-mast. The urge to sink into her heat was strong.

Relax. You'll have her again. Once more, or twice, before they went back to real life.

Piper walked back to him and sat on the arm of his chair, her fingers dancing across the screen of her phone. She passed it to him, and Jaeger looked down at the burst of blue on black velvet.

His heart stopped momentarily and his hand shook as he placed his glass on the table in front of him.

Jaeger enlarged the screen and focused on the biggest of the cut stones. The quality of the photo wasn't great, but the color was breathtakingly brilliant.

"Where did you say these came from?" he asked. *Tell me again that you think they're from Kashmir because, hell, you may be right.*

"Through a great-great-uncle on my mother's side.

He was a soldier in the British army. Family legend says they come from Kashmir."

Yes!

Be cool, Jaeger told himself. *If it sounds too good to be true then it usually is. But the color and her family history suggested there was a possibility of these stones being real.*

"What else do you know about the original owner?"

"Just what I told you," Piper said. She tapped her screen with the tip of her finger. "Well, what do you think? Could they be real? I've taken them to other gem dealers who say they aren't."

Of course they would say that. She was young and pretty and an easy mark. They'd make her a token offer, resell the gems and make a freakin' killing. "Stay away from dodgy dealers," he muttered.

"But do *you* think they could be worth anything?"

Maybe she'd been in Ballantyne and Company because she was thinking of selling them. If they were genuine, he was definitely interested in buying. He slid his habitual I'm-not-impressed expression onto his face—his excitement tended to inflate prices—and handed Piper a casual smile. "I don't know. It's really difficult to tell from a photograph. Let me look at them when we're back in the States. Can you send me the photo?"

"Sure."

Jaeger rattled off his number, and within twenty seconds he heard the beep telling him the photo was on his phone.

"I really hope they aren't real," Piper stated, her expression glum.

Now *there* was a statement he'd never heard from a prospective seller before. "Why on earth would you not want to be the owner of a collection of stones worth, potentially, a lot of money?" Jaeger demanded.

"Because then I'd feel morally obligated to sell them to help my...to help someone out of a financial jam."

"You have people in your life who owe millions?"

Piper wrinkled her nose. "They're worth as much as that? No, tell me they aren't!"

"They could be, possibly, *if* they are Kashmir sapphires. But don't bank on it," Jaeger warned

"Maybe I should've just taken the first offer I received. A grand a stone." Piper muttered.

Ten thousand dollars? Jaeger felt sick. Although he was trying to remain calm, trying not to overreact, he knew, somewhere deep inside him, that he'd might've made the discovery of a lifetime. If they were real, then hers were special stones.

"Will you promise to bring them to me, in New York? No one else?" He couldn't let the stones slip through his fingers.

Piper nodded. "Sure."

"I'll call you to set up a time."

Piper swung her legs around and placed the balls of her feet on Jaeger's bare thigh. Their eyes met and sparks flew.

Seeing desire flash and burn in her eyes, he slid his hand between her thighs, sighing at the smooth, warm flesh. He opened his mouth to ask whether he could see her again like this, not just at Ballantyne, when they both returned to New York. Then he frowned. Why her and why now?

For more than a decade, since his early twenties—after crawling out of the deep, dark mine shaft that grief and loss tossed him into—he'd seldom pursued a woman beyond three or four nights. He didn't want to raise expectations, didn't want any of his very temporary lovers to think there could be a chance of them becoming permanent fixtures in his life. He'd worn permanence once. He'd—briefly—been a father, and when his daughter Jess died, he'd lost his lover, too.

Permanence now felt like an itchy, scratchy, ill-fitting coat.

Why was he thinking about losing his baby girl and the woman he'd once loved while he was with this sexy stranger? He'd thoroughly enjoyed his easy conversation with Piper, loved her offbeat sense of humor and, hell, the sex was off-the-charts amazing. Three damn fine reasons he couldn't see her again when they both returned to the city.

He liked her a bit too much…and that meant he had to move on.

"When are you going back to the city?" Jaeger asked.

"My flight leaves in the morning. You?"

He'd leave as soon as she did; she was the only reason he was still in Milan. "Tomorrow, as well." Jaeger moved the pad of his thumb up her smooth calf.

"When we meet in the city," she said, "let's be all business."

Whoa! What?

Piper's toes dug into the bare skin of his thigh.

"Don't look so shocked, Jaeger. If not for the sapphires, I'd never hear from you again," Piper stated, her voice not accusing.

Jaeger dropped his hand from her thigh.

"It's okay, Jaeger, I get it. It's not what you do." Piper continued. "The problem with being the biggest playboy on the East Coast, one of the famous Ballantyne siblings, is that the world knows how you operate. You date a girl for a couple of days, maybe for a couple of weeks if she's really, really lucky, and then you move on." Piper lifted her hand when he opened his mouth to respond. "Don't look so worried. I knew the deal going in."

"The deal?"

"This was fun, a moment in time, an unexpected encounter. So when we meet again, we'll just chat about the stones and pretend we never saw each other naked."

Jaeger didn't know he was going to speak the words until they flew out of his mouth. "What if I wanted to? See you naked again, that is," he clarified.

Surprise flashed across Piper's face, but it was quickly followed by a healthy dose of doubt.

"I'd probably ask you not to."

Okay. *So* not what he'd expected to hear.

Piper tipped her head to the side, her expression thoughtful. "Jaeger, I'm a normal woman who has her feet firmly on the ground. I enjoy my job as an art appraiser. I date. I have a full life. I don't need you to sweep me away and into your world. I don't *like* your world."

"My world?"

"Big money, Manhattan, socialite city. It's not me. It'll never be me," Piper said, her tone and expression earnest.

"I'm not asking you to marry me, Piper, or even date me," Jaeger replied, feeling irritated. This wasn't how the conversation normally went. Usually he fielded the demands about when he'd be calling, when their next date would be. He didn't particularly like that the shoe was very firmly, and uncomfortably, on the other foot. "I was just wondering if you'd like to—"

"—hook up again sometime?" Piper cocked her head,

the corners of her mouth lifting. When she exposed her neck, he wanted to nibble on her collar bone, kiss that spot under her jaw. "Thanks, but no. Hooking up is not something I make a habit of. This interlude will be a lovely memory, but recreating this back home won't work for me."

Piper tucked a long curl behind her ear. "There's something about Italy that's sexy and seductive. It's a place that subliminally encourages you to seize the day and act out of character, and this—" Piper waved her hand at his bare chest "—is very out of character for me. In the real world, I sleep with guys only if I think we are going somewhere, if the man has the potential to become important to me. Thanks to the tabloids, we all know you don't do commitment, so that rules you out."

Okay, sure, that was true but... *But?* There was no *but*. She had him pegged!

Piper stood up and pulled the knot on her robe, allowing the sides to fall open. The fabric framed her pretty breasts, and the moisture in his mouth evaporated. With a small shrug the robe slid down her arms and then to the floor, and she stood in front of him gloriously naked. She straddled his thighs and gently touched his mouth with hers. "If this is all the time we have, then we're wasting it, Ballantyne."

Jaeger gripped her butt in his hands and stood up, holding her. Her legs locked around his waist as he carried her to the bedroom.

She was the perfect one-night stand; she'd let him off the hook with no drama and little fanfare, and he should feel grateful, he thought, lowering her to the bed.

So, then, why didn't he?

One

Piper Mills pulled her reading glasses from her face and tossed them onto her desk. Rubbing the bridge of her nose, she pushed her chair back from her Georgian mahogany writing desk and scowled at her laptop screen, where the offer of an exciting consultation sat in her inbox, waiting for her response.

Of course she would like to appraise a recently discovered Daniel Glutz. She'd written her master's thesis on the German painter. But it was impossible. The painting was in Berlin, and since Ty's birth nine months ago, she was restricted to appraising art on the East Coast, to trips she could undertake in a day or less. Although she loved and trusted her nanny, Ceri, and Ceri's twin brother, Rainn, who was also good with Ty, she still didn't feel comfortable leaving her precious child for extended periods. She couldn't leave Ty overnight. Not yet.

Maybe when he was in college.

Piper stood up and went to the curved bow window of her three-story redbrick Victorian. She folded her arms across her chest and looked down onto the street below. Fall was nearly over, winter was rushing in and the seasons seemed to be flying past. She'd conceived Ty in spring, lost Mick in late summer, given birth to Ty in midwinter. This summer, unlike the previous one, passed by uneventfully.

Mick's death last year was a smack rather than a blow, but one she was still wrapping her head around. Even though she and her father rarely spoke, she liked knowing there was somebody she was connected to, some family she could call her own—even if it was only in the quiet depths of her soul, since Mick never publicly acknowledged her as his daughter.

Or acknowledged her at all.

Growing up, she'd never thought she'd be glad he publicly ignored her and her mother, his longtime mistress. But when the most flamboyant and driven personality on the New York social scene, one of the most respected stockbrokers and investment advisors in the world, was arrested for fraud, Piper was very glad not to be linked to him.

Over decades, Mick convinced thousands of people to invest in funds he recommended, promising solid returns. He then used money from new investors to pay off existing investors, all while living the high life. It was no surprise he'd demanded she hand over her sapphires in the months leading up to, and after, his arrest.

He'd needed to raise some money to buy a shovel so he could dig himself out of a very big hole.

The press attention over his arrest was intense, and Mick's ex-wife was constantly harassed by reporters. Mick's child bride/trophy wife conveniently left the States for Colombia two days before his arrest, never to return, not even to attend Mick's funeral.

Ah, such a demonstration of true love.

Since neither of Mick's wives knew of Piper's existence, she'd just stayed in Park Slope, Brooklyn, living in the house Mick bought for her mother, watching the Mick-induced craziness from a distance. She was grateful her mother never witnessed the man she loved fall from the very high and gilded pedestal she'd placed him on. His death, from a heart attack two-and-a-half months after first being arrested, would've killed her if cancer had not.

Piper heard a snuffle from the baby monitor on her desk and smiled. Her boy was awake and would be wanting some lunch. Piper walked out of her study and ran up the stairs to the third floor of her building, which served as the second floor of her home. The first floor was an apartment she rented to Ceri and Rainn. She padded into the smaller of two bedrooms and across to the wooden crib she'd slept in as a child. Ty turned to look at her, and love flooded her system.

He was all Jaeger, she thought, picking him up and cuddling him to her chest. He had Jaeger's light blue eyes, his facial structure and his dark sable hair. Ty would also, she was sure, have Jaeger's height and naturally muscular build.

Ty was a Ballantyne, she thought, in everything but name.

"There's my big boy," she crooned, rubbing her chin across the top of his head. Piper carried Ty to his changing mat and deftly undressed him, taking a moment, as she always did, to kiss his foot, to nibble his heel. The actions caused Ty to release a belly laugh which, in turn, made her laugh. God, she'd never thought she could love someone this much…

Piper whipped a disposable diaper from the box on the chest of drawers and slid it under Ty's clean bottom. Under the pile of diapers was the black velvet roll of fabric, and inside the roll were the ten sapphires she'd discussed with Jaeger.

In Milan, he'd promised he'd call her so he could examine the sapphires, but he never did. When six weeks passed without hearing from him, and she'd realized condoms weren't a hundred percent foolproof, she'd tried to contact him. Every call she made to his cell phone went directly to voice mail.

He couldn't be hard to reach, she'd thought, so she'd tried to contact him through Ballantyne and Company. Ha! That was like trying to speak directly with one of the Windsor boys. She'd left countless messages, sent a dozen emails to the group secretary, but nothing. When she'd visited the flagship store, asking to see Jaeger, her requests to speak to someone higher up the food chain were dismissed. When she refused to leave until either Jaeger or one of his three siblings spoke with her, security escorted her off the premises.

She'd been on the internet a few days later and found an in-depth article on him in which he was quoted saying that he had no intention of ever marrying, that he did not want children. The world needed innovators and adventurers and discoverers, not more mouths to feed.

Besides, kids would seriously cramp his style…

By midnight of that awful day, she'd finally received the message that Jaeger wasn't interested in her or her sapphires or hearing she was pregnant.

Ty, she decided, was hers; she wasn't obliged to share his existence with a man who would not be excited or interested in her child. Mick had ignored her, and she'd always wondered why he didn't love her. There was no way she would burden her son with an uninterested, un-enthusiastic father.

Piper desperately wished she could forget about Jaeger, but that was impossible when she lived with a miniature version of the man. In Ty she saw Jaeger's gorgeous, fallen-angel face—light eyes a perfect foil for his olive skin and dark, wavy hair—and then she remembered the scrape of his two-day-old beard against her skin, the breadth of his shoulders, the ridges of his corrugated stomach, the peace she felt in his clever assured touch.

Some nights she woke up from a deep sleep, her heart pounding, an orgasm hovering, her thoughts full of him. On occasion she rolled over looking for him, wanting him to take her to that place where only he could—a diz-zying, sparkling place where time stood still and magic lived. When reality crashed down—she was a single mother and he wasn't interested in her or her son—the following hours were dark and dismal, long on tears and short on sleep.

Ty gurgled and Piper dropped her head to nuzzle his tummy, feeling his tiny hands in her curls. When she'd first found out she was pregnant with Manhat-tan's Main Man's baby, she'd cursed God and Fate and wept and wailed. Now she couldn't imagine her life without her little man; he was the beginning and the end of her universe.

"What about some lunch and then a walk in the park? It's cold but sunny." Piper put Ty on her hip and walked downstairs, ignoring her study to head for the kitchen. "You up for that, Ty?"

Ty shoved his fist in his mouth, and Piper took that to be a yes. Handing Ty a sippy cup filled with water, she pulled out a jar of organic baby food and heard her doorbell buzz. Frowning, she looked at the small screen in her kitchen and saw a man in a suit standing by the front door to her building. He looked very...lawyerly, Piper decided.

Piper lifted the receiver to her intercom, and when she heard he represented the law firm in charge of administering her father's estate, she buzzed her visitor into the building.

Five minutes later, Mr. Simms sat at her kitchen table as she fed Ty his lunch.

"I understand that you're a fine arts appraiser, you work from home and you have a steady clientele of both art gallery owners and private collectors."

Accurate enough. Piper nodded as she spooned sweet potato and carrots into Ty's welcoming mouth. Wanting to get outside and into the fresh air, she lifted her eyebrows. "All true. But I doubt you came here to talk about my business, so what can I do for you?"

"I also understand you are Michael Shuttle's daughter?"

There was no point denying it. "I am. My mother and Mick were together for over thirty years. My relationship to Mick is not public knowledge, and I'd prefer it stayed private."

Piper wiped Ty's face and hands and handed him oversize plastic house keys to play with. They immediately went to his mouth. "Why are you here?"

Simms nodded. "Unlike his business, your father's personal assets were very well-documented. On his list were numerous pieces of furniture, with annotations that they are in this house. There is a Georgian desk, a painting by Zabinski, a sculpture by Barry Jackson. A Frida Kahlo painting."

"He gave those to my mother. They were gifts."

"The spreadsheet states the items were on loan to Gail Mills." Mr. Simms looked sympathetic.

From the kitchen she could see into the living room, where the bronze sculpture of a ballet dancer sat on the credenza. "Are you telling me they have to be sold?"

Simms nodded. "Yes. They are part of his estate."

Piper bit her bottom lip to keep her curses from escaping. "On loan, my ass! They were gifts. I was there when he gave them to her." Feeling sad and a little sick, Piper stood up to release Ty from his high chair.

Simms made a note in a small black notepad and looked at her as she swayed side to side, Ty on her hip. "I'll send a crew to collect the table, the art and the bronze. They'll go up for auction and you can buy them back."

Yeah, right, that wasn't going to happen. "I'll keep that in mind. Thank you." Piper looked at the door, hinting that she'd like him gone.

"There's just one more thing, Miss Mills."

Oh, God, judging by his serious face, whatever he was about to say would be a kick to the gut. She tightened her grip on Ty and waited for the hammer to fall.

"This property is owned by one of your father's companies and will definitely have to be sold to repay some of his creditors."

Piper felt her knees buckle, and she dropped to a chair, Ty landing on her lap. "What? But he left this house to my mom, who left it to me. I've requested a copy of the deed but I've received nothing."

"That's because he left the right for your mom to live in it. He didn't leave the asset. It's definitely not yours to live in. It will be sold. That is indisputable."

Indisputable? That sounded pretty damn final. Piper pushed past the panic and forced herself to think. "Would I be able to buy it?" she asked, her voice breaking.

"Do you have around three million dollars?" Simms asked. "Or a way to raise three million dollars?"

No, but she had some stones that might be worth that much, if they were real. This was her home, Ty's home! She'd lost her mother; she couldn't lose her house, too. If she could raise money from the sapphires, she might be able to get a mortgage for the rest...

"I can try to find the money. How much time do I have?"

Mr. Simms's face softened. "Your father left a hell of a mess, and you're being punished for it. That's not right. I'll push the sale of the property down my list of priorities and hope like hell I don't get caught. What about three months?"

Piper nodded, tears in her eyes. "Three months to raise three million. Holy crack-a-doodle."

Simms cocked his head at her. "If anyone can do it, Michael Shuttle's daughter can."

Piper didn't bother explaining that, while she carried Mick's DNA, she'd been anything but his daughter. But she *was* Gail's daughter and Ty's mom, and she had a life she loved, a life now under threat. Piper looked around her colorful, cozy home, and her stomach twisted into a sailor's knot. This was her nest, the center of her life. It was her refuge, her cave, her son's playpen. It was where she felt safe.

Leaving her house and her life wasn't an option, so she had to fight for it, and that meant... God. Piper pushed her hand against her flat stomach, ordering her lungs to work.

Fighting for her life and her home meant selling her stones. And selling her stones meant going back to see Jaeger, the only man who'd ever tempted her to walk on the wild side. It didn't matter that she was still furious that he'd refused to see her, still hurt that she was so easily forgotten. She needed him.

Dammit. She needed Jaeger.

Only, she quickly qualified, to buy her sapphires so she could save her and Ty's home. She didn't need Jaeger to be her lover or Ty's dad or even to rehash the past and explain his actions.

It was a simple transaction: she'd give him ten sapphires and he'd give her a considerable amount of money.

It would be swift and simple.

With her rising stress levels, she didn't think she could cope with anything *but* swift and simple.

Sitting in the reception area, three floors up from the magnificent flagship jewelry store on Fifth Avenue, Piper took in the details of the Ballantyne and Company headquarters.

Unlike the restrained elegance of the jewelry store below, where the furnishings were top quality but designed to play second fiddle to the magnificent jewels, the corporate offices were modern, light and airy. Orange backless couches sat on polished cement floors, and wide windows allowed visitors to watch the Manhattan traffic below. Modern artwork—Piper instantly recognized the massive monochromatic Pinz—dominated the wall above a light wood credenza holding a coffee machine.

The knowledge that she was in danger of losing her house had galvanized her, and she'd swung into action. She had no choice; she had to establish whether the stones were valuable or not.

Piper hadn't wasted her energy trying to get an appointment with Jaeger directly, choosing instead to use her contacts in the art world. Art collectors had deep pockets, and many of them, including her old client Mr. Hendricks, purchased jewelry as well. She'd once saved him from purchasing a fraudulent Dali, and he'd quickly agreed to facilitate a meeting between her and Jaeger.

She would've saved herself a lot of heartache if she'd had this brainwave last year. Baby brain, she decided. Those pregnancy hormones had a lot to answer for!

Despite Jaeger acting like a toad after Milan, she trusted him professionally to tell her the truth about the stones. His reputation as an honest dealer was vitally important to him. Ballantyne and Company was also reputed to pay the highest prices for quality gems. Three very good, very *business-y* reasons for her to be here. Piper felt a drop of perspiration run down her spine. Her heart was bouncing off her rib cage and the air seemed thin.

She had to calm down.

She was going to see Jaeger again. Her one-time lover, the father of her child, the man she'd spent the past eighteen months fantasizing about. In Milan she hadn't been able to look at him without wanting to kiss him deeply, madly, without wanting to get naked with him as soon as humanly possible.

Jaeger, the same man who'd blocked her from his life.

Piper sucked in as much air as she could. She had to pull herself together! She was a few months shy of thirty, a mother, She was not a gauche girl about to meet her first crush. She had sapphires to sell, her house to save, a child to raise. She was being utterly ridiculous! This meeting had nothing to do with Ty or Milan. This meeting was about her gems and her need to raise the cash to keep her home. Ty's home.

Unable to sit still, Piper walked down the hall to examine another painting, this one by Crouch. Not his best work, she decided. Piper turned when male voices drifted toward her, and she immediately recognized Jaeger's deep timbre. Her skin prickled and burned and her heart flew out of her chest.

"Miss Mills?"

Piper hauled in a deep breath and looked at Jaeger. His hair was slightly shorter, she noticed, his stubble a little heavier. His eyes were still the same arresting blue, but his shoulders seemed broader, his arms under the sleeves of the black oxford shirt more defined. A soft leather belt was threaded through the loops of black chinos.

The corner of his mouth tipped up, the same way it had the first time they'd met, and like before, the butterflies in her stomach took flight and crashed into one another. Heat ran up her neck and into her cheeks and she bit her bottom lip, frantically telling herself she couldn't, wouldn't, throw herself into his arms and tell him that her mouth had missed his, that her body still craved his.

He held out his hand. "I'm Jaeger Ballantyne."

Yes, I know. We did several things to each other that, when I remember Milan, still make me blush.

What had she said in Italy? *"When we meet again, we'll pretend we never saw each other naked."*

Oh, God! Was he really going to take her statement literally?

Jaeger shoved his hand into the pocket of his pants and rocked on his heels, his expression wary. "Okay, skipping the pleasantries. I understand you have some sapphires you'd like me to see?"

His words instantly reminded her of her mission. It shouldn't—*it didn't!*—matter that he was being a hemorrhoid. She'd spent one night with the Playboy of Park Avenue and he'd unknowingly given her the best gift of her life, but that wasn't why she was here. She needed him to look at her stones and, ideally, confirm they were valuable. She needed him to buy the gems so she could keep her house.

Piper nodded. "Right. Yes, I have sapphires."

"I only deal in exceptional stones, Ms. Mills." Jaeger told her, his expression guarded.

Tired of wasting time, and feeling like an idiot, Piper reached into the side pocket of her tote bag and hauled out a knuckle-size cut sapphire.

"This exceptional enough for you, Ballantyne?"

Two

Jaeger lowered his loupe and looked at the sapphire he held between his thumb and index finger. It was a small stone, barely four carats, but its color and quality, like those of the rest of the ten stones, were off the charts.

Like the woman who owned them.

Jaeger turned his head to the right and looked toward the window where she stood, watching the traffic on the famous street below. Like the stones, something in her called to him. She wasn't beautiful, precisely, but she was...*dazzling*. With her naturally curly hair and cat-like green eyes, her stubborn chin and long, lean swimmer's body, she was exotic, interesting. Utterly feminine...

And majorly pissed off with him.

Jaeger knew women. He should—he'd had enough experience dealing with them. He knew when they were moody or sad. He could recognize manipulation and desperation from a mile away, could see calculation and greed with one glance. He could read body language like other people read text, and Piper Mills was five feet seven inches of pure pissiness.

Directed at him.

He wanted to ask if they'd met before, but he knew that couldn't be possible. Apart from those two months last year, his memory was impeccable, and he knew they'd never crossed paths before that. The probability of them meeting during his lost months was slim indeed. Credit cards, air tickets and a private investigator had filled in the blanks for the majority of the time he'd lost.

He'd spent July in Burma and Thailand, on the trail of a fantastic ruby he'd subsequently lost in an auction held in the back rooms of Bangkok. From Bangkok, he'd flown to Milan, where he visited Ballantyne and Company and examined and purchased some inexpensive art deco jewelry. He'd spent some extra time in Milan, not unusual since it was his favorite city, but the visit had ended badly. On his way to the airport, the taxi he'd traveled in was T-boned by a delivery truck, and he'd become the human filling in a vehicular sandwich. He'd sustained a broken clavicle and bleeding on the brain.

They'd stabilized him in Milan. Then Linc sent their private plane and a team of doctors to Italy, and Jaeger was transferred back to New York. After operating to stem the bleeding on his brain, they'd kept him in an induced coma until the swelling in his brain subsided. He woke up to the news he'd lost ten weeks of his life, and his beloved uncle, the man who'd raised the Ballantyne siblings, was dead.

Jaeger pulled his eyes from the long-legged beauty at the window and turned back to the stones. Kashmir Blues...why did that phrase keep jumping into his brain?

Jaeger picked up his desk phone and punched in a number, impatient for Beckett to answer. His brother had
a computer-like brain and remembered most of their
uncle's many stories. From the age of ten, he, Beckett
and Sage, along with the housekeeper's son, Linc—who
Connor adopted along with the rest of them—listened
to Connor's gemstone-related tales. Beckett always remembered the finer details.

"You're calling because you can't handle the hot chick
and you need my help?"

Jaeger scowled at his brother's greeting. "Yeah, *that's*
why I'm calling," he sarcastically replied.

"Thought so. Hang on, sweetheart. I'll be right there
to rescue you."

If he'd been alone, he would have told his cocky
younger brother exactly what he thought of his comment.
Because he wasn't, Jaeger just asked him what jumped
into his head when he heard the phrase *Kashmir Blues*.

It took Beckett less than ten seconds to respond.
"Great-Grandfather Mac called a cache of sapphires
he saw in the London store the Kashmir Blues. Fifteen
brilliant stones. Because other gem dealers, like Jim
Moreau, also saw them, we know they definitely existed and weren't just a figment of Mac's whiskey-soaked
imagination. Strangely, they've never, as far as I know,
turned up again."

Until, maybe, today. Could these ten stones be part
of the original fifteen? If they were, Jaeger was staring
at a hell of a find. He placed the handset back into its
cradle. Good God. Could he really be looking at the biggest gem discovery of the last fifty years?

"Well, are they worth anything?" Piper demanded, her
hands on her slim hips. Jaeger couldn't help noticing the

sun shone through her thin silk blouse. He could see the curve of her breast, the lace of her bra. He wanted her stones but, by God, he also wanted her with a ferocity that roared and clawed.

Pull yourself together, Ballantyne. This is not the time to think about sex.

"Yeah, they are worth something," Jaeger slowly replied. "But how much, right now, I'm not sure. I need to do some tests. I'd like other experts to look at them."

"I thought *you* were an expert."

"I am. But with stones like these—" magnificent, important, breathtaking, *expensive* stones "—I like to make doubly sure."

"I'd prefer to keep this between us," Piper said, lifting a stubborn, sexy chin.

"My other experts are my two brothers, Linc and Beckett, and my sister, Sage. They are all Ballantyne directors, and we don't discuss our clients with anyone else."

Piper folded her arms across her chest and stared down at the floor, lifting one hand to hold her riotous hair back from her face. When she looked up at him, her expression was fierce. "No games, no lies...if I wanted to sell them right now, what would you offer me?"

"Do you need the money?" She didn't look like she did. Her clothes were fashionable, her shoes new.

Piper dropped her hand and sent him a hard stare. "I know you might not realize this, but some people do."

Jaeger held her hot eyes, not bothering to tell her he'd seen more poverty on one trip to Southeast Asia than she could ever comprehend. He knew what people would do for money; he'd witnessed what people would do for money.

He couldn't help that he was the heir to a dynasty, that he was wealthy beyond belief, but he worked damn hard every day of his life. He didn't lie or cheat people out of their stones. He paid good prices for good gems. He didn't deal in blood diamonds, and he boycotted mines and miners using child labor. Like his parents, like Connor, he operated ethically, dammit!

Annoyingly, the urge to explain was strong.

What *was it* about this woman? And why did he care what she thought about him?

"Give me a number," Piper demanded, but he heard the fear in her voice, and her hope that the gems would solve a very big problem.

"I'd give you a million," Jaeger said, just to test her. Actually, he'd consider paying her double, but he wanted to see what her reaction would be.

Her shoulders slumped and she bit the inside of her lip. So a million was short of what she needed.

"Three?" Piper asked.

So three was what she needed. For what?

"Maybe two," Jaeger said, pretending to think about her offer.

Again, there was a flash of disappointment in her green eyes. God, such beautiful eyes. Eyes that tempted him to cut her a check for the full three mil and then kiss her senseless before ripping off her clothes.

"Can I think about that?" Piper asked, placing her thumbnail between her teeth.

Jaeger slowly rolled up the velvet, capturing the gems inside. "Sure, but I'm not making the offer today, Ms. Mills. Or tomorrow."

Because, despite the party in his pants, he wasn't a

novice dealer who could be swayed by a pretty face, a rocking body and sad, possibly desperate, eyes.

Piper's luscious mouth fell open, and he wondered what she tasted like, whether her lips were as soft and plump, as sweet, as they looked. He knew her smile would be dynamite. He wanted to see it, feel it on his skin. *God, Ballantyne, get a frickin' grip.*

"But…but…you said—"

Jaeger stood up and placed his hands on his desk, leaning down so their eyes were level. "I'm not making a million-plus offer on gems I know next to nothing about. I do that in the field when I have nothing to rely on but my gut. But I'm not prepared to do that now when I don't need to take the risk." Jaeger stood up and pushed his hand through his hair. "I'll make you a solid offer after I've done some research—"

"What type of research?" Piper asked, obviously frustrated.

"We use various databases, including those set up by Interpol and the FBI, to check whether any similar gems are reported stolen. I want my siblings to look at the stones."

"How long will it take?"

Jaeger shrugged. "As long as it takes."

"I can always take them to Moreau's."

Ballantyne and Company's biggest competition.

"That's your prerogative, but you won't," Jaeger said, watching her eyes, watching frustration chase fear through all the green. "You won't because you want me to buy these stones. For some reason you want me to have them. Why?"

Piper tried to dismiss his statement, but he saw the flash of agreement in her eyes. Why did he think there was so much more happening here than her wanting to sell the stones? He felt like she had a story and he was part of it.

"You have two weeks to make me a solid offer," Piper told him, picking up her bag and pulling it over her shoulder. "After that, I start shopping around."

Jaeger nodded. "I need your contact information. If you'll give me a little time, I'll enter the details of the stones into our database and print you a receipt, stating that they are in our custody."

"I'll give you my card. Just send the receipt. I know you won't steal them or swap them."

Her instinctive trust in him made him feel warm.

"All I need is for you to keep my name, and the fact that I have these jewels, confidential. Can you do that?"

Why was she so concerned about privacy and confidentiality? Could these sapphires be stolen? God, he hoped not. If they were, he'd have to report her, and he did not want to see Piper arrested and jailed for handling stolen property.

The only thing she should handle was him.

Jaeger gave himself a mental punch to the head. It was time to act like an adult, a partner in Ballantyne and Company, like the hard-ass gem hunter he was reputed to be.

"You did hear me say I'll be running these stones through the Interpol and FBI databases, didn't you?"

Piper's only response was a searing look. Shaking her head, she pulled a business card out of her bag and handed it over.

Jaeger looked down at the card and flicked the edge with his finger. "You're an art appraiser?"

Piper shook her head. "You really did take my words to heart, didn't you?"

Jaeger frowned. What did that odd comment mean? From the moment she'd walked into his office, he'd seen half-formed statements on her lips, in her eyes. She'd start to speak, but then she'd bite the words back, acting as if there was something she needed to say but wouldn't. What was going on behind those pretty eyes?

Mind your own business, Ballantyne. She's a client, nothing more.

But there was definitely something odd about the very gorgeous Ms. Mills, Jaeger decided as he watched her walk across his office and yank open the door. She turned back to look at him and lifted her index finger to point at him. "I'm trusting you to look after my stones. Trusting you, after everything that's happened, is a very big deal for me, Ballantyne."

Before he could reply, she walked out of his office. Jaeger stared at his half-open door, feeling like she was leaving him with just a few pieces of a puzzle.

He'd find the missing pieces, he thought, sitting back down behind his desk. He'd start by running her name through as many databases as he had access to and see what popped up.

Because, he was damn sure, something would.

Why hadn't she called Jaeger on his BS?

The question played on repeat in her head, like nails on a chalkboard, since she'd hurried out of Jaeger's office eight hours before. Why hadn't she mentioned their past to get it out in the open? Why did she go along with his I've-never-met-you-before attitude?

Piper turned the corner onto her street, her tote over

one shoulder and her arms around two brown sacks of baby food and diapers. And chocolate… After a day like today, she needed chocolate. Baby food, diapers and chocolate… God, her life was so exciting.

Not.

Well, it had been! Back when she was with that six-foot-something slab of sexiness… No, that wasn't what she meant to think! Dammit! *So why didn't you say anything about the time you spent together in Milan, Mills? What was with that nonsense?*

Piper shifted her sacks and tried to blow a curl out of her eye. Pride…pride was a factor. She'd wanted *him* to mention Milan, to be the one to go there, to say how nice it was to see her again. She'd wanted him to ask if he could take her to dinner…to bed. She'd never thought, not once, not even after he'd shut her out completely, that she'd be so utterly forgettable.

And, man, it killed her—in a dagger-to-the-heart way—that he didn't remember her. Spending the night with him was a highlight of her life. Conversely, she was, for him, a forgettable experience in what was obviously a long line of sexual encounters.

And Jaeger forgetting her, forgetting about Milan, made all her feelings around her father and his neglect bubble to the surface. She was an adult, and she should have been over feeling hurt by Mick's actions, but she couldn't help remembering the times she'd opened the door to him and watched him struggle to remember her name. Her mother and whatever she gave Mick were important to him, not Piper. When her mom died, her father stopped visiting the house in Brooklyn altogether, and the only time he'd spoken to Piper after the funeral was to demand she give him the sapphires.

She'd lived with rejection all her life. Jaeger not re-membering her was just another version of the same thing.

That being said, Jaeger's actions still didn't make sense. Why the pretense? They'd agreed to keep it busi-nesslike when they met again, so why not take her calls right after Milan? Why did he go to such lengths to ig-nore her and then pretend not to remember her?

What game was he playing?

Maybe she should've avoided Jaeger altogether and gone directly to Moreau's. Why hadn't she?

Jaeger paid better, according to Mr. Hendricks, than all the other gem dealers. She'd also, in Milan, prom-ised Jaeger she'd bring the stones to him. Thanks to her father being a thief, it was important that she kept her promises. Piper strongly believed in keeping her word, in doing the right thing.

So, was not telling Jaeger about Ty the right thing to do?

The thought slammed into her, holding all the power of a rogue wave. Of course it was. Meeting Jaeger again changed nothing! She knew, everyone knew, that Jaeger wasn't daddy material. He'd openly admitted a wife and kids weren't part of his plans.

There was nothing worse than knowing who your parent was and knowing he didn't care enough to be a part of your life. Piper wouldn't put her son in the same position she'd been in.

Approaching her house, she pushed the wrought iron gate open with her hip and noticed her lemon verbena and geraniums needed water and the pots needed re-painting. Yeah, that probably wouldn't be happening anytime soon.

"Piper!"

Standing on the top step, Piper whirled around quickly. She wobbled, her bags tipped and she struggled to find her balance.

"Dammit, Ballantyne!"

Jaeger walked up to her, his hands in the air. "Why so jumpy? I just called your name."

He didn't need to know she'd been thinking about him and felt like she'd conjured him out of thin air. "It's been a long day. Why are you here?"

Her skin prickled as Jaeger slowly approached her, his long legs eating up the space between them. As he came closer, she caught a hint of masculine cologne, warm skin. God, she remembered the smell and texture and taste of him—spicy, warm...

He interrupted that train of thought by taking her groceries from her and looking into the bags. "Wine, baby food, diapers, a popular men's magazine, tampons, chocolate and hummus. That's quite a mixed bag."

Piper blushed, then frowned. "Stop examining my shopping. It's rude."

"Are you going to invite me inside?" Jaeger demanded, and Piper knew it wasn't a suggestion but an order.

Piper shifted from foot to foot as she thought about what to say. Ceri, her nanny and good friend, was upstairs with Ty, and Piper really, really didn't want Jaeger and Ty meeting. She didn't know what game Jaeger was playing by pretending not to remember her, but until she'd figured out the rules, she wasn't going to introduce a new player into the arena. Especially when that new player was her innocent son.

The decision was taken from her when the front door

opened behind them and Piper turned to see Ceri and Rainn standing there, each with a hand on Ty's stroller. Piper immediately dropped to her haunches and kissed her son's cheek. "Hey, there's my favorite guy."

Ty wasn't as excited to see her as usual, but he did pat her face before pushing her away so he could look around to see who was out and about.

Piper stood up, glanced at Jaeger and saw nothing but mild interest on his face when he looked at Ty. Her heart slowed down when she realized he didn't see what she did; he didn't see anything of himself in Ty. *Thank you, God.*

"We all needed some air, so we're going to take a walk," Ceri said, worried. Her eyes bounced off Piper's face, onto Jaeger's and her mouth fell open. "Wow, you're—"

"Jaeger Ballantyne." Jaeger smiled at Ceri, his eyes crinkled and Piper's stomach flipped over once, twice. She'd forgotten how sexy his smile was, how it transformed his face from hard-ass to gorgeous. Jaeger shook hands with Rainn after the twins carried Ty's stroller down the steps.

"I'm Ceri Brown, and that's Rainn. And the cutie is Ty."

Piper started to explain that Ceri was her nanny, that Rainn was her twin and that they lived in the apartment below hers, but she stopped. She didn't owe him explanations of any kind!

Ceri managed to pull her admiring gaze off Jaeger to look at Piper. "Do you want to join us? We'll be back in about a half hour."

Piper bit her lip and shook her head. "I think I'll skip. Jaeger needs to have a word."

Ceri tipped her head to the side, curious. "How do you two know each other?"

"That's a long and complicated story," Piper replied. So long and so complicated. "I'll see you in a bit, okay?"

Piper and Jaeger stood on the top step and watched Rainn tip the stroller back on two wheels. Ty's belly laugh drifted over to her; it was another of his favorite games. There went her heart, she thought. Her kid and the two people as close to her as siblings.

"Cute family," Jaeger said. "They are young to have a kid."

Piper started to tell him Ty was hers, not theirs, but she just managed to catch the words. She darted a look at him, her interest caught by the emotion in his eyes. Longing, sadness, pain? Why would Jaeger Ballantyne—who'd routinely told the world he would follow in his uncle Connor's footsteps and remain resolutely single—look envious of what he erroneously assumed was a young family on their way to a park? She had to be misinterpreting his look and his emotions, Piper decided. This was Jaeger Ballantyne, after all, who thought the world was overpopulated.

Who'd refused her calls and pretended not to know who she was.

He didn't deserve her explanations.

At the corner, Ceri waved at them, and Piper rolled her shoulders.

"Are you here to make an offer for my stones?" Piper asked, wincing at the eagerness in her voice. Maybe this ordeal would be done sooner than she'd expected.

"I'm no closer to offering you a deal than I was earlier," Jaeger replied.

Damn.

"Invite me in, Piper." Jaeger reached past her to push

open her front door. "We both know that we have a lot more than sapphires to talk about."

Now he wanted to talk about what happened in Milan? And really, after all her unanswered phone calls, what was there to discuss? Apparently everything they'd needed to say had been captured in the last kiss they'd shared outside the hotel entrance. It had been tender and sweet, regretful and poignant but very, very final.

Thank you and goodbye, think of me occasionally, remember this time we spent together with a smile. Have a wonderful life.

A silent but powerful acknowledgment that when they met again, they would not pick up where they left off…

They hadn't agreed to treat each other like strangers… but maybe it was better if they did. Jaeger still had the ability to keep her off balance.

"You're giving me the silent treatment again. I can't decide if it's because your mind is revving or because you are being stubborn." Jaeger bent his knees so their eyes were level. "Either way, we are doing this. We can talk either here or over a cup of coffee or, if the gods are smiling on me, a glass of whiskey. But we are going to have a conversation, Ms. Mills."

Yeah, they were. Piper saw the determination in his eyes, saw the hard-ass negotiator who bought and sold valuable gemstones on six continents. Jaeger wasn't going anywhere until he'd said whatever was on his mind. She had to be very careful to keep control of this conversation; they had to stay on topic. She wanted to know why he'd blocked her from contacting him after Milan, but Ty was firmly off-limits. As was the fact that she wanted him naked and panting.

Why did she keep thinking that?

She felt like she was standing in a field planted with land mines and she needed to carefully pick a path to safety.

"I would give a rare red diamond to know what you are thinking," Jaeger said, breaking into her thoughts.

Piper blinked and refocused. She pushed her hair back and briefly closed her eyes.

"I'll make us coffee," Piper capitulated, resigned.

Jaeger put a hand on her lower back and pushed her toward the stairs leading up to her living quarters. "Sounds good. It would sound better if you offered a shot of whiskey with it. I've had a rough day, too."

Three

Piper took her cup of coffee into her den-slash-office and found Jaeger standing in front of the fireplace, admiring a series of ink and pencil drawings hanging on the wall, a tumbler of whiskey in his hand.

Piper hesitated in the doorway, taking a moment to catch her breath. Every inch of Jaeger's six-foot-something frame reflected his masculinity; his legs were long and muscled, his hands were broad and his fingers blunt-tipped, his chest wide. He made her feel smaller, feminine and sexier.

Smoking hot she could deal with, sort of, but he looked so at ease in her messy space—and it felt so right for him be here, with her… The thought liquefied her knees.

"These are fantastic. Who is the artist?"

"She's Danish. I bought those from a gallery in Copenhagen, and I've never found any more of her work.

Pity, because she's fabulous." Wanting to delay the subject of Milan and her unanswered calls, she gestured to an oil seascape on the opposite wall. "That's Joonie Paul, also unknown, equally fabulous."

Jaeger, tall and broad and a work of art she could look at all day long, turned so those fabulous eyes met hers. "You obviously love art," he stated.

"I'm an art appraiser. It comes with the job."

Jaeger sat down on the ottoman, rested his forearms on his thighs, the glass almost disappearing in his big hand. He stared at the multicolored Persian carpet between his feet before raising his face. Under his gaze, Piper felt like a deer caught in the headlights, his eyes pinning her to her spot on the couch.

"Let's talk about Milan."

Okay, here we go. She was finally going to get an explanation about why he'd acted like a hemorrhoid. And his explanation had better be good...

"Apparently we met in Milan, at Ballantyne's, in late April?"

Met? Is that what the most elusive, popular bachelors in Manhattan were calling three fun, fabulous dates and a night of off-the-charts sex? Geez, things were different across the Brooklyn Bridge. Piper nodded. What else could she do? It was the truth, after all.

"I presume we discussed your sapphires in Milan, and that's why you left so many messages for me in the fall of last year?"

Yeah, *that's* what happened. It took all of her willpower not to roll her eyes. Piper watched as Jaeger shot to his feet and swiftly walked over to the window, pushing the heavy drape away to look outside. His big shoulders were up around his ears and tension radiated from him. Okay, what was happening here?

"Why are you asking me these questions? You were *there*."

Jaeger turned and pushed the ball of his shoulder into the wall, crossing his foot over his ankle in an attempt to look relaxed. The expression on his masculine face was inscrutable, but she saw the emotion churning in his eyes, the tension in his sexy mouth. His clever lips were thin and tight. Jaeger looked confused and unsettled.

Why? Why would he...?

"You don't remember?" she asked. It was the only plausible scenario she could think of.

Jaeger pointed his index finger at her in a you've-nailed-it gesture. Piper sucked in a long breath. Jaeger, tall, ripped and oh-so-sexy, genuinely didn't remember her, Milan, their dates, the stones. Or that they slept together. God, Italy was so fantastic, and he didn't remember? Piper's mind raced. Was that a curse or a blessing?

But how could he not remember?

"Seriously? You don't remember anything about Milan?" Piper clarified. "You don't remember us meeting? Going to dinner—"

You don't remember anything about the night we spent in your hotel room? Me kissing my way down your body, the last time in the shower when we shook the foundations of the hotel? Your gasps, my screams? The way we struggled to say goodbye the following morning?

She scratched her forehead. "What happened, Jaeger?"

Jaeger linked his hands behind his head. His big biceps pulled the cotton fabric tight across his arms. The shirt gaped open and she saw a hint of tanned, muscled flesh above his belt. And just above his belt buckle would be a thin strip of hair. Her lips had traced that line of hair, going lower and…

Jaeger dropped his arms and jammed his hands into the pockets of his pants. His straight black brows pulled together. "I'll tell you why I don't remember, but would you mind telling me about us meeting in Milan first?"

Piper crossed her legs and linked her arms around her knee. How much to say? *Keep it simple*…

"I had some free time in Milan and I walked into your store, wondering if someone could tell me about the stones, even though I only had a photo on my phone. You were there and, because you're you and you work fast, you invited me to dinner."

"We ate at a trattoria I often go to, the one in Linate?" He saw her confused expression and explained. "Credit card receipts. I paid. The date was April the twenty-ninth. Is that right?"

Sure was; she remembered the date she conceived Ty as well as she knew his birth date. Since it was also the last time she'd had sex in, oh, about *forever*, it wasn't a date easy to forget. Piper started to explain they'd met the day before, but Jaeger interrupted her. "Will you tell me about that night?"

Should she tell him they slept together? No! If she did then he might do some math and suspect Ty could be his. He'd see the resemblance between him and his son and then he'd know. Six hours after meeting him again, she wasn't ready to go there, to deal with Jaeger's reaction to having a son he didn't want.

One problem at a time, she decided.

She'd delay—or even avoid—the issue, but she

wouldn't lie to Jaeger. If he asked whether they'd slept together, she'd answer and roll the dice.

She might not believe in lying, but she did believe in distraction. Besides, she was being eaten alive by curiosity. "Jaeger, why don't you remember?"

Jaeger walked back toward her, picked up his glass, took a sip and stared at her over the rim, as if he were trying to decide what to tell her. "I was leaving Milan, on my way to the airport. The police reports said that a..."

"Police reports?" Piper interjected, her voice rising.

Jaeger frowned at her interruption. "I was in a taxi when a truck slammed into us. I was in its direct path."

Piper just stared at him, not sure whether she was hearing him properly. Jaeger was in a car accident the morning they'd said goodbye? "But—"

"Do you want to hear this or are you going to keep interrupting?" Jaeger muttered. "I was in a bad way. I had various injuries, the most serious of which was swelling and bleeding on the brain."

"God, Jaeger." Piper placed her hand over her mouth, horrified. She stood up and faced him, wishing she could touch him. It wasn't enough that he was standing in front of her looking healthy and fit—deliciously healthy and fit. She needed to examine him to make sure, dammit!

The thought of him being so injured made her world tilt upside down.

"My siblings and a medical team came to Italy and accompanied me back to the States. I had a couple of surgeries, and then they kept me in an induced coma for six weeks. When I woke up, the last thing I remembered was landing in Bangkok a month before the accident. After that, nothing."

"God, I'm so sorry. I had no idea!"

"Nobody did. We kept it very quiet. My siblings put the word out that I was hunting for an emerald in a very remote area of Colombia where communications were dicey. They told anyone who asked that they weren't sure when I would return."

"Why didn't you just tell the world what really happened?"

Jaeger grimaced. "There were a few reasons. Most important, my siblings were trying to keep the news of my accident from our uncle Connor. He raised me and my sibs from the time I was ten, and when the accident happened, he was in a scary stage of Alzheimer's. The stage when everything is upsetting and confusing. Knowing I was so injured possibly would've accelerated his mental deterioration."

Piper tipped her head to the side, thinking back. "But…didn't he pass on around that time?"

Jaeger nodded, his expression grim. "He died ten days before they pulled me out of the coma. God, the weeks following were hell."

"I'm glad you're okay, and I'm sorry about your uncle."

Jaeger ran a hand over the back of his head, obviously uncomfortable. "Yeah, thanks."

Piper pulled her bottom lip with her finger and thumb. "Well, that explains a hell of a lot. What it doesn't explain is how you linked me to Milan," she said, curious.

"This morning, I knew there was something you weren't telling me. It made me curious."

Oh, there was quite a bit she still wasn't telling him…

"I did a Google search on you, but I didn't realize I was also searching my own computer and the Ballantyne server. I had the usual Google hits, but it was what was on my computer that I found interesting."

Piper bit the inside of her lip. "Pray tell."

"I hired a PI after the accident. He dug deep into that month I spent overseas, and he mentioned in his report that you and I had dinner." Piper opened her mouth to speak, but Jaeger beat her to it. "No, I don't know how he found out who you were and how we met."

"And how did you find out about the calls and messages I sent to you?"

Amusement sparked in Jaeger's eyes. "My family is fairly high-profile, and we work in a high-risk business. Security logs all calls, messages and emails coming in. If we don't respond to the calls and emails, and if they are ongoing, the person making contact is put on a special list."

Piper narrowed her eyes at him. "A special list?"

"The kooks and crazies list." Jaeger grinned, and Piper felt like she was standing in a beam of pure sunlight.

Oh, God, not good. When he smiled, her hands itched to undo the buttons on his shirt, to spread the fabric apart and rediscover his hard chest, the ridges of his stomach. She wanted to unbuckle his belt, unzip his fly, take his...

Whoa! Alrighty, that's enough now.

Piper tapped the tip of her finger against her bottom lip. He should have been the last man in the world to rev her engine; he was a commitment-phobic playboy who would never change. But from the moment she'd met him, Jaeger had the ability to short-circuit her brain.

She wasn't the carefree woman she'd been a year and a half back, though. She had responsibilities now. This wasn't about her and what she wanted—hot, curl-her-toes and burn-her-sheets sex.

So stop imagining him naked and think!

He had an ironclad good excuse for not contacting her after Milan, and his explanation went some way toward erasing the anger and hurt she'd lived with for so long. But did it fundamentally change anything?

Piper couldn't see that it did.

She still needed to sell her sapphires to save her house and provide the stable, calm environment she needed to raise Ty. Her life before Simms's visit was good for a single mom juggling a career. She loved living in this house; she paid the bills; she had people she trusted with Ty.

She needed to keep doing that.

Should she tell Jaeger about Ty?

Not now, was her gut instinct. She needed to tackle one problem at a time. Securing her house was her priority, and she didn't want the negotiations around her stones clouded by any emotions—panic, guilt, responsibility—that Jaeger might experience after hearing she was the mother of his son.

Unlike her own mother, she would not spend her life waiting for the father of her child to discover his daddy-and-husband instincts.

"I'm sorry about your hassles with security, but they had no way of knowing you were trying to sell me some stunning sapphires."

Piper forced her attention back to their conversation and slowly nodded. Sure, *that. Let's go with the sapphire excuse and pretend I wasn't also trying to find the courage to tell you I was carrying your baby.*

"Wonderful."

Jaeger's hand pushing a curl behind her ear jerked her

attention back to reality. Oh, God, he was now standing a couple of inches from her, and with every breath she took, she inhaled his soap and cologne smell, his Jaegerness. So close she could see the flecks of silver in his eyes, the tiny scar bisecting his right eyebrow, another on his top lip...

How could she still be so attracted to him? Why was she desperate to feel his lips on hers, his hands on her bare skin? Yet she wanted nothing more than to stand on her tiptoes and rest her lips against his.

Once more, just once...

"That night? Did we—?"

She couldn't allow him to finish the question. She didn't want to lie to him, so she stopped his words the only way she knew how: she pushed up onto her toes and slammed her lips on his.

Jaeger pulled away, looked at her in surprise, blinked once, then grabbed the front of her shirt and yanked her back into him. Piper sighed when his mouth moved against hers, expertly, seductively. Without thought, she moved closer to him, her hands lifting to hold his strong neck, her fingers playing with the waves at the back of his head.

She sighed. This was what she'd been missing, dreaming of—enjoying Jaeger's broad hands on her hips, his erection pushing into her stomach. Piper made a tiny noise in the back of her throat, and Jaeger dialed the kiss up from immensely enjoyable to combustible. His tongue swept into her mouth and his hand on the top of her butt pulled her into him, so close a piece of paper couldn't have slid between them. His mouth created havoc on hers, and she felt herself falling into the magical space she'd visited eighteen months ago.

Jaeger was kissing her—his hand was holding the curve of her butt, his other hand was holding the back of her head—and he was kissing her with equal parts skill and desperation.

Then Piper felt one of Jaeger's hands sneak under her shirt, dance over her skin, and she shivered. His fingers moved slowly up her rib cage and flirted with the sides of her breasts. His thumb swiped her nipple through the lace of her bra, and God, he felt so incredibly good...

The front door opened. Ceri's "We're home" had Piper jerking away from Jaeger. Whirling around and stepping away from Jaeger, she looked across the living room to the front door, to where Ceri stood, Ty on her hip.

Something was wrong, Piper thought, instantly morphing from lover to mother. She narrowed her eyes. Ty had his head on Ceri's shoulder and he looked a little pale, almost listless. Ignoring Jaeger, Piper hurried toward them. Ty saw her and held his arms out, leaning forward, a silent plea for her to take him. Piper gathered him into her and held his head against her shoulder. "Hey, baby boy. What's the matter, huh?"

Ceri bit her bottom lip. "I think he might have an earache. He's bumping his hand against his ear. He doesn't have a fever, but he's not himself." Ceri looked at her watch and grimaced. "I need to go, but call me if I can help or if he gets worse."

"Thanks, Ceri."

Ceri closed the front door behind her as Piper held the back of her hand to Ty's forehead, to his cheek. Ceri was right, he didn't have a fever, but his eyes seemed dull. She cuddled him close and rocked on her feet, inhaling his little boy smell, feeling his breath against her neck.

"Love you to the moon and back," she murmured,

her hand rubbing circles on his back. "My beautiful, beautiful, boy."

"Everything okay?"

The deep voice drifted over, and Piper spun around. Jaeger pressed his shoulder into the door frame of the den, his face inscrutable. Her boy got all his beauty from his father, she thought again. Piper rested her cheek on Ty's head. "Ty isn't feeling too well."

"So he's yours and doesn't belong to the kids downstairs?"

"Yep." Being Ty's mommy wasn't something she could keep secret, even if she wanted to. Being a mother, Ty's mother, was her biggest achievement. Everything— her master's degree in art history, her pre-Ty career, traveling the world looking at great art—paled to insignificance beside the importance of raising her son.

"So, who was the young guy?"

"Ceri and Rainn are twins. Ceri is my nanny, but Rainn also helps out. They live in the apartment downstairs," Piper replied, pulling a curl from Ty's fist. "In between being a nanny, she works as an illustrator for children's books. Rainn is studying medicine. I give them a kick-ass subsidy on their rent and they look after Ty when I need to work. They have six brothers and sisters, all a lot younger than them, and their parents also take in foster kids. They've taught me more about babies than I've learned from books."

Piper looked at her watch. She needed to feed and bathe Ty. She and Ty had a schedule, and Jaeger's presence messed with her routine and with—well—her head.

She'd just kissed the hell out of her baby's daddy in her den. What was wrong with her?

Uh, sexy guy, good kisser, been a long drought?

She needed to give Ty her full attention. He was, thank God, the easiest child on the planet, but he was rarely sick. She felt a surge of panic hit the back of her throat. He was just a little off-color right now and if he became sicker, she could handle it. That was why God made drugs and doctor's offices. She was in Brooklyn, dammit, not in a shack in outer Mongolia.

Piper picked up a soft toy from out of Ty's playpen, handed it to Ty and closed her eyes.

Needing some space and distance between her and Jaeger, she patted Ty's bottom. "I need to change him." She darted a look at Jaeger and silently cursed when she saw he was as cool and composed as he always was, like he hadn't had a wild woman sucking the life out of him just a few moments before. "Can you let yourself out?"

Jaeger's eyes bounced between her and Ty, and he eventually nodded his head. "Yeah." He gestured to Ty. "I hope he'll be okay."

"He'll be fine," Piper said. Piper looked at her feet before forcing her eyes back to Jaeger's. She glanced at his mouth, sighed and wished he'd kiss her again.

No kissing Jaeger, she told herself. This was a complicated situation as it was. She didn't need to add a truckload of sexual tension to the growing pile of craziness.

"Look," she said, "I think we need to forget that kiss, pretend it never happened."

Jaeger slowly shook his head. "Not an option. There are too many things I've already forgotten. I'm not adding kissing you to that list."

Four

In his West Street penthouse, Jaeger rolled out of his empty bed and padded to the kitchen, glancing at the Hudson River through the massive windows that were a key feature of the apartment. This place was ridiculously big for one person, but he liked returning to light and space and quiet after his trips abroad.

A lot of light, space and quiet, Jaeger thought. *Thanks, Uncle Connor.*

Connor had left everything he owned to his four adopted children, including property and equal shares in Ballantyne International, with its many subsidiaries, the most important of which were the exclusive jewelry stores around the world. Their childhood home, a brownstone on the Upper East Side, was also jointly owned by the four of them, but he and Beckett retained their own residences. Beckett had offered his place to fam-

ly friends from London visiting the city for a month,
so he was temporarily living in Jaeger's apartment. Jaeger didn't mind. It wasn't like he didn't have the room.

He liked this apartment, but its designer perfection
was wasted on him. He was hardly here, and it felt sterile and cold. He preferred Piper's relaxed bohemian
style, a mishmash of old and new furniture, interesting
art and the ordinary household items indicating people
used the space, lived and loved there. An open book, a
corked wine bottle, magnets on the fridge, a playpen in
the corner...

God, she had a kid.

He'd met her yesterday, so he couldn't exactly ask,
but Jaeger wondered who Ty's father was and whether
he was in the picture. Were they together when he and
Piper had dinner in Milan? Piper didn't seem like the
type to cheat on her man, but Jaeger knew how wrong
he could be when he made assumptions.

He'd thought Jess would live past six weeks, never
imagined she'd be a victim of sudden infant death syn-
drome. He'd assumed he and Andrea needed time to
grieve and they'd find their way back to each other.

And he'd never believed that he could forget a chunk
of his life.

God, he'd been so lucky. What if he'd forgotten more?
What if he'd had no memories of his parents, his childhood, Connor... God, no memories of Jess? As it always did when he thought too long about his amnesia,
panic bubbled and boiled. It was a couple of months of
his life lost, but to Jaeger, it was symbolic of everything
that went away.

Like his parents, Jess, Connor...those memories were
inaccessible.

His body had healed quickly, but his mind hadn't. He coped with the uncertainty by minimizing risk, particularly in his personal life. No relationships, no kids, no connections. He was never going to bring someone new into his life, since life had this habit of whisking away the people he loved.

Few people knew what it felt like when grief plunged its icy hand into your rib cage and ripped out your heart. He couldn't even call it pain; it went beyond that. He'd had his heart replaced with an organ pumping cold regret, hot anger, crippling guilt and searing agony all at the same time. Those emotions gradually faded, but he remembered enough to want not to go there again.

Besides, even if he desired to revisit that madness—he didn't; he'd rather have been stabbed in the eye with a red-hot poker—the nature of his work made it difficult to sustain a relationship. He dropped in and out of New York like a yo-yo, and his schedule could turn on a dime. If he received a tip from any of his numerous contacts around the world, he was on the next plane out, hoping to be the first to do the deal. He had no illusions about the loyalty of his contacts—they passed the same information to his rivals—but they generally gave him a head start, probably because he paid them a slightly higher commission than his competitors did.

International gem dealing was a cutthroat business, and Jaeger cut throats, metaphorically, very well indeed. He was ruthless, demanding and persistent. He liked his life, liked the opportunity to see places few people did, to meet with people from different cultures, to visit villages where time stood still. He liked the freedom his work gave him, and he loved the adrenaline of making a deal.

He'd never, not for a single second, thought he'd find

the same adrenaline kissing Piper, someone he'd met before but whom he couldn't remember, a woman with a kid.

A baby…a species he'd vowed to avoid after he'd chosen a tiny white coffin painted with delicate pink roses.

"Bro."

Jaeger turned to see his younger brother walking into his kitchen, scratching his bare chest. Beckett looked like someone had dragged him backward through a bush, but his blue eyes, darker than Jaeger's, looked lazy and satisfied.

"Is she still here?"

Beck shook his head. "Nope, she left a half hour ago."

Thank God, Jaeger thought, not in the mood to make small talk with one of Beckett's short-term women. *Hypocrite*, his inner voice mocked. Until eighteen months ago, their women would've bumped into each other in the kitchen. But since his accident, the revolving door to his bedroom was broken, and he'd slept with only a select few. He hadn't lost his libido—it was working just fine—but he wanted something more than a quick bang, a roll in the sack.

He didn't want a relationship, though, which left him in no man's—or little sex—land.

"Jay, coffee?"

Jaeger nodded and walked into the kitchen. He sat on one of the uncomfortable seats at the sleek granite island separating the kitchen from the rest of the open-plan apartment.

Jaeger watched Beckett, who was far more at home in his kitchen than he was, make coffee.

"Do you really think those sapphires you saw yesterday could be part of the Kashmir Blues?" Beckett asked, pushing a cup of coffee over the counter toward him. Jaeger nodded his thanks and lifted the cup to his mouth.

"There's a good possibility." Jaeger smiled as excitement jumped into Beckett's eyes. Although he was their director of finance and their master strategist, Beck loved the hunt for gems as much as Jaeger did. He knew finding the Kashmir Blues was a freakin' big deal.

"Holy crap, Jay, that's unbelievable."

Jaeger told Beck about Piper, about them meeting in Milan, that Ballantyne security had kept her away when he'd been in the hospital and afterward.

"She must've been desperate to sell those sapphires," Beck stated, leaning against a counter and crossing his legs at the ankles. "But if she was, why didn't she sell them to someone else?"

"It would be easier to answer that question if I could remember meeting her in Milan."

"The doctors say you probably never will."

And that pissed him off. He wanted to remember Piper, wanted to remember what they spoke about, talked about, whether there was something else he was missing. And dammit, he really felt like he was missing something. Something huge.

"Could the sapphires be stolen?" Beck asked, pulling Jaeger back to the present.

He wanted to say no, but he wasn't sure. "I'm running a background check."

"If the sapphs are the Kashmir Blues then we are looking at paying her five million or more. That's a hell of a payout, but we'd make a massive return."

Yeah, he was aware.

Beck tapped Jaeger's shoulder as he walked out of the kitchen to shower and dress. Jaeger thought he should get ready, too. He had a busy day ahead. He was valuing a collection of vintage jewelry belonging to a rapacious, childless scion of New York society. He couldn't wait to see what Amelia Grant-Childs had in her vault.

His thoughts wandered back to his own vault and the sapphires within it. From there it was a mini-jump to Piper, remembering her slim body in his arms, her soft lips, her spicy mouth, the passion that flashed and ignited when he kissed her.

No married women. No kids.

He ignored the mantra in his head, walked back into his bedroom and picked up his phone off the credenza where he'd left it to recharge. Piper's card was under the phone, and he quickly dialed her number and waited for it to ring. Calling her just because he wanted to hear her voice was *pathetic*.

That didn't stop him.

"Hello?" She sounded exhausted, Jaeger realized.

"Hi, it's me... Jaeger."

"Oh, hi. Listen, it's really not a good time for me. We're just walking in, Ty is screaming for me and I need to give him some medicine."

"Walking in from where?" It was barely seven, for God's sake!

"Ty took a turn for the worse late last night. I took him to an after-hours clinic at around four this morning. He had a miserable night."

"Is he okay?" Jaeger asked, his heart lurching. His thoughts immediately went to a tiny white coffin with pink painted roses.

"He has an ear infection and it's nothing serious," Piper replied. "Ceri says he'll be fine in a day or so."

"I find it incredible that your source for all things

baby is a twenty-year-old with a nose ring," Jaeger said, smiling as he sat on the edge of his bed.

"My parents are dead and I'm a single mom. My friends, the ones who didn't ease away after I became pregnant, have even less experience with babies than I do. I don't have time to attend mommy groups, so Ceri, Rainn, the internet and a massive book on the subject are what I use."

She shouldn't be dealing with this alone, Jaeger thought.

"Anyway, you called me. How can I help you?"

Jaeger did some fast thinking to come up with an excuse. "I was wondering if you have any documentation on the sapphires?"

"Provenance. I should have thought of that. Well, there are boxes of stuff my mom inherited from her mom in the attic. I'll go up there and get them down. She was a hoarder, so if she had anything on the sapphires, then it'll be in there. Actually, I might need Rainn's help to get the boxes down, so depending on his schedule, I'll let you know when I've been through them."

"Don't bother the kid. I'll help you."

Piper's silence indicated her surprise. "It's pretty chaotic and dirty up there."

"And the jungles and villages I wander into are perfectly pristine? I'm capable of digging through a dirty attic, Piper," Jaeger said, gripping the bridge of his nose, irritated. Yeah, he lived in a fancy apartment and wore designer threads, but God, he wasn't a wuss.

Not that he really wanted to dig in a dirty attic, but he did want to see her again. As soon as possible...

He'd obviously picked up a brain-eating bug on his

st trip abroad. It was the only explanation for the ab-
urd way he was acting.

"Oh, okay. Thanks," Piper said, and Jaeger heard Ty's
ail in the background. "Sorry, I really have to go."

"Sure. Try to sleep this morning."

Piper's laugh was strained. "It's better if I don't sleep.
'll push through and sleep tonight. The trick is finding
ays to keep myself awake."

He could think of more than a few ways to keep her
rom falling asleep. All of them involved being naked.

Jaeger banged his hand against his forehead, hoping
smack the sexy images of Piper out of his mind. Why
as he going there? He couldn't have a relationship with
er; he didn't *have* relationships. And even if he did, a
elationship—an *anything*—with a single mom was ab-
olutely out of the question.

Yet he still wanted to see her again.

"Jaeger, are you there?"

Physically holding his phone? Sure. Mentally, he had
is doubts.

"Yes. Well, I hope your little guy feels better soon."

Piper thanked him and disconnected the call. Jae-
er, sitting on his massive bed in his stupidly expensive
partment, looked at his top-of-the-line phone. Nobody
hould have to rely on a book and two kids to help her
vith her baby. It was in complete contrast to what was
appening at the Ballantyne family home. Linc was a
ingle dad raising four-year-old Shaw with Linc's moth-
r's help. Their sister, Sage, still lived at home, and she
elped out with Shaw, too. Beck pitched in when they
eeded him to. It took a village of Ballantynes to raise
haw.

Because being with Shaw, being with babies, made

Jaeger break out in hives, or unshed tears, he was th
village idiot. Linc understood how hard it was for him t
be around Shaw… At least, Jaeger hoped he understoo
It wasn't like they'd had a heart-to-heart on the subjec

His siblings knew about Jess and Andrea but sinc
Jess's funeral, he never discussed her, or Andrea, wit
anyone. Ever.

Piper, despite her book and babysitters, was raisin
Ty on her own. That was incredibly brave. His bachelc
uncle often said that raising three Ballantyne boys, an
Sage, was one long, epic party. There was screaminț
vomiting, drinking straight from the bottle and the od
brush with blood.

No wonder Connor absconded to his gentlemen's clư
every Wednesday and Saturday night, leaving them wit
Jo, Linc's mom and their nanny-cum-housekeeper.

Did Piper ever get to take a break, to step out of th
madness of raising a baby on her own? Maybe he coul
earn some karmic points by inviting her to see Ameli
Grant-Childs's art collection. She'd enjoy the art, an
the break, and he'd enjoy her…

Was he really using karma as an excuse to see
woman?

Crap.

Brain-eating bugs. It was the only logical explanatior

If it wasn't for the fact that Amelia Grant-Child
used her fingerprint to unlock the door, Piper would'v
thought the large, windowless room was just anothe
immaculately decorated space in the enormous mansio
owned by the timber heiress.

Piper, trying to look secretarial, held Jaeger's tab
let to her chest, her eyes growing wider and wider a

he took in the treasures in the glass-front cabinets and hanging on the wall.

Dear God, was that a Manet? And a Warhol?

"I am really not happy you failed to inform me you were bringing your assistant, Jaeger," Amelia said, frowning. "I'd hoped to show you my collection in private."

Amelia was somewhere in her seventies, looked fifty, and had a reputation for inventing the concept *cougar*. Her fondness for young men was legendary. Piper looked at the large red chaise longue in the middle of the room and knew her presence severely compromised Amelia's plans to do wicked things to Jaeger on that piece of furniture.

"I thought I did inform you, Ms. Grant-Childs. I apologize, but Piper's presence makes this process so much more efficient."

And it keeps your clothes on, Piper thought. Jaeger's next message, sent shortly before eight that morning, now made complete sense.

Amelia Grant-Childs has a collection of jewelry she wants me to value. In her younger days—as my uncle once warned me—she had a thing for younger men and I'm scared nothing has changed. Would you like to accompany me to protect my virtue? Oh, she also, apparently, has a helluva art collection.

Another text came through ten seconds later.

And it will keep you awake.

After a hellish night with Ty, she deserved a little treat, and Jaeger plus wonderful art was a near-perfect

combination. Ceri offered to sit with the sleeping Ty
and after a long internal debate—she really did want t
see Amelia's art—Piper agreed to act as his assistant.

As for why Jaeger really had invited her, who knew

Pulling her focus back to their host, Piper watche
Amelia lift a hand to touch the massive diamond in he
earlobe. "This safe room was specially commissioned b
my recently deceased to house his treasures. It's bomb
proof, theft-proof, sound-and fireproof. I need to get th
contents appraised. The coins and the art have been va
ued. I just need you to look at the jewelry."

"If you don't mind me asking, who did the valuatio
for the art?" Piper asked, darting a look at the Manet.

"None of your business," Amelia snapped.

Alrighty then. Amelia drifted toward the door. "M
butler is on the premises. Push this button to call him
I'll be upstairs and I do not wish to be disturbed." Ame
lia rested her hand on the door frame. "Send the valua
tion and bill to my lawyer, Jaeger. God, you do look lik
your uncle. He was such a handsome man." She glance
from Jaeger to Piper and sniffed. "It's such a pity yo
brought her."

When Amelia closed the door behind them, Pipe
tried to look regretful. "You missed out on a good time
Jaeger," she teased. "I'm *so* sorry."

Jaeger made a face. "Funny."

His eyes turned a deeper blue, and Piper felt heat bub
ble in her stomach. He lifted his hand and swiped hi
thumb across her lower lip. "There's only one woma
I want in my bed, and she's standing in front of me, a
sexy as sin."

"Jaeger—" Piper closed her eyes, feeling his heat a
his other hand gripped her hip and pulled her into him

His chest brushed hers and he slid a hard thigh between her legs.

"You look tired," he murmured.

"I am," Piper admitted.

"You need a shot of energy," Jaeger said, his lips brushing hers, once, twice, so softly she wondered if she was imagining his kiss. "The other night, after we kissed, I felt like I could hurdle mountains, swim oceans. Want to see if it works for you?"

She had to think, to be sensible. "Here?"

"Where better?" Jaeger replied, his hand cradling her face. "Amelia is upstairs, the door is closed, the place is soundproof. Because of the couch, I doubt there are hidden cameras. It's just a kiss, Piper. We're not going to get naked."

Damn, Piper thought. "One kiss?"

"One long, sexy, hot, deep, crazy kiss."

She didn't have enough willpower to say no; she didn't have any willpower at all. Kissing Jaeger wasn't something any sane woman with a pulse would walk away from. Not wanting to wait a half second longer, she placed her hands flat against Jaeger's chest and tilted her head back in a silent, powerful plea.

Jaeger heard her, answered, and Piper felt her knees buckle when his mouth touched hers. He pulled her into a whirlwind that swiftly built into a tornado. As she flew on its winds of sensation, she oriented herself by clinging to him, by pushing her breasts into his hard chest, her fingers gripping his belt to keep her from falling down.

Or flying away.

God, he was good at this, Piper thought as he nipped her bottom lip before smoothing the sting with a slide of his tongue. One minute he was all power and determination. Then he brought the kiss down to soft and gentle before pulling her back up to hot and crazy. His hand didn't move off her face, and the other stayed on her hip, yet Piper felt like he was touching her most erogenous zones, bringing all her heat to the surface.

She'd never thought she could get so hot, feel so wanton—like she was about to burst out of her skin—from just a kiss. It was a kiss on crack and she was addicted.

This, kissing Jaeger, was what she wanted to do for the rest of—

Bang! Bang! Bang!

Jaeger pulled his mouth off hers and eased back, turning his head to look at the door. Piper followed her gaze. Her eyes widened as a young man dressed in solid black stepped into the room. He held a silver tray containing a carafe of coffee and thin china cups. He grinned and dropped his hand from the door.

"'Sorry!" the butler called.

Piper tried to step away from Jaeger, but he quickly placed both hands on her hips and kept her against him. When she felt his rock-hard erection, she realized why, and heat climbed up her neck and into her cheeks. She looked at Jaeger through lowered lids, lifting her eyebrows as if to say, "Really?"

"Your fault," Jaeger muttered. "Just stay where you are, okay?"

The butler placed his tray on the credenza against the back wall. "Help yourself. I'll bring you a light lunch if you are still here later."

Piper nodded and rested her forehead against Jaeger's collarbone. Ack! Could this be more embarrassing?

The butler grinned. "I'll leave you with the strong

suggestion that you avoid the couch. It's seen a lot of action."

"Dear Lord," Piper murmured, feeling laughter running through Jaeger's body. Hearing the door close, she lifted her bright pink face and saw amusement dancing in his eyes.

"We'll avoid the couch," he said, his tone teasing.

"We'll avoid each other," Piper firmly stated, stepping away and crossing her arms.

In order to break the arc of pure attraction linking them, she walked over to the drop-leg table where she'd put her bag, her phone and Jaeger's tablet. Pretending to be interested in her phone and trying to get her breathing and heartbeat under control, she ran her finger over the screen and immediately noticed she had no signal.

Panic flared. "Jaeger, there's no cell service here. What if Ceri is looking for me?" Guilt flooded her system.

She shouldn't have been here, doing this. Her kid was sick with an ear infection. What if they had tried to reach her while she was kissing Jaeger?

Ty was her first priority, *always*.

"This room is reinforced, which drops the strength of the signal," Jaeger explained. "If you go back into the hall, you'll get a signal in there." Jaeger pushed his hands into the pockets of his pants, his eyes steady on hers. "You and Ceri agreed Ty was well enough for you to accompany me. He didn't have a fever, he'd eaten earlier today and he was definitely feeling better. When you last checked fifteen minutes ago, Ty was sound asleep."

Jaeger's voice didn't hold reproach or irritation, and his recital of the facts calmed her. She looked down at her phone and waved it back and forth. "I'm still not comfortable not having a signal."

"Okay." Jaeger pulled out his phone and looked at the display. "I have a signal. Not a lot, but some. Text Ceri my number and tell her to call me if she can't reach you. Or I can call a taxi to take you back home."

She so appreciated his calm attitude. Piper looked at Jaeger standing with his hands in his pockets, patiently waiting for her to make up her mind. He wore a beige linen blazer over a light blue long-sleeve shirt, blue jeans threaded with a burgundy leather belt. Designer sunglasses rested in his hair.

"Look, Piper, if you don't want to stay, it's okay," Jaeger said. His mouth lifted at the corners. "Of course, if you leave, I'll be at Amelia's mercy, but I'm sure I can fight her off."

Piper managed a smile, but she sent an anxious look toward the hall. "It's just…he's so little and he's sick."

Jaeger lifted his hands. "It's your call."

Piper bit her lip. She really wanted to see Amelia's collection, and Ty *had* seemed better. She wouldn't have left otherwise. Walking into the hall, she sent Ceri a quick message with Jaeger's number. Ceri's thumbs-up emoji was instantaneous. Her next message, Ty's fine, still asleep, will text you and Jaeger when he wakes up, came a few seconds later, and Piper exhaled her tension.

She dropped her hunched shoulders and walked back into the collector's room. Jaeger was examining a pencil drawing on the wall next to the reinforced door.

"We good?" he asked.

"Very. He's fine, and Ceri now has your number." Piper wrinkled her nose. "I suppose you think I am a neurotic mother and overly anxious."

Jaeger's eyes dropped from hers to her mouth and back up again. "I think you are a good mom who is, naturally, worried about her kid."

His easy acceptance touched her; it wasn't what she'd expected from Manhattan's Main Man. She'd thought he'd be impatient and dismissive, not kind and accepting. His eyes darted to her mouth again, and he shook his head. "God, I could so take up where we just stopped."

"We can't," Piper murmured, touching her tongue to her bottom lip and sighing when she tasted him there.

"If you don't stop looking at me like that, I'm going to have you up against the nearest wall," Jaeger said, his voice almost a growl. He placed his hand on her shoulder and turned her so she faced the sketch he'd been examining. "I think that's a Degas."

Instead of the ballerina the artist was famous for, this sketch was of a naked woman lying on her back, her legs open. Degas didn't go into a lot of anatomical detail, but her sprawling, boneless posture suggested she'd been well loved. Piper had seen a lot of erotic art, much of it designed to titillate, but looking at this sketch, knowing Jaeger was watching her reaction, heated her from the inside out. Her skin prickled, her saliva disappeared and she could feel the insistent throb between her legs. Her libido screamed that she wanted this man. That she had to have him. Again. Soon. Now.

"Not the most appropriate sketch to show me when we're trying to cool down the situation, Ballantyne," Piper pointed out.

"That is what a woman should look like after making love," Jaeger said, his voice low and supersexy. "I want to make you look like that."

She was sure he had.

After Jaeger rocketed her from orgasm to orgasm in Milan, she'd *felt* sexy and sated. He'd made her feel incredibly feminine and wonderful, and if she turned and faced him, she wouldn't be able to hide her desire from him. He'd know exactly how he'd made her feel then and how much she wanted him now. He'd kiss her. They wouldn't stop. Because their chemistry was so combustible, he'd take her up against the nearest wall.

God, that sounded so good.

Calm the hell down, Mills, and think!

Getting involved with Jaeger, even just for a hookup, was asking for a heap of trouble.

She had to keep her head on straight and her thoughts clear. The priority was to sell the sapphires, buy her house back from her father's estate. Then she would have security for herself and Ty. She'd be able to stay in the house where she'd been raised, the place that held a million memories for her.

It was her home, her link to the parent who'd adored her. The only home she, and Ty, knew.

Selling the sapphires was important. Buying her house was important.

Protecting Ty was vital.

Making love to her son's father was, sadly, not.

But, hell and dammit, she really, really wanted to.

Jaeger dropped a kiss on her shoulder before walking away. She slowly turned and watched as he tossed his sunglasses next to her bag and picked up his tablet. He hauled in a deep breath and made the shift from lover to businessman.

He looked up and sent her a quick smile. "The jewelry isn't going to value itself, so I'd better get to work." He opened the doors to a floor-to-ceiling cupboard and pulled out a drawer. On the molded foam rested a choker with five rows of huge round diamonds in descending sizes from the center, separated by smaller emeralds.

Piper hurried over to get a closer look and whistled her appreciation. "Oh...wow."

Jaeger picked up the necklace, diamonds literally dripping from his fingers. He tapped his tablet, activated the voice app and spoke. "Five-row platinum, diamond and emerald necklace, 1980s, worth about two-point-five."

Piper gasped, her eyes wide. "Two-point-five million?"

Jaeger grinned. "And that's just the first piece. I've heard rumors there's a massive green diamond ring in this collection. First one to find it buys pizza tomorrow evening."

Piper looked at him, puzzled. "Tomorrow? That's Sunday. What's happening tomorrow?"

"We're going through your mother's boxes, looking for documentation about the sapphires." Jaeger replaced the diamond necklace and shut the drawer. "Is that a problem? You did give me a two-week deadline to make an offer, and the rest of my week is crazy. I don't have any plans tomorrow except for the ritual Ballantyne Sunday evening supper at the Den."

The Den, as everyone who read the society pages knew, was Connor's huge brownstone on Eighty-Fifth Street. Sage Ballantyne and Linc Taylor-Ballantyne—Connor, Piper remembered, adopted the Ballantyne siblings and Linc in their teens—shared the townhome with Linc's mother, Jo, and his son, Shaw.

"Tomorrow is good. Ty will be there, obviously."

Piper saw the muscle in Jaeger's jaw tense, noticed his grip on the drawer tighten. Well, tough. Ty was a part of her life, and it wasn't her problem if Jaeger didn't like being around kids. He'd simply have to suck it up.

"Tell me something," Jaeger said, releasing the handle to the drawer and leaning his shoulder into the collector's cupboard. Piper looked at him, knowing an opening like that usually meant an awkward question was about to follow.

"You were desperate to contact me last year," he said, "presumably because you wanted to sell the stones. Then your calls and messages stopped—"

"I was threatened with a restraining order if I didn't leave you alone," Piper interjected, her voice dry.

Jaeger winced. "Is that what happened? Damn, I'm sorry."

"I'm over it."

"Yet you didn't sell the stones. You could've sold them to Moreau's or to another high-end jewelry store, but you didn't. Now you want to sell them again, but this time you seem to have a very real deadline. Why?"

Piper stared at the Manet painting—her eyes immediately assessing the brush strokes and his masterful use of light.

"My circumstances are different. Can we leave it at that?" Without waiting for his answer, she changed the subject. "Tell me what you know about Manet."

"Are you avoiding the subject?" Jaeger asked.

"Sure," she answered truthfully, obviously surprising him. "We spent a short time together in Milan and we reconnected *yesterday*, Jaeger. There are things I don't feel comfortable sharing."

"Fair point."

Piper noticed his sensual mouth had turned grim. His tone was equally hard when he spoke again. "Okay, just tell me the sapphires weren't illegally acquired by either you or one of your ancestors."

That was a question she could answer. "The gems are not stolen."

Jaeger stood up straight, removed his jacket and rolled the cuffs of his shirt up to reveal strong wrists and corded forearms. "Okay, that's a relief. I can deal with the rest. Let's get to work."

Happy they were off the land mine subject, Piper gestured to the Manet. "So, about Manet?"

Jaeger's eyes darted from the painting to her face and back again. "I know absolutely nothing about art except what I like. Why?"

"Because it's a fake."

Jaeger winced before shrugging. "Not my problem."

Piper rubbed her hands together and approached the collector's cupboard containing what seemed like a hundred drawers.

"So, you're going to buy me pizza if I find you a green diamond ring?" Piper clarified as she pulled out a drawer filled with rings nestled in foam rows.

She chuckled, reached for a ring and lifted the green gorgeousness up to the light. "Anchovies, capers and olives on mine, please."

Five

Jaeger, sitting on the Persian carpet in Piper's den, grabbed a cold slice of pizza and placed another file back in the box, frustrated at not finding anything so far pertaining to the sapphires or Piper's great-uncle.

Shoeless, he crossed his feet at the ankles as he munched his way through the slice. He'd arrived at Piper's place midafternoon and she'd immediately sent him to the attic.

He should've agreed to let Rainn do the work, he thought. The space was dusty, overfull and dark, and he now had a backache from bending his too-long frame trying to shift boxes. Yet despite hauling boxes, Piper's dishwater-tasting coffee—how could anyone mess up coffee?—and there being a baby in the house, he felt relaxed, at ease. The moment he'd stepped through her front door and into her slightly chaotic home, he'd felt his shoulders drop and the knots in his muscles loosen. He hadn't felt this way about a house, a space, since he'd left the family brownstone to go off to college.

He liked being here, and he didn't like it that he liked it. Dammit.

He'd ordered pizza while Piper fed and bathed Ty, trying his best to stay out of their way. Ty was, as Piper informed him, not fully well and unusually fussy, which meant Piper had him on her hip for much of the afternoon. It had taken her ages to get Ty to settle, and when she returned, she'd eaten one slice of pizza and curled up on the couch. She'd fallen asleep about an hour ago. Jaeger glanced at his watch; it was a little past seven and he needed to leave for dinner at the Den. His family was expecting him.

Standing up, he stretched before shutting the pizza box and picking up the papers below Piper's hand. He placed them back in the folder and put it on the coffee table, staring down at the sleeping beauty below him.

She wasn't classically beautiful, he thought. Her chin was a bit too stubborn and her cheekbones a little too pronounced, but she was fascinating. Strong, charismatic, interesting.

Interesting was far more dangerous than beautiful, he thought, and a lot harder to resist.

Brain injury or not, how could he have forgotten meeting her before? They'd had dinner—he knew that—but what else? Had he kissed her? Did he try to take her to bed? Was this a new attraction, or had he felt the same in Milan? Jaeger cursed, frustrated. He *needed* to remember her.

God, she was hot…

Two fiery kisses were nowhere near enough. He

wanted to kneel on the wide couch and wake her up with kisses along the cords of her throat. He would suck her plump lower lip into his mouth, giving it a light nip, followed by a soothing swipe of his tongue. He wanted to know how her breasts filled his hands, whether her nipples were as succulent as he suspected. He wanted to taste her, stroke her, slide into her. Thoughts of doing all three constantly snuck up on him, and at night, his fantasies took flight. When he did sleep, it was to dream of her.

She'd told him she hadn't slept much last night, but he knew Ty had kept her up, not thoughts of him. She had blue stripes under her eyes, and her skin looked a shade or two paler than her normal creamy complexion. Interesting be damned—she *was* beautiful. She was *his* type of beautiful.

Jaeger turned as he heard a low cry coming from the baby monitor on the coffee table. He quickly scooped it up, hoping to muffle the noise. Leaving Piper to sleep, and asking himself what the hell he was doing, he carried the monitor with him and ran up the stairs to the second floor of her home. He passed a larger bedroom—obviously Piper's, judging by the hot-pink bra on the floor by her door—and stopped at the door to Ty's room.

You can do this. You have to do this. Beckett and Sage will have kids one day, and you can't keep avoiding Shaw forever. Go inside. It's a baby, not a bomb. Piper's baby...

That Ty was hers didn't matter, shouldn't matter. He had to conquer this fear at some point and it might as well be now. *And if you have a panic attack and start dry heaving, Ty won't tell anyone.*

Just try, dammit.

Jaeger pushed open the door. In the glow from the night-light next to the crib, he saw Ty sitting up, rubbing his eyes. Hoping Ty wouldn't yell, and ignoring his hummingbird heart, Jaeger lifted the baby and held him under his arms, his chubby legs dangling. "Hey, you. Why aren't you asleep?"

Ty blinked at him, his eyes wide. He spat out his pacifier and grinned at Jaeger. So far, so good. Shaking hands and a tight chest, but he wasn't about to have a heart attack.

Jaeger returned Ty's smile. "Yeah, you're cute. So, why aren't you asleep?"

Jaeger caught a whiff of something very unpleasant and grimaced. "Aw, c'mon, you're kidding me!"

Ty kicked his legs, gurgled and waved his hands in the air as if to say, *Let's see how tough you are, big guy.*

He wasn't that tough.

He should take Ty downstairs, wake Piper up and ask her to deal with her son's full diaper. That would be the most efficient and least disgusting way to handle the situation. But Piper was exhausted and she really needed to sleep...

But Ty wouldn't go back to sleep until he was clean and changed. Dammit. Jaeger didn't change diapers; he hadn't even changed any of Jess's diapers. Andrea had insisted on doing everything for Jess, and being young and thinking he was dodging a bullet, he'd let her. Now he had no idea where to start...

Piper—he'd wake her up. He made the decision and then shook his head. If he could negotiate, fight and scheme his way out of various dicey situations in third world countries, he could change a baby's diaper. Billions of people did it every day; it couldn't be rocket science.

All he needed was instructions, and he knew someone who could give him some.

Tucking Ty against his hip as he'd seen Piper and Ceri do, he dug into the back pocket of his jeans and pulled out his phone. He placed it on the table next to the changing pad and used his voice app to instruct the phone to call Linc. His brother answered within two rings.

"Where are you, Jay?" he demanded. "We're starving!"

Jaeger lowered Ty onto the changing table and flipped on the lamp next to his phone. Ty rolled, and Jaeger slapped his hand on his rump to keep him from falling off. "Hold still, dammit."

"Um…what are you doing?" Linc asked in his what-are-you-up-to voice.

"Trying to change a diaper on a wriggling baby," Jaeger replied. "I need you to talk me through it."

Linc didn't reply, and Jaeger wondered if he'd lost the connection. Then he heard Linc's voice and knew that he was on speaker. "He said he is changing a baby's diaper."

Beck's voice rose from the mobile. "Tell him that's he's drunk and to catch a cab home." Beneath their laughter, Jaeger heard amazement and concern. Yeah, well, he was concerned, too. He'd intended to avoid babies and kids for the rest of his life.

Okay, yes, Piper needed to sleep, but his decision to deal with Ty went deeper than that. There was something about this warm house in Brooklyn, and Piper, and being here with her, that made him feel stronger, better, able to face his past. Or at least, feel that it was time to try. "I'm being serious, and take me off speaker!"

"Not a chance in hell," Linc said. "First, why are you changing a diaper and second, who does the baby belong to? Third, are you sure you are not drunk?"

"Long story. Come on, I'm dying here. It's not… pleasant," Jaeger said.

"Tell us what we want to know and I'll guide you through it," Linc drawled.

Bastard! "It's Piper Mills's kid and she's downstairs asleep. The kid has had an ear infection and she's had no rest two nights running. I heard the kid and came up here and was rewarded with this mess in its pants."

"You could just wake her up," Beck suggested.

He'd covered that ground several times. "Are you going to help me or not?"

"Only if you agree to watch Shaw this week so Beck and I can go watch the Knicks kick ass."

Jaeger glared at his phone. He also had a ticket to that game, the asshat.

"I don't babysit, Linc. You know that," Jaeger said, his hand on Ty's thigh. Ty was looking past him to the ceiling. Jaeger glanced up, too, and noticed the glow-in-the-dark stickers of cartoon characters on the ceiling. *Pretty cool, Piper.*

"You're changing a diaper on a baby belonging to a woman you barely know, but you won't babysit your own nephew?" Linc asked.

Crap! But he was changing a freakin' diaper, so he'd might as well go all-in and babysit too. Essentially, Linc had him between a rock and a dirty diaper, so he reluctantly agreed. Linc walked him through the process. Because Piper was organized, he found everything he needed quickly. Within five minutes, Ty was clean, creamed and powdered. After listening to his brothers' sarcastic congratulations, he disconnected the call.

He'd survived.

Jaeger felt like he needed a strong drink. To normal

people, changing a diaper was an oft-repeated action. To Jaeger it felt like he'd negotiated a mental Mount Everest. He'd been hiding from kids, from babies, scared to deal with the memories of Jess he thought would drop him to his knees.

He hadn't realized how much pain he'd buried until, four years ago, he'd seen Linc rock a tiny Shaw to sleep, unaware that Jaeger was standing in the doorway. When Linc rested his lips against his son's head, Jaeger felt the burn of hot, unwelcome and acidic tears on his skin.

He'd had this; he'd lost this. And he'd known that although he loved Linc, he couldn't watch Linc raise Shaw. It would hurt too damn much.

He'd had to leave, to run. Before dawn he was on a plane to Colombia, trying to outpace his past.

He now accepted that, while he could face down warlords and hardened criminals, he'd lacked the courage to push past his own loss and be there for his brother in raising Shaw. It was one of his deepest regrets. He loved his sibs and enjoyed spending time with them. Someday there would be more Ballantyne children, and he wouldn't make the same mistake with Beckett and Sage. He wouldn't distance himself from his family to avoid their babies. Or hide from his past.

Ty was a good way to become reacquainted with the smaller species. With Ty, he could take it as fast or as slow as he liked.

Best of all, when he felt overwhelmed, he could hand the baby back to Piper and walk away. Jaeger placed his hands on either side of Ty's body and looked down into his happy face. The little guy was seriously cute.

"That was a hell of a way to get to know you, dude," he murmured. Ty gave him a gummy smile, and Jaeger couldn't help smiling in return. "You don't have much of your pretty mom in you, Ty. Now, Jess, she looked just like her mom. Same pointed chin, triangular face, black hair. Deep brown eyes. Pretty, you know."

He was talking to a baby about his baby, Jaeger thought. Talking about Jess wasn't something he did. But he figured he was safe since Ty wasn't going to blab. "She had a birthmark on the inside of her thigh." Jaeger pressed a spot on Ty's pudgy thigh and the kid laughed. "Just here, and it was shaped like a butterfly."

Jaeger squeezed Ty's thigh and he laughed again. Ah, so he was ticklish. Jaeger allowed his fingers to dance his way up the sides of Ty's ribs, and Ty's belly laugh rumbled over his skin. "Would she have laughed like this? Would she be ticklish?"

Ty shoved his hand into his mouth and stared at Jaeger with his owl-like eyes.

"She would be a teenager now. Probably wearing a bra and talking about boys. God!"

How could he miss her so much when he'd hardly known her? He'd spent his days at work, a lot of time traveling, and he'd had an hour or two with her on weekdays, slightly more on weekends. Yet her death created a hole in both his and Andrea's hearts, a hole that widened until it became so big they fell into it and were lost. As individuals and as a couple.

"Hey, sorry. I didn't hear him."

Keeping his hand on Ty so he remained on the table, Jaeger looked around. Piper's hair was a mess of curls, her mascara was smudged and she had a pillow crease on her cheek. She looked tired but, hell, still hot. She walked into the room and saw the dirty diaper, the pile of baby wipes on the counter.

"You changed him? Why didn't you call me?" she asked, picking Ty up and dropping a kiss on his head.

Jaeger shrugged. "I thought you needed to sleep," Jaeger replied, his voice rough. Oh, God, he prayed she hadn't heard him talking about Jess. It was one thing facing your past; it was another confessing it.

Ty leaned away from Piper as if silently asking Jaeger to hold him. Jaeger stepped back and lifted up his hands. "Sorry, I don't do babies."

Piper looked at the dirty diaper, the open jar of cream and the powder and lifted her eyebrows. "You changed his diaper but you don't do babies? Do you know how nuts that sounds?"

Of course he did. But it wasn't like he could tell her the truth. Jaeger shrugged and made a production of looking at his watch. "I have to go. I'm late for dinner."

Piper nodded and cocked her head. "Nobody is keeping you here, Jaeger," she murmured, her voice soft and nonaccusatory.

Yeah, fair point. Yet it still took everything Jaeger had to get his feet to move.

Six

On the following Thursday, the flight from Washington was delayed and Piper, in a taxi heading into the city from JFK, looked at her watch and sighed. Ceri would've bathed and put Ty to bed by now, and he'd be asleep. She hated the days when she didn't see Ty. She'd left before he woke this morning, and her appraisal of a private collection of Cuban art had taken longer than she'd anticipated, which necessitated her taking a later flight back to New York.

She wanted to go home, have a glass of wine and chill out. Actually, what she really wanted was to go home, kiss her baby and climb into bed with a ripped man with amazing blue eyes and a quirky smile. She hadn't seen or heard from Jaeger since Sunday—how could four days feel like a decade?—and the time apart only seemed to heat her fantasies from hot to scorching.

She had so much to lose. This was the worst time ever to fall back in lust with her one time ex-lover—the provider of all her son's boy genes! Despite this, she desperately wanted a repeat of eighteen months ago. She wanted Jaeger's clever mouth trailing kisses over her body, his hands exploring every inch of her, his voice rumbling across her skin, whispering hot, naughty, sexy words in her ear.

"You're so hot."

"God, you turn me on"

"You feel so damn good."

Piper wanted those words; she *needed* those words. For just one evening she wanted to forget she was a single mother, that she was in danger of losing her house, that she was the daughter Michael Shuttle had never acknowledged. That her life was insanely complicated. She wanted to be anyone other than a frazzled, stressed, almost thirty-year-old who hadn't had sex for eighteen months. She wanted wine. She wanted heat. She wanted...

Jaeger.

Again. Would a time ever come when she didn't want him? Probably not. Her pheromones liked his... It was that simple.

And that problematic.

Piper's heavy sigh filled the back of the cab. Was it even ethical to be thinking of diving back into bed with Jaeger when she was keeping such a huge secret from him? And she had to consider how her actions would affect Ty.

Ty came first. He always had and he always would. If she slept with Jaeger and if they reignited, she would still have to protect Ty.

To do that, she had to continue keeping his parentage a secret.

To do *that*, she had to withhold information from Jaeger, and that felt like she was lying. Aaargh!

And while she was torturing herself with difficult scenarios, what exactly did she want from Ballantyne? Just sex? Sex with friendship? Sex and a relationship? Exactly what type of explosion did she want to detonate?

Realistically, Jaeger wasn't the type of guy she should have been thinking about, the type of guy she needed in her life. He was a rolling stone, someone who openly and consistently said he wasn't interested in settling down, or in relationships, or in being a husband or father. He did not want to be tied down.

Just like her own father.

Piper pushed the tips of her fingers into her temples to release the tension building behind her eyes. She had to stop thinking about Jaeger. He was someone who'd dropped back into her life last week and was going to drop out again when Ballantyne and Company bought her stones.

Maybe her intense reaction to him was a sign she should start dating again. Maybe if she'd had a relationship with someone else, had dated someone other than herself since Milan, she wouldn't be feeling so, *jeez*, horny. Crazy. Frustrated.

And if she started dating again, maybe, one day, she might meet a guy who would love both her and Ty, who'd be an amazing husband, a superb lover, her best friend and a man who'd be prepared to be Ty's dad, too.

Yeah, and a purple unicorn wearing sparkly red shoes and a tiara just flew past the window of her taxi.

Piper heard her phone ringing and pulled it out of her purse, frowning when she didn't recognize the number.

"Ms. Mills, it's Simms."

The lawyer handling her father's estate. Piper felt the pain behind her left eye increase and pushed her fingers into her temple, hoping to push the ache away.

"I'm sorry to call you so late, but I thought it important you know that I can't delay putting the Park Slope house up for auction. It will have to be sold as soon as possible, just like your father's other properties."

It took Piper a moment for his words to make sense, and when they did, a cold hand squeezed her heart. No! She needed more time to raise the cash.

"What's changed?" Piper asked, grimacing at the wobble in her voice.

"We've discovered your father owes more to creditors than we thought, and we're auctioning off the properties as soon as possible."

God! "When?"

"I don't have a definite date but…soon," Simms replied, sounding sympathetic. "I'm sorry. I really wanted to give you some time."

"Could I make an offer on the property before it goes to auction?" Piper asked.

"We'll entertain an offer, but it will have to be for the full market value. Or else you'd have to bid at the auction and take your chances."

Piper exhaled. "How much do they want?"

"It's in a good area, on a good street. It's a very desirable property. Three point two million but I'm sure you could beat them down."

"And my deadline?"

"Yesterday."

Piper couldn't believe this was happening. With acid churning in her stomach, she told Simms she'd get back to him and disconnected.

Taking a deep breath, she dialed Jaeger's number. When he answered, she said, "I need to see you. Now."

Jaeger opened his door to a white-faced Piper. Tension tightened her amazing eyes, and her wide mouth was a slash in her face. She looked on the verge of snapping.

She needed a large glass of wine or some fantastic sex. He could provide both, at the same time if necessary. He was talented that way.

Jaeger gestured her inside and took her coat, which he hung on a steel-and-wood coat stand by the door. She wore a tight black turtleneck tucked into a gray-and-black tartan skirt and long leather boots. Her penny-colored curls were pulled off her face into a tight knot, and she wore black-rimmed glasses. She looked like a hot professor. Jaeger mentally stripped her of the skirt and sweater, loosened her hair and left her in those glasses and boots. He instantly went from interested to aching.

Like he always did when she stepped into the room. Or looked at him. Or breathed.

Jaeger walked away from her and headed to the fridge, hoping the cavernous empty space would distract him from thoughts of leading Piper straight to his bedroom.

"Would you like some wine?"

"No, but thanks. What I do need is three million for the sapphires. Preferably by yesterday."

What? Jaeger straightened and turned, lust temporarily pushed aside. His brain clicked into gear and he frowned. "I thought I had another week before I had to make an offer."

"That was then. Today I need three million or I'm going to have to find another buyer," Piper stated, hugging herself and staring at the floor.

Most visitors to his apartment said something about the space or the kickass view. Piper, who instinctively appreciated beauty, didn't comment. She was so taut she didn't even notice her surroundings. And that told him exactly how upset she was.

Jaeger slammed the fridge door shut, turned to another cupboard and pulled down a crystal tumbler. He found a bottle of Scotch and poured a healthy two fingers. She looked cold and upset, and whiskey would help for both.

"Take a seat." Jaeger led her to the streamlined sofa next to the window and gestured for her to sit down. Piper sat and crossed her legs. Jaeger tried not to notice how her skirt rode up, revealing four inches of a very sexy, silky thigh. He handed her the whiskey and sighed when she just held it between her palms.

"It'll help only if you drink it," he murmured.

Piper took an obligatory sip, took another and placed her elbow on her knee, her hand on her forehead. Jaeger waited for her explanation. When she eventually lifted her eyes to his, she looked shattered. "I'm sorry. I don't mean to be difficult or to go back on my word, but I need to sell those sapphires. Quickly."

Yeah, okay. But why?

She asked, "Are the stones, right now, worth three million?"

Jaeger sat down next to her and lifted his thigh onto the blocky cushion. "Piper, we suspect the gems are from Kashmir, probably mined in the late 1800s. If this was a back room in Bombay, I'd offer you three million right now and trust my gut. Here in New York, I don't need to take the risk. Tomorrow a gemologist will test the stones, and in a few days we will have a detailed report, including color, clarity and carats. After I receive the report, I will have a better idea of what to offer. They might be worth three, four times what you're asking. I like making a good deal, but I don't want you to be cheated out of the true value because you are in a hurry."

Piper stared at the toes of her leather boots. "But I need the money...*now*."

"Surely a week or two won't matter?"

"You'd be surprised." Piper placed her whiskey on the glass-and-wood coffee table and stood up, crossing her arms over her chest. "I need to sell them, Jaeger. If you as the Ballantyne representative won't buy them from me, then maybe Moreau's will."

Of course they would. If Piper walked into Moreau's tomorrow and asked for three million, James Moreau probably wouldn't hesitate. And Ballantyne would lose the find of the century.

He supposed he could offer Piper three million for the stones right now and be done with it. Three million and Piper could walk out the door, and he'd never have to see her again...

He wasn't ready to do that, not yet.

Since his accident he'd been playing it safe, trying to take fewer risks, measuring the reward before charging into a situation. He'd been lucky to escape that accident with his memory mostly intact. He now thought before he acted, sometimes too much.

But Piper tempted him to step out of the safe zone and live a little. She made him feel like the man he'd been when he was younger—fearless and invincible. Interacting with Piper was akin to surfing a sixty-foot wave, incredibly exciting and ridiculously dangerous.

And, he noted with wry amusement, he hadn't even made love to her yet. He wasn't letting her walk away until that had happened.

He had many regrets, and he was damned if he would add *never slept with Piper Mills* to that list.

He would make love to Piper. Of that he was dead certain.

"Jaeger, I'm about to lose my house, the house I grew up in. It's going up for auction unless I make a substantial offer," Piper told him, her voice sounding infinitely weary. "That house is my home, Ty's home. The area has great schools and great amenities, and I don't want to live anywhere else! Besides, where will I find another place that can fit the four of us, that gives Ceri and Rainn their privacy, but where they are a minute away when I need them?" Piper's voice rose. "That house is a part of me. It's mine."

Jaeger frowned. "If it's yours, then why is it going up for auction?"

Piper stared out of the custom windows, still not seeing the view. "I've just found out it was owned by my father through a company, and it's now part of his estate. It has to be sold to repay some of his debts."

Fair enough. Jaeger picked up her glass of whiskey, drained it and stared across to New Jersey, his mind tumbling. Essentially, he needed those sapphs; Piper needed the money. He wasn't prepared for Ballantyne and Company to take the risk, but *he* could.

Along with this property, Connor had also made him—and his siblings—a beneficiary on a multimillion-dollar insurance policy. Adding up the money he'd received from the policy, his personal savings and the money he'd inherited as his share of his parent's estate, he had a heap of cash sitting in the bank, doing nothing.

He could offer Piper a loan against the future sale of the sapphires provided she sold the sapphires to Ballantyne and Company. If she reneged on the agreement, which he doubted she would, he could afford to lose the three million. Hell, he could afford to lose a lot more.

His offer would secure the sapphires, and it would get Piper out of a hole. It was *one* risk he felt reasonably comfortable taking. This way, he and Piper could keep looking for provenance, which would ensure a bigger profit for all of them.

And it would keep Piper from walking out of his life...

It was a no-brainer.

Jaeger calmly made the offer and watched the emotions dance through Piper's eyes. He saw relief and temptation and suspicion.

"You're offering to buy the stones? Yourself?"

"I am offering you an advance against the sale of the sapphires," Jaeger replied, trying not to use the word *loan*. He thought the word would make Piper twitchy.

He was right. "It's a *loan*, Jaeger."

"It's a temporary advance, Piper." Jaeger pushed his hand through his hair. "Once the gemology report comes back, Ballantyne will offer you a lot more for those stones, and you will repay me the money. It's not rocket science."

Piper opened her mouth to argue, shut it again and repeated the action. He lifted his eyebrows and waited another thirty seconds before speaking again. "Okay, that's settled. I'll get the money to you, maybe by the end of day tomorrow, but definitely by Monday."

That sexy mouth opened again, and Jaeger thought she was the most gorgeous goldfish he'd ever seen. Deciding it was past time to change the subject, he leaned back against the couch and folded his arms. "You're looking very businesslike, Miss Mills. How's Ty feeling?"

"He's fine, back to normal. I haven't seen him today and when I get home he'll be asleep."

Piper fingered the hem of her skirt. "I was in Washington earlier and on my way home when I got a call from the lawyers telling me about the house." She licked her top lip, and Jaeger nearly offered to do it for her. "Um, thank you. For the advance. I promise I'll pay you back."

"I know you will," Jaeger replied. "That's a given." If she kept looking at him like that, all soft and grateful, then he wouldn't be able to stop himself from taking her in his arms and seeing exactly how she looked wearing just boots and glasses and crazy curls. "Tell me about the art you saw today."

Piper looked at him. "Why are you doing this? You don't even know me."

Jaeger stood up and walked around the couch to the window, resting his forearm on the glass and his head on his arm. He felt the air behind him move, inhaled Piper's perfume as she joined him. She placed her hand on the center of his back. He felt connected, for the first time in a long time, to something bigger and deeper than himself. It scared the crap out of him.

He swallowed, thinking he could tell her he didn't want the gems to go to Moreau's, that securing the sapphires was all he cared about. The sapphs were important—of course they were—but he didn't want her to lose her house, lose her connection to her mother. He suspected emotional connections were vitally important to Piper. It wasn't necessary for her to be this stressed, this worried. This was a solution he could well afford. But his impulse to offer the money went deeper than business; he was trying to protect her. Seeing her so frazzled caused his intestines to knot.

That sixty-foot wave was swelling to eighty feet. Why was he on this crazy ride with her? His gut wasn't screaming that the risk was too great. What if this wasn't just about getting her into bed? What if he wanted more? God, he was risking emotional annihilation if he couldn't master this ride, but he still didn't pull the offer, didn't back away.

He couldn't.

He forced the words out. "It's just money, Piper."

It could only be about money; he couldn't afford anything else—like his future or his heart—to be at stake.

Piper rested her forehead on his biceps, and he looked down at her bright hair. He wanted her, and his raging desire had nothing to do with gemstones or money or houses in Brooklyn.

He just flat-out wanted her under him, naked and panting. He had since she'd walked into his life a little less than a week ago.

Jaeger dropped his arm, turned to face her and waited for her to meet his eyes. She would; he knew she would. She couldn't resist temptation any more than he could. That he wasn't alone in this madness made him feel, strangely, a little less like he was surfing that wave.

"Don't take this the wrong way," he said, his voice gruff, "but I want you."

Piper lifted her hand to touch his chest, and he felt her warmth through the thin layer of his cotton T-shirt. "Don't take this the wrong way, but I want you back."

He knew that. He was old enough to recognize mutual attraction when it was standing between them, doing the tango. Sex was just sex, a good way to blow off steam. They weren't kids, and he was sure Piper wouldn't think this could be the start of something that went deeper than mutual pleasure. He didn't want her getting the wrong idea. Hell, he didn't want either of them getting swept up in the moment and thinking this was more than it could be.

"Sex is all that's on the table, Piper." Jaeger jammed his hands in the pockets of his jeans so he didn't reach for that big button that held her wraparound skirt together.

"I never thought anything else was on offer," Piper replied, her eyes steady on his. "Apart from the fact that we've known each other for a *week*, I'm a single mother who has got more than enough to deal with without the complication of a relationship. I'd like to be with you, for an hour or two, so I can step out of my crazy life.

"I want to do nothing but touch you and have you touch me, think of nothing more than how much pleasure you are going to give me. I need to escape and I think I could, with you. A lover is what I need tonight." Piper looked at her watch and grimaced. "Well, for the next hour or so."

Jaeger felt the air leave his body, and he lifted his hands so he could frame her face. His fingers speared into her curls and she gripped his wrists, looking up at him with big eyes. He couldn't wait to touch her, to kiss her, but first things first.

He moved his hand to the back of her head and found

the pins restraining her curls. He pulled them out one by one and tossed them to the floor, allowing her hair to fall over his hands and wrists. "That's better. Now let's get rid of the skirt and shirt."

Piper started to remove her glasses, but Jaeger captured her hand and pulled it back to her side. "Nope, the boots and glasses stay on…"

This was what she needed, Piper thought as Jaeger pulled her turtleneck over her head, being careful not to dislodge her glasses, and dropped the garment to the couch.

Jaeger ran his finger over the edges of her pale green lacy bra, from one side to the other and back again. It felt like he was running a gentle firecracker over her skin. Every cell in her body woke up and did a hello-there-darling stretch.

Yeah, Jaeger touching her was exactly what she needed, what she wanted. For eighteen months she'd thought of little more than Ty and his needs—whether he was thriving, growing, happy. She hadn't had a date, or sex, in far too long, and she'd forgotten how amazing it felt to be the object of a man's attention —a very sexy man's attention.

It was a fantastically bad idea. That was indubitable. But she wanted him. So—what the hell?—she was going for it.

Jaeger undid the button on her skirt, and the length of fabric dropped to the floor. She stood before him dressed in her lingerie, glasses and boots. She thought she'd feel ridiculous, self-conscious, but Jaeger's frank appreciation chased embarrassment away. The open admiration on his face, and the massive rod in his pants, told her he really, *really* liked what he was seeing. Feeling more confident now and a little naughty, Piper slowly spun around, showing off her teeny tiny thong.

"God, Piper, you're killing me," Jaeger muttered. When she faced him again, her hand on her hip, he shook his head. "You are truly spectacular."

"Keep talking dirty and I'll let you have your way with me," Piper breathlessly quipped. She pushed her glasses up her nose and thought the dorky gesture was in complete contrast with the vamp she so longed to be. She pulled her glasses off and threw them onto the couch.

Jaeger smiled, stepped toward her and scooped her up to hold her against his chest. Piper linked her arms around his neck, reveling in his hard thighs beneath hers, his wide chest. His masculinity made her feel so utterly feminine.

"Let's take this to the bedroom. As much as I want to make love to you on this couch in front of these windows, I'd hate for Beck to walk in and get an eyeful."

"Your brother lives here too?" Piper asked, pulling back.

"Temporarily," Jaeger told her, walking down the hallway to what she presumed to be the master bedroom. Piper dropped her eyes from Jaeger's face to look ahead, and her mouth fell open when she looked right to the glass wall of the hall and noticed the view of the Hudson River flowing between two sets of city lights. Dear God, she had been so worried, so focused on her problems, she'd missed this amazing view!

"Oh my God, your view is phenomenal!"

What else had she missed? Piper stretched her neck to look over Jaeger's shoulder, back into his apartment, and she noticed the oversize, vibrant artworks, the clean lines of his modern, very expensive furniture, a metal sculpture. She realized the sculpture was of a horse and the artist had captured the elegance of the animal's movement. Only one artist had the chops to do that; it had to be Latimore, one of her favorite artists.

Ever.

"Is that a Latimore?"

"Now she notices the art," Jaeger muttered."No more talking about art or views or anything else. Got it?"

"Then I'm going to have to find something else to do with my mouth."

Above hers, Jaeger's lips curved into a bone-dissolving smile. "I most definitely can help you with that."

His big arms tightened his hold on her, melding her to his muscled body. The art could, very definitely, wait.

She couldn't. "Kiss me, Jaeger."

At the end of the hall Jaeger dropped her to her feet and pushed her up against a door, his mouth slanting over hers, his tongue sliding into her mouth. All thoughts of art and views were forgotten, and Piper released a deep groan in the back of her throat.

This was what she wanted, needed.

One of Jaeger's hands fumbled for the knob behind her back, and the door opened. He banded an arm around her waist and pulled her up and into him, holding her against his body as he walked her into the room. Piper felt the edges of the bed against her calves, and Jaeger gently lowered her and followed her down. As her back hit the cool covers, he lifted his head, and his eyes glittered with desire and need.

Jaeger lowered his mouth to hers, sucking on her bottom lip and sliding his tongue into her mouth. His hands skimmed her sides, his knuckles rubbing over her ribs, and she arched her back in a silent plea for him to touch her breasts, to pay attention to her aching nipples. When Jaeger finally, finally, sucked her lace-covered nipple into his mouth, she let out a low sound and clasped her hand behind his head to keep him in place.

This was what she'd craved during those long, lonely nights—this hot, delicious, mindless sex. She needed him to touch her everywhere, to slide into those neglected, lonely places and chase away the doubts and the darkness. She needed the oblivion, to step out of her life. But even as he touched her, as his mouth moved down her body to explore her belly button, to drag warmth over her lace-covered mound, she knew she couldn't, mustn't, become addicted to him, to this.

He was a temporary fix, not a permanent repair. She couldn't rely on him to be there in the future, not for her and certainly not for Ty.

He was about pleasure, and he did pleasure so well.

Jaeger quickly divested her of her underwear and, sitting on his heels, he looked at her, naked except for her boots. "As sexy as these are, I want to see you, all of you."

He grabbed the heel of one boot, pulled it off and repeated the action for the other. There was something incredibly intimate about being naked when your lover was still fully dressed, Piper thought. She kept her eyes on his face, watching the emotions sliding in and out of his eyes. Lust, desire, crazy attraction, they were all there, but the romantic in her thought that under the crazy, she could see affection, a little fear, a lot of anticipation.

Romance had no part in this. Tonight was about sex and escapism.

Jaeger pulled away from her to stand between her legs

and lifted his hand to grip the back of his shirt. He pulled it over his head in one easy, fluid movement. His wide chest was lightly touched with hair, hard with muscle. Long, lean hips disappeared beneath the low band of his pants, and Piper sucked in her breath when he hooked his thumbs into the waistband and pushed his jeans down long, muscled thighs. And there he was, utterly masculine, hard, proud—needing her.

Naked, Jaeger grabbed her around the waist and boosted her up the bed. When she was where he wanted her, he lay down on top of her, chest to chest, his erection finding its natural place between her thighs. He reached across her to yank on the bedside drawer. Ten seconds later he'd pulled a condom out of its packaging.

Oh, God, she didn't have much faith in Jaeger's condoms. Somehow—who knew how?—she'd managed to become pregnant despite him wearing one. It wouldn't happen a second time, would it? That would be like winning the lottery twice, Piper thought.

Jaeger sheathed himself and skimmed his thumb over the spot between her eyes. "Second thoughts?" he asked.

Uh, no. Her ankles were already curved around his calves and she was lifting her hips, trying to push his tip further into her. She needed him now, immediately.

Pregnancy and condoms flew out of her mind as his chest brushed hers, her nipples teased by his chest hair.

"Quick question?" she asked.

His eyes bored into her. "Make it very damn quick."

"I was just wondering how long you are going to tease me?"

"This long." Jaeger entered her with one fluid stroke, burying himself to the hilt. Yeah, this was what she remembered, this feeling of being filled, completed. Then

Jaeger kissed her, his mouth echoing his body's movements and Piper forgot to think.

All she could concentrate on was the warm, sparkly sensation building, each spark igniting the rest until a million tiny fires danced under her skin. When Jaeger placed his hand under her back and yanked her up as he plunged inside, those fires joined and created an explosion burning her from the inside out. She thought Jaeger stepped into the fire with her, but she didn't care. All she wanted was this heat and light and warmth.

She hadn't thought sex could be better than what they'd shared in Milan. But it was—better, hotter, brighter. And that, Piper thought when she crashed back down to earth, was a big, huge, freakin' *enormous* problem.

Seven

Version one of fantastic sex was pretty much immediately followed by version two—Jaeger hadn't needed much time to recover. But as much as she wanted to, Piper knew she couldn't hang around for version three. Ceri had agreed to watch Ty for a few more hours, but Piper had to get home; Ty was her first priority.

Piper slid out from under Jaeger's arm and sat on the edge of the bed, looking down at the floor. She needed to call a taxi, dress and gather her scattered thoughts and belongings. Piper felt his hand on her back, his knuckles running down her spine.

"I'll drive you home when you're ready."

Piper spun around and looked at him, long-limbed and naked, sleepy and satisfied. "That's not necessary. I can take a cab."

"You can, but you won't." Jaeger stretched, sat up,

dropped a kiss on her shoulder blade and rolled out of bed. He reached for his jeans and tossed her panties and bra onto the bed beside her. Then he nodded to his en suite bathroom. "Would you like to take a shower before you go?"

She should, but she knew if she did, there was a good chance they'd get distracted and she'd be even later than she already was. Piper cradled her lingerie against her chest and shook her head.

She stepped into the modern, luxurious bathroom and quickly cleaned up. She pulled on her lingerie, ran her fingers through her curls and touched her puffy lips. Yeah, the fact she'd had sex—fantastic, mind-blowing sex—was written all over her face. On the plus side, she had taken nearly a week to fall into Jaeger's bed and arms instead of thirty-six hours. In a century or so, she might be able to resist him altogether.

Piper splashed some water on her face in an attempt to take her color down, and when the water didn't help, she stuck out her tongue at her reflection. When she stepped back into the bedroom, Jaeger was shoving his feet into a pair of scuffed sneakers. Her skirt and shirt lay on the rumpled bedding, and Piper murmured a quick thank-you to him for retrieving the garments for her.

Jaeger seemed lost in thought, and his silence made Piper uncomfortable. But really, what was there to say? *"Thanks, that was great. I've got to get home to your son?"*

Earlier she'd thought that keeping Ty a secret was the right thing to do, but now…she'd somehow crossed a line she hadn't intended to cross. She felt downright guilty. Maybe Jaeger had a right to know he was a father…

But she had the right—no, the duty—to protect Ty

from anyone or anything that would harm him, physically and emotionally. Even his own father.

Having a father who didn't want him would hurt Ty, just as it had hurt her as a girl, and she wasn't going to let that happen.

But if she continued sleeping with Jaeger and she kept the truth from him, the guilt would devour her. And now that they'd become intimate again, how would he react if he ever found out about Ty? Would he be hurt, livid, disinterested?

God, she didn't know. Piper recalled Fuseli's eighteenth-century painting and sympathized with Odysseus facing the sea monsters Scylla and Charybdis. Like the Greek god, both options sucked, but which choice would hurt the least?

Piper quickly dressed and finally felt a little more like herself, a lot more in control. As they walked into his living area, her eyes were again drawn to the horse sculpture. She walked over to it, her hands running over the smooth metal shaping the horse's rump. "Oh my God, he's fantastic."

"Yeah, I like him. My siblings bought him for me for my birthday," Jaeger said, picking up his phone and keys from the wide, shallow pottery bowl on the granite island separating the kitchen from the living area.

"Lucky you," Piper murmured, envious.

"Latimore's new exhibition is opening tomorrow night," Jaeger said, walking to the door and picking up her coat.

Piper got her laptop bag and sent the metal horse a final look. "I know. I plan to go in a couple of weeks."

"I've been invited to the opening. Do you want to go?" Jaeger opened the coat for her, and Piper slid her arms into the sleeves. Jaeger lifted her hair over her collar as she turned to face him, his eyes amused.

"Yes, I'd like to go! Are you kidding me? That would be awesome…" Piper mentally flipped through her schedule and scrunched up her face, disappointed. "I can't. Ceri has plans and Rainn has to study. I have no one to look after Ty."

And really, by accepting Jaeger's offer, was she not adding another layer of complication to the crazy? She and Jaeger weren't dating!

But it was Latimore, her inner art tart replied. *Latimore!*

Jaeger pulled her laptop bag off her shoulder and opened his front door, standing back to let her pass. When he stepped into the private elevator after her, she sighed heavily. "Damn, I would love to go with you. Latimore is always innovative and controversial."

"Oh, I'm not going."

Piper raised her eyebrows. If he wasn't going, then why did he invite her? Before she could ask for an explanation, he spoke again. "Linc strong-armed me into babysitting my four-year-old nephew, Shaw, for the evening. My brothers are going to see the Knicks game without me, the bastards."

"You have tickets to that, too?"

Jaeger scowled. "Courtside tickets. I am not happy." The doors to the elevator swished open, and Piper realized they were in the parking garage. Except the garage only held Jaeger's luxury SUV and a dangerous-looking superbike. "You have a private garage?"

Jaeger nodded as the lights on his vehicle flashed. He placed his hand on Piper's back as she moved between him and the open passenger door of his very expensive car. "Sage, my sister, is going. I think you'd like her, and she'll definitely like you. I'll get the name on the invitation changed to yours in case you manage to find someone to sit with Ty."

Jaeger slammed her door closed and walked around the hood of the car. When he was behind the wheel, Piper turned in her seat. "I really appreciate the offer, but—"

"Just think about it. I can see how much you want to go, so consider taking a couple of hours for yourself."

"Thanks, but I can't," Piper said, her decision made. She'd taken a couple of hours for herself just now. She'd see the exhibition when the rest of the art lovers of the city did. Her place was at home, with Ty.

She had decisions to make, a path through the sea monsters of guilt and duty to navigate. In one night he'd advanced her three million dollars—gulp!—rocked her sexual world and offered her an opportunity to see her favorite artist's new show. She had to find a way to simplify this complicated and convoluted situation.

Keeping her distance and not getting naked with Jaeger again would be a very good place to start.

The next evening, Piper sent an anxious look toward her phone and wondered, for the hundredth time, whether she'd imagined the conversation with Jaeger about the advance. He hadn't mentioned it again when he dropped her off last night, and he hadn't contacted her today.

She needed to make a firm offer for the house, but she didn't want to call Simms until she spoke to Jaeger. She didn't think he'd go back on his word, but until she had something tangible—money in her bank account would work—her hands were tied.

Could she call Jaeger and ask him? Piper rested her

forehead against the cool door of her fridge and wished she hadn't slept with him. Sleeping together made the conversation about money so awkward...

"Thanks for the Big O's, but can we talk money?"

"It was a fantastic night, but can you transfer the cash?"

Man, being with Jaeger spun her world off its axis. Being in his arms, being kissed and touched by him, changed her internal universe. Nothing mattered but being naked with Ballantyne. Hell, being with Ballantyne, naked or not, terminated all rational thought.

Not clever when she was risking Ty's emotional well-being and her battered heart.

Piper banged her head on the door and closed her eyes. And that was why sex and business shouldn't mix. If she hadn't heard from him by early Monday morning, she would have to initiate another conversation about the sapphires. For now she had a baby to feed and laundry to do. Reports to write. Friday night excitement, she wryly thought.

As she tossed vegetables and chicken into the blender for Ty's supper, she thought about Jaeger's invitation to Latimore's exhibition. If their affair in Milan had ended differently, she'd be in her bedroom now, pulling on her sexiest thong, her strapless bra. She would feel Jaeger's hot eyes on her as he watched her dress. When she sat down in front of her dressing table in her lingerie to put on her makeup, she'd watch him button his shirt behind her.

She could see him in gray suit pants, a light gray shirt with his sleeves rolled up and a gray vest. Black tie. She would pull on her stretchy LBD with its skinny spaghetti straps, liking the way the darted triangle bodice showed off her boobs. She'd slowly, oh so slowly, bend over to put on her sexy silver sandals, and Jaeger would run his hands between her thighs. His finger would sneak under her thong and he'd be touching her and, damn, she could feel the heat spearing into her stomach…

The doorbell interrupted her very far-fetched X-rated fantasy, and she jumped, inadvertently flipping the switch to the lidless blender. Vegetables volcanoed across the kitchen, splattering her white T-shirt, the counter and the floor.

Puree dripped off her chin, so she grabbed a kitchen towel. She shook her head at the mess. Behind her in his playpen, Ty was chattering to his soft toys, incomprehensible baby talk.

She looked at the screen and saw Jaeger standing at her front door, hands in the pockets of his leather jacket, looking hot enough to melt glass. She, on the other hand, looked like hell.

Yes, she needed to speak to Jaeger, but not when she was looking like a refugee from the Baby Feeding Wars.

The doorbell chimed again, and Piper hit the button to unlock the main door. She wanted to clean up the mess and change her shirt, but before she had time to do either, Piper heard a knock on the apartment door.

She reluctantly opened it. "Hi. I wasn't expecting to see you tonight."

Jaeger looked at the streaks on her shirt and lifted a curl from her right breast, the ends coated in splatters of chicken and carrots. "Hi. You look like you had a food fight with Ty and you lost."

"Close." Piper shut the door behind him and looked at his most excellent bum in nicely fitting jeans. Apart from her grungy shirt, she was also wearing yoga pants hanging low on her hips, and she wasn't wearing any shoes.

"Just another exciting Friday night," Piper muttered, following him into the living room.

"That's actually why I'm here," Jaeger said, standing next to Ty's playpen. The tips of his fingers brushed Ty's dark head, and Ty grinned up at him. How could he not see the resemblance? Piper wondered. They had the same eyes, the same hair and the same smile.

"I've been let off babysitting duty. Shaw has tonsillitis and Linc is staying home with him," Jaeger explained. "So I thought you might want to go to Latimore's exhibition."

Piper frowned, confused. Jeans, a long-sleeve cobalt T-shirt and a battered leather jacket were not what she would have expected him to wear to an opening night of such importance. "With you?"

"Nope, with my sister Sage." Jaeger pulled an invitation from the inside pocket of his jacket and handed it to her. He shrugged out of the leather and tossed it over the back of a chair. "She says she'll meet you there. She's as big a fan of art as you are, so you should like each other."

"But Ty…"

Jaeger bent over the side of the playpen, and Piper couldn't help admiring his hard, tight butt as he picked up Ty and settled the baby on his hip. "This little dude and I will drink beer and watch ESPN."

"But—"

"Piper, it seems to me that you don't have a lot of people to rely on. I understand that Ty is your priority, but you deserve to have some fun, too. Let me make you happy. Let me do this for you."

No, this was too much! On top of the advance and

the great sex, she didn't think she could cope with him being so ridiculously thoughtful. How was she supposed to resist him?

"Look, I admit I don't have a hell of a lot of experience with babies, but I can now change a diaper. I'm pretty sure I can make a bottle if you tell me how. Besides, I checked in with Ceri, and she said Rainn will be downstairs because he's studying, so if Ty starts screaming his head off, I'll call him to give me a hand."

Piper bit the inside of her lip, still undecided. She flicked her finger against the edges of the card. "I can't, Jaeger. I haven't fed Ty yet. I'd need to shower, put on makeup, a dress. Get into the city."

Ty's little hand reached up to grab Jaeger's ear, then his hair. Jaeger just flashed him a quick smile and allowed Ty's little hands to explore.

"Sage is going to start looking for you later. I knew you'd need time to sort Ty out and to give me a long lecture on what to do and what not to do." Ty shouted, and Jaeger followed his eyes to the playpen. He frowned at the pile of toys on the floor. "You're going to have to be more specific, dude."

"The yellow duck," Piper told him. "It's his favorite."

Jaeger picked up the duck and handed it over. Ty waved the skinny animal around, its beak scraping along Jaeger's jaw. "Take a break, Piper. Go meet my sister, talk art, have some wine."

"I took a break last night," Piper said, staring at the floor.

"Is there a law somewhere stating single moms can't go out two nights in a row?" Jaeger asked.

"But…you could be watching basketball!"

"I could also be at a cocktail party, having dinner,

seeing a show on Broadway." Jaeger held her eyes. "If I wanted to be there, I would be. I choose to be here."

"But why?"

Jaeger shrugged, and Ty loved the up-and-down movement. "Because I can do any of those things on any other night. What you can't do every night is be one of the first people in the world to see Latimore's new work. I like his art, but you love it. You appreciate it at a depth I don't. So, I'd like you to go, even though you had a—" the corners of his mouth turned up "—break last night."

Piper looked from Jaeger to Ty and back again. Could she leave Ty with him? Could she trust him?

On the other hand, she didn't have a reason *not* to trust him. He was Ty's dad, even though he didn't know it, and if he came to like Ty a little, maybe that would dilute his shocked reaction when the time came to tell him the truth.

If the time came to tell him about Ty, she silently amended.

"I've got this, Piper. Really."

Ty looked happy enough with Jaeger, she thought. He was a pretty easygoing child and as sociable as a golden retriever. Provided he was fed, was clean and had company, he wouldn't fuss. She'd be gone only two hours, three at the most. For most of those hours Ty would be asleep. Rainn was five seconds away if something went wrong or if Jaeger found himself out of his depth.

She could be home by half-past ten if she hustled. Jaeger was right. How often did one get to meet the reclusive artist, be the first to see his new work? She was also quite curious to meet Jaeger's sister...

If their lives hadn't taken such a U-turn, if they had been two normal people looking for love, was this what living with Jaeger would have been like? Spontaneity and fun? The giving and receiving of pleasure, both in bed and out?

"I can see the capitulation in your eyes." Jaeger grinned. "Get moving, honey."

Piper looked at the mess in the kitchen and pushed her curls back. "I need to clean the kitchen first."

"I can handle the kitchen. You need to shower." Jaeger reached out and touched the tip of his finger to the ends of her hair. Then, wrapping a curl around his fist, he nudged her chin up with his knuckle. "But first... this."

Still holding Ty, he leaned in and touched his mouth to hers, his lips cool and assured. He kept a lid on the kiss, not allowing the churning heat to run away from them. Piper heard Ty's chortle at this new game, felt his small hand bouncing off her head as she closed her eyes and took this moment.

It was over too soon. Piper watched as Jaeger pulled back from her and looked at his son, their son.

"Kissing your mommy is fun. Even when she smells like chicken."

Ty cocked his head and grinned up at Jaeger. Jaeger smiled back, and Piper's heart stopped as the two identical smiles held.

God, how much longer could she keep this from him? One of these days he would look at Ty and think *This kid looks like me*, and then she'd be up the proverbial creek without a paddle and with holes in her canoe.

After tonight she would have to limit the amount of contact Ty and Jaeger had. She would keep them apart. Jaeger had dropped into her life and within another week, maybe two, he'd be gone. He would buy the stones and move on and forget about them both.

She couldn't, *wouldn't*, fall into the trap of playing happy family. It was too easy to lean on him, to be a part of something bigger and better than just her and Ty. But Jaeger wasn't the type who hunkered down for the long term, and if she thought he might change, she was kidding herself.

Her mother had spent all of her adult life hoping that her father would change, that he'd commit to her, that he'd show interest in the daughter they'd made together.

Jaeger nodded to the stairs. "Get a move on. You are going to be late. Oh, and remind me to give you your check before I go."

Piper held back her relieved sigh. So their deal was still on. Her shoulders dropped three inches. "Thank you. Really. For everything. I'm very grateful."

"No worries," Jaeger replied, his tone relaxed. He turned away and walked toward the kitchen, stopping in the doorway when he saw the mess. "That was your dinner, Ty? Yuck. Let's order pizza. Pepperoni, anchovies, olives? What's your poison?"

"There's some baby food in the freezer. He's too young to eat pizza," Piper said, still hovering at the bottom of the stairs.

Jaeger made a production of looking at Ty and rolling his eyes. "Your mommy thinks I'm an idiot. Of course I know babies can't eat pizza. But Chinese—you can eat Chinese, can't you?"

Jaeger, his hands clammy and his breathing shallow, decided to keep his eyes on Ty for every second he was in charge. If he did, then nothing would happen to the kid.

When Ty fell asleep, he'd keep watching him, make sure he was breathing. Ty would be safe on his watch.

He'd debated long and hard whether he wanted to do this—whether he could spend concentrated alone-time with a baby. But the excitement he'd seen earlier on Piper's face was worth a little cold sweat.

He liked making Piper happy, both in bed and out, and that fact made his blood run freezing cold. Between Piper and her son, Jaeger was six-foot-plus of scared.

One step at a time, Ballantyne. Keep Ty safe for the next couple of hours.

He could do that if he didn't panic. Rainn was his safety net, just as much as he was Piper's. If Rainn hadn't been a yell away, there was no way Jaeger could have sat here with Ty, on his own.

But he could do this; he *had* to do this. The chances of this happy, healthy little boy dying of SIDS, or anything else, were a gajillion to one. His mind knew that; his heart still was in fight-or-flight mode.

Calm the hell down, Ballantyne. You can do this.

Jaeger looked out the window of the den and saw Piper climbing into a taxi, her long legs catching an appreciative glance from a pedestrian walking by.

He'd fed Ty, made some coffee and intended to tackle the mess on the kitchen floor, but then Piper walked down the stairs, and the sight of her nearly dropped him to his knees. The dress was black and skimmed across her sexy body, stopping midthigh. He'd just stared at her as she pulled on her coat, wondering whether he could dump Ty in his playpen and take her back upstairs. The dress was enough to give any red-blooded male a heart attack, and like her boots from last night, those silver ice pick heels made him think of her wearing nothing else.

He was seriously worried he might have a shoe fetish. He was seriously worried, period. Jaeger released a long sigh, holding Ty against his chest as he watched Ty's mommy drive away.

"Your mother is driving me nuts, dude," Jaeger told Ty, sitting in the wingback chair by the window, Ty straddling his knee. He jiggled, and Ty laughed and waved his yellow duck around. "I just look at her and my IQ drops by twenty points."

Ty blew him a raspberry, and Jaeger bounced his knee again. "I'm supposed to be risk-averse and yet I do this. I mean, what idiot agrees to give a woman he barely knows a loan against the sale of her gems? From his own friggin' money, no less. She makes me do things I would never normally consider, just to make her smile. I'm teetering on the edge of a cliff and it's a long way down."

But he had yet to take a step back.

Ty cocked his head and gave Jaeger a look he couldn't read. Was he supposed to keep talking or keep bouncing? Hedging his bets, Jaeger did both. "The gems will definitely sell for three million, and if they are the Kashmir Blues, they'll sell for a lot more. But I have to trust her to pay me back. I can trust her, right?"

Jaeger nodded and Ty nodded, too, liking this new game. Jaeger chose to believe the kid knew exactly what he was talking about.

"And every time she walks into the room, I just want to strip her naked and slide on home." Jaeger heard what he'd said and winced, suddenly remembering he was talking not only to a baby but also about the kid's *mother*. "Hearing me talk this way about your mom isn't going to scar you for life and send you into therapy, is it?"

Ty tipped his head sideways and waved his hands

after noticing a fabric ball on the carpet by the foot of the chair. Jaeger lowered the baby to the floor and placed the ball between his chubby legs. Then Jaeger moved off the chair to sit on the carpet next to Ty, his legs bent at the knees.

Thanks to the long windows, he could still look at the street below. He rather liked Brooklyn, he thought. Stylistically it was a million miles from his luxurious but cold penthouse. There were trees and families and schools. It was all a little more real, a lot more normal.

"But normal isn't me," Jaeger said, watching a couple and their three young kids walking down the street. A golden Labrador, looking like he'd taken a hit of doggy crack, walked a young boy.

"I'm a vagabond, a drifter, someone who is perfectly happy with a designer apartment, with all the amenities of city living. God knows I deserve a little luxury after some of the hellholes I visit and sleep in."

Ty pushed the ball away from him, Jaeger rolled it back and Ty shouted his approval. This was such a happy kid. Everything made him laugh.

Outside, the dog wrapped his leash around the legs of the kid, and the entire family laughed as they tried to separate the kid and the dog. Dad took control of the dog but not before he dropped a hot openmouthed kiss on Mom. Jaeger grinned when the boy made a "gross" face.

"But really, this house, this place, it's for families, and I'm not a family guy," Jaeger said, resting his head back against the cushion of the chair. He watched the street for a couple of minutes, enjoying the changing light. "I was going to be, but I never got the chance. I had my shot at having a happy family, and losing it nearly killed me. I'm not interested. No matter how sexy your mom is.

No matter how much I like her, this is a one-shot deal. It's not forever. So don't think it is," Jaeger warned Ty, dropping his head to the right to look at Piper's son.

Except Ty wasn't where he'd left him.

Jaeger's heart stopped. He'd been watching Ty for what, ten minutes, and he'd already lost him? He shot to his feet, his heart pounding as his eyes scanned the den. His head told him the kid wasn't that fast, but his heart went into panic mode. Jaeger looked at the front door—locked, thank God. Ty had to be somewhere in the apartment. Babies didn't just vaporize! Then Jaeger caught the movement of a socked foot as it disappeared into the kitchen.

Gotcha. Jaeger put his hands on his thighs and took a few calming, deep breaths. *Relax or you'll give yourself a heart attack.*

After a couple of moments, after his heart slowed from a gallop to a jog, Jaeger walked toward the kitchen and found Ty sitting in the mess on the floor—the mess he'd promised Piper he'd clean up. Ty's little fingers went straight into the goop and up to his mouth. He sucked his digits and dove back in.

By the time Jaeger reached him, the baby had smeared the goop over his face, into his hair, down his clothing and around his neck. The kid had the ability to cause major mayhem in the shortest time possible. Jaeger rather admired that about him.

Jaeger stood in the doorway to the kitchen, pulled his phone from his back pocket and, keeping his eyes on the tiny troublemaker, lifted the phone to his ear.

"Linc? How do you bathe a baby?"

"With soap and water, moron."

Eight

Piper stepped into the dark hallway of her apartment and sent a guilty glance at her watch. It was after midnight; she'd intended to be back home hours ago, but Latimore's new work was spectacular and thought-provoking and mesmerizing. She'd spent far more time in the gallery than she'd planned on.

What an evening, Piper thought as she slipped off her shoes. At around ten, the very sexy sculptor finally emerged from a back room, walked directly over to Sage and, without greeting a single soul or saying a word, planted a smokin' hot kiss on Sage's mouth. Sage responded by slapping him, and they'd both stormed out of the gallery. Neither returned, much to the consternation of the gallery owner and his guests. Latimore and Sage were the only topic of conversation for the rest of the evening.

Piper, who'd immediately bonded with the quiet but

wickedly funny Sage, was annoyed by the crowd's fascination with something that had absolutely nothing to do with them. She'd blocked out the snippets of gossip drifting her way and immersed herself in Latimore's art. The steel and carved wood elements remained but the sculptures weren't as heavy, as masculine as before. There was fluidity in his work and an unexpected femininity that hadn't been present in his earlier works.

Latimore might be a jerk—he had to have done something more than kiss Sage to earn a slap like that—but dear God, he was a brilliant artist.

Piper dropped her clutch onto the hallway table and jerked when the bag hit the floor. Dammit, she still wasn't used to the empty space where the blue marble side table had stood for thirty-odd years. Piper stared at the empty space and slowly raised her eyes to the blank space on the wall. Her Mom's favorite possession, an early Frida Kahlo, was also gone. So was her beloved eighteenth-century rolltop desk and the ballerina bronze. The items had left her apartment a few days before, soon to be sold to make a teeny tiny dent in her father's debts.

Tears stung Piper's eyes and she placed her hand beneath her rib cage, fighting the wave of pain. It wasn't fair. They were her mother's possessions, the only proof Piper had that her father loved her mother, that he felt enough for her to buy her a very expensive gift occasionally.

But was that love? Piper wrapped her arms around her waist and stared at the empty spaces on the floor and on the wall and in her heart. Was it still an expression of love when it wasn't freely given? These gifts, like her father's affection, were on loan to her mom, always able to be pulled back, to be used for something else.

It was typical Mick, Piper thought. He always had a backup plan, a way to cover his ass. Even in death, he came first. Selfish bastard.

While she could live with losing the paintings and a couple of pieces of furniture, she couldn't handle losing her house. Thanks to Jaeger, she wouldn't have to. Resolved to get back into the attic and to contact the few relatives left on her mother's side to see if they knew anything about her great-uncle—without mentioning the stones—and whether they had any family papers, Piper turned and walked into the dark living room.

In the light spilling from the hall, she saw Jaeger lying on her couch, one foot on the floor and his other bent leg resting on the cushions. Her son—their son—was sprawled over Jaeger's broad chest, his mouth a scant inch from Jaeger's strong neck. One of Jaeger's hands covered Ty's small back. His other arm was firmly under the baby's little butt.

Piper sat on the table next to the couch and looked at her son and his father. Two peas in a pod, she thought, examining their faces.

She should tell Jaeger, Piper thought. He had a right to know, and if she was a better, braver person, she would share the miracle of her son with this man.

But…there were so many buts.

If she wanted to tell Jaeger about Ty, then she would have to come clean about why she'd felt she needed to keep the secret in the first place. She'd have to tell him about Mick, her illegitimacy, and admit that her mother was her father's lifelong mistress and Piper was the daughter he never wanted.

If it came out that she was Mick's daughter, his bad reputation would taint hers and could badly damage her career. Her client's faith in her would be tested—the apple didn't fall far from the tree and all that.

If she told Jaeger about Ty, she'd have to trust him on all levels. Trust him to keep her paternity to himself. Trust him to understand why it was so important to her that Ty have an involved father, or no father at all.

Trust him to be that kind of father for Ty.

She really liked Jaeger—hell, she was halfway to falling in love with him! He was funny and smart and generous and hot. Any woman with a pulse would fall a little in love with Jaeger. Maybe he wouldn't care that she was Mick's daughter. Maybe he would understand her reasons, and maybe he would even like Ty. But none of those reactions would change the fact that Jaeger didn't want children.

When Jaeger recovered from the shock of the truth, what sort of dad would he be? Would he ignore Ty for the rest of his life? Would he be a half-there dad, visiting Ty when he felt like it? Would he be the type of parent who bought expensive presents instead of spending time with him?

Ty needed Jaeger to be fully involved, to love him with everything he had. He needed to be the most important person in Jaeger's life. Ty deserved everything a father could give, and she wouldn't accept anything less than amazing for her son. She would not allow Ty to spend his life questioning his father's love, second-guessing himself, wondering why his dad chose his career and his freedom above his son.

Not happening. Not to Ty.

Jaeger didn't want a family, didn't want children.

Ty needed, deserved, a crazy-about-him dad.

But still...didn't Jaeger deserve to know?

God, she was so confused. Her heart and brain were at odds, and she really didn't know what to do.

He's only been back in your life, in Ty's life, for a week. You don't need to make this decision now.

Piper latched on to the thought. So much had happened, she kept forgetting Jaeger had reentered her life only a week ago today; she was allowed to slow down, to take a breath. She was feeling emotional and stressed. It was very late. She didn't need to deal with this now.

Piper watched as Jaeger's eyes opened. He yawned and turned his head, his eyes connecting with hers. Desire flared, and Piper felt the moisture drying up in her mouth. The special spot between her legs started to tingle, and she briefly wished his mouth was licking her to a fiery orgasm. He would be naked, she would be naked and she would climb on top of him…

"Hey, how was the exhibition?" Jaeger asked in a sexy, sleep-roughened voice.

Exhibition? What exhibition? Piper sent him a blank look.

Jaeger lifted an amused eyebrow. "You did go to see Latimore's latest work, didn't you?"

Oh, right. Latimore. Sculptures. Sage slapping him.

God, Piper wished she wasn't so ridiculously attracted to her baby's father. Earlier she'd stared at one of Latimore's pieces for more than twenty minutes, because it reminded her of this man.

"Ah, yes. The exhibition was—" Piper hesitated "—interesting."

Jaeger's hand moved up Ty's back to hold his head. Ty, fast asleep, didn't react. "A good or bad interesting?" Jaeger asked, his voice a low rumble.

"His works were dynamic and flat-out brilliant. Supersexy."

Jaeger lifted an amused, and interested, eyebrow. "Really?"

"Mmm. There was one piece I couldn't stop looking at. It reminded me of you...naked."

Jaeger flashed his heart-stopping smile. "Were you having naughty thoughts about me, Ms. Mills?"

"I was."

"I like it."

"I thought you might," Piper said, her tone dry. "Oh, and Latimore kissed Sage and she slapped him, hard," Piper reluctantly admitted.

Jaeger's low laugh surprised her.

Piper frowned at him. "You're not upset? The incident is going to be breaking news in the morning."

Jaeger managed a quick shrug. "If you're worried about being in the news then you have no business being a Ballantyne." The corners of his mouth kicked up in amusement. "You are dying to know their history, aren't you?"

She wished she could deny it but...of course she was. "It was a hell of a kiss and a hell of a slap," Piper admitted. "Anyone would be curious—in fact, rumors were flying—but if it's a big secret, then I can live without knowing what it is." She wasn't a hypocrite. Sage was entitled to keep her past buried, just as Piper was.

"It's not a big deal," Jaeger explained. "They had a thing and something went wrong."

Piper looked at Jaeger, waiting for more. What went wrong? What happened? "That's it? That's all you're going to tell me?"

"Shh." Jaeger pointed to the sleeping Ty. "That's all I know because that's all she told us."

"And you didn't pry?"

"Uh, no. She cried, we threatened to kill him, she threatened to kill us if we interfered and Connor told us to stay out of it, so we did."

Rats, Piper thought. She wouldn't know anything more than the gossip she'd heard. Damn these Ballantynes for being so damn intriguing, and interesting. And contrary.

Talking about contrary...

"Why is Ty sleeping on your chest and not in his crib?" Piper asked.

Jaeger twisted his neck to look down at Ty, his mouth curving into a grin. "Ah, that. Well, we were drinking beer and smoking cigars and watching a porno horror flick—"

"You were not," Piper interrupted, unable to keep the amusement out of her voice.

"Okay, we were watching the game, and midway through me explaining how a technical foul worked, he conked out. Blam! Lights out."

"He's always done that," Piper admitted. "He goes flat-out and then drops like a stone."

"It could be because he motors over the floor like a Formula One racer."

Piper lifted her hands, not understanding. "What are you talking about?"

"His crawling."

Piper shook her head. "He isn't crawling yet."

"He crawled from the den into the kitchen and spent the evening crawling all over the floor," Jaeger said, both hands on Ty as he swung his legs down and sat up in a fluid, easy movement.

"That really sucks," Piper muttered, standing up.

"Shouldn't I have let him crawl? Is that a problem?"

Piper heard the worry in Jaeger's voice, the self-doubt, and her feelings of resentment instantly disappeared. "No, of course not. I would've just loved to see him crawl for the first time. It's a big deal, and I wanted to be here."

"I'm sorry," Jaeger said, still holding her sleeping son—their son—in his brawny arms.

"It's okay." And it was. Jaeger had missed out on so much; she could give him this moment with Ty. And if she didn't tell him about Ty, soon, he'd miss out on him walking and talking, his first day at school…

Cool your jets, Mills. It all depended on whether he was prepared to be part of Ty's life or not.

You weren't going to think about that again tonight, remember?

Piper stepped forward to take Ty from Jaeger, but Jaeger shook his head. "I'll put him in his crib if that's okay."

"Sure." Piper nodded and watched as Jaeger left the room, the gift he'd given her in his arms.

As Jaeger stepped into the hallway, Piper saw him duck down to drop a soft kiss on Ty's head. The gesture of affection made the urge to tell him he was Ty's father rise within her once more.

It was one kiss, Mills. You can't spill your guts because of one spontaneous gesture in the middle of the night.

Ty looked angelic. Anyone with a heart would want to kiss his gorgeous face. It didn't mean Jaeger would be a good dad, that he would be there for Ty every step of the way.

Midnight kisses given to sleeping babies were easy; kisses after grueling days were a lot more difficult to dole out.

It didn't matter. Jaeger wasn't going to be around long enough to prove anything to anybody. In a couple of weeks, this would all be over. The stones would be sold, she'd own her house and Jaeger would be on the road again, searching for amazing jewels. The order of the universe would be restored.

If that was what she wanted, what she craved, then why did she feel sick at the thought of a life without Jaeger in it?

Nine

Jaeger placed a kiss in the center of Piper's back and glanced at the weak sunlight behind the curtains. Piper didn't stir, so Jaeger pulled back and rested his head in his hand, his other hand sweeping over the smooth, creamy skin of Piper's back and butt.

He should leave soon, and he knew he should let her sleep, but part of him wanted to wake Piper up and make love to her again. After putting Ty to bed last night, he'd kept her busy until the early hours of this morning. So, yeah, he should let her sleep.

Jaeger released a frustrated sigh and looked around her bedroom. It was full of color—bold, bright jewel tones ranging from the dark teal wall behind him to the scarlet chair in the corner, the multicolored cushions he'd tossed from the bed to the floor before he'd lowered her naked body to the multihued comforter. Her love of art was revealed by a collection of sketches grouped on the far wall and the sexy abstract painting above their heads. It was wild and bright and bold, perfect adjectives to describe his lover.

His temporary lover, Jaeger amended. This wasn't going anywhere, couldn't go anywhere. He was in the country only until he'd finalized the deal to buy the Kashmir Blues. To complete the deal, he needed to find something proving where the stones came from and explaining Piper's connection to the sapphires. After he'd dotted those *i*'s and crossed those *t*'s, he was out of here; there were Colombian emeralds to find, deep blue tanzanite to discover in Kenya, alexandrite in Siberia. He had places to visit, stones to buy.

Piper and her very cute kid were not reason enough to stop traveling, to make changes to his life. He really liked Piper and he adored her body—couldn't seem to get enough of her, actually—but there was something else besides his commitment phobia making him gun-shy.

Piper was like a very fine Zultanite. The rare gemstone had the ability to change from a kiwi green in the sun to a raspberry-purple-pink in candlelight. Like Piper, the stone didn't stop there. It could also be a dull green and morph into a sage green before changing to a whiskey-shaded pink. Zultanite, like Piper, had a million shades and a dozen secrets.

He needed to know Piper's secrets, needed to know what she was hiding. Oh, she'd told him a little—just enough, she thought, to satisfy his curiosity. Her eyes reflected her soul and he saw all her colors, and, like Zultanite, each color was a revelation.

Thanks to his missing memory—and his experience with Jess and Andrea—he couldn't deal in half truths and evasions. Yeah, he knew some of what had happened directly before the accident, but he couldn't see the full picture, and that scorched his soul.

Thoughts of what he'd missed tortured him. How did he and Piper meet? What did they speak about? It was like looking at a photograph that was out of focus.

He needed details and...

He needed the truth, the whole truth.

Last night, after rocking each other's world, he'd tried to ask Piper again about Milan, but she'd changed the subject by rolling onto him and kissing her way down his chest, his stomach...

When she'd run her tongue down his erection, talking seemed like a highly overrated activity. This morning he could see her actions more clearly; she'd wanted to distract him and, yeah, sex was a fantastic way to side-track the conversation. But she'd shut him down, shut him out. She wasn't letting him see the full picture...

Why didn't she trust him? He wanted her to trust him.

But what would he do with that trust? It wasn't like he could take their relationship any further. He wasn't prepared to risk his heart on someone who would walk away and take his love with her. That wasn't part of his plan.

Okay, yeah, being around Ty was curing him of his baby phobia, and he rather enjoyed the little guy, but he knew there was a hell of a difference between baby-sitting for a night and being an ongoing and consistent part of a kid's life. Piper was a package deal. If Jaeger wanted her, then he had to take on her kid, too. And... no, he wasn't up to being a part-time dad.

When his folks died, Connor had jumped into raising Jaeger and his sibs with enthusiasm. He'd never doubted Connor's love or commitment to them. Jaeger wasn't prepared to take on a kid unless he could do the same. First because whatever he did, he did properly, and second because doing a half-assed job of parenting would be an insult to Connor's memory.

If he fell in love with Piper then he had to fall in love with Ty—so easy to do!—and that would mean losing not one but two people he cared for if—when—the deal went south.

Because with love, the deal always went south.

Piper sighed and rolled over, her big eyes widening when she saw him. Her look of confusion was easily interpreted. She wasn't used to waking up with a man in her bed, and he liked the idea that she didn't treat sex casually. Yeah, double standards, yada yada. He was a man and he liked knowing no one else slept on her sheets.

"Hey, you're still here," Piper said, her voice deeper and sexier.

Jaeger used his index finger to push a curl from the corner of her mouth. "Were you expecting me to leave without saying goodbye?"

"I—um—" Piper glanced at the door as she pushed herself up. Then she glanced down, realized she was naked and yanked the comforter over her breasts.

Jaeger responded by tugging the material down again. "You're too pretty to be shy."

Piper just pulled the covers up again and Jaeger let her, wishing she could see herself through his eyes. Messy hair, wide eyes, perfect skin. So hot it hurt.

"I need to check on Ty," Piper said, sounding flustered.

"He's fast asleep, Piper. Relax."

"But what if he sees you in my bed? What will he think?"

Jaeger grinned. "He'll high-five me and tell me I scored?" When Piper didn't smile at his joke, he sighed. "Honey, he's still a baby. He's not going to remember a damn thing."

Piper's blush started on her chest and inched up her throat. "Sorry. I'm not good at this morning-after stuff."

Jaeger squeezed her knee as he sat up. "Just relax, okay? It's all good." He stood up, walked over to the window and pulled the drape, keeping to the side so he didn't show the good residents of Brooklyn everything he had to offer. And because he was in Piper's bed and she was hot, what he had was impressive.

He loved fresh air, so he cracked the window an inch and sighed at the gush of rain-tinged wind drifting into the room. Piper pulled the comforter up around her shoulders and tossed him an are-you-crazy look.

"I've spent too many hours in dank, moldy, stuffy caves and tunnels, so fresh air is like perfume to me."

"City air isn't the freshest air on the planet," Piper pointed out.

Jaeger smiled and took another deep breath before closing the window. He walked back to her, told her to scoot over and slid into bed, shoulder to shoulder and thigh to thigh with her. He felt her tremble, one of those little shudders that rushed through women when they were turned on, and he swallowed his smile. He knew how she felt. All she had to do was breathe and he wanted to slip inside.

"So, what's on your to-do list today?" Jaeger asked, his hand on her slim thigh. He felt her sharp intake of breath and smiled. Yeah, by the grace of God and sleeping babies, he'd have her again shortly.

"Um, not a lot. I thought I'd take Ty running if it doesn't rain."

"He's just started to crawl, so aren't you expecting a bit much?"

"I run. He's in his stroller… Oh, you're joking," Piper said, shaking her head. "Sorry, it's a bit early and I need coffee to wake me up."

Or you need a man to make you smile more, someone you can laugh with, to tease you. Not that he could be that man, but the thought of another man doing that made him… God, *enough!*

"I also need to contact my mom's relatives. Maybe they have some info on my great-uncle, something to help us understand how he came to own the stones."

"That's a good idea."

"Um, so do you want to, uh, maybe come back later and we can look through some more boxes?" Piper asked.

He wished he could, but Moreau's Ball was that night, a must-attend event. Yeah, the Moreaus were their closest competitors, but the Ballantynes and the Moreaus had a cordial though competitive relationship. Each Ballantyne sibling had received one of the coveted invitations, and not to attend would be, in Connor's words, very bad form. Jaeger would love to take Piper as his date; apart from the fact that he enjoyed being with her, he knew she'd enjoy the spectacle of the ball, the elaborate designs and the drama Morgan and Riley Moreau brought to the event.

But that was impossible. Piper didn't socialize in those circles, and there would be a lot of speculation about who she was and why she was with him. The press would want to know, and if he didn't give them the information, they'd go and dig for it. He couldn't risk anyone finding out about the stones before they sold, and neither did he want anyone digging into Piper's life. They'd realize she was a single mom, which would raise a dozen more questions, the biggest one being why he would be dating a single mom when he'd told the world, on numerous occasions, he wasn't the marrying and daddy type.

God, it would be a nightmare and a headache he didn't need. No, it was better to keep his relationship—or whatever this was—with Piper a secret for as long as possible.

"Sorry, Piper, but I have plans. I could come around tomorrow afternoon. I have a breakfast date with my siblings in the morning."

"Oh." He felt her sigh and sensed she wanted to ask what his plans were, whether he was seeing someone else. He braced himself, waiting for the questions.

Instead of speaking, Piper dropped her head and rested her temple on the ball of his shoulder. "Okay, no worries. I'll see you if and when I see you."

Why was she okay with him dropping in and out of her life? Didn't she realize that she deserved more, that she had a right to ask for what she wanted? Maybe this loose arrangement was all she wanted…and why did that irritate him?

He was losing it. Jaeger placed a kiss on her forehead and deliberately pushed his frustration away. "You're easy to be with, Piper Mills," he murmured into her hair, his words so low he wasn't sure if she heard him. "And I still have the morning free."

Piper stretched her neck and her lips grazed the underside of his jaw, painting streaks of fire on his skin. He closed his eyes and felt her move away, and he hissed his disappointment. His eyes opened when he felt the bed covers move off his chest and then his thighs, to be replaced with a slim, sexy, fragrant woman.

Piper straddled his legs, her knees against his hips

and her hands on his chest, her happy place an inch away from his. He swelled beneath her and his hands skimmed up the sides of her rib cage, his thumbs swiping across her nipples. Piper's eyes darkened and her mouth opened, but she didn't break eye contact.

She dropped her hips and her heat met his hardness. Jaeger groaned, thinking this was the best type of torture, the sweetest hell. She could spend the next day—year, decade—just sliding up and down his shaft and he would be content to stare into her eyes, wondering what it was about this woman that captured his fascination.

Oh, her long, slim body was a turn-on, and she was as beautiful without makeup as she was with it. Her hair was soft and silky. He picked up the curl skimming the top of her breast and wound it around his finger. He brushed her nipple with her own hair. Piper shuddered and he watched her, desperately trying to ignore her slick, wet heat sliding across him.

He wanted to delay this, wanted to slow down and watch her enjoy him. He wanted to figure out what made this woman so different.

Maybe it was the fleeting emotions flashing in her eyes, which were the exact green of a tsavorite garnet. But the emotions were there and gone before he could identify them. Lust and desire were easy to recognize; she wanted him as much as he wanted her. But behind those feelings he sensed her desire to connect, to push away loneliness, to feel wanted in a nonsexual way.

He understood.

Jaeger lifted his hand and cradled her face. As her eyes closed, he watched her turn her face into his hand, seeking more. Yeah, Piper needed tenderness, affection, a connection...

He couldn't give it to her.

She wasn't asking for a lifetime commitment, Jaeger argued with his inner cynic. All she was silently asking for was a brief moment to pretend this was more than an exchange of pleasure, more than a big bang on a Saturday morning.

Or is a connection what you want?

Did he want a different sexual experience that had nothing to do with sex and everything to do with giving and receiving emotion, appreciation, acceptance, affection?

Jaeger skimmed his thumb across her lower lip. When her eyes connected with his, he saw his need for more—just this one time—reflected in those pure green depths. Unable to resist, he placed his hands on her hips and flipped her under him, holding himself up and away to keep from touching her. He just needed a moment to look at her, to burn the memory of her—so soft, so feminine, so open—into his brain.

"I need to love you."

Dammit, he didn't mean to say the words out loud.

Piper gave him a look he couldn't decipher. Then she linked her arms around his neck and pulled him down so they lay hip to hip, chest to breast. Her legs fell open. He nudged at her opening and groaned, feeling her fiery welcome on his tip.

He wanted more, he wanted to explore, but Piper lifted her hips and slid onto him, hot and tight. When he tried to pull out, she locked her legs around his hips to hold him in place. She surged upward again, and he was buried so deep inside her that his brain shut down and instinct took over.

He didn't need to move. Piper was moving enough

for both of them, setting the pace. All he had to do was hold on for the ride. It was a strange experience, letting her take control, but it was massively erotic. With every thrust, she squeezed and he felt the pressure build. He gritted his teeth, willing himself to let her drive, knowing the orgasm she pulled from him would be one of the best of his life.

He felt her internal muscles contract, heard her intake of breath, and when heat coursed over him, he thrust once, then twice and followed her into a deep blinding light he never wanted to leave.

At the Ninth Street entrance to Prospect Park, Jaeger pushed the handle of Ty's stroller into her hand, walked over to the hot dog stand and ordered a dog fully loaded. God, he'd already had two bowls of cereal back at her apartment, two cups of coffee and three of Ty's baby biscuits. She'd forgotten how much men ate. Especially ripped, fit men who burned calories like a hot rocket.

Piper leaned down and checked on Ty. As she'd suspected, he'd pulled off his beanie, both his shoes and one sock. Piper replaced his footwear and tried to tug his beanie back over his ears. Within five seconds, Ty had it off again and in his mouth. Okay, Piper decided, this was a battle she wasn't going to win. The hat could stay off, but the socks and baby shoes had to stay on.

Piper watched as Jaeger lifted his hot dog to his mouth and took an enormous bite. She'd expected him to leave right after they made love, but after a trip to the bathroom, he'd climbed back into bed and wrapped his arms around her. Within a few minutes he'd fallen asleep.

She woke up around eight. Her bed was empty but her kitchen wasn't. Jaeger had Ty in his high chair, making buzzing noises as he directed a spoon of yogurt toward Ty's open mouth. Ty would not eat if his diaper was soggy, so that meant Jaeger had changed him while she slept.

Any other man, she suspected, would've nudged her awake, and told her Ty was awake and yelling for her—when Ty woke up he immediately demanded company. Any other man would've buried his head in the pillow and left her to sort out her son. Not Jaeger Ballantyne; he'd heard Ty, went to him, changed him and fed him breakfast, allowing her another hour of precious sleep.

If he ever needed a kidney, or blood, she was his girl. Hell, she suspected her heart already belonged to him, anyway. What was another organ or two?

Every minute she spent with him deepened her connection to him; what a fool she had been for thinking she could stop herself from falling for him. Maybe that was why, in Milan, she'd insisted they not hook up again. She'd subconsciously known they could never be just bed buddies.

Jaeger was a good guy. In fact, he was one of the best she'd ever known.

He deserved to know about Ty, to be the dad her father had never been.

Ty deserved to know him. It wasn't fair to either of them to keep this a secret.

So how to tell him? And when?

Jaeger approached her and lifted up his half-eaten dog. "Want a bite?" he offered.

Piper shook her head. "God, no. Processed food and carbs and preservatives."

Jaeger looked at his hot dog, then at her, and took an-

other enormous bite, his eyes reflecting pure mischief.
He chewed and swallowed. "Tastes damn good."

"Smells good, too," Piper reluctantly admitted.

Jaeger popped the last piece of his third breakfast into
his mouth, and they walked into the park, her pushing
the stroller with one hand. She loved this park. It was
her favorite place to walk or run, with Ty or not. Both
she and Ty loved being in the fresh air, and in the summer she'd spent a lot of time lounging on a blanket with
Ty in the Long Meadow. She turned her head to watch
Jaeger, who was looking around with interest.

"Have you been here before?" she asked.

"I'm ashamed to admit I haven't. It's stunning."

"In summer it's a riot of green, but I think it's prettiest in fall, still pretty in winter. A little starker, a little
emptier, but..." Piper shrugged, suddenly embarrassed.
"I think it's awesome. I've been coming here since I was
a kid, so I consider it my personal playground."

Ty shouted and Jaeger jumped, his face instantly worried. Piper laughed. "He's fine. It's his way of telling me
he's happy to be outside."

Jaeger turned around and walked backward, looking
at Ty. "He's missing a sock and a shoe," Jaeger pointed
out.

Piper stopped the stroller and let out a long sigh. Jaeger bent down and lifted a tiny sock. "The sock is here.
One shoe is definitely AWOL."

Piper looked back to see if she could find it on the
path. There it was, about sixty feet from them. Jaeger
spotted it and immediately jogged away to pick it up.
When he returned, she tucked it into her tote bag. "I can't
tell you how many shoes I've lost in this park."

She walked around to the front of the stroller and

pulled Ty's sock back onto his foot, tucking his blanket around his feet to keep him warm. Ty held up his arms and sent her his patented, hard-to-resist, please-pick-me-up smile. Without asking her, Jaeger reached down, popped the button to release his five-strap safety belt and lifted the baby to his chest. Ty sent her a *See how irresistible I am?* look, happy to perch on Jaeger's forearm. Jaeger pulled Ty's blanket from the stroller, draped it over Ty's shoulders and tucked it under the baby's butt. Ty just patted Jaeger's face with tiny, excited hands.

Jaeger smiled at him. "Happy now?"

Ty blew him a raspberry and shouted at a pigeon flying past. His hand narrowly missed hitting Jaeger's nose.

"He's happy," Piper said, her tone dry. "And you're a sucker."

"He's a very cute kid," Jaeger said as they resumed their walk.

"I think so," Piper softly replied.

Jaeger ran his free hand down her hair, over her back. "I think you are pretty awesome, you know. You're raising a kid on your own, and you seem to have it all under control."

"I don't have a choice," Piper stated. "Life gives you what it gives you, and you have to handle it as best you can."

"And his father? Does he have any contact with Ty?"

She'd dodged this question last night, and here it was again. After Jaeger fell asleep last night, she'd rehearsed answers for when he asked again. All those carefully constructed responses were forgotten as she stared at the pathway in front of her.

She didn't know how to tell him the truth.

"I never told him," she admitted.

Jaeger jerked to a stop. She knew that behind his aviator sunglasses, he was frowning. "Why not?"

Piper rocked on her heels, unable to look into his face. "It's complicated."

Jaeger transferred Ty to his other arm and turned him around so Ty faced the road, Jaeger's strong arm across the baby's chest. Ty yelled his approval at his new view, and Jaeger rubbed his chin across the baby's head.

How would he react if she blurted out the news that he was holding his son, that he'd provided half Ty's genes? It still amazed her that nobody could see they shared the same eyes, the same face.

But if she did blurt it out, everything between them would change immediately. She had a week, maybe two left with him before the sapphires sold. Was it so wrong to want to delay the inevitable so she could enjoy being with him, just for a little while?

The memories she made now would have to last a lifetime. He'd never see her the same way once he knew.

She'd tell him. She would. Soon. Just…not today.

"When my girlfriend told me she was pregnant, I was furious. But under the anger, I was soul-deep scared."

It was Piper's turn to stop, and the stroller jerked when she slammed on the brakes. "You have a child?" She shook her head to clear it, not sure whether her ears were playing tricks on her.

Jaeger ran his free hand through his hair before shoving his sunglasses on top of his head. His eyes were a shade of blue she'd never seen before—colder, harder, full of pain. "I was twenty-one. She was twenty. I wasn't as careful about protection as I am now—"

Piper told herself to keep her mouth shut.

"I was in college. So was she. Luckily I'd come into

some money a few months before—money from a trust my parents set up for us—so I could house and feed us and still attend college."

"What did you study?"

"Geology, gemology, business," Jaeger replied. "Andrea dropped out and moved in with me, and we got engaged. It was…difficult."

Piper watched as his mouth tightened and the tension in his jaw increased. Ty felt it, too, and he immediately twisted his head to look at Jaeger. Jaeger turned Ty around to face him, and Ty immediately dropped his forehead into Jaeger's neck and closed his eyes.

Within ten seconds he was asleep.

"He's asleep?" Jaeger asked, his eyes wide with surprise. "How does he do that?"

Piper smiled. "That's—" she pulled back the *your* just in time "—my son. Want me to put him back into his stroller?"

Jaeger shook his head. "I'll carry him."

They resumed walking, and Piper flicked a glance at him. "You were telling me about Andrea?" she prompted him.

"Yeah." Jaeger blew out his breath. "One minute we were college students. The next we were about to be parents with no friggin' idea what we were doing. Andy threw herself into being a stay-at-home mom, spending money and preparing for the baby. It was all she could think about, all she could talk about."

"She was excited?"

"Insanely." Jaeger's bottom lip disappeared between his teeth. "Her entire focus became the baby. She couldn't think about anyone else, even me. I was competing for her affection with our unborn child and I was losing."

"You loved her," Piper stated.

"I did. She was my world. Then Jess arrived and we seemed to gel into a family. I was working part-time for the company, still studying, but life was good. Andy was happy being a mom, Jess was amazing and things smoothed out."

Jealousy oozed into Piper's veins. Lucky, lucky, *lucky* Andrea to be the first and probably only woman to be loved by this amazing man. "What happened?"

Jaeger placed his hand on Ty's back, his jaw brushing the top of Ty's head. "It was a Sunday morning. Andy nursed Jess and put her down in her crib. I went to check on her fifteen, twenty minutes later and she was gone. Just…gone."

Piper placed her hand across her mouth, knowing what was coming. "Oh, God." she murmured. "SIDS?"

Jaeger nodded. "I tried to resuscitate her, but I knew my efforts were useless."

Piper blinked her tears away. What an absolutely horrible thing to have happened. "I'm so sorry, Jaeger."

"Yeah. It was rough. Andy fell apart. Our relationship fell apart. Everything fell apart," Jaeger stated. "It was a very bad time."

"Could you not stay together?" Piper asked, hearing the pain in his voice and wishing she could crawl inside him and fix his cracked heart.

"I tried. For about six months, we tried to go back to what we were, what we had, but she was in a very bad place. Eventually we split up. She went back to live with her folks, and it took her a while to deal with the loss, to conquer the depression."

There was still more to this story, Piper thought. "Did you ever see her again?"

Jaeger nodded. "About four years later, I called her to see how she was doing, and we met up. She told me that she missed me, that she still loved me."

"And you still loved her?"

"Yeah. I wanted her to move in with me, to pick up where we left off, but she refused. She said we had to take it slow, get to know each other again. I hated waiting. I wanted to live with her, be with her. But I was thrilled she was coming back to New York. To me."

Piper felt a cold fist squeezing her heart. "Oh, Lord. What happened?"

"Out of the blue she up and married a guy she'd been seeing since she moved back home. She sent me a text message ten minutes before she walked down the aisle, saying she loved me but every time she looked at me, she remembered Jess and it hurt too much. That she couldn't live her life like that," Jaeger said, his voice flat.

"Oh, sweetie." Piper had to touch him. She snuck her hand under his leather jacket and placed it directly over his heart. She knew there was nothing she could say, nothing that would help. She just kept looking into his eyes with her hand on his chest.

His antimarriage, antikids stance made sense now. He'd almost had it all, and then his dreams for love and a family were ripped away. He wasn't a selfish man, or a selfish father. He was just a guy trying to protect himself. Who could blame him?

Him not wanting children or not wanting to make a commitment had nothing to do with wanting to be free. Jaeger wasn't shallow, and she was embarrassed she'd bought the tale he'd told the world, even if it was the tale he'd spun so well.

He'd told her the truth. Wasn't it time she did the

same? It took courage to open up, to lay his cards—battered, ripped and stained—on the table. Could she be as brave? Maybe it was time for her to try.

"I can't believe that I am rehashing this!" The words sounded harsh on his lips, but Piper understood that feeling angry was better than feeling sad. "I trust you will keep this to yourself? I've never told anyone, not even my siblings, about that attempt at reconciliation."

"Why not?"

Jaeger shrugged, and the smallest smile touched his lips. "Those two months with Andy and Jess, they were—" he tipped his head up and looked for a word. "—magical. I just wanted to keep those memories of her and I, together again, to myself."

Piper nodded. She understood the need to hold a memory close, not to rob it of its magic. That was the way she felt about Milan and the time they'd spent together last summer. It didn't matter that he didn't remember her, didn't recall the magic they'd shared.

It was enough that she did.

She had to tell him. She would tell him. She just had to find her words.

"Jay, I—" God, this was so hard. Tears burned her eyes and she looked at the ground, softly blowing air over her lips. "God, I—that is…"

Jaeger bent down and placed Ty back in the stroller, pulling the straps over his sleeping frame. Jaeger tested the lock to make sure Ty was strapped in tight and looked up at her. "Can we walk and talk? I need to head back to Manhattan. I've got to whip Beck's ass at racquetball."

Piper jerked her head back. "Oh! Well, um, I thought—okay." Explaining about Ty would take some time, and it wasn't a conversation they should have while rushing. No matter what his reaction was, he'd have, at the very least, questions.

"I interrupted you," Jaeger said, using his free hand to hold hers. "What were you going to say?"

"It'll keep," Piper replied.

This wasn't news that she wanted to blurt out, especially so soon after hearing about his daughter's death. She didn't want Jaeger to feel she was presenting Ty as a replacement for Jess. She didn't want to diminish his loss.

She understood that Jess was irreplaceable.

But now she knew she had to tell Jaeger the truth. And soon.

Ten

Crawling exhausted Ty. He was in bed a half hour sooner than normal, and Piper was intensely grateful. His crawling exhausted her, too, and Jaeger keeping her up most of last night didn't help. She was finished with her work, and all she wanted was to lie down on her couch, watch some mindless TV and drift off. Jaeger hadn't said whether he was coming back and a small part of her hoped he didn't. She could use a solid night's sleep.

She also needed some emotional distance and a chance to rehearse how to tell him about Ty. She needed to present him with a coherent, logical explanation why she'd kept Ty a secret, how convinced she'd been that he'd be a disinterested father. If they managed to have a rational conversation about all of that, she'd tell him she was Mick's daughter. She wanted to open up to Jaeger completely and explain how her nonrelationship with Mick had deeply scarred her.

She might also tell Jaeger she loved him. She'd explain that she'd loved him from the first time she'd seen him in Milan and she hadn't stopped loving him since. Love, to her, meant going all in, risking everything. Love had to stand in the light of truth to flourish. If she loved Jaeger then she had to trust him with her secrets, with her past, her thoughts and her insecurities.

Yeah, telling him the truth was scary, but she had no choice.

Piper took a sip of wine, tapped her finger against the glass and tried not to worry about how he'd respond. Jaeger had never once intimated that they had anything more than a sexual connection and a fond friendship. Was she setting herself up for a fall? And if he did feel something for her, would their oh-so-fragile relationship survive the truth?

But love wasn't love when it lived in the dark.

God, thinking so much was exhausting. It had been a hell of a week, one of the craziest of her life. She picked up the remote to start her downtime when her phone rang. Digging it out of the back pocket of her jeans, she frowned at the unfamiliar number on the screen before answering.

"Is that you then, Piper Mills?"

"Um, yes, who am I talking to?"

Piper listened to a rambling explanation. This was Maeve Cummings, once Mills. She was Piper's mom's oldest cousin. Piper dropped the remote and leaned forward, surprised the many messages she'd sent to the email addresses in her mom's address book had finally received a response.

"You and I are the closest living relatives of John Carter Mills. Your email said you need information about him?"

"I do. Do you have anything of his?"

"I have some gems and his diary. A few papers."

"You have...sorry...what?" Piper asked, her breath catching in her throat.

"Three blue stones that are supposed to be worth something," Maeve replied. Maeve had the missing Blues...maybe.

"And you haven't had them valued?" Piper asked, trying to keep up.

"Never needed to. I'm as old as dirt and as rich as sin."

God, her cousin was a character! Why hadn't her mother kept in touch with this feisty old woman? Thinking it couldn't hurt to ask, Piper did.

Maeve snorted her displeasure. "I didn't like your father, and I told your mother he was bad news. Your mother didn't appreciate my frank assessment of the situation and broke off contact. How is she coping without him? She loved that thieving son-of-a gun."

"She died years ago. I don't know if she would've managed without him, so maybe it was better she went first," Piper admitted, pushing her fingers into her forehead.

"I'm sorry to hear that. So, you're *his* daughter?"

"Yep."

"The fact your surname is Mills tells me all I need to know about how good he was at being a father."

Maeve sniffed her disapproval and let out a hacking cough. Piper waited, listening as Maeve eventually caught her breath. "I live in Sag Harbor. Come and take them when you're ready."

"Take what?" Piper asked, confused.

"John Carter's diary and the rest of the stones. They might as well go to you and not to charity."

Piper shook her head wildly before realizing Maeve couldn't see her. "No! Really, I'll borrow the diary, if I may. That's all I need."

"Fine. Changing my will would be a pain in the ass, anyway."

Dear Lord, this woman was batty. "Have you read the diary?"

"Yes, sixty years ago."

"Do you possibly remember how he acquired the stones?" Piper asked, holding her breath.

"I'm old but not senile," Maeve snapped. "There was a landslide in a village to the north of Srinagar, and he pulled some local people out from under a pile of rocks. The villagers thanked him by giving him the sapphires. Three quarters of the way through the book, if I remember correctly, is his description of the landslide and the rescue. A little further along is a detailed description of the stones."

Piper's heart flipped over with excitement. Surely that was all the proof and provenance she needed?

"Come and get the book and the stones. I'm here all the time. If I'm not, I'm dead."

"I don't want your stones, Cousin Maeve. Just the diary."

"Don't argue with me, my girl. The stones belong together, and what would I do with them anyway?"

"Jaeger Ballantyne would buy them from you," Piper told her.

"Come and see me. Bring vodka, preferably Russian. I'll send you my address. Don't wait too long. I'm going to die soon," Maeve snapped out the commands before disconnecting the call.

Piper stared at her phone before letting out a squeal of excitement. If she and Jaeger could shoot up to the Hamptons tomorrow, they would have what they needed and could finalize the sale. She'd tell Jaeger about Ty and sell Ballantyne and Company the stones. Maybe, if she was very lucky, they could start a new chapter with no secrets between them.

Jaeger's phone went straight to voice mail and Piper nearly howled with frustration. "Jaeger, can you call me? As soon as possible? I think I've found the provenance we need. It's in the Hamptons with an old relative. She's batty, but she has a diary, and I think she has more Kashmir Blues. We need to get there, like, tomorrow! Seriously, I need you to call me! Now! Please?"

Piper tossed the phone onto the cushions of her couch. So excited she was unable to sit down, she walked the carpet in front of her blank TV, holding her wine and willing Jaeger to call her back. God, she was bursting with excitement, and there was no one else she could tell about this... There was no one else she wanted to tell.

Piper pushed her fist into her sternum. No matter what, Jaeger would always be the person she wanted to talk to first. Whether it was about Ty, or a piece of art that excited her, or a memory that made her cry or laugh, Jaeger was the only person she wanted to tell.

He was the one she wanted to go to bed with. His was the voice she wanted to listen to for the rest of her life. She wanted to watch him interact with Ty, wanted to make another child with him. She wanted to grow old with him, laugh with him, love him.

God, she loved him.

Loved. Him.

Her cell phone buzzed and Piper, seeing the light indicating a message, felt her heart go into overdrive. Jaeger! Yay. Her clumsy fingers pulled up the message, and her heart plummeted when she saw it was from Ceri, telling Piper to tune in to a local TV channel. The ten exclamation points indicated that tuning in was vitally important, so Piper pointed the remote at the TV and found the right station.

It was a typical scene from any entertainment show—velvet ropes holding the peasants away from the popular folks, the bright and beautiful of New York working the red carpet. Piper looked at the headline and realized it was the entrance to Moreau's Ball, the most glamorous social event on the city's calendar.

"As I promised earlier," the slick presenter stated, "I'm about to chat with Jaeger Ballantyne. He's just leaving the limousine with the rest of the Ballantyne clan. Dear Lord, they are a good-looking bunch! Jaeger, over here!"

Piper watched, fascinated, as Jaeger fastened the button of his designer tuxedo and ran a hand down his solid black tie. Sage stood just behind him, wearing a gold gown and to-die-for shoes, dwarfed by her bigger, brawnier brothers. The siblings started to make their way up the carpet, and paparazzi cameras flashed.

Jaeger stepped up to the presenter, who stroked Jaeger's biceps. Piper glared at the screen. "How nice to see you, Jaeger."

"Annette, how are you doing?" Jaeger replied.

"Why, just wonderful. Thank you for asking." Annette's voice slid into a drawl, and Piper rolled her eyes.

After a lot of sickening simpering and inane questions, Annette went in for the kill. "This is the premier event on the social calendar. I would've expected you to have a date on your arm. So why are you here alone?"

Jaeger sighed and shrugged. "It's a special event and, as per usual, there's no one special in my life. So I thought I'd do this solo."

There's no one special in his life...

Wait! Stop! Think! You're an adult and you know how dangerous the press can be. You're intelligent enough to know that what is said isn't always what is meant. Jaeger might not be in love with you, but he's been fairly damn wonderful.

Before you hang, draw and quarter him, give him the benefit of the doubt. That's what adults do.

But why those words?

Of all the billions of words he could've thrown together, why did he choose the one phrase that had the ability to unravel her?

Piper stared at Jaeger's image on the screen, watched him give Annette an air kiss and kept her eyes on him as he walked down the red carpet and disappeared into the venue. Piper licked her lips as her heart shriveled up and died. The annoying presenter was talking, but Piper couldn't hear anything but Jaeger's words on a continuous loop.

There's no one special in his life...

Piper knew she was on a downward spiral, losing her grip on rationality, but she couldn't help it. Destructive emotions flooded her system as her inner insecure girl started to panic.

She was nothing to him. What she'd thought they had was nothing. Sleeping with her was okay but taking her out in public, being seen with her, was another kettle of stinky fish. Piper felt herself rolling back in time, asking her father to take her to the park and him refusing.

Asking if she could take his name and him refusing.

Asking him to take her out to dinner, to his home, to the circus, to a father-daughter dance, to attend her graduation…

Mick always said no.

She was someone Mick only barely acknowledged in this house, in this space. Outside these four walls she hadn't existed, not for Mick, and apparently not for Jaeger, either.

Piper felt the tip of a red-hot knife punching holes in her heart. She felt the burn and the piercing pain, and the remote fell to the floor. She watched as tears splashed onto the black plastic, and she heard a buzzing in her ears. She placed her shaking hands under her armpits and cursed her father and cursed Jaeger, cursed these two men she'd loved but couldn't, wouldn't, love her in return.

"Hey, it's me. I've tried to call a couple of times, but your phone keeps going to voice mail. Very excited about the provenance. I won't be able to talk for a while, but text me, okay?"

Jaeger closed his phone and frowned. Piper had sounded excited and she'd asked him to call right away, so why was her phone off?

God, he hoped that everything was okay, that nothing had happened to her or Ty. Jaeger pulled out his seat at the round table and sent his siblings a distracted smile as he sat down.

Sage, sitting opposite him, leaned forward to speak across the table. "What's wrong?"

Jaeger picked up his tumbler of whiskey and shrugged. "Piper found the provenance for the stones."

Linc sat up straighter, immediately eager to hear more. "Seriously? Where?"

"A relative has a diary, and Piper thinks there might be more Blues." Jaeger pitched his voice low and kept his sentences brief, not wanting to give anything away.

"More?" Beckett's demanded. "How many?"

"Three. Piper wants us to go up to the Hamptons tomorrow to take a look."

Linc pointed a finger at him. "You'd better let us know as soon as you do."

Jaeger nodded, still uneasy that he couldn't reach Piper. He looked around the richly decorated ballroom and saw the reporter from earlier, Annette, looking at him from a neighboring table.

He'd lied to her earlier. There *was* someone special in his life. He didn't want there to be, would feel a great deal more comfortable if Piper wasn't so important, but she was. The uncomfortable feeling in his chest when he couldn't reach her just proved it.

He could deny his feelings until the freakin' cows came home, but what was the point? It didn't change the fact that he had feelings for a woman for the first time since Andy, and they were growing bigger and bolder.

He'd known her only a week, for God's sake.

Yet he knew Piper was the source of his recent happiness. When he allowed himself to dream, he saw himself in her house, a baby monitor on the table next to them, listening to Ty's occasional snuffle, cocking their heads to hear if it turned into a whimper or a cry. He wanted to stretch out on her couch and watch the game, a beer in his hand, her head on his thigh as she read one of her weighty art books. He wanted to listen to her explain cubism and Picasso, take her to Europe and watch her face as she explored the great art on that continent.

Eat hot croissants in Paris.

Sit in the teacups with Ty in his lap at Disneyland.

Read Ty a bedtime story.

Tell Piper another story using his mouth and hands.

She should have been here, with him, at his side where she belonged. His fear and her secrets and the stones and the press be damned. Her next to him, him next to her— that's the way it should be.

Jaeger felt a broad hand on his shoulder, and he looked up. Jaeger smiled at his friend and rival, James Moreau, and shook his hand.

"Sorry I missed out on poker the other night," James told Beckett after he'd greeted all the Ballantyne brothers and kissed Sage's cheek.

"I get it. You were scared. Perfectly understandable," Beckett taunted him.

"Up yours," James genially replied.

"I heard you lodged a claim with Mick Shuttle's estate to recover the money he owes you," Linc stated as James slid into the empty chair.

"Shuttle bought many pieces from us over the years. I never thought his damned check would bounce," James muttered.

"Glad he was your client and not ours," Beckett cheerfully stated.

"I'm sure you are," James wryly replied. "Ballantyne and Company definitely dodged a bullet. Shuttle's Colombian honey flew south the night before he was arrested. With, I presume, my diamond choker."

"Judging by his long list of creditors, you'll be lucky

if you get money back from his estate," Jaeger commented.

James placed his elbows on the table and tapped his finger against the bloodred tablecloth. "And that's what I can't understand. Thirty years ago, my father bought two stones off Shuttle, two exceptional sapphires my father paid top dollar for. Shuttle boasted he had many more and, no matter what happened, the rest of the stones were his backup plan."

Jaeger felt his heart stop, start and bump against his rib cage.

"My mother sold two stones thirty years ago to give him the capital to start his business."

Piper's house, he remembered, was owned by her father through a company, and the reason she had to sell was because it was part of his estate. The cash raised would go toward repaying her father's debts.

Piper Mills was Mick Shuttle's daughter.

That was a hell of a secret and raised the question: Why hadn't she told him?

And what else was she holding back?

Eleven

Piper wasn't surprised when Jaeger pushed the button to her intercom sometime after midnight. The message she'd left on his phone was intriguing. He'd want to know more, want to know everything.

She stood and placed her hand on her stomach, pulling in a deep breath. Silly of her to think they'd have a little more time before the situation detonated. In Milan, they'd hurtled from dinner to breakfast to dinner to bed in record time, and over the past week she'd reconnected, slept with and fallen in love with Jaeger.

Everything with Jaeger happened at warp speed.

Piper walked to the kitchen to buzz him up. God, she was tired and pissed and so in love with him it hurt.

Ask him about the interview, tell him about Ty and get it done. Throw your cards on the table and stop second-guessing him and yourself.

Honesty is always better than sugar-coated BS.

Honesty was the foundation of trust, and she'd short-changed Jaeger by not being totally up-front. About everything.

But she had to be prepared for him to be honest back. Maybe he meant every word he'd said to that television presenter; there might be nothing more between them than a bit of great sex. Jaeger might genuinely not be interested in Ty, and she'd have to deal with that.

She was stronger than she felt; she had to be if she was going to survive the worst consequences of this conversation. She'd survived her father's lack of interest; she could survive Jaeger's, too.

Straightening her shoulders, she walked to the hallway, unlocked her front door and there he was, his hand raised to knock. Jaeger sent her a cool look and walked past her, shrugging off his thigh-length coat and tossing it over the back of the nearest chair. His tuxedo jacket followed, and he ripped his tie from his neck and snapped open the top button of his shirt.

Piper folded her arms and watched as he rolled back the cuffs of his dress shirt in short, snappy movements. His eyes were ice blue, his shoulders tense, his jaw rockhard.

Jaeger looked as out of sorts as she was. But she had no idea why.

"Why didn't you answer your phone?" Jaeger demanded, slapping his hands on his hips.

Piper tipped her head to the side. Her rugby jersey reached to midthigh. Woolen socks covered her feet. She looked ridiculous and wished she was better dressed.

"I needed some time alone," Piper replied.

"Why?" Jaeger asked, as if talking to him was the

beginning and end of her existence. It was, but he didn't need to know that.

"Well, I'd just heard you tell the world there was nobody special enough in your life to take to Moreau's Ball. Considering you'd spent the last night making love to me, your statement made me feel cheap and inconsequential." Piper perched on the arm of a chair and crossed her legs. She looked up at him, keeping her face blank. "I was trying to work through my hurt and anger so we could have a rational conversation."

Jaeger ran an agitated hand across his jaw. "You saw the interview?"

"I did."

Jaeger's curse bounced off the walls of her apartment. "I never, for one moment, thought you would see that. You don't even watch television!"

"And that makes what you said okay?" Piper heard her voice rising and reached for control. She pulled in a calming breath and linked her shaking hands around her knees. It didn't escape her notice that he'd yet to deny the truth of what she'd said.

She couldn't help that a little sarcasm leached through her rationality. "Silly me. I'd started to think I might be more than a warm, willing body and a source of some very fine stones."

"That's not fair. I've never treated you that way." Jaeger jammed his hands into his pockets and scowled at her. "I don't know what you want me to say, Piper. I never discuss my love life with the press."

That wasn't a denial, either, Piper thought as she moved to sit in the chair. "What are we doing, Jaeger?"

"Right now? Having a fruitless conversation."

Despite her questions, he hadn't said anything to make

her think there was anything serious between them. She wasn't going to beg him to be with her. And she couldn't stay with him, vacillating between love and hope, waiting for him to become bored with her, waking up each day wondering how much time they had together.

It was better to live without him than to live in limbo. She was better, stronger than that.

She was not her mother.

Piper stood up, found her bag and pulled his check from her wallet. She handed it to him, ignoring the fire in his eyes. "I don't need this anymore. My uncle's diary will prove that the stones are from Kashmir, mined in the late nineteenth century. I'll get the diary tomorrow and I'll drop it off at your office on Monday morning. Ballantyne and Company can cut me a check." She sucked in a deep breath. "I would be grateful if you'd contact the lawyers administering my father's estate. With your assurance that I have funds coming in, they might not sell my house from under me."

Piper opened her mouth to tell him about Ty when he spoke again. "Who is your father?"

Those were the last words she'd expected from his mouth. Why was he asking her that? And why now? Piper felt a prickle of unease dance up her spine. "Why is that important?"

"Is your father Michael Shuttle?"

How had he found out? Piper forced herself to hold Jaeger's demanding stare.

Jaeger pointed his index finger at her. "Don't even try to lie to me! I know he's your father, Piper."

"How?" Piper asked.

"Because Shuttle sold two Kashmir sapphires to Moreau's thirty years ago to fund his business and said he had more. Your mother sold two sapphires to kick-start your father's business. Your father's estate is in administration and in debt. So is Shuttle's." Jaeger paced the area between her living room and hallway.

"Yes. He's my father."

Jaeger stopped pacing, and his direct look pinned her to her seat. "Okay, so why is that such a secret?"

"You're kidding me, right?" Piper heard her voice rising and thought, *To hell with control and rationality.* Jaeger was a big boy. He could handle a little shouting. Oh, damn, she couldn't shout, she had a baby in the house. "Why would I want to tell anyone about him? Why would I want to invite the attention and the scrutiny?"

"I'm not talking about telling the world. I'm talking about telling me!" Jaeger shot a look at the stairs and kept his voice low as well. "What else aren't you telling me? What else have you lied to me about?" Jaeger closed the gap between them, and his hands gripped her biceps. "What else, Piper?"

Piper wrenched herself from Jaeger's grip and wrapped her arms around her waist, feeling cold and hot at the same time. "You and I met in Milan and yes, we did go out a couple of times. What I didn't tell you is that we slept together."

She risked a peek at Jaeger's face. As she expected, he looked confused. "Okay. Why not tell me? It's not a big deal."

Piper let out a low, humorless laugh. "Yeah, it is." Gathering every bit of courage she could find, she looked him in the eye. "Ty is the result."

Piper watched as her words sank in and the color faded from Jaeger's face. He spoke through bloodless lips, the words rough. "I always use condoms."

"You did that night, too," Piper admitted. "I can't explain how it happened, but he's yours."

"He can't be!"

"Oh, for God's sake! He has your eyes, your chin, your face, your build. He has a dimple in his butt, just like you do. He has your body, your hands, your smile. He is a carbon copy of you!" Piper cried.

"He's not. He can't be."

She wasn't going to try to convince him. "Okay, he's not. Believe whatever you want to believe, Jaeger."

Jaeger gripped the back of the couch and looked at her, his eyes bleak. "Why didn't you tell me? Why did you keep this from me?"

"After Milan, I tried to tell you I was pregnant, Jaeger, but I couldn't reach you! I was kicked out of Ballantyne and Company and put on the kooks and crazies list!" Piper retorted. "We reconnected a week ago. When, exactly, was I supposed to blurt this out? While we were discussing the stones, after sex, before sex?"

"Yes!"

"I started to tell you today, at the park, but you had just told me about your daughter, and then you had a game with your brother, a ball to attend," Piper said, her voice bitter. "I needed time to explain, but you had better things to do."

"I would've blown off both if you'd said it was important," Jaeger countered.

"I didn't want you to reject Ty." There, she'd said it.

"I freely admit that I have no experience with babies, but I've given you no reason to think I would reject him!"

"Jaeger, for years you've been telling anyone with a microphone that you're not cut out to be a husband or a father. I believed that! I believed you!"

"You still should've told me," Jaeger said, his voice hard and stubborn.

"Of course I should've, but I was scared."

"Of what?"

"You rejecting Ty. You rejecting me." Unaware her face was wet with tears, she forced herself to meet his hard, angry eyes.

Face it, Piper. Demand the truth. Take the hit. You'll survive it. Maybe.

"Are you going to do that?" she asked.

Jaeger didn't flinch. His eyes remained steady on her face as he shook his head. "I can't be with someone I can't trust. I can't do that again."

His words felt like a blow. She managed to nod, and then she forced the next sentence up her constricted throat. "And Ty?"

"I don't know. I need to think about him."

Piper lifted her chin and scowled at him. "The fact that you have to think about loving him, accepting him, tells me everything I need to know." Piper heard her voice break, and she placed one hand over her eyes. She swallowed and blinked back tears. "I really need you to leave."

"Fine." Piper heard Jaeger's footsteps and felt the brush of his coat on her bare legs as he walked past. Then she heard the door close behind him. She dropped to the floor, placed her head between her knees and felt the chopped up pieces of her heart shatter into tiny shards.

It was Monday morning and Jaeger propped his feet up on the corner of his desk and stared out his rain-streaked office window. Thanksgiving was a week away, and some stores already had their Christmas decorations

in place. The creative designer would change the Ballantyne windows at the end of the month, and then the crazy
season would start. But all he could think about was...

He had a son.

He had a son with a beautiful, smart, funny woman
who'd cheated him out of the first months of his son's
life.

She should've tried harder to reach him...

But, as much as this annoyed him to admit, there had
been little more she could do. He dimly recalled that he'd
been presented with a list of people who'd tried to reach
him while he was in hospital but he'd trashed the document, figuring that if the matter was important, they'd
reach out to him again.

Piper hadn't. Not once.

Jaeger dropped his feet to the ground and placed his
forearms on his knees, staring at the expensive flooring below his feet. If he and Piper hadn't fought, would
she have told him? Ty was his son, a Ballantyne, his
flesh and blood. She had no right to keep Jaeger from
his child.

He wanted to rewind time. He wanted to recall how
it felt making love to Piper that first time, remember the
moment Ty was conceived. He wanted to watch Piper
grow round and full, see Ty on the sonar screen, be the
one to catch him as he entered the world.

Maybe he was being unfair but he didn't care... Piper
had cheated him out of those moments and the following nine months. He'd never forgive her. Forgiveness
wasn't possible.

He'd lost time he could never recover, and not because of amnesia. Piper had made the decision to keep
Ty from him, to keep him in the dark—a state he couldn't

stand—and Jaeger's anger was a living, breathing entity, crawling under his skin.

But he had to find a way to deal with her, because he had every intention of being in his son's life. He wasn't interested in an hour here or a weekend there. Feeling a little more clearheaded than he had on Saturday night, he now knew that he wanted to see Ty every damned day.

Jaeger glanced up as his computer beeped, notifying him of a new message. Jaeger rubbed his jaw, acknowledging that being Ty's dad would impact his career. It would change how he sourced gems from all over the globe. He couldn't be a full-time parent if he was crisscrossing the world. Would he have to choose between his career and his son? Could he give up the job he loved to spend more time with Ty?

Yeah. If it came to that, he would. He'd had so little time with his own parents before their deaths, but as an adult reflecting on that period, he clearly remembered how much he was loved. They'd adored being with him and his siblings. He wanted to give Ty that kind of family. He wanted his son to know nothing was more important to Jaeger than him.

Jaeger had thought Piper might be as important, but that just showed him how ridiculous he could be when it came to women. He'd started to fall in love with her... Thank God he'd managed to pull himself back from the ledge.

Oh, who was he kidding? He'd tumbled off that cliff the day she'd walked into his office a little less than two weeks back. He'd probably fallen in love with her back in Milan when they first made love. She'd snuck under his skin, climbed into his head and staged a takeover of his heart.

He loved her, but he couldn't trust her.

First Andy, now Piper. Why couldn't he find a woman he could love *and* trust?

Jaeger stood up and jammed his hands into his suit pockets. Piper would be here in ten minutes to finalize the purchase of her stones, and he had to pull himself together.

He couldn't let her know how much she affected him, how seasick he felt. She'd flipped his heart and his world and his life upside down, and he now had to find a new type of normal.

Normal. Jaeger snorted. As if anything could ever be normal again.

Piper walked into the imposing conference room at Ballantyne and Company, clutching her uncle's diary against her chest. She placed the old book and her bag on the sleek conference table and refused the offer of a cup of coffee from Linc. Beckett, Jaeger's younger brother, shook her hand, and Sage gave her a quick hug. Jaeger, standing across the room at the head of the table, lifted his chin to acknowledge her presence and turned his attention back to the phone in his hand.

So, his feelings hadn't changed between Saturday night and now. That was the price she had to pay for wanting to protect her son. She'd lied to Jaeger, and he wasn't going to forgive her.

Piper took a seat at the table and admitted to herself that Jaeger had a right to be angry. Despite trying to contact him, many times, she'd still kept him from his son and that, in his eyes, was reprehensible. He'd tossed her a quick, hot question about her motivations but he hadn't pushed her for an explanation. If he cared for her, even a little, shouldn't he have, at the very least, tried to understand her choices?

Piper darted a look at Jaeger's hard face and sighed. Dressed in solid black—dress shirt, tie and suit pants— he looked as accessible as a black hole. And as cuddly. Suddenly she saw the hard-eyed, edgy businessman who confidently walked into dangerous situations to buy gemstones. No matter his clothing, if she were selling him something and she was faced with that granite face, she wouldn't mess with him either. Hard, silent, dangerous. But, dammit, still so sexy.

Linc cleared his throat, and Piper looked up. Jaeger took a seat as far away from her as possible. Piper sighed at his nonverbal slap.

Yeah, I get it, Ballantyne. You want nothing to do with me.

Linc tapped his pen on the table, and Piper told herself to concentrate. What was about to be discussed would impact her future for a very long time, and she needed to be on her game.

"Thank you for sending us copies of the relevant pages of the diary, Piper," Linc said, his deep voice rumbling through the room. "I'm fully satisfied you are the legitimate owner of the stones. We've matched the description of the sapphires with some of the stones mentioned in the book, but we seem to be missing five stones from the original fifteen."

"I know where they are." Piper pulled in a deep breath. "May I have your assurance that whatever we discuss here will not leave the confines of this room?"

"You have it," Linc replied.

Piper nodded her thanks. "Jaeger knows this already, but Michael Shuttle was my father. My mother sold two stones thirty years ago to give him the capital to start his business."

Linc exchanged a long look with Jaeger, and Piper turned her head to look at Beckett and Sage. Beckett looked surprised and Sage sympathetic.

"Oh, honey. Nobody knows?" Sage asked.

Piper lifted one shoulder in a tiny shrug. "Mick never acknowledged me as his daughter."

Sage frowned. "In a way, I can sort of understand why he wouldn't want that to be public. You would've grown up with a million cameras on you and your life."

Ah, Sage, you are so far off base.

Piper didn't give any further explanations; she didn't need empty platitudes and false sympathy. Beckett's measured voice pulled her attention back to the business at hand. "Okay, so that's twelve stones. Where are the missing three?"

"My cousin Maeve has them," Piper told him and instantly saw the excitement flash in their eyes. Even the rock at the end of the table reacted to her statement. The air crackled with anticipation as long looks were exchanged between the siblings.

Piper made herself concentrate on Jaeger. This was his wheelhouse, after all. "She offered to give them to me, but I refused." Mick would've taken the stones in a flash, but Piper didn't feel she had any right to them. Cousin or not, she'd only spent a morning with Maeve, and that didn't entitle her to a couple of million in gems. "I told her about you, Jaeger, and she'll probably sell you the stones. If I were you, I'd ask to see what else she has. She was sporting a stunning ten-carat-plus diamond when I met her. She doesn't have any heirs, and she's going to leave her wealth to various foundations."

"She won't leave it to you?" Beckett asked when Jaeger didn't acknowledge her suggestion.

Piper shook her head. "I met her for the first time yesterday. I don't feel like I can take the money. I didn't earn it."

In this regard, she was *not* her father's daughter.

"Piper, that money could pay for Ty's education, could make your life a lot easier," Sage said, leaning forward.

"I just need enough to pay for my house. The rest I will earn," Piper said, hearing the stubborn in her voice. "I will be fine. Speaking of your offer..." Piper hinted. She couldn't sit here for much longer with Jaeger tossing accusing looks her way.

Linc nodded. "We're prepared to offer you seven million."

Seven million? More than she needed and much more than she'd hoped for. Piper felt tears prick her eyes, and she stared down at the table. "Thank you."

"If our offer is acceptable, I'll arrange for payment to be made," Linc said.

"Very acceptable. Thank you very much," Piper replied, her voice low. Seven million would secure her house, would pay for Ty's schooling and would give her a lot of financial security.

It was done. All that remained between her and Jaeger was their son.

Sage walked around the table to Piper's chair. She turned Piper's chair, bent down and brushed her lips across her cheek. "Let's get together sometime soon, okay?"

Sadly that would never happen, not now. Linc stood up and held out his hand for her to shake. "Nice doing business with you, Piper. I'll get your money to you by the end of the day."

Linc squeezed her shoulder as he followed Beckett out of the room. Jaeger just sat where he was, one ankle on his knee, his face a thundercloud.

When they were alone, she stood up and pulled her bag over her shoulder. She was suddenly exhausted, emotionally and physically wiped out. Wishing Jaeger would say something and then hoping he wouldn't, she pushed her chair under the table and turned to leave.

"My lawyers will contact you with regard to custody of Ty," he said.

Piper stiffened. That was too much. He was not going to take her son from her. He wanted custody? Oh, hell, no!

Piper felt white-hot anger flash over her as she went into full, rabid momma-bear mode. She slapped both hands on the conference table, her face burning.

"Know this, Jaeger Ballantyne. No matter how much I love you, how much I want you in my life, if you ever so much as mention taking my son from me again, I will take every cent of those millions and I will vanish! I will go so deep and so dark you will never find him again. No one, not even you, will come between me and my son!"

Jaeger sat up straighter, and a small frown appeared between his eyes. "Whoa, hold on—"

"My mother loved me, but she loved my father more. My father didn't love me at all. Ty is my only family, my world. I love you, but God, I will fight you with every breath I have if you try to take him from me."

Piper lifted a shaking finger in the general direction of his face. Tears burned hot passages down her cheeks as she continued, "I should've told you about him when I first saw you again. I know that now. I know you hate me, but please, taking Ty from me would be a death sentence for me. Please don't make me do something drastic to keep him. I'll share him with you—he deserves to know you—but please don't try to take it all. Don't make me do something irreversible."

"Piper, I—"

She couldn't withstand any more. Piper felt the last chunk of her heart rip into shreds. She dashed her hands over her wet cheeks and whirled around, seeing the blurred outline of the door. Needing to escape, to run, she bolted from the room, ignoring Jaeger's command for her to stay.

Earlier, when she'd walked into this room, she didn't think the situation between her and Jaeger could get worse, but it had.

Be strong, Piper. Be brave. Your love wasn't enough, not this time, not for this man.

There was no point in thinking about what-could-have-beens. No point in mourning a future she'd wanted but he didn't. It was over. By threatening to take her son from her, he'd killed the last fragment of hope she'd been clinging to that they could work something out.

What they had, what they could've had, was impossible, a shattered dream.

Piper walked out of Ballantyne and Company for the final time and begged her hopes, her dreams and her love for Jaeger not to follow her home.

Twelve

Jaeger pushed his hand under his suit jacket and felt the padded outline of the stones he'd just purchased. There was another fortune in jewelry in his briefcase, but he felt the need to keep the three cabochon-cut sapphires, twenty-five carats of corundum, on his person. With the addition of these stones purchased an hour ago from Piper's cousin Maeve, the Kashmir Blues collection was as complete as they could hope it to be.

Linc was excited, Beckett quietly thrilled, Sage loudly ecstatic.

Jaeger felt like his head was about to explode.

He pulled his SUV into the fast lane to pass a slow-moving sedan and, through his expensive shades, glared at the asphalt of Route 27. A headache pulsed behind his right eye and his chest felt tight. He instructed the on-board computer to find a radio station playing hard rock, hoping the strident music would distract him from his thoughts. He made it through the first verse before shouting at the computer to turn the music off.

He was losing his temper with technology, a new low.

He eased his foot off the gas and pushed his free hand through his hair. He wasn't sleeping, he was mainlining coffee and he couldn't remember when he last ate. His office felt claustrophobic, his apartment like a sophisticated jail cell. The sun seemed to be dimmer and the air thinner and...

And he missed his son.

Yeah, he missed Ty, but he yearned for Piper.

Yearned? God! Whatever label he gave the emotion—yearning, pining, longing—he was feeling it every miserable second. His head and heart ached. He wanted to go back to Park Slope, to that red Victorian, and beat on her door until she let him inside.

Because he was a man, his fantasy included skipping the talking and taking her straight to bed. After he'd reacquainted himself with every inch of her body, through mental telepathy she'd understand that they belonged together, that she was his, that Ty was his and that they were in it for the long haul.

Yeah, and he had more chance of finding the missing Kashmir Blues.

He loved her.

He loved her because she was funny and smart and had legs that made his mouth water. Because she was an amazing mother, a wild lover and a loyal friend. He loved her because he now understood her better, thanks to the pithy, and direct, lecture he'd endured from her acerbic elderly cousin.

It turned out Mick Shuttle wasn't only a criminal, he'd

also been a crappy father. According to Maeve, Shuttle had been an utter bastard to Piper and her mom, starting with the deal he'd struck with Piper's mom when she'd told him she was pregnant.

After kicking her out of their apartment in a rage, Mick waited for more than two months before tracking Gail down at Maeve's house. Mick, the bastard, made a deal with Gail: she could have full custody of the baby if she sold two of her sapphires and gave him the money to set up his business. Mick would keep her on as his mistress, would house and clothe and support her as long as she lived, but he wanted nothing to do with Piper. Ever.

It was a stance he'd never deviated from. Knowing that, and taking into account Jaeger's own oft-repeated statements about not wanting a wife or children, Jaeger now better understood why Piper had kept Ty from him. She'd wanted to protect Ty from a father who'd openly admitted he wasn't interested in children. She'd thought he was like Mick—the thought turned his stomach—and she didn't want Ty to go through what she did. Jaeger wasn't anything like Mick, but how was she to know that?

She'd been protecting his son; he couldn't fault her for that.

Piper, Maeve informed him, was a Mills, and Mills women loved hard and loved fast. Their men never, not for a fraction of a second, questioned that love. It was just there, a living, breathing, tangible entity.

He wanted that love, Piper's love. But he'd been too damn scared or too busy protecting himself to realize he'd been given a second chance at being happy. If he didn't fix this, he might never know what being loved by Piper would feel like.

He'd lost his daughter, lost Andy and lost his parents. He'd lost Connor and a month of memories. Every loss rocked his world, but the thought of not having Piper and Ty in his life froze the blood in his veins.

He'd crawled through jungles, braved blizzards, talked his way past thieves and bargained with warlords to acquire the gemstones he wanted, but Piper and Ty were his biggest treasures, his ultimate find. He'd do anything to become part of their world, to share their lives. Ty allowed his shoulders to drop, and he stretched his spine to work out some tension.

It might take some swift negotiating, some smooth talking and fast thinking, but they were his biggest quest.

This had all started because Piper wanted to sell her stones to keep her house, and just like that, Jaeger knew what he had to do to win her back.

He smiled.

Oh, yeah, this was going to be *fun*.

Piper, convinced that she was about to burst a blood vessel in her brain, kept one hand on the handle of Ty's stroller and slapped her other hand on the expensive counter between her and a robot wearing a black suit. She peered at the robot's badge. Johnson, Chief of Security, Ballantyne and Co. "Mr. Johnson—"

"Just Johnson, ma'am."

"I'm sure if you just call Jaeger and tell him I am here, why I am here—"

"Why are you here, ma'am?"

Because Simms told me to come!

Because the lawyer representing Mick's estate now, for some odd reason, wouldn't take her money, wouldn't allow her to buy her house. Simms had told her to talk to Jaeger Ballantyne and to get back to him when she had.

Why did she care so much, anyway? Two weeks ago the house was her refuge, her link to her childhood and her mom, a place of safety. Now it felt empty without Jaeger, just rooms and walls and stuff. Her home was in Jaeger's arms; she felt grounded when she looked into his eyes, energized when he kissed her, connected to the universe when he loved her.

Wherever he was, that was where she wanted to be.

He didn't feel the same.

Piper pushed her fist into her sternum and breathed through her mouth, physically pushing the painful emotions back. She would not cry, not now, but she acknowledged that she couldn't live like this for much longer. She was falling apart. Worry was eating her from the inside out. It wasn't good for her or for Ty.

She'd spent the last four nights not sleeping, trying to act normal around Ty, Ceri and Rainn, but falling apart when she was alone. She didn't think she was fooling anyone. Ty had picked up on her stress. He was clingier than usual and a lot crankier. She'd wanted to leave him with Ceri earlier, but he'd refused to let Piper go, and she didn't have the heart to leave him. It was as if he was also suffering from a bad case of missing Jaeger.

"Ma'am, I asked you a question. What is the nature of your business with Mr. Ballantyne?"

I love him but he doesn't love me or our son? The words hovered on her lips, but she pulled them back. "It's personal business."

Johnson did not look convinced.

"It really is. I am—" God, what was she? His ex-lover, the mother of his child, his casual fling?

He was the only man she wanted in her life. He was the only man she could imagine in her life. Piper pushed her hands through her tangled curls and blew air over her bottom lip. Even if she told Johnson that, she doubted he'd believe her.

She looked like what she was—a frazzled single mother barely keeping her life together. A young woman wearing faded jeans, battered sneakers and a cinnamon knee-length trench coat. No makeup, eyes red from too many tears and minimal sleep.

"Ma'am. Can I see some identification?" Johnson asked, his voice low and patient.

"For the love of God," Piper whimpered. Piper let go of the stroller and yanked her wallet out of her bag, slamming it onto the counter. Sending the implacable Johnson a narrow-eyed, you're-high-on-my-hit-list look, she handed over her driver's license and tapped her fingers as he typed her name into his database.

Johnson looked at the screen, frowned and looked at the screen again.

"Problem?" she asked, her tone sarcastic.

Johnson rubbed the back of his neck as he passed her license back to her.

"What?" Piper demanded. "Am I still on the kooks and crazies list?"

Déjà vu, Piper thought, feeling the walls of the lobby closing in on her. She'd been here before. Jaeger had, once again, restricted access to himself. She'd backed away once before, turned tail and run—a habit she'd carried over from her childhood. Instead of fighting her father, making him notice her, she'd retreated and allowed him to control the situation.

She wasn't a child anymore.

She was done with running, slinking off, hiding out, trying not to rock the boat. She wanted a definitive answer about what Jaeger was planning, whether he intended to sue for custody or not. She wanted to know why he'd spoken to Simms, the lawyer dealing with Mick's estate. What business did Jaeger have discussing her house? And why the hell hadn't he taken her off the kooks and crazies list?

She was done with playing nice. Piper looked around and noticed the cameras in the corners of the lobby. Two, three, another over the door, all of them recording her interaction with Johnson. She'd bet a Kashmir Blue that there was a microphone picking up every word she uttered. "I want to leave a message for Jaeger, Johnson."

Johnson reached for a message pad, but she shook her head. "I'm not an idiot. I know every move I make is being recorded." Slapping her hands on her hips, Piper looked directly up into the camera above the desk, opening her mouth to blast him.

"I heard you are looking for me."

"Hey, bud." Jaeger dropped to his haunches in front of Ty, and a look of love crossed his face that liquefied Piper's knees.

Breathe, Mills, dammit. Ty, immediately leaned forward, dropping his duck and shouting his approval. His favorite person, Piper thought, was back and all was right with his world.

Jaeger pushed the button to release Ty from his safety belts and lifted the baby into his arms, placing his mouth on Ty's temple and inhaling his special baby smell. Then Jaeger grimaced and held Ty away from him, shaking his head at his son.

"Is that your way of punishing me for staying away? By greeting me with a loaded diaper?" Jaeger asked, smiling. "That's a highly effective reprimand. Respect, dude."

Jaeger tucked Ty against his side, grabbed the stroller and finally, finally looked at her, his eyes guarded. "Hi."

Piper lifted her hand to hold her throat, wishing she could get more air into her lungs. He was dressed in navy pants, a brown leather belt that matched his shoes and a plain white shirt. He looked insanely hot. Situation normal, then.

Piper looked again and noticed his ragged edges. His beard was days past trendy, and his olive complexion looked a shade lighter. His hair suggested that his hands lived in it, and his eyes were as bloodshot as hers.

Jaeger nodded at Johnson. "I've got this, thanks. Thanks for letting me know she was here."

It took a moment for Jaeger's words to sink in, and when they did, Piper spun around and glared at Johnson. "You alerted him I was here? Why did you let me think I was on the kooks and crazies list?"

"Stop giving my staff a hard time, Piper, and let's go up."

Piper gave the now openly amused Johnson a slitty-eyed glare as Jaeger pulled Ty's diaper bag from the storage area below his seat. He asked Johnson to park the stroller, and Piper followed Jaeger and Ty to the bank of elevators. Jaeger stopped in front of a smaller single elevator she hadn't noticed the last time she was here and watched as he placed his thumb on a scanner. Within seconds the doors opened, and Jaeger waited for her to enter first.

As the elevator lifted, Piper turned to him. "What have you done with my house?"

The smallest smile touched Jaeger's face. "We'll get to that."

Piper started to argue, but then the elevator doors opened. Instead of seeing a hallway, Piper faced a wall of Jaeger's siblings. Their eyes bounced from Jaeger's face to Ty's, and they instantly made the connection. Oh, crap! Piper took a step back and then another until she reached the back of the elevator.

"Linc, Beck, Sage, meet Ty. Your nephew."

Sage squealed, Linc laughed and Beck grinned. Three sets of hands reached to take Ty. Ty, who didn't have a shy or retiring bone in his body, laughed and blew raspberries.

"You take him, you change him. Warning, he's ripe," Jaeger said, and those eager hands disappeared. Jaeger rolled his eyes. "Thought so."

With the hand not holding Ty, Jaeger reached out, grabbed Piper by the wrist and tugged her into the hall. "We'll be in my office, my *locked* office. Leave us alone." Jaeger threw the words over his shoulder as he led her to his office. Piper looked back at their bemused expressions and lifted her shoulders in a tiny shrug. At least Jaeger had publicly acknowledged his son. Maybe that meant he wanted to claim Ty as his own.

Jaeger locked the door behind him and nodded to the sofa in the corner. "Take a seat while I change Ty."

"I can do it," Piper protested.

Using just one hand, Jaeger cleared a space on his desk, pulled a blanket from the diaper bag and spread it over the sleek wood. He put Ty on his back and quickly and efficiently changed him. She stood by the door, listening to the rumble of his voice as he spoke to his son, his tone too low to make out his words. Judging by Ty's soft chuckles, he was enjoying their conversation. Within minutes, the diaper was disposed of, Ty was back in his arms and Jaeger rubbed his cheek against Ty's head, closing his eyes as he inhaled Ty's scent. "God, I missed you," he said.

Piper swallowed, trying to dispel the knot of emotion in her throat. Jaeger loved Ty, absolutely adored him. She just wished he felt a fraction of that love for her.

"I want to share custody of Ty," Jaeger stated, looking at her.

This was progress. He wasn't professing his deep and abiding love, but it was obvious that he loved Ty and wanted to be his dad.

Piper walked toward her son and his father. "I appreciate the sentiment, but he's too young to deal with the upheaval of spending some nights with you and some nights with me. Maybe when he's older."

"I'm not waiting that long," Jaeger firmly stated. "Not for him, and not for you."

Piper felt the world rock beneath her feet. Oh, God, she couldn't cope with false hope. "What, exactly, does that mean?"

The corners of Jaeger's mouth tipped up. Jaeger walked toward her and picked up her hand, which she immediately snatched away. If he touched her she'd cave—beg him to love her—and she wouldn't allow herself to do that.

Piper stepped away from him, ordering herself to think. "Explain that! Right now."

Ty batted Jaeger's face with his hand, and Jaeger captured the baby's fingers, pretending to bite them. Ty's laughter rang out loud and clear.

"Jaeger!"

Jaeger sent her a half smile. "I want to share cus-tody of Ty with you, but in the only way it makes sense. You and me, together. I want Ty, but I need you. I need you in my bed and in my arms and in my life. I need to wake up with you, fall asleep with you, make more ba-bies with you. I need you. I love you. Frankly, my life is crap without you."

Piper felt love, hot and strong, well up inside her, but she forced it back down, not willing to allow it to cloud her thinking. "But you said you'd never trust me again."

Jaeger led her to the sofa and Piper sat down on the edge, grateful, because she wasn't sure whether her legs would hold her for much longer. Jaeger loved her, wanted her and Ty in his life.

God, was she hallucinating? Not sure, she touched his hard thigh as he sat down and bounced Ty on his knee.

"I went to see your cousin in Sag Harbor. I bought her sapphs."

She didn't care about the sapphires. She wanted to hear more about how much he loved her, whether there was some way, any way, they could make this work.

"She's the sharpest geriatric I've ever met, and she also has a magnificent jewelry collection."

Piper really didn't care.

"You obviously had a heart-to-heart with Maeve be-cause she immediately tagged me as Ty's father, as the man you were having issues with. I told her I wouldn't discuss you, and she told me she wouldn't sell me the sapphs if I didn't."

Piper sneaked a look at him. "So, what did you tell her?"

"That I was confused, that I loved you but I couldn't understand why you kept Ty from me. Maeve told me about your nonrelationship with your father, and I understand a bit better. Maybe we can talk about it more?"

Piper waved her hand in the air. "I shouldn't have let my issues with Mick affect my decision." Piper lifted her hand and rested her fingers on his cheek. "I didn't want to hurt you, Jaeger, and I wanted to tell you. After Milan, I really did try to tell you. I couldn't get hold of you, and I thought you didn't want anything to do with me." Piper rubbed her hand up and down his thigh. "And then I read about your lack of interest in kids, and I took it at face value. Afterward, and subconsciously, it was also a way for me to justify my decision not to tell you about Ty."

"I'm not like your father, Piper."

God, she knew that! "Jaeger, you're the best man I know and nothing like Mick. You've walked through hell and it's just made you stronger, and better. You're a good man and God knows, I need one of those in my life. I need you. Another reason I didn't tell you about Ty was that I knew I would lose you when I did." Her voice cracked. "I didn't want to lose you, Jay."

"I'm here now, Piper, asking if we can move beyond this, whether we can move forward, together." Jaeger's voice was low and deep and laced with emotion. And love. So much love. "I trust you. With my heart, my life, my son. Be with me. Love me."

Tears welled and ran down her face. "I do. I will."

Jaeger raised his hand and cradled her cheek, his own eyes bright with moisture. "I love you so much."

"And I you," Piper whispered against his lips.

Jaeger's kiss was soft, sweet and so very, very sexy. He broke their kiss to speak. "I have a little something for you."

"You gave me our marvelous son. He, and you, are the only gifts I'll ever need."

His eyes danced with pleasure. "Well, I have two more," he said, his voice gruff as he handed Ty to her. "Go to your mom for a sec, bud."

Ty bellowed his outrage, waving his hands at his dad. Ty had fallen in love with Jaeger, Piper realized. She could understand it; she was head over heels in love with him herself.

Jaeger stood up, walked to his desk and picked up some papers. He handed them to Piper. She looked at Jaeger, confused. "This looks like an agreement for you to buy my house."

"It is. I want to buy it for you. Well, for us. I'd like to put it in your name, but I was hoping you'd share it with me," Jaeger said, taking Ty back into his arms. "I want to live with you and Ty. I'll still have to travel, but instead of prolonging my trips, I'll make them as short as possible. And if I live with you, then I can look after Ty when you travel. Or we can come with you, or you and Ty can travel with me. We can work it out. We can work anything out."

"We can," Piper agreed. "Anything."

"So, are you agreeing to marry me?" Jaeger asked.

Piper laughed. "I don't recall you asking me. But when you get around to it, the answer will be yes."

Jaeger smiled, his face softer with happiness. He ducked his hand into the right pocket of his pants and pulled out a rich, sleepy blue stone. "I bought this from the collection of Kashmir Blues, and it was worth every penny Linc extorted from me. It's practically flawless, fabulously rare and infinitely precious. Just like you. Want it?"

"If it comes with a proposal, then hell yes, I want it."

Ty rested his head on his dad's shoulder, and Piper looked at her two men, pure love pumping through her veins. She lifted her lips to be kissed. "I love you, Jaeger. I have since the moment I caught you ogling my legs in Milan."

Jaeger's lips brushed hers. "Can you blame me? They are fabulous legs, sweetheart." Sadness came and went in his eyes. "I'm sorry I don't remember our first meeting. I want to, but…" He shrugged.

Piper dropped her face into his neck. "Maybe you can take me back and I'll show you what we did, where we ate, how we loved each other. We can reconstruct that time."

"I'm up for that." Jaeger kissed her forehead and looked at their son. "And maybe this time, we can try to make a pink one?"

Piper sent him a long, loving, I-can't-wait-to-get-you-naked look.

Jaeger grinned, bounced up from his seat and, still holding Ty, quickly walked over to the door. He yanked it open and yelled down the hallway. "Yo, family! Linc, Sage, Beck! I need one of you to spend some quality time with your brand-new nephew so I can kiss his mama. He's clean and happy. Any takers?"

It took ten long and very frustrating minutes to referee the argument around who got to hold the newest Ballantyne first before Piper got her hands on the newest Ballantyne's daddy.

* * * * *

MILLS & BOON®

Desire™

PASSIONATE AND DRAMATIC LOVE STORIES

A sneak peek at next month's titles...

In stores from 6th April 2017:

- **The Marriage Contract** – Kat Cantrell *and*
  The Rancher's Cinderella Bride – Sara Orwig

- **Triplets for the Texan** – Janice Maynard *and*
  The Magnate's Marriage Merger – Joanne Rock

- **Little Secret, Red Hot Scandal** – Cat Schield *and*
  Tycoon Cowboy's Baby Surprise – Katherine Garber

Just can't wait?
Buy our books online before they hit the shops!
www.millsandboon.co.uk

Also available as eBooks.